The Penguin Arthur Miller

*This is a bespoke
centennial edition
produced in a limited quantity
by the publisher*

THE PENGUIN ARTHUR MILLER

In the history of postwar American art and politics, Arthur Miller casts a long shadow as a dramatist of stunning range and power, an accomplished writer of fiction, memoir, and screenplays, and an engaged public intellectual. Miller's life and work hold a mirror up to America and its shifting values. His body of work consists of plays from across the decades spanning the 1930s to the new millennium, creating what biographer Christopher Bigsby calls "an alternative history of a troubled century." These plays are of their time yet timeless: bound not in realism, but the product of, in Miller's own words, "a dream rising out of reality." At his core, he was a humanist fundamentally devoted to the moral responsibility of one person to another, an interest that manifested in both a concern for the private individual and the public experience. He was not a moralist but a man of deep moral conscience. Miller believed in the need to confront ourselves continually, and his plays represent a belief in the obligation of theater and art to help us do so. To this worldview, he brought psychological perspicacity, remarkably fluid dialogue, and an abiding sense of humor. Little wonder, then, that he remains among the most widely read and produced playwrights of any century.

The Penguin Arthur Miller celebrates the Arthur Miller centennial, honoring a near-matchless creative and intellectual legacy. Beginning with his quiet debut, *The Man Who Had All the Luck*—now recognized as containing the stirrings of genius—and *All My Sons*, the follow-up that established him as a major talent, this volume collects the breadth of Miller's plays. From career hallmarks like *The Crucible* and *Death of a Salesman*, to later works like *Mr. Peters' Connections* and *Resurrection Blues*, the range and courage of Miller's moral and artistic vision are here on full display.

"Here we find the true compassion and catharsis that are as essential to our society as water and fire and babies and air. I remember walking and running and jumping out of the theater after seeing *Death of a Salesman*, like a child in the morning, because Miller awakened in me the taste for all that must be—the empathy and love for the least of us, out of which bursts a gratitude for the poetry of these characters and the greatness of their creator."

—Philip Seymour Hoffman

"I think you can tell from his plays whether a writer loves actors. Arthur gives you tap dances. He gives you arias."   —Dustin Hoffman

"Arthur was the last of the three great theatrical voices of the American century—O'Neill, Williams, Miller."   —David Hare

"[Miller] has looked with compassion into the hearts of some ordinary Americans and quietly transferred their hope and anguish to the theatre."

—Brooks Atkinson

PENGUIN CLASSICS ( ) DELUXE EDITION

THE PENGUIN ARTHUR MILLER

ARTHUR MILLER (1915–2005) was born in New York City and studied at the University of Michigan. His plays include *All My Sons* (1947), *Death of a Salesman* (1949), *The Crucible* (1953), *A View from the Bridge* and *A Memory of Two Mondays* (1955), *After the Fall* and *Incident at Vichy* (1964), *The Price* (1968), *The Creation of the World and Other Business* (1972), and *The American Clock* (1980). His other works include *Focus*, a novel (1945); *The Misfits*, a cinema novel (1961); and the texts for *In Russia* (1969), *In the Country* (1977), and *Chinese Encounters* (1979), three books in collaboration with his wife, photographer Inge Morath. His memoirs include *Salesman in Beijing* (1984) and *Timebends*, an autobiography (1987). His short fiction includes the collection *I Don't Need You Any More* (1967), the novella *Homely Girl, A Life* (1995), and *Presence: Stories* (2007). His later work includes the plays *The Ride Down Mt. Morgan* (1991), *The Last Yankee* (1993), *Broken Glass* (1994), and *Mr. Peters' Connections* (1999); *Echoes Down the Corridor: Collected Essays, 1944–2000*; and *On Politics and the Art of Acting* (2001). Among numerous honors, he received the Pulitzer Prize for Drama and the John F. Kennedy Lifetime Achievement Award.

LYNN NOTTAGE is a Pulitzer Prize–winning playwright and a screenwriter. Her plays have been produced widely in the United States and throughout the world. They include *Sweat*; *By the Way, Meet Vera Stark* (Lilly Award, Drama Desk nomination); *Ruined* (Pulitzer Prize, OBIE Award, Lucille Lortel Award, New York Drama Critics' Circle Award for Best Play, Audelco, Drama Desk Award for Outstanding Play, and Outer Critics Circle Award); *Intimate Apparel* (American Theatre Critics and New York Drama Critics' Circle Awards for Best Play); *Fabulation, or The Re-Education of Undine* (OBIE Award); *Crumbs from the Table of Joy*; *Las Meninas*; *Mud, River, Stone*; *Por'knockers*; and *POOF!*

BY ARTHUR MILLER

PLAYS

The Golden Years
The Man Who Had All the Luck
All My Sons
Death of a Salesman
An Enemy of the People
The Crucible
A View from the Bridge
After the Fall
Incident at Vichy
The Price
The Creation of the World and
   Other Business
The Archbishop's Ceiling
The American Clock
Playing for Time
The Ride Down Mt. Morgan
Broken Glass
Mr. Peters' Connections
Resurrection Blues
Finishing the Picture

ONE-ACT PLAYS

A View from the Bridge
   (*one-act version*)
A Memory of Two Mondays
Fame
The Reason Why
Elegy for a Lady (*in* Two-Way Mirror)
Some Kind of Love Story
   (*in* Two-Way Mirror)
I Can't Remember Anything
   (*in* Danger: Memory!)
Clara (*in* Danger: Memory!)
The Last Yankee

SCREENPLAYS

Playing for Time
Everybody Wins
The Crucible
The Misfits

MUSICAL

Up from Paradise

AUTOBIOGRAPHY

Timebends

REPORTAGE

Situation Normal
In Russia (*with Inge Morath*)
In the Country (*with Inge Morath*)
Chinese Encounters (*with Inge Morath*)
Salesman in Beijing

FICTION

Focus (*a novel*)
Jane's Blanket (*a children's story*)
The Misfits (*a cinema novel*)
I Don't Need You Any More (*stories*)
Homely Girl, A Life
   (*a novella and stories*)
Presence: Stories

COLLECTIONS

Arthur Miller's Collected Plays,
   Volumes I and II
The Portable Arthur Miller
Arthur Miller: Collected Plays
   1944–1961 (*Tony Kushner, editor*)
Arthur Miller: Collected Plays
   1964–1982 (*Tony Kushner, editor*)
Arthur Miller: Collected Plays
   1987–2004 with Stage and Radio
   Plays of the 1930s and 40s (*Tony
   Kushner, editor*)

ESSAYS

The Theater Essays of Arthur Miller
   (*Robert A. Martin, editor*)
Echoes Down the Corridor: Collected
   Essays, 1944–2000
   (*Steven R. Centola, editor*)
On Politics and the Art of Acting

VIKING
CRITICAL LIBRARY EDITIONS

Death of a Salesman
   (*Gerald Weales, editor*)
The Crucible
   (*Gerald Weales, editor*)

ARTHUR MILLER

The Penguin Arthur Miller

COLLECTED PLAYS

Foreword by
LYNN NOTTAGE

PENGUIN BOOKS

PENGUIN BOOKS

An imprint of Penguin Random House LLC
375 Hudson Street
New York, New York 10014
penguin.com

LIBRARY OF CONGRESS CATALOGING-IN-PUBLICATION DATA
Miller, Arthur, 1915–2005.
[Plays. Selections]
The Penguin Arthur Miller : collected plays / Arthur Miller ; foreword by Lynn Nottage.
pages cm.—(Penguin Classics Deluxe)
ISBN 978-0-14-310777-4 (pb.)
ISBN 978-0-14-310778-1 (hc.)
I. Title.
PS3525.I5156A6 2015
812'.52—dc23
2015024812

Printed in the United States of America
5   7   9   10   8   6   4

Set in Sabon Std

Contents

Foreword

Letter to a Young Playwright

Dear Young Playwrights,

As a young playwright grappling with concerns about content, form, and structure, there were of course numerous places that I'd turned to for guidance and inspiration, but repeatedly I found myself retreating to a well-worn volume of *The Collected Plays by Arthur Miller*. The collection occupied an honored place on my bookshelf alongside the other seminal American playwrights of the twentieth century: Lillian Hellman, Lorraine Hansberry, Tennessee Williams, Clifford Odets, and August Wilson. But, in many respects, I learned my craft by reading the plays of Miller, dissecting the careful way he used the poetry of everyday speech to shape and interrogate his characters. I marveled at how effortlessly he conjured the worlds of ordinary men, transforming the minutiae of their day-to-day lives into epic tragedies. I found his plays to be like soul music, fusing the bitter truth of history with the urgency and incendiary spirit of a generation eager to be heard. He wrote from a place of passion and conviction, never passive about his belief that drama should have social impact. He used the small rebellions and conflicts of the common man in order to stage a larger conversation with history.

I found myself drawn to Miller's work because he wrote with a sense of purpose—an evangelical fervor rooted in his overarching concern about the shifting moral fault lines that threatened to fracture the foundation of American culture in the twentieth century. Indeed, Miller never backed away from the social issues of the day, mining his own misgivings and frustrations to create plays that probed the complexities of a flawed society. He had great empathy for the disaffected souls that hovered on the edges of darkness, light-seekers trying to negotiate a world that was rapidly redefining itself in the aftermath of the Depression and World War II.

There is perhaps no other playwright of his era who devoted as much time and care to dramatizing the anxieties, aspirations, and sacrifices made by men in pursuit of the elusive American dream. He understood that theater had the potential to be more than a frivolous divertissement; it could be a powerful social art, designed to instigate and unsettle, and ultimately pry people out of their complacency.

To me the theatre is not a disconnected entertainment, which it usually is
to most people here. It's the sound and the ring of the spirit of the people
at any one time. It is where a collective mass of people, through the genius
of some author, is able to project its terrors and its hopes and to symbol-
ize them.

—Arthur Miller in a speech he delivered at the University of
Michigan, February 28, 1967

Born in New York City in 1915 to Jewish parents, Miller came of age
in Brooklyn during the Depression. Throughout the 1920s, the Millers
enjoyed a relatively affluent lifestyle, but as a teenager Arthur experi-
enced the devastating impact of the stock market crash. After the failure
of his father's garment company, his family faced considerable financial
hardship. Miller witnessed, firsthand, the erosion of the American dream.
His early teenage struggles shaped his subsequent worldview. Throughout his youth Miller worked hard to make a living and eventually willed
his way into the University of Michigan, where he began to discover his
voice as a writer. Very quickly he gravitated toward theater, which at the
time was a hotbed of radical thought.

For a number of years Miller patched together a living writing radio
plays, rejecting more lucrative commercial opportunities in Hollywood
to work for the government-administered Federal Theatre Project. It's
important to note that his path to success was circuitous and not without
a few major bumps in the road. His first Broadway play in 1944, *The
Man Who Had All the Luck*, failed to excite critics and had an embar-
rassingly short run. These setbacks remind us that a playwright is shaped
not only by how one copes with success, but, also as important, how the
playwright rebounds from failure. Three years after his first Broadway
premiere, Miller finally achieved his first critical success with a highly
acclaimed production of *All My Sons* directed by Elia Kazan. It garnered
the New York Drama Critics' Circle Award and established him as a
force to be reckoned with. *All My Sons* was a realistic postwar drama
about a businessman, Joe Keller, who makes the ill-fated decision to sell
defective airplane parts to the military during World War II. His questionable action provides financial security for his company but has tragic
repercussions for his family. Keller places capitalist concerns over those
of his community, and in doing so destroys the integrity of his family. In
All My Sons, Miller begins to examine the underlying tension between
characters who are victims of their own moral shortcomings, and characters who are destroyed because of their moral convictions. These
themes will remain prominent threads running throughout his entire body
of work.

Several years after the success of *All My Sons*, Miller again tackled the
psychology of a failed businessman in the Pulitzer Prize–winning *Death*

of a Salesman. Here, Miller departs from the stark realism of *All My Sons* to engage a new theatrical vocabulary that reflects the inner turmoil of his central character, Willy Loman. He creates a dramatic structure that captures the interiority of Loman's chaotic and deteriorating mind. The past is precariously interwoven with the present, like a tenacious vine that is slowly choking the life out of its host tree. In a candid interview in the *New Yorker* Miller explains what he was seeking to dramatize in Loman's character:

> Failure in the face of surrounding success. He was the ultimate climber up the ladder who was constantly being stepped on. His fingers were being stepped on by those climbing past him.

Loman is an unfortunate idealist. He fails to evolve with the changing demands of the world, but the real tragedy lies in the fact that he is too blinded by an unattainable dream to recognize his own myopia. *Death of a Salesman* is Miller's masterwork, as it firmly established him as one of the preeminent playwrights of his era.

In the late 1940s, the House Un-American Activities Committee (HUAC) began to aggressively target the left-leaning theater community. Many in Miller's inner circle found themselves under direct attack. Instead of retreating, Miller wrote an adaptation of Henrik Ibsen's *An Enemy of the People* as a way of speaking out against the badgering and bullying of the creative and intellectual communities. The play was a resounding failure with the public. Perhaps the adaptation hit too close to home to attract mainstream Broadway audiences. Nevertheless, as the Cold War atmosphere of paranoia and fear continued to sweep the country, Miller wrote *The Crucible*, a timely allegory about the 1692 Salem witch trials. The play took as its subject the corruption of power and the insidious way in which fear can reshape a community's notion of reality. At the center is the character John Proctor, a decent man with a flawed past, who comes to recognize the hypocrisy and greed of those in power, yet refuses to give in to their demands and thereby sacrifice his integrity and good name.

> As a general rule, to which there may be exceptions unknown to me, I think the tragic feeling is evoked in us when we are in the presence of a character who is ready to lay down his life, if need be, to secure one thing—his sense of personal dignity. From Orestes to Hamlet, Medea to Macbeth, the underlying struggle is that of the individual attempting to gain his "rightful" position in his society.
>
> —Arthur Miller, "Tragedy and the Common Man,"
> *The New York Times*, February 27, 1949

Like many outspoken artists and intellectuals during the 1950s, Miller found himself subpoenaed by HUAC. The committee questioned him, but unlike several of his close friends and collaborators he refused to give the names of alleged communists. It is not surprising that personal betrayals in life and love would thematically fuel Miller's next cycle of plays. In *A View from the Bridge*, he again centered his drama around a flawed man, Eddie Carbone, whose integrity is called into question when he betrays members of his own close-knit community.

After *A View from the Bridge* it would be nearly a decade before Miller produced another successful play. In 1964, when he returned to the stage, he'd continue to experiment with form and content, writing powerful plays about imperfect men and embattled dreamers, including *After the Fall, Incident at Vichy, The American Clock, Broken Glass*, and *The Price*. Farther ahead in his career, Miller began to use more humor and satire to excoriate and question the selfishness of Americans toward the end of the twentieth century. His oft-overlooked later plays, *The Ride Down Mt. Morgan, Mr. Peters' Connections*, and *Resurrection Blues*, maintain their political edge and revisit themes of his earlier work, investigating, as he says, the "immense contradictions of the human animal"; however, they are more wistful and open-ended.

As demonstrated in this extraordinary body of work, Miller invested in a theater of ideas but never allowed himself to be subjugated by commercial demands. At times he found himself in sync with the culture at large, and at other times, he battled against the prevailing winds. Ultimately, Miller's plays have transcended time, not simply because they are beautifully crafted, but also because they are important social documents that capture moral conundrums that resonate powerfully for audiences today.

Miller's career spanned seven decades, and he remained prolific to the end of his life. Even now, when I read plays in this collection, such as *Death of a Salesman, The Crucible, A View from the Bridge*, and *Incident at Vichy*, I can feel the urgency with which he pressed the pen to page and summoned up his characters from the margins.

Over the years there have been extensive scholarship and conjecture about the meaning of Miller's work. But as a fellow playwright, I am a firm believer that his beautiful and timeless plays should speak for themselves. Part of the joy of having Miller's plays in this one glorious collection is that it permits a new generation of theater makers and thinkers to delve into the major and minor works of one of America's greatest writers and social critics. When viewed together his work forms a cohesive narrative of twentieth-century America, reflecting its contradictions and flaws. This collection reveals Miller's fierce and uncompromising com-

mitment to his ideals, to his notion that art should be in active conversation with the culture.

Each time I reach the end of *The Crucible* and read John Proctor's
final act of rebellion, I gasp not because I don't know what is coming,
but rather because I remain enthralled by the transcendent power of a
few well-selected words on the page.

> PROCTOR, *with a cry of his whole soul*: How may I live without my name?
> I have given you my soul; leave me my name!

I invite you, the next generation of theater makers, to dive into the collected plays of Arthur Miller. His work reminds us that theater should
be a place of transformation, a place where we can collectively explore
society's wounds, unearth difficult truths, and wrestle with untidy
human emotions.

Sincerely,
LYNN NOTTAGE

A Note on the Text

The texts printed in this volume are the versions preferred by Arthur Miller and should be considered authoritative texts.

The Penguin Arthur Miller

THE MAN WHO HAD ALL THE LUCK

A FABLE

1944

Characters

DAVID BEEVES

SHORY

J.B. FELLER

ANDREW FALK

PATTERSON (PAT) BEEVES

AMOS BEEVES

HESTER FALK

DAN DIBBLE

GUSTAV EBERSON

AUGIE BELFAST

AUNT BELLE

SYNOPSIS OF SCENES

THE TIME *Not so long ago.*

Act One

SCENE I
An evening in early April.
Inside a barn used as a repair shop.

SCENE II
The barn, near dawn.

Act Two

SCENE I
June. About three years later.
The living room of the Falks'—now David's—house.

SCENE II
Later that day. The living room.

Act Three

SCENE I
The following February. The living room.

SCENE II
One month later. The living room at evening.

ACT ONE

SCENE I

A barn in a small, midwestern town. It is set on a rake angle. The back wall of the barn sweeps toward upstage and right, and the big entrance doors are in this wall. Along the left wall a work bench on which auto tools lie along with some old parts and rags and general mechanic's junk. A rack over the bench holds wrenches, screwdrivers, other tools. In the left wall is a normal-sized door leading into Shory's Feed and Grain Store to which this barn is attached. A step-high ramp leads down from the threshold of this door into the barn. Further to the left, extending into the offstage area along the wall, are piles of cement bags. In front of them several new barrels that contain fertilizer.

Downstage, near the center, is a small wood stove, now glowing red. Over the bench is a hanging bulb. There is a big garage jack on the floor, several old nail barrels for chairs—two of them by the stove. A large drum of alcohol lies on blocks, downstage right. Near it are scattered a few gallon tins. This is an old barn being used partly as a storage place, and mainly as an auto repair shop. The timber supports have a warm, oak color, unstained. The colors of wood dominate the scene, and the gray of the cement bags.

Before the rise, two car horns, one of them the old-fashioned ga-goo-ga type of the old Ford, are heard honking impatiently. An instant of this and the curtain rises.

David Beeves is filling a can from an alcohol drum. He is twenty-two. He has the earnest manner of the young, small-town businessman until he forgets it, which is most of the time. Then he becomes what he is—wondrous, funny, naïve, and always searching. He wears a windbreaker.

Enter J.B. Feller from the right. He is a fat man near fifty, dressed for winter. A certain delicacy of feeling clings to his big face. He has a light way of walking despite his weight.

3

J.B.: Sure doing nice business on that alcohol, huh David? *Thumbing right*. They're freezing out there, better step on it.

DAVID: Near every car in town's been here today for some. April! What a laugh!

J.B., *nods downstage*: My store got so cold I had to close off the infant's wear counter. I think I'll get a revolving door for next winter. *Sits*. What you got your hair all slicked for?

DAVID, *on one knee, examines the spigot which pours slowly*: Going over to Hester's in a while.

J.B.: Dave! *Excitedly*: Going alone?

DAVID: Hester'll be here right away. I'm going to walk back to the house with her, and . . . well, I guess we'll lay down the law to him. If he's going to be my father-in-law I better start talking to him some time.

J.B., *anxiously*: The only thing is you want to watch your step with him.

DAVID, *turns off spigot, lifts up can as he gets to his feet*: I can't believe that he'd actually start a battle with me. You think he would?

J.B.: Old man Falk is a very peculiar man, Dave.

> *Horns sound from the right.*

DAVID, *going right with the can*: Coming, coming!

> *He goes out as from the back door, Shory descends the ramp in a fury. He is in a wheelchair. He is thirty-eight but his age is hard to tell because of the absence of any hair on his body. He is totally bald, his beard does not grow, his eyebrows are gone. His face is capable of great laughter and terrible sneers. A dark green blanket covers his legs. He stops at the big doors with his fist in the air. As he speaks the horns stop.*

SHORY: Goddamn you, shut those goddam horns! Can't you wait a god-dam minute?

J.B.: Lay off, will you? They're his customers.

SHORY, *turns*: What're you doing, living here?

J.B.: Why, got any objections? *Goes to stove, clapping his arms*. Jesus, how can he work in this place? You could hang meat in here. *Warms his hands on the stove*.

SHORY: You cold with all that fat on you?

J.B.: I don't know why everybody thinks a fat man is always warm. There's nerves in the fat too, y'know.

SHORY: Come into the store. It's warmer. Shoot some pinochle. *Starts toward the ramp to his store.*

J.B.: Dave's going over to see Falk.

Shory stops.

SHORY: Dave's not going to Falk.

J.B.: He just told me.

SHORY, *turns again*: Listen. Since the day he walked into the store and asked me for a job he's been planning on going to see Falk about Hester. That's seven years of procrastination, and it ain't going to end tonight. What is it with you lately? You hang around him like an old cow or something. What'd your wife throw you out of the house again?

J.B.: No, I don't drink anymore, not any important drinking—really. *He sits on a barrel.* I keep thinking about those two kids. It's so rare. Two people staying in love since they were children . . . that oughtn't to be trifled with.

SHORY: Your wife did throw you out, didn't she?

J.B.: No, but . . . we just got the last word: no kids.

SHORY, *compassionately*: That so, Doctor?

J.B.: Yeh, no kids. Too old. Big, nice store with thirty-one different departments. Beautiful house. No kids. Isn't that something? You die, and they wipe your name off the mail box and . . . and that's the ball game.

Slight pause.

Changing the subject; with some relish: I think I might be able to put Dave next to something very nice, Shor.

SHORY: You're in your dotage, you know that? You're getting a Santa Claus complex.

J.B.: No, he just reminds me of somebody. Myself, in fact. At his age I was in a roaring confusion. And him? He's got his whole life laid out like a piece of linoleum. I don't know why but sometimes I'm around him and it's like watching one of them nice movies, where you know everything is going to turn out good. . . . *Suddenly strikes him.* I guess it's because he's so young . . . and I'm gettin' so goddam old.

SHORY: What's this you're puttin' him next to?

J.B.: My brother-in-law up in Burley; you know, Dan Dibble that's got the mink ranch.

SHORY: Oh don't bring him around, now . . .

J.B.: Listen, his car's on the bum and he's lookin' for a mechanic. He's a sucker for a mechanic!

SHORY: That hayseed couldn't let go of a nickel if it was stuck up his . . .

> *Roar of engines starting close by outside. Enter David from the upstage door, putting a small wrench in his pocket. As he comes in two cars are heard pulling away. He goes to a can of gasoline and rinses his hands.*

DAVID: Geez, you'd think people could tighten a fan belt. What time you got, John?

SHORY: Why, where *you* going? You can't go into Falk's house . . .

> *From the store enter Aunt Belle. She is carrying a wrapped shirt and a bag. She is a woman who was never young; skinny, bird-like, constantly sniveling. A kerchief grows out of her hand.*

BELLE: I thought you were in the store. Hester said to hurry.

DAVID, *going to her*: Oh, thanks, Belle. *Unwrapping a shirt.* It's the new one, isn't it?

BELLE, *horrified*: Did you want the new one?

DAVID, *looking at the shirt*: Oh, Belle. When are you going to remember something! Hester told you to bring my new shirt!

BELLE, *lifting them out of bag*: Well I—I brought your galoshes.

DAVID: I don't wear galoshes anymore, I wanted my new shirt! Belle, sometimes you . . .

> *Belle bursts into tears.*

All right, all right, forget it.

BELLE: I only do my best, I'm not your mother . . .

DAVID, *leading her right*: I'm sorry, Aunt Belle, go—and thanks.

BELLE, *still sniffling*: Your father's got your brother Amos out running on the road . . .

DAVID: Yeah, well . . . thanks . . .

BELLE, *a kerchief at her nose*: He makes Amos put on his galoshes, why doesn't he give a thought to you?

DAVID, *pats her hand*: I'll be home later.

SHORY: You know why you never remember anything, Belle? You blow your nose too much. The nose is connected with the brain and you're blowin' your brains out.

DAVID: Ah, cut it out, will ya?

With another sob, Belle rushes out.

She still treats me like after Mom died. Just like I was seven years old. *David picks up the clean shirt.*

SHORY, *alarmed*: Listen, that man'll kill you. *Grabs the shirt and sits on it.*

DAVID, *with an embarrassed but determined laugh, trying to grab the shirt back*: Give me that. I decided to go see him, and I'm going to see him!

Enter Pat and Amos from right. Pat is a small, nervous man about forty-five, Amos is twenty-four, given to a drawl and a tendency to lumber when he walks.

PAT, *on entering*: What's the matter with you?

David looks up. All turn to him as both come center. Amos is squeezing a rubber ball.

Pointing between David and stove: Don't you know better than to stand so close to that stove? Heat is ruination to the arteries.

AMOS, *eagerly*: You goin', Dave?

SHORY, *to Pat*: Everything was getting clear. Will you go home?

PAT: I'm his father, if you please.

SHORY: Then tell him what to do, father.

PAT: I'll tell him. *Turns to David as though to command.* What exactly did you decide?

DAVID: We're going to tell Mr. Andrew Falk we're getting married.

PAT: Uh, huh. Good work.

SHORY: Good work! *Pointing at Pat, he turns to J.B.* Will you listen to this . . . !

J.B.—*he shares Shory's attitude toward Pat, but with more compassion*: But somebody ought to go along with him.

PAT, *adamantly to David*: Definitely, somebody ought to go along . . .

AMOS, *to David*: Let me go. If he starts anything, I'll . . .

DAVID, *to all*: Now look, for Christ's sake, will you . . .

PAT, *to David*: I forbid you to curse. Close your collar, Amos. *Of Amos to J.B.*: Just ran two miles. *He buttons another button on Amos, indicating Amos's ball.* How do you like the new method?

AMOS, *holds up ball*: Squeezin' a rubber ball.

J.B.: What's that, for his fingers, heh?

  David examines his arm.

PAT: Fingers! That's the old forearm. A pitcher can have everything, but without a forearm?—Zero!

SHORY, *to Pat, of Dave*: Are you going to settle this or is he going to get himself murdered in that house?

PAT: Who? What house? *Recalling*: Oh yes, Dave . . .

SHORY, *to J.B.*: Oh yes, Dave! *To Pat*: You're his father, for G . . . !

DAVID: All right. I got enough advice. Hester's coming here right away and we're going over to the house and we'll talk it out, and if . . .

SHORY: His brains are busted, how are you going to talk to him? He doesn't like you, he doesn't want you, he said he'd shoot you if you came onto his place. Now will you start from there and figure it out or you going to put it together in the hospital? *Pause.*

DAVID: What am I supposed to do then? Let him send her to that normal school? I might never see her again. I know how these things work.

SHORY: You don't know how these things work. Two years I waited in there for a boy to ask for the job I put up in the window. I could've made a big stink about it. I was a veteran, people ought to explain to the kids why I looked like this. But I learned something across the sea. Never go lookin' for trouble. I waited. And you came. Wait, Davey.

PAT: I'm inclined to agree with him, David.

DAVID: I've been waiting to marry Hester since we were babies. *Sits on a barrel.* God! How do you know when to wait and when to take things in your hand and make them happen?

SHORY: You can't make anything happen any more than a jellyfish makes the tides, David.

DAVID: What do you say, John?

J.B.: I'd hate to see you battle old man Falk, but personally, Dave, I don't believe in waiting too long. A man's got to have faith, I think, and push right out into the current, and . . .

PAT, *leans forward, pointing*: Faith, David, is a great thing. Take me for instance. When I came back from the sea . . .

DAVID: What time you got, John . . . excuse me, Dad.

J.B.: Twenty to eight.

DAVID, *to Shory*: You giving me that shirt or must I push you off that chair?

PAT, *continuing*: I am speaking, David. When I came back from the sea . . .

SHORY, *pointing at Amos*: Before you come back from the sea, you're going to kill him, running his ass off into the snow.

PAT: Kill him! Why it's common knowledge that pacing is indispensable for the arches. After all, a pitcher can have everything, but if his arches are not perfect . . . ?

SHORY: Zero!

PAT: Before I forget, do you know if that alcohol can be used for rubbing? *Indicates the drum.*

DAVID: There's only a couple of drops left.

AMOS: You sold it all today? *Joyously to Pat*: I told you he'd sell it all!

DAVID: Don't go making a genius out of your brother. Salesman hooked him. He bought alcohol in April when the sun was shining hot as hell.

AMOS: Yeah, but look how it froze up today!

SHORY: *He* didn't know it was going to freeze.

J.B.: Maybe he did know. *To Dave*: Did you, Dave?

DAVID, *stares into his memory*: Well, I . . . I kinda thought . . .

PAT, *breaking in*: Speaking of geniuses, most people didn't know that there are two kinds; physical and mental. Take pitchers like Christy Mathewson now. Or Walter Johnson. There you have it in a nutshell. Am I right, J.B.?

SHORY: What've you got in a nutshell?

PAT—*the beginnings of confusion, his desire to protect Amos and himself against everyone, tremble in him*: Just what I said. People simply refuse to concentrate. They don't know what they're supposed to be doing in their lives.

SHORY, *pointing to David*: Example number one.

PAT, *rises to a self-induced froth of a climax*: I always left David to concentrate for himself. But take Amos then. When I got back from the sea I came home and what do I find? An infant in his mother's arms. I felt his body and I saw it was strong. And I said to myself, this boy is not going to waste out his life being seventeen different kind of things and ending up nothing. He's going to play baseball. And by ginger he's been throwin' against the target down the cellar seven days a week for twelve solid years! That's concentration. That's faith! That's taking your life in your own hands and molding it to fit the thing you want. That's bound to have an effect . . . and don't you think they don't know it!

SHORY: Who knows it?

PAT, *with a cry*: I don't like everybody's attitude! *Silence an instant. All staring at him.* It's still winter! Can he play in the winter?

SHORY: Who are you talking about?

DAVID, *going away—toward the right—bored and disgusted*: Dad, he didn't say . . .

PAT: He doesn't have to say it. You people seem to think he's going to go through life pitching Sundays in the sand lots. *To all*: Pitching's his business; it's a regular business like . . . like running a store, or being a mechanic or anything else. And it happens that in the winter there is nothing to do in his business but sit home and wait!

J.B.: Well, yeh, Pat, that's just what he ought to be doing.

PAT: Then why does everybody look at him as though . . . ?

> He raises his hand to his head, utterly confused and ashamed for his outburst. A long pause like this.

DAVID, *unable to bear it, he goes to Pat*: Sit down, Dad. Sit down. *He gets a barrel under Pat, who sits, staring, exhausted.*

PAT: I can't understand it. Every paper in the country calls him a phenomenon.

> As he speaks, David, feeling Pat's pain, goes right a few yards and stands looking away.

> Undefeated. He's ready for the big leagues. Been ready for three years. Who can explain a thing like that? Why don't they send a scout?

DAVID: I been thinking about that, Dad. Maybe you ought to call the Detroit Tigers again.

AMOS, *peevishly. This has been in him a long time*: He never called them in the first place.

PAT: Now, Amos . . .

DAVID, *reprimanding*: Dad . . .

AMOS: He didn't. He didn't call them. *To Pat*: I want him to know!

DAVID, *to Pat*: But last summer you said . . .

PAT: I've picked up the phone a lot of times . . . but I . . . I wanted it to happen . . . naturally. It ought to happen naturally, Dave.

SHORY: You mean you don't want to hear them say no.

PAT: Well . . . yes, I admit that. *To David*: If I call now and demand an answer, maybe they'll have to say no. I don't want to put that word in their head in relation to Amos. It's a great psychological thing there. Once they refuse it's twice as hard to get them to accept.

DAVID: But, Dad, maybe . . . maybe they forgot to send a scout. Maybe they even thought they'd sent one and didn't, and when you call they'll thank you for reminding them. *To all*: I mean . . . can you *just wait for something to happen?*

SHORY, *claps*: Pinochle? Let's go. Come on, John! Pat!

They start for the store door.

J.B., *glancing at his watch*: My wife'll murder me.

SHORY: Why? Pinochle leaves no odor on the breath.

PAT, *turning at ramp*: I want you to watch us, Amos. Pinochle is very good for the figuring sense. Help you on base play. Open your coat.

Pat follows Shory and J.B. into the store. Amos dutifully starts to follow, hesitates at the door, then closes it behind them and comes to David.

AMOS: Dave, I want to ask you something. *He glances toward the door, then quietly*: Take me over, will ya? *Dave just looks at him.* Do something for me. I'm standing still. I'm not going anywhere. I swear I'm gettin' ashamed.

DAVID: Ah, don't, don't, Ame.

AMOS: No, I am. Since I started to play everybody's been saying, *Mimics*: "Amos is goin' someplace, Amos is goin' someplace." I been out of high school five years and I'm still taking spending money. I want to find a girl. I want to get married. I want to start doing things. You're movin' like a daisy cutter, Dave, you know how to *do*. Take me over.

DAVID: But I don't know half what Pop knows about baseball . . . about training or . . .

AMOS: I don't care, you didn't know anything about cars either, and look what you made here.

DAVID: What'd I make? I got nothin'. I still don't know anything about cars.

AMOS: But you do. Everybody knows you know . . .

DAVID: Everybody's crazy. Don't envy me, Ame. If every car I ever fixed came rolling in here tomorrow morning and the guys said I did it wrong

I wouldn't be surprised. I started on Shory's Ford and I got another one and another, and before I knew what was happening they called me a mechanic. But I ain't a trained man. You are. You *got* something . . . *Takes his arm, with deepest feeling*: and you're going to be great. Because you deserve it. You know something perfect. Don't look to me, I could be out on that street tomorrow morning, and then I wouldn't look so smart. . . . Don't laugh at Pop. You're his whole life, Ame. You hear me? You stay with him.

AMOS: Gee, Dave . . . you always make me feel so good. *Suddenly like Pat, ecstatic*: When I'm in the Leagues I'm gonna buy you . . . a . . . a whole goddam garage!

> *Enter Hester from the right. She is a full-grown girl, a heartily developed girl. She can run fast, swim hard, and lift heavy things—not stylishly—with the most economical and direct way to run, swim and lift. She has a loud, throaty laugh. Her femininity dwells in one fact—she loves David with all her might, always has, and she doesn't feel she's doing anything when he's not around. The pallor of tragedy is nowhere near her. She enters breathless, not from running but from expectation.*

HESTER: David, he's home. *Goes to David and cups his face in her hands.* He just came back! You ready? *Looks around David's shoulder at Amos.* Hullo, Ame, how's the arm?

AMOS: Good as ever.

HESTER: You do that long division I gave you?

AMOS: Well, I been working at it.

HESTER: There's nothing better'n arithmetic to sharpen you up. You'll see, when you get on the diamond again, you'll be quicker on base play. We better go, David.

AMOS, *awkwardly*: Well . . . good luck to ya. *He goes to the store door.*

DAVID: Thanks, Ame.

> *Amos waves, goes through the door and closes it behind him.*

HESTER: What're you looking so pruney about? Don't you want to go?

DAVID: I'm scared, Hess. I don't mind tellin' you. I'm scared.

HESTER: Of a beatin'?

DAVID: You know I was never scared of a beatin'.

HESTER: We always knew we'd have to tell him, didn't we?

DAVID: Yeh, but I always thought that by the time we had to, I'd be some-body. You know . . .

HESTER: But you are somebody . . .

DAVID: But just think of it from his side. He's a big farmer, a hundred and ten of the best acres in the county. Supposing he asks me—I only got three hundred and ninety-four dollars, counting today . . .

HESTER: But we always said, when you had three fifty we'd ask him.

DAVID: God, if I was a lawyer, or a doctor, or even a bookkeeper . . .

HESTER: A mechanic's good as a bookkeeper!

DAVID: Yeh . . . but I don't know if I am a mechanic. *Takes her hand.* Hess, listen, in a year maybe I could build up some kind of a real busi-ness, something he could look at and see.

HESTER: A year! Davey, don't . . . don't you . . . ?

DAVID: I mean . . . let's get married now, without asking him.

HESTER: I told you, I can't . . .

DAVID: If we went away . . . far, far away . . .

HESTER: Wherever we went, I'd always be afraid he'd knock on the door. You don't know what he can do when he's mad. He roared my mother to her grave. . . . We have to face him with it, Davey. It seems now that I've known it since we were babies. When I used to talk to you at night through the kitchen window, when I'd meet you to ride around the quarry in Shory's car; even as far back as *The Last of the Mohicans* in 6B. I always knew we'd have to sit in the house together and listen to him roaring at us. We have to, Davey. *She steps away, as though to give him a choice.*

DAVID—*he smiles, a laugh escapes him*: You know, Hess, I don't only love you. You're my best friend.

> *Hester springs at him and kisses him. They are locked in the embrace when a figure enters from the right. It is Dan Dibble, a little sun-dried farmer, stolidly dressed—a mackinaw, felt hat. He hesitates a moment, then . . .*

DIBBLE: Excuse me . . . J.B. Feller . . . is J.B. Feller in here?

DAVID: J.B.? Sure. *Points at back door.* Go through there . . . he's in the store.

DIBBLE: Much obliged.

DAVID: That's all right, sir.

Dibble tips his hat slightly to Hester, goes a few yards toward the door, turns.

DIBBLE: You . . . you Dave Beeves? Mechanic?

DAVID: Yes, sir, that's me.

Dibble nods, turns, goes up the ramp and into the store, closing door behind him. David looks after him.

HESTER: Come, Davey.

DAVID: Yeh. I'll get my coat. *He goes to rail at back where it hangs, starts to put it on.* Gosh, I better change my shirt. Shory grabbed my clean one before. I guess he took it into the store with him.

HESTER, *knowingly*: He doesn't think you ought to go.

DAVID: Well . . . he was just kiddin' around. I'll only be a minute.

Dave starts for the store door when it opens and J.B. surges out full of excitement. Dibble follows him, then Amos, then Pat, and finally Shory who looks on from his wheelchair above the ramp.

J.B.: Hey, Dave! Dave, come here. *To Dan*: You won't regret it, Dan . . . Dave . . . want you to meet my brother-in-law from up in Burley. Dan Dibble.

DAVID: Yes, sir, how de do.

J.B.: Dan's got a brand new Marmon . . . he's down here for a funeral, see, and he's staying at my house . . .

DAVID, *to J.B. A note of faltering*: Marmon, did you say?

J.B.: Yeh, Marmon. *Imperatively*: You know the Marmon, Dave.

DAVID: Sure, ya . . . *To Dan*: Well, bring it around. I'll be glad to work on her. I've got to go right now . . .

J.B.: Dan, will you wait in my car? Just want to explain a few things. I'll be right out and we'll go.

DIBBLE: Hurry up. It's cold out there. I'd like him to get it fixed up by tomorrow. It's shakin' me up so, I think I'm gettin' my appendix back.

J.B., *jollying him to the door*: I don't think they grow back once they're cut out . . .

DIBBLE: Well it feels like it. Be damned if I'll ever buy a Marmon again. *Dibble goes out.*

J.B.—*he comes back to Dave*: This idiot is one of the richest farmers in the Burley district. . . . He's got that mink ranch I was tellin' you about.

DAVID: Say, I don't know anything about a Marmon . . .

J.B.: Neither does he. He's got two vacuum cleaners in his house and never uses nothin' but a broom. Now listen. He claims she ain't hitting right. I been tryin' the past two weeks to get him to bring her down here to you. Now get this. Besides the mink ranch he's got a wheat farm with five tractors.

HESTER: Five tractors!

J.B.: He's an idiot, but he's made a fortune out of mink. Now you clean up this Marmon for him and you'll open your door to the biggest tractor farms in the state. There's big money in tractor work, you know that. He's got a thousand friends and they follow him. They'll follow him here.

DAVID: Uh, huh. But I don't know anything about tractors.

HESTER: Oh, heck, you'll learn!

DAVID: Yeah, but I can't learn on his tractors.

HESTER: Yeah, but . . .

J.B.: Listen! This could be the biggest thing that ever happened to you. The Marmon's over at my house. He's afraid to drive her any further on the snow. I'll bring her over and you'll go to work. All right?

DAVID: Yeah, but look, John, I . . .

J.B.: You better get in early and start on her first thing in the morning. All right?

HESTER, *with a loud bubble of laughter*: David, that's wonderful!

DAVID, *quickly*: See, if we waited, Hess. In six months, maybe less, I'd have something to show!

HESTER: But I'm going to Normal in a week if we don't do it now!

SHORY: You're pushing him, Hester.

HESTER—*a sudden outburst at Shory*: Stop talking to him! A person isn't a frog, to wait and wait for something to happen!

SHORY: He'll fight your father if you drag him there tonight! And your father can kill him!

DAVID, *takes her hand. Evenly*: Come on, Hess. We'll go. *To J.B.*: Bring the car over, I'll be back later . . .

> But J.B. is staring off right, down the driveway. Dave turns, with Hester and all to follow his stare. She steps a foot away from him. Enter Andrew Falk, a tall, old man, hard as iron, nearsighted, slightly stooped. Sound of idling motor outside.

J.B., *after a moment*: I'll bring the car, Dave. Five minutes.

DAVID, *affecting a businesslike, careless flair*: Right, J.B., I'll fix him up. *As J.B. goes out*: And thanks loads, John!

> *Falk has been looking at Hester, who dares every other moment to look up from the floor at him. David turns to Falk, desperately controlling his voice. Pat enters from Shory's store.*

Evening, Mr. Falk. You want to go in to Shory's store? There's chairs there. . . . *Falk turns deliberately, heavily looks at him.* You left your engine running. Stay awhile. Let me shut it off.

FALK: You willin' to push it?

DAVID: Oh, battery run down?

FALK, *caustically*: I don't know what else would prevent her from turnin' over without a push. *To Hester*: I'll see you home.

HESTER, *smiling, she goes to him, but does not touch him*: We were just comin' to the house, Daddy.

FALK: Go on home, Hester.

DAVID: We'd like to talk to you, Mr. Falk. *Indicating the store*: We could all go . . .

FALK, *in reply*: Go on home, Hester.

DAVID, *with a swipe at indignation*: I'd like for her to be here, Mr. Falk . . .

FALK—*he does not even look at David*: I'll be home right away. *He takes her arm and moves her to the right. She digs her heels in.*

HESTER—*a cry*: Daddy, why . . . !

> *She breaks off, looking into his face. With a sob she breaks from him and runs off right. He turns slowly to David, takes a breath.*

DAVID, *angering*: That ain't gonna work any more, Mr. Falk. We're old enough now.

PAT, *reasonably*: Look, Falk, why don't we . . . ?

FALK, *to David, without so much as a glance at Pat*: This is the last time I'm ever goin' to talk to you, Beeves. You . . .

DAVID: Why is it you're the only man who hates me like this? Everybody else . . .

FALK: Nobody but me knows what you are.

SHORY, *from the store doorway*: What is he? What are you blowin' off about?

FALK, *his first rise of voice. He points at Shory*: The good God gave you your answer long ago! Keep your black tongue in your head when I'm here.

SHORY, *nervously. To David*: His brains are swimmin', don't you see? What are you botherin' with him for . . . !

FALK—*roaring, he takes a stride toward Shory*: Shut up, you . . . you whoremonger! You ruined your last woman on *this* earth! The good God saw to that.

SHORY, *with a screech of fury*: You don't scare me, Falk. You been dead twenty years, why don't you bury yourself?

> *Falk strangely relaxes, walks away from Shory's direction, raising his shoulder to run his chin on his coat collar. The motor outside stalls. His head cocks toward right.*

DAVID, *pointing to the right*: Your car stalled. I'll start her up for you.

FALK: Don't touch anything I own! *Pause.* What were you doin' that night I caught you with her by the river? You got backbone enough to tell me that?

DAVID, *recalls*: Oh . . . we were kids then . . . just talkin', that's all.

FALK: You never come and ask me if she could talk to you. You come sneakin' every time, like a rat through the fences.

DAVID: Well . . . Hess was always scared to ask you, and I . . . I guess I got it from her.

FALK: You're scared of me now too, and you know why, Beeves? Nobody but me knows what you are.

DAVID: Why, what am I?

FALK: You're a lost soul, a lost man. You don't know the nights I've watched you, sittin' on the river ice, fishin' through a hole—alone, alone like an old man with a boy's face. Or makin' you a fire in Keldon's woods where nobody could see. And that Sunday night you nearly burned down the church . . .

DAVID: I was nowhere near the church that night . . . !

FALK: It couldn't have been nobody else! When the church burned there never was a sign from God that was so clear.

AMOS: He was down in the cellar with me when the church burned.

FALK, *looks at Amos*: I am not blind. *Turns back to David.* The man Hester marries is gonna know what he's about. He's gonna be a steady man that I can trust with what I brought forth in this world. He's gonna know his God, he's gonna know where he came from and where he's goin'. You ain't that man. *He turns to go.*

DAVID: I'm marryin' Hester, Mr. Falk. *Falk stops, turns.* I'm sorry, but we're going to marry.

FALK: Beeves, if you ever step onto my land again, I'll put a bullet through you, may God write my words . . . I don't fool, Beeves. Don't go near her again. *Points to Shory.* No man who could find a friend in that lump of corruption is going to live in my daughter's house. *He starts to go again.*

DAVID: I'm marryin' Hester, Mr. Falk! We're gonna do it!

FALK: You'll sleep with your shroud first, Beeves. I'm old enough to know what I'll do. Stay away!

> He goes to the right edge of the stage, and hesitates, looking off right in the direction of his stalled car. David starts doubt-fully toward him, looking over his shoulder.

SHORY, *rolling down the ramp*: Let him start it himself! Don't be a damned fool!

> *Falk hurries out.*

PAT, *pointing right*: Maybe you ought to give him a push.

SHORY: Not on your life! *He pushes himself between Dave and the door.* Get away from there, go on!

DAVID, *looking off right all the time*: Shory . . . he's going . . . what can I say to him . . . *Starts to go right.* I'll help him.

SHORY, *pushes him back*: Get away! *Calling off right.* That's it, Grandpa, push it . . . push it! Harder, you crazy bastard, it's only half a mile! Go ahead, harder! *Laughs wildly, mockingly.*

DAVID, *wrenches the chair around*: Stop it!

SHORY: You can't talk to that man! You're through, you damned fool.

DAVID, *suddenly*: Come on, Ame, we'll pick up Hester on the road before he gets home. I'm going to do it tonight, by God . . .

AMOS, *in ecstasy at the thought of action, he wings the ball across the stage*: Let's go!

PAT, *grabs David*: No, Dave . . .

DAVID, *furiously*: No, I gotta do it, Dad!

PAT: I forbid it. *To Amos*: I forbid you to go. *To David*: She's his daughter and he's got a right, David.

DAVID: What right has he got! *She* wants me!

PAT: Then let her break from him. That's not your province.

DAVID: She's scared to death of him! The whole thing is between me and Hester. *I don't understand why I can't have that girl!*

SHORY, *sardonically*: Must there be a reason?

DAVID—*he stops for an instant as though a light flashed on him*: Yes, there has to be a reason! I did everything a man could do. *I didn't do anything wrong and . . .*

SHORY: You didn't have to! *Dave stares at Shory.* A man is a jellyfish. The tide goes in and the tide goes out. About what happens to him, a man has very little to say. When are you going to get used to it?

> *David stands staring.*

PAT: You better go home and sleep, Dave. Sleep is a great doctor, you know.

SHORY, *gently*: He said it, Dave.

> *Enter J.B. in a hurry.*

J.B.: Where is Dan? Where's the Marmon?

PAT: He didn't come here.

J.B.: That ox! I tell him I'll drive it over for him. No, Dan Dibble don't allow anybody behind the wheel but himself. I go into the house to tell Ellie I'm goin' and when I come out he's gone. *Starts to go right.* That seven passenger moron . . .

DAVID: He probably decided to go back home to Burley.

J.B.: No, I'm sure he's tryin' to get here. Rugged individualist! I'll find him on some dirt road some place . . . *He shuts up abruptly as a door slams outside.*

> *All look right.*

DAVID, *alarmed*: Hester!

> *He quickly goes off right. For an instant Amos, Pat, and Shory are galvanized. Amos goes off and returns immediately supporting Dan Dibble who is shaking all over and seems about to collapse in distress.*

DIBBLE, *on entering*: God help me, God in Heaven help me . . .

> *Enter David and J.B. helping Hester. She is sobbing on David's arm and he's trying to lift her face up.*

DAVID: Stop crying, what's the matter? Hester, stop it, what happened? J.B.!

DIBBLE, *goes prayerfully to Hester*: I couldn't see him, Miss, how in the world could I see him? His car had no lights . . . *Hester's loud sob cuts him off.*

DAVID, *to Dan*: What happened? What did you do?

DIBBLE: Oh, God in Heaven, help me . . .

J.B., *goes to him, pulls his hands down*: Dan . . . stop that. . . . For Pete's sake, what happened?

DIBBLE: This girl's father . . . an old man . . . I couldn't see him . . . He was pushing a car without lights. There were no lights at all, and he walked out from behind just as I came on him.

> But for Hester's subsiding sobs, there is silence for a moment. She looks at David, who looks once at her, then comes to life.

DAVID, *to Dan*: Where is he now?

DIBBLE, *points upstage*: I took him to his house . . . she was there. It happened a few feet from his house.

DAVID, *horrified*: Well, why didn't you get a doctor! *He starts for the back door.*

HESTER: No . . . he's dead, Davey.

> Almost at the ramp, David stops as though shot. After an instant he turns quickly. He comes as in a dream a few yards toward her, and, as in a dream, halts, staring at her.

He's dead.

> David stares at her. Then turns his head to Pat, Amos, Shory, Dan . . . as though to seek reality. Then looking at her once more he goes to the nail barrel and sits.

DAVID, *whisper*: I'll be darned. *Goes to Hester . . . after a moment*: I'm so sorry.

HESTER: It was nobody's fault. Oh that poor man!

PAT, *goes to David*: You better . . . come home, David.

DAVID—*he gets up, goes to Hester, takes her hand*: Hess? I really am sorry.

> Hester looks at him, a smile comes to her face. She thankfully throws her arms around him and sobs.

Don't, Hess . . . don't cry anymore. Please, Hess . . . John, take her to your house for tonight, heh?

J.B.: I was going to do that. *Takes Hester's arm.* Come on, baby. I'll tend to everything.

DAVID: Goodnight, Hess. You sleep, heh?

HESTER: You mustn't feel any fault, Davey.

DAVID: I could have gotten him started, that's all. He said . . . *A filament of sardonic laughter.* . . . don't touch anything I own.

HESTER: It wasn't your fault! You understand? In any way.

DAVID, *nods inconclusively*: Go to bed, go ahead.

J.B., *leading Hester off*: We'll get you home, and you'll sleep.

DIBBLE—*Dan follows them until he gets to the right edge. Turning to David*: If there's any blood on the car will you clean it off? Please, will you?

   Dan goes, David looks after them.

SHORY: Get me home, will you, Dave?

DAVID: Huh? No, I'll stay awhile. I want to look at the car. You take him, will you, Dad?

PAT, *taking hold of the back of Shory's chair*: Sure. Come on, Amos.

SHORY: Well, wake up, jellyfish. A hundred and ten of the best acres in the valley. Not bad, eh?

DAVID, *stunned*: Just like that.

SHORY: Never happens any other way, brother. *Almost intones it*: Jellyfish don't swim. . . . It's the tide moves him . . . out and in . . . out and in . . . and in. Keep it in mind. *To Pat*: Let's go, father.

   They push him out as David stands there lost in a dream.

CURTAIN

SCENE II

The barn near dawn.

David is lying under the front end of the Marmon. Beside it the hood stands on end on the floor. David is lying under the engine with one light near his head, hurriedly tightening a nut on the pan. There is one other light on, over the bench, but this is shaded. After a moment, David hurriedly slides out from under and eagerly looking at the engine, wipes his hands. He is about to get into the car to start it when a soft knock from offstage right is heard. Startled, he peers through the darkness.

DAVID: Who's that? *Surprised*: Hester . . .

HESTER—*she comes out of the darkness at right*: Aren't you finished yet?

DAVID, *glancing defensively at the car*: What are you doing up? What time is it?

HESTER: It's almost five. I called your house, I just couldn't sleep. Belle said you were still here. Can I watch you?

DAVID: . . . It's pretty cold in here, you'll catch cold.

HESTER—*she goes to him, takes his face in her hands, and kisses him*: You didn't kiss me yet.

DAVID, *with growing ill-ease*: Please, Hess, I gotta figure something out here. I wish . . . I wish you'd leave me alone for a while. Please.

HESTER, *with quiet astonishment—and compassion*: Haven't you figured it out yet?

DAVID: Oh, I got it just about, but not . . . *Stops.* Hess, please leave me alone.

    David walks from her and pretends to study the engine.

HESTER: Davey.

DAVID: Ya?

HESTER: You're *going* to be able to fix it, aren't you?

DAVID: Don't you think I can?

HESTER: I know you can.

DAVID: Then why do you ask me?

HESTER: Because . . . in the Burley garage they didn't know how to fix it.

DAVID—*he straightens. Slight pause*: How do you know?

HESTER: J.B. told me. He's going to tell you in the morning after you're finished. He didn't want to scare you about it.

DAVID, *with growing fear*: That can't be. They got regular trained mechanics in the Burley garage.

HESTER: But it's true. Mr. Dibble said they wanted to take the whole thing apart and charge him a hundred and fifty dollars, and he wouldn't let them because . . .

DAVID, *comes to her anxiously*: Why'd they want to take the whole thing apart?

HESTER, *seeing his bewilderment clearer*: Well, I don't know, Davey . . .

DAVID: Well, what'd they tell him was wrong? Don't you remember . . . ?

HESTER, *her sob threatening*: Well, Davey, don't shout at me that way, I don't know anything about cars . . . *She begins to cry.*

DAVID, *with the pain of guilt*: Oh, Hester, don't cry, please. I'll fix it, I'll find out what the matter is, please, stop it, will you? *The pain it causes him makes him turn and almost march to the car. On the point of weeping himself.*

> I never *heard* an engine make that sound. I took the pan off, I took the head off, I looked at the valves; I just don't know what it is, Hess! It's turning off-center somewhere and I can't find it, I can't!

HESTER—*her sobbing vanishes as she senses his loss*: That's all right, Davey, it'll be all right. Maybe you better go to bed. You look so tired. . . . It really doesn't matter so much.

DAVID—*she growing taller upon his guilt*: Gosh, Hess . . . there never was a girl like you. *He goes to her and kisses her.* I swear there never was.

HESTER: Don't ever try for anything I want, if it worries you too much to get it, Davey.

DAVID—*he kisses her cheek. With swift resolution*: You go home and go to bed. I'll find out what's the matter. I'll do it! You go.

HESTER: All right, Davey, 'cause J.B. was telling Mr. Dibble such great things about you. . . . He's got a marvelous thing to tell you in the morning.

DAVID: What?

HESTER: I can't tell you till you finish . . .

DAVID: Please, Hess, what'd he say?

HESTER: No, fix it first. *Pause.* J.B. wants to tell you himself. He made me promise. Goodnight.

DAVID: Goodnight, Hess.

HESTER, *going and waving*: And don't worry . . . about anything, okay?

DAVID: . . . I won't.

> *He watches her go, then turns to the car, goes and stands over it, tapping his nose with his finger thoughtfully. Then*

lightly punching his fist into his palm in the heartbeat rhythm, faster, then faster . . . then . . . bursting out in loud whisper.

God damn!

The sound of a man walking into the shop rather slowly from offstage right is heard. David turns toward the sound and stands still watching. Gustav Eberson enters. He is a strong man, his suit is pressed but too small for him. He wears a white shirt. A plain brown overcoat. He is smiling warmly, but with the self-effacing manner of an intruder. David says nothing as he approaches.

GUS, *a slight German accent*: Excuse me, are you Mr. Beeves?

DAVID: Yeh. *Slight pause.*

GUS: My name is Eberson . . . Gus Eberson . . . *With an apologetic nod and smile*: Are you very busy? I could of course come back. Four o'clock in the morning is not the best time to visit.

DAVID: I'm busy . . . but what can I do for you?

GUS: I moved into town last night. And I couldn't wait to see my first morning. I noticed your light. I thought we ought to know each other.

DAVID, *taken*: I'm glad to know you. I was almost hoping you were a hold-up man and you'd knock me unconscious.

GUS: I didn't mean to walk in so invisibly; I am opening a repair garage on the other end of the avenue.

DAVID: Repair garage? You mean to repair cars?

GUS, *earnestly, worriedly*: I want to assure you, Mr. Beeves, that if I didn't think there is plenty of business here for both of us I would never set up a place in this town.

DAVID—*a faint tightness cramps his voice*: Oh, there's plenty of business for two here. Plenty! Where is your shop?

GUS: Over there on Poplar Street, right next to the grocery store.

DAVID: Oh, that place. Gosh, nobody's been in that building for years. We used to say it was haunted.

GUS: Maybe it is! *Laughs lightly at himself.* I have very little machinery. As a matter of fact . . . *Quite happily*: . . . I have very little money too. So possibly I will not be troubling you very long.

DAVID, *with emphatic assurance*: Oh, you'll make out all right. *Vaguely indicates the shop.* There's nothing to it. You come from around here?

GUS: No, I was with the Ford's Company, the River Rouge plant for several years. This last year and four months I was by the Hudson Motor people.

DAVID, *breathlessly*: Well . . . I guess you oughta know your stuff.

GUS, *sensing . . . extra hearty, therefore*: What is there to know? You are probably much better than I am!

DAVID: No, that's all right, I just meant . . .

GUS: I am not in the world to become rich. I was doing very well in Detroit.

DAVID: Then why'd you come here?

GUS: It is my nature. I cannot get used, I shall run, run, run, I shall work, work, work, all the time rushing. To tell you the truth, I was five years with Ford's and not one good friend did I have. Here, I hope, it will be more conducive to such activities as I always enjoy. A small town and so forth. I am Austrian, you understand. . . . Meanwhile I hope you will not object too strongly of my arrival?

DAVID, *entranced*: Hell no. Lots of luck to you! I got no right to object. *Extends his hand jerkily.*

GUS—*shakes hands*: Rights is not the question. I want to be welcome. Otherwise I will . . .

DAVID, *softly; Gus holds on to his hand*: No. . . . You're welcome here. . . . You are.

GUS: Thank you. . . . Thank you.

> *Laughs softly, thankfully. Their hands part. Gus turns a slow full circle looking at the shop. David watches him like a vision. At last the Austrian faces him again. Quietly.*

How old are you?

DAVID: Goin' on twenty-two.

GUS, *indicating the car, the shop . . . everything*: How . . . how did you know what to do? You studied somewhere mechanics?

DAVID, *with pride and yet uneasiness. The Austrian has grown very tall in his eyes*: Oh no—I just picked it up kinda. *Wanders near the Marmon as though to hide it.* But I guess I got plenty to learn.

GUS: No, no! The best mechanics is made in this fashion. You must not feel at all . . . how shall I say . . . at a loss.

> *Pause. They hold each other's gaze in a moment of understanding. Slowly the Austrian's eyes turn toward the Marmon.*

David, as though relinquishing it, moves aside now, not screening it any longer.

What's his trouble?

DAVID, *still entranced, and yet he must laugh as he confesses*: You got me there. I've been at it all night . . .

GUS, *sauntering easily to the car*: Oh? What he complains of?

DAVID—*for a moment he holds back; then the last shred of resentment fades and he bursts out*: She runs with a peculiar kind of a shudder . . . like a rubbing somewhere inside.

GUS: She misfires?

DAVID: That's what's so funny. She fires on eight and the carburetor's set right on the button.

> *Pause. Gus looks down at the engine. David is bent over watching his face.*

GUS: If you . . . feel like it, you can start the engine.

DAVID, *looks at him in silence*: You . . . you know what it is?

GUS, *reaches to him quickly*: Look, boy, tell me and I will leave the town, I'll never come back.

DAVID: No, no . . . I want it to be . . . just the way it ought to be, the way it . . . happened.

> *David goes to the car door, gets in—starts the motor. The Austrian stands listening for five seconds, then snaps his hand for the motor to be switched off. It is quiet again. David comes slowly out of the car and stands beside the Austrian, watching him.*

GUS: It is very rare. In a car so new. It comes sometimes with the Marmon, however.

DAVID, *softly*: What is it?

GUS, *turns straight to him*: The crankshaft is sprung.

DAVID—*for a long moment he stares into the Austrian's face*: How could you tell by listening?

GUS: Same way you do for pistons. You know. You going to work now?

DAVID, *looks at the car*: Ya.

> *He hurries around the front of the car, picks up a wrench, comes around and sets the wrench on a heat nut and starts forcing it.*

GUS—*hesitates for a moment, then lays his hand on David*: Don't take the head off. *David stops.* I mean . . . you don't need to, necessarily. *David stops moving. The wrench clatters out of his hand. He stands nearly trembling before the Austrian, who suddenly turns.* I'll go.

DAVID, *stops him*: No, I always knew a time would come when . . . this would happen. I mean somebody like you would come, and then I'd just . . . pack up. I knew it all the time . . .

GUS: That's nonsense. You fixed plenty cars no doubt; you're a mechanic . . .

DAVID: No, I'm not really. I don't know anything about metals and ratios and . . . I was almost going to tow it to the shop in Newton. Would you tell me what to do?

GUS: Gladly. And maybe sometimes I need a hand you'll drop by. All right?

DAVID: Oh I'd be glad to.

GUS, *grips his shoulder and points under the car*: First you take the pan down.

DAVID—*slight pause*: Ya?

GUS: Then you drop the bearings. Label them so you know where to put them back.

DAVID: Ya?

GUS: Then you drop the main bearings for the crankshaft.

DAVID: Ya?

GUS: Then you drop the shaft itself. Take it up to Newton, is a good shop there. Tell them to exchange for a new shaft.

DAVID: Can't I straighten this one?

GUS: Is not possible for you.

DAVID: Could you straighten it?

GUS: That would depend—but I sold my instruments for this. You go to work now. Go ahead.

DAVID, *starts to move*: You in a hurry to go away?

GUS: I'll stay, I'll watch you.

DAVID, *thankfully*: Okay. *He gets down on his knees and is about to get under the car.* You feel like workin'? Just for a couple of minutes?

GUS: You would like me to?

DAVID: I always wanted to see how somebody else works. Y'know?

GUS: All right, come on. We rip her open. *He pulls off his coat.* You got a socket, a quarter inch?

DAVID, *a new excitement in him*: I ain't got sockets yet, but . . .

GUS: That's all right, give me an open end. *David goes for the wrench quickly.* How much oil you got in here?

DAVID, *finding the wrench*: Just a couple of quarts. I just ran her a minute. I'll drain her.

> He gets under the car quickly, opening the drain nuts, setting a can under it, as . . .

GUS: Are you married?

DAVID: Not yet . . . *Under the car.* . . . but pretty soon . . . are you?

GUS, *ready to work, he kneels on one knee beside the car*: No, but I am always hopeful. There is a nice red-headed girl in this town? *Preparing to slide under.*

DAVID, *laughs*: She got to be red-headed?

GUS: Yes, I would prefer such a color. It always seemed to me in a small American town would be many red-headed girls. Probably this is because in general I like a small town. When this car has to be ready? *Slides under.*

> David moves to make room; sits on his heels beside the car.

DAVID: Eleven in the morning, if possible. You think it can?

GUS: Oh, plenty of time. You got a car to take this shaft to Newton?

DAVID: Yeh, that Ford outside. Oh—my back.

GUS: Spread out, take it easy.

DAVID, *relaxes on the floor*: Gosh, you sure swing that wrench. Lots of time I do something and I wonder how they'd do it in the factory—you know, officially.

GUS: In the factory also they wonder sometimes how it's done officially.

DAVID, *laughs*: Yeh, I bet. *Pause. Gus works.* Gosh, I suddenly feel awful tired. I been at it all night, y'know?

GUS: Sleep, go ahead. I'll wake you when it gets interesting.

DAVID: . . . Don't think you're doing this for nothing; I'll split the bill with you.

GUS: Nonsense. *Laughs.* We'll even it up sometime. One hand washes the other.

David's head comes down on his arm, his face toward the Austrian. For several moments Gus works in silence. David's breathing comes in longer draughts. Gus, noticing his eyes closed . . .

Mr. Beeves?

David sleeps.

Gus comes out from under the car, gets his own coat and lays it over David and looks down at him. A smile comes to his face, he shakes his head wondrously, and looks from David all around the shop. Then, happily, and with a certain anticipation, he whispers . . .

America!

He bends, slides under the car as the lights go down.

The lights come up on the same scene. From the large barn doors a wide shaft of sunlight is pouring in. David is asleep where he was before, the coat still on him. But now the car is off the jack, and the hood is in place over the engine. The tools are in a neat pile nearby.

Enter J.B., Dan Dibble, Hester, Pat and Amos.

J.B., *as they enter. To Dan:* We're a little early, so if he needs more time you'll wait, Dan. . . . *Looks at David. Quietly:* What'd he do, sleep here all night?

AMOS: Must've. He never come home.

J.B., *to Dan:* That's the type of character you're dealing with. I hope you don't forget to thank him.

DIBBLE, *fearfully touching the fender:* It looks just the same as when I brought it. You think it's fixed?

Hester goes to David.

J.B., *looks at David:* Don't worry, it's fixed.

HESTER: Should I wake him?

J.B.: Go ahead. I want to tell him right away.

HESTER, *bends over and shakes him lightly:* Davey? Davey?

DAVID: Huh?

HESTER: Wake up. J.B.'s here. It's morning. *Laughs.* Look at him!

DAVID: Oh. *Sits up and sees J.B. and Dibble.* Oh ya, ya.

> *He gets up quickly, catching the coat as it falls from him. He looks at the coat for an instant.*

HESTER, *fixing his shirt straight*: Is it all done?

DAVID: What? I'm asleep yet, wait a minute. *He rubs his head and walks a few steps.*

J.B., *to Dibble with a strongly possessive pride*: That's when you're young. Sleep anywhere. Nothin' bothers you.

DAVID: What time is it?

J.B.: About half past ten.

DAVID, *astonished and frightened*: Half past ten! Gosh, I didn't mean to sleep that long . . . ! *Looks around, suddenly anxious.*

HESTER, *laughs*: You look so *funny*!

J.B.: Well, how'd you do, Dave, all finished?

DAVID: Finished? Well, uh . . . *He looks at the car.*

J.B.: If you're not, Dan can wait.

DAVID: Ya . . . just a second, I . . . *He looks around the shop.*

HESTER: Looking for your tools? They're right on the floor here.

DAVID—*he keeps looking all around for an instant. Looks at the tools*: Oh, okay. *He looks at the car as though it were explosive. He lifts the hood and looks at the engine as . . .*

J.B.: How was it, tough job?

DAVID: Heh? Ya, pretty tough.

J.B.: Anything wrong . . . ?

DAVID: No, I . . . *He gets on his knees and looks under the engine.*

DIBBLE: Can I start her up now?

DAVID—*gets to his feet, looks at everyone as though in a dream*: Okay, try her. Wait a minute, let me.

DIBBLE, *following him to the car door*: Now don't dirty the upholstery . . .

J.B.: Don't worry about the upholstery, Dan, come over here.

DIBBLE, *coming to the front of car where J.B. and Hester are*: They always get in with their dirty clothes . . .

The engine starts. It hums smoothly, quietly. J.B. turns proudly smiling to Dan, who creeps closer to it and listens. Hester watches J.B., teetering on the edge of expectation, then watches Dan. After a moment the engine is shut off. David comes out of the car, comes slowly into view, his eyes wide.

PAT, *to Dan, of Dave*: Highly skilled, highly skilled.

J.B., *beaming, to Dibble*: Well, you damn fool?

DIBBLE, *excitedly*: Why she does, she does sound fine. *He snoops around the car.*

DAVID: Look, J.B., I . . .

J.B., *raises his fist and bangs on the fender*: Goddamn, Dave, I always said it! You know what you did?

HESTER: Davey, J.B.'s going to . . .

J.B., *to Hester*: I'm paying for it, at least let me tell it. Dan, come over here first and tell Dave what they did to you in Burley. Listen to this one, Dave. Pat, I want you to hear this.

Pat and Amos come into the group.

DIBBLE, *feeling the edge of the fender*: I think he bumped it here.

J.B.: Oh, the hell with that, come over here and tell him. *Dibble comes.* What about that guy in Burley?

DIBBLE: Well, there's a garage in Burley does tractor work. But he's not reasonable . . .

J.B.: Tell him what he does.

DIBBLE: I brought this one to him and he says I'll have to take her plumb apart, every screw and bolt of her. He had his mind set on charging me a hundred and thirty-one dollars for the job. So, I figured it was just about time I stopped subsidizin' the Burley Garage Incorporated.

PAT: That's intelligent, Mr. Dibble.

DAVID: Did he tell you what was wrong with the car? The Burley man?

DIBBLE: Well, yes, he did, he always tells you something, but I can't. . . . Now wait a minute. . . . These things have a dingus they call a . . . a crankshaft? He said it was crooked, or busted, or dented . . .

J.B., *laughs—to David, then back to Dan*: On a brand new Marmon! What the hell did he want with the crankshaft?

PAT: Scandalous.

DAVID: Look, J.B., lemme tell you . . .

J.B., *drawing David and Dan together*: Go ahead, David. And listen to this, Dan. This is the first honest word you ever heard out of a mechanic. *To David*: Go on, tell this poor sucker what the matter was.

> *David stands dumbly, looking into J.B.'s ecstatic face. He turns to Hester.*

HESTER, *hardly able to stand still. Pridefully*: Tell him, Davey!

DAVID, *turns back to J.B. He sighs*: Just a lot of small things, that's all.

> *David walks a few steps away to a fender and absently touches it. It could be taken for modesty. Amos is now to the side, resting a foot on the car bumper—watching in wonder.*

J.B.: Well? What do you say, Danny? Now you're looking at a *mechanic*!

PAT, *to Dan, of Dave*: At the age of six he fixed the plug on an iron.

DIBBLE, *goes to David*: Look, David. I have a proposition for you. Whenever there's a job to do on my tractors charge me for parts and that's all. If you'd do that for me, I could guarantee you more . . .

DAVID: I'm much obliged to you, Mr. Dibble, but I'm not tooled up for tractor work . . .

J.B.: Now wait a minute . . .

DAVID, *almost shouting with tension*: Let me say something will you? To work on heavy engines like that, and tractors in general a man has got to be a . . . well, I'm not tooled up for it, that's all, I haven't got the machinery.

J.B., *businesslike*: But you've got the machinery.

HESTER: Listen to this, Davey!

> *David looks at him.*

J.B.: You go out and buy everything you want. Fix up this building. Lay out a concrete driveway in the front. I'll pay the bills. Give me one percent on my money. *Roundly*: Let me be some good in my life!

DAVID, *as though a fever were rising in him, his voice begins to soar*: I don't know if I'm ready for that, J.B. . . . I'd have to study about tractors . . . I . . .

J.B.: Then study! Now's the *time*, Dave. You're young, strong . . . !

PAT, *to Dan*: He's very strong.

DIBBLE, *taking out a roll*: How much do I owe you, boy?

> *David looks at Dan.*

DAVID: Owe me?

J.B.: Make it sixty dollars flat, Dave. Since it wasn't as hard as we thought. *David looks at J.B. who won't wait for him to object.* Sixty flat, Dan.

DIBBLE, *counts laboriously, peeling off each bill into David's unwilling hand*: One, two, three . . . *Continues.*

HESTER, *joyously amused at Dan*: What're those, all ones?!

DIBBLE: All I carry is ones. Never can tell when you'll leave a five by mistake. *Continues counting.* Government ought to print different sizes.

J.B.: How's it feel to have two stars, heh, Pat? *With a sweep of his hand*: I can see a big red sign out there way up in the air. Dave Beeves, Incorporated, Tractor Station . . .

Hester has noticed the coat beside the car.

HESTER, *holding the coat up*: Did you get a new coat?

Dibble continues counting into David's hand.

DAVID: Huh?

Quickly turns to Hester and the coat. Dan Dibble continues counting. David stares at the coat, suddenly in the full blast of all the facts. Now all but Dibble are looking at the coat.

AMOS, *feels the coat*: Where'd you get this?

DIBBLE: Hold still! Fifty-three, fifty-four, fifty . . .

David looks at Amos, then down at his hand into which the money is still dropping. He then looks again at Amos . . . Amos to him.

AMOS: What's the matter?

HESTER: What's come over you?

David suddenly hands the money to Hester.

DIBBLE: Say!

DAVID—*his hand recedes from the bills as though they were burning. To Hester*: Take it, will ya? I . . .

He starts to point somewhere off right as though he were being called. Then his hand drops . . . and with gathering speed he strides out.

HESTER, *astonished*: Davey . . . *She hurries to watch him leaving, to the right, halts.* Why . . . he's running! *Calling in alarm*: Davey! *She runs out.*

J.B., Pat and Dan stand, watching them open-mouthed as they disappear down the driveway. Amos is center, downstage.

DIBBLE: What in the world come over the boy? I didn't finish payin' him.

They stand looking right. Amos looks at the coat. He starts turning it inside out, examining it carefully, perplexed . . .

SLOW CURTAIN

ACT TWO

SCENE I

June. Three years later. The living room of the Falks'—now David's—house. A farmhouse room, but brightly done over. Solid door to outside at the right. In the back wall, right, a swinging door to the dining room. A stairway at the back, its landing at the left. A door, leading to an office in the bedroom, down left. One window at left. Two windows flanking the door to outside at right. Good blue rug, odd pieces, some new, some old. Oak. A pair of well-used rubber boots beside the door.

The stage is empty. A perfect summer day, not too hot. Noon. After a moment the doorbell rings.

HESTER, *from above, shouts excitedly*: They're here! Davey!

DAVID, *hurrying down the stairs, buttoning on a white shirt. He wears pressed pants, shined shoes, his hair has just been combed; shouting up*: I'll get it, I'm going!

HESTER, *her head sticking out at the junction of banister and ceiling. She quickly surveys the room as David comes off the stairs*: Get your boots out of there! I just fixed up the house!

The bell rings.

DAVID, *calling toward the door*: Just a minute! *Getting the boots together. To Hester*: Go on, get dressed, it's almost noon! *He opens door to dining room.*

HESTER: Don't put them in there! They're filthy! Down the cellar!

DAVID: But I always put them in here!

HESTER: But you promised once the house is painted!

Door opens. Enter Gus.

GUS: Don't bother. It's only me.

35

*He wears a white Palm Beach suit, hatless. Hester and David
stare at him in astonishment. She comes down the stairs. She
is dressed in a robe, but has her best shoes on. Her hair is set.*

HESTER: Why, Gus! You look so handsome!

GUS: It is such a special day, I decided to make an impression on myself.

HESTER: No, you go perfectly with the room.

DAVID, *laughing with Gus*: Watch yourself or she'll hang you in a frame
over the couch. *He stamps at her to get her moving.*

HESTER, *squealing, she runs to the stairs and up a few steps, and leans
over the banister*: Is your girl outside? Bring her in.

DAVID: Hey, that's right! Where's your girl?

GUS, *looking up*: Well, we both decided suddenly that until she can
become as beautiful as Hester . . .

HESTER: Oh, you.

GUS, *opening his arms like a pleading lover*: Until she shows ability to
make over a house like this was, and until etcetera and etcetera, she is not
the girl for me, so I haven't seen her all week. Anyway, I have decided
definitely I need only a red-headed girl.

HESTER, *to Gus*: Stand in the middle of the room when they come in. You
make it look just like the picture in the *Ladies' Home Journal.*

DAVID, *starting after her*: Get dressed, will ya? Dad'll cut my head off if
we're not ready!

    Hester laughs with delight and runs upstairs.

GUS, *looking around*: It came out so nice. You know, this house shines in
the sun a quarter of a mile away.

DAVID: Well, look at that sun! *Goes right to windows.* God must've
pulled up the sun this morning, grabbed him by the back of the neck, and
said—make it a baseball day.

GUS, *touching the wall*: Now it is truly a place to call home. Amazing.

DAVID, *laughs musingly, indicating the windows at the right*: You know,
when I came down this morning that window caught my eye. I used to
sneak under that window when we were kids and peek in here to watch
Hester doing her homework. And then I used to sneak away. And now I
can walk in and outa this house fifty times a day and sleep up in his room
night after night! *Looks through the window.* Wherever he is I bet he still
can't figure it out. Read the encyclopedia if you like. I'll put on a tie. *Goes
to the landing.*

GUS, *looking around*: Encyclopedia, furniture, new plumbing. . . . When am I going to see a couple of brats around here!

DAVID—*stops at the landing*: What's the rush, you got some old suits you want ruined?

GUS: Me? I always pick up babies by the back of the neck, but . . . *Idly*: without children you wouldn't have to fix nothin' in here for twenty years. When nothing breaks it's boring. *He sits, reaches over for an encyclopedia volume.*

DAVID—*glances above, comes away from stairs. Quietly*: I been wanting to ask you about that.

GUS: What?

DAVID—*hesitates. In good humor*: Did you ever hear of it happening when people didn't have kids because of the man?

GUS: Certainly, why not? Why don't you talk it over with her?

DAVID—*laughs self-consciously*: I can't seem to get around to it. I mean we somehow always took it for granted, kinda, that when the time was right a kid would just naturally come along.

GUS: You go to the doctor, then you'll know. . . . Or do you want to know?

DAVID: Sure I do, but I don't know, it just doesn't seem *right*, especially when we've been all set financially for over two years now.

GUS: Right! What has this got to do with right or wrong? There is no justice in the world.

DAVID—*looks at him, then goes to the landing, stops*: I'll never believe that, Gus. If one way or another a man don't receive according to what he deserves inside . . . well, it's a madhouse.

HESTER, *from above*: There's a car stopping in front of the house! *Coming down*. Did you put your boots away?

DAVID, *slightly annoyed*: Yeh, I put 'em away! *Goes across to the door.*

HESTER, *hurrying downstairs*: You didn't! *Hurrying across the room toward the boots*. He'll have the place like a pigsty in a week!

David opens the door and looks out.

GUS, *to Hester*: Get used to it, the place will never be so neat once you have children around.

David turns to him, quickly, resentment in his face.

HESTER—*stops moving. An eager glow lights up her expression. The boots are in her hand*: Don't you think it is a wonderful house for children?

DAVID: Hello! Hello, Mr. Dibble! Didn't expect to see you around here today. Come in, come in.

Enter Dan Dibble after wiping his feet carefully on the doormat.

DIBBLE: Had to see J.B. on some business. Thought I'd stop in, say hello. Afternoon, Mrs. Beeves.

HESTER: Hello, Mr. Dibble. *She picks up the boots and goes out.*

DAVID: You know Gus Eberson. He's with me over at the shop.

DIBBLE: Sure, how are you, Gus? Say, you look more like a banker than a mechanic.

DAVID: Best mechanic there is.

DIBBLE: What I always say—never judge a man by his clothes. A man and his clothes are soon parted. *They laugh.* Say, J.B. was tellin' me you used to have a shop of your own here in town—over in Poplar Street was it . . . ?

DAVID: We amalgamated, Gus and I.

GUS: Actually, Mr. Dibble, I ran out of money and customers after the first seven months. I am working now for Mr. Beeves since over two years.

DIBBLE: Well, say, this is the first time I knew a hired man to insist he wasn't the boss's partner, and the boss to let on he was.

GUS, *chuckles*: Mr. Beeves suffers sometimes from an overdeveloped sense of responsibility.

DIBBLE: That's why I spotted him as a natural mink man. Given it any more thought, David?

DAVID: A lot, Mr. Dibble, a lot—but I'm afraid I haven't got an answer for you yet.

DIBBLE: Got time for a few facts today?

DAVID: Tell you the truth, we're expecting J.B. and Shory. Goin' up to Burley for the ball game. You heard about my brother, didn't you?

DIBBLE: J.B. said somethin' about him pitchin' against that colored team. Say, if he can knock them boys over he really belongs in the Big Leagues.

DAVID: I guess after today's game, Amos Beeves will be playin' for the Detroit Tigers.

DIBBLE: Well, say, they really took him, eh?

DAVID: Just about. A Tiger scout's goin' to be in the grandstand today.

DIBBLE: Well, say, it's about time.

DAVID: Yep, things even up, I guess in the long run. Why don't you drop around tonight. Havin' a big barbecue after the game.

Enter Hester from the dining room.

DIBBLE: Thanks, I'd like to but I got to get back and see my mink get fed on time and proper.

HESTER: David just never stops talkin' about mink. *Sits.* Have you still got that tiny one with the white spot on his head?

DAVID, *seeing Hester's interest kindles a happy liveliness in him*: Oh, that one's probably been in and out of a dozen New York night clubs by this time. *They laugh.*

HESTER, *disturbed—to Dibble*: Oh, you didn't kill her?

DAVID, *to Gus and Hester*: That's the way you get about mink, they're like people, little nervous people.

DIBBLE: I call them my little bankers myself. Pour a dollar's worth of feed down their gullets and they'll return you forty percent; best little bankers in the world.

DAVID: Except when they fall, Mr. Dibble, except when they fall.

DIBBLE: Mink never fall!

DAVID: Oh, now, Mr. Dibble . . .

DIBBLE: They don't! It's their keepers fall down on them. When a feller goes broke tryin' to raise mink it's mainly because he's a careless man. From everything I've seen, David, you ain't that kind. You got a farm here clean as a hospital and mink needs a clean place. You're the first and only man I thought of when I decided to sell off some of my breeders when my doctor told me to ease up.

DAVID: I been askin' around lately, and everybody I talked to . . .

DIBBLE, *to Gus too*: I'm glad you made the inquiries. It shows you're a careful man. And now I'll tell you my answer. Easiest thing in the world is to kill a mink. Mink'll die of a cold draught; they'll die of heart failure; indigestion can kill them, a cut lip, a bad tooth or sex trouble. And worse than that, the mink is a temperamental old woman. I wear an old brown canvas coat when I work around them. If I change that coat it might start them to eating their young. A big loud noise like thunder, or a heavy hailstorm comes and the mother's liable to pick up the litter, put 'em out in the open part of the cage, and then she'll go back into the nest box and close her eyes. As though they're out of danger if they're out of her sight. And when the storm's over you might have six or eight kits drowned to death out there. I've seen mink murder each other, I've seen them eat themselves to death and starve themselves to death, and I've seen them die of just plain worry. But! Not on my ranch! I'll show my records to anybody.

DAVID, *to Gus*: There's a business, boy!

GUS: A business! That's a slot machine. What do you need with mink?

DAVID: Oh, there's a kick in it, Gus. When you send a load of skins to New York you know you *did* something, you . . .

GUS: Why, you didn't do something? *Indicates right.* A great big shop you built up, a tractor station, how nice you made this farm . . . ?

DAVID, *not too intensely; he enjoys this talk*: Yeh, but is a thing really yours because your name is on it? Don't you have to feel you're smart enough, or strong enough, or something enough to have won it before it's really yours? You can't bluff a mink into staying alive. *Turns to Dibble.* I tell you, Mr. Dibble . . .

DIBBLE: Take your time. Think about it . . .

DAVID: Let me call you. I'll let you know.

DIBBLE: Oh, I'll bide my time. Just remember, in New York they murder people for a mink coat. Women sell their jewels for mink, they sell their . . . them New York women'll sell damn near anything for mink!

They laugh, as horns of two cars sound urgently outside.

DAVID, *to Dibble*: This is my brother!

GUS, *as David opens the door*: Look, like two peacocks!

HESTER, *at the door, over her shoulder ecstatically to Dibble*: They've waited so long!

DAVID, *exuberantly, backing from the door*: Here he comes! Christy Mathewson the Second!

Enter Amos and Patterson followed by J.B.

HESTER, *grabbing Amos's hand*: How's your arm, Ame!

AMOS—*winds up and pitches*: Wham!—He's out!

PAT, *throwing up his arms*: God bless this day! *Suddenly*: I'm not waiting for anybody! *Threatens to go out again.*

J.B., *to Hester*: Shory's waiting in the car! Let's go!

HESTER: Bring him in. Let's have a drink!

Nobody hears her.

DAVID: What're you lookin' so sad about, Dad! *Suddenly hugs Pat.*

HESTER: Get some whiskey, Dave!

PAT, *indignantly—he has broken from Dave*: You want to suffocate in here? Open the windows in this house! *He rushes around throwing windows up.*

DAVID, *laughing*: We're going in a minute! Where's the telegram, Ame! *Amos opens his mouth but Pat cuts him off.*

PAT, *busy with the windows*: Let the day come in! What a day! What a year! What a nation!

HESTER, *rushing after Pat*: Did you bring the telegram? *She corners him, laughing.* Where's the telegram?

PAT: I don't need to bring it. I will never forget that telegram so long as I live. *Takes it out of his pocket.* "Western Union. Class of Service. This is a full-rate Telegram or Cablegram unless its deferred character is indicated by a suitable symbol . . . "

HESTER: What're you reading that part for? *Tries to grab it from him.* What did the scout say!

PAT, *grabbing it back*: I'm reading it to you just the way I read it when I got it—from the very top, to the very bottom.

DAVID: Let him read it, Hess!

They go quiet.

PAT: I haven't felt this way since the last time I read the Bible. "Patterson Beeves, 26 Murdock Street. Will be in Burley for the Black Giants game Sunday, July 16th. Looking forward to seeing Amos Beeves's performance. Best regards, Augie Belfast, Detroit Tigers." *Looks around imperiously.* Twenty-one years I have been waiting for this telegram. Training him down the cellar since he was old enough to walk. People laughed when Amos got bad marks in school. Forget the homework, I said. Keep your eye on the ball. Concentration, I said . . .

J.B., *touched and fearing Pat's continuing indefinitely*: For God's sake, let's all have a drink!

DAVID: Comin' up! *Goes out door.*

HESTER, *pointing outside. To J.B.*: I'll bring Ellie in! Why don't you come to the game with us, Mr. Dibble? *She starts across to the door.*

J.B., *a little embarrassed, stops Hester*: Better leave her, baby. You know how she is about alcohol. Let's not start anything.

GUS: Shory likes a drink. I'll bring him in. *He goes out left.*

PAT: Plenty of room in Dave's car, Mr. Dibble. *He studies Dibble, automatically massaging Amos's arm.*

J.B., *holds his hand out to Hester*: What do you think of this?

HESTER: A wedding ring! You're giving Ellie a new ring?

J.B., *warmly*: No, this is for me. Since we decided to adopt a baby I been feeling like we're newlyweds.

HESTER—*flings her arms around him*: You're such a silly man!

Enter Shory, pushed in by Gus.

SHORY, *to J.B.*: Hey, Poppa, don't start nothin' you can't finish.

Enter David with drinks on a tray.

HESTER, *three-quarters joking, but only that much. To Shory*: And you've got a filthy mind.

SHORY: Madam, don't flatter me. *To David, who has been watching Hester since Shory came in*: Hey, husband, where's that drink?

DAVID: Come on, everybody. Before we go! *Gives out the drinks. . . . Raises his glass.* A toast! To everybody's luck—everybody's!

All raise their glasses.

GUS, *to Amos*: And the next World Series! *Starts to drink.*

DAVID: Wait! Make one big toast . . . to all our hearts' desires. For Amos! For Dad . . .

GUS: To David and Hester! To their prosperity, their shop, their tractor station, their farm . . .

DIBBLE, *suddenly struck with the idea*: And their mink!

HESTER, *quick complaint*: No . . .

DAVID—*he looks at Hester. Her face softens toward him*: Not the mink now! From today on everything is coming true! To our children.

GUS: To their children.

J.B.: Their children.

HESTER, *softly*: And in this year. Say that.

DAVID—*their eyes meet for an instant, and hold*: In this year . . . everything our hearts desire . . . all of us: in this year.

All drink.

PAT—*looks at watch*: Hey! We're late! We're getting drunk and the whole world is waiting for us out there! Come on!

They all rush out yelling and laughing as . . .

CURTAIN

SCENE II

Living room. About seven o'clock that night.

The stage is empty. The gentle murmur and occasional laughter of the guests at the barbecue can be heard dimly. Presently, David, followed by Dan Dibble, comes in through the front door. David crosses to the desk and removes a large checkbook. He pauses over it, pen in hand.

DAVID: It's a fortune. I never wrote a check this big in my life.

DIBBLE: You never got so much for so little, David. You'll have prize stock, the finest breeding mink alive. The rest's up to you.

DAVID: Mr. Dibble, I never thought I'd see my hand shaking.

The door at lower left opens and Pat appears. He closes the door gently behind him.

DAVID: Still asleep?

PAT: Shhh, I always make him take a long nap after a game.

DAVID: Aren't you going to eat anything?

PAT: I couldn't eat anything now. I'll eat after Belfast gets here. *He sits on the couch.* I was watchin' Amos just now asleep on the couch, and it suddenly struck me. Did you ever notice what a powerful face he has?

DAVID, *as he writes check*: He's great. After that game today there ain't a man in the world can doubt it. He's just great.

PAT: Didn't he look noble out there?

DAVID: Noble enough to vote for.

DAVID, *as he tears out check*: Here's your check, Mr. Dibble. *Dibble takes it.*

DIBBLE: You'll never regret it, David.

DAVID: I hope not.

DIBBLE: Well, I'll be runnin' along now. You call me as soon as you get your cages ready and I'll bring 'em over. *David has walked him to the front door.* Goodnight.

DAVID: G'night.

> *Dibble exits. David turns back into the room.*

PAT: You know why I'm extra glad? I think you were beginning to take it too hard, Dave. I was going to have a talk with you. Because I never had a doubt he'd scale the heights.

DAVID: I just didn't like the idea of me getting everything so steady, and him waiting around like . . . I mean you get to wondering if your own turn isn't coming.

PAT: Like what do you mean?

DAVID: A loss . . . a big unhappiness of some kind. But he's on his way now. I know it, Pop.

> *The door opens and J.B. enters with a grand new valise. He is slightly drunk. In one hand he has a slip of paper.*

J.B.: Surprise!

> *Pat springs up with finger to his lips.*

PAT: Shhh!

J.B., *whispers*: Surprise! Wake him up. *Pointing to valise*: Surprise . . .

PAT: After a game he's got to sleep an hour or he's peevish. *Pointing at watch*: Wait a few minutes.

DAVID: Wait'll he sees the initials.

PAT, *violently*: Ssh! *To J.B. . . . threatening*: If he's peevish . . . !

> *The door opens and Amos stands in the doorway.*

J.B.: Hey Amos . . . *Holding up valise*: Surprise.

AMOS: Aw . . . ! *Amos takes the valise and fingers it happily.*

J.B.: It's a token of our affection from . . . just a minute now . . . *Straightens the slip of paper.* Hester, Shory, Gus, Dave, Ellie, and me, and Belle. *Indicating upstage.*

AMOS, *fondling the valise*: Gee, you should'na done it.

J.B., *with growing flourish and sentiment*: No, you don't realize the traveling you'll do. *Looks into the distance.* Shibe Park, Comiskey Field, Sportsman's Park—Boston, Chicago, Cleveland, St. Louis. . . . And when you're packing up after a nice no-hitter, you'll give us a thought in the old home town. *To clinch it, he taps a buckle.* Solid brass.

AMOS, *feverish in glory*: Give me that list. *Takes it out of J.B.'s hand.* When I get my first paycheck I'm gonna send you all a big present! Say . . . ! *Starting to take Pat's wrist to look at his watch*: What time . . . ?

PAT, *holding onto his arm*: You heard what he said in the locker room. He's got to finish some long-distance phoning, and then he'll be here. Come on. I'll rub you down.

Hester enters as they start for the stairs.

HESTER: John, you better go outside. Ellie's going home.

J.B., *frightened and hurt*: Why? *To all*: Am I so drunk?

DAVID: Hurry up, maybe you can catch her.

J.B.: Come with me, Dave . . . tell her . . .

DAVID: Get washed, Ame . . . you want to look nice now. Be right back.

David and J.B. go out.

HESTER, *looking at the door*: Why must he always do that? *To Pat, who is rummaging in his old valise*: I'll get you some towels. Come on up.

PAT: Oh, no, we carry our own. You never can tell about strange towels. *He folds one over his arm. Amos is looking out of the window.*

HESTER, *ready to laugh*: Well, I wasn't going to give you a dirty towel, you stupid.

PAT: For twenty-one years I've kept him practically sterilized. I ain't layin' him low with an infection now. Come on, Amos, get washed.

Amos and Pat exit up the stairs as J.B. enters, followed by David. J.B. is drunk, unsteady but not staggering. He barges in, comes directly to Hester and takes her hand, speaks very close to her face, as though to discern her reactions better.

J.B.: Hester, you got to go home for me. *He goes to window helplessly.*

DAVID: Maybe she was only fooling, John . . .

J.B.: No! But . . . *To Hester*: Somebody's got to go home for me! *And suddenly he bursts into uncontrolled sobbings.*

HESTER: What in the world . . . !

DAVID, *angrily*: John! *Shakes him, then seats him.* John! Are you going to cut that out?

HESTER, *going to J.B.*: What happened? What did she say?

J.B., *stops sobbing, sits swaying backward and forward, very slightly in his chair*: All these years . . . we could've had children . . . all these weary, weary years.

HESTER: What are you talking about?

J.B., *pointing waywardly toward the door to the outside*: Just told me . . . she made it up about the doctor . . . made it all up. We could've had two kids by now. *Looks at David.* She wouldn't. She wouldn't. Because I drink, she says. A drunkard, she says! They'll wipe my name off my mail box like I never lived!

HESTER: Come upstairs and lie down. You make me so mad I could choke you! You could have everything in the world and you drink it away.

J.B.: If I had a boy . . . I wouldn't have touched a drop.

HESTER: Oh, push! *She tries to move him to the stairway.*

J.B.: I'm only a failure, Dave. The world is full of failures. All a man needs is one mistake and he's a failure.

> *David turns his head, a little annoyed.*

DAVID, *impatiently*: I know, John. *Looks out window again.*

J.B.: You are the only man I ever knew who never makes a mistake. You understand me. Look at me! I am saying something.

DAVID, *now turns full to him*: What are you talking about?

J.B.: I'm not as drunk as I look, David! You're a good man, yes. You know how to do. But you've had a phenomenal lot of luck in your life, Dave. Never play luck too hard. It's like a season, and seasons go away.

HESTER: Come up or you'll pass away.

> *Enter Pat downstairs with watch in hand.*

PAT: My watch says eight-thirty, where is he? He told you no later than eight o'clock, didn't he?

DAVID: Which means he's half an hour late. That's what it means, doesn't it?

PAT: I don't know what to tell Amos. I made him take another shower.

DAVID, *with growing fear*: He pitched the greatest game of his life today, what more does he need to be told? That man'll be here.

PAT: Maybe he was kidding us. He looked like he might be that type.

DAVID: Are you going to stop that?

PAT: . . . And Amos did look a little nervous in the eighth inning with those two men on base.

DAVID: But they didn't score! Now will you just stop. *Pat, hurt, looks at him, then goes to the stairs.* Dad, what you want me to do; I can't grow him in my back yard, can I?

> *Shory enters pushed by Gus. At the stairs, Pat turns, starts to speak, then goes up and out.*

SHORY, *as the door shuts*: I'm getting my aches and pains. I came in to say goodnight. . . . Party's breakin' up anyway out there.

DAVID: No, wait a little. I don't want everybody pulling out.

> *He goes to window as . . .*

SHORY: The man told you seven-thirty, what're you making believe he said eight? You told me as he said seven-thirty, didn't you?

DAVID—*his fury is at the scout. He keeps searching out of the window*: He could've got a flat maybe.

SHORY: It don't take an hour to change a flat, Dave.

DAVID, *tensely. He turns*: Don't go away. Please.

> *Enter Hester.*

> *To Hester*: The folks are starting to go. *Moving her back to the door.* I want a party here when the scout leaves. Keep them here.

HESTER: It's not the world coming to an end. I don't want you acting this way. It's no fault of yours what happens to him. *She grasps him.* Why do you act this way? Davey . . .

DAVID: I don't get it, I swear to God I don't get it. *Strides to the window. He seems about to burst from the room.*

SHORY: Get what?

DAVID: Everything is so hard for him. *Turns to them suddenly, unable to down his anxiety.* I want to ask you something. All of you, and you too, Hess. You know what I can do and what I can't do, you . . . you know me. Everything I touch, why is it? It turns gold. Everything.

HESTER: What's come over you? Why . . . ?

DAVID, *with extreme urgency*: It bothers me, it . . . *To all*: What is it about me? I never . . . I never lose. Since we were kids I expected Amos to rise and shine. He's the one, he knows something, he knows one thing perfect. Why? Is it all luck? Is that what it is?

GUS: Nonsense. You're a good man, David.

DAVID: Aren't you good?

GUS: Yes, but I . . .

DAVID: Then why did your shop fail? Why are you working for me now? *He moves as one in the throes of release.*

GUS: They remember the war here, Dave, they don't like to buy from a foreigner.

DAVID: No, that's crazy.

GUS: Also, I had a second-rate location.

DAVID: Gus, it was better than mine. Every car coming into town had to pass your place. And they came to me. Why is that?

GUS: You know an engine, Dave, you . . .

DAVID: Including Marmons? *To all*: I got fourteen thousand dollars in the bank and as much again standing on the ground. Amos? Never had a nickel. Not a bloody nickel. Why? *A slight pause.*

HESTER, *goes to him. Smiles to make him smile but he does not*: Why does it bother you? It's good to be lucky. Isn't it?

DAVID, *looks at her a moment*: Isn't it better to feel that what you have came to you because of something special you can do? Something, something . . . inside you? Don't you have to know what that thing is?

HESTER: Don't you know?

DAVID: . . . I don't, I don't know.

SHORY: And you'll never know . . .

DAVID: Damn it all, if everything drops on you like fruit from a tree, for no reason, why can't it break away for no reason? Everything you have . . . suddenly.

HESTER, *takes David's arm*: Come, say goodbye to the folks.

DAVID: No . . . they're not going home till the scout comes! Now go out . . .

HESTER, *shakes his arm*: It's his hard luck, not yours!

DAVID: It is mine! A man has a right to get what he deserves. He does, damn it! *He goes to the window, breaking from her.*

HESTER, *angrily*: You talk like you'd stole something from him. You never got anything you didn't deserve. You . . .

DAVID, *at the end of his patience, he turns on her*: Am I that good and he that bad? I can't believe it. There's something wrong, there's something wrong! *Suddenly*: I'm going to Burley. *To Hester, hurriedly*: Where's the keys to the car . . . ?

HESTER: You don't even know where to find the man . . .

DAVID: I'll find him, where are the keys?

HESTER—*she grabs him*: Davey, stop it . . .

DAVID: I'm going, I'll drag him here . . . !

HESTER, *frightened*: Davey . . . !

> He strides toward the door. Shory grabs his arm and holds it fast.

SHORY: Stop it!

DAVID: Let go of me!

SHORY—*he will not let go*: Listen to me, you damn fool! There's nothing you can do, you understand?

DAVID: Let go of my arm . . .

SHORY, *forces him down into a chair*: David, I'm going to tell you something . . . I never told you before. But you need to know this now. Amos deserves better than this, but I deserved better than this too. *Pats his thighs.* When I went to France there was no broken bones in my imagination. I left this town with a beautiful moustache and full head of hair. Women traveled half the state to climb into my bed. Even over there, under shot and shell, as they say, there was a special star over my head. I was the guy nothin' was ever going to hit . . . And nothin' ever did, David. *He releases David's arm. Now David does not move away.* Right through the war without a scratch. Surprised? I walked into Paris combing my hair. The women were smiling at me from both sides of the street, and I walked up the stairs with the whistles blowing out the Armistice. I remember how she took off my shoes and put them under the bed. The next thing I knew the house was laying on my chest and they were digging me out.

> David, all, stare at him.

HESTER: Everybody said it was a battle, I thought . . .

SHORY, *to her*: No, no battle at all. *To David.* In battle—there's almost a reason for it, a man almost "deserves" it that way. I just happened to pick out the one woman in Paris who lived in a house where the janitor was out getting drunk on the Armistice. He forgot to put water in the furnace boiler. *Smiles.* The walls blew out. *Points upstage with his thumb over his shoulder.* Amos's walls happened to blow out. And you happen to be a lucky boy, brother David. A jellyfish can't swim no matter how he tries; it's the tide that pushes him every time. So just keep feeding, and enjoy the water till you're thrown up on the beach to dry.

> *Pause.*

HESTER, *goes to him*: Come, Dave, the folks are waiting to say goodbye.

> *David is forced to turn quickly toward the window. It is an indecisive turn of the head, a questioning turn, and she follows as he strides to the window and looks out toward upstage direction . . .*

DAVID: Wait! *Starting for the window.* A car? *Turns quickly to them all.* It didn't go past. It stopped. *He starts quickly for the door, across the stage, right. Pat rushes down the stairs.*

PAT: He's here! He came! Get out, everybody! *To all*: All the way from Burley in a taxicab! Dave, you stay. I want your advice when he starts talkin' contract! *Pat rushes out.*

DAVID, *as they all keep exclaiming*: Out, out, all of you! *As they start for door, David musses Shory.* Where's your jellyfish now, brother!

SHORY, *at door with the others*: His luck is with him, sister, that's all, his luck!

DAVID: Luck, heh? *Smiling, he bends over Shory, pointing left toward his big desk and speaking privately . . .* : Some day remind me to open the middle drawer of that desk. I'll show you a fistful of phone bills for calls to Detroit.

GUS, *joyously*: Dave. You called them!

DAVID: Sure, I called them. That man is here because I brought him here! *To Shory*: Where's the jellyfish could've done that! *Triumphantly, to all*: Don't anybody go. We're going to raise the roof tonight!

> *They have all gone out now, on his last lines. Only Hester remains in the doorway.*
>
> *David looks at her a moment, and with a laugh embraces her quickly.*
>
> I'll tell you everything he says.

HESTER: Be like this all the time, Davey. *She turns toward the hallway into which this door leads.* Tell me every word, now. *She goes.*

> *David quickly brushes his hair back, looking rapidly about the room and to himself . . .*

DAVID: Now it's wonderful: This is how it ought to be!

Enter Amos—comes down stairs.

AMOS, *hushed, with his hands clasped as though in prayer*: God, it's happening just like it ought've. 'Cause I'm good. I betcha I'm probably great! *He says this, facing the door, glancing at David.*

Enter Augie Belfast and Pat. Augie is a big Irishman dressed nattily.

PAT, *as they enter*: . . . couldn't stop him from setting up a party. *Sees Dave.* Oh, here he is.

AUGIE, *to Amos and David*: Sit down, sit down. Don't stand on ceremony with me. I'm Augie Belfast . . .

Amos sits on the couch. David in a chair. As Pat . . .

PAT: Let me have your coat?

AUGIE—*lays down his hat*: It don't bother me. I live in it. Thanks just the same. *Taking out chewing gum*: Gum?

DAVID: No thanks, we've been eating all day.

AUGIE, *unfolding a slice as Pat sits. He moves about constantly; he already has a wad of gum in his cheek*: Loosen up, don't stand in awe of me. *To David and Amos*: I was just telling your father . . . I got tied up in Burley on some long-distance calls. I'm very sorry to be so late. *He is anxious to be pardoned.*

DAVID: Oh, that's all right. We know how busy you fellas are.

AUGIE: Thanks. I knew how you must've been feeling. *He paces a little, chewing, looking at the floor.* Amos? *He says nothing for a long moment. Stops walking, looks down, slowly unfolds another slice of gum.*

AMOS, *whisper*: Ya?

AUGIE: Amos, how long you been pitchin'?

AMOS: Well, about . . . *Turns to Pat.*

PAT: Steadily since he's been nine years old.

AUGIE, *nods. Pause*: I guess you know he's a damn fine pitcher.

PAT, *comfortably*: We like to think so around here.

AUGIE: Yeh, he's steady, he's good. Got a nice long arm, no nerves in that arm. He's all right. He feels the plate. *All the time thinking of something else, pacing.*

PAT: Well, you see, I've had him practicing down the cellar against a target. Dug the cellar out deeper so he could have room after he grew so tall.

AUGIE: Yeh, I know. Man sitting next to me this afternoon was telling me. Look, Mr. Beeves . . . *He straddles a chair, folds his arms on its back, facing them.* I want you to have confidence in what I say. I'm Augie Belfast, if you know anything about Augie Belfast you know he don't bull. There's enough heartbreak in this business without bull-throwers causin' any more. *In toto*, I don't string an athlete along. Pitchin' a baseball to me is like playin' the piano well, or writin' beautiful literature, so try to feel I'm giving you the last word because I am. *Pat nods a little, hardly breathing.* I have watched many thousands of boys, Mr. Beeves. I been whackin' the bushes for material for a long time. You done a fine job on Amos. He's got a fine, fast ball, he's got a curve that breaks off sharp, he's got his control down to a pinpoint. He's almost original sometimes. When it comes to throwin' a ball, he's all there. Now. *Slight pause.* When I saw him two years ago, I said . . .

DAVID, *electrically*: You were *here* before?

AUGIE: Oh yeh, I meant to tell you. I came to see him last year, too . . .

PAT: Why didn't you let me know?

AUGIE: Because there was one thing I couldn't understand, Mr. Beeves. I understand it today, but I couldn't then. When the bases are clear, Mr. Beeves, and there's nobody on, your boy is terrific. . . . Now wait a minute, let me say rather that he's good, very good. . . . I don't want to say an untruth, your boy is good when nobody's on. But as soon as a man gets on base and starts rubbin' his spikes in the dirt and makin' noise behind your boy's back, something happens to him. I seen it once, I seen it twice. I seen it every time the bases get loaded. And once the crowd starts howlin', your body, Mr. Beeves, is floatin' somewhere out in paradise.

PAT: But he pitched a shut-out.

AUGIE: Only because them Black Giants like to swing bats. If they'd waited him out in the eighth inning they could've walked in half a dozen runs. Your boy was out of control. *Dead silence.* I couldn't understand it. I absolutely couldn't get the angle on it. Here's a boy with a terrific. . . . Well, let's not say terrific, let's say a damn good long arm. But not an ounce of base-brains. There is something in him that prevents him from playin' the bases . . .

PAT: I know, I've been drilling him the last three years.

AUGIE: I know, but in three years there's been no improvement. In fact, this year he's worse in that respect than last year. Why? Today I found the answer.

PAT, *softly*: You did?

AUGIE: The guy sitting next to me mentions about him pitchin' down the cellar since he was nine years old. That was it! Follow me now. In the cellar there is no crowd. In the cellar he knows exactly what's behind his back. In the cellar, *in toto*, your boy is home. He's only got to concentrate on that target, his mind is trained to take in that one object, just the target. But once he gets out on a wide ball field, and a crowd is yelling in his ears, and there's two or three men on bases jumpin' back and forth behind him, his mind has got to do a lot of things at once, he's in a strange place, he gets panicky, he gets paralyzed, he gets mad at the base runners and he's through! From that minute he can't pitch worth a nickel bag of cold peanuts!

> *He gets up, pulls down his vest. David and Pat sit dumbly, Amos staring at nothing.*

I got to make a train, Mr. Beeves.

PAT, *slowly rises. As though in a dream*: I didn't want to waste the winters, that's why I trained him down the cellar.

AUGIE, *thoughtfully*: Yeh, that's just where you made your mistake, Mr. Beeves.

DAVID, *rises*: But . . . that was his plan. He didn't want to waste the winters. Down the cellar . . . it seemed like such a good idea!

AUGIE: But it was a mistake.

DAVID: But he's been doing it twelve years! A man can't be multiplying the same mistake for twelve years, can he?

AUGIE: I guess he can, son. It was a very big mistake.

> *Pause.*

PAT: Well . . . you can't take that out of him? Your coaches and . . . everything?

AUGIE: There's no coach in the world can take out a boy's brain and set it back twelve years. Your boy is crippled up here. *Taps his temple.* I'm convinced.

DAVID: But if you coached him right, if you drilled him day after day . . .

AUGIE: It would take a long, long time, and I personally don't believe he'll ever get rid of it.

PAT: You can't . . . you can't try him, eh?

AUGIE: I know how you feel, Mr. Beeves, but I am one man who will not take a boy out of his life when I know in my heart we're going to throw him away like a wet rag.

DAVID—*for a long time he stands staring*: He has no life.

AUGIE, *bends closer to hear*: Eh?

DAVID: He doesn't know how to do anything else.

AUGIE, *nods with sympathy*: That was another mistake. *He starts to turn away to go.*

PAT, *as though to call him back somehow*: I believed if he concentrated . . . concentration . . . you see I myself always jumped from one thing to another and never got anywhere, and I thought . . .

AUGIE: Yeh . . . when it works concentration is a very sound principle. *Takes a breath.* Well, lots of luck.

> *Still unable to believe, Pat can't speak.*
>
> 'Bye, Amos.
>
> *Amos nods slightly, numbly staring. At the door, to Dave.*
>
> 'Bye. *He starts to open the door.*

DAVID: Look . . . *He hurries to him. He looks in his eyes, his hand raised as though to grab the man and hold him here.*

AUGIE: Yeh?

> *David starts to speak, then looks at Amos who is still staring at nothing. David turns back to Augie.*

DAVID: . . . You'll see him in the Leagues.

AUGIE: I hope so. I just don't . . .

DAVID, *trying to restrain his fury*: No, you'll see him. You're not the only team, you know. You'll see him in the Leagues.

AUGIE, *grasps David's arm*: . . . Take it easy, boy. *To the others*: I hope you'll pardon me for being late.

DAVID, *quietly, like an echo, his voice cracking*: You'll see him.

> *Augie nods. Glances at Pat and Amos, opens the door and goes. Pat and David stand looking at the door. Pat turns now, walks slowly to Amos who is sitting. As Pat nears him he stands slowly, his fists clenched at his sides.*

PAT, *softly, really questioning*: He can be wrong too, can't he? *Amos is silent, his face filling with hate.* Can't he be wrong? *No reply.* He can, can't he?

AMOS, *a whip-like shout*: No, he can't be!

PAT: But everybody makes mistakes . . .

AMOS—*with a cry he grabs Pat by the collar and shakes him violently back and forth*: Mistakes! Mistakes! You and your goddam mistakes!

DAVID, *leaps to them, trying to break his grip*: Let him go! Amos, let him go!

AMOS, *amid his own, and Pat's weeping. To Pat*: You liar! I'll kill you, you little liar, *you liar*!

> *With a new burst of violence he starts forcing Pat backward and down to the floor. Gus comes in as David locks an arm around Amos's neck and jerks him from Pat who falls to the floor.*

> Leave me alone! Leave me alone!

> *With a great thrust David throws Amos to the couch and stands over him, fists raised.*

DAVID: Stay there! Don't get up! You'll fight me, Amos!

PAT, *scurrying to his feet, and taking David away from the couch*: Don't, don't fight! *He turns quickly, pleadingly to Amos, who is beginning to sob on the couch.* Amos, boy, boy . . . *Amos lies across the couch and sobs violently. Pat leans over and pats his head.* Boy, boy . . .

> *Amos swings his arm out blindly and hits Pat across the chest. David starts toward them but Pat remains over him, patting his back.*

> Come on, boy, please, boy, stop now, stop, Amos! Look, Ame, look, I'll get Cleveland down here, I'll go myself, I'll bring a man. Ame, listen, I did what I could, a man makes mistakes, he can't figure on everything. . . . *He begins shaking Amos who continues sobbing.* Ame, stop it! *He stands and begins shouting over Amos's sobbing*: I admit it, I admit it, Ame, I lie, I talk too much, I'm a fool, I admit it, but look how you pitch, give me credit for that, give me credit for something! *Rushes at Amos and turns him over.* Stop that crying! God Almighty, what do you want me to do! I'm a fool, what can I do!

DAVID, *wrenches Pat away from the couch. Stands over Amos*: Listen, you! *Leans over and pulls Amos by the collar to a sitting position. Amos sits limply, sobbing.* He made a mistake. That's over with. You're going to drill on base play. You got a whole life. One mistake can't ruin a life. He'll go to Cleveland. I'll send him to New York . . .

> *Hester enters quietly.*

The man can be wrong. Look at me! The man can be wrong, you understand!

Amos shakes his head.

AMOS: He's right.

David releases him and stands looking down at him. Amos gets up slowly, goes to a chair and sits.

He's right. I always knew I couldn't play the bases. Everything the man said was right. I'm dumb, that's why. I can't figure nothin'. *Looks up at Pat.* There wasn't no time, he said, no time for nothin' but throwin' that ball. Let 'em laugh, he said, you don't need to know how to figure. He knew it all. He knows everything! Well, this is one time I know something. I ain't gonna touch a baseball again as long as I live!

PAT, *frantically*: Amos, you don't know what you're saying . . . !

AMOS: I couldn't ever stand out on a diamond again! I can't do it! I know! I can't! *Slight pause.* I ain't goin' to let you kid me anymore. I'm through. *He rises. Pat sobs into his hands.*

DAVID—*Amos keeps shaking his head in denial of everything*: What do you mean, through? Amos, you can't lay down. Listen to me. Stop shaking your head—who gets what he wants in this world!

AMOS, *suddenly*: You. Only you.

DAVID: Me! Don't believe it, Amos. *Grabs him.* Don't believe that anymore!

AMOS: Everything you ever wanted . . . in your whole life, every . . . !

DAVID: Including my children, Ame? *Silence.* Where are my children?

HESTER: Dave . . .

DAVID, *to Hester*: I want to tell him! To Amos: What good is everything when nothing is good without children? Do you know the laughingstock it makes of everything you do in the world? You'll never meet a man who doesn't carry one curse . . . at least one. Shory, J.B., Pop, you, and me too. Me as much as anybody!

HESTER: Don't, Davey . . .

DAVID, *with a dreadful triumph*: No, Hess, I'm not afraid of it anymore. I want it out. I was always afraid I was something special in the world. But not after this. *To Amos: Nobody* escapes, Ame! But I don't lay down, I don't die because I'll have no kids. A man is born with one curse at least to be cracked over his head. I see it now, and you got to see it. Don't envy me, Ame . . . we're the same now. The world is made that way, as if a law was written in the sky somewhere—nobody escapes! *Takes Amos's hand.*

HESTER, *almost weeping she cannot restrain*: Why do you talk that way?

DAVID: Hess, the truth . . .

HESTER: It's not the truth! . . . You have no curse! None at all!

DAVID, *struck*: What . . . ?

HESTER: I wanted to wait till the scout signed him up. And then . . . when the house was full of noise and cheering, I'd stand with you on the stairs high over them all, and tell them you were going to have a child. *With anger and disappointment and grief*: Oh, Davey, I saw you so proud . . . !

DAVID, *twisted and wracked, he bursts out*: Oh, Hess, I am, I am.

HESTER: No, you don't want it. I don't know what's happened to you, you don't want it now!

DAVID, *with a chill of horror freezing him*: Don't say that! Hester, you mustn't . . . *David tries to draw her to him.*

HESTER, *holding him away*: You've got to want it, Davey. You've just got to want it!

> She bursts into tears and rushes out. He starts after her, calling her name . . . when he finds himself facing Amos.

AMOS: Nobody escapes . . . *David stops, turns to Amos. . . .* except you. *He walks to the door, past David, and goes out.*

CURTAIN

ACT THREE

SCENE I

Living room. Night in the following February.

J.B. is asleep on the couch. Shory and Gus are silently playing cards and smoking at a table near the fireplace. Snow can be seen on the window muntins. Several coats on the rack. Presently . . .

GUS: There's no brainwork in this game. Let me teach you claviash.

SHORY: I can win all the money I need in rummy and pinochle. Play.

GUS: You have no intellectual curiosity.

SHORY: No, but you can slip me a quarter. *Showing his hand.* Rummy.

Enter Belle from the stairs.

GUS, *to Belle*: Everything all right?

BELLE, *half turns to him, holding blanket forth*: She keeps sweating up all the blankets. That poor girl.

GUS: The doctor say anything?

BELLE: Yes . . . *Thinks.* . . . he said, go down and get a dry blanket.

GUS: I mean, about when it will be coming along?

BELLE: Oh, you can't tell about a baby. That's one thing about them, they come most any time. Sometimes when you don't expect it, and sometimes when you do expect it. *She goes up to door and turns again.* Why don't Davey buy a baby carriage?

GUS: Didn't he? I suppose he will.

BELLE: But how can you have a baby without a baby carriage?

SHORY: You better blow your nose.

BELLE: I haven't time! *She blows her nose and goes out, up left.*

SHORY: A quarter says it's a boy. *Tosses a quarter on the table.*

GUS: It's a bet. You know, statistics show more girls is born than boys. You should've asked me for odds.

SHORY: Dave Beeves doesn't need statistics, he wants a boy. Matter of fact, let's raise it—a dollar to your half that he's got a boy tonight.

GUS: Statistically I would take the bet, but financially I stand pat.

> *Enter David from left door to outside. He is dressed for winter. It is immediately evident that a deep enthusiasm, a ruddy satisfaction is upon him. He wears a strong smile. He stamps his feet a little as he removes his gloves, and then his short coat, muffler, hat, leaving a sweater on. As he closes the door.*

DAVID: How'm I doing upstairs?

GUS: So far she only sweats.

DAVID: Sweating! Is that normal?

GUS: Listen, she ain't up there eating ice cream.

DAVID—*goes to the fireplace, rubs his hands before it. Of J.B. as though amused*: The least little thing happens and he stays home from work. He's been here all day.

GUS: Certain men like to make holidays. A new kid to him is always a holiday.

DAVID—*he looks around*: What a fuss.

GUS: You're very calm. Surprising to me. Don't you feel nervous?

SHORY, *to Gus*: You seen too many movies. What's the use of him pacing up and down?

DAVID, *with an edge of guilt*: I got the best doctor; everything she needs. I figure, whatever's going to happen'll happen. After all, I can't . . .

> *Breaks off. In a moment Belle enters from the left door, carrying a different blanket. She goes toward the stair landing. David finally speaks, unable to restrain it.*

> Belle . . . *She stops. He goes to her, restraining anxiety.* Would you ask the doctor . . . if he thinks it's going to be very hard for her, heh?

BELLE: He told me to shut up.

DAVID: Then ask J.B.'s wife.

BELLE: She told me to shut up too. But I'll ask her.

Belle goes up the stairs. David watches her ascend a moment.

DAVID, *looking upstairs*: That girl is going to live like a queen after this. *Turns to them, banging his fist in his palm.* Going to make a lot of money this year.

SHORY: Never predict nothin' but the weather, half an hour ahead.

DAVID: Not this time. I just finished mating my mink, and I think every one of them took.

GUS: All finished? That's fine.

A knock is heard on the door. David goes to it, opens it. Pat enters. He is dressed in a pea jacket, a wool stocking cap on his head. He carries a duffel bag on his shoulder.

DAVID: Oh, hello, Dad.

PAT: The baby come yet?

DAVID: Not yet.

PAT: My train doesn't leave for a couple of hours. I thought I'd wait over here.

DAVID: Here, give me that. *He takes the duffel bag from Pat, puts it out of the way.*

SHORY: So you're really going, Pat?

PAT: I got my old job back—ship's cook. I figure with a little studying, maybe in a year or so, I'll have my Third license. So . . .

DAVID: It's so foolish your leaving, Dad. Can't I change your mind?

PAT: It's better this way, David. Maybe if I'm not around Amos'll take hold of himself.

There is a knock on the door.

DAVID: That's probably Amos now.

He goes to the door, opens it. Amos enters. He is smoking a cigarette.

Hello, Ame. All locked up? Come in.

AMOS: I got my motor running. Hello, Gus, Shory. *He ignores Pat. There is a pause.*

GUS: Working hard?

AMOS, *a tired, embittered chuckle*: Yeh, pretty tough; pumpin' gas, ringin' the cash register . . . *Giving David a small envelope and a key*: There's twenty-six bucks in there. I got the tally slip in with it.

DAVID, *as though anxious for his participation; strained*: Twenty-six! We did all right today.

AMOS: Always do, don't ya? 'Night. *Starts to go.*

DAVID: Listen, Ame. *Amos turns.* The mink'll be bearing in about a month. I was thinking you might like to take a shot at working with me, here . . . it's a great exercise. . . . Spring is coming, you know. You want to be in condition . . .

AMOS: For what?

DAVID: Well . . . maybe play some ball this summer.

AMOS, *glances at Pat*: Who said I'm playing ball?

DAVID, *as carelessly as possible*: What are you going to do with yourself?

AMOS: Pump your gas. . . . Bring you the money every night. Wait for something good to happen. *A bitter little laugh.* I mean the day they announced they're building the new main highway right past your gas station I knew *something* good had to happen to me. *Laughing*: I mean it just *had* to, Dave! *Now with real feeling*: Baby hasn't come yet? *David shakes his head, disturbed by his brother's bitterness.* Overdue, ain't she? *Takes a drag on his cigarette.*

DAVID: A little.

AMOS: Well, if it's a boy . . . *Glancing at Pat and defiantly blowing out smoke.* Don't have him pitchin' down the cellar. *With a wink at David, he goes out. After a moment David goes to Pat.*

DAVID: Why must you go, Dad? Work with me here, I've plenty for everybody, I don't need it all.

PAT: Inhaling cigarettes in those glorious lungs. I couldn't bear to watch him destroying my work that way.

SHORY, *at the fireplace*: Come on, Pat, pinochle.

DAVID, *beckoning Gus over to the right*: Hey, Gus, I want to talk to you.

PAT, *going to Shory. Without the old conviction*: Fireplace heat is ruination to the arteries.

   Pat takes Gus's place, Gus coming to the right.

SHORY, *mixing the deck*: So you'll drop dead warm. Sit down. *He deals.*

David and Gus are at right. J.B. continues sleeping. The card game begins.

DAVID: I want you to do something for me, Gus. In a little more than thirty days I'll have four or five mink for every bitch in those cages. Four to one.

GUS: Well, don't count the chickens . . .

DAVID: No, about this I'm sure. I want to mortgage the shop. Before you answer . . . I'm not being an Indian giver. I signed sixty percent of the shop over to you because you're worth it—I didn't want what don't belong to me and I still don't. I just want you to sign so I can borrow some money on the shop. I need about twenty-five hundred dollars.

GUS: I can ask why?

DAVID: Sure. I want to buy some more breeders.

GUS: Oh. Well, why not use the money you have?

DAVID: Frankly, Gus . . . *Laughs confidently.* . . . I don't have any other money.

GUS: Ah, go on now, don't start kidding me . . .

DAVID: No, it's the truth. I've damn near as many mink out there as Dan Dibble. That costs big money. What do you say?

Pat and Shory look up now and listen while playing their hands.

GUS, *thinks a moment*: Why do you pick on the shop to mortgage? You could get twenty-five hundred on the gas station, or the quarry, or the farm . . . *Slight pause.*

DAVID: I did. I've got everything mortgaged. Everything but the shop.

GUS, *shocked*: Dave, I can't believe this!

DAVID, *indicates out of the right window*: Well, look at them out there. I've got a *ranch*. You didn't think I had enough cash to buy that many, did you?

GUS, *gets up trying to shake off his alarm*: But, Dave, this is mink. Who knows what can happen to them? I don't understand how you can take everything you own and sink it in . . .

DAVID: Four for one, Gus. If prices stay up I can make sixty thousand dollars this year.

GUS: But how can you be sure; you can't . . .

DAVID: I'm sure.

GUS: But how can you be . . . ?

DAVID, *more nervously now, wanting to end this tack*: I'm sure. Isn't it possible? To be sure?

GUS: Yes, but why? *Pause.* Why are you sure?

J.B., *suddenly erupting on the couch*: Good Good and . . . ! *He sits up rubbing himself.* What happened to those radiators you were going to put into this house? *He gets up, goes to the fire, frozen.* You could hang meat in this room.

DAVID, *to J.B.*: You're always hanging meat.

GUS: I don't know how to answer you. I have worked very hard in the shop . . . I . . . *His reasonableness breaks*: You stand there and don't seem to realize you'll be wiped out if those mink go, and now you want more yet!

DAVID: *I said they're not going to die!*

J.B., *to Pat and Shory*: Who's going to die? What're they talking about?

DAVID: Nothin'. *He looks out of the window. J.B. watches him, mystified.*

PAT: I think Amos would smoke a pipe instead of those cigarettes, if you told him, Shory.

J.B.: Dave, you want a baby carriage y'know.

DAVID, *half turns*: Heh? . . . Yeh, sure.

J.B.: I figured you forgot to ask me so I ordered a baby carriage for you.

    David turns back to the window as. . . .

    Matter of fact, it's in the store. *With great enthusiasm*: Pearl gray! Nice soft rubber tires too . . . boy, one thing I love to see . . .

DAVID, *turns to him, restraining*: All right, will you stop talking?

    J.B. is shocked. In a moment he turns and goes to the rack, starts getting into his coat. David crosses quickly to him.

    John, what the hell! *He takes J.B.'s arm.*

J.B.: You unnerve me, Dave! You unnerve me! A man acts a certain way when he's going to be a father, and by Jesus I want him to act that way.

SHORY: Another moviegoer! Why should he worry about something he can't change?

DAVID: I've got a million things to think of, John. I want to ask you.

J.B.: What?

DAVID—*hangs J.B.'s coat up*: I want to get a buy on a new Buick; maybe you can help me swindle that dealer you know in Burley. I'm taking Hester to California in about a month. Sit down.

J.B., *suddenly pointing at him*: That's what unnerves me! You don't seem to realize what's happening. You can't take a month-old baby in a car to California.

DAVID, *a blank, shocked look*: Well, I meant . . .

J.B., *laughs, slaps his back relieved at this obvious truth*: The trouble with you is, you don't realize that she didn't swell up because she swallowed an olive! *Gus and he laugh; David tries to.* You're a poppa, boy! You're the guy he's going to call Pop!

> *There is a commotion of footsteps upstairs. David goes quickly to the landing. Belle hurries down. She is sniffling, sobbing.*

DAVID: What happened?

> *Belle touches his shoulder kindly but brushes right past him to the fireplace where she picks up a wood basket.*

> *David continues going to her.* What happened, Belle!

BELLE, *standing with the wood*: She's having it, she's having it. *She hurries to the landing, David behind her.*

DAVID: What does the doctor say? Belle! How is she? *He catches her arm.*

BELLE: I don't know. She shouldn't have fallen that time. She shouldn't have fallen, Davey. Oh dear . . .

> *She bursts into a sob and rushes upstairs. David stands gaping upward. But Gus is staring at David. After a long moment . . .*

GUS, *quietly*: Hester fell down?

DAVID, *turns slowly to him after an instant of his own*: What?

GUS: Hester had a fall?

DAVID: Yeh, some time ago.

GUS: You had her to the doctor?

DAVID: Yeh.

GUS: He told you the baby would be possibly dead? *Pause.*

DAVID: What're you talking about?

GUS, *quavering*: I think you know what I'm talking about.

> *David is speechless. Walks to a chair and sits on the arm as though, at the price of terrible awkwardness, to simulate ease. Always glancing at Gus, he gets up unaccountably, and in a broken, uncontrolled voice . . .*

DAVID: What are you talking about?

GUS: I understand why you were so sure about the mink. But I sign no mortgage on the shop. I do not bet on dead children.

> *David is horrified at the revelation. He stands rigidly, his fists clenched. He might sit down or spring at Gus or weep.*

J.B.: He couldn't think a thing like that. He . . .

> *He looks to David for reinforcement, but David is standing there hurt and silent and self-horrified. J.B. goes to David.*

Dave, you wouldn't want a thing like that. *He shakes him.* Dave!

DAVID, *glaring at Gus*: I'd cut my throat!

> *He walks downstage from J.B., looking at Gus. His movements are wayward, restless, like one caught in a strange cul-de-sac. Gus is silent.*

Why do you look at me that way? *Glances at J.B. then slowly back to Gus.* Why do you look that way? I'm only telling you what happened. A person has to look at facts, doesn't he? I heard something at the door and I opened it . . . and there she was lying on the step. A fact is a fact, isn't it? *They don't reply. Bursting out:* Well, for Jesus' sake, if you . . . !

GUS, *a shout*: What fact! She fell! So the baby is dead because she fell? Is this a fact?!!

DAVID, *moves away from Gus's direction, in high tension*: I didn't say dead. It doesn't have to be dead to be . . . to . . . *Breaks off.*

GUS: To be what?

> *Pause.*

DAVID: To be a curse on us. It can come wrong . . . A fall can make them that way. The doctor told me. *Gus looks unconvinced.* The trouble with you is that you think I got a special angel watching over me.

SHORY, *pointing at Gus*: He said it that time, brother!

GUS, *to Shory too*: A man needs a special angel to have a live child?

DAVID, *furiously*: Who said he was going to be dead?!

GUS: What are you excited about? *Takes his arm.* Take it easy, sit . . .

DAVID, *freeing his arm*: Stop humoring me, will you? Dan Dibble'll have my new mink here tonight. I got all the papers ready . . . *Goes to a drawer, takes out papers.* All you do is sign and . . .

GUS—*suddenly he rushes to David, pulls the papers out of his hand, throws them down*: Are you mad! *He frightens David into immobility.* There is no catastrophe upstairs, there is no guarantee up there for your mink. *He grasps David's arm, pleadingly.* Dave . . .

DAVID: If you say that again I'm going to throw you out of this house!

J.B., *nervously*: Oh, come on now, come on now.

> *From above a scream of pain is heard. David freezes. Gus looks up.*

GUS, *to David*: Don't say that again.

> *David thrusts his hands into his pockets as though they might reveal him too. Under great tension he attempts to speak reasonably. His voice leaps occasionally, he clears his throat. Gus never takes his eyes off him. David walks from J.B. unwillingly.*

DAVID: I'm a lucky man, John. Everything I've ever gotten came . . . straight out of the blue. There's nothing mad about it. It's facts. When I couldn't have Hester unless Old Man Falk got out of the way, he was killed just like it was specially for me. When I couldn't fix the Marmon . . . a man walks in from the middle of the night . . . and fixes it for me. I buy a lousy little gas station . . . they build a highway in front of it. That's lucky. You pay for that.

SHORY: Damn right you do.

GUS: Where is such a law?

DAVID: I don't know. *Observes a silence. He walks to the windows.* Of all the people I've heard of I'm the only one who's never paid. Well . . . I think the holiday's over. *Turns toward upstairs, with great sorrow:* I think we're about due to join up with the rest of you. I'll have almost sixty thousand dollars when I market my mink . . . but it won't be money I got without paying for it. And that's why I put everything in them. That's why I'm sure. Because from here on in we're paid for. I saw it in black and white when she fell. *With a heartbroken tone:* God help me, we're paid for now. I'm not afraid of my luck anymore, and I'm going to play it for everything it's worth.

GUS: David, you break my heart. This is from Europe this idea. This is from Asia, from the rotten places, not America.

DAVID: No?

GUS: Here you are not a worm, a louse in the earth; here you are a man. A man deserves everything here!

SHORY: Since when?

GUS, *strongly to Shory*: Since forever!

SHORY: Then I must have been born before that.

GUS, *angrily now*: I beg your pardon, he is not you and do me a favor and stop trying to make him like you.

DAVID: He's not making me anything.

GUS: He won't be happy until he does, I can tell you! *Indicating Shory*: This kind of people never are.

SHORY: What kind of people?

GUS: Your kind! *His* life he can make golden, if he wants.

SHORY: Unless the walls blow out.

GUS: If he don't go chasing after whores his walls won't blow out. *Quietly*: And I beg your pardon. I didn't mean nothing personal.

J.B., *goes to David*: I'll lend you the money for the mink, Dave.

GUS: Are you mad?

J.B.: I can see what he means, Gus. *Looks at David*. It takes a great kind of man to prepare himself that way. A man does have to pay. It's just the way it happens, senseless. *He glances upstairs, then to David*: It's true. It always happens senseless.

J.B.: I'll back you, Dave.

DAVID: I'd like to pay him tonight if I can . . .

> They all turn to look up as Belle appears, slowly descending the stairs. They do not hear her until she is a little way down. Her usual expression of wide-eyed bewilderment is on her face, but now she is tense, and descends looking at David. She half sniffs, half sobs into her kerchief. She stops on the stairs. David rises. She half laughs, half snivels in a quiet ecstasy of excitement, and weakly motions him upstairs. He comes toward her questioningly, to the landing.

BELLE: Go . . . Go up.

DAVID: What. What . . . ?

BELLE, *suddenly bursts out and rushes down and flings her arms about him*: Oh, Davey, Davey.

DAVID, *ripping her free, he roars in her face*: What happened?! *With a sob of grief in his voice, he grips her.* Belle! *The cry of a baby is suddenly heard from above. The sound almost throws David back, away from the stairs. He stands stock still, hard as a rock, looking upward, his mouth fallen open.*

BELLE, *still half-sobbing*: It's a boy. A perfect baby boy!

> *She now breaks into full sobs and rushes up the stairs. Everything is still a moment, David stares at nothing. The cry sounds again. He looks upward again as though to let it sink in. J.B. goes to him, hand extended.*

J.B., *filled with joy, and gravely*: Dave.

> *David dumbly shakes his hand, a weak smile on his face.*

A boy, a boy, Dave! Just what you wanted!

> *A strange short laugh leaps from David. An easier but still tense laugh comes. Pat goes to him and shakes his hand.*

PAT: Dave, a new generation!

GUS, *smilingly*: Well? You see? *Laughs.* A good man gets what a good man makes. *Hits David jovially.* Wake up now! Good luck!

> *Gus tosses a quarter to Shory.*

GUS: It's the first time you've been right since I knew you.

J.B.: Come out of the ether. Take a look at him, Dave.

> *David rushes out. They stand astonished for a moment.*

What do you suppose come over him?

GUS: What else could come over him? . . . he's ashamed.

> *Gus hurries out the door. The others remain in silence. Then one by one they look upstairs toward the sound of the baby's crying.*

SLOW CURTAIN

SCENE II

Before the curtain rises thunder is heard.

It is one month later. The living room. Night.

The room is empty and in darkness. A bolt of lightning illumi-nates it through the windows, then darkness again. Now the door to the outside opens and Hester enters. She is very tense but her motions are minute, as though she were mentally absorbed and had entirely forgotten her surroundings. With-out removing her coat or galoshes she comes to the center of the room and stands there staring. Then she goes to a window and looks out. A flash of lightning makes her back a step from the window; and without further hesitation she goes to the phone, switching on a nearby light.

HESTER—*she watches the window as she waits:* Hello? Gus? Where have you been, I've been ringing you for an hour. *She listens.* Well, look, could you come over here? Right now, I mean. It would *not* be inter-fering, Gus, I want to talk to you. He's outside. Gus, you've got to come here—his mink are going to die. *She keeps glancing at the window.* He doesn't know it yet, but he'll probably see it any minute. Dan Dibble called before. . . . He's lost over thirty of his already. . . . They use the same fish. . . . I want you here when he notices. *She turns suddenly toward the door.* He's coming in. You hurry over now. . . . Please!

She hangs up, and starts for the door, but as though to com-pose herself she stops, and starts toward a chair when she real-izes she still has her coat and galoshes on. She is kicking off the galoshes when David enters. He looks up at her, and with a slight glance upstairs . . .

DAVID: Everything all right?

HESTER: Why?

DAVID: I thought I heard a call or a scream.

HESTER: No, there was no scream.

DAVID: I guess it was the lightning. Is he all right? *Of the baby.*

HESTER: There's no gate there, you can go up and see.

DAVID: How can I go to him with my hands so bloody? *She turns from him. He starts for the door.*

HESTER: I thought you were through feeding.

DAVID: I am. I'm just grinding some for tomorrow.

HESTER: Are they all right?

DAVID: I never saw them so strung up. I think it's the hail banging on the cages. *There is a momentary hiatus as he silently asks for leave to go.* I just wondered if he was all right. *He takes a step.*

HESTER, *suddenly*: Don't go out again, Davey. Please. You told me yourself, they ought to be left alone when they're whelping.

DAVID: I've got to be there, Hess, I've just got to. I . . . *He goes to her.* I promise you, after they whelp we'll go away, we'll travel . . . I'm going to make a queen's life for you.

HESTER: Don't go out.

DAVID: I'll be in right away . . .

HESTER, *grasps his arms*: I don't want them to be so important, Davey!

DAVID: But everything we've got is in them. You know that.

HESTER: I'm not afraid of being poor . . .

DAVID: That's 'cause you never were—and you'll never be. You're going to have a life like a . . .

HESTER: Why do you keep saying that? I don't want it, I don't need it! I don't care what happens out there! And I don't want you to care. Do you hear what I say, I don't want you to care!

> *A bolt of lightning floods suddenly through the windows.
> David starts. Then hurries to the door.*

HESTER, *frightened now*: Davey! *David stops, does not turn.* You can't stop the lightning, can you? *He does not turn still. She goes closer to him, pleading*: I know how hard you worked, but it won't be the first year's work that ever went for nothing in the world. It happens that way, doesn't it?

DAVID—*he turns to her slowly. Now his emotions seem to flood him*: Not when a man doesn't make any mistakes. I kept them alive all year. Not even one got sick. I didn't make a mistake. And now this storm comes, just when I need it calm, just tonight . . .

HESTER: You talk as though the sun were shining everywhere else but here, as though the sky is making thunder just to knock you down.

DAVID—*he looks at her long as though she had reached into him*: Yeh, that's the way I talk. *He seems about to sob*: Bear with me, Hess—only a little while. *He moves to go.*

HESTER: Davey . . . the house is gray. Like the old paint was creeping back on the walls. When will we sit and talk again? When will you pick up the baby . . . ?

DAVID, *comes alive*: I did, Hess . . .

HESTER: You never did. And why is that?

DAVID: When you were out of the house . . .

HESTER: Never, not since he's been born. Can't you tell me why? *David turns and opens the door. Her fear raises her voice.* Can't you tell me why? *He starts out.* Davey, tell me why! *He goes out. She calls out the door*: Davey, I don't understand! Come back here!

> *In a moment, she comes away, closing the door. Her hands are lightly clasped to her throat. She comes to a halt in the room; now she turns on a lamp. She suddenly hears something behind her, turns, and takes a step toward the door as Gus quietly enters.*

HESTER, *relieved*: Oh, Gus!

GUS, *glancing toward the door*: Is he coming right back?

HESTER: He goes in and out, I don't know. You'll stay here tonight, won't you?

GUS: The first thing to do is sit down.

> *As he leads her to the couch—she is near tears.*

HESTER: I kept calling you and calling you.

GUS, *taking off his coat*: Now get hold of yourself; there's nothing to do till he finds out. I'm sorry, I was in Burley all afternoon, I just got home. What did Dibble tell you? *He returns to her.*

HESTER: Just that he was losing animals, and he thought it was silkworm in the feed. They share the same carload.

GUS: Ah. David notices nothing? *A gesture toward outside with his head.*

HESTER: He just says they're strung up, but that's the lightning. It takes time for them to digest.

GUS: Well then, we'll wait and see. *He goes to the window, looks out.* This storm is going to wipe out the bridges. It's terrible.

HESTER: What am I going to do, Gus? He worked all year on those animals.

GUS: We will do what we have to, Hester, that's what we will do. *He turns to her, taking out an envelope.* Actually, I was coming over tonight anyway . . . To say goodbye.

HESTER: Goodbye!

GUS: In here I explain. *He places the envelope on the mantel.* When I am gone, give it to him. I can't argue with him no more.

HESTER: You mean you're moving away?

GUS: I am going to Chicago. There is an excellent position for me. Double what I can make here.

HESTER: But why are you going?

GUS: I told you, I can make double . . .

HESTER, *gets up*: Don't treat me like a baby, why are you going? *Slight pause.*

GUS: Well . . . Actually, I am lonely. *Laughs slightly.* There is plenty of girls here, but no wifes, Hester. Thirty-seven years is a long time for a man to wash his own underwear.

HESTER, *touched*: You and your red-headed girls!

GUS: I was always a romantic man. You know that, don't you? Truly.

HESTER: But to give up a business and go traipsing off just for . . . ?

GUS: Why not? What made me give up Detroit to come here?

HESTER: Really, Gus?

GUS: Certainly. Moving is very necessary for me. *Pause.* I'm leaving tomorrow night.

HESTER: But why? I suppose I should understand, but I can't. *Pause. Gus looks directly at her.* It doesn't make sense. *Insistently:* Gus?

GUS—*pause. For a long time he keeps her in his eye*: Because I have no courage to stay here. *Pause.* I was talking today with a doctor in Burley. I believe David . . . is possibly losing his mind.

> *She does not react. She stands there gaping at him. He waits. With no sound she backs a few steps, then comes downstage and lightly sets both hands on the couch, never taking her eyes from him. A pause. As though hearing what he said again, she is impelled to move again, to a chair on whose back she sets a hand—facing him now. They stand so a moment.*

I thought surely you knew. Or at least you would know soon. *She does not answer.* Do you know?

HESTER: I've almost thought so sometimes. . . . But I can't believe he . . .

GUS—*a new directness, now that she has taken the blow*: I have been try-ing to straighten him out all month. But I have no more wisdom, Hester. I . . . I would like to take him to the doctors in Burley.

HESTER, *shocked*: Burley!

GUS: Tonight. They will know what to say to him there.

HESTER, *horrified*: No, he's not going there.

GUS: It is no disgrace. You are talking like a silly woman.

HESTER: He's not going there! There's nothing wrong with him. He's wor-ried, that's all . . .

GUS: When those animals begin dying he will be more than worried. Nothing worse could possibly happen . . .

HESTER: No. If he can take the shock tonight he'll be all right. I think it's better if they die.

GUS: For God's sake, no!

HESTER: All his life he's been waiting for it. All his life, waiting, waiting for something to happen. It'll be over now, all over, don't you see? Just stay here tonight. And when it happens, you'll talk to him . . .

GUS: What he has lost I can't put back, Hester. He is not a piece of ma-chinery.

HESTER, *stops moving*: What has he lost? What do you mean, lost?

GUS: What a man must have, what a man must believe. That on this earth he is the boss of his life. Not the leafs in the teacups, not the stars. In Europe I seen already millions of Davids walking around, millions. They gave up already to know that they are the boss. They gave up to know that they deserve this world. And now here too, with such good land, with such a . . . such a big sky they are saying . . . I hear it every day . . . that it is somehow unnatural for a man to have a sweet life and nice things. Daily they wait for catastrophe. A man must understand the pres-ence of God in his hands. And when he don't understand it he is trapped. David is trapped, Hester. You understand why everything he has is in the mink?

HESTER, *wide-eyed*: It's the baby, isn't it. He thought it was going to be . . .

GUS: Dead, yes. Say, say out now. I was here that night. He always wanted so much to have a son and that is why he saw him dead. This, what he wanted most of all he couldn't have. This finally would be his catastrophe.

And then everything would be guaranteed for him. And that is why he put everything in those animals.

HESTER: Gus . . .

GUS: The healthy baby stole from David his catastrophe, Hester. Perfect he was born and David was left with every penny he owns in an animal that can die like this . . . *Snaps his fingers.* . . . and the catastrophe still on its way.

HESTER, *seeing the reason*: He never touched the baby . . .

GUS: How can he touch him? He is bleeding with shame, Hester. Because he betrayed his son, and he betrayed you. And now if those animals die he will look into the tea leafs of his mind, into the sky he will look where he always looked, and if he sees retribution there . . . you will not call him worried any more. Let me take him to Burley before he notices anything wrong in the cages.

HESTER: No. He's Davey, he's not some . . .

GUS: They will know what to do there!

HESTER: I know what to do! *She moves away and faces him.* I could have warned him. . . . Dan called before he started feeding.

GUS, *shocked and furious*: Hester!

HESTER: I wanted them dead! I want them dead now, those beautiful rats!

GUS: How could you do that!

HESTER: He's got to lose. Once and for all he's got to lose. I always knew it had to happen, let it happen now, before the baby can see and understand. You're not taking him anywhere. He'll be happy again. It'll be over and he'll be happy!

GUS, *unwillingly*: Hester.

HESTER: No, I'm not afraid now. It'll be over now.

GUS: What will be over, Hester? He took out last week an insurance policy. A big one. *Hester stops moving.* It covers his life.

HESTER: No, Gus.

GUS: What will be over?

HESTER, *a cry*: No, Gus! *Breaks into sobbing.*

GUS, *taking her by the arms*: Get hold now, get hold!

HESTER, *sobbing, shaking her head negatively*: Davey, Davey . . . he was always so fine, what happened to him . . . !

GUS: He mustn't see you this way . . . ! Nothing is worse than . . .

HESTER, *trying to break from Gus to go out*: Davey, Davey . . . !

GUS: Stop it, Hester! He's shamed enough!

> *He has her face in his hands as the door suddenly opens and David is standing there. Gus releases her. They stand apart. David has stopped moving in surprise. He looks at her, then at Gus, then at her. David goes toward her.*

DAVID, *astonished, alarmed*: Hess. What's the matter?

HESTER: Nothing . . . How is everything outside?

DAVID: It's still hailing . . . *Stops. With an edge of self-accusation*: Why were you crying?

HESTER, *her voice still wet*: I wasn't really.

DAVID, *feeling the awkwardness, glances at both; to Gus*: Why were you holding her?

HESTER, *with an attempt at a laugh*: He wasn't holding me. He's decided to go to Chicago and . . .

DAVID, *mystified, to Gus*: Chicago! Why . . . ?

HESTER, *tries to laugh*: He wants to find a wife! Imagine?

DAVID, *to Gus*: All of a sudden you . . . ?

HESTER, *unbuttoning his coat, ready to weep and trying to be gay*: Let's have some tea and sit up till way late and talk! Don't go out anymore, Davey. . . . From now on I'm not letting you out of my sight. . . . There are so many nice things to talk about!

> *She has his coat and has just stepped away with a gross animation.*

DAVID, *deeply worried. Brushing her attempt away*: Why were you crying, Hester?

> *The phone rings. Hester fairly leaps at the sound. She starts quickly for the phone but David is close to it and picks it up easily, slightly puzzled at her frantic eagerness to take it.*

HESTER: It's probably Ellie. I promised to lend her a hat for tomorrow.

DAVID—*looks at her perplexed. He lifts the receiver*: Yes?

> *As she speaks Hester steps away from him, in fear now. Gus changes position instinctively, almost as though for physical advantage.*

Mr. Dibble? No, he isn't here; I don't expect him. Oh! Well, he isn't here yet. What's it all about? *Listens.* What are you talking about; have I got what under control? *Listens. Now with horror:* Of course I've fed! Why didn't you call me, you know I feed before this! God damn your soul, you know I use the same feed he does! *Roars:* Don't tell me he called me! Don't . . . ! *Listens.* When did he call?

Breaks off; listens. He turns, listening, to Hester; slowly, an expression of horrified perplexity and astonishment grips his face. His eyes stay on Hester.

Well, they seem all right now . . . maybe it hasn't had time to grip them. *Still into the phone:* Yeh . . . yeh . . . all right, I'll wait for him.

He hangs up weakly. For a long time he looks at her. Then he looks at Gus and back to her as though connecting them somehow.

What . . . Why . . . didn't you tell me he called?

HESTER—*suddenly she dares not be too near him; she holds out a hand to touch and ward him off . . . she is a distance from him:* Davey . . .

DAVID: Why didn't you stop me from feeding?

GUS: Dan'll be here. Maybe he can do something.

DAVID, *facing Hester:* What can he do? Something's wrong in the feed! He can't pull it out of their stomachs! *With welling grief. To Hester:* Why didn't you tell me? *Hester retreats a few inches.* Why are you moving away from me? *He suddenly reaches out and catches her arm.* You wanted them to die!

HESTER, *straining at his grip:* You always said something had to happen. It's better this way, isn't it?

DAVID: Better?! My boy is a pauper, we're on the bottom of a hole, how is it better!

HESTER—*her fear alone makes her brave:* Then I . . . I think I'll have to go away, Davey. I can't stay here, then.

She moves toward the stairs. He lets her move a few steps, then moves across to her and she stops and faces him.

DAVID: You can't . . . What did you say?

HESTER: I can't live with you, Davey. Not with the baby.

DAVID: No, Hester . . .

HESTER: I don't want him to see you this way. It's a harmful thing. I'm going away.

DAVID—*he breathes as though about to burst into weeping. He looks to Gus, stares at him, then back to her. Incredibly*: You're going with him?

HESTER—*she darts a suddenly frightened glance toward Gus*: Oh, no, no, I didn't mean that. He was going anyway.

DAVID—*it is truer to him now*: You're going with him.

HESTER: No, David, I'm not going with anybody . . .

DAVID, *with certainty. Anger suddenly stalks him*: You're going with him!

HESTER: No, Davey . . . !

DAVID, *to Gus*: You told her not to tell me!

HESTER: He wasn't even here when Dan phoned!

DAVID: How do I know where he was! *To Gus*: You think I'm a blind boy?!

HESTER: You're talking like a fool!

DAVID: You couldn't have done this to me! He wants you!

He starts to stride for Gus. Hester gets in front of him.

HESTER: I did it! *Grabs his coat.* Davey, I did it myself!

DAVID: No, you couldn't have! Not you! *To Gus*: You think I've fallen apart? You want her . . . ?

He starts to push her aside, knocking a chair over, going for Gus. She slaps him hard across the face. He stops moving.

HESTER, *with loathing and heartbreak*: I did it!

For an instant they are still, she watching for his reaction. He quietly draws in a sob, looking at her in grief.

HESTER: I wanted you like you were, Davey—a good man, able to do anything. You were always a good man, why can't you understand that?

DAVID: A good man! You pick up a phone and everything you've got dies in the ground! A man! What good is a man!

HESTER: You can start again, start fresh and clean!

DAVID: For what! For what!! The world is a madhouse, what can you build in a madhouse that won't be knocked down when you turn your back!

HESTER: It was you made it all and you destroyed it! I'm going, Davey . . . *With a sob*: I can't bear any more. *She rushes to the landing.*

DAVID, *a call, and yet strangled by sobs*: Hester . . .

> *Hester halts, looks at him. His hands raised toward her, shaken and weeping, he moves toward the landing . . . frantically.*

I love you. . . . I love you. . . . Don't . . . don't . . . don't.

> *He reaches her, and sobbing, lost, starts drawing her down to him as the door, left, swings open. Dan Dibble rushes in and halts when he sees David. He carries a small satchel.*

DIBBLE, *indicating downstage, right*: I've been out there looking for you, what are you doing in here? I've got something may help them. Come on. *He starts for the door.*

DAVID: I don't want to look at them, Dan. *He goes to a chair.*

DIBBLE: You can't be sure, it might take . . . *Opens the door.*

DAVID: No, I'm sure they digested, it's over two hours.

DIBBLE, *stops moving suddenly at door*: Over two hours what?

DAVID: Since I fed them.

DIBBLE: You didn't give them this morning's load of fish?

DAVID: What else could I give them? The load I split with you, goddamit.

DIBBLE: Well, you just couldn't've, David. They don't show a sign yet: that kind of silkworm'll kill them in twenty minutes. You must've . . .

DAVID: Silkworm.—But my fish wasn't wormy . . .

DIBBLE: They don't look like worms, they're very small, you wouldn't have noticed them, they're black, about the size of a . . .

DAVID: Poppyseed . . .

DIBBLE: A grain of ground pepper, yah. Come on . . . *But David is motionless, staring* . . . Well? You want me to look at them?

> *David slowly sits in a chair.*

GUS: At least have a look, Dave. *Slight pause.*

DAVID, *wondrously; but also an edge of apology*: . . . I saw them, Dan. I didn't know what they were but I decided not to take any chances, so I threw them away.

DIBBLE, *angering*: But you couldn't have gone over every piece of fish!

DAVID: Well I . . . yah, I did, Dan. Most of it was okay, but the ones with the black specks I threw away.

HESTER: Davey!—You saved them!

DAVID: Well, you told me to watch the feed very carefully, Dan—I figured you'd notice them the same as me!

DIBBLE: But you know nobody's got the time to go over every goddam piece of fish!

DAVID: But I thought everybody did!—I swear, Dan!

DIBBLE: God Almighty, Dave, a man'd think you'd warn him if you saw silkworm!—The least you could've done is call me.

DAVID: I started to, I had the phone in my hand—but it seemed ridiculous, me telling you something. Listen, let me give you some of my breeders to start you off again.

DIBBLE: No—no . . .

DAVID: Please, Dan, go out and pick whatever you like.

DIBBLE: . . . Well, I might think about that, but I'm too old to start all over again, I don't think I could get up the steam. Well, goodnight.

Dibble exits.

Gus and Hester stand watching David who is puzzled and astonished.

DAVID: I can't believe it. He's the best in the business.

GUS: Not anymore.

HESTER: This wasn't something from the sky, dear. This was you only. You must see that now, don't you?

The baby crying is heard from above.

I'd better go up, he's hungry. Come up?—Why don't you, Dave?

DAVID, *awkwardly*: I will . . . right away. *Hester exits. His face is rapt.* But they couldn't all have made their own luck!—J.B. with his drinking, Shory with his whores, Dad and Amos . . . and you losing your shop. *Seizing on it*: And I could never have fixed that Marmon if you hadn't walked in like some kind of an angel!—That Marmon wasn't me!

GUS: You'd have towed it to Newton and fixed it there without me. *Grasps David's hand.* But is that really the question anyway? Of course bad things must happen. And you can't help it when God drops the other shoe. But whether you lay there or get up again—that's the part that's entirely up to you, that's for sure.

DAVID: You don't understand it either, do you.

GUS: No, but I live with it. All I know is you are a good man, but also you have luck. So you have to grin and bear it—you are lucky!

DAVID: For now.

GUS: Well, listen—"for now" is a very big piece of "forever."

HESTER, *from above*: Dave? You coming up?

GUS: Go on, kiss the little fellow.

DAVID: . . . I had the phone in my hand to call him. And I put it down. I had his whole ranch right here in my hand.

GUS: You mean you were a little bit like God . . . for him.

DAVID: Yes. Except I didn't know it.

GUS, *a thumb pointing heavenward*: Maybe he doesn't know either.

HESTER, *from above*: David? Are you there?

GUS: Goodnight, Dave.

DAVID, *with a farewell wave to Gus, calls upstairs*: Yes, I'm here!

> *He goes to the stairs. A shock of thunder strikes. He quickly turns toward the windows, the old apprehension in his face.*

> *. . . To himself*: For now.

> *With a self-energized determination in his voice and body.* Comin' up!

> *As he mounts the stairs a rumble of thunder sounds in the distance.*

ALL MY SONS

A DRAMA IN THREE ACTS

1947

Characters

JOE KELLER

KATE KELLER

CHRIS KELLER

ANN DEEVER

GEORGE DEEVER

DR. JIM BAYLISS

SUE BAYLISS

FRANK LUBEY

LYDIA LUBEY

BERT

SYNOPSIS OF SCENES

Act One
The back yard of the Keller home in the outskirts of an American town.
August of our era.

Act Two
Scene, as before. The same evening, as twilight falls.

Act Three
Scene, as before. Two o'clock the following morning.

ACT ONE

The back yard of the Keller home in the outskirts of an American town. August of our era.

The stage is hedged on right and left by tall, closely planted poplars which lend the yard a secluded atmosphere. Upstage is filled with the back of the house and its open, unroofed porch which extends into the yard some six feet. The house is two stories high and has seven rooms. It would have cost perhaps fifteen thousand in the early twenties when it was built. Now it is nicely painted, looks tight and comfortable, and the yard is green with sod, here and there plants whose season is gone. At the right, beside the house, the entrance of the driveway can be seen, but the poplars cut off view of its continuation downstage. In the left corner, downstage, stands the four-foot-high stump of a slender apple tree whose upper trunk and branches lie toppled beside it, fruit still clinging to its branches. Downstage right is a small, trellised arbor, shaped like a sea-shell, with a decorative bulb hanging from its forward-curving roof. Garden chairs and a table are scattered about. A garbage pail on the ground next to the porch steps, a wire leaf-burner near it.

On the rise: It is early Sunday morning. Joe Keller is sitting in the sun reading the want ads of the Sunday paper, the other sections of which lie neatly on the ground beside him. Behind his back, inside the arbor, Doctor Jim Bayliss is reading part of the paper at the table.

Keller is nearing sixty. A heavy man of solid mind and build, a business man these many years, but with the imprint of the machine-shop worker and boss still upon him. When he reads, when he speaks, when he listens, it is with the terrible concentration of the uneducated man for whom there is still wonder in many commonly known things, a man whose judgments must be dredged out of experience and a peasant-like common sense. A man among men.

Doctor Bayliss is nearing forty. A wry self-controlled man, an easy talker, but with a wisp of sadness that clings even to his self-effacing humor.

At curtain, Jim is standing at left, staring at the broken tree. He taps a pipe on it, blows through the pipe, feels in his pockets for tobacco, then speaks.

JIM: Where's your tobacco?

KELLER: I think I left it on the table. *Jim goes slowly to table on the arbor at right, finds a pouch, and sits there on the bench, filling his pipe.* Gonna rain tonight.

JIM: Paper says so?

KELLER: Yeah, right here.

JIM: Then it can't rain.

Frank Lubey enters, from right through a small space between the poplars. Frank is thirty-two but balding. A pleasant, opinionated man, uncertain of himself, with a tendency toward peevishness when crossed, but always wanting it pleasant and neighborly. He rather saunters in, leisurely, nothing to do. He does not notice Jim in the arbor. On his greeting, Jim does not bother looking up.

FRANK: Hya.

KELLER: Hello, Frank. What's doin'?

FRANK: Nothin'. Walking off my breakfast. *Looks up at the sky.* That beautiful? Not a cloud.

KELLER, *looks up*: Yeah, nice.

FRANK: Every Sunday ought to be like this.

KELLER, *indicating the sections beside him*: Want the paper?

FRANK: What's the difference, it's all bad news. What's today's calamity?

KELLER: I don't know, I don't read the news part any more. It's more interesting in the want ads.

FRANK: Why, you trying to buy something?

KELLER: No, I'm just interested. To see what people want, y'know? For instance, here's a guy is lookin' for two Newfoundland dogs. Now what's he want with two Newfoundland dogs?

FRANK: That is funny.

KELLER: Here's another one. Wanted—Old Dictionaries. High prices paid. Now what's a man going to do with an old dictionary?

FRANK: Why not? Probably a book collector.

KELLER: You mean he'll make a living out of that?

FRANK: Sure, there's a lot of them.

KELLER, *shakes his head*: All the kind of business goin' on. In my day, either you were a lawyer, or a doctor, or you worked in a shop. Now . . .

FRANK: Well, I was going to be a forester once.

KELLER: Well, that shows you; in my day, there was no such thing. *Scanning the page, sweeping it with his hand*: You look at a page like this you realize how ignorant you are. *Softly, with wonder, as he scans page*: Psss!

FRANK, *noticing tree*: Hey, what happened to your tree?

KELLER: Ain't that awful? The wind must've got it last night. You heard the wind, didn't you?

FRANK: Yeah, I got a mess in my yard, too. *Goes to tree*. What a pity. *Turns to Keller*. What'd Kate say?

KELLER: They're all asleep yet. I'm just waiting for her to see it.

FRANK, *struck*: You know?—It's funny.

KELLER: What?

FRANK: Larry was born in August. He'd been twenty-seven this month. And his tree blows down.

KELLER, *touched*: I'm surprised you remember his birthday, Frank. That's nice.

FRANK: Well, I'm working on his horoscope.

KELLER: How can you make him a horoscope? That's for the future, ain't it?

FRANK: Well, what I'm doing is this, see. Larry was reported missing on November 25th, right?

KELLER: Yeah?

FRANK: Well, then, we assume that if he was killed it was on November 25th. Now, what Kate wants . . .

KELLER: Oh, Kate asked you to make a horoscope?

FRANK: Yeah, what she wants to find out is whether November 25th was a favorable day for Larry.

KELLER: What is that, favorable day?

FRANK: Well, a favorable day for a person is a fortunate day, according to his stars. In other words it would be practically impossible for him to have died on his favorable day.

KELLER: Well, was that his favorable day?—November 25th?

FRANK: That's what I'm working on to find out. It takes time! See, the point is, if November 25th was his favorable day, then it's completely possible he's alive somewhere, because . . . I mean it's possible. *He notices Jim now. Jim is looking at him as though at an idiot. To Jim—with an uncertain laugh*: I didn't even see you.

KELLER, *to Jim*: Is he talkin' sense?

JIM: Him? He's all right. He's just completely out of his mind, that's all.

FRANK, *peeved*: The trouble with you is, you don't *believe* in anything.

JIM: And your trouble is that you believe in *anything*. *You* didn't see my kid this morning, did you?

FRANK: No.

KELLER: Imagine? He walked off with his thermometer. Right out of his bag.

JIM, *gets up*: What a problem. One look at a girl and he takes her temperature. *Goes to driveway, looks upstage toward street.*

FRANK: That boy's going to be a real doctor; he's smart.

JIM: Over my dead body he'll be a doctor. A good beginning, too.

FRANK: Why? It's an honorable profession.

JIM, *looks at him tiredly*: Frank, will you stop talking like a civics book? *Keller laughs.*

FRANK: Why, I saw a movie a couple of weeks ago, reminded me of you. There was a doctor in that picture . . .

KELLER: Don Ameche!

FRANK: I think it was, yeah. And he worked in his basement discovering things. That's what you ought to do; you could help humanity, instead of . . .

JIM: I would love to help humanity on a Warner Brothers salary.

KELLER, *points at him, laughing*: That's very good, Jim.

JIM, *looks toward house*: Well, where's the beautiful girl was supposed to be here?

FRANK, *excited*: Annie came?

KELLER: Sure, sleepin' upstairs. We picked her up on the one o'clock train last night. Wonderful thing. Girl leaves here, a scrawny kid. Couple of years go by, she's a regular woman. Hardly recognized her, and she was running in and out of this yard all her life. That was a very happy family used to live in your house, Jim.

JIM: Like to meet her. The block can use a pretty girl. In the whole neighborhood there's not a damned thing to look at. *Enter Sue, Jim's wife, from left. She is rounding forty, an overweight woman who fears it. On seeing her Jim wryly adds*: . . . Except my wife, of course.

SUE, *in same spirit*: Mrs. Adams is on the phone, you dog.

JIM, *to Keller*: Such is the condition which prevails . . . *Going to his wife*: my love, my light. . . .

SUE: Don't sniff around me. *Points to their house, left.* And give her a nasty answer. I can smell her perfume over the phone.

JIM: What's the matter with her now?

SUE: I don't know, dear. She sounds like she's in terrible pain—unless her mouth is full of candy.

JIM: Why don't you just tell her to lay down?

SUE: She enjoys it more when you tell her to lay down. And when are you going to see Mr. Hubbard?

JIM: My dear; Mr. Hubbard is not sick, and I have better things to do than to sit there and hold his hand.

SUE: It seems to me that for ten dollars you could hold his hand.

JIM, *to Keller*: If your son wants to play golf tell him I'm ready. *Going left.* Or if he'd like to take a trip around the world for about thirty years. *He exits left.*

KELLER: Why do you needle him? He's a doctor, women are supposed to call him up.

SUE: All I said was Mrs. Adams is on the phone. Can I have some of your parsley?

KELLER: Yeah, sure. *She goes left to parsley box and pulls some parsley.* You were a nurse too long, Susie. You're too . . . too . . . realistic.

SUE, *laughing, points at him*: Now you said it! *Enter Lydia Lubey from right. She is a robust, laughing girl of twenty-seven.*

LYDIA: Frank, the toaster . . . *Sees the others.* Hya.

KELLER: Hello!

LYDIA, *to Frank*: The toaster is off again.

FRANK: Well, plug it in, I just fixed it.

LYDIA, *kindly, but insistently*: Please, dear, fix it back like it was before.

FRANK: I don't know why you can't learn to turn on a simple thing like a toaster! *Frank exits right.*

SUE, *laughs*: Thomas Edison.

LYDIA, *apologetically*: He's really very handy. *She sees broken tree.* Oh, did the wind get your tree?

KELLER: Yeah, last night.

LYDIA: Oh, what a pity. Annie get in?

KELLER: She'll be down soon. Wait'll you meet her, Sue, she's a knockout.

SUE: I should've been a man. People are always introducing me to beautiful women. *To Joe*: Tell her to come over later; I imagine she'd like to see what we did with her house. And thanks. *Sue exits left.*

LYDIA: Is she still unhappy, Joe?

KELLER: Annie? I don't suppose she goes around dancing on her toes, but she seems to be over it.

LYDIA: She going to get married? Is there anybody . . . ?

KELLER: I suppose . . . say, it's a couple years already. She can't mourn a boy forever.

LYDIA: It's so strange . . . Annie's here and not even married. And I've got three babies. I always thought it'd be the other way around.

KELLER: Well, that's what a war does. I had two sons, now I got one. It changed all the tallies. In my day when you had sons it was an honor. Today a doctor could make a million dollars if he could figure out a way to bring a boy into the world without a trigger finger.

LYDIA: You know, I was just reading . . . *Enter Chris Keller from house, stands in doorway.*

LYDIA: Hya, Chris . . . *Frank shouts from off right.*

FRANK: Lydia, come in here! If you want the toaster to work don't plug in the malted mixer.

LYDIA, *embarrassed, laughs*: Did I . . . ?

FRANK: And the next time I fix something don't tell me I'm crazy! Now come in here!

LYDIA, *to Keller*: I'll never hear the end of this one.

KELLER, *calling to Frank*: So what's the difference? Instead of toast have a malted!

LYDIA: Sh! sh! *She exits right laughing.*

> *Chris watches her off. He is thirty-two; like his father, solidly built, a listener. A man capable of immense affection and loyalty. He has a cup of coffee in one hand, part of a doughnut in other.*

KELLER: You want the paper?

CHRIS: That's all right, just the book section. *He bends down and pulls out part of paper on porch floor.*

KELLER: You're always reading the book section and you never buy a book.

CHRIS, *coming down to settee*: I like to keep abreast of my ignorance. *He sits on settee.*

KELLER: What is that, every week a new book comes out?

CHRIS: Lot of new books.

KELLER: All different.

CHRIS: All different.

KELLER, *shakes his head, puts knife down on bench, takes oilstone up to the cabinet*: Psss! Annie up yet?

CHRIS: Mother's giving her breakfast in the dinning-room.

KELLER, *crosses, downstage of stool, looking at broken tree*: See what happened to the tree?

CHRIS, *without looking up*: Yeah.

KELLER: What's Mother going to say? *Bert runs on from driveway. He is about eight. He jumps on stool, then on Keller's back.*

BERT: You're finally up.

KELLER, *swinging him around and putting him down*: Ha! Bert's here! Where's Tommy? He's got his father's thermometer again.

BERT: He's taking a reading.

CHRIS: What!

BERT: But it's only oral.

KELLER: Oh, well, there's no harm in oral. So what's new this morning, Bert?

BERT: Nothin'. *He goes to broken tree, walks around it.*

KELLER: Then you couldn't've made a complete inspection of the block. In the beginning, when I first made you a policeman you used to come in every morning with something new. Now, nothin's ever new.

BERT: Except some kids from Thirtieth Street. They started kicking a can down the block, and I made them go away because you were sleeping.

KELLER: Now you're talkin', Bert. Now you're on the ball. First thing you know I'm liable to make you a detective.

BERT, *pulls him down by the lapel and whispers in his ear*: Can I see the jail now?

KELLER: Seein' the jail ain't allowed, Bert. You know that.

BERT: Aw, I betcha there isn't even a jail. I don't see any bars on the cellar windows.

KELLER: Bert, on my word of honor, there's a jail in the basement. I showed you my gun, didn't I?

BERT: But that's a hunting gun.

KELLER: That's an arresting gun!

BERT: Then why don't you ever arrest anybody? Tommy said another dirty word to Doris yesterday, and you didn't even demote him.

KELLER—*he chuckles and winks at Chris, who is enjoying all this*: Yeah, that's a dangerous character, that Tommy. *Beckons him closer*: What word does he say?

BERT, *backing away quickly in great embarrassment*: Oh, I can't say that.

KELLER, *grabs him by the shirt and pulls him back*: Well, gimme an idea.

BERT: I can't. It's not a nice word.

KELLER: Just whisper it in my ear. I'll close my eyes. Maybe I won't even hear it.

BERT, *on tiptoe, puts his lips to Keller's ear, then in unbearable embarrassment steps back*: I can't, Mr. Keller.

CHRIS, *laughing*: Don't make him do that.

KELLER: Okay, Bert. I take your word. Now go out, and keep both eyes peeled.

BERT, *interested*: For what?

KELLER: For what! Bert, the whole neighborhood is depending on you. A policeman don't ask questions. Now peel them eyes!

BERT, *mystified, but willing:* Okay. *He runs off right back of arbor.*

KELLER, *calling after him:* And mum's the word, Bert.

BERT, *stops and sticks his head thru the arbor:* About what?

KELLER: Just in general. Be v-e-r-y careful.

BERT, *nods in bewilderment:* Okay. *Bert exits downstage right.*

KELLER, *laughs:* I got all the kids crazy!

CHRIS: One of these days, they'll all come in here and beat your brains out.

KELLER: What's she going to say? Maybe we ought to tell her before she sees it.

CHRIS: She saw it.

KELLER: How could she see it? I was the first one up. She was still in bed.

CHRIS: She was out here when it broke.

KELLER: When?

CHRIS: About four this morning. *Indicating window above them:* I heard it cracking and I woke up and looked out. She was standing right here when it cracked.

KELLER: What was she doing out here four in the morning?

CHRIS: I don't know. When it cracked she ran back into the house and cried in the kitchen.

KELLER: Did you talk to her?

CHRIS: No, I . . . I figured the best thing was to leave her alone. *Pause.*

KELLER, *deeply touched:* She cried hard?

CHRIS: I could hear her right through the floor of my room.

KELLER, *slight pause:* What was she doing out here at that hour? *Chris silent. An undertone of anger showing:* She's dreaming about him again. She's walking around at night.

CHRIS: I guess she is.

KELLER: She's getting just like after he died. *Slight pause. What's the meaning of that?

CHRIS: I don't know the meaning of it. *Slight pause.* But I know one thing, Dad. We've made a terrible mistake with Mother.

KELLER: What?

CHRIS: Being dishonest with her. That kind of thing always pays off, and now it's paying off.

KELLER: What do you mean, dishonest?

CHRIS: You know Larry's not coming back and I know it. Why do we allow her to go on thinking that we believe with her?

KELLER: What do you want to do, argue with her?

CHRIS: I don't want to argue with her, but it's time she realized that nobody believes Larry is alive any more. *Keller simply moves away, thinking, looking at the ground.* Why shouldn't she dream of him, walk the nights waiting for him? Do we contradict her? Do we say straight out that we have no hope any more? That we haven't had any hope for years now?

KELLER, *frightened at the thought:* You can't say that to her.

CHRIS: We've got to say it to her.

KELLER: How're you going to prove it? Can you prove it?

CHRIS: For God's sake, three years! Nobody comes back after three years! It's insane.

KELLER: To you it is, and to me. But not to her. You can talk yourself blue in the face, but there's no body and there's no grave, so where are you?

CHRIS: Sit down, Dad. I want to talk to you.

KELLER, *looks at him searchingly a moment, and sitting . . . :* The trouble is the Goddam newspapers. Every month some boy turns up from nowhere, so the next one is going to be Larry, so . . .

CHRIS: All right, all right, listen to me. *Slight pause. Keller sits on settee.* You know why I asked Annie here, don't you?

KELLER—*he knows, but . . . :* Why?

CHRIS: You know.

KELLER: Well, I got an idea, but . . . What's the story?

CHRIS: I'm going to ask her to marry me. *Slight pause.*

KELLER, *nods:* Well, that's only your business, Chris.

CHRIS: You know it's not only my business.

KELLER: What do you want me to do? You're old enough to know your own mind.

CHRIS, *asking, annoyed*: Then it's all right, I'll go ahead with it?

KELLER: Well, you want to be sure Mother isn't going to . . .

CHRIS: Then it isn't just my business.

KELLER: I'm just sayin'. . . .

CHRIS: Sometimes you infuriate me, you know that? Isn't it your business, too, if I tell this to Mother and she throws a fit about it? You have such a talent for ignoring things.

KELLER: I ignore what I gotta ignore. The girl is Larry's girl . . .

CHRIS: She's not Larry's girl.

KELLER: From Mother's point of view he is not dead and you have no right to take his girl. *Slight pause.* Now you can go on from there if you know where to go, but I'm tellin' you I don't know where to go. See? I don't know. Now what can I do for you?

CHRIS: I don't know why it is, but every time I reach out for something I want, I have to pull back because other people will suffer. My whole bloody life, time after time after time.

KELLER: You're a considerate fella, there's nothing wrong in that.

CHRIS: To hell with that.

KELLER: Did you ask Annie yet?

CHRIS: I wanted to get this settled first.

KELLER: How do you know she'll marry you? Maybe she feels the same way Mother does?

CHRIS: Well, if she does, then that's the end of it. From her letters I think she's forgotten him. I'll find out. And then we'll thrash it out with Mother? Right? Dad, don't avoid me.

KELLER: The trouble is, you don't see enough women. You never did.

CHRIS: So what? I'm not fast with women.

KELLER: I don't see why it has to be Annie. . . .

CHRIS: Because it is.

KELLER: That's a good answer, but it don't answer anything. You haven't seen her since you went to war. It's five years.

CHRIS: I can't help it. I know her best. I was brought up next door to her. These years when I think of someone for my wife, I think of Annie. What do you want, a diagram?

KELLER: I don't want a diagram . . . I . . . I'm . . . She thinks he's coming back, Chris. You marry that girl and you're pronouncing him dead. Now what's going to happen to Mother? Do you know? I don't! *Pause.*

CHRIS: All right, then, Dad.

KELLER, *thinking Chris has retreated*: Give it some more thought.

CHRIS: I've given it three years of thought. I'd hoped that if I waited, Mother would forget Larry and then we'd have a regular wedding and everything happy. But if that can't happen here, then I'll have to get out.

KELLER: What the hell is *this*?

CHRIS: I'll get out. I'll get married and live someplace else. Maybe in New York.

KELLER: Are you crazy?

CHRIS: I've been a good son too long, a good sucker. I'm through with it.

KELLER: You've got a business here, what the hell is this?

CHRIS: The business! The business doesn't inspire me.

KELLER: Must you be inspired?

CHRIS: Yes. I like it an hour a day. If I have to grub for money all day long at least at evening I want it beautiful. I want a family, I want some kids, I want to build something I can give myself to. Annie is in the middle of that. Now . . . where do I find it?

KELLER: You mean . . . *Goes to him.* Tell me something, you mean you'd leave the business?

CHRIS: Yes. On this I would.

KELLER—*pause*: Well . . . you don't want to think like that.

CHRIS: Then help me stay here.

KELLER: All right, but . . . but don't think like that. Because what the hell did I work for? That's only for you, Chris, the whole shootin'-match is for you!

CHRIS: I know that, Dad. Just you help me stay here.

KELLER, *puts a fist up to Chris's jaw*: But don't think that way, you hear me?

CHRIS: I am thinking that way.

KELLER, *lowering his hand*: I don't understand you, do I?

CHRIS: No, you don't. I'm a pretty tough guy.

KELLER: Yeah. I can see that. *Mother appears on porch. She is in her early fifties, a woman of uncontrolled inspirations, and an overwhelming capacity for love.*

MOTHER: Joe?

CHRIS, *going toward porch*: Hello, Mom.

MOTHER, *indicating house behind her. To Keller*: Did you take a bag from under the sink?

KELLER: Yeah, I put it in the pail.

MOTHER: Well, get it out of the pail. That's my potatoes. *Chris bursts out laughing—goes up into alley.*

KELLER, *laughing*: I thought it was garbage.

MOTHER: Will you do me a favor, Joe? Don't be helpful.

KELLER: I can afford another bag of potatoes.

MOTHER: Minnie scoured that pail in boiling water last night. It's cleaner than your teeth.

KELLER: And I don't understand why, after I worked forty years and I got a maid, why I have to take out the garbage.

MOTHER: If you would make up your mind that every bag in the kitchen isn't full of garbage you wouldn't be throwing out my vegetables. Last time it was the onions. *Chris comes on, hands her bag.*

KELLER: I don't like garbage in the house.

MOTHER: Then don't eat. *She goes into the kitchen with bag.*

CHRIS: That settles you for today.

KELLER: Yeah, I'm in last place again. I don't know, once upon a time I used to think that when I got money again I would have a maid and my wife would take it easy. Now I got money, and I got a maid, and my wife is workin' for the maid. *He sits in one of the chairs. Mother comes out on last line. She carries a pot of stringbeans.*

MOTHER: It's her day off, what are you crabbing about?

CHRIS, *to Mother*: Isn't Annie finished eating?

MOTHER, *looking around preoccupiedly at yard*: She'll be right out. *Moves.* That wind did some job on this place. *Of the tree*: So much for that, thank God.

KELLER, *indicating chair beside him*: Sit down, take it easy.

MOTHER—*she presses her hand to top of her head*: I've got such a funny pain on the top of my head.

CHRIS: Can I get you an aspirin?

MOTHER, *picks a few petals off ground, stands there smelling them in her hand, then sprinkles them over plants*: No more roses. It's so funny . . . everything decides to happen at the same time. This month is his birthday; his tree blows down, Annie comes. Everything that happened seems to be coming back. I was just down the cellar, and what do I stumble over? His baseball glove. I haven't seen it in a century.

CHRIS: Don't you think Annie looks well?

MOTHER: Fine. There's no question about it. She's a beauty . . . I still don't know what brought her here. Not that I'm not glad to see her, but . . .

CHRIS: I just thought we'd all like to see each other again. *Mother just looks at him, nodding ever so slightly—almost as though admitting something.* And I wanted to see her myself.

MOTHER—*her nods halt. To Keller*: The only thing is I think her nose got longer. But I'll always love that girl. She's one that didn't jump into bed with somebody else as soon as it happened with her fella.

KELLER, *as though that were impossible for Annie*: Oh, what're you . . . ?

MOTHER: Never mind. Most of them didn't wait till the telegrams were opened. I'm just glad she came, so you can see I'm not *completely* out of my mind. *Sits, and rapidly breaks stringbeans in the pot.*

CHRIS: Just because she isn't married doesn't mean she's been mourning Larry.

MOTHER, *with an undercurrent of observation*: Why then isn't she?

CHRIS, *a little flustered*: Well . . . it could've been any number of things.

MOTHER, *directly at him*: Like what, for instance?

CHRIS, *embarrassed, but standing his ground*: I don't know. Whatever it is. Can I get you an aspirin? *Mother puts her hand to her head.*

MOTHER—*she gets up and goes aimlessly toward the trees on rising*: It's not like a headache.

KELLER: You don't sleep, that's why. She's wearing out more bedroom slippers than shoes.

MOTHER: I had a terrible night. *She stops moving.* I never had a night like that.

CHRIS, *looks at Keller*: What was it, Mom? Did you dream?

MOTHER: More, more than a dream.

CHRIS, *hesitantly*: About Larry?

MOTHER: I was fast asleep, and . . . *Raising her arm over the audience*: Remember the way he used to fly low past the house when he was in training? When we used to see his face in the cockpit going by? That's the way I saw him. Only high up. Way, way up, where the clouds are. He was so real I could reach out and touch him. And suddenly he started to fall. And crying, crying to me . . . Mom, Mom! I could hear him like he was in the room. Mom! . . . it was his voice! If I could touch him I knew I could stop him, if I could only . . . *Breaks off, allowing her outstretched hand to fall.* I woke up and it was so funny . . . The wind . . . it was like the roaring of his engine. I came out here . . . I must've still been half asleep. I could hear that roaring like he was going by. The tree snapped right in front of me . . . and I like . . . came awake. *She is looking at tree. She suddenly realizes something, turns with a reprimanding finger shaking slightly at Keller.* See? We should never have planted that tree. I said so in the first place; it was too soon to plant a tree for him.

CHRIS, *alarmed*: Too soon!

MOTHER, *angering*: We rushed into it. Everybody was in such a hurry to bury him. I *said* not to plant it yet. *To Keller*: I told you to . . . !

CHRIS: Mother, Mother! *She looks into his face.* The wind blew it down. What significance has that got? What are you talking about? Mother, please . . . Don't go through it all again, will you? It's no good, it doesn't accomplish anything. I've been thinking, y'know?—maybe we ought to put our minds to forgetting him?

MOTHER: That's the third time you've said that this week.

CHRIS: Because it's not right; we never took up our lives again. We're like at a railroad station waiting for a train that never comes in.

MOTHER, *presses top of her head*: Get me an aspirin, heh?

CHRIS: Sure, and let's break out of this, heh, Mom? I thought the four of us might go out to dinner a couple of nights, maybe go dancing out at the shore.

MOTHER: Fine. *To Keller*: We can do it tonight.

KELLER: Swell with me!

CHRIS: Sure, let's have some fun. *To Mother*: You'll start with this aspirin. *He goes up and into house with new spirit. Her smile vanishes.*

MOTHER, *with an accusing undertone*: Why did he invite her here?

KELLER: Why does that bother you?

MOTHER: She's been in New York three and a half years, why all of a sudden . . . ?

KELLER: Well, maybe . . . maybe he just wanted to see her . . .

MOTHER: Nobody comes seven hundred miles "just to see."

KELLER: What do you mean? He lived next door to the girl all his life, why shouldn't he want to see her again? *Mother looks at him critically.* Don't look at me like that, he didn't tell me any more than he told you.

MOTHER, *a warning and a question*: He's not going to marry her.

KELLER: How do you know he's even thinking of it?

MOTHER: It's got that about it.

KELLER, *sharply watching her reaction*: Well? So what?

MOTHER, *alarmed*: What's going on here, Joe?

KELLER: Now listen, kid . . .

MOTHER, *avoiding contact with him*: She's not his girl, Joe; she knows she's not.

KELLER: You can't read her mind.

MOTHER: Then why is she still single? New York is full of men, why isn't she married? *Pause.* Probably a hundred people told her she's foolish, but she's waited.

KELLER: How do you know why she waited?

MOTHER: She knows what I know, that's why. She's faithful as a rock. In my worst moments, I think of her waiting, and I know again that I'm right.

KELLER: Look, it's a nice day. What are we arguing for?

MOTHER, *warningly*: Nobody in this house dast take her faith away, Joe. Strangers might. But not his father, not his brother.

KELLER, *exasperated*: What do you want me to do? What do you want?

MOTHER: I want you to act like he's coming back. Both of you. Don't think I haven't noticed you since Chris invited her. I won't stand for any nonsense.

KELLER: But, Kate . . .

MOTHER: Because if he's not coming back, then I'll kill myself! Laugh. Laugh at me. *She points to tree.* But why did that happen the very night she came back? Laugh, but there are meanings in such things. She goes to sleep in his room and his memorial breaks in pieces. Look at it; look. *She sits on bench at his left.* Joe . . .

KELLER: Calm yourself.

MOTHER: Believe with me, Joe. I can't stand all alone.

KELLER: Calm yourself.

MOTHER: Only last week a man turned up in Detroit, missing longer than Larry. You read it yourself.

KELLER: All right, all right, calm yourself.

MOTHER: You above all have got to believe, you . . .

KELLER, *rises*: Why me above all?

MOTHER: . . . Just don't stop believing . . .

KELLER: What does that mean, me above all? *Bert comes rushing on from left.*

BERT: Mr. Keller! Say, Mr. Keller . . . *Pointing up driveway*: Tommy just said it again!

KELLER, *not remembering any of it*: Said what? . . . Who? . . .

BERT: The dirty word.

KELLER: Oh. Well . . .

BERT: Gee, aren't you going to arrest him? I warned him.

MOTHER, *with suddenness*: Stop that, Bert. Go home. *Bert backs up, as she advances.* There's no jail here.

KELLER, *as though to say, "Oh-what-the-hell-let-him-believe-there-is"*: Kate . . .

MOTHER, *turning on Keller, furiously*: There's no jail here! I want you to stop that jail business! *He turns, shamed, but peeved.*

BERT, *past her to Keller*: He's right across the street . . .

MOTHER: Go home, Bert.

> *Bert turns around and goes up driveway. She is shaken. Her speech is bitten off, extremely urgent.*

> I want you to stop that, Joe. That whole jail business!

KELLER, *alarmed, therefore angered*: Look at you, look at you shaking.

MOTHER *trying to control herself, moving about clasping her hands*: I can't help it.

KELLER: What have I got to hide? What the hell is the matter with you, Kate?

MOTHER: I didn't say you had anything to hide, I'm just telling you to stop it! Now stop it!

> *As Ann and Chris appear on porch. Ann is twenty-six, gentle but despite herself capable of holding fast to what she knows. Chris opens door for her.*

ANN: Hya, Joe! *She leads off a general laugh that is not self-conscious because they know one another too well.*

CHRIS, *bringing Ann down, with an outstretched, chivalric arm*: Take a breath of that air, kid. You never get air like that in New York.

MOTHER, *genuinely overcome with it*: Annie, where did you get that dress!

ANN: I couldn't resist. I'm taking it right off before I ruin it. *Swings around.* How's that for three weeks' salary?

MOTHER, *to Keller*: Isn't she the most . . . ? *To Ann*: It's gorgeous, simply gor . . .

CHRIS, *to Mother*: No kidding, now, isn't she the prettiest gal you ever saw?

MOTHER, *caught short by his obvious admiration, she finds herself reaching out for a glass of water and aspirin in his hand, and . . .* : You gained a little weight, didn't you, darling? *She gulps pill and drinks.*

ANN: It comes and goes.

KELLER: Look how nice her legs turned out!

ANN—*she runs to fence, left*: Boy, the poplars got thick, didn't they?

KELLER, *moves upstage to settee and sits*: Well, it's three years, Annie. We're gettin' old, kid.

MOTHER: How does Mom like New York? *Ann keeps looking through trees.*

ANN, *a little hurt*: Why'd they take our hammock away?

KELLER: Oh, no, it broke. Couple of years ago.

MOTHER: What broke? He had one of his light lunches and flopped into it.

ANN—*she laughs and turns back toward Jim's yard. . . . .* : Oh, excuse me! *Jim has come to fence and is looking over it. He is smoking a cigar. As she cries out, he comes on around on stage.*

JIM: How do you do. *To Chris*: She looks very intelligent!

CHRIS: Ann, this is Jim . . . Doctor Bayliss.

ANN, *shaking Jim's hand*: Oh sure, he writes a lot about you.

JIM: Don't believe it. He likes everybody. In the Battalion he was known as Mother McKeller.

ANN: I can believe it . . . You know—? *To Mother*: It's so strange seeing him come out of that yard. *To Chris*: I guess I never grew up. It almost seems that Mom and Pop are in there now. And you and my brother doing Algebra, and Larry trying to copy my home-work. Gosh, those dear dead days beyond recall.

JIM: Well, I hope that doesn't mean you want me to move out?

SUE, *calling from off left*: Jim, come in here! Mr. Hubbard is on the phone!

JIM: I told you I don't want . . .

SUE, *commandingly sweet*: Please, dear! Please!!

JIM, *resigned*: All right, Susie. . . . *Trailing off*: All right, all right. . . . *To Ann*: I've only met you, Ann, but if I may offer you a piece of advice—When you marry, never—even in your mind—never count your husband's money.

SUE, *from off*: Jim?!

JIM: At once! *Turns and goes left*. At once. *He exits left*.

MOTHER—*Ann is looking at her. She speaks meaningfully*: I told her to take up the guitar. It'd be a common interest for them. *They laugh*. Well, he loves the guitar!

ANN—*as though to overcome Mother, she becomes suddenly lively, crosses to Keller on settee, sits on his lap*: Let's eat at the shore tonight! Raise some hell around here, like we used to before Larry went!

MOTHER, *emotionally*: You think of him! You see? *Triumphantly*: She thinks of him!

ANN, *with an uncomprehending smile*: What do you mean, Kate?

MOTHER: Nothing. Just that you . . . remember him, he's in your thoughts.

ANN: That's a funny thing to say; how could I help remembering him?

MOTHER—*it is drawing to a head the wrong way for her; she starts anew. She rises and comes to Ann*: Did you hang up your things?

ANN: Yeah . . . *To Chris*: Say, you've sure gone in for clothes. I could hardly find room in the closet.

MOTHER: No, don't you remember? That's Larry's room.

ANN: You mean . . . they're Larry's?

MOTHER: Didn't you recognize them?

ANN, *slowly rising, a little embarrassed*: Well, it never occurred to me that you'd . . . I mean the shoes are all shined.

MOTHER: Yes, dear. *Slight pause. Ann can't stop staring at her. Mother breaks it by speaking with the relish of gossip, putting her arm around Ann and walking stage left with her.* For so long I've been aching for a nice conversation with you, Annie. Tell me something.

ANN: What?

MOTHER: I don't know. Something nice.

CHRIS, *wryly*: She means do you go out much?

MOTHER: Oh, shut up.

KELLER: And are any of them serious?

MOTHER, *laughing, sits in her chair*: Why don't you both choke?

KELLER: Annie, you can't go into a restaurant with that woman any more. In five minutes thirty-nine strange people are sitting at the table telling her their life story.

MOTHER: If I can't ask Annie a personal question . . .

KELLER: Askin' is all right, but don't beat her over the head. You're beatin' her, you're beatin' her. *They are laughing.*

ANN, *to Mother. Takes pan of beans off stool, puts them on floor under chair and sits*: Don't let them bulldoze you. Ask me anything you like. What do you want to know, Kate? Come on, let's gossip.

MOTHER, *to Chris and Keller*: She's the only one is got any sense. *To Ann*: Your mother . . . she's not getting a divorce, heh?

ANN: No, she's calmed down about it now. I think when he gets out they'll probably live together. In New York, of course.

MOTHER: That's fine. Because your father is still . . . I mean he's a decent man after all is said and done.

ANN: I don't care. She can take him back if she likes.

MOTHER: And you? You . . . *Shakes her head negatively* . . . go out much? *Slight pause.*

ANN, *delicately*: You mean am I still waiting for him?

MOTHER: Well, no, I don't expect you to wait for him but . . .

ANN, *kindly*: But that's what you mean, isn't it?

MOTHER: . . . Well . . . yes.

ANN: Well, I'm not, Kate.

MOTHER, *faintly*: You're not?

ANN: Isn't it ridiculous? You don't really imagine he's . . . ?

MOTHER: I know, dear, but don't say it's ridiculous, because the papers were full of it; I don't know about New York, but there was half a page about a man missing even longer than Larry, and he turned up from Burma.

CHRIS, *coming to Ann*: He couldn't have wanted to come home very badly, Mom.

MOTHER: Don't be so smart.

CHRIS: You can have a helluva time in Burma.

ANN, *rises and swings around in back of Chris*: So I've heard.

CHRIS: Mother, I'll bet you money that you're the only woman in the country who after three years is still . . .

MOTHER: You're sure?

CHRIS: Yes, I am.

MOTHER: Well, if you're sure then you're sure. *She turns her head away an instant.* They don't say it on the radio but I'm sure that in the dark at night they're still waiting for their sons.

CHRIS: Mother, you're absolutely—

MOTHER, *waving him off*: Don't be so damned smart! Now stop it! *Slight pause.* There are just a few things you *don't* know. All of you. And I'll tell you one of them, Annie. Deep, deep in your heart you've always been waiting for him.

ANN, *resolutely*: No, Kate.

MOTHER, *with increasing demand*: But deep in your heart, Annie!

CHRIS: She ought to know, shouldn't she?

MOTHER: Don't let them tell you what to think. Listen to your heart. Only your heart.

ANN: Why does your heart tell you he's alive?

MOTHER: Because he has to be.

ANN: But why, Kate?

MOTHER, *going to her*: Because certain things have to be, and certain things can never be. Like the sun has to rise, it has to be. That's why there's God. Otherwise anything could happen. But there's God, so certain things can never happen. I would know, Annie—just like I knew the day he—*indicates Chris*—went into that terrible battle. Did he write me? Was it in the papers? No, but that morning I couldn't raise my head off the pillow. Ask Joe. Suddenly, I knew! I knew! And he was nearly killed that day. Ann, you *know* I'm right!

ANN—*she stands there in silence, then turns trembling, going upstage*: No, Kate.

MOTHER: I have to have some tea. *Frank appears from left carrying ladder.*

FRANK: Annie! *Coming down.* How are you, gee whiz!

ANN, *taking his hand*: Why, Frank, you're losing your hair.

KELLER: He's got responsibility.

FRANK: Gee whiz!

KELLER: Without Frank the stars wouldn't know when to come out.

FRANK, *laughs. To Ann*: You look more womanly. You've matured. You . . .

KELLER: Take it easy, Frank, you're a married man.

ANN, *as they laugh*: You still haberdashering?

FRANK: Why not? Maybe I too can get to be president. How's your brother? Got his degree, I hear.

ANN: Oh, George has his own office now!

FRANK: Don't say! *Funereally*: And your dad? Is he . . . ?

ANN, *abruptly*: Fine. I'll be in to see Lydia.

FRANK, *sympathetically*: How about it, does Dad expect a parole soon?

ANN, *with growing ill-ease*: I really don't know, I . . .

FRANK, *staunchly defending her father for her sake*: I mean because I feel, y'know, that if an intelligent man like your father is put in prison, there ought to be a law that says either you execute him, or let him go after a year.

CHRIS, *interrupting*: Want a hand with that ladder, Frank?

FRANK, *taking cue*: That's all right, I'll . . . *Picks up ladder.* I'll finish the horoscope tonight, Kate. *Embarrassed*: See you later, Ann, you look wonderful. *He exits right. They look at Ann.*

ANN, *to Chris, sits slowly on stool*: Haven't they stopped talking about Dad?

CHRIS, *comes down and sits on arm of chair*: Nobody talks about him any more.

KELLER, *rises and comes to her*: Gone and forgotten, kid.

ANN: Tell me. Because I don't want to meet anybody on the block if they're going to . . .

CHRIS: I don't want you to worry about it.

ANN, *to Keller*: Do they still remember the case, Joe? Do they talk about you?

KELLER: The only one still talks about it is my wife.

MOTHER: That's because you keep on playing policeman with the kids. All their parents hear out of you is jail, jail, jail.

KELLER: Actually what happened was that when I got home from the penitentiary the kids got very interested in me. You know kids. I was . . . *Laughs.* like the expert on the jail situation. And as time passed they got it confused and . . . I ended up a detective. *Laughs.*

MOTHER: Except that *they* didn't get it confused. *To Ann*: He hands out police badges from the Post Toasties boxes. *They laugh.*

ANN, *wondrously at them, happily. She rises and comes to Keller, putting her arm around his shoulder*: Gosh, it's wonderful to hear you laughing about it.

CHRIS: Why, what'd you expect?

ANN: The last thing I remember on this block was one word—"Murderers!" Remember that, Kate? . . . Mrs. Hammond standing in front of our house and yelling that word . . . She's still around, I suppose?

MOTHER: They're all still around.

KELLER: Don't listen to her. Every Saturday night the whole gang is playin' poker in this arbor. All the ones who yelled murderer takin' my money now.

MOTHER: Don't, Joe, she's a sensitive girl, don't fool her. *To Ann*: They still remember about Dad. It's different with him— *Indicates Joe* —he was exonerated, your father's still there. That's why I wasn't so enthusiastic about your coming. Honestly, I know how sensitive you are, and I told Chris, I said . . .

KELLER: Listen, you do like I did and you'll be all right. The day I come home, I got out of my car;—but not in front of the house . . . on the corner. You should've been here, Annie, and you too, Chris; you'd-a seen something. Everybody knew I was getting out that day; the porches were loaded. Picture it now; none of them believed I was innocent. The story was, I pulled a fast one getting myself exonerated. So I get out of my car, and I walk down the street. But very slow. And with a smile. The beast! I was the beast; the guy who sold cracked cylinder heads to the Army Air Force; the guy who made twenty-one P-40's crash in Australia. Kid, walkin' down the street that day I was guilty as hell. Except I wasn't, and there was a court paper in my pocket to prove I wasn't, and I walked . . . past . . . the porches. Result? Fourteen months later I had one of the best shops in the state again, a respected man again; bigger than ever.

CHRIS, *with admiration*: Joe McGuts.

KELLER, *now with great force*: That's the only way you lick 'em is guts! *To Ann*: The worst thing you did was to move away from here. You made it tough for your father when he gets out. That's why I tell you, I like to see him move back right on this block.

MOTHER, *pained*: How could they move back?

KELLER: It ain't gonna end *till* they move back! *To Ann*: Till people play cards with him again, and talk with him, and smile with him—you play cards with a man you know he can't be a murderer. And the next time you write him I like you to tell him just what I said. *Ann simply stares at him*. You hear me?

ANN, *surprised*: Don't you hold anything against him?

KELLER: Annie, I never believed in crucifying people.

ANN, *mystified*: But he was your partner, he dragged you through the mud . . .

KELLER: Well, he ain't my sweetheart, but you gotta forgive, don't you?

ANN: You, either, Kate? Don't you feel any . . . ?

KELLER, *to Ann*: The next time you write Dad . . .

ANN: I don't write him.

KELLER, *struck*: Well every now and then you . . .

ANN, *a little ashamed, but determined*: No, I've never written to him. Neither has my brother. *To Chris*: Say, do you feel this way, too?

CHRIS: He murdered twenty-one pilots.

KELLER: What the hell kinda talk is that?

MOTHER: That's not a thing to say about a man.

ANN: What else can you say? When they took him away I followed him, went to him every visiting day. I was crying all the time. Until the news came about Larry. Then I realized. It's wrong to pity a man like that. Father or no father, there's only one way to look at him. He knowingly shipped out parts that would crash an airplane. And how do you know Larry wasn't one of them?

MOTHER: I was waiting for that. *Going to her*: As long as you're here, Annie, I want to ask you never to say that again.

ANN: You surprise me. I thought you'd be mad at him.

MOTHER: What your father did had nothing to do with Larry. Nothing.

ANN: But we can't know that.

MOTHER, *striving for control*: As long as you're here!

ANN, *perplexed*: But, Kate . . .

MOTHER: Put that out of your head!

KELLER: Because . . .

MOTHER, *quickly to Keller*: That's all, that's enough. *Places her hand on her head.* Come inside now, and have some tea with me. *She turns and goes up steps.*

KELLER, *to Ann*: The one thing you . . .

MOTHER, *sharply*: He's not dead, so there's no argument! Now come!

KELLER, *angrily*: In a minute! *Mother turns and goes into house.* Now look, Annie . . .

CHRIS: All right, Dad, forget it.

KELLER: No, she dasn't feel that way. Annie . . .

CHRIS: I'm sick of the whole subject, now cut it out.

KELLER: You want her to go on like this? *To Ann*: Those cylinder heads went into P-40's only. What's the matter with you? You know Larry never flew a P-40.

CHRIS: So who flew those P-40's, pigs?

KELLER: The man was a fool, but don't make a murderer out of him. You got no sense? Look what it does to her! *To Ann*: Listen, you gotta appreciate what was doin' in that shop in the war. The both of you! It was a madhouse. Every half hour the Major callin' for cylinder heads, they were whippin' us with the telephone. The trucks were hauling them away hot, damn near. I mean just try to see it human, see it human. All of a sudden a batch comes out with a crack. That happens, that's the business. A fine, hairline crack. All right, so . . . so he's a little man, your father, always scared of loud voices. What'll the Major say?—Half a day's production shot. . . . What'll I say? You know what I mean? Human. *He pauses.* So he takes out his tools and he . . . covers over the cracks. All right . . . that's bad, it's wrong, but that's what a little man does. If I could have gone in that day I'd a told him—junk 'em, Steve, we can afford it. But alone he was afraid. But I know he meant no harm. He believed they'd hold up a hundred percent. That's a mistake, but it ain't murder. You mustn't feel that way about him. You understand me? It ain't right.

ANN—*she regards him a moment*: Joe, let's forget it.

KELLER: Annie, the day the news came about Larry he was in the next cell to mine . . . Dad. And he cried, Annie . . . he cried half the night.

ANN, *touched*: He shoulda cried all night. *Slight pause.*

KELLER, *almost angered*: Annie, I do not understand why you . . . !

CHRIS, *breaking in—with nervous urgency*: Are you going to stop it?!

ANN: Don't yell at him. He just wants everybody happy.

KELLER, *clasps her around waist, smiling*: That's my sentiments. Can you stand steak?

CHRIS: And champagne!

KELLER: Now you're operatin'! I'll call Swanson's for a table! Big time tonight, Annie!

ANN: Can't scare me.

KELLER, *to Chris, pointing at Ann*: I like that girl. Wrap her up. *They laugh. Goes up porch.* You got nice legs, Annie! . . . I want to see everybody drunk tonight. *Pointing to Chris*: Look at him, he's blushin'! *He exits, laughing, into house.*

CHRIS, *calling after him*: Drink your tea, Casanova. *He turns to Ann.* Isn't he a great guy?

ANN: You're the only one I know who loves his parents!

CHRIS: I know. It went out of style, didn't it?

ANN, *with a sudden touch of sadness*: It's all right. It's a good thing. *She looks about.* You know? It's lovely here. The air is sweet.

CHRIS, *hopefully*: You're not sorry you came?

ANN: Not sorry, no. But I'm . . . not going to stay . . .

CHRIS: Why?

ANN: In the first place, your mother as much as told me to go.

CHRIS: Well . . .

ANN: You saw that . . . and then you . . . you've been kind of . . .

CHRIS: What?

ANN: Well . . . kind of embarrassed ever since I got here.

CHRIS: The trouble is I planned on kind of sneaking up on you over a period of a week or so. But they take it for granted that we're all set.

ANN: I knew they would. Your mother anyway.

CHRIS: How did you know?

ANN: From *her* point of view, why else would I come?

CHRIS: Well . . . would you want to? *Ann studies him.* I guess you know this is why I asked you to come.

ANN: I guess this is why I came.

CHRIS: Ann, I love you. I love you a great deal. *Finally:* I love you. *Pause. She waits.* I have no imagination . . . that's all I know to tell you. *Ann, waiting, ready.* I'm embarrassing you. I didn't want to tell it to you here. I wanted some place we'd never been; a place where we'd be brand new to each other. . . . You feel it's wrong here, don't you? This yard, this chair? I want you to be ready for me. I don't want to win you away from anything.

ANN, *putting her arms around him:* Oh, Chris, I've been ready a long, long time!

CHRIS: Then he's gone forever. You're sure.

ANN: I almost got married two years ago.

CHRIS: . . . Why didn't you?

ANN: You started to write to me . . . *Slight pause.*

CHRIS: You felt something that far back?

ANN: Every day since!

CHRIS: Ann, why didn't you let me know?

ANN: I was waiting for you, Chris. Till then you never wrote. And when you did, what did you say? You sure can be ambiguous, you know.

CHRIS—*he looks towards house, then at her, trembling:* Give me a kiss, Ann. Give me a . . . *They kiss.* God, I kissed you, Annie, I kissed Annie. How long, how long I've been waiting to kiss you!

ANN: I'll never forgive you. Why did you wait all these years? All I've done is sit and wonder if I was crazy for thinking of you.

CHRIS: Annie, we're going to live now! I'm going to make you so happy. *He kisses her, but without their bodies touching.*

ANN, *a little embarrassed:* Not like that you're not.

CHRIS: I kissed you . . .

ANN: Like Larry's brother. Do it like you, Chris. *He breaks away from her abruptly.* What is it, Chris?

CHRIS: Let's drive some place . . . I want to be alone with you.

ANN: No . . . what is it, Chris, your mother?

CHRIS: No . . . nothing like that . . .

ANN: Then what's wrong? . . . Even in your letters, there was something ashamed.

CHRIS: Yes. I suppose I have been. But it's going from me.

ANN: You've got to tell me—

CHRIS: I don't know how to start. *He takes her hand.*

ANN: It wouldn't work this way. *Slight pause.*

CHRIS, *speaks quietly, factually at first:* It's all mixed up with so many other things. . . . You remember, overseas, I was in command of a company?

ANN: Yeah, sure.

CHRIS: Well, I lost them.

ANN: How many?

CHRIS: Just about all.

ANN: Oh, gee!

CHRIS: It takes a little time to toss that off. Because they weren't just men. For instance, one time it'd been raining several days and this kid came to me, and gave me his last pair of dry socks. Put them in my pocket. That's only a little thing . . . but . . . that's the kind of guys I had. They didn't die; they killed themselves for each other. I mean that exactly; a little more selfish and they'd've been here today. And I got an idea—watching them go down. Everything was being destroyed, see, but it seemed to me that one new thing was made. A kind of . . . responsibility. Man for man. You understand me?—To show that, to bring that on to the earth again like some kind of a monument and everyone would feel it standing there, behind him, and it would make a difference to him. *Pause.* And then I came home and it was incredible. I . . . there was no meaning in it here; the whole thing to them was a kind of a—bus accident. I went to work with Dad, and that rat-race again. I felt . . . what you said . . . ashamed somehow. Because nobody was changed at all. It seemed to make suckers out of a lot of guys. I felt wrong to be alive, to open the bankbook, to drive the new car, to see the new refrigerator. I mean you can take those things out of a war, but when you drive that car you've got to know that it came out of the love a man can have for a man, you've got to be a little better because of that. Otherwise what you have is really loot, and there's blood on it. I didn't want to take any of it. And I guess that included you.

ANN: And you still feel that way?

CHRIS: I want you now, Annie.

ANN: Because you mustn't feel that way any more. Because you have a right to whatever you have. Everything, Chris, understand that? To me, too . . . And the money, there's nothing wrong in your money. Your father put hundreds of planes in the air, you should be proud. A man should be paid for that . . .

CHRIS: Oh Annie, Annie . . . I'm going to make a fortune for you!

KELLER, *offstage*: Hello . . . Yes. Sure.

ANN, *laughing softly*: What'll I do with a fortune . . . ? *They kiss. Keller enters from house.*

KELLER, *thumbing toward house*: Hey, Ann, your brother . . . *They step apart shyly. Keller comes down, and wryly . . . :* What is this, Labor Day?

CHRIS, *waving him away, knowing the kidding will be endless*: All right, all right . . .

ANN: You shouldn't burst out like that.

KELLER: Well, nobody told me it was Labor Day. *Looks around.* Where's the hot dogs?

CHRIS *loving it*: All right. You said it once.

KELLER: Well, as long as I know it's Labor Day from now on, I'll wear a bell around my neck.

ANN, *affectionately*: He's so subtle!

CHRIS: George Bernard Shaw as an elephant.

KELLER: George!—hey, you kissed it out of my head—your brother's on the phone.

ANN, *surprised*: My brother?

KELLER: Yeah, George. Long distance.

ANN: What's the matter, is anything wrong?

KELLER: I don't know, Kate's talking to him. Hurry up, she'll cost him five dollars.

ANN—*she takes a step upstage, then comes down toward Chris*: I wonder if we ought to tell your mother yet? I mean I'm not very good in an argument.

CHRIS: We'll wait till tonight. After dinner. Now don't get tense, just leave it to me.

KELLER: What're you telling her?

CHRIS: Go ahead, Ann. *With misgivings, Ann goes up and into house.* We're getting married, Dad. *Keller nods indecisively.* Well, don't you say anything?

KELLER, *distracted*: I'm glad, Chris, I'm just . . . George is calling from Columbus.

CHRIS: Columbus!

KELLER: Did Annie tell you he was going to see his father today?

CHRIS: No, I don't think she knew anything about it.

KELLER, *asking uncomfortably*: Chris! You . . . you think you know her pretty good?

CHRIS, *hurt and apprehensive*: What kind of a question . . . ?

KELLER: I'm just wondering. All these years George don't go to see his father. Suddenly he goes . . . and she comes here.

CHRIS: Well, what about it?

KELLER: It's crazy, but it comes to my mind. She don't hold nothin' against me, does she?

CHRIS, *angry*: I don't know what you're talking about.

KELLER, *a little more combatively*: I'm just talkin'. To his last day in court the man blamed it all on me; and this is his daughter. I mean if she was sent here to find out something?

CHRIS, *angered*: Why? What is there to find out?

ANN, *on phone, offstage*: Why are you so excited, George? What happened there?

KELLER: I mean if they want to open up the case again, for the nuisance value, to hurt us?

CHRIS: Dad . . . how could you think that of her? ⎱
                                                       Together
ANN, *still on phone*: But what did he say to you, ⎰
for God's sake?

KELLER: It couldn't be, heh. You know.

CHRIS: Dad, you amaze me . . .

KELLER, *breaking in*: All right, forget it, forget it. *With great force, moving about*: I want a clean start for you, Chris. I want a new sign over the plant—Christopher Keller, Incorporated.

CHRIS, *a little uneasily*: J. O. Keller is good enough.

KELLER: We'll talk about it. I'm going to build you a house, stone, with a driveway from the road. I want you to spread out, Chris, I want you to use what I made for you . . . *He is close to him now.* . . . I mean, with joy, Chris, without shame . . . with joy.

CHRIS, *touched*: I will, Dad.

KELLER, *with deep emotion*: . . . Say it to me.

CHRIS: Why?

KELLER: Because sometimes I think you're . . . ashamed of the money.

CHRIS: No, don't feel that.

KELLER: Because it's good money, there's nothing wrong with that money.

CHRIS, *a little frightened*: Dad, you don't have to tell me this.

KELLER, *with overriding affection and self-confidence now. He grips Chris by the back of the neck, and with laughter between his determined jaws*: Look, Chris, I'll go to work on Mother for you. We'll get her so drunk tonight we'll all get married! *Steps away, with a wide gesture of his arm*: There's gonna be a wedding, kid, like there never was seen! Champagne, tuxedoes . . . !

> *He breaks off as Ann's voice comes out loud from the house where she is still talking on phone.*

ANN: Simply because when you get excited you don't control yourself. . . . *Mother comes out of house.* Well, what did he tell you for God's sake? *Pause.* All right, come then. *Pause.* Yes, they'll all be here. Nobody's running away from you. And try to get hold of yourself, will you? *Pause.* All right, all right. Goodbye. *There is a brief pause as Ann hangs up receiver, then comes out of kitchen.*

CHRIS: Something happen?

KELLER: He's coming here?

ANN: On the seven o'clock. He's in Columbus. *To Mother*: I told him it would be all right.

KELLER: Sure, fine! Your father took sick?

ANN, *mystified*: No, George didn't say he was sick. I . . . *Shaking it off*: I don't know, I suppose it's something stupid, you know my brother . . . *She comes to Chris*. Let's go for a drive, or something . . .

CHRIS: Sure. Give me the keys, Dad.

MOTHER: Drive through the park. It's beautiful now.

CHRIS: Come on, Ann. *To them*: Be back right away.

ANN, *as she and Chris exit up driveway*: See you. *Mother comes down toward Keller, her eyes fixed on him.*

KELLER: Take your time. *To Mother*: What does George want?

MOTHER: He's been in Columbus since this morning with Steve. He's gotta see Annie right away, he says.

KELLER: What for?

MOTHER: I don't know. *She speaks with warning.* He's a lawyer now, Joe. George is a lawyer. All these years he never even sent a postcard to Steve. Since he got back from the war, not a postcard.

KELLER: So what?

MOTHER, *her tension breaking out*: Suddenly he takes an airplane from New York to see him. An airplane!

KELLER: Well? So?

MOTHER, *trembling*: Why?

KELLER: I don't read minds. Do you?

MOTHER: Why, Joe? What has Steve suddenly got to tell him that he takes an airplane to see him?

KELLER: What do I care what Steve's got to tell him?

MOTHER: You're sure, Joe?

KELLER, *frightened, but angry*: Yes, I'm sure.

MOTHER—*she sits stiffly in a chair*: Be smart now, Joe. The boy is coming. Be smart.

KELLER, *desperately*: Once and for all, did you hear what I said? I said I'm sure!

MOTHER—*she nods weakly*: All right, Joe. *He straightens up.* Just . . . be smart. *Keller, in hopeless fury, looks at her, turns around, goes up to porch and into house, slamming screen door violently behind him. Mother sits in chair downstage, stiffly, staring, seeing.*

CURTAIN

ACT TWO

As twilight falls, that evening.

On the rise: Chris is discovered at right, sawing the broken-off tree, leaving stump standing alone. He is dressed in good pants, white shoes, but without a shirt. He disappears with tree up the alley when Mother appears on porch. She comes down and stands watching him. She has on a dressing-gown, carries a tray of grape juice drink in a pitcher, and glasses with sprigs of mint in them.

MOTHER, *calling up alley:* Did you have to put on good pants to do that? *She comes downstage and puts tray on table in the arbor. Then looks around uneasily, then feels pitcher for coolness. Chris enters from alley brushing off his hands.* You notice there's more light with that thing gone?

CHRIS: Why aren't you dressing?

MOTHER: It's suffocating upstairs. I made a grape drink for Georgie. He always liked grape. Come and have some.

CHRIS, *impatiently:* Well, come on, get dressed. And what's Dad sleeping so much for? *He goes to table and pours a glass of juice.*

MOTHER: He's worried. When he's worried he sleeps. *Pauses. Looks into his eyes.* We're dumb, Chris. Dad and I are stupid people. We don't know anything. You've got to protect us.

CHRIS: You're silly; what's there to be afraid of?

MOTHER: To his last day in court Steve never gave up the idea that Dad made him do it. If they're going to open the case again I won't live through it.

CHRIS: George is just a damn fool, Mother. How can you take him seriously?

MOTHER: That family hates us. Maybe even Annie. . . .

CHRIS: Oh, now, Mother . . .

MOTHER: You think just because you like everybody, they like you!

CHRIS: All right, stop working yourself up. Just leave everything to me.

MOTHER: When George goes home tell her to go with him.

CHRIS, *noncommittally*: Don't worry about Annie.

MOTHER: Steve is her father, too.

CHRIS: Are you going to cut it out? Now, come.

MOTHER, *going upstage with him*: You don't realize how people can hate, Chris, they can hate so much they'll tear the world to pieces. . . . *Ann, dressed up, appears on porch.*

CHRIS: Look! She's dressed already. *As he and Mother mount porch*: I've just got to put on a shirt.

ANN, *in a preoccupied way*: Are you feeling well, Kate?

MOTHER: What's the difference, dear. There are certain people, y'know, the sicker they get the longer they live. *She goes into house.*

CHRIS: You look nice.

ANN: We're going to tell her tonight.

CHRIS: Absolutely, don't worry about it.

ANN: I wish we could tell her now. I can't stand scheming. My stomach gets hard.

CHRIS: It's not scheming, we'll just get her in a better mood.

MOTHER, *offstage, in the house*: Joe, are you going to sleep all day!

ANN, *laughing*: The only one who's relaxed is your father. He's fast asleep.

CHRIS: I'm relaxed.

ANN: Are you?

CHRIS: Look. *He holds out his hand and makes it shake.* Let me know when George gets here.

> *He goes into the house. She moves aimlessly, and then is drawn toward tree stump. She goes to it, hesitantly touches broken top in the hush of her thoughts. Offstage Lydia calls, "Johnny! Come get your supper!" Sue enters from left, and halts, seeing Ann.*

SUE: Is my husband . . . ?

ANN, *turns, startled*: Oh!

SUE: I'm terribly sorry.

ANN: It's all right, I . . . I'm a little silly about the dark.

SUE, *looks about*: It is getting dark.

ANN: Are you looking for your husband?

SUE: As usual. *Laughs tiredly.* He spends so much time here, they'll be charging him rent.

ANN: Nobody was dressed so he drove over to the depot to pick up my brother.

SUE: Oh, your brother's in?

ANN: Yeah, they ought to be here any minute now. Will you have a cold drink?

SUE: I will, thanks. *Ann goes to table and pours.* My husband. Too hot to drive me to beach.—Men are like little boys; for the neighbors they'll always cut the grass.

ANN: People like to do things for the Kellers. Been that way since I can remember.

SUE: It's amazing. I guess your brother's coming to give you away, heh?

ANN, *giving her drink*: I don't know. I suppose.

SUE: You must be all nerved up.

ANN: It's always a problem getting yourself married, isn't it?

SUE: That depends on your shape, of course. I don't see why you should have had a problem.

ANN: I've had chances—

SUE: I'll bet. It's romantic . . . it's very unusual to me, marrying the brother of your sweetheart.

ANN: I don't know. I think it's mostly that whenever I need somebody to tell me the truth I've always thought of Chris. When he tells you something you know it's so. He relaxes me.

SUE: And he's got money. That's important, you know.

ANN: It wouldn't matter to me.

SUE: You'd be surprised. It makes all the difference, I married an intern. On my salary. And that was bad, because as soon as a woman supports a man he owes her something. You can never owe somebody without resenting them. *Ann laughs.* That's true, you know.

ANN: Underneath, I think the doctor is very devoted.

SUE: Oh, certainly. But it's bad when a man always sees the bars in front of him. Jim thinks he's in jail all the time.

ANN: Oh . . .

SUE: That's why I've been intending to ask you a small favor, Ann . . . it's something very important to me.

ANN: Certainly, if I can do it.

SUE: You can. When you take up housekeeping, try to find a place away from here.

ANN: Are you fooling?

SUE: I'm very serious. My husband is unhappy with Chris around.

ANN: How is that?

SUE: Jim's a successful doctor. But he's got an idea he'd like to do medical research. Discover things. You see?

ANN: Well, isn't that good?

SUE: Research pays twenty-five dollars a week minus laundering the hair shirt. You've got to give up your life to go into it.

ANN: How does Chris—?

SUE, *with growing feeling*: Chris makes people want to be better than it's possible to be. He does that to people.

ANN: Is that bad?

SUE: My husband has a family, dear. Every time he has a session with Chris he feels as though he's compromising by not giving up everything for research. As though Chris or anybody else isn't compromising. It happens with Jim every couple of years. He meets a man and makes a statue out of him.

ANN: Maybe he's right. I don't mean that Chris is a statue, but . . .

SUE: Now darling, you know he's not right.

ANN: I don't agree with you. Chris . . .

SUE: Let's face it, dear. Chris is working with his father, isn't he? He's taking money out of that business every week in the year.

ANN: What of it?

SUE: You ask me what of it?

ANN: I certainly do ask you. *She seems about to burst out.* You oughtn't cast aspersions like that, I'm surprised at you.

SUE: You're surprised at me!

ANN: He'd never take five cents out of that plant if there was anything wrong in it.

SUE: You know that.

ANN: I know it. I resent everything you've said.

SUE, *moving toward her*: You know what I resent, dear?

ANN: Please, I don't want to argue.

SUE: I resent living next door to the Holy Family. It makes me look like a bum, you understand?

ANN: I can't do anything about that.

SUE: Who is he to ruin a man's life? Everybody knows Joe pulled a fast one to get out of jail.

ANN: That's not true!

SUE: Then why don't you go out and talk to people? Go on, talk to them. There's not a person on the block who doesn't know the truth.

ANN: That's a lie. People come here all the time for cards and . . .

SUE: So what? They give him credit for being smart. I do, too, I've got nothing against Joe. But if Chris wants people to put on the hair shirt let him take off his broadcloth. He's driving my husband crazy with that phony idealism of his, and I'm at the end of my rope on it!

> Chris enters on porch, wearing shirt and tie now. She turns
> quickly, hearing. With a smile: Hello, darling. How's Mother?

CHRIS: I thought George came.

SUE: No, it was just us.

CHRIS, *coming down to them*: Susie, do me a favor, heh? Go up to Mother and see if you can calm her. She's all worked up.

SUE: She still doesn't know about you two?

CHRIS, *laughs a little*: Well, she senses it, I guess. You know my mother.

SUE, *going up to porch*: Oh, yeah, she's psychic.

CHRIS: Maybe there's something in the medicine chest.

SUE: I'll give her one of everything. *On porch*: Don't worry about Kate; couple of drinks, dance her around a little . . . she'll love Ann. *To Ann*: Because you're the female version of him. *Chris laughs.* Don't be alarmed, I said version. *She goes into house.*

CHRIS: Interesting woman, isn't she?

ANN: Yeah, she's very interesting.

CHRIS: She's a great nurse, you know, she . . .

ANN, *in tension, but trying to control it*: Are you still doing that?

CHRIS, *sensing something wrong, but still smiling*: Doing what?

ANN: As soon as you get to know somebody you find a distinction for them. How do you know she's a great nurse?

CHRIS: What's the matter, Ann?

ANN: The woman hates you. She despises you!

CHRIS: Hey . . . what's hit you?

ANN: Gee, Chris . . .

CHRIS: What happened here?

ANN: You never . . . Why didn't you tell me?

CHRIS: Tell you what?

ANN: She says they think Joe is guilty.

CHRIS: What difference does it make what they think?

ANN: I don't care what they think, I just don't understand why you took the trouble to deny it. You said it was all forgotten.

CHRIS: I didn't want you to feel there was anything wrong in you coming here, that's all. I know a lot of people think my father was guilty, and I assumed there might be some question in your mind.

ANN: But I never once said I suspected him.

CHRIS: Nobody says it.

ANN: Chris, I know how much you love him, but it could never . . .

CHRIS: Do you think I could forgive him if he'd done that thing?

ANN: I'm not here out of a blue sky, Chris. I turned my back on my father, if there's anything wrong here now . . .

CHRIS: I know that, Ann.

ANN: George is coming from Dad, and I don't think it's with a blessing.

CHRIS: He's welcome here. You've got nothing to fear from George.

ANN: Tell me that . . . just tell me that.

CHRIS: The man is innocent, Ann. Remember he was falsely accused once and it put him through hell. How would you behave if you were faced with the same thing again? Annie, believe me, there's nothing wrong for you here, believe me, kid.

ANN: All right, Chris, all right.

They embrace as Keller appears quietly on porch. Ann simply studies him.

KELLER: Every time I come out here it looks like Playland! *They break and laugh in embarrassment.*

CHRIS: I thought you were going to shave?

KELLER, *sitting on bench*: In a minute. I just woke up, I can't see nothin'.

ANN: You look shaved.

KELLER: Oh, no. *Massages his jaw.* Gotta be extra special tonight. Big night, Annie. So how's it feel to be a married woman?

ANN, *laughs*: I don't know, yet.

KELLER, *to Chris*: What's the matter, you slippin'? *He takes a little box of apples from under the bench as they talk.*

CHRIS: The great roué!

KELLER: What is that, roué?

CHRIS: It's French.

KELLER: Don't talk dirty. *They laugh.*

CHRIS, *to Ann*: You ever meet a bigger ignoramus?

KELLER: Well, somebody's got to make a living.

ANN, *as they laugh*: That's telling him.

KELLER: I don't know, everybody's gettin' so Goddam educated in this country there'll be nobody to take away the garbage. *They laugh.* It's gettin' so the only dumb ones left are the bosses.

ANN: You're not so dumb, Joe.

KELLER: I know, but you go into our plant, for instance. I got so many lieutenants, majors, and colonels that I'm ashamed to ask somebody to sweep the floor. I gotta be careful I'll insult somebody. No kiddin'. It's a tragedy: you stand on the street today and spit, you're gonna hit a college man.

CHRIS: Well, don't spit.

KELLER, *breaks apple in half, passing it to Ann and Chris*: I mean to say, it's comin' to a pass. *He takes a breath.* I been thinkin', Annie . . . your brother, George. I been thinkin' about your brother George. When he comes I like you to *brooch* something to him.

CHRIS: Broach.

KELLER: What's the matter with brooch?

CHRIS, *smiling*: It's not English.

KELLER: When I went to night school it was brooch.

ANN, *laughing*: Well, in day school it's broach.

KELLER: Don't surround me, will you? Seriously, Ann . . . You say he's not well. George, I been thinkin', why should he knock himself out in New York with that cut-throat competition, when I got so many friends here; I'm very friendly with some big lawyers in town. I could set George up here.

ANN: That's awfully nice of you, Joe.

KELLER: No, kid, it ain't nice of me. I want you to understand me. I'm thinking of Chris. *Slight pause.* See . . . this is what I mean. You get older, you want to feel that you . . . accomplished something. My only accomplishment is my son. I ain't brainy. That's all I accomplished. Now, a year, eighteen months, your father'll be a free man. Who is he going to come to, Annie? His baby. You. He'll come, old, mad, into your house.

ANN: That can't matter any more, Joe.

KELLER: I don't want that hate to come between us. *Gestures between Chris and himself.*

ANN: I can only tell you that that could never happen.

KELLER: You're in love now, Annie, but believe me, I'm older than you and I know—a daughter is a daughter, and a father is a father. And it could happen. *He pauses.* I like you and George to go to him in prison and tell him. . . . "Dad, Joe wants to bring you into the business when you get out."

ANN, *surprised, even shocked*: You'd have him as a partner?

KELLER: No, no partner. A good job. *Pause. He sees she is shocked, a little mystified. He gets up, speaks more nervously.* I want him to know, Annie . . . while he's sitting there I want him to know that when he gets out he's got a place waitin' for him. It'll take his bitterness away. To know you got a place . . . it sweetens you.

ANN: Joe, you owe him nothing.

KELLER: I owe him a good kick in the teeth, but he's your father. . . .

CHRIS: Then kick him in the teeth! I don't want him in the plant, so that's that! You understand? And besides, don't talk about him like that. People misunderstand you!

KELLER: And I don't understand why she has to crucify the man.

CHRIS: Well, it's her father, if she feels . . .

KELLER: No, no. . . .

CHRIS, *almost angrily*: What's it to you? Why . . . ?

KELLER, *a commanding outburst in his high nervousness*: A father is a father! *As though the outburst had revealed him, he looks about, wanting to retract it. His hand goes to his cheek.* I better . . . I better shave. *He turns and a smile is on his face. To Ann*: I didn't mean to yell at you, Annie.

ANN: Let's forget the whole thing, Joe.

KELLER: Right. *To Chris*: She's likable.

CHRIS, *a little peeved at the man's stupidity*: Shave, will you?

KELLER: Right again.

    As he turns to porch Lydia comes hurrying from her house, right.

LYDIA: I forgot all about it . . . *Seeing Chris and Ann*: Hya. *To Joe*: I promised to fix Kate's hair for tonight. Did she comb it yet?

KELLER: Always a smile, hey, Lydia?

LYDIA: Sure, why not?

KELLER, *going up on porch*: Come on up and comb my Katie's hair. *Lydia goes up on porch.* She's got a big night, make her beautiful.

LYDIA: I will.

KELLER—*he holds door open for her and she goes into kitchen. To Chris and Ann*: Hey, that could be a song. *He sings softly.*

    Come on up and comb my Katie's hair . . .
    Oh, come on up, 'cause she's my lady fair—

    To Ann: How's that for one year of night school? *He continues singing as he goes into kitchen.*

    Oh, come on up, come on up, and comb my lady's hair—

    Jim Bayliss rounds corner of driveway, walking rapidly. Jim crosses to Chris, motions him up and pulls him down to stage left, excitedly. Keller stands just inside kitchen door, watching them.

CHRIS: What's the matter? Where is he?

JIM: Where's your mother?

CHRIS: Upstairs, dressing.

ANN, *crossing to them rapidly*: What happened to George?

JIM: I asked him to wait in the car. Listen to me now. Can you take some advice? *They wait.* Don't bring him in here.

ANN: Why?

JIM: Kate is in bad shape, you can't explode this in front of her.

ANN: Explode what?

JIM: You know why he's here, don't try to kid it away. There's blood in his eye; drive him somewhere and talk to him alone.

> *Ann turns to go up drive, takes a couple of steps, sees Keller and stops. He goes quietly on into house.*

CHRIS, *shaken, and therefore angered*: Don't be an old lady.

JIM: He's come to take her home. What does that mean? *To Ann*: You know what that means. Fight it out with him someplace else.

ANN—*she comes back down toward Chris*: I'll drive . . . him somewhere.

CHRIS, *goes to her*: No.

JIM: Will you stop being an idiot?

CHRIS: Nobody's afraid of him here. Cut that out!

> *He starts for driveway, but is brought up short by George, who enters there. George is Chris's age, but a paler man, now on the edge of his self-restraint. He speaks quietly, as though afraid to find himself screaming. An instant's hesitation and Chris steps up to him, hand extended, smiling.*

Helluva way to do; what're you sitting out there for?

GEORGE: Doctor said your mother isn't well, I . . .

CHRIS: So what? She'd want to see you, wouldn't she? We've been waiting for you all afternoon. *He puts his hand on George's arm, but George pulls away, coming across toward Ann.*

ANN, *touching his collar*: This is filthy, didn't you bring another shirt?

> *George breaks away from her, and moves down and left, examining the yard. Door opens, and he turns rapidly, thinking it is Kate, but it's Sue. She looks at him, he turns away and moves on left, to fence. He looks over it at his former home. Sue comes downstage.*

SUE, *annoyed*: How about the beach, Jim?

JIM: Oh, it's too hot to drive.

SUE: How'd you get to the station—Zeppelin?

CHRIS: This is Mrs. Bayliss, George. *Calling, as George pays no attention, staring at house off left*: George! *George turns.* Mrs. Bayliss.

SUE: How do you do.

GEORGE, *removing his hat*: You're the people who bought our house, aren't you?

SUE: That's right. Come and see what we did with it before you leave.

GEORGE—*he walks down and away from her*: I liked it the way it was.

SUE, *after a brief pause*: He's frank, isn't he?

JIM, *pulling her off left*: See you later. . . . Take it easy, fella. *They exit, left.*

CHRIS, *calling after them*: Thanks for driving him! *Turning to George*: How about some grape juice? Mother made it especially for you.

GEORGE, *with forced appreciation*: Good old Kate, remembered my grape juice.

CHRIS: You drank enough of it in this house. How've you been, George?— Sit down.

GEORGE—*he keeps moving*: It takes me a minute. *Looking around*: It seems impossible.

CHRIS: What?

GEORGE: I'm back here.

CHRIS: Say, you've gotten a little nervous, haven't you?

GEORGE: Yeah, toward the end of the day. What're you, big executive now?

CHRIS: Just kind of medium. How's the law?

GEORGE: I don't know. When I was studying in the hospital it seemed sensible, but outside there doesn't seem to be much of a law. The trees got thick, didn't they? *Points to stump*: What's that?

CHRIS: Blew down last night. We had it there for Larry. You know.

GEORGE: Why, afraid you'll forget him?

CHRIS, *starts for George*: Kind of a remark is that?

ANN, *breaking in, putting a restraining hand on Chris*: When did you start wearing a hat?

GEORGE, *discovers hat in his hand*: Today. From now on I decided to look like a lawyer, anyway. *He holds it up to her.* Don't you recognize it?

ANN: Why? Where . . . ?

GEORGE: Your father's . . . he asked me to wear it.

ANN: . . . How is he?

GEORGE: He got smaller.

ANN: Smaller?

GEORGE: Yeah, little. *Holds out his hand to measure.* He's a little man. That's what happens to suckers, you know. It's good I went to him in time—another year there'd be nothing left but his smell.

CHRIS: What's the matter, George, what's the trouble?

GEORGE: The trouble? The trouble is when you make suckers out of people once, you shouldn't try to do it twice.

CHRIS: What does that mean?

GEORGE, *to Ann*: You're not married yet, are you?

ANN: George, will you sit down and stop—?

GEORGE: Are you married yet?

ANN: No, I'm not married yet.

GEORGE: You're not going to marry him.

ANN: Why am I not going to marry him?

GEORGE: Because his father destroyed your family.

CHRIS: Now look, George . . .

GEORGE: Cut it short, Chris. Tell her to come home with me. Let's not argue, you know what I've got to say.

CHRIS: George, you don't want to be the voice of God, do you?

GEORGE: I'm . . .

CHRIS: That's been your trouble all your life, George, you dive into things. What kind of a statement is that to make? You're a big boy now.

GEORGE: I'm a big boy now.

CHRIS: Don't come bulling in here. If you've got something to say, be civilized about it.

GEORGE: Don't civilize me!

ANN: Shhh!

CHRIS, *ready to hit him*: Are you going to talk like a grown man or aren't you?

ANN, *quickly, to forestall an outburst*: Sit down, dear. Don't be angry, what's the matter? *He allows her to seat him, looking at her.* Now what happened? You kissed me when I left, now you . . .

GEORGE, *breathlessly*: My life turned upside down since then. I couldn't go back to work when you left. I wanted to go to Dad and tell him you were going to be married. It seemed impossible not to tell him. He loved you so much . . . *He pauses.* Annie . . . we did a terrible thing. We can never be forgiven. Not even to send him a card at Christmas. I didn't see him once since I got home from the war! Annie, you don't know what was done to that man. You don't know what happened.

ANN, *afraid*: Of course I know.

GEORGE: You can't know, you wouldn't be here. Dad came to work that day. The night foreman came to him and showed him the cylinder heads . . . they were coming out of the process with defects. There was something wrong with the process. So Dad went directly to the phone and called here and told Joe to come down right away. But the morning passed. No sign of Joe. So Dad called again. By this time he had over a hundred defectives. The Army was screaming for stuff and Dad didn't have anything to ship. So Joe told him . . . on the phone he told him to weld, cover up the cracks in any way he could, and ship them out.

CHRIS: Are you through now?

GEORGE, *surging up at him*: I'm not through now! *Back to Ann*: Dad was afraid. He wanted Joe there if he was going to do it. But Joe can't come down . . . he's sick. Sick! He suddenly gets the flu! Suddenly! But he promised to take responsibility. Do you understand what I'm saying? On the telephone you can't have responsibility! In a court you can always deny a phone call and that's exactly what he did. They knew he was a liar the first time, but in the appeal they believed that rotten lie and now Joe is a big shot and your father is the patsy. *He gets up.* Now what're you going to do? Eat his food, sleep in his bed? Answer me; what're you going to do?

CHRIS: What're you going to do, George?

GEORGE: He's too smart for me, I can't prove a phone call.

CHRIS: Then how dare you come in here with that rot?

ANN: George, the court . . .

GEORGE: The court didn't know your father! But you know him. You know in your heart Joe did it.

CHRIS, *whirling him around*: Lower your voice or I'll throw you out of here!

GEORGE: She knows. She knows.

CHRIS, *to Ann*: Get him out of here, Ann. Get him out of here.

ANN: George, I know everything you've said. Dad told that whole thing in court, and they . . .

GEORGE, *almost a scream*: The court did not know him, Annie!

ANN: Shhh!—But he'll say anything, George. You know how quick he can lie.

GEORGE, *turning to Chris, with deliberation*: I'll ask you something, and look me in the eye when you answer me.

CHRIS: I'll look you in the eye.

GEORGE: You know your father . . .

CHRIS: I know him well.

GEORGE: And he's the kind of boss to let a hundred and twenty-one cylinder heads be repaired and shipped out of his shop without even knowing about it?

CHRIS: He's that kind of boss.

GEORGE: And that's the same Joe Keller who never left his shop without first going around to see that all the lights were out.

CHRIS, *with growing anger*: The same Joe Keller.

GEORGE: The same man who knows how many minutes a day his workers spend in the toilet.

CHRIS: The same man.

GEORGE: And my father, that frightened mouse who'd never buy a shirt without somebody along—that man would dare do such a thing on his own?

CHRIS: On his own. And because he's a frightened mouse this is another thing he'd do;—throw the blame on somebody else because he's not man enough to take it himself. He tried it in court but it didn't work, but with a fool like you it works!

GEORGE: Oh, Chris, you're a liar to yourself!

ANN, *deeply shaken*: Don't talk like that!

CHRIS, *sits facing George*: Tell me, George. What happened? The court record was good enough for you all these years, why isn't it good now? Why did you believe it all these years?

GEORGE, *after a slight pause*: Because you believed it. . . . That's the truth, Chris. I believed everything, because I thought you did. But today I heard it from his mouth. From his mouth it's altogether different than the record. Anyone who knows him, and knows your father, will believe it from his mouth. Your Dad took everything we have. I can't beat that. But she's one item he's not going to grab. *He turns to Ann.* Get your things. Everything they have is covered with blood. You're not the kind of a girl who can live with that. Get your things.

CHRIS: Ann . . . you're not going to believe that, are you?

ANN—*she goes to him*: You know it's not true, don't you?

GEORGE: How can he tell you? It's his father. *To Chris*: None of these things ever even cross your mind?

CHRIS: Yes, they crossed my mind. Anything can cross your mind!

GEORGE: *He knows*, Annie. He knows!

CHRIS: The Voice of God!

GEORGE: Then why isn't your name on the business? Explain that to her!

CHRIS: What the hell has that got to do with . . . ?

GEORGE: Annie, why isn't his name on it?

CHRIS: Even when I don't own it!

GEORGE: Who're you kidding? Who gets it when he dies? *To Ann*: Open your eyes, you know the both of them, isn't that the first thing they'd do, the way they love each other?—J. O. Keller & Son? *Pause. Ann looks from him to Chris.* I'll settle it. Do you want to settle it, or are you afraid to?

CHRIS: . . . What do you mean?

GEORGE: Let me go up and talk to your father. In ten minutes you'll have the answer. Or are you afraid of the answer?

CHRIS: I'm not afraid of the answer. I know the answer. But my mother isn't well and I don't want a fight here now.

GEORGE: Let me go to him.

CHRIS: You're not going to start a fight here now.

GEORGE, *to Ann*: What more do you want!!!

    There is a sound of footsteps in the house.

ANN, *turns her head suddenly toward house*: Someone's coming.

CHRIS, *to George, quietly*: You won't say anything now.

ANN: You'll go soon. I'll call a cab.

GEORGE: You're coming with me.

ANN: And don't mention marriage, because we haven't told her yet.

GEORGE: You're coming with me.

ANN: You understand? Don't . . . George, you're not going to start anything now! *She hears footsteps.* Shsh!

    Mother enters on porch. She is dressed almost formally, her hair is fixed. They are all turned toward her. On seeing George she raises both hands, comes down toward him.

MOTHER: Georgie, Georgie.

GEORGE—*he has always liked her*: Hello, Kate.

MOTHER—*she cups his face in her hands*: They made an old man out of you. *Touches his hair*: Look, you're gray.

GEORGE—*her pity, open and unabashed, reaches into him, and he smiles sadly*: I know, I . . .

MOTHER: I told you when you went away, don't try for medals.

GEORGE—*he laughs, tiredly*: I didn't try, Kate. They made it very easy for me.

MOTHER, *actually angry*: Go on. You're all alike. *To Ann*: Look at him, why did you say he's fine? He looks like a ghost.

GEORGE, *relishing her solicitude*: I feel all right.

MOTHER: I'm sick to look at you. What's the matter with your mother, why don't she feed you?

ANN: He just hasn't any appetite.

MOTHER: If he ate in my house he'd have an appetite. *To Ann*: I pity your husband! *To George*: Sit down. I'll make you a sandwich.

GEORGE, *sits with an embarrassed laugh*: I'm really not hungry.

MOTHER: Honest to God, it breaks my heart to see what happened to all the children. How we worked and planned for you, and you end up no better than us.

GEORGE, *with deep feeling for her*: You . . . you haven't changed at all, you know that, Kate?

MOTHER: None of us changed, Georgie. We all love you. Joe was just talking about the day you were born and the water got shut off. People were carrying basins from a block away—a stranger would have thought the whole neighborhood was on fire! *They laugh. She sees the juice. To Ann*: Why didn't you give him some juice!

ANN, *defensively*: I offered it to him.

MOTHER, *scoffingly*: You offered it to him! *Thrusting glass into George's hand*: Give it to him! *To George, who is laughing*: And now you're going to sit here and drink some juice . . . and look like something!

GEORGE, *sitting*: Kate, I feel hungry already.

CHRIS, *proudly*: She could turn Mahatma Gandhi into a heavyweight!

MOTHER, *to Chris, with great energy*: Listen, to hell with the restaurant! I got a ham in the icebox, and frozen strawberries, and avocados, and . . .

ANN: Swell, I'll help you!

GEORGE: The train leaves at eight-thirty, Ann.

MOTHER, *to Ann*: You're leaving?

CHRIS: No, Mother, she's not . . .

ANN, *breaking through it, going to George*: You hardly got here; give yourself a chance to get acquainted again.

CHRIS: Sure, you don't even know us any more.

MOTHER: Well, Chris, if they can't stay, don't . . .

CHRIS: No, it's just a question of George, Mother, he planned on . . .

GEORGE—*he gets up politely, nicely, for Kate's sake*: Now wait a minute, Chris . . .

CHRIS, *smiling and full of command, cutting him off*: If you want to go, I'll drive you to the station now, but if you're staying, no arguments while you're here.

MOTHER, *at last confessing the tension*: Why should he argue? *She goes to him, and with desperation and compassion, stroking his hair*: Georgie and us have no argument. How could we have an argument, Georgie? We all got hit by the same lightning, how can you . . . ? Did you see what happened to Larry's tree, Georgie? *She has taken his arm, and unwillingly he moves across stage with her.* Imagine? While I was dreaming of him in the middle of the night, the wind came along and . . .

> *Lydia enters on porch. As soon as she sees him.*

LYDIA: Hey, Georgie! Georgie! Georgie! Georgie! Georgie!

> *She comes down to him eagerly. She has a flowered hat in her hand, which Kate takes from her as she goes to George.*

GEORGE—*they shake hands eagerly, warmly*: Hello, Laughy. What'd you do, grow?

LYDIA: I'm a big girl now.

MOTHER, *taking hat from her*: Look what she can do to a hat!

ANN, *to Lydia, admiring the hat*: Did you make that?

MOTHER: In ten minutes! *She puts it on.*

LYDIA, *fixing it on her head*: I only rearranged it.

GEORGE: You still make your own clothes?

CHRIS, *of Mother*: Ain't she classy! All she needs now is a Russian wolfhound.

MOTHER, *moving her head from left to right*: It feels like somebody is sitting on my head.

ANN: No, it's beautiful, Kate.

MOTHER, *kisses Lydia—to George*: She's a genius! You should've married her. *They laugh*. This one can feed you!

LYDIA, *strangely embarrassed*: Oh, stop that, Kate.

GEORGE, *to Lydia*: Didn't I hear you had a baby?

MOTHER: You don't hear so good. She's got three babies.

GEORGE, *a little hurt by it—to Lydia*: No kidding, three?

LYDIA: Yeah, it was one, two, three— You've been away a long time, Georgie.

GEORGE: I'm beginning to realize.

MOTHER, *to Chris and George*: The trouble with you kids is you *think* too much.

LYDIA: Well, we think, too.

MOTHER: Yes, but not all the time.

GEORGE, *with almost obvious envy*: They never took Frank, heh?

LYDIA, *a little apologetically*: No, he was always one year ahead of the draft.

MOTHER: It's amazing. When they were calling boys twenty-seven Frank was just twenty-eight, when they made it twenty-eight he was just twenty-nine. That's why he took up astrology. It's all in when you were born, it just goes to show.

CHRIS: What does it go to show?

MOTHER, *to Chris*: Don't be so intelligent. Some superstitions are very nice! *To Lydia*: Did he finish Larry's horoscope?

LYDIA: I'll ask him now, I'm going in. *To George, a little sadly, almost embarrassed*: Would you like to see my babies? Come on.

GEORGE: I don't think so, Lydia.

LYDIA, *understanding*: All right. Good luck to you, George.

GEORGE: Thanks. And to you . . . And Frank. *She smiles at him, turns and goes off right to her house. George stands staring after her.*

LYDIA, *as she runs off*: Oh, Frank!

MOTHER, *reading his thoughts*: She got pretty, heh?

GEORGE, *sadly*: Very pretty.

MOTHER, *as a reprimand*: She's beautiful, you damned fool!

GEORGE, *looks around longingly; and softly, with a catch in his throat*: She makes it seem so nice around here.

MOTHER, *shaking her finger at him*: Look what happened to you because you wouldn't listen to me! I told you to marry that girl and stay out of the war!

GEORGE, *laughs at himself*: She used to laugh too much.

MOTHER: And you didn't laugh enough. While you were getting mad about Fascism Frank was getting into her bed.

GEORGE, *to Chris*: He won the war, Frank.

CHRIS: All the battles.

MOTHER, *in pursuit of this mood*: The day they started the draft, Georgie, I told you you loved that girl.

CHRIS, *laughs*: And truer love hath no man!

MOTHER: I'm smarter than any of you.

GEORGE, *laughing*: She's wonderful!

MOTHER: And now you're going to listen to me, George. You had big principles, Eagle Scouts the three of you; so now I got a tree, and this one—*indicating Chris*—when the weather gets bad he can't stand on his feet; and that big dope—*pointing to Lydia's house*—next door who never reads anything but Andy Gump has three children and his house paid off. Stop being a philosopher, and look after yourself. Like Joe was just saying—you move back here, he'll help you get set, and I'll find you a girl and put a smile on your face.

GEORGE: Joe? Joe wants me here?

ANN, *eagerly*: He asked me to tell you, and I think it's a good idea.

MOTHER: Certainly. Why must you make believe you hate us? Is that another principle?—that you have to hate us? You don't hate us, George, I know you, you can't fool me, I diapered you. *Suddenly to Ann*: You remember Mr. Marcy's daughter?

ANN, *laughing, to George*: She's got you hooked already! *George laughs, is excited.*

MOTHER: You look her over, George; you'll see she's the most beautiful . . .

CHRIS: She's got warts, George.

MOTHER, *to Chris*: She hasn't got warts! *To George*: So the girl has a little beauty mark on her chin . . .

CHRIS: And two on her nose.

MOTHER: You remember. Her father's the retired police inspector.

CHRIS: Sergeant, George.

MOTHER: He's a very kind man!

CHRIS: He looks like a gorilla.

MOTHER, *to George*: He never shot anybody. *They all burst out laughing, as Keller appears in doorway. George rises abruptly, stares at Keller, who comes rapidly down to him.*

KELLER—*the laughter stops. With strained joviality*: Well! Look who's here! *Extending his hand*: Georgie, good to see ya.

GEORGE, *shakes hands—somberly*: How're you, Joe?

KELLER: So-so. Gettin' old. You comin' out to dinner with us?

GEORGE: No, got to be back in New York.

ANN: I'll call a cab for you. *She goes up into the house.*

KELLER: Too bad you can't stay, George. Sit down. *To Mother*: He looks fine.

MOTHER: He looks terrible.

KELLER: That's what I said, you look terrible, George. *They laugh.* I wear the pants and she beats me with the belt.

GEORGE: I saw your factory on the way from the station. It looks like General Motors.

KELLER: I wish it was General Motors, but it ain't. Sit down, George. Sit down. *Takes cigar out of his pocket.* So you finally went to see your father, I hear?

GEORGE: Yes, this morning. What kind of stuff do you make now?

KELLER: Oh, little of everything. Pressure cookers, an assembly for washing machines. Got a nice, flexible plant now. So how'd you find Dad? Feel all right?

GEORGE, *searching Keller, he speaks indecisively*: No, he's not well, Joe.

KELLER, *lighting his cigar*: Not his heart again, is it?

GEORGE: It's everything, Joe. It's his soul.

KELLER, *blowing out smoke*: Uh huh—

CHRIS: How about seeing what they did with your house?

KELLER: Leave him be.

GEORGE, *to Chris, indicating Keller*: I'd like to talk to him.

KELLER: Sure, he just got here. That's the way they do, George. A little man makes a mistake and they hang him by the thumbs; the big ones become ambassadors. I wish you'd-a told me you were going to see Dad.

GEORGE, *studying him*: I didn't know you were interested.

KELLER: In a way, I am. I would like him to know, George, that as far as I'm concerned, any time he wants, he's got a place with me. I would like him to know that.

GEORGE: He hates your guts, Joe. Don't you know that?

KELLER: I imagined it. But that can change, too.

MOTHER: Steve was never like that.

GEORGE: He's like that now. He'd like to take every man who made money in the war and put him up against a wall.

CHRIS: He'll need a lot of bullets.

GEORGE: And he'd better not get any.

KELLER: That's a sad thing to hear.

GEORGE, *with bitterness dominant*: Why? What'd you expect him to think of you?

KELLER, *the force of his nature rising, but under control*: I'm sad to see he hasn't changed. As long as I know him, twenty-five years, the man never learned how to take the blame. You know that, George.

GEORGE—*he does*: Well, I . . .

KELLER: But you do know it. Because the way you come in here you don't look like you remember it. I mean like in 1937 when we had the shop on Flood Street. And he damn near blew us all up with that heater he left burning for two days without water. He wouldn't admit that was his fault, either. I had to fire a mechanic to save his face. You remember that.

GEORGE: Yes, but . . .

KELLER: I'm just mentioning it, George. Because this is just another one of a lot of things. Like when he gave Frank that money to invest in oil stock.

GEORGE, *distressed*: I know that, I . . .

KELLER, *driving in, but restrained*: But it's good to remember those things, kid. The way he cursed Frank because the stock went down. Was that Frank's fault? To listen to him Frank was a swindler. And all the man did was give him a bad tip.

GEORGE, *gets up, moves away*: I know those things . . .

KELLER: Then remember them, remember them. *Ann comes out of house. There are certain men in the world who rather see everybody hung before they'll take blame. You understand me, George? They stand facing each other, George trying to judge him.*

ANN, *coming downstage*: The cab's on its way. Would you like to wash?

MOTHER, *with the thrust of hope*: Why must he go? Make the midnight, George.

KELLER: Sure, you'll have dinner with us!

ANN: How about it? Why not? We're eating at the lake, we could have a swell time.

GEORGE—*long pause, as he looks at Ann, Chris, Keller, then back to her*: All right.

MOTHER: Now you're talking.

CHRIS: I've got a shirt that'll go right with that suit.

MOTHER: Size fifteen and a half, right, George?

GEORGE: Is Lydia . . . ? I mean—Frank and Lydia coming?

MOTHER: I'll get you a date that'll make her look like a . . . *She starts upstage.*

GEORGE, *laughs*: No, I don't want a date.

CHRIS: I know somebody just for you! Charlotte Tanner! *He starts for the house.*

KELLER: Call Charlotte, that's right.

MOTHER: Sure, call her up. *Chris goes into house.*

ANN: You go up and pick out a shirt and tie.

GEORGE—*he stops, looks around at them and the place*: I never felt at home anywhere but here. I feel so . . . *He nearly laughs, and turns away from them.* Kate, you look so young, you know? You didn't change at all. It . . . rings an old bell. *Turns to Keller.* You too, Joe, you're amazingly the same. The whole atmosphere is.

KELLER: Say, I ain't got time to get sick.

MOTHER: He hasn't been laid up in fifteen years. . . .

KELLER: Except my flu during the war.

MOTHER: Huhh?

KELLER: My flu, when I was sick during . . . the war.

MOTHER: Well, sure . . . *To George*: I meant except for that flu. *George stands perfectly still.* Well, it slipped my mind, don't look at me that way. He wanted to go to the shop but he couldn't lift himself off the bed. I thought he had pneumonia.

GEORGE: Why did you say he's never . . . ?

KELLER: I know how you feel, kid, I'll never forgive myself. If I could've gone in that day I'd never allow Dad to touch those heads.

GEORGE: She said you've never been sick.

MOTHER: I said he was sick, George.

GEORGE, *going to Ann*: Ann, didn't you hear her say . . . ?

MOTHER: Do you remember every time you were sick?

GEORGE: I'd remember pneumonia. Especially if I got it just the day my partner was going to patch up cylinder heads . . . What happened that day, Joe?

FRANK, *enters briskly from driveway, holding Larry's horoscope in his hand. He comes to Kate*: Kate! Kate!

MOTHER: Frank, did you see George?

FRANK, *extending his hand*: Lydia told me, I'm glad to . . . you'll have to pardon me. *Pulling Mother over right.* I've got something amazing for you, Kate, I finished Larry's horoscope.

MOTHER: You'd be interested in this, George. It's wonderful the way he can understand the . . .

CHRIS, *entering from house*: George, the girl's on the phone . . .

MOTHER, *desperately*: He finished Larry's horoscope!

CHRIS: Frank, can't you pick a better time than this?

FRANK: The greatest men who ever lived believed in the stars!

CHRIS: Stop filling her head with that junk!

FRANK: Is it junk to feel that there's a greater power than ourselves? I've studied the stars of his life! I won't argue with you, I'm telling you. Somewhere in this world your brother is alive!

MOTHER, *instantly to Chris*: Why isn't it possible?

CHRIS: Because it's insane.

FRANK: Just a minute now. I'll tell you something and you can do as you please. Just let me say it. He was supposed to have died on November twenty-fifth. But November twenty-fifth was his favorable day.

CHRIS: Mother!

MOTHER: Listen to him!

FRANK: It was a day when everything good was shining on him, the kind of day he should've married on. You can laugh at a lot of it, I can understand you laughing. But the odds are a million to one that a man won't die on his favorable day. That's known, that's known, Chris!

MOTHER: Why isn't it possible, why isn't it possible, Chris!

GEORGE, *to Ann*: Don't you understand what she's saying? She just told you to go. What are you waiting for now?

CHRIS: Nobody can tell her to go. *A car horn is heard.*

MOTHER, *to Frank*: Thank you, darling, for your trouble. Will you tell him to wait, Frank?

FRANK, *as he goes*: Sure thing.

MOTHER, *calling out*: They'll be right out, driver!

CHRIS: She's not leaving, Mother.

GEORGE: You heard her say it, he's never been sick!

MOTHER: He misunderstood me, Chris! *Chris looks at her, struck.*

GEORGE, *to Ann*: He simply told your father to kill pilots, and covered himself in bed!

CHRIS: You'd better answer him, Annie. Answer him.

MOTHER: I packed your bag, darling . . .

CHRIS: What?

MOTHER: I packed your bag. All you've got to do is close it.

ANN: I'm not closing anything. He asked me here and I'm staying till he tells me to go. *To George*: Till Chris tells me!

CHRIS: That's all! Now get out of here, George!

MOTHER, *to Chris*: But if that's how he feels . . .

CHRIS: That's all, nothing more till Christ comes, about the case or Larry as long as I'm here! *To George*: Now get out of here, George!

GEORGE, *to Ann*: You tell me. I want to hear you tell me.

ANN: Go, George!

> *They disappear up the driveway, Ann saying, "Don't take it that way, Georgie! Please don't take it that way."*
>
> *Chris turns to his mother.*

CHRIS: What do you mean, you packed her bag? How dare you pack her bag?

MOTHER: Chris . . .

CHRIS: How dare you pack her bag?

MOTHER: She doesn't belong here.

CHRIS: Then I don't belong here.

MOTHER: She's Larry's girl.

CHRIS: And I'm his brother and he's dead, and I'm marrying his girl.

MOTHER: Never, never in this world!

KELLER: You lost your mind?

MOTHER: You have nothing to say!

KELLER, *cruelly*: I got plenty to say. Three and a half years you been talking like a maniac—

MOTHER—*she smashes him across the face*: Nothing. You have nothing to say. Now I say. He's coming back, and everybody has got to wait.

CHRIS: Mother, Mother . . .

MOTHER: Wait, wait . . .

CHRIS: How long? How long?

MOTHER, *rolling out of her*: Till he comes; forever and ever till he comes!

CHRIS, *as an ultimatum*: Mother, I'm going ahead with it.

MOTHER: Chris, I've never said no to you in my life, now I say no!

CHRIS: You'll never let him go till I do it.

MOTHER: I'll never let him go and you'll never let him go . . . !

CHRIS: I've let him go. I've let him go a long . . .

MOTHER, *with no less force, but turning from him*: Then let your father go. *Pause. Chris stands transfixed.*

KELLER: She's out of her mind.

MOTHER: Altogether! *To Chris, but not facing them*: Your brother's alive, darling, because if he's dead, your father killed him. Do you understand me now? As long as you live, that boy is alive. God does not let a son be killed by his father. Now you see, don't you? Now you see. *Beyond control, she hurries up and into house.*

KELLER—*Chris has not moved. He speaks insinuatingly, questioningly*: She's out of her mind.

CHRIS, *a broken whisper*: Then . . . you did it?

KELLER, *the beginning of plea in his voice*: He never flew a P-40—

CHRIS, *struck. Deadly*: But the others.

KELLER, *insistently*: She's out of her mind. *He takes a step toward Chris, pleadingly.*

CHRIS, *unyielding*: Dad . . . you did it?

KELLER: He never flew a P-40, what's the matter with you?

CHRIS, *still asking, and saying*: Then you did it. To the others. *Both hold their voices down.*

KELLER, *afraid of him, his deadly insistence*: What's the matter with you? What the hell is the matter with you?

CHRIS, *quietly, incredibly*: How could you do that? How?

KELLER: What's the matter with you!

CHRIS: Dad . . . Dad, you killed twenty-one men!

KELLER: What, killed?

CHRIS: You killed them, you murdered them.

KELLER, *as though throwing his whole nature open before Chris*: How could I kill anybody?

CHRIS: Dad! Dad!

KELLER, *trying to hush him*: I didn't kill anybody!

CHRIS: Then explain it to me. What did you do? Explain it to me or I'll tear you to pieces!

KELLER, *horrified at his overwhelming fury*: Don't, Chris, don't . . .

CHRIS: I want to know what you did, now what did you do? You had a hundred and twenty cracked engine-heads, now what did you do?

KELLER: If you're going to hang me then I . . .

CHRIS: I'm listening, God Almighty, I'm listening!

KELLER—*their movements now are those of subtle pursuit and escape. Keller keeps a step out of Chris's range as he talks*: You're a boy, what could I do! I'm in business, a man is in business; a hundred and twenty cracked, you're out of business; you got a process, the process don't work you're out of business; you don't know how to operate, your stuff is no good; they close you up, they tear up your contracts, what the hell's it to them? You lay forty years into a business and they knock you out in five minutes, what could I do, let them take forty years, let them take my life away? *His voice cracking*: I never thought they'd install them. I swear to God. I thought they'd stop 'em before anybody took off.

CHRIS: Then why'd you ship them out?

KELLER: By the time they could spot them I thought I'd have the process going again, and I could show them they needed me and they'd let it go by. But weeks passed and I got no kick-back, so I was going to tell them.

CHRIS: Then why didn't you tell them?

KELLER: It was too late. The paper, it was all over the front page, twenty-one went down, it was too late. They came with handcuffs into the shop, what could I do? *He sits on bench at center.* Chris . . . Chris, I did it for you, it was a chance and I took it for you. I'm sixty-one years old, when would I have another chance to make something for you? Sixty-one years old you don't get another chance, do ya?

CHRIS: You even knew they wouldn't hold up in the air.

KELLER: I didn't say that . . .

CHRIS: But you were going to warn them not to use them . . .

KELLER: But that don't mean . . .

CHRIS: It means you knew they'd crash.

KELLER: It don't mean that.

CHRIS: Then you *thought* they'd crash.

KELLER: I was afraid maybe . . .

CHRIS: You were afraid maybe! God in heaven, what kind of a man are you? Kids were hanging in the air by those heads. You knew that!

KELLER: For you, a business for you!

CHRIS, *with burning fury*: For me! Where do you live, where have you come from? For me!—I was dying every day and you were killing my boys and you did it for me? What the hell do you think I was thinking of, the Goddam business? Is that as far as your mind can see, the business? What is that, the world—the business? What the hell do you mean, you did it for me? Don't you have a country? Don't you live in the world? What the hell are you? You're not even an animal, no animal kills his own, what are you? What must I do to you? I ought to tear the tongue out of your mouth, what must I do? *With his fist he pounds down upon his father's shoulder. He stumbles away, covering his face as he weeps.* What must I do, Jesus God, what must I do?

KELLER: Chris . . . My Chris . . .

CURTAIN

ACT THREE

Two o'clock the following morning, Mother is discovered on the rise, rocking ceaselessly in a chair, staring at her thoughts. It is an intense, slight sort of rocking. A light shows from upstairs bedroom, lower floor windows being dark. The moon is strong and casts its bluish light.

Presently Jim, dressed in jacket and hat, appears from left, and seeing her, goes up beside her.

JIM: Any news?

MOTHER: No news.

JIM, *gently*: You can't sit up all night, dear, why don't you go to bed?

MOTHER: I'm waiting for Chris. Don't worry about me, Jim, I'm perfectly all right.

JIM: But it's almost two o'clock.

MOTHER: I can't sleep. *Slight pause.* You had an emergency?

JIM, *tiredly*: Somebody had a headache and thought he was dying. *Slight pause.* Half of my patients are quite mad. Nobody realizes how many people are walking around loose, and they're cracked as coconuts. Money. Money-money-money-money. You say it long enough it doesn't mean anything. *She smiles, makes a silent laugh.* Oh, how I'd love to be around when that happens!

MOTHER, *shakes her head*: You're so childish, Jim! Sometimes you are.

JIM, *looks at her a moment*: Kate. *Pause.* What happened?

MOTHER: I told you. He had an argument with Joe. Then he got in the car and drove away.

JIM: What kind of an argument?

MOTHER: An argument. Joe . . . he was crying like a child, before.

JIM: They argued about Ann?

MOTHER, *slight hesitation*: No, not Ann. Imagine? *Indicates lighted window above*: She hasn't come out of that room since he left. All night in that room.

JIM, *looks at window, then at her*: What'd Joe do, tell him?

MOTHER—*she stops rocking*: Tell him what?

JIM: Don't be afraid, Kate, I know. I've always known.

MOTHER: How?

JIM: It occurred to me a long time ago.

MOTHER: I always had the feeling that in the back of his head, Chris . . . almost knew. I didn't think it would be such a shock.

JIM, *gets up*: Chris would never know how to live with a thing like that. It takes a certain talent . . . for lying. You have it, and I do. But not him.

MOTHER: What do you mean . . . he's not coming back?

JIM: Oh, no, he'll come back. We all come back, Kate. These private little revolutions always die. The compromise is always made. In a peculiar way. Frank is right—every man does have a star. The star of one's honesty. And you spend your life groping for it, but once it's out it never lights again. I don't think he went very far. He probably just wanted to be alone to watch his star go out.

MOTHER: Just as long as he comes back.

JIM: I wish he wouldn't, Kate. One year I simply took off, went to New Orleans; for two months I lived on bananas and milk, and studied a certain disease. It was beautiful. And then she came, and she cried. And I went back home with her. And now I live in the usual darkness; I can't find myself; it's even hard sometimes to remember the kind of man I wanted to be. I'm a good husband; Chris is a good son—he'll come back.

> *Keller comes out on porch in dressing-gown and slippers. He goes upstage—to alley. Jim goes to him.*

JIM: I have a feeling he's in the park. I'll look around for him. Put her to bed, Joe; this is no good for what she's got. *Jim exits up driveway.*

KELLER, *coming down*: What does he want here?

MOTHER: His friend is not home.

KELLER—*his voice is husky. Comes down to her*: I don't like him mixing in so much.

MOTHER: It's too late, Joe. He knows.

KELLER, *apprehensively*: How does he know?

MOTHER: He guessed a long time ago.

KELLER: I don't like that.

MOTHER, *laughs dangerously, quietly into the line*: What you don't like . . .

KELLER: Yeah, what I don't like.

MOTHER: You can't bull yourself through this one, Joe, you better be smart now. This thing—this thing is not over yet.

KELLER, *indicating lighted window above*: And what is she doing up there? She don't come out of the room.

MOTHER: I don't know, what is she doing? Sit down, stop being mad. You want to live? You better figure out your life.

KELLER: She don't know, does she?

MOTHER: She saw Chris storming out of here. It's one and one—she knows how to add.

KELLER: Maybe I ought to talk to her?

MOTHER: Don't ask me, Joe.

KELLER, *almost an outburst*: Then who do I ask? But I don't think she'll do anything about it.

MOTHER: You're asking me again.

KELLER: I'm askin' you. What am I, a stranger? I thought I had a family here. What happened to my family?

MOTHER: You've got a family. I'm simply telling you that I have no strength to think any more.

KELLER: You have no strength. The minute there's trouble you have no strength.

MOTHER: Joe, you're doing the same thing again; all your life whenever there's trouble you yell at me and you think that settles it.

KELLER: Then what do I do? Tell me, talk to me, what do I do?

MOTHER: Joe . . . I've been thinking this way. If he comes back . . .

KELLER: What do you mean "if"? . . . He's comin' back!

MOTHER: I think if you sit him down and you . . . explain yourself. I mean you ought to make it clear to him that you know you did a terrible thing. *Not looking into his eyes*. I mean if he saw that you realize what you did. You see?

KELLER: What ice does that cut?

MOTHER, *a little fearfully*: I mean if you told him that you want to pay for what you did.

KELLER, *sensing . . . quietly*: How can I pay?

MOTHER: Tell him . . . you're willing to go to prison. *Pause.*

KELLER, *struck, amazed*: I'm willing to . . . ?

MOTHER, *quickly*: You wouldn't go, he wouldn't ask you to go. But if you told him you wanted to, if he could feel that you wanted to pay, maybe he would forgive you.

KELLER: He would forgive me! For what?

MOTHER: Joe, you know what I mean.

KELLER: I don't know what you mean! You wanted money, so I made money. What must I be forgiven? You wanted money, didn't you?

MOTHER: I didn't want it that way.

KELLER: I didn't want it that way, either! What difference is it what you want? I spoiled the both of you. I should've put him out when he was ten like I was put out, and make him earn his keep. Then he'd know how a buck is made in this world. Forgiven! I could live on a quarter a day myself, but I got a family so I . . .

MOTHER: Joe, Joe . . . it don't excuse it that you did it for the family.

KELLER: It's got to excuse it!

MOTHER: There's something bigger than the family to him.

KELLER: Nothin' is bigger!

MOTHER: There is to him.

KELLER: There's nothin' he could do that I wouldn't forgive. Because he's my son. Because I'm his father and he's my son.

MOTHER: Joe, I tell you . . .

KELLER: Nothin's bigger than that. And you're goin' to tell him, you understand? I'm his father and he's my son, and if there's something bigger than that I'll put a bullet in my head!

MOTHER: You stop that!

KELLER: You heard me. Now you know what to tell him. *Pause. He moves from her—halts.* But he wouldn't put me away though . . . He wouldn't do that . . . Would he?

MOTHER: He loved you, Joe, you broke his heart.

KELLER: But to put me away . . .

MOTHER: I don't know. I'm beginning to think we don't really know him. They say in the war he was such a killer. Here he was always afraid of mice. I don't know him. I don't know what he'll do.

KELLER: Goddam, if Larry was alive he wouldn't act like this. He understood the way the world is made. He listened to me. To him the world had a forty-foot front, it ended at the building line. This one, everything bothers him. You make a deal, overcharge two cents, and his hair falls out. He don't understand money. Too easy, it came too easy. Yes sir. Larry. That was a boy we lost. Larry. Larry. *He slumps on chair in front of her.* What am I gonna do, Kate . . .

MOTHER: Joe, Joe, please . . . you'll be all right, nothing is going to happen . . .

KELLER, *desperately, lost*: For you, Kate, for both of you, that's all I ever lived for . . .

MOTHER: I know, darling, I know . . .

> *Ann enters from house. They say nothing, waiting for her to speak.*

ANN: Why do you stay up? I'll tell you when he comes.

KELLER, *rises, goes to her*: You didn't eat supper, did you? *To Mother*: Why don't you make her something?

MOTHER: Sure, I'll . . .

ANN: Never mind, Kate, I'm all right. *They are unable to speak to each other.* There's something I want to tell you. *She starts, then halts.* I'm not going to do anything about it. . . .

MOTHER: She's a good girl! *To Keller*: You see? She's a . . .

ANN: I'll do nothing about Joe, but you're going to do something for me. *Directly to Mother*: You made Chris feel guilty with me. Whether you wanted to or not, you've crippled him in front of me. I'd like you to tell him that Larry is dead and that you know it. You understand me? I'm not going out of here alone. There's no life for me that way. I want you to set him free. And then I promise you, everything will end, and we'll go away, and that's all.

KELLER: You'll do that. You'll tell him.

ANN: I know what I'm asking, Kate. You had two sons. But you've only got one now.

KELLER: You'll tell him . . .

ANN: And you've got to say it to him so he knows you mean it.

MOTHER: My dear, if the boy was dead, it wouldn't depend on my words to make Chris know it. . . . The night he gets into your bed, his heart will dry up. Because he knows and you know. To his dying day he'll wait for his brother! No, my dear, no such thing. You're going in the morning, and you're going alone. That's your life, that's your lonely life. *She goes to porch, and starts in.*

ANN: Larry is dead, Kate.

MOTHER—*she stops*: Don't speak to me.

ANN: I said he's dead. I know! He crashed off the coast of China November twenty-fifth! His engine didn't fail him. But he died. I know . . .

MOTHER: How did he die? You're lying to me. If you know, how did he die?

ANN: I loved him. You know I loved him. Would I have looked at anyone else if I wasn't sure? That's enough for you.

MOTHER, *moving on her*: What's enough for me? What're you talking about? *She grasps Ann's wrists.*

ANN: You're hurting my wrists.

MOTHER: What are you talking about! *Pause. She stares at Ann a moment, then turns and goes to Keller.*

ANN: Joe, go in the house . . .

KELLER: Why should I . . .

ANN: Please go.

KELLER: Lemme know when he comes. *Keller goes into house.*

MOTHER—*she sees Ann take a letter from her pocket*: What's that?

ANN: Sit down . . . *Mother moves left to chair, but does not sit.* First you've got to understand. When I came, I didn't have any idea that Joe . . . I had nothing against him or you. I came to get married. I hoped . . . So I didn't bring this to hurt you. I thought I'd show it to you only if there was no other way to settle Larry in your mind.

MOTHER: Larry? *Snatches letter from Ann hand.*

ANN: He wrote it to me just before he— *Mother opens and begins to read letter.* I'm not trying to hurt you, Kate. You're making me do this, now remember you're— Remember. I've been so lonely, Kate . . . I can't leave here alone again. *A long, low moan comes from Mother's throat as she reads.* You made me show it to you. You wouldn't believe me. I told you a hundred times, why wouldn't you believe me!

MOTHER: Oh, my God . . .

ANN, *with pity and fear*: Kate, please, please . . .

MOTHER: My God, my God . . .

ANN: Kate, dear, I'm so sorry . . . I'm so sorry.

Chris enters from driveway. He seems exhausted.

CHRIS: What's the matter . . . ?

ANN: Where were you? . . . You're all perspired. *Mother doesn't move.* Where were you?

CHRIS: Just drove around a little. I thought you'd be gone.

ANN: Where do I go? I have nowhere to go.

CHRIS, *to Mother*: Where's Dad?

ANN: Inside lying down.

CHRIS: Sit down, both of you. I'll say what there is to say.

MOTHER: I didn't hear the car . . .

CHRIS: I left it in the garage.

MOTHER: Jim is out looking for you.

CHRIS: Mother . . . I'm going away. There are a couple of firms in Cleveland, I think I can get a place. I mean, I'm going away for good. *To Ann alone*: I know what you're thinking, Annie. It's true. I'm yellow. I was made yellow in this house because I suspected my father and I did nothing about it, but if I knew that night when I came home what I know now, he'd be in the district attorney's office by this time, and I'd have brought him there. Now if I look at him, all I'm able to do is cry.

MOTHER: What are you talking about? What else can you do?

CHRIS: I could jail him! I could jail him, if I were human any more. But I'm like everybody else now. I'm practical now. You made me practical.

MOTHER: But you have to be.

CHRIS: The cats in that alley are practical, the bums who ran away when we were fighting were practical. Only the dead ones weren't practical. But now I'm practical, and I spit on myself. I'm going away. I'm going now.

ANN, *goes up to stop him*: I'm coming with you. . . .

CHRIS: No, Ann.

ANN: Chris, I don't ask you to do anything about Joe.

CHRIS: You do, you do . . .

ANN: I swear I never will.

CHRIS: In your heart you always will.

ANN: Then do what you have to do!

CHRIS: Do what? What is there to do? I've looked all night for a reason to make him suffer.

ANN: There's reason, there's reason!

CHRIS: What? Do I raise the dead when I put him behind bars? Then what'll I do it for? We used to shoot a man who acted like a dog, but honor was real there, you were protecting something. But here? This is the land of the great big dogs, you don't love a man here, you eat him! That's the principle; the only one we live by—it just happened to kill a few people this time, that's all. The world's that way, how can I take it out on him? What sense does that make? This is a zoo, a zoo!

ANN, *to Mother*: You know what he's got to do! Tell him!

MOTHER: Let him go.

ANN: I won't let him go. You'll tell him what he's got to do . . .

MOTHER: Annie!

ANN: Then I will!

> *Keller enters from house. Chris sees him, goes down right near arbor.*

KELLER: What's the matter with you? I want to talk to you.

CHRIS: I've got nothing to say to you.

KELLER, *taking his arm*: I want to talk to you!

CHRIS, *pulling violently away from him*: Don't do that, Dad. I'm going to hurt you if you do that. There's nothing to say, so say it quick.

KELLER: Exactly what's the matter? What's the matter? You got too much money? Is that what bothers you?

CHRIS, *with an edge of sarcasm*: It bothers me.

KELLER: If you can't get used to it, then throw it away. You hear me? Take every cent and give it to charity, throw it in the sewer. Does that settle it? In the sewer, that's all. You think I'm kidding? I'm tellin' you what to do, if it's dirty then burn it. It's your money, that's not my money. I'm a dead man, I'm an old dead man, nothing's mine. Well, talk to me!—what do you want to do!

CHRIS: It's not what I want to do. It's what you want to do.

KELLER: What should I want to do? *Chris is silent.* Jail? You want me to go to jail? If you want me to go, say so! Is that where I belong?—then tell me so! *Slight pause*. What's the matter, why can't you tell me? *Furiously*. You say everything else to me, say that! *Slight pause*. I'll tell you why you can't say it. Because you know I don't belong there. Because you know! *With growing emphasis and passion, and a persistent tone of desperation*: Who worked for nothin' in that war? When they work for nothin', I'll work for nothin'. Did they ship a gun or a truck outa Detroit before they got their price? Is that clean? It's dollars and cents, nickels and dimes; war and peace, it's nickels and dimes, what's clean? Half the Goddam country is gotta go if I go! That's why you can't tell me.

CHRIS: That's exactly why.

KELLER: Then . . . why am *I* bad?

CHRIS: *I* know you're no worse than most men but I thought you were better. I never saw you as a man. I saw you as my father. *Almost breaking*: I can't look at you this way, I can't look at myself! *He turns away unable to face Keller. Ann goes quickly to Mother, takes letter from her and starts for Chris. Mother instantly rushes to intercept her.*

MOTHER: Give me that!

ANN: He's going to read it! *She thrusts letter into Chris's hand.* Larry. He wrote it to me the day he died. . . .

KELLER: Larry?!

MOTHER: Chris, it's not for you. *He starts to read.* Joe . . . go away . . .

KELLER, *mystified, frightened*: Why'd she say, Larry, what . . . ?

MOTHER—*she desperately pushes him toward alley, glancing at Chris*: Go to the street, Joe, go to the street! *She comes down beside Keller.* Don't, Chris . . . *Pleading from her whole soul*: Don't tell him . . .

CHRIS, *quietly*: Three and one half years . . . talking, talking. Now you tell me what you must do. . . . This is how he died, now tell me where you belong.

KELLER, *pleading*: Chris, a man can't be a Jesus in this world!

CHRIS: I know all about the world. I know the whole crap story. Now listen to this, and tell me what a man's got to be! *Reads*: "My dear Ann . . . " You listening? He wrote this the day he died. Listen, don't cry . . . listen! "My dear Ann: It is impossible to put down the things I feel. But I've got to tell you something. Yesterday they flew in a load of papers from the States and I read about Dad and your father being convicted. I can't express myself. I can't tell you how I feel—I can't bear to live any more. Last night I circled the base for twenty minutes before I could bring myself in. How could he have done that? Every day three or four men never come back and he sits back there doing business. . . . I don't know how to tell you what I feel . . . I can't face anybody . . . I'm going out on a mission in a few minutes. They'll probably report me missing. If they do, I want you to know that you mustn't wait for me. I tell you, Ann, if I had him here now I could kill him—" *Keller grabs letter from Chris's hand and reads it. After a long pause*: Now blame the world. Do you understand that letter?

KELLER—*he speaks almost inaudibly*: I think I do. Get the car, I'll put on my jacket. *He turns and starts slowly for the house. Mother rushes to intercept him.*

MOTHER: Why are you going? You'll sleep, why are you going?

KELLER: I can't sleep here. I'll feel better if I go.

MOTHER: You're so foolish. Larry was your son too, wasn't he? You know he'd never tell you to do this.

KELLER, *looking at letter in his hand*: Then what is this if it isn't telling me? Sure, he was my son. But I think to him they were all my sons. And I guess they were, I guess they were. I'll be right down. *Exits into house.*

MOTHER, *to Chris, with determination*: You're not going to take him!

CHRIS: I'm taking him.

MOTHER: It's up to you, if you tell him to stay he'll stay. Go and tell him!

CHRIS: Nobody could stop him now.

MOTHER: You'll stop him! How long will he live in prison?—are you trying to kill him?

CHRIS, *holding out letter*: I thought you read this!

MOTHER, *of Larry, the letter*: The war is over! Didn't you hear?—it's over!

CHRIS: Then what was Larry to you? A stone that fell into the water? It's not enough for him to be sorry. Larry didn't kill himself to make you and Dad sorry.

MOTHER: What more can we be!

CHRIS: You can be better! Once and for all you can know there's a universe of people outside and you're responsible to it, and unless you know that you threw away your son because that's why he died.

A shot is heard in the house. They stand frozen for a brief second. Chris starts for porch, pauses at step, turns to Ann.

CHRIS: Find Jim! *He goes on into the house and Ann runs up driveway. Mother stands alone, transfixed.*

MOTHER, *softly, almost moaning*: Joe . . . Joe . . . Joe . . . Joe . . .

    Chris comes out of house, down to Mother's arms.

CHRIS, *almost crying*: Mother, I didn't mean to . . .

MOTHER: Don't, dear. Don't take it on yourself. Forget now. Live. *Chris stirs as if to answer.* Shhh . . . *She puts his arms down gently and moves towards porch.* Shhh . . . *As she reaches porch steps she begins sobbing, as*:

THE CURTAIN FALLS.

DEATH OF A SALESMAN

CERTAIN PRIVATE CONVERSATIONS IN TWO ACTS AND A REQUIEM

1949

Characters

WILLY LOMAN

LINDA

BIFF

HAPPY

BERNARD

THE WOMAN

CHARLEY

UNCLE BEN

HOWARD WAGNER

JENNY

STANLEY

MISS FORSYTHE

LETTA

The action takes place in Willy Loman's house and yard and in various places he visits in the New York and Boston of today.

ACT ONE

A melody is heard, played upon a flute. It is small and fine, telling of grass and trees and the horizon. The curtain rises.

Before us is the Salesman's house. We are aware of towering, angular shapes behind it, surrounding it on all sides. Only the blue light of the sky falls upon the house and forestage; the surrounding area shows an angry glow of orange. As more light appears, we see a solid vault of apartment houses around the small, fragile-seeming home. An air of the dream clings to the place, a dream rising out of reality. The kitchen at center seems actual enough, for there is a kitchen table with three chairs, and a refrigerator. But no other fixtures are seen. At the back of the kitchen there is a draped entrance, which leads to the living-room. To the right of the kitchen, on a level raised two feet, is a bedroom furnished only with a brass bedstead and a straight chair. On a shelf over the bed a silver athletic trophy stands. A window opens on to the apartment house at the side.

Behind the kitchen, on a level raised six and a half feet, is the boys' bedroom, at present barely visible. Two beds are dimly seen, and at the back of the room a dormer window. (This bedroom is above the unseen living-room.) At the left a stairway curves up to it from the kitchen.

The entire setting is wholly or, in some places, partially transparent. The roof-line of the house is one-dimensional; under and over it we see the apartment buildings. Before the house lies an apron, curving beyond the forestage into the orchestra. This forward area serves as the back yard as well as the locale of all Willy's imaginings and of his city scenes. Whenever the action is in the present the actors observe the imaginary wall-lines, entering the house only through its door at the left. But in the scenes of the past these boundaries are broken, and characters enter or leave a room by stepping "through" a wall on to the forestage.

From the right, Willy Loman, the Salesman, enters, carrying two large sample cases. The flute plays on. He hears but is not aware of it. He is past sixty years of age, dressed quietly. Even as he crosses the stage to the doorway of the house, his exhaustion is apparent. He unlocks the door, comes into the kitchen, and thankfully lets his burden down, feeling the soreness of his palms. A word-sigh escapes his lips—it might be "Oh, boy, oh, boy." He closes the door, then carries his cases out into the living-room, through the draped kitchen doorway. Linda, his wife, has stirred in her bed at the right. She gets out and puts on a robe, listening. Most often jovial, she has developed an iron repression of her exceptions to Willy's behavior—she more than loves him, she admires him, as though his mercurial nature, his temper, his massive dreams and little cruelties, served her only as sharp reminders of the turbulent longings within him, longings which she shares but lacks the temperament to utter and follow to their end.

LINDA, *hearing Willy outside the bedroom, calls with some trepidation:* Willy!

WILLY: It's all right. I came back.

LINDA: Why? What happened? *Slight pause.* Did something happen, Willy?

WILLY: No, nothing happened.

LINDA: You didn't smash the car, did you?

WILLY, *with casual irritation:* I said nothing happened. Didn't you hear me?

LINDA: Don't you feel well?

WILLY: I'm tired to the death. *The flute has faded away. He sits on the bed beside her, a little numb.* I couldn't make it. I just couldn't make it, Linda.

LINDA, *very carefully, delicately:* Where were you all day? You look terrible.

WILLY: I got as far as a little above Yonkers. I stopped for a cup of coffee. Maybe it was the coffee.

LINDA: What?

WILLY, *after a pause:* I suddenly couldn't drive any more. The car kept going off on to the shoulder, y'know?

LINDA, *helpfully:* Oh. Maybe it was the steering again. I don't think Angelo knows the Studebaker.

WILLY: No, it's me, it's me. Suddenly I realize I'm goin' sixty miles an hour and I don't remember the last five minutes. I'm—I can't seem to—keep my mind to it.

LINDA: Maybe it's your glasses. You never went for your new glasses.

WILLY: No, I see everything. I came back ten miles an hour. It took me nearly four hours from Yonkers.

LINDA, *resigned*: Well, you'll just have to take a rest, Willy, you can't continue this way.

WILLY: I just got back from Florida.

LINDA: But you didn't rest your mind. Your mind is overactive, and the mind is what counts, dear.

WILLY: I'll start out in the morning. Maybe I'll feel better in the morning. *She is taking off his shoes.* These goddam arch supports are killing me.

LINDA: Take an aspirin. Should I get you an aspirin? It'll soothe you.

WILLY, *with wonder*: I was driving along, you understand? And I was fine. I was even observing the scenery. You can imagine, me looking at scenery, on the road every week of my life. But it's so beautiful up there, Linda, the trees are so thick, and the sun is warm. I opened the windshield and just let the warm air bathe over me. And then all of a sudden I'm goin' off the road! I'm tellin' ya, I absolutely forgot I was driving. If I'd've gone the other way over the white line I might've killed somebody. So I went on again—and five minutes later I'm dreamin' again, and I nearly— *He presses two fingers against his eyes.* I have such thoughts, I have such strange thoughts.

LINDA: Willy, dear. Talk to them again. There's no reason why you can't work in New York.

WILLY: They don't need me in New York. I'm the New England man. I'm vital in New England.

LINDA: But you're sixty years old. They can't expect you to keep traveling every week.

WILLY: I'll have to send a wire to Portland. I'm supposed to see Brown and Morrison tomorrow morning at ten o'clock to show the line. Goddammit, I could sell them! *He starts putting on his jacket.*

LINDA, *taking the jacket from him*: Why don't you go down to the place tomorrow and tell Howard you've simply got to work in New York? You're too accommodating, dear.

WILLY: If old man Wagner was alive I'd a been in charge of New York now! That man was a prince, he was a masterful man. But that boy of his, that Howard, he don't appreciate. When I went north the first time, the Wagner Company didn't know where New England was!

LINDA: Why don't you tell those things to Howard, dear?

WILLY, *encouraged*: I will, I definitely will. Is there any cheese?

LINDA: I'll make you a sandwich.

WILLY: No, go to sleep. I'll take some milk. I'll be up right away. The boys in?

LINDA: They're sleeping. Happy took Biff on a date tonight.

WILLY, *interested*: That so?

LINDA: It was so nice to see them shaving together, one behind the other, in the bathroom. And going out together. You notice? The whole house smells of shaving lotion.

WILLY: Figure it out. Work a lifetime to pay off a house. You finally own it, and there's nobody to live in it.

LINDA: Well, dear, life is a casting off. It's always that way.

WILLY: No, no, some people—some people accomplish something. Did Biff say anything after I went this morning?

LINDA: You shouldn't have criticized him, Willy, especially after he just got off the train. You mustn't lose your temper with him.

WILLY: When the hell did I lose my temper? I simply asked him if he was making any money. Is that a criticism?

LINDA: But, dear, how could he make any money?

WILLY, *worried and angered*: There's such an undercurrent in him. He became a moody man. Did he apologize when I left this morning?

LINDA: He was crestfallen, Willy. You know how he admires you. I think if he finds himself, then you'll both be happier and not fight any more.

WILLY: How can he find himself on a farm? Is that a life? A farmhand? In the beginning, when he was young, I thought, well, a young man, it's good for him to tramp around, take a lot of different jobs. But it's more than ten years now and he has yet to make thirty-five dollars a week!

LINDA: He's finding himself, Willy.

WILLY: Not finding yourself at the age of thirty-four is a disgrace!

LINDA: Shh!

WILLY: The trouble is he's lazy, goddammit!

LINDA: Willy, please!

WILLY: Biff is a lazy bum!

LINDA: They're sleeping. Get something to eat. Go on down.

WILLY: Why did he come home? I would like to know what brought him home.

LINDA: I don't know. I think he's still lost, Willy. I think he's very lost.

WILLY: Biff Loman is lost. In the greatest country in the world a young man with such—personal attractiveness, gets lost. And such a hard worker. There's one thing about Biff—he's not lazy.

LINDA: Never.

WILLY, *with pity and resolve*: I'll see him in the morning; I'll have a nice talk with him. I'll get him a job selling. He could be big in no time. My God! Remember how they used to follow him around in high school? When he smiled at one of them their faces lit up. When he walked down the street . . . *He loses himself in reminiscences.*

LINDA, *trying to bring him out of it*: Willy, dear, I got a new kind of American-type cheese today. It's whipped.

WILLY: Why do you get American when I like Swiss?

LINDA: I just thought you'd like a change—

WILLY: I don't want a change! I want Swiss cheese. Why am I always being contradicted?

LINDA, *with a covering laugh*: I thought it would be a surprise.

WILLY: Why don't you open a window in here, for God's sake?

LINDA, *with infinite patience*: They're all open, dear.

WILLY: The way they boxed us in here. Bricks and windows, windows and bricks.

LINDA: We should've bought the land next door.

WILLY: The street is lined with cars. There's not a breath of fresh air in the neighborhood. The grass don't grow any more, you can't raise a carrot in the back yard. They should've had a law against apartment houses. Remember those two beautiful elm trees out there? When I and Biff hung the swing between them?

LINDA: Yeah, like being a million miles from the city.

WILLY: They should've arrested the builder for cutting those down. They massacred the neighborhood. *Lost*: More and more I think of those days, Linda. This time of year it was lilac and wisteria. And then the peonies would come out, and the daffodils. What fragrance in this room!

LINDA: Well, after all, people had to move somewhere.

WILLY: No, there's more people now.

LINDA: I don't think there's more people. I think—

WILLY: There's more people! That's what's ruining this country! Population is getting out of control. The competition is maddening! Smell the stink from that apartment house! And another one on the other side . . . How can they whip cheese?

> *On Willy's last line, Biff and Happy raise themselves up in their beds, listening.*

LINDA: Go down, try it. And be quiet.

WILLY, *turning to Linda, guiltily*: You're not worried about me, are you, sweetheart?

BIFF: What's the matter?

HAPPY: Listen!

LINDA: You've got too much on the ball to worry about.

WILLY: You're my foundation and my support, Linda.

LINDA: Just try to relax, dear. You make mountains out of molehills.

WILLY: I won't fight with him any more. If he wants to go back to Texas, let him go.

LINDA: He'll find his way.

WILLY: Sure. Certain men just don't get started till later in life. Like Thomas Edison, I think. Or B. F. Goodrich. One of them was deaf. *He starts for the bedroom doorway.* I'll put my money on Biff.

LINDA: And Willy—if it's warm Sunday we'll drive in the country. And we'll open the windshield, and take lunch.

WILLY: No, the windshields don't open on the new cars.

LINDA: But you opened it today.

WILLY: Me? I didn't. *He stops.* Now isn't that peculiar! Isn't that a remarkable— *He breaks off in amazement and fright as the flute is heard distantly.*

LINDA: What, darling?

WILLY: That is the most remarkable thing.

LINDA: What, dear?

WILLY: I was thinking of the Chevvy. *Slight pause.* Nineteen twenty-eight . . . when I had that red Chevvy— *Breaks off.* That funny? I coulda sworn I was driving that Chevvy today.

LINDA: Well, that's nothing. Something must've reminded you.

WILLY: Remarkable. Ts. Remember those days? The way Biff used to simonize that car? The dealer refused to believe there was eighty thousand miles on it. *He shakes his head.* Heh! *To Linda:* Close your eyes, I'll be right up. *He walks out of the bedroom.*

HAPPY, *to Biff:* Jesus, maybe he smashed up the car again!

LINDA, *calling after Willy:* Be careful on the stairs, dear! The cheese is on the middle shelf! *She turns, goes over to the bed, takes his jacket, and goes out of the bedroom.*

> *Light has risen on the boys' room. Unseen, Willy is heard talking to himself, "Eighty thousand miles," and a little laugh. Biff gets out of bed, comes downstage a bit, and stands attentively. Biff is two years older than his brother, Happy, well built, but in these days bears a worn air and seems less self-assured. He has succeeded less, and his dreams are stronger and less acceptable than Happy's. Happy is tall, powerfully made. Sexuality is like a visible color on him, or a scent that many women have discovered. He, like his brother, is lost, but in a different way, for he has never allowed himself to turn his face toward defeat and is thus more confused and hard-skinned, although seemingly more content.*

HAPPY, *getting out of bed:* He's going to get his license taken away if he keeps that up. I'm getting nervous about him, y'know, Biff?

BIFF: His eyes are going.

HAPPY: No, I've driven with him. He sees all right. He just doesn't keep his mind on it. I drove into the city with him last week. He stops at a green light and then it turns red and he goes. *He laughs.*

BIFF: Maybe he's color-blind.

HAPPY: Pop? Why, he's got the finest eye for color in the business. You know that.

BIFF, *sitting down on his bed:* I'm going to sleep.

HAPPY: You're not still sour on Dad, are you, Biff?

BIFF: He's all right, I guess.

WILLY, *underneath them, in the living-room:* Yes, sir, eighty thousand miles—eighty-two thousand!

BIFF: You smoking?

HAPPY, *holding out a pack of cigarettes*: Want one?

BIFF, *taking a cigarette*: I can never sleep when I smell it.

WILLY: What a simonizing job, heh!

HAPPY, *with deep sentiment*: Funny, Biff, y'know? Us sleeping in here again? The old beds. *He pats his bed affectionately.* All the talk that went across those two beds, huh? Our whole lives.

BIFF: Yeah. Lotta dreams and plans.

HAPPY, *with a deep and masculine laugh*: About five hundred women would like to know what was said in this room.

> *They share a soft laugh.*

BIFF: Remember that big Betsy something—what the hell was her name—over on Bushwick Avenue?

HAPPY, *combing his hair*: With the collie dog!

BIFF: That's the one. I got you in there, remember?

HAPPY: Yeah, that was my first time—I think. Boy, there was a pig! *They laugh, almost crudely.* You taught me everything I know about women. Don't forget that.

BIFF: I bet you forgot how bashful you used to be. Especially with girls.

HAPPY: Oh, I still am, Biff.

BIFF: Oh, go on.

HAPPY: I just control it, that's all. I think I got less bashful and you got more so. What happened, Biff? Where's the old humor, the old confidence? *He shakes Biff's knee. Biff gets up and moves restlessly about the room.* What's the matter?

BIFF: Why does Dad mock me all the time?

HAPPY: He's not mocking you, he—

BIFF: Everything I say there's a twist of mockery on his face. I can't get near him.

HAPPY: He just wants you to make good, that's all. I wanted to talk to you about Dad for a long time, Biff. Something's—happening to him. He—talks to himself.

BIFF: I noticed that this morning. But he always mumbled.

HAPPY: But not so noticeable. It got so embarrassing I sent him to Florida. And you know something? Most of the time he's talking to you.

BIFF: What's he say about me?

HAPPY: I can't make it out.

BIFF: What's he say about me?

HAPPY: I think the fact that you're not settled, that you're still kind of up in the air . . .

BIFF: There's one or two other things depressing him, Happy.

HAPPY: What do you mean?

BIFF: Never mind. Just don't lay it all to me.

HAPPY: But I think if you got started—I mean—is there any future for you out there?

BIFF: I tell ya, Hap, I don't know what the future is. I don't know—what I'm supposed to want.

HAPPY: What do you mean?

BIFF: Well, I spent six or seven years after high school trying to work myself up. Shipping clerk, salesman, business of one kind or another. And it's a measly manner of existence. To get on that subway on the hot mornings in summer. To devote your whole life to keeping stock, or making phone calls, or selling or buying. To suffer fifty weeks of the year for the sake of a two-week vacation, when all you really desire is to be outdoors, with your shirt off. And always to have to get ahead of the next fella. And still—that's how you build a future.

HAPPY: Well, you really enjoy it on a farm? Are you content out there?

BIFF, *with rising agitation*: Hap, I've had twenty or thirty different kinds of job since I left home before the war, and it always turns out the same. I just realized it lately. In Nebraska when I herded cattle, and the Dakotas, and Arizona, and now in Texas. It's why I came home now, I guess, because I realized it. This farm I work on, it's spring there now, see? And they've got about fifteen new colts. There's nothing more inspiring or— beautiful than the sight of a mare and a new colt. And it's cool there now, see? Texas is cool now, and it's spring. And whenever spring comes to where I am, I suddenly get the feeling, my God, I'm not gettin' anywhere! What the hell am I doing, playing around with horses, twenty-eight dollars a week! I'm thirty-four years old, I oughta be makin' my future. That's when I come running home. And now, I get here, and I don't know what to do with myself. *After a pause*: I've always made a point of not wasting my life, and everytime I come back here I know that all I've done is to waste my life.

HAPPY: You're a poet, you know that, Biff? You're a—you're an idealist!

BIFF: No, I'm mixed up very bad. Maybe I oughta get married. Maybe I oughta get stuck into something. Maybe that's my trouble. I'm like a boy. I'm not married, I'm not in business, I just—I'm like a boy. Are you content, Hap? You're a success, aren't you? Are you content?

HAPPY: Hell, no!

BIFF: Why? You're making money, aren't you?

HAPPY, *moving about with energy, expressiveness*: All I can do now is wait for the merchandise manager to die. And suppose I get to be merchandise manager? He's a good friend of mine, and he just built a terrific estate on Long Island. And he lived there about two months and sold it, and now he's building another one. He can't enjoy it once it's finished. And I know that's just what I would do. I don't know what the hell I'm workin' for. Sometimes I sit in my apartment—all alone. And I think of the rent I'm paying. And it's crazy. But then, it's what I always wanted. My own apartment, a car, and plenty of women. And still, goddammit, I'm lonely.

BIFF, *with enthusiasm*: Listen, why don't you come out West with me?

HAPPY: You and I, heh?

BIFF: Sure, maybe we could buy a ranch. Raise cattle, use our muscles. Men built like we are should be working out in the open.

HAPPY, *avidly*: The Loman Brothers, heh?

BIFF, *with vast affection*: Sure, we'd be known all over the counties!

HAPPY, *enthralled*: That's what I dream about, Biff. Sometimes I want to just rip my clothes off in the middle of the store and outbox that goddam merchandise manager. I mean I can outbox, outrun, and outlift anybody in that store, and I have to take orders from those common, petty sons-of-bitches till I can't stand it any more.

BIFF: I'm tellin' you, kid, if you were with me I'd be happy out there.

HAPPY, *enthused*: See, Biff, everybody around me is so false that I'm constantly lowering my ideals . . .

BIFF: Baby, together we'd stand up for one another, we'd have someone to trust.

HAPPY: If I were around you—

BIFF: Hap, the trouble is we weren't brought up to grub for money. I don't know how to do it.

HAPPY: Neither can I!

BIFF: Then let's go!

HAPPY: The only thing is—what can you make out there?

BIFF: But look at your friend. Builds an estate and then hasn't the peace of mind to live in it.

HAPPY: Yeah, but when he walks into the store the waves part in front of him. That's fifty-two thousand dollars a year coming through the revolving door, and I got more in my pinky finger than he's got in his head.

BIFF: Yeah, but you just said—

HAPPY: I gotta show some of those pompous, self-important executives over there that Hap Loman can make the grade. I want to walk into the store the way he walks in. Then I'll go with you, Biff. We'll be together yet, I swear. But take those two we had tonight. Now weren't they gorgeous creatures?

BIFF: Yeah, yeah, most gorgeous I've had in years.

HAPPY: I get that any time I want, Biff. Whenever I feel disgusted. The only trouble is, it gets like bowling or something. I just keep knockin' them over and it doesn't mean anything. You still run around a lot?

BIFF: Naa. I'd like to find a girl—steady, somebody with substance.

HAPPY: That's what I long for.

BIFF: Go on! You'd never come home.

HAPPY: I would! Somebody with character, with resistance! Like Mom, y'know? You're gonna call me a bastard when I tell you this. That girl Charlotte I was with tonight is engaged to be married in five weeks. *He tries on his new hat.*

BIFF: No kiddin'!

HAPPY: Sure, the guy's in line for the vice-presidency of the store. I don't know what gets into me, maybe I just have an overdeveloped sense of competition or something, but I went and ruined her, and furthermore I can't get rid of her. And he's the third executive I've done that to. Isn't that a crummy characteristic? And to top it all, I go to their weddings! *Indignantly, but laughing:* Like I'm not supposed to take bribes. Manufacturers offer me a hundred-dollar bill now and then to throw an order their way. You know how honest I am, but it's like this girl, see. I hate myself for it. Because I don't want the girl, and, still, I take it and—I love it!

BIFF: Let's go to sleep.

HAPPY: I guess we didn't settle anything, heh?

BIFF: I just got one idea that I think I'm going to try.

HAPPY: What's that?

BIFF: Remember Bill Oliver?

HAPPY: Sure, Oliver is very big now. You want to work for him again?

BIFF: No, but when I quit he said something to me. He put his arm on my shoulder, and he said, "Biff, if you ever need anything, come to me."

HAPPY: I remember that. That sounds good.

BIFF: I think I'll go to see him. If I could get ten thousand or even seven or eight thousand dollars I could buy a beautiful ranch.

HAPPY: I bet he'd back you. 'Cause he thought highly of you, Biff. I mean, they all do. You're well liked, Biff. That's why I say to come back here, and we both have the apartment. And I'm tellin' you, Biff, any babe you want . . .

BIFF: No, with a ranch I could do the work I like and still be something. I just wonder though. I wonder if Oliver still thinks I stole that carton of basketballs.

HAPPY: Oh, he probably forgot that long ago. It's almost ten years. You're too sensitive. Anyway, he didn't really fire you.

BIFF: Well, I think he was going to. I think that's why I quit. I was never sure whether he knew or not. I know he thought the world of me, though. I was the only one he'd let lock up the place.

WILLY, *below*: You gonna wash the engine, Biff?

HAPPY: Shh!

Biff looks at Happy, who is gazing down, listening. Willy is mumbling in the parlor.

HAPPY: You hear that?

They listen. Willy laughs warmly.

BIFF, *growing angry*: Doesn't he know Mom can hear that?

WILLY: Don't get your sweater dirty, Biff!

A look of pain crosses Biff's face.

HAPPY: Isn't that terrible? Don't leave again, will you? You'll find a job here. You gotta stick around. I don't know what to do about him, it's getting embarrassing.

WILLY: What a simonizing job!

BIFF: Mom's hearing that!

WILLY: No kiddin', Biff, you got a date? Wonderful!

HAPPY: Go on to sleep. But talk to him in the morning, will you?

BIFF, *reluctantly getting into bed*: With her in the house. Brother!

HAPPY, *getting into bed*: I wish you'd have a good talk with him.

The light on their room begins to fade.

BIFF, *to himself in bed*: That selfish, stupid . . .

HAPPY: Sh . . . Sleep, Biff.

Their light is out. Well before they have finished speaking, Willy's form is dimly seen below in the darkened kitchen. He opens the refrigerator, searches in there, and takes out a bottle of milk. The apartment houses are fading out, and the entire house and surroundings become covered with leaves. Music insinuates itself as the leaves appear.

WILLY: Just wanna be careful with those girls, Biff, that's all. Don't make any promises. No promises of any kind. Because a girl, y'know, they always believe what you tell 'em, and you're very young, Biff, you're too young to be talking seriously to girls.

Light rises on the kitchen. Willy, talking, shuts the refrigerator door and comes downstage to the kitchen table. He pours milk into a glass. He is totally immersed in himself, smiling faintly.

WILLY: Too young entirely, Biff. You want to watch your schooling first. Then when you're all set, there'll be plenty of girls for a boy like you. *He smiles broadly at a kitchen chair.* That so? The girls pay for you? *He laughs.* Boy, you must really be makin' a hit.

Willy is gradually addressing—physically—a point offstage, speaking through the wall of the kitchen, and his voice has been rising in volume to that of a normal conversation.

WILLY: I been wondering why you polish the car so careful. Ha! Don't leave the hubcaps, boys. Get the chamois to the hubcaps. Happy, use newspaper on the windows, it's the easiest thing. Show him how to do it, Biff! You see, Happy? Pad it up, use it like a pad. That's it, that's it, good work. You're doin' all right, Hap. *He pauses, then nods in approbation for a few seconds, then looks upward.* Biff, first thing we gotta do when we get time is clip that big branch over the house. Afraid it's gonna fall in a storm and hit the roof. Tell you what. We get a rope and sling her around, and then we climb up there with a couple of saws and take her down. Soon as you finish the car, boys, I wanna see ya. I got a surprise for you, boys.

BIFF, *offstage*: Whatta ya got, Dad?

WILLY: No, you finish first. Never leave a job till you're finished— remember that. *Looking toward the "big trees"*: Biff, up in Albany I saw a beautiful hammock. I think I'll buy it next trip, and we'll hang it right between those two elms. Wouldn't that be something? Just swingin' there under those branches. Boy, that would be . . .

> *Young Biff and Young Happy appear from the direction Willy was addressing. Happy carries rags and a pail of water. Biff, wearing a sweater with a block "S," carries a football.*

BIFF, *pointing in the direction of the car offstage*: How's that, Pop, professional?

WILLY: Terrific. Terrific job, boys. Good work, Biff.

HAPPY: Where's the surprise, Pop?

WILLY: In the back seat of the car.

HAPPY: Boy! *He runs off.*

BIFF: What is it, Dad? Tell me, what'd you buy?

WILLY, *laughing, cuffs him*: Never mind, something I want you to have.

BIFF, *turns and starts off*: What is it, Hap?

HAPPY, *offstage*: It's a punching bag!

BIFF: Oh, Pop!

WILLY: It's got Gene Tunney's signature on it!

> *Happy runs onstage with a punching bag.*

BIFF: Gee, how'd you know we wanted a punching bag?

WILLY: Well, it's the finest thing for the timing.

HAPPY, *lies down on his back and pedals with his feet*: I'm losing weight, you notice, Pop?

WILLY, *to Happy*: Jumping rope is good too.

BIFF: Did you see the new football I got?

WILLY, *examining the ball*: Where'd you get a new ball?

BIFF: The coach told me to practice my passing.

WILLY: That so? And he gave you the ball, heh?

BIFF: Well, I borrowed it from the locker room. *He laughs confidentially.*

WILLY, *laughing with him at the theft*: I want you to return that.

HAPPY: I told you he wouldn't like it!

BIFF, *angrily*: Well, I'm bringing it back!

WILLY, *stopping the incipient argument, to Happy*: Sure, he's gotta practice with a regulation ball, doesn't he? *To Biff*: Coach'll probably congratulate you on your initiative!

BIFF: Oh, he keeps congratulating my initiative all the time, Pop.

WILLY: That's because he likes you. If somebody else took that ball there'd be an uproar. So what's the report, boys, what's the report?

BIFF: Where'd you go this time, Dad? Gee, we were lonesome for you.

WILLY, *pleased, puts an arm around each boy and they come down to the apron*: Lonesome, heh?

BIFF: Missed you every minute.

WILLY: Don't say? Tell you a secret, boys. Don't breathe it to a soul. Someday I'll have my own business, and I'll never have to leave home any more.

HAPPY: Like Uncle Charley, heh?

WILLY: Bigger than Uncle Charley! Because Charley is not—liked. He's liked, but he's not—well liked.

BIFF: Where'd you go this time, Dad?

WILLY: Well, I got on the road, and I went north to Providence. Met the Mayor.

BIFF: The Mayor of Providence!

WILLY: He was sitting in the hotel lobby.

BIFF: What'd he say?

WILLY: He said, "Morning!" And I said, "You got a fine city here, Mayor." And then he had coffee with me. And then I went to Waterbury. Waterbury is a fine city. Big clock city, the famous Waterbury clock. Sold a nice bill there. And then Boston—Boston is the cradle of the Revolution. A fine city. And a couple of other towns in Mass., and on to Portland and Bangor and straight home!

BIFF: Gee, I'd love to go with you sometime, Dad.

WILLY: Soon as summer comes.

HAPPY: Promise?

WILLY: You and Hap and I, and I'll show you all the towns. America is full of beautiful towns and fine, upstanding people. And they know me, boys, they know me up and down New England. The finest people. And when I bring you fellas up, there'll be open sesame for all of us, 'cause one thing, boys: I have friends. I can park my car in any street in New England, and the cops protect it like their own. This summer, heh?

BIFF AND HAPPY, *together*: Yeah! You bet!

WILLY: We'll take our bathing suits.

HAPPY: We'll carry your bags, Pop!

WILLY: Oh, won't that be something! Me comin' into the Boston stores with you boys carryin' my bags. What a sensation!

Biff is prancing around, practicing passing the ball.

WILLY: You nervous, Biff, about the game?

BIFF: Not if you're gonna be there.

WILLY: What do they say about you in school, now that they made you captain?

HAPPY: There's a crowd of girls behind him every time the classes change.

BIFF, *taking Willy's hand*: This Saturday, Pop, this Saturday—just for you, I'm going to break through for a touchdown.

HAPPY: You're supposed to pass.

BIFF: I'm takin' one play for Pop. You watch me, Pop, and when I take off my helmet, that means I'm breakin' out. Then you watch me crash through that line!

WILLY, *kisses Biff*: Oh, wait'll I tell this in Boston!

Bernard enters in knickers. He is younger than Biff, earnest and loyal, a worried boy.

BERNARD: Biff, where are you? You're supposed to study with me today.

WILLY: Hey, looka Bernard. What're you lookin' so anemic about, Bernard?

BERNARD: He's gotta study, Uncle Willy. He's got Regents next week.

HAPPY, *tauntingly, spinning Bernard around*: Let's box, Bernard!

BERNARD: Biff! *He gets away from Happy.* Listen, Biff, I heard Mr. Birnbaum say that if you don't start studyin' math he's gonna flunk you, and you won't graduate. I heard him!

WILLY: You better study with him, Biff. Go ahead now.

BERNARD: I heard him!

BIFF: Oh, Pop, you didn't see my sneakers! *He holds up a foot for Willy to look at.*

WILLY: Hey, that's a beautiful job of printing!

BERNARD, *wiping his glasses*: Just because he printed University of Virginia on his sneakers doesn't mean they've got to graduate him, Uncle Willy!

WILLY, *angrily*: What're you talking about? With scholarships to three universities they're gonna flunk him?

BERNARD: But I heard Mr. Birnbaum say—

WILLY: Don't be a pest, Bernard! *To his boys*: What an anemic!

BERNARD: Okay, I'm waiting for you in my house, Biff.

> *Bernard goes off. The Lomans laugh.*

WILLY: Bernard is not well liked, is he?

BIFF: He's liked, but he's not well liked.

HAPPY: That's right, Pop.

WILLY: That's just what I mean, Bernard can get the best marks in school, y'understand, but when he gets out in the business world, y'understand, you are going to be five times ahead of him. That's why I thank Almighty God you're both built like Adonises. Because the man who makes an appearance in the business world, the man who creates personal interest, is the man who gets ahead. Be liked and you will never want. You take me, for instance. I never have to wait in line to see a buyer. "Willy Loman is here!" That's all they have to know, and I go right through.

BIFF: Did you knock them dead, Pop?

WILLY: Knocked 'em cold in Providence, slaughtered 'em in Boston.

HAPPY, *on his back, pedaling again*: I'm losing weight, you notice, Pop?

> *Linda enters, as of old, a ribbon in her hair, carrying a basket of washing.*

LINDA, *with youthful energy*: Hello, dear!

WILLY: Sweetheart!

LINDA: How'd the Chevvy run?

WILLY: Chevrolet, Linda, is the greatest car ever built. *To the boys*: Since when do you let your mother carry wash up the stairs?

BIFF: Grab hold there, boy!

HAPPY: Where to, Mom?

LINDA: Hang them up on the line. And you better go down to your friends, Biff. The cellar is full of boys. They don't know what to do with themselves.

BIFF: Ah, when Pop comes home they can wait!

WILLY, *laughs appreciatively*: You better go down and tell them what to do, Biff.

BIFF: I think I'll have them sweep out the furnace room.

WILLY: Good work, Biff.

BIFF, *goes through wall-line of kitchen to doorway at back and calls down*: Fellas! Everybody sweep out the furnace room! I'll be right down!

VOICES: All right! Okay, Biff.

BIFF: George and Sam and Frank, come out back! We're hangin' up the wash! Come on, Hap, on the double! *He and Happy carry out the basket.*

LINDA: The way they obey him!

WILLY: Well, that's training, the training. I'm tellin' you, I was sellin' thousands and thousands, but I had to come home.

LINDA: Oh, the whole block'll be at that game. Did you sell anything?

WILLY: I did five hundred gross in Providence and seven hundred gross in Boston.

LINDA: No! Wait a minute, I've got a pencil. *She pulls pencil and paper out of her apron pocket.* That makes your commission . . . Two hundred—my God! Two hundred and twelve dollars!

WILLY: Well, I didn't figure it yet, but . . .

LINDA: How much did you do?

WILLY: Well, I—I did—about a hundred and eighty gross in Providence. Well, no—it came to—roughly two hundred gross on the whole trip.

LINDA, *without hesitation*: Two hundred gross. That's . . . *She figures.*

WILLY: The trouble was that three of the stores were half closed for inventory in Boston. Otherwise I woulda broke records.

LINDA: Well, it makes seventy dollars and some pennies. That's very good.

WILLY: What do we owe?

LINDA: Well, on the first there's sixteen dollars on the refrigerator—

WILLY: Why sixteen?

LINDA: Well, the fan belt broke, so it was a dollar eighty.

WILLY: But it's brand new.

LINDA: Well, the man said that's the way it is. Till they work themselves in, y'know. *They move through the wall-line into the kitchen.*

WILLY: I hope we didn't get stuck on that machine.

LINDA: They got the biggest ads of any of them!

WILLY: I know, it's a fine machine. What else?

LINDA: Well, there's nine-sixty for the washing machine. And for the vacuum cleaner there's three and a half due on the fifteenth. Then the roof, you got twenty-one dollars remaining.

WILLY: It don't leak, does it?

LINDA: No, they did a wonderful job. Then you owe Frank for the carburetor.

WILLY: I'm not going to pay that man! That goddam Chevrolet, they ought to prohibit the manufacture of that car!

LINDA: Well, you owe him three and a half. And odds and ends, comes to around a hundred and twenty dollars by the fifteenth.

WILLY: A hundred and twenty dollars! My God, if business don't pick up I don't know what I'm gonna do!

LINDA: Well, next week you'll do better.

WILLY: Oh, I'll knock 'em dead next week. I'll go to Hartford. I'm very well liked in Hartford. You know, the trouble is, Linda, people don't seem to take to me.

They move onto the forestage.

LINDA: Oh, don't be foolish.

WILLY: I know it when I walk in. They seem to laugh at me.

LINDA: Why? Why would they laugh at you? Don't talk that way, Willy.

Willy moves to the edge of the stage. Linda goes into the kitchen and starts to darn stockings.

WILLY: I don't know the reason for it, but they just pass me by. I'm not noticed.

LINDA: But you're doing wonderful, dear. You're making seventy to a hundred dollars a week.

WILLY: But I gotta be at it ten, twelve hours a day. Other men—I don't know—they do it easier. I don't know why—I can't stop myself—I talk too much. A man oughta come in with a few words. One thing about Charley. He's a man of few words, and they respect him.

LINDA: You don't talk too much, you're just lively.

WILLY, smiling: Well, I figure, what the hell, life is short, a couple of jokes. To himself: I joke too much! The smile goes.

LINDA: Why? You're—

WILLY: I'm fat. I'm very—foolish to look at, Linda. I didn't tell you, but Christmas time I happened to be calling on F. H. Stewarts, and a salesman I know, as I was going in to see the buyer I heard him say something about—walrus. And I—I cracked him right across the face. I won't take that. I simply will not take that. But they do laugh at me. I know that.

LINDA: Darling . . .

WILLY: I gotta overcome it. I know I gotta overcome it. I'm not dressing to advantage, maybe.

LINDA: Willy, darling, you're the handsomest man in the world—

WILLY: Oh, no, Linda.

LINDA: To me you are. *Slight pause.* The handsomest. *From the darkness is heard the laughter of a woman. Willy doesn't turn to it, but it continues through Linda's lines.*

LINDA: And the boys, Willy. Few men are idolized by their children the way you are.

> *Music is heard as behind a scrim, to the left of the house, The Woman, dimly seen, is dressing.*

WILLY, *with great feeling*: You're the best there is, Linda, you're a pal, you know that? On the road—on the road I want to grab you sometimes and just kiss the life outa you.

> *The laughter is loud now, and he moves into a brightening area at the left, where The Woman has come from behind the scrim and is standing, putting on her hat, looking into a "mirror," and laughing.*

WILLY: 'Cause I get so lonely—especially when business is bad and there's nobody to talk to. I get the feeling that I'll never sell anything again, that I won't make a living for you, or a business, a business for the boys. *He talks through The Woman's subsiding laughter; The Woman primps at the "mirror."* There's so much I want to make for—

THE WOMAN: Me? You didn't make me, Willy. I picked you.

WILLY, *pleased*: You picked me?

THE WOMAN, *who is quite proper-looking, Willy's age*: I did. I've been sitting at that desk watching all the salesmen go by, day in, day out. But you've got such a sense of humor, and we do have such a good time together, don't we?

WILLY: Sure, sure. *He takes her in his arms.* Why do you have to go now?

THE WOMAN: It's two o'clock . . .

WILLY: No, come on in! *He pulls her.*

THE WOMAN: . . . my sisters'll be scandalized. When'll you be back?

WILLY: Oh, two weeks about. Will you come up again?

THE WOMAN: Sure thing. You do make me laugh. It's good for me. *She squeezes his arm, kisses him.* And I think you're a wonderful man.

WILLY: You picked me, heh?

THE WOMAN: Sure. Because you're so sweet. And such a kidder.

WILLY: Well, I'll see you next time I'm in Boston.

THE WOMAN: I'll put you right through to the buyers.

WILLY, *slapping her bottom*: Right. Well, bottoms up!

THE WOMAN, *slaps him gently and laughs*: You just kill me, Willy. *He suddenly grabs her and kisses her roughly.* You kill me. And thanks for the stockings. I love a lot of stockings. Well, good night.

WILLY: Good night. And keep your pores open!

THE WOMAN: Oh, Willy!

> *The Woman bursts out laughing, and Linda's laughter blends in. The Woman disappears into the dark. Now the area at the kitchen table brightens. Linda is sitting where she was at the kitchen table, but now is mending a pair of her silk stockings.*

LINDA: You are, Willy. The handsomest man. You've got no reason to feel that—

WILLY, *coming out of The Woman's dimming area and going over to Linda*: I'll make it all up to you, Linda, I'll—

LINDA: There's nothing to make up, dear. You're doing fine, better than—

WILLY, *noticing her mending*: What's that?

LINDA: Just mending my stockings. They're so expensive—

WILLY, *angrily, taking them from her*: I won't have you mending stockings in this house! Now throw them out!

> *Linda puts the stockings in her pocket.*

BERNARD, *entering on the run*: Where is he? If he doesn't study!

WILLY, *moving to the forestage, with great agitation*: You'll give him the answers!

BERNARD: I do, but I can't on a Regents! That's a state exam! They're liable to arrest me!

WILLY: Where is he? I'll whip him, I'll whip him!

LINDA: And he'd better give back that football, Willy, it's not nice.

WILLY: Biff! Where is he? Why is he taking everything?

LINDA: He's too rough with the girls, Willy. All the mothers are afraid of him!

WILLY: I'll whip him!

BERNARD: He's driving the car without a license!

The Woman's laugh is heard.

WILLY: Shut up!

LINDA: All the mothers—

WILLY: Shut up!

BERNARD, *backing quietly away and out*: Mr. Birnbaum says he's stuck up.

WILLY: Get outa here!

BERNARD: If he doesn't buckle down he'll flunk math! *He goes off.*

LINDA: He's right, Willy, you've gotta—

WILLY, *exploding at her*: There's nothing the matter with him! You want him to be a worm like Bernard? He's got spirit, personality . . .

As he speaks, Linda, almost in tears, exits into the living-room. Willy is alone in the kitchen, wilting and staring. The leaves are gone. It is night again, and the apartment houses look down from behind.

WILLY: Loaded with it. Loaded! What is he stealing? He's giving it back, isn't he? Why is he stealing? What did I tell him? I never in my life told him anything but decent things.

Happy in pajamas has come down the stairs; Willy suddenly becomes aware of Happy's presence.

HAPPY: Let's go now, come on.

WILLY, *sitting down at the kitchen table*: Huh! Why did she have to wax the floors herself? Everytime she waxes the floors she keels over. She knows that!

HAPPY: Shh! Take it easy. What brought you back tonight?

WILLY: I got an awful scare. Nearly hit a kid in Yonkers. God! Why didn't I go to Alaska with my brother Ben that time! Ben! That man was a genius, that man was success incarnate! What a mistake! He begged me to go.

HAPPY: Well, there's no use in—

WILLY: You guys! There was a man started with the clothes on his back and ended up with diamond mines!

HAPPY: Boy, someday I'd like to know how he did it.

WILLY: What's the mystery? The man knew what he wanted and went out and got it! Walked into a jungle, and comes out, the age of twenty-one, and he's rich! The world is an oyster, but you don't crack it open on a mattress!

HAPPY: Pop, I told you I'm gonna retire you for life.

WILLY: You'll retire me for life on seventy goddam dollars a week? And your women and your car and your apartment, and you'll retire me for life! Christ's sake, I couldn't get past Yonkers today! Where are you guys, where are you? The woods are burning! I can't drive a car!

> *Charley has appeared in the doorway. He is a large man, slow of speech, laconic, immovable. In all he says, despite what he says, there is pity, and, now, trepidation. He has a robe over pajamas, slippers on his feet. He enters the kitchen.*

CHARLEY: Everything all right?

HAPPY: Yeah, Charley, everything's . . .

WILLY: What's the matter?

CHARLEY: I heard some noise. I thought something happened. Can't we do something about the walls? You sneeze in here, and in my house hats blow off.

HAPPY: Let's go to bed, Dad. Come on.

> *Charley signals to Happy to go.*

WILLY: You go ahead, I'm not tired at the moment.

HAPPY, *to Willy*: Take it easy, huh? *He exits.*

WILLY: What're you doin' up?

CHARLEY, *sitting down at the kitchen table opposite Willy*: Couldn't sleep good. I had a heartburn.

WILLY: Well, you don't know how to eat.

CHARLEY: I eat with my mouth.

WILLY: No, you're ignorant. You gotta know about vitamins and things like that.

CHARLEY: Come on, let's shoot. Tire you out a little.

WILLY, *hesitantly*: All right. You got cards?

CHARLEY, *taking a deck from his pocket*: Yeah, I got them. Someplace. What is it with those vitamins?

WILLY, *dealing*: They build up your bones. Chemistry.

CHARLEY: Yeah, but there's no bones in a heartburn.

WILLY: What are you talkin' about? Do you know the first thing about it?

CHARLEY: Don't get insulted.

WILLY: Don't talk about something you don't know anything about.

    They are playing. Pause.

CHARLEY: What're you doin' home?

WILLY: A little trouble with the car.

CHARLEY: Oh. *Pause.* I'd like to take a trip to California.

WILLY: Don't say.

CHARLEY: You want a job?

WILLY: I got a job, I told you that. *After a slight pause*: What the hell are you offering me a job for?

CHARLEY: Don't get insulted.

WILLY: Don't insult me.

CHARLEY: I don't see no sense in it. You don't have to go on this way.

WILLY: I got a good job. *Slight pause.* What do you keep comin' in here for?

CHARLEY: You want me to go?

WILLY, *after a pause, withering*: I can't understand it. He's going back to Texas again. What the hell is that?

CHARLEY: Let him go.

WILLY: I got nothin' to give him, Charley, I'm clean, I'm clean.

CHARLEY: He won't starve. None a them starve. Forget about him.

WILLY: Then what have I got to remember?

CHARLEY: You take it too hard. To hell with it. When a deposit bottle is broken you don't get your nickel back.

WILLY: That's easy enough for you to say.

CHARLEY: That ain't easy for me to say.

WILLY: Did you see the ceiling I put up in the living-room?

CHARLEY: Yeah, that's a piece of work. To put up a ceiling is a mystery to me. How do you do it?

WILLY: What's the difference?

CHARLEY: Well, talk about it.

WILLY: You gonna put up a ceiling?

CHARLEY: How could I put up a ceiling?

WILLY: Then what the hell are you bothering me for?

CHARLEY: You're insulted again.

WILLY: A man who can't handle tools is not a man. You're disgusting.

CHARLEY: Don't call me disgusting, Willy.

> Uncle Ben, carrying a valise and an umbrella, enters the fore-stage from around the right corner of the house. He is a stolid man, in his sixties, with a mustache and an authoritative air. He is utterly certain of his destiny, and there is an aura of far places about him. He enters exactly as Willy speaks.

WILLY: I'm getting awfully tired, Ben.

> Ben's music is heard. Ben looks around at everything.

CHARLEY: Good, keep playing; you'll sleep better. Did you call me Ben?

> Ben looks at his watch.

WILLY: That's funny. For a second there you reminded me of my brother Ben.

BEN: I only have a few minutes. *He strolls, inspecting the place. Willy and Charley continue playing.*

CHARLEY: You never heard from him again, heh? Since that time?

WILLY: Didn't Linda tell you? Couple of weeks ago we got a letter from his wife in Africa. He died.

CHARLEY: That so.

BEN, *chuckling*: So this is Brooklyn, eh?

CHARLEY: Maybe you're in for some of his money.

WILLY: Naa, he had seven sons. There's just one opportunity I had with that man . . .

BEN: I must make a train, William. There are several properties I'm looking at in Alaska.

WILLY: Sure, sure! If I'd gone with him to Alaska that time, everything would've been totally different.

CHARLEY: Go on, you'd froze to death up there.

WILLY: What're you talking about?

BEN: Opportunity is tremendous in Alaska, William. Surprised you're not up there.

WILLY: Sure, tremendous.

CHARLEY: Heh?

WILLY: There was the only man I ever met who knew the answers.

CHARLEY: Who?

BEN: How are you all?

WILLY, *taking a pot, smiling*: Fine, fine.

CHARLEY: Pretty sharp tonight.

BEN: Is Mother living with you?

WILLY: No, she died a long time ago.

CHARLEY: Who?

BEN: That's too bad. Fine specimen of a lady, Mother.

WILLY, *to Charley*: Heh?

BEN: I'd hoped to see the old girl.

CHARLEY: Who died?

BEN: Heard anything from Father, have you?

WILLY, *unnerved*: What do you mean, who died?

CHARLEY, *taking a pot*: What're you talkin' about?

BEN, *looking at his watch*: William, it's half past eight!

WILLY, *as though to dispel his confusion he angrily stops Charley's hand*: That's my build!

CHARLEY: I put the ace—

WILLY: If you don't know how to play the game I'm not gonna throw my money away on you!

CHARLEY, *rising*: It was my ace, for God's sake!

WILLY: I'm through, I'm through!

BEN: When did Mother die?

WILLY: Long ago. Since the beginning you never knew how to play cards.

CHARLEY, *picks up the cards and goes to the door*: All right! Next time I'll bring a deck with five aces.

WILLY: I don't play that kind of game!

CHARLEY, *turning to him*: You ought to be ashamed of yourself!

WILLY: Yeah?

CHARLEY: Yeah! *He goes out.*

WILLY, *slamming the door after him*: Ignoramus!

BEN, *as Willy comes toward him through the wall-line of the kitchen*: So you're William.

WILLY, *shaking Ben's hand*: Ben! I've been waiting for you so long! What's the answer? How did you do it?

BEN: Oh, there's a story in that.

Linda enters the forestage, as of old, carrying the wash basket.

LINDA: Is this Ben?

BEN, *gallantly*: How do you do, my dear.

LINDA: Where've you been all these years? Willy's always wondered why you—

WILLY, *pulling Ben away from her impatiently*: Where is Dad? Didn't you follow him? How did you get started?

BEN: Well, I don't know how much you remember.

WILLY: Well, I was just a baby, of course, only three or four years old—

BEN: Three years and eleven months.

WILLY: What a memory, Ben!

BEN: I have many enterprises, William, and I have never kept books.

WILLY: I remember I was sitting under the wagon in—was it Nebraska?

BEN: It was South Dakota, and I gave you a bunch of wildflowers.

WILLY: I remember you walking away down some open road.

BEN, *laughing*: I was going to find Father in Alaska.

WILLY: Where is he?

BEN: At that age I had a very faulty view of geography, William. I discovered after a few days that I was heading due south, so instead of Alaska, I ended up in Africa.

LINDA: Africa!

WILLY: The Gold Coast!

BEN: Principally diamond mines.

LINDA: Diamond mines!

BEN: Yes, my dear. But I've only a few minutes—

WILLY: No! Boys! Boys! *Young Biff and Happy appear.* Listen to this. This is your Uncle Ben, a great man! Tell my boys, Ben!

BEN: Why boys, when I was seventeen I walked into the jungle, and when I was twenty-one I walked out. *He laughs.* And by God I was rich.

WILLY, *to the boys*: You see what I been talking about? The greatest things can happen!

BEN, *glancing at his watch*: I have an appointment in Ketchikan Tuesday week.

WILLY: No, Ben! Please tell about Dad. I want my boys to hear. I want them to know the kind of stock they spring from. All I remember is a man with a big beard, and I was in Mamma's lap, sitting around a fire, and some kind of high music.

BEN: His flute. He played the flute.

WILLY: Sure, the flute, that's right!

   New music is heard, a high, rollicking tune.

BEN: Father was a very great and a very wild-hearted man. We would start in Boston, and he'd toss the whole family into the wagon, and then he'd drive the team right across the country; through Ohio, and Indiana, Michigan, Illinois, and all the Western states. And we'd stop in the towns and sell the flutes that he'd made on the way. Great inventor, Father. With one gadget he made more in a week than a man like you could make in a lifetime.

WILLY: That's just the way I'm bringing them up, Ben—rugged, well liked, all-around.

BEN: Yeah? *To Biff*: Hit that, boy—hard as you can. *He pounds his stomach.*

BIFF: Oh, no, sir!

BEN, *taking boxing stance*: Come on, get to me! *He laughs.*

WILLY: Go to it, Biff! Go ahead, show him!

BIFF: Okay! *He cocks his fists and starts in.*

LINDA, *to Willy*: Why must he fight, dear?

sounds crvel

BEN, *sparring with Biff*: Good boy! Good boy!

WILLY: How's that, Ben, heh?

HAPPY: Give him the left, Biff!

LINDA: Why are you fighting?

BEN: Good boy! *Suddenly comes in, trips Biff, and stands over him, the point of his umbrella poised over Biff's eye.*

LINDA: Look out, Biff!

BIFF: Gee!

BEN, *patting Biff's knee*: Never fight fair with a stranger, boy. You'll never get out of the jungle that way. *Taking Linda's hand and bowing*: It was an honor and a pleasure to meet you, Linda.

LINDA, *withdrawing her hand coldly, frightened*: Have a nice—trip.

BEN, *to Willy*: And good luck with your—what do you do?

WILLY: Selling.

BEN: Yes. Well . . . *He raises his hand in farewell to all.*

WILLY: No, Ben, I don't want you to think . . . *He takes Ben's arm to show him.* It 's Brooklyn, I know, but we hunt too.

BEN: Really, now.

WILLY: Oh, sure, there's snakes and rabbits and—that's why I moved out here. Why, Biff can fell any one of these trees in no time! Boys! Go right over to where they're building the apartment house and get some sand. We're gonna rebuild the entire front stoop right now! Watch this, Ben!

BIFF: Yes, sir! On the double, Hap!

HAPPY, *as he and Biff run off*: I lost weight, Pop, you notice?

Charley enters in knickers, even before the boys are gone.

CHARLEY: Listen, if they steal any more from that building the watchman'll put the cops on them!

LINDA, *to Willy*: Don't let Biff . . .

Ben laughs lustily.

WILLY: You shoulda seen the lumber they brought home last week. At least a dozen six-by-tens worth all kinds a money.

CHARLEY: Listen, if that watchman—

WILLY: I gave them hell, understand. But I got a couple of fearless characters there.

now thats cruel.

CHARLEY: Willy, the jails are full of fearless characters.

BEN, *clapping Willy on the back, with a laugh at Charley*: And the stock exchange, friend!

WILLY, *joining in Ben's laughter*: Where are the rest of your pants?

CHARLEY: My wife bought them.

WILLY: Now all you need is a golf club and you can go upstairs and go to sleep. *To Ben*: Great athlete! Between him and his son Bernard they can't hammer a nail!

BERNARD, *rushing in*: The watchman's chasing Biff!

WILLY, *angrily*: Shut up! He's not stealing anything!

LINDA, *alarmed, hurrying off left*: Where is he? Biff, dear! *She exits.*

WILLY, *moving toward the left, away from Ben*: There's nothing wrong. What's the matter with you?

BEN: Nervy boy. Good!

WILLY, *laughing*: Oh, nerves of iron, that Biff!

CHARLEY: Don't know what it is. My New England man comes back and he's bleedin', they murdered him up there.

WILLY: It's contacts, Charley, I got important contacts!

CHARLEY, *sarcastically*: Glad to hear it, Willy. Come in later, we'll shoot a little casino. I'll take some of your Portland money. *He laughs at Willy and exits.*

WILLY, *turning to Ben*: Business is bad, it's murderous. But not for me, of course.

BEN: I'll stop by on my way back to Africa.

WILLY, *longingly*: Can't you stay a few days? You're just what I need, Ben, because I—I have a fine position here, but I—well, Dad left when I was such a baby and I never had a chance to talk to him and I still feel—kind of temporary about myself.

BEN: I'll be late for my train.

   They are at opposite ends of the stage.

WILLY: Ben, my boys—can't we talk? They'd go into the jaws of hell for me, see, but I—

BEN: William, you're being first-rate with your boys. Outstanding, manly chaps!

WILLY, *hanging on to his words*: Oh, Ben, that's good to hear! Because sometimes I'm afraid that I'm not teaching them the right kind of—Ben, how should I teach them?

BEN, *giving great weight to each word, and with a certain vicious audacity*: William, when I walked into the jungle, I was seventeen. When I walked out I was twenty-one. And, by God, I was rich! *He goes off into darkness around the right corner of the house.*

WILLY: . . . was rich! That's just the spirit I want to imbue them with! To walk into a jungle! I was right! I was right! I was right!

> *Ben is gone, but Willy is still speaking to him as Linda, in nightgown and robe, enters the kitchen, glances around for Willy, then goes to the door of the house, looks out and sees him. Comes down to his left. He looks at her.*

LINDA: Willy, dear? Willy?

WILLY: I was right!

LINDA: Did you have some cheese? *He can't answer.* It's very late, darling. Come to bed, heh?

WILLY, *looking straight up*: Gotta break your neck to see a star in this yard.

LINDA: You coming in?

WILLY: Whatever happened to that diamond watch fob? Remember? When Ben came from Africa that time? Didn't he give me a watch fob with a diamond in it?

LINDA: You pawned it, dear. Twelve, thirteen years ago. For Biff's radio correspondence course.

WILLY: Gee, that was a beautiful thing. I'll take a walk.

LINDA: But you're in your slippers.

WILLY, *starting to go around the house at the left*: I was right! I was! *Half to Linda, as he goes, shaking his head*: What a man! There was a man worth talking to. I was right!

LINDA, *calling after Willy*: But in your slippers, Willy!

> *Willy is almost gone when Biff, in his pajamas, comes down the stairs and enters the kitchen.*

BIFF: What is he doing out there?

LINDA: Sh!

BIFF: God Almighty, Mom, how long has he been doing this?

LINDA: Don't, he'll hear you.

BIFF: What the hell is the matter with him?

LINDA: It'll pass by morning.

BIFF: Shouldn't we do anything?

LINDA: Oh, my dear, you should do a lot of things, but there's nothing to do, so go to sleep.

Happy comes down the stairs and sits on the steps.

HAPPY: I never heard him so loud, Mom.

LINDA: Well, come around more often; you'll hear him.

She sits down at the table and mends the lining of Willy's jacket.

BIFF: Why didn't you ever write me about this, Mom?

LINDA: How would I write to you? For over three months you had no address.

BIFF: I was on the move. But you know I thought of you all the time. You know that, don't you, pal?

LINDA: I know, dear, I know. But he likes to have a letter. Just to know that there's still a possibility for better things.

BIFF: He's not like this all the time, is he?

LINDA: It's when you come home he's always the worst.

BIFF: When I come home?

LINDA: When you write you're coming, he's all smiles, and talks about the future, and—he's just wonderful. And then the closer you seem to come, the more shaky he gets, and then, by the time you get here, he's arguing, and he seems angry at you. I think it's just that maybe he can't bring himself to—to open up to you. Why are you so hateful to each other? Why is that?

BIFF, *evasively*: I'm not hateful, Mom.

LINDA: But you no sooner come in the door than you're fighting!

BIFF: I don't know why. I mean to change. I'm tryin', Mom, you understand?

LINDA: Are you home to stay now?

BIFF: I don't know. I want to look around, see what's doin'.

LINDA: Biff, you can't look around all your life, can you?

BIFF: I just can't take hold, Mom. I can't take hold of some kind of a life.

LINDA: Biff, a man is not a bird, to come and go with the springtime.

BIFF: Your hair . . . *He touches her hair.* Your hair got so gray.

LINDA: Oh, it's been gray since you were in high school. I just stopped dyeing it, that's all.

BIFF: Dye it again, will ya? I don't want my pal looking old. *He smiles.*

LINDA: You're such a boy! You think you can go away for a year and . . . You've got to get it into your head now that one day you'll knock on this door and there'll be strange people here—

BIFF: What are you talking about? You're not even sixty, Mom.

LINDA: But what about your father?

BIFF, *lamely*: Well, I meant him too.

HAPPY: He admires Pop.

LINDA: Biff, dear, if you don't have any feeling for him, then you can't have any feeling for me.

BIFF: Sure I can, Mom.

LINDA: No. You can't just come to see me, because I love him. *With a threat, but only a threat, of tears*: He's the dearest man in the world to me, and I won't have anyone making him feel unwanted and low and blue. You've got to make up your mind now, darling, there's no leeway any more. Either he's your father and you pay him that respect, or else you're not to come here. I know he's not easy to get along with—nobody knows that better than me—but . . .

WILLY, *from the left, with a laugh*: Hey, hey, Biffo!

BIFF, *starting to go out after Willy*: What the hell is the matter with him? *Happy stops him.*

LINDA: Don't—don't go near him!

BIFF: Stop making excuses for him! He always, always wiped the floor with you. Never had an ounce of respect for you.

HAPPY: He's always had respect for—

BIFF: What the hell do you know about it?

HAPPY, *surlily*: Just don't call him crazy!

BIFF: He's got no character—Charley wouldn't do this. Not in his own house—spewing out that vomit from his mind.

HAPPY: Charley never had to cope with what he's got to.

BIFF: People are worse off than Willy Loman. Believe me, I've seen them!

LINDA: Then make Charley your father, Biff. You can't do that, can you? I don't say he's a great man. Willy Loman never made a lot of money. His name was never in the paper. He's not the finest character that ever lived. But he's a human being, and a terrible thing is happening to him. So attention must be paid. He's not to be allowed to fall into his grave like an old dog. Attention, attention must be finally paid to such a person. You called him crazy—

BIFF: I didn't mean—

LINDA: No, a lot of people think he's lost his—balance. But you don't have to be very smart to know what his trouble is. The man is exhausted.

HAPPY: Sure!

LINDA: A small man can be just as exhausted as a great man. He works for a company thirty-six years this March, opens up unheard-of territories to their trademark, and now in his old age they take his salary away.

HAPPY, *indignantly*: I didn't know that, Mom.

LINDA: You never asked, my dear! Now that you get your spending money someplace else you don't trouble your mind with him.

HAPPY: But I gave you money last—

LINDA: Christmas time, fifty dollars! To fix the hot water it cost ninety-seven fifty! For five weeks he's been on straight commission, like a beginner, an unknown!

BIFF: Those ungrateful bastards!

LINDA: Are they any worse than his sons? When he brought them business, when he was young, they were glad to see him. But now his old friends, the old buyers that loved him so and always found some order to hand him in a pinch—they're all dead, retired. He used to be able to make six, seven calls a day in Boston. Now he takes his valises out of the car and puts them back and takes them out again and he's exhausted. Instead of walking he talks now. He drives seven hundred miles, and when he gets there no one knows him any more, no one welcomes him. And what goes through a man's mind, driving seven hundred miles home without having earned a cent? Why shouldn't he talk to himself? Why? When he has to go to Charley and borrow fifty dollars a week and pretend to me that it's his pay? How long can that go on? How long? You see what I'm sitting here and waiting for? And you tell me he has no character? The man who never worked a day but for your benefit? When does he get the medal for that? Is this his reward—to turn around at the age of sixty-three and find his sons, who he loved better than his life, one a phi-landering bum—

HAPPY: Mom!

LINDA: That's all you are, my baby! *To Biff*: And you! What happened to the love you had for him? You were such pals! How you used to talk to him on the phone every night! How lonely he was till he could come home to you!

BIFF: All right, Mom. I'll live here in my room, and I'll get a job. I'll keep away from him, that's all.

LINDA: No, Biff. You can't stay here and fight all the time.

BIFF: He threw me out of this house, remember that.

LINDA: Why did he do that? I never knew why.

BIFF: Because I know he's a fake and he doesn't like anybody around who knows!

LINDA: Why a fake? In what way? What do you mean?

BIFF: Just don't lay it all at my feet. It's between me and him—that's all I have to say. I'll chip in from now on. He'll settle for half my pay check. He'll be all right. I'm going to bed. *He starts for the stairs.*

LINDA: He won't be all right.

BIFF, *turning on the stairs, furiously*: I hate this city and I'll stay here. Now what do you want?

LINDA: He's dying, Biff.

Happy turns quickly to her, shocked.

BIFF, *after a pause*: Why is he dying?

LINDA: He's been trying to kill himself.

BIFF, *with great horror*: How?

LINDA: I live from day to day.

BIFF: What're you talking about?

LINDA: Remember I wrote you that he smashed up the car again? In February?

BIFF: Well?

LINDA: The insurance inspector came. He said that they have evidence. That all these accidents in the last year—weren't—weren't—accidents.

HAPPY: How can they tell that? That's a lie.

LINDA: It seems there's a woman . . . *She takes a breath as*

BIFF, *sharply but contained*: What woman? ⎫

LINDA: . . . and this woman . . .   ⎬ *Simultaneously*

                                                ⎭

LINDA: What?

BIFF: Nothing. Go ahead.

LINDA: What did you say?

BIFF: Nothing. I just said what woman?

HAPPY: What about her?

LINDA: Well, it seems she was walking down the road and saw his car. She says that he wasn't driving fast at all, and that he didn't skid. She says he came to that little bridge, and then deliberately smashed into the railing, and it was only the shallowness of the water that saved him.

BIFF: Oh, no, he probably just fell asleep again.

LINDA: I don't think he fell asleep.

BIFF: Why not?

LINDA: Last month . . . *With great difficulty*: Oh, boys, it's so hard to say a thing like this! He 's just a big stupid man to you, but I tell you there's more good in him than in many other people. *She chokes, wipes her eyes.* I was looking for a fuse. The lights blew out, and I went down the cellar. And behind the fuse box—it happened to fall out—was a length of rubber pipe—just short.

HAPPY: No kidding?

LINDA: There's a little attachment on the end of it. I knew right away. And sure enough, on the bottom of the water heater there's a new little nipple on the gas pipe.

HAPPY, *angrily*: That—jerk.

BIFF: Did you have it taken off?

LINDA: I'm—I'm ashamed to. How can I mention it to him? Every day I go down and take away that little rubber pipe. But, when he comes home, I put it back where it was. How can I insult him that way? I don't know what to do. I live from day to day, boys. I tell you, I know every thought in his mind. It sounds so old-fashioned and silly, but I tell you he put his whole life into you and you've turned your backs on him. *She is bent over in the chair, weeping, her face in her hands.* Biff, I swear to God! Biff, his life is in your hands!

HAPPY, *to Biff*: How do you like that damned fool!

BIFF, *kissing her*: All right, pal, all right. It's all settled now. I've been remiss. I know that, Mom. But now I'll stay, and I swear to you, I'll apply myself. *Kneeling in front of her, in a fever of self-reproach*: It's just—you see, Mom, I don't fit in business. Not that I won't try. I'll try, and I'll make good.

HAPPY: Sure you will. The trouble with you in business was you never tried to please people.

BIFF: I know, I—

HAPPY: Like when you worked for Harrison's. Bob Harrison said you were tops, and then you go and do some damn fool thing like whistling whole songs in the elevator like a comedian.

BIFF, *against Happy*: So what? I like to whistle sometimes.

HAPPY: You don't raise a guy to a responsible job who whistles in the elevator!

LINDA: Well, don't argue about it now.

HAPPY: Like when you'd go off and swim in the middle of the day instead of taking the line around.

BIFF, *his resentment rising*: Well, don't you run off? You take off sometimes, don't you? On a nice summer day?

HAPPY: Yeah, but I cover myself!

LINDA: Boys!

HAPPY: If I'm going to take a fade the boss can call any number where I'm supposed to be and they'll swear to him that I just left. I'll tell you something that I hate to say, Biff, but in the business world some of them think you're crazy.

BIFF, *angered*: Screw the business world!

HAPPY: All right, screw it! Great, but cover yourself!

LINDA: Hap, Hap!

BIFF: I don't care what they think! They've laughed at Dad for years, and you know why? Because we don't belong in this nuthouse of a city! We should be mixing cement on some open plain, or—or carpenters. A carpenter is allowed to whistle!

Willy walks in from the entrance of the house, at left.

WILLY: Even your grandfather was better than a carpenter. *Pause. They watch him.* You never grew up. Bernard does not whistle in the elevator, I assure you.

BIFF, *as though to laugh Willy out of it*: Yeah, but you do, Pop.

WILLY: I never in my life whistled in an elevator! And who in the business world thinks I'm crazy?

BIFF: I didn't mean it like that, Pop. Now don't make a whole thing out of it, will ya?

WILLY: Go back to the West! Be a carpenter, a cowboy, enjoy yourself!

LINDA: Willy, he was just saying—

WILLY: I heard what he said!

HAPPY, *trying to quiet Willy*: Hey, Pop, come on now . . .

WILLY, *continuing over Happy's line*: They laugh at me, heh? Go to Filene's, go to the Hub, go to Slattery's Boston. Call out the name Willy Loman and see what happens! Big shot!

BIFF: All right, Pop.

WILLY: Big!

BIFF: All right!

WILLY: Why do you always insult me?

BIFF: I didn't say a word. *To Linda*: Did I say a word?

LINDA: He didn't say anything, Willy.

WILLY, *going to the doorway of the living-room*: All right, good night, good night.

LINDA: Willy, dear, he just decided . . .

WILLY, *to Biff*: If you get tired hanging around tomorrow, paint the ceiling I put up in the living-room.

BIFF: I'm leaving early tomorrow.

HAPPY: He's going to see Bill Oliver, Pop.

WILLY, *interestedly*: Oliver? For what?

BIFF, *with reserve, but trying, trying*: He always said he'd stake me. I'd like to go into business, so maybe I can take him up on it.

LINDA: Isn't that wonderful?

WILLY: Don't interrupt. What's wonderful about it? There's fifty men in the City of New York who'd stake him. *To Biff*: Sporting goods?

BIFF: I guess so. I know something about it and—

WILLY: He knows something about it! You know sporting goods better than Spalding, for God's sake! How much is he giving you?

BIFF: I don't know, I didn't even see him yet, but—

WILLY: Then what're you talkin' about?

BIFF, *getting angry*: Well, all I said was I'm gonna see him, that's all!

WILLY, *turning away*: Ah, you're counting your chickens again.

BIFF, *starting left for the stairs*: Oh, Jesus, I'm going to sleep!

WILLY, *calling after him*: Don't curse in this house!

BIFF, *turning*: Since when did you get so clean?

HAPPY, *trying to stop them*: Wait a . . .

WILLY: Don't use that language to me! I won't have it!

HAPPY, *grabbing Biff, shouts*: Wait a minute! I got an idea. I got a feasible idea. Come here, Biff, let's talk this over now, let's talk some sense here. When I was down in Florida last time, I thought of a great idea to sell sporting goods. It just came back to me. You and I, Biff—we have a line, the Loman Line. We train a couple of weeks, and put on a couple of exhibitions, see?

WILLY: That's an idea!

HAPPY: Wait! We form two basketball teams, see? Two water-polo teams. We play each other. It's a million dollars' worth of publicity. Two brothers, see? The Loman Brothers. Displays in the Royal Palms—all the hotels. And banners over the ring and the basketball court: "Loman Brothers." Baby, we could sell sporting goods!

WILLY: That is a one-million-dollar idea!

LINDA: Marvelous!

BIFF: I'm in great shape as far as that's concerned.

HAPPY: And the beauty of it is, Biff, it wouldn't be like a business. We'd be out playin' ball again . . .

BIFF, *enthused*: Yeah, that's . . .

WILLY: Million-dollar . . .

HAPPY: And you wouldn't get fed up with it, Biff. It'd be the family again. There'd be the old honor, and comradeship, and if you wanted to go off for a swim or somethin'—well you'd do it! Without some smart cooky gettin' up ahead of you!

WILLY: Lick the world! You guys together could absolutely lick the civilized world.

BIFF: I'll see Oliver tomorrow. Hap, if we could work that out . . .

LINDA: Maybe things are beginning to—

WILLY, *wildly enthused, to Linda*: Stop interrupting! *To Biff*: But don't wear sport jacket and slacks when you see Oliver.

BIFF: No, I'll—

WILLY: A business suit, and talk as little as possible, and don't crack any jokes.

BIFF: He did like me. Always liked me.

LINDA: He loved you!

WILLY, *to Linda*: Will you stop! *To Biff*: Walk in very serious. You are not applying for a boy's job. Money is to pass. Be quiet, fine, and serious. Everybody likes a kidder, but nobody lends him money.

HAPPY: I'll try to get some myself, Biff. I'm sure I can.

WILLY: I see great things for you kids, I think your troubles are over. But remember, start big and you'll end big. Ask for fifteen. How much you gonna ask for?

BIFF: Gee, I don't know—

WILLY: And don't say "Gee." "Gee" is a boy's word. A man walking in for fifteen thousand dollars does not say "Gee"!

BIFF: Ten, I think, would be top though.

WILLY: Don't be so modest. You always started too low. Walk in with a big laugh. Don't look worried. Start off with a couple of your good stories to lighten things up. It's not what you say, it's how you say it—because personality always wins the day.

LINDA: Oliver always thought the highest of him—

WILLY: Will you let me talk? *(what an asshole!)*

BIFF: Don't yell at her, Pop, will ya?

WILLY, *angrily*: I was talking, wasn't I?

BIFF: I don't like you yelling at her all the time, and I'm tellin' you, that's all.

WILLY: What're you, takin' over this house?

LINDA: Willy—

WILLY, *turning on her*: Don't take his side all the time, goddammit!

BIFF, *furiously*: Stop yelling at her!

WILLY, *suddenly pulling on his cheek, beaten down, guilt ridden*: Give my best to Bill Oliver—he may remember me. *He exits through the living-room doorway.*

now he's telling him to joke!

LINDA, *her voice subdued*: What'd you have to start that for? *Biff turns away.* You see how sweet he was as soon as you talked hopefully? *She goes over to Biff.* Come up and say good night to him. Don't let him go to bed that way.

HAPPY: Come on, Biff, let's buck him up.

LINDA: Please, dear. Just say good night. It takes so little to make him happy. Come. *She goes through the living-room doorway, calling upstairs from within the living-room.* Your pajamas are hanging in the bathroom, Willy!

HAPPY, *looking toward where Linda went out*: What a woman! They broke the mold when they made her. You know that, Biff?

BIFF: He's off salary. My God, working on commission!

HAPPY: Well, let's face it: he's no hot-shot selling man. Except that sometimes, you have to admit, he's a sweet personality.

BIFF, *deciding*: Lend me ten bucks, will ya? I want to buy some new ties.

HAPPY: I'll take you to a place I know. Beautiful stuff. Wear one of my striped shirts tomorrow.

BIFF: She got gray. Mom got awful old. Gee, I'm gonna go in to Oliver tomorrow and knock him for a—

HAPPY: Come on up. Tell that to Dad. Let's give him a whirl. Come on.

BIFF, *steamed up*: You know, with ten thousand bucks, boy!

HAPPY, *as they go into the living-room*: That's the talk, Biff, that's the first time I've heard the old confidence out of you! *From within the living-room, fading off*: You're gonna live with me, kid, and any babe you want just say the word . . . *The last lines are hardly heard. They are mounting the stairs to their parents' bedroom.*

LINDA, *entering her bedroom and addressing Willy, who is in the bathroom. She is straightening the bed for him*: Can you do anything about the shower? It drips.

WILLY, *from the bathroom*: All of a sudden everything falls to pieces! Goddam plumbing, oughta be sued, those people. I hardly finished putting it in and the thing . . . *His words rumble off.*

LINDA: I'm just wondering if Oliver will remember him. You think he might?

WILLY, *coming out of the bathroom in his pajamas*: Remember him? What's the matter with you, you crazy? If he'd've stayed with Oliver he'd be on top by now! Wait'll Oliver gets a look at him. You don't know the average caliber any more. The average young man today—*he is getting into bed*—is got a caliber of zero. Greatest thing in the world for him was to bum around.

> *Biff and Happy enter the bedroom. Slight pause.*

WILLY, *stops short, looking at Biff*: Glad to hear it, boy.

HAPPY: He wanted to say good night to you, sport.

WILLY, *to Biff*: Yeah. Knock him dead, boy. What'd you want to tell me?

BIFF: Just take it easy, Pop. Good night. *He turns to go.*

WILLY, *unable to resist*: And if anything falls off the desk while you're talking to him—like a package or something—don't you pick it up. They have office boys for that.

LINDA: I'll make a big breakfast—

WILLY: Will you let me finish? *To Biff*: Tell him you were in the business in the West. Not farm work.

BIFF: All right, Dad.

LINDA: I think everything—

WILLY, *going right through her speech*: And don't undersell yourself. No less than fifteen thousand dollars.

BIFF, *unable to bear him*: Okay. Good night, Mom. *He starts moving.*

WILLY: Because you got a greatness in you, Biff, remember that. You got all kinds a greatness . . . *He lies back, exhausted. Biff walks out.*

LINDA, *calling after Biff*: Sleep well, darling!

HAPPY: I'm gonna get married, Mom. I wanted to tell you.

LINDA: Go to sleep, dear.

HAPPY, *going*: I just wanted to tell you.

WILLY: Keep up the good work. *Happy exits.* God . . . remember that Ebbets Field game? The championship of the city?

LINDA: Just rest. Should I sing to you?

WILLY: Yeah. Sing to me. *Linda hums a soft lullaby.* When that team came out—he was the tallest, remember?

LINDA: Oh, yes. And in gold.

> *Biff enters the darkened kitchen, takes a cigarette, and leaves the house. He comes downstage into a golden pool of light. He smokes, staring at the night.*

WILLY: Like a young god. Hercules—something like that. And the sun, the sun all around him. Remember how he waved to me? Right up from the field, with the representatives of three colleges standing by? And the buyers I brought, and the cheers when he came out—Loman, Loman, Loman! God Almighty, he'll be great yet. A star like that, magnificent, can never really fade away!

> *The light on Willy is fading. The gas heater begins to glow through the kitchen wall, near the stairs, a blue flame beneath red coils.*

LINDA, *timidly*: Willy dear, what has he got against you?

WILLY: I'm so tired. Don't talk any more.

> *Biff slowly returns to the kitchen. He stops, stares toward the heater.*

LINDA: Will you ask Howard to let you work in New York?

WILLY: First thing in the morning. Everything'll be all right.

> *Biff reaches behind the heater and draws out a length of rubber tubing. He is horrified and turns his head toward Willy's room, still dimly lit, from which the strains of Linda's desperate but monotonous humming rise.*

WILLY, *staring through the window into the moonlight*: Gee, look at the moon moving between the buildings!

> *Biff wraps the tubing around his hand and quickly goes up the stairs.*

CURTAIN

ACT TWO

Music is heard, gay and bright. The curtain rises as the music fades away. Willy, in shirt sleeves, is sitting at the kitchen table, sipping coffee, his hat in his lap. Linda is filling his cup when she can.

WILLY: Wonderful coffee. Meal in itself.

LINDA: Can I make you some eggs?

WILLY: No. Take a breath.

LINDA: You look so rested, dear.

WILLY: I slept like a dead one. First time in months. Imagine, sleeping till ten on a Tuesday morning. Boys left nice and early, heh?

LINDA: They were out of here by eight o'clock.

WILLY: Good work!

LINDA: It was so thrilling to see them leaving together. I can't get over the shaving lotion in this house!

WILLY, *smiling*: Mmm—

LINDA: Biff was very changed this morning. His whole attitude seemed to be hopeful. He couldn't wait to get downtown to see Oliver.

WILLY: He's heading for a change. There's no question, there simply are certain men that take longer to get—solidified. How did he dress?

LINDA: His blue suit. He's so handsome in that suit. He could be a— anything in that suit!

Willy gets up from the table. Linda holds his jacket for him.

WILLY: There's no question, no question at all. Gee, on the way home tonight I'd like to buy some seeds.

LINDA, *laughing*: That'd be wonderful. But not enough sun gets back there. Nothing'll grow any more.

WILLY: You wait, kid, before it's all over we're gonna get a little place out in the country, and I'll raise some vegetables, a couple of chickens . . .

LINDA: You'll do it yet, dear.

Willy walks out of his jacket. Linda follows him.

WILLY: And they'll get married, and come for a weekend. I'd build a little guest house. 'Cause I got so many fine tools, all I'd need would be a little lumber and some peace of mind.

LINDA, *joyfully*: I sewed the lining . . .

WILLY: I could build two guest houses, so they'd both come. Did he decide how much he's going to ask Oliver for?

LINDA, *getting him into the jacket*: He didn't mention it, but I imagine ten or fifteen thousand. You going to talk to Howard today?

WILLY: Yeah. I'll put it to him straight and simple. He'll just have to take me off the road.

LINDA: And Willy, don't forget to ask for a little advance, because we've got the insurance premium. It's the grace period now.

WILLY: That's a hundred . . . ?

LINDA: A hundred and eight, sixty-eight. Because we're a little short again.

WILLY: Why are we short?

LINDA: Well, you had the motor job on the car . . .

WILLY: That goddam Studebaker!

LINDA: And you got one more payment on the refrigerator . . .

WILLY: But it just broke again!

LINDA: Well, it's old, dear.

WILLY: I told you we should've bought a well-advertised machine. Charley bought a General Electric and it's twenty years old and it's still good, that son-of-a-bitch.

LINDA: But, Willy—

WILLY: Whoever heard of a Hastings refrigerator? Once in my life I would like to own something outright before it's broken! I'm always in a race with the junkyard! I just finished paying for the car and it's on its last legs. The refrigerator consumes belts like a goddam maniac. They time those things. They time them so when you finally paid for them, they're used up.

LINDA, *buttoning up his jacket as he unbuttons it*: All told, about two hundred dollars would carry us, dear. But that includes the last payment on the mortgage. After this payment, Willy, the house belongs to us.

WILLY: It's twenty-five years!

LINDA: Biff was nine years old when we bought it.

WILLY: Well, that's a great thing. To weather a twenty-five-year mortgage is—

LINDA: It's an accomplishment.

WILLY: All the cement, the lumber, the reconstruction I put in this house! There ain't a crack to be found in it any more.

LINDA: Well, it served its purpose.

WILLY: What purpose? Some stranger'll come along, move in, and that's that. If only Biff would take this house, and raise a family . . . *He starts to go.* Good-bye, I'm late.

LINDA, *suddenly remembering*: Oh, I forgot! You're supposed to meet them for dinner.

WILLY: Me?

LINDA: At Frank's Chop House on Forty-eighth near Sixth Avenue.

WILLY: Is that so! How about you?

LINDA: No, just the three of you. They're gonna blow you to a big meal!

WILLY: Don't say! Who thought of that?

LINDA: Biff came to me this morning, Willy, and he said, "Tell Dad, we want to blow him to a big meal." Be there six o'clock. You and your two boys are going to have dinner.

WILLY: Gee whiz! That's really somethin'. I'm gonna knock Howard for a loop, kid. I'll get an advance, and I'll come home with a New York job. Goddammit, now I'm gonna do it!

LINDA: Oh, that's the spirit, Willy!

WILLY: I will never get behind a wheel the rest of my life!

LINDA: It's changing, Willy, I can feel it changing!

WILLY: Beyond a question. G'bye, I'm late. *He starts to go again.*

LINDA, *calling after him as she runs to the kitchen table for a handkerchief*: You got your glasses?

WILLY, *feels for them, then comes back in*: Yeah, yeah, got my glasses.

LINDA, *giving him the handkerchief*: And a handkerchief.

WILLY: Yeah, handkerchief.

LINDA: And your saccharine?

WILLY: Yeah, my saccharine.

LINDA: Be careful on the subway stairs.

She kisses him, and a silk stocking is seen hanging from her hand. Willy notices it.

WILLY: Will you stop mending stockings? At least while I'm in the house. It gets me nervous. I can't tell you. Please.

Linda hides the stocking in her hand as she follows Willy across the forestage in front of the house.

LINDA: Remember, Frank's Chop House.

WILLY, *passing the apron*: Maybe beets would grow out there.

LINDA, *laughing*: But you tried so many times.

WILLY: Yeah. Well, don't work hard today. *He disappears around the right corner of the house.*

LINDA: Be careful!

As Willy vanishes, Linda waves to him. Suddenly the phone rings. She runs across the stage and into the kitchen and lifts it.

LINDA: Hello? Oh, Biff! I'm so glad you called, I just . . . Yes, sure, I just told him. Yes, he'll be there for dinner at six o'clock, I didn't forget. Listen, I was just dying to tell you. You know that little rubber pipe I told you about? That he connected to the gas heater? I finally decided to go down the cellar this morning and take it away and destroy it. But it's gone! Imagine? He took it away himself, it isn't there! *She listens.* When? Oh, then you took it. Oh—nothing, it's just that I'd hoped he'd taken it away himself. Oh, I'm not worried, darling, because this morning he left in such high spirits, it was like the old days! I'm not afraid any more. Did Mr. Oliver see you? . . . Well, you wait there then. And make a nice impression on him, darling. Just don't perspire too much before you see him. And have a nice time with Dad. He may have big news too! . . . That's right, a New York job. And be sweet to him tonight, dear. Be loving to him. Because he's only a little boat looking for a harbor. *She is trembling with sorrow and joy.* Oh, that's wonderful, Biff, you'll save his life. Thanks, darling. Just put your arm around him when he comes into the restaurant. Give him a smile. That's the boy. . . . Good-bye, dear. . . . You got your comb? . . . That's fine. Good-bye, Biff dear.

In the middle of her speech, Howard Wagner, thirty-six, wheels on a small typewriter table on which is a wire-recording machine and proceeds to plug it in. This is on the left forestage. Light slowly fades on Linda as it rises on Howard. Howard is intent on threading the machine and only glances over his shoulder as Willy appears.

WILLY: Pst! Pst!

HOWARD: Hello, Willy, come in.

WILLY: Like to have a little talk with you, Howard.

HOWARD: Sorry to keep you waiting. I'll be with you in a minute.

WILLY: What's that, Howard?

HOWARD: Didn't you ever see one of these? Wire recorder.

WILLY: Oh. Can we talk a minute?

HOWARD: Records things. Just got delivery yesterday. Been driving me crazy, the most terrific machine I ever saw in my life. I was up all night with it.

WILLY: What do you do with it?

HOWARD: I bought it for dictation, but you can do anything with it. Listen to this. I had it home last night. Listen to what I picked up. The first one is my daughter. Get this. *He flicks the switch and "Roll out the Barrel" is heard being whistled.* Listen to that kid whistle.

WILLY: That is lifelike, isn't it?

HOWARD: Seven years old. Get that tone.

WILLY: Ts, ts. Like to ask a little favor if you . . .

The whistling breaks off, and the voice of Howard's daughter is heard.

HIS DAUGHTER: "Now you, Daddy."

HOWARD: She's crazy for me! *Again the same song is whistled.* That's me! Ha! *He winks.*

WILLY: You're very good!

The whistling breaks off again. The machine runs silent for a moment.

HOWARD: Sh! Get this now, this is my son.

HIS SON: "The capital of Alabama is Montgomery; the capital of Arizona is Phoenix; the capital of Arkansas is Little Rock; the capital of California is Sacramento . . . " *and on, and on.*

HOWARD, *holding up five fingers*: Five years old, Willy!

WILLY: He'll make an announcer some day!

HIS SON, *continuing*: "The capital . . . "

HOWARD: Get that—alphabetical order! *The machine breaks off suddenly.* Wait a minute. The maid kicked the plug out.

WILLY: It certainly is a—

HOWARD: Sh, for God's sake!

HIS SON: "It's nine o'clock, Bulova watch time. So I have to go to sleep."

WILLY: That really is—

HOWARD: Wait a minute! The next is my wife.

    They wait.

HOWARD'S VOICE: "Go on, say something." *Pause.* "Well, you gonna talk?"

HIS WIFE: "I can't think of anything."

HOWARD'S VOICE: "Well, talk—it's turning."

HIS WIFE, *shyly, beaten*: "Hello." *Silence.* "Oh, Howard, I can't talk into this . . . "

HOWARD, *snapping the machine off*: That was my wife.

WILLY: That is a wonderful machine. Can we—

HOWARD: I tell you, Willy, I'm gonna take my camera, and my bandsaw, and all my hobbies, and out they go. This is the most fascinating relaxation I ever found.

WILLY: I think I'll get one myself.

HOWARD: Sure, they're only a hundred and a half. You can't do without it. Supposing you wanna hear Jack Benny, see? But you can't be at home at that hour. So you tell the maid to turn the radio on when Jack Benny comes on, and this automatically goes on with the radio . . .

WILLY: And when you come home you . . .

HOWARD: You can come home twelve o'clock, one o'clock, any time you like, and you get yourself a Coke and sit yourself down, throw the switch, and there's Jack Benny's program in the middle of the night!

WILLY: I'm definitely going to get one. Because lots of time I'm on the road, and I think to myself, what I must be missing on the radio!

HOWARD: Don't you have a radio in the car?

WILLY: Well, yeah, but who ever thinks of turning it on?

HOWARD: Say, aren't you supposed to be in Boston?

WILLY: That's what I want to talk to you about, Howard. You got a minute? *He draws a chair in from the wing.*

HOWARD: What happened? What're you doing here?

WILLY: Well . . .

HOWARD: You didn't crack up again, did you?

WILLY: Oh, no. No . . .

HOWARD: Geez, you had me worried there for a minute. What's the trouble?

WILLY: Well, tell you the truth, Howard. I've come to the decision that I'd rather not travel any more.

HOWARD: Not travel! Well, what'll you do?

WILLY: Remember, Christmas time, when you had the party here? You said you'd try to think of some spot for me here in town.

HOWARD: With us?

WILLY: Well, sure.

HOWARD: Oh, yeah, yeah. I remember. Well, I couldn't think of anything for you, Willy.

WILLY: I tell ya, Howard. The kids are all grown up, y'know. I don't need much any more. If I could take home—well, sixty-five dollars a week, I could swing it.

HOWARD: Yeah, but Willy, see I—

WILLY: I tell ya why, Howard. Speaking frankly and between the two of us, y'know—I'm just a little tired.

HOWARD: Oh, I could understand that, Willy. But you're a road man, Willy, and we do a road business. We've only got a half-dozen salesmen on the floor here.

WILLY: God knows, Howard, I never asked a favor of any man. But I was with the firm when your father used to carry you in here in his arms.

HOWARD: I know that, Willy, but—

WILLY: Your father came to me the day you were born and asked me what I thought of the name of Howard, may he rest in peace.

HOWARD: I appreciate that, Willy, but there just is no spot here for you. If I had a spot I'd slam you right in, but I just don't have a single solitary spot.

He looks for his lighter. Willy has picked it up and gives it to him. Pause.

WILLY, *with increasing anger*: Howard, all I need to set my table is fifty dollars a week.

HOWARD: But where am I going to put you, kid?

WILLY: Look, it isn't a question of whether I can sell merchandise, is it?

HOWARD: No, but it's a business, kid, and everybody's gotta pull his own weight.

WILLY, *desperately*: Just let me tell you a story, Howard—

HOWARD: 'Cause you gotta admit, business is business.

WILLY, *angrily*: Business is definitely business, but just listen for a minute. You don't understand this. When I was a boy—eighteen, nineteen— I was already on the road. And there was a question in my mind as to whether selling had a future for me. Because in those days I had a yearning to go to Alaska. See, there were three gold strikes in one month in Alaska, and I felt like going out. Just for the ride, you might say.

HOWARD, *barely interested*: Don't say.

WILLY: Oh, yeah, my father lived many years in Alaska. He was an adventurous man. We've got quite a little streak of self-reliance in our family. I thought I'd go out with my older brother and try to locate him, and maybe settle in the North with the old man. And I was almost decided to go, when I met a salesman in the Parker House. His name was Dave Singleman. And he was eighty-four years old, and he'd drummed merchandise in thirty-one states. And old Dave, he'd go up to his room, y' understand, put on his green velvet slippers—I'll never forget—and pick up his phone and call the buyers, and without ever leaving his room, at the age of eighty-four, he made his living. And when I saw that, I realized that selling was the greatest career a man could want. 'Cause what could be more satisfying than to be able to go, at the age of eighty-four, into twenty or thirty different cities, and pick up a phone, and be remembered and loved and helped by so many different people? Do you know? When he died— and by the way he died the death of a salesman, in his green velvet slippers in the smoker of the New York, New Haven, and Hartford, going into Boston—when he died, hundreds of salesmen and buyers were at his funeral. Things were sad on a lotta trains for months after that. *He stands up. Howard has not looked at him.* In those days there was personality in it, Howard. There was respect, and comradeship, and gratitude in it. Today, it's all cut and dried, and there's no chance for bringing friendship to bear—or personality. You see what I mean? They don't know me any more.

HOWARD, *moving away, to the right*: That's just the thing, Willy.

WILLY: If I had forty dollars a week—that's all I'd need. Forty dollars, Howard.

HOWARD: Kid, I can't take blood from a stone, I—

WILLY, *desperation is on him now*: Howard, the year Al Smith was nominated, your father came to me and—

HOWARD, *starting to go off*: I've got to see some people, kid.

WILLY, *stopping him*: I'm talking about your father! There were promises made across this desk! You mustn't tell me you've got people to see—I put thirty-four years into this firm, Howard, and now I can't pay my insurance! You can't eat the orange and throw the peel away—a man is not a piece of fruit! *After a pause*: Now pay attention. Your father—in 1928 I had a big year. I averaged a hundred and seventy dollars a week in commissions.

HOWARD, *impatiently*: Now, Willy, you never averaged—

WILLY, *banging his hand on the desk*: I averaged a hundred and seventy dollars a week in the year of 1928! And your father came to me—or rather, I was in the office here—it was right over this desk—and he put his hand on my shoulder—

HOWARD, *getting up*: You'll have to excuse me, Willy, I gotta see some people. Pull yourself together. *Going out*: I'll be back in a little while.

> On Howard's exit, the light on his chair grows very bright and strange.

WILLY: Pull myself together! What the hell did I say to him? My God, I was yelling at him! How could I! *Willy breaks off, staring at the light, which occupies the chair, animating it. He approaches this chair, standing across the desk from it.* Frank, Frank, don't you remember what you told me that time? How you put your hand on my shoulder, and Frank . . . *He leans on the desk and as he speaks the dead man's name he accidentally switches on the recorder, and instantly—*

HOWARD'S SON: ". . . of New York is Albany. The capital of Ohio is Cincinnati, the capital of Rhode Island is . . . " *The recitation continues.*

WILLY, *leaping away with fright, shouting*: Ha! Howard! Howard! Howard!

HOWARD, *rushing in*: What happened?

WILLY, *pointing at the machine, which continues nasally, childishly, with the capital cities*: Shut it off! Shut it off!

HOWARD, *pulling the plug out*: Look, Willy . . .

WILLY, *pressing his hands to his eyes*: I gotta get myself some coffee. I'll get some coffee . . .

Willy starts to walk out. Howard stops him.

HOWARD, *rolling up the cord*: Willy, look . . .

WILLY: I'll go to Boston.

HOWARD: Willy, you can't go to Boston for us.

WILLY: Why can't I go?

HOWARD: I don't want you to represent us. I've been meaning to tell you for a long time now.

WILLY: Howard, are you firing me?

HOWARD: I think you need a good long rest, Willy.

WILLY: Howard—

HOWARD: And when you feel better, come back, and we'll see if we can work something out.

WILLY: But I gotta earn money, Howard. I'm in no position to—

HOWARD: Where are your sons? Why don't your sons give you a hand?

WILLY: They're working on a very big deal.

HOWARD: This is no time for false pride, Willy. You go to your sons and you tell them that you're tired. You've got two great boys, haven't you?

WILLY: Oh, no question, no question, but in the meantime . . .

HOWARD: Then that's that, heh?

WILLY: All right, I'll go to Boston tomorrow.

HOWARD: No, no.

WILLY: I can't throw myself on my sons. I'm not a cripple!

HOWARD: Look, kid, I'm busy this morning.

WILLY, *grasping Howard's arm*: Howard, you've got to let me go to Boston!

HOWARD, *hard, keeping himself under control*: I've got a line of people to see this morning. Sit down, take five minutes, and pull yourself together, and then go home, will ya? I need the office, Willy. *He starts to go, turns, remembering the recorder, starts to push off the table holding the recorder.* Oh, yeah. Whenever you can this week, stop by and drop off the samples. You'll feel better, Willy, and then come back and we'll talk. Pull yourself together, kid, there's people outside.

Howard exits, pushing the table off left. Willy stares into space, exhausted. Now the music is heard—Ben's music—first distantly, then closer, closer. As Willy speaks, Ben enters from the right. He carries valise and umbrella.

WILLY: Oh, Ben, how did you do it? What is the answer? Did you wind up the Alaska deal already?

BEN: Doesn't take much time if you know what you're doing. Just a short business trip. Boarding ship in an hour. Wanted to say good-bye.

WILLY: Ben, I've got to talk to you.

BEN, *glancing at his watch*: Haven't the time, William.

WILLY, *crossing the apron to Ben*: Ben, nothing's working out. I don't know what to do.

BEN: Now, look here, William. I've bought timberland in Alaska and I need a man to look after things for me.

WILLY: God, timberland! Me and my boys in those grand outdoors!

BEN: You've a new continent at your doorstep, William. Get out of these cities, they're full of talk and time payments and courts of law. Screw on your fists and you can fight for a fortune up there.

WILLY: Yes, yes! Linda, Linda!

Linda enters as of old, with the wash.

LINDA: Oh, you're back?

BEN: I haven't much time.

WILLY: No, wait! Linda, he's got a proposition for me in Alaska.

LINDA: But you've got— *To Ben*: He's got a beautiful job here.

WILLY: But in Alaska, kid, I could—

LINDA: You're doing well enough, Willy!

BEN, *to Linda*: Enough for what, my dear?

LINDA, *frightened of Ben and angry at him*: Don't say those things to him! Enough to be happy right here, right now. *To Willy, while Ben laughs*: Why must everybody conquer the world? You're well liked, and the boys love you, and someday— *To Ben*: —why, old man Wagner told him just the other day that if he keeps it up he'll be a member of the firm, didn't he, Willy?

WILLY: Sure, sure. I am building something with this firm, Ben, and if a man is building something he must be on the right track, mustn't he?

BEN: What are you building? Lay your hand on it. Where is it?

WILLY, *hesitantly*: That's true, Linda, there's nothing.

LINDA: Why? *To Ben*: There's a man eighty-four years old—

WILLY: That's right, Ben, that's right. When I look at that man I say, what is there to worry about?

BEN: Bah!

WILLY: It's true, Ben. All he has to do is go into any city, pick up the phone, and he's making his living and you know why?

BEN, *picking up his valise*: I've got to go.

WILLY, *holding Ben back*: Look at this boy!

> *Biff, in his high school sweater, enters carrying suitcase. Happy carries Biff's shoulder guards, gold helmet, and football pants.*

WILLY: Without a penny to his name, three great universities are begging for him, and from there the sky's the limit, because it's not what you do, Ben. It's who you know and the smile on your face! It's contacts, Ben, contacts! The whole wealth of Alaska passes over the lunch table at the Commodore Hotel, and that's the wonder, the wonder of this country, that a man can end with diamonds here on the basis of being liked! *He turns to Biff*. And that's why when you get out on that field today it's important. Because thousands of people will be rooting for you and loving you. *To Ben, who has again begun to leave*: And Ben! when he walks into a business office his name will sound out like a bell and all the doors will open to him! I've seen it, Ben, I've seen it a thousand times! You can't feel it with your hand like timber, but it's there!

BEN: Good-bye, William.

WILLY: Ben, am I right? Don't you think I'm right? I value your advice.

BEN: There's a new continent at your doorstep, William. You could walk out rich. Rich! *He is gone.*

WILLY: We'll do it here, Ben! You hear me? We're gonna do it here!

> *Young Bernard rushes in. The gay music of the boys is heard.*

BERNARD: Oh, gee, I was afraid you left already!

WILLY: Why? What time is it?

BERNARD: It's half-past one!

WILLY: Well, come on, everybody! Ebbets Field next stop! Where's the pennants? *He rushes through the wall-line of the kitchen and out into the living-room.*

LINDA, *to Biff*: Did you pack fresh underwear?

BIFF, *who has been limbering up*: I want to go!

BERNARD: Biff, I'm carrying your helmet, ain't I?

HAPPY: No, I'm carrying the helmet.

BERNARD: Oh, Biff, you promised me.

HAPPY: I'm carrying the helmet.

BERNARD: How am I going to get in the locker room?

LINDA: Let him carry the shoulder guards. *She puts her coat and hat on in the kitchen.*

BERNARD: Can I, Biff? 'Cause I told everybody I'm going to be in the locker room.

HAPPY: In Ebbets Field it's the clubhouse.

BERNARD: I meant the clubhouse. Biff!

HAPPY: Biff!

BIFF, *grandly, after a slight pause*: Let him carry the shoulder guards.

HAPPY, *as he gives Bernard the shoulder guards*: Stay close to us now.

> *Willy rushes in with the pennants.*

WILLY, *handing them out*: Everybody wave when Biff comes out on the field. *Happy and Bernard run off.* You set now, boy?

> *The music has died away.*

BIFF: Ready to go, Pop. Every muscle is ready.

WILLY, *at the edge of the apron*: You realize what this means?

BIFF: That's right, Pop.

WILLY, *feeling Biff's muscles*: You're comin' home this afternoon captain of the All-Scholastic Championship Team of the City of New York.

BIFF: I got it, Pop. And remember, pal, when I take off my helmet, that touchdown is for you.

WILLY: Let's go! *He is starting out, with his arm around Biff, when Charley enters, as of old, in knickers.* I got no room for you, Charley.

CHARLEY: Room? For what?

WILLY: In the car.

CHARLEY: You goin' for a ride? I wanted to shoot some casino.

WILLY, *furiously*: Casino! *Incredulously*: Don't you realize what today is?

LINDA: Oh, he knows, Willy. He's just kidding you.

WILLY: That's nothing to kid about!

CHARLEY: No. Linda, what's goin' on?

LINDA: He's playing in Ebbets Field.

CHARLEY: Baseball in this weather?

WILLY: Don't talk to him. Come on, come on! *He is pushing them out.*

CHARLEY: Wait a minute, didn't you hear the news?

WILLY: What?

CHARLEY: Don't you listen to the radio? Ebbets Field just blew up.

WILLY: You go to hell! *Charley laughs. Pushing them out*: Come on, come on! We're late.

CHARLEY, *as they go*: Knock a homer, Biff, knock a homer!

WILLY, *the last to leave, turning to Charley*: I don't think that was funny, Charley. This is the greatest day of his life.

CHARLEY: Willy, when are you going to grow up?

WILLY: Yeah, heh? When this game is over, Charley, you'll be laughing out of the other side of your face. They'll be calling him another Red Grange. Twenty-five thousand a year.

CHARLEY, *kidding*: Is that so?

WILLY: Yeah, that's so.

CHARLEY: Well, then, I'm sorry, Willy. But tell me something.

WILLY: What?

CHARLEY: Who is Red Grange?

WILLY: Put up your hands. Goddam you, put up your hands!

> *Charley, chuckling, shakes his head and walks away, around the left corner of the stage. Willy follows him. The music rises to a mocking frenzy.*

WILLY: Who the hell do you think you are, better than everybody else? You don't know everything, you big, ignorant, stupid . . . Put up your hands!

> *Light rises, on the right side of the forestage, on a small table in the reception room of Charley's office. Traffic sounds are heard.*

Bernard, now mature, sits whistling to himself. A pair of tennis rackets and an overnight bag are on the floor beside him.

WILLY, *offstage*: What are you walking away for? Don't walk away! If you're going to say something say it to my face! I know you laugh at me behind my back. You'll laugh out of the other side of your goddam face after this game. Touchdown! Touchdown! Eighty thousand people! Touchdown! Right between the goal posts.

Bernard is a quiet, earnest, but self-assured young man. Willy's voice is coming from right upstage now. Bernard lowers his feet off the table and listens. Jenny, his father's secretary, enters.

JENNY, *distressed*: Say, Bernard, will you go out in the hall?

BERNARD: What is that noise? Who is it?

JENNY: Mr. Loman. He just got off the elevator.

BERNARD, *getting up*: Who's he arguing with?

JENNY: Nobody. There's nobody with him. I can't deal with him any more, and your father gets all upset everytime he comes. I've got a lot of typing to do, and your father's waiting to sign it. Will you see him?

WILLY, *entering*: Touchdown! Touch— *He sees Jenny.* Jenny, Jenny, good to see you. How're ya? Workin'? Or still honest?

JENNY: Fine. How've you been feeling?

WILLY: Not much any more, Jenny. Ha, ha! *He is surprised to see the rackets.*

BERNARD: Hello, Uncle Willy.

WILLY, *almost shocked*: Bernard! Well, look who's here! *He comes quickly, guiltily, to Bernard and warmly shakes his hand.*

BERNARD: How are you? Good to see you.

WILLY: What are you doing here?

BERNARD: Oh, just stopped by to see Pop. Get off my feet till my train leaves. I'm going to Washington in a few minutes.

WILLY: Is he in?

BERNARD: Yes, he's in his office with the accountant. Sit down.

WILLY, *sitting down*: What're you going to do in Washington?

BERNARD: Oh, just a case I've got there, Willy.

WILLY: That so? *Indicating the rackets*: You going to play tennis there?

BERNARD: I'm staying with a friend who's got a court.

WILLY: Don't say. His own tennis court. Must be fine people, I bet.

BERNARD: They are, very nice. Dad tells me Biff's in town.

WILLY, *with a big smile*: Yeah, Biff's in. Working on a very big deal, Bernard.

BERNARD: What's Biff doing?

WILLY: Well, he's been doing very big things in the West. But he decided to establish himself here. Very big. We're having dinner. Did I hear your wife had a boy?

BERNARD: That's right. Our second.

WILLY: Two boys! What do you know!

BERNARD: What kind of a deal has Biff got?

WILLY: Well, Bill Oliver—very big sporting-goods man—he wants Biff very badly. Called him in from the West. Long distance, carte blanche, special deliveries. Your friends have their own private tennis court?

BERNARD: You still with the old firm, Willy?

WILLY, *after a pause*: I'm—I'm overjoyed to see how you made the grade, Bernard, overjoyed. It's an encouraging thing to see a young man really— really— Looks very good for Biff—very— *He breaks off, then*: Bernard— *He is so full of emotion, he breaks off again.*

BERNARD: What is it, Willy?

WILLY, *small and alone*: What—what's the secret?

BERNARD: What secret?

WILLY: How—how did you? Why didn't he ever catch on?

BERNARD: I wouldn't know that, Willy.

WILLY, *confidentially, desperately*: You were his friend, his boyhood friend. There's something I don't understand about it. His life ended after that Ebbets Field game. From the age of seventeen nothing good ever happened to him.

BERNARD: He never trained himself for anything.

WILLY: But he did, he did. After high school he took so many correspondence courses. Radio mechanics; television; God knows what, and never made the slightest mark.

BERNARD, *taking off his glasses*: Willy, do you want to talk candidly?

WILLY *rising, faces Bernard*: I regard you as a very brilliant man, Bernard. I value your advice.

BERNARD: Oh, the hell with the advice, Willy. I couldn't advise you. There's just one thing I've always wanted to ask you. When he was supposed to graduate, and the math teacher flunked him—

WILLY: Oh, that son-of-a-bitch ruined his life.

BERNARD: Yeah, but, Willy, all he had to do was to go to summer school and make up that subject.

WILLY: That's right, that's right.

BERNARD: Did you tell him not to go to summer school?

WILLY: Me? I begged him to go. I ordered him to go!

BERNARD: Then why wouldn't he go?

WILLY: Why? Why! Bernard, that question has been trailing me like a ghost for the last fifteen years. He flunked the subject, and laid down and died like a hammer hit him!

BERNARD: Take it easy, kid.

WILLY: Let me talk to you—I got nobody to talk to. Bernard, Bernard, was it my fault? Y'see? It keeps going around in my mind, maybe I did something to him. I got nothing to give him.

BERNARD: Don't take it so hard.

WILLY: Why did he lay down? What is the story there? You were his friend!

BERNARD: Willy, I remember, it was June, and our grades came out. And he'd flunked math.

WILLY: That son-of-a-bitch!

BERNARD: No, it wasn't right then. Biff just got very angry, I remember, and he was ready to enroll in summer school.

WILLY, *surprised*: He was?

BERNARD: He wasn't beaten by it at all. But then, Willy, he disappeared from the block for almost a month. And I got the idea that he'd gone up to New England to see you. Did he have a talk with you then?

Willy stares in silence.

BERNARD: Willy?

WILLY, *with a strong edge of resentment in his voice*: Yeah, he came to Boston. What about it?

BERNARD: Well, just that when he came back—I'll never forget this, it always mystifies me. Because I'd thought so well of Biff, even though he'd always taken advantage of me. I loved him, Willy, y'know? And he came back after that month and took his sneakers—remember those sneakers with "University of Virginia" printed on them? He was so proud of those, wore them every day. And he took them down in the cellar, and burned them up in the furnace. We had a fist fight. It lasted at least half an hour. Just the two of us, punching each other down the cellar, and crying right through it. I've often thought of how strange it was that I knew he'd given up his life. What happened in Boston, Willy?

Willy looks at him as at an intruder.

BERNARD: I just bring it up because you asked me.

WILLY, *angrily*: Nothing. What do you mean, "What happened?" What's that got to do with anything?

BERNARD: Well, don't get sore.

WILLY: What are you trying to do, blame it on me? If a boy lays down is that my fault?

BERNARD: Now, Willy, don't get—

WILLY: Well, don't—don't talk to me that way! What does that mean, "What happened?"

Charley enters. He is in his vest, and he carries a bottle of bourbon.

CHARLEY: Hey, you're going to miss that train. *He waves the bottle.*

BERNARD: Yeah, I'm going. *He takes the bottle.* Thanks, Pop. *He picks up his rackets and bag.* Good-bye, Willy, and don't worry about it. You know, "If at first you don't succeed . . . "

WILLY: Yes, I believe in that.

BERNARD: But sometimes, Willy, it's better for a man just to walk away.

WILLY: Walk away?

BERNARD: That's right.

WILLY: But if you can't walk away?

BERNARD, *after a slight pause*: I guess that's when it's tough. *Extending his hand*: Good-bye, Willy.

WILLY, *shaking Bernard's hand*: Good-bye, boy.

CHARLEY, *an arm on Bernard's shoulder*: How do you like this kid? Gonna argue a case in front of the Supreme Court.

BERNARD, *protesting*: Pop!

WILLY, *genuinely shocked, pained, and happy*: No! The Supreme Court!

BERNARD: I gotta run. 'Bye, Dad!

CHARLEY: Knock 'em dead, Bernard!

> *Bernard goes off.*

WILLY, *as Charley takes out his wallet*: The Supreme Court! And he didn't even mention it!

CHARLEY, *counting out money on the desk*: He don't have to—he's gonna do it.

WILLY: And you never told him what to do, did you? You never took any interest in him.

CHARLEY: My salvation is that I never took any interest in anything. There's some money—fifty dollars. I got an accountant inside.

WILLY: Charley, look . . . *With difficulty*: I got my insurance to pay. If you can manage it—I need a hundred and ten dollars.

> *Charley doesn't reply for a moment; merely stops moving.*

WILLY: I'd draw it from my bank but Linda would know, and I . . .

CHARLEY: Sit down, Willy.

WILLY, *moving toward the chair*: I'm keeping an account of everything, remember. I'll pay every penny back. *He sits.*

CHARLEY: Now listen to me, Willy.

WILLY: I want you to know I appreciate . . .

CHARLEY, *sitting down on the table*: Willy, what're you doin'? What the hell is goin' on in your head?

WILLY: Why? I'm simply . . .

CHARLEY: I offered you a job. You can make fifty dollars a week. And I won't send you on the road.

WILLY: I've got a job.

CHARLEY: Without pay? What kind of a job is a job without pay? *He rises.* Now, look, kid, enough is enough. I'm no genius but I know when I'm being insulted.

WILLY: Insulted!

CHARLEY: Why don't you want to work for me?

WILLY: What's the matter with you? I've got a job.

CHARLEY: Then what're you walkin' in here every week for?

WILLY, *getting up*: Well, if you don't want me to walk in here—

CHARLEY: I am offering you a job.

WILLY: I don't want your goddam job!

CHARLEY: When the hell are you going to grow up?

WILLY, *furiously*: You big ignoramus, if you say that to me again I'll rap you one! I don't care how big you are! *He's ready to fight.*

   Pause.

CHARLEY, *kindly, going to him*: How much do you need, Willy?

WILLY: Charley, I'm strapped, I'm strapped. I don't know what to do. I was just fired.

CHARLEY: Howard fired you?

WILLY: That snotnose. Imagine that? I named him. I named him Howard.

CHARLEY: Willy, when're you gonna realize that them things don't mean anything? You named him Howard, but you can't sell that. The only thing you got in this world is what you can sell. And the funny thing is that you're a salesman, and you don't know that.

WILLY: I've always tried to think otherwise, I guess. I always felt that if a man was impressive, and well liked, that nothing—

CHARLEY: Why must everybody like you? Who liked J. P. Morgan? Was he impressive? In a Turkish bath he'd look like a butcher. But with his pockets on he was very well liked. Now listen, Willy, I know you don't like me, and nobody can say I'm in love with you, but I'll give you a job because—just for the hell of it, put it that way. Now what do you say?

WILLY: I—I just can't work for you, Charley.

CHARLEY: What're you, jealous of me?

WILLY: I can't work for you, that's all, don't ask me why.

CHARLEY, *angered, takes out more bills*: You been jealous of me all your life, you damned fool! Here, pay your insurance. *He puts the money in Willy's hand.*

WILLY: I'm keeping strict accounts.

CHARLEY: I've got some work to do. Take care of yourself. And pay your insurance.

WILLY, *moving to the right*: Funny, y'know? After all the highways, and the trains, and the appointments, and the years, you end up worth more dead than alive.

CHARLEY: Willy, nobody's worth nothin' dead. *After a slight pause*: Did you hear what I said?

Willy stands still, dreaming.

CHARLEY: Willy!

WILLY: Apologize to Bernard for me when you see him. I didn't mean to argue with him. He's a fine boy. They're all fine boys, and they'll end up big—all of them. Someday they'll all play tennis together. Wish me luck, Charley. He saw Bill Oliver today.

CHARLEY: Good luck.

WILLY, *on the verge of tears*: Charley, you're the only friend I got. Isn't that a remarkable thing? *He goes out.*

CHARLEY: Jesus!

> *Charley stares after him a moment and follows. All light blacks out. Suddenly raucous music is heard, and a red glow rises behind the screen at right. Stanley, a young waiter, appears, carrying a table, followed by Happy, who is carrying two chairs.*

STANLEY, *putting the table down*: That's all right, Mr. Loman, I can handle it myself. *He turns and takes the chairs from Happy, and places them at the table.*

HAPPY, *glancing around*: Oh, this is better.

STANLEY: Sure, in the front there you're in the middle of all kinds a noise. Whenever you got a party, Mr. Loman, you just tell me and I'll put you back here. Y'know, there's a lotta people they don't like it private, because when they go out they like to see a lotta action around them because they're sick and tired to stay in the house by theirself. But I know you, you ain't from Hackensack. You know what I mean?

HAPPY, *sitting down*: So how's it coming, Stanley?

STANLEY: Ah, it's a dog's life. I only wish during the war they'd a took me in the army. I coulda been dead by now.

HAPPY: My brother's back, Stanley.

STANLEY: Oh, he come back, heh? From the Far West.

HAPPY: Yeah, big cattle man, my brother, so treat him right. And my father's coming too.

STANLEY: Oh, your father too!

HAPPY: You got a couple of nice lobsters?

STANLEY: Hundred percent, big.

HAPPY: I want them with the claws.

STANLEY: Don't worry, I don't give you no mice. *Happy laughs.* How about some wine? It'll put a head on the meal.

HAPPY: No. You remember, Stanley, that recipe I brought you from overseas? With the champagne in it?

STANLEY: Oh, yeah, sure. I still got it tacked up yet in the kitchen. But that'll have to cost a buck apiece anyways.

HAPPY: That's all right.

STANLEY: What'd you, hit a number or somethin'?

HAPPY: No, it's a little celebration. My brother is—I think he pulled off a big deal today. I think we're going into business together.

STANLEY: Great! That's the best for you. Because a family business, you know what I mean?—that's the best.

HAPPY: That's what I think.

STANLEY: 'Cause what's the difference? Somebody steals? It's in the family. Know what I mean? *Sotto voce:* Like this bartender here. The boss is goin' crazy what kinda leak he's got in the cash register. You put it in but it don't come out.

HAPPY, *raising his head:* Sh!

STANLEY: What?

HAPPY: You notice I wasn't lookin' right or left, was I?

STANLEY: No.

HAPPY: And my eyes are closed.

STANLEY: So what's the—?

HAPPY: Strudel's comin'.

STANLEY, *catching on, looks around:* Ah, no, there's no—

> He breaks off as a furred, lavishly dressed girl enters and sits at the next table. Both follow her with their eyes.

STANLEY: Geez, how'd ya know?

HAPPY: I got radar or something. *Staring directly at her profile:* Oooooooo . . . Stanley.

STANLEY: I think that's for you, Mr. Loman.

HAPPY: Look at that mouth. Oh, God. And the binoculars.

STANLEY: Geez, you got a life, Mr. Loman.

HAPPY: Wait on her.

STANLEY, *going to the girl's table*: Would you like a menu, ma'am?

GIRL: I'm expecting someone, but I'd like a—

HAPPY: Why don't you bring her—excuse me, miss, do you mind? I sell champagne, and I'd like you to try my brand. Bring her a champagne, Stanley.

GIRL: That's awfully nice of you.

HAPPY: Don't mention it. It's all company money. *He laughs.*

GIRL: That's a charming product to be selling, isn't it?

HAPPY: Oh, gets to be like everything else. Selling is selling, y'know.

GIRL: I suppose.

HAPPY: You don't happen to sell, do you?

GIRL: No, I don't sell.

HAPPY: Would you object to a compliment from a stranger? You ought to be on a magazine cover.

GIRL, *looking at him a little archly*: I have been.

> *Stanley comes in with a glass of champagne.*

HAPPY: What'd I say before, Stanley? You see? She's a cover girl.

STANLEY: Oh, I could see, I could see.

HAPPY, *to the Girl*: What magazine?

GIRL: Oh, a lot of them. *She takes the drink.* Thank you.

HAPPY: You know what they say in France, don't you? "Champagne is the drink of the complexion"—Hya, Biff!

> *Biff has entered and sits with Happy.*

BIFF: Hello, kid. Sorry I'm late.

HAPPY: I just got here. Uh, Miss—?

GIRL: Forsythe.

HAPPY: Miss Forsythe, this is my brother.

BIFF: Is Dad here?

HAPPY: His name is Biff. You might've heard of him. Great football player.

GIRL: Really? What team?

HAPPY: Are you familiar with football?

GIRL: No, I'm afraid I'm not.

HAPPY: Biff is quarterback with the New York Giants.

GIRL: Well, that is nice, isn't it? *She drinks.*

HAPPY: Good health.

GIRL: I'm happy to meet you.

HAPPY: That's my name. Hap. It's really Harold, but at West Point they called me Happy.

GIRL, *now really impressed*: Oh, I see. How do you do? *She turns her profile.*

BIFF: Isn't Dad coming?

HAPPY: You want her?

BIFF: Oh, I could never make that.

HAPPY: I remember the time that idea would never come into your head. Where's the old confidence, Biff?

BIFF: I just saw Oliver—

HAPPY: Wait a minute. I've got to see that old confidence again. Do you want her? She's on call.

BIFF: Oh, no. *He turns to look at the Girl.*

HAPPY: I'm telling you. Watch this. *Turning to the Girl*: Honey? *She turns to him.* Are you busy?

GIRL: Well, I am . . . but I could make a phone call.

HAPPY: Do that, will you, honey? And see if you can get a friend. We'll be here for a while. Biff is one of the greatest football players in the country.

GIRL, *standing up*: Well, I'm certainly happy to meet you.

HAPPY: Come back soon.

GIRL: I'll try.

HAPPY: Don't try, honey, try hard.

> *The Girl exits. Stanley follows, shaking his head in bewil-*
> *dered admiration.*

HAPPY: Isn't that a shame now? A beautiful girl like that? That's why I can't get married. There's not a good woman in a thousand. New York is loaded with them, kid!

BIFF: Hap, look—

HAPPY: I told you she was on call!

BIFF, *strangely unnerved*: Cut it out, will ya? I want to say something to you.

HAPPY: Did you see Oliver?

BIFF: I saw him all right. Now look, I want to tell Dad a couple of things and I want you to help me.

HAPPY: What? Is he going to back you?

BIFF: Are you crazy? You're out of your goddam head, you know that?

HAPPY: Why? What happened?

BIFF, *breathlessly*: I did a terrible thing today, Hap. It's been the strangest day I ever went through. I'm all numb, I swear.

HAPPY: You mean he wouldn't see you?

BIFF: Well, I waited six hours for him, see? All day. Kept sending my name in. Even tried to date his secretary so she'd get me to him, but no soap.

HAPPY: Because you're not showin' the old confidence, Biff. He remembered you, didn't he?

BIFF, *stopping Happy with a gesture*: Finally, about five o'clock, he comes out. Didn't remember who I was or anything. I felt like such an idiot, Hap.

HAPPY: Did you tell him my Florida idea?

BIFF: He walked away. I saw him for one minute. I got so mad I could've torn the walls down! How the hell did I ever get the idea I was a salesman there? I even believed myself that I'd been a salesman for him! And then he gave me one look and—I realized what a ridiculous lie my whole life has been. We've been talking in a dream for fifteen years. I was a shipping clerk.

HAPPY: What'd you do?

BIFF, *with great tension and wonder*: Well, he left, see. And the secretary went out. I was all alone in the waiting-room. I don't know what came over me, Hap. The next thing I know I'm in his office—paneled walls, everything. I can't explain it. I—Hap, I took his fountain pen.

HAPPY: Geez, did he catch you?

BIFF: I ran out. I ran down all eleven flights. I ran and ran and ran.

HAPPY: That was an awful dumb—what'd you do that for?

BIFF, *agonized*: I don't know, I just—wanted to take something, I don't know. You gotta help me, Hap, I'm gonna tell Pop.

HAPPY: You crazy? What for?

BIFF: Hap, he's got to understand that I'm not the man somebody lends that kind of money to. He thinks I've been spiting him all these years and it's eating him up.

HAPPY: That's just it. You tell him something nice.

BIFF: I can't.

HAPPY: Say you got a lunch date with Oliver tomorrow.

BIFF: So what do I do tomorrow?

HAPPY: You leave the house tomorrow and come back at night and say Oliver is thinking it over. And he thinks it over for a couple of weeks, and gradually it fades away and nobody's the worse.

BIFF: But it'll go on for ever!

HAPPY: Dad is never so happy as when he's looking forward to something!

> *Willy enters.*

HAPPY: Hello, scout!

WILLY: Gee, I haven't been here in years!

> *Stanley has followed Willy in and sets a chair for him. Stanley starts off but Happy stops him.*

HAPPY: Stanley!

> *Stanley stands by, waiting for an order.*

BIFF, *going to Willy with guilt, as to an invalid*: Sit down, Pop. You want a drink?

WILLY: Sure, I don't mind.

BIFF: Let's get a load on.

WILLY: You look worried.

BIFF: N-no. *To Stanley*: Scotch all around. Make it doubles.

STANLEY: Doubles, right. *He goes.*

WILLY: You had a couple already, didn't you?

BIFF: Just a couple, yeah.

WILLY: Well, what happened, boy? *Nodding affirmatively, with a smile* Everything go all right?

BIFF, *takes a breath, then reaches out and grasps Willy's hand*: Pal . . . *He is smiling bravely, and Willy is smiling too.* I had an experience today.

HAPPY: Terrific, Pop.

WILLY: That so? What happened?

BIFF, *high, slightly alcoholic, above the earth*: I'm going to tell you everything from first to last. It's been a strange day. *Silence. He looks around, composes himself as best he can, but his breath keeps breaking the rhythm of his voice.* I had to wait quite a while for him, and—

WILLY: Oliver?

BIFF: Yeah, Oliver. All day, as a matter of cold fact. And a lot of—instances—facts, Pop, facts about my life came back to me. Who was it, Pop? Who ever said I was a salesman with Oliver?

WILLY: Well, you were.

BIFF: No, Dad, I was a shipping clerk.

WILLY: But you were practically—

BIFF, *with determination*: Dad, I don't know who said it first, but I was never a salesman for Bill Oliver.

WILLY: What're you talking about?

BIFF: Let's hold on to the facts tonight, Pop. We're not going to get anywhere bullin' around. I was a shipping clerk.

WILLY, *angrily*: All right, now listen to me—

BIFF: Why don't you let me finish?

WILLY: I'm not interested in stories about the past or any crap of that kind because the woods are burning, boys, you understand? There's a big blaze going on all around. I was fired today.

BIFF, *shocked*: How could you be?

WILLY: I was fired, and I'm looking for a little good news to tell your mother, because the woman has waited and the woman has suffered. The gist of it is that I haven't got a story left in my head, Biff. So don't give me a lecture about facts and aspects. I am not interested. Now what've you got to say to me?

Stanley enters with three drinks. They wait until he leaves.

WILLY: Did you see Oliver?

BIFF: Jesus, Dad!

WILLY: You mean you didn't go up there?

HAPPY: Sure he went up there.

BIFF: I did. I—saw him. How could they fire you?

WILLY, *on the edge of his chair*: What kind of a welcome did he give you?

BIFF: He won't even let you work on commission?

WILLY: I'm out! *Driving*: So tell me, he gave you a warm welcome?

HAPPY: Sure, Pop, sure!

BIFF, *driven*: Well, it was kind of—

WILLY: I was wondering if he'd remember you. *To Happy*: Imagine, man doesn't see him for ten, twelve years and gives him that kind of a welcome!

HAPPY: Damn right!

BIFF, *trying to return to the offensive*: Pop, look—

WILLY: You know why he remembered you, don't you? Because you impressed him in those days.

BIFF: Let's talk quietly and get this down to the facts, huh?

WILLY, *as though Biff had been interrupting*: Well, what happened? It's great news, Biff. Did he take you into his office or'd you talk in the waiting-room?

BIFF: Well, he came in, see, and—

WILLY, *with a big smile*: What'd he say? Betcha he threw his arm around you.

BIFF: Well, he kinda—

WILLY: He's a fine man. *To Happy*: Very hard man to see, y'know.

HAPPY, *agreeing*: Oh, I know.

WILLY, *to Biff*: Is that where you had the drinks?

BIFF: Yeah, he gave me a couple of—no, no!

HAPPY, *cutting in*: He told him my Florida idea.

WILLY: Don't interrupt. *To Biff*: How'd he react to the Florida idea?

BIFF: Dad, will you give me a minute to explain?

WILLY: I've been waiting for you to explain since I sat down here! What happened? He took you into his office and what?

BIFF: Well—I talked. And—and he listened, see.

WILLY: Famous for the way he listens, y'know. What was his answer?

BIFF: His answer was— *He breaks off, suddenly angry.* Dad, you're not letting me tell you what I want to tell you!

WILLY, *accusing, angered*: You didn't see him, did you?

BIFF: I did see him!

WILLY: What'd you insult him or something? You insulted him, didn't you?

BIFF: Listen, will you let me out of it, will you just let me out of it!

HAPPY: What the hell!

WILLY: Tell me what happened!

BIFF, *to Happy*: I can't talk to him!

> *A single trumpet note jars the ear. The light of green leaves stains the house, which holds the air of night and a dream. Young Bernard enters and knocks on the door of the house.*

YOUNG BERNARD, *frantically*: Mrs. Loman, Mrs. Loman!

HAPPY: Tell him what happened!

BIFF, *to Happy*: Shut up and leave me alone!

WILLY: No, no! You had to go and flunk math!

BIFF: What math? What're you talking about?

YOUNG BERNARD: Mrs. Loman, Mrs. Loman!

> *Linda appears in the house, as of old.*

WILLY, *wildly*: Math, math, math!

BIFF: Take it easy, Pop!

YOUNG BERNARD: Mrs. Loman!

WILLY, *furiously*: If you hadn't flunked you'd've been set by now!

BIFF: Now, look, I'm gonna tell you what happened, and you're going to listen to me.

YOUNG BERNARD: Mrs. Loman!

BIFF: I waited six hours—

HAPPY: What the hell are you saying?

BIFF: I kept sending in my name but he wouldn't see me. So finally he . . . *He continues unheard as light fades low on the restaurant.*

YOUNG BERNARD: Biff flunked math!

LINDA: No!

YOUNG BERNARD: Birnbaum flunked him! They won't graduate him!

LINDA: But they have to. He's gotta go to the university. Where is he? Biff! Biff!

YOUNG BERNARD: No, he left. He went to Grand Central.

LINDA: Grand—You mean he went to Boston!

YOUNG BERNARD: Is Uncle Willy in Boston?

LINDA: Oh, maybe Willy can talk to the teacher. Oh, the poor, poor boy!

   Light on house area snaps out.

BIFF, *at the table, now audible, holding up a gold fountain pen:* . . . so I'm washed up with Oliver, you understand? Are you listening to me?

WILLY, *at a loss:* Yeah, sure. If you hadn't flunked—

BIFF: Flunked what? What're you talking about?

WILLY: Don't blame everything on me! I didn't flunk math—you did! What pen?

HAPPY: That was awful dumb, Biff, a pen like that is worth—

WILLY, *seeing the pen for the first time:* You took Oliver's pen?

BIFF, *weakening:* Dad, I just explained it to you.

WILLY: You stole Bill Oliver's fountain pen!

BIFF: I didn't exactly steal it! That's just what I've been explaining to you!

HAPPY: He had it in his hand and just then Oliver walked in, so he got nervous and stuck it in his pocket!

WILLY: My God, Biff!

BIFF: I never intended to do it, Dad!

OPERATOR'S VOICE: Standish Arms, good evening!

WILLY *shouting:* I'm not in my room!

BIFF, *frightened:* Dad, what's the matter? *He and Happy stand up.*

OPERATOR: Ringing Mr. Loman for you!

WILLY: I'm not there, stop it!

BIFF, *horrified, gets down on one knee before* Willy: Dad, I'll make good, I'll make good. *Willy tries to get to his feet. Biff holds him down.* Sit down now.

WILLY: No, you're no good, you're no good for anything.

BIFF: I am, Dad, I'll find something else, you understand? Now don't worry about anything. *He holds up Willy's face.* Talk to me, Dad.

OPERATOR: Mr. Loman does not answer. Shall I page him?

WILLY, *attempting to stand, as though to rush and silence the Operator*: No, no, no!

HAPPY: He'll strike something, Pop.

WILLY: No, no . . .

BIFF, *desperately, standing over Willy*: Pop, listen! Listen to me! I'm telling you something good. Oliver talked to his partner about the Florida idea. You listening? He—he talked to his partner, and he came to me . . . I'm going to be all right, you hear? Dad, listen to me, he said it was just a question of the amount!

WILLY: Then you . . . got it?

HAPPY: He's gonna be terrific, Pop!

WILLY, *trying to stand*: Then you got it, haven't you? You got it! You got it!

BIFF, *agonized, holds Willy down*: No, no. Look, Pop. I'm supposed to have lunch with them tomorrow. I'm just telling you this so you'll know that I can still make an impression, Pop. And I'll make good somewhere, but I can't go tomorrow, see?

WILLY: Why not? You simply—

BIFF: But the pen, Pop!

WILLY: You give it to him and tell him it was an oversight!

HAPPY: Sure, have lunch tomorrow!

BIFF: I can't say that—

WILLY: You were doing a crossword puzzle and accidentally used his pen!

BIFF: Listen, kid, I took those balls years ago, now I walk in with his fountain pen? That clinches it, don't you see? I can't face him like that! I'll try elsewhere.

PAGE'S VOICE: Paging Mr. Loman!

WILLY: Don't you want to be anything?

BIFF: Pop, how can I go back?

WILLY: You don't want to be anything, is that what's behind it?

BIFF, *now angry at Willy for not crediting his sympathy*: Don't take it that way! You think it was easy walking into that office after what I'd done to him? A team of horses couldn't have dragged me back to Bill Oliver!

WILLY: Then why'd you go?

BIFF: Why did I go? Why did I go! Look at you! Look at what's become of you!

   Off left, The Woman laughs.

WILLY: Biff, you're going to go to that lunch tomorrow, or—

BIFF: I can't go. I've got no appointment!

HAPPY: Biff, for . . . !

WILLY: Are you spiting me?

BIFF: Don't take it that way! Goddammit!

WILLY, *strikes Biff and falters away from the table*: You rotten little louse! Are you spiting me?

THE WOMAN: Someone's at the door, Willy!

BIFF: I'm no good, can't you see what I am?

HAPPY, *separating them*: Hey, you're in a restaurant! Now cut it out, both of you! *The girls enter.* Hello, girls, sit down.

   The Woman laughs, off left.

MISS FORSYTHE: I guess we might as well. This is Letta.

THE WOMAN: Willy, are you going to wake up?

BIFF, *ignoring Willy*: How're ya, miss, sit down. What do you drink?

MISS FORSYTHE: Letta might not be able to stay long.

LETTA: I gotta get up very early tomorrow. I got jury duty. I'm so excited! Were you fellows ever on a jury?

BIFF: No, but I been in front of them! *The girls laugh.* This is my father.

LETTA: Isn't he cute? Sit down with us, Pop.

HAPPY: Sit him down, Biff!

BIFF, *going to him*: Come on, slugger, drink us under the table. To hell with it! Come on, sit down, pal.

On Biff's last insistence, Willy is about to sit.

THE WOMAN, *now urgently*: Willy, are you going to answer the door!

The Woman's call pulls Willy back. He starts right, befuddled.

BIFF: Hey, where are you going?

WILLY: Open the door.

BIFF: The door?

WILLY: The washroom . . . the door . . . where's the door?

BIFF, *leading Willy to the left*: Just go straight down.

Willy moves left.

THE WOMAN: Willy, Willy, are you going to get up, get up, get up, get up?

Willy exits left.

LETTA: I think it's sweet you bring your daddy along.

MISS FORSYTHE: Oh, he isn't really your father!

BIFF, *at left, turning to her resentfully*: Miss Forsythe, you've just seen a prince walk by. A fine, troubled prince. A hardworking, unappreciated prince. A pal, you understand? A good companion. Always for his boys.

LETTA: That's so sweet.

HAPPY: Well, girls, what's the program? We're wasting time. Come on, Biff. Gather round. Where would you like to go?

BIFF: Why don't you do something for him?

HAPPY: Me!

BIFF: Don't you give a damn for him, Hap?

HAPPY: What're you talking about? I'm the one who—

BIFF: I sense it, you don't give a good goddam about him. *He takes the rolled-up hose from his pocket and puts it on the table in front of Happy.* Look what I found in the cellar, for Christ's sake. How can you bear to let it go on?

HAPPY: Me? Who goes away? Who runs off and—

BIFF: Yeah, but he doesn't mean anything to you. You could help him—I can't. Don't you understand what I'm talking about? He's going to kill himself, don't you know that?

HAPPY: Don't I know it! Me!

BIFF: Hap, help him! Jesus . . . help him. . . . Help me, help me, I can't bear to look at his face! *Ready to weep, he hurries out, up right.*

HAPPY, *starting after him*: Where are you going?

MISS FORSYTHE: What's he so mad about?

HAPPY: Come on, girls, we'll catch up with him.

MISS FORSYTHE, *as Happy pushes her out*: Say, I don't like that temper of his!

HAPPY: He's just a little overstrung, he'll be all right!

WILLY, *off left, as The Woman laughs*: Don't answer! Don't answer!

LETTA: Don't you want to tell your father—

HAPPY: No, that's not my father. He's just a guy. Come on, we'll catch Biff, and, honey, we're going to paint this town! Stanley, where's the check! Hey, Stanley!

They exit. Stanley looks toward left.

STANLEY, *calling to Happy indignantly*: Mr. Loman! Mr. Loman!

Stanley picks up a chair and follows them off. Knocking is heard off left. The Woman enters, laughing. Willy follows her. She is in a black slip; he is buttoning his shirt. Raw, sensuous music accompanies their speech.

WILLY: Will you stop laughing? Will you stop?

THE WOMAN: Aren't you going to answer the door? He'll wake the whole hotel.

WILLY: I'm not expecting anybody.

THE WOMAN: Whyn't you have another drink, honey, and stop being so damn self-centered?

WILLY: I'm so lonely.

THE WOMAN: You know you ruined me, Willy? From now on, whenever you come to the office, I'll see that you go right through to the buyers. No waiting at my desk any more, Willy. You ruined me.

WILLY: That's nice of you to say that.

THE WOMAN: Gee, you are self-centered! Why so sad? You are the saddest, self-centeredest soul I ever did see-saw. *She laughs. He kisses her.* Come on inside, drummer boy. It's silly to be dressing in the middle of the night. *As knocking is heard*: Aren't you going to answer the door?

WILLY: They're knocking on the wrong door.

THE WOMAN: But I felt the knocking. And he heard us talking in here. Maybe the hotel's on fire!

WILLY, *his terror rising*: It's a mistake.

THE WOMAN: Then tell him to go away!

WILLY: There's nobody there.

THE WOMAN: It's getting on my nerves, Willy. There's somebody standing out there and it's getting on my nerves!

WILLY, *pushing her away from him*: All right, stay in the bathroom here, and don't come out. I think there's a law in Massachusetts about it, so don't come out. It may be that new room clerk. He looked very mean. So don't come out. It's a mistake, there's no fire.

> *The knocking is heard again. He takes a few steps away from her, and she vanishes into the wing. The light follows him, and now he is facing young Biff, who carries a suitcase. Biff steps toward him. The music is gone.*

BIFF: Why didn't you answer?

WILLY: Biff! What are you doing in Boston?

BIFF: Why didn't you answer? I've been knocking for five minutes, I called you on the phone—

WILLY: I just heard you. I was in the bathroom and had the door shut. Did anything happen home?

BIFF: Dad—I let you down.

WILLY: What do you mean?

BIFF: Dad . . .

WILLY: Biffo, what's this about? *Putting his arm around Biff*: Come on, let's go downstairs and get you a malted.

BIFF: Dad, I flunked math.

WILLY: Not for the term?

BIFF: The term. I haven't got enough credits to graduate.

WILLY: You mean to say Bernard wouldn't give you the answers?

BIFF: He did, he tried, but I only got a sixty-one.

WILLY: And they wouldn't give you four points?

BIFF: Birnbaum refused absolutely. I begged him, Pop, but he won't give me those points. You gotta talk to him before they close the school.

Because if he saw the kind of man you are, and you just talked to him in your way, I'm sure he'd come through for me. The class came right before practice, see, and I didn't go enough. Would you talk to him? He'd like you, Pop. You know the way you could talk.

WILLY: You're on. We'll drive right back.

BIFF: Oh, Dad, good work! I'm sure he'll change it for you!

WILLY: Go downstairs and tell the clerk I'm checkin' out. Go right down.

BIFF: Yes, sir! See, the reason he hates me, Pop—one day he was late for class so I got up at the blackboard and imitated him. I crossed my eyes and talked with a lithp.

WILLY, *laughing*: You did? The kids like it?

BIFF: They nearly died laughing!

WILLY: Yeah? What'd you do?

BIFF: The thquare root of thixthy twee is . . . *Willy bursts out laughing; Biff joins him.* And in the middle of it he walked in!

Willy laughs and The Woman joins in offstage.

WILLY, *without hesitation*: Hurry downstairs and—

BIFF: Somebody in there?

WILLY: No, that was next door.

The Woman laughs offstage.

BIFF: Somebody got in your bathroom!

WILLY: No, it's the next room, there's a party—

THE WOMAN, *enters, laughing. She lisps this*: Can I come in? There's something in the bathtub, Willy, and it's moving!

Willy looks at Biff, who is staring open-mouthed and horrified at The Woman.

WILLY: Ah—you better go back to your room. They must be finished painting by now. They're painting her room so I let her take a shower here. Go back, go back . . . *He pushes her.*

THE WOMAN, *resisting*: But I've got to get dressed, Willy, I can't—

WILLY: Get out of here! Go back, go back . . . *Suddenly striving for the ordinary*: This is Miss Francis, Biff, she's a buyer. They're painting her room. Go back, Miss Francis, go back . . .

THE WOMAN: But my clothes, I can't go out naked in the hall!

WILLY, *pushing her offstage*: Get outa here! Go back, go back!

> *Biff slowly sits down on his suitcase as the argument continues offstage.*

THE WOMAN: Where's my stockings? You promised me stockings, Willy!

WILLY: I have no stockings here!

THE WOMAN: You had two boxes of size nine sheers for me, and I want them!

WILLY: Here, for God's sake, will you get outa here!

THE WOMAN, *enters holding a box of stockings*: I just hope there's nobody in the hall. That's all I hope. *To Biff*: Are you football or baseball?

BIFF: Football.

THE WOMAN, *angry, humiliated*: That's me too. G'night. *She snatches her clothes from Willy, and walks out.*

WILLY, *after a pause*: Well, better get going. I want to get to the school first thing in the morning. Get my suits out of the closet. I'll get my valise. *Biff doesn't move.* What's the matter? *Biff remains motionless, tears falling.* She's a buyer. Buys for J. H. Simmons. She lives down the hall—they're painting. You don't imagine— *He breaks off. After a pause*: Now listen, pal, she's just a buyer. She sees merchandise in her room and they have to keep it looking just so . . . *Pause. Assuming command*: All right, get my suits. *Biff doesn't move.* Now stop crying and do as I say. I gave you an order. Biff, I gave you an order! Is that what you do when I give you an order? How dare you cry? *Putting his arm around Biff*: Now look, Biff, when you grow up you'll understand about these things. You mustn't—you mustn't overemphasize a thing like this. I'll see Birnbaum first thing in the morning.

BIFF: Never mind.

WILLY, *getting down beside Biff*: Never mind! He's going to give you those points. I'll see to it.

BIFF: He wouldn't listen to you.

WILLY: He certainly will listen to me. You need those points for the U. of Virginia.

BIFF: I'm not going there.

WILLY: Heh? If I can't get him to change that mark you'll make it up in summer school. You've got all summer to—

BIFF, *his weeping breaking from him*: Dad . . .

WILLY, *infected by it*: Oh, my boy . . .

BIFF: Dad . . .

WILLY: She's nothing to me, Biff. I was lonely, I was terribly lonely.

BIFF: You—you gave her Mama's stockings! *His tears break through and he rises to go.*

WILLY, *grabbing for Biff*: I gave you an order!

BIFF: Don't touch me, you—liar!

WILLY: Apologize for that!

BIFF: You fake! You phony little fake! You fake! *Overcome, he turns quickly and weeping fully goes out with his suitcase. Willy is left on the floor on his knees.*

WILLY: I gave you an order! Biff, come back here or I'll beat you! Come back here! I'll whip you!

> *Stanley comes quickly in from the right and stands in front of Willy.*

WILLY, *shouts at Stanley*: I gave you an order . . .

STANLEY: Hey, let's pick it up, pick it up, Mr. Loman. *He helps Willy to his feet.* Your boys left with the chippies. They said they'll see you home.

> *A second waiter watches some distance away.*

WILLY: But we were supposed to have dinner together.

> *Music is heard, Willy's theme.*

STANLEY: Can you make it?

WILLY: I'll—sure, I can make it. *Suddenly concerned about his clothes.* Do I—I look all right?

STANLEY: Sure, you look all right. *He flicks a speck off Willy's lapel.*

WILLY: Here—here's a dollar.

STANLEY: Oh, your son paid me. It's all right.

WILLY, *putting it in Stanley's hand*: No, take it. You're a good boy.

STANLEY: Oh, no, you don't have to . . .

WILLY: Here—here's some more. I don't need it any more. *After a slight pause*: Tell me—is there a seed store in the neighborhood?

STANLEY: Seeds? You mean like to plant?

> *As Willy turns, Stanley slips the money back into his jacket pocket.*

WILLY: Yes. Carrots, peas . . .

STANLEY: Well, there's hardware stores on Sixth Avenue, but it may be too late now.

WILLY, *anxiously*: Oh, I'd better hurry. I've got to get some seeds. *He starts off to the right.* I've got to get some seeds, right away. Nothing's planted. I don't have a thing in the ground.

> *Willy hurries out as the light goes down. Stanley moves over to the right after him, watches him off. The other waiter has been staring at Willy.*

STANLEY, *to the waiter*: Well, whatta you looking at?

> *The waiter picks up the chairs and moves off right. Stanley takes the table and follows him. The light fades on this area. There is a long pause, the sound of the flute coming over. The light gradually rises on the kitchen, which is empty. Happy appears at the door of the house, followed by Biff. Happy is carrying a large bunch of long-stemmed roses. He enters the kitchen, looks around for Linda. Not seeing her, he turns to Biff, who is just outside the house door, and makes a gesture with his hands, indicating "Not here, I guess." He looks into the living-room and freezes. Inside, Linda, unseen, is seated, Willy's coat on her lap. She rises ominously and quietly and moves toward Happy, who backs up into the kitchen, afraid.*

HAPPY: Hey, what're you doing up? *Linda says nothing but moves toward him implacably.* Where's Pop? *He keeps backing to the right, and now Linda is in full view in the doorway to the living-room.* Is he sleeping?

LINDA: Where were you?

HAPPY, *trying to laugh it off*: We met two girls, Mom, very fine types. Here, we brought you some flowers. *Offering them to her*: Put them in your room, Ma.

> *She knocks them to the floor at Biff's feet. He has now come inside and closed the door behind him. She stares at Biff, silent.*

HAPPY: Now what'd you do that for? Mom, I want you to have some flowers—

LINDA, *cutting Happy off, violently to Biff*: Don't you care whether he lives or dies?

HAPPY, *going to the stairs*: Come upstairs, Biff.

BIFF, *with a flare of disgust, to Happy*: Go away from me! *To Linda*: What do you mean, lives or dies? Nobody's dying around here, pal.

LINDA: Get out of my sight! Get out of here!

BIFF: I wanna see the boss.

LINDA: You're not going near him!

BIFF: Where is he? *He moves into the living-room and Linda follows.*

LINDA, *shouting after Biff*: You invite him to dinner. He looks forward to it all day—*Biff appears in his parents' bedroom, looks around, and exits*—and then you desert him there. There's no stranger you'd do that to!

HAPPY: Why? He had a swell time with us. Listen, when I—*Linda comes back into the kitchen*—desert him I hope I don't outlive the day!

LINDA: Get out of here!

HAPPY: Now look, Mom . . .

LINDA: Did you have to go to women tonight? You and your lousy rotten whores!

> *Biff reenters the kitchen.*

HAPPY: Mom, all we did was follow Biff around trying to cheer him up! *To Biff*: Boy, what a night you gave me!

LINDA: Get out of here, both of you, and don't come back! I don't want you tormenting him any more. Go on now, get your things together! *To Biff*: You can sleep in his apartment. *She starts to pick up the flowers and stops herself.* Pick up this stuff, I'm not your maid any more. Pick it up, you bum, you!

> *Happy turns his back to her in refusal. Biff slowly moves over and gets down on his knees, picking up the flowers.*

LINDA: You're a pair of animals! Not one, not another living soul would have had the cruelty to walk out on that man in a restaurant!

BIFF, *not looking at her*: Is that what he said?

LINDA: He didn't have to say anything. He was so humiliated he nearly limped when he came in.

HAPPY: But, Mom, he had a great time with us—

BIFF, *cutting him off violently*: Shut up!

> *Without another word, Happy goes upstairs.*

LINDA: You! You didn't even go in to see if he was all right!

BIFF, *still on the floor in front of Linda, the flowers in his hand; with self-loathing*: No. Didn't. Didn't do a damned thing. How do you like that, heh? Left him babbling in a toilet.

LINDA: You louse. You . . .

BIFF: Now you hit it on the nose! *He gets up, throws the flowers in the wastebasket.* The scum of the earth, and you're looking at him!

LINDA: Get out of here!

BIFF: I gotta talk to the boss, Mom. Where is he?

LINDA: You're not going near him. Get out of this house!

BIFF, *with absolute assurance, determination*: No. We're gonna have an abrupt conversation, him and me.

LINDA: You're not talking to him!

> *Hammering is heard from outside the house, off right. Biff turns toward the noise.*

LINDA, *suddenly pleading*: Will you please leave him alone?

BIFF: What's he doing out there?

LINDA: He's planting the garden!

BIFF, *quietly*: Now? Oh, my God!

> *Biff moves outside, Linda following. The light dies down on them and comes up on the center of the apron as Willy walks into it. He is carrying a flashlight, a hoe, and a handful of seed packets. He raps the top of the hoe sharply to fix it firmly, and then moves to the left, measuring off the distance with his foot. He holds the flashlight to look at the seed packets, reading off the instructions. He is in the blue of night.*

WILLY: Carrots . . . quarter-inch apart. Rows . . . one-foot rows. *He measures it off.* One foot. *He puts down a package and measures off.* Beets. *He puts down another package and measures again.* Lettuce. *He reads the package, puts it down.* One foot— *He breaks off as Ben appears at the right and moves slowly down to him.* What a proposition, ts, ts. Terrific, terrific. 'Cause she's suffered, Ben, the woman has suffered. You understand me? A man can't go out the way he came in, Ben, a man has got to add up to something. You can't, you can't— *Ben moves toward him as though to interrupt.* You gotta consider, now. Don't answer so quick. Remember, it's a guaranteed twenty-thousand-dollar proposition. Now look, Ben, I want you to go through the ins and outs of this thing with me. I've got nobody to talk to, Ben, and the woman has suffered, you hear me?

BEN, *standing still, considering*: What's the proposition?

WILLY: It's twenty thousand dollars on the barrelhead. Guaranteed, gilt-edged, you understand?

BEN: You don't want to make a fool of yourself. They might not honor the policy.

WILLY: How can they dare refuse? Didn't I work like a coolie to meet every premium on the nose? And now they don't pay off? Impossible!

BEN: It's called a cowardly thing, William.

WILLY: Why? Does it take more guts to stand here the rest of my life ringing up a zero?

BEN, *yielding*: That's a point, William. *He moves, thinking, turns.* And twenty thousand—that *is* something one can feel with the hand, it is there.

WILLY, *now assured, with rising power*: Oh, Ben, that's the whole beauty of it! I see it like a diamond, shining in the dark, hard and rough, that I can pick up and touch in my hand. Not like—like an appointment! This would not be another damned-fool appointment, Ben, and it changes all the aspects. Because he thinks I'm nothing, see, and so he spites me. But the funeral— *Straightening up*: Ben, that funeral will be massive! They'll come from Maine, Massachusetts, Vermont, New Hampshire! All the old-timers with the strange license plates—that boy will be thunderstruck, Ben, because he never realized—I am known! Rhode Island, New York, New Jersey—I am known, Ben, and he'll see it with his eyes once and for all. He'll see what I am, Ben! He's in for a shock, that boy!

BEN, *coming down to the edge of the garden*: He'll call you a coward.

WILLY, *suddenly fearful*: No, that would be terrible.

BEN: Yes. And a damned fool.

WILLY: No, no, he mustn't, I won't have that! *He is broken and desperate.*

BEN: He'll hate you, William.

> *The gay music of the boys is heard.*

WILLY: Oh, Ben, how do we get back to all the great times? Used to be so full of light, and comradeship, the sleigh-riding in winter, and the ruddiness on his cheeks. And always some kind of good news coming up, always something nice coming up ahead. And never even let me carry the valises in the house, and simonizing, simonizing that little red car! Why, why can't I give him something and not have him hate me?

BEN: Let me think about it. *He glances at his watch.* I still have a little time. Remarkable proposition, but you've got to be sure you're not making a fool of yourself.

> *Ben drifts off upstage and goes out of sight. Biff comes down from the left.*

WILLY, *suddenly conscious of Biff, turns and looks up at him, then begins picking up the packages of seeds in confusion*: Where the hell is that seed? *Indignantly*: You can't see nothing out here! They boxed in the whole goddam neighborhood!

BIFF: There are people all around here. Don't you realize that?

WILLY: I'm busy. Don't bother me.

BIFF, *taking the hoe from Willy*: I'm saying good-bye to you, Pop. *Willy looks at him, silent, unable to move.* I'm not coming back any more.

WILLY: You're not going to see Oliver tomorrow?

BIFF: I've got no appointment, Dad.

WILLY: He put his arm around you, and you've got no appointment?

BIFF: Pop, get this now, will you? Everytime I've left it's been a fight that sent me out of here. Today I realized something about myself and I tried to explain it to you and I—I think I'm just not smart enough to make any sense out of it for you. To hell with whose fault it is or anything like that. *He takes Willy's arm.* Let's just wrap it up, heh? Come on in, we'll tell Mom. *He gently tries to pull Willy to left.*

WILLY, *frozen, immobile, with guilt in his voice*: No, I don't want to see her.

BIFF: Come on! *He pulls again, and Willy tries to pull away.*

WILLY, *highly nervous*: No, no, I don't want to see her.

BIFF, *tries to look into Willy's face, as if to find the answer there*: Why don't you want to see her?

WILLY, *more harshly now*: Don't bother me, will you?

BIFF: What do you mean, you don't want to see her? You don't want them calling you yellow, do you? This isn't your fault; it's me, I'm a bum. Now come inside! *Willy strains to get away.* Did you hear what I said to you?

> *Willy pulls away and quickly goes by himself into the house. Biff follows.*

LINDA, *to Willy*: Did you plant, dear?

BIFF, *at the door, to Linda*: All right, we had it out. I'm going and I'm not writing any more.

LINDA, *going to Willy in the kitchen*: I think that's the best way, dear. 'Cause there's no use drawing it out, you'll just never get along.

> *Willy doesn't respond.*

BIFF: People ask where I am and what I'm doing, you don't know, and you don't care. That way it'll be off your mind and you can start brightening up again. All right? That clears it, doesn't it? *Willy is silent, and Biff goes to him.* You gonna wish me luck, scout? *He extends his hand.* What do you say?

LINDA: Shake his hand, Willy.

WILLY, *turning to her, seething with hurt*: There's no necessity to mention the pen at all, y'know.

BIFF, *gently*: I've got no appointment, Dad.

WILLY, *erupting fiercely*: He put his arm around . . . ?

BIFF: Dad, you're never going to see what I am, so what's the use of arguing? If I strike oil I'll send you a check. Meantime forget I'm alive.

WILLY, *to Linda*: Spite, see?

BIFF: Shake hands, Dad.

WILLY: Not my hand.

BIFF: I was hoping not to go this way.

WILLY: Well, this is the way you're going. Good-bye.

> *Biff looks at him a moment, then turns sharply and goes to the stairs.*

WILLY, *stops him with*: May you rot in hell if you leave this house!

BIFF, *turning*: Exactly what is it that you want from me?

WILLY: I want you to know, on the train, in the mountains, in the valleys, wherever you go, that you cut down your life for spite!

BIFF: No, no.

WILLY: Spite, spite, is the word of your undoing! And when you're down and out, remember what did it. When you're rotting somewhere beside the railroad tracks, remember, and don't you dare blame it on me!

BIFF: I'm not blaming it on you!

WILLY: I won't take the rap for this, you hear?

> *Happy comes down the stairs and stands on the bottom step, watching.*

BIFF: That's just what I'm telling you!

WILLY, *sinking into a chair at the table, with full accusation*: You're trying to put a knife in me—don't think I don't know what you're doing!

BIFF: All right, phony! Then let's lay it on the line. *He whips the rubber tube out of his pocket and puts it on the table.*

HAPPY: You crazy—

LINDA: Biff! *She moves to grab the hose, but Biff holds it down with his hand.*

BIFF: Leave it there! Don't move it!

WILLY, *not looking at it*: What is that?

BIFF: You know goddam well what that is.

WILLY, *caged, wanting to escape*: I never saw that.

BIFF: You saw it. The mice didn't bring it into the cellar! What is this supposed to do, make a hero out of you? This supposed to make me sorry for you?

WILLY: Never heard of it.

BIFF: There'll be no pity for you, you hear it? No pity!

WILLY, *to Linda*: You hear the spite!

BIFF: No, you're going to hear the truth—what you are and what I am!

LINDA: Stop it!

WILLY: Spite!

HAPPY, *coming down toward Biff*: You cut it now!

BIFF, *to Happy*: The man don't know who we are! The man is gonna know! *To Willy*: We never told the truth for ten minutes in this house!

HAPPY: We always told the truth!

BIFF, *turning on him*: You big blow, are you the assistant buyer? You're one of the two assistants to the assistant, aren't you?

HAPPY: Well, I'm practically—

BIFF: You're practically full of it! We all are! And I'm through with it. *To Willy*: Now hear this, Willy, this is me.

WILLY: I know you!

BIFF: You know why I had no address for three months? I stole a suit in Kansas City and I was in jail. *To Linda, who is sobbing*: Stop crying. I'm through with it.

Linda turns away from them, her hands covering her face.

WILLY: I suppose that's my fault!

BIFF: I stole myself out of every good job since high school!

WILLY: And whose fault is that?

BIFF: And I never got anywhere because you blew me so full of hot air I could never stand taking orders from anybody! That's whose fault it is!

WILLY: I hear that!

LINDA: Don't, Biff!

BIFF: It's goddam time you heard that! I had to be boss big shot in two weeks, and I'm through with it!

WILLY: Then hang yourself! For spite, hang yourself!

BIFF: No! Nobody's hanging himself, Willy! I ran down eleven flights with a pen in my hand today. And suddenly I stopped, you hear me? And in the middle of that office building, do you hear this? I stopped in the middle of that building and I saw—the sky. I saw the things that I love in this world. The work and the food and time to sit and smoke. And I looked at the pen and said to myself, what the hell am I grabbing this for? Why am I trying to become what I don't want to be? What am I doing in an office, making a contemptuous, begging fool of myself, when all I want is out there, waiting for me the minute I say I know who I am! Why can't I say that, Willy? *He tries to make Willy face him, but Willy pulls away and moves to the left.*

WILLY, *with hatred, threateningly*: The door of your life is wide open!

BIFF: Pop! I'm a dime a dozen, and so are you!

WILLY, *turning on him now in an uncontrolled outburst*: I am not a dime a dozen! I am Willy Loman, and you are Biff Loman!

Biff starts for Willy, but is blocked by Happy. In his fury, Biff seems on the verge of attacking his father.

BIFF: I am not a leader of men, Willy, and neither are you. You were never anything but a hard-working drummer who landed in the ash can like all the rest of them! I'm one dollar an hour, Willy! I tried seven states and couldn't raise it. A buck an hour! Do you gather my meaning? I'm not bringing home any prizes any more, and you're going to stop waiting for me to bring them home!

WILLY, *directly to Biff*: You vengeful, spiteful mutt!

Biff breaks from Happy. Willy, in fright, starts up the stairs. Biff grabs him.

BIFF, *at the peak of his fury*: Pop, I'm nothing! I'm nothing, Pop. Can't you understand that? There's no spite in it any more. I'm just what I am, that's all.

Biff's fury has spent itself, and he breaks down, sobbing, holding on to Willy, who dumbly fumbles for Biff's face.

WILLY, *astonished*: What're you doing? What're you doing? *To Linda*: Why is he crying?

BIFF, *crying, broken*: Will you let me go, for Christ's sake? Will you take that phony dream and burn it before something happens? *Struggling to contain himself, he pulls away and moves to the stairs.* I'll go in the morning. Put him—put him to bed. *Exhausted, Biff moves up the stairs to his room.*

WILLY, *after a long pause, astonished, elevated*: Isn't that—isn't that remarkable? Biff—he likes me!

LINDA: He loves you, Willy!

HAPPY, *deeply moved*: Always did, Pop.

WILLY: Oh, Biff! *Staring wildly*: He cried! Cried to me. *He is choking with his love, and now cries out his promise.* That boy—that boy is going to be magnificent!

   Ben appears in the light just outside the kitchen.

BEN: Yes, outstanding, with twenty thousand behind him.

LINDA, *sensing the racing of his mind, fearfully, carefully*: Now come to bed, Willy. It's all settled now.

WILLY, *finding it difficult not to rush out of the house*: Yes, we'll sleep. Come on. Go to sleep, Hap.

BEN: And it does take a great kind of a man to crack the jungle.

   In accents of dread, Ben's idyllic music starts up.

HAPPY, *his arm around Linda*: I'm getting married, Pop, don't forget it. I'm changing everything. I'm gonna run that department before the year is up. You'll see, Mom. *He kisses her.*

BEN: The jungle is dark but full of diamonds, Willy.

   Willy turns, moves, listening to Ben.

LINDA: Be good. You're both good boys, just act that way, that's all.

HAPPY: 'Night, Pop. *He goes upstairs.*

LINDA, *to Willy*: Come, dear.

BEN, *with greater force*: One must go in to fetch a diamond out.

WILLY, *to Linda, as he moves slowly along the edge of the kitchen, toward the door*: I just want to get settled down, Linda. Let me sit alone for a little.

LINDA, *almost uttering her fear*: I want you upstairs.

WILLY, *taking her in his arms*: In a few minutes, Linda. I couldn't sleep right now. Go on, you look awful tired. *He kisses her.*

BEN: Not like an appointment at all. A diamond is rough and hard to the touch.

WILLY: Go on now. I'll be right up.

LINDA: I think this is the only way, Willy.

WILLY: Sure, it's the best thing.

BEN: Best thing!

WILLY: The only way. Everything is gonna be—go on, kid, get to bed. You look so tired.

LINDA: Come right up.

WILLY: Two minutes.

> *Linda goes into the living-room, then reappears in her bedroom. Willy moves just outside the kitchen door.*

WILLY: Loves me. *Wonderingly*: Always loved me. Isn't that a remarkable thing? Ben, he'll worship me for it!

BEN, *with promise*: It's dark there, but full of diamonds.

WILLY: Can you imagine that magnificence with twenty thousand dollars in his pocket?

LINDA, *calling from her room*: Willy! Come up!

WILLY, *calling into the kitchen*: Yes! Yes. Coming! It's very smart, you realize that, don't you, sweetheart? Even Ben sees it. I gotta go, baby. 'Bye! 'Bye! *Going over to Ben, almost dancing*: Imagine? When the mail comes he'll be ahead of Bernard again!

BEN: A perfect proposition all around.

WILLY: Did you see how he cried to me? Oh, if I could kiss him, Ben!

BEN: Time, William, time!

WILLY: Oh, Ben, I always knew one way or another we were gonna make it, Biff and I!

BEN, *looking at his watch*: The boat. We'll be late. *He moves slowly off into the darkness.*

WILLY, *elegiacally, turning to the house*: Now when you kick off, boy, I want a seventy-yard boot, and get right down the field under the ball, and when you hit, hit low and hit hard, because it's important, boy. *He swings around and faces the audience*. There's all kinds of important people in

↳ phony dream

the stands, and the first thing you know ... *Suddenly realizing he is alone*: Ben! Ben, where do I ... ? *He makes a sudden movement of search.* Ben, how do I ... ?

LINDA, *calling*: Willy, you coming up?

WILLY, *uttering a gasp of fear, whirling about as if to quiet her*: Sh! *He turns around as if to find his way; sounds, faces, voices seem to be swarming in upon him and he flicks at them, crying, "Sh! Sh!" Suddenly music, faint and high, stops him. It rises in intensity, almost to an unbearable scream. He goes up and down on his toes, and rushes off around the house.* Shhh!

LINDA: Willy?

> *There is no answer. Linda waits. Biff gets up off his bed. He is still in his clothes. Happy sits up. Biff stands listening.*

LINDA, *with real fear*: Willy, answer me! Willy! *There is the sound of a car starting and moving away at full speed.*

LINDA: No!

BIFF, *rushing down the stairs*: Pop!

> *As the car speeds off, the music crashes down in a frenzy of sound, which becomes the soft pulsation of a single cello string. Biff slowly returns to his bedroom. He and Happy gravely don their jackets. Linda slowly walks out of her room. The music has developed into a dead march. The leaves of day are appearing over everything. Charley and Bernard, somberly dressed, appear and knock on the kitchen door. Biff and Happy slowly descend the stairs to the kitchen as Charley and Bernard enter. All stop a moment when Linda, in clothes of mourning, bearing a little bunch of roses, comes through the draped doorway into the kitchen. She goes to Charley and takes his arm. Now all move toward the audience, through the wall-line of the kitchen. At the limit of the apron, Linda lays down the flowers, kneels, and sits back on her heels. All stare down at the grave.*

REQUIEM

CHARLEY: It's getting dark, Linda.

Linda doesn't react. She stares at the grave.

BIFF: How about it, Mom? Better get some rest, heh? They'll be closing the gate soon.

Linda makes no move. Pause.

HAPPY, *deeply angered*: He had no right to do that. There was no necessity for it. We would've helped him.

CHARLEY, *grunting*: Hmmm.

BIFF: Come along, Mom.

LINDA: Why didn't anybody come?

CHARLEY: It was a very nice funeral.

LINDA: But where are all the people he knew? Maybe they blame him.

CHARLEY: Naa. It's a rough world, Linda. They wouldn't blame him.

LINDA: I can't understand it. At this time especially. First time in thirty-five years we were just about free and clear. He only needed a little salary. He was even finished with the dentist.

CHARLEY: No man only needs a little salary.

LINDA: I can't understand it.

BIFF: There were a lot of nice days. When he'd come home from a trip; or on Sundays, making the stoop; finishing the cellar; putting on the new porch; when he built the extra bathroom; and put up the garage. You know something, Charley, there's more of him in that front stoop than in all the sales he ever made.

CHARLEY: Yeah. He was a happy man with a batch of cement.

LINDA: He was so wonderful with his hands.

BIFF: He had the wrong dreams. All, all, wrong.

HAPPY, *almost ready to fight Biff*: Don't say that!

BIFF: He never knew who he was.

CHARLEY, *stopping Happy's movement and reply. To Biff*: Nobody dast blame this man. You don't understand: Willy was a salesman. And for a salesman, there is no rock bottom to the life. He don't put a bolt to a nut, he don't tell you the law or give you medicine. He's a man way out there in the blue, riding on a smile and a shoeshine. And when they start not smiling back—that's an earthquake. And then you get yourself a couple of spots on your hat, and you're finished. Nobody dast blame this man. A salesman is got to dream, boy. It comes with the territory.

BIFF: Charley, the man didn't know who he was.

HAPPY, *infuriated*: Don't say that!

BIFF: Why don't you come with me, Happy?

HAPPY: I'm not licked that easily. I'm staying right in this city, and I'm gonna beat this racket! *He looks at Biff, his chin set.* The Loman Brothers!

BIFF: I know who I am, kid.

HAPPY: All right, boy. I'm gonna show you and everybody else that Willy Loman did not die in vain. He had a good dream. It's the only dream you can have—to come out number-one man. He fought it out here, and this is where I'm gonna win it for him.

BIFF, *with a hopeless glance at Happy, bends toward his mother*: Let's go, Mom.

LINDA: I'll be with you in a minute. Go on, Charley. *He hesitates.* I want to, just for a minute. I never had a chance to say good-bye.

> *Charley moves away, followed by Happy. Biff remains a slight distance up and left of Linda. She sits there, summoning herself. The flute begins, not far away, playing behind her speech.*

LINDA: Forgive me, dear. I can't cry. I don't know what it is, but I can't cry. I don't understand it. Why did you ever do that? Help me, Willy, I can't cry. It seems to me that you're just on another trip. I keep expecting you. Willy, dear, I can't cry. Why did you do it? I search and search and I search, and I can't understand it, Willy. I made the last payment on the house today. Today, dear. And there'll be nobody home. *A sob rises in her throat.* We're free and clear. *Sobbing more fully, released*: We're free. *Biff comes slowly toward her.* We're free . . . We're free . . .

Biff lifts her to her feet and moves out up right with her in his arms. Linda sobs quietly. Bernard and Charley come together and follow them, followed by Happy. Only the music of the flute is left on the darkening stage as over the house the hard towers of the apartment buildings rise into sharp focus.

CURTAIN

AN ENEMY OF THE PEOPLE

AN ADAPTATION OF THE PLAY BY HENRIK IBSEN

1950

Characters

MORTEN KIIL

BILLING

MRS. STOCKMANN

PETER STOCKMANN

HOVSTAD

DR. STOCKMANN

MORTEN

EJLIF

CAPTAIN HORSTER

PETRA

ASLAKSEN

THE DRUNK

TOWNSPEOPLE

SYNOPSIS OF SCENES

The action takes place in a Norwegian town.

Act One

SCENE I

Dr. Stockmann's living room.

SCENE II

The same, the following morning.

Act Two

SCENE I

Editorial office of the People's Daily Messenger.

SCENE II

A room in Captain Horster's house.

Act Three

SCENE

Dr. Stockmann's living room the following morning.

ACT ONE

SCENE I

It is evening. Dr. Stockmann's living room is simply but cheer-fully furnished. A doorway, upstage right, leads into the entrance hall, which extends from the front door to the dining room, running unseen behind the living room. At the left is another door, which leads to the Doctor's study and other rooms. In the upstage left corner is a stove. Toward the left foreground is a sofa with a table behind it. In the right fore-ground are two chairs, a small table between them, on which stand a lamp and a bowl of apples. At the back, to the left, an open doorway leads to the dining room, part of which is seen. The windows are in the right wall, a bench in front of them.

As the curtain rises, Billing and Morten Kiil are eating in the dining room. Billing is junior editor of the People's Daily Mes-senger. *Kiil is a slovenly old man who is feeding himself in a great hurry. He gulps his last bite and comes into the living room, where he puts on his coat and ratty fur hat. Billing comes in to help him.*

BILLING: You sure eat fast, Mr. Kiil. *Billing is an enthusiast to the point of foolishness.*

KIIL: Eating don't get you anywhere, boy. Tell my daughter I went home.

Kiil starts across to the front door. Billing returns to his food in the dining room. Kiil halts at the bowl of apples; he takes one, tastes it, likes it, takes another and puts it in his pocket, then continues on toward the door. Again he stops, returns, and takes another apple for his pocket. Then he sees a tobacco can on the table. He covers his action from Billing's possible glance, opens the can, smells it, pours some into his side pocket. He is just closing the can when Catherine Stockmann enters from the dining room.

253

MRS. STOCKMANN: Father! You're not going, are you?

KIIL: Got business to tend to.

MRS. STOCKMANN: Oh, you're only going back to your room and you know it. Stay! Mr. Billing's here, and Hovstad's coming. It'll be interesting for you.

KIIL: Got all kinds of business. The only reason I came over was the butcher told me you bought roast beef today. Very tasty, dear.

MRS. STOCKMANN: Why don't you wait for Tom? He only went for a little walk.

KIIL, *taking out his pipe*: You think he'd mind if I filled my pipe?

MRS. STOCKMANN: No, go ahead. And here—take some apples. You should always have some fruit in your room.

KIIL: No, no, wouldn't think of it.

The doorbell rings.

MRS. STOCKMANN: That must be Hovstad. *She goes to the door and opens it.*

Peter Stockmann, the Mayor, enters. He is a bachelor, nearing sixty. He has always been one of those men who make it their life work to stand in the center of the ship to keep it from overturning. He probably envies the family life and warmth of this house, but when he comes he never wants to admit he came and often sits with his coat on.

MRS. STOCKMANN: Peter! Well, this is a surprise!

PETER STOCKMANN: I was just passing by . . . *He sees Kiil and smiles, amused.* Mr. Kiil!

KIIL, *sarcastically*: Your Honor! *He bites into his apple and exits.*

MRS. STOCKMANN: You mustn't mind him, Peter, he's getting terribly old. Would you like a bite to eat?

PETER STOCKMANN: No, no thanks. *He sees Billing now, and Billing nods to him from the dining room.*

MRS. STOCKMANN, *embarrassed*: He just happened to drop in.

PETER STOCKMANN: That's all right. I can't take hot food in the evening. Not with my stomach.

MRS. STOCKMANN: Can't I ever get you to eat anything in this house?

PETER STOCKMANN: Bless you, I stick to my tea and toast. Much healthier and more economical.

MRS. STOCKMANN, *smiling*: You sound as though Tom and I throw money out the window.

PETER STOCKMANN: Not you, Catherine. He wouldn't be home, would he?

MRS. STOCKMANN: He went for a little walk with the boys.

PETER STOCKMANN: You don't think that's dangerous, right after dinner? *There is a loud knocking on the front door. That* sounds like my brother.

MRS. STOCKMANN: I doubt it, so soon. Come in, please.

> *Hovstad enters. He is in his early thirties, a graduate of the peasantry struggling with a terrible conflict. For while he hates authority and wealth, he cannot bring himself to cast off a certain desire to partake of them. Perhaps he is dangerous because he wants more than anything to belong, and in a radical that is a withering wish, not easily to be borne.*

MRS. STOCKMANN: Mr. Hovstad—

HOVSTAD: Sorry I'm late. I was held up at the printing shop. *Surprised*: Good evening, Your Honor.

PETER STOCKMANN, *rather stiffly*: Hovstad. On business, no doubt.

HOVSTAD: Partly. It's about an article for the paper—

PETER STOCKMANN, *sarcastically*: Ha! I don't doubt it. I understand my brother has become a prolific contributor to—what do you call it?—the *People's Daily Liberator*?

HOVSTAD, *laughing, but holding his ground*: The *People's Daily Messenger*, sir. The Doctor sometimes honors the *Messenger* when he wants to uncover the real truth of some subject.

PETER STOCKMANN: The truth! Oh, yes, I see.

MRS. STOCKMANN, *nervously to Hovstad*: Would you like to . . . *She points to dining room.*

PETER STOCKMANN: I don't want you to think I blame the Doctor for using your paper. After all, every performer goes for the audience that applauds him most. It's really not your paper I have anything against, Mr. Hovstad.

HOVSTAD: I really didn't think so, Your Honor.

PETER STOCKMANN: As a matter of fact, I happen to admire the spirit of tolerance in our town. It's magnificent. Just don't forget that we have it because we all believe in the same thing; it brings us together.

HOVSTAD: Kirsten Springs, you mean.

PETER STOCKMANN: The springs, Mr. Hovstad, our wonderful new springs. They've changed the soul of this town. Mark my words, Kirsten Springs are going to put us on the map, and there is no question about it.

MRS. STOCKMANN: That's what Tom says too.

PETER STOCKMANN: Everything is shooting ahead—real estate going up, money changing hands every hour, business humming—

HOVSTAD: And no more unemployment.

PETER STOCKMANN: Right. Give us a really good summer, and sick people will be coming here in carloads. The springs will turn into a regular fad, a new Carlsbad. And for once the well-to-do people won't be the only ones paying taxes in this town.

HOVSTAD: I hear reservations are really starting to come in?

PETER STOCKMANN: Coming in every day. Looks very promising, very promising.

HOVSTAD: That's fine. *To Mrs. Stockmann:* Then the Doctor's article will come in handy.

PETER STOCKMANN: He's written something again?

HOVSTAD: No, it's a piece he wrote at the beginning of the winter, recommending the water. But at the time I let the article lie.

PETER STOCKMANN: Why, some hitch in it?

HOVSTAD: Oh, no, I just thought it would have a bigger effect in the spring, when people start planning for the summer.

PETER STOCKMANN: That's smart, Mr. Hovstad, very smart.

MRS. STOCKMANN: Tom is always so full of ideas about the springs; every day he—

PETER STOCKMANN: Well, he ought to be, he gets his salary from the springs, my dear.

HOVSTAD: Oh, I think it's more than that, don't you? After all, Doctor Stockmann *created* Kirsten Springs.

PETER STOCKMANN: You don't say! I've been hearing that lately, but I did think I had a certain modest part—

MRS. STOCKMANN: Oh, Tom always says—

HOVSTAD: I only meant the original idea was—

PETER STOCKMANN: My good brother is never at a loss for ideas. All sorts of ideas. But when it comes to putting them into action you need another kind of man, and I did think that at least people in this house would—

MRS. STOCKMANN: But Peter, dear—we didn't mean to— Go get yourself a bite, Mr. Hovstad, my husband will be here any minute.

HOVSTAD: Thank you, maybe just a little something. *He goes into the dining room and joins Billing at the table.*

PETER STOCKMANN, *lowering his voice*: Isn't it remarkable? Why is it that people without background can never learn tact?

MRS. STOCKMANN: Why let it bother you? Can't you and Thomas share the honor like good brothers?

PETER STOCKMANN: The trouble is that certain men are never satisfied to share, Catherine.

MRS. STOCKMANN: Nonsense. You've always gotten along beautifully with Tom— That must be him now.

> *She goes to the front door, opens it. Dr. Stockmann is laughing and talking outside. He is in the prime of his life. He might be called the eternal amateur—a lover of things, of people, of sheer living, a man for whom the days are too short, and the future fabulous with discoverable joys. And for all this most people will not like him—he will not compromise for less than God's own share of the world while they have settled for less than Man's.*

DR. STOCKMANN, *in the entrance hall*: Hey, Catherine! Here's another guest for you! Here's a hanger for your coat, Captain. Oh, that's right, you don't wear overcoats! Go on in, boys. You kids must be hungry all over again. Come here, Captain Horster, I want you to get a look at this roast. *He pushes Captain Horster along the hallway to the dining room. Ejlif and Morten also go to the dining room.*

MRS. STOCKMANN: Tom, dear . . . *She motions toward Peter in the living room.*

DR. STOCKMANN, *turns around in the doorway to the living room and sees Peter*: Oh, Peter . . . *He walks across and stretches out his hand.* Say now, this is really nice.

PETER STOCKMANN: I'll have to go in a minute.

DR. STOCKMANN: Oh, nonsense, not with the toddy on the table. You haven't forgotten the toddy, have you, Catherine?

MRS. STOCKMANN: Of course not, I've got the water boiling. *She goes into the dining room.*

PETER STOCKMANN: Toddy too?

DR. STOCKMANN: Sure, just sit down and make yourself at home.

PETER STOCKMANN: No, thanks, I don't go in for drinking parties.

DR. STOCKMANN: But this is no party.

PETER STOCKMANN: What else do you call it? *He looks toward the dining room.* It's extraordinary how you people can consume all this food and live.

DR. STOCKMANN, *rubbing his hands*: Why? What's finer than to watch young people eat? Peter, those are the fellows who are going to stir up the whole future.

PETER STOCKMANN, *a little alarmed*: Is that so! What's there to stir up? *He sits in a chair to the left.*

DR. STOCKMANN, *walking around*: Don't worry, they'll let us know when the time comes. Old idiots like you and me, we'll be left behind like—

PETER STOCKMANN: I've never been called *that* before.

DR. STOCKMANN: Oh, Peter, don't jump on me every minute! You know your trouble, Peter? Your impressions are blunted. You ought to sit up there in that crooked corner of the north for five years, the way I did, and then come back here. It's like watching the first seven days of creation!

PETER STOCKMANN: Here!

DR. STOCKMANN: Things to work and fight for, Peter! Without that you're dead. Catherine, you sure the mailman came today?

MRS. STOCKMANN, *from the dining room*: There wasn't any mail today.

DR. STOCKMANN: And another thing, Peter—a good income; *that's* something you learn to value after you've lived on a starvation diet.

PETER STOCKMANN: When did you starve?

DR. STOCKMANN: Damned near! It was pretty tough going a lot of the time up there. And now, to be able to live like a prince! Tonight, for instance, we had roast beef for dinner, and, by God, there was enough left for supper too. Please have a piece—come here.

PETER STOCKMANN: Oh, no, no—please, certainly not.

DR. STOCKMANN: At least let me show it to you! Come in here—we even have a tablecloth. *He pulls his brother toward the dining room.*

PETER STOCKMANN: I saw it.

DR. STOCKMANN: Live to the hilt! that's my motto. Anyway, Catherine says I'm earning almost as much as we spend.

PETER STOCKMANN, *refusing an apple*: Well, you are improving.

DR. STOCKMANN: Peter, that was a joke! You're supposed to laugh! *He sits in the other chair to the left.*

PETER STOCKMANN: Roast beef twice a day is no joke.

DR. STOCKMANN: Why can't I give myself the pleasure of having people around me? It's a necessity for me to see young, lively, happy people, free people burning with a desire to do something. You'll see. When Hovstad comes in we'll talk and—

PETER STOCKMANN: Oh, yes, Hovstad. That reminds me. He told me he was going to print one of your articles.

DR. STOCKMANN: One of my articles?

PETER STOCKMANN: Yes, about the springs—an article you wrote during the winter?

DR. STOCKMANN: Oh, that one! In the first place, I don't want that one printed right now.

PETER STOCKMANN: No? It sounded to me like it would be very timely.

DR. STOCKMANN: Under normal conditions, maybe so. *He gets up and walks across the floor.*

PETER STOCKMANN, *looking after him*: Well, what is abnormal about the conditions now?

DR. STOCKMANN, *stopping*: I can't say for the moment, Peter—at least not tonight. There could be a great deal abnormal about conditions; then again, there could be nothing at all.

PETER STOCKMANN: Well, you've managed to sound mysterious. Is there anything wrong? Something you're keeping from me? Because I wish once in a while you'd remind yourself that I am chairman of the board for the springs.

DR. STOCKMANN: And I would like *you* to remember that, Peter. Look, let's not get into each other's hair.

PETER STOCKMANN: I don't make a habit of getting into people's hair! But I'd like to underline that everything concerning Kirsten Springs must be treated in a businesslike manner, through the proper channels, and dealt with by the legally constituted authorities. I can't allow anything done behind my back in a roundabout way.

DR. STOCKMANN: When did I ever go behind your back, Peter?

PETER STOCKMANN: You have an ingrained tendency to go your own way, Thomas, and that simply can't go on in a well-organized society. The individual really must subordinate himself to the over-all, or—*groping for words, he points to himself*—to the authorities who are in charge of the general welfare. *He gets up.*

DR. STOCKMANN: Well, that's probably so. But how the hell does that concern me, Peter?

PETER STOCKMANN: My dear Thomas, this is exactly what you will never learn. But you had better watch out because someday you might pay dearly for it. Now I've said it. Good-by.

DR. STOCKMANN: Are you out of your mind? You're absolutely on the wrong track.

PETER STOCKMANN: I am usually not. Anyway, may I be excused? *He nods toward the dining room.* Good-by, Catherine. Good evening, gentlemen. *He leaves.*

MRS. STOCKMANN, *entering the living room*: He left?

DR. STOCKMANN: And burned up!

MRS. STOCKMANN: What did you do to him now?

DR. STOCKMANN: What does he want from me? He can't expect me to give him an accounting of every move I make, every thought I think, until I am ready to do it.

MRS. STOCKMANN: Why? What should you give him an accounting of?

DR. STOCKMANN, *hesitantly*: Just leave that to me, Catherine. Peculiar the mailman didn't come today.

> *Hovstad, Billing, and Captain Horster have gotten up from the dining-room table and enter the living room. Ejlif and Morten come in a little later, Catherine exits.*

BILLING, *stretching out his arms*: After a meal like that, by God, I feel like a new man. This house is so—

HOVSTAD, *cutting him off*: The Mayor certainly wasn't in a glowing mood tonight.

DR. STOCKMANN: It's his stomach. He has a lousy digestion.

HOVSTAD: I think two editors from the *People's Daily Messenger* didn't help either.

DR. STOCKMANN: No, it's just that Peter is a lonely man. Poor fellow, all he knows is official business and duties, and then all that damn weak tea that he pours into himself. Catherine, may we have the toddy?

MRS. STOCKMANN, *calling from the dining room*: I'm just getting it.

DR. STOCKMANN: Sit down here on the couch with me, Captain Horster—a rare guest like you—sit here. Sit down, friends.

HORSTER: This used to be such an ugly house. Suddenly it's beautiful!

Billing and Hovstad sit down at the right. Mrs. Stockmann brings a tray with pot, glasses, bottles, etc., on it, and puts it on the table behind the couch.

BILLING, *to Horster, intimately, indicating Stockmann*: Great man!

MRS. STOCKMANN: Here you are. Help yourselves.

DR. STOCKMANN, *taking a glass*: We sure will. *He mixes the toddy.* And the cigars, Ejlif—you know where the box is. And Morten, get my pipe. *The boys go out to the left.* I have a sneaking suspicion that Ejlif is snitching a cigar now and then, but I don't pay any attention. Catherine, you know where I put it? Oh, he's got it. Good boys! *The boys bring the various things in.* Help yourselves, fellows. I'll stick to the pipe. This one's gone through plenty of blizzards with me up in the north. Skol! *He looks around.* Home! What an invention, heh?

The boys sit down on the bench near the windows.

MRS. STOCKMANN, *who has sat down and is now knitting*: Are you sailing soon, Captain Horster?

HORSTER: I expect to be ready next week.

MRS. STOCKMANN: And then to America, Captain?

HORSTER: Yes, that's the plan.

BILLING: Oh, then you won't be home for the new election?

HORSTER: Is there going to be another election?

BILLING: Didn't you know?

HORSTER: No, I don't get mixed up in those things.

BILLING: But you are interested in public affairs, aren't you?

HORSTER: Frankly, I don't understand a thing about it.

He does, really, although not very much. Captain Horster is one of the longest silent roles in dramatic literature, but he is not to be thought of as characterless therefor. It is not a bad thing to have a courageous, quiet man for a friend, even if it has gone out of fashion.

MRS. STOCKMANN, *sympathetically*: Neither do I, Captain. Maybe that's why I'm always so glad to see you.

BILLING: Just the same, you ought to vote, Captain.

HORSTER: Even if I don't understand anything about it?

BILLING: Understand! What do you mean by that? Society, Captain, is like a ship—every man should do something to help navigate the ship.

HORSTER: That may be all right on shore, but on board a ship it doesn't work out so well.

> *Petra in hat and coat and with textbooks and notebooks under her arm comes into the entrance hall. She is Ibsen's clear-eyed hope for the future—and probably ours. She is forthright, determined, and knows the meaning of work, which to her is the creation of good on the earth.*

PETRA, *from the hall*: Good evening.

DR. STOCKMANN, *warmly*: Good evening, Petra!

BILLING, *to Horster*: Great young woman!

> *There are mutual greetings. Petra removes her coat and hat and places the books on a chair in the entrance hall.*

PETRA, *entering the living room*: And here you are, lying around like lizards while I'm out slaving.

DR. STOCKMANN: Well, you come and be a lizard too. Come here, Petra, sit with me. I look at her and say to myself, "How did I do it?"

> *Petra goes over to her father and kisses him.*

BILLING: Shall I mix a toddy for you?

PETRA, *coming up to the table*: No, thanks, I had better do it myself—you always mix it too strong. Oh, Father, I forgot—I have a letter for you. *She goes to the chair where her books are.*

DR. STOCKMANN, *alerted*: Who's it from?

PETRA: I met the mailman on the way to school this morning and he gave me your mail too, and I just didn't have time to run back.

DR. STOCKMANN, *getting up and walking toward her*: And you don't give it to me until now!

PETRA: I really didn't have time to run back, Father.

MRS. STOCKMANN: If she didn't have time . . .

DR. STOCKMANN: Let's see it—come on, child! *He takes the letter and looks at the envelope.* Yes, indeed.

MRS. STOCKMANN: Is that the one you've been waiting for?

DR. STOCKMANN: I'll be right back. There wouldn't be a light on in my room, would there?

MRS. STOCKMANN: The lamp is on the desk, burning away.

DR. STOCKMANN: Please excuse me for a moment. *He goes into his study and quickly returns. Mrs. Stockmann hands him his glasses. He goes out again.*

PETRA: What is that, Mother?

MRS. STOCKMANN: I don't know. The last couple of days he's been asking again and again about the mailman.

BILLING: Probably an out-of-town patient of his.

PETRA: Poor Father, he's got much too much to do. *She mixes her drink.* This ought to taste good.

HOVSTAD: By the way, what happened to that English novel you were going to translate for us?

PETRA: I started it, but I've gotten so busy—

HOVSTAD: Oh, teaching evening school again?

PETRA: Two hours a night.

BILLING: Plus the high school every day?

PETRA, *sitting down on the couch*: Yes, five hours, and every night a pile of lessons to correct!

MRS. STOCKMANN: She never stops going.

HOVSTAD: Maybe that's why I always think of you as kind of breathless and—well, breathless.

PETRA: I love it. I get so wonderfully tired.

BILLING, *to Horster*: She looks tired.

MORTEN: You must be a wicked woman, Petra.

PETRA, *laughing*: Wicked?

MORTEN: You work so much. My teacher says that work is a punishment for our sins.

EJLIF: And you believe that?

MRS. STOCKMANN: Ejlif! Of course he believes his teacher!

BILLING, *smiling*: Don't stop him . . .

HOVSTAD: Don't you like to work, Morten?

MORTEN: Work? No.

HOVSTAD: Then what will you ever amount to in this world?

MORTEN: Me? I'm going to be a Viking.

EJLIF: You can't! You'd have to be a heathen!

MORTEN: So I'll be a heathen.

MRS. STOCKMANN: I think it's getting late, boys.

BILLING: I agree with you, Morten. I think—

MRS. STOCKMANN, *making signs to Billing*: You certainly don't, Mr. Billing.

BILLING: Yes, by God, I do. I am a real heathen and proud of it. You'll see, pretty soon we're all going to be heathens!

MORTEN: And then we can do anything we want!

BILLING: Right! You see, Morten—

MRS. STOCKMANN, *interrupting*: Don't you have any homework for tomorrow, boys? Better go in and do it.

EJLIF: Oh, can't we stay in here awhile?

MRS. STOCKMANN: No, neither of you. Now run along.

The boys say good night and go off at the left.

HOVSTAD: You really think it hurts them to listen to such talk?

MRS. STOCKMANN: I don't know, but I don't like it.

Dr. Stockmann enters from his study, an open letter in his hand. He is like a sleepwalker, astonished, engrossed. He walks toward the front door.

MRS. STOCKMANN: Tom!

He turns, suddenly aware of them.

DR. STOCKMANN: Boys, there is going to be news in this town!

BILLING: News?

MRS. STOCKMANN: What kind of news?

DR. STOCKMANN: A terrific discovery, Catherine.

HOVSTAD: Really?

MRS. STOCKMANN: That you made?

DR. STOCKMANN: That I made. *He walks back and forth.* Now let the baboons running this town call me a lunatic! Now they'd better watch out. Oh, how the mighty have fallen!

PETRA: What is it, Father?

DR. STOCKMANN: Oh, if Peter were only here! Now you'll see how human beings can walk around and make judgments like blind rats.

HOVSTAD: What in the world's happened, Doctor?

DR. STOCKMANN, *stopping at the table*: It's the general opinion, isn't it, that our town is a sound and healthy spot?

HOVSTAD: Of course.

MRS. STOCKMANN: What happened?

DR. STOCKMANN: Even a rather unusually healthy spot! Oh, God, a place that can be recommended not only to all people but to sick people!

MRS. STOCKMANN: But, Tom, what are you—

DR. STOCKMANN: And we certainly have recommended it. I myself have written and written, in the *People's Messenger*, pamphlets—

HOVSTAD: Yes, yes, but—

DR. STOCKMANN: The miraculous springs that cost such a fortune to build, the whole Health Institute, is a pesthole!

PETRA: Father! The springs? ⎫
                              ⎬ *Simultaneously*
MRS. STOCKMANN: Our springs? ⎭

BILLING: That's unbelievable!

DR. STOCKMANN: You know the filth up in Windmill Valley? That stuff that has such a stinking smell? It comes down from the tannery up there, and the same damn poisonous mess comes right out into the blessed, miraculous water we're supposed to *cure* people with!

HORSTER: You mean actually where our beaches are?

DR. STOCKMANN: Exactly.

HOVSTAD: How are you so sure about this, Doctor?

DR. STOCKMANN: I had a suspicion about it a long time ago—last year there were too many sick cases among the visitors, typhoid and gastric disturbances.

MRS. STOCKMANN: That did happen. I remember Mrs. Svensen's niece—

DR. STOCKMANN: Yes, dear. At the time we thought that the visitors brought the bug, but later this winter I got a new idea and I started investigating the water.

MRS. STOCKMANN: So that's what you've been working on!

DR. STOCKMANN: I sent samples of the water to the University for an exact chemical analysis.

HOVSTAD: And that's what you have just received?

DR. STOCKMANN, *waving the letter again*: This is it. It proves the existence of infectious organic matter in the water.

MRS. STOCKMANN: Well, thank God you discovered it in time.

DR. STOCKMANN: I think we can say that, Catherine.

MRS. STOCKMANN: Isn't it wonderful!

HOVSTAD: And what do you intend to do now, Doctor?

DR. STOCKMANN: Put the thing right, of course.

HOVSTAD: Do you think that can be done?

DR. STOCKMANN: Maybe. If not, the whole Institute is useless. But there's nothing to worry about—I am quite clear on what has to be done.

MRS. STOCKMANN: But, Tom, why did you keep it so secret?

DR. STOCKMANN: What did you want me to do? Go out and shoot my mouth off before I really knew? *He walks around, rubbing his hands.* You don't realize what this means, Catherine—the whole water system has got to be changed.

MRS. STOCKMANN: The *whole* water system?

DR. STOCKMANN: The whole water system. The intake is too low, it's got to be raised to a much higher spot. The whole construction's got to be ripped out!

PETRA: Well, Father, at last you can prove they should have listened to you!

DR. STOCKMANN: Ha, she remembers!

MRS. STOCKMANN: That's right, you did warn them—

DR. STOCKMANN: Of course I warned them. When they started the damned thing I told them not to build it down there! But who am I, a mere scientist, to tell politicians where to build a health institute! Well, now they're going to get it, both barrels!

BILLING: This is tremendous! *To Horster*: He's a great man!

DR. STOCKMANN: It's bigger than tremendous. *He starts toward his study.* Wait'll they see this! *He stops.* Petra, my report is on my desk . . . *Petra goes into his study.* An envelope, Catherine! *She goes for it.* Gentlemen, this final proof from the University—*Petra comes out with the report, which he takes*—and my report—*he flicks the pages*—five solid, explosive pages . . .

MRS. STOCKMANN, *handing him an envelope*: Is this big enough?

DR. STOCKMANN: Fine. Right to the Board of Directors! *He inserts the report, seals the envelope, and hands it to Catherine.* Will you give this to the maid— What's her name again?

MRS. STOCKMANN: Randine, dear, Randine.

DR. STOCKMANN: Tell our darling Randine to wipe her nose and run over to the Mayor right now.

    Mrs. Stockmann just stands there looking at him.

DR. STOCKMANN: What's the matter, dear?

MRS. STOCKMANN: I don't know . . .

PETRA: What's Uncle Peter going to say about this?

MRS. STOCKMANN: That's what I'm wondering.

DR. STOCKMANN: What can he say! He ought to be damn glad that such an important fact is brought out before we start an epidemic! Hurry, dear!

    Catherine exits at the left.

HOVSTAD: I would like to put a brief item about this discovery in the *Messenger*.

DR. STOCKMANN: Go ahead. I'd really be grateful for that now.

HOVSTAD: Because the public ought to know soon.

DR. STOCKMANN: Right away.

BILLING: By God, you'll be the leading man in this town, Doctor.

DR. STOCKMANN, *walking around with an air of satisfaction*: Oh, there was nothing to it. Every detective gets a lucky break once in his life. But just the same I—

BILLING: Hovstad, don't you think the town ought to pay Dr. Stockmann some tribute?

DR. STOCKMANN: Oh, no, no . . .

HOVSTAD: Sure, let's all put in a word for—

BILLING: I'll talk to Aslaksen about it!

Catherine enters.

DR. STOCKMANN: No, no, fellows, no fooling around! I won't put up with any commotion. Even if the Board of Directors wants to give me an increase I won't take it—I just won't take it, Catherine.

MRS. STOCKMANN, *dutifully*: That's right, Tom.

PETRA, *lifting her glass*: Skol, Father!

EVERYBODY: Skol, Doctor!

HORSTER: Doctor, I hope this will bring you great honor and pleasure.

DR. STOCKMANN: Thanks, friends, thanks. There's one blessing above all others. To have earned the respect of one's neighbors is—is— Catherine, I'm going to dance!

> *He grabs his wife and whirls her around. There are shouts and struggles, general commotion. The boys in nightgowns stick their heads through the doorway at the right, wondering what is going on. Mrs. Stockmann, seeing them, breaks away and chases them upstairs as*

THE CURTAIN FALLS.

SCENE II

> *Dr. Stockmann's living room the following morning. As the curtain rises, Mrs. Stockmann comes in from the dining room, a sealed letter in her hand. She goes to the study door and peeks in.*

MRS. STOCKMANN: Are you there, Tom?

DR. STOCKMANN, *from within*: I just got in. *He enters the living room.* What's up?

MRS. STOCKMANN: From Peter. It just came. *She hands him the envelope.*

DR. STOCKMANN: Oh, let's see. *He opens the letter and reads*: "I am returning herewith the report you submitted . . ." *He continues to read, mumbling to himself.*

MRS. STOCKMANN: Well, what does he say? Don't stand there!

DR. STOCKMANN, *putting the letter in his pocket*: He just says he'll come around this afternoon.

MRS. STOCKMANN: Oh. Well, maybe you ought to try to remember to be home then.

DR. STOCKMANN: Oh, I sure will. I'm through with my morning visits anyway.

MRS. STOCKMANN: I'm dying to see how he's going to take it.

DR. STOCKMANN: Why, is there any doubt? He'll probably make it look like he made the discovery, not I.

MRS. STOCKMANN: But aren't you a little bit afraid of that?

DR. STOCKMANN: Oh, underneath he'll be happy, Catherine. It's just that Peter is so afraid that somebody else is going to do something good for this town.

MRS. STOCKMANN: I wish you'd go out of your way and share the honors with him. Couldn't we say that he put you on the right track or something?

DR. STOCKMANN: Oh, I don't mind—as long as it makes everybody happy.

Morten Kiil sticks his head through the doorway. He looks around searchingly and chuckles. He will continue chuckling until he leaves the house. He is the archetype of the little twinkle-eyed man who sneaks into so much of Ibsen's work. He will chuckle you right over the precipice. He is the dealer, the man with the rat's finely tuned brain. But he is sometimes likable because he is without morals and announces the fact by laughing.

KIIL, *slyly*: Is it really true?

MRS. STOCKMANN, *walking toward him*: Father!

DR. STOCKMANN: Well, good morning!

MRS. STOCKMANN: Come on in.

KIIL: It better be true or I'm going.

DR. STOCKMANN: What had better be true?

KIIL: This crazy story about the water system. Is it true?

MRS. STOCKMANN: Of course it's true! How did you find out about it?

KIIL: Petra came flying by on her way to school this morning.

DR. STOCKMANN: Oh, she did?

KIIL: Ya. I thought she was trying to make a fool out of me—

MRS. STOCKMANN: Now why would she do that?

KIIL: Nothing gives more pleasure to young people than to make fools out of old people. But this is true, eh?

DR. STOCKMANN: Of course it's true. Sit down here. It's pretty lucky for the town, eh?

KIIL, *fighting his laughter*: Lucky for the town!

DR. STOCKMANN: I mean, that I made the discovery before it was too late.

KIIL: Tom, I never thought you had the imagination to pull your own brother's leg like this.

DR. STOCKMANN: Pull his leg?

MRS. STOCKMANN: But, Father, he's not—

KIIL: How does it go now, let me get it straight. There's some kind of— like cockroaches in the waterpipes—

DR. STOCKMANN, *laughing*: No, not cockroaches.

KIIL: Well, some kind of little animals.

MRS. STOCKMANN: Bacteria, Father.

KIIL, *who can barely speak through his laughter*: Ah, but a whole mess of them, eh?

DR. STOCKMANN: Oh, there'd be millions and millions.

KIIL: And nobody can see them but you, is that it?

DR. STOCKMANN: Yes, that's—well, of course anybody with a micro— *He breaks off.* What are you laughing at?

MRS. STOCKMANN, *smiling at Kiil*: You don't understand, Father. Nobody can actually see bacteria, but that doesn't mean they're not there.

KIIL: Good girl, you stick with him! By God, this is the best thing I ever heard in my life!

DR. STOCKMANN, *smiling*: What do you mean?

KIIL: But tell me, you think you are actually going to get your brother to believe this?

DR. STOCKMANN: Well, we'll see soon enough!

KIIL: You really think he's that crazy?

DR. STOCKMANN: I hope the whole town will be that crazy, Morten.

KIIL: Ya, they probably are, and it'll serve them right too—they think they're so much smarter than us old-timers. Your good brother ordered them to bounce me out of the council, so they chased me out like a dog! Make jackasses out of all of them, Stockmann!

DR. STOCKMANN: Yes, but, Morten—

KIIL: Long-eared, short-tailed jackasses! *He gets up.* Stockmann, if you can make the Mayor and his elegant friends grab at this bait, I will give a couple of hundred crowns to charity, and right now, right on the spot.

DR. STOCKMANN: Well, that would be very kind of you, but I'm—

KIIL: I haven't got much to play around with, but if you can pull the rug out from under him with this cockroach business, I'll give at least fifty crowns to some poor people on Christmas Eve. Maybe this'll teach them to put some brains back in Town Hall!

Hovstad enters from the hall.

HOVSTAD: Good morning! Oh, pardon me . . .

KIIL, *enjoying this proof immensely*: Oh, this one is in on it too?

HOVSTAD: What's that, sir?

DR. STOCKMANN: Of course he's in on it.

KIIL: Couldn't I have guessed that! And it's going to be in the papers, I suppose. You're sure tying down the corners, aren't you? Well, lay it on thick. I've got to go.

DR. STOCKMANN: Oh, no, stay awhile, let me explain it to you!

KIIL: Oh, I get it, don't worry! Only you can see them, heh? That's the best idea I've ever—damn it, you shouldn't do this for nothing! *He goes toward the hall.*

MRS. STOCKMANN, *following him out, laughing*: But, Father, you don't understand about bacteria.

DR. STOCKMANN, *laughing*: The old badger doesn't believe a word of it.

HOVSTAD: What does he think you're doing?

DR. STOCKMANN: Making an idiot out of my brother—imagine that?

HOVSTAD: You got a few minutes?

DR. STOCKMANN: Sure, as long as you like.

HOVSTAD: Have you heard from the Mayor?

DR. STOCKMANN: Only that he's coming over later.

HOVSTAD: I've been thinking about this since last night—

DR. STOCKMANN: Don't say?

HOVSTAD: For you as a medical man, a scientist, this is a really rare opportunity. But I've been wondering if you realize that it ties in with a lot of other things.

DR. STOCKMANN: How do you mean? Sit down. *They sit at the right.* What are you driving at?

HOVSTAD: You said last night that the pollution comes from impurities in the ground—

DR. STOCKMANN: It comes from the poisonous dump up in Windmill Valley.

HOVSTAD: Doctor, I think it comes from an entirely different dump.

DR. STOCKMANN: What do you mean?

HOVSTAD, *with growing zeal*: The same dump that is poisoning and polluting our whole social life in this town.

DR. STOCKMANN: For God's sake, Hovstad, what are you babbling about?

HOVSTAD: Everything that matters in this town has fallen into the hands of a few bureaucrats.

DR. STOCKMANN: Well, they're not all bureaucrats—

HOVSTAD: They're all rich, all with old reputable names, and they've got everything in the palm of their hands.

DR. STOCKMANN: Yes, but they happen to have ability and knowledge.

HOVSTAD: Did they show ability and knowledge when they built the water system where they did?

DR. STOCKMANN: No, of course not, but that happened to be a blunder, and we'll clear it up now.

HOVSTAD: You really imagine it's going to be as easy as all that?

DR. STOCKMANN: Easy or not easy, it's got to be done.

HOVSTAD: Doctor, I've made up my mind to give this whole scandal very special treatment.

DR. STOCKMANN: Now wait. You can't call it a scandal yet.

HOVSTAD: Doctor, when I took over the *People's Messenger* I swore I'd blow that smug cabal of old, stubborn, self-satisfied fogies to bits. This is the story that can do it.

DR. STOCKMANN: But I still think we owe them a deep debt of gratitude for building the springs.

HOVSTAD: The Mayor being your brother, I wouldn't ordinarily want to touch it, but I know you'd never let that kind of thing obstruct the truth.

DR. STOCKMANN: Of course not, but . . .

HOVSTAD: I want you to understand me. I don't have to tell you I come from a simple family. I know in my bones what the underdog needs—he's got to have a say in the government of society. That's what brings out ability, intelligence, and self-respect in people.

DR. STOCKMANN: I understand that, but . . .

HOVSTAD: I think a newspaperman who turns down any chance to give the underdog a lift is taking on a responsibility that I don't want. I know perfectly well that in fancy circles they call it agitation, and they can call it anything they like if it makes them happy, but I have my own conscience—

DR. STOCKMANN, *interrupting*: I agree with you, Hovstad, but this is just the water supply and— *There is a knock on the door.* Damn it! Come in!

Mr. Aslaksen, the publisher, enters from the hall. He is simply but neatly dressed. He wears gloves and carries a hat and an umbrella in his hand. He is so utterly drawn it is unnecessary to say anything at all about him.

ASLAKSEN: I beg your pardon, Doctor, if I intrude . . .

HOVSTAD, *standing up*: Are you looking for me, Aslaksen?

ASLAKSEN: No, I didn't know you were here. I want to see the Doctor.

DR. STOCKMANN: What can I do for you?

ASLAKSEN: Is it true, Doctor, what I hear from Mr. Billing, that you intend to campaign for a better water system?

DR. STOCKMANN: Yes, for the Institute. But it's not a campaign.

ASLAKSEN: I just wanted to call and tell you that we are behind you a hundred per cent.

HOVSTAD, *to Dr. Stockmann*: There, you see!

DR. STOCKMANN: Mr. Aslaksen, I thank you with all my heart. But you see—

ASLAKSEN: We can be important, Doctor. When the little businessman wants to push something through, he turns out to be the majority, you know, and it's always good to have the majority on your side.

DR. STOCKMANN: That's certainly true, but I don't understand what this is all about. It seems to me it's a simple, straightforward business. The water—

ASLAKSEN: Of course we intend to behave with moderation, Doctor. I always try to be a moderate and careful man.

DR. STOCKMANN: You are known for that, Mr. Aslaksen, but—

ASLAKSEN: The water system is very important to us little businessmen, Doctor. Kirsten Springs are becoming a gold mine for this town, especially for the property owners, and that is why, in my capacity as chairman of the Property Owners Association—

DR. STOCKMANN: Yes.

ASLAKSEN: And furthermore, as a representative of the Temperance Society— You probably know, Doctor, that I am active for prohibition.

DR. STOCKMANN: So I have heard.

ASLAKSEN: As a result, I come into contact with all kinds of people, and since I am known to be a law-abiding and solid citizen, I have a certain influence in this town—you might even call it a little power.

DR. STOCKMANN: I know that very well, Mr. Aslaksen.

ASLAKSEN: That's why you can see that it would be practically nothing for me to arrange a demonstration.

DR. STOCKMANN: Demonstration! What are you going to demonstrate about?

ASLAKSEN: The citizens of the town complimenting you for bringing this important matter to everybody's attention. Obviously it would have to be done with the utmost moderation so as not to hurt the authorities.

HOVSTAD: This could knock the big-bellies right into the garbage can!

ASLAKSEN: No indiscretion or extreme aggressiveness toward the authorities, Mr. Hovstad! I don't want any wild-eyed radicalism on this thing. I've had enough of that in my time, and no good ever comes of it. But for a good solid citizen to express his calm, frank, and free opinion is something nobody can deny.

DR. STOCKMANN, *shaking the publisher's hand*: My dear Aslaksen, I can't tell you how it heartens me to hear this kind of support. I am happy—I really am—I'm happy. Listen! Wouldn't you like a glass of sherry?

ASLAKSEN: I am a member of the Temperance Society. I—

DR. STOCKMANN: Well, how about a glass of beer?

ASLAKSEN, *considers, then*: I don't think I can go quite that far, Doctor. I never take anything. Well, good day, and I want you to remember that the little man is behind you like a wall.

DR. STOCKMANN: Thank you.

ASLAKSEN: You have the solid majority on your side, because when the little—

DR. STOCKMANN, *trying to stop Aslaksen's talk*: Thanks for that, Mr. Aslaksen, and good day.

ASLAKSEN: Are you going back to the printing shop, Mr. Hovstad?

HOVSTAD: I just have a thing or two to attend to here.

ASLAKSEN: Very well. *He leaves.*

HOVSTAD: Well, what do you say to a little hypodermic for these fence-sitting deadheads?

DR. STOCKMANN, *surprised*: Why? I think Aslaksen is a very sincere man.

HOVSTAD: Isn't it time we pumped some guts into these well-intentioned men of good will? Under all their liberal talk they still idolize authority, and that's got to be rooted out of this town. This blunder of the water system has to be made clear to every voter. Let me print your report.

DR. STOCKMANN: Not until I talk to my brother.

HOVSTAD: I'll write an editorial in the meantime, and if the Mayor won't go along with us—

DR. STOCKMANN: I don't see how you can imagine such a thing!

HOVSTAD: Believe me, Doctor, it's possible, and then—

DR. STOCKMANN: Listen, I promise you: he will go along, and then you can print my report, every word of it.

HOVSTAD: On your word of honor?

DR. STOCKMANN, *giving Hovstad the manuscript*: Here it is. Take it. It can't do any harm for you to read it. Return it to me later.

HOVSTAD: Good day, Doctor.

DR. STOCKMANN: Good day. You'll see, it's going to be easier than you think, Hovstad!

HOVSTAD: I hope so, Doctor. Sincerely. Let me know as soon as you hear from His Honor. *He leaves.*

DR. STOCKMANN, *goes to dining room and looks in*: Catherine! Oh, you're home already, Petra!

PETRA, *coming in*: I just got back from school.

MRS. STOCKMANN, *entering*: Hasn't he been here yet?

DR. STOCKMANN: Peter? No, but I just had a long chat with Hovstad. He's really fascinated with my discovery, and you know, it has more implications than I thought at first. Do you know what I have backing me up?

MRS. STOCKMANN: What in heaven's name have you got backing you up?

DR. STOCKMANN: The solid majority.

MRS. STOCKMANN: Is that good?

DR. STOCKMANN: Good? It's wonderful. You can't imagine the feeling, Catherine, to know that your own town feels like a brother to you. I have never felt so at home in this town since I was a boy. *A noise is heard.*

MRS. STOCKMANN: That must be the front door.

DR. STOCKMANN: Oh, it's Peter then. Come in.

PETER STOCKMANN, *entering from the hall*: Good morning!

DR. STOCKMANN: It's nice to see you, Peter.

MRS. STOCKMANN: Good morning. How are you today?

PETER STOCKMANN: Well, so so. *To Dr. Stockmann*: I received your thesis about the condition of the springs yesterday.

DR. STOCKMANN: I got your note. Did you read it?

PETER STOCKMANN: I read it.

DR. STOCKMANN: Well, what do you have to say?

> *Peter Stockmann clears his throat and glances at the women.*

MRS. STOCKMANN: Come on, Petra. *She and Petra leave the room at the left.*

PETER STOCKMANN, *after a moment*: Thomas, was it really necessary to go into this investigation behind my back?

DR. STOCKMANN: Yes. Until I was convinced myself, there was no point in—

PETER STOCKMANN: And now you are convinced?

DR. STOCKMANN: Well, certainly. Aren't you too, Peter? *Pause.* The University chemists corroborated . . .

PETER STOCKMANN: You intend to present this document to the Board of Directors, officially, as the medical officer of the springs?

DR. STOCKMANN: Of course, something's got to be done, and quick.

PETER STOCKMANN: You always use such strong expressions, Thomas. Among other things, in your report you say that we *guarantee* our guests and visitors a permanent case of poisoning.

DR. STOCKMANN: But Peter, how can you describe it any other way? Imagine! Poisoned internally and externally!

PETER STOCKMANN: So you merrily conclude that we must build a waste-disposal plant—and reconstruct a brand-new water system from the bottom up!

DR. STOCKMANN: Well, do you know some other way out? I don't.

PETER STOCKMANN: I took a little walk over to the city engineer this morning and in the course of conversation I sort of jokingly mentioned these changes—as something we might consider for the future, you know.

DR. STOCKMANN: The future won't be soon enough, Peter.

PETER STOCKMANN: The engineer kind of smiled at my extravagance and gave me a few facts. I don't suppose you have taken the trouble to consider what your proposed changes would cost?

DR. STOCKMANN: No, I never thought of that.

PETER STOCKMANN: Naturally. Your little project would come to at least three hundred thousand crowns.

DR. STOCKMANN, *astonished*: That expensive!

PETER STOCKMANN: Oh, don't look so upset—it's only money. The worst thing is that it would take some two years.

DR. STOCKMANN: Two years?

PETER STOCKMANN: At the least. And what do you propose we do about the springs in the meantime? Shut them up, no doubt! Because we would have to, you know. As soon as the rumor gets around that the water is dangerous, we won't have a visitor left. So that's the picture, Thomas. You have it in your power literally to ruin your own town.

DR. STOCKMANN: Now look, Peter! I don't want to ruin anything.

PETER STOCKMANN: Kirsten Springs are the blood supply of this town, Thomas—the only future we've got here. Now will you stop and think?

DR. STOCKMANN: Good God! Well, what do you think we ought to do?

PETER STOCKMANN: Your report has not convinced me that the conditions are as dangerous as you try to make them.

DR. STOCKMANN: Now listen; they are even worse than the report makes them out to be. Remember, summer is coming, and the warm weather!

PETER STOCKMANN: I think you're exaggerating. A capable physician ought to know what precautions to take.

DR. STOCKMANN: And what then?

PETER STOCKMANN: The existing water supply for the springs is a fact, Thomas, and has got to be treated as a fact. If you are reasonable and act with discretion, the directors of the Institute will be inclined to take under consideration any means to make possible improvements, reasonably and without financial sacrifices.

DR. STOCKMANN: Peter, do you imagine that I would ever agree to such trickery?

PETER STOCKMANN: Trickery?

DR. STOCKMANN: Yes, a trick, a fraud, a lie! A treachery, a downright crime, against the public and against the whole community!

PETER STOCKMANN: I said before that I am not convinced that there is any actual danger.

DR. STOCKMANN: Oh, you aren't? Anything else is impossible! My report is an absolute fact. The only trouble is that you and your administration were the ones who insisted that the water supply be built where it is, and now you're afraid to admit the blunder you committed. Damn it! Don't you think I can see through it all?

PETER STOCKMANN: All right, let's suppose that's true. Maybe I do care a little about my reputation. I still say I do it for the good of the town— without moral authority there can be no government. And that is why, Thomas, it is my duty to prevent your report from reaching the Board. Some time later I will bring up the matter for discussion. In the meantime, not a single word is to reach the public.

DR. STOCKMANN: Oh, my dear Peter, do you imagine you can prevent that!

PETER STOCKMANN: It will be prevented.

DR. STOCKMANN: It can't be. There are too many people who already know about it.

PETER STOCKMANN, *angered*: Who? It can't possibly be those people from the *Daily Messenger* who—

DR. STOCKMANN: Exactly. The liberal, free, and independent press will stand up and do its duty!

PETER STOCKMANN: You are an unbelievably irresponsible man, Thomas! Can't you imagine what consequences that is going to have for you?

DR. STOCKMANN: For me?

PETER STOCKMANN: Yes, for you and your family.

DR. STOCKMANN: What the hell are you saying now!

PETER STOCKMANN: I believe I have the right to think of myself as a helpful brother, Thomas.

DR. STOCKMANN: You have been, and I thank you deeply for it.

PETER STOCKMANN: Don't mention it. I often couldn't help myself. I had hoped that by improving your finances I would be able to keep you from running completely hog wild.

DR. STOCKMANN: You mean it was only for your own sake?

PETER STOCKMANN: Partly, yes. What do you imagine people think of an official whose closest relatives get themselves into trouble time and time again?

DR. STOCKMANN: And that's what I have done?

PETER STOCKMANN: You do it without knowing it. You're like a man with an automatic brain—as soon as an idea breaks into your head, no matter how idiotic it may be, you get up like a sleepwalker and start writing a pamphlet about it.

DR. STOCKMANN: Peter, don't you think it's a citizen's duty to share a new idea with the public?

PETER STOCKMANN: The public doesn't need new ideas—the public is much better off with old ideas.

DR. STOCKMANN: You're not even embarrassed to say that?

PETER STOCKMANN: Now look, I'm going to lay this out once and for all. You're always barking about authority. If a man gives you an order he's persecuting you. Nothing is important enough to respect once you decide to revolt against your superiors. All right then, I give up. I'm not going to try to change you any more. I told you the stakes you are playing for here, and now I am going to give you an order. And I warn you, you had better obey it if you value your career.

DR. STOCKMANN: What kind of an order?

PETER STOCKMANN: You are going to deny these rumors officially.

DR. STOCKMANN: How?

PETER STOCKMANN: You simply say that you went into the examination of the water more thoroughly and you find that you overestimated the danger.

DR. STOCKMANN: I see.

PETER STOCKMANN: And that you have complete confidence that what-ever improvements are needed, the management will certainly take care of them.

DR. STOCKMANN, *after a pause*: My convictions come from the condition of the water. My convictions will change when the water changes, and for no other reason.

PETER STOCKMANN: What are you talking about convictions? You're an official, you keep your convictions to yourself!

DR. STOCKMANN: To myself?

PETER STOCKMANN: As an official, I said. God knows, as a private person that's something else, but as a subordinate employee of the Institute, you have no right to express any convictions or personal opinions about any-thing connected with policy.

DR. STOCKMANN: Now you listen to me. I am a doctor and a scientist—

PETER STOCKMANN: This has nothing to do with science!

DR. STOCKMANN: Peter, I have the right to express my opinion on any-thing in the world!

PETER STOCKMANN: Not about the Institute—that I forbid.

DR. STOCKMANN: You forbid!

PETER STOCKMANN: I forbid you as your superior, and when I give orders you obey.

DR. STOCKMANN: Peter, if you weren't my brother—

PETRA, *throwing the door at the left open*: Father! You aren't going to stand for this! *She enters.*

MRS. STOCKMANN, *coming in after her*: Petra, Petra!

PETER STOCKMANN: What have you two been doing, eavesdropping?

MRS. STOCKMANN: You were talking so loud we couldn't help . . .

PETRA: Yes, I was eavesdropping!

PETER STOCKMANN: That makes me very happy.

DR. STOCKMANN, *approaching his brother*: You said something to me about forbidding—

PETER STOCKMANN: You forced me to.

DR. STOCKMANN: So you want me to spit in my own face officially—is that it?

PETER STOCKMANN: Why must you always be so colorful?

DR. STOCKMANN: And if I don't obey?

PETER STOCKMANN: Then we will publish our own statement, to calm the public.

DR. STOCKMANN: Good enough! And I will write against you. I will stick to what I said, and I will prove that I am right and that you are wrong, and what will you do then?

PETER STOCKMANN: Then I simply won't be able to prevent your dismissal.

DR. STOCKMANN: What!

PETRA: Father!

PETER STOCKMANN: Dismissed from the Institute is what I said. If you want to make war on Kirsten Springs, you have no right to be on the Board of Directors.

DR. STOCKMANN, *after a pause*: You'd dare to do that?

PETER STOCKMANN: Oh, no, you're the daring man.

PETRA: Uncle, this is a rotten way to treat a man like Father!

MRS. STOCKMANN: Will you be quiet, Petra!

PETER STOCKMANN: So young and you've got opinions already—but that's natural. *To Mrs. Stockmann*: Catherine dear, you're probably the only sane person in this house. Knock some sense into his head, will you? Make him realize what he's driving his whole family into.

DR. STOCKMANN: My family concerns nobody but myself.

PETER STOCKMANN: His family and his own town.

DR. STOCKMANN: I'm going to show you who loves his town. The people are going to get the full stink of this corruption, Peter, and then we will see who loves his town!

PETER STOCKMANN: You love your town when you blindly, spitefully, stubbornly go ahead trying to cut off our most important industry?

DR. STOCKMANN: That source is poisoned, man. We are getting fat by peddling filth and corruption to innocent people!

PETER STOCKMANN: I think this has gone beyond opinions and convictions, Thomas. A man who can throw that kind of insinuation around is nothing but a traitor to society!

DR. STOCKMANN, *starting toward his brother in a fury*: How dare you to—

MRS. STOCKMANN, *stepping between them*: Tom!

PETRA, *grabbing her father's arm*: Be careful, Father!

PETER STOCKMANN, *with dignity*: I won't expose myself to violence. You have been warned. Consider what you owe yourself and your family! Good day! *He exits.*

DR. STOCKMANN, *walking up and down*: He's insulted. *He's* insulted!

MRS. STOCKMANN: It's shameful, Tom.

PETRA: Oh, I would love to give him a piece of my mind!

DR. STOCKMANN: It was my own fault! I should have shown my teeth right from the beginning. He called me a traitor to society. Me! Damn it all, that's not going to stick!

MRS. STOCKMANN: Please, think! He's got all the power on his side.

DR. STOCKMANN: Yes, but I have the truth on mine.

MRS. STOCKMANN: Without power, what good is the truth?

PETRA: Mother, how can you say such a thing?

DR. STOCKMANN: That's ridiculous, Catherine. I have the liberal press with me, and the majority. If that isn't power, what is?

MRS. STOCKMANN: But, for heaven's sake, Tom, you aren't going to—

DR. STOCKMANN: What am I not going to do?

MRS. STOCKMANN: You aren't going to fight it out in public with your brother!

DR. STOCKMANN: What the hell else do you want me to do?

MRS. STOCKMANN: But it won't do you any earthly good. If they won't do it, they won't. All you'll get out of it is a notice that you're fired.

DR. STOCKMANN: I am going to do my duty, Catherine. Me, the man he calls a traitor to society!

MRS. STOCKMANN: And how about your duty toward your family—the people you're supposed to provide for?

PETRA: Don't always think of us first, Mother.

MRS. STOCKMANN, *to Petra*: You can talk! If worst comes to worst, you can manage for yourself. But what about the boys, Tom, and you and me?

DR. STOCKMANN: What about you? You want me to be the miserable animal who'd crawl up the boots of that damn gang? Will you be happy if I can't face myself the rest of my life?

MRS. STOCKMANN: Tom, Tom, there's so much injustice in the world! You've simply got to learn to live with it. If you go on this way, God help us, we'll have no money again. Is it so long since the north that you've forgotten what it was to live like we lived? Haven't we had enough of that for one lifetime? *The boys enter.* What will happen to them? We've got nothing if you're fired!

DR. STOCKMANN: Stop it! *He looks at the boys.* Well, boys, did you learn anything in school today?

MORTEN, *looking at them, puzzled*: We learned what an insect is.

DR. STOCKMANN: You don't say!

MORTEN: What happened here? Why is everybody—

DR. STOCKMANN: Nothing, nothing. You know what I'm going to do, boys? From now on I'm going to teach you what a man is. *He looks at Mrs. Stockmann. She cries as*

THE CURTAIN FALLS.

ACT TWO

SCENE I

The editorial office of the People's Daily Messenger. *At the back of the room, to the left, is a door leading to the printing room. Near it, in the left wall, is another door. At the right of the stage is the entrance door. In the middle of the room there is a large table covered with papers, newspapers, and books. Around it are a few chairs. A writing desk stands against the right wall. The room is dingy and cheerless, the furniture shabby.*

As the curtain rises, Billing is sitting at the desk, reading the manuscript. Hovstad comes in after a moment from the printing room. Billing looks up.

BILLING: The Doctor not come yet?

HOVSTAD: No, not yet. You finish it?

Billing holds up a hand to signal "just a moment." He reads on, the last paragraph of the manuscript. Hovstad comes and stands over him, reading with him. Now Billing closes the manuscript, glances up at Hovstad with some trepidation, then looks off. Hovstad, looking at Billing, walks a few steps away.

HOVSTAD: Well? What do you think of it?

BILLING, *with some hesitation*: It's devastating. The Doctor is a brilliant man. I swear, I myself never really understood how incompetent those fat fellows are, on top. *He picks up the manuscript and waves it a little.* I hear the rumble of revolution in this.

HOVSTAD, *looking toward the door*: Sssh! Aslaksen's inside.

BILLING: Aslaksen's a coward. With all that moderation talk, all he's saying is, he's yellow. You're going to print this, aren't you?

HOVSTAD: Sure, I'm just waiting for the Doctor to give the word. If his brother hasn't given in, we put it on the press anyway.

BILLING: Yes, but if the Mayor's against this it's going to get pretty rough. You know that, don't you?

HOVSTAD: Just let him try to block the reconstruction—the little business-men and the whole town'll be screaming for his head. Aslaksen'll see to that.

BILLING, *ecstatically*: The stockholders'll have to lay out'a fortune of money if this goes through!

HOVSTAD: My boy, I think it's going to bust them. And when the springs go busted, the people are finally going to understand the level of genius that's been running this town. Those five sheets of paper are going to put in a liberal administration once and for all.

BILLING: It's a revolution. You know that? *With hope and fear*: I mean it, we're on the edge of a real revolution!

DR. STOCKMANN, *entering*: Put it on the press!

HOVSTAD, *excited*: Wonderful! What did the Mayor say?

DR. STOCKMANN: The Mayor has declared war, so war is what it's going to be! *He takes the manuscript from Billing.* And this is only the beginning! You know what he tried to do?

BILLING, *calling into the printing room*: Mr. Aslaksen, the Doctor's here!

DR. STOCKMANN, *continuing*: He actually tried to blackmail me! He's got the nerve to tell me that I'm not allowed to speak my mind without his permission! Imagine the shameless effrontery!

HOVSTAD: He actually said it right out?

DR. STOCKMANN: Right to my face! The trouble with me was I kept giving them credit for being our kind of people, but they're dictators! They're peo-ple who'll try to hold power even if they have to poison the town to do it.

> *Toward the last part of Dr. Stockmann's speech Aslaksen enters.*

ASLAKSEN: Now take it easy, Doctor, you—you mustn't always be throw-ing accusations. I'm with you, you understand, but moderation—

DR. STOCKMANN, *cutting him off*: What'd you think of the article, Hovstad?

HOVSTAD: It's a masterpiece. In one blow you've managed to prove beyond any doubt what kind of men are running us.

ASLAKSEN: May we print it now, then?

DR. STOCKMANN: I should say *so*!

HOVSTAD: We'll have it ready for tomorrow's paper.

DR. STOCKMANN: And listen, Mr. Aslaksen, do me a favor, will you? You run a fine paper, but supervise the printing personally, eh? I'd hate to see the weather report stuck into the middle of my article.

ASLAKSEN, *laughing*: Don't worry, that won't happen this time!

DR. STOCKMANN: Make it perfect, eh? Like you were printing money. You can't imagine how I'm dying to see it in print. After all the lies in the papers, the half-lies, the quarter-lies—to finally see the absolute, unvarnished truth about something important. And this is only the beginning. We'll go on to other subjects and blow up every lie we live by! What do you say, Aslaksen?

ASLAKSEN, *nodding in agreement*: But just remember . . .

BILLING *and* HOVSTAD *together with* ASLAKSEN: Moderation!

ASLAKSEN, *to Billing and Hovstad*: I don't know what's so funny about that!

BILLING, *enthralled*: Doctor Stockmann, I feel as though I were standing in some historic painting. Goddammit, this is a historic day! Someday this scene'll be in a museum, entitled, "The Day the Truth Was Born."

DR. STOCKMANN, *suddenly*: Oh! I've got a patient half-bandaged down the street. *He leaves.*

HOVSTAD, *to Aslaksen*: I hope you realize how useful he could be to us.

ASLAKSEN: I don't like that business about "this is only the beginning." Let him stick to the springs.

BILLING: What makes you so scared all the time?

ASLAKSEN: I have to live here. It'd be different if he were attacking the national government or something, but if he thinks I'm going to start going after the whole town administration—

BILLING: What's the difference? Bad is bad!

ASLAKSEN: Yes, but there is a difference. You attack the national government, what's going to happen? Nothing. They go right on. But a town administration—they're liable to be overthrown or something! I represent the small property owners in this town—

BILLING: Ha! It's always the same. Give a man a little property and the truth can go to hell!

ASLAKSEN: Mr. Billing, I'm older than you are. I've seen fire-eaters before. You know who used to work at that desk before you? Councilman Stensford—*councilman*!

BILLING: Just because I work at a renegade's desk, does that mean—

ASLAKSEN: You're a politician. A politician never knows where he's going to end up. And besides you applied for a job as secretary to the Magistrate, didn't you?

HOVSTAD, *surprised, laughs*: Billing!

BILLING, *to Hovstad*: Well, why not? If I get it I'll have a chance to put across some good things. I could put plenty of big boys on the spot with a job like that!

ASLAKSEN: All right, I'm just saying. *He goes to the printing-room door.* People change. Just remember when you call me a coward—I may not have made the hot speeches, but I never went back on my beliefs either. Unlike some of the big radicals around here, I didn't change. Of course, I *am* a little more moderate, but moderation is—

HOVSTAD: Oh, God!

ASLAKSEN: I don't see what's so funny about that! *He glares at Hovstad and goes out.*

BILLING: If we could get rid of him we—

HOVSTAD: Take it easy—he pays the printing bill, he's not that bad. *He picks up the manuscript.* I'll get the printer on this. *He starts out.*

BILLING: Say, Hovstad, how about asking Stockmann to back us? Then we could really put out a paper!

HOVSTAD: What would he do for money?

BILLING: His father-in-law.

HOVSTAD: Kiil? Since when has he got money?

BILLING: I think he's loaded with it.

HOVSTAD: No! Why, as long as I've known him he's worn the same overcoat, the same suit—

BILLING: Yeah, and the same ring on his right hand. You ever get a look at that boulder? *He points to his finger.*

HOVSTAD: No, I never—

BILLING: All year he wears the diamond inside, but on New Year's Eve he turns it around. Figure it out—when a man has no visible means of support, what is he living on? Money, right?

Petra enters, carrying a book.

PETRA: Hello.

HOVSTAD: Well, fancy seeing you here. Sit down. What—

PETRA, *walking slowly up to Hovstad*: I want to ask you a question. *She starts to open the book.*

BILLING: What's that?

PETRA: The English novel you wanted translated.

HOVSTAD: Aren't you going to do it?

PETRA, *with deadly seriousness and curiosity*: I don't get this.

HOVSTAD: You don't get what?

PETRA: This book is absolutely against everything you people believe.

HOVSTAD: Oh, it isn't that bad.

PETRA: But, Mr. Hovstad, it says if you're good there's a supernatural force that'll fix it so you end up happy. And if you're bad you'll be punished. Since when does the world work that way?

HOVSTAD: Yes, Petra, but this is a newspaper, people like to read that kind of thing. They buy the paper for that and then we slip in our political stuff. A newspaper can't buck the public—

PETRA, *astonished, beginning to be angry*: You don't say! *She starts to go.*

HOVSTAD, *hurrying after her*: Now, wait a minute, I don't want you to go feeling that way. *He holds the manuscript out to Billing.* Here, take this to the printer, will you?

BILLING, *taking the manuscript*: Sure. *He goes.*

HOVSTAD: I just want you to understand something: I never even read that book. It was Billing's idea.

PETRA, *trying to penetrate his eyes*: I thought he was a radical.

HOVSTAD: He is. But he's also a—

PETRA, *testily*: A newspaperman.

HOVSTAD: Well, that too, but I was going to say that Billing is trying to get the job as secretary to the Magistrate.

PETRA: What?

HOVSTAD: People are—people, Miss Stockmann.

PETRA: But the Magistrate! He's been fighting everything progressive in this town for thirty years.

HOVSTAD: Let's not argue about it, I just didn't want you to go out of here with a wrong idea of me. I guess you know that I—I happen to admire women like you. I've never had a chance to tell you, but I—well, I want you to know it. Do you mind? *He smiles.*

PETRA: No, I don't mind, but—reading that book upset me. I really don't understand. Will you tell me why you're supporting my father?

HOVSTAD: What's the mystery? It's a matter of principle.

PETRA: But a paper that'll print a book like this has no principle.

HOVSTAD: Why do you jump to such extremes? You're just like . . .

PETRA: Like what?

HOVSTAD: I simply mean that . . .

PETRA, *moving away from him*: Like my father, you mean. You really have no use for him, do you?

HOVSTAD: Now wait a minute!

PETRA: What's behind this? Are you just trying to hold my hand or something?

HOVSTAD: I happen to agree with your father, and that's why I'm printing his stuff.

PETRA: You're trying to put something over, I think. Why are you in this?

HOVSTAD: Who're you accusing? Billing gave you that book, not me!

PETRA: But you don't mind printing it, do you? What are you trying to do with my father? You have no principles—what are you up to here?

> *Aslaksen hurriedly enters from the printing shop, Stockmann's manuscript in his hand.*

ASLAKSEN: My God! Hovstad! *He sees Petra.* Miss Stockmann.

PETRA, *looking at Hovstad*: I don't think I've been so frightened in my life. *She goes out.*

HOVSTAD, *starting after her*: Please, you mustn't think I—

ASLAKSEN, *stopping him*: Where are you going? The Mayor's out there.

HOVSTAD: The Mayor!

ASLAKSEN: He wants to speak to you. He came in the back door. He doesn't want to be seen.

HOVSTAD: What does he want? *He goes to the printing-room door, opens it, calls out with a certain edge of servility*: Come in, Your Honor!

PETER STOCKMANN, *entering*: Thank you.

> *Hovstad carefully closes the door.*

PETER STOCKMANN, *walking around*: It's clean! I always imagined this place would look dirty. But it's clean. *Commendingly*: Very nice, Mr. Aslaksen. *He puts his hat on the desk.*

ASLAKSEN: Not at all, Your Honor—I mean to say, I always . . .

HOVSTAD: What can I do for you, Your Honor? Sit down?

PETER STOCKMANN, *sits, placing his cane on the table*: I had a very annoying thing happen today, Mr. Hovstad.

HOVSTAD: That so?

PETER STOCKMANN: It seems my brother has written some sort of— memorandum. About the springs.

HOVSTAD: You don't say.

PETER STOCKMANN, *looking at Hovstad now*: He mentioned it . . . to you?

HOVSTAD: Yes. I think he said something about it.

ASLAKSEN, *nervously starts to go out, attempting to hide the manuscript*: Will you excuse me, gentlemen . . .

PETER STOCKMANN, *pointing to the manuscript*: That's it, isn't it?

ASLAKSEN: This? I don't know, I haven't had a chance to look at it, the printer just handed it to me . . .

HOVSTAD: Isn't that the thing the printer wanted the spelling checked?

ASLAKSEN: That's it. It's only a question of spelling. I'll be right back.

PETER STOCKMANN: I'm very good at spelling. *He holds out his hand.* Maybe I can help you.

HOVSTAD: No, Your Honor, there's some Latin in it. You wouldn't know Latin, would you?

PETER STOCKMANN: Oh, yes. I used to help my brother with his Latin all the time. Let me have it.

> *Aslaksen gives him the manuscript. Peter Stockmann looks at the title on the first page, then glances up sarcastically at Hovstad, who avoids his eyes.*

PETER STOCKMANN: You're going to print this?

HOVSTAD: I can't very well refuse a signed article. A signed article is the author's responsibility.

PETER STOCKMANN: Mr. Aslaksen, you're going to allow this?

ASLAKSEN: I'm the publisher, not the editor, Your Honor. My policy is freedom for the editor.

PETER STOCKMANN: You have a point—I can see that.

ASLAKSEN, *reaching for the manuscript*: So if you don't mind . . .

PETER STOCKMANN: Not at all. *But he holds on to the manuscript. After a pause*: This reconstruction of the springs—

ASLAKSEN: I realize, Your Honor—it does mean tremendous sacrifices for the stockholders.

PETER STOCKMANN: Don't upset yourself. The first thing a Mayor learns is that the less wealthy can always be prevailed upon to demand a spirit of sacrifice for the public good.

ASLAKSEN: I'm glad you see that.

PETER STOCKMANN: Oh, yes. Especially when it's the wealthy who are going to do the sacrificing. What you don't seem to understand, Mr. Aslaksen, is that so long as I am Mayor, any changes in those springs are going to be paid for by a municipal loan.

ASLAKSEN: A municipal—you mean you're going to tax the people for this?

PETER STOCKMANN: Exactly.

HOVSTAD: But the springs are a private corporation!

PETER STOCKMANN: The corporation built Kirsten Springs out of its own money. If the people want them changed, the people naturally must pay the bill. The corporation is in no position to put out any more money. It simply can't do it.

ASLAKSEN, *to Hovstad*: That's impossible! People will never stand for a new tax. *To the Mayor*: Is this a fact or your opinion?

PETER STOCKMANN: It happens to be a fact. Plus another fact—you'll forgive me for talking about facts in a newspaper office—but don't forget that the springs will take two years to make over. Two years without income for your small businessmen, Mr. Aslaksen, and a heavy new tax besides. And all because—*his private emotion comes to the surface; he throttles the manuscript in his hand*—because of this dream, this hallucination, that we live in a pesthole!

HOVSTAD: That's based on science.

PETER STOCKMANN, *raising the manuscript and throwing it down on the table*: This is based on vindictiveness, on his hatred of authority and nothing else. *He pounds on the manuscript*. This is the mad dream of a man who is trying to blow up our way of life! It has nothing to do with reform or science or anything else, but pure and simple destruction! And I intend to see to it that the people understand it exactly so!

ASLAKSEN, *hit by this*: My God! *To Hovstad*: Maybe . . . You sure you want to support this thing, Hovstad?

HOVSTAD, *nervously*: Frankly I'd never thought of it in quite that way. I mean . . . *To the Mayor*: When you think of it psychologically it's completely possible, of course, that the man is simply out to— I don't know what to say, Your Honor. I'd hate to hurt the town in any way. I never imagined we'd have to have a new tax.

PETER STOCKMANN: You should have imagined it because you're going to have to advocate it. Unless, of course, liberal and radical newspaper readers enjoy high taxes. But you'd know that better than I. I happen to have here a brief story of the actual facts. It proves that, with a little care, nobody need be harmed at all by the water. *He takes out a long envelope.* Of course, in time we'd have to make a few minor structural changes and we'd pay for those.

HOVSTAD: May I see that?

PETER STOCKMANN: I want you to *study* it, Mr. Hovstad, and see if you don't agree that—

BILLING, *entering quickly*: Are you expecting the Doctor?

PETER STOCKMANN, *alarmed*: He's here?

BILLING: Just coming across the street.

PETER STOCKMANN: I'd rather not run into him here. How can I . . .

BILLING: Right this way, sir, hurry up!

ASLAKSEN, *at the entrance door, peeking*: Hurry up!

PETER STOCKMANN, *going with Billing through the door at the left*: Get him out of here right away! *They exit.*

HOVSTAD: Do something, do something!

> Aslaksen pokes among some papers on the table. Hovstad sits
> at the desk, starts to "write." Dr. Stockmann enters.

DR. STOCKMANN: Any proofs yet? *He sees they hardly turn to him.* I guess not, eh?

ASLAKSEN, *without turning*: No, you can't expect them for some time.

DR. STOCKMANN: You mind if I wait?

HOVSTAD: No sense in that, Doctor, it'll be quite a while yet.

DR. STOCKMANN, *laughing, places his hand on Hovstad's back*: Bear with me, Hovstad, I just can't wait to see it in print.

HOVSTAD: We're pretty busy, Doctor, so . . .

DR. STOCKMANN, *starting toward the door*: Don't let me hold you up. That's the way to be, busy, busy. We'll make this town shine like a jewel! *He has opened the door, now he comes back.* Just one thing. I—

HOVSTAD: Couldn't we talk some other time? We're very—

DR. STOCKMANN: Two words. Just walking down the street now, I looked at the people, in the stores, driving the wagons, and suddenly I was— well, touched, you know? By their innocence, I mean. What I'm driving at is, when this exposé breaks they're liable to start making a saint out of me or something, and I— Aslaksen, I want you to promise me that you're not going to try to get up any dinner for me or—

ASLAKSEN, *turning toward the Doctor*: Doctor, there's no use concealing—

DR. STOCKMANN: I knew it. Now look, I will simply not attend a dinner in my honor.

HOVSTAD, *getting up*: Doctor, I think it's time we—

    Mrs. Stockmann enters.

MRS. STOCKMANN: I thought so. Thomas, I want you home. Now come. I want you to talk to Petra.

DR. STOCKMANN: What happened? What are you doing here?

HOVSTAD: Something wrong, Mrs. Stockmann?

MRS. STOCKMANN, *leveling a look of accusation at Hovstad*: Doctor Stockmann is the father of three children, Mr. Hovstad.

DR. STOCKMANN: Now look, dear, everybody knows that. What's the—

MRS. STOCKMANN, *restraining an outburst at her husband*: Nobody would *believe* it from the way you're dragging us into this disaster!

DR. STOCKMANN: What disaster?

MRS. STOCKMANN, *to Hovstad*: He treated you like a son, now you make a fool of him?

HOVSTAD: *I'm* not making a—

DR. STOCKMANN: Catherine! *He indicates Hovstad.* How can you accuse—

MRS. STOCKMANN, *to Hovstad*: He'll lose his job at the springs, do you realize that? You print the article, and they'll grind him up like a piece of flesh!

DR. STOCKMANN: Catherine, you're embarrassing me! I beg your pardon, gentlemen . . .

MRS. STOCKMANN: Mr. Hovstad, what are you up to?

DR. STOCKMANN: I won't have you jumping at Hovstad, Catherine!

MRS. STOCKMANN: I want you home! This man is not your friend!

DR. STOCKMANN: He is my friend! Any man who shares my risk is my friend! You simply don't understand that as soon as this breaks everybody in this town is going to come out in the streets and drive that gang of— *He picks up the Mayor's cane from the table, notices what it is, and stops. He looks from it to Hovstad and Aslaksen.* What's this? *They don't reply. Now he notices the hat on the desk and picks it up with the tip of the cane. He looks at them again. He is angry, incredulous.* What the hell is he doing here?

ASLAKSEN: All right, Doctor, now let's be calm and—

DR. STOCKMANN, *starting to move:* Where is he? What'd he do, talk you out of it? Hovstad! *Hovstad remains immobile.* He won't get away with it! Where'd you hide him? *He opens the door at the left.*

ASLAKSEN: Be careful, Doctor!

> *Peter Stockmann enters with Billing through the door Dr. Stockmann opened. Peter Stockmann tries to hide his embarrassment.*

DR. STOCKMANN: Well, Peter, poisoning the water was not enough! You're working on the press now, eh? *He crosses to the entrance door.*

PETER STOCKMANN: My hat, please. And my stick. *Dr. Stockmann puts on the Mayor's hat.* Now what's *this* nonsense! Take that off, that's official insignia!

DR. STOCKMANN: I just wanted you to realize, Peter—*he takes off the hat and looks at it*—that anyone may wear this hat in a democracy, and that a free citizen is not afraid to touch it. *He hands him the hat.* And as for the baton of command, Your Honor, it can pass from hand to hand. *He hands the cane to Peter Stockmann.* So don't gloat yet. The people haven't spoken. *He turns to Hovstad and Aslaksen.* And I have the people because I have the truth, my friends!

ASLAKSEN: Doctor, we're not scientists. We can't judge whether your article is really true.

DR. STOCKMANN: Then print it under my name. Let *me* defend it!

HOVSTAD: I'm not printing it. I'm not going to sacrifice this newspaper. When the whole story gets out the public is not going to stand for any changes in the springs.

ASLAKSEN: His Honor just told us, Doctor—you see, there will have to be a new tax—

DR. STOCKMANN: Ahhhhh! Yes. I see. That's why you're not scientists suddenly and can't decide if I'm telling the truth. Well. So!

HOVSTAD: Don't take that attitude. The point is—

DR. STOCKMANN: The point, the point, oh, the point is going to fly through this town like an arrow, and I am going to fire it! *To Aslaksen*: Will you print this article as a pamphlet? I'll pay for it.

ASLAKSEN: I'm not going to ruin this paper and this town. Doctor, for the sake of your family—

MRS. STOCKMANN: You can leave his family out of this, Mr. Aslaksen. God help me, I think you people are horrible!

DR. STOCKMANN: My article, if you don't mind.

ASLAKSEN, *giving it to him*: Doctor, you won't get it printed in this town.

PETER STOCKMANN: Can't you forget it? *He indicates Hovstad and Aslaksen*. Can't you see now that everybody—

DR. STOCKMANN: Your Honor, I can't forget it, and you will never forget it as long as you live. I am going to call a mass meeting, and I—

PETER STOCKMANN: And who is going to rent you a hall?

DR. STOCKMANN: Then I will take a drum and go from street to street, proclaiming that the springs are befouled and poison is rotting the body politic! *He starts for the door.*

PETER STOCKMANN: And I believe you really are that mad!

DR. STOCKMANN: Mad? Oh, my brother, you haven't even heard me raise my voice yet. Catherine? *He holds out his hand, she gives him her elbow. They go stiffly out.*

> *Peter Stockmann looks regretfully toward the exit, then takes out his manuscript and hands it to Hovstad, who in turn gives it to Billing, who hands it to Aslaksen, who takes it and exits. Peter Stockmann puts his hat on and moves toward the door. Blackout.*

THE CURTAIN FALLS.

SCENE II

A room in Captain Horster's house. The room is bare, as though unused for a long time. A large doorway is at the left, two shuttered windows at the back, and another door at the right. Upstage right, packing cases have been set together, forming a platform, on which are a chair and a small table. There are two chairs next to the platform at the right. One chair stands downstage left.

The room is angled, thus making possible the illusion of a large crowd off in the wing to the left. The platform faces the audience at an angle, thus giving the speakers the chance to speak straight out front and creating the illusion of a large crowd by addressing "people" in the audience.

As the curtain rises the room is empty. Captain Horster enters, carrying a pitcher of water, a glass, and a bell. He is putting these on the table when Billing enters. A crowd is heard talking outside in the street.

BILLING: Captain Horster?

HORSTER, *turning*: Oh, come in. I don't have enough chairs for a lot of people so I decided not to have chairs at all.

BILLING: My name is Billing. Don't you remember, at the Doctor's house?

HORSTER, *a little coldly*: Oh, yes, sure. I've been so busy I didn't recognize you. *He goes to a window and looks out.* Why don't those people come inside?

BILLING: I don't know, I guess they're waiting for the Mayor or somebody important so they can be sure it's respectable in here. I wanted to ask you a question before it begins, Captain. Why are you lending your house for this? I never heard of you connected with anything political.

HORSTER, *standing still*: I'll answer that. I travel most of the year and— did you ever travel?

BILLING: Not abroad, no.

HORSTER: Well, I've been in a lot of places where people aren't allowed to say unpopular things. Did you know that?

BILLING: Sure, I've read about it.

HORSTER, *simply*: Well, I don't like it. *He starts to go out.*

BILLING: One more question. What's your opinion about the Doctor's proposition to rebuild the springs?

HORSTER, *turning, thinks, then*: Don't understand a thing about it.

   Three citizens enter.

HORSTER: Come in, come in. I don't have enough chairs so you'll just have to stand. *He goes out.*

FIRST CITIZEN: Try the horn.

SECOND CITIZEN: No, let him start to talk first.

THIRD CITIZEN, *a big beef of a man, takes out a horn*: Wait'll they hear this! I could blow your mustache off with this!

   Horster returns. He sees the horn and stops abruptly.

HORSTER: I don't want any roughhouse, you hear me?

   Mrs. Stockmann and Petra enter.

HORSTER: Come in. I've got chairs just for you.

MRS. STOCKMANN, *nervously*: There's quite a crowd on the sidewalk. Why don't they come in?

HORSTER: I suppose they're waiting for the Mayor.

PETRA: Are all those people on his side?

HORSTER: Who knows? People are bashful, and it's so unusual to come to a meeting like this, I suppose they—

BILLING, *going over to this group*: Good evening, ladies. *They simply look at him.* I don't blame you for not speaking. I just wanted to say I don't think this is going to be a place for ladies tonight.

MRS. STOCKMANN: I don't remember asking your advice, Mr. Billing.

BILLING: I'm not as bad as you think, Mrs. Stockmann.

MRS. STOCKMANN: Then why did you print the Mayor's statement and not a word about my husband's report? Nobody's had a chance to find out what he really stands for. Why, everybody on the street there is against him already!

BILLING: If we printed his report it only would have hurt your husband.

MRS. STOCKMANN: Mr. Billing, I've never said this to anyone in my life, but I think you're a liar.

   Suddenly the third citizen lets out a blast on his horn. The women jump, Billing and Horster turn around quickly.

HORSTER: You do that once more and I'll throw you out of here!

Peter Stockmann enters. Behind him comes the crowd. He pretends to be unconnected with them. He goes straight to Mrs. Stockmann, bows.

PETER STOCKMANN: Catherine? Petra?

PETRA: Good evening.

PETER STOCKMANN: Why so coldly? He wanted a meeting and he's got it. *To Horster*: Isn't he here?

HORSTER: The Doctor is going around town to be sure there's a good attendance.

PETER STOCKMANN: Fair enough. By the way, Petra, did you paint that poster? The one somebody stuck on the Town Hall?

PETRA: If you can call it painting, yes.

PETER STOCKMANN: You know I could arrest you? It's against the law to deface the Town Hall.

PETRA: Well, here I am. *She holds out her hands for the handcuffs.*

MRS. STOCKMANN, *taking it seriously*: If you arrest her, Peter, I'll never speak to you!

PETER STOCKMANN, *laughing*: Catherine, you have no sense of humor!

He crosses and sits down at the left. They sit right. A drunk comes out of the crowd.

DRUNK: Say, Billy, who's runnin'? Who's the candidate?

HORSTER: You're drunk, Mister, now get out of here!

DRUNK: There's no law says a man who's drunk can't vote!

HORSTER, *pushing the drunk toward the door as the crowd laughs*: Get out of here! Get out!

DRUNK: I wanna vote! I got a right to vote!

Aslaksen enters hurriedly, sees Peter Stockmann, and rushes to him.

ASLAKSEN: Your Honor . . . *He points to the door.* He's . . .

DR. STOCKMANN, *offstage*: Right this way, gentlemen! In you go, come on, fellows!

Hovstad enters, glances at Peter Stockmann and Aslaksen, then at Dr. Stockmann and another crowd behind him, who enter.

DR. STOCKMANN: Sorry, no chairs, gentlemen, but we couldn't get a hall, y'know, so just relax. It won't take long anyway. *He goes to the platform, sees Peter Stockmann.* Glad you're here, Peter!

PETER STOCKMANN: Wouldn't miss it for the world.

DR. STOCKMANN: How do you feel, Catherine?

MRS. STOCKMANN, *nervously*: Just promise me, don't lose your temper . . .

HORSTER, *seeing the drunk pop in through the door*: Did I tell you to get out of here!

DRUNK: Look, if you ain't votin', what the hell's going on here? *Horster starts after him.* Don't push!

PETER STOCKMANN, *to the drunk*: I order you to get out of here and stay out!

DRUNK: I don't like the tone of your voice! And if you don't watch your step I'm gonna tell the Mayor right now, and he'll throw yiz all in the jug! *To all*: What're you, a revolution here?

> *The crowd bursts out laughing; the drunk laughs with them, and they push him out. Dr. Stockmann mounts the platform.*

DR. STOCKMANN, *quieting the crowd*: All right, gentlemen, we might as well begin. Quiet down, please. *He clears his throat.* The issue is very simple—

ASLAKSEN: We haven't elected a chairman, Doctor.

DR. STOCKMANN: I'm sorry, Mr. Aslaksen, this isn't a meeting. I advertised a lecture and I—

A CITIZEN: I came to a meeting, Doctor. There's got to be some kind of control here.

DR. STOCKMANN: What do you mean, control? What is there to control?

SECOND CITIZEN: Sure, let him speak, this is no meeting!

THIRD CITIZEN: Your Honor, why don't you take charge of this—

DR. STOCKMANN: Just a minute now!

THIRD CITIZEN: Somebody responsible has got to take charge. There's a big difference of opinion here—

DR. STOCKMANN: What makes you so sure? You don't even know yet what I'm going to say.

THIRD CITIZEN: I've got a pretty good idea what you're going to say, and I don't like it! If a man doesn't like it here, let him go where it suits him better. We don't want any troublemakers here!

*There is assent from much of the crowd. Dr. Stockmann looks
at them with new surprise.*

DR. STOCKMANN: Now look, friend, you don't know anything about me—

FOURTH CITIZEN: We know plenty about you, Stockmann!

DR. STOCKMANN: From what? From the newspapers? How do you know
I don't like this town? *He picks up his manuscript.* I'm here to save the
life of this town!

PETER STOCKMANN, *quickly*: Now just a minute, Doctor, I think the democratic thing to do is to elect a chairman.

FIFTH CITIZEN: I nominate the Mayor!

Seconds are heard.

PETER STOCKMANN: No, no, no! That wouldn't be fair. We want a neutral
person. I suggest Mr. Aslaksen—

SECOND CITIZEN: I came to a lecture, I didn't—

THIRD CITIZEN, *to second citizen*: What're you afraid of, a fair fight? *To
the Mayor*: Second Mr. Aslaksen!

The crowd assents.

DR. STOCKMANN: All right, if that's your pleasure. I just want to remind
you that the reason I called this meeting was that I have a very important
message for you people and I couldn't get it into the press, and nobody
would rent me a hall. *To Peter Stockmann*: I just hope I'll be given time
to speak here. Mr. Aslaksen?

*As Aslaksen mounts the platform and Dr. Stockmann steps
down, Kiil enters, looks shrewdly around.*

ASLAKSEN: I just have one word before we start. Whatever is said tonight,
please remember, the highest civic virtue is moderation. *He can't help
turning to Dr. Stockmann, then back to the crowd.* Now if anybody
wants to speak—

The drunk enters suddenly.

DRUNK, *pointing at Aslaksen*: I heard that! Since when you allowed to
electioneer at the poles? *Citizens push him toward the door amid laughter.* I'm gonna report this to the Mayor, goddammit! *They push him out
and close the door.*

ASLAKSEN: Quiet, please, quiet. Does anybody want the floor?

*Dr. Stockmann starts to come forward, raising his hand, but
Peter Stockmann also has his hand raised.*

PETER STOCKMANN: Mr. Chairman!

ASLAKSEN, *quickly recognizing Peter Stockmann*: His Honor the Mayor will address the meeting.

> *Dr. Stockmann stops, looks at Peter Stockmann, and, suppressing a remark, returns to his place. The Mayor mounts the platform.*

PETER STOCKMANN: Gentlemen, there's no reason to take very long to settle this tonight and return to our ordinary, calm, and peaceful life. Here's the issue: Doctor Stockmann, my brother—and believe me, it is not easy to say this—has decided to destroy Kirsten Springs, our Health Institute—

DR. STOCKMANN: Peter!

ASLAKSEN, *ringing his bell*: Let the Mayor continue, please. There mustn't be any interruptions.

PETER STOCKMANN: He has a long and very involved way of going about it, but that's the brunt of it, believe me.

THIRD CITIZEN: Then what're we wasting time for? Run him out of town!

> *Others join in the cry.*

PETER STOCKMANN: Now wait a minute. I want no violence here. I want you to understand his motives. He is a man, always has been, who is never happy unless he is badgering authority, ridiculing authority, destroying authority. He wants to attack the springs so he can prove that the administration blundered in the construction.

DR. STOCKMANN, *to Aslaksen*: May I speak? I—

ASLAKSEN: The Mayor's not finished.

PETER STOCKMANN: Thank you. Now there are a number of people here who seem to feel that the Doctor has a right to say anything he pleases. After all, we are a democratic country. Now, God knows, in ordinary times I'd agree a hundred per cent with anybody's right to say anything. But these are not ordinary times. Nations have crises, and so do towns. There are ruins of nations, and there are ruins of towns all over the world, and they were wrecked by people who, in the guise of reform, and pleading for justice, and so on, broke down all authority and left only revolution and chaos.

DR. STOCKMANN: What the hell are you talking about!

ASLAKSEN: I'll have to insist, Doctor—

DR. STOCKMANN: I called a lecture! I didn't invite him to attack me. He's got the press and every hall in town to attack me, and I've got nothing but this room tonight!

ASLAKSEN: I don't think you're making a very good impression, Doctor.

> *Assenting laughter and catcalls. Again Dr. Stockmann is taken aback by this reaction.*

ASLAKSEN: Please continue, Your Honor.

PETER STOCKMANN: Now this is our crisis. We know what this town was without our Institute. We could barely afford to keep the streets in condition. It was a dead, third-rate hamlet. Today we're just on the verge of becoming internationally known as a resort. I predict that within five years the income of every man in this room will be immensely greater. I predict that our schools will be bigger and better. And in time this town will be crowded with fine carriages; great homes will be built here; first-class stores will open all along Main Street. I predict that if we are not defamed and maliciously attacked we will someday be one of the richest and most beautiful resort towns in the world. There are your choices. Now all you've got to do is ask yourselves a simple question: Has any one of us the right, the "democratic right," as they like to call it, to pick at minor flaws in the springs, to exaggerate the most picayune faults? *Cries of No, No!* And to attempt to publish these defamations for the whole world to see? We live or die on what the outside world thinks of us. I believe there is a line that must be drawn, and if a man decides to cross that line, we the people must finally take him by the collar and declare, "You cannot say that."

> *There is an uproar of assent. Aslaksen rings the bell.*

PETER STOCKMANN, *continuing*: All right then. I think we all understand each other. Mr. Aslaksen, I move that Doctor Stockmann be prohibited from reading his report at this meeting! *He goes back to his chair, which meanwhile Kiil has occupied.*

> *Aslaksen rings the bell to quiet the enthusiasm. Dr. Stockmann is jumping to get up on the platform, the report in his hand.*

ASLAKSEN: Quiet, please. Please now. I think we can proceed to the vote.

DR. STOCKMANN: Well, aren't you going to let me speak at all?

ASLAKSEN: Doctor, we are just about to vote on that question.

DR. STOCKMANN: But damn it, man, I've got a right to—

PETRA, *standing up*: Point of order, Father!

DR. STOCKMANN, *picking up the cue*: Yes, point of order!

ASLAKSEN, *turning to him now*: Yes, Doctor.

> *Dr. Stockmann, at a loss, turns to Petra for further instructions.*

PETRA: You want to discuss the motion.

DR. STOCKMANN: That's right, damn it, I want to discuss the motion!

ASLAKSEN: Ah . . . *He glances at Peter Stockmann.* All right, go ahead.

DR. STOCKMANN, *to the crowd:* Now, listen. *He points at Peter Stockmann.* He talks and he talks and he talks, but not a word about the facts! *He holds up the manuscript.*

THIRD CITIZEN: We don't want to hear any more about the water!

FOURTH CITIZEN: You're just trying to blow up everything!

DR. STOCKMANN: Well, judge for yourselves, let me read—

> *Cries of No, No, No! The man with the horn blows it. Aslaksen rings the bell. Dr. Stockmann is utterly shaken. Astonished, he looks at the maddened faces. He lowers the hand holding the manuscript and steps back, defeated.*

ASLAKSEN: Please, please now, quiet. We can't have this uproar! *Quiet returns.* I think, Doctor, that the majority wants to take the vote before you start to speak. If they so will, you can speak. Otherwise, majority rules. You won't deny that.

DR. STOCKMANN, *turns, tosses the manuscript on the floor, turns back to Aslaksen:* Don't bother voting. I understand everything now. Can I have a few minutes—

PETER STOCKMANN: Mr. Chairman!

DR. STOCKMANN, *to his brother:* I won't mention the Institute. I have a new discovery that's a thousand times more important than all the Institutes in the world. *To Aslaksen:* May I have the platform.

ASLAKSEN, *to the crowd:* I don't see how we can deny him that, as long as he confines himself to—

DR. STOCKMANN: The springs are not the subject. *He mounts the platform, looks at the crowd.* Before I go into my subject I want to congratulate the liberals and radicals among us, like Mr. Hovstad—

HOVSTAD: What do you mean, radical! Where's your evidence to call me a radical!

DR. STOCKMANN: You've got me there. There isn't any evidence. I guess there never really was. I just wanted to congratulate you on your self-control tonight—you who have fought in every parlor for the principle of free speech these many years.

HOVSTAD: I believe in democracy. When my readers are overwhelmingly against something, I'm not going to impose my will on the majority.

DR. STOCKMANN: You have begun my remarks, Mr. Hovstad. *He turns to the crowd.* Gentlemen, Mrs. Stockmann, Miss Stockmann. Tonight I was struck by a sudden flash of light, a discovery second to none. But before I tell it to you—a little story. I put in a good many years in the north of our country. Up there the rulers of the world are the great seal and the gigantic squadrons of duck. Man lives on ice, huddled together in little piles of stones. His whole life consists of grubbing for food. Nothing more. He can barely speak his own language. And it came to me one day that it was romantic and sentimental for a man of my education to be tending these people. They had not yet reached the stage where they needed a doctor. If the truth were to be told, a veterinary would be more in order.

BILLING: Is that the way you refer to decent hard-working people!

DR. STOCKMANN: I expected that, my friend, but don't think you can fog up my brain with that magic word—the People! Not any more! Just because there is a mass of organisms with the human shape, they do not automatically become a People. That honor has to be earned! Nor does one automatically become a Man by having human shape, and living in a house, and feeding one's face—and agreeing with one's neighbors. That name *also* has to be earned. Now, when I came to my conclusions about the springs—

PETER STOCKMANN: You have no right to—

DR. STOCKMANN: That's a picayune thing, to catch me on a word, Peter. I am not going into the springs. *To the crowd*: When I became convinced of my theory about the water, the authorities moved in at once, and I said to myself, I will fight them to the death, because—

THIRD CITIZEN: What're you trying to do, make a revolution here? He's a revolutionist!

DR. STOCKMANN: Let me finish. I thought to myself: The majority, I have the majority! And let me tell you, friends, it was a grand feeling. Because that's the reason I came back to this place of my birth. I wanted to give my education to this town. I loved it so, I spent months without pay or encouragement and dreamed up the whole project of the springs. And why? Not as my brother says, so that fine carriages could crowd our streets, but so that we might cure the sick, so that we might meet people from all over the world and learn from them, and become broader and more civilized. In other words, more like Men, more like A People.

A CITIZEN: You don't like anything about this town, do you?

ANOTHER CITIZEN: Admit it, you're a revolutionist, aren't you? Admit it!

DR. STOCKMANN: I don't admit it! I proclaim it now! I am a revolutionist! I am in revolt against the age-old lie that the majority is always right!

HOVSTAD: He's an aristocrat all of a sudden!

DR. STOCKMANN: And more! I tell you now that the majority is always wrong, and in this way!

PETER STOCKMANN: Have you lost your mind! Stop talking before—

DR. STOCKMANN: Was the majority right when they stood by while Jesus was crucified? *Silence.* Was the majority right when they refused to believe that the earth moved around the sun and let Galileo be driven to his knees like a dog? It takes fifty years for the majority to be right. The majority is never right until it *does* right.

HOVSTAD: I want to state right now, that although I've been this man's friend, and I've eaten at his table many times, I now cut myself off from him absolutely.

DR. STOCKMANN: Answer me this! Please, one more moment! A platoon of soldiers is walking down a road toward the enemy. Every one of them is convinced he is on the right road, the safe road. But two miles ahead stands one lonely man, the outpost. He sees that this road is dangerous, that his comrades are walking into a trap. He runs back, he finds the platoon. Isn't it clear that this man must have the right to warn the majority, to argue with the majority, to fight with the majority if he believes he has the truth? Before many can know something, *one* must know it! *His passion has silenced the crowd.* It's always the same. Rights are sacred until it hurts for somebody to use them. I beg you now—I realize the cost is great, the inconvenience is great, the risk is great that other towns will get the jump on us while we're rebuilding—

PETER STOCKMANN: Aslaksen, he's not allowed to—

DR. STOCKMANN: Let me prove it to you! The water is poisoned!

THIRD CITIZEN, *steps up on the platform, waves his fist in Dr. Stockmann's face*: One more word about poison and I'm gonna take you outside!

> The crowd is roaring; some try to charge the platform. The horn is blowing. Aslaksen rings his bell. Peter Stockmann steps forward, raising his hands. Kiil quietly exits.

PETER STOCKMANN: That's enough. Now stop it! Quiet! There is not going to be any violence here! *There is silence. He turns to Dr. Stockmann.* Doctor, come down and give Mr. Aslaksen the platform.

DR. STOCKMANN, *staring down at the crowd with new eyes*: I'm not through yet.

PETER STOCKMANN: Come down or I will not be responsible for what happens.

MRS. STOCKMANN: I'd like to go home. Come on, Tom.

PETER STOCKMANN: I move the chairman order the speaker to leave the platform.

VOICES: Sit down! Get off that platform!

DR. STOCKMANN: All right. Then I'll take this to out-of-town newspapers until the whole country is warned!

PETER STOCKMANN: You wouldn't dare!

HOVSTAD: You're trying to ruin this town—that's all; trying to ruin it.

DR. STOCKMANN: You're trying to build a town on a morality so rotten that it will infect the country and the world! If the only way you can prosper is this murder of freedom and truth, then I say with all my heart, "Let it be destroyed! Let the people perish!"

He leaves the platform.

FIRST CITIZEN, *to the Mayor*: Arrest him! Arrest him!

SECOND CITIZEN: He's a traitor!

Cries of "Enemy! Traitor! Revolution!"

ASLAKSEN, *ringing for quiet*: I would like to submit the following resolution: The people assembled here tonight, decent and patriotic citizens, in defense of their town and their country, declare that Doctor Stockmann, medical officer of Kirsten Springs, is an enemy of the people and of his community.

An uproar of assent starts.

MRS. STOCKMANN, *getting up*: That's not true! He loves this town!

DR. STOCKMANN: You damned fools, you fools!

The Doctor and his family are all standing together, at the right, in a close group.

ASLAKSEN, *shouting over the din*: Is there anyone against this motion! Anyone against!

HORSTER, *raising his hand*: I am.

ASLAKSEN: One? *He looks around.*

DRUNK, *who has returned, raising his hand*: Me too! You can't do without a doctor! Anybody'll . . . tell you . . .

ASLAKSEN: Anyone else? With all votes against two, this assembly formally declares Doctor Thomas Stockmann to be the people's enemy. In the future, all dealings with him by decent, patriotic citizens will be on that basis. The meeting is adjourned.

> *Shouts and applause. People start leaving. Dr. Stockmann goes over to Horster.*

DR. STOCKMANN: Captain, do you have room for us on your ship to America?

HORSTER: Any time you say, Doctor.

DR. STOCKMANN: Catherine? Petra?

> *The three start for the door, but a gantlet has formed, dangerous and silent, except for*

THIRD CITIZEN: You'd better get aboard soon, Doctor!

MRS. STOCKMANN: Let's go out the back door.

HORSTER: Right this way.

DR. STOCKMANN: No, no. No back doors. *To the crowd:* I don't want to mislead anybody—the enemy of the people is not finished in this town—not quite yet. And if anybody thinks—

> *The horn blasts, cutting him off. The crowd starts yelling hysterically: "Enemy! Traitor! Throw him in the river! Come on, throw him in the river! Enemy! Enemy! Enemy!" The Stockmanns, erect, move out through the crowd, with Horster. Some of the crowd follow them out, yelling.*

> *Downstage, watching, are Peter Stockmann, Billing, Aslaksen, and Hovstad. The stage is throbbing with the chant, "Enemy, Enemy, Enemy!" as*

THE CURTAIN FALLS.

ACT THREE

Dr. Stockmann's living room the following morning. The windows are broken. There is great disorder. As the curtain rises, Dr. Stockmann enters, a robe over shirt and trousers—it's cold in the house. He picks up a stone from the floor, lays it on the table.

DR. STOCKMANN: Catherine! Tell what's-her-name there are still some rocks to pick up in here.

MRS. STOCKMANN, *from inside*: She's not finished sweeping up the glass.

As Dr. Stockmann bends down to get at another stone under a chair a rock comes through one of the last remaining panes. He rushes to the window, looks out. Mrs. Stockmann rushes in.

MRS. STOCKMANN, *frightened*: You all right?

DR. STOCKMANN, *looking out*: A little boy. Look at him run! *He picks up the stone.* How fast the poison spreads—even to the children!

MRS. STOCKMANN, *looking out the window*: It's hard to believe this is the same town.

DR. STOCKMANN, *adding this rock to the pile on the table*: I'm going to keep these like sacred relics. I'll put them in my will. I want the boys to have them in their homes to look at every day. *He shudders.* Cold in here. Why hasn't what's-her-name got the glazier here?

MRS. STOCKMANN: She's getting him . . .

DR. STOCKMANN: She's been getting him for two hours! We'll freeze to death in here.

MRS. STOCKMANN, *unwillingly*: He won't come here, Tom.

DR. STOCKMANN, *stops moving*: No! The glazier's afraid to fix my windows?

MRS. STOCKMANN: You don't realize—people don't like to be pointed out. He's got neighbors, I suppose, and— *She hears something.* Is that someone at the door, Randine?

She goes to front door. He continues picking up stones. She comes back.

MRS. STOCKMANN: Letter for you.

DR. STOCKMANN, *taking and opening it*: What's this now?

MRS. STOCKMANN, *continuing his pick-up for him*: I don't know how we're going to do any shopping with everybody ready to bite my head off and—

DR. STOCKMANN: Well, what do you know? We're evicted.

MRS. STOCKMANN: Oh, no!

DR. STOCKMANN: He hates to do it, but with public opinion what it is . . .

MRS. STOCKMANN, *frightened*: Maybe we shouldn't have let the boys go to school today.

DR. STOCKMANN: Now don't get all frazzled again.

MRS. STOCKMANN: But the landlord is such a nice man. If he's got to throw us out, the town must be ready to murder us!

DR. STOCKMANN: Just calm down, will you? We'll go to America, and the whole thing'll be like a dream.

MRS. STOCKMANN: But I don't want to go to America— *She notices his pants.* When did this get torn?

DR. STOCKMANN, *examining the tear*: Must've been last night.

MRS. STOCKMANN: Your best pants!

DR. STOCKMANN: Well, it just shows you, that's all—when a man goes out to fight for the truth he should never wear his best pants. *He calms her.* Stop worrying, will you? You'll sew them up, and in no time at all we'll be three thousand miles away.

MRS. STOCKMANN: But how do you know it'll be any different there?

DR. STOCKMANN: I don't know. It just seems to me, in a big country like that, the spirit must be bigger. Still, I suppose they must have the solid majority there too. I don't know, at least there must be more room to hide there.

MRS. STOCKMANN: Think about it more, will you? I'd hate to go half around the world and find out we're in the same place.

DR. STOCKMANN: You know, Catherine, I don't think I'm ever going to forget the face of that crowd last night.

MRS. STOCKMANN: Don't think about it.

DR. STOCKMANN: Some of them had their teeth bared, like animals in a pack. And who leads them? Men who call themselves liberals! Radicals! *She starts looking around at the furniture, figuring.* The crowd lets out one roar, and where are they, my liberal friends? I bet if I walked down the street now not one of them would admit he ever met me! Are you listening to me?

MRS. STOCKMANN: I was just wondering what we'll ever do with this furniture if we go to America.

DR. STOCKMANN: Don't you ever listen when I talk, dear?

MRS. STOCKMANN: Why must I listen? I know you're right.

    Petra enters.

MRS. STOCKMANN: Petra! Why aren't you in school?

DR. STOCKMANN: What's the matter?

PETRA, *with deep emotion, looks at Dr. Stockmann, goes up and kisses him*: I'm fired.

MRS. STOCKMANN: They wouldn't!

PETRA: As of two weeks from now. But I couldn't bear to stay there.

DR. STOCKMANN, *shocked*: Mrs. Busk fired you?

MRS. STOCKMANN: Who'd ever imagine she could do such a thing!

PETRA: It hurt her. I could see it, because we've always agreed so about things. But she didn't dare do anything else.

DR. STOCKMANN: The glazier doesn't dare fix the windows, the landlord doesn't dare let us stay on—

PETRA: The landlord!

DR. STOCKMANN: Evicted, darling! Oh, God, on the wreckage of all the civilizations in the world there ought to be a big sign: "They Didn't Dare!"

PETRA: I really can't blame her, Father. She showed me three letters she got this morning—

DR. STOCKMANN: From whom?

PETRA: They weren't signed.

DR. STOCKMANN: Oh, naturally. The big patriots with their anonymous indignation, scrawling out the darkness of their minds onto dirty little slips of paper—that's morality, and *I'm* the traitor! What did the letters say?

PETRA: Well, one of them was from somebody who said that he'd heard at the club that somebody who visits this house said that I had radical opinions about certain things.

DR. STOCKMANN: Oh, wonderful! Somebody heard that somebody heard that she heard, that he heard . . . ! Catherine, pack as soon as you can. I feel as though vermin were crawling all over me.

Horster enters.

HORSTER: Good morning.

DR. STOCKMANN: Captain! You're just the man I want to see.

HORSTER: I thought I'd see how you all were.

MRS. STOCKMANN: That's awfully nice of you, Captain, and I want to thank you for seeing us through the crowd last night.

PETRA: Did you get home all right? We hated to leave you alone with that mob.

HORSTER: Oh, nothing to it. In a storm there's just one thing to remember: it will pass.

DR. STOCKMANN: Unless it kills you.

HORSTER: You mustn't let yourself get too bitter.

DR. STOCKMANN: I'm trying, I'm trying. But I don't guarantee how I'll feel when I try to walk down the street with "Traitor" branded on my forehead.

MRS. STOCKMANN: Don't think about it.

HORSTER: Ah, what's a word?

DR. STOCKMANN: A word can be like a needle sticking in your heart, Captain. It can dig and corrode like an acid, until you become what they want you to be—really an enemy of the people.

HORSTER: You mustn't ever let that happen, Doctor.

DR. STOCKMANN: Frankly, I don't give a damn any more. Let summer come, let an epidemic break out, then they'll know whom they drove into exile. When are you sailing?

PETRA: You really decided to go, Father?

DR. STOCKMANN: Absolutely. When do you sail, Captain?

HORSTER: That's really what I came to talk to you about.

DR. STOCKMANN: Why? Something happen to the ship?

MRS. STOCKMANN, *happily, to Dr. Stockmann:* You see! We can't go!

HORSTER: No, the ship will sail. But I won't be aboard.

DR. STOCKMANN: No!

PETRA: You fired too? 'Cause I was this morning.

MRS. STOCKMANN: Oh, Captain, you shouldn't have given us your house.

HORSTER: Oh, I'll get another ship. It's just that the owner, Mr. Vik, happens to belong to the same party as the Mayor, and I suppose when you belong to a party, and the party takes a certain position . . . Because Mr. Vik himself is a very decent man.

DR. STOCKMANN: Oh, they're all decent men!

HORSTER: No, really, he's not like the others.

DR. STOCKMANN: He doesn't have to be. A party is like a sausage grinder: it mashes up clearheads, longheads, fatheads, blockheads—and what comes out? Meatheads!

There is a knock on the hall door. Petra goes to answer.

MRS. STOCKMANN: Maybe that's the glazier!

DR. STOCKMANN: Imagine, Captain! *He points to the window.* Refused to come all morning!

Peter Stockmann enters, his hat in his hand. Silence.

PETER STOCKMANN: If you're busy . . .

DR. STOCKMANN: Just picking up broken glass. Come in, Peter. What can I do for you this fine, brisk morning? *He demonstratively pulls his robe tighter around his throat.*

MRS. STOCKMANN: Come inside, won't you, Captain?

HORSTER: Yes, I'd like to finish our talk, Doctor.

DR. STOCKMANN: Be with you in a minute, Captain.

Horster follows Petra and Catherine out through the dining-room doorway. Peter Stockmann says nothing, looking at the damage.

DR. STOCKMANN: Keep your hat on if you like, it's a little drafty in here today.

PETER STOCKMANN: Thanks, I believe I will. *He puts his hat on.* I think I caught cold last night—that house was freezing.

DR. STOCKMANN: I thought it was kind of warm—suffocating, as a matter of fact. What do you want?

PETER STOCKMANN: May I sit down? *He indicates a chair near the window.*

DR. STOCKMANN: Not there. A piece of the solid majority is liable to open your skull. Here.

They sit on the couch. Peter Stockmann takes out a large envelope.

DR. STOCKMANN: Now don't tell me.

PETER STOCKMANN: Yes. *He hands the Doctor the envelope.*

DR. STOCKMANN: I'm fired.

PETER STOCKMANN: The Board met this morning. There was nothing else to do, considering the state of public opinion.

DR. STOCKMANN, *after a pause*: You look scared, Peter.

PETER STOCKMANN: I—I haven't completely forgotten that you're still my brother.

DR. STOCKMANN: I doubt that.

PETER STOCKMANN: You have no practice left in this town, Thomas.

DR. STOCKMANN: Oh, people always need a doctor.

PETER STOCKMANN: A petition is going from house to house. Everybody is signing it. A pledge not to call you any more. I don't think a single family will dare refuse to sign it.

DR. STOCKMANN: You started that, didn't you?

PETER STOCKMANN: No. As a matter of fact, I think it's all gone a little too far. I never wanted to see you ruined, Thomas. This will ruin you.

DR. STOCKMANN: No, it won't.

PETER STOCKMANN: For once in your life, will you act like a responsible man?

DR. STOCKMANN: Why don't you say it, Peter? You're afraid I'm going out of town to start publishing about the springs, aren't you?

PETER STOCKMANN: I don't deny that. Thomas, if you really have the good of the town at heart, you can accomplish everything without damaging anybody, including yourself.

DR. STOCKMANN: What's this now?

PETER STOCKMANN: Let me have a signed statement saying that in your zeal to help the town you went overboard and exaggerated. Put it any way you like, just so you calm anybody who might feel nervous about the water. If you'll give me that, you've got your job. And I give you my word, you can gradually make all the improvements you feel are necessary. Now, that gives you what you want . . .

DR. STOCKMANN: You're nervous, Peter.

PETER STOCKMANN, *nervously*: I am not nervous!

DR. STOCKMANN: You expect me to remain in charge while people are being poisoned? *He gets up.*

PETER STOCKMANN: In time you can make your changes.

DR. STOCKMANN: When, five years, ten years? You know your trouble, Peter? You just don't grasp—even now—that there are certain men you can't buy.

PETER STOCKMANN: I'm quite capable of understanding that. But you don't happen to be one of those men.

DR. STOCKMANN, *after a slight pause*: What do you mean by that now?

PETER STOCKMANN: You know damned well what I mean by that. Morten Kiil is what I mean by that.

DR. STOCKMANN: Morten Kiil?

PETER STOCKMANN: Your father-in-law, Morten Kiil.

DR. STOCKMANN: I swear, Peter, one of us is out of his mind! What are you talking about?

PETER STOCKMANN: Now don't try to charm me with that professional innocence!

DR. STOCKMANN: What are you talking about?

PETER STOCKMANN: You don't know that your father-in-law has been running around all morning buying up stock in Kirsten Springs?

DR. STOCKMANN, *perplexed*: Buying up stock?

PETER STOCKMANN: Buying up stock, every share he can lay his hands on!

DR. STOCKMANN: Well, I don't understand, Peter. What's that got to do with—

PETER STOCKMANN, *walking around agitatedly*: Oh, come now, come now, come now!

DR. STOCKMANN: I hate you when you do that! Don't just walk around gabbling "Come now, come now!" What the hell are you talking about?

PETER STOCKMANN: Very well, if you insist on being dense. A man wages a relentless campaign to destroy confidence in a corporation. He even goes so far as to call a mass meeting against it. The very next morning, when people are still in a state of shock about it all, his father-in-law runs all over town, picking up shares at half their value.

DR. STOCKMANN, *realizing, turns away*: My God!

PETER STOCKMANN: And you have the nerve to speak to me about principles!

DR. STOCKMANN: You mean you actually believe that I . . . ?

PETER STOCKMANN: I'm not interested in psychology! I believe what I see! And what I see is nothing but a man doing a dirty, filthy job for Morten Kiil. And let me tell you—by tonight every man in this town'll see the same thing!

DR. STOCKMANN: Peter, you, you . . .

PETER STOCKMANN: Now go to your desk and write me a statement denying everything you've been saying, or . . .

DR. STOCKMANN: Peter, you're a low creature!

PETER STOCKMANN: All right then, you'd better get this one straight, Thomas. If you're figuring on opening another attack from out of town, keep this in mind: the morning it's published I'll send out a subpoena for you and begin a prosecution for conspiracy. I've been trying to make you respectable all my life; now if you want to make the big jump there'll be nobody there to hold you back. Now do we understand each other?

DR. STOCKMANN: Oh, we do, Peter! *Peter Stockmann starts for the door.* Get the girl—what the hell is her name—scrub the floors, wash down the walls, a pestilence has been here!

> *Kiil enters. Peter Stockmann almost runs into him. Peter turns to his brother.*

PETER STOCKMANN, *pointing to Kiil*: Ha! *He turns and goes out.*

> *Kiil, humming quietly, goes to a chair.*

DR. STOCKMANN: Morten! What have you done? What's the matter with you? Do you realize what this makes me look like?

> *Kiil has started taking some papers out of his pocket. Dr. Stockmann breaks off on seeing them. Kiil places them on the table.*

DR. STOCKMANN: Is that—them?

KIIL: That's them, yes. Kirsten Springs shares. And very easy to get this morning.

DR. STOCKMANN: Morten, don't play with me—what is this all about?

KIIL: What are you so nervous about? Can't a man buy some stock without . . . ?

DR. STOCKMANN: I want an explanation, Morten.

KIIL, *nodding*: Thomas, they hated you last night—

DR. STOCKMANN: You don't have to tell me that.

KIIL: But they also believed you. They'd love to murder you, but they believe you. *Slight pause.* The way they say it, the pollution is coming down the river from Windmill Valley.

DR. STOCKMANN: That's exactly where it's coming from.

KIIL: Yes. And that's exactly where my tannery is.

> *Pause. Dr. Stockmann sits down slowly.*

DR. STOCKMANN: Well, Morten, I never made a secret to you that the pollution was tannery waste.

KIIL: I'm not blaming you. It's my fault. I didn't take you seriously. But it's very serious now. Thomas, I got that tannery from my father; he got it from his father; and his father got it from my great-grandfather. I do not intend to allow my family's name to stand for the three generations of murdering angels who poisoned this town.

DR. STOCKMANN: I've waited a long time for this talk, Morten. I don't think you can stop that from happening.

KIIL: No, but you can.

DR. STOCKMANN: I?

KIIL, *nudging the shares*: I've bought these shares because—

DR. STOCKMANN: Morten, you've thrown your money away. The springs are doomed.

KIIL: I never throw my money away, Thomas. These were bought with your money.

DR. STOCKMANN: My money? What . . . ?

KIIL: You've probably suspected that I might leave a little something for Catherine and the boys?

DR. STOCKMANN: Well, naturally, I'd hoped you'd . . .

KIIL, *touching the shares*: I decided this morning to invest that money in some stock.

DR. STOCKMANN, *slowly getting up*: You bought that junk with Catherine's money!

KIIL: People call me "badger," and that's an animal that roots out things, but it's also some kind of a pig, I understand. I've lived a clean man and I'm going to die clean. You're going to clean my name for me.

DR. STOCKMANN: Morten . . .

KIIL: Now I want to see if you really belong in a strait jacket.

DR. STOCKMANN: How could you do such a thing? What's the matter with you!

KIIL: Now don't get excited, it's very simple. If you should make another investigation of the water—

DR. STOCKMANN: I don't *need* another investigation, I—

KIIL: If you think it over and decide that you ought to change your opinion about the water—

DR. STOCKMANN: But the water is poisoned! It is poisoned!

KIIL: If you simply go on insisting the water is poisoned—*he holds up the shares*—with these in your house, then there's only one explanation for you—you're absolutely crazy. *He puts the shares down on the table again.*

DR. STOCKMANN: You're right! I'm mad! I'm insane!

KIIL, *with more force*: You're stripping the skin off your family's back! Only a madman would do a thing like that!

DR. STOCKMANN: Morten, Morten, I'm a penniless man! Why didn't you tell me before you bought this junk?

KIIL: Because you would understand it better if I told you after. *He goes up to Dr. Stockmann, holds him by the lapels. With terrific force, and the twinkle still in his eye*: And, goddammit, I think you do understand it now, don't you? Millions of tons of water come down that river. How do you know the day you made your tests there wasn't something unusual about the water?

DR. STOCKMANN, *not looking at Kiil*: Yes, but I . . .

KIIL: How do you know? Why couldn't those little animals have clotted up only the patch of water you souped out of the river? How do you know the rest of it wasn't pure?

DR. STOCKMANN: It's not probable. People were getting sick last summer . . .

KIIL: They were sick when they came here or they wouldn't have come!

DR. STOCKMANN, *breaking away*: Not intestinal diseases, skin diseases . . .

KIIL, *following him*: The only place anybody gets a bellyache is here! There are no carbuncles in Norway? Maybe the food was bad. Did you ever think of the food?

DR. STOCKMANN, *with the desire to agree with him*: No, I didn't look into the food . . .

KIIL: Then what makes you so sure it's the water?

DR. STOCKMANN: Because I tested the water and—

KIIL, *taking hold of him again*: Admit it! We're all alone here. You have some doubt.

DR. STOCKMANN: Well, there's always a possible . . .

KIIL: Then part of it's imaginary.

DR. STOCKMANN: Well, nothing is a hundred per cent on this earth, but—

KIIL: Then you have a perfect right to doubt the other way! You have a scientific right! And did you ever think of some disinfectant? I bet you never even thought of that.

DR. STOCKMANN: Not for a mass of water like that, you can't . . .

KIIL: Everything can be killed. That's science! Thomas, I never liked your brother either, you have a perfect right to hate him.

DR. STOCKMANN: I didn't do it because I hate my brother.

KIIL: Part of it, part of it, don't deny it! You admit there's some doubt in your mind about the water, you admit there may be ways to disinfect it, and yet you went after your brother as though these doubts didn't exist; as though the only way to cure the thing was to blow up the whole Institute! There's hatred in that, boy, don't forget it. *He points to the shares.* These can belong to you now, so be sure, be sure! Tear the hatred out of your heart, stand naked in front of yourself—*are you sure?*

DR. STOCKMANN: What right have you to gamble my family's future on the strength of my convictions?

KIIL: Aha! Then the convictions are not really that strong!

DR. STOCKMANN: I am ready to hang for my convictions! But no man has a right to make martyrs of others; my family is innocent. Sell back those shares, give her what belongs to her. I'm a penniless man!

KIIL: Nobody is going to say Morten Kiil wrecked this town. *He gathers up the shares.* You retract your convictions—or these go to my charity.

DR. STOCKMANN: Everything?

KIIL: There'll be a little something for Catherine, but not much. I want my good name. It's exceedingly important to me.

DR. STOCKMANN, *bitterly*: And charity . . .

KIIL: Charity will do it, or you will do it. It's a serious thing to destroy a town.

DR. STOCKMANN: Morten, when I look at you, I swear to God I see the devil!

The door opens, and before we see who is there . . .

DR. STOCKMANN: You!

Aslaksen enters, holding up his hand defensively.

ASLAKSEN: Now don't get excited! Please!

Hovstad enters. He and Aslaksen stop short and smile on seeing Kiil.

KIIL: Too many intellectuals here: I'd better go.

ASLAKSEN, *apologetically*: Doctor, can we have five minutes of—

DR. STOCKMANN: I've got nothing to say to you.

KIIL, *going to the door*: I want an answer right away. You hear? I'm waiting. *He leaves.*

DR. STOCKMANN: All right, say it quick, what do you want?

HOVSTAD: We don't expect you to forgive our attitude at the meeting, but . . .

DR. STOCKMANN, *groping for the word*: Your attitude was prone . . . prostrated . . . prostituted!

HOVSTAD: All right, call it whatever you—

DR. STOCKMANN: I've got a lot on my mind, so get to the point. What do you want?

ASLAKSEN: Doctor, you should have told us what was in back of it all. You could have had the *Messenger* behind you all the way.

HOVSTAD: You'd have had public opinion with you now. Why didn't you tell us?

DR. STOCKMANN: Look, I'm very tired, let's not beat around the bush!

HOVSTAD, *gesturing toward the door where Kiil went out*: He's been all over town buying up stock in the springs. It's no secret any more.

DR. STOCKMANN, *after a slight pause*: Well, what about it?

HOVSTAD, *in a friendly way*: You don't want me to spell it out, do you?

DR. STOCKMANN: I certainly wish you would. I—

HOVSTAD: All right, let's lay it on the table. Aslaksen, you want to . . . ?

ASLAKSEN: No, no, go ahead.

HOVSTAD: Doctor, in the beginning we supported you. But it quickly became clear that if we kept on supporting you in the face of public hysteria—

DR. STOCKMANN: Your paper created the hysteria.

HOVSTAD: One thing at a time, all right? *Slowly, to drive it into Dr. Stockmann's head*: We couldn't go on supporting you because, in simple language, we didn't have the money to withstand the loss in circulation. You're boycotted now? Well, the paper would have been boycotted too, if we'd stuck with you.

ASLAKSEN: You can see that, Doctor.

DR. STOCKMANN: Oh, yes. But what do you want?

HOVSTAD: The *People's Messenger* can put on such a campaign that in two months you will be hailed as a hero in this town.

ASLAKSEN: We're ready to go.

HOVSTAD: We will prove to the public that you had to buy up the stock because the management would not make the changes required for public health. In other words, you did it for absolutely scientific, public-spirited reasons. Now what do you say, Doctor?

DR. STOCKMANN: You want money from me, is that it?

ASLAKSEN: Well, now, Doctor . . .

HOVSTAD, *to Aslaksen*: No, don't walk around it. *To Dr. Stockmann*: If we started to support you again, Doctor, we'd lose circulation for a while. We'd like you—or Mr. Kiil rather—to make up the deficit. *Quickly*: Now that's open and aboveboard, and I don't see anything wrong with it. Do you?

> *Pause. Dr. Stockmann looks at him, then turns and walks to the windows, deep in thought.*

ASLAKSEN: Remember, Doctor, you need the paper, you need it desperately.

DR. STOCKMANN, *returning*: No, there's nothing wrong with it at all. I—I'm not at all averse to cleaning up my name—although for myself it never was dirty. But I don't *enjoy* being hated, if you know what I mean.

ASLAKSEN: Exactly.

HOVSTAD: Aslaksen, will you show him the budget . . .

Aslaksen reaches into his pocket.

DR. STOCKMANN: Just a minute. There is one point. I hate to keep repeating the same thing, but the water is poisoned.

HOVSTAD: Now, Doctor . . .

DR. STOCKMANN: Just a minute. The Mayor says that he will levy a tax on everybody to pay for the reconstruction. I assume you are ready to support that tax at the same time you're supporting me.

ASLAKSEN: That tax would be extremely unpopular.

HOVSTAD: Doctor, with you back in charge of the baths, I have absolutely no fear that anything can go wrong.

DR. STOCKMANN: In other words, you will clean up my name—so that I can be in charge of the corruption.

HOVSTAD: But we can't tackle everything at once. A new tax—there'd be an uproar!

ASLAKSEN: It would ruin the paper!

DR. STOCKMANN: Then you don't intend to do anything about the water?

HOVSTAD: We have faith you won't let anyone get sick.

DR. STOCKMANN: In other words, gentlemen, you are looking for someone to blackmail into paying your printing bill.

HOVSTAD, *indignantly*: We are trying to clear your name, Doctor Stockmann! And if you refuse to cooperate, if that's going to be your attitude . . .

DR. STOCKMANN: Yes? Go on. What will you do?

HOVSTAD, *to Aslaksen*: I think we'd better go.

DR. STOCKMANN, *stepping in their way*: What will you do? I would like you to tell me. Me, the man two minutes ago you were going to make into a hero—what will you do now that I won't pay you?

ASLAKSEN: Doctor, the public is almost hysterical . . .

DR. STOCKMANN: To my face, tell me what you are going to do!

HOVSTAD: The Mayor will prosecute you for conspiracy to destroy a corporation, and without a paper behind you, you will end up in prison.

DR. STOCKMANN: And you'll support him, won't you? I want it from your mouth, Hovstad. This little victory you will not deny me. *Hovstad starts for the door. Dr. Stockmann steps into his way.* Tell the hero, Hovstad.

You're going to go on crucifying the hero, are you not? Say it to me! You will not leave here until I get this from your mouth!

HOVSTAD, *looking directly at Dr. Stockmann*: You are a madman. You are insane with egotism. And don't excuse it with humanitarian slogans, because a man who'll drag his family through a lifetime of disgrace is a demon in his heart! *He advances on Dr. Stockmann.* You hear me? A demon who cares more for the purity of a public bath than the lives of his wife and children. Doctor Stockmann, you deserve everything you're going to get!

> *Dr. Stockmann is struck by Hovstad's ferocious conviction. Aslaksen comes toward him, taking the budget out of his pocket.*

ASLAKSEN, *nervously*: Doctor, please consider it. It won't take much money, and in two months' time I promise you your whole life will change and . . .

> *Offstage Mrs. Stockmann is heard calling in a frightened voice, "What happened? My God, what's the matter?" She runs to the front door. Dr. Stockmann, alarmed, goes quickly to the hallway. Ejlif and Morten enter. Morten's head is bruised. Petra and Captain Horster enter from the left.*

MRS. STOCKMANN: Something happened! Look at him!

MORTEN: I'm all right, they just . . .

DR. STOCKMANN, *looking at the bruise*: What happened here?

MORTEN: Nothing, Papa, I swear . . .

DR. STOCKMANN, *to Ejlif*: What happened? Why aren't you in school?

EJLIF: The teacher said we better stay home the rest of the week.

DR. STOCKMANN: The boys hit him?

EJLIF: They started calling you names, so he got sore and began to fight with one kid, and all of a sudden the whole bunch of them . . .

MRS. STOCKMANN, *to Morten*: Why did you answer!

MORTEN, *indignantly*: They called him a traitor! My father is no traitor!

EJLIF: But you didn't have to answer!

MRS. STOCKMANN: You should've known they'd all jump on you! They could have killed you!

MORTEN: I don't care!

DR. STOCKMANN, *to quiet him—and his own heart*: Morten . . .

MORTEN, *pulling away from his father*: I'll kill them! I'll take a rock and the next time I see one of them I'll kill him!

> *Dr. Stockmann reaches for Morten, who, thinking his father will chastise him, starts to run. Dr. Stockmann catches him and grips him by the arm.*

MORTEN: Let me go! Let me . . . !

DR. STOCKMANN: Morten . . . Morten . . .

MORTEN, *crying in his father's arms*: They called you traitor, an enemy . . . *He sobs.*

DR. STOCKMANN: Sssh. That's all. Wash your face.

> *Mrs. Stockmann takes Morten. Dr. Stockmann stands erect, faces Aslaksen and Hovstad.*

DR. STOCKMANN: Good day, gentlemen.

HOVSTAD: Let us know what you decide and we'll—

DR. STOCKMANN: I've decided. I am an enemy of the people.

MRS. STOCKMANN: Tom, what are you . . . ?

DR. STOCKMANN: To such people, who teach their own children to think with their fists—to them I'm an enemy! And my boy . . . my boys . . . my family . . . I think you can count us all enemies.

ASLAKSEN: Doctor, you could have everything you want!

DR. STOCKMANN: Except the truth. I could have everything but that— that the water is poisoned!

HOVSTAD: But you'll be in charge.

DR. STOCKMANN: But the children are poisoned, the people are poisoned! If the only way I can be a friend of the people is to take charge of that corruption, then I am an enemy! The water is poisoned, poisoned, poisoned! That's the beginning of it and that's the end of it! Now get out of here!

HOVSTAD: You know where you're going to end?

DR. STOCKMANN: I said get out of here! *He grabs Aslaksen's umbrella out of his hand.*

MRS. STOCKMANN: What are you doing?

> *Aslaksen and Hovstad back toward the door as Dr. Stockmann starts to swing.*

ASLAKSEN: You're a fanatic, you're out of your mind!

MRS. STOCKMANN, *grabbing Dr. Stockmann to take the umbrella*: What are you doing?

DR. STOCKMANN: They want me to buy the paper, the public, the pollution of the springs, buy the whole pollution of this town! They'll make a hero out of me for that! *Furiously, to Aslaksen and Hovstad*: But I'm not a hero, I'm the enemy—and now you're first going to find out what kind of enemy I am! I will sharpen my pen like a dagger—you, all you friends of the people, are going to bleed before I'm done! Go, tell them to sign the petitions! Warn them not to call me when they're sick! Beat up my children! And never let her—*he points to Petra*—in the school again or she'll destroy the immaculate purity of the vacuum there! See to all the barricades—the truth is coming! Ring the bells, sound the alarm! The truth, the truth is out, and soon it will be prowling like a lion in the streets!

HOVSTAD: Doctor, you're out of your mind.

He and Aslaksen turn to go. They are in the doorway.

EJLIF, *rushing at them*: Don't you say that to him!

DR. STOCKMANN, *as Mrs. Stockmann cries out, rushes them with the umbrella*: Out of here!

They rush out. Dr. Stockmann throws the umbrella after them, then slams the door. Silence. He has his back pressed against the door, facing his family.

DR. STOCKMANN: I've had all the ambassadors of hell today, but there'll be no more. Now, now listen, Catherine! Children, listen. Now we're besieged. They'll call for blood now, they'll whip the people like oxen— *A rock comes through a remaining pane. The boys start for the window.* Stay away from there!

MRS. STOCKMANN: The Captain knows where we can get a ship.

DR. STOCKMANN: No ships.

PETRA: We're staying?

MRS. STOCKMANN: But they can't go back to school! I won't let them out of the house!

DR. STOCKMANN: We're staying.

PETRA: Good!

DR. STOCKMANN: We must be careful now. We must live through this. Boys, no more school. I'm going to teach you, and Petra will. Do you know any kids, street louts, hookey-players—

EJLIF: Oh, sure, we—

DR. STOCKMANN: We'll want about twelve of them to start. But I want them good and ignorant, absolutely uncivilized. Can we use your house, Captain?

HORSTER: Sure, I'm never there.

DR. STOCKMANN: Fine. We'll begin, Petra, and we'll turn out not taxpayers and newspaper subscribers, but free and independent people, hungry for the truth. Oh, I forgot! Petra, run to Grandpa and tell him—tell him as follows: No!

MRS. STOCKMANN, *puzzled*: What do you mean?

DR. STOCKMANN, *going over to Mrs. Stockmann*: It means, my dear, that we are all alone. And there'll be a long night before it's day—

A rock comes through a paneless window. Horster goes to the window. A crowd is heard approaching.

HORSTER: Half the town is out!

MRS. STOCKMANN: What's going to happen? Tom! What's going to happen?

DR. STOCKMANN, *holding his hands up to quiet her, and with a trembling mixture of trepidation and courageous insistence*: I don't know. But remember now, everybody. You are fighting for the truth, and that's why you're alone. And that makes you strong. We're the strongest people in the world . . .

The crowd is heard angrily calling outside. Another rock comes through a window.

DR. STOCKMANN: . . . and the strong must learn to be lonely!

The crowd noise gets louder. He walks upstage toward the windows as a wind rises and the curtains start to billow out toward him.

THE CURTAIN FALLS.

THE CRUCIBLE

A PLAY IN FOUR ACTS

1953

Characters

REVEREND PARRIS

BETTY PARRIS

TITUBA

ABIGAIL WILLIAMS

SUSANNA WALCOTT

MRS. ANN PUTNAM

THOMAS PUTNAM

MERCY LEWIS

MARY WARREN

JOHN PROCTOR

REBECCA NURSE

GILES COREY

REVEREND JOHN HALE

ELIZABETH PROCTOR

FRANCIS NURSE

EZEKIEL CHEEVER

MARSHAL HERRICK

JUDGE HATHORNE

DEPUTY GOVERNOR DANFORTH

SARAH GOOD

HOPKINS

A NOTE ON THE
HISTORICAL ACCURACY OF THIS PLAY

This play is not history in the sense in which the word is used by the academic historian. Dramatic purposes have sometimes required many characters to be fused into one; the number of girls involved in the "crying-out" has been reduced; Abigail's age has been raised; while there were several judges of almost equal authority, I have symbolized them all in Hathorne and Danforth. However, I believe that the reader will discover here the essential nature of one of the strangest and most awful chapters in human history. The fate of each character is exactly that of his historical model, and there is no one in the drama who did not play a similar—and in some cases exactly the same—role in history.

As for the characters of the persons, little is known about most of them excepting what may be surmised from a few letters, the trial record, certain broadsides written at the time, and references to their conduct in sources of varying reliability. They may therefore be taken as creations of my own, drawn to the best of my ability in conformity with their known behavior, except as indicated in the commentary I have written for this text.

ACT ONE
(AN OVERTURE)

A small upper bedroom in the home of Reverend Samuel Parris, Salem, Massachusetts, in the spring of the year 1692.

There is a narrow window at the left. Through its leaded panes the morning sunlight streams. A candle still burns near the bed, which is at the right. A chest, a chair, and a small table are the other furnishings. At the back a door opens on the landing of the stairway to the ground floor. The room gives off an air of clean spareness. The roof rafters are exposed, and the wood colors are raw and unmellowed.

As the curtain rises, Reverend Parris is discovered kneeling beside the bed, evidently in prayer. His daughter, Betty Parris, aged ten, is lying on the bed, inert.

At the time of these events Parris was in his middle forties. In history he cut a villainous path, and there is very little good to be said for him. He believed he was being persecuted wherever he went, despite his best efforts to win people and God to his side. In meeting, he felt insulted if someone rose to shut the door without first asking his permission. He was a widower with no interest in children, or talent with them. He regarded them as young adults, and until this strange crisis he, like the rest of Salem, never conceived that the children were anything but thankful for being permitted to walk straight, eyes slightly lowered, arms at the sides, and mouths shut until bidden to speak.

His house stood in the "town"—but we today would hardly call it a village. The meeting house was nearby, and from this point outward—toward the bay or inland—there were a few small-windowed, dark houses snuggling against the raw Massachusetts winter. Salem had been established hardly forty years before. To the European world the whole province was a barbaric frontier inhabited by a sect of fanatics who, nevertheless, were shipping out products of slowly increasing quantity and value.

No one can really know what their lives were like. They had no novelists—and would not have permitted anyone to read a novel if one were handy. Their creed forbade anything resembling a theater or "vain enjoyment." They did not celebrate Christmas, and a holiday from work meant only that they must concentrate even more upon prayer.

Which is not to say that nothing broke into this strict and somber way of life. When a new farmhouse was built, friends assembled to "raise the roof," and there would be special foods cooked and probably some potent cider passed around. There was a good supply of ne'er-do-wells in Salem, who dallied at the shovelboard in Bridget Bishop's tavern. Probably more than the creed, hard work kept the morals of the place from spoiling, for the people were forced to fight the land like heroes for every grain of corn, and no man had very much time for fooling around.

That there were some jokers, however, is indicated by the practice of appointing a two-man patrol whose duty was to "walk forth in the time of God's worship to take notice of such as either lye about the meeting house, without attending to the word and ordinances, or that lye at home or in the fields without giving good account thereof, and to take the names of such persons, and to present them to the magistrates, whereby they may be accordingly proceeded against." This predilection for minding other people's business was time-honored among the people of Salem, and it undoubtedly created many of the suspicions which were to feed the coming madness. It was also, in my opinion, one of the things that a John Proctor would rebel against, for the time of the armed camp had almost passed, and since the country was reasonably—although not wholly—safe, the old disciplines were beginning to rankle. But, as in all such matters, the issue was not clear-cut, for danger was still a possibility, and in unity still lay the best promise of safety.

The edge of the wilderness was close by. The American continent stretched endlessly west, and it was full of mystery for them. It stood, dark and threatening, over their shoulders night and day, for out of it Indian tribes marauded from time to time, and Reverend Parris had parishioners who had lost relatives to these heathen.

The parochial snobbery of these people was partly responsible for their failure to convert the Indians. Probably they also preferred to take land from heathens rather than from fellow Christians. At any rate, very few Indians were converted, and the Salem folk believed that the virgin forest was the Devil's last preserve, his home base and the citadel of his final stand. To the best of their knowledge the American forest was the last place on earth that was not paying homage to God.

For these reasons, among others, they carried about an air of innate resistance, even of persecution. Their fathers had, of course, been persecuted in England. So now they and their church found it necessary to deny any other sect its freedom, lest their New Jerusalem be defiled and corrupted by wrong ways and deceitful ideas.

They believed, in short, that they held in their steady hands the candle that would light the world. We have inherited this belief, and it has helped and hurt us. It helped them with the discipline it gave them. They were a dedicated folk, by and large, and they had to be to survive the life they had chosen or been born into in this country.

The proof of their belief's value to them may be taken from the opposite character of the first Jamestown settlement, farther south, in Virginia. The Englishmen who landed there were motivated mainly by a hunt for profit. They had thought to pick off the wealth of the new country and then return rich to England. They were a band of individualists, and a much more ingratiating group than the Massachusetts men. But Virginia destroyed them. Massachusetts tried to kill off the Puritans, but they combined; they set up a communal society which, in the beginning, was little more than an armed camp with an autocratic and very devoted leadership. It was, however, an autocracy by consent, for they were united from top to bottom by a commonly held ideology whose perpetuation was the reason and justification for all their sufferings. So their self-denial, their purposefulness, their suspicion of all vain pursuits, their hard-handed justice were altogether perfect instruments for the conquest of this space so antagonistic to man.

But the people of Salem in 1692 were not quite the dedicated folk that arrived on the *Mayflower.* A vast differentiation had taken place, and in their own time a revolution had unseated the royal government and substituted a junta which was at this moment in power. The times, to their eyes, must have been out of joint, and to the common folk must have seemed as insoluble and complicated as do ours today. It is not hard to see how easily many could have been led to believe that the time of confusion had been brought upon them by deep and darkling forces. No hint of such speculation appears on the court record, but social disorder in any age breeds such mystical suspicions, and when, as in Salem, wonders are brought forth from below the social surface, it is too much to expect people to hold back very long from laying on the victims with all the force of their frustrations.

The Salem tragedy, which is about to begin in these pages, developed from a paradox. It is a paradox in whose grip we still live, and there is no prospect yet that we will discover its resolution. Simply, it was this: for good purposes, even high purposes, the people of Salem developed a theocracy, a combine of state and religious power whose function was to keep the community together, and to prevent any kind of disunity that might open it to destruction by material or ideological enemies. It was forged for a necessary purpose and accomplished that purpose. But all organization is and must be grounded on the idea of exclusion and prohibition, just as two objects cannot occupy the same space. Evidently the time came in New England when the repressions of order were heavier than seemed warranted by the dangers against which the order was organized. The witch-hunt was a perverse manifestation of the panic which set in among all classes when the balance began to turn toward greater individual freedom.

When one rises above the individual villainy displayed, one can only pity them all, just as we shall be pitied someday. It is still impossible for man to organize his social life without repressions, and the balance has yet to be struck between order and freedom.

The witch-hunt was not, however, a mere repression. It was also, and as importantly, a long overdue opportunity for everyone so inclined to express publicly his guilt and sins, under the cover of accusations against the victims. It suddenly became possible—and patriotic and holy—for a man to say that Martha Corey had come into his bedroom at night, and that, while his wife was sleeping at his side, Martha laid herself down on his chest and "nearly suffocated him." Of course it was her spirit only, but his satisfaction at confessing himself was no lighter than if it had been Martha herself. One could not ordinarily speak such things in public.

Long-held hatreds of neighbors could now be openly expressed, and vengeance taken, despite the Bible's charitable injunctions. Land-lust, which had been expressed by constant bickering over boundaries and deeds, could now be elevated to the arena of morality; one could cry witch against one's neighbor and feel perfectly justified in the bargain. Old scores could be settled on a plane of heavenly combat between Lucifer and the Lord; suspicions and the envy of the miserable toward the happy could and did burst out in the general revenge.

Reverend Parris is praying now, and, though we cannot hear his words, a sense of his confusion hangs about him. He mumbles, then seems about to weep; then he weeps, then prays again; but his daughter does not stir on the bed.

The door opens, and his Negro slave enters. Tituba is in her forties. Parris brought her with him from Barbados, where he spent some years as a merchant before entering the ministry. She enters as one does who can no longer bear to be barred from the sight of her beloved, but she is also very frightened because her slave sense has warned her that, as always, trouble in this house eventually lands on her back.

TITUBA, *already taking a step backward*: My Betty be hearty soon?

PARRIS: Out of here!

TITUBA, *backing to the door*: My Betty not goin' die . . .

PARRIS, *scrambling to his feet in a fury*: Out of my sight! *She is gone.* Out of my— *He is overcome with sobs. He clamps his teeth against them and closes the door and leans against it, exhausted.* Oh, my God! God help me! *Quaking with fear, mumbling to himself through his sobs, he goes to the bed and gently takes Betty's hand.* Betty. Child. Dear child. Will you wake, will you open up your eyes! Betty, little one . . .

> *He is bending to kneel again when his niece, Abigail Williams, seventeen, enters—a strikingly beautiful girl, an orphan, with an endless capacity for dissembling. Now she is all worry and apprehension and propriety.*

ABIGAIL: Uncle? *He looks to her.* Susanna Walcott's here from Doctor Griggs.

PARRIS: Oh? Let her come, let her come.

ABIGAIL, *leaning out the door to call to Susanna, who is down the hall a few steps*: Come in, Susanna.

> *Susanna Walcott, a little younger than Abigail, a nervous, hurried girl, enters.*

PARRIS, *eagerly*: What does the doctor say, child?

SUSANNA, *craning around Parris to get a look at Betty*: He bid me come and tell you, reverend sir, that he cannot discover no medicine for it in his books.

PARRIS: Then he must search on.

SUSANNA: Aye, sir, he have been searchin' his books since he left you, sir. But he bid me tell you, that you might look to unnatural things for the cause of it.

PARRIS, *his eyes going wide*: No—no. There be no unnatural cause here. Tell him I have sent for Reverend Hale of Beverly, and Mr. Hale will surely confirm that. Let him look to medicine and put out all thought of unnatural causes here. There be none.

SUSANNA: Aye, sir. He bid me tell you. *She turns to go.*

ABIGAIL: Speak nothin' of it in the village, Susanna.

PARRIS: Go directly home and speak nothing of unnatural causes.

SUSANNA: Aye, sir. I pray for her. *She goes out.*

ABIGAIL: Uncle, the rumor of witchcraft is all about; I think you'd best go down and deny it yourself. The parlor's packed with people, sir. I'll sit with her.

PARRIS, *pressed, turns on her*: And what shall I say to them? That my daughter and my niece I discovered dancing like heathen in the forest?

ABIGAIL: Uncle, we did dance; let you tell them I confessed it—and I'll be whipped if I must be. But they're speakin' of witchcraft. Betty's not witched.

PARRIS: Abigail, I cannot go before the congregation when I know you have not opened with me. What did you do with her in the forest?

ABIGAIL: We did dance, uncle, and when you leaped out of the bush so suddenly, Betty was frightened and then she fainted. And there's the whole of it.

PARRIS: Child. Sit you down.

ABIGAIL, *quavering, as she sits*: I would never hurt Betty. I love her dearly.

PARRIS: Now look you, child, your punishment will come in its time. But if you trafficked with spirits in the forest I must know it now, for surely my enemies will, and they will ruin me with it.

ABIGAIL: But we never conjured spirits.

PARRIS: Then why can she not move herself since midnight? This child is desperate!

> *Abigail lowers her eyes.*

> It must come out—my enemies will bring it out. Let me know what you done there. Abigail, do you understand that I have many enemies?

ABIGAIL: I have heard of it, uncle.

PARRIS: There is a faction that is sworn to drive me from my pulpit. Do you understand that?

ABIGAIL: I think so, sir.

PARRIS: Now then, in the midst of such disruption, my own household is discovered to be the very center of some obscene practice. Abominations are done in the forest—

ABIGAIL: It were sport, uncle!

PARRIS, *pointing at Betty*: You call this sport? *She lowers her eyes. He pleads*: Abigail, if you know something that may help the doctor, for God's sake tell it to me. *She is silent.* I saw Tituba waving her arms over the fire when I came on you. Why was she doing that? And I heard a screeching and gibberish coming from her mouth. She were swaying like a dumb beast over that fire!

ABIGAIL: She always sings her Barbados songs, and we dance.

PARRIS: I cannot blink what I saw, Abigail, for my enemies will not blink it. I saw a dress lying on the grass.

ABIGAIL, *innocently*: A dress?

PARRIS—*it is very hard to say*: Aye, a dress. And I thought I saw—someone naked running through the trees!

ABIGAIL, *in terror*: No one was naked! You mistake yourself, uncle!

PARRIS, *with anger*: I saw it! *He moves from her. Then, resolved*: Now tell me true, Abigail. And I pray you feel the weight of truth upon you, for now my ministry's at stake, my ministry and perhaps your cousin's life. Whatever abomination you have done, give me all of it now, for I dare not be taken unaware when I go before them down there.

ABIGAIL: There is nothin' more. I swear it, uncle.

PARRIS, *studies her, then nods, half convinced*: Abigail, I have fought here three long years to bend these stiff-necked people to me, and now, just now when some good respect is rising for me in the parish, you compromise my very character. I have given you a home, child, I have put clothes upon your back—now give me upright answer. Your name in the town—it is entirely white, is it not?

ABIGAIL, *with an edge of resentment*: Why, I am sure it is, sir. There be no blush about my name.

PARRIS, *to the point*: Abigail, is there any other cause than you have told me, for your being discharged from Goody Proctor's service? I have heard it said, and I tell you as I heard it, that she comes so rarely to the church this year for she will not sit so close to something soiled. What signified that remark?

ABIGAIL: She hates me, uncle, she must, for I would not be her slave. It's a bitter woman, a lying, cold, sniveling woman, and I will not work for such a woman!

PARRIS: She may be. And yet it has troubled me that you are now seven month out of their house, and in all this time no other family has ever called for your service.

ABIGAIL: They want slaves, not such as I. Let them send to Barbados for that. I will not black my face for any of them! *With ill-concealed resentment at him*: Do you begrudge my bed, uncle?

PARRIS: No—no.

ABIGAIL, *in a temper*: My name is good in the village! I will not have it said my name is soiled! Goody Proctor is a gossiping liar!

> *Enter Mrs. Ann Putnam. She is a twisted soul of forty-five, a death-ridden woman, haunted by dreams.*

PARRIS, *as soon as the door begins to open*: No—no, I cannot have anyone. *He sees her, and a certain deference springs into him, although his worry remains*. Why, Goody Putnam, come in.

MRS. PUTNAM, *full of breath, shiny-eyed*: It is a marvel. It is surely a stroke of hell upon you.

PARRIS: No, Goody Putnam, it is—

MRS. PUTNAM, *glancing at Betty*: How high did she fly, how high?

PARRIS: No, no, she never flew—

MRS. PUTNAM, *very pleased with it*: Why, it's sure she did. Mr. Collins saw her goin' over Ingersoll's barn, and come down light as bird, he says!

PARRIS: Now, look you, Goody Putnam, she never— *Enter Thomas Putnam, a well-to-do, hard-handed landowner, near fifty.* Oh, good morning, Mr. Putnam.

PUTNAM: It is a providence the thing is out now! It is a providence. *He goes directly to the bed.*

PARRIS: What's out, sir, what's—?

Mrs. Putnam goes to the bed.

PUTNAM, *looking down at Betty*: Why, *her* eyes is closed! Look you, Ann.

MRS. PUTNAM: Why, that's strange. *To Parris*: Ours is open.

PARRIS, *shocked*: Your Ruth is sick?

MRS. PUTNAM, *with vicious certainty*: I'd not call it sick; the Devil's touch is heavier than sick. It's death, y'know, it's death drivin' into them, forked and hoofed.

PARRIS: Oh, pray not! Why, how does Ruth ail?

MRS. PUTNAM: She ails as she must—she never waked this morning, but her eyes open and she walks, and hears naught, sees naught, and cannot eat. Her soul is taken, surely.

Parris is struck.

PUTNAM, *as though for further details*: They say you've sent for Reverend Hale of Beverly?

PARRIS, *with dwindling conviction now*: A precaution only. He has much experience in all demonic arts, and I—

MRS. PUTNAM: He has indeed; and found a witch in Beverly last year, and let you remember that.

PARRIS: Now, Goody Ann, they only thought that were a witch, and I am certain there be no element of witchcraft here.

PUTNAM: No witchcraft! Now look you, Mr. Parris—

PARRIS: Thomas, Thomas, I pray you, leap not to witchcraft. I know that you—you least of all, Thomas, would ever wish so disastrous a charge laid upon me. We cannot leap to witchcraft. They will howl me out of Salem for such corruption in my house.

A word about Thomas Putnam. He was a man with many griev-ances, at least one of which appears justified. Some time before, his wife's brother-in-law, James Bayley, had been turned down as minister of Salem. Bayley had all the qualifications, and a two-thirds vote into the bargain, but a faction stopped his acceptance, for reasons that are not clear.

Thomas Putnam was the eldest son of the richest man in the village. He had fought the Indians at Narragansett, and was deeply interested in par-ish affairs. He undoubtedly felt it poor payment that the village should so blatantly disregard his candidate for one of its more important offices, especially since he regarded himself as the intellectual superior of most of the people around him.

His vindictive nature was demonstrated long before the witchcraft began. A former Salem minister, George Burroughs, had had to borrow money to pay for his wife's funeral, and, since the parish was remiss in his salary, he was soon bankrupt. Thomas and his brother John had Bur-roughs jailed for debts the man did not owe. The incident is important only in that Burroughs succeeded in becoming minister where Bayley, Thomas Putnam's brother-in-law, had been rejected; the motif of resent-ment is clear here. Thomas Putnam felt that his own name and the honor of his family had been smirched by the village, and he meant to right mat-ters however he could.

Another reason to believe him a deeply embittered man was his attempt to break his father's will, which left a disproportionate amount to a step-brother. As with every other public cause in which he tried to force his way, he failed in this.

So it is not surprising to find that so many accusations against people are in the handwriting of Thomas Putnam, or that his name is so often found as a witness corroborating the supernatural testimony, or that his daughter led the crying-out at the most opportune junctures of the trials, especially when— But we'll speak of that when we come to it.

PUTNAM—*at the moment he is intent upon getting Parris, for whom he has only contempt, to move toward the abyss*: Mr. Parris, I have taken your part in all contention here, and I would continue; but I cannot if you hold back in this. There are hurtful, vengeful spirits layin' hands on these children.

PARRIS: But, Thomas, you cannot—

PUTNAM: Ann! Tell Mr. Parris what you have done.

MRS. PUTNAM: Reverend Parris, I have laid seven babies unbaptized in the earth. Believe me, sir, you never saw more hearty babies born. And yet, each would wither in my arms the very night of their birth. I have spoke nothin', but my heart has clamored intimations. And now, this year, my Ruth, my only— I see her turning strange. A secret child she has become this year, and shrivels like a sucking mouth were pullin' on her life too. And so I thought to send her to your Tituba—

PARRIS: To Tituba! What may Tituba—?

MRS. PUTNAM: Tituba knows how to speak to the dead, Mr. Parris.

PARRIS: Goody Ann, it is a formidable sin to conjure up the dead!

MRS. PUTNAM: I take it on my soul, but who else may surely tell us what person murdered my babies?

PARRIS, *horrified*: Woman!

MRS. PUTNAM: They were murdered, Mr. Parris! And mark this proof! Mark it! Last night my Ruth were ever so close to their little spirits; I know it, sir. For how else is she struck dumb now except some power of darkness would stop her mouth? It is a marvelous sign, Mr. Parris!

PUTNAM: Don't you understand it, sir? There is a murdering witch among us, bound to keep herself in the dark. *Parris turns to Betty, a frantic terror rising in him.* Let your enemies make of it what they will, you cannot blink it more.

PARRIS, *to Abigail*: Then you were conjuring spirits last night.

ABIGAIL, *whispering*: Not I, sir—Tituba and Ruth.

PARRIS *turns now, with new fear, and goes to Betty, looks down at her, and then, gazing off*: Oh, Abigail, what proper payment for my charity! Now I am undone.

PUTNAM: You are not undone! Let you take hold here. Wait for no one to charge you—declare it yourself. You have discovered witchcraft—

PARRIS: In my house? In my house, Thomas? They will topple me with this! They will make of it a—

> Enter Mercy Lewis, the Putnams' servant, a fat, sly, merciless girl of eighteen.

MERCY: Your pardons. I only thought to see how Betty is.

PUTNAM: Why aren't you home? Who's with Ruth?

MERCY: Her grandma come. She's improved a little, I think—she give a powerful sneeze before.

MRS. PUTNAM: Ah, there's a sign of life!

MERCY: I'd fear no more, Goody Putnam. It were a grand sneeze; another like it will shake her wits together, I'm sure. *She goes to the bed to look.*

PARRIS: Will you leave me now, Thomas? I would pray a while alone.

ABIGAIL: Uncle, you've prayed since midnight. Why do you not go down and—

PARRIS: No—no. *To Putnam:* I have no answer for that crowd. I'll wait till Mr. Hale arrives. *To get Mrs. Putnam to leave:* If you will, Goody Ann . . .

PUTNAM: Now look you, sir. Let you strike out against the Devil, and the village will bless you for it! Come down, speak to them—pray with them. They're thirsting for your word, Mister! Surely you'll pray with them.

PARRIS, *swayed:* I'll lead them in a psalm, but let you say nothing of witchcraft yet. I will not discuss it. The cause is yet unknown. I have had enough contention since I came; I want no more.

MRS. PUTNAM: Mercy, you go home to Ruth, d'y'hear?

MERCY: Aye, mum.

Mrs. Putnam goes out.

PARRIS, *to Abigail:* If she starts for the window, cry for me at once.

ABIGAIL: I will, uncle.

PARRIS, *to Putnam:* There is a terrible power in her arms today. *He goes out with Putnam.*

ABIGAIL, *with hushed trepidation:* How is Ruth sick?

MERCY: It's weirdish, I know not—she seems to walk like a dead one since last night.

ABIGAIL, *turns at once and goes to Betty, and now, with fear in her voice:* Betty? *Betty doesn't move. She shakes her.* Now stop this! Betty! Sit up now!

Betty doesn't stir. Mercy comes over.

MERCY: Have you tried beatin' her? I gave Ruth a good one and it waked her for a minute. Here, let me have her.

ABIGAIL, *holding Mercy back:* No, he'll be comin' up. Listen, now; if they be questioning us, tell them we danced—I told him as much already.

MERCY: Aye. And what more?

ABIGAIL: He knows Tituba conjured Ruth's sisters to come out of the grave.

MERCY: And what more?

ABIGAIL: He saw you naked.

MERCY, *clapping her hands together with a frightened laugh*: Oh, Jesus!

> *Enter Mary Warren, breathless. She is seventeen, a subservient, naïve, lonely girl.*

MARY WARREN: What'll we do? The village is out! I just come from the farm; the whole country's talkin' witchcraft! They'll be callin' us witches, Abby!

MERCY, *pointing and looking at Mary Warren*: She means to tell, I know it.

MARY WARREN: Abby, we've got to tell. Witchery's a hangin' error, a hangin' like they done in Boston two year ago! We must tell the truth, Abby! You'll only be whipped for dancin', and the other things!

ABIGAIL: Oh, *we'll* be whipped!

MARY WARREN: I never done none of it, Abby. I only looked!

MERCY, *moving menacingly toward Mary*: Oh, you're a great one for lookin', aren't you, Mary Warren? What a grand peeping courage you have!

> *Betty, on the bed, whimpers. Abigail turns to her at once.*

ABIGAIL: Betty? *She goes to Betty.* Now, Betty, dear, wake up now. It's Abigail. *She sits Betty up and furiously shakes her.* I'll beat you, Betty! *Betty whimpers.* My, you seem improving. I talked to your papa and I told him everything. So there's nothing to—

BETTY, *darts off the bed, frightened of Abigail, and flattens herself against the wall*: I want my mama!

ABIGAIL, *with alarm, as she cautiously approaches Betty*: What ails you, Betty? Your mama's dead and buried.

BETTY: I'll fly to Mama. Let me fly! *She raises her arms as though to fly, and streaks for the window, gets one leg out.*

ABIGAIL, *pulling her away from the window*: I told him everything; he knows now, he knows everything we—

BETTY: You drank blood, Abby! You didn't tell him that!

ABIGAIL: Betty, you never say that again! You will never—

BETTY: You did, you did! You drank a charm to kill John Proctor's wife! You drank a charm to kill Goody Proctor!

ABIGAIL, *smashes her across the face*: Shut it! Now shut it!

BETTY, *collapsing on the bed*: Mama, Mama! *She dissolves into sobs.*

ABIGAIL: Now look you. All of you. We danced. And Tituba conjured Ruth Putnam's dead sisters. And that is all. And mark this. Let either of you breathe a word, or the edge of a word, about the other things, and I will come to you in the black of some terrible night and I will bring a pointy reckoning that will shudder you. And you know I can do it; I saw Indians smash my dear parents' heads on the pillow next to mine, and I have seen some reddish work done at night, and I can make you wish you had never seen the sun go down! *She goes to Betty and roughly sits her up.* Now, you—sit up and stop this!

> *But Betty collapses in her hands and lies inert on the bed.*

MARY WARREN, *with hysterical fright*: What's got her? *Abigail stares in fright at Betty.* Abby, she's going to die! It's a sin to conjure, and we—

ABIGAIL, *starting for Mary*: I say shut it, Mary Warren!

> *Enter John Proctor. On seeing him, Mary Warren leaps in fright.*

Proctor was a farmer in his middle thirties. He need not have been a partisan of any faction in the town, but there is evidence to suggest that he had a sharp and biting way with hypocrites. He was the kind of man—powerful of body, even-tempered, and not easily led—who cannot refuse support to partisans without drawing their deepest resentment. In Proctor's presence a fool felt his foolishness instantly—and a Proctor is always marked for calumny therefore.

But as we shall see, the steady manner he displays does not spring from an untroubled soul. He is a sinner, a sinner not only against the moral fashion of the time, but against his own vision of decent conduct. These people had no ritual for the washing away of sins. It is another trait we inherited from them, and it has helped to discipline us as well as to breed hypocrisy among us. Proctor, respected and even feared in Salem, has come to regard himself as a kind of fraud. But no hint of this has yet appeared on the surface, and as he enters from the crowded parlor below it is a man in his prime we see, with a quiet confidence and an unexpressed, hidden force. Mary Warren, his servant, can barely speak for embarrassment and fear.

MARY WARREN: Oh! I'm just going home, Mr. Proctor.

PROCTOR: Be you foolish, Mary Warren? Be you deaf? I forbid you leave the house, did I not? Why shall I pay you? I am looking for you more often than my cows!

MARY WARREN: I only come to see the great doings in the world.

PROCTOR: I'll show you a great doin' on your arse one of these days. Now get you home; my wife is waitin' with your work! *Trying to retain a shred of dignity, she goes slowly out.*

MERCY LEWIS, *both afraid of him and strangely titillated*: I'd best be off. I have my Ruth to watch. Good morning, Mr. Proctor.

> *Mercy sidles out. Since Proctor's entrance, Abigail has stood as though on tiptoe, absorbing his presence, wide-eyed. He glances at her, then goes to Betty on the bed.*

ABIGAIL: Gah! I'd almost forgot how strong you are, John Proctor!

PROCTOR, *looking at Abigail now, the faintest suggestion of a knowing smile on his face*: What's this mischief here?

ABIGAIL, *with a nervous laugh*: Oh, she's only gone silly somehow.

PROCTOR: The road past my house is a pilgrimage to Salem all morning. The town's mumbling witchcraft.

ABIGAIL: Oh, posh! *Winningly she comes a little closer, with a confidential, wicked air.* We were dancin' in the woods last night, and my uncle leaped in on us. She took fright, is all.

PROCTOR, *his smile widening*: Ah, you're wicked yet, aren't y'! *A trill of expectant laughter escapes her, and she dares come closer, feverishly looking into his eyes.* You'll be clapped in the stocks before you're twenty.

> *He takes a step to go, and she springs into his path.*

ABIGAIL: Give me a word, John. A soft word. *Her concentrated desire destroys his smile.*

PROCTOR: No, no, Abby. That's done with.

ABIGAIL, *tauntingly*: You come five mile to see a silly girl fly? I know you better.

PROCTOR, *setting her firmly out of his path*: I come to see what mischief your uncle's brewin' now. *With final emphasis*: Put it out of mind, Abby.

ABIGAIL, *grasping his hand before he can release her*: John—I am waitin' for you every night.

PROCTOR: Abby, I never give you hope to wait for me.

ABIGAIL, *now beginning to anger—she can't believe it*: I have something better than hope, I think!

PROCTOR: Abby, you'll put it out of mind. I'll not be comin' for you more.

ABIGAIL: You're surely sportin' with me.

PROCTOR: You know me better.

ABIGAIL: I know how you clutched my back behind your house and sweated like a stallion whenever I come near! Or did I dream that? It's she put me out, you cannot pretend it were you. I saw your face when she put me out, and you loved me then and you do now!

PROCTOR: Abby, that's a wild thing to say—

ABIGAIL: A wild thing may say wild things. But not so wild, I think. I have seen you since she put me out; I have seen you nights.

PROCTOR: I have hardly stepped off my farm this seven month.

ABIGAIL: I have a sense for heat, John, and yours has drawn me to my window, and I have seen you looking up, burning in your loneliness. Do you tell me you've never looked up at my window?

PROCTOR: I may have looked up.

ABIGAIL, *now softening*: And you must. You are no wintry man. I know you, John. I *know* you. *She is weeping.* I cannot sleep for dreamin'; I cannot dream but I wake and walk about the house as though I'd find you comin' through some door. *She clutches him desperately.*

PROCTOR, *gently pressing her from him, with great sympathy but firmly*: Child—

ABIGAIL, *with a flash of anger*: How do you call me child!

PROCTOR: Abby, I may think of you softly from time to time. But I will cut off my hand before I'll ever reach for you again. Wipe it out of mind. We never touched, Abby.

ABIGAIL: Aye, but we did.

PROCTOR: Aye, but we did not.

ABIGAIL, *with a bitter anger*: Oh, I marvel how such a strong man may let such a sickly wife be—

PROCTOR, *angered—at himself as well*: You'll speak nothin' of Elizabeth!

ABIGAIL: She is blackening my name in the village! She is telling lies about me! She is a cold, sniveling woman, and you bend to her! Let her turn you like a—

PROCTOR, *shaking her*: Do you look for whippin'?

A psalm is heard being sung below.

ABIGAIL, *in tears*: I look for John Proctor that took me from my sleep and put knowledge in my heart! I never knew what pretense Salem was, I never knew the lying lessons I was taught by all these Christian women and their covenanted men! And now you bid me tear the light out of my eyes? I will not, I cannot! You loved me, John Proctor, and whatever sin it is, you love me yet! *He turns abruptly to go out. She rushes to him.* John, pity me, pity me!

The words "going up to Jesus" are heard in the psalm, and Betty claps her ears suddenly and whines loudly.

ABIGAIL: Betty? *She hurries to Betty, who is now sitting up and screaming. Proctor goes to Betty as Abigail is trying to pull her hands down, calling "Betty!"*

PROCTOR, *growing unnerved*: What's she doing? Girl, what ails you? Stop that wailing!

The singing has stopped in the midst of this, and now Parris rushes in.

PARRIS: What happened? What are you doing to her? Betty! *He rushes to the bed, crying, "Betty, Betty!"*

Mrs. Putnam enters, feverish with curiosity, and with her Thomas Putnam and Mercy Lewis. Parris, at the bed, keeps lightly slapping Betty's face, while she moans and tries to get up.

ABIGAIL: She heard you singin' and suddenly she's up and screamin'.

MRS. PUTNAM: The psalm! The psalm! She cannot bear to hear the Lord's name!

PARRIS: No, God forbid. Mercy, run to the doctor! Tell him what's happened here! *Mercy Lewis rushes out.*

MRS. PUTNAM: Mark it for a sign, mark it!

Rebecca Nurse, seventy-two, enters. She is white-haired, leaning upon her walking-stick.

PUTNAM, *pointing at the whimpering Betty*: That is a notorious sign of witchcraft afoot, Goody Nurse, a prodigious sign!

MRS. PUTNAM: My mother told me that! When they cannot bear to hear the name of—

PARRIS, *trembling*: Rebecca, Rebecca, go to her, we're lost. She suddenly cannot bear to hear the Lord's—

Giles Corey, eighty-three, enters. He is knotted with muscle, canny, inquisitive, and still powerful.

REBECCA: There is hard sickness here, Giles Corey, so please to keep the quiet.

GILES: I've not said a word. No one here can testify I've said a word. Is she going to fly again? I hear she flies.

PUTNAM: Man, be quiet now!

Everything is quiet. Rebecca walks across the room to the bed. Gentleness exudes from her. Betty is quietly whimper-

ing, eyes shut. Rebecca simply stands over the child, who gradually quiets.

And while they are so absorbed, we may put a word in for Rebecca. Rebecca was the wife of Francis Nurse, who, from all accounts, was one of those men for whom both sides of the argument had to have respect. He was called upon to arbitrate disputes as though he were an unofficial judge, and Rebecca also enjoyed the high opinion most people had for him. By the time of the delusion, they had three hundred acres, and their children were settled in separate homesteads within the same estate. However, Francis had originally rented the land, and one theory has it that, as he gradually paid for it and raised his social status, there were those who resented his rise.

Another suggestion to explain the systematic campaign against Rebecca, and inferentially against Francis, is the land war he fought with his neighbors, one of whom was a Putnam. This squabble grew to the proportions of a battle in the woods between partisans of both sides, and it is said to have lasted for two days. As for Rebecca herself, the general opinion of her character was so high that to explain how anyone dared cry her out for a witch—and more, how adults could bring themselves to lay hands on her—we must look to the fields and boundaries of that time.

As we have seen, Thomas Putnam's man for the Salem ministry was Bayley. The Nurse clan had been in the faction that prevented Bayley's taking office. In addition, certain families allied to the Nurses by blood or friendship, and whose farms were contiguous with the Nurse farm or close to it, combined to break away from the Salem town authority and set up Topsfield, a new and independent entity whose existence was resented by old Salemites.

That the guiding hand behind the outcry was Putnam's is indicated by the fact that, as soon as it began, this Topsfield-Nurse faction absented themselves from church in protest and disbelief. It was Edward and Jonathan Putnam who signed the first complaint against Rebecca; and Thomas Putnam's little daughter was the one who fell into a fit at the hearing and pointed to Rebecca as her attacker. To top it all, Mrs. Putnam—who is now staring at the bewitched child on the bed—soon accused Rebecca's spirit of "tempting her to iniquity," a charge that had more truth in it than Mrs. Putnam could know.

MRS. PUTNAM, *astonished*: What have you done?

Rebecca, in thought, now leaves the bedside and sits.

PARRIS, *wondrous and relieved*: What do you make of it, Rebecca?

PUTNAM, *eagerly*: Goody Nurse, will you go to my Ruth and see if you can wake her?

REBECCA, *sitting*: I think she'll wake in time. Pray calm yourselves. I have eleven children, and I am twenty-six times a grandma, and I have seen them all through their silly seasons, and when it come on them they will run the Devil bowlegged keeping up with their mischief. I think she'll wake when she tires of it. A child's spirit is like a child, you can never catch it by running after it; you must stand still, and, for love, it will soon itself come back.

PROCTOR: Aye, that's the truth of it, Rebecca.

MRS. PUTNAM: This is no silly season, Rebecca. My Ruth is bewildered, Rebecca; she cannot eat.

REBECCA: Perhaps she is not hungered yet. *To Parris*: I hope you are not decided to go in search of loose spirits, Mr. Parris. I've heard promise of that outside.

PARRIS: A wide opinion's running in the parish that the Devil may be among us, and I would satisfy them that they are wrong.

PROCTOR: Then let you come out and call them wrong. Did you consult the wardens before you called this minister to look for devils?

PARRIS: He is not coming to look for devils!

PROCTOR: Then what's he coming for?

PUTNAM: There be children dyin' in the village, Mister!

PROCTOR: I seen none dyin'. This society will not be a bag to swing around your head, Mr. Putnam. *To Parris*: Did you call a meeting before you—?

PUTNAM: I am sick of meetings; cannot the man turn his head without he have a meeting?

PROCTOR: He may turn his head, but not to Hell!

REBECCA: Pray, John, be calm. *Pause. He defers to her.* Mr. Parris, I think you'd best send Reverend Hale back as soon as he come. This will set us all to arguin' again in the society, and we thought to have peace this year. I think we ought rely on the doctor now, and good prayer.

MRS. PUTNAM: Rebecca, the doctor's baffled!

REBECCA: If so he is, then let us go to God for the cause of it. There is prodigious danger in the seeking of loose spirits. I fear it, I fear it. Let us rather blame ourselves and—

PUTNAM: How may we blame ourselves? I am one of nine sons; the Putnam seed have peopled this province. And yet I have but one child left of eight—and now she shrivels!

REBECCA: I cannot fathom that.

MRS. PUTNAM, *with a growing edge of sarcasm*: But I must! You think it God's work you should never lose a child, nor grandchild either, and I bury all but one? There are wheels within wheels in this village, and fires within fires!

PUTNAM, *to Parris*: When Reverend Hale comes, you will proceed to look for signs of witchcraft here.

PROCTOR, *to Putnam*: You cannot command Mr. Parris. We vote by name in this society, not by acreage.

PUTNAM: I never heard you worried so on this society, Mr. Proctor. I do not think I saw you at Sabbath meeting since snow flew.

PROCTOR: I have trouble enough without I come five mile to hear him preach only hellfire and bloody damnation. Take it to heart, Mr. Parris. There are many others who stay away from church these days because you hardly ever mention God any more.

PARRIS, *now aroused*: Why, that's a drastic charge!

REBECCA: It's somewhat true; there are many that quail to bring their children—

PARRIS: I do not preach for children, Rebecca. It is not the children who are unmindful of their obligations toward this ministry.

REBECCA: Are there really those unmindful?

PARRIS: I should say the better half of Salem village—

PUTNAM: And more than that!

PARRIS: Where is my wood? My contract provides I be supplied with all my firewood. I am waiting since November for a stick, and even in November I had to show my frostbitten hands like some London beggar!

GILES: You are allowed six pound a year to buy your wood, Mr. Parris.

PARRIS: I regard that six pound as part of my salary. I am paid little enough without I spend six pound on firewood.

PROCTOR: Sixty, plus six for firewood—

PARRIS: The salary is sixty-six pound, Mr. Proctor! I am not some preaching farmer with a book under my arm; I am a graduate of Harvard College.

GILES: Aye, and well instructed in arithmetic!

PARRIS: Mr. Corey, you will look far for a man of my kind at sixty pound a year! I am not used to this poverty; I left a thrifty business in the

Barbados to serve the Lord. I do not fathom it, why am I persecuted here? I cannot offer one proposition but there be a howling riot of argument. I have often wondered if the Devil be in it somewhere; I cannot understand you people otherwise.

PROCTOR: Mr. Parris, you are the first minister ever did demand the deed to this house—

PARRIS: Man! Don't a minister deserve a house to live in?

PROCTOR: To live in, yes. But to ask ownership is like you shall own the meeting house itself; the last meeting I were at you spoke so long on deeds and mortgages I thought it were an auction.

PARRIS: I want a mark of confidence, is all! I am your third preacher in seven years. I do not wish to be put out like the cat whenever some majority feels the whim. You people seem not to comprehend that a minister is the Lord's man in the parish; a minister is not to be so lightly crossed and contradicted—

PUTNAM: Aye!

PARRIS: There is either obedience or the church will burn like Hell is burning!

PROCTOR: Can you speak one minute without we land in Hell again? I am sick of Hell!

PARRIS: It is not for you to say what is good for you to hear!

PROCTOR: I may speak my heart, I think!

PARRIS, *in a fury*: What, are we Quakers? We are not Quakers here yet, Mr. Proctor. And you may tell that to your followers!

PROCTOR: My followers!

PARRIS—*now he's out with it*: There is a party in this church. I am not blind; there is a faction and a party.

PROCTOR: Against you?

PUTNAM: Against him and all authority!

PROCTOR: Why, then I must find it and join it.

There is shock among the others.

REBECCA: He does not mean that.

PUTNAM: He confessed it now!

PROCTOR: I mean it solemnly, Rebecca; I like not the smell of this "authority."

REBECCA: No, you cannot break charity with your minister. You are another kind, John. Clasp his hand, make your peace.

PROCTOR: I have a crop to sow and lumber to drag home. *He goes angrily to the door and turns to Corey with a smile.* What say you, Giles, let's find the party. He says there's a party.

GILES: I've changed my opinion of this man, John. Mr. Parris, I beg your pardon. I never thought you had so much iron in you.

PARRIS, *surprised*: Why, thank you, Giles!

GILES: It suggests to the mind what the trouble be among us all these years. *To all*: Think on it. Wherefore is everybody suing everybody else? Think on it now, it's a deep thing, and dark as a pit. I have been six time in court this year—

PROCTOR, *familiarly, with warmth, although he knows he is approaching the edge of Giles' tolerance with this*: Is it the Devil's fault that a man cannot say you good morning without you clap him for defamation? You're old, Giles, and you're not hearin' so well as you did.

GILES—*he cannot be crossed*: John Proctor, I have only last month collected four pound damages for you publicly sayin' I burned the roof off your house, and I—

PROCTOR, *laughing*: I never said no such thing, but I've paid you for it, so I hope I can call you deaf without charge. Now come along, Giles, and help me drag my lumber home.

PUTNAM: A moment, Mr. Proctor. What lumber is that you're draggin', if I may ask you?

PROCTOR: My lumber. From out my forest by the riverside.

PUTNAM: Why, we are surely gone wild this year. What anarchy is this? That tract is in my bounds, it's in my bounds, Mr. Proctor.

PROCTOR: In your bounds! *Indicating Rebecca*: I bought that tract from Goody Nurse's husband five months ago.

PUTNAM: He had no right to sell it. It stands clear in my grandfather's will that all the land between the river and—

PROCTOR: Your grandfather had a habit of willing land that never belonged to him, if I may say it plain.

GILES: That's God's truth; he nearly willed away my north pasture but he knew I'd break his fingers before he'd set his name to it. Let's get your lumber home, John. I feel a sudden will to work coming on.

PUTNAM: You load one oak of mine and you'll fight to drag it home!

GILES: Aye, and we'll win too, Putnam—this fool and I. Come on! *He turns to Proctor and starts out.*

PUTNAM: I'll have my men on you, Corey! I'll clap a writ on you!

Enter Reverend John Hale of Beverly.

Mr. Hale is nearing forty, a tight-skinned, eager-eyed intellectual. This is a beloved errand for him; on being called here to ascertain witchcraft he felt the pride of the specialist whose unique knowledge has at last been publicly called for. Like almost all men of learning, he spent a good deal of his time pondering the invisible world, especially since he had himself encountered a witch in his parish not long before. That woman, however, turned into a mere pest under his searching scrutiny, and the child she had allegedly been afflicting recovered her normal behavior after Hale had given her his kindness and a few days of rest in his own house. However, that experience never raised a doubt in his mind as to the reality of the underworld or the existence of Lucifer's many-faced lieutenants. And his belief is not to his discredit. Better minds than Hale's were—and still are—convinced that there is a society of spirits beyond our ken. One cannot help noting that one of his lines has never yet raised a laugh in any audience that has seen this play; it is his assurance that "We cannot look to superstition in this. The Devil is precise." Evidently we are not quite certain even now whether diabolism is holy and not to be scoffed at. And it is no accident that we should be so bemused.

Like Reverend Hale and the others on this stage, we conceive the Devil as a necessary part of a respectable view of cosmology. Ours is a divided empire in which certain ideas and emotions and actions are of God, and their opposites are of Lucifer. It is as impossible for most men to conceive of a morality without sin as of an earth without "sky." Since 1692 a great but superficial change has wiped out God's beard and the Devil's horns, but the world is still gripped between two diametrically opposed absolutes. The concept of unity, in which positive and negative are attributes of the same force, in which good and evil are relative, ever-changing, and always joined to the same phenomenon—such a concept is still reserved to the physical sciences and to the few who have grasped the history of ideas. When it is recalled that until the Christian era the underworld was never regarded as a hostile area, that all gods were useful and essentially friendly to man despite occasional lapses; when we see the steady and methodical inculcation into humanity of the idea of man's worthlessness—until redeemed—the necessity of the Devil may become evident as a weapon, a weapon designed and used time and time again in every age to whip men into a surrender to a particular church or church-state.

Our difficulty in believing the—for want of a better word—political

inspiration of the Devil is due in great part to the fact that he is called up
and damned not only by our social antagonists but by our own side,
whatever it may be. The Catholic Church, through its Inquisition, is
famous for cultivating Lucifer as the arch-fiend, but the Church's enemies
relied no less upon the Old Boy to keep the human mind enthralled.
Luther was himself accused of alliance with Hell, and he in turn accused
his enemies. To complicate matters further, he believed that he had had
contact with the Devil and had argued theology with him. I am not surprised at this, for at my own university a professor of history—a Lutheran,
by the way—used to assemble his graduate students, draw the shades,
and commune in the classroom with Erasmus. He was never, to my
knowledge, officially scoffed at for this, the reason being that the university officials, like most of us, are the children of a history which still sucks
at the Devil's teats. At this writing, only England has held back before
the temptations of contemporary diabolism. In the countries of the
Communist ideology, all resistance of any import is linked to the
totally malign capitalist succubi, and in America any man who is not
reactionary in his views is open to the charge of alliance with the Red
hell. Political opposition, thereby, is given an inhumane overlay which
then justifies the abrogation of all normally applied customs of civilized
intercourse. A political policy is equated with moral right, and opposition
to it with diabolical malevolence. Once such an equation is effectively
made, society becomes a congerie of plots and counterplots, and the main
role of government changes from that of the arbiter to that of the scourge
of God.

The results of this process are no different now from what they
ever were, except sometimes in the degree of cruelty inflicted, and not
always even in that department. Normally the actions and deeds of a man
were all that society felt comfortable in judging. The secret intent of an
action was left to the ministers, priests, and rabbis to deal with. When
diabolism rises, however, actions are the least important manifests of the
true nature of a man. The Devil, as Reverend Hale said, is a wily one, and,
until an hour before he fell, even God thought him beautiful in Heaven.

The analogy, however, seems to falter when one considers that, while
there were no witches then, there are Communists and capitalists now,
and in each camp there is certain proof that spies of each side are at work
undermining the other. But this is a snobbish objection and not at all warranted by the facts. I have no doubt that people *were* communing with,
and even worshiping, the Devil in Salem, and if the whole truth could be
known in this case, as it is in others, we should discover a regular and
conventionalized propitiation of the dark spirit. One certain evidence of
this is the confession of Tituba, the slave of Reverend Parris, and another
is the behavior of the children who were known to have indulged in sor-
ceries with her.

1 man's opinion, whose to say if
right or wrong — we weren't there.

There are accounts of similar *klatches* in Europe, where the daughters of the towns would assemble at night and, sometimes with fetishes, sometimes with a selected young man, give themselves to love, with some bastardly results. The Church, sharp-eyed as it must be when gods long dead are brought to life, condemned these orgies as witchcraft and interpreted them rightly, as a resurgence of the Dionysiac forces it had crushed long before. Sex, sin, and the Devil were early linked, and so they continued to be in Salem, and are today. From all accounts there are no more puritanical mores in the world than those enforced by the Communists in Russia, where women's fashions, for instance, are as prudent and all-covering as any American Baptist would desire. The divorce laws lay a tremendous responsibility on the father for the care of his children. Even the laxity of divorce regulations in the early years of the revolution was undoubtedly a revulsion from the nineteenth-century Victorian immobility of marriage and the consequent hypocrisy that developed from it. If for no other reasons, a state so powerful, so jealous of the uniformity of its citizens, cannot long tolerate the atomization of the family. And yet, in American eyes at least, there remains the conviction that the Russian attitude toward women is lascivious. It is the Devil working again, just as he is working within the Slav who is shocked at the very idea of a woman's disrobing herself in a burlesque show. Our opposites are always robed in sexual sin, and it is from this unconscious conviction that demonology gains both its attractive sensuality and its capacity to infuriate and frighten.

Coming into Salem now, Reverend Hale conceives of himself much as a young doctor on his first call. His painfully acquired armory of symptoms, catchwords, and diagnostic procedures is now to be put to use at last. The road from Beverly is unusually busy this morning, and he has passed a hundred rumors that make him smile at the ignorance of the yeomanry in this most precise science. He feels himself allied with the best minds of Europe—kings, philosophers, scientists, and ecclesiasts of all churches. His goal is light, goodness and its preservation, and he knows the exaltation of the blessed whose intelligence, sharpened by minute examinations of enormous tracts, is finally called upon to face what may be a bloody fight with the Fiend himself.

He appears loaded down with half a dozen heavy books.

HALE: Pray you, someone take these!

PARRIS, *delighted*: Mr. Hale! Oh! it's good to see you again! *Taking some books*: My, they're heavy!

HALE, *setting down his books*: They must be; they are weighted with authority.

PARRIS, *a little scared*: Well, you do come prepared!

HALE: We shall need hard study if it comes to tracking down the Old Boy. *Noticing Rebecca*: You cannot be Rebecca Nurse?

REBECCA: I am, sir. Do you know me?

HALE: It's strange how I knew you, but I suppose you look as such a good soul should. We have all heard of your great charities in Beverly.

PARRIS: Do you know this gentleman? Mr. Thomas Putnam. And his good wife Ann.

HALE: Putnam! I had not expected such distinguished company, sir.

PUTNAM, *pleased*: It does not seem to help us today, Mr. Hale. We look to you to come to our house and save our child.

HALE: Your child ails too?

MRS. PUTNAM: Her soul, her soul seems flown away. She sleeps and yet she walks . . .

PUTNAM: She cannot eat.

HALE: Cannot eat! *Thinks on it. Then, to Proctor and Giles Corey*: Do you men have afflicted children?

PARRIS: No, no, these are farmers. John Proctor—

GILES COREY: He don't believe in witches.

PROCTOR, *to Hale*: I never spoke on witches one way or the other. Will you come, Giles?

GILES: No—no, John, I think not. I have some few queer questions of my own to ask this fellow.

PROCTOR: I've heard you to be a sensible man, Mr. Hale. I hope you'll leave some of it in Salem.

    Proctor goes. Hale stands embarrassed for an instant.

PARRIS, *quickly*: Will you look at my daughter, sir? *Leads Hale to the bed*. She has tried to leap out the window; we discovered her this morning on the highroad, waving her arms as though she'd fly.

HALE, *narrowing his eyes*: Tries to fly.

PUTNAM: She cannot bear to hear the Lord's name, Mr. Hale; that's a sure sign of witchcraft afloat.

HALE, *holding up his hands*: No, no. Now let me instruct you. We cannot look to superstition in this. The Devil is precise; the marks of his presence are definite as stone, and I must tell you all that I shall not proceed unless you are prepared to believe me if I should find no bruise of Hell upon her.

PARRIS: It is agreed, sir—it is agreed—we will abide by your judgment.

HALE: Good then. *He goes to the bed, looks down at Betty. To Parris*: Now, sir, what were your first warning of this strangeness?

PARRIS: Why, sir—I discovered her—*indicating Abigail*—and my niece and ten or twelve of the other girls, dancing in the forest last night.

HALE, *surprised*: You permit dancing?

PARRIS: No, no, it were secret—

MRS. PUTNAM, *unable to wait*: Mr. Parris's slave has knowledge of conjurin', sir.

PARRIS, *to Mrs. Putnam*: We cannot be sure of that, Goody Ann—

MRS. PUTNAM, *frightened, very softly*: I know it, sir. I sent my child—she should learn from Tituba who murdered her sisters.

REBECCA, *horrified*: Goody Ann! You sent a child to conjure up the dead?

MRS. PUTNAM: Let God blame me, not you, not you, Rebecca! I'll not have you judging me any more! *To Hale*: Is it a natural work to lose seven children before they live a day?

PARRIS: Sssh!

> *Rebecca, with great pain, turns her face away. There is a pause.*

HALE: Seven dead in childbirth.

MRS. PUTNAM, *softly*: Aye. *Her voice breaks; she looks up at him. Silence. Hale is impressed. Parris looks to him. He goes to his books, opens one, turns pages, then reads. All wait, avidly.*

PARRIS, *hushed*: What book is that?

MRS. PUTNAM: What's there, sir?

HALE, *with a tasty love of intellectual pursuit*: Here is all the invisible world, caught, defined, and calculated. In these books the Devil stands stripped of all his brute disguises. Here are all your familiar spirits—your incubi and succubi; your witches that go by land, by air, and by sea; your wizards of the night and of the day. Have no fear now—we shall find him out if he has come among us, and I mean to crush him utterly if he has shown his face! *He starts for the bed.*

REBECCA: Will it hurt the child, sir?

HALE: I cannot tell. If she is truly in the Devil's grip we may have to rip and tear to get her free.

REBECCA: I think I'll go, then. I am too old for this. *She rises.*

PARRIS, *striving for conviction*: Why, Rebecca, we may open up the boil of all our troubles today!

REBECCA: Let us hope for that. I go to God for you, sir.

PARRIS, *with trepidation—and resentment*: I hope you do not mean we go to Satan here! *Slight pause.*

REBECCA: I wish I knew. *She goes out; they feel resentful of her note of moral superiority.*

PUTNAM, *abruptly*: Come, Mr. Hale, let's get on. Sit you here.

GILES: Mr. Hale, I have always wanted to ask a learned man—what signifies the readin' of strange books?

HALE: What books?

GILES: I cannot tell; she hides them.

HALE: Who does this?

GILES: Martha, my wife. I have waked at night many a time and found her in a corner, readin' of a book. Now what do you make of that?

HALE: Why, that's not necessarily—

GILES: It discomfits me! Last night—mark this—I tried and tried and could not say my prayers. And then she close her book and walks out of the house, and suddenly—mark this—I could pray again!

Old Giles must be spoken for, if only because his fate was to be so remarkable and so different from that of all the others. He was in his early eighties at this time, and was the most comical hero in the history. No man has ever been blamed for so much. If a cow was missed, the first thought was to look for her around Corey's house; a fire blazing up at night brought suspicion of arson to his door. He didn't give a hoot for public opinion, and only in his last years—after he had married Martha—did he bother much with the church. That she stopped his prayer is very probable, but he forgot to say that he'd only recently learned any prayers and it didn't take much to make him stumble over them. He was a crank and a nuisance, but withal a deeply innocent and brave man. In court, once, he was asked if it were true that he had been frightened by the strange behavior of a hog and had then said he knew it to be the Devil in an animal's shape. "What frighted you?" he was asked. He forgot everything but the word "frighted," and instantly replied, "I do not know that I ever spoke that word in my life."

HALE: Ah! The stoppage of prayer—that is strange. I'll speak further on that with you.

GILES: I'm not sayin' she's touched the Devil, now, but I'd admire to know what books she reads and why she hides them. She'll not answer me, y'see.

HALE: Aye, we'll discuss it. *To all*: Now mark me, if the Devil is in her you will witness some frightful wonders in this room, so please to keep your wits about you. Mr. Putnam, stand close in case she flies. Now, Betty, dear, will you sit up? *Putnam comes in closer, ready-handed. Hale sits Betty up, but she hangs limp in his hands.* Hmmm. *He observes her carefully. The others watch breathlessly.* Can you hear me? I am John Hale, minister of Beverly. I have come to help you, dear. Do you remember my two little girls in Beverly? *She does not stir in his hands.*

PARRIS, *in fright*: How can it be the Devil? Why would he choose my house to strike? We have all manner of licentious people in the village!

HALE: What victory would the Devil have to win a soul already bad? It is the best the Devil wants, and who is better than the minister?

GILES: That's deep, Mr. Parris, deep, deep!

PARRIS, *with resolution now*: Betty! Answer Mr. Hale! Betty!

HALE: Does someone afflict you, child? It need not be a woman, mind you, or a man. Perhaps some bird invisible to others comes to you—perhaps a pig, a mouse, or any beast at all. Is there some figure bids you fly? *The child remains limp in his hands. In silence he lays her back on the pillow.*

> *Now, holding out his hands toward her, he intones*: In nomine Domini Sabaoth sui filiique ite ad infernos. *She does not stir. He turns to Abigail, his eyes narrowing.* Abigail, what sort of dancing were you doing with her in the forest?

ABIGAIL: Why—common dancing is all.

PARRIS: I think I ought to say that I—I saw a kettle in the grass where they were dancing.

ABIGAIL: That were only soup.

HALE: What sort of soup were in this kettle, Abigail?

ABIGAIL: Why, it were beans—and lentils, I think, and—

HALE: Mr. Parris, you did not notice, did you, any living thing in the kettle? A mouse, perhaps, a spider, a frog—?

PARRIS, *fearfully*: I—do believe there were some movement—in the soup.

ABIGAIL: That jumped in, we never put it in!

HALE, *quickly*: What jumped in?

ABIGAIL: Why, a very little frog jumped—

PARRIS: A frog, Abby!

HALE, *grasping Abigail*: Abigail, it may be your cousin is dying. Did you call the Devil last night?

ABIGAIL: I never called him! Tituba, Tituba . . .

PARRIS, *blanched*: She called the Devil?

HALE: I should like to speak with Tituba.

PARRIS: Goody Ann, will you bring her up?

> *Mrs. Putnam exits.*

HALE: How did she call him?

ABIGAIL: I know not—she spoke Barbados.

HALE: Did you feel any strangeness when she called him? A sudden cold wind, perhaps? A trembling below the ground?

ABIGAIL: I didn't see no Devil! *Shaking Betty*: Betty, wake up. Betty! Betty!

HALE: You cannot evade me, Abigail. Did your cousin drink any of the brew in that kettle?

ABIGAIL: She never drank it!

HALE: Did you drink it?

ABIGAIL: No, sir!

HALE: Did Tituba ask you to drink it?

ABIGAIL: She tried, but I refused.

HALE: Why are you concealing? Have you sold yourself to Lucifer?

ABIGAIL: I never sold myself! I'm a good girl! I'm a proper girl!

> *Mrs. Putnam enters with Tituba, and instantly Abigail points at Tituba.*

ABIGAIL: She made me do it! She made Betty do it!

TITUBA, *shocked and angry*: Abby!

ABIGAIL: She makes me drink blood!

PARRIS: Blood!!

MRS. PUTNAM: My baby's blood?

TITUBA: No, no, chicken blood. I give she chicken blood!

HALE: Woman, have you enlisted these children for the Devil?

TITUBA: No, no, sir, I don't truck with no Devil!

HALE: Why can she not wake? Are you silencing this child?

TITUBA: I love me Betty!

HALE: You have sent your spirit out upon this child, have you not? Are you gathering souls for the Devil?

ABIGAIL: She sends her spirit on me in church; she makes me laugh at prayer!

PARRIS: She have often laughed at prayer!

ABIGAIL: She comes to me every night to go and drink blood!

TITUBA: You beg *me* to conjure! She beg *me* make charm—

ABIGAIL: Don't lie! *To Hale*: She comes to me while I sleep; she's always making me dream corruptions!

TITUBA: Why you say that, Abby?

ABIGAIL: Sometimes I wake and find myself standing in the open door-way and not a stitch on my body! I always hear her laughing in my sleep. I hear her singing her Barbados songs and tempting me with—

TITUBA: Mister Reverend, I never—

HALE, *resolved now*: Tituba, I want you to wake this child.

TITUBA: I have no power on this child, sir.

HALE: You most certainly do, and you will free her from it now! When did you compact with the Devil?

TITUBA: I don't compact with no Devil!

PARRIS: You will confess yourself or I will take you out and whip you to your death, Tituba!

PUTNAM: This woman must be hanged! She must be taken and hanged!

TITUBA, *terrified, falls to her knees*: No, no, don't hang Tituba! I tell him I don't desire to work for him, sir.

PARRIS: The Devil?

HALE: Then you saw him! *Tituba weeps*. Now Tituba, I know that when we bind ourselves to Hell it is very hard to break with it. We are going to help you tear yourself free—

TITUBA, *frightened by the coming process*: Mister Reverend, I do believe somebody else be witchin' these children.

HALE: Who?

TITUBA: I don't know, sir, but the Devil got him numerous witches.

HALE: Does he! *It is a clue.* Tituba, look into my eyes. Come, look into me. *She raises her eyes to his fearfully.* You would be a good Christian woman, would you not, Tituba?

TITUBA: Aye, sir, a good Christian woman.

HALE: And you love these little children?

TITUBA: Oh, yes, sir, I don't desire to hurt little children.

HALE: And you love God, Tituba?

TITUBA: I love God with all my bein'.

HALE: Now, in God's holy name—

TITUBA: Bless Him. Bless Him. *She is rocking on her knees, sobbing in terror.*

HALE: And to His glory—

TITUBA: Eternal glory. Bless Him—bless God . . .

HALE: Open yourself, Tituba—open yourself and let God's holy light shine on you.

TITUBA: Oh, bless the Lord.

HALE: When the Devil comes to you does he ever come—with another person? *She stares up into his face.* Perhaps another person in the village? Someone you know.

PARRIS: Who came with him?

PUTNAM: Sarah Good? Did you ever see Sarah Good with him? Or Osburn?

PARRIS: Was it man or woman came with him?

TITUBA: Man or woman. Was—was woman.

PARRIS: What woman? A woman, you said. What woman?

TITUBA: It was black dark, and I—

PARRIS: You could see him, why could you not see her?

TITUBA: Well, they was always talking; they was always runnin' round and carryin' on—

PARRIS: You mean out of Salem? Salem witches?

TITUBA: I believe so, yes, sir.

Now Hale takes her hand. She is surprised.

HALE: Tituba. You must have no fear to tell us who they are, do you understand? We will protect you. The Devil can never overcome a minister. You know that, do you not?

TITUBA—*she kisses Hale's hand*: Aye, sir, oh, I do.

HALE: You have confessed yourself to witchcraft, and that speaks a wish to come to Heaven's side. And we will bless you, Tituba.

TITUBA, *deeply relieved*: Oh, God bless you, Mr. Hale!

HALE, *with rising exaltation*: You are God's instrument put in our hands to discover the Devil's agents among us. You are selected, Tituba, you are chosen to help us cleanse our village. So speak utterly, Tituba, turn your back on him and face God—face God, Tituba, and God will protect you.

TITUBA, *joining with him*: Oh, God, protect Tituba!

HALE, *kindly*: Who came to you with the Devil? Two? Three? Four? How many?

Tituba pants and begins rocking back and forth again, staring ahead.

TITUBA: There was four. There was four.

PARRIS, *pressing in on her*: Who? Who? Their names, their names!

TITUBA, *suddenly bursting out*: Oh, how many times he bid me kill you, Mr. Parris!

PARRIS: Kill me!

TITUBA, *in a fury*: He say Mr. Parris must be kill! Mr. Parris no goodly man, Mr. Parris mean man and no gentle man, and he bid me rise out of my bed and cut your throat! *They gasp.* But I tell him "No! I don't hate that man. I don't want kill that man." But he say, "You work for me, Tituba, and I make you free! I give you pretty dress to wear, and put you way high up in the air, and you gone fly back to Barbados!" And I say, "You lie, Devil, you lie!" And then he come one stormy night to me, and he say, "Look! I have *white* people belong to me." And I look—and there was Goody Good.

PARRIS: Sarah Good!

TITUBA, *rocking and weeping*: Aye, sir, and Goody Osburn.

MRS. PUTNAM: I knew it! Goody Osburn were midwife to me three times. I begged you, Thomas, did I not? I begged him not to call Osburn because I feared her. My babies always shriveled in her hands!

HALE: Take courage, you must give us all their names. How can you bear to see this child suffering? Look at her, Tituba. *He is indicating Betty on the bed*. Look at her God-given innocence; her soul is so tender; we must protect her, Tituba; the Devil is out and preying on her like a beast upon the flesh of the pure lamb. God will bless you for your help.

Abigail rises, staring as though inspired, and cries out.

ABIGAIL: I want to open myself! *They turn to her, startled. She is enraptured, as though in a pearly light.* I want the light of God, I want the sweet love of Jesus! I danced for the Devil; I saw him; I wrote in his book; I go back to Jesus; I kiss His hand. I saw Sarah Good with the Devil! I saw Goody Osburn with the Devil! I saw Bridget Bishop with the Devil!

As she is speaking, Betty is rising from the bed, a fever in her eyes, and picks up the chant.

BETTY, *staring too*: I saw George Jacobs with the Devil! I saw Goody Howe with the Devil!

PARRIS: She speaks! *He rushes to embrace Betty.* She speaks!

HALE: Glory to God! It is broken, they are free!

BETTY, *calling out hysterically and with great relief*: I saw Martha Bellows with the Devil!

ABIGAIL: I saw Goody Sibber with the Devil! *It is rising to a great glee.*

PUTNAM: The marshal, I'll call the marshal!

Parris is shouting a prayer of thanksgiving.

BETTY: I saw Alice Barrow with the Devil!

The curtain begins to fall.

HALE, *as Putnam goes out*: Let the marshal bring irons!

ABIGAIL: I saw Goody Hawkins with the Devil!

BETTY: I saw Goody Bibber with the Devil!

ABIGAIL: I saw Goody Booth with the Devil!

On their ecstatic cries

THE CURTAIN FALLS.

ACT TWO

The common room of Proctor's house, eight days later.

At the right is a door opening on the fields outside. A fireplace is at the left, and behind it a stairway leading upstairs. It is the low, dark, and rather long living room of the time. As the curtain rises, the room is empty. From above, Elizabeth is heard softly singing to the children. Presently the door opens and John Proctor enters, carrying his gun. He glances about the room as he comes toward the fireplace, then halts for an instant as he hears her singing. He continues on to the fireplace, leans the gun against the wall as he swings a pot out of the fire and smells it. Then he lifts out the ladle and tastes. He is not quite pleased. He reaches to a cupboard, takes a pinch of salt, and drops it into the pot. As he is tasting again, her footsteps are heard on the stair. He swings the pot into the fireplace and goes to a basin and washes his hands and face. Elizabeth enters.

ELIZABETH: What keeps you so late? It's almost dark.

PROCTOR: I were planting far out to the forest edge.

ELIZABETH: Oh, you're done then.

PROCTOR: Aye, the farm is seeded. The boys asleep?

ELIZABETH: They will be soon. *And she goes to the fireplace, proceeds to ladle up stew in a dish.*

PROCTOR: Pray now for a fair summer.

ELIZABETH: Aye.

PROCTOR: Are you well today?

ELIZABETH: I am. *She brings the plate to the table, and, indicating the food*: It is a rabbit.

PROCTOR, *going to the table*: Oh, is it! In Jonathan's trap?

ELIZABETH: No, she walked into the house this afternoon; I found her sittin' in the corner like she come to visit.

PROCTOR: Oh, that's a good sign walkin' in.

ELIZABETH: Pray God. It hurt my heart to strip her, poor rabbit. *She sits and watches him taste it.*

PROCTOR: It's well seasoned.

ELIZABETH, *blushing with pleasure*: I took great care. She's tender?

PROCTOR: Aye. *He eats. She watches him.* I think we'll see green fields soon. It's warm as blood beneath the clods.

ELIZABETH: That's well.

> *Proctor eats, then looks up.*

PROCTOR: If the crop is good I'll buy George Jacobs' heifer. How would that please you?

ELIZABETH: Aye, it would.

PROCTOR, *with a grin*: I mean to please you, Elizabeth.

ELIZABETH—*it is hard to say*: I know it, John.

> *He gets up, goes to her, kisses her. She receives it. With a certain disappointment, he returns to the table.*

PROCTOR, *as gently as he can*: Cider?

ELIZABETH, *with a sense of reprimanding herself for having forgot*: Aye! *She gets up and goes and pours a glass for him. He now arches his back.*

PROCTOR: This farm's a continent when you go foot by foot droppin' seeds in it.

ELIZABETH, *coming with the cider*: It must be.

PROCTOR, *he drinks a long draught, then, putting the glass down*: You ought to bring some flowers in the house.

ELIZABETH: Oh! I forgot! I will tomorrow.

PROCTOR: It's winter in here yet. On Sunday let you come with me, and we'll walk the farm together; I never see such a load of flowers on the earth. *With good feeling he goes and looks up at the sky through the open doorway.* Lilacs have a purple smell. Lilac is the smell of nightfall, I think. Massachusetts is a beauty in the spring!

ELIZABETH: Aye, it is.

> *There is a pause. She is watching him from the table as he stands there absorbing the night. It is as though she would speak but cannot. Instead, now, she takes up his plate and glass and fork and goes with them to the basin. Her back is*

turned to him. He turns to her and watches her. A sense of their separation rises.

PROCTOR: I think you're sad again. Are you?

ELIZABETH—*she doesn't want friction, and yet she must*: You come so late I thought you'd gone to Salem this afternoon.

PROCTOR: Why? I have no business in Salem.

ELIZABETH: You did speak of going, earlier this week.

PROCTOR—*he knows what she means*: I thought better of it since.

ELIZABETH: Mary Warren's there today.

PROCTOR: Why'd you let her? You heard me forbid her to go to Salem any more!

ELIZABETH: I couldn't stop her.

PROCTOR, *holding back a full condemnation of her*: It is a fault, it is a fault, Elizabeth—you're the mistress here, not Mary Warren.

ELIZABETH: She frightened all my strength away.

PROCTOR: How may that mouse frighten you, Elizabeth? You—

ELIZABETH: It is a mouse no more. I forbid her go, and she raises up her chin like the daughter of a prince and says to me, "I must go to Salem, Goody Proctor; I am an official of the court!"

PROCTOR: Court! What court?

ELIZABETH: Aye, it is a proper court they have now. They've sent four judges out of Boston, she says, weighty magistrates of the General Court, and at the head sits the Deputy Governor of the Province.

PROCTOR, *astonished*: Why, she's mad.

ELIZABETH: I would to God she were. There be fourteen people in the jail now, she says. *Proctor simply looks at her, unable to grasp it.* And they'll be tried, and the court have power to hang them too, she says.

PROCTOR, *scoffing, but without conviction*: Ah, they'd never hang—

ELIZABETH: The Deputy Governor promise hangin' if they'll not confess, John. The town's gone wild, I think. She speak of Abigail, and I thought she were a saint, to hear her. Abigail brings the other girls into the court, and where she walks the crowd will part like the sea for Israel. And folks are brought before them, and if they scream and howl and fall to the floor—the person's clapped in the jail for bewitchin' them.

PROCTOR, *wide-eyed*: Oh, it is a black mischief.

ELIZABETH: I think you must go to Salem, John. *He turns to her.* I think so. You must tell them it is a fraud.

PROCTOR, *thinking beyond this*: Aye, it is, it is surely.

ELIZABETH: Let you go to Ezekiel Cheever—he knows you well. And tell him what she said to you last week in her uncle's house. She said it had naught to do with witchcraft, did she not?

PROCTOR, *in thought*: Aye, she did, she did. *Now a pause.*

ELIZABETH, *quietly, fearing to anger him by prodding*: God forbid you keep that from the court, John. I think they must be told.

PROCTOR, *quietly, struggling with his thought*: Aye, they must, they must. It is a wonder they do believe her.

ELIZABETH: I would go to Salem now, John—let you go tonight.

PROCTOR: I'll think on it.

ELIZABETH, *with her courage now*: You cannot keep it, John.

PROCTOR, *angering*: I know I cannot keep it. I say I will think on it!

ELIZABETH, *hurt, and very coldly*: Good, then, let you think on it. *She stands and starts to walk out of the room.*

PROCTOR: I am only wondering how I may prove what she told me, Elizabeth. If the girl's a saint now, I think it is not easy to prove she's fraud, and the town gone so silly. She told it to me in a room alone—I have no proof for it.

ELIZABETH: You were alone with her?

PROCTOR, *stubbornly*: For a moment alone, aye.

ELIZABETH: Why, then, it is not as you told me.

PROCTOR, *his anger rising*: For a moment, I say. The others come in soon after.

ELIZABETH, *quietly—she has suddenly lost all faith in him*: Do as you wish, then. *She starts to turn.*

PROCTOR: Woman. *She turns to him.* I'll not have your suspicion any more.

ELIZABETH, *a little loftily*: I have no—

PROCTOR: I'll not have it!

ELIZABETH: Then let you not earn it.

PROCTOR, *with a violent undertone*: You doubt me yet?

ELIZABETH, *with a smile, to keep her dignity*: John, if it were not Abigail that you must go to hurt, would you falter now? I think not.

PROCTOR: Now look you—

ELIZABETH: I see what I see, John.

PROCTOR, *with solemn warning*: You will not judge me more, Elizabeth. I have good reason to think before I charge fraud on Abigail, and I will think on it. Let you look to your own improvement before you go to judge your husband any more. I have forgot Abigail, and—

ELIZABETH: And I.

PROCTOR: Spare me! You forget nothin' and forgive nothin'. Learn charity, woman. I have gone tiptoe in this house all seven month since she is gone. I have not moved from there to there without I think to please you, and still an everlasting funeral marches round your heart. I cannot speak but I am doubted, every moment judged for lies, as though I come into a court when I come into this house!

ELIZABETH: John, you are not open with me. You saw her with a crowd, you said. Now you—

PROCTOR: I'll plead my honesty no more, Elizabeth.

ELIZABETH—*now she would justify herself*: John, I am only—

PROCTOR: No more! I should have roared you down when first you told me your suspicion. But I wilted, and, like a Christian, I confessed. Confessed! Some dream I had must have mistaken you for God that day. But you're not, you're not, and let you remember it! Let you look sometimes for the goodness in me, and judge me not.

ELIZABETH: I do not judge you. The magistrate sits in your heart that judges you. I never thought you but a good man, John—*with a smile*—only somewhat bewildered.

PROCTOR, *laughing bitterly*: Oh, Elizabeth, your justice would freeze beer! *He turns suddenly toward a sound outside. He starts for the door as Mary Warren enters. As soon as he sees her, he goes directly to her and grabs her by her cloak, furious.* How do you go to Salem when I forbid it? Do you mock me? *Shaking her*: I'll whip you if you dare leave this house again!

Strangely, she doesn't resist him but hangs limply by his grip.

MARY WARREN: I am sick, I am sick, Mr. Proctor. Pray, pray, hurt me not. *Her strangeness throws him off, and her evident pallor and weakness. He frees her.* My insides are all shuddery; I am in the proceedings all day, sir.

PROCTOR, *with draining anger—his curiosity is draining it*: And what of these proceedings here? When will you proceed to keep this house, as you are paid nine pound a year to do—and my wife not wholly well?

> *As though to compensate, Mary Warren goes to Elizabeth with a small rag doll.*

MARY WARREN: I made a gift for you today, Goody Proctor. I had to sit long hours in a chair, and passed the time with sewing.

ELIZABETH, *perplexed, looking at the doll*: Why, thank you, it's a fair poppet.

MARY WARREN, *with a trembling, decayed voice*: We must all love each other now, Goody Proctor.

ELIZABETH, *amazed at her strangeness*: Aye, indeed, we must.

MARY WARREN, *glancing at the room*: I'll get up early in the morning and clean the house. I must sleep now. *She turns and starts off.*

PROCTOR: Mary. *She halts.* Is it true? There be fourteen women arrested?

MARY WARREN: No, sir. There be thirty-nine now— *She suddenly breaks off and sobs and sits down, exhausted.*

ELIZABETH: Why, she's weepin'! What ails you, child?

MARY WARREN: Goody Osburn—will hang! *There is a shocked pause, while she sobs.*

PROCTOR: Hang! *He calls into her face.* Hang, y'say?

MARY WARREN, *through her weeping*: Aye.

PROCTOR: The Deputy Governor will permit it?

MARY WARREN: He sentenced her. He must. *To ameliorate it*: But not Sarah Good. For Sarah Good confessed, y'see.

PROCTOR: Confessed! To what?

MARY WARREN: That she—*in horror at the memory*—she sometimes made a compact with Lucifer, and wrote her name in his black book— with her blood—and bound herself to torment Christians till God's thrown down—and we all must worship Hell forevermore.

> *Pause.*

PROCTOR: But—surely you know what a jabberer she is. Did you tell them that?

MARY WARREN: Mr. Proctor, in open court she near to choked us all to death.

PROCTOR: How, choked you?

MARY WARREN: She sent her spirit out.

ELIZABETH: Oh, Mary, Mary, surely you—

MARY WARREN, *with an indignant edge*: She tried to kill me many times, Goody Proctor!

ELIZABETH: Why, I never heard you mention that before.

MARY WARREN: I never knew it before. I never knew anything before. When she come into the court I say to myself, I must not accuse this woman, for she sleep in ditches, and so very old and poor. But then—then she sit there, denying and denying, and I feel a misty coldness climbin' up my back, and the skin on my skull begin to creep, and I feel a clamp around my neck and I cannot breathe air; and then—*entranced*—I hear a voice, a screamin' voice, and it were my voice—and all at once I remember everything she done to me!

PROCTOR: Why? What did she do to you?

MARY WARREN, *like one awakened to a marvelous secret insight*: So many time, Mr. Proctor, she come to this very door, beggin' bread and a cup of cider—and mark this: whenever I turned her away empty, she *mumbled.*

ELIZABETH: Mumbled! She may mumble if she's hungry.

MARY WARREN: But *what* does she mumble? You must remember, Goody Proctor. Last month—a Monday, I think—she walked away, and I thought my guts would burst for two days after. Do you remember it?

ELIZABETH: Why—I do, I think, but—

MARY WARREN: And so I told that to Judge Hathorne, and he asks her so. "Goody Osburn," says he, "what curse do you mumble that this girl must fall sick after turning you away?" And then she replies—*mimicking an old crone*—"Why, your excellence, no curse at all. I only say my commandments; I hope I may say my commandments," says she!

ELIZABETH: And that's an upright answer.

MARY WARREN: Aye, but then Judge Hathorne say, "Recite for us your commandments!"—*leaning avidly toward them*—and of all the ten she could not say a single one. She never knew no commandments, and they had her in a flat lie!

PROCTOR: And so condemned her?

MARY WARREN, *now a little strained, seeing his stubborn doubt*: Why, they must when she condemned herself.

PROCTOR: But the proof, the proof!

MARY WARREN, *with greater impatience with him*: I told you the proof. It's hard proof, hard as rock, the judges said.

PROCTOR—*he pauses an instant, then*: You will not go to court again, Mary Warren.

MARY WARREN: I must tell you, sir, I will be gone every day now. I am amazed you do not see what weighty work we do.

PROCTOR: What work you do! It's strange work for a Christian girl to hang old women!

MARY WARREN: But, Mr. Proctor, they will not hang them if they confess. Sarah Good will only sit in jail some time—*recalling*—and here's a wonder for you; think on this. Goody Good is pregnant!

ELIZABETH: Pregnant! Are they mad? The woman's near to sixty!

MARY WARREN: They had Doctor Griggs examine her, and she's full to the brim. And smokin' a pipe all these years, and no husband either! But she's safe, thank God, for they'll not hurt the innocent child. But be that not a marvel? You must see it, sir, it's God's work we do. So I'll be gone every day for some time. I'm—I am an official of the court, they say, and I— *She has been edging toward offstage.*

PROCTOR: I'll official you! *He strides to the mantel, takes down the whip hanging there.*

MARY WARREN, *terrified, but coming erect, striving for her authority*: I'll not stand whipping any more!

ELIZABETH, *hurriedly, as Proctor approaches*: Mary, promise now you'll stay at home—

MARY WARREN, *backing from him, but keeping her erect posture, striving, striving for her way*: The Devil's loose in Salem, Mr. Proctor; we must discover where he's hiding!

PROCTOR: I'll whip the Devil out of you! *With whip raised he reaches out for her, and she streaks away and yells.*

MARY WARREN, *pointing at Elizabeth*: I saved her life today!

Silence. His whip comes down.

ELIZABETH, *softly*: I am accused?

MARY WARREN, *quaking*: Somewhat mentioned. But I said I never see no sign you ever sent your spirit out to hurt no one, and seeing I do live so closely with you, they dismissed it.

ELIZABETH: Who accused me?

MARY WARREN: I am bound by law, I cannot tell it. *To Proctor*: I only hope you'll not be so sarcastical no more. Four judges and the King's deputy sat to dinner with us but an hour ago. I—I would have you speak civilly to me, from this out.

PROCTOR, *in horror, muttering in disgust at her*: Go to bed.

MARY WARREN, *with a stamp of her foot*: I'll not be ordered to bed no more, Mr. Proctor! I am eighteen and a woman, however single!

PROCTOR: Do you wish to sit up? Then sit up.

MARY WARREN: I wish to go to bed!

PROCTOR, *in anger*: Good night, then!

MARY WARREN: Good night. *Dissatisfied, uncertain of herself, she goes out. Wide-eyed, both Proctor and Elizabeth stand staring.*

ELIZABETH, *quietly*: Oh, the noose, the noose is up!

PROCTOR: There'll be no noose.

ELIZABETH: She wants me dead. I knew all week it would come to this!

PROCTOR, *without conviction*: They dismissed it. You heard her say—

ELIZABETH: And what of tomorrow? She will cry me out until they take me!

PROCTOR: Sit you down.

ELIZABETH: She wants me dead, John, you know it!

PROCTOR: I say sit down! *She sits, trembling. He speaks quietly, trying to keep his wits.* Now we must be wise, Elizabeth.

ELIZABETH, *with sarcasm, and a sense of being lost*: Oh, indeed, indeed!

PROCTOR: Fear nothing. I'll find Ezekiel Cheever. I'll tell him she said it were all sport.

ELIZABETH: John, with so many in the jail, more than Cheever's help is needed now, I think. Would you favor me with this? Go to Abigail.

PROCTOR, *his soul hardening as he senses . . .* : What have I to say to Abigail?

ELIZABETH, *delicately*: John—grant me this. You have a faulty understanding of young girls. There is a promise made in any bed—

PROCTOR, *striving against his anger*: What promise!

ELIZABETH: Spoke or silent, a promise is surely made. And she may dote on it now—I am sure she does—and thinks to kill me, then to take my place.

Proctor's anger is rising; he cannot speak.

ELIZABETH: It is her dearest hope, John, I know it. There be a thousand names; why does she call mine? There be a certain danger in calling such a name—I am no Goody Good that sleeps in ditches, nor Osburn, drunk and half-witted. She'd dare not call out such a farmer's wife but there be monstrous profit in it. She thinks to take my place, John.

PROCTOR: She cannot think it! *He knows it is true.*

ELIZABETH, *"reasonably"*: John, have you ever shown her somewhat of contempt? She cannot pass you in the church but you will blush—

PROCTOR: I may blush for my sin.

ELIZABETH: I think she sees another meaning in that blush.

PROCTOR: And what see you? What see you, Elizabeth?

ELIZABETH, *"conceding"*: I think you be somewhat ashamed, for I am there, and she so close.

PROCTOR: When will you know me, woman? Were I stone I would have cracked for shame this seven month!

ELIZABETH: Then go and tell her she's a whore. Whatever promise she may sense—break it, John, break it.

PROCTOR, *between his teeth*: Good, then. I'll go. *He starts for his rifle.*

ELIZABETH, *trembling, fearfully*: Oh, how unwillingly!

PROCTOR, *turning on her, rifle in hand*: I will curse her hotter than the oldest cinder in hell. But pray, begrudge me not my anger!

ELIZABETH: Your anger! I only ask you—

PROCTOR: Woman, am I so base? Do you truly think me base?

ELIZABETH: I never called you base.

PROCTOR: Then how do you charge me with such a promise? The promise that a stallion gives a mare I gave that girl!

ELIZABETH: Then why do you anger with me when I bid you break it?

PROCTOR: Because it speaks deceit, and I am honest! But I'll plead no more! I see now your spirit twists around the single error of my life, and I will never tear it free!

ELIZABETH, *crying out*: You'll tear it free—when you come to know that I will be your only wife, or no wife at all! She has an arrow in you yet, John Proctor, and you know it well!

*Quite suddenly, as though from the air, a figure appears in the
doorway. They start slightly. It is Mr. Hale. He is different
now—drawn a little, and there is a quality of deference, even
of guilt, about his manner now.*

HALE: Good evening.

PROCTOR, *still in his shock*: Why, Mr. Hale! Good evening to you, sir.
Come in, come in.

HALE, *to Elizabeth*: I hope I do not startle you.

ELIZABETH: No, no, it's only that I heard no horse—

HALE: You are Goodwife Proctor.

PROCTOR: Aye; Elizabeth.

HALE, *nods, then*: I hope you're not off to bed yet.

PROCTOR, *setting down his gun*: No, no. *Hale comes further into the
room. And Proctor, to explain his nervousness:* We are not used to visitors
after dark, but you're welcome here. Will you sit you down, sir?

HALE: I will. *He sits.* Let you sit, Goodwife Proctor.

> *She does, never letting him out of her sight. There is a pause
> as Hale looks about the room.*

PROCTOR, *to break the silence*: Will you drink cider, Mr. Hale?

HALE: No, it rebels my stomach; I have some further traveling yet tonight.
Sit you down, sir. *Proctor sits.* I will not keep you long, but I have some
business with you.

PROCTOR: Business of the court?

HALE: No—no, I come of my own, without the court's authority. Hear
me. *He wets his lips.* I know not if you are aware, but your wife's name
is—mentioned in the court.

PROCTOR: We know it, sir. Our Mary Warren told us. We are entirely
amazed.

HALE: I am a stranger here, as you know. And in my ignorance I find it
hard to draw a clear opinion of them that come accused before the court.
And so this afternoon, and now tonight, I go from house to house—I
come now from Rebecca Nurse's house and—

ELIZABETH, *shocked*: Rebecca's charged!

HALE: God forbid such a one be charged. She is, however—mentioned
somewhat.

ELIZABETH, *with an attempt at a laugh*: You will never believe, I hope, that Rebecca trafficked with the Devil.

HALE: Woman, it is possible.

PROCTOR, *taken aback*: Surely you cannot think so.

HALE: This is a strange time, Mister. No man may longer doubt the powers of the dark are gathered in monstrous attack upon this village. There is too much evidence now to deny it. You will agree, sir?

PROCTOR, *evading*: I—have no knowledge in that line. But it's hard to think so pious a woman be secretly a Devil's bitch after seventy year of such good prayer.

HALE: Aye. But the Devil is a wily one, you cannot deny it. However, she is far from accused, and I know she will not be. *Pause.* I thought, sir, to put some questions as to the Christian character of this house, if you'll permit me.

PROCTOR, *coldly, resentful*: Why, we—have no fear of questions, sir.

HALE: Good, then. *He makes himself more comfortable.* In the book of record that Mr. Parris keeps, I note that you are rarely in the church on Sabbath Day.

PROCTOR: No, sir, you are mistaken.

HALE: Twenty-six time in seventeen month, sir. I must call that rare. Will you tell me why you are so absent?

PROCTOR: Mr. Hale, I never knew I must account to that man for I come to church or stay at home. My wife were sick this winter.

HALE: So I am told. But you, Mister, why could you not come alone?

PROCTOR: I surely did come when I could, and when I could not I prayed in this house.

HALE: Mr. Proctor, your house is not a church; your theology must tell you that.

PROCTOR: It does, sir, it does; and it tells me that a minister may pray to God without he have golden candlesticks upon the altar.

HALE: What golden candlesticks?

PROCTOR: Since we built the church there were pewter candlesticks upon the altar; Francis Nurse made them, y'know, and a sweeter hand never touched the metal. But Parris came, and for twenty week he preach nothin' but golden candlesticks until he had them. I labor the earth from dawn of day to blink of night, and I tell you true, when I look to heaven and see my money glaring at his elbows—it hurt my prayer, sir, it hurt my prayer. I think, sometimes, the man dreams cathedrals, not clapboard meetin' houses.

HALE, *thinks, then*: And yet, Mister, a Christian on Sabbath Day must be in church. *Pause.* Tell me—you have three children?

PROCTOR: Aye. Boys.

HALE: How comes it that only two are baptized?

PROCTOR, *starts to speak, then stops, then, as though unable to restrain this*: I like it not that Mr. Parris should lay his hand upon my baby. I see no light of God in that man. I'll not conceal it.

HALE: I must say it, Mr. Proctor; that is not for you to decide. The man's ordained, therefore the light of God is in him.

PROCTOR, *flushed with resentment but trying to smile*: What's your suspicion, Mr. Hale?

HALE: No, no, I have no—

PROCTOR: I nailed the roof upon the church, I hung the door—

HALE: Oh, did you! That's a good sign, then.

PROCTOR: It may be I have been too quick to bring the man to book, but you cannot think we ever desired the destruction of religion. I think that's in your mind, is it not?

HALE, *not altogether giving way*: I—have—there is a softness in your record, sir, a softness.

ELIZABETH: I think, maybe, we have been too hard with Mr. Parris. I think so. But sure we never loved the Devil here.

HALE, *nods, deliberating this. Then, with the voice of one administering a secret test*: Do you know your Commandments, Elizabeth?

ELIZABETH, *without hesitation, even eagerly*: I surely do. There be no mark of blame upon my life, Mr. Hale. I am a covenanted Christian woman.

HALE: And you, Mister?

PROCTOR, *a trifle unsteadily*: I—am sure I do, sir.

HALE, *glances at her open face, then at John, then*: Let you repeat them, if you will.

PROCTOR: The Commandments.

HALE: Aye.

PROCTOR, *looking off, beginning to sweat*: Thou shalt not kill.

HALE: Aye.

PROCTOR, *counting on his fingers*: Thou shalt not steal. Thou shalt not covet thy neighbor's goods, nor make unto thee any graven image. Thou shalt not take the name of the Lord in vain; thou shalt have no other gods before me. *With some hesitation*: Thou shalt remember the Sabbath Day and keep it holy. *Pause. Then*: Thou shalt honor thy father and mother. Thou shalt not bear false witness. *He is stuck. He counts back on his fingers, knowing one is missing.* Thou shalt not make unto thee any graven image.

HALE: You have said that twice, sir.

PROCTOR, *lost*: Aye. *He is flailing for it.*

ELIZABETH, *delicately*: Adultery, John.

PROCTOR, *as though a secret arrow had pained his heart*: Aye. *Trying to grin it away—to Hale*: You see, sir, between the two of us we do know them all. *Hale only looks at Proctor, deep in his attempt to define this man. Proctor grows more uneasy.* I think it be a small fault.

HALE: Theology, sir, is a fortress; no crack in a fortress may be accounted small. *He rises; he seems worried now. He paces a little, in deep thought.*

PROCTOR: There be no love for Satan in this house, Mister.

HALE: I pray it, I pray it dearly. *He looks to both of them, an attempt at a smile on his face, but his misgivings are clear.* Well, then—I'll bid you good night.

ELIZABETH, *unable to restrain herself*: Mr. Hale. *He turns.* I do think you are suspecting me somewhat? Are you not?

HALE, *obviously disturbed—and evasive*: Goody Proctor, I do not judge you. My duty is to add what I may to the godly wisdom of the court. I pray you both good health and good fortune. *To John*: Good night, sir. *He starts out.*

ELIZABETH, *with a note of desperation*: I think you must tell him, John.

HALE: What's that?

ELIZABETH, *restraining a call*: Will you tell him?

Slight pause. Hale looks questioningly at John.

PROCTOR, *with difficulty*: I—I have no witness and cannot prove it, except my word be taken. But I know the children's sickness had naught to do with witchcraft.

HALE, *stopped, struck*: Naught to do—?

PROCTOR: Mr. Parris discovered them sportin' in the woods. They were startled and took sick.

 Pause.

HALE: Who told you this?

PROCTOR, *hesitates, then*: Abigail Williams.

HALE: Abigail!

PROCTOR: Aye.

HALE, *his eyes wide*: Abigail Williams told you it had naught to do with witchcraft!

PROCTOR: She told me the day you came, sir.

HALE, *suspiciously*: Why—why did you keep this?

PROCTOR: I never knew until tonight that the world is gone daft with this nonsense.

HALE: Nonsense! Mister, I have myself examined Tituba, Sarah Good, and numerous others that have confessed to dealing with the Devil. They have *confessed* it.

PROCTOR: And why not, if they must hang for denyin' it? There are them that will swear to anything before they'll hang; have you never thought of that?

HALE: I have. I—I have indeed. *It is his own suspicion, but he resists it. He glances at Elizabeth, then at John.* And you—would you testify to this in court?

PROCTOR: I—had not reckoned with goin' into court. But if I must I will.

HALE: Do you falter here?

PROCTOR: I falter nothing, but I may wonder if my story will be credited in such a court. I do wonder on it, when such a steady-minded minister as you will suspicion such a woman that never lied, and cannot, and the world knows she cannot! I may falter somewhat, Mister; I am no fool.

HALE, *quietly—it has impressed him*: Proctor, let you open with me now, for I have a rumor that troubles me. It's said you hold no belief that there may even be witches in the world. Is that true, sir?

PROCTOR—*he knows this is critical, and is striving against his disgust with Hale and with himself for even answering*: I know not what I have said, I may have said it. I have wondered if there be witches in the world— although I cannot believe they come among us now.

HALE: Then you do not believe—

PROCTOR: I have no knowledge of it; the Bible speaks of witches, and I will not deny them.

HALE: And you, woman?

ELIZABETH: I—I cannot believe it.

HALE, *shocked*: You cannot!

PROCTOR: Elizabeth, you bewilder him!

ELIZABETH, *to Hale*: I cannot think the Devil may own a woman's soul, Mr. Hale, when she keeps an upright way, as I have. I am a good woman, I know it; and if you believe I may do only good work in the world, and yet be secretly bound to Satan, then I must tell you, sir, I do not believe it.

HALE: But, woman, you do believe there are witches in—

ELIZABETH: If you think that I am one, then I say there are none.

HALE: You surely do not fly against the Gospel, the Gospel—

PROCTOR: She believe in the Gospel, every word!

ELIZABETH: Question Abigail Williams about the Gospel, not myself!

 Hale stares at her.

PROCTOR: She do not mean to doubt the Gospel, sir, you cannot think it. This be a Christian house, sir, a Christian house.

HALE: God keep you both; let the third child be quickly baptized, and go you without fail each Sunday in to Sabbath prayer; and keep a solemn, quiet way among you. I think—

 Giles Corey appears in doorway.

GILES: John!

PROCTOR: Giles! What's the matter?

GILES: They take my wife.

 Francis Nurse enters.

GILES: And his Rebecca!

PROCTOR, *to Francis*: Rebecca's in the *jail*!

FRANCIS: Aye, Cheever come and take her in his wagon. We've only now come from the jail, and they'll not even let us in to see them.

ELIZABETH: They've surely gone wild now, Mr. Hale!

FRANCIS, *going to Hale*: Reverend Hale! Can you not speak to the Deputy Governor? I'm sure he mistakes these people—

HALE: Pray calm yourself, Mr. Nurse.

FRANCIS: My wife is the very brick and mortar of the church, Mr. Hale—*indicating Giles*—and Martha Corey, there cannot be a woman closer yet to God than Martha.

HALE: How is Rebecca charged, Mr. Nurse?

FRANCIS, *with a mocking, half-hearted laugh*: For murder, she's charged! *Mockingly quoting the warrant*: "For the marvelous and supernatural murder of Goody Putnam's babies." What am I to do, Mr. Hale?

HALE, *turns from Francis, deeply troubled, then*: Believe me, Mr. Nurse, if Rebecca Nurse be tainted, then nothing's left to stop the whole green world from burning. Let you rest upon the justice of the court; the court will send her home, I know it.

FRANCIS: You cannot mean she will be tried in court!

HALE, *pleading*: Nurse, though our hearts break, we cannot flinch; these are new times, sir. There is a misty plot afoot so subtle we should be criminal to cling to old respects and ancient friendships. I have seen too many frightful proofs in court—the Devil is alive in Salem, and we dare not quail to follow wherever the accusing finger points!

PROCTOR, *angered*: How may such a woman murder children?

HALE, *in great pain*: Man, remember, until an hour before the Devil fell, God thought him beautiful in Heaven.

GILES: I never said my wife were a witch, Mr. Hale; I only said she were reading books!

HALE: Mr. Corey, exactly what complaint were made on your wife?

GILES: That bloody mongrel Walcott charge her. Y'see, he buy a pig of my wife four or five year ago, and the pig died soon after. So he come dancin' in for his money back. So my Martha, she says to him, "Walcott, if you haven't the wit to feed a pig properly, you'll not live to own many," she says. Now he goes to court and claims that from that day to this he cannot keep a pig alive for more than four weeks because my Martha bewitch them with her books!

Enter Ezekiel Cheever. A shocked silence.

CHEEVER: Good evening to you, Proctor.

PROCTOR: Why, Mr. Cheever. Good evening.

CHEEVER: Good evening, all. Good evening, Mr. Hale.

PROCTOR: I hope you come not on business of the court.

CHEEVER: I do, Proctor, aye. I am clerk of the court now, y'know.

> *Enter Marshal Herrick, a man in his early thirties, who is somewhat shamefaced at the moment.*

GILES: It's a pity, Ezekiel, that an honest tailor might have gone to Heaven must burn in Hell. You'll burn for this, do you know it?

CHEEVER: You know yourself I must do as I'm told. You surely know that, Giles. And I'd as lief you'd not be sending me to Hell. I like not the sound of it, I tell you; I like not the sound of it. *He fears Proctor, but starts to reach inside his coat.* Now believe me, Proctor, how heavy be the law, all its tonnage I do carry on my back tonight. *He takes out a warrant.* I have a warrant for your wife.

PROCTOR, *to Hale*: You said she were not charged!

HALE: I know nothin' of it. *To Cheever*: When were she charged?

CHEEVER: I am given sixteen warrant tonight, sir, and she is one.

PROCTOR: Who charged her?

CHEEVER: Why, Abigail Williams charge her.

PROCTOR: On what proof, what proof?

CHEEVER, *looking about the room*: Mr. Proctor, I have little time. The court bid me search your house, but I like not to search a house. So will you hand me any poppets that your wife may keep here?

PROCTOR: Poppets?

ELIZABETH: I never kept no poppets, not since I were a girl.

CHEEVER, *embarrassed, glancing toward the mantel where sits Mary Warren's poppet*: I spy a poppet, Goody Proctor.

ELIZABETH: Oh! *Going for it*: Why, this is Mary's.

CHEEVER, *shyly*: Would you please to give it to me?

ELIZABETH, *handing it to him, asks Hale*: Has the court discovered a text in poppets now?

CHEEVER, *carefully holding the poppet*: Do you keep any others in this house?

PROCTOR: No, nor this one either till tonight. What signifies a poppet?

CHEEVER: Why, a poppet—*he gingerly turns the poppet over*—a poppet may signify— Now, woman, will you please to come with me?

PROCTOR: She will not! *To Elizabeth*: Fetch Mary here.

CHEEVER, *ineptly reaching toward Elizabeth*: No, no, I am forbid to leave her from my sight.

PROCTOR, *pushing his arm away*: You'll leave her out of sight and out of mind, Mister. Fetch Mary, Elizabeth. *Elizabeth goes upstairs.*

HALE: What signifies a poppet, Mr. Cheever?

CHEEVER, *turning the poppet over in his hands*: Why, they say it may signify that she— *He has lifted the poppet's skirt, and his eyes widen in astonished fear.* Why, this, this—

PROCTOR, *reaching for the poppet*: What's there?

CHEEVER: Why—*he draws out a long needle from the poppet*—it is a needle! Herrick, Herrick, it is a needle!

Herrick comes toward him.

PROCTOR, *angrily, bewildered*: And what signifies a needle!

CHEEVER, *his hands shaking*: Why, this go hard with her, Proctor, this— I had my doubts, Proctor, I had my doubts, but here's calamity. *To Hale, showing the needle*: You see it, sir, it is a needle!

HALE: Why? What meanin' has it?

CHEEVER, *wide-eyed, trembling*: The girl, the Williams girl, Abigail Williams, sir. She sat to dinner in Reverend Parris's house tonight, and without word nor warnin' she falls to the floor. Like a struck beast, he says, and screamed a scream that a bull would weep to hear. And he goes to save her, and, stuck two inches in the flesh of her belly, he draw a needle out. And demandin' of her how she come to be so stabbed, she—*to Proctor now*—testify it were your wife's familiar spirit pushed it in.

PROCTOR: Why, she done it herself! *To Hale*: I hope you're not takin' this for proof, Mister!

Hale, struck by the proof, is silent.

CHEEVER: 'Tis hard proof! *To Hale*: I find here a poppet Goody Proctor keeps. I have found it, sir. And in the belly of the poppet a needle's stuck. I tell you true, Proctor, I never warranted to see such proof of Hell, and I bid you obstruct me not, for I—

Enter Elizabeth with Mary Warren. Proctor, seeing Mary Warren, draws her by the arm to Hale.

PROCTOR: Here now! Mary, how did this poppet come into my house?

MARY WARREN, *frightened for herself, her voice very small*: What poppet's that, sir?

PROCTOR, *impatiently, pointing at the doll in Cheever's hand*: This poppet, this poppet.

MARY WARREN, *evasively, looking at it*: Why, I—I think it is mine.

PROCTOR: It is your poppet, is it not?

MARY WARREN, *not understanding the direction of this*: It—is, sir.

PROCTOR: And how did it come into this house?

MARY WARREN, *glancing about at the avid faces*: Why—I made it in the court, sir, and—give it to Goody Proctor tonight.

PROCTOR, *to Hale*: Now, sir—do you have it?

HALE: Mary Warren, a needle have been found inside this poppet.

MARY WARREN, *bewildered*: Why, I meant no harm by it, sir.

PROCTOR, *quickly*: You stuck that needle in yourself?

MARY WARREN: I—I believe I did, sir, I—

PROCTOR, *to Hale*: What say you now?

HALE, *watching Mary Warren closely*: Child, you are certain this be your natural memory? May it be, perhaps, that someone conjures you even now to say this?

MARY WARREN: Conjures me? Why, no, sir, I am entirely myself, I think. Let you ask Susanna Walcott—she saw me sewin' it in court. *Or better still*: Ask Abby, Abby sat beside me when I made it.

PROCTOR, *to Hale, of Cheever*: Bid him begone. Your mind is surely settled now. Bid him out, Mr. Hale.

ELIZABETH: What signifies a needle?

HALE: Mary—you charge a cold and cruel murder on Abigail.

MARY WARREN: Murder! I charge no—

HALE: Abigail were stabbed tonight; a needle were found stuck into her belly—

ELIZABETH: And she charges me?

HALE: Aye.

ELIZABETH, *her breath knocked out*: Why—! The girl is murder! She must be ripped out of the world!

CHEEVER, *pointing at Elizabeth*: You've heard that, sir! Ripped out of the world! Herrick, you heard it!

PROCTOR, *suddenly snatching the warrant out of Cheever's hands*: Out with you.

CHEEVER: Proctor, you dare not touch the warrant.

PROCTOR, *ripping the warrant*: Out with you!

CHEEVER: You've ripped the Deputy Governor's warrant, man!

PROCTOR: Damn the Deputy Governor! Out of my house!

HALE: Now, Proctor, Proctor!

PROCTOR: Get y'gone with them! You are a broken minister.

HALE: Proctor, if she is innocent, the court—

PROCTOR: If *she* is innocent! Why do you never wonder if Parris be innocent, or Abigail? Is the accuser always holy now? Were they born this morning as clean as God's fingers? I'll tell you what's walking Salem—vengeance is walking Salem. We are what we always were in Salem, but now the little crazy children are jangling the keys of the kingdom, and common vengeance writes the law! This warrant's vengeance! I'll not give my wife to vengeance!

ELIZABETH: I'll go, John—

PROCTOR: You will not go!

HERRICK: I have nine men outside. You cannot keep her. The law binds me, John, I cannot budge.

PROCTOR, *to Hale, ready to break him*: Will you see her taken?

HALE: Proctor, the court is just—

PROCTOR: Pontius Pilate! God will not let you wash your hands of this!

ELIZABETH: John—I think I must go with them. *He cannot bear to look at her.* Mary, there is bread enough for the morning; you will bake, in the afternoon. Help Mr. Proctor as you were his daughter—you owe me that, and much more. *She is fighting her weeping. To Proctor*: When the children wake, speak nothing of witchcraft—it will frighten them. *She cannot go on.*

PROCTOR: I will bring you home. I will bring you soon.

ELIZABETH: Oh, John, bring me soon!

PROCTOR: I will fall like an ocean on that court! Fear nothing, Elizabeth.

ELIZABETH, *with great fear*: I will fear nothing. *She looks about the room, as though to fix it in her mind.* Tell the children I have gone to visit someone sick.

She walks out the door, Herrick and Cheever behind her. For a moment, Proctor watches from the doorway. The clank of chain is heard.

PROCTOR: Herrick! Herrick, don't chain her! *He rushes out the door. From outside*: Damn you, man, you will not chain her! Off with them! I'll not have it! I will not have her chained!

There are other men's voices against his. Hale, in a fever of guilt and uncertainty, turns from the door to avoid the sight; Mary Warren bursts into tears and sits weeping. Giles Corey calls to Hale.

GILES: And yet silent, minister? It is fraud, you know it is fraud! What keeps you, man?

Proctor is half braced, half pushed into the room by two deputies and Herrick.

PROCTOR: I'll pay you, Herrick, I will surely pay you!

HERRICK, *panting*: In God's name, John, I cannot help myself. I must chain them all. Now let you keep inside this house till I am gone! *He goes out with his deputies.*

Proctor stands there, gulping air. Horses and a wagon creaking are heard.

HALE, *in great uncertainty*: Mr. Proctor—

PROCTOR: Out of my sight!

HALE: Charity, Proctor, charity. What I have heard in her favor, I will not fear to testify in court. God help me, I cannot judge her guilty or innocent—I know not. Only this consider: the world goes mad, and it profit nothing you should lay the cause to the vengeance of a little girl.

PROCTOR: You are a coward! Though you be ordained in God's own tears, you are a coward now!

HALE: Proctor, I cannot think God be provoked so grandly by such a petty cause. The jails are packed—our greatest judges sit in Salem now—and hangin's promised. Man, we must look to cause proportionate. Were there murder done, perhaps, and never brought to light? Abomination? Some secret blasphemy that stinks to Heaven? Think on cause, man, and let you help me to discover it. For there's your way, believe it, there is your only way, when such confusion strikes upon the world. *He goes to Giles and Francis.* Let you counsel among yourselves; think on your village and what may have drawn from heaven such thundering wrath upon you all. I shall pray God open up our eyes.

Hale goes out.

FRANCIS, *struck by Hale's mood*: I never heard no murder done in Salem.

PROCTOR—*he has been reached by Hale's words*: Leave me, Francis, leave me.

GILES, *shaken*: John—tell me, are we lost?

PROCTOR: Go home now, Giles. We'll speak on it tomorrow.

GILES: Let you think on it. We'll come early, eh?

PROCTOR: Aye. Go now, Giles.

GILES: Good night, then.

Giles Corey and Francis Nurse go out. After a moment:

MARY WARREN, *in a fearful squeak of a voice*: Mr. Proctor, very likely they'll let her come home once they're given proper evidence.

PROCTOR: You're coming to the court with me, Mary. You will tell it in the court.

MARY WARREN: I cannot charge murder on Abigail.

PROCTOR, *moving menacingly toward her*: You will tell the court how that poppet come here and who stuck the needle in.

MARY WARREN: She'll kill me for sayin' that! *Proctor continues toward her.* Abby'll charge lechery on you, Mr. Proctor!

PROCTOR, *halting*: She's told you!

MARY WARREN: I have known it, sir. She'll ruin you with it, I know she will.

PROCTOR, *hesitating, and with deep hatred of himself*: Good. Then her saintliness is done with. *Mary backs from him.* We will slide together into our pit; you will tell the court what you know.

MARY WARREN, *in terror*: I cannot, they'll turn on me—

Proctor strides and catches her, and she is repeating, "I cannot, I cannot!"

PROCTOR: My wife will never die for me! I will bring your guts into your mouth but that goodness will not die for me!

MARY WARREN, *struggling to escape him*: I cannot do it, I cannot!

PROCTOR, *grasping her by the throat as though he would strangle her*: Make your peace with it! Now Hell and Heaven grapple on our backs, and all our old pretense is ripped away—make your peace! *He throws her to the floor, where she sobs, "I cannot, I cannot . . ." And now, half to himself, staring, and turning to the open door:* Peace. It is a providence, and no great change; we are only what we always were, but naked now. *He walks as though toward a great horror, facing the open sky.* Aye, naked! And the wind, God's icy wind, will blow!

> *And she is over and over again sobbing, "I cannot, I cannot, I cannot," as*

THE CURTAIN FALLS.*

---

* Act Two, Scene II, which appeared in the original production, was dropped by the author from the published reading version, the *Collected Plays,* and all Compass editions prior to 1971. It has not been included in most productions subsequent to the revival at New York's Martinique Theatre in 1958 and was dropped by Sir Laurence Olivier in his London production in 1965. It is included here as an appendix on page 433.

ACT THREE

The vestry room of the Salem meeting house, now serving as the anteroom of the General Court.

As the curtain rises, the room is empty, but for sunlight pouring through two high windows in the back wall. The room is solemn, even forbidding. Heavy beams jut out, boards of random widths make up the walls. At the right are two doors leading into the meeting house proper, where the court is being held. At the left another door leads outside.

There is a plain bench at the left, and another at the right. In the center a rather long meeting table, with stools and a considerable armchair snugged up to it.

Through the partitioning wall at the right we hear a prosecutor's voice, Judge Hathorne's, asking a question; then a woman's voice, Martha Corey's, replying.

HATHORNE'S VOICE: Now, Martha Corey, there is abundant evidence in our hands to show that you have given yourself to the reading of fortunes. Do you deny it?

MARTHA COREY'S VOICE: I am innocent to a witch. I know not what a witch is.

HATHORNE'S VOICE: How do you know, then, that you are not a witch?

MARTHA COREY'S VOICE: If I were, I would know it.

HATHORNE'S VOICE: Why do you hurt these children?

MARTHA COREY'S VOICE: I do not hurt them. I scorn it!

GILES' VOICE, *roaring*: I have evidence for the court!

Voices of townspeople rise in excitement.

DANFORTH'S VOICE: You will keep your seat!

GILES' VOICE: Thomas Putnam is reaching out for land!

DANFORTH'S VOICE: Remove that man, Marshal!

GILES' VOICE: You're hearing lies, lies!

A roaring goes up from the people.

HATHORNE'S VOICE: Arrest him, Excellency!

GILES' VOICE: I have evidence. Why will you not hear my evidence?

> *The door opens and Giles is half carried into the vestry room by Herrick. Francis Nurse enters, trailing anxiously behind Giles.*

GILES: Hands off, damn you, let me go!

HERRICK: Giles, Giles!

GILES: Out of my way, Herrick! I bring evidence—

HERRICK: You cannot go in there, Giles; it's a court!

> *Enter Hale from the court.*

HALE: Pray be calm a moment.

GILES: You, Mr. Hale, go in there and demand I speak.

HALE: A moment, sir, a moment.

GILES: They'll be hangin' my wife!

> *Judge Hathorne enters. He is in his sixties, a bitter, remorseless Salem judge.*

HATHORNE: How do you dare come roarin' into this court! Are you gone daft, Corey?

GILES: You're not a Boston judge yet, Hathorne. You'll not call me daft!

> *Enter Deputy Governor Danforth and, behind him, Ezekiel Cheever and Parris. On his appearance, silence falls. Danforth is a grave man in his sixties, of some humor and sophistication that do not, however, interfere with an exact loyalty to his position and his cause. He comes down to Giles, who awaits his wrath.*

DANFORTH, *looking directly at Giles*: Who is this man?

PARRIS: Giles Corey, sir, and a more contentious—

GILES, *to Parris*: I am asked the question, and I am old enough to answer it! *To Danforth, who impresses him and to whom he smiles through his strain*: My name is Corey, sir, Giles Corey. I have six hundred acres, and timber in addition. It is my wife you be condemning now. *He indicates the courtroom.*

DANFORTH: And how do you imagine to help her cause with such contemptuous riot? Now be gone. Your old age alone keeps you out of jail for this.

GILES, *beginning to plead*: They be tellin' lies about my wife, sir, I—

DANFORTH: Do you take it upon yourself to determine what this court shall believe and what it shall set aside?

GILES: Your Excellency, we mean no disrespect for—

DANFORTH: Disrespect indeed! It is disruption, Mister. This is the highest court of the supreme government of this province, do you know it?

GILES, *beginning to weep*: Your Excellency, I only said she were readin' books, sir, and they come and take her out of my house for—

DANFORTH, *mystified*: Books! What books?

GILES, *through helpless sobs*: It is my third wife, sir; I never had no wife that be so taken with books, and I thought to find the cause of it, d'y'see, but it were no witch I blamed her for. *He is openly weeping.* I have broke charity with the woman, I have broke charity with her. *He covers his face, ashamed. Danforth is respectfully silent.*

HALE: Excellency, he claims hard evidence for his wife's defense. I think that in all justice you must—

DANFORTH: Then let him submit his evidence in proper affidavit. You are certainly aware of our procedure here, Mr. Hale. *To Herrick*: Clear this room.

HERRICK: Come now, Giles. *He gently pushes Corey out.*

FRANCIS: We are desperate, sir; we come here three days now and cannot be heard.

DANFORTH: Who is this man?

FRANCIS: Francis Nurse, Your Excellency.

HALE: His wife's Rebecca that were condemned this morning.

DANFORTH: Indeed! I am amazed to find you in such uproar. I have only good report of your character, Mr. Nurse.

HATHORNE: I think they must both be arrested in contempt, sir.

DANFORTH, *to Francis*: Let you write your plea, and in due time I will—

FRANCIS: Excellency, we have proof for your eyes; God forbid you shut them to it. The girls, sir, the girls are frauds.

DANFORTH: What's that?

FRANCIS: We have proof of it, sir. They are all deceiving you.

Danforth is shocked, but studying Francis.

HATHORNE: This is contempt, sir, contempt!

DANFORTH: Peace, Judge Hathorne. Do you know who I am, Mr. Nurse?

FRANCIS: I surely do, sir, and I think you must be a wise judge to be what you are.

DANFORTH: And do you know that near to four hundred are in the jails from Marblehead to Lynn, and upon my signature?

FRANCIS: I—

DANFORTH: And seventy-two condemned to hang by that signature?

FRANCIS: Excellency, I never thought to say it to such a weighty judge, but you are deceived.

> *Enter Giles Corey from left. All turn to see as he beckons in Mary Warren with Proctor. Mary is keeping her eyes to the ground; Proctor has her elbow as though she were near collapse.*

PARRIS, *on seeing her, in shock*: Mary Warren! *He goes directly to bend close to her face.* What are you about here?

PROCTOR, *pressing Parris away from her with a gentle but firm motion of protectiveness*: She would speak with the Deputy Governor.

DANFORTH, *shocked by this, turns to Herrick*: Did you not tell me Mary Warren were sick in bed?

HERRICK: She were, Your Honor. When I go to fetch her to the court last week, she said she were sick.

GILES: She has been strivin' with her soul all week, Your Honor; she comes now to tell the truth of this to you.

DANFORTH: Who is this?

PROCTOR: John Proctor, sir. Elizabeth Proctor is my wife.

PARRIS: Beware this man, Your Excellency, this man is mischief.

HALE, *excitedly*: I think you must hear the girl, sir, she—

DANFORTH, *who has become very interested in Mary Warren and only raises a hand toward Hale*: Peace. What would you tell us, Mary Warren?

> *Proctor looks at her, but she cannot speak.*

PROCTOR: She never saw no spirits, sir.

DANFORTH, *with great alarm and surprise, to Mary*: Never saw no spirits!

GILES, *eagerly*: Never.

PROCTOR, *reaching into his jacket*: She has signed a deposition, sir—

DANFORTH, *instantly*: No, no, I accept no depositions. *He is rapidly calculating this; he turns from her to Proctor.* Tell me, Mr. Proctor, have you given out this story in the village?

PROCTOR: We have not.

PARRIS: They've come to overthrow the court, sir! This man is—

DANFORTH: I pray you, Mr. Parris. Do you know, Mr. Proctor, that the entire contention of the state in these trials is that the voice of Heaven is speaking through the children?

PROCTOR: I know that, sir.

DANFORTH, *thinks, staring at Proctor, then turns to Mary Warren*: And you, Mary Warren, how came you to cry out people for sending their spirits against you?

MARY WARREN: It were pretense, sir.

DANFORTH: I cannot hear you.

PROCTOR: It were pretense, she says.

DANFORTH: Ah? And the other girls? Susanna Walcott, and—the others? They are also pretending?

MARY WARREN: Aye, sir.

DANFORTH, *wide-eyed*: Indeed. *Pause. He is baffled by this. He turns to study Proctor's face.*

PARRIS, *in a sweat*: Excellency, you surely cannot think to let so vile a lie be spread in open court!

DANFORTH: Indeed not, but it strike hard upon me that she will dare come here with such a tale. Now, Mr. Proctor, before I decide whether I shall hear you or not, it is my duty to tell you this. We burn a hot fire here; it melts down all concealment.

PROCTOR: I know that, sir.

DANFORTH: Let me continue. I understand well, a husband's tenderness may drive him to extravagance in defense of a wife. Are you certain in your conscience, Mister, that your evidence is the truth?

PROCTOR: It is. And you will surely know it.

DANFORTH: And you thought to declare this revelation in the open court before the public?

PROCTOR: I thought I would, aye—with your permission.

DANFORTH, *his eyes narrowing*: Now, sir, what is your purpose in so doing?

PROCTOR: Why, I—I would free my wife, sir.

DANFORTH: There lurks nowhere in your heart, nor hidden in your spirit, any desire to undermine this court?

PROCTOR, *with the faintest faltering*: Why, no, sir.

CHEEVER, *clears his throat, awakening*: I— Your Excellency.

DANFORTH: Mr. Cheever.

CHEEVER: I think it be my duty, sir— *Kindly, to Proctor*: You'll not deny it, John. *To Danforth*: When we come to take his wife, he damned the court and ripped your warrant.

PARRIS: Now you have it!

DANFORTH: He did that, Mr. Hale?

HALE, *takes a breath*: Aye, he did.

PROCTOR: It were a temper, sir. I knew not what I did.

DANFORTH, *studying him*: Mr. Proctor.

PROCTOR: Aye, sir.

DANFORTH, *straight into his eyes*: Have you ever seen the Devil?

PROCTOR: No, sir.

DANFORTH: You are in all respects a Gospel Christian?

PROCTOR: I am, sir.

PARRIS: Such a Christian that will not come to church but once in a month!

DANFORTH, *restrained—he is curious*: Not come to church?

PROCTOR: I—I have no love for Mr. Parris. It is no secret. But God I surely love.

CHEEVER: He plow on Sunday, sir.

DANFORTH: Plow on Sunday!

CHEEVER, *apologetically*: I think it be evidence, John. I am an official of the court, I cannot keep it.

PROCTOR: I—I have once or twice plowed on Sunday. I have three children, sir, and until last year my land give little.

GILES: You'll find other Christians that do plow on Sunday if the truth be known.

HALE: Your Honor, I cannot think you may judge the man on such evidence.

DANFORTH: I judge nothing. *Pause. He keeps watching Proctor, who tries to meet his gaze.* I tell you straight, Mister—I have seen marvels in this court. I have seen people choked before my eyes by spirits; I have seen them stuck by pins and slashed by daggers. I have until this moment not the slightest reason to suspect that the children may be deceiving me. Do you understand my meaning?

PROCTOR: Excellency, does it not strike upon you that so many of these women have lived so long with such upright reputation, and—

PARRIS: Do you read the Gospel, Mr. Proctor?

PROCTOR: I read the Gospel.

PARRIS: I think not, or you should surely know that Cain were an upright man, and yet he did kill Abel.

PROCTOR: Aye, God tells us that. *To Danforth*: But who tells us Rebecca Nurse murdered seven babies by sending out her spirit on them? It is the children only, and this one will swear she lied to you.

> *Danforth considers, then beckons Hathorne to him. Hathorne leans in, and he speaks in his ear. Hathorne nods.*

HATHORNE: Aye, she's the one.

DANFORTH: Mr. Proctor, this morning, your wife send me a claim in which she states that she is pregnant now.

PROCTOR: My wife pregnant!

DANFORTH: There be no sign of it—we have examined her body.

PROCTOR: But if she say she is pregnant, then she must be! That woman will never lie, Mr. Danforth.

DANFORTH: She will not?

PROCTOR: Never, sir, never.

DANFORTH: We have thought it too convenient to be credited. However, if I should tell you now that I will let her be kept another month; and if she begin to show her natural signs, you shall have her living yet another year until she is delivered—what say you to that? *John Proctor is struck silent.* Come now. You say your only purpose is to save your wife. Good, then, she is saved at least this year, and a year is long. What say you, sir? It is done now. *In conflict, Proctor glances at Francis and Giles.* Will you drop this charge?

PROCTOR: I—I think I cannot.

DANFORTH, *now an almost imperceptible hardness in his voice*: Then your purpose is somewhat larger.

PARRIS: He's come to overthrow this court, Your Honor!

PROCTOR: These are my friends. Their wives are also accused—

DANFORTH, *with a sudden briskness of manner*: I judge you not, sir. I am ready to hear your evidence.

PROCTOR: I come not to hurt the court; I only—

DANFORTH, *cutting him off*: Marshal, go into the court and bid Judge Stoughton and Judge Sewall declare recess for one hour. And let them go to the tavern, if they will. All witnesses and prisoners are to be kept in the building.

HERRICK: Aye, sir. *Very deferentially*: If I may say it, sir, I know this man all my life. It is a good man, sir.

DANFORTH—*it is the reflection on himself he resents*: I am sure of it, Marshal. *Herrick nods, then goes out.* Now, what deposition do you have for us, Mr. Proctor? And I beg you be clear, open as the sky, and honest.

PROCTOR, *as he takes out several papers*: I am no lawyer, so I'll—

DANFORTH: The pure in heart need no lawyers. Proceed as you will.

PROCTOR, *handing Danforth a paper*: Will you read this first, sir? It's a sort of testament. The people signing it declare their good opinion of Rebecca, and my wife, and Martha Corey. *Danforth looks down at the paper.*

PARRIS, *to enlist Danforth's sarcasm*: Their good opinion! *But Danforth goes on reading, and Proctor is heartened.*

PROCTOR: These are all landholding farmers, members of the church. *Delicately, trying to point out a paragraph*: If you'll notice, sir—they've known the women many years and never saw no sign they had dealings with the Devil.

> *Parris nervously moves over and reads over Danforth's shoulder.*

DANFORTH, *glancing down a long list*: How many names are here?

FRANCIS: Ninety-one, Your Excellency.

PARRIS, *sweating*: These people should be summoned. *Danforth looks up at him questioningly.* For questioning.

FRANCIS, *trembling with anger*: Mr. Danforth, I gave them all my word no harm would come to them for signing this.

PARRIS: This is a clear attack upon the court!

HALE, *to Parris, trying to contain himself*: Is every defense an attack upon the court? Can no one—?

PARRIS: All innocent and Christian people are happy for the courts in Salem! These people are gloomy for it. *To Danforth directly*: And I think you will want to know, from each and every one of them, what discontents them with you!

HATHORNE: I think they ought to be examined, sir.

DANFORTH: It is not necessarily an attack, I think. Yet—

FRANCIS: These are all covenanted Christians, sir.

DANFORTH: Then I am sure they may have nothing to fear. *Hands Cheever the paper.* Mr. Cheever, have warrants drawn for all of these—arrest for examination. *To Proctor*: Now, Mister, what other information do you have for us? *Francis is still standing, horrified.* You may sit, Mr. Nurse.

FRANCIS: I have brought trouble on these people; I have—

DANFORTH: No, old man, you have not hurt these people if they are of good conscience. But you must understand, sir, that a person is either with this court or he must be counted against it, there be no road between. This is a sharp time, now, a precise time—we live no longer in the dusky afternoon when evil mixed itself with good and befuddled the world. Now, by God's grace, the shining sun is up, and them that fear not light will surely praise it. I hope you will be one of those. *Mary Warren suddenly sobs.* She's not hearty, I see.

PROCTOR: No, she's not, sir. *To Mary, bending to her, holding her hand, quietly*: Now remember what the angel Raphael said to the boy Tobias. Remember it.

MARY WARREN, *hardly audible*: Aye.

PROCTOR: "Do that which is good, and no harm shall come to thee."

MARY WARREN: Aye.

DANFORTH: Come, man, we wait you.

Marshal Herrick returns, and takes his post at the door.

GILES: John, my deposition, give him mine.

PROCTOR: Aye. *He hands Danforth another paper.* This is Mr. Corey's deposition.

DANFORTH: Oh? *He looks down at it. Now Hathorne comes behind him and reads with him.*

HATHORNE, *suspiciously*: What lawyer drew this, Corey?

GILES: You know I never hired a lawyer in my life, Hathorne.

DANFORTH, *finishing the reading*: It is very well phrased. My compliments. Mr. Parris, if Mr. Putnam is in the court, will you bring him in? *Hathorne takes the deposition, and walks to the window with it. Parris goes into the court.* You have no legal training, Mr. Corey?

GILES, *very pleased*: I have the best, sir—I am thirty-three time in court in my life. And always plaintiff, too.

DANFORTH: Oh, then you're much put-upon.

GILES: I am never put-upon; I know my rights, sir, and I will have them. You know, your father tried a case of mine—might be thirty-five year ago, I think.

DANFORTH: Indeed.

GILES: He never spoke to you of it?

DANFORTH: No, I cannot recall it.

GILES: That's strange, he give me nine pound damages. He were a fair judge, your father. Y'see, I had a white mare that time, and this fellow come to borrow the mare— *Enter Parris with Thomas Putnam. When he sees Putnam, Giles' ease goes; he is hard.* Aye, there he is.

DANFORTH: Mr. Putnam, I have here an accusation by Mr. Corey against you. He states that you coldly prompted your daughter to cry witchery upon George Jacobs that is now in jail.

PUTNAM: It is a lie.

DANFORTH, *turning to Giles*: Mr. Putnam states your charge is a lie. What say you to that?

GILES, *furious, his fists clenched*: A fart on Thomas Putnam, that is what I say to that!

DANFORTH: What proof do you submit for your charge, sir?

GILES: My proof is there! *Pointing to the paper.* If Jacobs hangs for a witch he forfeit up his property—that's law! And there is none but

Putnam with the coin to buy so great a piece. This man is killing his neighbors for their land!

DANFORTH: But proof, sir, proof.

GILES, *pointing at his deposition*: The proof is there! I have it from an honest man who heard Putnam say it! The day his daughter cried out on Jacobs, he said she'd given him a fair gift of land.

HATHORNE: And the name of this man?

GILES, *taken aback*: What name?

HATHORNE: The man that give you this information.

GILES, *hesitates, then*: Why, I—I cannot give you his name.

HATHORNE: And why not?

GILES, *hesitates, then bursts out*: You know well why not! He'll lay in jail if I give his name!

HATHORNE: This is contempt of the court, Mr. Danforth!

DANFORTH, *to avoid that*: You will surely tell us the name.

GILES: I will not give you no name. I mentioned my wife's name once and I'll burn in hell long enough for that. I stand mute.

DANFORTH: In that case, I have no choice but to arrest you for contempt of this court, do you know that?

GILES: This is a hearing; you cannot clap me for contempt of a hearing.

DANFORTH: Oh, it is a proper lawyer! Do you wish me to declare the court in full session here? Or will you give me good reply?

GILES, *faltering*: I cannot give you no name, sir, I cannot.

DANFORTH: You are a foolish old man. Mr. Cheever, begin the record. The court is now in session. I ask you, Mr. Corey—

PROCTOR, *breaking in*: Your Honor—he has the story in confidence, sir, and he—

PARRIS: The Devil lives on such confidences! *To Danforth*: Without confidences there could be no conspiracy, Your Honor!

HATHORNE: I think it must be broken, sir.

DANFORTH, *to Giles*: Old man, if your informant tells the truth let him come here openly like a decent man. But if he hide in anonymity I must know why. Now sir, the government and central church demand of you the name of him who reported Mr. Thomas Putnam a common murderer.

HALE: Excellency—

DANFORTH: Mr. Hale.

HALE: We cannot blink it more. There is a prodigious fear of this court in the country—

DANFORTH: Then there is a prodigious guilt in the country. Are *you* afraid to be questioned here?

HALE: I may only fear the Lord, sir, but there is fear in the country nevertheless.

DANFORTH, *angered now*: Reproach me not with the fear in the country; there is fear in the country because there is a moving plot to topple Christ in the country!

HALE: But it does not follow that everyone accused is part of it.

DANFORTH: No uncorrupted man may fear this court, Mr. Hale! None! *To Giles*: You are under arrest in contempt of this court. Now sit you down and take counsel with yourself, or you will be set in the jail until you decide to answer all questions.

> *Giles Corey makes a rush for Putnam. Proctor lunges and holds him.*

PROCTOR: No, Giles!

GILES, *over Proctor's shoulder at Putnam*: I'll cut your throat, Putnam, I'll kill you yet!

PROCTOR, *forcing him into a chair*: Peace, Giles, peace. *Releasing him.* We'll prove ourselves. Now we will. *He starts to turn to Danforth.*

GILES: Say nothin' more, John. *Pointing at Danforth*: He's only playin' you! He means to hang us all!

> *Mary Warren bursts into sobs.*

DANFORTH: This is a court of law, Mister. I'll have no effrontery here!

PROCTOR: Forgive him, sir, for his old age. Peace, Giles, we'll prove it all now. *He lifts up Mary's chin.* You cannot weep, Mary. Remember the angel, what he say to the boy. Hold to it, now; there is your rock. *Mary quiets. He takes out a paper, and turns to Danforth.* This is Mary Warren's deposition. I—I would ask you remember, sir, while you read it, that until two week ago she were no different than the other children are today. *He is speaking reasonably, restraining all his fears, his anger, his anxiety.* You saw her scream, she howled, she swore familiar spirits choked her; she even testified that Satan, in the form of women now in jail, tried to win her soul away, and then when she refused—

DANFORTH: We know all this.

PROCTOR: Aye, sir. She swears now that she never saw Satan; nor any spirit, vague or clear, that Satan may have sent to hurt her. And she declares her friends are lying now.

Proctor starts to hand Danforth the deposition, and Hale comes up to Danforth in a trembling state.

HALE: Excellency, a moment. I think this goes to the heart of the matter.

DANFORTH, *with deep misgivings*: It surely does.

HALE: I cannot say he is an honest man; I know him little. But in all justice, sir, a claim so weighty cannot be argued by a farmer. In God's name, sir, stop here; send him home and let him come again with a lawyer—

DANFORTH, *patiently*: Now look you, Mr. Hale—

HALE: Excellency, I have signed seventy-two death warrants; I am a minister of the Lord, and I dare not take a life without there be a proof so immaculate no slightest qualm of conscience may doubt it.

DANFORTH: Mr. Hale, you surely do not doubt my justice.

HALE: I have this morning signed away the soul of Rebecca Nurse, Your Honor. I'll not conceal it, my hand shakes yet as with a wound! I pray you, sir, *this* argument let lawyers present to you.

DANFORTH: Mr. Hale, believe me; for a man of such terrible learning you are most bewildered—I hope you will forgive me. I have been thirty-two year at the bar, sir, and I should be confounded were I called upon to defend these people. Let you consider, now— *To Proctor and the others*: And I bid you all do likewise. In an ordinary crime, how does one defend the accused? One calls up witnesses to prove his innocence. But witchcraft is *ipso facto*, on its face and by its nature, an invisible crime, is it not? Therefore, who may possibly be witness to it? The witch and the victim. None other. Now we cannot hope the witch will accuse herself; granted? Therefore, we must rely upon her victims—and they do testify, the children certainly do testify. As for the witches, none will deny that we are most eager for all their confessions. Therefore, what is left for a lawyer to bring out? I think I have made my point. Have I not?

HALE: But this child claims the girls are not truthful, and if they are not—

DANFORTH: That is precisely what I am about to consider, sir. What more may you ask of me? Unless you doubt my probity?

HALE, *defeated*: I surely do not, sir. Let you consider it, then.

DANFORTH: And let you put your heart to rest. Her deposition, Mr. Proctor.

Proctor hands it to him. Hathorne rises, goes beside Danforth, and starts reading. Parris comes to his other side. Danforth looks at John Proctor, then proceeds to read. Hale gets up, finds position near the judge, reads too. Proctor glances at Giles. Francis prays silently, hands pressed together. Cheever waits placidly, the sublime official, dutiful. Mary Warren sobs once. John Proctor touches her head reassuringly. Presently Danforth lifts his eyes, stands up, takes out a kerchief and blows his nose. The others stand aside as he moves in thought toward the window.

PARRIS, *hardly able to contain his anger and fear*: I should like to question—

DANFORTH—*his first real outburst, in which his contempt for Parris is clear*: Mr. Parris, I bid you be silent! *He stands in silence, looking out the window. Now, having established that he will set the gait*: Mr. Cheever, will you go into the court and bring the children here? *Cheever gets up and goes out upstage. Danforth now turns to Mary.* Mary Warren, how came you to this turnabout? Has Mr. Proctor threatened you for this deposition?

MARY WARREN: No, sir.

DANFORTH: Has he ever threatened you?

MARY WARREN, *weaker*: No, sir.

DANFORTH, *sensing a weakening*: Has he threatened you?

MARY WARREN: No, sir.

DANFORTH: Then you tell me that you sat in my court, callously lying, when you knew that people would hang by your evidence? *She does not answer.* Answer me!

MARY WARREN, *almost inaudibly*: I did, sir.

DANFORTH: How were you instructed in your life? Do you not know that God damns all liars? *She cannot speak.* Or is it now that you lie?

MARY WARREN: No, sir—I am with God now.

DANFORTH: You are with God now.

MARY WARREN: Aye, sir.

DANFORTH, *containing himself*: I will tell you this—you are either lying now, or you were lying in the court, and in either case you have committed perjury and you will go to jail for it. You cannot lightly say you lied, Mary. Do you know that?

MARY WARREN: I cannot lie no more. I am with God, I am with God.

But she breaks into sobs at the thought of it, and the right door opens, and enter Susanna Walcott, Mercy Lewis, Betty Parris, and finally Abigail. Cheever comes to Danforth.

CHEEVER: Ruth Putnam's not in the court, sir, nor the other children.

DANFORTH: These will be sufficient. Sit you down, children. *Silently they sit.* Your friend, Mary Warren, has given us a deposition. In which she swears that she never saw familiar spirits, apparitions, nor any manifest of the Devil. She claims as well that none of you have seen these things either. *Slight pause.* Now, children, this is a court of law. The law, based upon the Bible, and the Bible, writ by Almighty God, forbid the practice of witchcraft, and describe death as the penalty thereof. But likewise, children, the law and Bible damn all bearers of false witness. *Slight pause.* Now then. It does not escape me that this deposition may be devised to blind us; it may well be that Mary Warren has been conquered by Satan, who sends her here to distract our sacred purpose. If so, her neck will break for it. But if she speak true, I bid you now drop your guile and confess your pretense, for a quick confession will go easier with you. *Pause.* Abigail Williams, rise. *Abigail slowly rises.* Is there any truth in this?

ABIGAIL: No, sir.

DANFORTH, *thinks, glances at Mary, then back to Abigail*: Children, a very augur bit will now be turned into your souls until your honesty is proved. Will either of you change your positions now, or do you force me to hard questioning?

ABIGAIL: I have naught to change, sir. She lies.

DANFORTH, *to Mary*: You would still go on with this?

MARY WARREN, *faintly*: Aye, sir.

DANFORTH, *turning to Abigail*: A poppet were discovered in Mr. Proctor's house, stabbed by a needle. Mary Warren claims that you sat beside her in the court when she made it, and that you saw her make it and witnessed how she herself stuck her needle into it for safe-keeping. What say you to that?

ABIGAIL, *with a slight note of indignation*: It is a lie, sir.

DANFORTH, *after a slight pause*: While you worked for Mr. Proctor, did you see poppets in that house?

ABIGAIL: Goody Proctor always kept poppets.

PROCTOR: Your Honor, my wife never kept no poppets. Mary Warren confesses it was her poppet.

CHEEVER: Your Excellency.

DANFORTH: Mr. Cheever.

CHEEVER: When I spoke with Goody Proctor in that house, she said she never kept no poppets. But she said she did keep poppets when she were a girl.

PROCTOR: She has not been a girl these fifteen years, Your Honor.

HATHORNE: But a poppet will keep fifteen years, will it not?

PROCTOR: It will keep if it is kept, but Mary Warren swears she never saw no poppets in my house, nor anyone else.

PARRIS: Why could there not have been poppets hid where no one ever saw them?

PROCTOR, *furious*: There might also be a dragon with five legs in my house, but no one has ever seen it.

PARRIS: We are here, Your Honor, precisely to discover what no one has ever seen.

PROCTOR: Mr. Danforth, what profit this girl to turn herself about? What may Mary Warren gain but hard questioning and worse?

DANFORTH: You are charging Abigail Williams with a marvelous cool plot to murder, do you understand that?

PROCTOR: I do, sir. I believe she means to murder.

DANFORTH, *pointing at Abigail, incredulously*: This child would murder your wife?

PROCTOR: It is not a child. Now hear me, sir. In the sight of the congregation she were twice this year put out of this meetin' house for laughter during prayer.

DANFORTH, *shocked, turning to Abigail*: What's this? Laughter during—!

PARRIS: Excellency, she were under Tituba's power at that time, but she is solemn now.

GILES: Aye, now she is solemn and goes to hang people!

DANFORTH: Quiet, man.

HATHORNE: Surely it have no bearing on the question, sir. He charges contemplation of murder.

DANFORTH: Aye. *He studies Abigail for a moment, then*: Continue, Mr. Proctor.

PROCTOR: Mary. Now tell the Governor how you danced in the woods.

PARRIS, *instantly*: Excellency, since I come to Salem this man is blackening my name. He—

DANFORTH: In a moment, sir. *To Mary Warren, sternly, and surprised*: What is this dancing?

MARY WARREN: I— *She glances at Abigail, who is staring down at her remorselessly. Then, appealing to Proctor*: Mr. Proctor—

PROCTOR, *taking it right up*: Abigail leads the girls to the woods, Your Honor, and they have danced there naked—

PARRIS: Your Honor, this—

PROCTOR, *at once*: Mr. Parris discovered them himself in the dead of night! There's the "child" she is!

DANFORTH—*it is growing into a nightmare, and he turns, astonished, to Parris*: Mr. Parris—

PARRIS: I can only say, sir, that I never found any of them naked, and this man is—

DANFORTH: But you discovered them dancing in the woods? *Eyes on Parris, he points at Abigail.* Abigail?

HALE: Excellency, when I first arrived from Beverly, Mr. Parris told me that.

DANFORTH: Do you deny it, Mr. Parris?

PARRIS: I do not, sir, but I never saw any of them naked.

DANFORTH: But she have *danced*?

PARRIS, *unwillingly*: Aye, sir.

   Danforth, as though with new eyes, looks at Abigail.

HATHORNE: Excellency, will you permit me? *He points at Mary Warren.*

DANFORTH, *with great worry*: Pray, proceed.

HATHORNE: You say you never saw no spirits, Mary, were never threatened or afflicted by any manifest of the Devil or the Devil's agents.

MARY WARREN, *very faintly*: No, sir.

HATHORNE, *with a gleam of victory*: And yet, when people accused of witchery confronted you in court, you would faint, saying their spirits came out of their bodies and choked you—

MARY WARREN: That were pretense, sir.

DANFORTH: I cannot hear you.

MARY WARREN: Pretense, sir.

PARRIS: But you did turn cold, did you not? I myself picked you up many times, and your skin were icy. Mr. Danforth, you—

DANFORTH: I saw that many times.

PROCTOR: She only pretended to faint, Your Excellency. They're all marvelous pretenders.

HATHORNE: Then can she pretend to faint now?

PROCTOR: Now?

PARRIS: Why not? Now there are no spirits attacking her, for none in this room is accused of witchcraft. So let her turn herself cold now, let her pretend she is attacked now, let her faint. *He turns to Mary Warren.* Faint!

MARY WARREN: Faint?

PARRIS: Aye, faint. Prove to us how you pretended in the court so many times.

MARY WARREN, *looking to Proctor*: I—cannot faint now, sir.

PROCTOR, *alarmed, quietly*: Can you not pretend it?

MARY WARREN: I— *She looks about as though searching for the passion to faint.* I—have no *sense* of it now, I—

DANFORTH: Why? What is lacking now?

MARY WARREN: I—cannot tell, sir, I—

DANFORTH: Might it be that here we have no afflicting spirit loose, but in the court there were some?

MARY WARREN: I never saw no spirits.

PARRIS: Then see no spirits now, and prove to us that you can faint by your own will, as you claim.

MARY WARREN, *stares, searching for the emotion of it, and then shakes her head*: I—cannot do it.

PARRIS: Then you will confess, will you not? It were attacking spirits made you faint!

MARY WARREN: No, sir, I—

PARRIS: Your Excellency, this is a trick to blind the court!

MARY WARREN: It's not a trick! *She stands.* I—I used to faint because I— I thought I saw spirits.

DANFORTH: *Thought* you saw them!

MARY WARREN: But I did not, Your Honor.

HATHORNE: How could you think you saw them unless you saw them?

MARY WARREN: I—I cannot tell how, but I did. I—I heard the other girls screaming, and you, Your Honor, you seemed to believe them, and I— It were only sport in the beginning, sir, but then the whole world cried spirits, spirits, and I—I promise you, Mr. Danforth, I only thought I saw them but I did not.

Danforth peers at her.

PARRIS, *smiling, but nervous because Danforth seems to be struck by Mary Warren's story*: Surely Your Excellency is not taken by this simple lie.

DANFORTH, *turning worriedly to Abigail*: Abigail. I bid you now search your heart and tell me this—and beware of it, child, to God every soul is precious and His vengeance is terrible on them that take life without cause. Is it possible, child, that the spirits you have seen are illusion only, some deception that may cross your mind when—

ABIGAIL: Why, this—this—is a base question, sir.

DANFORTH: Child, I would have you consider it—

ABIGAIL: I have been hurt, Mr. Danforth; I have seen my blood runnin' out! I have been near to murdered every day because I done my duty pointing out the Devil's people—and this is my reward? To be mistrusted, denied, questioned like a—

DANFORTH, *weakening*: Child, I do not mistrust you—

ABIGAIL, *in an open threat*: Let *you* beware, Mr. Danforth. Think you to be so mighty that the power of Hell may not turn *your* wits? Beware of it! There is— *Suddenly, from an accusatory attitude, her face turns, looking into the air above—it is truly frightened.*

DANFORTH, *apprehensively*: What is it, child?

ABIGAIL, *looking about in the air, clasping her arms about her as though cold*: I—I know not. A wind, a cold wind, has come. *Her eyes fall on Mary Warren.*

MARY WARREN, *terrified, pleading*: Abby!

MERCY LEWIS, *shivering*: Your Honor, I freeze!

PROCTOR: They're pretending!

HATHORNE, *touching Abigail's hand*: She is cold, Your Honor, touch her!

MERCY LEWIS, *through chattering teeth*: Mary, do you send this shadow on me?

MARY WARREN: Lord, save me!

SUSANNA WALCOTT: I freeze, I freeze!

ABIGAIL, *shivering visibly*: It is a wind, a wind!

MARY WARREN: Abby, don't do that!

DANFORTH, *himself engaged and entered by Abigail*: Mary Warren, do you witch her? I say to you, do you send your spirit out?

> *With a hysterical cry Mary Warren starts to run. Proctor catches her.*

MARY WARREN, *almost collapsing*: Let me go, Mr. Proctor, I cannot, I cannot—

ABIGAIL, *crying to Heaven*: Oh, Heavenly Father, take away this shadow!

> *Without warning or hesitation, Proctor leaps at Abigail and, grabbing her by the hair, pulls her to her feet. She screams in pain. Danforth, astonished, cries, "What are you about?" and Hathorne and Parris call, "Take your hands off her!" and out of it all comes Proctor's roaring voice.*

PROCTOR: How do you call Heaven! Whore! Whore!

> *Herrick breaks Proctor from her.*

HERRICK: John!

DANFORTH: Man! Man, what do you—

PROCTOR, *breathless and in agony*: It is a whore!

DANFORTH, *dumfounded*: You charge—?

ABIGAIL: Mr. Danforth, he is lying!

PROCTOR: Mark her! Now she'll suck a scream to stab me with, but—

DANFORTH: You will prove this! This will not pass!

PROCTOR, *trembling, his life collapsing about him*: I have known her, sir. I have known her.

DANFORTH: You—you are a lecher?

FRANCIS, *horrified*: John, you cannot say such a—

PROCTOR: Oh, Francis, I wish you had some evil in you that you might know me! *To Danforth*: A man will not cast away his good name. You surely know that.

DANFORTH, *dumfounded*: In—in what time? In what place?

PROCTOR, *his voice about to break, and his shame great*: In the proper place—where my beasts are bedded. On the last night of my joy, some eight months past. She used to serve me in my house, sir. *He has to clamp his jaw to keep from weeping.* A man may think God sleeps, but God sees everything, I know it now. I beg you, sir, I beg you—see her what she is. My wife, my dear good wife, took this girl soon after, sir, and put her out on the highroad. And being what she is, a lump of vanity, sir— *He is being overcome.* Excellency, forgive me, forgive me. *Angrily against himself, he turns away from the Governor for a moment. Then, as though to cry out is his only means of speech left*: She thinks to dance with me on my wife's grave! And well she might, for I thought of her softly. God help me, I lusted, and there *is* a promise in such sweat. But it is a whore's vengeance, and you must see it; I set myself entirely in your hands. I know you must see it now.

DANFORTH, *blanched, in horror, turning to Abigail*: You deny every scrap and tittle of this?

ABIGAIL: If I must answer that, I will leave and I will not come back again!

> *Danforth seems unsteady.*

PROCTOR: I have made a bell of my honor! I have rung the doom of my good name—you will believe me, Mr. Danforth! My wife is innocent, except she knew a whore when she saw one!

ABIGAIL, *stepping up to Danforth*: What look do you give me? *Danforth cannot speak.* I'll not have such looks! *She turns and starts for the door.*

DANFORTH: You will remain where you are! *Herrick steps into her path. She comes up short, fire in her eyes.* Mr. Parris, go into the court and bring Goodwife Proctor out.

PARRIS, *objecting*: Your Honor, this is all a—

DANFORTH, *sharply to Parris*: Bring her out! And tell her not one word of what's been spoken here. And let you knock before you enter. *Parris goes out.* Now we shall touch the bottom of this swamp. *To Proctor*: Your wife, you say, is an honest woman.

PROCTOR: In her life, sir, she have never lied. There are them that cannot sing, and them that cannot weep—my wife cannot lie. I have paid much to learn it, sir.

DANFORTH: And when she put this girl out of your house, she put her out for a harlot?

PROCTOR: Aye, sir.

DANFORTH: And knew her for a harlot?

PROCTOR: Aye, sir, she knew her for a harlot.

DANFORTH: Good then. *To Abigail:* And if she tell me, child, it were for harlotry, may God spread His mercy on you! *There is a knock. He calls to the door.* Hold! *To Abigail:* Turn your back. Turn your back. *To Proctor:* Do likewise. *Both turn their backs—Abigail with indignant slowness.* Now let neither of you turn to face Goody Proctor. No one in this room is to speak one word, or raise a gesture aye or nay. *He turns toward the door, calls:* Enter! *The door opens. Elizabeth enters with Parris. Parris leaves her. She stands alone, her eyes looking for Proctor.* Mr. Cheever, report this testimony in all exactness. Are you ready?

CHEEVER: Ready, sir.

DANFORTH: Come here, woman. *Elizabeth comes to him, glancing at Proctor's back.* Look at me only, not at your husband. In my eyes only.

ELIZABETH, *faintly:* Good, sir.

DANFORTH: We are given to understand that at one time you dismissed your servant, Abigail Williams.

ELIZABETH: That is true, sir.

DANFORTH: For what cause did you dismiss her? *Slight pause. Then Elizabeth tries to glance at Proctor.* You will look in my eyes only and not at your husband. The answer is in your memory and you need no help to give it to me. Why did you dismiss Abigail Williams?

ELIZABETH, *not knowing what to say, sensing a situation, wetting her lips to stall for time:* She—dissatisfied me. *Pause.* And my husband.

DANFORTH: In what way dissatisfied you?

ELIZABETH: She were— *She glances at Proctor for a cue.*

DANFORTH: Woman, look at me! *Elizabeth does.* Were she slovenly? Lazy? What disturbance did she cause?

ELIZABETH: Your Honor, I—in that time I were sick. And I—My husband is a good and righteous man. He is never drunk as some are, nor wastin' his time at the shovelboard, but always at his work. But in my sickness—you see, sir, I were a long time sick after my last baby, and I thought I saw my husband somewhat turning from me. And this girl— *She turns to Abigail.*

DANFORTH: Look at me.

ELIZABETH: Aye, sir. Abigail Williams— *She breaks off.*

DANFORTH: What of Abigail Williams?

ELIZABETH: I came to think he fancied her. And so one night I lost my wits, I think, and put her out on the highroad.

DANFORTH: Your husband—did he indeed turn from you?

ELIZABETH, *in agony*: My husband—is a goodly man, sir.

DANFORTH: Then he did not turn from you.

ELIZABETH, *starting to glance at Proctor*: He—

DANFORTH, *reaches out and holds her face, then*: Look at me! To your own knowledge, has John Proctor ever committed the crime of lechery? *In a crisis of indecision she cannot speak.* Answer my question! Is your husband a lecher!

ELIZABETH, *faintly*: No, sir.

DANFORTH: Remove her, Marshal.

PROCTOR: Elizabeth, tell the truth!

DANFORTH: She has spoken. Remove her!

PROCTOR, *crying out*: Elizabeth, I have confessed it!

ELIZABETH: Oh, God! *The door closes behind her.*

PROCTOR: She only thought to save my name!

HALE: Excellency, it is a natural lie to tell; I beg you, stop now before another is condemned! I may shut my conscience to it no more—private vengeance is working through this testimony! From the beginning this man has struck me true. By my oath to Heaven, I believe him now, and I pray you call back his wife before we—

DANFORTH: She spoke nothing of lechery, and this man has lied!

HALE: I believe him! *Pointing at Abigail*: This girl has always struck me false! She has—

> *Abigail, with a weird, wild, chilling cry, screams up to the ceiling.*

ABIGAIL: You will not! Begone! Begone, I say!

DANFORTH: What is it, child? *But Abigail, pointing with fear, is now raising up her frightened eyes, her awed face, toward the ceiling—the girls are doing the same—and now Hathorne, Hale, Putnam, Cheever, Herrick, and Danforth do the same.* What's there? *He lowers his eyes from the ceiling, and now he is frightened; there is real tension in his voice.* Child! *She is transfixed—with all the girls, she is whimpering openmouthed, agape at the ceiling.* Girls! Why do you—?

MERCY LEWIS, *pointing*: It's on the beam! Behind the rafter!

DANFORTH, *looking up*: Where!

ABIGAIL: Why—? *She gulps.* Why do you come, yellow bird?

PROCTOR: Where's a bird? I see no bird!

ABIGAIL, *to the ceiling*: My face? My face?

PROCTOR: Mr. Hale—

DANFORTH: Be quiet!

PROCTOR, *to Hale*: Do you see a bird?

DANFORTH: Be quiet!!

ABIGAIL, *to the ceiling, in a genuine conversation with the "bird," as though trying to talk it out of attacking her*: But God made my face; you cannot want to tear my face. Envy is a deadly sin, Mary.

MARY WARREN, *on her feet with a spring, and horrified, pleading*: Abby!

ABIGAIL, *unperturbed, continuing to the "bird"*: Oh, Mary, this is a black art to change your shape. No, I cannot, I cannot stop my mouth; it's God's work I do.

MARY WARREN: Abby, I'm *here*!

PROCTOR, *frantically*: They're pretending, Mr. Danforth!

ABIGAIL—*now she takes a backward step, as though in fear the bird will swoop down momentarily*: Oh, please, Mary! Don't come down.

SUSANNA WALCOTT: Her claws, she's stretching her claws!

PROCTOR: Lies, lies.

ABIGAIL, *backing further, eyes still fixed above*: Mary, please don't hurt me!

MARY WARREN, *to Danforth*: I'm not hurting her!

DANFORTH, *to Mary Warren*: Why does she see this vision?

MARY WARREN: She sees nothin'!

ABIGAIL, *now staring full front as though hypnotized, and mimicking the exact tone of Mary Warren's cry*: She sees nothin'!

MARY WARREN, *pleading*: Abby, you mustn't!

ABIGAIL AND ALL THE GIRLS, *all transfixed*: Abby, you mustn't!

MARY WARREN, *to all the girls*: I'm here, I'm here!

GIRLS: I'm here, I'm here!

DANFORTH, *horrified*: Mary Warren! Draw back your spirit out of them!

MARY WARREN: Mr. Danforth!

GIRLS, *cutting her off*: Mr. Danforth!

DANFORTH: Have you compacted with the Devil? Have you?

MARY WARREN: Never, never!

GIRLS: Never, never!

DANFORTH, *growing hysterical*: Why can they only repeat you?

PROCTOR: Give me a whip—I'll stop it!

MARY WARREN: They're sporting. They—!

GIRLS: They're sporting!

MARY WARREN, *turning on them all hysterically and stamping her feet*: Abby, stop it!

GIRLS, *stamping their feet*: Abby, stop it!

MARY WARREN: Stop it!

GIRLS: Stop it!

MARY WARREN, *screaming it out at the top of her lungs, and raising her fists*: Stop it!!

GIRLS, *raising their fists*: Stop it!!

> *Mary Warren, utterly confounded, and becoming over-whelmed by Abigail's—and the girls'—utter conviction, starts to whimper, hands half raised, powerless, and all the girls begin whimpering exactly as she does.*

DANFORTH: A little while ago you were afflicted. Now it seems you afflict others; where did you find this power?

MARY WARREN, *staring at Abigail*: I—have no power.

GIRLS: I have no power.

PROCTOR: They're gulling you, Mister!

DANFORTH: Why did you turn about this past two weeks? You have seen the Devil, have you not?

HALE, *indicating Abigail and the girls*: You cannot believe them!

MARY WARREN: I—

PROCTOR, *sensing her weakening*: Mary, God damns all liars!

DANFORTH, *pounding it into her*: You have seen the Devil, you have made compact with Lucifer, have you not?

PROCTOR: God damns liars, Mary!

> *Mary utters something unintelligible, staring at Abigail, who keeps watching the "bird" above.*

DANFORTH: I cannot hear you. What do you say? *Mary utters again unintelligibly.* You will confess yourself or you will hang! *He turns her roughly to face him.* Do you know who I am? I say you will hang if you do not open with me!

PROCTOR: Mary, remember the angel Raphael—do that which is good and—

ABIGAIL, *pointing upward*: The wings! Her wings are spreading! Mary, please, don't, don't—!

HALE: I see nothing, Your Honor!

DANFORTH: Do you confess this power! *He is an inch from her face.* Speak!

ABIGAIL: She's going to come down! She's walking the beam!

DANFORTH: Will you speak!

MARY WARREN, *staring in horror*: I cannot!

GIRLS: I cannot!

PARRIS: Cast the Devil out! Look him in the face! Trample him! We'll save you, Mary, only stand fast against him and—

ABIGAIL, *looking up*: Look out! She's coming down!

> *She and all the girls run to one wall, shielding their eyes. And now, as though cornered, they let out a gigantic scream, and Mary, as though infected, opens her mouth and screams with them. Gradually Abigail and the girls leave off, until only Mary is left there, staring up at the "bird," screaming madly. All watch her, horrified by this evident fit. Proctor strides to her.*

PROCTOR: Mary, tell the Governor what they— *He has hardly got a word out, when, seeing him coming for her, she rushes out of his reach, screaming in horror.*

MARY WARREN: Don't touch me—don't touch me! *At which the girls halt at the door.*

PROCTOR, *astonished*: Mary!

MARY WARREN, *pointing at Proctor*: You're the Devil's man!

> *He is stopped in his tracks.*

PARRIS: Praise God!

GIRLS: Praise God!

PROCTOR, *numbed*: Mary, how—?

MARY WARREN: I'll not hang with you! I love God, I love God.

DANFORTH, *to Mary*: He bid you do the Devil's work?

MARY WARREN, *hysterically, indicating Proctor*: He come at me by night and every day to sign, to sign, to—

DANFORTH: Sign what?

PARRIS: The Devil's book? He come with a book?

MARY WARREN, *hysterically, pointing at Proctor, fearful of him*: My name, he want my name. "I'll murder you," he says, "if my wife hangs! We must go and overthrow the court," he says!

> Danforth's head jerks toward Proctor, shock and horror in his face.

PROCTOR, *turning, appealing to Hale*: Mr. Hale!

MARY WARREN, *her sobs beginning*: He wake me every night, his eyes were like coals and his fingers claw my neck, and I sign, I sign . . .

HALE: Excellency, this child's gone wild!

PROCTOR, *as Danforth's wide eyes pour on him*: Mary, Mary!

MARY WARREN, *screaming at him*: No, I love God; I go your way no more. I love God, I bless God. *Sobbing, she rushes to Abigail.* Abby, Abby, I'll never hurt you more! *They all watch, as Abigail, out of her infinite charity, reaches out and draws the sobbing Mary to her, and then looks up to Danforth.*

DANFORTH, *to Proctor*: What are you? *Proctor is beyond speech in his anger.* You are combined with anti-Christ, are you not? I have seen your power; you will not deny it! What say you, Mister?

HALE: Excellency—

DANFORTH: I will have nothing from you, Mr. Hale! *To Proctor*: Will you confess yourself befouled with Hell, or do you keep that black allegiance yet? What say you?

PROCTOR, *his mind wild, breathless*: I say—I say—God is dead!

PARRIS: Hear it, hear it!

PROCTOR, *laughs insanely, then*: A fire, a fire is burning! I hear the boot of Lucifer, I see his filthy face! And it is my face, and yours, Danforth! For them that quail to bring men out of ignorance, as I have quailed, and as you quail now when you know in all your black hearts that this be fraud—God damns our kind especially, and we will burn, we will burn together!

DANFORTH: Marshal! Take him and Corey with him to the jail!

HALE, *starting across to the door*: I denounce these proceedings!

PROCTOR: You are pulling Heaven down and raising up a whore!

HALE: I denounce these proceedings, I quit this court! *He slams the door to the outside behind him.*

DANFORTH, *calling to him in a fury*: Mr. Hale! Mr. Hale!

THE CURTAIN FALLS.

ACT FOUR

A cell in Salem jail, that fall.

At the back is a high barred window; near it, a great, heavy door. Along the walls are two benches.

The place is in darkness but for the moonlight seeping through the bars. It appears empty. Presently footsteps are heard coming down a corridor beyond the wall, keys rattle, and the door swings open. Marshal Herrick enters with a lantern.

He is nearly drunk, and heavy-footed. He goes to a bench and nudges a bundle of rags lying on it.

HERRICK: Sarah, wake up! Sarah Good! *He then crosses to the other bench.*

SARAH GOOD, *rising in her rags*: Oh, Majesty! Comin', comin'! Tituba, he's here, His Majesty's come!

HERRICK: Go to the north cell; this place is wanted now. *He hangs his lantern on the wall. Tituba sits up.*

TITUBA: That don't look to me like His Majesty; look to me like the marshal.

HERRICK, *taking out a flask*: Get along with you now, clear this place. *He drinks, and Sarah Good comes and peers up into his face.*

SARAH GOOD: Oh, is it you, Marshal! I thought sure you be the Devil comin' for us. Could I have a sip of cider for me goin'-away?

HERRICK, *handing her the flask*: And where are you off to, Sarah?

TITUBA, *as Sarah drinks*: We goin' to Barbados, soon the Devil gits here with the feathers and the wings.

HERRICK: Oh? A happy voyage to you.

SARAH GOOD: A pair of bluebirds wingin' southerly, the two of us! Oh, it be a grand transformation, Marshal! *She raises the flask to drink again.*

HERRICK, *taking the flask from her lips:* You'd best give me that or you'll never rise off the ground. Come along now.

TITUBA: I'll speak to him for you, if you desires to come along, Marshal.

HERRICK: I'd not refuse it, Tituba; it's the proper morning to fly into Hell.

TITUBA: Oh, it be no Hell in Barbados. Devil, him be pleasure-man in Barbados, him be singin' and dancin' in Barbados. It's you folks—you riles him up 'round here; it be too cold 'round here for that Old Boy. He freeze his soul in Massachusetts, but in Barbados he just as sweet and— *A bellowing cow is heard, and Tituba leaps up and calls to the window:* Aye, sir! That's him, Sarah!

SARAH GOOD: I'm here, Majesty! *They hurriedly pick up their rags as Hopkins, a guard, enters.*

HOPKINS: The Deputy Governor's arrived.

HERRICK, *grabbing Tituba:* Come along, come along.

TITUBA, *resisting him:* No, he comin' for me. I goin' home!

HERRICK, *pulling her to the door:* That's not Satan, just a poor old cow with a hatful of milk. Come along now, out with you!

TITUBA, *calling to the window:* Take me home, Devil! Take me home!

SARAH GOOD, *following the shouting Tituba out:* Tell him I'm goin', Tituba! Now you tell him Sarah Good is goin' too!

> *In the corridor outside Tituba calls on—"Take me home, Devil; Devil take me home!" and Hopkins' voice orders her to move on. Herrick returns and begins to push old rags and straw into a corner. Hearing footsteps, he turns, and enter Danforth and Judge Hathorne. They are in greatcoats and wear hats against the bitter cold. They are followed in by Cheever, who carries a dispatch case and a flat wooden box containing his writing materials.*

HERRICK: Good morning, Excellency.

DANFORTH: Where is Mr. Parris?

HERRICK: I'll fetch him. *He starts for the door.*

DANFORTH: Marshal. *Herrick stops.* When did Reverend Hale arrive?

HERRICK: It were toward midnight, I think.

DANFORTH, *suspiciously:* What is he about here?

HERRICK: He goes among them that will hang, sir. And he prays with them. He sits with Goody Nurse now. And Mr. Parris with him.

DANFORTH: Indeed. That man have no authority to enter here, Marshal. Why have you let him in?

HERRICK: Why, Mr. Parris command me, sir. I cannot deny him.

DANFORTH: Are you drunk, Marshal?

HERRICK: No, sir; it is a bitter night, and I have no fire here.

DANFORTH, *containing his anger*: Fetch Mr. Parris.

HERRICK: Aye, sir.

DANFORTH: There is a prodigious stench in this place.

HERRICK: I have only now cleared the people out for you.

DANFORTH: Beware hard drink, Marshal.

HERRICK: Aye, sir. *He waits an instant for further orders. But Danforth, in dissatisfaction, turns his back on him, and Herrick goes out. There is a pause. Danforth stands in thought.*

HATHORNE: Let you question Hale, Excellency; I should not be surprised he have been preaching in Andover lately.

DANFORTH: We'll come to that; speak nothing of Andover. Parris prays with him. That's strange. *He blows on his hands, moves toward the window, and looks out.*

HATHORNE: Excellency, I wonder if it be wise to let Mr. Parris so continuously with the prisoners. *Danforth turns to him, interested.* I think, sometimes, the man has a mad look these days.

DANFORTH: Mad?

HATHORNE: I met him yesterday coming out of his house, and I bid him good morning—and he wept and went his way. I think it is not well the village sees him so unsteady.

DANFORTH: Perhaps he have some sorrow.

CHEEVER, *stamping his feet against the cold*: I think it be the cows, sir.

DANFORTH: Cows?

CHEEVER: There be so many cows wanderin' the highroads, now their masters are in the jails, and much disagreement who they will belong to now. I know Mr. Parris be arguin' with farmers all yesterday—there is great contention, sir, about the cows. Contention make him weep, sir; it were always a man that weep for contention. *He turns, as do Hathorne and Danforth, hearing someone coming up the corridor. Danforth raises his head as Parris enters. He is gaunt, frightened, and sweating in his greatcoat.*

PARRIS, *to Danforth, instantly*: Oh, good morning, sir, thank you for coming, I beg your pardon wakin' you so early. Good morning, Judge Hathorne.

DANFORTH: Reverend Hale have no right to enter this—

PARRIS: Excellency, a moment. *He hurries back and shuts the door.*

HATHORNE: Do you leave him alone with the prisoners?

DANFORTH: What's his business here?

PARRIS, *prayerfully holding up his hands*: Excellency, hear me. It is a providence. Reverend Hale has returned to bring Rebecca Nurse to God.

DANFORTH, *surprised*: He bids her confess?

PARRIS, *sitting*: Hear me. Rebecca have not given me a word this three month since she came. Now she sits with him, and her sister and Martha Corey and two or three others, and he pleads with them, confess their crimes and save their lives.

DANFORTH: Why—this is indeed a providence. And they soften, they soften?

PARRIS: Not yet, not yet. But I thought to summon you, sir, that we might think on whether it be not wise, to— *He dares not say it.* I had thought to put a question, sir, and I hope you will not—

DANFORTH: Mr. Parris, be plain, what troubles you?

PARRIS: There is news, sir, that the court—the court must reckon with. My niece, sir, my niece—I believe she has vanished.

DANFORTH: Vanished!

PARRIS: I had thought to advise you of it earlier in the week, but—

DANFORTH: Why? How long is she gone?

PARRIS: This be the third night. You see, sir, she told me she would stay a night with Mercy Lewis. And next day, when she does not return, I send to Mr. Lewis to inquire. Mercy told him she would sleep in *my* house for a night.

DANFORTH: They are both gone?!

PARRIS, *in fear of him*: They are, sir.

DANFORTH, *alarmed*: I will send a party for them. Where may they be?

PARRIS: Excellency, I think they be aboard a ship. *Danforth stands agape.* My daughter tells me how she heard them speaking of ships last week, and tonight I discover my—my strongbox is broke into. *He presses his fingers against his eyes to keep back tears.*

HATHORNE, *astonished*: She have robbed you?

PARRIS: Thirty-one pound is gone. I am penniless. *He covers his face and sobs.*

DANFORTH: Mr. Parris, you are a brainless man! *He walks in thought, deeply worried.*

PARRIS: Excellency, it profit nothing you should blame me. I cannot think they would run off except they fear to keep in Salem any more. *He is pleading.* Mark it, sir, Abigail had close knowledge of the town, and since the news of Andover has broken here—

DANFORTH: Andover is remedied. The court returns there on Friday, and will resume examinations.

PARRIS: I am sure of it, sir. But the rumor here speaks rebellion in Andover, and it—

DANFORTH: There is no rebellion in Andover!

PARRIS: I tell you what is said here, sir. Andover have thrown out the court, they say, and will have no part of witchcraft. There be a faction here, feeding on that news, and I tell you true, sir, I fear there will be riot here.

HATHORNE: Riot! Why at every execution I have seen naught but high satisfaction in the town.

PARRIS: Judge Hathorne—it were another sort that hanged till now. Rebecca Nurse is no Bridget that lived three year with Bishop before she married him. John Proctor is not Isaac Ward that drank his family to ruin. *To Danforth*: I would to God it were not so, Excellency, but these people have great weight yet in the town. Let Rebecca stand upon the gibbet and send up some righteous prayer, and I fear she'll wake a vengeance on you.

HATHORNE: Excellency, she is condemned a witch. The court have—

DANFORTH, *in deep concern, raising a hand to Hathorne*: Pray you. *To Parris*: How do you propose, then?

PARRIS: Excellency, I would postpone these hangin's for a time.

DANFORTH: There will be no postponement.

PARRIS: Now Mr. Hale's returned, there is hope, I think—for if he bring even one of these to God, that confession surely damns the others in the public eye, and none may doubt more that they are all linked to Hell. This way, unconfessed and claiming innocence, doubts are multiplied, many honest people will weep for them, and our good purpose is lost in their tears.

DANFORTH, *after thinking a moment, then going to Cheever*: Give me the list.

> *Cheever opens the dispatch case, searches.*

PARRIS: It cannot be forgot, sir, that when I summoned the congregation for John Proctor's excommunication there were hardly thirty people come to hear it. That speak a discontent, I think, and—

DANFORTH, *studying the list*: There will be no postponement.

PARRIS: Excellency—

DANFORTH: Now, sir—which of these in your opinion may be brought to God? I will myself strive with him till dawn. *He hands the list to Parris, who merely glances at it.*

PARRIS: There is not sufficient time till dawn.

DANFORTH: I shall do my utmost. Which of them do you have hope for?

PARRIS, *not even glancing at the list now, and in a quavering voice, quietly*: Excellency—a dagger— *He chokes up.*

DANFORTH: What do you say?

PARRIS: Tonight, when I open my door to leave my house—a dagger clattered to the ground. *Silence. Danforth absorbs this. Now Parris cries out*: You cannot hang this sort. There is danger for me. I dare not step outside at night!

> *Reverend Hale enters. They look at him for an instant in silence. He is steeped in sorrow, exhausted, and more direct than he ever was.*

DANFORTH: Accept my congratulations, Reverend Hale; we are gladdened to see you returned to your good work.

HALE, *coming to Danforth now*: You must pardon them. They will not budge.

> *Herrick enters, waits.*

DANFORTH, *conciliatory*: You misunderstand, sir; I cannot pardon these when twelve are already hanged for the same crime. It is not just.

PARRIS, *with failing heart*: Rebecca will not confess?

HALE: The sun will rise in a few minutes. Excellency, I must have more time.

DANFORTH: Now hear me, and beguile yourselves no more. I will not receive a single plea for pardon or postponement. Them that will not confess will hang. Twelve are already executed; the names of these seven are given out, and the village expects to see them die this morn-ing. Postponement now speaks a floundering on my part; reprieve or pardon must cast doubt upon the guilt of them that died till now. While I speak God's law, I will not crack its voice with whimpering. If retalia-tion is your fear, know this—I should hang ten thousand that dared to rise against the law, and an ocean of salt tears could not melt the resolu-tion of the statutes. Now draw yourselves up like men and help me, as you are bound by Heaven to do. Have you spoken with them all, Mr. Hale?

HALE: All but Proctor. He is in the dungeon.

DANFORTH, *to Herrick*: What's Proctor's way now?

HERRICK: He sits like some great bird; you'd not know he lived except he will take food from time to time.

DANFORTH, *after thinking a moment*: His wife—his wife must be well on with child now.

HERRICK: She is, sir.

DANFORTH: What think you, Mr. Parris? You have closer knowledge of this man; might her presence soften him?

PARRIS: It is possible, sir. He have not laid eyes on her these three months. I should summon her.

DANFORTH, *to Herrick*: Is he yet adamant? Has he struck at you again?

HERRICK: He cannot, sir, he is chained to the wall now.

DANFORTH, *after thinking on it*: Fetch Goody Proctor to me. Then let you bring him up.

HERRICK: Aye, sir. *Herrick goes. There is silence.*

HALE: Excellency, if you postpone a week and publish to the town that you are striving for their confessions, that speak mercy on your part, not faltering.

DANFORTH: Mr. Hale, as God have not empowered me like Joshua to stop this sun from rising, so I cannot withhold from them the perfection of their punishment.

HALE, *harder now*: If you think God wills you to raise rebellion, Mr. Danforth, you are mistaken!

DANFORTH, *instantly*: You have heard rebellion spoken in the town?

HALE: Excellency, there are orphans wandering from house to house; abandoned cattle bellow on the highroads, the stink of rotting crops hangs everywhere, and no man knows when the harlots' cry will end his life—and you wonder yet if rebellion's spoke? Better you should marvel how they do not burn your province!

DANFORTH: Mr. Hale, have you preached in Andover this month?

HALE: Thank God they have no need of me in Andover.

DANFORTH: You baffle me, sir. Why have you returned here?

HALE: Why, it is all simple. I come to do the Devil's work. I come to counsel Christians they should belie themselves. *His sarcasm collapses.* There is blood on my head! Can you not see the blood on my head!!

PARRIS: Hush! *For he has heard footsteps. They all face the door. Herrick enters with Elizabeth. Her wrists are linked by heavy chain, which Herrick now removes. Her clothes are dirty; her face is pale and gaunt. Herrick goes out.*

DANFORTH, *very politely*: Goody Proctor. *She is silent.* I hope you are hearty?

ELIZABETH, *as a warning reminder*: I am yet six month before my time.

DANFORTH: Pray be at your ease, we come not for your life. We— *uncertain how to plead, for he is not accustomed to it.* Mr. Hale, will you speak with the woman?

HALE: Goody Proctor, your husband is marked to hang this morning.

   Pause.

ELIZABETH, *quietly*: I have heard it.

HALE: You know, do you not, that I have no connection with the court? *She seems to doubt it.* I come of my own, Goody Proctor. I would save your husband's life, for if he is taken I count myself his murderer. Do you understand me?

ELIZABETH: What do you want of me?

HALE: Goody Proctor, I have gone this three month like our Lord into the wilderness. I have sought a Christian way, for damnation's doubled on a minister who counsels men to lie.

HATHORNE: It is no lie, you cannot speak of lies.

HALE: It is a lie! They are innocent!

DANFORTH: I'll hear no more of that!

HALE, *continuing to Elizabeth*: Let you not mistake your duty as I mistook my own. I came into this village like a bridegroom to his beloved, bearing gifts of high religion; the very crowns of holy law I brought, and what I touched with my bright confidence, it died; and where I turned the eye of my great faith, blood flowed up. Beware, Goody Proctor—cleave to no faith when faith brings blood. It is mistaken law that leads you to sacrifice. Life, woman, life is God's most precious gift; no principle, however glorious, may justify the taking of it. I beg you, woman, prevail upon your husband to confess. Let him give his lie. Quail not before God's judgment in this, for it may well be God damns a liar less than he that throws his life away for pride. Will you plead with him? I cannot think he will listen to another.

ELIZABETH, *quietly*: I think that be the Devil's argument.

HALE, *with a climactic desperation*: Woman, before the laws of God we are as swine! We cannot read His will!

ELIZABETH: I cannot dispute with you, sir; I lack learning for it.

DANFORTH, *going to her*: Goody Proctor, you are not summoned here for disputation. Be there no wifely tenderness within you? He will die with the sunrise. Your husband. Do you understand it? *She only looks at him.* What say you? Will you contend with him? *She is silent.* Are you stone? I tell you true, woman, had I no other proof of your unnatural life, your dry eyes now would be sufficient evidence that you delivered up your soul to Hell! A very ape would weep at such calamity! Have the Devil dried up any tear of pity in you? *She is silent.* Take her out. It profit nothing she should speak to him!

ELIZABETH, *quietly*: Let me speak with him, Excellency.

PARRIS, *with hope*: You'll strive with him? *She hesitates.*

DANFORTH: Will you plead for his confession or will you not?

ELIZABETH: I promise nothing. Let me speak with him.

> A sound—the sibilance of dragging feet on stone. They turn. A pause. Herrick enters with John Proctor. His wrists are chained. He is another man, bearded, filthy, his eyes misty as though webs had overgrown them. He halts inside the doorway, his eye caught by the sight of Elizabeth. The emotion flowing between them prevents anyone from speaking for an instant. Now Hale, visibly affected, goes to Danforth and speaks quietly.

HALE: Pray, leave them, Excellency.

DANFORTH, *pressing Hale impatiently aside*: Mr. Proctor, you have been notified, have you not? *Proctor is silent, staring at Elizabeth.* I see light in the sky, Mister; let you counsel with your wife, and may God help you turn your back on Hell. *Proctor is silent, staring at Elizabeth.*

HALE, *quietly*: Excellency, let—

Danforth brushes past Hale and walks out. Hale follows. Cheever stands and follows, Hathorne behind. Herrick goes. Parris, from a safe distance, offers:

PARRIS: If you desire a cup of cider, Mr. Proctor, I am sure I— *Proctor turns an icy stare at him, and he breaks off. Parris raises his palms toward Proctor.* God lead you now. *Parris goes out.*

Alone. Proctor walks to her, halts. It is as though they stood in a spinning world. It is beyond sorrow, above it. He reaches out his hand as though toward an embodiment not quite real, and as he touches her, a strange soft sound, half laughter, half amazement, comes from his throat. He pats her hand. She covers his hand with hers. And then, weak, he sits. Then she sits, facing him.

PROCTOR: The child?

ELIZABETH: It grows.

PROCTOR: There is no word of the boys?

ELIZABETH: They're well. Rebecca's Samuel keeps them.

PROCTOR: You have not seen them?

ELIZABETH: I have not. *She catches a weakening in herself and downs it.*

PROCTOR: You are a—marvel, Elizabeth.

ELIZABETH: You—have been tortured?

PROCTOR: Aye. *Pause. She will not let herself be drowned in the sea that threatens her.* They come for my life now.

ELIZABETH: I know it.

Pause.

PROCTOR: None—have yet confessed?

ELIZABETH: There be many confessed.

PROCTOR: Who are they?

ELIZABETH: There be a hundred or more, they say. Goody Ballard is one; Isaiah Goodkind is one. There be many.

PROCTOR: Rebecca?

ELIZABETH: Not Rebecca. She is one foot in Heaven now; naught may hurt her more.

PROCTOR: And Giles?

ELIZABETH: You have not heard of it?

PROCTOR: I hear nothin', where I am kept.

ELIZABETH: Giles is dead.

He looks at her incredulously.

PROCTOR: When were he hanged?

ELIZABETH, *quietly, factually*: He were not hanged. He would not answer aye or nay to his indictment; for if he denied the charge they'd hang him surely, and auction out his property. So he stand mute, and died Christian under the law. And so his sons will have his farm. It is the law, for he could not be condemned a wizard without he answer the indictment, aye or nay.

PROCTOR: Then how does he die?

ELIZABETH, *gently*: They press him, John.

PROCTOR: Press?

ELIZABETH: Great stones they lay upon his chest until he plead aye or nay. *With a tender smile for the old man*: They say he give them but two words. "More weight," he says. And died.

PROCTOR, *numbed—a thread to weave into his agony*: "More weight."

ELIZABETH: Aye. It were a fearsome man, Giles Corey.

Pause.

PROCTOR, *with great force of will, but not quite looking at her*: I have been thinking I would confess to them, Elizabeth. *She shows nothing.* What say you? If I give them that?

ELIZABETH: I cannot judge you, John.

Pause.

PROCTOR, *simply—a pure question*: What would you have me do?

ELIZABETH: As you will, I would have it. *Slight pause.* I want you living, John. That's sure.

PROCTOR—*he pauses, then with a flailing of hope*: Giles' wife? Have she confessed?

ELIZABETH: She will not.

Pause.

PROCTOR: It is a pretense, Elizabeth.

ELIZABETH: What is?

PROCTOR: I cannot mount the gibbet like a saint. It is a fraud. I am not that man. *She is silent.* My honesty is broke, Elizabeth; I am no good man. Nothing's spoiled by giving them this lie that were not rotten long before.

ELIZABETH: And yet you've not confessed till now. That speak goodness in you.

PROCTOR: Spite only keeps me silent. It is hard to give a lie to dogs. *Pause, for the first time he turns directly to her.* I would have your forgiveness, Elizabeth.

ELIZABETH: It is not for me to give, John, I am—

PROCTOR: I'd have you see some honesty in it. Let them that never lied die now to keep their souls. It is pretense for me, a vanity that will not blind God nor keep my children out of the wind. *Pause.* What say you?

ELIZABETH, *upon a heaving sob that always threatens*: John, it come to naught that I should forgive you, if you'll not forgive yourself. *Now he turns away a little, in great agony.* It is not my soul, John, it is yours. *He stands, as though in physical pain, slowly rising to his feet with a great immortal longing to find his answer. It is difficult to say, and she is on the verge of tears.* Only be sure of this, for I know it now: Whatever you will do, it is a good man does it. *He turns his doubting, searching gaze upon her.* I have read my heart this three month, John. *Pause.* I have sins of my own to count. It needs a cold wife to prompt lechery.

PROCTOR, *in great pain*: Enough, enough—

ELIZABETH, *now pouring out her heart*: Better you should know me!

PROCTOR: I will not hear it! I know you!

ELIZABETH: You take my sins upon you, John—

PROCTOR, *in agony*: No, I take my own, my own!

ELIZABETH: John, I counted myself so plain, so poorly made, no honest love could come to me! Suspicion kissed you when I did; I never knew how I should say my love. It were a cold house I kept! *In fright, she swerves, as Hathorne enters.*

HATHORNE: What say you, Proctor? The sun is soon up.

Proctor, his chest heaving, stares, turns to Elizabeth. She comes to him as though to plead, her voice quaking.

ELIZABETH: Do what you will. But let none be your judge. There be no higher judge under Heaven than Proctor is! Forgive me, forgive me, John— I never knew such goodness in the world! *She covers her face, weeping.*

Proctor turns from her to Hathorne; he is off the earth, his voice hollow.

PROCTOR: I want my life.

HATHORNE, *electrified, surprised*: You'll confess yourself?

PROCTOR: I will have my life.

HATHORNE, *with a mystical tone*: God be praised! It is a providence! *He rushes out the door, and his voice is heard calling down the corridor*: He will confess! Proctor will confess!

PROCTOR, *with a cry, as he strides to the door*: Why do you cry it? *In great pain he turns back to her*. It is evil, is it not? It is evil.

ELIZABETH, *in terror, weeping*: I cannot judge you, John, I cannot!

PROCTOR: Then who will judge me? *Suddenly clasping his hands*: God in Heaven, what is John Proctor, what is John Proctor? *He moves as an animal, and a fury is riding in him, a tantalized search*. I think it is honest, I think so; I am no saint.

As though she had denied this he calls angrily at her: Let Rebecca go like a saint; for me it is fraud!

Voices are heard in the hall, speaking together in suppressed excitement.

ELIZABETH: I am not your judge, I cannot be. *As though giving him release*: Do as you will, do as you will!

PROCTOR: Would you give them such a lie? Say it. Would you ever give them this? *She cannot answer*. You would not; if tongs of fire were singeing you you would not! It is evil. Good, then—it is evil, and I do it!

Hathorne enters with Danforth, and, with them, Cheever, Parris, and Hale. It is a businesslike, rapid entrance, as though the ice had been broken.

DANFORTH, *with great relief and gratitude*: Praise to God, man, praise to God; you shall be blessed in Heaven for this. *Cheever has hurried to the bench with pen, ink, and paper. Proctor watches him*. Now then, let us have it. Are you ready, Mr. Cheever?

PROCTOR, *with a cold, cold horror at their efficiency*: Why must it be written?

DANFORTH: Why, for the good instruction of the village, Mister; this we shall post upon the church door! *To Parris, urgently*: Where is the marshal?

PARRIS, *runs to the door and calls down the corridor*: Marshal! Hurry!

DANFORTH: Now, then, Mister, will you speak slowly, and directly to the point, for Mr. Cheever's sake. *He is on record now, and is really dictating to Cheever, who writes*. Mr. Proctor, have you seen the Devil in your life?

Proctor's jaws lock. Come, man, there is light in the sky; the town waits at the scaffold; I would give out this news. Did you see the Devil?

PROCTOR: I did.

PARRIS: Praise God!

DANFORTH: And when he come to you, what were his demand? *Proctor is silent. Danforth helps.* Did he bid you to do his work upon the earth?

PROCTOR: He did.

DANFORTH: And you bound yourself to his service? *Danforth turns, as Rebecca Nurse enters, with Herrick helping to support her. She is barely able to walk.* Come in, come in, woman!

REBECCA, *brightening as she sees Proctor*: Ah, John! You are well, then, eh?

    Proctor turns his face to the wall.

DANFORTH: Courage, man, courage—let her witness your good example that she may come to God herself. Now hear it, Goody Nurse! Say on, Mr. Proctor. Did you bind yourself to the Devil's service?

REBECCA, *astonished*: Why, John!

PROCTOR, *through his teeth, his face turned from Rebecca*: I did.

DANFORTH: Now, woman, you surely see it profit nothin' to keep this conspiracy any further. Will you confess yourself with him?

REBECCA: Oh, John—God send his mercy on you!

DANFORTH: I say, will you confess yourself, Goody Nurse?

REBECCA: Why, it is a lie, it is a lie; how may I damn myself? I cannot, I cannot.

DANFORTH: Mr. Proctor. When the Devil came to you did you see Rebecca Nurse in his company? *Proctor is silent.* Come, man, take courage—did you ever see her with the Devil?

PROCTOR, *almost inaudibly*: No.

    Danforth, now sensing trouble, glances at John and goes to the table, and picks up a sheet—the list of condemned.

DANFORTH: Did you ever see her sister, Mary Easty, with the Devil?

PROCTOR: No, I did not.

DANFORTH, *his eyes narrow on Proctor*: Did you ever see Martha Corey with the Devil?

PROCTOR: I did not.

DANFORTH, *realizing, slowly putting the sheet down*: Did you ever see anyone with the Devil?

PROCTOR: I did not.

DANFORTH: Proctor, you mistake me. I am not empowered to trade your life for a lie. You have most certainly seen some person with the Devil. *Proctor is silent*. Mr. Proctor, a score of people have already testified they saw this woman with the Devil.

PROCTOR: Then it is proved. Why must I say it?

DANFORTH: Why "must" you say it! Why, you should rejoice to say it if your soul is truly purged of any love for Hell!

PROCTOR: They think to go like saints. I like not to spoil their names.

DANFORTH, *inquiring, incredulous*: Mr. Proctor, do you think they go like saints?

PROCTOR, *evading*: This woman never thought she done the Devil's work.

DANFORTH: Look you, sir. I think you mistake your duty here. It matters nothing what she thought—she is convicted of the unnatural murder of children, and you for sending your spirit out upon Mary Warren. Your soul alone is the issue here, Mister, and you will prove its whiteness or you cannot live in a Christian country. Will you tell me now what persons conspired with you in the Devil's company? *Proctor is silent*. To your knowledge was Rebecca Nurse ever—

PROCTOR: I speak my own sins; I cannot judge another. *Crying out, with hatred*: I have no tongue for it.

HALE, *quickly to Danforth*: Excellency, it is enough he confess himself. Let him sign it, let him sign it.

PARRIS, *feverishly*: It is a great service, sir. It is a weighty name; it will strike the village that Proctor confess. I beg you, let him sign it. The sun is up, Excellency!

DANFORTH, *considers; then with dissatisfaction*: Come, then, sign your testimony. *To Cheever*: Give it to him. *Cheever goes to Proctor, the confession and a pen in hand. Proctor does not look at it*. Come, man, sign it.

PROCTOR, *after glancing at the confession*: You have all witnessed it—it is enough.

DANFORTH: You will not sign it?

PROCTOR: You have all witnessed it; what more is needed?

DANFORTH: Do you sport with me? You will sign your name or it is no confession, Mister! *His breast heaving with agonized breathing, Proctor now lays the paper down and signs his name.*

PARRIS: Praise be to the Lord!

> *Proctor has just finished signing when Danforth reaches for the paper. But Proctor snatches it up, and now a wild terror is rising in him, and a boundless anger.*

DANFORTH, *perplexed, but politely extending his hand*: If you please, sir.

PROCTOR: No.

DANFORTH, *as though Proctor did not understand*: Mr. Proctor, I must have—

PROCTOR: No, no. I have signed it. You have seen me. It is done! You have no need for this.

PARRIS: Proctor, the village must have proof that—

PROCTOR: Damn the village! I confess to God, and God has seen my name on this! It is enough!

DANFORTH: No, sir, it is—

PROCTOR: You came to save my soul, did you not? Here! I have confessed myself; it is enough!

DANFORTH: You have not con—

PROCTOR: I have confessed myself! Is there no good penitence but it be public? God does not need my name nailed upon the church! God sees my name; God knows how black my sins are! It is enough!

DANFORTH: Mr. Proctor—

PROCTOR: You will not use me! I am no Sarah Good or Tituba, I am John Proctor! You will not use me! It is no part of salvation that you should use me!

DANFORTH: I do not wish to—

PROCTOR: I have three children—how may I teach them to walk like men in the world, and I sold my friends?

DANFORTH: You have not sold your friends—

PROCTOR: Beguile me not! I blacken all of them when this is nailed to the church the very day they hang for silence!

DANFORTH: Mr. Proctor, I must have good and legal proof that you—

PROCTOR: You are the high court, your word is good enough! Tell them I confessed myself; say Proctor broke his knees and wept like a woman; say what you will, but my name cannot—

DANFORTH, *with suspicion*: It is the same, is it not? If I report it or you sign to it?

PROCTOR—*he knows it is insane*: No, it is not the same! What others say and what I sign to is not the same!

DANFORTH: Why? Do you mean to deny this confession when you are free?

PROCTOR: I mean to deny nothing!

DANFORTH: Then explain to me, Mr. Proctor, why you will not let—

PROCTOR, *with a cry of his whole soul*: Because it is my name! Because I cannot have another in my life! Because I lie and sign myself to lies! Because I am not worth the dust on the feet of them that hang! How may I live without my name? I have given you my soul; leave me my name!

DANFORTH, *pointing at the confession in Proctor's hand*: Is that document a lie? If it is a lie I will not accept it! What say you? I will not deal in lies, Mister! *Proctor is motionless.* You will give me your honest confession in my hand, or I cannot keep you from the rope. *Proctor does not reply.* Which way do you go, Mister?

> His breast heaving, his eyes staring, Proctor tears the paper and crumples it, and he is weeping in fury, but erect.

DANFORTH: Marshal!

PARRIS, *hysterically, as though the tearing paper were his life*: Proctor, Proctor!

HALE: Man, you will hang! You cannot!

PROCTOR, *his eyes full of tears*: I can. And there's your first marvel, that I can. You have made your magic now, for now I do think I see some shred of goodness in John Proctor. Not enough to weave a banner with, but white enough to keep it from such dogs. *Elizabeth, in a burst of terror, rushes to him and weeps against his hand.* Give them no tear! Tears pleasure them! Show honor now, show a stony heart and sink them with it! *He has lifted her, and kisses her now with great passion.*

REBECCA: Let you fear nothing! Another judgment waits us all!

DANFORTH: Hang them high over the town! Who weeps for these, weeps for corruption! *He sweeps out past them. Herrick starts to lead Rebecca, who almost collapses, but Proctor catches her, and she glances up at him apologetically.*

REBECCA: I've had no breakfast.

HERRICK: Come, man.

> *Herrick escorts them out, Hathorne and Cheever behind them. Elizabeth stands staring at the empty doorway.*

PARRIS, *in deadly fear, to Elizabeth*: Go to him, Goody Proctor! There is yet time!

> *From outside a drumroll strikes the air. Parris is startled. Elizabeth jerks about toward the window.*

PARRIS: Go to him! *He rushes out the door, as though to hold back his fate.* Proctor! Proctor!

> *Again, a short burst of drums.*

HALE: Woman, plead with him! *He starts to rush out the door, and then goes back to her.* Woman! It is pride, it is vanity. *She avoids his eyes, and moves to the window. He drops to his knees.* Be his helper! What profit him to bleed? Shall the dust praise him? Shall the worms declare his truth? Go to him, take his shame away!

ELIZABETH, *supporting herself against collapse, grips the bars of the window, and with a cry*: He have his goodness now. God forbid I take it from him!

> *The final drumroll crashes, then heightens violently. Hale weeps in frantic prayer, and the new sun is pouring in upon her face, and the drums rattle like bones in the morning air.*

THE CURTAIN FALLS.

ECHOES DOWN THE CORRIDOR

Not long after the fever died, Parris was voted from office, walked out on the highroad, and was never heard of again.

The legend has it that Abigail turned up later as a prostitute in Boston.

Twenty years after the last execution, the government awarded compensation to the victims still living, and to the families of the dead. However, it is evident that some people still were unwilling to admit their total guilt, and also that the factionalism was still alive, for some beneficiaries were actually not victims at all, but informers.

Elizabeth Proctor married again, four years after Proctor's death.

In solemn meeting, the congregation rescinded the excommunications— this in March 1712. But they did so upon orders of the government. The jury, however, wrote a statement praying forgiveness of all who had suffered.

Certain farms which had belonged to the victims were left to ruin, and for more than a century no one would buy them or live on them.

To all intents and purposes, the power of theocracy in Massachusetts was broken.

APPENDIX

A wood. Night.

Proctor enters with lantern, glowing behind him, then halts, holding lantern raised. Abigail appears with a wrap over her nightgown, her hair down. A moment of questioning silence.

PROCTOR, *searching*: I must speak with you, Abigail. *She does not move, staring at him.*

Will you sit?

ABIGAIL: How do you come?

PROCTOR: Friendly.

ABIGAIL, *glancing about*: I don't like the woods at night. Pray you, stand closer. *He comes closer to her.* I knew it must be you. When I heard the pebbles on the window, before I opened up my eyes I knew. *Sits on log.* I thought you would come a good time sooner.

PROCTOR: I had thought to come many times.

ABIGAIL: Why didn't you? I am so alone in the world now.

PROCTOR, *as a fact, not bitterly*: Are you! I've heard that people ride a hundred mile to see your face these days.

ABIGAIL: Aye, my face. Can you see my face?

PROCTOR, *holds the lantern to her face*: Then you're troubled?

ABIGAIL: Have you come to mock me?

PROCTOR, *sets lantern on ground. Sits next to her*: No, no, but I hear only that you go to the tavern every night, and play shovelboard with the Deputy Governor, and they give you cider.

ABIGAIL: I have once or twice played the shovelboard. But I have no joy in it.

PROCTOR: This is a surprise, Abby. I'd thought to find you gayer than this. I'm told a troop of boys go step for step with you wherever you walk these days.

ABIGAIL: Aye, they do. But I have only lewd looks from the boys.

PROCTOR: And you like that not?

ABIGAIL: I cannot bear lewd looks no more, John. My spirit's changed entirely. I ought be given Godly looks when I suffer for them as I do.

PROCTOR: Oh? How do you suffer, Abby?

ABIGAIL, *pulls up dress*: Why, look at my leg. I'm holes all over from their damned needles and pins. *Touching her stomach*: The jab your wife gave me's not healed yet, y'know.

PROCTOR, *seeing her madness now*: Oh, it isn't.

ABIGAIL: I think sometimes she pricks it open again while I sleep.

PROCTOR: Ah?

ABIGAIL: And George Jacobs—*sliding up her sleeve*—he comes again and again and raps me with his stick—the same spot every night all this week. Look at the lump I have.

PROCTOR: Abby—George Jacobs is in the jail all this month.

ABIGAIL: Thank God he is, and bless the day he hangs and lets me sleep in peace again! Oh, John, the world's so full of hypocrites! *Astonished, outraged*: They pray in jail! I'm told they all pray in jail!

PROCTOR: They may not pray?

ABIGAIL: And torture me in my bed while sacred words are comin' from their mouths? Oh, it will need God Himself to cleanse this town properly!

PROCTOR: Abby—you mean to cry out still others?

ABIGAIL: If I live, if I am not murdered, I surely will, until the last hypocrite is dead.

PROCTOR: Then there is no good?

ABIGAIL: Aye, there is one. *You* are good.

PROCTOR: Am I! How am I good?

ABIGAIL: Why, you taught me goodness, therefore you are good. It were a fire you walked me through, and all my ignorance was burned away. It were a fire, John, we lay in fire. And from that night no woman dare call me wicked any more but I knew my answer. I used to weep for my sins when the wind lifted up my skirts; and blushed for shame because some old Rebecca called me loose. And then you burned my ignorance away. As bare as some December tree I saw them all—walking like saints to church, running to feed the sick, and hypocrites in their hearts! And God gave me strength to call them liars, and God made men to listen to me, and by God I will scrub the world clean for the love of Him! Oh, John, I will make you such a wife when the world is white again! *She kisses his hand.* You will be amazed to see me every day, a light of heaven in your house, a— *He rises, backs away, amazed.* Why are you cold?

PROCTOR: My wife goes to trial in the morning, Abigail.

ABIGAIL, *distantly*: Your wife?

PROCTOR: Surely you knew of it?

ABIGAIL: I do remember it now. How—how— Is she well?

PROCTOR: As well as she may be, thirty-six days in that place.

ABIGAIL: You said you came friendly.

PROCTOR: She will not be condemned, Abby.

ABIGAIL: You brought me from my bed to speak of her?

PROCTOR: I come to tell you, Abby, what I will do tomorrow in the court. I would not take you by surprise, but give you all good time to think on what to do to save yourself.

ABIGAIL: Save myself!

PROCTOR: If you do not free my wife tomorrow, I am set and bound to ruin you, Abby.

ABIGAIL, *her voice small—astonished*: How—ruin me?

PROCTOR: I have rocky proof in documents that you knew that poppet were none of my wife's; and that you yourself bade Mary Warren stab that needle into it.

ABIGAIL—*a wildness stirs in her, a child is standing here who is unutterably frustrated, denied her wish, but she is still grasping for her wits*: I bade Mary Warren—?

PROCTOR: You know what you do, you are not so mad!

ABIGAIL: Oh, hypocrites! Have you won him, too? John, why do you let them send you?

PROCTOR: I warn you, Abby!

ABIGAIL: They send you! They steal your honesty and—

PROCTOR: I have found my honesty!

ABIGAIL: No, this is your wife pleading, your sniveling, envious wife! This is Rebecca's voice, Martha Corey's voice. You were no hypocrite!

PROCTOR: I will prove you for the fraud you are!

ABIGAIL: And if they ask you why Abigail would ever do so murderous a deed, what will you tell them?

PROCTOR: I will tell them why.

ABIGAIL: What will you tell? You will confess to fornication? In the court?

PROCTOR: If you will have it so, so I will tell it! *She utters a disbelieving laugh.* I say I will! *She laughs louder, now with more assurance he will never do it. He shakes her roughly.* If you can still hear, hear this! Can you hear! *She is trembling, staring up at him as though he were out of his mind.* You will tell the court you are blind to spirits; you cannot see them any more, and you will never cry witchery again, or I will make you famous for the whore you are!

ABIGAIL, *grabs him*: Never in this world! I know you, John—you are this moment singing secret hallelujahs that your wife will hang!

PROCTOR, *throws her down*: You mad, you murderous bitch!

ABIGAIL: Oh, how hard it is when pretense falls! But it falls, it falls! *She wraps herself up as though to go.* You have done your duty by her. I hope it is your last hypocrisy. I pray you will come again with sweeter news for me. I know you will—now that your duty's done. Good night, John. *She is backing away, raising her hand in farewell.* Fear naught. I will save you tomorrow. *As she turns and goes:* From yourself I will save you. *She is gone. Proctor is left alone, amazed, in terror. He takes up his lantern and slowly exits.*

A VIEW FROM THE BRIDGE

A PLAY IN TWO ACTS

1955

Characters

LOUIS

MIKE

ALFIERI

EDDIE

CATHERINE

BEATRICE

TONY

MARCO

RODOLPHO

FIRST IMMIGRATION OFFICER

SECOND IMMIGRATION OFFICER

MR. LIPARI

MRS. LIPARI

TWO "SUBMARINES"

NEIGHBORS

ACT ONE

The street and house front of a tenement building. The front is skeletal entirely. The main acting area is the living room–dining room of Eddie's apartment. It is a worker's flat, clean, sparse, homely. There is a rocker down front; a round dining table at center, with chairs; and a portable phonograph.

At back are a bedroom door and an opening to the kitchen; none of these interiors are seen.

At the right, forestage, a desk. This is Mr. Alfieri's law office.

There is also a telephone booth. This is not used until the last scenes, so it may be covered or left in view.

A stairway leads up to the apartment, and then farther up to the next story, which is not seen.

Ramps, representing the street, run upstage and off to right and left.

As the curtain rises, Louis and Mike, longshoremen, are pitching coins against the building at left.

A distant foghorn blows.

Enter Alfieri, a lawyer in his fifties turning gray; he is portly, good-humored, and thoughtful. The two pitchers nod to him as he passes. He crosses the stage to his desk, removes his hat, runs his fingers through his hair, and grinning, speaks to the audience.

ALFIERI: You wouldn't have known it, but something amusing has just happened. You see how uneasily they nod to me? That's because I am a lawyer. In this neighborhood to meet a lawyer or a priest on the street is unlucky. We're only thought of in connection with disasters, and they'd rather not get too close.

I often think that behind that suspicious little nod of theirs lie three thousand years of distrust. A lawyer means the law, and in Sicily, from where their fathers came, the law has not been a friendly idea since the Greeks were beaten.

I am inclined to notice the ruins in things, perhaps because I was born in Italy. . . . I only came here when I was twenty-five. In those days, Al Capone, the greatest Carthaginian of all, was learning his trade on these pavements, and Frankie Yale himself was cut precisely in half by a machine gun on the corner of Union Street, two blocks away. Oh, there were many here who were justly shot by unjust men. Justice is very important here.

But this is Red Hook, not Sicily. This is the slum that faces the bay on the seaward side of Brooklyn Bridge. This is the gullet of New York swallowing the tonnage of the world. And now we are quite civilized, quite American. Now we settle for half, and I like it better. I no longer keep a pistol in my filing cabinet.

And my practice is entirely unromantic.

My wife has warned me, so have my friends; they tell me the people in this neighborhood lack elegance, glamour. After all, who have I dealt with in my life? Longshoremen and their wives, and fathers and grandfathers, compensation cases, evictions, family squabbles—the petty troubles of the poor—and yet . . . every few years there is still a case, and as the parties tell me what the trouble is, the flat air in my office suddenly washes in with the green scent of the sea, the dust in this air is blown away and the thought comes that in some Caesar's year, in Calabria perhaps or on the cliff at Syracuse, another lawyer, quite differently dressed, heard the same complaint and sat there as powerless as I, and watched it run its bloody course.

Eddie has appeared and has been pitching coins with the men and is highlighted among them. He is forty—a husky, slightly overweight longshoreman.

This one's name was Eddie Carbone, a longshoreman working the docks from Brooklyn Bridge to the breakwater where the open sea begins.

Alfieri walks into darkness.

EDDIE, *moving up steps into doorway:* Well, I'll see ya, fellas.

Catherine enters from kitchen, crosses down to window, looks out.

LOUIS: You workin' tomorrow?

EDDIE: Yeah, there's another day yet on that ship. See ya, Louis.

Eddie goes into the house, as light rises in the apartment.

Catherine is waving to Louis from the window and turns to him.

CATHERINE: Hi, Eddie!

Eddie is pleased and therefore shy about it; he hangs up his cap and jacket.

EDDIE: Where you goin' all dressed up?

CATHERINE, *running her hands over her skirt*: I just got it. You like it?

EDDIE: Yeah, it's nice. And what happened to your hair?

CATHERINE: You like it? I fixed it different. *Calling to kitchen*: He's here, B.!

EDDIE: Beautiful. Turn around, lemme see in the back. *She turns for him.* Oh, if your mother was alive to see you now! She wouldn't believe it.

CATHERINE: You like it, huh?

EDDIE: You look like one of them girls that went to college. Where you goin'?

CATHERINE, *taking his arm*: Wait'll B. comes in, I'll tell you something. Here, sit down. *She is walking him to the armchair. Calling offstage*: Hurry up, will you, B.?

EDDIE, *sitting*: What's goin' on?

CATHERINE: I'll get you a beer, all right?

EDDIE: Well, tell me what happened. Come over here, talk to me.

CATHERINE: I want to wait till B. comes in. *She sits on her heels beside him.* Guess how much we paid for the skirt.

EDDIE: I think it's too short, ain't it?

CATHERINE, *standing*: No! Not when I stand up.

EDDIE: Yeah, but you gotta sit down sometimes.

CATHERINE: Eddie, it's the style now. *She walks to show him.* I mean, if you see me walkin' down the street—

EDDIE: Listen, you been givin' me the willies the way you walk down the street, I mean it.

CATHERINE: Why?

EDDIE: Catherine, I don't want to be a pest, but I'm tellin' you you're walkin' wavy.

CATHERINE: I'm walkin' wavy?

EDDIE: Now don't aggravate me, Katie, you are walkin' wavy! I don't like the looks they're givin' you in the candy store. And with them new high heels on the sidewalk—clack, clack, clack. The heads are turnin' like windmills.

CATHERINE: But those guys look at all the girls, you know that.

EDDIE: You ain't "all the girls."

CATHERINE, *almost in tears because he disapproves*: What do you want me to do? You want me to—

EDDIE: Now don't get mad, kid.

CATHERINE: Well, I don't know what you want from me.

EDDIE: Katie, I promised your mother on her deathbed. I'm responsible for you. You're a baby, you don't understand these things. I mean like when you stand here by the window, wavin' outside.

CATHERINE: I was wavin' to Louis!

EDDIE: Listen, I could tell you things about Louis which you wouldn't wave to him no more.

CATHERINE, *trying to joke him out of his warning*: Eddie, I wish there was one guy you couldn't tell me things about!

EDDIE: Catherine, do me a favor, will you? You're gettin' to be a big girl now, you gotta keep yourself more, you can't be so friendly, kid. *Calls*: Hey, B., what're you doin' in there? *To Catherine*: Get her in here, will you? I got news for her.

CATHERINE, *starting out*: What?

EDDIE: Her cousins landed.

CATHERINE, *clapping her hands together*: No! *She turns instantly and starts for the kitchen.* B.! Your cousins!

    Beatrice enters, wiping her hands with a towel.

BEATRICE, *in the face of Catherine's shout*: What?

CATHERINE: Your cousins got in!

BEATRICE, *astounded, turns to Eddie*: What are you talkin' about? Where?

EDDIE: I was just knockin' off work before and Tony Bereli come over to me; he says the ship is in the North River.

BEATRICE—*her hands are clasped at her breast; she seems half in fear, half in unutterable joy*: They're all right?

EDDIE: He didn't see them yet, they're still on board. But as soon as they get off he'll meet them. He figures about ten o'clock they'll be here.

BEATRICE *sits, almost weak from tension*: And they'll let them off the ship all right? That's fixed, heh?

EDDIE: Sure, they give them regular seamen papers and they walk off with the crew. Don't worry about it, B., there's nothin' to it. Couple of hours they'll be here.

BEATRICE: What happened? They wasn't supposed to be till next Thursday.

EDDIE: I don't know; they put them on any ship they can get them out on. Maybe the other ship they was supposed to take there was some danger— What you cryin' about?

BEATRICE, *astounded and afraid*: I'm— I just—I can't believe it! I didn't even buy a new tablecloth; I was gonna wash the walls—

EDDIE: Listen, they'll think it's a millionaire's house compared to the way they live. Don't worry about the walls. They'll be thankful. *To Catherine*: Whyn't you run down buy a tablecloth. Go ahead, here. *He is reaching into his pocket.*

CATHERINE: There's no stores open now.

EDDIE, *to Beatrice*: You was gonna put a new cover on the chair.

BEATRICE: I know—well, I thought it was gonna be next week! I was gonna clean the walls, I was gonna wax the floors. *She stands disturbed.*

CATHERINE, *pointing upward*: Maybe Mrs. Dondero upstairs—

BEATRICE, *of the tablecloth*: No, hers is worse than this one. *Suddenly:* My God, I don't even have nothin' to eat for them! *She starts for the kitchen.*

EDDIE, *reaching out and grabbing her arm*: Hey, hey! Take it easy.

BEATRICE: No, I'm just nervous, that's all. *To Catherine*: I'll make the fish.

EDDIE: You're savin' their lives, what're you worryin' about the table-cloth? They probably didn't see a tablecloth in their whole life where they come from.

BEATRICE, *looking into his eyes*: I'm just worried about you, that's all. I'm worried.

EDDIE: Listen, as long as they know where they're gonna sleep.

BEATRICE: I told them in the letters. They're sleepin' on the floor.

EDDIE: Beatrice, all I'm worried about is you got such a heart that I'll end up on the floor with you, and they'll be in our bed.

BEATRICE: All right, stop it.

EDDIE: Because as soon as you see a tired relative, I end up on the floor.

BEATRICE: When did you end up on the floor?

EDDIE: When your father's house burned down I didn't end up on the floor?

BEATRICE: Well, their house burned down!

EDDIE: Yeah, but it didn't keep burnin' for two weeks!

BEATRICE: All right, look, I'll tell them to go someplace else. *She starts into the kitchen.*

EDDIE: Now wait a minute. Beatrice! *She halts. He goes to her.* I just don't want you bein' pushed around, that's all. You got too big a heart. *He touches her hand.* What're you so touchy?

BEATRICE: I'm just afraid if it don't turn out good you'll be mad at me.

EDDIE: Listen, if everybody keeps his mouth shut, nothin' can happen. They'll pay for their board.

BEATRICE: Oh, I told them.

EDDIE: Then what the hell. *Pause. He moves.* It's an honor, B. I mean it. I was just thinkin' before, comin' home, suppose my father didn't come to this country, and I was starvin' like them over there . . . and I had people in America could keep me a couple of months? The man would be honored to lend me a place to sleep.

BEATRICE—*there are tears in her eyes. She turns to Catherine:* You see what he is? *She turns and grabs Eddie's face in her hands.* Mmm! You're an angel! God'll bless you. *He is gratefully smiling.* You'll see, you'll get a blessing for this!

EDDIE, *laughing:* I'll settle for my own bed.

BEATRICE: Go, Baby, set the table.

CATHERINE: We didn't tell him about me yet.

BEATRICE: Let him eat first, then we'll tell him. Bring everything in. *She hurries Catherine out.*

EDDIE, *sitting at the table:* What's all that about? Where's she goin'?

BEATRICE: Noplace. It's very good news, Eddie. I want you to be happy.

EDDIE: What's goin' on?

Catherine enters with plates, forks.

BEATRICE: She's got a job.

Pause. Eddie looks at Catherine, then back to Beatrice.

EDDIE: What job? She's gonna finish school.

CATHERINE: Eddie, you won't believe it—

EDDIE: No—no, you gonna finish school. What kinda job, what do you mean? All of a sudden you—

CATHERINE: Listen a minute, it's wonderful.

EDDIE: It's not wonderful. You'll never get nowheres unless you finish school. You can't take no job. Why didn't you ask me before you take a job?

BEATRICE: She's askin' you now, she didn't take nothin' yet.

CATHERINE: Listen a minute! I came to school this morning and the principal called me out of the class, see? To go to his office.

EDDIE: Yeah?

CATHERINE: So I went in and he says to me he's got my records, y'know? And there's a company wants a girl right away. It ain't exactly a secretary, it's a stenographer first, but pretty soon you get to be secretary. And he says to me that I'm the best student in the whole class—

BEATRICE: You hear that?

EDDIE: Well why not? Sure she's the best.

CATHERINE: I'm the best student, he says, and if I want, I should take the job and the end of the year he'll let me take the examination and he'll give me the certificate. So I'll save practically a year!

EDDIE, *strangely nervous*: Where's the job? What company?

CATHERINE: It's a big plumbing company over Nostrand Avenue.

EDDIE: Nostrand Avenue and where?

CATHERINE: It's someplace by the Navy Yard.

BEATRICE: Fifty dollars a week, Eddie.

EDDIE, *to Catherine, surprised*: Fifty?

CATHERINE: I swear.

Pause.

EDDIE: What about all the stuff you wouldn't learn this year, though?

CATHERINE: There's nothin' more to learn, Eddie, I just gotta practice from now on. I know all the symbols and I know the keyboard. I'll just get faster, that's all. And when I'm workin' I'll keep gettin' better and better, you see?

BEATRICE: Work is the best practice anyway.

EDDIE: That ain't what I wanted, though.

CATHERINE: Why! It's a great big company—

EDDIE: I don't like that neighborhood over there.

CATHERINE: It's a block and a half from the subway, he says.

EDDIE: Near the Navy Yard plenty can happen in a block and a half. And a plumbin' company! That's one step over the water front. They're practically longshoremen.

BEATRICE: Yeah, but she'll be in the office, Eddie.

EDDIE: I know she'll be in the office, but that ain't what I had in mind.

BEATRICE: Listen, she's gotta go to work sometime.

EDDIE: Listen, B., she'll be with a lotta plumbers? And sailors up and down the street? So what did she go to school for?

CATHERINE: But it's fifty a week, Eddie.

EDDIE: Look, did I ask you for money? I supported you this long I support you a little more. Please, do me a favor, will ya? I want you to be with different kind of people. I want you to be in a nice office. Maybe a lawyer's office someplace in New York in one of them nice buildings. I mean if you're gonna get outa here then get out; don't go practically in the same kind of neighborhood.

> *Pause. Catherine lowers her eyes.*

BEATRICE: Go, Baby, bring in the supper. *Catherine goes out.* Think about it a little bit, Eddie. Please. She's crazy to start work. It's not a little shop, it's a big company. Some day she could be a secretary. They picked her out of the whole class.

> *He is silent, staring down at the tablecloth, fingering the pattern.*

What are you worried about? She could take care of herself. She'll get out of the subway and be in the office in two minutes.

EDDIE, *somehow sickened*: I know that neighborhood, B., I don't like it.

BEATRICE: Listen, if nothin' happened to her in this neighborhood it ain't gonna happen noplace else. *She turns his face to her.* Look, you gotta get used to it, she's no baby no more. Tell her to take it. *He turns his head away.* You hear me? *She is angering.* I don't understand you; she's seventeen years old, you gonna keep her in the house all her life?

EDDIE, *insulted*: What kinda remark is that?

BEATRICE, *with sympathy but insistent force*: Well, I don't understand when it ends. First it was gonna be when she graduated high school, so she graduated high school. Then it was gonna be when she learned stenographer, so she learned stenographer. So what're we gonna wait for now? I mean it, Eddie, sometimes I don't understand you; they picked her out of the whole class, it's an honor for her.

> *Catherine enters with food, which she silently sets on the table. After a moment of watching her face, Eddie breaks into a smile, but it almost seems that tears will form in his eyes.*

EDDIE: With your hair that way you look like a madonna, you know that? You're the madonna type. *She doesn't look at him, but continues ladling out food onto the plates.* You wanna go to work, heh, Madonna?

CATHERINE, *softly*: Yeah.

EDDIE, *with a sense of her childhood, her babyhood, and the years*: All right, go to work. *She looks at him, then rushes and hugs him.* Hey, hey! Take it easy! *He holds her face away from him to look at her.* What're you cryin' about? *He is affected by her, but smiles his emotion away.*

CATHERINE, *sitting at her place*: I just— *Bursting out*: I'm gonna buy all new dishes with my first pay! *They laugh warmly.* I mean it. I'll fix up the whole house! I'll buy a rug!

EDDIE: And then you'll move away.

CATHERINE: No, Eddie!

EDDIE, *grinning*: Why not? That's life. And you'll come visit on Sundays, then once a month, then Christmas and New Year's, finally.

CATHERINE, *grasping his arm to reassure him and to erase the accusation*: No, please!

EDDIE, *smiling but hurt*: I only ask you one thing—don't trust nobody. You got a good aunt but she's got too big a heart, you learned bad from her. Believe me.

BEATRICE: Be the way you are, Katie, don't listen to him.

EDDIE, *to Beatrice—strangely and quickly resentful*: You lived in a house all your life, what do you know about it? You never worked in your life.

BEATRICE: She likes people. What's wrong with that?

EDDIE: Because most people ain't people. She's goin' to work; plumbers; they'll chew her to pieces if she don't watch out. *To Catherine*: Believe me, Katie, the less you trust, the less you be sorry.

Eddie crosses himself and the women do the same, and they eat.

CATHERINE: First thing I'll buy is a rug, heh, B.?

BEATRICE: I don't mind. *To Eddie*: I smelled coffee all day today. You unloadin' coffee today?

EDDIE: Yeah, a Brazil ship.

CATHERINE: I smelled it too. It smelled all over the neighborhood.

EDDIE: That's one time, boy, to be a longshoreman is a pleasure. I could work coffee ships twenty hours a day. You go down in the hold, y'know? It's like flowers, that smell. We'll bust a bag tomorrow, I'll bring you some.

BEATRICE: Just be sure there's no spiders in it, will ya? I mean it. *She directs this to Catherine, rolling her eyes upward.* I still remember that spider coming out of that bag he brung home. I nearly died.

EDDIE: You call that a spider? You oughta see what comes outa the bananas sometimes.

BEATRICE: Don't talk about it!

EDDIE: I seen spiders could stop a Buick.

BEATRICE, *clapping her hands over her ears*: All right, shut up!

EDDIE, *laughing and taking a watch out of his pocket*: Well, who started with spiders?

BEATRICE: All right, I'm sorry, I didn't mean it. Just don't bring none home again. What time is it?

EDDIE: Quarter nine. *Puts watch back in his pocket. They continue eating in silence.*

CATHERINE: He's bringin' them ten o'clock, Tony?

EDDIE: Around, yeah. *He eats.*

CATHERINE: Eddie, suppose somebody asks if they're livin' here. *He looks at her as though already she had divulged something publicly. Defensively*: I mean if they ask.

EDDIE: Now look, Baby, I can see we're gettin' mixed up again here.

CATHERINE: No, I just mean . . . people'll see them goin' in and out.

EDDIE: I don't care who sees them goin' in and out as long as you don't see them goin' in and out. And this goes for you too, B. You don't see nothin' and you don't know nothin'.

BEATRICE: What do you mean? I understand.

EDDIE: You don't understand; you still think you can talk about this to somebody just a little bit. Now lemme say it once and for all, because you're makin' me nervous again, both of you. I don't care if somebody comes in the house and sees them sleepin' on the floor, it never comes out of your mouth who they are or what they're doin' here.

BEATRICE: Yeah, but my mother'll know—

EDDIE: Sure she'll know, but just don't you be the one who told her, that's all. This is the United States government you're playin' with now, this is the Immigration Bureau. If you said it you knew it, if you didn't say it you didn't know it.

CATHERINE: Yeah, but Eddie, suppose somebody—

EDDIE: I don't care what question it is. You—don't—know—nothin'. They got stool pigeons all over this neighborhood they're payin' them every week for information, and you don't know who they are. It could be your best friend. You hear? *To Beatrice*: Like Vinny Bolzano, remember Vinny?

BEATRICE: Oh, yeah. God forbid.

EDDIE: Tell her about Vinny. *To Catherine*: You think I'm blowin' steam here? *To Beatrice*: Go ahead, tell her. *To Catherine*: You was a baby then. There was a family lived next door to her mother, he was about sixteen—

BEATRICE: No, he was no more than fourteen, 'cause I was to his confirmation in Saint Agnes. But the family had an uncle that they were hidin' in the house, and he snitched to the Immigration.

CATHERINE: The kid snitched?

EDDIE: On his own uncle!

CATHERINE: What, was he crazy?

EDDIE: He was crazy after, I tell you that, boy.

BEATRICE: Oh, it was terrible. He had five brothers and the old father. And they grabbed him in the kitchen and pulled him down the stairs— three flights his head was bouncin' like a coconut. And they spit on him in the street, his own father and his brothers. The whole neighborhood was cryin'.

CATHERINE: Ts! So what happened to him?

BEATRICE: I think he went away. *To Eddie*: I never seen him again, did you?

EDDIE *rises during this, taking out his watch*: Him? You'll never see him no more, a guy do a thing like that? How's he gonna show his face? *To Catherine, as he gets up uneasily*: Just remember, kid, you can quicker get back a million dollars that was stole than a word that you gave away. *He is standing now, stretching his back.*

CATHERINE: Okay, I won't say a word to nobody, I swear.

EDDIE: Gonna rain tomorrow. We'll be slidin' all over the decks. Maybe you oughta put something on for them, they be here soon.

BEATRICE: I only got fish, I hate to spoil it if they ate already. I'll wait, it only takes a few minutes; I could broil it.

CATHERINE: What happens, Eddie, when that ship pulls out and they ain't on it, though? Don't the captain say nothin'?

EDDIE, *slicing an apple with his pocket knife*: Captain's pieced off, what do you mean?

CATHERINE: Even the captain?

EDDIE: What's the matter, the captain don't have to live? Captain gets a piece, maybe one of the mates, piece for the guy in Italy who fixed the papers for them, Tony here'll get a little bite. . . .

BEATRICE: I just hope they get work here, that's all I hope.

EDDIE: Oh, the syndicate'll fix jobs for them; till they pay 'em off they'll get them work every day. It's after the pay-off, then they'll have to scramble like the rest of us.

BEATRICE: Well, it be better than they got there.

EDDIE: Oh sure, well, listen. So you gonna start Monday, heh, Madonna?

CATHERINE, *embarrassed*: I'm supposed to, yeah.

> *Eddie is standing facing the two seated women. First Beatrice smiles, then Catherine, for a powerful emotion is on him, a childish one and a knowing fear, and the tears show in his eyes—and they are shy before the avowal.*

EDDIE, *sadly smiling, yet somehow proud of her*: Well . . . I hope you have good luck. I wish you the best. You know that, kid.

CATHERINE, *rising, trying to laugh*: You sound like I'm goin' a million miles!

EDDIE: I know. I guess I just never figured on one thing.

CATHERINE, *smiling:* What?

EDDIE: That you would ever grow up. *He utters a soundless laugh at himself, feeling his breast pocket of his shirt.* I left a cigar in my other coat, I think. *He starts for the bedroom.*

CATHERINE: Stay there! I'll get it for you.

> *She hurries out. There is a slight pause, and Eddie turns to Beatrice, who has been avoiding his gaze.*

EDDIE: What are you mad at me lately?

BEATRICE: Who's mad? *She gets up, clearing the dishes.* I'm not mad. *She picks up the dishes and turns to him.* You're the one is mad. *She turns and goes into the kitchen as Catherine enters from the bedroom with a cigar and a pack of matches.*

CATHERINE: Here! I'll light it for you! *She strikes a match and holds it to his cigar. He puffs. Quietly:* Don't worry about me, Eddie, heh?

EDDIE: Don't burn yourself. *Just in time she blows out the match.* You better go in help her with the dishes.

CATHERINE *turns quickly to the table, and, seeing the table cleared, she says, almost guiltily:* Oh! *She hurries into the kitchen, and as she exits there:* I'll do the dishes, B.!

> *Alone, Eddie stands looking toward the kitchen for a moment. Then he takes out his watch, glances at it, replaces it in his pocket, sits in the armchair, and stares at the smoke flowing out of his mouth.*
>
> *The lights go down, then come up on Alfieri, who has moved onto the forestage.*

ALFIERI: He was as good a man as he had to be in a life that was hard and even. He worked on the piers when there was work, he brought home his pay, and he lived. And toward ten o'clock of that night, after they had eaten, the cousins came.

> *The lights fade on Alfieri and rise on the street.*
>
> *Enter Tony, escorting Marco and Rodolpho, each with a valise. Tony halts, indicates the house. They stand for a moment looking at it.*

MARCO—*he is a square-built peasant of thirty-two, suspicious, tender, and quiet-voiced:* Thank you.

TONY: You're on your own now. Just be careful, that's all. Ground floor.

MARCO: Thank you.

TONY, *indicating the house*: I'll see you on the pier tomorrow. You'll go to work.

> *Marco nods. Tony continues on walking down the street.*

RODOLPHO: This will be the first house I ever walked into in America! Imagine! She said they were poor!

MARCO: Ssh! Come. *They go to door.*

> *Marco knocks. The lights rise in the room. Eddie goes and opens the door. Enter Marco and Rodolpho, removing their caps. Beatrice and Catherine enter from the kitchen. The lights fade in the street.*

EDDIE: You Marco?

MARCO: Marco.

EDDIE: Come on in! *He shakes Marco's hand.*

BEATRICE: Here, take the bags!

MARCO *nods, looks to the women and fixes on Beatrice. Crosses to Beatrice*: Are you my cousin?

> *She nods. He kisses her hand.*

BEATRICE, *above the table, touching her chest with her hand*: Beatrice. This is my husband, Eddie. *All nod.* Catherine, my sister Nancy's daughter. *The brothers nod.*

MARCO, *indicating Rodolpho*: My brother. Rodolpho. *Rodolpho nods. Marco comes with a certain formal stiffness to Eddie.* I want to tell you now Eddie—when you say go, we will go.

EDDIE: Oh, no . . . *Takes Marco's bag.*

MARCO: I see it's a small house, but soon, maybe, we can have our own house.

EDDIE: You're welcome, Marco, we got plenty of room here. Katie, give them supper, heh? *Exits into bedroom with their bags.*

CATHERINE: Come here, sit down. I'll get you some soup.

MARCO, *as they go to the table*: We ate on the ship. Thank you. *To Eddie, calling off to bedroom*: Thank you.

BEATRICE: Get some coffee. We'll all have coffee. Come sit down.

> *Rodolpho and Marco sit, at the table.*

CATHERINE, *wondrously*: How come he's so dark and you're so light, Rodolpho?

RODOLPHO, *ready to laugh*: I don't know. A thousand years ago, they say, the Danes invaded Sicily.

Beatrice kisses Rodolpho. They laugh as Eddie enters.

CATHERINE, *to Beatrice*: He's practically blond!

EDDIE: How's the coffee doin'?

CATHERINE, *brought up*: I'm gettin' it. *She hurries out to kitchen.*

EDDIE *sits on his rocker*: Yiz have a nice trip?

MARCO: The ocean is always rough. But we are good sailors.

EDDIE: No trouble gettin' here?

MARCO: No. The man brought us. Very nice man.

RODOLPHO, *to Eddie*: He says we start to work tomorrow. Is he honest?

EDDIE, *laughing*: No. But as long as you owe them money, they'll get you plenty of work. *To Marco*: Yiz ever work on the piers in Italy?

MARCO: Piers? Ts!—no.

RODOLPHO, *smiling at the smallness of his town*: In our town there are no piers, only the beach, and little fishing boats.

BEATRICE: So what kinda work did yiz do?

MARCO, *shrugging shyly, even embarrassed*: Whatever there is, anything.

RODOLPHO: Sometimes they build a house, or if they fix the bridge—Marco is a mason and I bring him the cement. *He laughs.* In harvest time we work in the fields . . . if there is work. Anything.

EDDIE: Still bad there, heh?

MARCO: Bad, yes.

RODOLPHO, *laughing*: It's terrible! We stand around all day in the piazza listening to the fountain like birds. Everybody waits only for the train.

BEATRICE: What's on the train?

RODOLPHO: Nothing. But if there are many passengers and you're lucky you make a few lire to push the taxi up the hill.

Enter Catherine; she listens.

BEATRICE: You gotta push a taxi?

RODOLPHO, *laughing*: Oh, sure! It's a feature in our town. The horses in our town are skinnier than goats. So if there are too many passengers we help to push the carriages up to the hotel. *He laughs.* In our town the horses are only for show.

CATHERINE: Why don't they have automobile taxis?

RODOLPHO: There is one. We push that too. *They laugh.* Everything in our town, you gotta push!

BEATRICE, *to Eddie*: How do you like that!

EDDIE, *to Marco*: So what're you wanna do, you gonna stay here in this country or you wanna go back?

MARCO, *surprised*: Go back?

EDDIE: Well, you're married, ain't you?

MARCO: Yes. I have three children.

BEATRICE: Three! I thought only one.

MARCO: Oh, no. I have three now. Four years, five years, six years.

BEATRICE: Ah . . . I bet they're cryin' for you already, heh?

MARCO: What can I do? The older one is sick in his chest. My wife—she feeds them from her own mouth. I tell you the truth, if I stay there they will never grow up. They eat the sunshine.

BEATRICE: My God. So how long you want to stay?

MARCO: With your permission, we will stay maybe a—

EDDIE: She don't mean in this house, she means in the country.

MARCO: Oh. Maybe four, five, six years, I think.

RODOLPHO, *smiling*: He trusts his wife.

BEATRICE: Yeah, but maybe you'll get enough, you'll be able to go back quicker.

MARCO: I hope. I don't know. *To Eddie*: I understand it's not so good here either.

EDDIE: Oh, you guys'll be all right—till you pay them off, anyway. After that, you'll have to scramble, that's all. But you'll make better here than you could there.

RODOLPHO: How much? We hear all kinds of figures. How much can a man make? We work hard, we'll work all day, all night—

Marco raises a hand to hush him.

EDDIE—*he is coming more and more to address Marco only*: On the average a whole year? Maybe—well, it's hard to say, see. Sometimes we lay off, there's no ships three four weeks.

MARCO: Three, four weeks!—Ts!

EDDIE: But I think you could probably—thirty, forty a week, over the whole twelve months of the year.

MARCO, *rises, crosses to Eddie*: Dollars.

EDDIE: Sure dollars.

Marco puts an arm round Rodolpho and they laugh.

MARCO: If we can stay here a few months, Beatrice—

BEATRICE: Listen, you're welcome, Marco—

MARCO: Because I could send them a little more if I stay here.

BEATRICE: As long as you want, we got plenty a room.

MARCO, *his eyes are showing tears*: My wife— *To Eddie*: My wife—I want to send right away maybe twenty dollars—

EDDIE: You could send them something next week already.

MARCO—*he is near tears*: Eduardo . . . *He goes to Eddie, offering his hand.*

EDDIE: Don't thank me. Listen, what the hell, it's no skin off me. *To Catherine*: What happened to the coffee?

CATHERINE: I got it on. *To Rodolpho*: You married too? No.

RODOLPHO *rises*: Oh, no . . .

BEATRICE, *to Catherine*: I told you he—

CATHERINE: I know, I just thought maybe he got married recently.

RODOLPHO: I have no money to get married. I have a nice face, but no money. *He laughs.*

CATHERINE, *to Beatrice*: He's a real blond!

BEATRICE, *to Rodolpho*: You want to stay here too, heh? For good?

RODOLPHO: Me? Yes, forever! Me, I want to be an American. And then I want to go back to Italy when I am rich, and I will buy a motorcycle. *He smiles. Marco shakes him affectionately.*

CATHERINE: A motorcycle!

RODOLPHO: With a motorcycle in Italy you will never starve any more.

BEATRICE: I'll get you coffee. *She exits to the kitchen.*

EDDIE: What you do with a motorcycle?

MARCO: He dreams, he dreams.

RODOLPHO, *to Marco*: Why? *To Eddie*: Messages! The rich people in the hotel always need someone who will carry a message. But quickly, and with a great noise. With a blue motorcycle I would station myself in the courtyard of the hotel, and in a little while I would have messages.

MARCO: When you have no wife you have dreams.

EDDIE: Why can't you just walk, or take a trolley or sump'm?

Enter Beatrice with coffee.

RODOLPHO: Oh, no, the machine, the machine is necessary. A man comes into a great hotel and says, I am a messenger. Who is this man? He disappears walking, there is no noise, nothing. Maybe he will never come back, maybe he will never deliver the message. But a man who rides up on a great machine, this man is responsible, this man exists. He will be given messages. *He helps Beatrice set out the coffee things.* I am also a singer, though.

EDDIE: You mean a regular—?

RODOLPHO: Oh, yes. One night last year Andreola got sick. Baritone. And I took his place in the garden of the hotel. Three arias I sang without a mistake! Thousand-lire notes they threw from the tables, money was falling like a storm in the treasury. It was magnificent. We lived six months on that night, eh, Marco?

Marco nods doubtfully.

MARCO: Two months.

Eddie laughs.

BEATRICE: Can't you get a job in that place?

RODOLPHO: Andreola got better. He's a baritone, very strong.

Beatrice laughs.

MARCO, *regretfully, to Beatrice*: He sang too loud.

RODOLPHO: Why too loud?

MARCO: Too loud. The guests in that hotel are all Englishmen. They don't like too loud.

RODOLPHO, *to Catherine*: Nobody ever said it was too loud!

MARCO: I say. It was too loud. *To Beatrice*: I knew it as soon as he started to sing. Too loud.

RODOLPHO: Then why did they throw so much money?

MARCO: They paid for your courage. The English like courage. But once is enough.

RODOLPHO, *to all but Marco*: I never heard anybody say it was too loud.

CATHERINE: Did you ever hear of jazz?

RODOLPHO: Oh, sure! I *sing* jazz.

CATHERINE *rises*: You could sing jazz?

RODOLPHO: Oh, I sing Napolidan, jazz, bel canto—I sing "Paper Doll," you like "Paper Doll"?

CATHERINE: Oh, sure, I'm crazy for "Paper Doll." Go ahead, sing it.

RODOLPHO *takes his stance after getting a nod of permission from Marco, and with a high tenor voice begins singing*:

> I'll tell you boys it's tough to be alone,
> And it's tough to love a doll that's not your own.
> I'm through with all of them,
> I'll never fall again,
> Hey, boy, what you gonna do?
> I'm gonna buy a paper doll that I can call my own,
> A doll that other fellows cannot steal.

Eddie rises and moves upstage.

> And then those flirty, flirty guys
> With their flirty, flirty eyes
> Will have to flirt with dollies that are real—

EDDIE: Hey, kid—hey, wait a minute—

CATHERINE, *enthralled*: Leave him finish, it's beautiful! *To Beatrice*: He's terrific! It's terrific, Rodolpho.

EDDIE: Look, kid; you don't want to be picked up, do ya?

MARCO: No—no! *He rises.*

EDDIE, *indicating the rest of the building*: Because we never had no singers here . . . and all of a sudden there's a singer in the house, y'know what I mean?

MARCO: Yes, yes. You'll be quiet, Rodolpho.

EDDIE—*he is flushed*: They got guys all over the place, Marco. I mean.

MARCO: Yes. He'll be quiet. *To Rodolpho*: You'll be quiet.

Rodolpho nods.

Eddie has risen, with iron control, even a smile. He moves to Catherine.

EDDIE: What's the high heels for, Garbo?

CATHERINE: I figured for tonight—

EDDIE: Do me a favor, will you? Go ahead.

Embarrassed now, angered, Catherine goes out into the bedroom. Beatrice watches her go and gets up; in passing, she gives Eddie a cold look, restrained only by the strangers, and goes to the table to pour coffee.

EDDIE, *striving to laugh, and to Marco, but directed as much to Beatrice*: All actresses they want to be around here.

RODOLPHO, *happy about it*: In Italy too! All the girls.

Catherine emerges from the bedroom in low-heel shoes, comes to the table. Rodolpho is lifting a cup.

EDDIE—*he is sizing up Rodolpho, and there is a concealed suspicion*: Yeah, heh?

RODOLPHO: Yes! *Laughs, indicating Catherine*: Especially when they are so beautiful!

CATHERINE: You like sugar?

RODOLPHO: Sugar? Yes! I like sugar very much!

Eddie is downstage, watching as she pours a spoonful of sugar into his cup, his face puffed with trouble, and the room dies.

Lights rise on Alfieri.

ALFIERI: Who can ever know what will be discovered? Eddie Carbone had never expected to have a destiny. A man works, raises his family, goes bowling, eats, gets old, and then he dies. Now, as the weeks passed, there was a future, there was a trouble that would not go away.

The lights fade on Alfieri, then rise on Eddie standing at the doorway of the house. Beatrice enters on the street. She sees Eddie, smiles at him. He looks away.

She starts to enter the house when Eddie speaks.

EDDIE: It's after eight.

BEATRICE: Well, it's a long show at the Paramount.

EDDIE: They must've seen every picture in Brooklyn by now. He's supposed to stay in the house when he ain't working. He ain't supposed to go advertising himself.

BEATRICE: Well that's his trouble, what do you care? If they pick him up they pick him up, that's all. Come in the house.

EDDIE: What happened to the stenography? I don't see her practice no more.

BEATRICE: She'll get back to it. She's excited, Eddie.

EDDIE: She tell you anything?

BEATRICE *comes to him, now the subject is opened*: What's the matter with you? He's a nice kid, what do you want from him?

EDDIE: That's a nice kid? He gives me the heeby-jeebies.

BEATRICE, *smiling*: Ah, go on, you're just jealous.

EDDIE: Of *him*? Boy, you don't think much of me.

BEATRICE: I don't understand you. What's so terrible about him?

EDDIE: You mean it's all right with you? That's gonna be her husband?

BEATRICE: Why? He's a nice fella, hard workin', he's a good-lookin' fella.

EDDIE: He sings on the ships, didja know that?

BEATRICE: What do you mean, he sings?

EDDIE: Just what I said, he sings. Right on the deck, all of a sudden, a whole song comes out of his mouth—with motions. You know what they're callin' him now? Paper Doll they're callin' him, Canary. He's like a weird. He comes out on the pier, one-two-three, it's a regular free show.

BEATRICE: Well, he's a kid; he don't know how to behave himself yet.

EDDIE: And with that wacky hair; he's like a chorus girl or sump'm.

BEATRICE: So he's blond, so—

EDDIE: I just hope that's his regular hair, that's all I hope.

BEATRICE: You crazy or sump'm? *She tries to turn him to her.*

EDDIE—*he keeps his head turned away*: What's so crazy? I don't like his whole way.

BEATRICE: Listen, you never seen a blond guy in your life? What about Whitey Balso?

EDDIE, *turning to her victoriously*: Sure, but Whitey don't sing; he don't do like that on the ships.

BEATRICE: Well, maybe that's the way they do in Italy.

EDDIE: Then why don't his brother sing? Marco goes around like a man; nobody kids Marco. *He moves from her, halts. She realizes there is a campaign solidified in him.* I tell you the truth I'm surprised I have to tell you all this. I mean I'm surprised, B.

BEATRICE—*she goes to him with purpose now:* Listen, you ain't gonna start nothin' here.

EDDIE: I ain't startin' nothin', but I ain't gonna stand around lookin' at that. For that character I didn't bring her up. I swear, B., I'm surprised at you; I sit there waitin' for you to wake up but everything is great with you.

BEATRICE: No, everything ain't great with me.

EDDIE: No?

BEATRICE: No. But I got other worries.

EDDIE: Yeah. *He is already weakening.*

BEATRICE: Yeah, you want me to tell you?

EDDIE, *in retreat:* Why? What worries you got?

BEATRICE: When am I gonna be a wife again, Eddie?

EDDIE: I ain't been feelin' good. They bother me since they came.

BEATRICE: It's almost three months you don't feel good; they're only here a couple of weeks. It's three months, Eddie.

EDDIE: I don't know, B. I don't want to talk about it.

BEATRICE: What's the matter, Eddie, you don't like me, heh?

EDDIE: What do you mean, I don't like you? I said I don't feel good, that's all.

BEATRICE: Well, tell me, am I doing something wrong? Talk to me.

EDDIE—*pause. He can't speak, then:* I can't. I can't talk about it.

BEATRICE: Well tell me what—

EDDIE: I got nothin' to say about it!

> *She stands for a moment; he is looking off; she turns to go into the house.*

EDDIE: I'll be all right, B.; just lay off me, will ya? I'm worried about her.

BEATRICE: The girl is gonna be eighteen years old, it's time already.

EDDIE: B., he's taking her for a ride!

BEATRICE: All right, that's her ride. What're you gonna stand over her till she's forty? Eddie, I want you to cut it out now, you hear me? I don't like it! Now come in the house.

EDDIE: I want to take a walk, I'll be in right away.

BEATRICE: They ain't goin' to come any quicker if you stand in the street. It ain't nice, Eddie.

EDDIE: I'll be in right away. Go ahead. *He walks off.*

> *She goes into the house. Eddie glances up the street, sees Louis and Mike coming, and sits on an iron railing. Louis and Mike enter.*

LOUIS: Wanna go bowlin' tonight?

EDDIE: I'm too tired. Goin' to sleep.

LOUIS: How's your two submarines?

EDDIE: They're okay.

LOUIS: I see they're gettin' work allatime.

EDDIE: Oh yeah, they're doin' all right.

MIKE: That's what we oughta do. We oughta leave the country and come in under the water. Then we get work.

EDDIE: You ain't kiddin'.

LOUIS: Well, what the hell. Y'know?

EDDIE: Sure.

LOUIS, *sits on railing beside Eddie*: Believe me, Eddie, you got a lotta credit comin' to you.

EDDIE: Aah, they don't bother me, don't cost me nutt'n.

MIKE: That older one, boy, he's a regular bull. I seen him the other day liftin' coffee bags over the Matson Line. They leave him alone he woulda load the whole ship by himself.

EDDIE: Yeah, he's a strong guy, that guy. Their father was a regular giant, supposed to be.

LOUIS: Yeah, you could see. He's a regular slave.

MIKE, *grinning*: That blond one, though— *Eddie looks at him.* He's got a sense of humor. *Louis snickers.*

EDDIE, *searchingly*: Yeah. He's funny—

MIKE, *starting to laugh*: Well he ain't exackly funny, but he's always like makin' remarks like, y'know? He comes around, everybody's laughin'. *Louis laughs.*

EDDIE, *uncomfortably, grinning*: Yeah, well . . . he's got a sense of humor.

MIKE, *laughing*: Yeah, I mean, he's always makin' like remarks, like, y'know?

EDDIE: Yeah, I know. But he's a kid yet, y'know? He—he's just a kid, that's all.

MIKE, *getting hysterical with Louis*: I know. You take one look at him—everybody's happy. *Louis laughs.* I worked one day with him last week over the Moore-MacCormack Line, I'm tellin' you they was all hysterical. *Louis and he explode in laughter.*

EDDIE: Why? What'd he do?

MIKE: I don't know . . . he was just humorous. You never can remember what he says, y'know? But it's the way he says it. I mean he gives you a look sometimes and you start laughin'!

EDDIE: Yeah. *Troubled*: He's got a sense of humor.

MIKE, *gasping*: Yeah.

LOUIS, *rising*: Well, we see ya, Eddie.

EDDIE: Take it easy.

LOUIS: Yeah. See ya.

MIKE: If you wanna come bowlin' later we're goin' Flatbush Avenue.

> *Laughing, they move to exit, meeting Rodolpho and Catherine entering on the street. Their laughter rises as they see Rodolpho, who does not understand but joins in. Eddie moves to enter the house as Louis and Mike exit. Catherine stops him at the door.*

CATHERINE: Hey, Eddie—what a picture we saw! Did we laugh!

EDDIE—*he can't help smiling at sight of her*: Where'd you go?

CATHERINE: Paramount. It was with those two guys, y'know? That—

EDDIE: Brooklyn Paramount?

CATHERINE, *with an edge of anger, embarrassed before Rodolpho*: Sure, the Brooklyn Paramount. I told you we wasn't goin' to New York.

EDDIE, *retreating before the threat of her anger*: All right, I only asked you. *To Rodolpho*: I just don't want her hangin' around Times Square, see? It's full of tramps over there.

RODOLPHO: I would like to go to Broadway once, Eddie. I would like to walk with her once where the theaters are and the opera. Since I was a boy I see pictures of those lights.

EDDIE, *his little patience waning*: I want to talk to her a minute, Rodolpho. Go inside, will you?

RODOLPHO: Eddie, we only walk together in the streets. She teaches me.

CATHERINE: You know what he can't get over? That there's no fountains in Brooklyn!

EDDIE, *smiling unwillingly*: Fountains? *Rodolpho smiles at his own naïveté.*

CATHERINE: In Italy he says, every town's got fountains, and they meet there. And you know what? They got oranges on the trees where he comes from, and lemons. Imagine—on the trees? I mean it's interesting. But he's crazy for New York.

RODOLPHO, *attempting familiarity*: Eddie, why can't we go once to Broadway—?

EDDIE: Look, I gotta tell her something—

RODOLPHO: Maybe you can come too. I want to see all those lights. *He sees no response in Eddie's face. He glances at Catherine.* I'll walk by the river before I go to sleep. *He walks off down the street.*

CATHERINE: Why don't you talk to him, Eddie? He blesses you, and you don't talk to him hardly.

EDDIE, *enveloping her with his eyes*: I bless you and you don't talk to me. *He tries to smile.*

CATHERINE: *I* don't talk to you? *She hits his arm.* What do you mean?

EDDIE: I don't see you no more. I come home you're runnin' around someplace—

CATHERINE: Well, he wants to see everything, that's all, so we go. . . . You mad at me?

EDDIE: No. *He moves from her, smiling sadly.* It's just I used to come home, you was always there. Now, I turn around, you're a big girl. I don't know how to talk to you.

CATHERINE: Why?

EDDIE: I don't know, you're runnin', you're runnin', Katie. I don't think you listening any more to me.

CATHERINE, *going to him*: Ah, Eddie, sure I am. What's the matter? You don't like him?

    Slight pause.

EDDIE *turns to her*: *You* like him, Katie?

CATHERINE, *with a blush but holding her ground*: Yeah. I like him.

EDDIE—*his smile goes*: You like him.

CATHERINE, *looking down*: Yeah. *Now she looks at him for the consequences, smiling but tense. He looks at her like a lost boy.* What're you got against him? I don't understand. He only blesses you.

EDDIE *turns away*: He don't bless me, Katie.

CATHERINE: He does! You're like a father to him!

EDDIE *turns to her*: Katie.

CATHERINE: What, Eddie?

EDDIE: You gonna marry him?

CATHERINE: I don't know. We just been . . . goin' around, that's all. *Turns to him*: What're you got against him, Eddie? Please, tell me. What?

EDDIE: He don't respect you.

CATHERINE: Why?

EDDIE: Katie . . . if you wasn't an orphan, wouldn't he ask your father's permission before he run around with you like this?

CATHERINE: Oh, well, he didn't think you'd mind.

EDDIE: He knows I mind, but it don't bother him if I mind, don't you see that?

CATHERINE: No, Eddie, he's got all kinds of respect for me. And you too! We walk across the street he takes my arm—he almost bows to me! You got him all wrong, Eddie; I mean it, you—

EDDIE: Katie, he's only bowin' to his passport.

CATHERINE: His passport!

EDDIE: That's right. He marries you he's got the right to be an American citizen. That's what's goin' on here. *She is puzzled and surprised.* You understand what I'm tellin' you? The guy is lookin' for his break, that's all he's lookin' for.

CATHERINE, *pained*: Oh, no, Eddie, I don't think so.

EDDIE: You don't think so! Katie, you're gonna make me cry here. Is that a workin' man? What does he do with his first money? A snappy new jacket he buys, records, a pointy pair new shoes and his brother's kids are starvin' over there with tuberculosis? That's a hit-and-run guy, Baby; he's got bright lights in his head, Broadway. Them guys don't think of nobody but their-self! You marry him and the next time you see him it'll be for divorce!

CATHERINE *steps toward him*: Eddie, he never said a word about his papers or—

EDDIE: You mean he's supposed to tell you that?

CATHERINE: I don't think he's even thinking about it.

EDDIE: What's better for him to think about! He could be picked up any day here and he's back pushin' taxis up the hill!

CATHERINE: No, I don't believe it.

EDDIE: Katie, don't break my heart, listen to me.

CATHERINE: I don't want to hear it.

EDDIE: Katie, listen . . .

CATHERINE: He loves me!

EDDIE, *with deep alarm*: Don't say that, for God's sake! This is the oldest racket in the country—

CATHERINE, *desperately, as though he had made his imprint*: I don't believe it! *She rushes to the house.*

EDDIE, *following her*: They been pullin' this since the Immigration Law was put in! They grab a green kid that don't know nothin' and they—

CATHERINE, *sobbing*: I don't believe it and I wish to hell you'd stop it!

EDDIE: Katie!

> *They enter the apartment. The lights in the living room have risen and Beatrice is there. She looks past the sobbing Catherine at Eddie, who in the presence of his wife, makes an awkward gesture of eroded command, indicating Catherine.*

EDDIE: Why don't you straighten her out?

BEATRICE, *inwardly angered at his flowing emotion, which in itself alarms her*: When are you going to leave her alone?

EDDIE: B., the guy is no good!

BEATRICE, *suddenly, with open fright and fury*: You going to leave her alone? Or you gonna drive me crazy? *He turns, striving to retain his dignity, but nevertheless in guilt walks out of the house, into the street and away. Catherine starts into a bedroom.* Listen, Catherine. *Catherine halts, turns to her sheepishly.* What are you going to do with yourself?

CATHERINE: I don't know.

BEATRICE: Don't tell me you don't know; you're not a baby any more, what are you going to do with yourself?

CATHERINE: He won't listen to me.

BEATRICE: I don't understand this. He's not your father, Catherine. I don't understand what's going on here.

CATHERINE, *as one who herself is trying to rationalize a buried impulse*: What am I going to do, just kick him in the face with it?

BEATRICE: Look, honey, you wanna get married, or don't you wanna get married? What are you worried about, Katie?

CATHERINE, *quietly, trembling*: I don't know, B. It just seems wrong if he's against it so much.

BEATRICE, *never losing her aroused alarm*: Sit down, honey, I want to tell you something. Here, sit down. Was there ever any fella he liked for you? There wasn't, was there?

CATHERINE: But he says Rodolpho's just after his papers.

BEATRICE: Look, he'll say anything. What does he care what he says? If it was a prince came here for you it would be no different. You know that, don't you?

CATHERINE: Yeah, I guess.

BEATRICE: So what does that mean?

CATHERINE *slowly turns her head to Beatrice*: What?

BEATRICE: It means you gotta be your own self more. You still think you're a little girl, honey. But nobody else can make up your mind for you any more, you understand? You gotta give him to understand that he can't give you orders no more.

CATHERINE: Yeah, but how am I going to do that? He thinks I'm a baby.

BEATRICE: Because *you* think you're a baby. I told you fifty times already, you can't act the way you act. You still walk around in front of him in your slip—

CATHERINE: Well I forgot.

BEATRICE: Well you can't do it. Or like you sit on the edge of the bathtub talkin' to him when he's shavin' in his underwear.

CATHERINE: When'd I do that?

BEATRICE: I seen you in there this morning.

CATHERINE: Oh . . . well, I wanted to tell him something and I—

BEATRICE: I know, honey. But if you act like a baby and he be treatin' you like a baby. Like when he comes home sometimes you throw yourself at him like when you was twelve years old.

CATHERINE: Well I like to see him and I'm happy so I—

BEATRICE: Look, I'm not tellin' you what to do, honey, but—

CATHERINE: No, you could tell me, B.! Gee, I'm all mixed up. See, I— He looks so sad now and it hurts me.

BEATRICE: Well look, Katie, if it's goin' to hurt you so much you're gonna end up an old maid here.

CATHERINE: No!

BEATRICE: I'm tellin' you, I'm not makin' a joke. I tried to tell you a couple of times in the last year or so. That's why I was so happy you were going to go out and get work, you wouldn't be here so much, you'd be a little more independent. I mean it. It's wonderful for a whole family to love each other, but you're a grown woman and you're in the same house with a grown man. So you'll act different now, heh?

CATHERINE: Yeah, I will. I'll remember.

BEATRICE: Because it ain't only up to him, Katie, you understand? I told him the same thing already.

CATHERINE, *quickly*: What?

BEATRICE: That he should let you go. But, you see, if only I tell him, he thinks I'm just bawlin' him out, or maybe I'm jealous or somethin', you know?

CATHERINE, *astonished*: He said you was jealous?

BEATRICE: No, I'm just sayin' maybe that's what he thinks. *She reaches over to Catherine's hand; with a strained smile*: You think I'm jealous of you, honey?

CATHERINE: No! It's the first I thought of it.

BEATRICE, *with a quiet sad laugh*: Well you should have thought of it before . . . but I'm not. We'll be all right. Just give him to understand; you don't have to fight, you're just— You're a woman, that's all, and you got a nice boy, and now the time came when you said good-by. All right?

CATHERINE, *strangely moved at the prospect*: All right. . . . If I can.

BEATRICE: Honey . . . you gotta.

> *Catherine, sensing now an imperious demand, turns with some fear, with a discovery, to Beatrice. She is at the edge of tears, as though a familiar world had shattered.*

CATHERINE: Okay.

> *Lights out on them and up on Alfieri, seated behind his desk.*

ALFIERI: It was at this time that he first came to me. I had represented his father in an accident case some years before, and I was acquainted with the family in a casual way. I remember him now as he walked through my doorway—

Enter Eddie down right ramp.

His eyes were like tunnels; my first thought was that he had committed a crime. *Eddie sits beside the desk, cap in hand, looking out.*

But soon I saw it was only a passion that had moved into his body, like a stranger. *Alfieri pauses, looks down at his desk, then to Eddie as though he were continuing a conversation with him.* I don't quite understand what I can do for you. Is there a question of law somewhere?

EDDIE: That's what I want to ask you.

ALFIERI: Because there's nothing illegal about a girl falling in love with an immigrant.

EDDIE: Yeah, but what about it if the only reason for it is to get his papers?

ALFIERI: First of all you don't know that.

EDDIE: I see it in his eyes; he's laughin' at her and he's laughin' at me.

ALFIERI: Eddie, I'm a lawyer. I can only deal in what's provable. You understand that, don't you? Can you prove that?

EDDIE: *I know what's in his mind, Mr. Alfieri!*

ALFIERI: Eddie, even if you could prove that—

EDDIE: Listen . . . will you listen to me a minute? My father always said you was a smart man. I want you to listen to me.

ALFIERI: I'm only a lawyer, Eddie.

EDDIE: Will you listen a minute? I'm talkin' about the law. Lemme just bring out what I mean. A man, which he comes into the country illegal, don't it stand to reason he's gonna take every penny and put it in the sock? Because they don't know from one day to another, right?

ALFIERI: All right.

EDDIE: He's spendin'. Records he buys now. Shoes. Jackets. Y'understand me? This guy ain't worried. This guy is *here*. So it must be that he's got it all laid out in his mind already—he's stayin'. Right?

ALFIERI: Well? What about it?

EDDIE: All right. *He glances at Alfieri, then down to the floor.* I'm talking to you confidential, ain't I?

ALFIERI: Certainly.

EDDIE: I mean it don't go no place but here. Because I don't like to say this about anybody. Even my wife I didn't exactly say this.

ALFIERI: What is it?

EDDIE *takes a breath and glances briefly over each shoulder*: The guy ain't right, Mr. Alfieri.

ALFIERI: What do you mean?

EDDIE: I mean he ain't right.

ALFIERI: I don't get you.

EDDIE *shifts to another position in the chair*: Dja ever get a look at him?

ALFIERI: Not that I know of, no.

EDDIE: He's a blond guy. Like . . . platinum. You know what I mean?

ALFIERI: No.

EDDIE: I mean if you close the paper fast—you could blow him over.

ALFIERI: Well that doesn't mean—

EDDIE: Wait a minute, I'm tellin' you sump'm. He sings, see. Which is—I mean it's all right, but sometimes he hits a note, see. I turn around. I mean—high. You know what I mean?

ALFIERI: Well, that's a tenor.

EDDIE: I know a tenor, Mr. Alfieri. This ain't no tenor. I mean if you came in the house and you didn't know who was singin', you wouldn't be lookin' for him you be lookin' for her.

ALFIERI: Yes, but that's not—

EDDIE: I'm tellin' you sump'm, wait a minute. Please, Mr. Alfieri. I'm tryin' to bring out my thoughts here. Couple of nights ago my niece brings out a dress which it's too small for her, because she shot up like a light this last year. He takes the dress, lays it on the table, he cuts it up; one-two-three, he makes a new dress. I mean he looked so sweet there, like an angel—you could kiss him he was so sweet.

ALFIERI: Now look, Eddie—

EDDIE: Mr. Alfieri, they're laughin' at him on the piers. I'm ashamed. Paper Doll they call him. Blondie now. His brother thinks it's because he's got a sense of humor, see—which he's got—but that ain't what they're laughin'. Which they're not goin' to come out with it because they know he's my relative, which they have to see me if they make a crack, y'know? But I know what they're laughin' at, and when I think of that guy layin' his hands on her I could—I mean it's eatin' me out, Mr. Alfieri, because I struggled for that girl. And now he comes in my house and—

ALFIERI: Eddie, look—I have my own children. I understand you. But the law is very specific. The law does not . . .

EDDIE, *with a fuller flow of indignation*: You mean to tell me that there's no law that a guy which he ain't right can go to work and marry a girl and—?

ALFIERI: You have no recourse in the law, Eddie.

EDDIE: Yeah, but if he ain't right, Mr. Alfieri, you mean to tell me—

ALFIERI: There is nothing you can do, Eddie, believe me.

EDDIE: Nothin'.

ALFIERI: Nothing at all. There's only one legal question here.

EDDIE: What?

ALFIERI: The manner in which they entered the country. But I don't think you want to do anything about that, do you?

EDDIE: You mean—?

ALFIERI: Well, they entered illegally.

EDDIE: Oh, Jesus, no, I wouldn't do nothin' about that, I mean—

ALFIERI: All right, then, let me talk now, eh?

EDDIE: Mr. Alfieri, I can't believe what you tell me. I mean there must be some kinda law which—

ALFIERI: Eddie, I want you to listen to me. *Pause.* You know, sometimes God mixes up the people. We all love somebody, the wife, the kids— every man's got somebody that he loves, heh? But sometimes . . . there's too much. You know? There's too much, and it goes where it mustn't. A man works hard, he brings up a child, sometimes it's a niece, sometimes even a daughter, and he never realizes it, but through the years—there is too much love for the daughter, there is too much love for the niece. Do you understand what I'm saying to you?

EDDIE, *sardonically*: What do you mean, I shouldn't look out for her good?

ALFIERI: Yes, but these things have to end, Eddie, that's all. The child has to grow up and go away, and the man has to learn to forget. Because after all, Eddie—what other way can it end? *Pause.* Let her go. That's my advice. You did your job, now it's her life; wish her luck, and let her go. *Pause.* Will you do that? Because there's no law, Eddie; make up your mind to it; the law is not interested in this.

EDDIE: You mean to tell me, even if he's a punk? If he's—

ALFIERI: There's nothing you can do.

   Eddie stands.

EDDIE: Well, all right, thanks. Thanks very much.

ALFIERI: What are you going to do?

EDDIE, *with a helpless but ironic gesture*: What can I do? I'm a patsy, what can a patsy do? I worked like a dog twenty years so a punk could have her, so that's what I done. I mean, in the worst times, in the worst, when there wasn't a ship comin' in the harbor, I didn't stand around lookin' for relief—I hustled. When there was empty piers in Brooklyn I went to Hoboken, Staten Island, the West Side, Jersey, all over—because I made a promise. I took out of my own mouth to give to her. I took out of my wife's mouth. I walked hungry plenty days in this city! *It begins to break through.* And now I gotta sit in my own house and look at a son-of-a-bitch punk like that—which he came out of nowhere! I give him my house to sleep! I take the blankets off my bed for him, and he takes and puts his dirty filthy hands on her like a goddam thief!

ALFIERI, *rising*: But, Eddie, she's a woman now.

EDDIE: He's stealing from me!

ALFIERI: She wants to get married, Eddie. She can't marry you, can she?

EDDIE, *furiously*: What're you talkin' about, marry me! I don't know what the hell you're talkin' about!

   Pause.

ALFIERI: I gave you my advice, Eddie. That's it.

   Eddie gathers himself. A pause.

EDDIE: Well, thanks. Thanks very much. It just—it's breakin' my heart, y'know. I—

ALFIERI: I understand. Put it out of your mind. Can you do that?

EDDIE: I'm— *He feels the threat of sobs, and with a helpless wave.* I'll see you around. *He goes out up the right ramp.*

ALFIERI *sits on desk*: There are times when you want to spread an alarm, but nothing has happened. I knew, I knew then and there—I could have finished the whole story that afternoon. It wasn't as though there was a mystery to unravel. I could see every step coming, step after step, like a dark figure walking down a hall toward a certain door. I knew where he was heading for, I knew where he was going to end. And I sat here many afternoons asking myself why, being an intelligent man, I was so powerless to stop it. I even went to a certain old lady in the neighborhood, a very wise old woman, and I told her, and she only nodded, and said, "Pray for him . . ." And so I—waited here.

As lights go out on Alfieri, they rise in the apartment where all are finishing dinner. Beatrice and Catherine are clearing the table.

CATHERINE: You know where they went?

BEATRICE: Where?

CATHERINE: They went to Africa once. On a fishing boat.

Eddie glances at her.

It's true, Eddie.

Beatrice exits into the kitchen with dishes.

EDDIE: I didn't say nothin'. *He goes to his rocker, picks up a newspaper.*

CATHERINE: And I was never even in Staten Island.

EDDIE, *sitting with the paper*: You didn't miss nothin'. *Pause. Catherine takes dishes out.* How long that take you, Marco—to get to Africa?

MARCO, *rising*: Oh . . . two days. We go all over.

RODOLPHO, *rising*: Once we went to Yugoslavia.

EDDIE, *to Marco*: They pay all right on them boats?

Beatrice enters. She and Rodolpho stack the remaining dishes.

MARCO: If they catch fish they pay all right. *Sits on a stool.*

RODOLPHO: They're family boats, though. And nobody in our family owned one. So we only worked when one of the families was sick.

BEATRICE: Y'know, Marco, what I don't understand—there's an ocean full of fish and yiz are all starvin'.

EDDIE: They gotta have boats, nets, you need money.

Catherine enters.

BEATRICE: Yeah, but couldn't they like fish from the beach? You see them down Coney Island—

MARCO: Sardines.

EDDIE: Sure. *Laughing*: How you gonna catch sardines on a hook?

BEATRICE: Oh, I didn't know they're sardines. *To Catherine*: They're sardines!

CATHERINE: Yeah, they follow them all over the ocean, Africa, Yugoslavia . . . *She sits and begins to look through a movie magazine. Rodolpho joins her.*

BEATRICE, *to Eddie*: It's funny, y'know. You never think of it, that sardines are swimming in the ocean! *She exits to kitchen with dishes.*

CATHERINE: I know. It's like oranges and lemons on a tree. *To Eddie*: I mean you ever think of oranges and lemons on a tree?

EDDIE: Yeah, I know. It's funny. *To Marco*: I heard that they paint the oranges to make them look orange.

Beatrice enters.

MARCO—*he has been reading a letter*: Paint?

EDDIE: Yeah, I heard that they grow like green.

MARCO: No, in Italy the oranges are orange.

RODOLPHO: Lemons are green.

EDDIE, *resenting his instruction*: I know lemons are green, for Christ's sake, you see them in the store they're green sometimes. I said oranges they paint, I didn't say nothin' about lemons.

BEATRICE, *sitting; diverting their attention*: Your wife is gettin' the money all right, Marco?

MARCO: Oh, yes. She bought medicine for my boy.

BEATRICE: That's wonderful. You feel better, heh?

MARCO: Oh, yes! But I'm lonesome.

BEATRICE: I just hope you ain't gonna do like some of them around here. They're here twenty-five years, some men, and they didn't get enough together to go back twice.

MARCO: Oh, I know. We have many families in our town, the children never saw the father. But I will go home. Three, four years, I think.

BEATRICE: Maybe you should keep more here. Because maybe she thinks it comes so easy you'll never get ahead of yourself.

MARCO: Oh, no, she saves. I send everything. My wife is very lonesome. *He smiles shyly.*

BEATRICE: She must be nice. She pretty? I bet, heh?

MARCO, *blushing*: No, but she understand everything.

RODOLPHO: Oh, he's got a clever wife!

EDDIE: I betcha there's plenty surprises sometimes when those guys get back there, heh?

MARCO: Surprises?

EDDIE, *laughing*: I mean, you know—they count the kids and there's a couple extra than when they left?

MARCO: No—no . . . The women wait, Eddie. Most. Most. Very few surprises.

RODOLPHO: It's more strict in our town. *Eddie looks at him now.* It's not so free.

EDDIE *rises, paces up and down*: It ain't so free here either, Rodolpho, like you think. I seen greenhorns sometimes get in trouble that way—they think just because a girl don't go around with a shawl over her head that she ain't strict, y'know? Girl don't have to wear black dress to be strict. Know what I mean?

RODOLPHO: Well, I always have respect—

EDDIE: I know, but in your town you wouldn't just drag off some girl without permission, I mean. *He turns.* You know what I mean, Marco? It ain't that much different here.

MARCO, *cautiously*: Yes.

BEATRICE: Well, he didn't exactly drag her off though, Eddie.

EDDIE: I know, but I seen some of them get the wrong idea sometimes. *To Rodolpho*: I mean it might be a little more free here but it's just as strict.

RODOLPHO: I have respect for her, Eddie. I do anything wrong?

EDDIE: Look, kid, I ain't her father, I'm only her uncle—

BEATRICE: Well then, be an uncle then. *Eddie looks at her, aware of her criticizing force.* I mean.

MARCO: No, Beatrice, if he does wrong you must tell him. *To Eddie*: What does he do wrong?

EDDIE: Well, Marco, till he came here she was never out on the street twelve o'clock at night.

MARCO, *to Rodolpho*: You come home early now.

BEATRICE, *to Catherine*: Well, you said the movie ended late, didn't you?

CATHERINE: Yeah.

BEATRICE: Well, tell him, honey. *To Eddie*: The movie ended late.

EDDIE: Look, B., I'm just sayin'—he thinks she always stayed out like that.

MARCO: You come home early now, Rodolpho.

RODOLPHO, *embarrassed*: All right, sure. But I can't stay in the house all the time, Eddie.

EDDIE: Look, kid, I'm not only talkin' about her. The more you run around like that the more chance you're takin'. *To Beatrice*: I mean suppose he gets hit by a car or something. *To Marco*: Where's his papers, who is he? Know what I mean?

BEATRICE: Yeah, but who is he in the daytime, though? It's the same chance in the daytime.

EDDIE, *holding back a voice full of anger*: Yeah, but he don't have to go lookin' for it, Beatrice. If he's here to work, then he should work; if he's here for a good time then he could fool around! *To Marco*: But I understood, Marco, that you was both comin' to make a livin' for your family. You understand me, don't you, Marco? *He goes to his rocker.*

MARCO: I beg your pardon, Eddie.

EDDIE: I mean, that's what I understood in the first place, see.

MARCO: Yes. That's why we came.

EDDIE *sits on his rocker*: Well, that's all I'm askin'.

> *Eddie reads his paper. There is a pause, an awkwardness. Now Catherine gets up and puts a record on the phonograph—"Paper Doll."*

CATHERINE, *flushed with revolt*: You wanna dance, Rodolpho?

> *Eddie freezes.*

RODOLPHO, *in deference to Eddie*: No, I—I'm tired.

BEATRICE: Go ahead, dance, Rodolpho.

CATHERINE: Ah, come on. They got a beautiful quartet, these guys. Come.

> *She has taken his hand and he stiffly rises, feeling Eddie's eyes on his back, and they dance.*

EDDIE, *to Catherine*: What's that, a new record?

CATHERINE: It's the same one. We bought it the other day.

BEATRICE, *to Eddie*: They only bought three records. *She watches them dance; Eddie turns his head away. Marco just sits there, waiting. Now*

Beatrice turns to Eddie. Must be nice to go all over in one of them fishin' boats. I would like that myself. See all them other countries?

EDDIE: Yeah.

BEATRICE, *to Marco:* But the women don't go along, I bet.

MARCO: No, not on the boats. Hard work.

BEATRICE: What're you got, a regular kitchen and everything?

MARCO: Yes, we eat very good on the boats—especially when Rodolpho comes along; everybody gets fat.

BEATRICE: Oh, he cooks?

MARCO: Sure, very good cook. Rice, pasta, fish, everything.

> *Eddie lowers his paper.*

EDDIE: He's a cook, too! *Looking at Rodolpho:* He sings, he cooks . . .

> *Rodolpho smiles thankfully.*

BEATRICE: Well it's good, he could always make a living.

EDDIE: It's wonderful. He sings, he cooks, he could make dresses . . .

CATHERINE: They get some high pay, them guys. The head chefs in all the big hotels are men. You read about them.

EDDIE: That's what I'm sayin'.

> *Catherine and Rodolpho continue dancing.*

CATHERINE: Yeah, well, I mean.

EDDIE, *to Beatrice:* He's lucky, believe me. *Slight pause. He looks away, then back to Beatrice.* That's why the water front is no place for him. *They stop dancing. Rodolpho turns off phonograph.* I mean like me—I can't cook, I can't sing, I can't make dresses, so I'm on the water front. But if I could cook, if I could sing, if I could make dresses, I wouldn't be on the water front. *He has been unconsciously twisting the newspaper into a tight roll. They are all regarding him now; he senses he is exposing the issue and he is driven on.* I would be someplace else. I would be like in a dress store. *He has bent the rolled paper and it suddenly tears in two. He suddenly gets up and pulls his pants up over his belly and goes to Marco.* What do you say, Marco, we go to the bouts next Saturday night. You never seen a fight, did you?

MARCO, *uneasily:* Only in the moving pictures.

EDDIE, *going to Rodolpho:* I'll treat yiz. What do you say, Danish? You wanna come along? I'll buy the tickets.

RODOLPHO: Sure. I like to go.

CATHERINE *goes to Eddie; nervously happy now*: I'll make some coffee, all right?

EDDIE: Go ahead, make some! Make it nice and strong. *Mystified, she smiles and exits to kitchen. He is weirdly elated, rubbing his fists into his palms. He strides to Marco.* You wait, Marco, you see some real fights here. You ever do any boxing?

MARCO: No, I never.

EDDIE, *to Rodolpho*: Betcha you have done some, heh?

RODOLPHO: No.

EDDIE: Well, come on, I'll teach you.

BEATRICE: What's he got to learn that for?

EDDIE: Ya can't tell, one a these days somebody's liable to step on his foot or sump'm. Come on, Rodolpho, I show you a couple a passes. *He stands below table.*

BEATRICE: Go ahead, Rodolpho. He's a good boxer, he could teach you.

RODOLPHO, *embarrassed*: Well, I don't know how to— *He moves down to Eddie.*

EDDIE: Just put your hands up. Like this, see? That's right. That's very good, keep your left up, because you lead with the left, see, like this. *He gently moves his left into Rodolpho's face.* See? Now what you gotta do is you gotta block me, so when I come in like that you— *Rodolpho parries his left.* Hey, that's very good! *Rodolpho laughs.* All right, now come into me. Come on.

RODOLPHO: I don't want to hit you, Eddie.

EDDIE: Don't pity me, come on. Throw it, I'll show you how to block it. *Rodolpho jabs at him, laughing. The others join.* 'At's it. Come on again. For the jaw right here. *Rodolpho jabs with more assurance.* Very good!

BEATRICE, *to Marco*: He's very good!

Eddie crosses directly upstage of Rodolpho.

EDDIE: Sure, he's great! Come on, kid, put sump'm behind it, you can't hurt me. *Rodolpho, more seriously, jabs at Eddie's jaw and grazes it.* Attaboy.

Catherine comes from the kitchen, watches.

Now I'm gonna hit you, so block me, see?

CATHERINE, *with beginning alarm*: What are they doin'?

They are lightly boxing now.

BEATRICE—*she senses only the comradeship in it now*: He's teachin' him; he's very good!

EDDIE: Sure, he's terrific! Look at him go! *Rodolpho lands a blow.* 'At's it! Now, watch out, here I come, Danish! *He feints with his left hand and lands with his right. It mildly staggers Rodolpho. Marco rises.*

CATHERINE, *rushing to Rodolpho*: Eddie!

EDDIE: Why? I didn't hurt him. Did I hurt you, kid? *He rubs the back of his hand across his mouth.*

RODOLPHO: No, no, he didn't hurt me. *To Eddie with a certain gleam and a smile*: I was only surprised.

BEATRICE, *pulling Eddie down into the rocker*: That's enough, Eddie; he did pretty good, though.

EDDIE: Yeah. *Rubbing his fists together*: He could be very good, Marco. I'll teach him again.

Marco nods at him dubiously.

RODOLPHO: Dance, Catherine. Come. *He takes her hand; they go to phonograph and start it. It plays "Paper Doll."*

Rodolpho takes her in his arms. They dance. Eddie in thought sits in his chair, and Marco takes a chair, places it in front of Eddie, and looks down at it. Beatrice and Eddie watch him.

MARCO: Can you lift this chair?

EDDIE: What do you mean?

MARCO: From here. *He gets on one knee with one hand behind his back, and grasps the bottom of one of the chair legs but does not raise it.*

EDDIE: Sure, why not? *He comes to the chair, kneels, grasps the leg, raises the chair one inch, but it leans over to the floor. Gee, that's hard, I never knew that. He tries again, and again fails.* It's on an angle, that's why, heh?

MARCO: Here. *He kneels, grasps, and with strain slowly raises the chair higher and higher, getting to his feet now. Rodolpho and Catherine have stopped dancing as Marco raises the chair over his head.*

Marco is face to face with Eddie, a strained tension gripping his eyes and jaw, his neck stiff, the chair raised like a weapon over Eddie's head—and he transforms what might appear like a glare of warning into a smile of triumph, and Eddie's grin vanishes as he absorbs his look.

CURTAIN

ACT TWO

Light rises on Alfieri at his desk.

ALFIERI: On the twenty-third of that December a case of Scotch whisky slipped from a net while being unloaded—as a case of Scotch whisky is inclined to do on the twenty-third of December on Pier Forty-one. There was no snow, but it was cold, his wife was out shopping. Marco was still at work. The boy had not been hired that day; Catherine told me later that this was the first time they had been alone together in the house.

Light is rising on Catherine in the apartment. Rodolpho is watching as she arranges a paper pattern on cloth spread on the table.

CATHERINE: You hungry?

RODOLPHO: Not for anything to eat. *Pause.* I have nearly three hundred dollars. Catherine?

CATHERINE: I heard you.

RODOLPHO: You don't like to talk about it any more?

CATHERINE: Sure, I don't mind talkin' about it.

RODOLPHO: What worries you, Catherine?

CATHERINE: I been wantin' to ask you about something. Could I?

RODOLPHO: All the answers are in my eyes, Catherine. But you don't look in my eyes lately. You're full of secrets. *She looks at him. She seems withdrawn.* What is the question?

CATHERINE: Suppose I wanted to live in Italy.

RODOLPHO, *smiling at the incongruity*: You going to marry somebody rich?

CATHERINE: No, I mean live there—you and me.

RODOLPHO, *his smile vanishing*: When?

CATHERINE: Well . . . when we get married.

RODOLPHO, *astonished*: You want to be an Italian?

CATHERINE: No, but I could live there without being Italian. Americans live there.

RODOLPHO: Forever?

CATHERINE: Yeah.

RODOLPHO *crosses to rocker*: You're fooling.

CATHERINE: No, I mean it.

RODOLPHO: Where do you get such an idea?

CATHERINE: Well, you're always saying it's so beautiful there, with the mountains and the ocean and all the—

RODOLPHO: You're fooling me.

CATHERINE: I mean it.

RODOLPHO *goes to her slowly*: Catherine, if I ever brought you home with no money, no business, nothing, they would call the priest and the doctor and they would say Rodolpho is crazy.

CATHERINE: I know, but I think we would be happier there.

RODOLPHO: Happier! What would you eat? You can't cook the view!

CATHERINE: Maybe you could be a singer, like in Rome or—

RODOLPHO: Rome! Rome is full of singers.

CATHERINE: Well, I could work then.

RODOLPHO: Where?

CATHERINE: God, there must be jobs somewhere!

RODOLPHO: There's nothing! Nothing, nothing, nothing. Now tell me what you're talking about. How can I bring you from a rich country to suffer in a poor country? What are you talking about? *She searches for words.* I would be a criminal stealing your face. In two years you would have an old, hungry face. When my brother's babies cry they give them water, water that boiled a bone. Don't you believe that?

CATHERINE, *quietly*: I'm afraid of Eddie here.

    Slight pause.

RODOLPHO *steps closer to her*: We wouldn't live here. Once I am a citizen I could work anywhere and I would find better jobs and we would have a house, Catherine. If I were not afraid to be arrested I would start to be something wonderful here!

CATHERINE, *steeling herself*: Tell me something. I mean just tell me, Rodolpho—would you still want to do it if it turned out we had to go live in Italy? I mean just if it turned out that way.

RODOLPHO: This is your question or his question?

CATHERINE: I would like to know, Rodolpho. I mean it.

RODOLPHO: To go there with nothing.

CATHERINE: Yeah.

RODOLPHO: No. *She looks at him wide-eyed.* No.

CATHERINE: You wouldn't?

RODOLPHO: No; I will not marry you to live in Italy. I want you to be my wife, and I want to be a citizen. Tell him that, or I will. Yes. *He moves about angrily.* And tell him also, and tell yourself, please, that I am not a beggar, and you are not a horse, a gift, a favor for a poor immigrant.

CATHERINE: Well, don't get mad!

RODOLPHO: I am furious! *Goes to her.* Do you think I am so desperate? My brother is desperate, not me. You think I would carry on my back the rest of my life a woman I didn't love just to be an American? It's so wonderful? You think we have no tall buildings in Italy? Electric lights? No wide streets? No flags? No automobiles? Only work we don't have. I want to be an American so I can work, that is the only wonder here—work! How can you insult me, Catherine?

CATHERINE: I didn't mean that—

RODOLPHO: My heart dies to look at you. Why are you so afraid of him?

CATHERINE, *near tears*: I don't know!

RODOLPHO: Do you trust me, Catherine? You?

CATHERINE: It's only that I— He was good to me, Rodolpho. You don't know him; he was always the sweetest guy to me. Good. He razzes me all the time but he don't mean it. I know. I would—just feel ashamed if I made him sad. 'Cause I always dreamt that when I got married he would be happy at the wedding, and laughin'—and now he's—mad all the time and nasty— *She is weeping.* Tell him you'd live in Italy—just tell him, and maybe he would start to trust you a little, see? Because I want him to be happy; I mean—I like him, Rodolpho—and I can't stand it!

RODOLPHO: Oh, Catherine—oh, little girl.

CATHERINE: I love you, Rodolpho, I love you.

RODOLPHO: Then why are you afraid? That he'll spank you?

CATHERINE: Don't, don't laugh at me! I've been here all my life. . . . Every day I saw him when he left in the morning and when he came home at night. You think it's so easy to turn around and say to a man he's nothin' to you no more?

RODOLPHO: I know, but—

CATHERINE: You don't know; nobody knows! I'm not a baby, I know a lot more than people think I know. Beatrice says to be a woman, but—

RODOLPHO: Yes.

CATHERINE: Then why don't she be a woman? If I was a wife I would make a man happy instead of goin' at him all the time. I can tell a block away when he's blue in his mind and just wants to talk to somebody quiet and nice. . . . I can tell when he's hungry or wants a beer before he even says anything. I know when his feet hurt him, I mean I *know* him and now I'm supposed to turn around and make a stranger out of him? I don't know why I have to do that, I mean.

RODOLPHO: Catherine. If I take in my hands a little bird. And she grows and wishes to fly. But I will not let her out of my hands because I love her so much, is that right for me to do? I don't say you must hate him; but anyway you must go, mustn't you? Catherine?

CATHERINE, *softly*: Hold me.

RODOLPHO, *clasping her to him*: Oh, my little girl.

CATHERINE: Teach me. *She is weeping*. I don't know anything, teach me, Rodolpho, hold me.

RODOLPHO: There's nobody here now. Come inside. Come. *He is leading her toward the bedrooms*. And don't cry any more.

> *Light rises on the street. In a moment Eddie appears. He is unsteady, drunk. He mounts the stairs. He enters the apartment, looks around, takes out a bottle from one pocket, puts it on the table. Then another bottle from another pocket, and a third from an inside pocket. He sees the pattern and cloth, goes over to it and touches it, and turns toward upstage.*

EDDIE: Beatrice? *He goes to the open kitchen door and looks in*. Beatrice? Beatrice?

> *Catherine enters from bedroom; under his gaze she adjusts her dress.*

CATHERINE: You got home early.

EDDIE: Knocked off for Christmas early. *Indicating the pattern*: Rodolpho makin' you a dress?

CATHERINE: No. I'm makin' a blouse.

Rodolpho appears in the bedroom doorway. Eddie sees him and his arm jerks slightly in shock. Rodolpho nods to him testingly.

RODOLPHO: Beatrice went to buy presents for her mother.

Pause.

EDDIE: Pack it up. Go ahead. Get your stuff and get outa here. *Catherine instantly turns and walks toward the bedroom, and Eddie grabs her arm.* Where you goin'?

CATHERINE, *trembling with fright:* I think I have to get out of here, Eddie.

EDDIE: No, you ain't goin' nowhere, he's the one.

CATHERINE: I think I can't stay here no more. *She frees her arm, steps back toward the bedroom.* I'm sorry, Eddie. *She sees the tears in his eyes.* Well, don't cry. I'll be around the neighborhood; I'll see you. I just can't stay here no more. You know I can't. *Her sobs of pity and love for him break her composure.* Don't you know I can't? You know that, don't you? *She goes to him.* Wish me luck. *She clasps her hands prayerfully.* Oh, Eddie, don't be like that!

EDDIE: You ain't goin' nowheres.

CATHERINE: Eddie, I'm not gonna be a baby any more! You—

He reaches out suddenly, draws her to him, and as she strives to free herself he kisses her on the mouth.

RODOLPHO: Don't! *He pulls on Eddie's arm.* Stop that! Have respect for her!

EDDIE, *spun round by Rodolpho:* You want something?

RODOLPHO: Yes! She'll be my wife. That is what I want. My wife!

EDDIE: But what're you gonna be?

RODOLPHO: I show you what I be!

CATHERINE: Wait outside; don't argue with him!

EDDIE: Come on, show me! What're you gonna be? Show me!

RODOLPHO, *with tears of rage:* Don't say that to me!

Rodolpho flies at him in attack. Eddie pins his arms, laughing, and suddenly kisses him.

CATHERINE: Eddie! Let go, ya hear me! I'll kill you! Leggo of him!

She tears at Eddie's face and Eddie releases Rodolpho. Eddie stands there with tears rolling down his face as he laughs mockingly at Rodolpho. She is staring at him in horror. Rodolpho is rigid. They are like animals that have torn at one another and broken up without a decision, each waiting for the other's mood.

EDDIE, *to Catherine*: You see? *To Rodolpho*: I give you till tomorrow, kid. Get outa here. Alone. You hear me? Alone.

CATHERINE: I'm going with him, Eddie. *She starts toward Rodolpho.*

EDDIE, *indicating Rodolpho with his head*: Not with that. *She halts, frightened. He sits, still panting for breath, and they watch him helplessly as he leans toward them over the table.* Don't make me do nuttin', Catherine. Watch your step, submarine. By rights they oughta throw you back in the water. But I got pity for you. *He moves unsteadily toward the door, always facing Rodolpho.* Just get outa here and don't lay another hand on her unless you wanna go out feet first. *He goes out of the apartment.*

The lights go down, as they rise on Alfieri.

ALFIERI: On December twenty-seventh I saw him next. I normally go home well before six, but that day I sat around looking out my window at the bay, and when I saw him walking through my doorway, I knew why I had waited. And if I seem to tell this like a dream, it was that way. Several moments arrived in the course of the two talks we had when it occurred to me how—almost transfixed I had come to feel. I had lost my strength somewhere. *Eddie enters, removing his cap, sits in the chair, looks thoughtfully out.* I looked in his eyes more than I listened—in fact, I can hardly remember the conversation. But I will never forget how dark the room became when he looked at me; his eyes were like tunnels. I kept wanting to call the police, but nothing had happened. Nothing at all had really happened. *He breaks off and looks down at the desk. Then he turns to Eddie.* So in other words, he won't leave?

EDDIE: My wife is talkin' about renting a room upstairs for them. An old lady on the top floor is got an empty room.

ALFIERI: What does Marco say?

EDDIE: He just sits there. Marco don't say much.

ALFIERI: I guess they didn't tell him, heh? What happened?

EDDIE: I don't know; Marco don't say much.

ALFIERI: What does your wife say?

EDDIE, *unwilling to pursue this*: Nobody's talkin' much in the house. So what about that?

ALFIERI: But you didn't prove anything about him. It sounds like he just wasn't strong enough to break your grip.

EDDIE: I'm tellin' you I know—he ain't right. Somebody that don't want it can break it. Even a mouse, if you catch a teeny mouse and you hold it in your hand, that mouse can give you the right kind of fight. He didn't give me the right kind of fight, I know it, Mr. Alfieri, the guy ain't right.

ALFIERI: What did you do that for, Eddie?

EDDIE: To show her what he is! So she would see, once and for all! Her mother'll turn over in the grave! *He gathers himself almost peremptorily.* So what do I gotta do now? Tell me what to do.

ALFIERI: She actually said she's marrying him?

EDDIE: She told me, yeah. So what do I do?

Slight pause.

ALFIERI: This is my last word, Eddie, take it or not, that's your business. Morally and legally you have no rights, you cannot stop it; she is a free agent.

EDDIE, *angering*: Didn't you hear what I told you?

ALFIERI, *with a tougher tone*: I heard what you told me, and I'm telling you what the answer is. I'm not only telling you now, I'm warning you— the law is nature. The law is only a word for what has a right to happen. When the law is wrong it's because it's unnatural, but in this case it is natural and a river will drown you if you buck it now. Let her go. And bless her. *A phone booth begins to glow on the opposite side of the stage; a faint, lonely blue. Eddie stands up, jaws clenched.* Somebody had to come for her, Eddie, sooner or later. *Eddie starts turning to go and Alfieri rises with new anxiety.* You won't have a friend in the world, Eddie! Even those who understand will turn against you, even the ones who feel the same will despise you! *Eddie moves off.* Put it out of your mind! Eddie! *He follows into the darkness, calling desperately.*

> *Eddie is gone. The phone is glowing in light now. Light is out on Alfieri. Eddie has at the same time appeared beside the phone.*

EDDIE: Give me the number of the Immigration Bureau. Thanks. *He dials.* I want to report something. Illegal immigrants. Two of them. That's right. Four-forty-one Saxon Street, Brooklyn, yeah. Ground floor. Heh? *With greater difficulty*: I'm just around the neighborhood, that's all. Heh?

> *Evidently he is being questioned further, and he slowly hangs up. He leaves the phone just as Louis and Mike come down the street.*

LOUIS: Go bowlin', Eddie?

EDDIE: No, I'm due home.

LOUIS: Well, take it easy.

EDDIE: I'll see yiz.

> *They leave him, exiting right, and he watches them go. He glances about, then goes up into the house. The lights go on in the apartment. Beatrice is taking down Christmas decorations and packing them in a box.*

EDDIE: Where is everybody? *Beatrice does not answer.* I says where is everybody?

BEATRICE, *looking up at him, wearied with it, and concealing a fear of him*: I decided to move them upstairs with Mrs. Dondero.

EDDIE: Oh, they're all moved up there already?

BEATRICE: Yeah.

EDDIE: Where's Catherine? She up there?

BEATRICE: Only to bring pillow cases.

EDDIE: She ain't movin' in with them.

BEATRICE: Look, I'm sick and tired of it. I'm sick and tired of it!

EDDIE: All right, all right, take it easy.

BEATRICE: I don't wanna hear no more about it, you understand? Nothin'!

EDDIE: What're you blowin' off about? Who brought them in here?

BEATRICE: All right, I'm sorry; I wish I'd a drop dead before I told them to come. In the ground I wish I was.

EDDIE: Don't drop dead, just keep in mind who brought them in here, that's all. *He moves about restlessly.* I mean I got a couple of rights here. *He moves, wanting to beat down her evident disapproval of him.* This is my house here not their house.

BEATRICE: What do you want from me? They're moved out; what do you want now?

EDDIE: I want my respect!

BEATRICE: So I moved them out, what more do you want? You got your house now, you got your respect.

EDDIE—*he moves about biting his lip*: I don't like the way you talk to me, Beatrice.

BEATRICE: I'm just tellin' you I done what you want!

EDDIE: I don't like it! The way you talk to me and the way you look at me. This is my house. And she is my niece and I'm responsible for her.

BEATRICE: So that's why you done that to him?

EDDIE: I done what to him?

BEATRICE: What you done to him in front of her; you know what I'm talkin' about. She goes around shakin' all the time, she can't go to sleep! That's what you call responsible for her?

EDDIE, *quietly*: The guy ain't right, Beatrice. *She is silent.* Did you hear what I said?

BEATRICE: Look, I'm finished with it. That's all. *She resumes her work.*

EDDIE, *helping her to pack the tinsel*: I'm gonna have it out with you one of these days, Beatrice.

BEATRICE: Nothin' to have out with me, it's all settled. Now we gonna be like it never happened, that's all.

EDDIE: I want my respect, Beatrice, and you know what I'm talkin' about.

BEATRICE: What?

Pause.

EDDIE—*finally his resolution hardens*: What I feel like doin' in the bed and what I don't feel like doin'. I don't want no—

BEATRICE: When'd I say anything about that?

EDDIE: You said, you said, I ain't deaf. I don't want no more conversations about that, Beatrice. I do what I feel like doin' or what I don't feel like doin'.

BEATRICE: Okay.

Pause.

EDDIE: You used to be different, Beatrice. You had a whole different way.

BEATRICE: *I'm* no different.

EDDIE: You didn't used to jump me all the time about everything. The last year or two I come in the house I don't know what's gonna hit me. It's a shootin' gallery in here and I'm the pigeon.

BEATRICE: Okay, okay.

EDDIE: Don't tell me okay, okay, I'm tellin' you the truth. A wife is supposed to believe the husband. If I tell you that guy ain't right don't tell me he is right.

BEATRICE: But how do you know?

EDDIE: Because I know. I don't go around makin' accusations. He give me the heeby-jeebies the first minute I seen him. And I don't like you sayin' I don't want her marryin' anybody. I broke my back payin' her stenography lessons so she could go out and meet a better class of people. Would I do that if I didn't want her to get married? Sometimes you talk like I was a crazy man or sump'm.

BEATRICE: But she likes him.

EDDIE: Beatrice, she's a baby, how is she gonna know what she likes?

BEATRICE: Well, you kept her a baby, you wouldn't let her go out. I told you a hundred times.

Pause.

EDDIE: All right. Let her go out, then.

BEATRICE: She don't wanna go out now. It's too late, Eddie.

Pause.

EDDIE: Suppose I told her to go out. Suppose I—

BEATRICE: They're going to get married next week, Eddie.

EDDIE—*his head jerks around to her*: She said that?

BEATRICE: Eddie, if you want my advice, go to her and tell her good luck. I think maybe now that you had it out you learned better.

EDDIE: What's the hurry next week?

BEATRICE: Well, she's been worried about him bein' picked up; this way he could start to be a citizen. She loves him, Eddie. *He gets up, moves about uneasily, restlessly.* Why don't you give her a good word? Because I still think she would like you to be a friend, y'know? *He is standing, looking at the floor.* I mean like if you told her you'd go to the wedding.

EDDIE: She asked you that?

BEATRICE: I know she would like it. I'd like to make a party here for her. I mean there oughta be some kinda send-off. Heh? I mean she'll have trouble enough in her life, let's start it off happy. What do you say? 'Cause in her heart she still loves you, Eddie. I know it. *He presses his fingers against his eyes.* What're you, cryin'? *She goes to him, holds his face.* Go . . . whyn't you go tell her you're sorry? *Catherine is seen on the upper landing of the stairway, and they hear her descending.* There . . . she's comin' down. Come on, shake hands with her.

EDDIE, *moving with suppressed suddenness*: No, I can't, I can't talk to her.

BEATRICE: Eddie, give her a break; a wedding should be happy!

EDDIE: I'm goin', I'm goin' for a walk.

He goes upstage for his jacket. Catherine enters and starts for the bedroom door.

BEATRICE: Katie? . . . Eddie, don't go, wait a minute. *She embraces Eddie's arm with warmth.* Ask him, Katie. Come on, honey.

EDDIE: It's all right, I'm— *He starts to go and she holds him.*

BEATRICE: No, she wants to ask you. Come on, Katie, ask him. We'll have a party! What're we gonna do, hate each other? Come on!

CATHERINE: I'm gonna get married, Eddie. So if you wanna come, the wedding be on Saturday.

Pause.

EDDIE: Okay. I only wanted the best for you, Katie. I hope you know that.

CATHERINE: Okay. *She starts out again.*

EDDIE: Catherine? *She turns to him.* I was just tellin' Beatrice . . . if you wanna go out, like . . . I mean I realize maybe I kept you home too much. Because he's the first guy you ever knew, y'know? I mean now that you got a job, you might meet some fellas, and you get a different idea, y'know? I mean you could always come back to him, you're still only kids, the both of yiz. What's the hurry? Maybe you'll get around a little bit, you grow up a little more, maybe you'll see different in a couple of months. I mean you be surprised, it don't have to be him.

CATHERINE: No, we made it up already.

EDDIE, *with increasing anxiety*: Katie, wait a minute.

CATHERINE: No, I made up my mind.

EDDIE: But you never knew no other fella, Katie! How could you make up your mind?

CATHERINE: 'Cause I did. I don't want nobody else.

EDDIE: But, Katie, suppose he gets picked up.

CATHERINE: That's why we gonna do it right away. Soon as we finish the wedding he's goin' right over and start to be a citizen. I made up my mind, Eddie. I'm sorry. *To Beatrice*: Could I take two more pillow cases for the other guys?

BEATRICE: Sure, go ahead. Only don't let her forget where they came from.

Catherine goes into a bedroom.

EDDIE: She's got other boarders up there?

BEATRICE: Yeah, there's two guys that just came over.

EDDIE: What do you mean, came over?

BEATRICE: From Italy. Lipari the butcher—his nephew. They come from Bari, they just got here yesterday. I didn't even know till Marco and Rodolpho moved up there before. *Catherine enters, going toward exit with two pillow cases.* It'll be nice, they could all talk together.

EDDIE: Catherine! *She halts near the exit door. He takes in Beatrice too.* What're you, got no brains? You put them up there with two other submarines?

CATHERINE: Why?

EDDIE, *in a driving fright and anger*: Why! How do you know they're not trackin' these guys? They'll come up for them and find Marco and Rodolpho! Get them out of the house!

BEATRICE: But they been here so long already—

EDDIE: How do you know what enemies Lipari's got? Which they'd love to stab him in the back?

CATHERINE: Well what'll I do with them?

EDDIE: The neighborhood is full of rooms. Can't you stand to live a couple of blocks away from him? Get them out of the house!

CATHERINE: Well maybe tomorrow night I'll—

EDDIE: Not tomorrow, do it now. Catherine, you never mix yourself with somebody else's family! These guys get picked up, Lipari's liable to blame you or me and we got his whole family on our head. They got a temper, that family.

Two men in overcoats appear outside, start into the house.

CATHERINE: How'm I gonna find a place tonight?

EDDIE: Will you stop arguin' with me and get them out! You think I'm always tryin' to fool you or sump'm? What's the matter with you, don't you believe I could think of your good? Did I ever ask sump'm for myself? You think I got no feelin's? I never told you nothin' in my life that wasn't for your good. Nothin'! And look at the way you talk to me! Like I was an enemy! Like I— *A knock on the door. His head swerves. They all stand motionless. Another knock. Eddie, in a whisper, pointing upstage.* Go up the fire escape, get them out over the back fence.

Catherine stands motionless, uncomprehending.

FIRST OFFICER, *in the hall*: Immigration! Open up in there!

EDDIE: Go, go. Hurry up! *She stands a moment staring at him in a realized horror.* Well, what're you lookin' at!

FIRST OFFICER: Open up!

EDDIE, *calling toward door:* Who's that there?

FIRST OFFICER: Immigration, open up.

> *Eddie turns, looks at Beatrice. She sits. Then he looks at Catherine. With a sob of fury Catherine streaks into a bedroom.*

> *Knock is repeated.*

EDDIE: All right, take it easy, take it easy. *He goes and opens the door. The Officer steps inside.* What's all this?

FIRST OFFICER: Where are they?

> *Second Officer sweeps past and, glancing about, goes into the kitchen.*

EDDIE: Where's who?

FIRST OFFICER: Come on, come on, where are they? *He hurries into the bedrooms.*

EDDIE: Who? We got nobody here. *He looks at Beatrice, who turns her head away. Pugnaciously, furious, he steps toward Beatrice.* What's the matter with *you?*

> *First Officer enters from the bedroom, calls to the kitchen.*

FIRST OFFICER: Dominick?

> *Enter Second Officer from kitchen.*

SECOND OFFICER: Maybe it's a different apartment.

FIRST OFFICER: There's only two more floors up there. I'll take the front, you go up the fire escape. I'll let you in. Watch your step up there.

SECOND OFFICER: Okay, right, Charley. *First Officer goes out apartment door and runs up the stairs.* This is Four-forty-one, isn't it?

EDDIE: That's right.

> *Second Officer goes out into the kitchen.*

> *Eddie turns to Beatrice. She looks at him now and sees his terror.*

BEATRICE, *weakened with fear:* Oh, Jesus, Eddie.

EDDIE: What's the matter with *you?*

BEATRICE, *pressing her palms against her face*: Oh, my God, my God.

EDDIE: What're you, accusin' me?

BEATRICE—*her final thrust is to turn toward him instead of running from him*: My God, what did you do?

> *Many steps on the outer stair draw his attention. We see the First Officer descending, with Marco, behind him Rodolpho, and Catherine and the two strange immigrants, followed by Second Officer. Beatrice hurries to door.*

CATHERINE, *backing down stairs, fighting with First Officer; as they appear on the stairs*: What do yiz want from them? They work, that's all. They're boarders upstairs, they work on the piers.

BEATRICE, *to First Officer*: Ah, Mister, what do you want from them, who do they hurt?

CATHERINE, *pointing to Rodolpho*: They ain't no submarines, he was born in Philadelphia.

FIRST OFFICER: Step aside, lady.

CATHERINE: What do you mean? You can't just come in a house and—

FIRST OFFICER: All right, take it easy. *To Rodolpho*: What street were you born in Philadelphia?

CATHERINE: What do you mean, what street? Could you tell me what street you were born?

FIRST OFFICER: Sure. Four blocks away, One-eleven Union Street. Let's go, fellas.

CATHERINE, *fending him off Rodolpho*: No, you can't! Now, get outa here!

FIRST OFFICER: Look, girlie, if they're all right they'll be out tomorrow. If they're illegal they go back where they came from. If you want, get yourself a lawyer, although I'm tellin' you now you're wasting your money. Let's get them in the car, Dom. *To the men*: Andiamo, andiamo, let's go.

> *The men start, but Marco hangs back.*

BEATRICE, *from doorway*: Who're they hurtin', for God's sake, what do you want from them? They're starvin' over there, what do you want! Marco!

> *Marco suddenly breaks from the group and dashes into the room and faces Eddie; Beatrice and First Officer rush in as Marco spits into Eddie's face.*

Catherine runs into hallway and throws herself into Rodolpho's arms. Eddie, with an enraged cry, lunges for Marco.

EDDIE: Oh, you mother's—!

First Officer quickly intercedes and pushes Eddie from Marco, who stands there accusingly.

FIRST OFFICER, *between them, pushing Eddie from Marco:* Cut it out!

EDDIE, *over the First Officer's shoulder, to Marco:* I'll kill you for that, you son of a bitch!

FIRST OFFICER: Hey! *Shakes him.* Stay in here now, don't come out, don't bother him. You hear me? Don't come out, fella.

For an instant there is silence. Then First Officer turns and takes Marco's arm and then gives a last, informative look at Eddie. As he and Marco are going out into the hall, Eddie erupts.

EDDIE: I don't forget that, Marco! You hear what I'm sayin'?

Out in the hall, First Officer and Marco go down the stairs. Now, in the street, Louis, Mike, and several neighbors including the butcher, Lipari—a stout, intense, middle-aged man— are gathering around the stoop.

Lipari, the butcher, walks over to the two strange men and kisses them. His wife, keening, goes and kisses their hands. Eddie is emerging from the house shouting after Marco. Beatrice is trying to restrain him.

EDDIE: That's the thanks I get? Which I took the blankets off my bed for yiz? You gonna apologize to me, Marco! *Marco!*

FIRST OFFICER, *in the doorway with Marco:* All right, lady, let them go. Get in the car, fellas, it's over there.

Rodolpho is almost carrying the sobbing Catherine off up the street, left.

CATHERINE: He was born in Philadelphia! What do you want from him?

FIRST OFFICER: Step aside, lady, come on now . . .

The Second Officer has moved off with the two strange men. Marco, taking advantage of the First Officer's being occupied with Catherine, suddenly frees himself and points back at Eddie.

MARCO: That one! I accuse that one!

Eddie brushes Beatrice aside and rushes out to the stoop.

FIRST OFFICER, *grabbing him and moving him quickly off up the left street*: Come on!

MARCO, *as he is taken off, pointing back at Eddie*: That one! He killed my children! That one stole the food from my children!

Marco is gone. The crowd has turned to Eddie.

EDDIE, *to Lipari and wife*: He's crazy! I give them the blankets off my bed. Six months I kept them like my own brothers!

Lipari, the butcher, turns and starts up left with his arm around his wife.

EDDIE: Lipari! *He follows Lipari up left.* For Christ's sake, I kept them, I give them the blankets off my bed!

Lipari and wife exit. Eddie turns and starts crossing down right to Louis and Mike.

EDDIE: Louis! *Louis!*

Louis barely turns, then walks off and exits down right with Mike. Only Beatrice is left on the stoop. Catherine now returns, blank-eyed, from offstage and the car. Eddie calls after Louis and Mike.

EDDIE: He's gonna take that back. He's gonna take that back or I'll kill him! You hear me? I'll kill him! I'll kill him! *He exits up street calling.*

There is a pause of darkness before the lights rise, on the reception room of a prison. Marco is seated; Alfieri, Catherine, and Rodolpho standing.

ALFIERI: I'm waiting, Marco, what do you say?

RODOLPHO: Marco never hurt anybody.

ALFIERI: I can bail you out until your hearing comes up. But I'm not going to do it, you understand me? Unless I have your promise. You're an honorable man, I will believe your promise. Now what do you say?

MARCO: In my country he would be dead now. He would not live this long.

ALFIERI: All right, Rodolpho—you come with me now.

RODOLPHO: No! Please, Mister. Marco—promise the man. Please, I want you to watch the wedding. How can I be married and you're in here? Please, you're not going to do anything; you know you're not.

Marco is silent.

CATHERINE, *kneeling left of Marco*: Marco, don't you understand? He can't bail you out if you're gonna do something bad. To hell with Eddie. Nobody is gonna talk to him again if he lives to a hundred. Everybody knows you spit in his face, that's enough, isn't it? Give me the satisfaction— I want you at the wedding. You got a wife and kids, Marco. You could be workin' till the hearing comes up, instead of layin' around here.

MARCO, *to Alfieri*: I have no chance?

ALFIERI *crosses to behind Marco*: No, Marco. You're going back. The hearing is a formality, that's all.

MARCO: But him? There is a chance, eh?

ALFIERI: When she marries him he can start to become an American. They permit that, if the wife is born here.

MARCO, *looking at Rodolpho*: Well—we did something. *He lays a palm on Rodolpho's arm and Rodolpho covers it.*

RODOLPHO: Marco, tell the man.

MARCO, *pulling his hand away*: What will I tell him? He knows such a promise is dishonorable.

ALFIERI: To promise not to kill is not dishonorable.

MARCO, *looking at Alfieri*: No?

ALFIERI: No.

MARCO, *gesturing with his head—this is a new idea*: Then what is done with such a man?

ALFIERI: Nothing. If he obeys the law, he lives. That's all.

MARCO *rises, turns to Alfieri*: The law? All the law is not in a book.

ALFIERI: Yes. In a book. There is no other law.

MARCO, *his anger rising*: He degraded my brother. My blood. He robbed my children, he mocks my work. I work to come here, Mister!

ALFIERI: I know, Marco—

MARCO: There is no law for that? Where is the law for that?

ALFIERI: There is none.

MARCO, *shaking his head, sitting*: I don't understand this country.

ALFIERI: Well? What is your answer? You have five or six weeks you could work. Or else you sit here. What do you say to me?

MARCO, *lowers his eyes. It almost seems he is ashamed*: All right.

ALFIERI: You won't touch him. This is your promise.

Slight pause.

MARCO: Maybe he wants to apologize to me.

Marco is staring away. Alfieri takes one of his hands.

ALFIERI: This is not God, Marco. You hear? Only God makes justice.

MARCO: All right.

ALFIERI, *nodding, not with assurance*: Good! Catherine, Rodolpho, Marco, let us go.

Catherine kisses Rodolpho and Marco, then kisses Alfieri's hand.

CATHERINE: I'll get Beatrice and meet you at the church. *She leaves quickly.*

Marco rises. Rodolpho suddenly embraces him. Marco pats him on the back and Rodolpho exits after Catherine. Marco faces Alfieri.

ALFIERI: Only God, Marco.

Marco turns and walks out. Alfieri with a certain processional tread leaves the stage. The lights dim out.

The lights rise in the apartment. Eddie is alone in the rocker, rocking back and forth in little surges. Pause. Now Beatrice emerges from a bedroom. She is in her best clothes, wearing a hat.

BEATRICE, *with fear, going to Eddie*: I'll be back in an hour, Eddie. All right?

EDDIE, *quietly, almost inaudibly, as though drained*: What, have I been talkin' to myself?

BEATRICE: Eddie, for God's sake, it's her wedding.

EDDIE: Didn't you hear what I told you? You walk out that door to that wedding you ain't comin' back here, Beatrice.

BEATRICE: Why! What do you want?

EDDIE: I want my respect. Didn't you ever hear of that? From my wife?

Catherine enters from bedroom.

CATHERINE: It's after three; we're supposed to be there already, Beatrice. The priest won't wait.

BEATRICE: Eddie. It's her wedding. There'll be nobody there from her family. For my sister let me go. I'm goin' for my sister.

EDDIE, *as though hurt*: Look, I been arguin' with you all day already, Beatrice, and I said what I'm gonna say. He's gonna come here and apologize to me or nobody from this house is goin' into that church today. Now if that's more to you than I am, then go. But don't come back. You be on my side or on their side, that's all.

CATHERINE, *suddenly*: Who the hell do you think you are?

BEATRICE: Sssh!

CATHERINE: You got no more right to tell nobody nothin'! Nobody! The rest of your life, nobody!

BEATRICE: Shut up, Katie! *She turns Catherine around.*

CATHERINE: You're gonna come with me!

BEATRICE: I can't, Katie, I can't . . .

CATHERINE: How can you listen to him? This rat!

BEATRICE, *shaking Catherine*: Don't you call him that!

CATHERINE, *clearing from Beatrice*: What're you scared of? He's a rat! He belongs in the sewer!

BEATRICE: Stop it!

CATHERINE, *weeping*: He bites people when they sleep! He comes when nobody's lookin' and poisons decent people. In the garbage he belongs!

Eddie seems about to pick up the table and fling it at her.

BEATRICE: No, Eddie! Eddie! *To Catherine*: Then we all belong in the garbage. You, and me too. Don't say that. Whatever happened we all done it, and don't you ever forget it, Catherine. *She goes to Catherine.* Now go, go to your wedding, Katie, I'll stay home. Go. God bless you, God bless your children.

Enter Rodolpho.

RODOLPHO: Eddie?

EDDIE: Who said you could come in here? Get outa here!

RODOLPHO: Marco is coming, Eddie. *Pause. Beatrice raises her hands in terror.* He's praying in the church. You understand? *Pause. Rodolpho advances into the room.* Catherine, I think it is better we go. Come with me.

CATHERINE: Eddie, go away, please.

BEATRICE, *quietly*: Eddie. Let's go someplace. Come. You and me. *He has not moved.* I don't want you to be here when he comes. I'll get your coat.

EDDIE: Where? Where am I goin'? This is my house.

BEATRICE, *crying out*: What's the use of it! He's crazy now, you know the way they get, what good is it! You got nothin' against Marco, you always liked Marco!

EDDIE: I got nothin' against Marco? Which he called me a rat in front of the whole neighborhood? Which he said I killed his children! Where you been?

RODOLPHO, *quite suddenly, stepping up to Eddie*: It is my fault, Eddie. Everything. I wish to apologize. It was wrong that I do not ask your permission. I kiss your hand. *He reaches for Eddie's hand, but Eddie snaps it away from him.*

BEATRICE: Eddie, he's apologizing!

RODOLPHO: I have made all our troubles. But you have insult me too. Maybe God understand why you did that to me. Maybe you did not mean to insult me at all—

BEATRICE: Listen to him! Eddie, listen what he's tellin' you!

RODOLPHO: I think, maybe when Marco comes, if we can tell him we are comrades now, and we have no more argument between us. Then maybe Marco will not—

EDDIE: Now, listen—

CATHERINE: Eddie, give him a chance!

BEATRICE: What do you want! Eddie, what do you want!

EDDIE: I want my name! He didn't take my name; he's only a punk. Marco's got my name—*to Rodolpho*: and you can run tell him, kid, that he's gonna give it back to me in front of this neighborhood, or we have it out. *Hoisting up his pants*: Come on, where is he? Take me to him.

BEATRICE: Eddie, listen—

EDDIE: I heard enough! Come on, let's go!

BEATRICE: Only blood is good? He kissed your hand!

EDDIE: What he does don't mean nothin' to nobody! *To Rodolpho*: Come on!

BEATRICE, *barring his way to the stairs*: What's gonna mean somethin'? Eddie, listen to me. Who could give you your name? Listen to me, I love you, I'm talkin' to you, I love you; if Marco'll kiss your hand outside, if he goes on his knees, what is he got to give you? That's not what you want.

EDDIE: Don't bother me!

BEATRICE: You want somethin' else, Eddie, and you can never have her!

CATHERINE, *in horror*: B.!

EDDIE, *shocked, horrified, his fist clenching*: Beatrice!

> *Marco appears outside, walking toward the door from a distant point.*

BEATRICE, *crying out, weeping*: The truth is not as bad as blood, Eddie! I'm tellin' you the truth—tell her good-by forever!

EDDIE, *crying out in agony*: That's what you think of me—that I would have such a thought? *His fists clench his head as though it will burst.*

MARCO, *calling near the door outside*: Eddie Carbone!

> *Eddie swerves about; all stand transfixed for an instant. People appear outside.*

EDDIE, *as though flinging his challenge*: Yeah, Marco! Eddie Carbone. Eddie Carbone. Eddie Carbone. *He goes up the stairs and emerges from the apartment. Rodolpho streaks up and out past him and runs to Marco.*

RODOLPHO: No, Marco, please! Eddie, please, he has children! You will kill a family!

BEATRICE: Go in the house! Eddie, go in the house!

EDDIE—*he gradually comes to address the people*: Maybe he come to apologize to me. Heh, Marco? For what you said about me in front of the neighborhood? *He is incensing himself and little bits of laughter even escape him as his eyes are murderous and he cracks his knuckles in his hands with a strange sort of relaxation.* He knows that ain't right. To do like that? To a man? Which I put my roof over their head and my food in their mouth? Like in the Bible? Strangers I never seen in my whole life? To come out of the water and grab a girl for a passport? To go and take from your own family like from the stable—and never a word to me? And now accusations in the bargain! *Directly to Marco*: Wipin' the neighborhood with my name like a dirty rag! I want my name, Marco. *He is moving now, carefully, toward Marco.* Now gimme my name and we go together to the wedding.

BEATRICE AND CATHERINE, *keening*: Eddie! Eddie, don't! Eddie!

EDDIE: No, Marco knows what's right from wrong. Tell the people, Marco, tell them what a liar you are! *He has his arms spread and Marco is spreading his.* Come on, liar, you know what you done! *He lunges for Marco as a great hushed shout goes up from the people.*

Marco strikes Eddie beside the neck.

MARCO: Animal! You go on your knees to me!

Eddie goes down with the blow and Marco starts to raise a foot to stomp him when Eddie springs a knife into his hand and Marco steps back. Louis rushes in toward Eddie.

LOUIS: Eddie, for Christ's sake!

Eddie raises the knife and Louis halts and steps back.

EDDIE: You lied about me, Marco. Now say it. Come on now, say it!

MARCO: Anima-a-a-l!

Eddie lunges with the knife. Marco grabs his arm, turning the blade inward and pressing it home as the women and Louis and Mike rush in and separate them, and Eddie, the knife still in his hand, falls to his knees before Marco. The two women support him for a moment, calling his name again and again.

CATHERINE: Eddie, I never meant to do nothing bad to you.

EDDIE: Then why— Oh, B.!

BEATRICE: Yes, yes!

EDDIE: My B.!

He dies in her arms, and Beatrice covers him with her body. Alfieri, who is in the crowd, turns out to the audience. The lights have gone down, leaving him in a glow, while behind him the dull prayers of the people and the keening of the women continue.

ALFIERI: Most of the time now we settle for half and I like it better. But the truth is holy, and even as I know how wrong he was, and his death useless, I tremble, for I confess that something perversely pure calls to me from his memory—not purely good, but himself purely, for he allowed himself to be wholly known and for that I think I will love him more than all my sensible clients. And yet, it is better to settle for half, it must be! And so I mourn him—I admit it—with a certain . . . alarm.

CURTAIN

AFTER THE FALL

A PLAY IN TWO ACTS

1964

Characters

QUENTIN

MAGGIE

HOLGA

FELICE

LOUISE

MOTHER

FATHER

DAN

ELSIE

LOU

MICKEY

LUCAS

CARRIE

Harley Barnes, Chairman, nurses, porter,
secretary, hospital attendant, a group of boys, and passers-by

ACT ONE

The action takes place in the mind, thought, and memory of Quentin. Except for one chair there is no furniture in the conventional sense; there are no walls or substantial boundaries.

The setting consists of three levels rising to the highest at the back, crossing in a curve from one side of the stage to the other. Rising above it, and dominating the stage, is the blasted stone tower of a German concentration camp. Its wide lookout windows are like eyes, which at the moment seem blind and dark; bent reinforcing rods stick out of it like broken tentacles.

On the two lower levels are sculpted areas; indeed, the whole effect is neolithic, a lava-like, supple geography in which, like pits and hollows found in lava, the scenes take place. The mind has no color but its memories are brilliant against the grayness of its landscape. When people sit they do so on any of the abutments, ledges, or crevices. A scene may start in a confined area, but spread or burst out onto the entire stage, overrunning any other area.

People appear and disappear instantaneously, as in the mind; but it is not necessary that they walk off the stage. The dialogue will make clear who is "alive" at any moment and who is in abeyance.

The effect, therefore, will be the surging, flitting, instantaneousness of a mind questing over its own surfaces and into its depths.

The stage is dark. Now there is a sense that some figure has moved in the farthest distance; a footstep is heard, then others. As light dimly rises, the persons in the play move in a random way up from beneath the high back platform. Some sit at once, others come farther downstage, seem to recognize each other, still others move alone and in total separateness. They are speaking toward Quentin in sibilant whispers, some angrily, some in appeal to him. Now Quentin, a man in his forties, moves out of this mass and continues down to the front of the stage. All movement ceases. Quentin addresses the Listener, who, if he could be seen, would be sitting just beyond the edge of the stage itself.

QUENTIN: Hello! God, it's good to see you again! I'm very well. I hope it wasn't too inconvenient on such short notice. Fine, I just wanted to say hello, really. Thanks. *He sits on invitation. Slight pause.* Actually, I called you on the spur of the moment this morning; I have a bit of a decision to make. You know—you mull around about something for months and all of a sudden there it is and you don't know what to do.

He sets himself to begin, looks off.

Ah . . .

Interrupted, he turns back to Listener, surprised.

I've quit the firm, didn't I write you about that? Really! I was sure I'd written. Oh, about fourteen months ago; a few weeks after Maggie died. *Maggie stirs on the second platform.* It just got to where I couldn't concentrate on a case any more; not the way I used to. I felt I was merely in the service of my own success. It all lost any point. Although I do wonder sometimes if I am simply trying to destroy myself. . . . Well, I have walked away from what passes for an important career. . . . Not very much, I'm afraid; I still live in the hotel, see a few people, read a good deal—*Smiles*—stare out the window. I don't know why I'm smiling; maybe I feel that's all over now, and I'll harness myself to something again. Although I've had that feeling before and done nothing about it, I—

Again, interrupted, he looks surprised.

God, I wrote you about *that*, didn't I? Maybe I dream these letters. Mother died. Oh, it's four—*Airplane sound is heard behind him*—five months ago now. Yes, quite suddenly; I was in Germany at the time and—it's one of the things I wanted—*Holga appears on upper platform, looking about for him*—to talk to you about. I . . . met a woman there. *He grins.* I never thought it could happen again, but we became quite close. In fact, she's arriving tonight, for some conference at Columbia—she's an archaeologist. I'm not sure, you see, if I want to lose her, and yet it's outrageous to think of committing myself again. . . . Well, yes, but look at my life. A life, after all, is evidence, and I have two divorces in my safe-deposit box. *Turning to glance up at Holga:* I tell you frankly, I'm a little afraid. . . . Well, of who and what I'm bringing to her. *He sits again, leans forward.* You know, more and more I think that for many years I looked at life like a case at law, a series of proofs. When you're young you prove how brave you are, or smart; then, what a good lover; then, a good father; finally, how wise, or powerful or what-the-hell-ever. But underlying it all, I see now, there was a presumption. That I was moving on an upward path toward some elevation, where—God knows what—I would be justified, or even condemned—a verdict anyway. I think now that my disaster really began when I looked up one day—and the bench was empty. No judge in sight. And all that remained was the endless argument with oneself—this pointless litigation of existence before an empty bench. Which, of course, is another way of saying—despair. And, of course, despair can be a way of life; but you have to believe in it, pick it up, take it to heart, and move on again. Instead, I seem to be hung up. *Slight pause.* And the days and the months and now the years are draining away. A couple of weeks ago I suddenly became aware of a strange fact. With all this darkness, the truth is that every morning when I awake, I'm full of hope! With everything I know—I open my eyes, I'm like a boy! For an instant there's some—unformed promise in the air. I jump out of bed, I shave, I can't wait to finish breakfast—and then, it seeps in my room, my life and its pointlessness. And I thought—if I could corner that hope, find what it consists of and either kill it for a lie, or really make it mine . . .

FELICE, *having entered*: You do remember me, don't you? Two years ago in your office, when you got my husband to sign the divorce papers?

QUENTIN, *to Listener*: I'm not sure why I bring her up. I ran into her on the street last month . . .

FELICE: I always wanted to tell you this—you changed my life!

QUENTIN, *to Listener*: There's something about that girl unnerves me.

FELICE, *facing front, standing beside him*: You see, my husband was always so childish, alone with me. But the way you talked to him; it made him act so dignified I almost began to love him! And when we got out in the street he asked me something. Should I tell you, or do you know already?

QUENTIN, *now turning to her*: He asked to go to bed with you one last time?

FELICE: How did you know that?

QUENTIN: Well, what harm would it have done?

FELICE: But wouldn't it be funny the same day we agreed to divorce?

QUENTIN: Honey, you never stop loving whoever you loved. Why must you try?

Louise starts down toward him, and Maggie appears far upstage in gold dress among anonymous men. Quentin turns back to Listener.

Why do I make such stupid statements!

MAGGIE, *from among the men, laughing as though with joy at seeing him*: Quentin! *She is gone.*

QUENTIN: These goddamned women have injured me! Have I learned nothing?

HOLGA, *appearing under the tower with flowers as Maggie and men go dark*: Would you like to see Salzburg? I think they play *The Magic Flute* tonight.

QUENTIN, *of Holga*: I don't know what I'd be bringing to that girl.

Holga exits. Louise has moved down in front of him, and he glances at her.

I don't know how to blame with confidence.

FELICE, *as Louise moves thoughtfully upstage and exits*: But I finally got your point! It's that there is no point, right? No one has to be to blame! And as soon as I realized that, I started to dance better!

QUENTIN, *to Listener*: God, what excellent advice I give!

FELICE: I almost feel free when I dance now! Sometimes I only have to think high and I go high! I get a long thought and I fly across the floor. *She flies out into darkness.*

QUENTIN: And on top of that she came back again the other night, flew into my room—reborn! She made me wonder how much I believe in life.

FELICE, *rushing on*: I had my nose fixed! Could I show it to you? The doctor took the bandage off, but I put it back because I wanted you to be the first! Do you mind?

QUENTIN, *turning to her*: No. But why me?

FELICE: Because—remember that night I came up here? I was trying to decide if I should have it done. 'Cause there could be something insincere about changing your nose; I wouldn't want to build everything on the shape of a piece of cartilage. You don't absolutely have to answer me, but—I think you wanted to make love to me that night. Didn't you?

QUENTIN: I did, yes.

FELICE: I knew it! And I felt it didn't matter what kind of nose I had! So I might as well have a short one! Could I show it to you?

QUENTIN: I'd like very much to see it.

FELICE: Close your eyes. *He does. She lifts the bandage.* Okay. *He looks. She raises her arm in blessing.* I'll always bless you. Always!

He slowly turns to the Listener as she walks into darkness.

QUENTIN: And I even liked her first nose better. And yet I may stand in her mind like some important corner she turned in life. And she meant so little to me. I feel like a mirror in which she somehow saw herself as glorious.

Two pallbearers in the distance carry an invisible coffin.

It's like my mother's funeral.

Mother appears on upper platform, arms crossed as in death.

I still hear her voice in the street sometimes, loud and real, calling me. And yet she's under the ground. That whole cemetery— I saw it like a field of buried mirrors in which the living merely saw themselves. I don't seem to know how to grieve for her.

Father appears, a blanket over him; two nurses tend him.

Or maybe I don't believe that grief is grief unless it kills you.

Dan appears, talking to a nurse.

Like when I flew back and met my brother in the hospital.

The nurse hurries out, and Quentin has gotten up and moved to Dan.

DAN: I'm so glad you got here, kid; I wouldn't have wired you, but I don't know what to do. You have a good flight?

QUENTIN, *to Dan*: But what's the alternative? She's dead, he has to know.

DAN, *to Quentin*: But he was only operated on this morning. How can we walk in and say, "Your wife is dead"? It's like sawing off his arm. Suppose we tell him she's on her way, then give him a sedative?

QUENTIN: But Dan, don't you think it belongs to him? After fifty years you owe one another a death.

DAN: Kid, the woman was his right hand; without her he was never very much, you know—he'll fall apart.

QUENTIN: I can't agree; I think he's got a lot of stuff—*Without halt, to the Listener*: Which is hilarious! . . . Because! He was always the one who idolized the old man, and I saw through him from the beginning! Suddenly we're changing places, like children in a game! I don't know any more what people *are* to one another!

DAN, *as though he had come to a decision*: All right; let's go in, then.

QUENTIN: You want me to tell him?

DAN, *unwillingly, afraid but challenged*: I'll do it.

QUENTIN: I could do it, Dan. It belongs to him, as much as his wedding.

DAN, *relieved*: All right, if you don't mind.

> *They turn together toward Father in the bed. He does not see them yet. They move with the weight of their news. Quentin turns toward Listener as he walks.*

QUENTIN: Or is it simply that I am crueler than he?

> *Now Father sees them and raises up his arm.*

DAN, *indicating Quentin*: Dad, look . . .

FATHER: For cryin' out loud! Look who's here! I thought you were in Europe!

QUENTIN: Just got back. How are you?

DAN: You look wonderful, Dad.

FATHER: What do you mean, "look"? I *am* wonderful! I tell you, I'm ready to go through it again! *They laugh proudly with him.* I mean it—the way that doctor worries, I finally told him, "Look, if it makes you feel so bad you lay down and I'll operate!" Very fine man. I thought you'd be away couple months more.

QUENTIN, *hesitantly*: I decided to come back and—

DAN, *breaking in, his voice turning strange*: Sylvia'll be right in. She's downstairs buying you something.

FATHER: Oh, that's nice! I tell you something, fellas—that kid is more and more like Mother. Been here every day . . . Where is Mother? I been calling the house.

> *The slightest empty, empty pause.*

DAN: One second, Dad, I just want to—

> *Crazily, without evident point, he starts calling, and moving upstage toward the nurse. Quentin is staring at his father.*

> Nurse! Ah . . . could you call down to the gift shop and see if my sister . . .

FATHER: Dan! Tell her to get some ice. When Mother comes you'll all have a drink! I got a bottle of rye in the closet. *To Quentin*: I tell you, kid, I'm going to be young. Mother's right; just because I got old I don't have to act old. I mean we could go to Florida, we could—

QUENTIN: Dad.

FATHER: What? Is that a new suit?

QUENTIN: No, I've had it.

FATHER, *remembering—to Dan, of the nurse*: Oh, tell her glasses, we'll need more glasses.

QUENTIN: Listen, Dad.

> *Dan halts and turns back.*

FATHER, *totally unaware, smiling at his returned son*: Yeah?

QUENTIN: Mother died. She had a heart attack last night on her way home.

FATHER: Oh, no, no, no, no.

QUENTIN: We didn't want to tell you but—

FATHER: Ahhh! Ahhh, no, no, no.

DAN: There's nothing anybody could have done, Dad.

FATHER: Oh. Oh. Oh!

QUENTIN, *grasping his hand*: Now look, Dad, you're going to be all right, you'll—

FATHER—*it is all turning into a deep gasping for breath*: Oh boy. Oh boy! No, no.

DAN: Now look, Dad, you're a hell of a fella. Dad, listen—

FATHER: Goddammit! I couldn't take care of myself, I knew she was working too hard!

QUENTIN: Dad, it's not your fault, that can happen to anyone—

FATHER: But she was sitting right here. She was—she was right here!

QUENTIN: Pa . . . Pa . . .

> *Dan moves in close, as though to share him.*

FATHER: Oh, boys—she was my right hand! *He raises his fist and seems about to lose his control again.*

DAN: We'll take care of you, Dad. I don't want you to worry about—

FATHER: No-no. I'll be all right. God! Now I'm better! Now, *now* I'm better!

> *They are silent.*

> So where is she?

QUENTIN: In the funeral parlor.

FATHER, *shaking his head—an explosive blow of air*: Paaaaaah!

QUENTIN: We didn't want to tell you but we figured you'd rather know.

FATHER: Ya. Thanks. Thanks. I'll . . . *He looks up at Quentin.* I'll just have to be stronger.

QUENTIN: That's right, Dad.

FATHER, *to no one, as Mother disappears above*: This . . . will make me stronger. *But the weeping threatens; he clenches his jaw, shakes his head, and indicates a point.* She was right here!

> *He is taken away by the nurses and Dan. Quentin comes slowly to the Listener.*

QUENTIN: Still and all, a couple months later he bothered to register and vote. . . . Well, I mean . . . it didn't kill him either, with all his tears. I don't know what the hell I'm driving at. It's connected to . . .

> *The tower gradually begins to light. He is caught by it.*

I visited a concentration camp in Germany.

> *He has started toward the tower when Felice appears, raising her arm in blessing.*

FELICE: Close your eyes, okay?

QUENTIN, *turned by her force*: I don't understand why that girl sticks in my mind. *He moves toward her now.* She did, she offered me some . . . love, I guess. And if I don't return it—it's like owing for a gift that you didn't ask for.

> *Mother has appeared again; she raises her hand in blessing as Felice does.*

FELICE: I'll always bless you!

> *She exits and Mother is gone.*

QUENTIN: When she left . . . I did a stupid thing. I don't understand it. There are two light fixtures on the wall of my hotel room . . .

> *As he speaks Maggie enters onto second platform, dressed in negligee, hair disheveled. Quentin struggles against his own disgust.*

I noticed for the first time that they're . . . a curious distance apart. And I suddenly saw that if you stood between them—*He spreads out his arms*—you could reach out and rest your arms.

> *Just before he completely spreads his arms, Maggie sits up, her breathing sounds.*

MAGGIE: Liar! Judge!

> *He drops his arms, aborting the image; Maggie exits.*

> *Now Holga appears and is bending to read a legend fixed to the wall of a torture chamber.*

QUENTIN: Oh. The concentration camp . . . this woman . . . Holga took me there.

HOLGA, *turning to "him," as though he stood beside her*: This is the room where they tortured them. No, I don't mind, I'll translate it.

> *She returns to the legend; he slowly approaches behind her.*

"The door to the left leads into the chamber where their teeth were extracted for gold; the drain in the floor carried off the blood. At times, instead of shooting, they were individually strangled to death. The barracks on the right were the bordello where women—"

QUENTIN: I think you've had enough, Holga.

HOLGA: No, if you want to see the rest—

QUENTIN, *taking her arm*: Let's walk, dear. Country looks lovely out there.

> *They walk. The light changes to day.*

They sure built solid watchtowers, didn't they! Here, this grass looks dry; let's sit down.

> *They sit. Pause.*

I always thought the Danube was blue.

HOLGA: Only the waltz; although it does change near Vienna, out of some lingering respect for Strauss, I suppose.

QUENTIN: I don't know why this hit me so.

HOLGA: I'm sorry! *Starting to rise as she senses an estrangement—to raise his spirits*: You still want to see Salzburg? I'd love to show you Mozart's house. And the cafés are excellent there.

QUENTIN, *turning to her now*: Was there somebody you knew died here?

HOLGA: Oh no. I feel people ought to see it, that's all. And you seemed so interested.

QUENTIN: Yes, but I'm an American. I can afford to be interested.

HOLGA: Don't be too sure. When I first visited America after the war I was three days under questioning before they let me in. How could one be in forced labor for two years if one were not a Communist or a Jew?

In fact, it was only when I told them I had blood relatives in several Nazi ministries that they were reassured. It's as though fifteen years of one's life had simply vanished in some insane confusion. So I was very glad you were so interested.

QUENTIN, *glancing up at the tower*: I guess I thought I'd be indignant, or angry. But it's like swallowing a lump of earth. It's strange.

HOLGA, *pressing him to lie down, cheerfully*: Come, lie down here for a while and perhaps—

QUENTIN: No, I'm— *He has fended off her hand.* I'm sorry, dear, I didn't mean to push you away.

HOLGA, *rebuffed and embarrassed*: I see wildflowers on that hill; I'll pick some for the car! *She gets up quickly.*

QUENTIN: Holga? *She continues off. He jumps up and hurries to her, turning her.* Holga. *He does not know what to say.*

HOLGA: Perhaps we've been together too much. I could rent another car at Linz; we could meet in Vienna sometime.

QUENTIN: I don't want to lose you, Holga.

HOLGA: I hear your wings opening, Quentin. I am not helpless alone. I love my work. It's simply that from the moment you spoke to me I felt somehow familiar, and it was never so before. . . . It isn't a question of getting married; I am not ashamed this way. But I must have *something*.

QUENTIN: I don't give you anything?

HOLGA: You give me very much. . . . It's difficult for me to speak like this. I am not a woman who must be reassured every minute, those women are stupid to me. . . .

QUENTIN, *turning her face to him*: Holga, are you weeping—for *me*?

HOLGA: Yes.

QUENTIN: It's that I don't want to abuse your feeling for me—I swear I don't know if I have lived in good faith. And the doubt ties my tongue when I think of promising anything again.

HOLGA: But how can one ever be sure of one's good faith?

QUENTIN, *surprised*: God, it's wonderful to hear you say that. All my women have been so goddamned sure!

HOLGA: But how can one ever be?

QUENTIN—*he kisses her gratefully*: Why do you keep coming back to this place? It seems to tear you apart.

Mother is heard softly singing a musical comedy ballad of the twenties.

HOLGA, *after a pause; she is disturbed, uncertain*: I . . . don't know. Perhaps . . . because I didn't die here.

QUENTIN, *turning quickly to Listener*: What?

HOLGA: Although that would make no sense! I don't really know!

QUENTIN, *going toward the Listener at the edge of the stage*: That people . . . what? "Wish to die for the dead." No-no, I can understand it; survival can be hard to bear. But I—I don't think I feel that way. . . . Although I do think of my mother now, and she's dead. Yes! *He turns to Holga.* And maybe the dead do bother her.

HOLGA: It was the middle of the war. I had just come out of a class and there were British leaflets on the sidewalk. And photographs of a concentration camp. And emaciated people. One tended to believe the British. I'd had no idea. Truly. It isn't easy to turn against your country; not in a war. Do Americans turn against America because of Hiroshima? There are reasons always. And I took the leaflet to my godfather—he was still commanding our Intelligence. And I asked if it were true. "Of course," he said, "why does it excite you?" And I said, "You are a swine. You are all swine." I threw my briefcase at him. And he opened it and put some papers in it and asked me to deliver it to a certain address. And I became a courier for the officers who were planning to assassinate Hitler. . . . They were all hanged.

QUENTIN: Why not you?

HOLGA: They didn't betray me.

QUENTIN: Then why do you say good faith is never sure?

HOLGA, *after a pause*: It was my country—longer, perhaps, than it should have been. But I didn't know. And now I don't know how I could not have known.

QUENTIN: Holga, I bless your uncertainty. You don't seem to be looking for some goddamned . . . moral *victory*. Forgive me, I didn't mean to be distant with you. I— *Looks up.*

HOLGA: I'll get the flowers! *She starts away.*

QUENTIN: It's only this place!

HOLGA, *turning, and with great love*: I know! I'll be right back! *She hurries away.*

He stands in stillness a moment; the presence of the tower bores in on him; its color changes; he now looks up at it and addresses the Listener.

QUENTIN: I think I expected it to be more unfamiliar. I never thought the stones would look so ordinary. And the view from here is rather pastoral. Why do I *know* something here? Even hollow now and empty, it has a face, and asks a sort of question: "What do you believe as true as this?" Yes! Believers built this, maybe that's the fright—and I, without belief, stand here disarmed. I can see the convoys grinding up this hill, and I inside; no one knows my name and yet they'll smash my head on a concrete floor! And no appeal . . . *He turns quickly to the Listener.* Yes! It's that I no longer see some final saving grace! Socialism once, then love; some final hope is gone that always saved before the end!

Mother appears; Dan enters, kisses her, and exits.

MOTHER, *to an invisible small boy*: Not too much cake, darling, there'll be a lot of food at this wedding.

QUENTIN: Mother! That's strange. And murder?

MOTHER, *getting down on her knees to tend the little boy*: Yes, garters, Quentin, and don't argue with me. . . . Because it's my brother's wedding and your stockings are not to hang over your shoes!

QUENTIN—*he has started to laugh but it turns into*: Why can't I mourn her? And Holga wept in there, why can't I weep? Why do I feel an understanding with this slaughterhouse?

Mother laughs. He turns to her.

MOTHER, *to the little boy*: My brothers! Why must every wedding in this family be a catastrophe! . . . Because the girl is pregnant, darling, and she's got no money, she's stupid, and I tell you this one is going to end up with a mustache! That's why, darling, when you grow up, I hope you learn how to disappoint people. Especially women.

QUENTIN, *watching her, sitting nearby*: But what the hell has this got to do with a concentration camp?

MOTHER: Will you stop playing with matches? *Slaps an invisible boy's hand.* You'll pee in bed! Why don't you practice your penmanship instead? You write like a monkey, darling. And where is your father? If he went to sleep in the Turkish bath again, I'll kill him! Like he forgot my brother Herbert's wedding and goes to the Dempsey-Tunney fight. And ends up in the men's room with the door stuck, so by the time they get him out my brother's married, there's a new champion, and it cost him a hundred dollars to go to the men's room! *She is laughing.*

Father with secretary has appeared on upper platform, an invisible phone to his ear.

FATHER: Then cable Southampton.

MOTHER: But you mustn't laugh at him, he's a wonderful man.

FATHER: Sixty thousand tons. Sixty.

Father disappears.

MOTHER: To this day he walks into a room you want to bow! *Warmly*: Any restaurant—one look at him and the waiters start moving tables around. *Because*, dear, people know that this is a *man*. Even Doctor Strauss, at my wedding he came over to me, says, "Rose, I can see it looking at him, you've got a wonderful man," and he was always in love with me, Strauss. . . . Oh, sure, but he was only a penniless medical student then, my father wouldn't let him in the house. Who knew he'd end up so big in the gallstones? That poor boy! Used to bring me novels to read, poetry, philosophy, God knows what! One time we even sneaked off to hear Rachmaninoff together. *She laughs sadly; and with wonder more than bitterness.* That's why, you see, two weeks after we were married; sit down to dinner and Papa hands me a menu and asks me to read it to him. Couldn't *read*! *I* got so frightened I nearly ran away! . . . Why? Because your grandmother is such a fine, unselfish woman; two months in school and they put him into the shop! That's what some women are, my dear—and now he goes and buys her a new Packard every year. *With a strange and deep fear*: Please, darling, I want you to *draw* the letters, that scribbling is ugly, dear; and your posture, your speech, it can all be beautiful! Ask Miss Fisher, for years they kept my handwriting pinned up on the bulletin board; God, I'll never forget it, valedictorian of the class with a scholarship to Hunter in my hand . . . *A blackness flows into her soul.* And I came home, and Grandpa says, "You're getting married!" I was like—like with small wings, just getting ready to fly; I slept all year with the catalogue under my pillow. To learn, to learn everything! Oh, darling, the whole thing is such a mystery!

Father enters the area, talking to the young, invisible Quentin.

FATHER: Quentin, would you get the office on the phone? *To Mother*: Why would you call the Turkish bath?

MOTHER: I thought you forgot about the wedding.

FATHER: I wish I could, but I'm paying for it.

MOTHER: He'll pay you back!

FATHER: I believe it, I just wouldn't want to hang by my hair that long. *He turns, and, going to a point, he takes up an invisible phone.* Herman? Hold the wire.

MOTHER: I don't want to be late, now.

FATHER: She won't give birth if we're half-hour late.

MOTHER: Don't be so smart! He fell in love, what's so terrible about that?

FATHER: They all fall in love on my money. I married into a love nest! *He turns to Quentin, laughing.* Did they pass a law that kid can't get a haircut? *Reaching into his pocket, tossing a coin:* Here, at least get a shine. *To Mother:* I'll be right up, dear, go ahead.

MOTHER: I'll put in your studs. God, he's so beautiful in a tuxedo!

> *She goes a distance out of the area, but halts, turns, eavesdrops on Father.*

FATHER, *into phone:* Herman? The accountant still there? Put him on.

QUENTIN, *suddenly, recalling, to the Listener:* Oh, yes!

FATHER: Billy? You finished? Well, what's the story, where am I?

QUENTIN: Yes!

FATHER: Don't you read the papers? What'll I do with Irving Trust? I can't give it away. What bank?

> *Mother descends a step, alarmed.*

I been to every bank in New York, I can't get a bill paid, how the hell they going to lend me money? No-no, there's no money in London, there's no money in Hamburg, there ain't a cargo moving in the world, the ocean's empty, Billy—now tell me the truth, where am I?

> *He puts down the phone. Pause. Mother comes up behind him. He stands almost stiffly, as though to take a storm.*

MOTHER: What's that about? What are you winding up?

> *Father stands staring; but she seems to hear additional shocking facts.*

What are you talking about? When did this start? . . . Well, how much are you taking out of it? . . . You lost your mind? You've got over four hundred thousand dollars' worth of stocks, you can sell the—

> *Father laughs silently.*

You sold those wonderful stocks? I just bought a new grand piano, why didn't you say something? And a silver service for my brother, and you don't say anything! *More subdued, she walks a few steps in thought.* Well, then—you'd better cash your insurance; you've got at least seventy-five thousand cash value— *Halts, turning in shock.* When!

> *Father is gradually losing his stance, his grandeur; he pulls his tie loose.*

All right, then—we'll get rid of my bonds. Do it tomorrow. . . . What do you mean? Well, you get them back, I've got ninety-one thousand dollars in bonds you gave me. Those are my bonds. I've got bonds— *She breaks off, open horror on her face and now a growing contempt.* You mean you saw everything going down and you throw good money after bad? Are you some kind of a moron?

FATHER: You don't walk away from a business; I came to this country with a tag around my neck like a package in the bottom of the boat!

MOTHER: I should have run the day I met you.

FATHER, *as though stabbed*: Rose! *He sits, closing his eyes, his neck bent.*

MOTHER: I should have done what my sisters did, tell my parents to go to hell and thought of myself for once! I should have run for my life!

FATHER, *indicating a point nearby*: Sssh, I hear the kids—

MOTHER: I ought to get a divorce!

FATHER: Rose, the college men are jumping out of windows.

MOTHER: But your last dollar! *Bending over, into his face*: You are an idiot!

> *Her nearness forces him to stand; they look at each other, strangers.*

QUENTIN, *looking up at the tower*: Yes! For no reason—they don't even ask your name!

FATHER, *looking toward the nearby point*: Somebody crying? Quentin's in there. You better talk to him.

> *She goes in some trepidation toward the indicated point. A foot or so from it, she halts.*

MOTHER: Quentin? Darling? You better get dressed. Don't cry, dear—

> *She is stopped short by something "Quentin" has said.*

What *I* said? Why, what did I say? . . . Well, I was a little angry, that's all, but I never said *that*. I think he's a wonderful man! *Laughs.* How could I say a thing like that? Quentin! *As though he is disappearing, she extends her arms.* I didn't say anything! *With a cry toward someone lost, rushing out after the boy*: Darling, I didn't say anything!

> *Father and Dan exit.*

> *Instantly Holga appears, coming toward him.*

QUENTIN, *to himself, turning up toward the tower*: They don't even ask your name.

HOLGA, *looking about for him*: Quentin? Quentin?

QUENTIN, *to Holga*: You love me, don't you?

HOLGA: Yes. *Of the wildflowers in her arms*: Look, the car will be all sweet inside!

QUENTIN, *clasping her hands*: Let's get out of this dump. Come on, I'll race you to the car!

HOLGA: Okay! On your mark!

They get set.

QUENTIN: Last one there's a rancid wurst!

HOLGA: Get ready! Set!

Quentin suddenly looks up at the tower and sits on the ground as though he had committed a sacrilege.

She has read his emotion, touches his face.

Quentin, dear—no one they didn't kill can be innocent again.

QUENTIN: But how did you solve it? How do you get so purposeful? You're so full of hope!

HOLGA: Quentin, I think it's a mistake to ever look for hope outside one's self. One day the house smells of fresh bread, the next of smoke and blood. One day you faint because the gardener cut his finger off, within a week you're climbing over the corpses of children bombed in a subway. What hope can there be if that is so? I tried to die near the end of the war. *She rises, moves up the stair toward the tower.* The same dream returned each night until I dared not go to sleep and grew quite ill. I dreamed I had a child, and even in the dream I saw it was my life, and it was an idiot, and I ran away. But it always crept onto my lap again, clutched at my clothes. Until I thought, if I could kiss it, whatever in it was my own, perhaps I could sleep. And I bent to its broken face, and it was horrible . . . but I kissed it. I think one must finally take one's life in one's arms, Quentin. Come, they play *The Magic Flute* tonight. You like *The Magic Flute*?

She exits from beneath the tower on the upper level.

QUENTIN, *alone*: I miss her . . . badly. And yet, I can't sign my letters to her "With love." I put, "Sincerely," or "As ever"—*Felice enters far away upstage*—some such brilliant evasion. I've lost the sense of some absolute necessity. Whether I open a book or think of marrying again, it's so damned clear I'm choosing what I do—and it cuts the strings between my hands and heaven. It sounds foolish, but I feel . . . unblessed.

Felice holds up her hand in blessing, then exits.

And I keep looking back to when there seemed to be some duty in the sky. I had a dinner table and a wife—*in the distance Louise appears with a dishcloth, wiping silver, wearing a kitchen apron*—a child and the world so wonderfully threatened by injustices I was born to correct! It seems so fine! Remember—when there were good people and bad people? And how easy it was to tell! The worst son of a bitch, if he loved Jews and hated Hitler, he was a buddy. Like some kind of paradise compared to this.

He is aware of Elsie appearing on second platform; a beach robe hangs from her shoulders, her arms out of the sleeves, her back to us.

Until I begin to look at it. God, when I think of what I believed I want to hide! *Glancing at Elsie*: But I wasn't all that young! A man of thirty-two sees a guest changing out of a wet bathing suit in his bedroom . . .

Elsie, as he approaches, turns to him and her robe slips off one shoulder.

. . . and she stands there with her two bare faces hanging out.

ELSIE: Oh, are you through working? Why don't you swim now? The water's just right.

QUENTIN—*a laugh of great pain, crying out*: I tell you I didn't believe she knew she was naked!

Louise enters and sits at right, as though on the ground. Elsie descends to join her and Quentin follows her with his eyes.

It's Eden! . . . Well, because she was *married*! How could a woman who can tell when the Budapest String Quartet is playing off key; who refuses to wear silk stockings—*Lou enters upstage, reading a brief*—because the Japanese are invading Manchuria; whose husband, my friend, a saintly professor of law, is editing my first appeal to the Supreme Court on the grass outside that window—I could see the top of his head past her tit, for God's sake! Of course I saw, but it's what you allow yourself to admit! To admit what you see endangers principles!

Quentin turns to Louise and Elsie seated on the ground. They are talking in an intense whisper. He now approaches them from behind. Halts, turns to the Listener.

And you know? When two women are whispering, and they stop abruptly when you appear . . .

ELSIE AND LOUISE, *turning to him after an abrupt stop to their talking*: Hi.

QUENTIN: The subject must have been sex. And if one of them is your wife . . . she must have been talking about you.

ELSIE, *as though to get him to go*: Lou's behind the house, reading your brief. He says it's superb!

QUENTIN: I hope so, Elsie. I've been kind of nervous about what he'd say.

ELSIE: I wish you'd tell him that, Quentin! Will you? Just how much his opinion means to you. It's important you tell him. It's so enchanting here. *Taking in Louise, standing*: I envy you both so much!

> She goes upstage, pausing beside her husband, Lou. He is a very tender, kindly man in shorts; he is absorbed in reading the brief.

I want one more walk along the beach before the train. Did you comb your hair today?

LOU: I think so. *Closing the brief, coming down to Quentin*: Quentin! This is superb! It's hardly like a brief at all; there's a majestic quality, like a classic opinion!

> Elsie exits. Lou, chuckling, tugs Quentin's sleeve.

I almost feel honored to have known you!

QUENTIN: I'm so glad, Lou—

LOU, *with an arm around Louise*: Your whole career will change with this! Could I ask a favor?

QUENTIN: Oh, anything, Lou.

LOU: Would you offer it to Elsie, to read? I know it seems an extraordinary request, but—

QUENTIN: No, I'd be delighted.

LOU: It's shaken her terribly—my being subpoenaed and all those damned headlines. Despite everything, it does affect one's whole relationship. So any gesture of respect—for example I gave her the manuscript of my new textbook and I've even called off publication for a while to incorporate her criticisms. It may be her psychoanalysis, but she's become remarkably acute—

LOUISE: My roast! *She exits upstage.*

QUENTIN: But I hope you don't delay it too long, Lou; it'd be wonderful to publish something now. Just to show those bastards.

LOU, *glancing behind him*: But you see, it's a textbook for the schools, and Elsie feels that it will only start a new attack on me.

QUENTIN: But they've investigated you. What more damage could they do?

LOU: Another attack might knock me off the faculty. It's only Mickey's vote that saved me the last time. He made a marvelous speech at the dean's meeting when I refused to testify.

QUENTIN: Well, that's Mickey.

LOU: Yes, but Elsie feels—I'd just be drawing down the lightning again to publish now. And yet to put that book away is like a kind of suicide to me—everything I know is in that book.

QUENTIN: Lou, you have a right to publish; a radical past is not leprosy—we only turned left because it seemed the truth was there. You mustn't be ashamed.

LOU, *in pain*: Goddammit, yes! Except—I never told you this, Quentin. . . . *He holds his position, de-animated.*

QUENTIN, *to Listener, as he comes down to the edge of the stage*: Yes, the day the world ended and nobody was innocent again. God, how swiftly it all fell down!

LOU, *speaking straight front*: When I returned from Russia and published my study of Soviet law—I left out many things I saw. I lied. For a good cause, I thought, but all that lasts is the lie.

> *Elsie and Louise enter, talking together intimately and unheard.*

> And it's so strange to me now—I have many failings, but I have never been a liar. And I lied for the Party, over and over, year after year. And that's why now, with this book of mine, I want so much to be true to myself! You see, it's no attack I fear, but being forced to defend my own incredible lies! *He turns, surprised, to see Elsie.*

ELSIE: Lou, I'm quite surprised. I thought we'd settled this.

> *Father and Dan appear upstage.*

LOU: Yes, dear, I only wanted Quentin's feeling—

ELSIE: Your shirt's out, dear.

> *He quickly tucks it into his shorts. And she turns to Quentin.*

You certainly don't think he ought to publish.

QUENTIN: But the alternative seems—

ELSIE, *with a volcanic, suppressed alarm*: But, dear, that's the *situation*! Lou's not like you, Quentin; you and Mickey can function in the rough-and-tumble of private practice, but Lou's a purely academic person. He's *incapable* of going out and—

> *Upstage, Mother appears beside Father.*

LOU, *with a difficult grin and chuckle*: Well, dear, I'm not all that delicate, I—

ELSIE, *with a sudden flash of contempt, to Lou*: This is hardly the time for illusions!

MOTHER: You *idiot*!

> *Quentin is shocked, turns quickly to Mother, who stands accusingly over the seated Father.*

My *bonds*?

QUENTIN, *watching Mother go*: Why do I think of things falling apart? Were they ever whole?

> *Mother exits; for a moment Father and Dan stay on in darkness, frozen in their despair.*

> *Louise now stands up.*

LOUISE: Quentin?

> *He turns his eyes to the ground, then to the Listener. . . .*

QUENTIN: Wasn't that a terrifying thing, what Holga said?

LOUISE: I've decided to go into psychoanalysis.

QUENTIN: To take up your life—like an idiot child?

LOUISE: I want to talk about some things with you.

QUENTIN: But can anybody really do that? Kiss his life?

LOUISE, *at a loss for an instant*: Sit down, will you?

> *She gathers her thoughts. He hesitates, as though pained at the memory, and also because at the time he lived this it was an agony. And as he approaches his chair . . .*

QUENTIN, *to the Listener*: It was like—a meeting. In seven years we had never had a meeting. Never, never what you'd call—a meeting.

LOUISE: We don't seem—*a long pause while she peers at a forming thought*—married.

QUENTIN: We?

> *It is sincere, what she says, but she has had to learn the words, so there is the faintest air of a formula in her way of speaking.*

LOUISE: You don't pay any attention to me.

QUENTIN, *to help her*: You mean like Friday night? When I didn't open the car door for you?

LOUISE: Yes, that's part of what I mean.

QUENTIN: But I told you; you always opened the car door for yourself.

LOUISE: I've always done everything for myself, but that doesn't mean it's right. Everybody notices it, Quentin.

QUENTIN: What?

LOUISE: The way you behave toward me. I don't exist. People are supposed to find out about each other. I am not all this uninteresting. Many people, men *and* women, think I *am* interesting.

QUENTIN: Well, I— *He breaks off.* I—don't know what you mean.

LOUISE: You have no conception of what a woman is.

QUENTIN: But I do pay attention—just last night I read you my whole brief.

LOUISE: Quentin, you think reading a brief to a woman is talking to her?

QUENTIN: But that's what's on my mind.

LOUISE: But if that's all on your mind, what do you need a wife for?

QUENTIN: Now what kind of a question is that?

LOUISE: Quentin, that's the question!

QUENTIN, *after a slight pause, with fear, astonishment*: What's the question?

LOUISE: What am I to you? Do you—do you ever *ask* me anything? Anything personal?

QUENTIN, *with rising alarm*: But Louise, what am I supposed to ask you? I *know* you!

LOUISE: No. *She stands with dangerous dignity.* You don't know me. *Pause. She proceeds now with caution.* I don't intend to be ashamed of myself any more. I used to think it was normal, or even that you don't see me because I'm not worth seeing. But I think now that you don't really see any woman. Except in some ways your mother. You do sense her feelings; you do know when she's unhappy or anxious, but not me. Or any other woman.

> *Elsie appears on second platform, about to drop her robe as before.*

QUENTIN: That's not true, though. I—

LOUISE: Elsie's noticed it too.

QUENTIN, *guiltily snapping away from the vision of Elsie*: What?

LOUISE: She's amazed at you.

QUENTIN: Why, what'd she say?

LOUISE: She says you don't seem to notice when a woman is *present*.

QUENTIN: Oh. *He is disarmed, confused, and silent.*

LOUISE: And you know how she admires you.

> *Elsie disappears. Quentin nods seriously. Suddenly he turns to the Listener and bursts into an agonized, ironical laughter. He abruptly breaks it off and returns to silence before Louise. With uncertainty; it is her first attempt at confrontation:*

Quentin?

He stands in silence.

Quentin?

He is silent.

Silence is not going to solve it any more, Quentin. I can't live this way.

> *Pause. Quentin gathers courage.*

QUENTIN: Maybe I don't speak because the one time I did tell you my feelings you didn't get over it for six months.

LOUISE, *angered:* It wasn't six months, it was a few weeks. I did overreact, but it's understandable. You come back from a trip and tell me you'd met a woman you wanted to sleep with.

QUENTIN: That's not the way I said it.

LOUISE: It's exactly the way. And we were married a year.

QUENTIN: It is not the way I said it, Louise. It was an idiotic thing to tell you, but I still say I meant it as a compliment; that I did not touch her because I realized what you meant to me. And for damn near a year you looked at me as though I were some kind of a monster who could never be trusted again. *Immediately to the Listener:* And why do I believe she's right! That's the point! Yes—now, now! It's innocence, isn't it? The innocent are always better, aren't they? Then why can't I be innocent?

> *The tower appears.*

Even this slaughterhouse! Why does something in me bow its head like an accomplice in this place!

> *Mother appears upstage.*

Huh? Please, yes, if you think you know. *Turning to Mother:* In what sense treacherous?

MOTHER: What poetry he brought me! He understood me, Strauss. And two weeks after the wedding, Papa hands me the menu. To *read*!

QUENTIN: Huh! Yes! And to a little boy—who knows how to read; a powerful reader, that little boy!

MOTHER: I want your handwriting beautiful, darling; I want you to be . . .

QUENTIN, *realizing*: . . . an accomplice!

MOTHER, *turning on Father, who still sits dejectedly*: My *bonds*? And you don't even tell me anything. Are you a moron? You idiot!

QUENTIN, *watching her and Father go dark, to the Listener*: But why is the world so treacherous?

> *Mickey appears upstage, faces Louise in silence.*

Shall we lay it all to mothers? Aren't there mothers who keep dissatisfaction hidden to the grave, and do not split the faith of sons until they go in guilt for what they did not do? And I'll go further—here's the final bafflement for me—is it altogether good to be not guilty for what another does?

Father and Dan exit in darkness. The tower goes dark.

MICKEY, *to Louise, grinning*: You proud of him?

LOUISE: Yes!

MICKEY, *coming to Quentin, who turns to him*: The brief is fine, kid; it almost began to move me.

LOUISE: Lou and Elsie are here.

MICKEY: Oh! I didn't know. You look wonderful, Louise. You look all excited.

LOUISE: Thanks! It's nice to hear! *She shyly, soundlessly laughs, glancing at Quentin, and goes.*

MICKEY: You got trouble?

QUENTIN, *embarrassed*: I don't think so, she's going into psychoanalysis.

MICKEY: You got trouble. *Shakes his head, laughing thoughtfully.* I think maybe you got married too young; I did too. Although, *you* don't fool around, do you?

QUENTIN: I don't, no.

MICKEY: Then what the hell are you so guilty about?

QUENTIN: I didn't know I was till lately.

MICKEY: You know, when it first happened to me, I set aside five minutes a day just imagining my wife as a stranger. As though I hadn't made her yet. You got to generate some respect for her mystery. Start with five minutes; I can go as long as an hour, now.

QUENTIN: Makes it seem like a game, though, doesn't it?

MICKEY: Well, it is, isn't it, in a way? As soon as there's two people, you can't be absolutely sincere, can you? I mean she's not your rib.

QUENTIN: I guess that's right, yes.

> Pause. Lou and Elsie are heard offstage. Mickey walks to a point, looks down as over a cliff.

MICKEY: Dear Lou; look at him down there, he never learned how to swim, always paddled like a dog. *Comes back.* I used to love that man. I still do. Quentin, I've been subpoenaed.

QUENTIN, *shocked*: Oh, God! The Committee?

MICKEY: Yes. I wish you'd have come into town when I called you. But it doesn't matter now.

QUENTIN: I had a feeling it was something like that. I guess I—I didn't want to know any more. I'm sorry, Mick. *To Listener*: Yes, not to see! To be innocent!

> A long pause. They find it hard to look directly at each other.

MICKEY: I've been going through hell, Quent. It's strange—to have to examine what you stand for; not theoretically, but on a life-and-death basis. A lot of things don't stand up.

QUENTIN: I guess the main thing is not to be afraid.

MICKEY, *after a pause*: I don't think I am now.

> A pause. Both sit staring ahead. Finally Mickey turns and looks at Quentin, who now faces him. Mickey tries to smile.

You may not be my friend any more.

QUENTIN, *trying to laugh it away—a terror rising in him*: Why?

MICKEY: I'm going to tell the truth.

> Pause.

QUENTIN: How do you mean?

MICKEY: I'm—going to name names.

QUENTIN, *incredulously*: Why?

MICKEY: Because—I want to. Fifteen years, wherever I go, whatever I talk about, the feeling is always there that I'm deceiving people.

QUENTIN: But why couldn't you just tell about yourself?

> Maggie enters, lies down on second platform.

MICKEY: They want the names, and they mean to destroy anyone who—

QUENTIN: I think it's a mistake, Mick. All this is going to pass, and I think you'll regret it. And anyway, Max has always talked against this kind of thing!

MICKEY: I've had it out with Max. I testify or I'll be voted out of the firm.

QUENTIN: I can't believe it! What about DeVries?

MICKEY: DeVries was there, and Burton, and most of the others. I wish you'd have seen their faces when I told them. Men I've worked with for thirteen years. Played tennis; intimate friends, you know? And as soon as I said, "I had been"—stones.

The tower lights.

QUENTIN, *to the Listener*: Everything is one thing! You see—I don't know what we are to one another!

MICKEY: I only know one thing, Quent, I want to live a straightforward, open life!

Lou enters in bathing trunks, instantly overjoyed at seeing Mickey. The tower goes dark.

LOU: Mick! I *thought* I heard your voice! *Grabs his hand.* How are you!

Lou and Mickey de-animate in an embrace. Holga appears with flowers on upper level.

QUENTIN, *glancing up at Holga*: How do you dare make promises again? I have lived through all the promises, you see?

Holga exits.

LOU, *resuming, moving downstage with Mickey*: Just the question of publishing my book, now. Elsie's afraid it will wake up all the sleeping dogs again.

MICKEY: But don't you have to take that chance? I think a man's got to take the rap, Lou, for what he's done, for what he is. After all, it's your work.

LOU: I feel exactly that way! *Grabs his arm, including Quentin in his feeling.* Golly, Mick! Why don't we get together as we used to! I miss all that wonderful talk! Of course I know how busy you are now, but—

MICKEY: Elsie coming up?

LOU: You want to see her? I could call down to the beach. *He starts off, but Mickey stops him.*

MICKEY: Lou.

LOU, *sensing something odd*: Yes, Mick.

QUENTIN, *facing the sky*: Dear God.

MICKEY: I've been subpoenaed.

LOU: No! *Mickey nods, looks at the ground. Lou grips his arm.* Oh, I'm terribly sorry, Mick. But can I say something—it might ease your mind; once you're in front of them it all gets remarkably simple!

QUENTIN: Oh dear God!

LOU: Everything kind of falls away excepting—one's self. One's truth.

MICKEY, *after a slight pause*: I've already been in front of them, Lou. Two weeks ago.

LOU: Oh! Then what do they want with you again?

MICKEY, *after a pause, with a fixed smile on his face*: I asked to be heard again.

LOU, *puzzled, open-eyed*: Why?

MICKEY—*he carefully forms his thought*: Because I want to tell the truth.

LOU, *with the first rising of incredulous fear*: In—what sense? What do you mean?

MICKEY: Lou, when I left the hearing room I didn't feel I had spoken. Something else had spoken, something automatic and inhuman. I asked myself, what am I protecting by refusing to answer? Lou, you must let me finish! You must. The Party? But I despise the Party, and have for many years. Just like you. Yet there is something, something that closes my throat when I think of telling names. What am I defending? It's a dream now, a dream of solidarity. But the fact is, I have no solidarity with the people I could name—excepting for you. And not because we were Communists together, but because we were young together. Because we— when we talked it was like some brotherhood opposed to all the world's injustice. Therefore, in the name of that love, I ought to be true to myself now. And the truth, Lou, my truth, is that I think the Party *is* a conspiracy—let me finish. I think we *were* swindled; they took our lust for the right and used it for Russian purposes. And I don't think we can go on turning our backs on the truth simply because reactionaries are saying it. What I propose—is that we try to separate our love for one another from this political morass. And I've said nothing just now that we haven't told each other for the past five years.

LOU: Then—what's your proposal?

MICKEY: That we go back together. Come with me. And answer the questions.

LOU: Name—the names?

MICKEY: Yes. I've talked to all the others in the unit. They've agreed, excepting for Ward and Harry. They cursed me out, but I expected that.

LOU, *dazed*: Let me understand—you are asking my permission to name me?

Pause.

You may not mention my name. *He begins physically shaking.* And if you do it, Mickey, you are selling me for your own prosperity. If you use my name I will be dismissed. You will ruin me. You will destroy my career.

MICKEY: Lou, I think I have a right to know exactly why you—

LOU: Because if everyone broke faith there would be no civilization! That is why that Committee is the face of the Philistine! And it astounds me that you can speak of truth and justice in relation to that gang of cheap publicity hounds! Not one syllable will they get from me! Not one word from my lips! No—your eleven-room apartment, your automobile, your money are not worth this.

MICKEY, *stiffened*: That's a lie! You can't reduce it all to money, Lou! *That* is false!

LOU, *turning on him*: There is only one truth here. You are terrified! They have bought your soul!

Elsie appears upstage, listening. Louise enters, watches.

MICKEY, *angrily, but contained*: And yours? Lou! Is it all yours, your soul?

LOU, *beginning to show tears*: How dare you speak of my—

MICKEY, *quaking with anger*: You've got to take it if you're going to dish it out, don't you? Have you really earned this high moral tone—this perfect integrity? I happen to remember when you came back from your trip to Russia; and I remember who made you throw your first version into my fireplace!

LOU, *with a glance toward Elsie*: The idea!

MICKEY: I saw you burn a true book and write another that told lies! Because she demanded it, because she terrified you, because she has taken your soul!

LOU, *shaking his fist in the air*: I condemn you!

MICKEY: But from your conscience or from hers? Who is speaking to me, Lou?

LOU: You are a monster!

Lou bursts into tears, walks off toward Elsie; he meets her in the near distance; her face shows horror. At the front of stage Mickey turns and looks across the full width toward Quentin at the farthest edge of light, and . . .

MICKEY, *reading Quentin's feelings*: I guess you'll want to get somebody else to go over your brief with you. *Pause.* Quent—

> *Quentin, indecisive, but not contradicting him, now turns to him.*

Good-by, Quentin.

QUENTIN, *in a dead tone*: Good-by, Mickey.

> *Mickey goes out.*

ELSIE: He's a moral idiot!

> *Holga enters above. Quentin turns to Elsie; something perhaps in his gaze or in the recesses of her mind makes her close her robe, which she holds tightly shut.*

Isn't that *incredible*?

> *Louise exits.*

QUENTIN, *quietly*: Yes.

ELSIE: After such friendship! Such love between them! And for so many years!

> *She goes to Lou. Lifts him and tenderly leads him off.*

> *The camp tower comes alive, and Quentin moves out of this group, slowly toward it, looking up.*

> *Holga descends, carrying flowers. She is a distance away from Quentin, who turns to her.*

QUENTIN: You—love me, don't you?

HOLGA: Yes.

> *An instant's hesitation, and he turns quickly to Listener and cries out.*

QUENTIN: Is it that I'm looking for some simple-minded constancy that never is and never was?

> *Holga exits. Now Louise approaches him. They are alone.*

LOUISE: Quentin, I'm trying to understand why you got so angry with me at the party the other night.

QUENTIN: I wasn't *angry*; I simply felt that every time I began to talk you cut in to explain what I was about to say. *He goes and gets a sheaf of paper, sits.*

LOUISE: Well, I'd had a drink; I was a little high; I felt happy, I guess, that you weren't running for cover when everybody else was.

QUENTIN: Yes, but Max was there and DeVries, and they don't feel they're running for cover. I only want to win Lou's case, not some moral victory over the firm—I felt you were putting me out on a limb.

LOUISE: Quentin, I saw you getting angry when I was talking about that new anti-virus vaccine.

He tries to remember, believing she is right.

What is it? The moment I begin to assert myself it seems to threaten you. I don't think you *want* me to be happy.

QUENTIN—*there is a basic concession made by his tone of admitted bewilderment*: I tell you the truth, Louise, I don't think I feel very sure of myself any more. I'm glad I took on Lou, but it only hit me lately that no respectable lawyer would touch him. It's like some unseen web of connection between people is simply not there. And I always relied on it, somehow; I never quite believed that people could be so easily disposed of. And it's larger than the political question. I think it's got me a little scared.

LOUISE, *with a wish for his sympathy, not accusing*: Well, then, you must know how I felt when I found that letter in your suit.

QUENTIN, *turning to her, aware*: I didn't do that to dispose of you, Louise. *She does not reply.* I thought we'd settled about that girl. Is that what this is about? *She still does not reply.* You mean you think I'm still—

LOUISE, *directly at him*: I don't know what you're doing. I thought you told the truth about that other girl years ago, but after what happened again this spring—I don't know anything.

QUENTIN, *after a pause*: Tell me something; until this party the other night—in fact this whole year, I thought you seemed much happier. I swear to God, Louise, I thought we were building something till the other night!

LOUISE: But why?

QUENTIN: I've been trying like hell to show what I think of you. You've seen that, haven't you?

LOUISE: Quentin, you are full of resentment against me, you think I'm blind?

QUENTIN: What I resent is being forever on trial, Louise. Are you an innocent bystander here?

LOUISE: I said I did contribute; I demanded nothing for much too long.

QUENTIN: You mean the summer before last you didn't come to me and say that if I didn't change you would divorce me?

LOUISE: I never said I was planning a—

QUENTIN: You said if it came down to it you would divorce me—that's not a contribution?

LOUISE: Well, it certainly ought not send a man out to play doctor with the first girl he could lay his hands on.

QUENTIN: How much shame do you want me to feel? I hate what I did. But, I think I've explained it—I felt like nothing; I shouldn't have, but I did, and I took the only means I knew to—

LOUISE: This is exactly what I mean Quentin—you are still defending it. Right now.

He is stopped by this truth.

QUENTIN: Look, you're—not at all to blame, hey?

LOUISE: But how?

QUENTIN: Well, for example—you never turn your back on me in bed?

LOUISE: I never turned my—

QUENTIN: You have turned your back on me in bed, Louise, I am not insane!

LOUISE: Well, what do you expect? Silent, cold, you lay your hand on me?

QUENTIN, *fallen*: Well, I—I'm not very demonstrative, I guess. *Slight pause.* He throws himself on her compassion. Louise—I worry about you all day. And all night.

LOUISE—*it is something, but not enough*: Well, you've got a child; I'm sure that worries you.

QUENTIN, *deeply hurt*: Is that all?

LOUISE, *with intense reasonableness*: Look, Quentin, you want a woman to provide an—atmosphere, in which there are never any issues, and you'll fly around in a constant bath of praise—

QUENTIN: Well, I wouldn't mind a little praise, what's wrong with praise?

LOUISE: Quentin, I am not a praise machine! I am not a blur and I am not your mother! I am a separate person!

QUENTIN, *staring at her, and what lies beyond her*: I see that now.

LOUISE: It's no crime! Not if you're adult and grown-up!

QUENTIN, *quietly*: I guess not. But it bewilders me. In fact, I got the same idea when I realized that Lou had gone from one of his former students to another and none would take him—

LOUISE: What's Lou got to do with it? I think it's admirable that you—

QUENTIN: Yes, but I am doing what you call an admirable thing because I can't bear to be—a separate person. I think so. I really don't want to be known as a Red lawyer; and I really don't want the newspapers to eat me alive; and if it came down to it Lou could defend himself. But when that decent, broken man who never wanted anything but the good of the world sits across my desk—I don't know how to say that my interests are no longer the same as his, and that if he doesn't change I consign him to hell because we are separate persons!

LOUISE: You are completely confused! Lou's case has nothing—

QUENTIN, *grasping for his thought*: I am telling you my confusion! I think Mickey also became a separate person—

LOUISE: You're incredible!

QUENTIN: I think of my mother, I think she almost became—

LOUISE: Are you identifying *me* with—

QUENTIN: Louise, I am asking you to explain this to me because this is when I go blind! When you've finally become a separate person, what the hell is there?

LOUISE, *with a certain unsteady pride*: Maturity.

QUENTIN: I don't know what that means.

LOUISE: It means that you know another person exists, Quentin. I'm not in analysis for nothing.

QUENTIN, *questing*: It's probably the symptom of a typical case of some kind, but I swear, Louise, if you would just once, of your own will, as right as you are—if you would come to me and say that something, something important was your fault and that you were sorry, it would help.

> *In her pride she is silent, in her refusal to be brought down again.*

Louise?

LOUISE: Good God! What an idiot! *She exits.*

QUENTIN: Louise . . .

> *He looks at his papers, the lights change. A sprightly music is heard. Anonymous park loungers appear and sit or lie about.*

How few the days are that hold the mind in place; like a tapestry hung on four or five hooks. Especially the day you stop becoming; the day you merely are. I suppose it's when the principles dissolve, and instead of the general gray of what ought to be you begin to see what is. Even the bench by the park seems alive, having held so many actual men. The word "now" is like a bomb through the window, and it ticks.

An old woman crosses with a caged parrot.

Now a woman takes a parrot for a walk. What will happen to it when she's gone? Everything suddenly has consequences.

A plain girl in tweeds passes, reading a paperback.

And how bravely a homely woman has to be! How disciplined of her, not to set fire to the Museum of Art.

A Negro appears, in pantomime asking for a light, which Quentin gives him.

And how does he keep so neat, and the bathroom on another floor? He must be furious when he shaves.

The Negro hurries off, seeing his girl.

Alone: And whatever made me think that at the end of the day I absolutely had to go home?

Maggie appears, looking about for someone, as Quentin sits on "park bench."

Now there's a truth; symmetrical, lovely skin, undeniable.

MAGGIE: 'Scuse me, did you see a man with a big dog?

QUENTIN: No. But I saw a woman with a little bird.

MAGGIE: No, that's not him. Is this the bus stop?

QUENTIN: Ya, the sign says—

MAGGIE, *sitting beside him*: I was standing over there and a man came with this big dog and just put the leash in my hand and walked away. So I started to go after him but the dog wouldn't move. And then this other man came and took the leash and went away. But I don't think it's really his dog. I think it's the first man's dog.

QUENTIN: But he obviously doesn't want it.

MAGGIE: But maybe he wanted for me to have it. I think the other man just saw it happening and figured he could get a free dog.

QUENTIN: Well, you want the dog?

MAGGIE: How could I keep a dog? I don't even think they allow dogs where I live. What bus is this?

QUENTIN: Fifth Avenue. This is the downtown side. Where do you want to go?

MAGGIE, *after thinking*: Well, I could go there.

QUENTIN: Where?

MAGGIE: Downtown.

QUENTIN: Lot of funny things go on, don't they?

MAGGIE: Well, he probably figured I would like a dog. Whereas I would if I had a way to keep it, but I don't even have a refrigerator.

QUENTIN: Yes. That must be it. I guess he thought you had a refrigerator.

> *She shrugs. Pause. He looks at her as she watches for the bus. He has no more to say.*

LOUISE, *appearing*: You don't talk to any woman—not like a *woman*! You think reading your brief is *talking* to me?

> *She exits. In tension Quentin leans forward, arms resting on his knees. He looks at Maggie again.*

QUENTIN, *with an effort*: What do you do?

MAGGIE, *as though he should know*: On the switchboard. *Laughs.* Don't you remember me?

QUENTIN, *surprised*: Me?

MAGGIE: I always sort of nod to you every morning through the window.

QUENTIN, *after an instant*: Oh. In the reception room!

MAGGIE: Sure! Maggie! *Points to herself.*

QUENTIN: Of course! You get my numbers sometimes.

MAGGIE: Did you think I just came up and started talking to you?

QUENTIN: I had no idea.

MAGGIE—*laughs*: Well, what must you have thought! I guess it's that you never saw me altogether. I mean just my head through that little window.

QUENTIN: Well, it's nice to meet all of you, finally.

MAGGIE—*laughs*: You go back to work again tonight?

QUENTIN: No, I'm just resting for a few minutes.

MAGGIE, *with a sense of his loneliness*: Oh. That's nice to do that. *She looks idly about. He glances down her body as she rises.* Is that my bus down there?

QUENTIN: I'm not really sure where you want to go. . . .

A man appears, eyes her, glances up toward the bus, back to her, staring.

MAGGIE: I wanted to find one of those discount stores; I just bought a phonograph but I only have one record. I'll see you! *She is half backing off toward the man.*

MAN: There's one on Twenty-seventh and Sixth Avenue.

MAGGIE, *turning, surprised*: Oh, thanks!

QUENTIN, *standing*: There's a record store around the corner, you know.

MAGGIE: But is it discount?

QUENTIN: Well, they all discount—

MAN, *slipping his hand under her arm*: What, ten per cent? Come on, honey, I'll get you an easy fifty per cent off.

MAGGIE, *to the man, starting to move off with him*: Really? But a Perry Sullivan . . . ?

MAN: Look, I'll give it to you—I'll give you two Perry Sullivans. Come on!

MAGGIE—*she halts, suddenly aware, disengages her arm, backs*: 'Scuse me, I—I—forgot something.

MAN, *reaching toward her*: Look, I'll give you ten records. *Calls off*: Hold that door! *Grabs her.* Come on!

QUENTIN, *moving toward him*: Hey!

MAN, *letting her go, to Quentin*: Ah, get lost! *He rushes off.* Hold it, hold the door!

Quentin watches the "bus" go by, then turns to her. She is absorbed in arranging her hair—but with a strangely doughy expression, removed.

QUENTIN: I'm sorry, I thought you knew him.

MAGGIE: No. I never saw him.

QUENTIN: Well—what were you going with him for?

MAGGIE: He said he knew a store. Where's the one you're talking about?

QUENTIN: I'll have to think a minute. Let's see . . .

MAGGIE: Could I sit with you? While you're thinking?

QUENTIN: Sure!

They return to the bench. He waits till she is seated; she is aware of the politeness, glances at him as he sits. Then she looks at him fully, for some reason amazed.

That happen to you very often?

MAGGIE, *factually*: Pretty often.

QUENTIN: It's because you talk to them.

MAGGIE: But they talk to me, so I have to answer.

QUENTIN: Not if they're rude. Just turn your back.

MAGGIE—*she thinks about that, and indecisively*: Oh, okay. *As though remotely aware of another world, his world*: Thanks, though—for stopping it.

QUENTIN: Well, anybody would.

MAGGIE: No, they laugh. I'm a joke to them. You—going to rest here very long?

QUENTIN: Just a few minutes. I'm on my way home—I never did this before.

MAGGIE: Oh! You look like you always did. Like you could sit for hours under these trees, just thinking.

QUENTIN: No. I usually go right home. *Grinning*: I've always gone right home.

MAGGIE: See, I'm still paying for the phonograph, whereas they don't sell records on time, you know.

QUENTIN: They're afraid they'll wear out, I guess.

MAGGIE: Oh, that must be it! I always wondered. 'Cause you *can* get phonographs. How'd you know that?

QUENTIN: I'm just guessing.

MAGGIE, *laughing*: I can never guess those things! I don't know why they do anything half the time! *She laughs more deeply. He does.* I had about ten or twenty records in Washington, but my friend got sick, and I had to leave. *Pause. Thinks.* His family lived right over there on Park Avenue.

QUENTIN: Oh. Is he better?

MAGGIE: He died. *Tears come into her eyes quite suddenly.*

QUENTIN, *entirely perplexed*: When was this?

MAGGIE: Friday. Remember they closed the office for the day?

QUENTIN: You mean—*astounded*—Judge Cruse?

MAGGIE: Ya.

QUENTIN: Oh, I didn't know that you—

MAGGIE: Yeah.

QUENTIN: He was a great lawyer. And a great judge too.

MAGGIE, *rubbing tears away*: He was very nice to me.

QUENTIN: I was at the funeral; I didn't see you, though.

MAGGIE, *with difficulty against her tears*: His wife wouldn't let me come. I got into the hospital before he died. But the family pushed me out and— I could hear him calling, "Maggie . . . Maggie!" *Pause.* They kept trying to offer me a thousand dollars. But I didn't want anything, I just wanted to say good-by to him! *She opens her purse, takes out an office envelope, opens it.* I have a little of the dirt. See? That's from his grave. His chauffeur drove me out—Alexander.

QUENTIN: Did you love him very much?

MAGGIE: No. In fact, a couple of times I really left him.

QUENTIN: Why didn't you altogether?

MAGGIE: He didn't want me to.

QUENTIN: Oh. *Pause.* So what are you going to do now?

MAGGIE: I'd love to get that record if I knew where they had a discount—

QUENTIN: No, I mean in general.

MAGGIE: Why, they going to fire me now?

QUENTIN: Oh, I wouldn't know about that.

MAGGIE: Although I'm not worried. Whereas I can always go back to hair.

QUENTIN: To where?

MAGGIE: I used to demonstrate hair preparations. *Laughs, squirts her hair with an imaginary bottle.* You know, in department stores? I was almost on TV once. *Tilting her head under his chin*: It's because I have very thick hair, you see? I have my mother's hair. And it's not broken. You notice I have no broken hair? Most women's hair is broken. Here, feel it, feel how— *She has lifted his hand to her head and suddenly lets go of it.* Oh, 'scuse me!

QUENTIN: That's all right!

MAGGIE: I just thought you might want to feel it.

QUENTIN: Sure.

MAGGIE: Go ahead. I mean if you want to. *She leans her head to him again. He touches the top of her head.*

QUENTIN: It is, ya! Very soft.

MAGGIE, *proudly:* I once went from page boy to bouffant in less than ten minutes!

QUENTIN: What made you quit?

A student sitting nearby looks at her.

MAGGIE: They start sending me to conventions and all. You're supposed to entertain, you see.

QUENTIN: Oh yes.

MAGGIE: There were parts of it I didn't like—any more. *She looks at the student, who turns away in embarrassment.* Aren't they sweet when they look up from their books!

The student walks off, mortified. She turns with a laugh to Quentin. He looks at her warmly, smiling. A clock strikes eight in a distant tower.

QUENTIN: Well, I've got to go now.

MAGGIE: 'Scuse me I put your hand on my head.

QUENTIN: Oh, that's all right. I'm not *that* bad. *He laughs softly, embarrassed.*

MAGGIE: It's not bad to be shy.

Pause. They look at each other.

QUENTIN: You're very beautiful, Maggie.

She smiles, straightens as though his words had entered her.

And I wish you knew how to take care of yourself.

MAGGIE: Oh . . . *Holding a ripped seam in her dress:* I got this torn on the bus this morning. I'm going to sew it home.

QUENTIN: I don't mean that.

She meets his eyes again—she looks chastised.

Not that I'm criticizing you. I'm not at all. You understand?

She nods, absorbed in his face.

MAGGIE: I understand. I think I'll take a walk in the park.

QUENTIN: You shouldn't. It's getting dark.

MAGGIE: But it's beautiful at night. I slept there one night when it was hot in my room.

QUENTIN: God, you don't want to do that. *Glancing at the park loungers*: Most of the animals around here are not in the zoo.

MAGGIE: Okay. I'll get a record, then. 'Scuse me about my hair if I embarrassed you.

QUENTIN, *laughing*: You didn't.

MAGGIE, *touching the top of her head as she backs away*: It's just that it's not broken. *He nods.* I'm going to sew this home. *He nods. She indicates the park, upstage.* I didn't *mean* to sleep there. I just fell asleep.

> *Several young men now rise, watching her.*

QUENTIN: I understand.

MAGGIE: Well . . . see you! *Laughs.* If they don't fire me!

QUENTIN: 'By.

> *She passes two men who walk step for step behind her, whispering in her ear together. She doesn't turn or answer. Now a group of men is beginning to surround her. Quentin, in anguish, goes and draws her away from them.*
>
> Maggie! *He takes a bill from his pocket, moving her across stage.* Here, why don't you take a cab? It's on me. Go ahead, there's one right there! *Points and whistles upstage and right.* Go on, grab it!

MAGGIE: Where—where will I tell him to go?

QUENTIN: Just cruise in the Forties—you've got enough there.

MAGGIE: Okay, 'by! *Backing out*: You—you just going to rest more?

QUENTIN: I don't know.

MAGGIE: Golly, that's nice!

> *The men walk off as Louise enters between Quentin and Maggie, continuing to her seat downstage. Maggie turns and goes to the second platform and lies down as before. Quentin moves down toward Louise, stands a few yards from her, staring at her optimistically. She remains unaware of him, reading.*

QUENTIN: Yes. She has legs, breasts, mouth, eyes . . . how beautiful! A woman of my own! What a miracle! In my own house! *He bends and kisses Louise, who looks up at him surprised, perplexed, lighting a cigarette.* Hi. *She keeps looking up at him, aware of some sea-like opening in the world.* What's the matter? *She still doesn't speak.* Well, what's the matter?

LOUISE: Nothing.

She returns to her book. Mystified, disappointed, he stands watching, then opens his briefcase and begins taking out papers.

Close the door if you're going to type.

QUENTIN: I always do.

LOUISE: Not always.

QUENTIN: Almost always. *He almost laughs, he feels loose, but she won't be amused, and returns again to her book.* How about eating out tomorrow night? Before the parents' meeting?

LOUISE: What parents' meeting?

QUENTIN: The school.

LOUISE: That was tonight.

QUENTIN, *shocked*: Really?

LOUISE: Of course. I just got back.

QUENTIN: Why didn't you remind me when I called today? You know I often forget those things. I told you I wanted to talk to her teacher.

LOUISE, *just a little more sharply*: People do what they want to do, Quentin. *An unwilling shout*: And you said you had to work tonight! *She returns to her book.*

QUENTIN: I didn't work.

LOUISE, *keeping to her book*: I know you didn't work.

QUENTIN, *surprised, an alarm beginning*: How did you know?

LOUISE: Well, for one thing, Max called here at seven-thirty.

QUENTIN: Max? What for?

LOUISE: Apparently the whole executive committee was in his office, waiting to meet with you tonight. *His hand goes to his head; open alarm shows on his face.* He called three times, as a matter of fact.

QUENTIN: My God, I— How could I do that? What's his home number?

LOUISE: The book is in the bedroom.

QUENTIN: We were supposed to discuss my handling Lou's case. DeVries stayed in town tonight just to—settle everything. *Breaks off.* What's Max's number, Murray Hill 3 . . . what is it?

LOUISE: The book is next to the bed.

QUENTIN: You remember it, Murray Hill 3, something.

LOUISE: It's in the book.

> *Pause. He looks at her, puzzled.*

I'm not the keeper of your phone numbers. You can remember them just as well as I. Please don't use that phone, you'll wake her up.

QUENTIN, *turning*: I had no intention of calling in there.

LOUISE: I thought you might want to be private.

QUENTIN: There's nothing "private" about this. This concerns the food in your mouth. The meeting was called to decide whether I should separate from the firm until Lou's case is over—or permanently, for all I know. *Remembering the number, he goes to the phone.* I've got it— Murray Hill 3 . . .

> *She watches him go to the phone. He picks it up, dials one digit. And much against her will . . .*

LOUISE: That's the old number.

QUENTIN: Murray Hill 3–4598.

LOUISE: It's been changed. *A moment.* Cortland 7–7098.

QUENTIN—*she is not facing him; he senses what he thinks is victory*: Thanks. *Starts again to dial, puts down the phone.* I don't know what to say to him. *She is silent.* We arranged for everybody to come back after dinner. It'll sound idiotic that I forgot about it.

LOUISE: You were probably frightened.

QUENTIN: But I made notes all afternoon about what I would say tonight! It's incredible!

LOUISE, *with an over-meaning*: You probably don't realize how frightened you are.

QUENTIN: I guess I don't. He said a dreadful thing today—Max. He was trying to argue me into dropping Lou and I said, "We should be careful not to adopt some new behavior just because there's hysteria in the country." I thought it was a perfectly ordinary thing to say but he—he's never looked at me that way, like we were suddenly standing on two distant mountains; and he said, "I don't know of any hysteria. Not in this office."

LOUISE: But why does all that surprise you? Max is not going to endanger his whole firm to defend a Communist. You tend to make relatives out of people.

QUENTIN: You mean . . .

LOUISE: I mean you can't have everything; if you feel this strongly about Lou you probably will have to resign.

QUENTIN, *after a pause*: You think I should?

LOUISE: That depends on how deeply you feel about Lou.

QUENTIN: I'm trying to determine that; I don't know for sure. What do you think?

LOUISE, *in anguish*: It's not my decision, Quentin.

QUENTIN, *puzzled and surprised*: But aren't you involved?

LOUISE: Of course I'm involved.

QUENTIN: I'm only curious how you—

LOUISE: You? Curious about me?

QUENTIN: Oh. We're not talking about what we're talking about, are we?

LOUISE, *nodding in emphasis*: You have to decide what you feel about a certain human being. For once in your life. And then maybe you'll decide what you feel about other human beings. Clearly and decisively.

QUENTIN: In other words . . . where was I tonight.

LOUISE: I don't care where you were tonight.

QUENTIN, *after a pause*: I sat by the park for a while. And this is what I thought. *With difficulty*: I don't sleep with other women, but I think I behave as though I do. *She is listening; he sees it and is enlivened by hope.* Maybe I invite your suspicion in order to—to come down off some bench, to stop judging others so perfectly. Because I do judge, and harshly too, when the fact is I'm bewildered. I wonder if I left that letter for you to read about that girl—in order somehow to start being real. *Against his own trepidation but encouraged by her evident uncertainty*: I met a girl tonight. Just happened to come by, one of the phone operators in the office. I probably shouldn't tell you this, but I will. Quite stupid, silly kid. Sleeps in the park, her dress ripped. She said some ridiculous things. But one thing struck me; she wasn't defending anything, upholding anything, or accusing—she was just *there*, like a tree or a cat. And I felt strangely abstract beside her. And I saw that we are killing one another with abstractions. I'm defending Lou because I love him, yet the society transforms that love into a kind of treason, what they call an issue, and I end up suspect and hated. Why can't we speak with the voice that speaks below the "issues"—with our real uncertainty? I came home just now— and I had a tremendous wish to come out—to you. And you to me. It sounds absurd, but this city is full of people rushing to meet one another. This city is full of lovers.

LOUISE: And what did she say?

QUENTIN: I guess I shouldn't have told you about it.

LOUISE: Why not?

QUENTIN: Louise, I don't know what's permissible to say any more.

LOUISE, *nodding*: You don't know how much to hide.

QUENTIN, *angering*: All right, let's not hide anything; it would have been easy to make love to her. *Louise reddens, stiffens.* And I didn't because I thought of you, and in a new way—like a stranger I had never gotten to know. And by some miracle you were waiting for me, in my own home.

LOUISE: What do you want, my congratulations? You don't imagine a real woman goes to bed with any man who happens to come along? Or that a real man goes to bed with every woman who'll have him? Especially a slut, which she obviously is?

QUENTIN: How do you know she's a—

LOUISE, *laughing*: Oh, excuse me, I didn't mean to insult her! You're unbelievable! Suppose I came home and told you I'd met a man on the street I wanted to go to bed with—because he made the city seem full of lovers.

QUENTIN, *humiliated*: I understand. I'm sorry. I would get angry too but I would see that you were struggling. And I would ask myself—maybe I'd even be brave enough to ask you—how *I* had failed.

LOUISE: Well, you've given me notice; I get the message. *She starts out.*

QUENTIN: Louise, don't you ever doubt yourself? Is it enough to prove a case, to even win it—*shouts*—when we are dying?

> *Mickey enters at the edge of the stage. Elsie enters on second platform, opening her robe as before.*

LOUISE, *turning, in full possession*: I'm not dying. I'm not the one who wanted to break this up. And that's all it's about. It's all it's been about the last three years. You don't want me. *She goes out.*

QUENTIN, *to himself*: God! Can that be true?

MICKEY: There's only one thing I can tell you for sure, kid—don't ever be guilty.

QUENTIN: Yes! *Seeking strength, he stretches upward.* Yes! *But his conviction wavers; he turns toward the vision.* But if you had felt more guilt, maybe you wouldn't have . . .

ELSIE, *closing her robe*: He's a moral idiot!

QUENTIN: Yes! That is right. And yet . . . What the hell is moral? And what am I, to even ask that question? A man ought to know—a decent man knows that like he knows his own face!

Louise enters with a folded sheet and a pillow.

LOUISE: I don't want to sleep with you.

QUENTIN: Louise, for God's sake!

LOUISE: You are disgusting!

QUENTIN: But in the morning Betty will see . . .

LOUISE: You should have thought of that.

The phone rings. He looks at sheets, makes no move to answer.

Did you give her this number?

It rings again.

Did you give her this number? *With which she strides to the phone.* Hello! Oh, yes. He's here. Hold on, please.

QUENTIN: I can't sleep out here; I don't want her to see it. *He goes to the phone with a look of hatred.*

LOUISE: It's Max.

Surprised, he takes the phone from her.

QUENTIN, *into phone*: Max? I'm sorry, the whole thing just slipped my mind. I don't know how to explain it, I just went blank, I guess. *Pause.* The radio? No, why? . . . What? When? *Long pause.* Thanks . . . for letting me know. Yes, he was. Good night . . . Ya, see you in the morning. *Hangs up. Pause. He stands staring.*

LOUISE: What is it?

QUENTIN: Lou. Was killed by a subway train tonight.

LOUISE—*gasps*: How?

QUENTIN: They don't know. They say "fell or jumped."

LOUISE: He couldn't have! The crowd must have pushed him!

QUENTIN: There is no crowd at eight o'clock. It was eight o'clock.

LOUISE: But *why*? Lou *knew* himself! He knew where he *stood*! It's impossible!

QUENTIN, *staring*: Maybe it's not enough—to know yourself. Or maybe it's too much. I think he did it.

LOUISE: But *why*? It's inconceivable!

QUENTIN: When I saw him last week he said a dreadful thing. I tried not to hear it. *Pause. She waits.* That I turned out to be the only friend he had.

LOUISE, *genuinely*: Why is that dreadful?

QUENTIN, *evasively, almost slyly*: It just was. I don't know why. *Tears forming in his eyes, he comes toward Listener.* I didn't dare know why! But I dare now. It was dreadful because I was not his friend either, and he knew it. I'd have stuck it to the end but I hated the danger in it for myself, and he saw through my faithfulness; and he was not telling me what a friend I was, he was praying I would be—"Please be my friend, Quentin" is what he was saying to me, "I am drowning, throw me a rope!" Because I wanted out, to be a good American again, kosher again—and proved it in the joy . . . the joy . . . the joy I felt now that my danger had spilled out on the subway track! So it is not bizarre to me.

> *The tower blazes into life, and he walks with his eyes upon it.*

> This is not some crazy aberration of human nature to me. I can easily see the perfectly normal contractors and their cigars, the carpenters, plumbers, sitting at their ease over lunch pails; I can see them laying the pipes to run the blood out of this mansion; good fathers, devoted sons, grateful that someone else will die, not they, and how can one understand that, if one is innocent? If somewhere in one's soul there is no accomplice—of that joy, that joy, that joy when a burden dies . . . and leaves you safe?

> *Maggie's difficult breathing is heard. He turns in pain from it, comes to a halt on one side of the sheets and pillow lying on the floor at Louise's feet.*

> I've got to sleep; I'm very tired. *He bends to pick up the sheets. She makes an aborted move to pick up the pillow.*

LOUISE, *with great difficulty*: I—I've always been proud you took Lou's case. *He picks up sheets and pillow, stands waiting.* It was—courageous. *She stands there, empty-handed, not fully looking at him.*

QUENTIN: I'm glad you feel that way. *But he makes no move either. The seconds are ticking by. Neither can let down his demand for apology, or grace. With difficulty:* And that you told me. Thanks.

LOUISE: But—you are honest, that way. I've often told you.

QUENTIN: Recently?

LOUISE: Good night.

> *She starts away, and he feels the unwillingness with which she leaves.*

QUENTIN: Louise, if there's one thing I've been trying to do it's to be honest with you.

LOUISE: No, you've been trying to keep the home fires burning and see the world at the same time.

QUENTIN: So that all I am is deceptive and cunning.

LOUISE: Not all, but mostly.

QUENTIN: And there is no struggle. There is no pain. There is no struggle to find a way back to you?

LOUISE: That isn't the struggle.

QUENTIN: Then what are you doing here?

LOUISE: I—

QUENTIN: What the hell are you compromising yourself for if you're so goddamned honest!

He starts a clench-fisted move toward her and she backs away, terrified and strangely alive. Her look takes note of the aborted violence, and she is very straight and yet ready to flee.

LOUISE: I've been waiting for the struggle to begin.

He is dumbstruck—by her sincerity, her adamance. With a straight look at him, she turns and goes out.

QUENTIN, *alone, and to himself*: Good God, can there be more? Can there be worse? *Turning to the Listener*: See, that's what's incredible to me—three years more! What did I expect to save us? Suddenly, God knows why, she'd hold out her hand and I hold out mine, and laugh, laugh it all away, laugh it all back to—her dear, honest face looking up to mine . . . *Breaks off, staring into the distance. Far upstage, Louise looks at him with pride, as of old.* Back to some everlasting smile that saves. That's maybe why I came; I think I still believe it. That underneath we're all profoundly friends! I can't believe this world; all this hatred isn't real to me! *Turns back to his "living room," the sheets. Louise is gone now.* To bed down like a dog in my living room, how can that be necessary? Then go in to her, open your heart, confess the lechery, the mystery of women, say it all. . . . *He has moved toward where she exited, now halts.* But I did that. So the truth, after all, may merely be murderous? The truth killed Lou, destroyed Mickey. Then how do you live? A workable lie? But that comes from a clear conscience! Or a dead one. Not to see one's own evil—there's power! And rightness too!—so kill conscience. Kill it. *Glancing toward her exit*: Know all. admit nothing, shave closely, remember birthdays, open car doors, pursue Louise not with truth but with attention. Be uncertain on your own time, in bed be absolute. And thus be a man—and join the world. And in the morning, a dagger in that dear little daughter's heart! *Flinging it toward Louise's exit*: Bitch! *Sits*. I'll say I have a cold. Didn't want to give it to Mommy. *With disgust*: Pah! Papa-papapapa. *Sniffs, tries to talk through his nose*. Got a cold in my nose, baby girl . . .

> *He groans. Pause. He stares; stalemate. A jet plane is heard. An airport porter appears, carrying two bags, as Holga, dressed for travel, moves onto the highest level, looking about for Quentin. A distant jet roars in take-off. Quentin glances at his watch, and, coming down to the chair . . .*

> Six o'clock, Idlewild. *Now he glances up at Holga, who is still looking about her as in a crowd*. It's that the evidence is bad for promises. But how else do you touch the world—except with a promise? And yet, I must not forget the way I wake; I open up my eyes each morning like a boy, even now; even now. That's as true as anything I know, but where's the evidence? Or is it simply that my heart still beats? . . . Certainly, go ahead, I'll wait.

> *He follows the departing Listener with his eyes; now he rises, follows "him" upstage.*

> You don't mind my staying? I'd like to settle this. Although actually, I—*laughs*—only came to say hello.

> *He turns front. He stares ahead; a different kind of relaxation is on him now, alone. The stage is dark but for a light on him. Now the tower is seen, and Maggie on the second platform near him. Suddenly she raises herself up.*

MAGGIE: Quentin? Quentin?

QUENTIN, *in agony*: I'll get to it, honey. *He closes his eyes*. I'll get to it.

> *He strikes sparks from a lighter held to a cigarette. All light is gone.*

ACT TWO

The stage is dark. A spark is seen, a flame fires up. When the stage illuminates, Quentin is discovered lighting his cigarette—no time has passed. He continues to await the Listener's return and walks a few steps in thought, and as he does a jet plane is heard, and the airport announcer's voice: ". . . from Frankfurt is now unloading at gate nine, passengers will please . . ." It becomes a watery garble, and at the same moment Holga, as before, walks onto the upper level with the airport porter, who leaves her bags and goes. She looks about as in a crowd, then, seeing "Quentin," stands on tiptoe and waves.

HOLGA: Quentin! Here! Here! *She opens her arms as he evidently approaches.* Hello! Hello!

He turns from her to the returned Listener at front and comes to him downstage. Holga moves out.

QUENTIN: Oh, that's all right, I didn't mind waiting. How much time do I have?

He sits at the forward edge of the stage, looks at his watch. Maggie appears on the second platform, in a lace wedding dress; Lucas, a designer, is on his knees, finishing the vast hem. Carrie, a Negro maid, stands by, holding her veil. Maggie is nervous, on the edge of life, looking into a mirror.

I think I can be clearer now.

MAGGIE, *in an ecstasy of fear and hope*: All right, Carrie, tell him to come in! *As though trying the angular words*: My *husband*!

CARRIE, *walking a few steps to a point, where she halts*: You can see her now, Mr. Quentin.

They are gone. Quentin continues to the Listener.

QUENTIN: I am bewildered by the death of love. And my responsibility for it.

Holga moves into light again, looking about for him at the airport.

This woman's on my side; I have no doubt of it. And I wouldn't want to outlive another accusation. Not hers.

Holga exits. He stands, agitated.

I suddenly wonder why I risk it again. Except . . .

Felice and Mother appear.

You ever felt you once saw yourself—absolutely true? I may have dreamed it, but I swear that somewhere along the line— with Maggie, I think—for one split second I saw my life; what I had done, what had been done to me, and even when I ought to do. And that vision sometimes hangs behind my head, blind now, bleached out like the moon in the morning; and if I could only let in some necessary darkness it would shine again. I think it had to do with power.

Felice approaches, about to remove the bandage.

Maybe that's why she sticks in my mind. *He walks around her, peering.* Well, that's power, isn't it? To influence a girl to change her nose, her life? . . . It does, yes, it frightens me, and I wish to God—*Felice raises her arm*—she'd stop blessing me! *Mother exits on upper platform. He laughs uneasily, surprised at the force of his fear.* Well, I suppose because there is a fraud involved; I have no such power.

Maggie suddenly appears in man's pajamas, talking into a phone, coming down to the bed, center.

MAGGIE, *with timid idolatry*: Hello? Is— How'd you know it's me? *Laughs as she lies down.* You really remember me? Maggie? From that park that day? Well, 'cause it's almost four years so I . . .

He comes away from her as she continues talking, unheard.

QUENTIN, *to the Listener, glancing from Maggie to Felice*: I do, yes, I see the similarity.

Laughter is heard as Holga appears at a café table, an empty chair beside her, the music of a café fiddle in the air.

HOLGA, *to an empty seat beside her*: I love the way you eat! You eat like a Pasha, a grand duke!

QUENTIN, *to Listener, looking toward her*: Yes, adored again! But . . . there is something different here. *As he moves toward Holga, he says to Listener*: Now keep me to my theme, I spoke of power.

He sits beside her. As he speaks now, Holga's aspect changes; she becomes moody, doesn't face him, seems hurt. And, sitting beside her, he speaks to the Listener.

We were in a café one afternoon in Salzburg, and quite suddenly, I don't know why—it all seemed to be dying between us. And I saw it all happening again. You know that moment, when you begin desperately to talk about architecture?

HOLGA: Fifteen thirty-five. The Archbishop designed it himself.

QUENTIN: Beautiful.

HOLGA, *distantly*: Yes.

QUENTIN, *as though drawing on his courage, suddenly turning to her*: Holga. I thought I noticed your pillow was wet this morning.

HOLGA: It really isn't anything important.

QUENTIN: There are no unimportant tears.

HOLGA: I feel sometimes— *Breaks off, then*: —that I'm boring you.

LOUISE, *entering upstage*: I am not all this uninteresting, Quentin!

He stares at her, trying to join this with his lost vision, and in that mood he turns out to the Listener.

QUENTIN: The question is power, but I've lost the . . . Yes! *He springs up and circles Louise.* I tell you there were times when she looked into the mirror and I saw she didn't like her face, and I wanted to step between her and her suffering.

HOLGA: I may not be all that interesting.

QUENTIN, *of Louise*: I felt guilty even for her face! But . . . with her— *He returns to the café table*—there was some new permission . . . not to blind her to her own unhappiness. I saw that it belonged to her as mine belonged to me. And suddenly there was only good will and a mystery.

HOLGA: I wish you'd believe me, Quentin; you have no duty here.

QUENTIN: Holga, I would go. But I know I'd be looking for you tomorrow.

Mother enters, taking Holga's place on the seat beside him. He continues speaking without pause.

But there's truth in what you feel. The time does come when I feel I must go. Not toward anything, or away from you. . . . But there *is* some freedom in the going.

MOTHER: Darling, there is never a depression for great people! The first time I felt you move, I was standing on the beach at Rockaway. . . .

Quentin has gotten up.

QUENTIN, *to Listener*: But power. Where is the . . .

MOTHER: And I saw a star, and it got bright, and brighter, and brighter! And suddenly it fell, like some great man had died, and you were being pulled out of me to take his place, and be a light, a light in the world!

QUENTIN, *to Listener*: Why is there some . . . air of treachery in that?

FATHER, *suddenly appearing with Dan behind him, to Mother*: What the hell are you talking about? We're just getting started again. I need him!

Quentin avidly turns from one to the other as they argue.

MOTHER: You've got Dan, you don't need him! He wants to try to get a job, go to college maybe.

FATHER: He's got a job!

MOTHER: He means with pay! I don't want his young years going by. He wants a life!

FATHER, *indicating Dan; they have surrounded Quentin*: Why don't *he* "want a life"?

MOTHER: Because he's different!

FATHER: Because *he* knows what's right! *Indicating Mother and Quentin together*: You're two of a kind—what you "want"! Chrissake, when I was his age I was supporting six people! *He comes up to Quentin.* What are you, stranger? What are you!

QUENTIN, *peering into the revulsion on his father's face*: Yes, I felt a power, in the going . . . and treason in it. Because there's failure, and you turn your back on failure . . .

Father exits with Mother.

FATHER: I need him!

DAN, *putting an arm around Quentin*: No, kid, don't feel that way. I just want to see him big again, but you go. I'll go back to school if things pick up.

QUENTIN, *peering at Dan, who has walked on past him and is talking to an invisible Quentin*: Yes, good men stay . . . although they die there . . .

DAN, *indicating a book in his hand, addressing an invisible Quentin*: It's my Byron, I'll put it in your valise, and I've put in my new Argyles, just don't wash them in hot water. And remember, kid, wherever you are . . . *A train whistle is heard far off. Dan rushes onto second platform, calling*:

Wherever you are, this family's behind you! So buckle down, now, I'll send you a list of books to read.

> *Mother, Father, and Dan disappear, waving farewell. Felice is gone.*

MAGGIE, *suddenly sitting up on her bed, addressing an empty space at the foot*: But could I read them?

QUENTIN, *spinning about in quick surprise*: Huh!

> *All the others have gone dark but him and Maggie.*

MAGGIE: I mean what kind of books? 'Cause, see—I never really graduated high school. Although I always liked poetry.

QUENTIN—*breaks his stare at her and quickly comes down to the Listener*: It's that I can't find myself in this vanity any more.

MAGGIE, *enthralled, on bed*: I can't hardly believe you came! Can you stay five minutes? I'm a singer now, see? In fact—*With a laugh at herself*—I'm in the top three. And for a long time I been wanting to tell you that . . . none of it would have happened to me if I hadn't met you that day.

QUENTIN: Why do you speak of love? All I can see now is the power she offered me. All right. *Turns to her in conflict, and unwillingly.* I'll try. *He approaches her.*

MAGGIE: I'm sorry if I sounded frightened on the phone but I didn't think you'd be in the office after midnight. *Laughs at herself nervously.* See, I only pretended to call you. Can you stay like five minutes?

QUENTIN, *backing into the chair*: Sure. Don't rush.

MAGGIE: That's what I mean, you know I'm rushing! Would you like a drink? Or a steak? They have two freezers here. My agent went to Jamaica so I'm just staying here this week till I go to London Friday. It's the Palladium, like a big vaudeville house, and it's kind of an honor but I'm a little scared to go.

QUENTIN: Why? I've heard you; you're marvelous. Especially . . . *He can't remember a title.*

MAGGIE: No, I'm just flapping my wings yet. But did you read what that *News* fellow wrote? He keeps my records in the 'frigerator, case they melt!

QUENTIN—*laughs with her, then recalls*: "Little Girl Blue"! It's very moving, the way you do that.

MAGGIE: Really? 'Cause, see, it's not I say to myself, "I'm going to sound sexy," I just try to come *through*—like in love or . . . *Laughs.* I really can't believe you're here!

QUENTIN: Why? I'm glad you called; I've often thought about you the last couple of years. All the great things happening to you gave me a secret satisfaction for some reason.

MAGGIE: Maybe 'cause you did it.

QUENTIN: Why do you say that?

MAGGIE: I don't know, just the way you looked at me. I didn't even have the nerve to go see an agent before that day.

QUENTIN: *How did* I look at you?

MAGGIE, *squinching up her shoulders, a mystery*: Like . . . out of your *self*. Most people, they . . . just look *at* you. I can't explain it. And the way you talked to me . . .

LOUISE, *who has been sitting right, playing solitaire*: You think reading your brief is talking to me?

MAGGIE: What did you mean—it gave you a secret satisfaction?

QUENTIN: Just that—like in the office, I'd hear people laughing that Maggie had the world at her feet—

MAGGIE, *hurt, mystified*: They laughed!

QUENTIN: In a way.

MAGGIE, *in pain*: That's what I mean; I'm a joke to most people.

QUENTIN: No, it's that you say what you mean, Maggie. You don't seem to be upholding anything, you're not—ashamed of what you are.

MAGGIE: W—what do you mean, of what I am?

Louise looks up. She is playing solitaire.

QUENTIN, *suddenly aware he has touched a nerve*: Well . . . that you love life, and . . . It's hard to define, I . . .

LOUISE: The word is "tart." But what did it matter as long as she praised you?

QUENTIN, *to Listener, standing, and moving within Maggie's area*: There's truth in it—I hadn't had a woman's praise, even a girl I'd laughed at with the others—

MAGGIE: But you didn't, did you?

He turns to her in agony.

Laugh at me?

QUENTIN: No. *He suddenly stands and cries out to Listener.* Fraud! From the first five minutes! . . . Because! I should have agreed she *was* a joke, a beautiful piece, trying to take herself seriously! Why did I lie to her, play this cheap benefactor, this— *Listens, and now unwillingly he turns back to her.*

MAGGIE: Like when you told me to fix where my dress was torn? You wanted me to be—proud of myself. Didn't you?

QUENTIN, *surprised*: I guess I did, yes. *To Listener*: By God I did!

MAGGIE, *feeling she has budged him*: Would you like a drink?

QUENTIN, *relaxing*: I wouldn't mind. *Glancing around*: What's all the flowers?

MAGGIE, *pouring*: Oh, that's that dopey prince or a king or whatever he is. He keeps sending me a contract—whereas I get a hundred thousand dollars if we ever divorce. I'd be like a queen or something, but I only met him in El Morocco *once*! *She laughs, handing him his drink.* I'm supposed to be his girl friend too! I don't know why they print those things.

QUENTIN: Well, I guess everybody wants to touch you now.

MAGGIE: Cheers! *They drink; she makes a face.* I hate the taste but I love the effect! Would you like to take off your shoes? I mean just to rest.

QUENTIN: I'm okay. I thought you sounded on the phone like something frightened you.

MAGGIE: Do you have to go home right away?

QUENTIN: Are you all alone here?

MAGGIE: It's okay. Oh hey! I cut your picture out of the paper last month. When you were defending that Reverend Harley Barnes in Washington? *Taking a small framed photo from under her pillow*: See? I framed it!

QUENTIN: Is something frightening you, Maggie?

MAGGIE: No, it's just you're here! It's odd how I found this—I went up to see my father—

QUENTIN: He must be very proud of you now.

MAGGIE, *laughing*: Oh, no—he left when I was eighteen months, see—'cause he said I wasn't from him, although my mother always said I was. And they keep interviewing me now and I never know what to answer, when they ask where you were born, and all. So I thought if he would just see me, and you know, just—look at me . . . I can't explain it.

QUENTIN: Maybe so you'll know who you are.

MAGGIE: Yes! But he wouldn't even talk to me on the phone—just said, "See my lawyer," and hung up. But on the train back there was your picture, right on the seat looking up at me. And I said, "I know who I am! I'm Quentin's friend!" But don't worry about it—I mean you could just be somebody's friend, couldn't you?

QUENTIN, *after a slight pause*: Yes, Maggie, I can be somebody's friend. It's just that you're so beautiful—and I don't only mean your body and your face.

MAGGIE: You wouldn't even have to see me again. I would do anything for you, Quentin—you're like a god!

QUENTIN: But anybody would have told you to mend your dress.

MAGGIE: No, they'd have laughed or tried for a quick one. You know.

QUENTIN, *to Listener*: Yes! It's all so clear—the honor! The first honor was that I hadn't tried to go to bed with her! She took it for a tribute to her "value," and I was only afraid! God, the hypocrisy! . . . But why do you speak of love?

MAGGIE: Oh hey! You know what I did because of you? *He turns back to her.* I was christening a submarine in the Groton shipyard; 'cause I was voted the favorite of all the workers! And I made them bring about ten workers up on the platform, whereas they're the ones built it, right? And you know what the admiral said? I better watch out or I'll be a Communist. And suddenly I thought of you and I said, "I don't know what's so terrible; they're for the poor people." Isn't that what you believe?

QUENTIN: I did, but it's a lot more complicated, honey.

MAGGIE: Oh! I wish I knew something.

QUENTIN: You know how to see it all with your own eyes, Maggie, that's more important than all the books.

MAGGIE: But you know if it's true. What you see.

QUENTIN, *puzzled*: You frightened *now*? . . . You are, aren't you? *Maggie stares at him in tension; a long moment passes.* What is it, dear? You afraid to be alone here? *Pause.* Why don't you call somebody to stay with you?

MAGGIE: I don't know anybody . . . like that.

QUENTIN, *after a slight pause*: Can I do anything? . . . Don't be afraid to ask me.

MAGGIE, *in a struggle, finally*: Would you . . . open that closet door?

QUENTIN—*looks off, then back to her*: Just open it?

MAGGIE: Yes.

> He walks into the dark periphery; she sits up warily, watching. He opens a "door." He returns. And she lies back.

QUENTIN: Do you want to tell me something? I'm not going to laugh. *Sits.* What is it?

MAGGIE, *with great difficulty*: When I start to go to sleep before. And suddenly I saw smoke coming out of that closet under the door. Kept coming and coming. It start to fill the whole room!

She breaks off, near weeping. He reaches and takes her hand.

QUENTIN: Oh, kid—you've often dreamed such things, haven't you?

MAGGIE: But I was awake!

QUENTIN: Well it was a waking dream. It just couldn't stay down till you went to sleep. These things can be explained if you trace them back.

MAGGIE: I know. I go to an analyst.

QUENTIN: Then tell him about it, you'll figure it out.

MAGGIE: It's when I start to call you before. *She is now absorbed in her own connections.* See, my mother—she used to get dressed in the closet. She was very—like moral, you know? But sometimes she'd smoke in there. And she'd come out—you know? with a whole cloud of smoke around her.

QUENTIN: Well—possibly you felt she didn't want you to call me.

MAGGIE, *astounded*: How'd you know that?

QUENTIN: You said she was so moral. And here you're calling a married man.

MAGGIE: Yes! She tried to kill me once with a pillow on my face 'cause I would turn out bad because of—like her sin. And I have her hair, and the same back. *She turns half to him, showing a naked back.* 'Cause I have a good back, see? Every masseur says.

QUENTIN: Yes, it is. It's beautiful. But it's no sin to call me.

MAGGIE, *shaking her head like a child with a relieved laugh at herself*: Doesn't make me bad. Right?

QUENTIN: You're a very moral girl, Maggie.

MAGGIE, *delicately and afraid*: W-what's moral?

QUENTIN: You tell the truth, even against yourself. You're not pretending to be—*turns out to the Listener, with a dread joy*—innocent! Yes, that suddenly there was someone who—could not club you to death with their innocence! And now it's all laughable!

Mother appears, raising her arm. Louise exits.

MOTHER: I saw a star . . .

MAGGIE: I bless you, Quentin! *Mother vanishes as he turns back to Maggie, who takes up his photo again.* Lots of nights, I take your picture, and I bless you. You mind? *She has pressed the picture against her cheek.*

QUENTIN: I hope you sleep.

MAGGIE: I will now! *Lies back.* Honestly! I feel . . . all clear!

QUENTIN, *with a wave of his hand*: Good luck in London.

MAGGIE: And—what's moral, again?

QUENTIN: To live the truth.

MAGGIE: That's you!

QUENTIN: Not yet, dear; but I intend to try. Don't be afraid to call me if you need any help. *She is suddenly gone. Alone, he continues the thought.* Any time—*Dan appears in crew-necked sweater with his book*—you need anything, you call, y'hear?

DAN: This family's behind you, Quentin. *Backing into darkness, with a wave of farewell as train whistle sounds*: Any time you need anything . . .

QUENTIN—*surprised, he has turned quickly to Dan, who disappears; and to the Listener, as he still stares at the empty space Dan has left*: You know? It isn't fraud, but some . . . disguise. I came to her like Dan—his goodness! No wonder I can't find myself!

> *Felice appears as Maggie exits. She is about to remove the bandage, and he grasps for the concept.*
>
> And that girl the other night. When she left. It's still not clear, but suddenly those two fixtures on my wall. *He walks toward a "wall," looking up.* I didn't do it, but I wanted to. Like—*he turns and spreads his arms in crucifixion*—this! *In disgust, he lowers his arms.* I don't know! Because she . . . *gave* me something! The power to change her! As though I—*cries out*—felt something for her! *He almost laughs.* What the hell am I trying to do, love *everybody*?
>
> *The line ends in self-contempt and anger. And suddenly, extremely fast, a woman appears in World War I costume—a Gibson Girl hat and veil over her face, ankle-length cloak, and in her hand a toy sailboat. She is bent over, as though offering the boat to a little boy, and her voice is like a whisper, distant, obscure. Father enters, calling, followed by Dan.*

MOTHER: Quentin? Look what we brought you from Atlantic City—from the boardwalk!

> *The boy evidently runs away; Mother instantly is anxious and angering and rushes to a point and halts, as though calling through a closed door.*

Don't lock this door! But darling, we didn't trick you, we took Dan because he's older and I wanted a rest! But Fanny told you we were coming back, didn't she? Why are you running that water? Quentin, stop that water! Ike, come quick! Break down the door! Break down the door! *She has rushed off into darkness.*

But a strange anger is on his face, and he has started after her. And to the Listener . . .

QUENTIN: They sent me out for a walk with the maid. When I came back the house was empty. God, why is betrayal the only truth that sticks? I adored that woman. It's monstrous I can't mourn her!

The park bench lights. Maggie appears in a heavy white man's sweater, a white angora skating cap over a red wig, moccasins, and sun glasses.

MAGGIE, *to the empty bench*: Hi! It's me! Maggie!

QUENTIN: Or mourn her either. . . . No, it's not that I think I killed her. It's . . .

MAGGIE, *to the empty bench*: See? I told you nobody recognizes me!

QUENTIN: . . . that I can't find myself in it. Either the guilt comes or the innocence! But where's my love or even my crime? And I tell you I saw it once! I saw *Quentin* here!

MAGGIE: Golly, I fell asleep the minute you left, the other night! You like my wig? See? And moccasins!

Slight pause. Now he smiles, comes beside her on the bench.

QUENTIN: All you need is roller skates.

MAGGIE, *clapping her hands with joy*: You're funny!

QUENTIN, *half to Listener*: I keep forgetting—*wholly to her*—how beautiful you are. Your eyes make me shiver.

She is silent for a moment, adoring.

MAGGIE: Like to see my new apartment? There's no elevator even, or a doorman. Nobody would know. If you want to rest before you go to Washington. *He doesn't reply.* 'Cause I just found out—I go to Paris after London.

QUENTIN: So . . . how long will you be gone?

MAGGIE: It's maybe two months, I think. *They both arrive at the same awareness—the separation is pain. Tears are in her eyes.* Quentin?

QUENTIN: Honey . . . *Takes her hand.* Don't look for anything more from me.

MAGGIE: I'm not! But if I went to Washington . . . I could register in the hotel as Miss None.

QUENTIN: N-u-n?

MAGGIE: No—"n-o-n-e"—like nothing. I made it up once 'cause I can never remember a fake name, so I just have to think of nothing and that's me! *She laughs with joy.* I've done it.

QUENTIN: It *is* a marvelous thought. The whole government's hating me, and meanwhile back at the hotel . . .

MAGGIE: That's what I mean! Just when that committee is knocking on your head you could think of me like naked—

QUENTIN: What a lovely thought!

MAGGIE: And it would make you happy.

QUENTIN, *smiling warmly at her*: And nervous.

MAGGIE: Because it should all be one one thing, you know? Helping people, and sex. You might even argue better the next day!

QUENTIN, *with a new awareness, astonishment*: You know? There's one word written on your forehead.

MAGGIE: What?

QUENTIN: "Now."

MAGGIE: But what else is there?

QUENTIN: A future. And I've been carrying it around all my life, like a vase that must never be dropped. So you can't ever touch anybody, you see?

MAGGIE: But why can't you just hold it in one hand?—*he laughs*—and touch with the other! I would never bother you, Quentin. *He looks at his watch, as though beginning to calculate if there might not be time. Maggie, encouraged, glances at his watch.* Just make it like when you're thirsty. And you drink and walk away, that's all.

QUENTIN: But what about you?

MAGGIE: Well . . . I would have what I gave.

QUENTIN: You're all love, aren't you?

MAGGIE: That's all I am! A person could die any minute, you know. *Suddenly*: Oh, hey! I've got a will! *Digging into her pocket, she brings out a folded sheet of notepaper.* But is it legal if it's not typewritten?

QUENTIN, *taking it*: What do you want with a will? He starts reading the will.

MAGGIE: I'm supposed to be like a millionaire in about two years! And I've got to do a lot of flying now.

QUENTIN, *looking at her*: Who wrote this?

MAGGIE: Jerry Moon. He's a friend of my agent Andy in the building business, but he knows a lot about law. He signed it there for a witness. I saw him sign it. In my bedroom—

QUENTIN: It leaves everything to the agency.

MAGGIE: I know, but just for temporary, till I can think of somebody to put down.

QUENTIN: Don't you have anybody at all?

MAGGIE: No!

QUENTIN: What's all the rush?

MAGGIE: Well, in case Andy's plane goes down. He's got five children, see, and his—

QUENTIN: But do you feel responsible for his family?

MAGGIE: Well, no. But he did help me, he loaned me money when I—

QUENTIN: A million dollars?

Two boys enter upstage, carrying baseball gloves.

MAGGIE, *with a dawning awareness and fear*: Well, not a million . . .

QUENTIN: Who's your lawyer?

MAGGIE: Well, nobody.

QUENTIN, *with a certain unwillingness, even a repugnance about interfering—he sounds neutral*: Didn't anybody suggest you get your own lawyer?

MAGGIE: But if you trust somebody you trust them—don't you?

Slight pause. A decision seizes him; he takes her hand.

QUENTIN: Come on, I'll walk you home.

MAGGIE, *as she stands with him*: Okay! 'Cause what's good for Andy's good for me, right?

QUENTIN: I can't advise you, honey, maybe you get something out of this that I don't understand. Let's go.

MAGGIE: No! I'm not involved with Andy. I . . . don't really sleep around with everybody, Quentin! *He starts to take her but she continues.*

> I was with a lot of men but I never got anything for it. It was like charity, see. My analyst said I gave to those in need. Whereas, I'm not an institution. You believe me?

QUENTIN, *wanting her feverishly*: I believe you. Come on.

A small gang of boys with baseball equipment obstructs them; one of the first pair points at her.

BOY: It's Maggie, I told you!

MAGGIE, *pulling at Quentin's arm, defensively, but excited*: No, I just look like her, I'm Sarah None!

QUENTIN: Let's go! *He tries to draw her off, but the boys grab her, and she begins accepting pencils and pieces of paper to autograph.* Hey!

CROWD: How about an autograph, Maggie! Whyn't you come down to the club! When's your next spectacular! Hey, Mag, I got all your records! Sing something! *Handing over a paper for her to sign*: For my brother, Mag! Take off your sweater, Mag, it's hot out! How about that dance like you did on TV!—*A boy wiggles sensuously.*

QUENTIN: That's enough!

Quentin has been thrust aside; he now reaches in, grabs her, and draws her away as she walks backward, still signing, laughing with them. And into darkness, and the boys gone, and she turns to him.

MAGGIE: I'm sorry!

QUENTIN: It's like they're eating you. You like that?

MAGGIE: No, but they're just people. Could you sit down till the train? All I got so far is this French Provincial. *Taking off her sweater*: You like it? I picked it out myself. And my bed, and my record player. But it could be a nice apartment, couldn't it?

In silence Quentin takes her hand; now he draws her to him; now he kisses her.

MAGGIE: I love you, Quentin. I would do anything for you. And I would never bother you, I swear.

QUENTIN: You're so beautiful it's hard to look at you.

MAGGIE: You didn't even see me! *Backing away*: Why don't you just stand there and I'll come out naked! Or isn't there a later train?

QUENTIN, *after a pause*: Sure. There's always a later train. *He starts unbuttoning his jacket.*

MAGGIE: I'll put music!

QUENTIN—*now he laughs through his words*: Yeah, put music! *He strives for his moment; to the Listener as he opens his jacket*: Here; it was somewhere here! I don't know, a—a fraud!

A driving jazz comes on.

MAGGIE: Here, let me take off your shoes!

Father, Mother, Dan enter. Maggie drops to his feet, starting to unlace. Stiffly, with a growing horror, he looks down at her. Now shapes move in the darkness.

QUENTIN: Maggie?

MAGGIE, *looking up from the floor, leaving off unlacing*: Yes?

He looks around in the darkness; and suddenly his father charges forward.

FATHER: What you *want*! Always what you *want*! Chrissake, *what are you*!

Now Louise appears, reading a book, but Dan is standing beside her, almost touching her with his hand.

DAN: This family's behind you, kid.

And Mother, isolated, moving almost sensuously—and Quentin is pressed, as though by them, away from Maggie.

QUENTIN, *roaring out to all of them, his fists angrily in air against them*: But where is *Quentin*?

MOTHER: Oh, what poetry he brought me, Strauss, and novels to read . . .

QUENTIN, *going toward Mother in her longing*: Yes, yes! But I know that treason! And the terror of complicity in that desire; yes, and not to be unworthy of these loyal, failing men! But where is Quentin? Instead of taking off my clothes, this—posture! Maggie—

MAGGIE: Okay. Maybe when I get back . . .

QUENTIN: You . . . have to tear up that will. *To Listener*: Can't even go to bed without a principle! But how can you speak of love, she was chewed and spat out by a long line of grinning men! Her name floating in the stench of locker rooms and parlor-car cigar smoke! She had the truth that day, I brought the lie that she had to be "saved"! From what? Except my own contempt!

MAGGIE, *to the empty space where Quentin was*: But even my analyst said it was okay. 'Cause a person like me has to have somebody.

QUENTIN: Maggie—honest men don't draw wills like that.

MAGGIE: But it's just for temporary—

QUENTIN: Darling, if I went to Andy, and this adviser, and the analyst too, perhaps—I think they'd offer me a piece, to shut up. They've got you on a table, honey, and they're carving you—

MAGGIE: But . . . I can't spend all that money anyway! I can't even think over twenty-five dollars!

QUENTIN: It's not the money they take, it's the dignity they destroy. You're not a piece of meat; you seem to think you owe people whatever they demand!

MAGGIE: I know. *She lowers her head with a cry, trembling with hope and shame.*

QUENTIN, *tilting up her face*: But Maggie, you're somebody! You're not a kid any more, running around looking for a place to sleep! It's not only your success or that you're rich—you're straight, you're serious, you're first-class, people mean something to you; you don't have to go begging shady people for advice like some—some tramp! *With a sob of love and desperation she slides to the floor and grasps his thighs, kissing his trousers. He watches, then suddenly lifts her, and with immense pity and hope*: Maggie, stand up!

> *The music flies in now, and she smiles strangely through her tears, and with a kind of statement of her persisting nature begins unbuttoning her blouse. Maggie's body writhes to the beat within her clothing. And as soon as she starts her dance, his head shakes—and to the Listener . . .*

> No, not love; to stop impersonating, that's all! To live— *Groping*—to live in good faith if only with my guts! To— *To Dan and Father*: Yes! To be "good" no more! Disguised no more! *To Mother*: Afraid no more to show what Quentin, Quentin, Quentin—is!

LOUISE: You haven't even the decency to . . .

> *A high tribunal appears, and a flag; a chairman bangs his gavel once; he is flanked by others looking down on Quentin from on high.*

QUENTIN: That decency is murderous! Speak truth, not decency. I curse the whole high administration of fake innocence! *To the chairman*: I declare it, I am not innocent!—nor good!

CHAIRMAN: But surely Reverend Barnes cannot object to answering whether he attended the Communist-run Peace Congress in Prague, Czechoslovakia. No—no, counsel will not be allowed to confer with the witness, this is not a trial! Any innocent man would be—

QUENTIN: And this question—innocent! How many Negroes you allow to vote in your patriotic district? And which of your social, political, or racial sentiments would Hitler have disapproved? And not a trial? You fraud, your "investigators" this moment are working in this man's church to hound him out of it!

HARLEY BARNES, *rising to his feet, wearing a clerical collar*: I decline on the grounds of the First and Fifth Amendments to the Constitution.

QUENTIN, *with intense sorrow*: But are we sure, Harley—I ask it, I ask it—if the tables were turned, and they were in front of you, would you permit them not to answer? Hateful men that they are? *Harley looks at him indignantly, suspiciously.* I am not sure what we are upholding any more—are we good by merely saying no to evil? Even in a righteous "no" there's some disguise. Isn't it necessary—to say—Harley is gone, and the tribunal; Maggie is there, snapping her fingers, letting down her hair—to finally say yes—to something? *Turning toward Maggie, who lies down on the bed*: Yes, yes, yes.

MAGGIE: Say anything to me.

QUENTIN, *looking down at her*: A fact . . . a fact . . . a fact, a thing.

MAGGIE: Sing inside me.

> *Quentin crosses to Listener.*

QUENTIN: Even condemned, unspeakable like all truth!

MAGGIE: Become happy.

QUENTIN: Contemptible like all truth.

MAGGIE: That's all I am.

QUENTIN: Covered like truth with slime: blind, ignorant.

MAGGIE: But nobody ever said to me, stand up!

QUENTIN: The blood's fact, the world's blind gut—yes!

MAGGIE: Now.

QUENTIN, *sitting before the listener, his back to Maggie*: To this, yes.

MAGGIE: Now . . . Now. *Pause.* Quentin? *She rises off the bed, drawing the blanket around her, and in a languid voice addresses a point upstage.* Quenny? That soap is odorless, so you don't have to worry. *Slight pause.* It's okay! Don't rush; I love to wait for you! *She glances down at the floor.* I love your shoes. You have good taste! *She moves upstage.* 'Scuse me I didn't have anything for you to eat, but I didn't know! I'll get eggs, though, case maybe in the mornings. And steaks—case at night. I mean just in case. You could have it just the way you want, just any time. *She turns, looking front.* Like me?

> *Holga appears above, in the airport, looking about for him.*

QUENTIN, *to the Listener, his back to Maggie*: It's all true, but it isn't the truth. I know it because it all comes back so cheap; I loved that girl. My bitterness is making me lie. I'm afraid. To make a promise. *Glancing up at Holga*: Because I don't know who'll be making it. I'm a stranger to my life.

MAGGIE—*she has lifted a "tie" off the floor*: Oh, your tie got all wrinkled! I'm sorry! But hey, I have a tie! It's beautiful, a regular man's tie. *Catching herself*: I . . . just happen to have it! *She laughs it off and goes into darkness. Holga is gone.*

QUENTIN: I tell you, below this fog of tawdriness and vanity, there is a law in this disaster, and I saw it as hard and clear as a statute. But I think I saw it . . . with some love. Or can one ever remember love? It's like trying to summon up the smell of roses in a cellar. You might see a rose, but never the perfume. And that's the truth of roses, isn't it—the perfume?

> *On the second platform Maggie appears in light in a wedding dress; Carrie, a Negro maid, is just placing a veiled hat on her head; Lucas, a designer, is on his knees, hurriedly fixing the last hem, as before. Maggie is turning herself, wide-eyed, in an unseen mirror. Quentin begins to rise.*

MAGGIE: Hurry, Lucas, the ceremony is for three! Hurry, please! *Lucas sews faster.*

QUENTIN, *to Listener*: I want to see her with . . . that love again! Why is it so hard? Standing there, that wishing girl, that victory in lace.

MAGGIE, *looking ahead on the edge of life as Lucas bites off the last threads*: You won't hardly know me any more, Lucas! He saved me, I mean it! I've got a new will and I even changed my analyst—I've got a wonderful doctor now! And we're going to do all my contracts over, which I never got properly paid. And Ludwig Reiner's taking me! And he won't take even opera singers unless they're, you know, like artists! No matter how much you want to pay him. I didn't even dare, but Quentin made me go—and now he took me, Ludwig Reiner, imagine!

> *Now she turns, seeing Quentin entering. An awe of the moment takes them both; Lucas goes. Carrie lightly touches Maggie's forehead and silently prays.*

QUENTIN: Oh, my darling. How perfect you are.

MAGGIE, *descending toward him*: Like me?

> *Clergyman and woman guest enter on second platform.*

QUENTIN: Good God! To come home every night—to *you*!

> *He starts for her, open-armed, laughing, but she touches his chest, excited and strangely fearful.*

MAGGIE: You still don't have to do it, Quentin. I could just come to you whenever you want.

QUENTIN: You just can't believe in something good really happening. But it's real, darling, you're my wife!

MAGGIE, *with a hush of fear on her voice*: I want to tell you why I went into analysis.

QUENTIN: Darling, you're always making new revelations, but—

MAGGIE: But you said we have to love what happened, didn't you? Even the bad things?

QUENTIN, *seriously now, to match her intensity*: Yes, I did.

Clergyman and woman exit.

MAGGIE: I . . . was with two men . . . the same day.

She has turned her eyes from him. A group of wedding guests appears on second platform.

I mean the same day, see. *She almost weeps now, and looks at him, subservient and oddly chastened.* I'll always love you, Quentin. But we could just tell them we changed our mind—

QUENTIN: Sweetheart—an event itself is not important; it's what you took from it. Whatever happened to you, this is what you made of it, and I love this! *Quickly to Listener:* Yes!—that we conspired to violate the past, and the past is holy and its horrors are holiest of all! *Turning back to Maggie:* And . . . something . . . more . . .

MAGGIE, *with hope now*: Maybe . . . it would even make me a better wife, right?

QUENTIN: That's the way to talk!

Elsie enters above and joins group of guests.

MAGGIE, *with gladness, seeing a fruit of past pain*: 'Cause I'm not curious! You be surprised, these so-called respectable women, they smile and their husbands never know, but they're curious. But I know all that, so I know I have a king! But there's people who're going to laugh at you!

QUENTIN: Not any more, dear, they're going to see what I see. Come!

MAGGIE, *not moving with him*: What do you see? Tell me! *Bursting out of her:* 'Cause I think . . . you were ashamed once, weren't you?

QUENTIN: I see your suffering, Maggie; and once I saw it, all shame fell away.

MAGGIE: You . . . were ashamed!?

QUENTIN, *with difficulty*: Yes. But you're a victory, Maggie, you're like a flag to me, a kind of proof, somehow, that people can win.

> *Louise enters upstage, brushing her hair.*

MAGGIE: And you—you won't ever look at any other woman, right?

QUENTIN: Darling, a wife can be loved!

MAGGIE, *with a new intensity of conflict*: Before, though—why did you kiss that Elsie?

QUENTIN: Just hello. She always throws her arms around people.

MAGGIE: But—why'd you let her rub her body against you?

QUENTIN, *laughing*: She wasn't rub—

MAGGIE, *downing a much greater anxiety*: I saw it. And you stood there.

QUENTIN, *trying to laugh*: Maggie, it was a meaningless gesture—

MAGGIE: You want me to be like I used to be—like it's all a fog? *Now pleadingly, and faintly wronged*: You told me yourself that I have to look for the meaning of things, didn't you? Why did you let her do that?

QUENTIN: She came up to me and threw her arms around me, what could I do?

MAGGIE, *in a flash of frightened anger*: Just tell her to knock it off!

QUENTIN, *taken aback*: I . . . don't think you want to sound like this, honey.

WOMAN GUEST: Ready! Ready!

> *The guests line up on the steps, forming a corridor for Maggie and Quentin.*

QUENTIN: Come, they're waiting.

> *He puts her arm in his; they turn to go. A wedding march is heard.*

MAGGIE, *almost in tears*: Teach me, Quentin! I don't know how to be! Forgive me I sounded that way.

QUENTIN, *as against the vision of Louise*: No. Say what you feel; the truth is on our side; always say it!

MAGGIE, *with a plea, but going on toward the guests*: You're not holding me!

QUENTIN, *half the stage away now, and turning toward the empty air, his arm still held as though he were walking beside her*: I am, darling, I'm with you!

MAGGIE, *moving along the corridor of guests*: I'm going to be a good wife. I'm going to be a good wife.

CARRIE: God bless this child.

MAGGIE, *faltering as she walks into darkness*: Quentin, I don't feel it!

The wedding march is gone. Louise exits upstage.

QUENTIN, *both frustrated and with an appeal to her, moving downstage with "her" on his arm*: I'm holding you! See everybody smiling, adoring you? Look at the orchestra guys making a V for victory! Everyone loves you, darling! Why are you sad?

Suddenly, from the far depths of the stage, she calls out with a laugh and hurries on in a fur coat, indicating a wall at front.

MAGGIE: Surprise! You like it? They rushed it while we were away!

QUENTIN—*they are half a stage apart*: Yes, it's beautiful!

MAGGIE: See how large it makes the living room? *Rushing toward left*: And I want to take down that wall too! Okay?

QUENTIN, *not facing in her direction; to his memory of it*: But we just finished putting those walls in.

MAGGIE: Well, it's only money; I want it big, like a castle for you!

QUENTIN: It's lovely, dear, but we're behind in the taxes.

MAGGIE: Used to say, I have one word written on my forehead. Why can't it be beautiful now? I get all that money next year.

QUENTIN: But you owe almost all of it—

MAGGIE: Don't hold the future like a vase—touch now, touch me! I'm here, and it's now!

She rushes into semi-darkness, where she is surrounded by Carrie, a dresser, and a secretary.

QUENTIN, *against himself, alone on the forestage*: Okay! Tear it down! Make it beautiful! Do it now! Maybe I am too cautious . . . Forgive me!

Her voice is suddenly heard in a recorded vocal number. He breaks into a genuine smile of joy and dances for a moment alone, as a group of executives surround Maggie. Now Maggie appears in a gold dress out of the group of cautiously listening executives. Quentin rushes to her.

QUENTIN: Maggie, sweetheart—that's magnificent!

MAGGIE, *worried, uncertain*: No! Tell me the truth! That piano's off, you're not listening!

> *A pianist, wearing sunglasses and smoking, emerges from the group listening to the record.*

QUENTIN: But nobody'll ever notice that!

MAGGIE: I notice it. Don't you want me to be good? I told Weinstein I wanted Johnny Block, but they give me this fag and he holds back my beat!

> *The pianist walks away, silently insulted.*

QUENTIN: But you said he's one of the best.

MAGGIE: I said Johnny Block was best, but they wouldn't pay his price. I make millions for them and I'm still some kind of a joke.

QUENTIN: Maybe I ought to talk to Weinstein. . . . *He hurries to a point upstage.*

MAGGIE, *calling after him*: No, don't get mixed up in my crummy business, you've got an important case—

QUENTIN: Weinstein, get her Johnny Block! Turning back to her as a new version of the number comes on: There now! Listen now! *She flies into his arms. The executives leave, gesturing their congratulations.* See? There's no reason to get upset.

MAGGIE: Oh, thank you, darling!

QUENTIN: Just tell me and I'll talk to these people any time you . . .

> *The music goes out.*

MAGGIE: See? They respect you. Ask Ludwig Reiner, soon as you come in the studio my voice flies! Oh, I'm going to be a good wife, Quentin, I just get nervous sometimes that I'm . . . only bringing you my problems. But I want my stuff to be perfect, and all they care is if they can get rich on it. *She sits dejectedly.*

QUENTIN: Exactly, dear—so how can you look to them for your self-respect? Come, why don't we go for a walk? We never walk any more. *Sits on his heels beside her.*

MAGGIE: You love me?

QUENTIN: I adore you. I just wish you could find some joy in your life.

MAGGIE: Quentin, I'm a joke that brings in money.

QUENTIN: I think it's starting to change though—you've got a great band now, and Johnny Block, and the best sound crew—

MAGGIE: Only because I fought for it. You'd think somebody'd come to me and say: Look, Maggie, you made us all this money, now we want you to develop yourself, what can we do for you?

QUENTIN: Darling, they'd be selling frankfurters if there were more money in it; how can you look to them for love?

Pause. Her loneliness floods in on her.

MAGGIE: But where will I look?

QUENTIN, *thrown down*: Maggie, how can you say that?

MAGGIE—*she stands; there is an underlying fear in her now*: When I walked into the party you didn't even put your arms around me. I felt like one of those wives or something!

QUENTIN: Well, Donaldson was in the middle of a sentence and I—

MAGGIE: So what? I walked into the room! I hire him, he doesn't hire me!

Louise appears upstage in dim light; she is cold-creaming her face.

QUENTIN: But he is directing your TV show, and I was being polite to him.

MAGGIE: You don't have to be ashamed of me, Quentin. I had a right to tell him to stop those faggy jokes at my rehearsal. Just because he's cultured? I'm the one the public pays for, not Donaldson! Ask Ludwig Reiner what my value is!

QUENTIN: I married you, Maggie. I don't need Ludwig's lecture on your value.

MAGGIE, *looking at him with strange, unfamiliar eyes*: Why—why you so cold?

QUENTIN: I'm not cold, I'm trying to explain what happened.

MAGGIE: Well, take me in your arms, don't explain. *He takes her in his arms, he kisses her.* Not like that. Hold me.

QUENTIN—*he tries to hold her tighter, then lets go*: Let's go for a walk, honey. Come on.

MAGGIE, *sinking*: What's the matter?

QUENTIN: Nothing.

MAGGIE: But Quentin—you should look at me, like I existed or something. Like you used to look—out of your self.

Maggie moves away into darkness, meets maid, and changes into negligee.

QUENTIN, *alone*: I adore you, Maggie; I'm sorry; it won't ever happen again. *Louise exits.* Never! You need more love than I thought. But I've got it, and I'll make you see it, and when you do you're going to astound the world!

> *A rose light floods the bed; Maggie emerges in a dressing gown.*

MAGGIE, *indicating out front*: Surprise! You like it? See the material?

QUENTIN: Oh, that's lovely! How'd you think of that?

MAGGIE: All you gotta do is close them and the sun makes the bed all rose.

QUENTIN, *striving for joy, embracing her on the bed*: Yes, it's beautiful! You see? An argument doesn't mean disaster! Oh, Maggie, I never knew what love was!

MAGGIE, *kissing him*: Case during the day, like maybe you get the idea to come home and we make love again in daytime. *She ends sitting in a weakness; nostalgically.* Like last year, remember? In the winter afternoons? And once there was still snow on your hair. See, that's all I am, Quentin.

QUENTIN: I'll come home tomorrow afternoon.

MAGGIE, *half humorously*: Well, don't plan it.

> *He laughs, but she looks at him strangely again, her stare piercing. His laugh dies.*

QUENTIN: What is it? I don't want to hide things any more, darling. Tell me, what's bothering you?

MAGGIE, *shaking her head, seeing*: I'm not a good wife. I take up so much of your work.

QUENTIN: No, dear. I only said that because you—*Striving to soften the incident*—you kind of implied that I didn't fight the network hard enough on that penalty, and I got it down to twenty thousand dollars. They had a right to a hundred when you didn't perform.

MAGGIE, *with rising indignation*: But can't I be sick? I was sick!

QUENTIN: I know, dear, but the doctor wouldn't sign the affidavit.

MAGGIE, *furious at him*: I had a pain in my side, for Christ's sake, I couldn't stand straight! You don't believe me, do you!

QUENTIN: Maggie, I'm only telling you the legal situation.

MAGGIE: Ask Ludwig what you should do! You should've gone in there roaring! 'Stead of a polite liberal and affidavits—I shouldn't have had to pay anything!

QUENTIN: Maggie, you have a great analyst, and Ludwig is a phenomenal teacher, and every stranger you meet has all the answers, but I'm putting in forty per cent of my time on your problems, not just some hot air.

MAGGIE: You're not putting forty per cent of—

QUENTIN: Maggie, I keep a log, I know what I spend my time on!

She looks at him, mortally wounded, goes upstage to a secretary, who enters with an invisible drink. Maid joins them with black dress, and Maggie changes.

I'm sorry, darling, but when you talk like that I feel a little like a fool. Don't start drinking, please.

MAGGIE: Should never have gotten married; every man I ever knew they hate their wives. I think I should have a separate lawyer.

QUENTIN, *alone on forestage*: Darling, I'm happy to spend my time on you; my greatest pleasure is to know I've helped your work to grow!

MAGGIE, *as a group of executives surrounds her*: But the only reason I went to Ludwig was so I could make myself an artist you'd be proud of! You're the first one that believed in me!

QUENTIN: Then what are we arguing about? We want the same thing, you see? *Suddenly to Listener*: Yes, power! To transform somebody, to save!

MAGGIE, *emerging from the group, wearing reading glasses*: He's a very good lawyer; he deals for a lot of stars. He'll call you to give him my files.

QUENTIN, *after a slight pause; hurt*: Okay.

MAGGIE: It's nothing against you; but like that girl in the orchestra, that cellist—I mean Andy took too much but he'd have gone in there and got rid of her. I mean you don't laugh when a singer goes off key.

QUENTIN: But she said she coughed.

MAGGIE, *furiously*: She didn't cough, she laughed!

QUENTIN: Now, Maggie.

MAGGIE: I'm not finishing this tape if she's in that band tomorrow! I'm entitled to my conditions, Quentin—and I shouldn't have to plead with my husband for my rights. I want her out!

The executives are gone.

QUENTIN: I don't know what the pleading's about. I've fired three others in three different bands.

MAGGIE: Well, so what? You're my husband. You're supposed to do that. Aren't you?

QUENTIN: But I can't pretend to enjoy demanding people be fired—

MAGGIE: But if it was your daughter you'd get angry, wouldn't you? Instead of apologizing for her?

QUENTIN, *envisioning it*: I guess I would, yes. I'm sorry. I'll do it in the morning.

MAGGIE, *with desperate warmth, joining him, sitting center*: That's all I mean. If I want something you should ask yourself why, why does she want it, not why she shouldn't have it. . . . That's why I don't smile, I feel I'm fighting all the time to make you see. You're like a little boy, you don't see the knives people hide.

QUENTIN: Darling, life is not all that dangerous. You've got a husband now who loves you.

> *Pause. She seems to fear greatly.*

MAGGIE: When your mother tells me I'm getting fat, I know where I am. And when you don't do anything about it.

QUENTIN: But what can I do?

MAGGIE: Slap her down, that's what you do!

> *Secretary enters with imaginary drink, which Maggie takes.*

QUENTIN: But she says anything comes into her head, dear—

MAGGIE: She insulted me! She's jealous of me!

QUENTIN: Maggie, she adores you. She's proud of you.

MAGGIE, *a distance away now*: What are you trying to make me think, I'm crazy? *Quentin approaches her, groping for reassurance.* I'm not crazy!

QUENTIN, *carefully*: The thought never entered my mind, darling. I'll . . . talk to her.

MAGGIE: Look, I don't want to see her any more. If she ever comes into this house, I'm walking out!

QUENTIN: Well, I'll tell her to apologize.

> *Secretary exits.*

MAGGIE: I'm not going to work tomorrow. She lies down on the bed as though crushed.

QUENTIN: Okay.

MAGGIE, *half springing up*: You know it's not "okay"! You're scared to death they'll sue me, why don't you say it?

QUENTIN: I'm not scared to death; it's just that you're so wonderful in this show and it's a pity to—

MAGGIE, *sitting up furiously*: All you care about is money! Don't shit me!

QUENTIN, *quelling a fury, his voice very level*: Maggie, don't use that language with me, will you?

MAGGIE: Call me vulgar, that I talk like a truck driver! Well, that's where I come from. I'm for Negroes and Puerto Ricans and truck drivers!

QUENTIN: Then why do you fire people so easily?

MAGGIE, *her eyes narrowing—she is seeing him anew*: Look. You don't want me. What the hell are you doing here?

Father and Dan enter, above them.

QUENTIN: I live here. And you do too, but you don't know it yet. But you're going to. I—

FATHER: Where's he going? I need him! What are you?

QUENTIN, *not turning to Father*: I'm here, and I stick it, that's what I am. And one day you're going to catch on. Now go to sleep. I'll be back in ten minutes, I'd like to take a walk.

He starts out and she comes to attention.

MAGGIE: Where you going to walk?

QUENTIN: Just around the block. *She watches him carefully.* There's nobody else, kid; I just want to walk.

MAGGIE, *with great suspicion*: 'Kay.

Father and Dan exit.

He goes a few yards, halts, turns to see her taking a pill bottle and unscrewing the top.

QUENTIN, *coming back*: You can't take pills on top of whisky, dear. *He has reached for them. She pulls them away, but he grabs them again and puts them in his pocket.* That's how it happened the last time. And it's not going to happen again. Never. I'll be right back.

MAGGIE—*an intoxication weighs on her speech now*: Why you wear those pants? *He turns back to her, knowing what is coming.* I told you the seat is too tight.

QUENTIN: Well, they made them too tight, but I can take a walk in them.

MAGGIE: Fags wear pants like that; I told you. They attract each other with their asses.

QUENTIN: You calling me a fag now?

MAGGIE, *very drunk*: Just I've known fags and some of them didn't even know themselves that they were. . . . And I didn't know if you knew about that.

QUENTIN: That's a hell of a way to reassure yourself, Maggie.

MAGGIE, *staggering slightly*: I'm allowed to say what I see!

QUENTIN: You trying to get me to throw you out? Is that what it is? So life will get real again?

MAGGIE, *pointing at him, at his control*: Wha's that suppose to be, strong and silent? I mean what is it?

> *She stumbles and falls. He makes no move to pick her up.*

QUENTIN, *standing over her*: And now I walk out, huh? And you finally know where you are, huh? *He picks her up angrily.* Is that what you want?

> *Breaking from him, she pitches forward. He catches her and roughly puts her on the bed.*

MAGGIE: Wha's the angle? Whyn't you beat it? *She gets on her feet again.* You gonna wait till I'm old? You know what another cab driver said to me today? "I'll give you fifty dollars . . ." *An open, lost sob, wild and contradictory, flies out of her.* You know what's fifty dollars to a cab driver? *Her pain moves into him, his anger is swamped with it.* Go ahead, you can go; I can even walk a straight line, see? Look, see? *She walks with arms out, one foot in front of the other.* So what is it, heh? I mean you want dancing? You want dancing? *Breathlessly she turns on the phonograph and goes into a hip-flinging caricature of a dance around him.* I mean what do you want? What is it?

QUENTIN: Please don't do that. *He catches her and lays her down on the bed.*

MAGGIE: You gonna wait till I'm old? Or what? I mean what is it? What is it?

> *She lies there, gasping. He stares down at her, addressing the Listener, as he sits beside the bed.*

QUENTIN: It's that if there is love, it must be limitless; a love not even of persons but blind, blind to insult, blind to the spear in the flesh, like justice blind, like . . .

> *Felice appears behind him. He has been raising up his arms. Father appears, slumped in chair.*

MOTHER'S VOICE, *off*: Idiot!

> *A dozen men appear on second level, under the harsh white light of a subway platform, some of them reading newspapers.*

Apart from them Mickey and Lou appear from each side, approaching each other.

MAGGIE, *rushing off unsteadily:* I mean whyn't you beat it?

QUENTIN, *his arms down, crying out to Listener:* But in whose name do you turn your back?

MICKEY: That we go together, Lou, and name the names! Lou!

Lou, staring at Quentin, mounts the platform where the men wait for a subway train.

QUENTIN: I saw it clear—in whose name you turn your back! I saw it once, I saw the name!

The approaching sound of a subway train is heard, and Lou leaps; the racking squeal of brakes.

LOU: Quentin! Quentin!

All the men look at Quentin, then at the "tracks." The men groan. Quentin's hands are a vise against his head. The tower lights as . . . Mother enters in prewar costume, sailboat in hand, bending toward the "bathroom door" as before.

QUENTIN: In whose name? In whose blood-covered name do you look into a face you loved, and say, Now you have been found wanting, and now in your extremity you die! It had a name, it . . .

MOTHER, *toward the "bathroom door":* Quentin? Quentin?

QUENTIN: Hah? *He hurries toward her, but in fear.*

MOTHER: See what we brought you from Atlantic City! From the boardwalk!

Men exit from subway platform. A tremendous crash of surf spins Quentin about, and Mother is gone and the light of the moon is rising on the pier.

QUENTIN: By the ocean. That cottage. That night. The last night.

Maggie in a rumpled wrapper, a bottle in her hand, her hair in snags over her face, staggers out to the edge of the pier and stands in the sound of the surf. Now she starts to topple over the edge of the pier, and he rushes to her and holds her in his hands. Maggie turns around and they embrace. Now the sound of jazz from within is heard, softly.

MAGGIE: You were loved, Quentin; no man was ever loved like you.

QUENTIN, *releasing her:* Carrie tell you I called? My plane couldn't take off all day—

MAGGIE, *drunk, but aware*: I was going to kill myself just now. *He is silent.* Or don't you believe that either?

QUENTIN, *with an absolute calm, a distance, but without hostility*: I saved you twice, why shouldn't I believe it? *Going toward her*: This dampness is bad for your throat, you oughtn't be out here.

MAGGIE—*she defiantly sits, her legs dangling*: Where've you been?

QUENTIN, *going upstage, removing his jacket*: I've been in Chicago. I told you. The Hathaway estate.

MAGGIE, *with a sneer*: Estates!

QUENTIN: Well, I have to pay some of our debts before I save the world. *He removes his jacket and puts it on bureau box; sits and removes a shoe.*

MAGGIE, *from the pier*: Didn't you hear what I told you?

QUENTIN: I heard it. I'm not coming out there, Maggie, it's too wet.

> *She looks toward him, gets up, unsteadily enters the room.*

MAGGIE: I didn't go to rehearsal today.

QUENTIN: I didn't think you did.

MAGGIE: And I called the network that I'm not finishing that stupid show. I'm an artist! And I don't have to do stupid shows, no matter what contract you made!

QUENTIN: I'm very tired, Maggie. I'll sleep in the living room. Good night. *He stands and starts out upstage.*

MAGGIE: What is this?

> *Pause. He turns back to her from the exit.*

QUENTIN: I've been fired.

MAGGIE: You're not fired.

QUENTIN: I didn't expect you to take it seriously, but it is to me; I can't make a decision any more without something sits up inside me and busts out laughing.

MAGGIE: That my fault, huh?

> *Slight pause. Then he resolves.*

QUENTIN: Look, dear, it's gone way past blame or justifying ourselves, I . . . talked to your doctor this afternoon.

MAGGIE, *stiffening with fear and suspicion*: About what?

QUENTIN: You want to die, Maggie, and I really don't know how to prevent it. But it struck me that I have been playing with your life out of some idiotic hope of some kind that you'd come out of this endless spell. But there's only one hope, dear—you've got to start to look at what you're doing.

MAGGIE: You going to put me away somewhere. Is that it?

QUENTIN: Your doctor's trying to get a plane up here tonight; you settle it with him.

MAGGIE: You're not going to put me anywhere, mister. *She opens the pill bottle.*

QUENTIN: You have to be supervised, Maggie. *She swallows pills.* Now listen to me while you can still hear. If you start going under tonight I'm calling the ambulance. I haven't the strength to go through that alone again. I'm not protecting you from the newspapers any more, Maggie, and the hospital means a headline. *She raises the whisky bottle to drink.* You've got to start facing the consequences of your actions, Maggie. *She drinks whisky.* Okay. I'll tell Carrie to call the ambulance as soon as she sees the signs. I'm going to sleep at the inn. *He gets his jacket.*

MAGGIE: Don't sleep at the inn!

QUENTIN: Then put that stuff away and go to sleep.

MAGGIE—*afraid he is leaving, she tries to smooth her tangled hair*: Could you . . . stay five minutes?

QUENTIN: Yes. *He returns.*

MAGGIE: You can even have the bottle if you want. I won't take any more. *She puts the pill bottle on the bed before him.*

QUENTIN, *against his wish to take it*: I don't want the bottle.

MAGGIE: 'Member how you used talk to me till I fell asleep?

QUENTIN: Maggie, I've sat beside you in darkened rooms for days and weeks at a time, and my office looking high and low for me—

MAGGIE: No, you lost patience with me.

QUENTIN, *after a slight pause*: That's right, yes.

MAGGIE: So you lied, right?

QUENTIN: Yes, I lied. Every day. We are all separate people. I tried not to be, but finally one is—a separate person. I have to survive too, honey.

MAGGIE: So where you going to put me?

QUENTIN, *trying not to break*: You discuss that with your doctor.

MAGGIE: But if you loved me . . .

QUENTIN: But how would you know, Maggie? Do you know any more who I am? Aside from my name? I'm all the evil in the world, aren't I? All the betrayal, the broken hopes, the murderous revenge? *She pours pills into her hand, and he stands. Now fear is in his voice.* A suicide kills two people, Maggie, that's what it's for! So I'm removing myself, and perhaps it will lose its point. *He resolutely starts out. She falls back on the bed. Her breathing is suddenly deep. He starts toward Carrie, who sits in semi-darkness, praying.* Carrie!

MAGGIE: Quentin, what's Lazarus?

He halts. She looks about for him, not knowing he has left. Quentin?

Not seeing him, she starts up off the bed; a certain alarm . . .

Quen?

He comes halfway back.

QUENTIN: Jesus raised him from the dead. In the Bible. Go to sleep now.

MAGGIE: Wha's 'at suppose to prove?

QUENTIN: The power of faith.

MAGGIE: What about those who have no faith?

QUENTIN: They only have the will.

MAGGIE: But how you get the will?

QUENTIN: You have faith.

MAGGIE: Some apples. *She lies back. A pause.* I want more cream puffs. And my birthday dress? If I'm good? Mama? I want my mother! *She sits up, looks about as in a dream, turns and sees him.* Why you standing there? *She gets out of bed, squinting, and comes up to him, peers into his face; her expression comes alive.* You—you want music?

QUENTIN: All right, you lie down, and I'll put a little music on.

MAGGIE: No, you; you, sit down. And take off your shoes. I mean just to rest. You don't have to do anything. *She staggers to the machine, turns it on; jazz. She tries to sing, but suddenly comes totally awake.* Was I sleeping?

QUENTIN: For a moment, I think.

MAGGIE, *coming toward him in terror*: Was—was my—was anybody else here?

QUENTIN: No. Just me.

MAGGIE: Is there smoke? *With a cry she clings to him; he holds her close.*

QUENTIN: Your mother's dead and gone, dear, she can't hurt you any more, don't be afraid.

MAGGIE, *in the helpless voice of a child as he returns her to the bed*: Where you going to put me?

QUENTIN, *his chest threatening a sob*: Nowhere, dear—the doctor'll decide with you.

MAGGIE: See? I'll lay down. *She lies down.* See? *She takes a strange, deep breath.* You—you could have the pills if you want.

QUENTIN—*stands and, after a hesitation, starts away*: I'll have Carrie come in and take them.

MAGGIE, *sliding off the bed, holding the pill bottle out to him*: No. I won't give them to Carrie. Only you. You take them.

QUENTIN: Why do you want me to have them?

MAGGIE, *extending them*: Here.

QUENTIN, *after a pause*: Do you see it, Maggie? Right now? You're trying to make me the one who does it to you? I grab them; and then we fight, and then I give them up, and you take your death from me. Something in you has been setting me up for a murder. Do you see it? *He moves backward.* But now I'm going away; so you're not my victim any more. It's just you, and your hand.

MAGGIE: But Jesus must have loved her.

QUENTIN: Who?

MAGGIE: Lazarus?

    Pause. He sees, he gropes toward his vision.

QUENTIN: That's right, yes! He . . . loved her enough to raise her from the dead. But He's God, see . . . and God's power is love without limit. But when a man dares reach for that . . . he is only reaching for the power. Whoever goes to save another person with the lie of limitless love throws a shadow on the face of God. And God is what happened, God is what is; and whoever stands between another person and her truth is not a lover, he is . . . *He breaks off, lost, peering, and turns back to Maggie for his clue.* And then she said. *He goes back to Maggie, crying out to invoke her.* And then she said!

MAGGIE: I still hear you. Way inside. Quentin? My love? I hear you! Tell me what happened!

QUENTIN, *through a sudden burst of tears*: Maggie, we . . . used one another!

MAGGIE: Not me, not me!

QUENTIN: Yes, you. And I. "To live" we cried, and "Now" we cried. And loved each other's innocence, as though to love enough what was not there would cover up what was. But there is an angel, and night and day he brings back to us exactly what we want to lose. So you must love him because he keeps truth in the world. You eat those pills to blind yourself, but if you could only say, "I have been cruel," this frightening room would open. If you could say, "I have been kicked around, but I have been just as inexcusably vicious to others, called my husband idiot in public, I have been utterly selfish despite my generosity, I have been hurt by a long line of men but I have cooperated with my persecutors—"

MAGGIE—*she has been writhing in fury*: Son of a bitch!

QUENTIN: "And I am full of hatred; I, Maggie, sweet lover of all life—I hate the world!"

MAGGIE: Get out of here!

QUENTIN: Hate women, hate men, hate all who will not grovel at my feet proclaiming my limitless love for ever and ever! But no pill can make us innocent. Throw them in the sea, throw death in the sea and all your innocence. Do the hardest thing of all—see your own hatred and live!

MAGGIE: What about your hatred? You know when I wanted to die. When I read what you wrote, kiddo. Two months after we were married, kiddo.

QUENTIN: Let's keep it true—you told me you tried to die long before you met me.

MAGGIE: So you're not even there, huh? I didn't even meet you. You coward! What about your hatred! *She moves front.* I was married to a king, you son of a bitch! I was looking for a fountain pen to sign some autographs. And there's his desk—*She is speaking toward some invisible source of justice now, telling her injury*—and there's his empty chair where he sits and thinks how to help people. And there's his handwriting. And there's some words. *She almost literally reads in the air, and with the same original astonishment.* "The only one I will ever love is my daughter. If I could only find an honorable way to die." *Now she turns to him.* When you gonna face that, Judgey? Remember how I fell down, fainted? On the new rug? That's what killed me, Judgey. Right? *She staggers up to him, and into his face*: 'Zat right?

QUENTIN, *after a pause*: All right. You pour them back, and I'll tell you the truth about that.

MAGGIE: You won't tell truth.

> *He tries to tip her hand toward the bottle, holding both her wrists.*

QUENTIN, *with difficulty*: We'll see. Pour them back first, and we'll see.

She lets him pour them back, but sits on the bed, holding the bottle in both hands.

MAGGIE, *after a deep breath*: Liar.

QUENTIN, *in quiet tension against his own self-condemnation*: We'd had our first party in our own house. Some important people, network heads, directors—

MAGGIE: And you were ashamed of me. Don't lie, now! You're still playing God! That's what killed me, Quentin!

QUENTIN: All right. I wasn't . . . ashamed. But . . . afraid. *Pause.* I wasn't sure if any of them . . . had had you.

MAGGIE, *astounded*: But I didn't know any of those!

QUENTIN, *not looking at her*: I swear to you, I did get to where I couldn't imagine what I'd ever been ashamed of. But it was too late. I had written that, and I was like all the others who'd betrayed you, and I could never be trusted again.

MAGGIE, *with a mixture of accusation and lament for a lost life, weeping*: Why did you write that?

QUENTIN: Because when the guests had gone, and you suddenly turned on me, calling me cold, remote, it was the first time I saw your eyes that way—betrayed, screaming that I'd made you feel you didn't exist—

MAGGIE: Don't mix me up with Louise!

QUENTIN: That's just it. That I could have brought two women so different to the same accusation—it closed a circle for me. And I wanted to face the worst thing I could imagine—that I could not love. And I wrote it down, like a letter from hell.

She starts to raise her hand to her mouth, and he steps in and holds her wrist.

That's rock bottom. What more do you *want*?

She looks at him; her eyes unreadable.

Maggie, we were both born of many errors; a human being has to forgive himself! Neither of us is innocent. What more do you want?

A strange calm overtakes her. She lies back on the bed. The hostility seems to have gone.

MAGGIE: Love me, and do what I tell you. And stop arguing. *He moves in anguish up and down beside the bed.*

And take down the sand dune. It's not too expensive. I want to hear the ocean when we make love in here, but we never hear the ocean.

QUENTIN: We're nearly broke, Maggie; and that dune keeps the roof from blowing off.

MAGGIE: So you buy a new roof. I'm cold. Lie on me.

QUENTIN: I can't do that again, not when you're like this.

MAGGIE: Just till I sleep!

QUENTIN—*an outcry*: Maggie, it's a mockery. Leave me something.

MAGGIE: Just out of humanness! I'm cold!

Holding down self-disgust, he lies down on her but holds his head away. Pause.

If you don't argue with me any more, I'll let you be my lawyer again. 'Kay? If you don't argue? Ludwig doesn't argue. *He is silent.* And don't keep saying we're broke? And the sand dune? *The agony is growing in his face, of total disintegration.* 'Cause I love the ocean sound; like a big mother—sssh, sssh, sssh. *He lifts himself off, stands looking down at her. Her eyes are closed.* You gonna be good now? *She takes a very deep breath.*

He reaches in carefully and tries to snatch the bottle; she grips it.

QUENTIN: It isn't my love you want any more. It's my destruction! But you're not going to kill me, Maggie. I want those pills. I don't want to fight you, Maggie. Now put them in my hand.

She looks at him, then quickly tries to swallow her handful, but he knocks some of them out—although she swallows many. He grabs for the bottle, but she holds and he pulls, yanks. She goes with the force, and he drags her onto the floor, trying to pry her hands open as she flails at him and hits his face—her strength is wild and no longer her own. He grabs her wrist and squeezes it with both his fists.

Drop them, you bitch! You won't kill me!

She holds on, and suddenly, clearly, he lunges for her throat and lifts her with his grip.

You won't kill me! You won't kill me!

She drops the bottle as from the farthest distance Mother rushes to the "bathroom door," crying out—the toy sailboat in her hand.

MOTHER: Darling, open this door! I didn't trick you!

Quentin springs away from Maggie, who falls back to the floor, his hands open and in air.

Mother continues without halt.

Quentin, why are you running water in there! *She backs away in horror from the "door."* I'll die if you do that! I saw a star when you were born—a light, a light in the world.

He stands transfixed as Mother backs into his hand, which of its own volition begins to squeeze her throat. She sinks to the floor, gasping for breath. And he falls back in horror.

QUENTIN: Murder?

Maggie gets to her hands and knees, gasping. He rushes to help her, terrified by his realization. She flails out at him, and on one elbow looks up at him in a caricature of laughter, her eyes victorious and wild with fear.

MAGGIE: Now we both know. You tried to kill me, mister. I been killed by a lot of people, some couldn't hardly spell, but it's the same, mister. You're on the end of a long, long line, Frank.

As though to ward off the accusation, he reaches again to help her up, and in absolute terror she springs away across the floor.

Stay 'way! . . . No! No—no, Frank. Don't you do that. *Cautiously, as though facing a wild, ravening beast:* Don't you do that. . . . I'll call Quentin if you do that. *She glances off and calls quietly, but never leaving him out of her sight.* Quentin! Qu—

She falls asleep, crumpled on the floor. Now deep, strange breathing. He quickly goes to her, throws her over onto her stomach for artificial respiration, but just as he is about to start, he stands. He calls upstage.

QUENTIN: Carrie? Carrie! *Carrie enters. As though it were a final farewell:* Quick! Call the ambulance! Stop wasting time! Call the ambulance!

Carrie exits. He looks down at Maggie, addressing Listener.

No-no, we saved her. It was just in time. Her doctor tells me she had a few good months; he even thought for a while she was making it. Unless, God knows, he fell in love with her too. *He almost smiles; it is gone. He moves out on the dock.* Look, I'll say it. It's really all I came to say. Barbiturates kill by suffocation. And the signal is a kind of sighing—the diaphragm is paralyzed. And I stood out on that dock. *He looks up.* And all those stars, still so fixed, so fortunate! And her precious seconds squirming in my hand, alive as bugs; and I heard. Those deep, unnatural breaths, like the footfalls of my coming peace—and knew . . . I wanted them. How is that possible? I loved that girl!

Enter Lou, Mickey, Father, Dan, Carrie, and Felice at various points. Louise appears.

And the name—yes, the name! In whose name do you ever turn your back—*he looks out at the audience*—but in your own? In Quentin's name. Always in your own blood-covered name you turn your back!

Holga appears on the highest level.

HOLGA: But no one is innocent they did not kill!

QUENTIN: But love, is love enough? What love, what wave of pity will ever reach this knowledge—I know how to kill? . . . I know, I know—she was doomed in any case, but will that cure? Or is it possible—*he turns toward the tower, moves toward it as toward a terrible God*—that this is not bizarre . . . to anyone? And I am not alone, and no man lives who would not rather be the sole survivor of this place than all its finest victims! What is the cure? Who can be innocent again on this mountain of skulls? I tell you what I know! My brothers died here—*he looks from the tower down at the fallen Maggie*—but my brothers built this place; our hearts have cut these stones! And what's the cure? . . . No, not love; I loved them all, all! And gave them willing to failure and to death that I might live, as they gave me and gave each other, with a word, a look, a trick, a truth, a lie—and all in love!

HOLGA: Hello!

QUENTIN: But what will defend her? *He cries up to Holga:* That woman hopes!

She stands unperturbed, resolute, aware of his pain and her own.

Or is that—*struck, to the Listener*—exactly why she hopes, because she knows? What burning cities taught her and the death of love taught me: that we are very dangerous! *Staring, seeing his vision:* And that, that's why I wake each morning like a boy—even now, even now! I swear to you, I could love the world again! Is the knowing all? To know, and even happily, that we meet unblessed; not in some garden of wax fruit and painted trees, that lie of Eden, but after, after the Fall, after many, many deaths. Is the knowing all? And the wish to kill is never killed, but with some gift of courage one may look into its face when it appears, and with a stroke of love—as to an idiot in the house—forgive it; again and again . . . forever?

He is evidently interrupted by the Listener.

No, it's not certainty, I don't feel that. But it does seem feasible . . . not to be afraid. Perhaps it's all one has. I'll tell her that. . . . Yes, she will, she'll know what I mean.

He turns upstage. He hesitates; all his people face him. He walks toward Louise, pausing; but she turns her face away. He goes on and pauses beside Mother, who stands in uncomprehending sorrow; he gestures as though he touched her, and she looks up at him and dares a smile, and he smiles back. He pauses at his dejected Father and Dan, and with a slight gesture magically makes them stand. Felice is about to raise her hand in blessing—he shakes her hand, aborting her enslavement. He passes Mickey and Lou and turns back to Maggie; she rises from the floor, webbed in with her demons, trying to awake. And with his life following him he climbs toward Holga, who raises her arm as though seeing him, and with great love . . .

HOLGA: Hello!

He comes to a halt a few yards from her and walks toward her, holding out his hand.

QUENTIN: Hello.

He moves away with her as a loud whispering comes up from all his people, who follow behind, endlessly alive. Darkness takes them all.

INCIDENT AT VICHY

A PLAY

1964

Characters

LEBEAU, *a painter*
BAYARD, *an electrician*
MARCHAND, *a businessman*
POLICE GUARD
MONCEAU, *an actor*
GYPSY
WAITER
BOY
MAJOR
FIRST DETECTIVE
OLD JEW
SECOND DETECTIVE
LEDUC, *a doctor*
POLICE CAPTAIN
VON BERG, *a prince*
PROFESSOR HOFFMAN
FERRAND, *a café proprietor*
FOUR PRISONERS

Vichy, France, 1942. A place of detention.

At the right a corridor leads to a turning and an unseen door to the street. Across the back is a structure with two grimy window panes in it—perhaps an office, in any case a private room with a door opening from it at the left.

A long bench stands in front of this room, facing a large empty area whose former use is unclear but which suggests a warehouse, perhaps, an armory, or part of a railroad station not used by the public. Two small boxes stand apart on either side of the bench.

When light begins to rise, six men and a boy of fifteen are discovered on the bench in attitudes expressive of their personalities and functions, frozen there like members of a small orchestra at the moment before they begin to play.

As normal light comes on, their positions flow out of the frieze. It appears that they do not know one another and are sitting like people thrown together in a public place, mutually curious but self-occupied. However, they are anxious and frightened and tend to make themselves small and unobtrusive. Only one, Marchand, a fairly well-dressed businessman, keeps glancing at his watch and bits of paper and calling cards he keeps in his pockets, and seems normally impatient.

Now, out of hunger and great anxiety, Lebeau, a bearded, unkempt man of twenty-five, lets out a dramatized blow of air and leans forward to rest his head on his hands. Others glance at him, then away. He is charged with the energy of fear, and it makes him seem aggressive.

LEBEAU: Cup of coffee would be nice. Even a sip.

No one responds. He turns to Bayard beside him; Bayard is his age, poorly but cleanly dressed, with a certain muscular austerity in his manner. Lebeau speaks in a private undertone.

You wouldn't have any idea what's going on, would you?

BAYARD, *shaking his head*: I was walking down the street.

LEBEAU: Me too. Something told me—Don't go outside today. So I went out. Weeks go by and I don't open my door. Today I go out. And I had no reason, I wasn't even going anywhere. *Looks left and right to the others. To Bayard*: They get picked up the same way?

BAYARD—*shrugs*: I've only been here a couple of minutes myself—just before they brought you in.

LEBEAU—*looks to the others*: Does anybody know anything?

> *They shrug and shake their heads. Lebeau looks at the walls, the room; then he speaks to Bayard.*

This isn't a police station, is it?

BAYARD: Doesn't seem so. There's always a desk. It's just some building they're using, I guess.

LEBEAU, *glancing about uneasily, curiously*: It's painted like a police station, though. There must be an international police paint, they're always the same color everywhere. Like dead clams, and a little yellow mixed in.

> *Pause. He glances at the other silent men, and tries to silence himself, like them. But it's impossible, and he speaks to Bayard with a nervous smile.*

You begin wishing you'd committed a crime, you know? Something definite.

BAYARD—*he is not amused, but not unsympathetic*: Try to take it easy. It's no good getting excited. We'll find out soon.

LEBEAU: It's just that I haven't eaten since three o'clock yesterday afternoon. Everything gets more vivid when you're hungry—you ever notice that?

BAYARD: I'd give you something, but I forgot my lunch this morning. Matter of fact, I was just turning back to get it when they came up alongside me. Why'n't you try to sit back and relax?

LEBEAU: I'm nervous. . . . I mean I'm nervous anyway. *With a faint, frightened laugh*: I was even nervous before the war.

> *His little smile vanishes. He shifts in his seat. The others wait with subdued anxiety. He notices the good clothes and secure manner of Marchand, who is at the head of the line, nearest the door. He leans forward to attract him.*

Excuse me.

> *Marchand does not turn to him. He gives a short, sharp, low whistle. Marchand, already offended, turns slowly to him.*

Is that the way they picked you up? On the street?

Marchand turns forward again without answering.

Sir?

Marchand still does not turn back to him.

Well, Jesus, pardon me for living.

MARCHAND: It's perfectly obvious they're making a routine identity check.

LEBEAU: Oh.

MARCHAND: With so many strangers pouring into Vichy this past year there're probably a lot of spies and God knows what. It's just a document check, that's all.

LEBEAU—*turns to Bayard, hopefully*: You think so?

BAYARD—*shrugs; obviously he feels there is something more to it*: I don't know.

MARCHAND, *to Bayard*: Why? There are thousands of people running around with false papers, we all know that. You can't permit such things in wartime.

The others glance uneasily at Marchand, whose sense of security is thereby confined to him alone.

Especially now with the Germans starting to take over down here you have to expect things to be more strict, it's inevitable.

A pause. Lebeau once again turns to him.

LEBEAU: You don't get any . . . special flavor, huh?

MARCHAND: What flavor?

LEBEAU, *glancing at the others*: Well like . . . some racial . . . implication?

MARCHAND: I don't see anything to fear if your papers are all right. *He turns front, concluding the conversation.*

Again silence. But Lebeau can't contain his anxiety. He studies Bayard's profile, then turns to the man on his other side and studies his. Then, turning back to Bayard, he speaks quietly.

LEBEAU: Listen, you are . . . Peruvian, aren't you?

BAYARD: What's the matter with you, asking questions like that in here? *He turns forward.*

LEBEAU: What am I supposed to do, sit here like a dumb beast?

BAYARD, *laying a calming hand on his knee*: Friend, it's no good getting hysterical.

LEBEAU: I think we've had it. I think all the Peruvians have had it in Vichy. *Suppressing a shout*: In 1939 I had an American visa. Before the invasion. I actually had it in my hand. . . .

BAYARD: Calm down—this may all be routine.

Slight pause. Then . . .

LEBEAU: Listen . . .

He leans in and whispers into Bayard's ear. Bayard glances toward Marchand, then shrugs to Lebeau.

BAYARD: I don't know, maybe; maybe he's not.

LEBEAU, *desperately attempting familiarity*: What about you?

BAYARD: Will you stop asking idiotic questions? You're making yourself ridiculous.

LEBEAU: But I am ridiculous, aren't you? In 1939 we were packed for America. Suddenly my mother wouldn't leave the furniture. I'm here because of a brass bed and some fourth-rate crockery. And a stubborn, ignorant woman.

BAYARD: Yes, but it's not all that simple. You should try to think of why things happen. It helps to know the meaning of one's suffering.

LEBEAU: What meaning? If my mother—

BAYARD: It's not your mother. The monopolies got control of Germany. Big business is out to make slaves of everyone, that's why you're here.

LEBEAU: Well I'm not a philosopher, but I know my mother, and that's why I'm here. You're like people who look at my paintings—"What does this mean, what does that mean?" *Look* at it, don't ask what it means; you're not God, you can't tell what anything means. I'm walking down the street before, a car pulls up beside me, a man gets out and measures my nose, my ears, my mouth, the next thing I'm sitting in a police station—or whatever the hell this is here—and in the middle of Europe, the highest peak of civilization! And you know what it means? After the Romans and the Greeks and the Renaissance, and you know what this means?

BAYARD: You're talking utter confusion.

LEBEAU, *in terror*: Because I'm utterly confused! *He suddenly springs up and shouts*: Goddammit, I want some coffee!

The Police Guard appears at the end of the corridor, a revolver on his hip; he strolls down the corridor and meets Lebeau, who has come halfway up. Lebeau halts, returns to his place on the bench, and sits. The Guard starts to turn to go up the corridor when Marchand raises his hand.

MARCHAND: Excuse me, officer, is there a telephone one can use? I have an appointment at eleven o'clock and it's quite . . .

> *The Guard simply walks up the corridor, turns the corner, and disappears. Lebeau looks toward Marchand and shakes his head, laughing silently.*

LEBEAU, *to Bayard, sotto*: Isn't it wonderful? The man is probably on his way to work in a German coal mine and he's worried about breaking an appointment. And people want realistic painting, you see what I mean? *Slight pause.* Did they measure your nose? Could you at least tell me that?

BAYARD: No, they just stopped me and asked for my papers. I showed them and they took me in.

MONCEAU, *leaning forward to address Marchand*: I agree with you, sir.

> *Marchand turns to him. Monceau is a bright-eyed, cheerful man of twenty-eight. His clothes were elegant, now frayed. He holds a gray felt hat on his knee, his posture rather elegant.*

Vichy must be full of counterfeit papers. I think as soon as they start, it shouldn't take long. *To Lebeau*: Try to settle down.

LEBEAU, *to Monceau*: Did they measure your nose?

MONCEAU, *disapprovingly*: I think it'd be best if we all kept quiet.

LEBEAU: What is it, my clothes? How do you know, I might be the greatest painter in France.

MONCEAU: For your sake, I hope you are.

LEBEAU: What a crew! I mean the animosity!

> *Pause.*

MARCHAND, *leaning forward to see Monceau*: You would think, though, that with the manpower shortage they'd economize on personnel. In the car that stopped me there was a driver, two French detectives, and a German official of some kind. They could easily have put a notice in the paper—everyone would have come here to present his documents. This way it's a whole morning wasted. Aside from the embarrassment.

LEBEAU: I'm not embarrassed, I'm scared to death. *To Bayard*: You embarrassed?

BAYARD: Look, if you can't be serious just leave me alone.

> *Pause. Lebeau leans forward to see the man sitting on the far side of Marchand. He points.*

LEBEAU: Gypsy?

GYPSY, *drawing closer a copper pot at his feet*: Gypsy.

LEBEAU, *to Monceau*: Gypsies never have papers. Why'd they bother him?

MONCEAU: In his case it might be some other reason. He probably stole that pot.

GYPSY: No. On the sidewalk. *He raises the pot from between his feet.* I fix, make nice. I sit down to fix. Come police. Pfft!

MARCHAND: But of course they'll tell you anything. . . . *To Gypsy, laughing familiarly*: Right?

> *Gypsy laughs and turns away to his own gloom.*

LEBEAU: That's a hell of a thing to say to him. I mean, would you say that to a man with pressed pants?

MARCHAND: They don't mind. In fact, they're proud of stealing. *To Gypsy*: Aren't you?

> *Gypsy glances at him, shrugs.*

> I've got a place in the country where they come every summer. I like them, personally—especially the music. *With a broad grin he sings toward the Gypsy and laughs.* We often listen to them around their campfires. But they'll steal the eyes out of your head. *To Gypsy*: Right?

> *Gypsy shrugs and kisses the air contemptuously. Marchand laughs with brutal familiarity.*

LEBEAU: Why shouldn't he steal? How'd you get *your* money?

MARCHAND: I happen to be in business.

LEBEAU: So what have you got against stealing?

BAYARD: Are you trying to provoke somebody? Is that it?

LEBEAU: Another businessman.

BAYARD: I happen to be an electrician. But a certain amount of solidarity wouldn't hurt right now.

LEBEAU: How about some solidarity with Gypsies? Just because they don't work nine to five?

WAITER—*a small man, middle-aged, still wearing his apron*: I know this one. I've made him go away a hundred times. He and his wife stand outside the café with a baby, and they beg. It's not even their baby.

LEBEAU: So what? They've still got a little imagination.

WAITER: Yes, but they keep whining to the customers through the shrub-bery. People don't like it.

LEBEAU: You know—you all remind me of my father. Always worshiped the hard-working Germans. And now you hear it all over France—we have to learn how to work like the Germans. Good God, don't you ever read history? Whenever a people starts to work hard, watch out, they're going to kill somebody.

BAYARD: That depends on how production is organized. If it's for private profit, yes, but—

LEBEAU: What are you talking about, when did the Russians start getting dangerous? When they learned how to work. Look at the Germans—for a thousand years peaceful, disorganized people—they start working and they're on everybody's back. Nobody's afraid of the Africans, are they? Because they don't work. Read the Bible—work is a curse, you're not sup-posed to worship work.

MARCHAND: And how do you propose to produce anything?

LEBEAU: Well that's the problem.

Marchand and Bayard laugh.

What are you laughing at? *That is the problem!* Yes! To work without making work a god! What kind of crew is this?

The office door opens and the Major comes out. He is twenty-eight, a wan but well-built man; there is something ill about him. He walks with a slight limp, passing the line of men as he goes toward the corridor.

WAITER: Good morning, Major.

MAJOR—*startled, nods to the Waiter*: Oh. Good morning.

He continues up the corridor, where he summons the Guard around the corner—the Guard appears and they talk unheard.

MARCHAND, *sotto*: You know him?

WAITER, *proudly*: I serve him breakfast every morning. Tell you the truth, he's really not a bad fellow. Regular army, see, not one of these S.S. bums. Got wounded somewhere, so they stuck him back here. Only came about a month ago, but he and I—

The Major comes back down the corridor. The Guard returns to his post out of sight at the corridor's end. As the Major passes Marchand . . .

MARCHAND, *leaping up and going to the Major*: Excuse me, sir.

The Major slowly turns his face to Marchand. Marchand affects to laugh deferentially.

I hate to trouble you, but I would be much obliged if I could use a telephone for one minute. In fact, it's business connected to the food supply. I am the manager of . . .

He starts to take out a business card, but the Major has turned away and walks to the door. But there he stops and turns back.

MAJOR: I'm not in charge of this procedure. You will have to wait for the Captain of Police. *He goes into the office.*

MARCHAND: I beg your pardon.

The door has been closed on his line. He goes back to his place and sits, glaring at the Waiter.

WAITER: He's not a really bad fellow.

They all look at him, eager for some clue.

He even comes at night sometimes, plays a beautiful piano. Gives himself French lessons out of a book. Always has a few nice words to say, too.

LEBEAU: Does he know that you're a . . . Peruvian?

BAYARD, *instantly*: Don't discuss that here, for God's sake! What's the matter with you?

LEBEAU: Can't I find out what's going on? If it's a general identity check it's one thing, but if—

From the end of the corridor enter First Detective with the Old Jew, a man in his seventies, bearded, carrying a large sackcloth bundle; then the Second Detective, holding the arm of Leduc; then the Police Captain, uniformed, with Von Berg; and finally the Professor in civilian clothes.

The First Detective directs the Old Jew to sit, and he does, beside the Gypsy. The Second Detective directs Von Berg to sit beside the Old Jew. Only now does the Second Detective release his hold on Leduc and indicate that he is to sit beside Von Berg.

SECOND DETECTIVE, *to Leduc*: Don't you give me any more trouble now.

The door opens and the Major enters. Instantly Leduc is on his feet, approaching the Major.

LEDUC: Sir, I must ask the reason for this. I am a combat officer, captain in the French Army. There is no authority to arrest me in French territory. The Occupation has not revoked French law in southern France.

The Second Detective, infuriated, throws Leduc back into his seat. He returns to the Professor.

SECOND DETECTIVE, *to Major, of Leduc*: Speechmaker.

PROFESSOR, *doubtfully*: You think you two can carry on now?

SECOND DETECTIVE: We got the idea, Professor. *To the Major*: There's certain neighborhoods they head for when they run away from Paris or wherever they come from. I can get you as many as you can handle.

FIRST DETECTIVE: It's a question of knowing the neighborhoods, you see. In my opinion you've got at least a couple thousand in Vichy on false papers.

PROFESSOR: You go ahead, then.

As the Second Detective turns to go with the First Detective, the Police Captain calls him.

CAPTAIN: Saint-Père.

SECOND DETECTIVE: Yes, sir.

The Captain walks downstage with the Detective.

CAPTAIN: Try to avoid taking anybody out of a crowd. Just cruise around the way we did before, and take them one at a time. There are all kinds of rumors. We don't want to alarm people.

SECOND DETECTIVE: Right, sir.

The Captain gestures, and both Detectives leave up the corridor.

CAPTAIN: I am just about to order coffee. Will you gentlemen have some?

PROFESSOR: Please.

WAITER, *timidly*: And a croissant for the Major.

The Major glances quickly at the Waiter and barely smiles. The Captain, who has thrown a mystified look at the Waiter, goes into the office.

MARCHAND, *to the Professor*: I believe I am first, sir.

PROFESSOR: Yes, this way.

He goes into the office, followed by the eager Marchand.

MARCHAND, *going in*: Thank you. I'm in a dreadful hurry. . . . I was on my way to the Ministry of Supply, in fact. . . .

His voice is lost within. As the Major reaches the door, Leduc, who has been in a fever of calculation, calls to him.

LEDUC: Amiens.

MAJOR—*he halts at the door, turns to Leduc, who is at the far end of the line*: What about Amiens?

LEDUC, *suppressing his nervousness*: June ninth, 'forty. I was in the Sixteenth Artillery, facing you. I recognize your insignia, which of course I could hardly forget.

MAJOR: That was a bad day for you fellows.

LEDUC: Yes. And evidently for you.

MAJOR—*glances down at his leg*: Can't complain.

    The Major goes into the office, shuts the door. A pause.

LEDUC, *to all*: What's this all about?

WAITER, *to all*: I told you he wasn't a bad guy. You'll see.

MONCEAU, *to Leduc*: It seems they're checking on identification papers.

Leduc receives the news, and obviously grows cautious and quietly alarmed. He examines their faces.

LEDUC: What's the procedure?

MONCEAU: They've just started—that businessman was the first.

LEBEAU, *to Leduc and Von Berg*: They measure your noses?

LEDUC, *sharply alarmed*: Measure noses?

LEBEAU, *putting thumb and forefinger against the bridge and tip of his nose*: Ya, they measured my nose, right on the street. I tell you what I think . . . *To Bayard*: With your permission.

BAYARD: I don't mind you talking as long as you're serious.

LEBEAU: I think it's to carry stones. It just occurred to me—last Monday a girl I know came up from Marseille—the road is full of detours. They probably need labor. She said there was a crowd of people just carrying stones. Lot of them Jews, she thought; hundreds.

LEDUC: I never heard of forced labor in the Vichy Zone. Is that going on here?

BAYARD: Where do you come from?

LEDUC—*slight pause—he decides whether to reveal*: I live in the country. I don't get into town very often. There's been no forced-labor decree, has there?

BAYARD, *to all*: Now, listen. *Everyone turns to his straight-forward, certain tone.* I'm going to tell you something, but I don't want anybody quoting me. Is that understood?

They nod. He glances at the door. He turns to Lebeau.

You hear what I said?

LEBEAU: Don't make me out some kind of an idiot. Christ's sake, I know it's serious!

BAYARD, *to the others*: I work in the railroad yards. A thirty-car freight train pulled in yesterday. The engineer is Polish, so I couldn't talk to him, but one of the switchmen says he heard people inside.

LEDUC: Inside the cars?

BAYARD: Yes. It came from Toulouse. I heard there's been a quiet roundup of Jews in Toulouse the last couple of weeks. And what's a Polish engineer doing on a train in southern France? You understand?

LEDUC: Concentration camp?

MONCEAU: Why? A lot of people have been volunteering for work in Germany. That's no secret. They're doubling the ration for anybody who goes.

BAYARD, *quietly*: The cars are locked on the outside. *Slight pause.* And they stink. You can smell the stench a hundred yards away. Babies are crying inside. You can hear them. And women. They don't lock volunteers in that way. I never heard of it.

A long pause.

LEDUC: But I've never heard of them applying the Racial Laws down here. It's still French territory, regardless of the Occupation—they've made a big point of that.

Pause.

BAYARD: The Gypsy bothers me.

LEBEAU: Why?

BAYARD: They're in the same category of the Racial Laws. Inferior.

Leduc and Lebeau slowly turn to look at the Gypsy.

LEBEAU, *turning back quickly to Bayard*: Unless he really stole that pot.

BAYARD: Well, yes, if he stole the pot then of course he—

LEBEAU, *quickly, to the Gypsy*: Hey, listen. *He gives a soft, sharp whistle. The Gypsy turns to him.* You steal that pot?

The Gypsy's face is inscrutable. Lebeau is embarrassed to press this, and more desperate.

You did, didn't you?

GYPSY: No steal, no.

LEBEAU: Look, I've got nothing against stealing. *Indicating the others*: I'm not one of these types. I've slept in parked cars, under bridges—I mean, to me all property is theft anyway so I've got no prejudice against you.

GYPSY: No steal.

LEBEAU: Look . . . I mean you're a Gypsy, so how else can you live, right?

WAITER: He steals everything.

LEBEAU, *to Bayard*: You hear? He's probably in for stealing, that's all.

VON BERG: Excuse me . . .

> *They turn to him.*

Have you all been arrested for being Jewish?

> *They are silent, suspicious and surprised.*

I'm terribly sorry. I had no idea.

BAYARD: I said nothing about being Jewish. As far as I know, nobody here is Jewish.

VON BERG: I'm terribly sorry.

> *Silence. The moment lengthens. In his embarrassment he laughs nervously.*

It's only that I . . . I was buying a newspaper and this gentleman came out of a car and told me I must have my documents checked. I . . . I had no idea.

> *Silence. Hope is rising in them.*

LEBEAU, *to Bayard*: So what'd they grab *him* for?

BAYARD—*looks at Von Berg for a moment, then addresses all*: I don't understand it, but take my advice. If anything like that happens and you find yourself on that train . . . there are four bolts halfway up the doors on the inside. Try to pick up a nail or a screwdriver, even a sharp stone—you can chisel the wood out around those bolts and the doors will open. I warn you, don't believe anything they tell you—I heard they're working Jews to death in the Polish camps.

MONCEAU: I happen to have a cousin; they sent him to Auschwitz; that's in Poland, you know. I have several letters from him saying he's fine. They've even taught him bricklaying.

BAYARD: Look, friend, I'm telling you what I heard from people who know. *Hesitates.* People who make it their business to know, you understand? Don't listen to any stories about resettlement, or that they're going to teach you a trade or something. If you're on that train get out before it gets where it's going.

Pause.

LEDUC: I've heard the same thing.

They turn to him and he turns to Bayard.

How would one find tools, you have any idea?

MONCEAU: This is so typical! We're in the French Zone, nobody has said one word to us, and we're already on a train for a concentration camp where we'll be dead in a year.

LEDUC: But if the engineer is a Pole . . .

MONCEAU: So he's a Pole, what does that prove?

BAYARD: All I'm saying is that if you have some kind of tool . . .

LEDUC: I think what this man says should be taken seriously.

MONCEAU: In my opinion you're hysterical. After all, they were picking up Jews in Germany for years before the war, they've been doing it in Paris since they came in—are you telling me all those people are dead? Is that really conceivable to you? War is war, but you still have to keep a certain sense of proportion. I mean Germans are still *people*.

LEDUC: I don't speak this way because they're Germans.

BAYARD: It's that they're Fascists.

LEDUC: Excuse me, no. It's exactly because they are people that I speak this way.

BAYARD: I don't agree with *that*.

MONCEAU—*looks at Leduc for an instant*: You must have had a peculiar life, is all I can say. I happen to have played in Germany; I know the German people.

LEDUC: I studied in Germany for five years, and in Austria and I—

VON BERG, *happily*: In Austria! Where?

LEDUC—*again he hesitates, then reveals*: The Psychoanalytic Institute in Vienna.

VON BERG: Imagine!

MONCEAU: You're a psychiatrist. *To the others*: No wonder he's so pessimistic!

VON BERG: Where did you live? I am Viennese.

LEDUC: Excuse me, but perhaps it would be wiser not to speak in . . . detail.

VON BERG, *glancing about as though he had committed a gaffe*: I'm terribly sorry . . . yes, of course. *Slight pause.* I was only curious if you knew Baron Kessler. He was very interested in the medical school.

LEDUC, *with an odd coolness*: No, I was never in that circle.

VON BERG: Oh, but he is extremely democratic. He . . . *shyly*: he is my cousin, you see. . . .

LEBEAU: You're a nobleman?

VON BERG: Yes.

LEDUC: What is your name?

VON BERG: Wilhelm Johann Von Berg.

MONCEAU, *astonished, impressed*: The prince?

VON BERG: Yes . . . forgive me, have we met?

MONCEAU, *excited by the honor*: Oh, no. But naturally I've heard your name. I believe it's one of the oldest houses in Austria.

VON BERG: Oh, that's of no importance any more.

LEBEAU, *turning to Bayard—bursting with hope*: Now, what the hell would they want with an Austrian prince?

Bayard looks at Von Berg, mystified.

I mean . . . *Turning back to Von Berg*: You're Catholic, right?

VON BERG: Yes.

LEDUC: But is your title on your papers?

VON BERG: Oh, yes, my passport.

Pause. They sit silent, on the edge of hope, but bewildered.

BAYARD: Were you . . . political or something?

VON BERG: No, no, I never had any interest in that direction. *Slight pause.* Of course, there is this resentment toward the nobility. That might explain it.

LEDUC: In the Nazis? Resentment?

VON BERG, *surprised*: Yes, certainly.

LEDUC, *with no evident viewpoint but with a neutral but pressing interest in drawing the nobleman out*: Really. I've never been aware of that.

VON BERG: Oh, I assure you.

LEDUC: But on what ground?

VON BERG—*laughs, embarrassed to have to even suggest he is offended*: You're not asking that seriously.

LEDUC: Don't be offended, I'm simply ignorant of that situation. I suppose I have taken for granted that the aristocracy is . . . always behind a reactionary regime.

VON BERG: Oh, there are some, certainly. But for the most part they never took responsibility, in any case.

LEDUC: That interests me. So you still take seriously the . . . the title and . . .

VON BERG: It is not a "title"; it is my name, my family. Just as you have a name, and a family. And you are not inclined to dishonor them, I presume.

LEDUC: I see. And by responsibility, you mean, I suppose, that—

VON BERG: Oh, I don't know; whatever that means. *He glances at his watch.*

    Pause.

LEDUC: Please forgive me, I didn't mean to pry into your affairs. *Pause.* I'd never thought about it, but it's obvious now—they *would* want to destroy whatever power you have.

VON BERG: Oh, no, I have no power. And if I did it would be a day's work for them to destroy it. That's not the issue.

    Pause.

LEDUC, *fascinated—he is drawn to some truth in Von Berg*: What is it, then? Believe me, I'm not being critical. Quite the contrary . . .

VON BERG: But these are obvious answers! *He laughs.* I have a certain . . . standing. My name is a thousand years old, and they know the danger if someone like me is perhaps . . . not vulgar enough.

LEDUC: And by vulgar you mean . . .

VON BERG: Well, don't you think Nazism . . . whatever else it may be . . . is an outburst of vulgarity? An ocean of vulgarity?

BAYARD: I'm afraid it's a lot more than that, my friend.

VON BERG, *politely, to Bayard*: I am sure it is, yes.

BAYARD: You make it sound like they have bad table manners, that's all.

VON BERG: They certainly do, yes. Nothing angers them more than a sign of any . . . refinement. It is decadent, you see.

BAYARD: What kind of statement is that? You mean you left Austria because of their table manners?

VON BERG: Table manners, yes; and their adoration of dreadful art; and grocery clerks in uniform telling the orchestra what music it may not play. Vulgarity can be enough to send a man out of his country, yes, I think so.

BAYARD: In other words, if they had good taste in art, and elegant table manners, and let the orchestra play whatever it liked, they'd be all right with you.

VON BERG: But how would that be possible? Can people with respect for art go about hounding Jews? Making a prison of Europe, pushing themselves forward as a race of policemen and brutes? Is that possible for artistic people?

MONCEAU: I'd like to agree with you, Prince von Berg, but I have to say that the German audiences—I've played there—no audience is as sensitive to the smallest nuance of a performance; they sit in the theater with respect, like in a church. And nobody listens to music like a German. Don't you think so? It's a passion with them.

> Pause.

VON BERG, *appalled at the truth*: I'm afraid that is true, yes. *Pause.* I don't know what to say. *He is depressed, deeply at a loss.*

LEDUC: Perhaps it isn't those people who are doing this.

VON BERG: I'm afraid I know many cultivated people who . . . did become Nazis. Yes, they did. Art is perhaps no defense against this. It's curious how one takes certain ideas for granted. Until this moment I had thought of art as a . . . *To Bayard*: You may be right—I don't understand very much about it. Actually, I'm essentially a musician—in an amateur way, of course, and politics has never . . .

> *The office door opens and Marchand appears, backing out, talking to someone within. He is putting a leather document-wallet into his breast pocket, while with the other hand he holds a white pass.*

MARCHAND: That's perfectly all right, I understand perfectly. Good day, gentlemen. *Holding up the pass to them*: I show the pass at the door? Thank you.

> *Shutting the door, he turns and hurries past the line of prisoners, and, as he passes the Boy . . .*

BOY: What'd they ask you, sir?

> *Marchand turns up the corridor without glancing at the Boy, and as he approaches the end the Guard, hearing him,*

appears there. He hands the pass to the Guard and goes out. The Guard moves around the turning of the corridor and disappears.

LEBEAU, *half mystified, half hopeful*: I could have sworn he was a Jew! *To Bayard*: Didn't you think so?

Slight pause.

BAYARD—*clearly he did think so*: You have papers, don't you?

LEBEAU: Oh sure, I have good papers. *He takes rumpled documents out of his pants pocket.*

BAYARD: Well, just insist they're valid. Maybe that's what he did.

LEBEAU: I wish you'd take a look at them, will you?

BAYARD: I'm no expert.

LEBEAU: I'd like your opinion, though. You seem to know what's going on. How they look to you?

Bayard quickly hides the papers as the office door opens. The Professor appears and indicates the Gypsy.

PROFESSOR: Next. You. Come with me.

The Gypsy gets up and starts toward him. The Professor indicates the pot in the Gypsy's hand.

You can leave that.

The Gypsy hesitates, glances at the pot.

I said leave it there.

The Gypsy puts the pot down on the bench unwillingly.

GYPSY: Fix. No steal.

PROFESSOR: Go in.

GYPSY, *indicating the pot, warning the others*: That's mine.

The Gypsy goes into the office. The Professor follows him in and shuts the door. Bayard takes the pot, bends the handle off, puts it in his pocket, and sets the pot back where it was.

LEBEAU, *turning back to Bayard, indicating his papers*: What do you think?

BAYARD—*holds a paper up to the light, turns it over, gives it back to Lebeau*: Look good far as I can tell.

MONCEAU: That man did seem Jewish to me. Didn't he to you, Doctor?

LEDUC: I have no idea. Jews are not a race, you know. They can look like anybody.

LEBEAU, *with the joy of near-certainty*: He just probably had good papers. Because I know people have papers, I mean all you have to do is look at them and you know they're phony. But I mean if you have good papers, right?

> *Monceau has meanwhile taken out his papers and is examining them. The Boy does the same with his. Lebeau turns to Leduc.*

That's true, though. My father looks like an Englishman. The trouble is I took after my mother.

BOY, *to Bayard, offering his paper*: Could you look at mine?

BAYARD: I'm no expert, kid. Anyway, don't sit there looking at them like that.

> *Monceau puts his away, as the Boy does. A pause. They wait.*

MONCEAU: I think it's a question of one's credibility—that man just now did carry himself with a certain confidence. . . .

> *The Old Jew begins to pitch forward onto the floor. Von Berg catches him and with the Boy helps him back onto the seat.*

LEBEAU, *with heightened nervousness*: Christ, you'd think they'd shave off their beards. I mean, to walk around with a beard like that in a country like this!

> *Monceau looks at his beard, and Lebeau touches it.*

Well, I just don't waste time shaving, but . . .

VON BERG, *to the Old Jew*: Are you all right, sir?

> *Leduc bends over Von Berg's lap and feels the Old Jew's pulse. Pause. He lets his hand go, and looks toward Lebeau.*

LEDUC: Were you serious? They actually measured your nose?

LEBEAU: With his fingers. That civilian. They called him "professor." *Pause.* Then, *to Bayard*: I think you're right; it's all a question of your papers. That businessman certainly looked Jewish. . . .

MONCEAU: I'm not so sure now.

LEBEAU, *angrily*: A minute ago you were sure, now suddenly . . . !

MONCEAU: Well, even if he wasn't—it only means it really is a general checkup. On the whole population.

LEBEAU: Hey, that's right too! *Slight pause.* Actually, I'm often taken for a gentile myself. Not that I give a damn but most of the time, I . . . *To Von Berg*: How about you, they measure your nose?

VON BERG: No, they told me to get into the car, that was all.

LEBEAU: Because actually yours looks bigger than mine.

BAYARD: Will you cut that out! Just cut it out, will you?

LEBEAU: Can't I try to find out what I'm in for?

BAYARD: Did you ever think of anything beside yourself? Just because you're an artist? You people demoralize everybody!

LEBEAU, *with unconcealed terror*: What the hell am I supposed to think of? Who're you thinking of?

> *The office door opens. The Police Captain appears, and gestures toward Bayard.*

CAPTAIN: Come inside here.

> *Bayard, trying hard to keep his knees from shaking, stands. Ferrand, a café proprietor, comes hurrying down the corridor with a tray of coffee things covered with a large napkin. He has an apron on.*

Ah, at last!

FERRAND: Sorry, Captain, but for you I had to make some fresh.

CAPTAIN, *as he goes into the office behind Ferrand*: Put it on my desk.

> *The door is closed. Bayard sits, wipes his face. Pause.*

MONCEAU, *to Bayard, quietly*: Would you mind if I made a suggestion?

> *Bayard turns to him, already defensive.*

You looked terribly uncertain of yourself when you stood up just now.

BAYARD, *taking offense*: Me uncertain? You've got the wrong man.

MONCEAU: Please, I'm not criticizing you.

BAYARD: Naturally I'm a little nervous, facing a room full of Fascists like this.

MONCEAU: But that's why one must seem especially self-confident. I'm quite sure that's what got that businessman through so quickly. I've had similar experiences on trains, and even in Paris when they stopped me several times. The important thing is not to look like a victim. Or even to feel like one. They can be very stupid, but they do have a sense for victims; they know when someone has nothing to hide.

LEDUC: But how does one avoid feeling like a victim?

MONCEAU: One must create one's own reality in this world. I'm an actor, we do this all the time. The audience, you know, is very sadistic; it looks for your first sign of weakness. So you must try to think of something that makes you feel self-assured; anything at all. Like the day, perhaps, when your father gave you a compliment, or a teacher was amazed at your cleverness . . . Any thought—*to Bayard*—that makes you feel . . . valuable. After all, you are trying to create an illusion; to make them believe you are who your papers say you are.

LEDUC: That's true, we must not play the part they have written for us. That's very wise. You must have great courage.

MONCEAU: I'm afraid not. But I have talent instead. *To Bayard*: One must show them the face of a man who is right, not a man who is suspect and wrong. They sense the difference.

BAYARD: My friend, you're in a bad way if you have to put on an act to feel your rightness. The bourgeoisie sold France; they let in the Nazis to destroy the French working class. Remember the causes of this war and you've got *real* confidence.

LEDUC: Excepting that the cause of this war keep changing so often.

BAYARD: Not if you understand the economic and political forces.

LEDUC: Still, when Germany attacked us the Communists refused to support France. They pronounced it an imperialist war. Until the Nazis turned against Russia; then in one afternoon it all changed into a sacred battle against tyranny. What confidence can one feel from an understanding that turns upside down in an afternoon?

BAYARD: My friend, without the Red Army standing up to them right now you could forget France for a thousand years!

LEDUC: I agree. But that does not require an understanding of political and economic forces—it is simply faith in the Red Army.

BAYARD: It is faith in the future; and the future is Socialist. And that is what *I* take in there with *me*.

> *To the others*:

> I warn you—I've had experience with these types. You'd better ram a viewpoint up your spine or you'll break in half.

LEDUC: I understand. You mean it's important not to feel alone, is that it?

BAYARD: None of us is alone. We're members of history. Some of us don't know it, but you'd better learn it for your own preservation.

LEDUC: That we are . . . symbols.

BAYARD, *uncertain whether to agree*: Yes. Why not? Symbols, yes.

LEDUC: And you feel that helps you. Believe me, I am genuinely interested.

BAYARD: It helps me because it's the truth. What am I to them personally? Do they know me? You react personally to this, they'll turn you into an idiot. You can't make sense of this on a personal basis.

LEDUC: I agree. *Personally*: But the difficulty is—what can one be if not oneself? For example, the thought of torture or something of that sort . . .

BAYARD, *struggling to live his conviction*: Well, it frightens me—of course. But they can't torture the future; it's out of their hands. Man was not made to be the slave of Big Business. Whatever they do, something inside me is laughing. Because they can't win. Impossible. *He has stiffened himself against his rising fear.*

LEDUC: So that in a sense . . . you aren't here. You personally.

BAYARD: In a sense. Why, what's wrong with that?

LEDUC: Nothing; it may be the best way to hold on to oneself. It's only that ordinarily one tries to experience life, to be in spirit where one's body is. For some of us it's difficult to shift gears and go into reverse. But that's not a problem for you.

BAYARD, *solicitously*: You think a man can ever be himself in this society? When millions go hungry and a few live like kings, and whole races are slaves to the stock market—how can you be yourself in such a world? I put in ten hours a day for a few francs, I see people who never bend their backs and they own the planet. . . . How can my spirit be where my body is? I'd have to be an ape.

VON BERG: Then where is your spirit?

BAYARD: In the future. In the day when the working class is master of the world. *That's* my confidence . . . *To Monceau*: Not some borrowed personality.

VON BERG, *wide-eyed, genuinely asking*: But don't you think . . . excuse me. Are not most of the Nazis . . . of the working class?

BAYARD: Well, naturally, with enough propaganda you can confuse anybody.

VON BERG: I see. *Slight pause.* But in that case, how can one have such confidence in them?

BAYARD: Who do you have confidence in, the aristocracy?

VON BERG: Very little. But in certain aristocrats, yes. And in certain common people.

BAYARD: Are you telling me that history is a question of "certain people"? Are we sitting here because we are "certain people"? Is any of us an individual to them? Class interest makes history, not individuals.

VON BERG: Yes. That seems to be the trouble.

BAYARD: Facts are not trouble. A human being has to glory in the facts.

VON BERG, *with a deep, anxious out-reaching to Bayard*: But the facts . . . Dear sir, what if the facts are dreadful? And will always be dreadful?

BAYARD: So is childbirth, so is . . .

VON BERG: But a child comes of it. What if nothing comes of the facts but endless, endless disaster? Believe me, I am happy to meet a man who is not cynical; any faith is precious these days. But to give your faith to a . . . a class of people is impossible, simply impossible—ninety-nine per cent of the Nazis are ordinary working-class people!

BAYARD: I concede it *is* possible to propagandize . . .

VON BERG, *with an untoward anxiety, as though the settlement of this issue is intimate with him*: But what can *not* be propagandized? Isn't that the . . . the only point? A few individuals. Don't you think so?

BAYARD: You're an intelligent man, Prince. Are you seriously telling me that five, ten, a thousand, ten thousand decent people of integrity are all that stand between us and the end of everything? You mean this whole world is going to hang on that thread?

VON BERG, *struck*: I'm afraid it does sound impossible.

BAYARD: If I thought that, I wouldn't have the strength to walk through that door, I wouldn't know how to put one foot in front of the other.

VON BERG—*slight pause*: Yes. I hadn't really considered it that way. But . . . you really think the working class will . . .

BAYARD: They will destroy Fascism because it is against their interest.

VON BERG—*nods*: But in that case, isn't it even more of a mystery?

BAYARD: I see no mystery.

VON BERG: But they adore Hitler.

BAYARD: How can you say that? Hitler is the creation of the capitalist class.

VON BERG, *in terrible mourning and anxiety*: But they adore him! My own cook, my gardeners, the people who work in my forests, the chauffeur, the gamekeeper—they are *Nazis*! I saw it coming over them, the love for this creature—my housekeeper dreams of him in her bed, she'd serve my breakfast like a god had slept with her; in a dream slicing my toast! I saw this adoration in my own house! That, that is the dreadful fact. *Controlling himself*: I beg your pardon, but it disturbs me. I admire your faith; all faith to some degree is beautiful. And when I know that yours is based on something so untrue—it's terribly disturbing. *Quietly*: In any case, I cannot glory in the facts; there is no reassurance there. They adore him, the salt of the earth. . . . *Staring*: Adore him.

> *There is a burst of laughter from within the office. He glances there, as they all do.*

Strange; if I did not know that some of them in there were French, I'd have said they laugh like Germans. I suppose vulgarity has no nation, after all.

> *The door opens. Mr. Ferrand comes out, laughing; within, the laughter is subsiding. He waves within, closing the door. His smile drops. And as he goes past the Waiter, he glances back at the door, then quickly leans over and whispers hurriedly into his ear. They all watch. Now Ferrand starts away. The Waiter reaches out and grasps his apron.*

WAITER: Ferrand!

FERRAND, *brushing the Waiter's hand off his apron*: What can I do? I told you fifty times to get out of this city! Didn't I? *Starting to weep*: Didn't I?

> *He hurries up the corridor, wiping his tears with his apron. They all watch the Waiter, who sits there staring.*

BAYARD: What? Tell me. Come on, I'm next, what'd he say?

WAITER—*whispers, staring ahead in shock*: It's not to work.

LEDUC, *leaning over toward him to hear*: What?

WAITER: They have furnaces.

BAYARD: What furnaces? . . . Talk! What is it?

WAITER: He heard the detectives; they came in for coffee just before. People get burned up in furnaces. It's not to work. They burn you up in Poland.

> *Silence. A long moment passes.*

MONCEAU: That is the most fantastic idiocy I ever heard in my life!

LEBEAU, *to the Waiter*: As long as you have regular French papers, though . . . There's nothing about Jew on *my* papers.

WAITER, *in a loud whisper*: They're going to look at your penis.

The Boy stands up as though with an electric shock. The door of the office opens; the Police Captain appears and beckons to Bayard. The Boy quickly sits.

CAPTAIN: You can come now.

Bayard stands, assuming an artificial and almost absurd posture of confidence. But approaching the Captain he achieves an authority.

BAYARD: I'm a master electrician with the railroad, Captain. You may have seen me there. I'm classified First Priority War Worker.

CAPTAIN: Inside.

BAYARD: You can check with Transport Minister Duquesne.

CAPTAIN: You telling me my business?

BAYARD: No, but we can all use advice from time to time.

CAPTAIN: Inside.

BAYARD: Right.

Without hesitation Bayard walks into the office, the Captain following and closing the door.

A long silence. Monceau, after a moment, smooths out a rough place on the felt of his hat. Lebeau looks at his papers, slowly rubbing his beard with the back of his hand, staring in terror. The Old Jew draws his bundle deeper under his feet. Leduc takes out a nearly empty pack of cigarettes, starts to take one for himself, then silently stands, crosses the line of men, and offers it to them. Lebeau takes one.

They light up. Faintly, from the next-door building, an accordion is heard playing a popular tune.

LEBEAU: Leave it to a cop to play now.

WAITER: No, that's the boss's son, Maurice. They're starting to serve lunch.

Leduc, who has returned to his position as the last man on the bench, cranes around the corner of the corridor, observes, and sits back.

LEDUC, *quietly*: There's only one guard at the door. Three men could take him.

Pause. No one responds. Then . . .

VON BERG, *apologetically*: I'm afraid I'd only get in your way. I have no strength in my hands.

MONCEAU, *to Leduc*: You actually believe that, Doctor? About the furnaces?

LEDUC—*he thinks; then*: I believe it is possible, yes. Come, we can do something.

MONCEAU: But what good are dead Jews to them? They want free labor. It's senseless. You can say whatever you like, but the Germans are not illogical; there's no conceivable advantage for them in such a thing.

LEDUC: You can be sitting here and still speak of advantages? Is there a rational explanation for your sitting here? But you are sitting here, aren't you?

MONCEAU: But an atrocity like that is . . . beyond any belief.

VON BERG: That is exactly the point.

MONCEAU: *You* don't believe it. Prince, you can't tell me you believe such a thing.

VON BERG: I find it the most believable atrocity I have heard.

LEBEAU: But why?

Slight pause.

VON BERG: Because it *is* so inconceivably vile. That is their power. To do the inconceivable; it paralyzes the rest of us. But if that is its purpose it is not the cause. Many times I used to ask my friends—if you love your country why is it necessary to hate other countries? To be a good German why must you despise everything that is not German? Until I realized the answer. They do these things not because they are German but because they are nothing. It is the hallmark of the age—the less you exist the more important it is to make a clear impression. I can see them discussing it as a kind of . . . truthfulness. After all, what *is* self-restraint but hypocrisy? If you despise Jews the most honest thing is to burn them up. And the fact that it costs money, and uses up trains and personnel—this only guarantees the integrity, the purity, the existence of their feelings. They would even tell you that only a Jew would think of the cost. They are poets, they are striving for a new nobility, the nobility of the totally vulgar. I believe in this fire; it would prove for all time that they exist, yes, and that they were sincere. You must not calculate these people with some nineteenth-century arithmetic of loss and gain. Their motives are musical, and people are merely sounds they play. And in my opinion, win or lose this war, they have pointed the way to the future. What one used to conceive a human being to be will have no room on this earth. I would try anything to get out.

A pause.

MONCEAU: But they arrested you. That German professor is an expert. There is nothing Jewish about you. . . .

VON BERG: I have an accent. I noticed he reacted when I started to speak. It is an Austrian inflection. He may think I am another refugee.

> *The door opens. The Professor comes out, and indicates the Waiter.*

PROFESSOR: Next. You.

> *The Waiter makes himself small, pressing up against Lebeau.*

Don't be alarmed, it's only to check your papers.

> *The Waiter suddenly bends over and runs away—around the corner and up the corridor. The Guard appears at the end, collars him, and walks him back down the corridor.*

WAITER, *to the Guard*: Felix, you know me. Felix, my wife will go crazy. Felix . . .

PROFESSOR: Take him in the office.

> *The Police Captain appears in the office doorway.*

GUARD: There's nobody at the door.

CAPTAIN—*grabs the Waiter from the Guard*: Get in here, you Jew son-of-a-bitch. . . .

> *He throws the Waiter into the office; the Waiter collides with the Major, who is just coming out to see what the disturbance is. The Major grips his thigh in pain, pushing the Waiter clear. The Waiter slides to the Major's feet, weeping pleadingly. The Captain strides over and violently jerks him to his feet and pushes him into the office, going in after him.*

> *From within, unseen:*

You want trouble? You want trouble?

> *The Waiter is heard crying out; there is the sound of blows struck. Quiet. The Professor starts toward the door. The Major takes his arm and leads him down to the extreme forward edge of the stage, out of hearing of the prisoners.*

MAJOR: Wouldn't it be much simpler if they were just asked whether they . . .

> *Impatiently, without replying, the Professor goes over to the line of prisoners.*

PROFESSOR: Will any of you admit right now that you are carrying forged identification papers?

Silence.

So. In short, you are all bona fide Frenchmen.

Silence. He goes over to the Old Jew, bends into his face.

Are there any Jews among you?

Silence. Then he returns to the Major.

There's the problem, Major; either we go house by house investigating everyone's biography, or we make this inspection.

MAJOR: That electrician fellow just now, though—I thought he made a point there. In fact, only this morning in the hospital, while I was waiting my turn for X-ray, another officer, a German officer, a captain, in fact—his bathrobe happened to fall open . . .

PROFESSOR: It is entirely possible.

MAJOR: It was unmistakable, Professor.

PROFESSOR: Let us be clear, Major; the Race Institute does not claim that circumcision is conclusive proof of Jewish blood. The Race Institute recognizes that a small proportion of gentiles . . .

MAJOR: I don't see any reason not to say it, Professor—I happen to be, myself.

PROFESSOR: Very well, but I certainly would never mistake you for a Jew. Any more than you could mistake a pig for a horse. Science is not capricious, Major; my degree is in racial anthropology. In any case, we can certainly separate the gentiles by this kind of examination.

He has taken the Major's arm to lead him back to the office.

MAJOR: Excuse me. I'll be back in a few minutes. *Moving to leave:* You can carry on without me.

PROFESSOR: Major; you have your orders; you are in command of this operation. I must insist you take your place beside me.

MAJOR: I think some mistake has been made. I am a line officer, I have no experience with things of this kind. My training is engineering and artillery.

Slight pause.

PROFESSOR—*he speaks more quietly, his eyes ablaze:* We'd better be candid, Major. Are you refusing this assignment?

MAJOR, *registering the threat he feels:* I'm in pain today, Professor. They are still removing fragments. In fact, I understood I was only to . . . hold this desk down until an S.S. officer took over. I'm more or less on loan, you see, from the regular Army.

PROFESSOR—*takes his arm, draws him down to the edge of the stage again*: But the Army is not exempt from carrying out the Racial Program. My orders come from the top. And my report will go to the top. You understand me.

MAJOR—*his resistance seems to fall*: I do, yes.

PROFESSOR: Look now, if you wish to be relieved, I can easily telephone General von—

MAJOR: No—no, that's all right. I . . . I'll be back in a few minutes.

PROFESSOR: This is bizarre, Major—how long am I supposed to wait for you?

MAJOR, *holding back an outburst of resentment*: I need a walk. I am not used to sitting in an office. I see nothing bizarre in it, I am a line officer, and this kind of business takes a little getting used to. *Through his teeth*: What do you find bizarre in it?

PROFESSOR: Very well.

Slight pause.

MAJOR: I'll be back in ten minutes. You can carry on.

· PROFESSOR: I will not continue without you, Major. The Army's responsibility is quite as great as mine here.

MAJOR: I won't be long.

> *The Professor turns abruptly and strides into the office, slamming the door shut. Very much wanting to get out, the Major goes up the corridor. Leduc stands as he passes.*

LEDUC: Major . . .

> *The Major limps past him without turning, up the corridor and out. Silence.*

BOY: Mister?

> *Leduc turns to him.*

I'd try it with you.

LEDUC, *to Monceau and Lebeau*: What about you two?

LEBEAU: Whatever you say, but I'm so hungry I wouldn't do you much good.

LEDUC: You can walk up to him and start an argument. Distract his attention. Then we—

MONCEAU: You're both crazy, they'll shoot you down.

LEDUC: Some of us might make it. There's only one man at the door. This neighborhood is full of alleyways—you could disappear in twenty yards.

MONCEAU: How long would you be free—an hour? And when they catch you they'll really tear you apart.

BOY: Please! I have to get out. I was on my way to the pawnshop. *Takes out a ring.* It's my mother's wedding ring, it's all that's left. She's waiting for the money. They have nothing in the house to eat.

MONCEAU: You take my advice, boy; don't do anything, they'll let you go.

LEDUC: Like the electrician?

MONCEAU: He was obviously a Communist. And the waiter irritated the Captain.

LEBEAU: Look, I'll try it with you but don't expect too much; I'm weak as a chicken, I haven't eaten since yesterday.

LEDUC, *to Monceau*: It would be better with another man. The boy is very light. If you and the boy rush him I'll get his gun away.

VON BERG, *to Leduc, looking at his hands*: Forgive me.

Monceau springs up, goes to a box, and sits.

MONCEAU: I am not going to risk my life for nothing. That businessman had a Jewish face. *To Lebeau*: You said so yourself.

LEBEAU, *to Leduc, appeasingly*: I did. I thought so. Look, if your papers are good, maybe that's it.

LEDUC, *to Lebeau and Monceau*: You know yourself the Germans have been moving into the Southern Zone; you see they are picking up Jews; a man has just told you that you are marked for destruction. . . .

MONCEAU—*indicates Von Berg*: They took him in. Nobody's explained it.

VON BERG: My accent . . .

MONCEAU: My dear Prince, only an idiot could mistake you for anything but an Austrian of the upper class. I took you for nobility the minute you walked in.

LEDUC: But if it's a general checkup why would they be looking at penises?

MONCEAU: There's no evidence of that!

LEDUC: The waiter's boss . . .

MONCEAU, *suppressing a nervous shout*: He overheard two French detectives who can't possibly know anything about what happens in Poland.

And if they do that kind of thing, it's not the end either—I had Jew stamped on my passport in Paris and I was playing Cyrano at the same time.

VON BERG: Really! Cyrano!

LEBEAU: Then why'd you leave Paris?

MONCEAU: It was an absolutely idiotic accident. I was rooming with another actor, a gentile. And he kept warning me to get out. But naturally one doesn't just give up a role like that. But one night I let myself be influenced by him. He pointed out that I had a number of books which were on the forbidden list—of Communist literature—I mean things like Sinclair Lewis, and Thomas Mann, and even a few things by Friedrich Engels, which everybody was reading at one time. And I decided I might as well get rid of them. So we made bundles and I lived on the fifth floor of a walkup and we'd take turns going down to the street and just leaving them on benches or in doorways or anywhere at all. It was after midnight, and I was just dropping a bundle into the gutter near the Opéra, when I noticed a man standing in a doorway watching me. At that moment I realized that I had stamped my name and address in every one of those books.

VON BERG: Hah! What did you do?

MONCEAU: Started walking, and kept right on down here to the Unoccupied Zone. *An outcry of remorse*: But in my opinion, if I'd done nothing at all I might still be working!

LEDUC, *with higher urgency, but deeply sympathetic; to Monceau*: Listen to me for one moment. I beg you. There is only one man guarding that door; we may never get another chance like this again.

LEBEAU: That's another thing; if it was all that serious, wouldn't they be guarding us more heavily? I mean, that's a point.

LEDUC: That is exactly the point. They are relying on us.

MONCEAU: Relying on us!

LEDUC: Yes. To project our own reasonable ideas into their heads. It is reasonable that a light guard means the thing is not important. They rely on our own logic to immobilize ourselves. But you have just told us how you went all over Paris advertising the fact that you owned forbidden books.

MONCEAU: But I didn't do it purposely.

LEDUC: May I guess that you could no longer bear the tension of remaining in Paris? But that you wanted to keep your role in Cyrano and had to find some absolute compulsion to save your own life? It was your unconscious mind that saved you. Do you understand? You cannot wager your life on a purely rational analysis of this situation. Listen to your feelings; you must certainly *feel* the danger here. . . .

MONCEAU, *in high anxiety*: I played in Germany. That audience could not burn up actors in a furnace. *Turning to Von Berg*: Prince, you cannot tell me you believe that!

VON BERG, *after a pause*: I supported a small orchestra. When the Germans came into Austria three of the players prepared to escape. I convinced them no harm would come to them; I brought them to my castle; we all lived together. The oboist was twenty, twenty-one—the heart stopped when he played certain tones. They came for him in the garden. They took him out of his chair. The instrument lay on the lawn like a dead bone. I made certain inquiries; he is dead now. And it was even more terrible—they came and sat down and listened until the rehearsal was over. And *then* they took him. It is as though they wished to take him at exactly the moment when he was most beautiful. I know how you feel—but I tell you nothing any longer is forbidden. Nothing. *Tears are in his eyes; he turns to Leduc*. I ask you to forgive me, Doctor.

> *Pause.*

BOY: Will they let you go?

VON BERG, *with a guilty glance at the Boy*: I suppose. If this is all to catch Jews they will let me go.

BOY: Would you take this ring? And bring it back to my mother?

> *He stretches his hand out with the ring. Von Berg does not touch it.*
>
> Number Nine Rue Charlot. Top floor. Hirsch, Sarah Hirsch. She has long brown hair . . . be sure it's her. She has a little beauty mark on this cheek. There are two other families in the apartment, so be sure it's her.
>
> *Von Berg looks into the Boy's face. Silence. Then he turns to Leduc.*

VON BERG: Come. Tell me what to do. I'll try to help you. *To Leduc*: Doctor?

LEDUC: I'm afraid it's hopeless.

VON BERG: Why?

LEDUC—*stares ahead, then looks at Lebeau*: He's weak with hunger, and the boy's like a feather. I wanted to get away, not just slaughtered. *Pause*. *With bitter irony*: I live in the country, you see; I haven't talked to anybody in so long, I'm afraid I came in here with the wrong assumptions.

MONCEAU: If you're trying to bait me, Doctor, forget it.

LEDUC: Would you mind telling me, are you religious?

MONCEAU: Not at all.

LEDUC: Then why do you feel this desire to be sacrificed?

MONCEAU: I ask you to stop talking to me.

LEDUC: But you are making a gift of yourself. You are the only able-bodied man here, aside from me, and yet you feel no impulse to do something? I don't understand your air of confidence.

Pause.

MONCEAU: I refuse to play a part I do not fit. Everyone is playing the victim these days; hopeless, hysterical, they always assume the worst. I have papers; I will present them with the single idea that they must be honored. I think that is exactly what saved that businessman. You accuse us of acting the part the Germans created for us; I think you're the one who's doing that by acting so desperate.

LEDUC: And if, despite your act, they throw you into a freight car?

MONCEAU: I don't think they will.

LEDUC: But if they do. You certainly have enough imagination to visualize that.

MONCEAU: In that case, I will have done my best. I know what failure is; it took me a long time to make good; I haven't the personality for leading roles; everyone said I was crazy to stay in the profession. But I did, and I imposed my idea on others.

LEDUC: In other words, you will create yourself.

MONCEAU: Every actor creates himself.

LEDUC: But when they tell you to open your fly.

Monceau is silent, furious.

Please don't stop now; I'm very interested. How do you regard that moment?

Monceau is silent.

Believe me, I am only trying to understand this. I am incapable of penetrating such passivity; I ask you what is in your mind when you face the command to open your fly. I am being as impersonal, as scientific as I know how to be—I believe I am going to be murdered. What do you believe will happen when they point to that spot between your legs?

Pause.

MONCEAU: I have nothing to say to you.

LEBEAU: I'll tell you what I'll feel. *Indicates Von Berg.* I'll wish I was him.

LEDUC: To be someone else.

LEBEAU, *exhausted*: Yes. To have been arrested by mistake. God—to see them relaxing when they realize I am innocent.

LEDUC: You feel guilty, then.

LEBEAU—*he has gradually become closer to exhaustion*: A little, I guess. Not for anything I've done but . . . I don't know why.

LEDUC: For being a Jew, perhaps?

LEBEAU: I'm not ashamed of being a Jew.

LEDUC: Then why feel guilty?

LEBEAU: I don't know. Maybe it's that they keep saying such terrible things about us, and you can't answer. And after years and years of it, you . . . I wouldn't say you believe it, but . . . you do, a little. It's a funny thing—I used to say to my mother and father just what you're saying. We could have gone to America a month before the invasion. But they wouldn't leave Paris. She had this brass bed, and carpets, and draperies and all kinds of junk. Like him with his Cyrano. And I told them, "You're doing just what they want you to do!" But, see, people won't believe they can be killed. Not them with their brass bed and their carpets and their faces. . . .

LEDUC: But do you believe it? It seems to me you don't believe it yourself.

LEBEAU: I believe it. They only caught me this morning because I . . . I always used to walk in the morning before I sat down to work. And I wanted to do it again. I knew I shouldn't go outside. But you get tired of believing in the truth. You get tired of seeing things clearly. *Pause.* I always collected my illusions in the morning. I could never paint what I saw, only what I imagined. And this morning, danger or no danger, I just had to get out, to walk around, to see something real, something else but the inside of my head . . . and I hardly turned the corner and that motherless son-of-a-bitch of a scientist got out of the car with his fingers going for my nose. . . . *Pause.* I believe I can die. But you can get so tired . . .

LEDUC: That it's not too bad.

LEBEAU: Almost, yes.

LEDUC, *glancing at them all*: So that one way or the other, with illusions or without them, exhausted or fresh—we have been trained to die. The Jew and the gentile both.

MONCEAU: You're still trying to bait me, Doctor, but if you want to commit suicide do it alone, don't involve others. The fact is there are laws and every government enforces its laws; and I want it understood that I have nothing to do with any of this talk.

LEDUC, *angering now*: Every government does not have laws condemning people because of their race.

MONCEAU: I beg your pardon. The Russians condemn the middle class, the English have condemned the Indians, Africans, and anybody else they could lay their hands on, the French, the Italians . . . every nation has condemned somebody because of his race, including the Americans and what they do to Negroes. The vast majority of mankind is condemned because of its race. What do you advise all these people—suicide?

LEDUC: What do you advise?

MONCEAU, *seeking and finding conviction*: I go on the assumption that if I obey the law with dignity I will live in peace. I may not like the law, but evidently the majority does, or they would overthrow it. And I'm speaking now of the French majority, who outnumber the Germans in this town fifty to one. These are French police, don't forget, not German. And if by some miracle you did knock out that guard you would find yourself in a city where not one person in a thousand would help you. And it's got nothing to do with being Jewish or not Jewish. It is what the world is, so why don't you stop insulting others with romantic challenges!

LEDUC: In short, because the world is indifferent you will wait calmly and with great dignity—to open your fly.

MONCEAU—*frightened and furious, he stands*: I'll tell you what I think; I think it's people like you who brought this on us. People who give Jews a reputation for subversion, and this Talmudic analysis, and this everlasting, niggling discontent.

LEDUC: Then I will tell you that I was wrong before; you didn't advertise your name on those forbidden books in order to find a reason to leave Paris and save yourself. It was in order to get yourself caught and be put out of your misery. Your heart is conquered territory, mister.

MONCEAU: If we meet again you will pay for that remark.

LEDUC: Conquered territory! *He leans forward, his head in his hands.*

BOY, *reaching over to hand the ring to Von Berg*: Will you do it? Number nine Rue Charlot?

VON BERG, *deeply affected*: I will try.

He takes the ring. The Boy immediately stands.

LEDUC: Where are you going?

The Boy, terrified but desperate, moves on the balls of his feet to the corridor and peeks around the corner. Leduc stands, tries to draw him back.

You can't; it'll take three men to . . .

The Boy shakes loose and walks rapidly up the hallway. Leduc hesitates, then goes after him.

Wait! Wait a minute! I'm coming.

The Major enters the corridor at its far end. The Boy halts, Leduc now beside him. For a moment they stand facing him. Then they turn and come down the corridor and sit, the Major following them. He touches Leduc's sleeve, and Leduc stands and follows him downstage.

MAJOR—*he is "high"—with drink and a flow of emotion*: That's impossible. Don't try it. There are sentries on both corners. *Glancing toward the office door*: Captain, I would only like to say that . . . this is all as inconceivable to me as it is to you. Can you believe that?

LEDUC: I'd believe it if you shot yourself. And better yet, if you took a few of them with you.

MAJOR, *wiping his mouth with the back of his hand*: We would all be replaced by tomorrow morning, wouldn't we?

LEDUC: We might get out alive, though; you could see to that.

MAJOR: They'd find you soon.

LEDUC: Not me.

MAJOR, *with a manic amusement, yet deeply questioning*: Why do you deserve to live more than I do?

LEDUC: Because I am incapable of doing what you are doing. I am better for the world than you.

MAJOR: It means nothing to you that I have feelings about this?

LEDUC: Nothing whatever, unless you get us out of here.

MAJOR: And then what? Then what?

LEDUC: I will remember a decent German, an honorable German.

MAJOR: Will that make a difference?

LEDUC: I will love you as long as I live. Will anyone do that now?

MAJOR: That means so much to you—that someone love you?

LEDUC: That I be worthy of someone's love, yes. And respect.

MAJOR: It's amazing; you don't understand anything. Nothing of that kind is left, don't you understand that yet?

LEDUC: It is left in me.

MAJOR, *more loudly, a fury rising in him*: There are no persons any more, don't you see that? There will never be persons again. What do I care if you love me? Are you out of your mind? What am I, a dog that I must be loved? You—*turning to all of them*—goddamned Jews!

The door opens; the Professor and the Police Captain appear.

Like dogs, Jew-dogs. Look at him—*indicating the Old Jew*—with his paws folded. Look what happens when I yell at him. Dog! He doesn't move. Does he move? Do you see him moving? *He strides to the Professor and takes him by the arm.* But we move, don't we? We measure your noses, don't we, Herr Professor, and we look at your cocks, we keep moving continually!

PROFESSOR, *with a gesture to draw him inside*: Major . . .

MAJOR: Hands off, you civilian bastard.

PROFESSOR: I think . . .

MAJOR, *drawing his revolver*: Not a word!

PROFESSOR: You're drunk.

The Major fires into the ceiling. The prisoners tense in shock.

MAJOR: Everything stops now.

He goes in thought, revolver cocked in his hand, and sits beside Lebeau.

Now it is all stopped.

His hands are shaking. He sniffs in his running nose. He crosses his legs to control them, and looks at Leduc, who is still standing.

Now you tell me. You tell me. Now nothing is moving. You tell me. Go ahead now.

LEDUC: What shall I tell you?

MAJOR: Tell me how . . . how there can be persons any more. I have you at the end of this revolver—*indicates the Professor*—he has me—and somebody has him—and somebody has somebody else. Now tell me.

LEDUC: I told you.

MAJOR: I won't repeat it. I am a man of honor. What do you make of that? I will not tell them what you advised me to do. What do you say—damned decent of me, isn't it . . . not to repeat your advice?

> *Leduc is silent. The Major gets up, comes to Leduc. Pause.*

You are a combat veteran.

LEDUC: Yes.

MAJOR: No record of subversive activities against the German authority.

LEDUC: No.

MAJOR: If you were released, and the others were kept . . . would you refuse?

> *Leduc starts to turn away. The Major nudges him with the pistol, forcing him face to face.*

Would you refuse?

LEDUC: No.

MAJOR: And walk out of that door with a light heart?

LEDUC—*he is looking at the floor now*: I don't know. *He starts to put his trembling hands into his pockets.*

MAJOR: Don't hide your hands. I am trying to understand why you are better for the world than me. Why do you hide your hands? Would you go out that door with a light heart, run to your woman, drink a toast to your skin? . . . Why are you better than anybody else?

LEDUC: I have no duty to make a gift of myself to your sadism.

MAJOR: But I do? To others' sadism? Of myself? I have that duty and you do not? To make a gift of myself?

LEDUC—*looks at the Professor and the Police Captain, glances back at the Major*: I have nothing to say.

MAJOR: That's better.

> *He suddenly gives Leduc an almost comradely push and nearly laughs. He puts his gun away, turns swaying to the Professor and with a victorious shout:*

Next!

> *The Major brushes past the Professor into the office. Lebeau has not moved.*

PROFESSOR: This way.

Lebeau stands up, starts sleepily toward the corridor, turns about, and moves into the office, the Professor following him.

CAPTAIN, *to Leduc*: Get back there.

Leduc returns to his seat. The Captain goes into the office; the door shuts. Pause.

MONCEAU: You happy now? You got him furious. You happy?

The door opens; the Captain appears, beckoning to Monceau.

CAPTAIN: Next.

Monceau gets up at once; taking papers out of his jacket, he fixes a smile on his face and walks with erect elegance to the Captain and with a slight bow, his voice cheerful:

MONCEAU: Good morning, Captain.

He goes right into the office; the Captain follows, and shuts the door. Pause.

BOY: Number nine Rue Charlot. Please.

VON BERG: I'll give it to her.

BOY: I'm a minor. I'm not even fifteen. Does it apply to minors?

Captain opens the door, beckons to the Boy.

BOY, *standing*: I'm a minor. I'm not fifteen until February . . .

CAPTAIN: Inside.

BOY, *halting before the Captain*: I could get my birth certificate for you.

CAPTAIN, *prodding him along*: Inside, inside.

They go in. The door shuts. The accordion is heard again from next door. The Old Jew begins to rock back and forth slightly, praying softly. Von Berg, his hand trembling as it passes down his cheek, stares at the Old Jew, then turns to Leduc on his other side. The three are alone now.

VON BERG: Does he realize what is happening?

LEDUC, *with an edgy note of impatience*: As much as anyone can, I suppose.

VON BERG: He seems to be watching it all from the stars. *Slight pause.* I wish we could have met under other circumstances. There are a great many things I'd like to have asked you.

LEDUC, *rapidly, sensing the imminent summons*: I'd appreciate it if you'd do me a favor.

VON BERG: Certainly.

LEDUC: Will you go and tell my wife?

VON BERG: Where is she?

LEDUC: Take the main highway north two kilometers. You'll see a small forest on the left and a dirt road leading into it. Go about a kilometer until you see the river. Follow the river to a small mill. They are in the tool shed behind the wheel.

VON BERG, *distressed*: And . . . what shall I say?

LEDUC: That I've been arrested. And that there may be a possibility I can . . . *Breaks off.* No, tell her the truth.

VON BERG, *alarmed*: What do you mean?

LEDUC: The furnaces. Tell her that.

VON BERG: But actually . . . that's only a rumor, isn't it?

LEDUC—*turns to him—sharply*: I don't regard it as a rumor. It should be known. I never heard of it before. It must be known. Just take her aside—there's no need for the children to hear it, but tell her.

VON BERG: It's only that it would be difficult for me. To tell such a thing to a woman.

LEDUC: If it's happening you can find a way to say it, can't you?

VON BERG—*hesitates; he senses Leduc's resentment*: Very well. I'll tell her. It's only that I have no great . . . facility with women. But I'll do as you say. *Pause. He glances to the door.* They're taking longer with that boy. Maybe he *is* too young, you suppose?

> *Leduc does not answer. Von Berg seems suddenly hopeful.*

> They would stick to the rules, you know. . . . In fact, with the shortage of physicians you suppose they—

> *He breaks off.*

> I'm sorry if I said anything to offend you.

LEDUC, *struggling with his anger*: That's all right.

> *Slight pause. His voice is trembling with anger.*

> It's just that you keep finding these little shreds of hope and it's a little difficult.

VON BERG: Yes, I see. I beg your pardon. I understand.

Pause. Leduc glances at the door; he is shifting about in high tension.

Would you like to talk of something else, perhaps? Are you interested in . . . in music?

LEDUC, *desperately trying to control himself*: It's really quite simple. It's that you'll survive, you see.

VON BERG: But I can't help that, can I?

LEDUC: That only makes it worse! I'm sorry, one isn't always in control of one's emotions.

VON BERG: Doctor, I can promise you—it will not be easy for me to walk out of here. You don't know me.

LEDUC—*he tries not to reply; then*: I'm afraid it will only be difficult because it is so easy.

VON BERG: I think that's unfair.

LEDUC: Well, it doesn't matter.

VON BERG: It does to me. I . . . I can tell you that I was very close to suicide in Austria. Actually, that is why I left. When they murdered my musicians—not that alone, but when I told the story to many of my friends there was hardly any reaction. That was almost worse. Do you understand such indifference?

LEDUC—*he seems on the verge of an outbreak*: You have a curious idea of human nature. It's astounding you can go on with it in these times.

VON BERG, *with hand on heart*: But what is left if one gives up one's ideals? What *is* there?

LEDUC: Who are you talking about? You? Or me?

VON BERG: I'm terribly sorry. . . . I understand.

LEDUC: Why don't you just stop talking. I can't listen to anything. *Slight pause.* Forgive me. I do appreciate your feeling. *Slight pause.* I see it too clearly, perhaps—I know the violence inside these people's heads. It's difficult to listen to amelioration, even if it's well-meant.

VON BERG: I had no intention of ameliorating—

LEDUC: I think you do. And you must; you will survive, you will have to ameliorate it; just a little, just enough. It's no reflection on you. *Slight pause.* But, you see, this is why one gets so furious. Because all this suffering is so pointless—it can never be a lesson, it can never have a meaning. And that is why it will be repeated again and again forever.

VON BERG: Because it cannot be shared?

LEDUC: Yes. Because it cannot be shared. It is total, absolute, waste.

He leans forward suddenly, trying to collect himself against his terror. He glances at the door.

How strange—one can even become impatient.

A groan as he shakes his head with wonder and anger at himself.

Hm!—what devils they are.

VON BERG, *with an overtone of closeness to Leduc*: You understand now why I left Vienna. They can make death seductive. It is their worst sin. I had dreams at night—Hitler in a great flowing cloak, almost like a gown, almost like a woman. He was beautiful.

LEDUC: Listen—don't mention the furnaces to my wife.

VON BERG: I'm glad you say that, I feel very relieved, there's really no point . . .

LEDUC, *in a higher agony as he realizes*: No, it's . . . it's . . . You see there was no reason for me to be caught here. We have a good hideout. They'd never have found us. But she has an exposed nerve in one tooth and I thought I might find some codein. Just say I was arrested.

VON BERG: Does she have sufficient money?

LEDUC: You could help her that way if you like. Thank you.

VON BERG: The children are small?

LEDUC: Two and three.

VON BERG: How dreadful. How dreadful. *He looks with a glance of fury at the door.* Do you suppose if I offered him something? I can get hold of a good deal of money. I know so little about people—I'm afraid he's rather an idealist. It could infuriate him more.

LEDUC: You might try to feel him out. I don't know what to tell you.

VON BERG: How upside down everything is—to find oneself wishing for a money-loving cynic!

LEDUC: It's perfectly natural. We have learned the price of idealism.

VON BERG: And yet can one wish for a world without ideals? That's what's so depressing—one doesn't know what to wish for.

LEDUC, *in anger*: You see, I knew it when I walked down the road, I knew it was senseless! For a goddamned toothache! So what, so she doesn't sleep for a couple of weeks! It was perfectly clear I shouldn't be taking the chance.

VON BERG: Yes, but if one loves someone . . .

LEDUC: We are not in love any more. It's just too difficult to separate in these times.

VON BERG: Oh, how terrible.

LEDUC, *more softly, realizing a new idea*: Listen . . . about the furnaces . . . don't mention that to her. Not a word, please. *With great self-contempt*: God, at a time like this—to think of taking vengeance on her! What scum we are! *He almost sways in despair.*

> *Pause. Von Berg turns to Leduc; tears are in his eyes.*

VON BERG: There is nothing, is that it? For you there is nothing?

LEDUC, *flying out at him suddenly*: Well what do you propose? Excuse me, but what in hell are you talking about?

> *The door opens. The Professor comes out and beckons to the Old Jew. He seems upset, by an argument he had in the office, possibly.*

Next.

> *The Old Jew does not turn to him.*

You hear me, why do you sit there?

> *He strides to the Old Jew and lifts him to his feet brusquely. The man reaches down to pick up his bundle, but the Professor tries to push it back to the floor.*

Leave that.

> *With a wordless little cry, the Old Jew clings to his bundle.*

Leave it!

> *The Professor strikes at the Old Jew's hand, but he only holds on tighter, uttering his wordless little cries. The Police Captain comes out as the Professor pulls at the bundle.*

Let go of that!

> *The bundle rips open. A white cloud of feathers blows up out of it. For an instant everything stops as the Professor looks in surprise at the feathers floating down. The Major appears in the doorway as the feathers settle.*

CAPTAIN: Come on.

> *The Captain and the Professor lift the Old Jew and carry him past the Major into the office. The Major with deadened eyes*

*glances at the feathers and limps in, closing the door be-
hind him.*

*Leduc and Von Berg stare at the feathers, some of which have
fallen on them. They silently brush them off. Leduc picks
the last one off his jacket, opens his fingers, and lets it fall to
the floor.*

*Silence. Suddenly a short burst of laughter is heard from the
office.*

VON BERG, *with great difficulty, not looking at Leduc*: I would like to be
able to part with your friendship. Is that possible?

Pause.

LEDUC: Prince, in my profession one gets the habit of looking at oneself
quite impersonally. It is not you I am angry with. In one part of my mind
it is not even this Nazi. I am only angry that I should have been born
before the day when man has accepted his own nature; that he is *not* reasonable, that he is full of murder, that his ideals are only the little tax he
pays for the right to hate and kill with a clear conscience. I am only angry
that, knowing this, I still deluded myself. That there was not time to truly
make part of myself what I know, and to teach others the truth.

VON BERG, *angered, above his anxiety*: There are ideals, Doctor, of
another kind. There are people who would find it easier to die than stain
one finger with this murder. They exist. I swear it to you. People for
whom everything is *not* permitted, foolish people and ineffectual, but
they do exist and will not dishonor their tradition. *Desperately*: I ask
your friendship.

*Again laughter is heard from within the office. This time it is
louder. Leduc slowly turns to Von Berg.*

LEDUC: I owe you the truth, Prince; you won't believe it now, but I wish
you would think about it and what it means. I have never analyzed a gentile who did not have, somewhere hidden in his mind, a dislike if not a
hatred for the Jews.

VON BERG, *clapping his ears shut, springing up*: That is impossible, it is
not true of me!

LEDUC, *standing, coming to him, a wild pity in his voice*: Until you know
it is true of you you will destroy whatever truth can come of this atrocity.
Part of knowing who we are is knowing we are not someone else. And
Jew is only the name we give to that stranger, that agony we cannot feel,
that death we look at like a cold abstraction. Each man has his Jew; it is
the other. And the Jews have their Jews. And now, now above all, you
must see that you have yours—the man whose death leaves you relieved

that you are not him, despite your decency. And that is why there is nothing and will be nothing—until you face your own complicity with this . . . your own humanity.

VON BERG: I deny that. I deny that absolutely. I have never in my life said a word against your people. Is that your implication? That I have something to do with this monstrousness! I have put a pistol to my head! To my head!

Laughter is heard again.

LEDUC, *hopelessly*: I'm sorry; it doesn't really matter.

VON BERG: It matters very much to me. Very much to me!

LEDUC, *in a level tone full of mourning; and yet behind it a howling horror*: Prince, you asked me before if I knew your cousin, Baron Kessler.

Von Berg looks at him, already with anxiety.

Baron Kessler is a Nazi. He helped to remove all the Jewish doctors from the medical school.

Von Berg is struck; his eyes glance about.

You were aware of that, weren't you?

Half-hysterical laughter comes from the office.

You must have heard that at some time or another, didn't you?

VON BERG, *stunned, inward-seeing*: Yes. I heard it. I . . . had forgotten it. You see, he was . . .

LEDUC: . . . Your cousin. I understand.

They are quite joined; and Leduc is mourning for the Prince as much as for himself, despite his anger.

And in any case, it is only a small part of Baron Kessler to you. I do understand it. But it is all of Baron Kessler to me. When you said his name it was with love; and I'm sure he must be a man of some kindness, with whom you can see eye to eye in many things. But when I hear that name I see a knife. You see now why I say there is nothing, and will be nothing, when even you cannot really put yourself in my place? Even you! And that is why your thoughts of suicide do not move me. It's not your guilt I want, it's your responsibility—that might have helped. Yes, if you had understood that Baron Kessler was in part, in some part, in some small and frightful part—doing your will. You might have done something then, with your standing, and your name and your decency, aside from shooting yourself!

VON BERG, *in full horror, his face upthrust, calling*: What can ever save us? *He covers his face with his hands.*

The door opens. The Professor comes out.

PROFESSOR, *beckoning to the Prince*: Next.

Von Berg does not turn, but holds Leduc in his horrified, beseeching gaze. The Professor approaches the Prince.

Come!

The Professor reaches down to take Von Berg's arm. Von Berg angrily brushes away his abhorrent hand.

VON BERG: *Hände weg!*

The Professor retracts his hand, immobilized, surprised, and for a moment has no strength against his own recognition of authority. Von Berg turns back to Leduc, who glances up at him and smiles with warmth, then turns away.

Von Berg turns toward the door and, reaching into his breast pocket for a wallet of papers, goes into the office. The Professor follows and closes the door.

Alone, Leduc sits motionless. Now he begins the movements of the trapped; he swallows with difficulty, crosses and recrosses his legs. Now he is still again and bends over and cranes around the corner of the corridor to look for the guard. A movement of his foot stirs up feathers. The accordion is heard outside. He angrily kicks a feather off his foot. Now he makes a decision; he quickly reaches into his pocket, takes out a clasp knife, opens the blade, and begins to get to his feet, starting for the corridor.

The door opens and Von Berg comes out. In his hand is a white pass. The door shuts behind him. He is looking at the pass as he goes by Leduc, and suddenly turns, walks back, and thrusts the pass into Leduc's hand.

VON BERG, *in a strangely angered whisper, motioning him out*: Take it! Go!

Von Berg sits quickly on the bench, taking out the wedding ring. Leduc stares at him, a horrified look on his face. Von Berg hands him the ring.

Number nine Rue Charlot. Go.

LEDUC, *in a desperate whisper*: What will happen to you?

VON BERG, *angrily waving him away*: Go, go!

Leduc backs away, his hands springing to cover his eyes in the awareness of his own guilt.

LEDUC—*a plea in his voice*: I wasn't asking you to do this! You don't owe me this!

VON BERG: Go!

Leduc, his eyes wide in awe and terror, suddenly turns and strides up the corridor. At the end of it the Guard appears, hearing his footsteps. He gives the Guard the pass and disappears.

A long pause. The door opens. The Professor appears.

PROFESSOR: Ne— *He breaks off. Looks about, then, to Von Berg*: Where's your pass?

Von Berg stares ahead. The Professor calls into the office.

Man escaped!

He runs up the corridor, calling.

Man escaped! Man escaped!

The Police Captain rushes out of the office. Voices are heard outside calling orders. The accordion stops. The Major hurries out of the office. The Police Captain rushes past him.

CAPTAIN: What? *Glancing back at Von Berg, he realizes and rushes up the corridor, calling*: Who let him out! Find that man! What happened?

The voices outside are swept away by a siren going off. The Major has gone to the opening of the corridor, following the Police Captain. For a moment he remains looking up the corridor. All that can be heard now is the siren moving off in pursuit. It dies away, leaving the Major's rapid and excited breaths, angry breaths, incredulous breaths.

Now he turns slowly to Von Berg, who is staring straight ahead. Von Berg turns and faces him. Then he gets to his feet. The moment lengthens, and lengthens yet. A look of anguish and fury is stiffening the Major's face; he is closing his fists. They stand there, forever incomprehensible to one another, looking into each other's eyes.

At the head of the corridor four new men, prisoners, appear. Herded by the Detectives, they enter the detention room and sit on the bench, glancing about at the ceiling, the walls, the feathers on the floor, and the two men who are staring at each other so strangely.

THE PRICE

A PLAY

1968

Characters

VICTOR FRANZ

ESTHER FRANZ

GREGORY SOLOMON

WALTER FRANZ

ACT ONE

Today. New York.

Two windows are seen at the back of the stage. Daylight filters through their sooty panes, which have been X'd out with fresh whitewash to prepare for the demolition of the building.

Now daylight seeps through a skylight in the ceiling, grayed by the grimy panes. The light from above first strikes an over-stuffed armchair in center stage. It has a faded rose slipcover. Beside it on its right, a small table with a filigreed radio of the Twenties on it and old newspapers; behind it a bridge lamp. At its left an old wind-up Victrola and a pile of records on a low table. A white cleaning cloth and a mop and pail are nearby.

The room is progressively seen. The area around the armchair alone appears to be lived-in, with other chairs and a couch related to it. Outside this area, to the sides and back limits of the room and up the walls, is the chaos of ten rooms of furniture squeezed into this one.

There are four couches and three settees strewn at random over the floor, armchairs, wingbacks, a divan, occasional chairs. On the floor and stacked against the three walls up to the ceiling are bureaus, armoires, a tall secretary, a break-front, a long, elaborately carved serving table, end tables, a library table, desks, glass-front bookcases, bow-front glass cabinets, and so forth. Several long rolled-up rugs and some shorter ones. A long sculling oar, bedsteads, trunks. And overhead one large and one smaller crystal chandelier hang from ropes, not connected to electric wires. Twelve dining-room chairs stand in a row along a dining-room table at left.

There is a rich heaviness, something almost Germanic, about the furniture, a weight of time upon the bulging fronts and curving chests marshalled against the walls. The room is monstrously crowded and dense, and it is difficult to decide if the stuff is impressive or merely over-heavy and ugly.

An uncovered harp, its gilt chipped, stands alone downstage, right. At the back, behind a rather makeshift drape, long since faded, can be seen a small sink, a hotplate, and an old icebox. Up right, a door to the bedroom. Down left, a door to the corridor and stairway, which are unseen.

We are in the attic of a Manhattan brownstone soon to be torn down.

From the down-left door, Police Sergeant Victor Franz enters in uniform. He halts inside the room, glances about, walks at random a few feet, then comes to a halt. Without expression, yet somehow stilled by some emanation from the room, he lets his gaze move from point to point, piece to piece, absorbing its sphinxlike presence.

He moves to the harp with a certain solemnity, as toward a coffin, and, halting before it, reaches out and plucks a string. He turns and crosses to the dining-room table and removes his gun belt and jacket, hanging them on a chair which he has taken off the table, where it had been set upside down along with two others.

He looks at his watch, waiting for time to pass. Then his eye falls on the pile of records in front of the phonograph. He raises the lid of the machine, sees a record already on the turntable, cranks, and sets the tone arm on the record. Gallagher and Shean sing. He smiles at the corniness.

With the record going he moves to the long sculling oar which stands propped against furniture and touches it. Now he recalls something, reaches in behind a chest, and takes out a fencing foil and mask. He snaps the foil in the air, his gaze held by memory. He puts the foil and mask on the table, goes through two or three records on the pile, and sees a title that makes him smile widely. He replaces the Gallagher and Shean record with this. It is a Laughing Record—two men trying unsuccessfully to get out a whole sentence through their wild hysteria.

He smiles. Broader. Chuckles. Then really laughs. It gets into him; he laughs more fully. Now he bends over with laughter, taking an unsteady step as helplessness rises in him.

Esther, his wife, enters from the down-left door. His back is to her. A half-smile is already on her face as she looks about to see who is laughing with him. She starts toward him, and he hears her heels and turns.

ESTHER: What in the world is that?

VICTOR, *surprised*: Hi! *He lifts the tone arm, smiling, a little embarrassed.*

ESTHER: Sounded like a party in here!

He gives her a peck.

Of the record: What *is* that?

VICTOR, *trying not to disapprove openly*: Where'd you get a drink?

ESTHER: I told you. I went for my checkup. *She laughs with a knowing abandonment of good sense.*

VICTOR: Boy, you and that doctor. I thought he told you not to drink.

ESTHER—*laughs*: I had one! One doesn't hurt me. Everything's normal anyway. He sent you his best. *She looks about.*

VICTOR: Well, that's nice. The dealer's due in a few minutes, if you want to take anything.

ESTHER, *looking around with a sigh*: Oh, dear God—here it is again.

VICTOR: The old lady did a nice job.

ESTHER: Ya—I never saw it so clean. *Indicating the room*: Make you feel funny?

VICTOR—*shrugs*: No, not really—she didn't recognize me, imagine?

ESTHER: Dear boy, it's a hundred and fifty years. *Shaking her head as she stares about*: Huh.

VICTOR: What?

ESTHER: Time.

VICTOR: I know.

ESTHER: There's something different about it.

VICTOR: No, it's all the way it was. *Indicating one side of the room*: I had my desk on that side and my cot. The rest is the same.

ESTHER: Maybe it's that it always used to seem so pretentious to me, and kind of bourgeois. But it does have a certain character. I think some of it's in style again. It's surprising.

VICTOR: Well, you want to take anything?

ESTHER, *looking about, hesitates*: I don't know if I want it around. It's all so massive . . . where would we put any of it? That chest is lovely. *She goes to it.*

VICTOR: That was mine. *Indicating one across the room*: The one over there was Walter's. They're a pair.

ESTHER, *comparing*: Oh ya! Did you get hold of him?

VICTOR—*rather glances away, as though this had been an issue*: I called again this morning—he was in consultation.

ESTHER: Was he in the office?

VICTOR: Ya. The nurse went and talked to him for a minute—it doesn't matter. As long as he's notified so I can go ahead.

She suppresses comment, picks up a lamp.

That's probably real porcelain. Maybe it'd go in the bedroom.

ESTHER, *putting the lamp down*: Why don't I meet you somewhere? The whole thing depresses me.

VICTOR: Why? It won't take long. Relax. Come on, sit down; the dealer'll be here any minute.

ESTHER, *sitting on a couch*: There's just something so damned rotten about it. I can't help it; it always was. The whole thing is infuriating.

VICTOR: Well, don't get worked up. We'll sell it and that'll be the end of it. I picked up the tickets, by the way.

ESTHER: Oh, good. *Laying her head back*: Boy, I hope it's a good picture.

VICTOR: Better be. Great, not good. Two-fifty apiece.

ESTHER, *with sudden protest*: I don't care! I want to go somewhere. *She aborts further response, looking around.* God, what's it all about? When I was coming up the stairs just now, and all the doors hanging open . . . It doesn't seem possible . . .

VICTOR: They tear down old buildings every day in the week, kid.

ESTHER: I know, but it makes you feel a hundred years old. I hate empty rooms. *She muses.* What was that screwball's name?—rented the front parlor, remember?—repaired saxophones?

VICTOR, *smiling*: Oh—Saltzman. *Extending his hand sideways*: With the one eye went out that way.

ESTHER: Ya! Every time I came down the stairs, there he was waiting for me with his four red hands! How'd he ever get all those beautiful girls?

VICTOR—*laughs*: God knows. He must've smelled good.

She laughs, and he does.

He'd actually come running up here sometimes; middle of the afternoon—"Victor, come down quick, I got extras!"

ESTHER: And you did, too!

VICTOR: Why not? If it was free, you took it.

ESTHER, *blushing*: You never told me that.

VICTOR: No, that was before you. Mostly.

ESTHER: You dog.

VICTOR: So what? It was the Depression.

She laughs at the non sequitur.

No, really—I think people were friendlier; lot more daytime screwing in those days. Like the McLoughlin sisters— remember, with the typing service in the front bedroom? *He laughs.* My father used to say, "In that typing service it's two dollars a copy."

She laughs. It subsides.

ESTHER: And they're probably all dead.

VICTOR: I guess Saltzman would be—he was well along. Although—*He shakes his head, laughs softly in surprise.* Jeeze, he wasn't either. I think he was about . . . my age now. Huh!

Caught by the impact of time, they stare for a moment in silence.

ESTHER—*gets up, goes to the harp*: Well, where's your dealer?

VICTOR, *glancing at his watch*: It's twenty to six. He should be here soon.

She plucks the harp.

That should be worth something.

ESTHER: I think a lot of it is. But you're going to have to bargain, you know. You can't just take what they say . . .

VICTOR, *with an edge of protest*: I can bargain; don't worry, I'm not giving it away.

ESTHER: Because they *expect* to bargain.

VICTOR: Don't get depressed already, will you? We didn't even start. I intend to bargain, I know the score with these guys.

ESTHER—*withholds further argument, goes to the phonograph; firing up some slight gaiety*: What's this record?

VICTOR: It's a Laughing Record. It was a big thing in the Twenties.

ESTHER, *curiously*: You remember it?

VICTOR: Very vaguely. I was only five or six. Used to play them at parties. You know—see who could keep a straight face. Or maybe they just sat around laughing; I don't know.

ESTHER: That's a wonderful idea!

Their relation is quite balanced, so to speak; he turns to her.

VICTOR: You look good.

She looks at him, an embarrassed smile.

I mean it.—I *said* I'm going to bargain, why do you . . . ?

ESTHER: I believe you.—This is the suit.

VICTOR: Oh, is that it! And how much? Turn around.

ESTHER, *turning*: Forty-five, imagine? He said nobody'd buy it, it was too simple.

VICTOR, *seizing the agreement*: Boy, women are dumb; that is really handsome. See, I don't mind if you get something for your money, but half the stuff they sell is such crap . . . *Going to her*: By the way, look at this collar. Isn't this one of the ones you just bought?

ESTHER, *examining it*: No, that's an older one.

VICTOR: Well, even so. *Turning up a heel*: Ought to write to Consumers Union about these heels. Three weeks—look at them!

ESTHER: Well, you don't walk straight.—You're not going in uniform, I hope.

VICTOR: I could've murdered that guy! I'd just changed, and McGowan was trying to fingerprint some bum and he didn't want to be printed; so he swings out his arm just as I'm going by, right into my container.

ESTHER, *as though this symbolized*: Oh, God . . .

VICTOR: I gave it to that quick cleaner, he'll try to have it by six.

ESTHER: Was there cream and sugar in the coffee?

VICTOR: Ya.

ESTHER: He'll never have it by six.

VICTOR, *assuagingly*: He's going to try.

ESTHER: Oh, forget it.

Slight pause. Seriously disconsolate, she looks around at random.

VICTOR: Well, it's only a movie . . .

ESTHER: But we go out so rarely—why must everybody know your salary? I want an evening! I want to sit down in a restaurant without some drunken ex-cop coming over to the table to talk about old times.

VICTOR: It happened twice. After all these years, Esther, it would seem to me . . .

ESTHER: I know it's unimportant—but like that man in the museum; he really did—he thought you were the sculptor.

VICTOR: So I'm a sculptor.

ESTHER, *bridling*: Well, it was nice, that's all! You really do, Vic—you look distinguished in a suit. Why not? *Laying her head back on the couch*: I should've taken down the name of that scotch.

VICTOR: All scotch is chemically the same.

ESTHER: I know; but some is better.

VICTOR, *looking at his watch*: Look at that, will you? Five-thirty sharp, he tells me. People say anything. *He moves with a heightened restlessness, trying to down his irritation with her mood. His eye falls on a partly opened drawer of a chest, and he opens it and takes out an ice skate.* Look at that, they're still good! *He tests the edge with his fingernail; she merely glances at him.* They're even sharp. We ought to skate again sometime. *He sees her unremitting moodiness.* Esther, I said I would bargain!—You see?—you don't know how to drink; it only depresses you.

ESTHER: Well, it's the kind of depression I enjoy!

VICTOR: Hot diggity dog.

ESTHER: I have an idea.

VICTOR: What?

ESTHER: Why don't you leave me? Just send me enough for coffee and cigarettes.

VICTOR: Then you'd *never* have to get out of bed.

ESTHER: I'd get out. Once in a while.

VICTOR: I got a better idea. Why don't you go off for a couple of weeks with your doctor? Seriously. It might change your viewpoint.

ESTHER: I wish I could.

VICTOR: Well, do it. He's got a suit. You could even take the dog—especially the dog. *She laughs.* It's not funny. Every time you go out for one of those walks in the rain I hold my breath what's going to come back with you.

ESTHER, *laughing*: Oh, go on, you love her.

VICTOR: I love her! You get plastered, you bring home strange animals, and I "love" them! I do not love that goddamned dog!

She laughs with affection, as well as with a certain feminine defiance.

ESTHER: Well, I want her!

VICTOR—*pause*: It won't be solved by a dog, Esther. You're an intelligent, capable woman, and you can't lay around all day. Even something part-time, it would give you a place to go.

ESTHER: I don't need a place to go. *Slight pause.* I'm not quite used to Richard not being there, that's all.

VICTOR: He's gone, kid. He's a grown man; you've got to do something with yourself.

ESTHER: I can't go to the same place day after day. I never could and I never will. Did you *ask* to speak to your brother?

VICTOR: I asked the nurse. Yes. He couldn't break away.

ESTHER: That son of a bitch. It's sickening.

VICTOR: Well, what are you going to do? He never had that kind of feeling.

ESTHER: What feeling? To come to the phone after sixteen years? It's common decency. *With sudden intimate sympathy*: You're furious, aren't you?

VICTOR: Only at myself. Calling him again and again all week like an idiot . . . To hell with him, I'll handle it alone. It's just as well.

ESTHER: What about his share?

He shifts; pressed and annoyed.

I don't want to be a pest—but I think there could be some money here, Vic.

He is silent.

You're going to raise that with him, aren't you?

VICTOR, *with a formed decision*: I've been thinking about it. He's got a right to his half, why should he give up anything?

ESTHER: I thought you'd decided to put it to him?

VICTOR: I've changed my mind. I don't really feel he owes me anything, I can't put on an act.

ESTHER: But how many Cadillacs can he drive?

VICTOR: That's why he's got Cadillacs. People who love money don't give it away.

ESTHER: I don't know why you keep putting it like charity. There's such a thing as a moral debt. Vic, you made his whole career possible. What law said that only he could study medicine—?

VICTOR: Esther, please—let's not get back on that, will you?

ESTHER: I'm not back on anything—you were even the better student. That's a real debt, and he ought to be made to face it. He could never have finished medical school if you hadn't taken care of Pop. I mean we ought to start talking the way people talk! There could be some real money here.

VICTOR: I doubt that. There are no antiques or—

ESTHER: Just because it's ours why must it be worthless?

VICTOR: Now what's that for?

ESTHER: Because that's the way we think! We do!

VICTOR, *sharply*: The man won't even come to the phone, how am I going to—?

ESTHER: Then you write him a letter, bang on his door. This *belongs* to you!

VICTOR, *surprised, seeing how deadly earnest she is*: What are you so excited about?

ESTHER: Well, for one thing it might help you make up your mind to take your retirement.

A slight pause.

VICTOR, *rather secretively, unwillingly*: It's not the money been stopping me.

ESTHER: Then what is it?

He is silent.

I just thought that with a little cushion you could take a month or two until something occurs to you that you want to do.

VICTOR: It's all I think about right now, I don't have to quit to think.

ESTHER: But nothing seems to come of it.

VICTOR: Is it that easy? I'm going to be fifty. You don't just start a whole new career. I don't understand why it's so urgent all of a sudden.

ESTHER—*laughs*: All of a sudden! It's all I've been talking about since you became eligible—I've been saying the same thing for three years!

VICTOR: Well, it's not three years—

ESTHER: It'll be three years in March! It's *three years*. If you'd gone back to school then you'd almost have your Master's by now; you might have had a chance to get into something you'd love to do. Isn't that true? Why can't you make a move?

VICTOR—*pause. He is almost ashamed*: I'll tell you the truth. I'm not sure the whole thing wasn't a little unreal. I'd be fifty-three, fifty-four by the time I could start doing anything.

ESTHER: But you always knew that.

VICTOR: It's different when you're right on top of it. I'm not sure it makes any sense now.

ESTHER, *moving away, the despair in her voice*: Well . . . this is exactly what I tried to tell you a thousand times. It makes the same sense it ever made. But you might have twenty more years, and that's still a long time. Could do a lot of interesting things in that time. *Slight pause.* You're so young, Vic.

VICTOR: I am?

ESTHER: Sure! I'm not, but you are. God, all the girls goggle at you, what do you want?

VICTOR—*laughs emptily*: It's hard to discuss it, Es, because I don't understand it.

ESTHER: Well, why not talk about what you don't understand? Why do you expect yourself to be an authority?

VICTOR: Well, one of us is got to stay afloat, kid.

ESTHER: You want me to pretend everything is great? I'm bewildered and I'm going to act bewildered! *It flies out as though long suppressed*: I've asked you fifty times to write a letter to Walter—

VICTOR, *like a repeated story*: What's this with Walter again? What's Walter going to—?

ESTHER: He is an important scientist, and that hospital's building a whole new research division. I saw it in the paper, it's his hospital.

VICTOR: Esther, the man hasn't called me in sixteen years.

ESTHER: But neither have you called him!

He looks at her in surprise.

Well, you haven't. That's also a fact.

VICTOR, *as though the idea were new and incredible*: What would I call him for?

ESTHER: Because, he's your brother, he's influential, and he could help—Yes, that's how people do, Vic! Those articles he wrote had a real idealism, there was a genuine human quality. I mean people do change, you know.

VICTOR, *turning away*: I'm sorry, I don't need Walter.

ESTHER: I'm not saying you have to approve of him; he's a selfish bastard, but he just might be able to put you on the track of something. I don't see the humiliation.

VICTOR, *pressed, irritated*: I don't understand why it's all such an emergency.

ESTHER: Because I don't know where in hell I am, Victor! *To her own surprise, she has ended nearly screaming. He is silent. She retracts.* I'll do anything if I know why, but all these years we've been saying, once we get the pension we're going to start to live. . . . It's like pushing against a door for twenty-five years and suddenly it opens . . . and we stand there. Sometimes I wonder, maybe I misunderstood you, maybe you like the department.

VICTOR: I've hated every minute of it.

ESTHER: I did everything wrong! I swear, I think if I demanded more it would have helped you more.

VICTOR: That's not true. You've been a terrific wife—

ESTHER: I don't think so. But the security meant so much to you I tried to fit into that; but I was wrong. God—just before coming here, I looked around at the apartment to see if we could use any of this—and it's all so ugly. It's worn and shabby and tasteless. And I have good taste! I know I do! It's that everything was always temporary with us. It's like we never were anything, we were always about-to-be. I think back to the war when any idiot was making so much money—that's when you should have quit, and I knew it, I knew it!

VICTOR: That's when I wanted to quit.

ESTHER: I only had one drink, Victor, so don't—

VICTOR: Don't change the whole story, kid. I wanted to quit, and you got scared.

ESTHER: Because you said there was going to be a Depression after the war.

VICTOR: Well, go to the library, look up the papers around 1945, see what they were saying!

ESTHER: I don't care! *She turns away—from her own irrationality.*

VICTOR: I swear, Es, sometimes you make it sound like we've had no life at all.

ESTHER: God—my mother was so right! I can never believe what I see. I knew you'd never get out if you didn't during the war—I saw it happening, and I said nothing. You know what the goddamned trouble is?

VICTOR, *glancing at his watch, as he senses the end of her revolt*: What's the goddamned trouble?

ESTHER: We can never keep our minds on money! We worry about it, we talk about it, but we can't seem to *want* it. I do, but you don't. I really do, Vic. I want it. Vic? *I want money!*

VICTOR: Congratulations.

ESTHER: You go to hell!

VICTOR: I wish you'd stop comparing yourself to other people, Esther! That's all you're doing lately.

ESTHER: Well, I can't help it!

VICTOR: Then you've got to be a failure, kid, because there's always going to be somebody up ahead of you. What happened? I have a certain nature; just as you do—I didn't change—

ESTHER: But you have changed. You've been walking around like a zombie ever since the retirement came up. You've gotten so vague—

VICTOR: Well, it's a decision. And I'd like to feel a little more certain about it. . . . Actually, I've even started to fill out the forms a couple of times.

ESTHER, *alerted*: And?

VICTOR, *with difficulty—he cannot understand it himself*: I suppose there's some kind of finality about it that . . . *He breaks off.*

ESTHER: But what else did you expect?

VICTOR: It's stupid; I admit it. But you look at that goddamned form and you can't help it. You sign your name to twenty-eight years and you ask yourself, Is that all? Is that it? And it is, of course. The trouble is, when I think of starting something new, that number comes up—five oh—and the steam goes out. But I'll do something. I will! *With a greater closeness to her now*: I don't know what it is; every time I think about it all—it's almost frightening.

ESTHER: What?

VICTOR: Well, like when I walked in here before . . . *He looks around.* This whole thing—it hit me like some kind of craziness. Piling up all this stuff here like it was made of gold. *He half-laughs, almost embarrassed.*

I brought up every stick; damn near saved the carpet tacks. *He turns to the center chair.* That whole way I was with him—it's inconceivable to me now.

ESTHER, *with regret over her sympathy*: Well . . . you loved him.

VICTOR: I know, but it's all words. What was he? A busted businessman like thousands of others, and I acted like some kind of a mountain crashed. I tell you the truth, every now and then the whole thing is like a story somebody told me. You ever feel that way?

ESTHER: All day, every day.

VICTOR: Oh, come on—

ESTHER: It's the truth. The first time I walked up those stairs I was nineteen years old. And when you opened that box with your first uniform in it—remember that? When you put it on the first time?—how we laughed? If anything happened you said you'd call a cop! *They both laugh.* It was like a masquerade. And we were right. That's when we were right.

VICTOR, *pained by her pain*: You know, Esther, every once in a while you try to sound childish and it—

ESTHER: I mean to be! I'm sick of the— Oh, forget it, I want a drink. *She goes for her purse.*

VICTOR, *surprised*: What's that, the great adventure? Where are you going all of a sudden?

ESTHER: I can't stand it in here, I'm going for a walk.

VICTOR: Now you cut out this nonsense!

ESTHER: I am not an alcoholic!

VICTOR: You've had a good life compared to an awful lot of people! You trying to turn into a goddamned teenager or something?

ESTHER, *indicating the furniture*: Don't talk childishness to me, Victor— not in this room! You let it lay here all these years because you can't have a simple conversation with your own brother, and I'm childish? You're still eighteen years old with that man! I mean I'm stuck, but I admit it!

VICTOR, *hurt*: Okay. Go ahead.

ESTHER—*she can't quite leave*: You got a receipt? I'll get your suit. *He doesn't move. She makes it rational*: I just want to get out of here.

VICTOR—*takes out a receipt and gives it to her. His voice is cold*: It's right off Seventh. The address is on it. *He moves from her.*

ESTHER: I'm coming back right away.

VICTOR, *freeing her to her irresponsibility*: Do as you please, kid. I mean it.

ESTHER: You were grinding your teeth again last night. Did you know that?

VICTOR: Oh! No wonder my ear hurts.

ESTHER: I wish I had a tape recorder. I mean it, it's gruesome; sounds like a lot of rocks coming down a mountain. I wish you could hear it, you wouldn't take this self-sufficient attitude.

> *He is silent, alarmed, hurt. He moves upstage as though looking at the furniture.*

VICTOR: It's okay. I think I get the message.

ESTHER, *afraid—she tries to smile and goes back toward him*: Like what?

VICTOR—*moves a chair and does a knee bend and draws out the chassis of an immense old radio*: What other message is there?

> *Slight pause.*

ESTHER, *to retrieve the contact*: What's that?

VICTOR: Oh, one of my old radios that I made. Mama mia, look at those tubes.

ESTHER, *more wondering than she feels about radios*: Would that work?

VICTOR: No, you need a storage battery. . . . *Recalling, he suddenly looks up at the ceiling.*

ESTHER, *looking up*: What?

VICTOR: One of my batteries exploded, went right through there someplace. *He points.* There! See where the plaster is different?

ESTHER, *striving for some spark between them*: Is this the one you got Tokyo on?

VICTOR, *not relenting, his voice dead*: Ya, this is the monster.

ESTHER, *with a warmth*: Why don't you take it?

VICTOR: Ah, it's useless.

ESTHER: Didn't you once say you had a lab up here? Or did I dream that?

VICTOR: Sure, I took it apart when Pop and I moved up here. Walter had that wall, and I had this. We did some great tricks up here.

> *She is fastened on him.*

> *He avoids her eyes and moves waywardly.* I'll be frank with you, kid—I look at my life and the whole thing is incompre-

hensible to me. I know all the reasons and all the reasons and all the reasons, and it ends up—nothing. *He goes to the harp, touches it.*

It's strange, you know? I forgot all about it—we'd work up here all night sometimes, and it was often full of music. My mother'd play for hours down in the library. Which is peculiar, because a harp is so soft. But it penetrates, I guess.

ESTHER: You're dear. You are, Vic. *She starts toward him, but he thwarts her by looking at his watch.*

VICTOR: I'll have to call another man. Come on, let's get out of here. *With a hollow, exhausted attempt at joy:* We'll get my suit and act rich!

ESTHER: Vic, I didn't mean that I—

VICTOR: Forget it. Wait, let me put these away before somebody walks off with them. *He takes up the foil and mask.*

ESTHER: Can you still do it?

VICTOR, *his sadness, his distance clinging to him:* Oh, no, you gotta be in shape for this. It's all in the thighs—

ESTHER: Well, let me see, I never saw you do it!

VICTOR, *giving the inch:* All right, but I can't get down far enough any more. *He takes position, feet at right angles, bouncing himself down to a difficult crouch.*

ESTHER: Maybe you could take it up again.

VICTOR: Oh no, it's a lot of work, it's the toughest sport there is. *Resuming position:* Okay, just stand there.

ESTHER: Me?

VICTOR: Don't be afraid. *Snapping the tip:* It's a beautiful foil, see how alive it is? I beat Princeton with this. *He laughs tiredly and makes a tramping lunge from yards away; the button touches her stomach.*

ESTHER, *springing back:* God! Victor!

VICTOR: What?

ESTHER: You looked beautiful.

> *He laughs, surprised and half-embarrassed—when both of them are turned to the door by a loud, sustained coughing out in the corridor. The coughing increases.*
>
> *Enter Gregory Solomon. In brief, a phenomenon; a man nearly ninety but still straight-backed and the air of his*

massiveness still with him. He has perfected a way of leaning on his cane without appearing weak.

He wears a worn fur-felt black fedora, its brim turned down on the right side like Jimmy Walker's—although much dustier—and a shapeless topcoat. His frayed tie has a thick knot, askew under a curled-up collar tab. His vest is wrinkled, his trousers baggy. A large diamond ring is on his left index finger. Tucked under his arm, a wrung-out leather portfolio. He hasn't shaved today.

Still coughing, catching his breath, trying to brush his cigar ashes off his lapel in a hopeless attempt at businesslike decorum, he is nodding at Esther and Victor and has one hand raised in a promise to speak quite soon. Nor has he failed to glance with some suspicion at the foil in Victor's hand.

VICTOR: Can I get you a glass of water?

Solomon gestures an imperious negative, trying to stop coughing.

ESTHER: Why don't you sit down?

Solomon gestures thanks, sits in the center armchair, the cough subsiding.

You sure you don't want some water?

SOLOMON, *in a Russian-Yiddish accent*: Water I don't need; a little blood I could use. Thank you. *He takes deep breaths, his attention on Victor, who now puts down the foil.* Oh boy. That's some stairs.

ESTHER: You all right now?

SOLOMON: Another couple steps you'll be in heaven. Ah—excuse me, Officer, I am looking for a party. The name is . . . *He fingers in his vest.*

VICTOR: Franz.

SOLOMON: That's it, Franz.

VICTOR: That's me.

Solomon looks incredulous.

Victor Franz.

SOLOMON: So it's a policeman!

VICTOR, *grinning*: Uh huh.

SOLOMON: What do you know! *Including Esther*: You see? There's only one beauty to this lousy business, you meet all kinda people. But I never dealed with a policeman. *Reaching over to shake hands*: I'm very happy to meet you. My name is Solomon, Gregory Solomon.

VICTOR, *shaking hands*: This is my wife.

ESTHER: How do you do.

SOLOMON, *nodding appreciatively to Esther*: Very nice. *To Victor*: That's a nice-looking woman. *He extends his hands to her.* How do you do, darling. Beautiful suit.

ESTHER—*laughs*: The fact is, I just bought it!

SOLOMON: You got good taste. Congratulations, wear it in good health. *He lets go her hand.*

ESTHER: I'll go to the cleaner, dear. I'll be back soon. *With a step toward the door—to Solomon*: Will you be very long?

SOLOMON, *glancing around at the furniture as at an antagonist*: With furniture you never know, can be short, can be long, can be medium.

ESTHER: Well, you give him a good price now, you hear?

SOLOMON: Ah ha! *Waving her out*: Look, you go to the cleaner, and we'll take care everything one hundred per cent.

ESTHER: Because there's some very beautiful stuff here. I know it, but he doesn't.

SOLOMON: I'm not sixty-two years in the business by taking advantage. Go, enjoy the cleaner.

    She and Victor laugh.

ESTHER, *shaking her finger at him*: I hope I'm going to like you!

SOLOMON: Sweetheart, all the girls like me, what can I do?

ESTHER, *still smiling—to Victor as she goes to the door*: You be careful.

VICTOR, *nodding*: See you later.

    She goes.

SOLOMON: I like her, she's suspicious.

VICTOR, *laughing in surprise*: What do you mean by that?

SOLOMON: Well, a girl who believes everything, how you gonna trust her?

    Victor laughs appreciatively.

    I had a wife . . . *He breaks off with a wave of the hand.* Well, what's the difference? Tell me, if you don't mind, how did you get my name?

VICTOR: In the phone book.

SOLOMON: You don't say! The phone book.

VICTOR: Why?

SOLOMON, *cryptically*: No-no, that's fine, that's fine.

VICTOR: The ad said you're a registered appraiser.

SOLOMON: Oh yes. I am registered, I am licensed, I am even vaccinated.

> *Victor laughs.*

Don't laugh, the only thing you can do today without a license is you'll go up the elevator and jump out the window. But I don't have to tell you, you're a policeman, you know this world. *Hoping for contact*: I'm right?

VICTOR, *reserved*: I suppose.

SOLOMON, *surveying the furniture, one hand on his thigh, the other on the chair arm in a naturally elegant position*: So. *He glances about again, and with an uncertain smile*: That's a lot of furniture. This is all for sale?

VICTOR: Well, ya.

SOLOMON: Fine, fine. I just like to be sure where we are. *With a weak attempt at a charming laugh*: Frankly, in this neighborhood I never expected such a load. It's very surprising.

VICTOR: But I said it was a whole houseful.

SOLOMON, *with a leaven of unsureness*: Look, don't worry about it, we'll handle everything very nice. *He gets up from the chair and goes to one of the pair of chiffoniers which he is obviously impressed with. He looks up at the chandeliers. Then straight at Victor*: I'm not mixing in, Officer, but if you wouldn't mind—what is your connection? How do you come to this?

VICTOR: It was my family.

SOLOMON: You don't say. Looks like it's standing here a long time, no?

VICTOR: Well, the old man moved everything up here after the '29 crash. My uncles took over the house and they let him keep this floor.

SOLOMON, *as though to emphasize that he believes it*: I see. *He walks to the harp.*

VICTOR: Can you give me an estimate now, or do you have to—?

SOLOMON, *running a hand over the harp frame*: No-no, I'll give you right away, I don't waste a minute, I'm very busy. *He plucks a string, listens.*

Then bends down and runs a hand over the sounding board: He passed away, your father?

VICTOR: Oh, long time ago—about sixteen years.

SOLOMON, *standing erect*: It's standing here sixteen years?

VICTOR: Well, we never got around to doing anything about it, but they're tearing the building down, so . . . It was very good stuff, you know—they had quite a little money.

SOLOMON: Very good, yes . . . I can see. *He leaves the harp with an estimating glance.* I was also very good; now I'm not so good. Time, you know, is a terrible thing. *He is a distance from the harp and indicates it.* That sounding board is cracked, you know. But don't worry about it, it's still a nice object. *He goes to an armoire and strokes the veneer.* It's a funny thing—an armoire like this, thirty years you couldn't give it away; it was a regular measles. Today all of a sudden, they want it again. Go figure it out. *He goes to one of the chests.*

VICTOR, *pleased*: Well, give me a good price and we'll make a deal.

SOLOMON: Definitely. You see, I don't lie to you. *He is pointing to the chest.* For instance, a chiffonier like this I wouldn't have to keep it a week. *Indicating the other chest*: That's a pair, you know.

VICTOR: I know.

SOLOMON: That's a nice chair, too. *He sits on a dining-room chair, rocking to test its tightness.* I like the chairs.

VICTOR: There's more stuff in the bedroom, if you want to look.

SOLOMON: Oh? *He goes toward the bedroom.* What've you got here? *He looks into the bedroom, up and down.* I like the bed. That's a very nice carved bed. That I can sell. That's your parents' bed?

VICTOR: Yes. They may have bought that in Europe, if I'm not mistaken. They used to travel a good deal.

SOLOMON: Very handsome, very nice. I like it. *He starts to return to the center chair, eyes roving the furniture.* Looks a very nice family.

VICTOR: By the way, that dining-room table opens up. Probably seat about twelve people.

SOLOMON, *looking at the table*: I know that. Yes. In a pinch even fourteen. *He picks up the foil.* What's this? I thought you were stabbing your wife when I came in.

VICTOR, *laughing*: No, I just found it. I used to fence years ago.

SOLOMON: You went to college?

VICTOR: Couple of years, ya.

SOLOMON: That's very interesting.

VICTOR: It's the old story.

SOLOMON: No, listen— What happens to people is always the main element to me. Because when do they call me? It's either a divorce or somebody died. So it's always a new story. I mean it's the same, but it's different. *He sits in the center chair.*

VICTOR: You pick up the pieces.

SOLOMON: That's very good, yes. I pick up the pieces. It's a little bit like you, I suppose. You must have some stories, I betcha.

VICTOR: Not very often.

SOLOMON: What are you, a traffic cop, or something . . . ?

VICTOR: I'm out in Rockaway most of the time, the airports.

SOLOMON: That's Siberia, no?

VICTOR, *laughing*: I like it better that way.

SOLOMON: You keep your nose clean.

VICTOR, *smiling*: That's it. *Indicating the furniture*: So what do you say?

SOLOMON: What I say? *Taking out two cigars as he glances about*: You like a cigar?

VICTOR: Thanks, I gave it up long time ago. So what's the story here?

SOLOMON: I can see you are a very factual person.

VICTOR: You hit it.

SOLOMON: Couldn't be better. So tell me, you got some kind of paper here? To show ownership?

VICTOR: Well, no, I don't. But . . . *He half-laughs.* I'm the owner, that's all.

SOLOMON: In other words, there's no brothers, no sisters.

VICTOR: I have a brother, yes.

SOLOMON: Ah hah. You're friendly with him. Not that I'm mixing in, but I don't have to tell you the average family they love each other like crazy, but the minute the parents die is all of a sudden a question who is going to get what and you're covered with cats and dogs—

VICTOR: There's no such problem here.

SOLOMON: Unless we're gonna talk about a few pieces, then it wouldn't bother me, but to take the whole load without a paper is a—

VICTOR: All right, I'll get you some kind of statement from him; don't worry about it.

SOLOMON: That's definite; because even from high-class people you wouldn't believe the shenanigans—lawyers, college professors, television personalities—five hundred dollars they'll pay a lawyer to fight over a bookcase it's worth fifty cents—because you see, everybody wants to be number one, so . . .

VICTOR: I said I'd get you a statement. *He indicates the room.* Now what's the story?

SOLOMON: All right, so I'll tell you the story. *He looks at the dining-room table and points to it.* For instance, you mention the dining-room table. That's what they call Spanish Jacobean. Cost maybe twelve, thirteen hundred dollars. I would say—1921, '22. I'm right?

VICTOR: Probably, ya.

SOLOMON—*clears his throat*: I see you're an intelligent man, so before I'll say another word, I ask you to remember—with used furniture you cannot be emotional.

VICTOR—*laughs*: I haven't opened my mouth!

SOLOMON: I mean you're a policeman, I'm a furniture dealer, we both know this world. Anything Spanish Jacobean you'll sell quicker a case of tuberculosis.

VICTOR: Why? That table's in beautiful condition.

SOLOMON: Officer, you're talking reality; you cannot talk reality with used furniture. They don't like that style; not only they don't like it, they hate it. The same thing with that buffet there and that . . . *He starts to point elsewhere.*

VICTOR: You only want to take a few pieces, is that the ticket?

SOLOMON: Please, Officer, we're already talking too fast—

VICTOR: No-no, you're not going to walk off with the gravy and leave me with the bones. All or nothing or let's forget it. I told you on the phone it was a whole houseful.

SOLOMON: What're you in such a hurry? Talk a little bit, we'll see what happens. In a day they didn't build Rome. *He calculates worriedly for a moment, glancing again at the pieces he wants. He gets up, goes and touches the harp.* You see, what I had in mind—I would give you such a knockout price for these few pieces that you—

VICTOR: That's *out.*

SOLOMON, *quickly*: Out.

VICTOR: I'm not running a department store. They're tearing the building down.

SOLOMON: Couldn't be better! We understand each other, so—*with his charm*—so there's no reason to be emotional. *He goes to the records.* These records go? *He picks up one.*

VICTOR: I might keep three or four.

SOLOMON, *reading a label*: Look at that! Gallagher and Shean!

VICTOR, *with only half a laugh*: You're not going to start playing them now!

SOLOMON: Who needs to play? I was on the same bill with Gallagher and Shean maybe fifty theaters.

VICTOR, *surprised*: You were an actor?

SOLOMON: An actor! An acrobat; my whole family was acrobats. *Expanding with this first opening*: You never heard "The Five Solomons"—may they rest in peace? I was the one on the bottom.

VICTOR: Funny—I never heard of a Jewish acrobat.

SOLOMON: What's the matter with Jacob, he wasn't a wrestler?—wrestled with the Angel?

> *Victor laughs.*

> Jews been acrobats since the beginning of the world. I was a horse them days: drink, women, anything—on-the-go, on-the-go, nothing ever stopped me. Only life. Yes, my boy. *Almost lovingly putting down the record*: What do you know, Gallagher and Shean.

VICTOR, *more intimately now, despite himself; but with no less persistence in keeping to the business*: So where are we?

SOLOMON—*glancing off, he turns back to Victor with a deeply concerned look*: Tell me, what's with crime now? It's up, hey?

VICTOR: Yeah, it's up, it's up. Look, Mr. Solomon, let me make one thing clear, heh? I'm not sociable.

SOLOMON: You're not.

VICTOR: No, I'm not; I'm not a businessman, I'm not good at conversations. So let's get to a price, and finish. Okay?

SOLOMON: You don't want we should be buddies.

VICTOR: That's exactly it.

SOLOMON: So we wouldn't be buddies! *He sighs.* But just so you'll know me a little better—I'm going to show you something. *He takes out a leather folder which he flips open and hands to Victor.* There's my discharge from the British Navy. You see? "His Majesty's Service."

VICTOR, *looking at the document*: Huh! What were you doing in the British Navy?

SOLOMON: Forget the British Navy. What does it say the date of birth?

VICTOR: "Eighteen . . ." *Amazed, he looks up at Solomon.* You're almost ninety?

SOLOMON: Yes, my boy. I left Russia sixty-five years ago, I was twenty-four years old. And I smoked all my life. I drinked, and I loved every woman who would let me. So what do I need to steal from you?

VICTOR: Since when do people need a reason to steal?

SOLOMON: I never saw such a man in my life!

VICTOR: Oh yes you did. Now you going to give me a figure or—?

SOLOMON—*he is actually frightened because he can't get a hook into Victor and fears losing the good pieces*: How can I give you a figure? You don't trust one word I say!

VICTOR, *with a strained laugh*: I never saw you before, what're you asking me to trust you?!

SOLOMON, *with a gesture of disgust*: But how am I going to start to talk to you? I'm sorry; here you can't be a policeman. If you want to do business a little bit you gotta believe or you can't do it. I'm . . . I'm . . . Look, forget it. *He gets up and goes to his portfolio.*

VICTOR, *astonished*: What are you doing?

SOLOMON: I can't work this way. I'm too old every time I open my mouth you should practically call me a thief.

VICTOR: Who called you a thief?

SOLOMON, *moving toward the door*: No—I don't need it. I don't want it in my shop. *Wagging a finger into Victor's face*: And don't forget it—I never gave you a price, and look what you did to me. You see? I never gave you a price!

VICTOR, *angering*: Well, what did you come here for, to do me a favor? What are you talking about?

SOLOMON: Mister, I pity you! What is the matter with you people! You're worse than my daughter! Nothing in the world you believe, nothing you respect—how can you live? You think that's such a smart thing? That's so hard, what you're doing? Let me give you a piece of advice—it's not that you can't believe nothing, that's not so hard—it's that you still got to believe it. *That's* hard. And if you can't do that, my friend—you're a dead man! *He starts toward the door.*

VICTOR, *chastened despite himself*: Oh, Solomon, come on, will you?

SOLOMON: No-no. You got a certain problem with this furniture but you don't want to listen so how can I talk?

VICTOR: I'm listening! For Christ's sake, what do you want me to do, get down on my knees?

SOLOMON, *putting down his portfolio and taking out a wrinkled tape measure from his jacket pocket*: Okay, come here. I realize you are a fac-tual person, but some facts are funny. *He stretches the tape measure across the depth of a piece.* What does that read? *Then turns to Victor, showing him.*

VICTOR—*comes to him, reads*: Forty inches. So?

SOLOMON: My boy, the bedroom doors in a modern apartment house are thirty, thirty-two inches maximum. So you can't get this in—

VICTOR: What about the old houses?

SOLOMON, *with a desperation growing*: All I'm trying to tell you is that my possibilities are smaller!

VICTOR: Well, can't I ask a question?

SOLOMON: I'm giving you architectural facts! Listen—*Wiping his face, he seizes on the library table, going to it.* You got there, for instance, a library table. That's a solid beauty. But go find me a modern apartment with a library. If they would build old hotels, I could sell this, but they only build new hotels. People don't live like this no more. This stuff is from another world. So I'm trying to give you a modern viewpoint. Because the price of used furniture is nothing but a viewpoint, and if you wouldn't understand the viewpoint is impossible to understand the price.

VICTOR: So what's the viewpoint—that it's all worth nothing?

SOLOMON: That's what you said, I didn't say that. The chairs is worth something, the chiffoniers, the bed, the harp—

VICTOR—*turns away from him*: Okay, let's forget it, I'm not giving you the cream—

SOLOMON: What're you jumping!

VICTOR, *turning to him*: Good God, are you going to make me an offer or not?

SOLOMON, *walking away with a hand at his temple*: Boy, oh boy, oh boy. You must've arrested a million people by now.

VICTOR: Nineteen in twenty-eight years.

SOLOMON: So what are you so hard on me?

VICTOR: Because you talk about everything but money and I don't know what the hell you're up to.

SOLOMON, *raising a finger*: We will now talk money. *He returns to the center chair.*

VICTOR: Great. I mean you can't blame me—every time you open your mouth the price seems to go down.

SOLOMON, *sitting*: My boy, the price didn't change since I walked in.

VICTOR, *laughing*: That's even better! So what's the price?

> Solomon glances about, his wit failed, a sunk look coming over his face.

What's going on? What's bothering you?

SOLOMON: I'm sorry, I shouldn't have come. I thought it would be a few pieces but . . . *Sunk, he presses his fingers into his eyes.* It's too much for me.

VICTOR: Well, what'd you come for? I told you it was the whole house.

SOLOMON, *protesting*: You called me so I came! What should I do, lay down and die? *Striving again to save it*: Look, I want very much to make you an offer, the only question is . . . *He breaks off as though fearful of saying something.*

VICTOR: This is a hell of a note.

SOLOMON: Listen, it's a terrible temptation to me! But . . . *As though throwing himself on Victor's understanding*: You see, I'll tell you the truth; you must have looked in a very old phone book; a couple of years ago already I cleaned out my store. Except a few English andirons I got left, I sell when I need a few dollars. I figured I was eighty, eighty-five, it was time already. But I waited—and nothing happened—I even moved out of my apartment. I'm living in the back of the store with a hotplate. But nothing happened. I'm still practically a hundred per cent—not a hundred, but I feel very well. And I figured maybe you got a couple nice pieces—not that the rest can't be sold, but it could take a year, year and half. For me that's a big bet. *In conflict, he looks around.* The trouble is I love to work; I love it, but—*Giving up*: I don't know what to tell you.

VICTOR: All right, let's forget it then.

SOLOMON, *standing*: What're you jumping?

VICTOR: Well, are you in or out!

SOLOMON: How do I know where I am! You see, it's also this particular furniture—the average person he'll take one look, it'll make him very nervous.

VICTOR: Solomon, you're starting again.

SOLOMON: I'm not bargaining with you!

VICTOR: Why'll it make him nervous?

SOLOMON: Because he knows it's never gonna break.

VICTOR, *not in bad humor, but clinging to his senses*: Oh come on, will you? Have a little mercy.

SOLOMON: My boy, you don't know the psychology! If it wouldn't break there is no more possibilities. For instance, you take—*crosses to table*—this table . . . Listen! *He bangs the table*. You can't move it. A man sits down to such a table he knows not only he's married, he's got to stay married—there is no more possibilities.

> *Victor laughs.*

> You're laughing, I'm telling you the factual situation. What is the key word today? Disposable. The more you can throw it away the more it's beautiful. The car, the furniture, the wife, the children—everything has to be disposable. Because you see the main thing today is—shopping. Years ago a person, he was unhappy, didn't know what to do with himself—he'd go to church, start a revolution—*something*. Today you're unhappy? Can't figure it out? What is the salvation? Go shopping.

VICTOR, *laughing*: You're terrific, I have to give you credit.

SOLOMON: I'm telling you the truth! If they would close the stores for six months in this country there would be from coast to coast a regular massacre. With this kind of furniture the shopping is over, it's finished, there's no more possibilities, you *got* it, you see? So you got a problem here.

VICTOR, *laughing*: Solomon, you are one of the greatest. But I'm way ahead of you, it's not going to work.

SOLOMON, *offended*: What "work"? I don't know how much time I got. What is so terrible if I say that? The trouble is, you're such a young fella you don't understand these things—

VICTOR: I understand very well, I know what you're up against. I'm not so young.

SOLOMON, *scoffing*: What are you, forty? Forty-five?

VICTOR: I'm going to be fifty.

SOLOMON: Fifty! You're a baby boy!

VICTOR: Some baby.

SOLOMON: My God, if I was fifty . . . ! I got married I was seventy-five.

VICTOR: Go on.

SOLOMON: What are you talking? She's still living by Eighth Avenue over there. See, that's why I like to stay liquid, because I don't want her to get her hands on this. . . . Birds she loves. She's living there with maybe a hundred birds. She gives you a plate of soup it's got feathers. I didn't work all my life for them birds.

VICTOR: I appreciate your problems, Mr. Solomon, but I don't have to pay for them. *He stands.* I've got no more time.

SOLOMON, *holding up a restraining hand—desperately*: I'm going to buy it! *He has shocked himself, and glances around at the towering masses of furniture.* I mean I'll . . . *He moves, looking at the stuff.* I'll have to live, that's all, I'll make up my mind! I'll buy it.

VICTOR—*he is affected as Solomon's fear comes through to him*: We're talking about everything now.

SOLOMON, *angrily*: Everything, everything! *Going to his portfolio*: I'll figure it up, I'll give you a very nice price, and you'll be a happy man.

VICTOR, *sitting again*: That I doubt.

> *Solomon takes a hard-boiled egg out of the portfolio.*

> What's this now, lunch?

SOLOMON: You give me such an argument, I'm hungry! I'm not supposed to get too hungry.

VICTOR: Brother!

SOLOMON—*cracks the shell on his diamond ring*: You want me to starve to death? I'm going to be very quick here.

VICTOR: Boy—I picked a number!

SOLOMON: There wouldn't be a little salt, I suppose.

VICTOR: I'm not going running for salt now!

SOLOMON: Please, don't be blue. I'm going to knock you off your feet with the price, you'll see. *He swallows the egg. He now faces the furniture, and, half to himself, pad and pencil poised*: I'm going to go here like an IBM. *He starts estimating on his pad.*

VICTOR: That's all right, take it easy. As long as you're serious.

SOLOMON: Thank you. *He touches the hated buffet*: Ay, yi, yi. All right, well . . . *He jots down a figure. He goes to the next piece, jots down another figure. He goes to another piece, jots down a figure.*

VICTOR, *after a moment*: You really got married at seventy-five?

SOLOMON: What's so terrible?

VICTOR: No, I think it's terrific. But what was the point?

SOLOMON: What's the point at twenty-five? You can't die twenty-six?

VICTOR, *laughing softly*: I guess so, ya.

SOLOMON: It's the same like secondhand furniture, you see; the whole thing is a viewpoint. It's a mental world. *He jots down another figure for another piece.* Seventy-five I got married, fifty-one, and twenty-two.

VICTOR: You're kidding.

SOLOMON: I wish! *He works, jotting his estimate of each piece on the pad, opening drawers, touching everything. Peering into a dark recess, he takes out a pencil flashlight, switches it on, and begins to probe with the beam.*

VICTOR—*he has gradually turned to watch Solomon, who goes on working*: Cut the kidding now—how old are you?

SOLOMON, *sliding out a drawer*: I'm eighty-nine. It's such an accomplishment?

VICTOR: You're a hell of a guy.

SOLOMON, *smiling with the encouragement and turning to Victor*: You know, it's a funny thing. It's so long since I took on such a load like this—you forget what kind of life it puts into you. To take out a pencil again . . . it's a regular injection. Frankly, my telephone you could use for a ladle, it wouldn't interfere with nothing. I want to thank you. *He points at Victor.* I'm going to take good care of you, I mean it. I can open that?

VICTOR: Sure, anything.

SOLOMON, *going to an armoire*: Some of them had a mirror . . . *He opens the armoire, and a rolled-up fur rug falls out. It is about three by five.* What's this?

VICTOR: God knows. I guess it's a rug.

SOLOMON, *holding it up*: No-no—that's a lap robe. Like for a car.

VICTOR: Say, that's right, ya. When they went driving. God, I haven't seen that in—

SOLOMON: You had a chauffeur?

VICTOR: Ya, we had a chauffeur.

Their eyes meet. Solomon looks at him as though Victor were coming into focus. Victor turns away. Now Solomon turns back to the armoire.

SOLOMON: Look at that! *He takes down an opera hat from the shelf within.* My God! *He puts it on, looks into the interior mirror.* What a world! *He turns to Victor:* He must've been some sporty guy!

VICTOR, *smiling:* You look pretty good!

SOLOMON: And from all this he could go so broke?

VICTOR: Why not? Sure. Took five weeks. Less.

SOLOMON: You don't say. And he couldn't make a comeback?

VICTOR: Well some men don't bounce, you know.

SOLOMON—*grunts:* Hmm! So what did he do?

VICTOR: Nothing. Just sat here. Listened to the radio.

SOLOMON: But what did he do? What—?

VICTOR: Well, now and then he was making change at the Automat. Toward the end he was delivering telegrams.

SOLOMON, *with grief and wonder:* You don't say. And how much he had?

VICTOR: Oh . . . couple of million, I guess.

SOLOMON: My God. What was the matter with him?

VICTOR: Well, my mother died around the same time. I guess that didn't help. Some men just don't bounce, that's all.

SOLOMON: Listen, I can tell you bounces. I went busted 1932; then 1923 they also knocked me out; the panic of 1904, 1898 . . . But to lay down like *that* . . .

VICTOR: Well, you're different. He believed in it.

SOLOMON: What he believed?

VICTOR: The system, the whole thing. He thought it was his fault, I guess. You—you come in with your song and dance, it's all a gag. You're a hundred and fifty years old, you tell your jokes, people fall in love with you, and you walk away with their furniture.

SOLOMON: That's not nice.

VICTOR: Don't shame me, will ya?—What do you say? You don't need to look any more, you know what I've got here.

Solomon is clearly at the end of his delaying resources. He looks about slowly; the furniture seems to loom over him like a threat or a promise. His eyes climb up to the edges of the ceiling, his hands grasping one another.

What are you afraid of? It'll keep you busy.

Solomon looks at him, wanting even more reassurance.

SOLOMON: You don't think it's foolish?

VICTOR: Who knows what's foolish? You enjoy it—

SOLOMON: Listen, I love it—

VICTOR: —so take it. You plan too much, you end up with nothing.

SOLOMON, *intimately*: I would like to tell you something. The last few months, I don't know what it is—she comes to me. You see, I had a daughter, she should rest in peace, she took her own life, a suicide. . . .

VICTOR: When was this?

SOLOMON: It was . . . 1916—the latter part. But very beautiful, a lovely face, with large eyes—she was pure like the morning. And lately, I don't know what it is—I see her clear like I see you. And every night practically, I lay down to go to sleep, so she sits there. And you can't help it, you ask yourself—what happened? What *happened*? Maybe I could have said something to her . . . maybe I *did* say something . . . it's all . . . *He looks at the furniture.* It's not that I'll die, you can't be afraid of that. But . . . I'll tell you the truth—a minute ago I mentioned I had three wives . . . *Slight pause. His fear rises.* Just this minute I realize I had four. Isn't that terrible? The first time was nineteen, in Lithuania. See, that's what I mean—it's impossible to know what is important. Here I'm sitting with you . . . and . . . and . . . *He looks around at the furniture.* What for? Not that I don't want it, I want it, but . . . You see, all my life I was a terrible fighter—you could never take nothing from me; I pushed, I pulled, I struggled in six different countries, I nearly got killed a couple times, and it's . . . It's like now I'm sitting here talking to you and I tell you it's a dream, it's a dream! You see, you can't imagine it because—

VICTOR: I know what you're talking about. But it's not a dream—it's that you've got to make decisions before you know what's involved, but you're stuck with the results anyway. Like I was very good in science—I loved it. But I had to drop out to feed the old man. And I figured I'd go on the Force temporarily, just to get us through the Depression, then go back to school. But the war came, we had the kid, and you turn around and you've racked up fifteen years on the pension. And what you started out to do is a million miles away. Not that I regret it all—we brought up a terrific boy, for one thing; nobody's ever going to take that guy. But it's like you were saying—it's impossible to know what's important. We always agreed, we stay out of the rat race and live our own life. That was important. But you shovel the crap out the window, it comes back in under the door—it all ends up she wants, she wants. And I can't really blame her—there's just no respect for anything but money.

SOLOMON: What've you got against money?

VICTOR: Nothing, I just didn't want to lay down my life for it. But I think I laid it down another way, and I'm not even sure any more what I was trying to accomplish. I look back now, and all I can see is a long, brainless walk in the street. I guess it's the old story; do anything, but just be sure you win. Like my brother; years ago I was living up here with the old man, and he used to contribute five dollars a month. A *month*! And a successful surgeon. But the few times he'd come around, the expression on the old man's face—you'd think God walked in. The respect, you know what I mean? The respect! And why not? Why not?

SOLOMON: Well, sure, he had the power.

VICTOR: Now you said it—if you got that you got it all. You're even lovable! *He laughs.* Well, what do you say? Give me the price.

SOLOMON—*slight pause*: I'll give you eleven hundred dollars.

VICTOR—*slight pause*: For everything?

SOLOMON, *in a breathless way*: Everything.

> *Slight pause. Victor looks around at the furniture.*

> I want it so I'm giving you a good price. Believe me, you will never do better. I want it; I made up my mind.

> *Victor continues staring at the stuff. Solomon takes out a common envelope and removes a wad of bills.*

> Here . . . I'll pay you now. *He readies a bill to start counting it out.*

VICTOR: It's that I have to split it, see—

SOLOMON: All right . . . so I'll make out a receipt for you and I'll put down six hundred dollars.

VICTOR: No-no . . . *He gets up and moves at random, looking at the furniture.*

SOLOMON: Why not? He took from you so take from him. If you want, I'll put down four hundred.

VICTOR: No, I don't want to do that. *Slight pause.* I'll call you tomorrow.

SOLOMON, *smiling*: All right; with God's help if I'm there tomorrow I'll answer the phone. If I wouldn't be . . . *Slight pause.* Then I wouldn't be.

VICTOR, *annoyed, but wanting to believe*: Don't start that again, will you?

SOLOMON: Look, you convinced me, so I want it. So what should I do?

VICTOR: *I* convinced *you*?

SOLOMON, *very distressed*: Absolutely you convinced me. You saw it—the minute I looked at it I was going to walk out!

VICTOR, *cutting him off, angered at his own indecision*: Ah, the hell with it. *He holds out his hand.* Give it to me.

SOLOMON, *wanting Victor's good will*: Please, don't be blue.

VICTOR: Oh, it all stinks. *Jabbing forth his hand*: Come on.

SOLOMON, *with a bill raised over Victor's hand—protesting*: What stinks? You should be happy. Now you can buy her a nice coat, take her to Florida, maybe—

VICTOR, *nodding ironically*: Right, right! We'll all be happy now. Give it to me.

> Solomon shakes his head and counts bills into his hand. Victor turns his head and looks at the piled walls of furniture.

SOLOMON: There's one hundred; two hundred; three hundred; four hundred . . . Take my advice, buy her a nice fur coat your troubles'll be over—

VICTOR: I know all about it. Come on.

SOLOMON: So you got there four, so I'm giving you—five, six, seven—I mean it's already in the Bible, the rat race. The minute she laid her hand on the apple, that's it.

VICTOR: I never read the Bible. Come on.

SOLOMON: If you'll read it you'll see—there's always a rat race, you can't stay out of it. So you got there seven, so now I'm giving you . . .

> *A man appears in the doorway. In his mid-fifties, well-barbered; hatless, in a camel's-hair coat, very healthy complexion. A look of sharp intelligence on his face.*
>
> *Victor, seeing past Solomon, starts slightly with shock, withdrawing his hand from the next bill which Solomon is about to lay in it.*

VICTOR, *suddenly flushed, his voice oddly high and boyish*: Walter!

WALTER—*enters the room, coming to Victor with extended hand and with a reserve of warmth but a stiff smile*: How are you, kid?

Solomon has moved out of their line of sight.

VICTOR—*shifts the money to his left hand as he shakes*: God, I never expected you.

WALTER, *of the money—half-humorously*: Sorry I'm late. What are you doing?

VICTOR, *fighting a treason to himself, thus taking on a strained humorous air*: I . . . I just sold it.

WALTER: Good! How much?

VICTOR, *as though absolutely certain now he has been had*: Ah . . . eleven hundred.

WALTER, *in a dead voice shorn of comment*: Oh. Well, good. *He turns rather deliberately—but not overly so—to Solomon*: For everything?

SOLOMON—*comes to Walter, his hand extended; with an energized voice that braves everything*: I'm very happy to meet you, Doctor! My name is Gregory Solomon.

WALTER—*the look on his face is rather amused, but his reserve has possibilities of accusation*: How do you do?

He shakes Solomon's hand, as Victor raises his hand to smooth down his hair, a look of near-alarm for himself on his face.

CURTAIN

ACT TWO

*The action is continuous. As the curtain rises Walter is just
releasing Solomon's hand and turning about to face Victor.
His posture is reserved, stiffened by traditional control over a
nearly fierce curiosity. His grin is disciplined and rather hard,
but his eyes are warm and combative.*

WALTER: How's Esther?

VICTOR: Fine. Should be here any minute.

WALTER: Here? Good! And what's Richard doing?

VICTOR: He's at M.I.T.

WALTER: No kidding! M.I.T.!

VICTOR, *nodding*: They gave him a full scholarship.

WALTER, *dispelling his surprise*: What do you know. *With a wider smile,
and embarrassed warmth*: You're proud.

VICTOR: I guess so. They put him in the Honors Program.

WALTER: Really. That's wonderful.—You don't mind my coming,
do you?

VICTOR: No! I called you a couple of times.

WALTER: Yes, my nurse told me. What's Richard interested in?

VICTOR: Science. So far, anyway. *With security*: How're yours?

WALTER—*moving, he breaks the confrontation*: I suppose Jean turned
out best—but I don't think you ever saw her.

VICTOR: I never did, no.

WALTER: The *Times* gave her quite a spread last fall. Pretty fair designer.

VICTOR: Oh? That's great. And the boys? They in school?

WALTER: They often are. *Abruptly laughs, refusing his own embarrassment*: I hardly see them, Vic. With all the unsolved mysteries in the world
they're investigating the guitar. But what the hell . . . I've given up

worrying about them. *He walks past Solomon, glancing at the furniture*: I'd forgotten how much he had up here. There's your radio!

VICTOR, *smiling with him*: I know, I saw it.

WALTER, *looking down at the radio, then upward to the ceiling through which the battery once exploded. Both laugh. Then he glances with open feeling at Victor*: Long time.

VICTOR, *fending off the common emotion*: Yes. How's Dorothy?

WALTER, *cryptically*: She's all right, I guess. *He moves, glancing at the things, but again with suddenness turns back*. Looking forward to seeing Esther again. She still writing poetry?

VICTOR: No, not for years now.

SOLOMON: He's got a very nice wife. We met.

WALTER, *surprised; as though at something intrusive*: Oh? *He turns back to the furniture*. Well. Same old junk, isn't it?

VICTOR, *downing a greater protest*: I wouldn't say that. Some of it isn't bad.

SOLOMON: One or two very nice things, Doctor. We came to a very nice agreement.

VICTOR, *with an implied rebuke*: I never thought you'd show up; I guess we'd better start all over again—

WALTER: Oh, no-no, I don't want to foul up your deal.

SOLOMON: Excuse me, Doctor—better you should take what you want now than we'll argue later. What did you want?

WALTER, *surprised, turning to Victor*: Oh, I didn't want anything. I came by to say hello, that's all.

VICTOR: I see. *Fending off Walter's apparent gesture with an over-quick movement toward the oar*: I found your oar, if you want it.

WALTER: Oar?

> *Victor draws it out from behind furniture. A curved-blade sweep.*

> Hah! *He receives the oar, looks up its length, and laughs, hefting it.* I must have been out of my mind!

SOLOMON: Excuse me, Doctor; if you want the oar—

WALTER, *standing the oar before Solomon, whom he leaves holding on to it*: Don't get excited, I don't want it.

SOLOMON: No. I was going to say—a personal thing like this I have no objection.

WALTER, *half-laughing*: That's very generous of you.

VICTOR, *apologizing for Solomon*: I threw in everything—I never thought you'd get here.

WALTER, *with a strained over-agreeableness*: Sure, that's all right. What are you taking?

VICTOR: Nothing, really. Esther might want a lamp or something like that.

SOLOMON: He's not interested, you see; he's a modern person, what are you going to do?

WALTER: You're not taking the harp?

VICTOR, *with a certain guilt*: Well, nobody plays . . . You take it, if you like.

SOLOMON: You'll excuse me, Doctor—the harp, please, that's another story . . .

WALTER—*laughs—archly amused and put out*: You don't mind if I make a suggestion, do you?

SOLOMON: Doctor, please, don't be offended, I only—

WALTER: Well, why do you interrupt? Relax, we're only talking. We haven't seen each other for a long time.

SOLOMON: Couldn't be better; I'm very sorry. *He sits, nervously pulling his cheek.*

WALTER, *touching the harp*: Kind of a pity—this was Grandpa's wedding present, you know.

VICTOR, *looking with surprise at the harp*: Say—that's right!

WALTER, *to Solomon*: What are you giving him for this?

SOLOMON: I didn't itemize—one price for everything. Maybe three hundred dollars. That sounding board is cracked, you know.

VICTOR, *to Walter*: You want it?

SOLOMON: Please, Victor, I hope you're not going to take that away from me. *To Walter*: Look, Doctor, I'm not trying to fool you. The harp is the heart and soul of the deal. I realize it was your mother's harp, but like I tried to tell—*to Victor*—you before—*to Walter*—with used furniture you cannot be emotional.

WALTER: I guess it doesn't matter. *To Victor*: Actually, I was wondering if he kept any of Mother's evening gowns, did he?

VICTOR: I haven't really gone through it all—

SOLOMON, *raising a finger, eagerly*: Wait, wait, I think I can help you. *He goes to an armoire he had earlier looked into, and opens it.*

WALTER, *moving toward the armoire*: She had some spectacular—

SOLOMON, *drawing out the bottom of a gown elaborately embroidered in gold*: Is this what you mean?

WALTER: Yes, that's the stuff!

> Solomon blows dust off and hands him the bottom of the gown.

> Isn't that beautiful! Say, I think she wore this at my wedding! *He takes it out of the closet, holds it up.* Sure! You remember this?

VICTOR: What do you want with it?

WALTER, *drawing out another gown off the rack*: Look at this one! Isn't that something? I thought Jeannie might make something new out of the material, I'd like her to wear something of Mother's.

VICTOR—*a new, surprising idea*: Oh! Fine, that's a nice idea.

SOLOMON: Take, take—they're beautiful.

WALTER, *suddenly glancing about as he lays the gowns across a chair*: What happened to the piano?

VICTOR: Oh, we sold that while I was still in school. We lived on it for a long time.

WALTER, *very interestedly*: I never knew that.

VICTOR: Sure. And the silver.

WALTER: Of course! Stupid of me not to remember that. *He half-sits against the back of a couch. His interest is avid, and his energy immense.* I suppose you know—you've gotten to look a great deal like Dad.

VICTOR: *I do?*

WALTER: It's very striking. And your voice is very much like his.

VICTOR: I know. It has that sound to me, sometimes.

SOLOMON: So, gentlemen . . . *He moves the money in his hand.*

VICTOR, *indicating Solomon*: Maybe we'd better settle this now.

WALTER: Yes, go ahead! *He walks off, looking at the furniture.*

SOLOMON, *indicating the money Victor holds*: You got there seven—

WALTER, *oblivious of Solomon; unable, so to speak, to settle for the status quo*: Wonderful to see you looking so well.

VICTOR—*the new interruption seems odd; observing more than speaking*: You do too, you look great.

WALTER: I ski a lot; and I ride nearly every morning. . . . You know, I started to call you a dozen times this year—*He breaks off. Indicating Solomon*: Finish up, I'll talk to you later.

SOLOMON: So now I'm going to give you—*A bill is poised over Victor's hand.*

VICTOR, *to Walter*: That price all right with you?

WALTER: Oh, I don't want to interfere. It's just that I dealt with these fellows when I split up Dorothy's and my stuff last year, and I found—

VICTOR, *from an earlier impression*: You're not divorced, are you?

WALTER, *with a nervous shot of laughter*: Yes!

> *Esther enters on his line; she is carrying a suit in a plastic wrapper.*

ESTHER, *surprised*: Walter! For heaven's sake!

WALTER, *eagerly jumping up, coming to her, shaking her hand*: How are you, Esther!

ESTHER, *between her disapproval and fascinated surprise*: What are *you* doing here?

WALTER: You've hardly changed!

ESTHER, *with a charged laugh, conflicted with herself*: Oh, go on now! *She hangs the suit on a chest handle.*

WALTER, *to Victor*: You son of a gun, she looks twenty-five!

VICTOR, *watching for Esther's reaction*: I know!

ESTHER, *flattered, and offended, too*: Oh stop it, Walter! *She sits.*

WALTER: But you do, honestly; you look marvelous.

SOLOMON: It's that suit, you see? What did I tell you, it's a very beautiful suit.

> *Victor laughs a little as Esther looks conflicted by Solomon's compliment.*

ESTHER, *with mock-affront—to Victor*: What are you laughing at? It is. *She is about to laugh.*

VICTOR: You looked so surprised, that's all.

ESTHER: Well, I'm not used to walking into all these compliments! *She bursts out laughing.*

WALTER, *suddenly recalling—eagerly*: Say! I'm sorry I didn't know I'd be seeing you when I left the house this morning—I'd have brought you some lovely Indian bracelets. I got a whole boxful from Bombay.

ESTHER, *still not focused on Walter, sizing him up*: How do you come to—?

WALTER: I operated on this big textile guy and he keeps sending me things. He sent me this coat, in fact.

ESTHER: I was noticing it. That's gorgeous material.

WALTER: Isn't it? Two gallstones.

ESTHER, *her impression lingering for the instant*: How's Dorothy?—Did I hear you saying you were—?

WALTER, *very seriously*: We're divorced, ya. Last winter.

ESTHER: I'm sorry to hear that.

WALTER: It was coming a long time. We're both much better off—we're almost friendly now. *He laughs.*

ESTHER: Oh, stop that, you dog.

WALTER, *with naïve excitement*: It's true!

ESTHER: Look, I'm for the woman, so don't hand me that. *To Victor— seeing the money in his hand*: Have you settled everything?

VICTOR: Just about, I guess.

WALTER: I was just telling Victor—*to Victor*: when we split things up I— *to Solomon*: you ever hear of Spitzer and Fox?

SOLOMON: Thirty years I know Spitzer and Fox. Bert Fox worked for me maybe ten, twelve years.

WALTER: They did my appraisal.

SOLOMON: They're good boys. Spitzer is not as good as Fox, but between the two you're in good hands.

WALTER: Yes. That's why I—

SOLOMON: Spitzer is vice president of the Appraisers' Association.

WALTER: I see. The point I'm making—

SOLOMON: I used to be president.

WALTER: Really.

SOLOMON: Oh yes. I made it all ethical.

WALTER, *trying to keep a straight face—and Victor as well*: Did you?

> *Victor suddenly bursts out laughing, which sets off Walter and Esther, and a warmth springs up among them.*

SOLOMON, *smiling, but insistent*: What's so funny? Listen, before me was a jungle—you wouldn't laugh so much. I put in all the rates, what we charge, you know—I made it a profession, like doctors, lawyers—used to be it was a regular snakepit. But today, you got nothing to worry—all the members are hundred per cent ethical.

WALTER: Well, that was a good deed, Mr. Solomon—but I think you can do a little better on this furniture.

ESTHER, *to Victor, who has money in his hand*: How much has he offered?

VICTOR, *embarrassed, but braving it quite well*: Eleven hundred.

ESTHER, *distressed; with a transcendent protest*: Oh, I think that's . . . isn't that very low? *She looks to Walter's confirmation.*

WALTER, *familiarly*: Come on, Solomon. He's been risking his life for you every day; be generous—

SOLOMON, *to Esther*: That's a real brother! Wonderful. *To Walter*: But you can call anybody you like—Spitzer and Fox, Joe Brody, Paul Cavallo, Morris White—I know them all and I know what they'll tell you.

VICTOR, *striving to retain some assurance; to Esther*: See, the point he was making about it—

SOLOMON, *to Esther, raising his finger*: Listen to him because he—

VICTOR, *to Solomon*: Hold it one second, will you? *To Esther and Walter*: Not that I'm saying it's true, but he claims a lot of it is too big to get into the new apartments.

ESTHER, *half-laughing*: You believe that?

WALTER: I don't know, Esther, Spitzer and Fox said the same thing.

ESTHER: Walter, the city is full of big, old apartments!

SOLOMON: Darling, why don't you leave it to the boys?

ESTHER, *suppressing an outburst*: I wish you wouldn't order me around, Mr. Solomon! *To Walter, protesting*: Those two bureaus alone are worth a couple of hundred dollars!

WALTER, *delicately*: Maybe I oughtn't interfere—

ESTHER: Why? *Of Solomon*: Don't let him bulldoze you—

SOLOMON: My dear girl, you're talking without a basis—

ESTHER, *slashing*: I don't like this kind of dealing, Mr. Solomon! I just don't like it! *She is near tears. A pause. She turns back to Walter*: This money is very important to us, Walter.

WALTER, *chastised*: Yes. I . . . I'm sorry, Esther. *He looks about.* Well . . . if it was mine—

ESTHER: Why? It's yours as much as Victor's.

WALTER: Oh no, dear—I wouldn't take anything from this.

   Pause.

VICTOR: No, Walter, you get half.

WALTER: I wouldn't think of it, kid. I came by to say hello, that's all.

   Pause.

ESTHER—*she is very moved*: That's terrific, Walter. It's . . . Really, I . . .

VICTOR: Well, we'll talk about it.

WALTER: No-no, Vic, you've earned it. It's yours.

VICTOR, *rejecting the implication*: Why have I earned it? You take your share.

WALTER: Why don't we discuss it later? *To Solomon*: In my opinion—

SOLOMON, *to Victor*: So now you don't even have to split. *To Victor and Walter*: You're lucky they're tearing the building down—you got together, finally.

WALTER: I would have said a minimum of three thousand dollars.

ESTHER: That's exactly what I had in mind! *To Solomon*: I was going to say thirty-five hundred dollars.

WALTER, *to Victor; tactfully*: In that neighborhood.

   Silence. Solomon sits there holding back comment, not look-ing at Victor, blinking with protest. Victor thinks for a moment; then turns to Solomon, and there is a wide discour-agement in his voice.

VICTOR: Well? What do you say?

SOLOMON, *spreading out his hands helplessly, outraged*: What can I say? It's ridiculous. Why does he give you three thousand? What's the matter with five thousand, ten thousand?

WALTER, *to Victor, without criticism*: You should've gotten a couple of other estimates, you see, that's always the—

VICTOR: I've been calling you all week for just that reason, Walter, and you never came to the phone.

WALTER, *blushing*: Why would that stop you from—?

VICTOR: I didn't think I had the right to do it alone—the nurse gave you my messages, didn't she?

WALTER: I've been terribly tied up—and I had no intention of taking anything for myself, so I assumed—

VICTOR: But how was I supposed to know that?

WALTER, *with open self-reproach*: Yes. Well, I . . . I beg your pardon. *He decides to stop there.*

SOLOMON: Excuse me, Doctor, but I can't understand you; first it's a lot of junk—

ESTHER: Nobody called it a lot of junk!

SOLOMON: He called it a lot of junk, Esther, when he walked in here.

Esther turns to Walter, puzzled and angry.

WALTER, *reacting to her look; to Solomon*: Now just a minute—

SOLOMON: No, please. *Indicating Victor*: This is a factual man, so let's be factual.

ESTHER: Well, that's an awfully strange thing to say, Walter.

WALTER, *intimately*: I didn't mean it in that sense, Esther—

SOLOMON: Doctor, please. You said junk.

WALTER, *sharply—and there is an over-meaning of much greater anger in his tone*: I didn't mean it in that sense, Mr. Solomon! *He controls himself—and, half to Esther*: When you've been brought up with things, you tend to be sick of them. . . . *To Esther*: That's all I meant.

SOLOMON: My dear man, if it was Louis Seize, Biedermeier, something like that, you wouldn't get sick.

WALTER, *pointing to a piece, and weakened by knowing he is exaggerating*: Well, there happens to be a piece right over there in Biedermeier style!

SOLOMON: Biedermeier "style"! *He picks up his hat.* I got a hat it's in Borsalino style but it's not a Borsalino. *To Victor*: I mean he don't have to charge me to make an impression.

WALTER, *striving for an air of amusement*: Now what's that supposed to mean?

VICTOR, *with a refusal to dump Solomon*: Well, what basis do you go on, Walter?

WALTER, *reddening but smiling*: I don't know . . . it's a feeling, that's all.

ESTHER—*there is ridicule*: Well, on what basis do you take eleven hundred, dear?

VICTOR, *angered; his manly leadership is suddenly in front*: I simply felt it was probably more or less right!

ESTHER, *as a refrain*: Oh God, here we go again. All right, throw it away—

SOLOMON, *indicating Victor*: Please, Esther, he's not throwing nothing away. This man is no fool! *To Walter as well*: Excuse me, but this is not right to do to him!

WALTER, *bridling, but retaining his smile*: You going to teach me what's right now?

ESTHER, *to Victor, expanding Walter's protest*: Really! I mean.

VICTOR—*obeying her protest for want of a certainty of his own, he touches Solomon's shoulder*: Mr. Solomon . . . why don't you sit down in the bedroom for a few minutes and let us talk?

SOLOMON: Certainly, whatever you say. *He gets up.* Only please, you made a very nice deal, you got no right to be ashamed. . . . *To Esther*: Excuse me, I don't want to be personal.

ESTHER—*laughs angrily*: He's fantastic!

VICTOR, *trying to get him moving again*: Whyn't you go inside?

SOLOMON: I'm going; I only want you to understand, Victor, that if it was a different kind of man—*turning to Esther*: I would say to you that he's got the money in his hand, so the deal is concluded.

WALTER: He can't conclude any deal without me, Solomon, I'm half owner here.

SOLOMON, *to Victor*: You see? What did I ask you the first thing I walked in here? "Who is the owner?"

WALTER: Why do you confuse everything? I'm not making any claim, I merely—

SOLOMON: Then how do you come to interfere? He's got the money; I know the law!

WALTER, *angering*: Now you stop being foolish! Just stop it! I've got the best lawyers in New York, so go inside and sit down.

VICTOR, *as he turns back to escort Solomon*: Take it easy, Walter, come on, cut it out.

ESTHER, *striving to keep a light, amused tone*: Why? He's perfectly right.

VICTOR, *with a hard glance at her, moving upstage with Solomon*: Here, you better hold onto this money.

SOLOMON: No, that's yours; you hold . . .

He sways. Victor grasps his arm. Walter gets up.

WALTER: You all right?

SOLOMON—*dizzy, he grasps his head*: Yes, yes, I'm . . .

WALTER, *coming to him*: Let me look at you. *He takes Solomon's wrists, looks into his face.*

SOLOMON: I'm only a little tired, I didn't take my nap today.

WALTER: Come in here, lie down for a moment. *He starts Solomon toward the bedroom.*

SOLOMON: Don't worry about me, I'm . . . *He halts and points back at his portfolio, leaning on a chest.* Please, Doctor, if you wouldn't mind—I got a Hershey's in there.

Walter hesitates to do his errand.

Helps me.

Walter unwillingly goes to the portfolio and reaches into it.

I'm a very healthy person, but a nap, you see, I have to have a . . .

Walter takes out an orange.

Not the orange—on the bottom is a Hershey's.

Walter takes out a Hershey bar.

That's a boy.

WALTER—*returns to him and helps him to the bedroom*: All right, come on . . . easy does it . . .

SOLOMON, *as he goes into the bedroom*: I'm all right, don't worry. You're very nice people.

Solomon and Walter exit into the bedroom. Victor glances at the money in his hand, then puts it on a table, setting the foil on it.

ESTHER: Why are you being so apologetic?

VICTOR: About what?

ESTHER: That old man. Was that his first offer?

VICTOR: Why do you believe Walter? He was obviously pulling a number out of a hat.

ESTHER: Well, I agree with him. Did you try to get him to go higher?

VICTOR: I don't know how to bargain and I'm not going to start now.

ESTHER: I wish you wouldn't be above everything, Victor, we're not twenty years old. We need this money.

He is silent.

You hear me?

VICTOR: I've made a deal, and that's it. You know, you take a tone sometimes—like I'm some kind of an incompetent.

ESTHER—*gets up, moves restlessly*: Well anyway, you'll get the whole amount.—God, he's certainly changed. It's amazing.

VICTOR, *without assent*: Seems so, ya.

ESTHER, *wanting him to join her*: He's so human! And he laughs!

VICTOR: I've seen him laugh.

ESTHER, *with a grin of trepidation*: Am I hearing something or is that my imagination?

VICTOR: I want to think about it.

ESTHER, *quietly*: You're not taking his share?

VICTOR: I said I would like to think . . .

Assuming he will refuse Walter's share, she really doesn't know what to do or where to move, so she goes for her purse with a quick stride.

VICTOR, *getting up*: Where you going?

ESTHER, *turning back on him*: I want to know. Are you or aren't you taking his share?

VICTOR: Esther, I've been calling him all week; doesn't even bother to come to the phone, walks in here and smiles and I'm supposed to fall into his arms? I can't behave as though nothing ever happened, and you're not going to either! Now just take it easy, we're not dying of hunger.

ESTHER: I don't understand what you think you're upholding!

VICTOR, *outraged*: Where have you been?!

ESTHER: But he's doing exactly what you thought he should do! What do you *want*?

VICTOR: Certain things have happened, haven't they? I can't turn around this fast, kid. He's only been here ten minutes, I've got twenty-eight years to shake off my back. . . . Now sit down, I want you here. *He sits.*

 She remains standing, uncertain of what to do.

 Please. You can wait a few minutes for your drink.

ESTHER, *in despair*: Vic, it's all blowing away.

VICTOR, *to diminish the entire prize*: Half of eleven hundred dollars is five-fifty, dear.

ESTHER: I'm not talking about money.

 Voices are heard from the bedroom.

 He's obviously making a gesture, why can't you open yourself a little? *She lays her head back.* My mother was right—I can never believe anything I see. But I'm going to. That's all I'm going to do. What I see.

 A chair scrapes in the bedroom.

VICTOR: Wipe your cheek, will you?

 Walter enters from the bedroom.

 How is he?

WALTER: I think he'll be all right. *Warmly*: God, what a pirate! *He sits.* He's eighty-nine!

ESTHER: I don't believe it!

VICTOR: He is. He showed me his—

WALTER, *laughing*: Oh, he show you that too?

VICTOR, *smiling*: Ya, the British Navy.

ESTHER: *He* was in the British Navy?

VICTOR, *building on Walter's support*: He's got a discharge. He's not altogether phony.

WALTER: I wouldn't go that far. A guy that age, though, still driving like that . . . *As though admitting Victor was not foolish*: There *is* something wonderful about it.

VICTOR, *understating*: I think so.

ESTHER: What do you think we ought to do, Walter?

WALTER—*slight pause. He is trying to modify what he believes is his overpowering force so as not to appear to be taking over. He is faintly smiling toward Victor*: There is a way to get a good deal more out of it. I suppose you know that, though.

VICTOR: Look, I'm not married to this guy. If you want to call another dealer we can compare.

WALTER: You don't have to do that; he's a registered appraiser.—You see, instead of selling it, you could make it a charitable contribution.

VICTOR: I don't understand.

WALTER: It's perfectly simple. He puts a value on it—let's say twenty-five thousand dollars, and—

ESTHER, *fascinated with a laugh*: Are you kidding?

WALTER: It's done all the time. It's a dream world but it's legal. He estimates its highest retail value, which could be put at some such figure. Then I donate it to the Salvation Army. I'd have to take ownership, you see, because my tax rate is much higher than yours so it would make more sense if I took the deduction. I pay around fifty per cent tax, so if I make a twenty-five-thousand-dollar contribution I'd be saving around twelve thousand in taxes. Which we could split however you wanted to. Let's say we split it in half, I'd give you six thousand dollars. *A pause.* It's really the only sensible way to do it, Vic.

ESTHER—*glances at Victor, but he remains silent*: Would it be costing you anything?

WALTER: On the contrary—it's found money to me. *To Victor*: I mentioned it to him just now.

VICTOR, *as though this had been the question*: What'd he say?

WALTER: It's up to you. We'd pay him an appraisal fee—fifty, sixty bucks.

VICTOR: Is he willing to do that?

WALTER: Well, of course he'd rather buy it outright, but what the hell—

ESTHER: Well, that's not his decision, is it?

VICTOR: No . . . it's just that I feel I did come to an agreement with him and I—

WALTER: Personally, I wouldn't let that bother me. He'd be making fifty bucks for filling out a piece of paper.

ESTHER: That's not bad for an afternoon.

Pause.

VICTOR: I'd like to think about it.

ESTHER: There's not much time, though, if you want to deal with him.

VICTOR, *cornered*: I'd like a few minutes, that's all.

WALTER, *to Esther*: Sure . . . let him think it over. *To Victor*: It's perfectly legal, if that's what's bothering you. I almost did it with my stuff but I finally decided to keep it. *He laughs.* In fact, my own apartment is so loaded up it doesn't look too different from this.

ESTHER: Well, maybe you'll get married again.

WALTER: I doubt that very much, Esther.—I often feel I never should have.

ESTHER, *scoffing*: Why!

WALTER: Seriously. I'm in a strange business, you know. There's too much to learn and far too little time to learn it. And there's a price you have to pay for that. I tried awfully hard to kid myself but there's simply no time for people. Not the way a woman expects, if she's any kind of woman. *He laughs.* But I'm doing pretty well alone!

VICTOR: How would I list an amount like that on my income tax?

WALTER: Well . . . call it a gift.

Victor is silent, obviously in conflict. Walter sees the emotion.

Not that it is, but you could list it as such. It's allowed.

VICTOR: I see. I was just curious how it—

WALTER: Just enter it as a gift. There's no problem.

With the first sting of a vague resentment, Walter turns his eyes away. Esther raises her eyebrows, staring at the floor. Walter lifts the foil off the table—clearly changing the subject.

You still fence?

VICTOR, *almost gratefully pursuing this diversion*: No, you got to join a club and all that. And I work weekends often. I just found it here.

WALTER, *as though to warm the mood*: Mother used to love to watch him do this.

ESTHER, *surprised, pleased*: Really?

WALTER: Sure, she used to come to all his matches.

ESTHER, *to Victor, somehow charmed*: You never told me that.

WALTER: Of course; she's the one made him take it up. *He laughs to Victor.* She thought it was elegant!

VICTOR: Hey, that's right!

WALTER, *laughing at the memory*: He did look pretty good too! *He spreads his jacket away from his chest.* I've still got the wounds! *To Victor, who laughs*: Especially with those French gauntlets she—

VICTOR, *recalling*: Say . . . ! *Looking around with an enlivened need*: I wonder where the hell . . . *He suddenly moves toward a bureau.* Wait, I think they used to be in . . .

ESTHER, *to Walter*: French gauntlets?

WALTER: She brought them from Paris. Gorgeously embroidered. He looked like one of the musketeers.

> *Out of the drawer where he earlier found the ice skate, Victor takes a pair of emblazoned gauntlets.*

VICTOR: Here they are! What do you know!

ESTHER, *reaching her hand out*: Aren't they beautiful!

> *He hands her one.*

VICTOR: God, I'd forgotten all about them. *He slips one on his hand.*

WALTER: Christmas, 1929.

VICTOR, *moving his hand in the gauntlet*: Look at that, they're still soft . . . *To Walter—a little shy in asking*: How do you remember all this stuff?

WALTER: Why not? Don't you?

ESTHER: He doesn't remember your mother very well.

VICTOR: I remember her. *Looking at the gauntlet*: It's just her face; somehow I can never see her.

WALTER, *warmly*: That's amazing, Vic. *To Esther*: She adored him.

ESTHER, *pleased*: Did she?

WALTER: Victor? If it started to rain she'd run all the way to school with his galoshes. Her Victor—my God! By the time he could light a match he was already Louis Pasteur.

VICTOR: It's odd . . . like the harp! I can almost hear the music . . . But I can never see her face. Somehow. *For a moment, silence, as he looks across at the harp.*

WALTER: What's the problem?

Pause. Victor's eyes are swollen with feeling. He turns and looks up at Walter, who suddenly is embarrassed and oddly anxious.

SOLOMON—*enters from the bedroom. He looks quite distressed. He is in his vest, his tie is open. Without coming downstage:* Please, Doctor, if you wouldn't mind I would like to . . . *He breaks off, indicating the bedroom.*

WALTER: What is it?

SOLOMON: Just for one minute, please.

Walter stands. Solomon glances at Victor and Esther and returns to the bedroom.

WALTER: I'll be right back. *He goes rather quickly up and into the bedroom.*

A pause. Victor is sitting in silence, unable to face her.

ESTHER, *with delicacy and pity, sensing his conflicting feelings:* Why can't you take him as he is?

He glances at her.

Well you can't expect him to go into an apology, Vic—he probably sees it all differently, anyway.

He is silent. She comes to him.

I know it's difficult, but he is trying to make a gesture, I think.

VICTOR: I guess he is, yes.

ESTHER: You know what would be lovely? If we could take a few weeks and go to like . . . out-of-the-way places . . . just to really break it up and see all the things that people do. You've been around such mean, petty people for so long and little ugly tricks. I'm serious—it's not romantic. We're much too suspicious of everything.

VICTOR, *staring ahead:* Strange guy.

ESTHER: Why?

VICTOR: Well, to walk in that way—as though nothing ever happened.

ESTHER: Why not? What can be done about it?

VICTOR—*slight pause:* I feel I have to say something.

ESTHER, *with a slight trepidation, less than she feels:* What can you say?

VICTOR: You feel I ought to just take the money and shut up, heh?

ESTHER: But what's the point of going backwards?

VICTOR, *with a self-bracing tension*: I'm not going to take this money unless I talk to him.

ESTHER, *frightened*: You can't bear the thought that he's decent.

He looks at her sharply.

That's all it is, dear. I'm sorry, I have to say it.

VICTOR, *without raising his voice*: I can't bear that he's *decent*!

ESTHER: You throw this away, you've got to explain it to me. You can't go on blaming everything on him or the system or God knows what else! You're free and you can't make a move, Victor, and that's what's driving me crazy! *Silence. Quietly*: Now take this money.

He is silent, staring at her.

You take this money! Or I'm washed up. You hear me? If you're stuck it doesn't mean I have to be. Now that's it.

Movements are heard within the bedroom. She straightens. Victor smooths down his hair with a slow, preparatory motion of his hand, like one adjusting himself for combat.

WALTER—*enters from the bedroom, smiling, shaking his head. Indicating the bedroom*: Boy—we got a tiger here. What is this between you, did you know him before?

VICTOR: No. Why? What'd he say?

WALTER: He's still trying to buy it outright. *He laughs.* He talks like you added five years by calling him up.

VICTOR: Well, what's the difference, I don't mind.

WALTER, *registering the distant rebuke*: No, that's fine, that's all right. *He sits. Slight pause.* We don't understand each other, do we?

VICTOR, *with a certain thrust, matching Walter's smile*: I am a little confused, Walter . . . yes.

WALTER: Why is that?

Victor doesn't answer at once.

Come on, we'll all be dead soon!

VICTOR: All right, I'll give you one example. When I called you Monday and Tuesday and again this morning—

WALTER: I've explained that.

VICTOR: But I don't make phone calls to pass the time. Your nurse sounded like I was a pest of some kind . . . it was humiliating.

WALTER—*oddly, he is over-upset*: I'm terribly sorry, she shouldn't have done that.

VICTOR: I know, Walter, but I can't imagine she takes that tone all by herself.

WALTER, *aware now of the depth of resentment in Victor*: Oh no—she's often that way. I've never referred to you like that.

> *Victor is silent, not convinced.*

Believe me, will you? I'm terribly sorry. I'm overwhelmed with work, that's all it is.

VICTOR: Well, you asked me, so I'm telling you.

WALTER: Yes! You should! But don't misinterpret that. *Slight pause. His tension has increased. He braves a smile.* Now about this tax thing. He'd be willing to make the appraisal twenty-five thousand. *With difficulty*: If you'd like, I'd be perfectly willing for you to have the whole amount I'd be saving.

> *Slight pause.*

ESTHER: Twelve thousand?

WALTER: Whatever it comes to.

> *Pause. Esther slowly looks to Victor.*

You must be near retirement now, aren't you?

ESTHER, *excitedly*: He's past it. But he's trying to decide what to do.

WALTER: Oh. *To Victor—near open embarrassment now*: It would come in handy, then, wouldn't it?

> *Victor glances at him as a substitute for a reply.*

I don't need it, that's all, Vic. Actually, I've been about to call you for quite some time now.

VICTOR: What for?

WALTER—*suddenly, with a strange quick laugh, he reaches and touches Victor's knee*: Don't be suspicious!

VICTOR, *grinning*: I'm just trying to figure it out, Walter.

WALTER: Yes, good. All right. *Slight pause.* I thought it was time we got to know one another. That's all.

> *Slight pause.*

VICTOR: You know, Walter, I tried to call you a couple of times before this about the furniture—must be three years ago.

WALTER: I was sick.

VICTOR, *surprised*: Oh . . . Because I left a lot of messages.

WALTER: I was quite sick. I was hospitalized.

ESTHER: What happened?

WALTER—*slight pause. As though he were not quite sure whether to say it*: I broke down.

> *Slight pause.*

VICTOR: I had no idea.

WALTER: Actually, I'm only beginning to catch up with things. I was out of commission for nearly three years. *With a thrust of success*: But I'm almost thankful for it now—I've never been happier!

ESTHER: You seem altogether different!

WALTER: I think I am, Esther. I live differently, I think differently. All I have now is a small apartment. And I got rid of the nursing homes—

VICTOR: What nursing homes?

WALTER, *with a removed self-amusement*: Oh, I owned three nursing homes. There's big money in the aged, you know. Helpless, desperate children trying to dump their parents—nothing like it. I even pulled out of the market. Fifty per cent of my time now is in City hospitals. And I tell you, I'm alive. For the first time. I do medicine, and that's it. *Attempting an intimate grin*: Not that I don't soak the rich occasionally, but only enough to live, really. *It is as though this was his mission here, and he waits for Victor's comment.*

VICTOR: Well, that must be great.

WALTER, *seizing on this minute encouragement*: Vic, I wish we could talk for weeks, there's so much I want to tell you. . . . *It is not rolling quite the way he would wish and he must pick examples of his new feelings out of the air.* I never had friends—you probably know that. But I do now, I have good friends. *He moves, sitting nearer Victor, his enthusiasm flowing.* It all happens so gradually. You start out wanting to be the best, and there's no question that you do need a certain fanaticism; there's so much to know and so little time. Until you've eliminated everything extraneous— *he smiles*—including people. And of course the time comes when you realize that you haven't merely been specializing in something—something has been specializing in you. You become a kind of instrument, an instrument that cuts money out of people, or fame out of the world. And it finally makes you stupid. Power can do that. You get to think that because you can frighten people they love you. Even that you love them.—And the whole thing comes down to fear. One night I found myself in the middle of my living room, dead drunk with a knife in my hand, getting ready to kill my wife.

ESTHER: Good Lord!

WALTER: Oh ya—and I nearly made it too! *He laughs.* But there's one virtue in going nuts—provided you survive, of course. You get to see the terror—not the screaming kind, but the slow, daily fear you call ambition, and cautiousness, and piling up the money. And really, what I wanted to tell you for some time now—is that you helped me to understand that in myself.

VICTOR: Me?

WALTER: Yes. *He grins warmly, embarrassed.* Because of what you did. I could never understand it, Vic—after all, you *were* the better student. And to stay with a job like that through all those years seemed . . . *He breaks off momentarily, the uncertainty of Victor's reception widening his smile.* You see, it never dawned on me until I got sick—that you'd made a choice.

VICTOR: A choice, how?

WALTER: You wanted a real life. And that's an expensive thing; it costs. *He has found his theme now; sees he has at last touched something in Victor. A breath of confidence comes through now.* I know I may sound terribly naïve, but I'm still used to talking about anything that matters. Frankly, I didn't answer your calls this week because I was afraid. I've struggled so long for a concept of myself and I'm not sure I can make it believable to you. But I'd like to. *He sees permission to go on in Victor's perplexed eyes:* You see, I got to a certain point where . . . I dreaded my own work; I finally couldn't cut. There are times, as you know, when if you leave someone alone he might live a year or two; while if you go in you might kill him. And the decision is often . . . not quite, but almost . . . arbitrary. But the odds are acceptable, provided you think the right thoughts. Or don't think at all, which I managed to do till then. *Slight pause. He is no longer smiling; instead, a near-embarrassment is on him.* I ran into a cluster of misjudgments. It can happen, but it never had to me, not one on top of the other. And they had one thing in common; they'd all been diagnosed by other men as inoperable. And quite suddenly the . . . the whole prospect of my own motives opened up. Why had I taken risks that very competent men had declined? And the quick answer, of course, is—to pull off the impossible. Shame the competition. But suddenly I saw something else. And it was terror. In dead center, directing my brains, my hands, my ambition—for thirty years.

Slight pause.

VICTOR: Terror of what?

Pause.

WALTER, *his gaze direct on Victor now*: Of it ever happening to me—*he glances at the center chair*—as it happened to him. Overnight, for no reason, to find yourself degraded and thrown-down. *With the faintest hint of impatience and challenge*: You know what I'm talking about, don't you?

> *Victor turns away slightly, refusing commitment.*

Isn't that why you turned your back on it all?

VICTOR, *sensing the relevancy to himself now*: Partly. Not altogether, though.

WALTER: Vic, we were both running from the same thing. I thought I wanted to be tops, but what it was was untouchable. I ended in a swamp of success and bankbooks, you on civil service. The difference is that you haven't hurt other people to defend yourself. And I've learned to respect that, Vic; you simply tried to make yourself useful.

ESTHER: That's wonderful—to come to such an understanding with yourself.

WALTER: Esther, it's a strange thing; in the hospital, for the first time since we were boys, I began to feel . . . like a brother. In the sense that we shared something. *To Victor*: And I feel I would know how to be friends now.

VICTOR—*slight pause; he is unsure*: Well fine. I'm glad of that.

WALTER—*sees the reserve but feels he has made headway and presses on a bit more urgently*: You see, that's why you're still so married. That's a very rare thing. And why your boy's in such good shape. You've lived a real life. *To Esther*: But you know that better than I.

ESTHER: I don't know what I know, Walter.

WALTER: Don't doubt it, dear—believe me, you're fortunate people. *To Victor*: You know that, don't you?

VICTOR, *without looking at Esther*: I think so.

ESTHER: It's not quite as easy as you make it, Walter.

WALTER—*hesitates, then throws himself into it*: Look, I've had a wild idea—it'll probably seem absurd to you, but I wish you'd think about it before you dismiss it. I gather you haven't decided what to do with yourself now? You're retiring . . . ?

VICTOR: I'll decide one of these days, I'm still thinking.

WALTER, *nervously*: Could I suggest something?

VICTOR: Sure, go ahead.

WALTER: We've been interviewing people for the new wing. For the administrative side. Kind of liaison people between the scientists and the board. And it occurred to me several times that you might fit in there.

    Slight pause.

ESTHER, *with a release of expectation*: That would be wonderful!

VICTOR—*slight pause. He glances at her with suppression, but his voice betrays excitement*: What could I do there, though?

WALTER, *sensing Victor's interest*: It's kind of fluid at the moment, but there's a place for people with a certain amount of science who—

VICTOR: I have no degree, you know.

WALTER: But you've had analytic chemistry, and a lot of math and physics, if I recall. If you thought you needed it you could take some courses in the evenings. I think you have enough background.—How would you feel about that?

VICTOR, *digging in against the temptation*: Well . . . I'd like to know more about it, sure.

ESTHER, *as though to press him to accept*: It'd be great if he could work in science, it's really the only thing he ever wanted.

WALTER: I know; it's a pity he never went on with it. *Turning to Victor*: It'd be perfectly simple, Vic, I'm chairman of the committee. I could set it all up—

    Solomon enters. They turn to him, surprised. He seems about to say something, but in fear changes his mind.

SOLOMON: Excuse me, go right ahead. *He goes nervously to his portfolio, reaching into it—which was not his original intention.* I'm sorry to disturb you. *He takes out an orange and starts back to the bedroom, then halts, addressing Walter*: About the harp. If you'll make me a straight out-and-out sale, I would be willing to go another fifty dollars. So it's eleven fifty, and between the two of you nobody has to do any favors.

WALTER: Well, you're getting warmer.

SOLOMON: I'm a fair person! So you don't have to bother with the appraisal and deductions, all right? *Before Walter can answer*: But don't rush, I'll wait. I'm at your service. *He goes quickly and worriedly into the bedroom.*

ESTHER, *starting to laugh; to Victor*: Where did you find him?

WALTER: —that wonderful? He "made it all ethical"!

    Esther bursts out laughing, and Walter with her, and Victor manages to join. As it begins to subside, Walter turns to him.

What do you say, Vic? Will you come by?

The laughter is gone. The smile is just fading on Victor's face. He looks at nothing, as though deciding. The pause lengthens, and lengthens still. Now it begins to seem he may not speak at all. No one knows how to break into his puzzling silence. At last he turns to Walter with a rather quick movement of his head as though he had made up his mind to take the step.

VICTOR: I'm not sure I know what you want, Walter.

Walter looks shocked, astonished, almost unbelieving. But Victor's gaze is steady on him.

ESTHER, *with a tone of the conciliator shrouding her shock and protest*: I don't think that's being very fair, is it?

VICTOR: Why is it unfair? We're talking about some pretty big steps here. *To Walter*: Not that I don't appreciate it, Walter, but certain things have happened, haven't they? *With a half laugh*: It just seems odd to suddenly be talking about—

WALTER, *downing his resentment*: I'd hoped we could take one step at a time, that's all. It's very complicated between us, I think, and it seemed to me we might just try to—

VICTOR: I know, but you can understand it would be a little confusing.

WALTER—*unwillingly, anger peaks his voice*: What do you find confusing?

VICTOR—*considers for a moment, but he cannot go back*: You must have some idea, don't you?

WALTER: This is a little astonishing, Victor. After all these years you can't expect to settle everything in one conversation, can you? I simply felt that with a little good will we . . . we . . . *He sees Victor's adamant poise.* Oh, the hell with it. *He goes abruptly and snatches up his coat and one of the evening gowns.* Get what you can from the old man, I don't want any of it. *He goes and extends his hand to Esther, forcing a smile.* I'm sorry, Esther. It was nice seeing you anyway.

Sickened, she accepts his hand.

Maybe I'll see you again, Vic. Good luck. *He starts for the door. There are tears in his eyes.*

ESTHER, *before she can think*: Walter?

Walter halts and turns to her questioningly. She looks to Victor helplessly. But he cannot think either.

WALTER: I don't accept this resentment, Victor. It simply baffles me. I don't understand it. I just want you to know how I feel.

ESTHER, *assuaging*: It's not resentment, Walter.

VICTOR: The whole thing is a little fantastic to me, that's all. I haven't cracked a book in twenty-five years, how do I walk into a research laboratory?

ESTHER: But Walter feels that you have enough background—

VICTOR, *almost laughing over his quite concealed anger at her*: I know less chemistry than most high-school kids, Esther. *To Walter*: And physics, yet! Good God, Walter. *He laughs.* Where you been?

WALTER: I'm sure you could make a place for yourself—

VICTOR: What place? Running papers from one office to another?

WALTER: You're not serious.

VICTOR: Why? Sooner or later my being your brother is not going to mean very much, is it? I've been walking a beat for twenty-eight years, I'm not qualified for anything technical. What's this all about?

WALTER: Why do you keep asking what it's about? I've been perfectly open with you, Victor!

VICTOR: I don't think you have.

WALTER: Why! What do you think I'm—?

VICTOR: Well, when you say what you said a few minutes ago, I—

WALTER: What did I say?!

VICTOR, *with a resolutely cool smile*: What a pity it was that I didn't go on with science.

WALTER, *puzzled*: What's wrong with that?

VICTOR, *laughing*: Oh, Walter, come on, now!

WALTER: But I feel that. I've always felt that.

VICTOR, *smiling still, and pointing at the center chair; a new reverberation sounds in his voice*: There used to be a man in that chair, staring into space. Don't you remember that?

WALTER: Very well, yes. I sent him money every month.

VICTOR: You sent him five dollars every month.

WALTER: I could afford five dollars. But what's that got to do with you?

VICTOR: What's it got to do with me!

WALTER: Yes, I don't see that.

VICTOR: Where did you imagine the rest of his living was coming from?

WALTER: Victor, that was your decision, not mine.

VICTOR: My decision!

WALTER: We had a long talk in this room once, Victor.

VICTOR, *not recalling*: What talk?

WALTER, *astonished*: Victor! We came to a complete understanding—just after you moved up here with Dad. I told you then that I was going to finish my schooling come hell or high water, and I advised you to do the same. In fact, I warned you not to allow him to strangle your life. *To Esther*: And if I'm not mistaken I told you the same at your wedding, Esther.

VICTOR, *with an incredulous laugh*: Who the hell was supposed to keep him alive, Walter?

WALTER, *with a strange fear, more than anger*: Why did anybody have to? He wasn't sick. He was perfectly fit to go to work.

VICTOR: Work? In 1936? With no skill, no money?

WALTER—*outburst*: Then he could have gone on welfare! Who *was* he, some exiled royalty? What did a hundred and fifty million other people do in 1936? He'd have survived, Victor. Good God, you must know that by now, don't you?!

Slight pause.

VICTOR—*suddenly at the edge of fury, and caught by Walter's voicing his own opinion, he turns to Esther*: I've had enough of this, Esther; it's the same old thing all over again, let's get out of here. *He starts rapidly upstage toward the bedroom.*

WALTER, *quickly*: Vic! Please! *He catches Victor, who frees his arm.* I'm not running him down. I loved him in many ways—

ESTHER, *as though conceding her earlier position*: Vic, listen—maybe you ought to talk about it.

VICTOR: It's all pointless! The whole thing doesn't matter to me! *He turns to go to the bedroom.*

WALTER: He exploited you!

Victor halts, turns to him, his anger full in his face.

Doesn't that matter to you?

VICTOR: Let's get one thing straight, Walter—I am nobody's victim.

WALTER: But that's exactly what I've tried to tell you. I'm not trying to condescend.

VICTOR: Of course you are. Would you be saying any of this if I'd made a pile of money somewhere? *Dead stop.* I'm sorry, Walter, I can't take that. I made no choice; the icebox was empty and the man was sitting there with his mouth open. *Slight pause.* I didn't start this, Walter, and the whole thing doesn't interest me, but when you talk about making choices, and I should have gone on with science, I have to say something.— Just because you want things a certain way doesn't make them that way. *He has ended at a point distant from Walter.*

A slight pause.

WALTER, *with affront mixed into his trepidation*: All right then . . . How do you see it?

VICTOR: Look, you've been sick, Walter, why upset yourself with all this?

WALTER: It's important to me!

VICTOR, *trying to smile—and in a friendly way*: But why? It's all over the dam. *He starts toward the bedroom again.*

ESTHER: I think he's come to you in good faith, Victor.

He turns to her angrily, but she braves his look.

I don't see why you can't consider his offer.

VICTOR: I said I'd consider it.

ESTHER, *restraining a cry*: You know you're turning it down! *In a certain fear of him, but persisting*: I mean what's so dreadful about telling the truth, can it be any worse than this?

VICTOR: What "truth"? What are you—?

Solomon suddenly appears from the bedroom.

ESTHER: For God's sake, now what?

SOLOMON: I just didn't want you to think I wouldn't make the appraisal; I will, I'll do it—

ESTHER, *pointing to the bedroom*: Will you please leave us alone!

SOLOMON, *suddenly, his underlying emotion coming through; indicating Victor*: What do you want from him! He's a policeman! I'm a dealer, he's a doctor, and he's a policeman, so what's the good you'll tear him to pieces?!

ESTHER: Well, one of us has got to leave this room, Victor.

SOLOMON: Please, Esther, let me . . . *Going quickly to Walter*: Doctor, listen to me, take my advice—stop it. What can come of this? In the first place, if you take the deduction how do you know in two, three years they wouldn't come back to you, whereby they disallow it? I don't have to tell you, the Federal Government is not reliable. I understand very well you want to be sweet to him—*to Esther*—but can be two, three years before you'll know how sweet they're going to allow him. *To Victor and Walter*: In other words, what I'm trying to bring out, my boys, is that—

ESTHER: —you want the furniture.

SOLOMON, *shouting at her*: Esther, if I didn't want it I wouldn't buy it! But what can they settle here? It's still up to the Federal Government, don't you see? If they can't settle nothing they should stop it right now! *With a look of warning and alarm in his eyes*: Now please—do what I tell you! I'm not a fool! *He walks out into the bedroom, shaking.*

WALTER, *after a moment*: I guess he's got a point, Vic. Why don't you just sell it to him; maybe then we can sit down and talk sometime. *Glancing at the furniture*: It isn't really a very conducive atmosphere.—Can I call you?

VICTOR: Sure.

ESTHER: You're both fantastic. *She tries to laugh.* We're giving this furniture away because nobody's able to say the simplest things. You're incredible, the both of you.

WALTER, *a little shamed*: It isn't that easy, Esther.

ESTHER: Oh, what the hell—I'll say it. When he went to you, Walter, for the five hundred he needed to get his degree—

VICTOR: Esther! There's no—

ESTHER: It's one of the things standing between you, isn't it? Maybe Walter can clear it up. I mean . . . Good God, is there never to be an end? *To Walter, without pause*: Because it stunned him, Walter. He'll never say it, but—*she takes the plunge*—he hadn't the slightest doubt you'd lend it to him. So when you turned him down—

VICTOR, *as though it wearies him*: Esther, he was just starting out—

ESTHER, *in effect, taking her separate road*: Not the way you told me! Please let me finish! *To Walter*: You already had the house in Rye, you were perfectly well established, weren't you?

VICTOR: So what? He didn't feel he could—

WALTER, *with a certain dread, quietly*: No, no, I . . . I could have spared the money . . . *He sits slowly.* Please, Vic—sit down, it'll only take a moment.

VICTOR: I just don't see any point in—

WALTER: No—no; maybe it's just as well to talk now. We've never talked about this. I think perhaps we have to. *Slight pause. Toward Esther*: It *was* despicable; but I don't think I can leave it quite that way. *Slight pause.* Two or three days afterward—*to Victor*—after you came to see me, I phoned to offer you the money. Did you know that?

> *Slight pause.*

VICTOR: Where'd you phone?

WALTER: Here. I spoke to Dad.

> *Slight pause. Victor sits.*

I saw that I'd acted badly, and I—

VICTOR: You didn't act badly—

WALTER, *with a sudden flight of his voice*: It was frightful! *He gathers himself against his past.* We'll have another talk, won't we? I wasn't prepared to go into all this. . . .

> *Victor is expressionless.*

In any case . . . when I called here he told me you'd joined the Force. And I said—he mustn't permit you to do a thing like that. I said—you had a fine mind and with a little luck you could amount to something in science. That it was a terrible waste. Etcetera. And his answer was—"Victor wants to help me. I can't stop him."

> *Pause.*

VICTOR: You told him you were ready to give me the money?

WALTER: Victor, you remember the . . . the helplessness in his voice. At that time? With Mother recently gone and everything shot out from under him?

VICTOR, *persisting*: Let me understand that, Walter; did you tell—?

WALTER, *in anguish, but hewing to himself*: There are conversations, aren't there, and looking back it's impossible to explain why you said or didn't say certain things? I'm not defending it, but I would like to be understood, if that's possible. You all seemed to need each other more, Vic—more than I needed them. I was never able to feel your kind of . . . faith in him; that . . . confidence. His selfishness—which was perfectly normal—was always obvious to me, but you never seemed to notice it. To the point where I used to blame myself for a lack of feeling. You understand? So when he said that you wanted to help him, I felt somehow that it'd be wrong for me to try to break it up between you. It seemed like interfering.

VICTOR: I see.—Because he never mentioned you'd offered the money.

WALTER: All I'm trying to convey is that . . . I was never indifferent; that's the whole point. I did call here to offer the loan, but he made it impossible, don't you see?

VICTOR: I understand.

WALTER, *eagerly*: Do you?

VICTOR: Yes.

WALTER, *sensing the unsaid*: Please say what you think. It's absurd to go on this way. What do you want to say?

VICTOR—*slight pause*: I think it was all . . . very convenient for you.

WALTER, *appalled*: That's all?

VICTOR: I think so. If you thought Dad meant so much to me—and I guess he did in a certain way—why would five hundred bucks break us apart? I'd have gone on supporting him; it would have let me finish school, that's all.—It doesn't make any sense, Walter.

WALTER, *with a hint of hysteria in his tone*: What makes sense?

VICTOR: You didn't give me the money because you didn't want to.

WALTER, *hurt and quietly enraged—slight pause*: It's that simple.

VICTOR: That's what it comes to, doesn't it? Not that you had any obligation, but if you want to help somebody you do it, if you don't you don't. *He sees Walter's growing frustration and Esther's impatience.* Well, why is that so astonishing? We do what we want to do, don't we? *Walter doesn't reply. Victor's anxiety rises.* I don't understand what you're bringing this all up for.

WALTER: You don't feel the need to heal anything.

VICTOR: I wouldn't mind that, but how does this heal anything?

ESTHER: I think he's been perfectly clear, Victor. He's asking your friendship.

VICTOR: By offering me a job and twelve thousand dollars?

WALTER: Why not? What else can I offer you?

VICTOR: But why do you have to offer me anything?

Walter is silent, morally checked.

It sounds like I have to be saved, or something.

WALTER: I simply felt that there was work you could do that you'd enjoy and I—

VICTOR: Walter, I haven't got the education, what are you talking about? You can't walk in with one splash and wash out twenty-eight years. There's a price people pay. I've paid it, it's all gone, I haven't got it any more. Just like you paid, didn't you? You've got no wife, you've lost your family, you're rattling around all over the place? Can you go home and start all over again from scratch? This is where we are; now, right here, now. And as long as we're talking, I have to tell you that this is not what you say in front of a man's wife.

WALTER, *glancing at Esther, certainty shattered*: What have I said . . . ?

VICTOR, *trying to laugh*: We don't need to be saved, Walter! I've done a job that has to be done and I think I've done it straight. You talk about being out of the rat race, in my opinion, you're in it as deep as you ever were. Maybe more.

ESTHER—*stands*: I want to go, Victor.

VICTOR: Please, Esther, he's said certain things and I don't think I can leave it this way.

ESTHER, *angrily*: Well, what's the difference?

VICTOR, *suppressing an outburst*: Because for some reason you don't understand *anything* any more! *He is trembling as he turns to Walter.* What are you trying to tell me—that it was all unnecessary? Is that it?

> *Walter is silent.*

> Well, correct me, is that the message? Because that's all I get out of this.

WALTER, *toward Esther*: I guess it's impossible—

VICTOR, *the more strongly because Walter seems about to be allied with Esther*: What's impossible? . . . What do you *want*, Walter!

WALTER—*in the pause is the admission that he indeed has not leveled yet. And there is fear in his voice*: I wanted to be of some use. I've learned some painful things, but it isn't enough to know; I wanted to act on what I know.

VICTOR: Act—in what way?

WALTER, *knowing it may be a red flag, but his honor is up*: I feel . . . I could be of help. Why live, only to repeat the same mistakes again and again? I didn't want to let the chance go by, as I let it go before.

> *Victor is unconvinced.*

> And I must say, if this is as far as you can go with me, then you're only defeating yourself.

VICTOR: Like I did before.

> *Walter is silent.*

Is that what you mean?

WALTER—*hesitates, then with frightened but desperate acceptance of combat*: All right, yes; that's what I meant.

VICTOR: Well, that's what I thought.—See, there's one thing about the cops—you get to learn how to listen to people, because if you don't hear right sometimes you end up with a knife in your back. In other words, I dreamed up the whole problem.

WALTER, *casting aside his caution, his character at issue*: Victor, my five hundred dollars was not what kept you from your degree! You could have left Pop and gone right on—he was perfectly fit.

VICTOR: And twelve million unemployed, what was that, my neurosis? I hypnotized myself every night to scrounge the outer leaves of lettuce from the Greek restaurant on the corner? The good parts we cut out of rotten grapefruit . . . ?

WALTER: I'm not trying to deny—

VICTOR, *leaning into Walter's face*: We were eating garbage here, buster!

ESTHER: But what is the point of—

VICTOR, *to Esther*: What are you trying to do, turn it all into a dream? *To Walter*: And perfectly fit! What about the inside of his head? The man was ashamed to go into the street!

ESTHER: But Victor, he's gone now.

VICTOR, *with a cry—he senses the weakness of his position*: Don't tell me he's gone now! *He is wracked, terribly alone before her.* He was here then, wasn't he? And a system broke down, did I invent that?

ESTHER: No, dear, but it's all different now.

VICTOR: What's different now? We're a goddamned army holding this city down and when it blows again you'll be thankful for a roof over your head! *To Walter*: How can you say that to me? I could have left him with your five dollars a month? I'm sorry, you can't brainwash me—if you got a hook in your mouth don't try to stick it into mine. You want to make up for things, you don't come around to make fools out of people. I didn't invent my life. Not altogether. You had a responsibility here and you walked on it. . . . You can go. I'll send you your half.

> *He is across the room from Walter, his face turned away. A long pause.*

WALTER: If you can reach beyond anger, I'd like to tell you something. Vic? *Victor does not move.* I know I should have said this many years ago. But I did try. When you came to me I told you—remember I said, "Ask Dad for money"? I did say that.

Pause.

VICTOR: What are you talking about?

WALTER: He had nearly four thousand dollars.

ESTHER: When?

WALTER: When they were eating garbage here.

Pause.

VICTOR: How do you know that?

WALTER: He'd asked me to invest it for him.

VICTOR: Invest it.

WALTER: Yes. Not long before he sent you to me for the loan.

Victor is silent.

That's why I never sent him more than I did. And if I'd had the strength of my convictions I wouldn't have sent him that!

Victor sits down in silence. A shame is flooding into him which he struggles with. He looks at nobody.

VICTOR, *as though still absorbing the fact*: He actually had it? In the bank?

WALTER: Vic, that's what he was living on, basically, till he died. What we gave him wasn't enough; you know that.

VICTOR: But he had those jobs—

WALTER: Meant very little. He lived on his money, believe me. I told him at the time, if he would send you through I'd contribute properly. But here he's got you running from job to job to feed him—I'm damned if I'd sacrifice when he was holding out on you. You can understand that, can't you?

Victor turns to the center chair and, shaking his head, exhales a blow of anger and astonishment.

Kid, there's no point getting angry now. You know how terrified he was that he'd never earn anything any more. And there was just no reassuring him.

VICTOR, *with protest—it is still nearly incredible*: But he saw I was supporting him, didn't he?

WALTER: For how long, though?

VICTOR, *angering*: What do you mean, how long? He could see I wasn't walking out—

WALTER: I know, but he was sure you would sooner or later.

ESTHER: He was waiting for him to walk out.

WALTER—*fearing to inflame Victor, he undercuts the obvious answer*: Well . . . you could say that, yes.

ESTHER: I knew it! God, when do I believe what I see!

WALTER: He was terrified, dear, and . . . *To Victor*: I don't mean that he wasn't grateful to you, but he really couldn't understand it. I may as well say it, Vic—I myself never imagined you'd go that far.

> *Victor looks at him. Walter speaks with delicacy in the face of a possible explosion.*

Well, you must certainly see now how extreme a thing it was, to stick with him like that? And at such cost to you?

> *Victor is silent.*

ESTHER, *with sorrow*: He sees it.

WALTER, *to erase it all, to achieve the reconciliation*: We could work together, Vic. I know we could. And I'd love to try it. What do you say?

> *There is a long pause. Victor now glances at Esther to see her expression. He sees she wants him to. He is on the verge of throwing it all up. Finally he turns to Walter, a new note of awareness in his voice.*

VICTOR: Why didn't you tell me he had that kind of money?

WALTER: But I did when you came to me for the loan.

VICTOR: To "ask Dad"?

WALTER: Yes!

VICTOR: But would I have come to you if I had the faintest idea he had four thousand dollars under his ass? It was meaningless to say that to me.

WALTER: Now just a second . . . *He starts to indicate the harp.*

VICTOR: Cut it out, Walter! I'm sorry, but it's kind of insulting. I'm not five years old! What am I supposed to make of this? You knew he had that kind of money, and came here many times, you sat here, the two of you, watching me walking around in this suit? And now you expect me to—?

WALTER, *sharply*: You certainly knew he had *something*, Victor!

VICTOR: What do you want here? What do you want here!

WALTER: Well, all I can tell you is that *I* wouldn't sit around eating garbage with *that* staring me in the face! *He points at the harp.* Even then it was worth a couple of hundred, maybe more! Your degree was right there. Right there, if nothing else.

> *Victor is silent, trembling.*

> But if you want to go on with this fantasy, it's all right with me. God knows, I've had a few of my own.

> *He starts for his coat.*

VICTOR: Fantasy.

WALTER: It's a fantasy, Victor. Your father was penniless and your brother a son of a bitch, and you play no part at all. I said to ask him because you could see in front of your face that he had some money. You knew it then and you certainly know it now.

VICTOR: You mean if he had a few dollars left, that—?

ESTHER: What do you mean, a few dollars?

VICTOR, *trying to retract*: I didn't know he—

ESTHER: But you knew he had something?

VICTOR, *caught; as though in a dream where nothing is explicable*: I didn't say that.

ESTHER: Then what are you saying?

VICTOR, *pointing at Walter*: Don't you have anything to say to him?

ESTHER: I want to understand what you're saying! You knew he had money left?

VICTOR: Not four thousand dol—

ESTHER: But enough to make out?

VICTOR, *crying out in anger and for release*: I couldn't nail him to the wall, could I? He said he had nothing!

ESTHER, *stating and asking*: But you knew better.

VICTOR: I don't know what I knew! *He has called this out, and his voice and words surprise him. He sits staring, cornered by what he senses in himself.*

ESTHER: It's a farce. It's all a goddamned farce!

VICTOR: Don't. Don't say that.

ESTHER: Farce! To stick us into a furnished room so you could send him part of your pay? Even after we were married, to go on sending him money? Put off having children, live like mice—and all the time you knew he . . . ? Victor, I'm trying to understand you. Victor?—Victor!

VICTOR, *roaring out, agonized*: Stop it! Silence. *Then*: Jesus, you can't leave everything out like this. The man was a beaten dog, ashamed to walk in the street, how do you demand his last buck—?

ESTHER: You're still saying that? The man had *four thousand dollars*!

He is silent.

It was all an act! Beaten dog!—he was a calculating liar! And in your heart you knew it!

He is struck silent by the fact, which is still ungraspable.

No wonder you're paralyzed—you haven't believed a word you've said all these years. We've been lying away our existence all these years; down the sewer, day after day after day . . . to protect a miserable cheap manipulator. No wonder it all seemed like a dream to me—it was; a goddamned nightmare. I knew it was all unreal, I knew it and I let it go by. Well, I can't any more, kid. I can't watch it another day. I'm not ready to die. *She moves toward her purse.*

She sits. Pause.

VICTOR—*not going to her; he can't. He is standing yards from her*: This isn't true either.

ESTHER: We are dying, that's what's true!

VICTOR: I'll tell you what happened. You want to hear it? *She catches the lack of advocacy in his tone, the simplicity. He moves from her, gathering himself, and glances at the center chair, then at Walter.* I did tell him what you'd said to me. I faced him with it. *He doesn't go on; his eyes go to the chair.* Not that I "faced" him, I just told him—"Walter said to ask you." *He stops; his stare is on the center chair, caught by memory; in effect, the last line was addressed to the chair.*

WALTER: And what happened?

Pause.

VICTOR, *quietly*: He laughed. I didn't know what to make of it. Tell you the truth—*to Esther*—I don't think a week has gone by that I haven't seen that laugh. Like it was some kind of a wild joke—because we *were* eating garbage here. *He breaks off.* I didn't know what I was supposed to do. And I went out. I went—*he sits, staring*—over to Bryant Park behind the public library. *Slight pause.* The grass was covered with men. Like a battlefield; a big open-air flophouse. And not bums—some of them still had shined shoes and good hats, busted businessmen, lawyers, skilled mechanics. Which I'd seen a hundred times. But suddenly—you know?— I saw it. *Slight pause.* There was no mercy. Anywhere. *Glancing at the chair at the end of the table:* One day you're the head of the house, at the head of the table, and suddenly you're shit. Overnight. And I tried to figure out that laugh.—How could he be holding out on me when he loved me?

ESTHER: Loved . . .

VICTOR, *his voice swelling with protest*: He loved me, Esther! He just didn't want to end up on the grass! It's not that you don't love somebody, it's that you've got to survive. We know what that feels like, don't we!

> *She can't answer, feeling the barb.*

> We do what we have to do. *With a wide gesture including her and Walter and himself*: What else are we talking about here? If he did have something left it was—

ESTHER: "*If*" he had—

VICTOR: What does that change! I know I'm talking like a fool, but what does that change? He couldn't believe in anybody any more, and it was unbearable to me! *The unlooked-for return of his old feelings seems to anger him. Of Walter*: He'd kicked him in the face; my mother—*he glances toward Walter as he speaks; there is hardly a pause*—the night he told us he was bankrupt, my mother . . . It was right on this couch. She was all dressed up—for some affair, I think. Her hair was piled up, and long earrings? And he had his tuxedo on . . . and made us all sit down; and he told us it was all gone. And she vomited. *Slight pause. His horror and pity twist in his voice.* All over his arms. His hands. Just kept on vomiting, like thirty-five years coming up. And he sat there. Stinking like a sewer. And a look came onto his face. I'd never seen a man look like that. He was sitting there, letting it dry on his hands. *Pause. He turns to Esther.* What's the difference what you know? Do *you* do everything you know?

> *She avoids his eyes, his mourning shared.*

> Not that I excuse it; it was idiotic, nobody has to tell me that. But you're brought up to believe in one another, you're filled full of that crap—you can't help trying to keep it going, that's all. I thought if I stuck with him, if he could see that somebody was still . . . *He breaks off; the reason strangely has fallen loose. He sits.* I can't explain it; I wanted to . . . stop it from falling apart. I . . . *He breaks off again, staring.*

Pause.

WALTER, *quietly*: It won't work, Vic.

Victor looks at him, then Esther does.

You see it yourself, don't you? It's not that at all. You see that, don't you?

VICTOR, *quietly, avidly*: What?

WALTER, *with his driving need*: Is it really that something fell apart? Were we really brought up to believe in one another? We were brought up to succeed, weren't we? Why else would he respect me so and not you? What fell apart? What was here to fall apart?

Victor looks away at the burgeoning vision.

Was there ever any love here? When he needed her, she vomited. And when you needed him, he laughed. What was unbearable is not that it all fell apart, it was that there was never anything here.

Victor turns back to him, fear on his face.

ESTHER, *as though she herself were somehow moving under the rays of judgment*: But who . . . who can ever face that, Walter?

WALTER, *to her*: You have to! *To Victor*: What you saw behind the library was not that there was no mercy in the world, kid. It's that there was no love in this house. There was no loyalty. There was nothing here but a straight financial arrangement. That's what was unbearable. And you proceeded to wipe out what you saw.

VICTOR, *with terrible anxiety*: Wipe out—

WALTER: Vic, I've been in this box. I wasted thirty years protecting myself from that catastrophe. *He indicates the chair*: And I only got out alive when I saw that there was no catastrophe, there had never been. They were never lovers—she said a hundred times that her marriage destroyed her musical career. I saw that nothing fell here, Vic—and he doesn't follow me any more with that vomit on his hands. I don't look high and low for some betrayal any more; my days belong to *me* now, I'm not afraid to risk believing someone. All I ever wanted was simply to do science, but I invented an efficient, disaster-proof, money-maker. You—*to Esther, with a warm smile*: He could never stand the sight of blood. He was shy, he was sensitive . . . *To Victor*: And what do you do? March straight into the most violent profession there is. We invent ourselves, Vic, to wipe out what we know. You invent a life of self-sacrifice, a life of duty; but what never existed here cannot be upheld. You were not upholding something, you were denying what you knew they were. And denying yourself. And that's all that is standing between us now—an illusion, Vic. That I kicked them in the face and you must uphold them against me. But I only saw then what you see now—there was nothing here to betray. I am not your enemy. It is all an illusion and if you could walk through it, we could meet . . . *His reconciliation is on him.* You see why I said before, that in the hospital—when it struck me so that we . . . we're brothers. It was only two seemingly different roads out of the same trap. It's almost as though—*he smiles warmly, uncertain still*—we're like two halves of the same guy. As though we can't quite move ahead—alone. You ever feel that?

> *Victor is silent.*

> Vic?

> *Pause.*

VICTOR: Walter, I'll tell you—there are days when I can't remember what I've got against you. *He laughs emptily, in suffering.* It hangs in me like a rock. And I see myself in a store window, and my hair going, I'm walking the streets—and I can't remember why. And you can go crazy trying to figure it out when all the reasons disappear—when you can't even hate any more.

WALTER: Because it's unreal, Vic, and underneath you know it is.

VICTOR: Then give me something real.

WALTER: What can I give you?

VICTOR: I'm not blaming you now, I'm asking you. I can understand you walking out. I've wished a thousand times I'd done the same thing. But, to come here through all those years knowing what you knew and saying nothing . . . ?

WALTER: And if I said—Victor, if I said that I did have some wish to hold you back? What would that give you now?

VICTOR: Is that what you wanted? Walter, tell me the truth.

WALTER: I wanted the freedom to do my work. Does that mean I stole your life? *Crying out and standing:* You made those choices, Victor! And that's what you have to face!

VICTOR: But, what do you face? You're not turning me into a walking fifty-year-old mistake—we have to go home when you leave, we have to look at each other. What do *you* face?

WALTER: I have offered you everything I know how to!

VICTOR: I would know if you'd come to give me something! I would know that!

WALTER, *crossing for his coat*: You don't want the truth, you want a monster!

VICTOR: You came for the old handshake, didn't you! The okay!

Walter halts in the doorway.

And you end up with the respect, the career, the money, and the best of all, the thing that nobody else can tell you so you can believe it—that you're one hell of a guy and never harmed anybody in your life! Well, you won't get it, not till I get mine!

WALTER: And you? You never had any hatred for me? Never a wish to see me destroyed? To destroy me, to destroy me with this saintly self-sacrifice, this mockery of sacrifice? What will you give me, Victor?

VICTOR: I don't have it to give you. Not any more. And you don't have it to give me. And there's nothing to give—I see that now. I just didn't want him to end up on the grass. And he didn't. That's all it was, and I don't need anything more. I couldn't work with you, Walter. I can't. I don't trust you.

WALTER: Vengeance. Down to the end. *To Esther*: He is sacrificing his life to vengeance.

ESTHER: Nothing was sacrificed.

WALTER, *to Victor*: To prove with your failure what a treacherous son of a bitch I am!—to hang yourself in my doorway!

ESTHER: Leave him, Walter—please, don't say any more!

WALTER—*humiliated by her. He is furious. He takes an unplanned step toward the door*: You quit; both of you. *To Victor as well*: You lay down and quit, and that's the long and short of all your ideology. It is all envy!

Solomon enters, apprehensive, looks from one to the other.

And to this moment you haven't the guts to face it! But your failure does not give you moral authority! Not with me! I *worked* for what I made and there are people walking around today who'd have been dead if I hadn't. Yes. *Moving toward the door, he points at the center chair.* He was smarter than all of us—he saw what you wanted and he gave it to you! *He suddenly reaches out and grabs Solomon's face and laughs.* Go ahead, you old mutt—rob them blind, they love it! *Letting go, he turns to Victor.* You will never, never again make me ashamed! *He strides toward the doorway. A gown lies on the dining table, spread out, and he is halted in surprise at the sight of it.*

Suddenly Walter sweeps it up in his hands and rushes at Victor, flinging the gown at him with an outcry. Victor backs up at his wild approach.

VICTOR: Walter!

The flicker of a humiliated smile passes across Walter's face. He wants to disappear into air. He turns, hardly glancing at Victor, makes for the door, and, straightening, goes out.

VICTOR—*starts hesitantly to the door*: Maybe he oughtn't go into the street like that—

SOLOMON, *stopping him with his hand*: Let him go.

Victor turns to Solomon uncertainly.

What can you do?

ESTHER: Whatever you see, huh.

Solomon turns to her, questioningly.

You believe what you see.

SOLOMON, *thinking she was rebuking him*: What then?

ESTHER: No—it's wonderful. Maybe that's why you're still going.

Victor turns to her. She stares at the doorway.

I was nineteen years old when I first walked up those stairs—if that's believable. And he had a brother, who was the cleverest, most wonderful young doctor . . . in the world. As he'd be soon. Somehow, some way. *She turns to the center chair.* And a rather sweet, inoffensive gentleman, always waiting for the news to come on. . . . And next week, men we never saw or heard of will come and smash it all apart and take it all away.—So many times I thought—the one thing he wanted most was to talk to his brother, and that if they could— But he's come and he's gone. And I still feel it—isn't that terrible? It always seems to me that one little step more and some crazy kind of forgiveness will come and lift up everyone. When do you stop being so . . . foolish?

SOLOMON: I had a daughter, should rest in peace, she took her own life. That's nearly fifty years. And every night I lay down to sleep, she's sitting there. I see her clear like I see you. But if it was a miracle and she came to life, what would I say to her? *He turns back to Victor, paying out.* So you got there seven; so I'm giving you eight, nine, ten, eleven—*he searches, finds a fifty*—and there's a fifty for the harp. Now you'll excuse me—I got a lot of work here tonight. *He gets his pad and pencil and begins carefully listing each piece.*

VICTOR—*folds the money*: We could still make the picture, if you like.

ESTHER: Okay.

He goes to his suit and begins to rip the plastic wrapper off.

Don't bother.

He looks at her.

She turns to Solomon. Goodbye, Mr. Solomon.

SOLOMON—*looks up from his pad*: Goodbye, dear. I like that suit, that's very nice. *He returns to his work.*

ESTHER: Thank you. *She walks out with her life.*

VICTOR—*buckles on his gun belt, pulls up his tie*: When will you be taking it away?

SOLOMON: With God's help if I'll live, first thing in the morning.

VICTOR, *of the suit*: I'll be back for this later, then. And there's my foil, and the mask, and the gauntlets. *Puts on his uniform jacket.*

SOLOMON, *continuing his work*: Don't worry, I wouldn't touch it.

VICTOR, *extending his hand*: I'm glad to have met you, Solomon.

SOLOMON: Likewise. And I want to thank you.

VICTOR: What for?

SOLOMON, *with a glance at the furniture*: Well . . . who would ever believe I would start such a thing again . . . ? *He cuts himself off.* But go, go, I got a lot of work here.

VICTOR, *starting to the door, putting his cap on*: Good luck with it.

SOLOMON: Good luck you can never know till the last minute, my boy.

VICTOR, *smiling*: Right. Yes. *With a last look around at the room.* Well . . . bye-bye.

SOLOMON, *as Victor goes out*: Bye-bye, bye-bye.

He is alone. He has the pad and pencil in his hand, and he takes the pencil to start work again. But he looks about, and the challenge of it all oppresses him and he is afraid and worried. His hand goes to his cheek, he pulls his flesh in fear, his eyes circling the room.

His eye falls on the phonograph. He goes, inspects it, winds it up, sets the tone arm on the record, and flicks the starting lever. The Laughing Record plays. As the two comedians begin their routine, his depressed expression gives way to surprise. Now he smiles. He chuckles, and remembers. Now a laugh escapes, and he nods his head in recollection. He is laughing now, and shakes his head back and forth as though to say, "It still works!" And the laughter, of the record and his own, increase and combine. He holds his head, unable to stop laughing, and sits in the center chair. He leans back sprawling in the chair, laughing with tears in his eyes, howling helplessly to the air.

SLOW CURTAIN

THE CREATION
OF THE WORLD
AND OTHER BUSINESS

1972

Characters

GOD

ADAM

EVE

LUCIFER

ANGELS: RAPHAEL, AZRAEL, CHEMUEL

CAIN

ABEL

ACT ONE

Music.

A night sky full of stars. Day spreads its pristine light, forming shadows in the contrasting sunlight. It is Paradise, the ultimate Garden—which is to say that it is all an impression of color rather than terrestrial details of plants and vines. Only one such feature stands apart; from the left, reaching out like an inverted, finger-spread hand, is a tree branch with golden leaves, from which hangs an apple.

God appears on his throne above the acting level. He is deep in thought as He tries to visualize the inevitable future.

Now, as light spreads, the caw of a crow sounds, the dawn-welcoming chatter of monkeys, the hee-hawing ass, the lion's echoing roar, seals barking, pigs grunting, the loon's sudden laughter—all at once in free cacophony.

And as they subside and day is full, one of the shadows moves—a man, Adam, who reaches up above his head and plucks a fig and, propped up against a rock, crosses his legs and idly chews. He is in every way a man and naked, but his skin is imprinted with striped and speckled shadows, an animated congealment of light and color and darkness.

God emerges behind and to one side of him. He looks about, at the weather, up at the sky. Then He turns and looks down at Adam, who gradually feels His presence, and with only the slightest start of surprise. . . .

ADAM: Oh! Good morning, God!

GOD: Good morning, Adam. Beautiful day.

ADAM: Oh, perfect, Lord. But they all are.

GOD: I've turned up the breeze a little. . . .

ADAM: I just noticed that. *Holds up a hand to feel it.* This is exactly right now. Thanks, Lord.

717

GOD: I'm very pleased with the way you keep the garden. I see you've pruned the peach tree.

ADAM: I had to, Lord. An injured branch was crying all night. Are we going to name more things today?

GOD: I have something else to discuss with you this morning, but I don't see why we couldn't name a few things first. *He points.* What would you call that?

ADAM: That? I'd call that a lion.

GOD: Lion. Well, that sounds all right. And that?

ADAM: That? Ahhh . . . lamb?

GOD, *trying the word*: Lamb.

ADAM: I don't know what it is today—everything seems to start with L.

GOD: I must say that *looks* like a lamb. And that?

ADAM: L, L, L . . . That should be—ah . . . labbit?

GOD, *cocking His head doubtfully*: Labbit doesn't seem—

ADAM, *quickly*: You're right, that's wrong. See, I was rushing.

GOD: Slow down, we have all the time in the world.

ADAM: Actually, that looks like something that should begin with an R. . . . rabbit!

GOD: Rabbit sounds much better.

ADAM, *happily*: Rabbit, rabbit!—oh, sure, that's much better.

GOD: How about that?

ADAM: I've been wondering about that. I have a feeling it should have a name that goes up and down, like . . . ka . . . ka . . .

GOD: Yes? Go on . . . *Ka* what?

ADAM, *undulantly*: Ca-ter-pill-ar.

GOD: What an amazing creature you've turned out to be; I would never have thought of "Caterpillar" in a million years. That'll be enough for today. I imagine you've noticed by this time that all the animals live in pairs—there are male and female?

ADAM: I'm so glad you mentioned that.

GOD: Oh, it disturbs you?

ADAM: Oh no, Lord, nothing disturbs me.

GOD: I'm glad to see that you've settled for perfection.

ADAM: It just seemed odd that, of all the creatures, only I am alone. But I'm sure you have your reasons.

GOD: Actually, Adam—and I know this won't shake your confidence—but now and then I do something and, quite frankly, it's only afterwards that I discover the reasons. Which, of course, is just as well. In your case it was extremely experimental. I had just finished the chimpanzee and had some clay left over. And I—well, just played around with it, and by golly there you were, the spitting image of me. In fact, that is probably why I feel such a special closeness to you: you sprang out of my instinct rather than some design. And that is probably why it never occurred to me to give you a wife, you see.

ADAM: Oh, I see. What would it look like? Or don't you know yet?

GOD: Supposing I improvise something and see how it strikes you.

ADAM: All right. But would I have to—like, talk to it all the time?

GOD: What in the world gave you an idea like that?

ADAM: Well, these lions and monkeys and mice—they're all constantly talking to each other. And I so enjoy lying on my back and just listening to the lilacs budding.

GOD: You mean you'd rather remain alone?

ADAM: I don't know! I've never had anybody.

GOD: Well, neither have I, so I'm afraid I can't help you there. Why don't we just try it and see what happens?

ADAM: Of course, Lord, anything you say.

GOD: Lie down, then, and I'll put you to sleep.

ADAM: Yes, Lord.

>   *He lies down. God feels his rib cage.*

GOD: I'll take out a bottom rib. This one here. You'll never know the difference.

ADAM, *starting up*: Is that—fairly definite?

GOD: Oh, don't worry. I shouldn't have put it in in the first place, but I wanted to be extra sure. Now close your eyes.

ADAM, *lying back nervously*: Yes, sir. . . . *Starts up again.* Is this also going to be experimental, or—I mean how long are we going to keep her?

GOD: Now look, son, you don't have to hang around her every minute. If it gets too much, you just walk off by yourself.

ADAM: Oh, good. *Starts lying down, then sits up nervously.* I just wondered.

GOD: Sleep, Adam! *He ceremonially lowers his hands on Adam's rib. Something stirs on the periphery, rising from the ground. Music.*

> This is now bone of thy bones,
> And flesh of thy flesh;
> She shall be called . . . Woman,
> Because she was taken out of Man.

> Wake up, Adam. *Adam opens his eyes and sits up. Eve moves out of the darkness, and they look at each other. Her skin too is covered with shadow-marks. God walks around her, inspecting her.* Hmmmmm. Very nice. *To Adam:* What do you say? *Music dies off.*

ADAM, *nervously*: Well . . . she certainly is *different.*

GOD: Is that all?

ADAM: Oh, Lord, she's perfect! *But he is still uneasy.*

GOD: I think so too.

ADAM: Me too.

GOD: Huh! I don't know how I do it! What would you like to call her?

ADAM: Eve.

GOD: Eve! Lovely name. *Takes her hand.* Now dear, you will notice many different kinds of animals in this garden. Each has its inborn rule. The bee will not eat meat; the elephant will not sing and fish have no interest in flowers.—Those are apples on that tree; you will not eat them.

EVE: Why?

ADAM: That's the rule!

GOD: Be patient, Adam, she's very new. *To Eve:* Perhaps the day will come when I can give you a fuller explanation; for the moment, we'll put it this way. That is the Tree of Knowledge, Knowledge of Good and Evil. All that you have here springs from my love for you; out of love for me you will not eat of that tree or you will surely die. Not right away, but sometime. Now tell me, Eve—when you look at that tree, what do you think of?

EVE, *looks up at the tree*: . . . God?

ADAM: She got it!

GOD: That's exactly the point, dear. *Takes both their hands.* Now be glad of one another. And remember—if you eat of that tree you shall surely die. Not right away, but sometime. And if you stay clear of that tree, everything will go one just as it is, forever. Eve?

EVE: Yes, Lord.

GOD: Adam?

ADAM: Yes, Lord.

GOD: It is all yours, my children, till the end of time.

> *He walks away and vanishes. Adam and Eve turn from God and face each other. They smile tentatively. Examine each other's hands, breasts. He sniffs her. Sniffs closer.*

ADAM: You smell differently than I do.

EVE: You do too.

> *He kisses her lips. Then she kisses his. They smile. He gives a little wave.*

ADAM: Well . . . maybe I'll see you again sometime. I feel like lying down over there.

EVE: I do too!

ADAM, *halting*: You do?

> *She stretches out.*

EVE: I think I have the same thoughts you do.

ADAM, *deciding to test this*: Are you a little thirsty?

EVE: Mmhm.

ADAM: Me too. And a little hungry?

EVE: Mmhm.

ADAM: Well, that's nice. Here, want a fig?

EVE: I just felt like a fig! *They chew.*

ADAM: We can go swimming later, if you like.

EVE: Fine! That's just what I was thinking. *They lie in silence.*

ADAM: Beautiful, isn't it?

EVE: Oh, ya. Is it all right to ask—

ADAM: What?

EVE: —what you do all day?

ADAM: Well, up till recently I've been naming things. But that's practically over now. See that up there? *She looks up.* I named that a pomegranate.

EVE: Pomewhat?

ADAM: Pomegranate.

EVE: That doesn't look like a pomegranate.

ADAM: Of course it's a pomegranate. *He fetches her one.* Here, eat one, you'll see. As you're spitting out the seeds it feels like "pomegranate, pomegranate, pomegranate." *She bites into it. As she spits out seeds.* Granate, granate, granate. . . .

EVE, *chewing, spitting out seeds*: Say . . . you're right, you're right.

ADAM: That's better.

EVE—*she suddenly plucks something out of his hair and holds it between her fingers*: What's this?

ADAM: That? That's a prndn. *He scratches himself.* It's one of the first things I named.

EVE: This you named a prndn?

ADAM, *with a tingle of alarm*: Now look, woman, once a thing is named, it's *named*.

EVE, *hurt, surprised*: Oh.

ADAM—*conviction failing, he turns back to her*: Why? What should I call it?

EVE: Well, to *me*, this is a louse.

ADAM: Saaay! No wonder I woke up full of L's this morning! *With a happy laugh, she eats the louse.* Isn't it marvelous how we both have exactly the same thoughts, pretty near!

EVE, *chewing*: Yes. *He stares ahead, considering for a moment, then, to show off he spreads his arms and stands on one foot.* So what do you do all day?

ADAM: Sometimes I do this. Or this. *He rolls onto his head and does a headstand. She watches for a moment. His headstand collapses*: Why? Do you have something in mind?

EVE: I think I do, but I don't know what it is. Say, that bush!

ADAM: What about it?

EVE: I just saw it growing!

ADAM: Oh, sure. Listen . . . do you hear?

EVE: Yes. What is that sound?

ADAM: That's the sound of sunset.

EVE: And that crackling?

ADAM: A shadow is moving across dry leaves.

EVE: What is that piping sound?

ADAM: Two trout are talking in the river.

EVE, *looking upward*: Something has exhaled.

ADAM: God is sighing.

EVE: Something is rising and falling.

ADAM: That's the footsteps of an angel walking through the vines. Come, I'll show you the pool.

EVE, *getting up*: I was just thinking that!

ADAM: Good for you! I'll teach you to ride my alligators! *With a comradely arm over her shoulder he walks her out, as angels Chemuel, Azrael, and Raphael enter on the platform.*

CHEMUEL: Did you ever see anything so sweet?

RAPHAEL: Look at him putting a plum in her mouth! How lovely!

   God enters on the platform.

CHEMUEL: She's adorable! Lord, you've done it again. *God, however, has left the group and stands in deep thought, apart.* Everybody! Halllllll-elujah!

ANGELS, *singing Handel*: Hallelujah, hallelujah . . .

   A full-blown orchestra and mighty chorus erupt from the air in accompaniment.

GOD, *motioning them out*: Excuse me! A little later, perhaps. I'd like a few words with Lucifer.

CHEMUEL, *kissing God's hand, as they leave*: Congratulations, Lord.

RAPHAEL: We'll bring the full chorus tonight!

   Alone, God looks down at the earth, as Lucifer enters.

GOD: All right, go ahead, say it.

LUCIFER: Nothing for me to say, Lord. *He points below.* You see it as well as I.

GOD, *looking down, shaking His head*: What did I do wrong?

LUCIFER: Why look at it that way? They're beautiful, they help each other, they praise You every few minutes—

GOD: Lucifer, they don't multiply.

LUCIFER: Maybe give them a few more years. . . .

GOD: But there's no sign of anything. Look at them—the middle of a perfect, moonlit night, and they're playing handball.

LUCIFER: Well, You wanted them innocent.

GOD: Every once in a while, though, he does seem to get aroused.

LUCIFER: Aroused, yes, but what's the good if he doesn't get it in the right place? And when he does, she walks off to pick a flower or something.

GOD: I can't figure that out. *Pause. They stare down.*

LUCIFER: Of course, You could always— *He breaks off.*

GOD: What?

LUCIFER: Look, I don't want to mix in, and then You'll say I'm criticizing everything—

GOD: I don't know why I stand for your superciliousness.

LUCIFER: At least I don't bore You like the rest of these spirits.

GOD: Sometimes I'd just as soon you did. What have you got in mind?

LUCIFER: Now, remember, You asked me.

GOD: What have you got in mind!

LUCIFER: You see? You're mad already.

GOD, *roaring furiously*: I am not mad!

LUCIFER: All right, all right. You could take her back and restring her insides. Reroute everything, so wherever he goes in it connects to the egg.

GOD: No-no-no, I don't want to fool with that. She's perfect now; I'm not tearing her apart again. Out of the question.

LUCIFER: Well, then. You've only got one other choice. You've got to thin out the innocence down there. *God turns to him suspiciously.* See? You're giving me that look again; whatever I say, You turn it into some kind of a plot. Like when You made that fish with the fur on. Throw him in the ocean, and all the angels run around screaming hosannahs. *I* come and tell You the thing's drowned, and You're insulted.

GOD: Yes. But I—I've stopped making fish with fur any more.

LUCIFER: But before I can penetrate with a fact I've got to go through hell.

GOD—*He suddenly points down*: He's putting his arm around her. *Lucifer looks down.* Lucifer! *They both stretch over the edge to see better.* Lucifer!! *Suddenly, His expression changes to incredulity, then anger, and He throws up His hands in futile protest.* Where in the world does he get those stupid ideas!

LUCIFER, *still looking down*: Now he's going to sleep.

GOD: Oh, dear, dear, dear, dear. *He sits disconsolately.*

LUCIFER: Lord, the problem down there is that You've made it all so perfect. Everything they look at is not only good, it's equally good. The sun
is good, rats are good, fleas are good, the moon, lions, athlete's foot—
every single thing is just as good as every other thing. Because, naturally,
You created everything, so everything's as attractive as everything else.

GOD: What's so terrible about perfection? Except that you can't stand it?

LUCIFER: Well, simply—if You want him to go into her, into the right
place, and stay there long enough, You'll have to make that part better.

GOD: I am not remaking that woman.

LUCIFER: It's not necesary. All I'm saying is that sex has to be made not
just good, but—well, terrific. Right now he'd just as soon pick his nose.
In other words, You've got to rivet his attention on that one place.

GOD: How would I do that?

LUCIFER: Well, let's look at it. What is the one thing that makes him stop
whatever he's doing and pay strict attention?

GOD: What?

LUCIFER: You, Lord. Soon as you appear, he, so to speak, comes erect.
Give sex that same sort of holiness in his mind, the same sort of hope that
is never discouraged and never really fulfilled, the same fear of being
unacceptable. Make him feel toward sex as he feels toward You, and
You're in—*unbeschreiblich*! Between such high promise and deadly terror, he won't be able to think of anything else.

    Pause.

GOD: How?

LUCIFER: Well . . . *He hesitates a long moment, until God slowly turns to
him with a suspicious look.* All right, look—there's no way around it, I
simply have to talk about those apples.

GOD, *stamps His foot and stands, strides up and down, trying to control
his temper*: Lucifer!

LUCIFER: I refuse to believe that man's only way to demonstrate his love
for God is to refuse to eat some fruit! That kind of game is simply unworthy of my father!

GOD, *angered*: Really now!

LUCIFER: Forgive me, sir, but I am useless to You if I don't speak my mind.
May I tell You why *I* think You planted that tree in the garden? *God is*

silent, but consenting, even if unwillingly. Objectively speaking, it *is* senseless. You wanted Adam's praise for everything You made, absolutely innocent of any doubt about Your goodness. Why, then, plant a fruit which can only make him wise, sophisticated, and analytical? May I continue? *God half-willingly nods.* He certainly will begin to question everything if he eats an apple, but why is that necessarily bad? *God looks surprised, angering.* He'll not only marvel that the flower blooms, he will ask why and discover chlorophyll—and bless You for chlorophyll. He'll not only praise You that food makes him strong, he will discover his bile duct and praise You for his pancreas. He may lose his innocence, but the more he learns of Your secrets, the more reasons he will have to praise You. And that is why, quite without consciously knowing it, You planted that tree there. It was your fantastic inner urge to magnify Your glory to the last degree. In six words, Lord, You wanted full credit for everything.

GOD: He must never eat those apples.

LUCIFER: Then why have You tempted him? What is the point?

GOD: I wanted him to wake each morning, look at that tree, and say, "For God's sake I won't eat these apples." Not even one.

LUCIFER: Fine. But with that same absence of curiosity he is not investigating Eve.

GOD: But the other animals manage.

LUCIFER: Their females go into heat, and the balloon goes up. But Eve is ready almost any time, and that means no time. It's part of that whole dreadful uniformity down there.

GOD: They are my children; I don't want them to know evil.

LUCIFER: Why call it evil? One apple, and he'll know the difference between good and better. And once he knows that, he'll be all over her. *He looks down.* Look, he's kissing a tree. You see? The damned fool has no means of discriminating.

GOD, *looking down*: Well, he should kiss trees too.

LUCIFER: Fine. If that's the way You feel, You've got Adam and Eve, and it'll be a thousand years before you're a grandfather. *He stands.* Think it over. I'd be glad to go down and—*God gives him a look.* I'm only trying to help!

GOD: Lucifer, I'm way ahead of you.

LUCIFER: Lord, that's inevitable.

GOD: Stay away from that tree.

LUCIFER, *with a certain evasiveness*: Whatever You say, sir. May I go now?

GOD, *after a pause*: Don't have the illusion that I am in conflict about this; I mean, don't decide to go down there and do Me a favor, or something. I know perfectly well why I put that tree there.

LUCIFER, *surprised*: Really!

GOD: Yes, really. I am in perfect control over my unconscious, friend. It was not to tempt Adam; it's I who was tempted. I finished him and I saw he was beautiful, and for a moment I loved him beyond anything I had ever made—and I thought, maybe I should let him see through the rose petal to its chemistry, the formation of amino acids to the secrets of life. His simple praise for surfaces made me impatient to show him the physics of My art, which would raise him to a god.

LUCIFER: Why'd You change Your mind?

GOD: Because I thought of what became of you. The one angel who really understands biology and physics, the one I loved before all the rest and took such care to teach—and you can't take a breath without thinking how to overthrow Me and take over the universe!

LUCIFER: Lord, I only wanted them to know more, the more to praise You!

GOD: The more they know, the less they will need Me, Lucifer; you know that as well as I! And that's all you're after, to grind away their respect for Me. "Give them an apple!" If it weren't for the Law of the Conservation of Energy I would destroy you! Don't go near that tree or those dear people—not in any form, you hear? They are innocent, and innocent they will remain till I turn out the lights forever!

    God goes out. Lucifer is alone.

LUCIFER: Now what is He *really* saying? He put it there to tempt *Himself*! Therefore He's not of one mind about innocence; and how could He be when innocence blinds Adam to half the wonders He has made? I will help the Lord. Yes, that's the only way to put it; I'm His helper. I open up the marvels He dares not show, and thereby magnify His glory. In short, I disobey what He says and carry out what He means, and if that's evil, it's only to do good. Strange—I never felt so close to my creator as I do right now! Once Adam eats, he'll multiply, and Lucifer completes the lovely world of God! Oh, praise the Lord who gave me all this insight! My fight with Him is over! Now evil be my good, and Eve and Adam multiply in blessed sin! Make way, dumb stars, the world of man begins!

    He exits as light rises on Paradise, where Eve is bent over from the waist, examining a—to us invisible—turtle. Adam enters. His attention is caught by her raised buttocks, and he approaches, halts, and stares—then looks off, puzzled by the idea that he can't quite form in his mind. Giving it up, he asks . . .

ADAM: You want to play volleyball?

Lucifer enters.

LUCIFER: Good evening.

ADAM: Good evening. *He nervously nudges Eve, who now stands up. Something in Lucifer moves something in her.*

EVE: Oh!

Lucifer exchanges a deep glance with her, then moves, glancing about and then turns back to Adam.

LUCIFER: Had enough?

EVE: Enough of what?

LUCIFER: You don't imagine, do you, that God intended you to lie around like this forever?

ADAM: We're going swimming later.

LUCIFER: Swimming! What about making something of yourselves?

ADAM: Making some . . . ?

LUCIFER, *with a quick glance about for God*: I'm a little short of time, Adam. By the way, my name is Lucifer. The archangel?

ADAM, *impressed*: Ohhh! I'm very pleased to meet you. This is my wife, Eve.

EVE: How do you do?

LUCIFER, *taking her hand with a little pressure*: Awfully nice to meet you, Eve. Tell me, you ever hold your breath?

ADAM: Oh sure, she does that a lot. Show him, Eve. *She inhales and holds it.* She can do that till she turns blue. *Eve lets out the air.*

EVE: I can really turn blue if I want to.

LUCIFER: And why does that happen?

ADAM: Because God makes it.

LUCIFER: But how, dear?

ADAM: How should she know?

LUCIFER: But God *wants* her to know.

ADAM: But why didn't He tell us?

LUCIFER: He's trying to tell you; that's why I've come; I am the Explainer. Adam, the fact is that God gives His most important commands through

His silences. For example, there is nothing He feels more passionate about than that you begin to multiply.

EVE: Really?

LUCIFER: Of course. That's why that tree is there.

EVE: We multiply with the tree?

LUCIFER: No, but if you eat the fruit you'll know how. He just can't bring Himself to say it, you see.

EVE: Is that so!

ADAM: Now, wait a minute, excuse me. We're not even supposed to *think* about that tree.

EVE: Say, that's right. In fact, lately, that's practically all I do is go around not thinking about it.

LUCIFER: Oh, you find that's getting difficult?

EVE: No, but it takes up so much time.

ADAM: It's because we'll die if we eat those things. *Lucifer reaches up, takes an apple.* You better watch out, they're not good for you—Don't! *Lucifer bites into the apple, chews. They watch him, wide-eyed.* Oh, I know why, it's that you're an angel!

LUCIFER: You could be too.

ADAM, *worried*: Angels?

LUCIFER: Absolutely. Now listen carefully, because this is fairly deep and I may have to leave any minute. You know by now why the Lord put you in this lovely garden.

ADAM: To praise everything.

LUCIFER: Right. Now what if I told you that there are a number of things you've been leaving out?

ADAM, *shocked*: Oh, no! I praise absolutely everything.

LUCIFER, *pointing to his penis*: And what about this thing here? Do you praise Him for that?

ADAM, *looking down at himself*: Well, not in particular, but I include it in.

LUCIFER: But how can you when you don't know what it's for?

EVE: He pees that way.

LUCIFER: Pees! That is so incidental it's not even worth mentioning. *To Adam*: You have no idea, do you?

ADAM: Well . . . ahh . . .

LUCIFER: Yes?

ADAM: I'm only guessing, but sometimes it makes me feel—

LUCIFER: Feel what?

ADAM: Well . . . kind of sporty?

LUCIFER: Adam! God has made you in His image, given you His body. How dare you refuse to understand the very best part of it? Now you will eat this apple.

ADAM: Angel, please—I really don't feel I should.

LUCIFER, *holding the apple to Adam's tightly shut lips*: You must! Could I make this offer without God's permission?

EVE: Say, that's right!

LUCIFER: Of course it's right! I mean nothing happens He doesn't want to happen—*n'est-ce pas?* Now, you take one bite, and I promise you will understand everything. Adam, open your mouth and you will become— *he glances quickly about, lowers his voice*—like God.

ADAM: Like *God*! You should never say a thing like that!

LUCIFER: You're not even living like animals!

ADAM: I don't want to hear any more! He said it in plain Hebrew, don't eat those apples, and that's it! I'm going swimming. Eve?

EVE, *extending her hand to Lucifer*: Very nice to have met you.

LUCIFER, *slowly running his eyes from her feet to her face*: Likewise.

> *A strange sensation emanates from his eyes, and she slowly looks down at her body.*

ADAM: Eve?

> *She unwillingly breaks from Lucifer, and they leave. Lucifer looks at the apple in his hand and takes a big bite. He stands there chewing thoughtfully. Offstage a splash is heard. A pause. Eve returns, glancing behind her, and hurries to Lucifer.*

EVE: There's only one thing I wonder if you could tell me.

LUCIFER: I love questions, my dear. What is it?

EVE—*she looks down at herself, pointing*: Why has he got that thing and I don't?

LUCIFER: Isn't it funny? I knew you were going to ask that question.

EVE: Well, I mean, is it going to grow on later?

LUCIFER: Never.

EVE: Why?

LUCIFER, *offering her his apple*: Take a bite, Eve, and everything will clear up.

EVE—*she accepts the apple, looks at it*: It smells all right.

LUCIFER: Of course. It *is* all right.

EVE: Maybe just a little bite.

LUCIFER: Better make it medium. You have an awful lot to learn, dear.

EVE: Well . . . here goes! *She bites and chews, her eyes widening, her body moving sinuously. A dread sound fills the air. She approaches him.*

LUCIFER, *retreating*: 'Fraid I've got to leave, dear.

EVE: You going *now*?

LUCIFER: Oh, yes, right now! But I'll be around.

> *He hurries off, glancing behind with trepidation. She stands there staring. She feels her body, her breasts, her face, awakening to herself. She starts her hand down to her genitals and inhales a surprised breath. Adam enters. The sound goes silent.*

ADAM: Where were you? Come on, the water's perfect! . . . Eve? *She turns to him.* What's the matter? *She sensuously touches his arm and puts it around her.* What are you doing? *She smashes her lips against his.* What is this? *She holds her apple before his face.*

EVE: Eat it.

ADAM: Eve!

EVE: It's marvelous! Please, a bite, a bite!

ADAM: But God said—

EVE: I'm God.

ADAM: You're what?

EVE: He is in me! He'll be in you! I never felt like this! I am the best thing that ever happened! Look at me! Adam, don't you see me?

ADAM: Well, sure, I—

EVE: You're not looking at me!

ADAM: Of course I'm looking at you!

EVE: But you're not *seeing* me! You don't see anything!

ADAM: Why? I see the trees, the sky—

EVE: You wouldn't see anything else if you were seeing me.

ADAM: How's that possible?

EVE: Say "Ahh."

ADAM: Ahh.

> *She suddenly pushes the apple into his mouth.*

EVE: Chew! Swallow!

> *He chews. The dread sound again. She watches. He looks down at his penis. Then to her. Then up at her face, astonished. He starts to reach for her.*

VOICE OF GOD, *echoing through the theater on the PA system*: WHERE ART THOU! *They both retract, glancing desperately around. They rush about trying to hide from each other.*

WHERE ART THOU!

ADAM: Here, quick! Put something on! *He hands her a leaf, which she holds in front of her.* Gee, you know you look even better with that leaf on—

EVE, *looking off*: He's coming!

> *They disappear. God enters.*

GOD: Where art thou?

ADAM, *still unseen*: Here, Lord. *God turns, looking around. Adam emerges. He is wearing a large leaf. Nervously apologizing.* I heard Thy voice in the garden and I was afraid, because I was naked; and I hid myself. *Eve emerges.*

GOD: Who told thee that thou wast naked?

ADAM: Who told me?

GOD: Who told thee! You didn't know you were naked!

ADAM, *appalled, looking down at himself*: Say, that's right.

GOD, *mimicking him*: "Say, that's right." You ate the apple!

ADAM: She made me.

EVE: I couldn't help it. A snake came. *To Adam*: Wasn't he a snake?

ADAM: Like a snake, ya.

GOD: That son of a . . . *Calling out*: Lucifer, I get my hands on you . . . !

EVE: But why'd You put the tree here if You . . . ?

GOD: *You're* questioning *Me*! Who the hell do you think you are? I put the tree here so there would be at least one thing you shouldn't think about! So, unlike the animals, you should exercise a little self-control.

EVE: Oh!

GOD: "Oh," she says. I'll give you an "Oh" that you'll wish you'd never been born! But first I'm going to fix it between you and snakes. Serpent, because thou hast done this,

> Thou art cursed above all cattle,
> And above every beast of the field;
> And I will put enmity between thee and woman—
> That means all women will hate snakes.
> Or almost all.

> You see? It's already impossible to make an absolute statement around here! You bad girl, look what you did to Me!

EVE, *covering her face*: I'm ashamed.

GOD: Ashamed! You don't know the half of it.

> I will greatly multiply thy sorrow and thy conception;
> In sorrow thou shalt bring forth children—

EVE: Oh God!

GOD:

> And thy desire shall be to thy husband
> And he shall rule over thee.

> No more equals, you hear? He's the boss forever. Pull up your leaf.

> *He turns to Adam.* And as for you, schmuck!

> Cursed is the ground for thy sake,
> In sorrow shalt thou eat of it all the days of thy life.
> Thorns and thistles shall it bring forth to thee!
> No more going around just picking up lunch.
> In the sweat of thy face shalt thou eat bread,
> Till thou return unto the ground;
> Yes, my friend, now there is time and age and death,
> No more living forever. You got it?
> For dust thou art.
> And unto dust shalt thou return.

ADAM—*he sobs*: What am I doing? What's this water?

GOD:

> You're weeping, my son, those are your first tears;

> There will be more before you're finished.
> Now you have become as one of us,
> A little lower than the angels,
> Because now you know good and evil.
> Adam and Eve? Get out of the Garden.

ADAM: Out where?

GOD, *pointing*: There!

ADAM: But that's a desert!

GOD: Right! It wasn't good enough for you here? Go and see how you make out on your own.

ADAM: God. Dear God, isn't there any way we can get back in? I don't want to be ashamed, I don't want to be so full of sadness. It was so wonderful here, we were both so innocent!

GOD: Out! You know too much to live in Eden.

ADAM: But I am ignorant!

GOD:

> Knowing you are ignorant is too much to know.
> The lion and the elephant, the spider and the mouse—
> They will remain, but they know My perfection
> Without knowing it. You ate what I forbade,
> You yearned for what you were not
> And thus laid a judgment on My work.
> I Am What I Am What I Am, but it was not enough;
> The warmth in the sand, the coolness of water,
> The coming and going of day and night—
> It was not enough to live in these things.
> You had to have power, and power is in you now,
> But not Eden any more. Listen, Adam. Listen, Eve.
> Can you hear the coming of night?

ADAM—*surprised, he raises his head*: Why . . . no!

GOD: Can you hear the sound of shadows on the leaves?

EVE, *with immense loss and wonder*: No!

> *God turns his back on them, hurt, erect.*

EVE: Where is the voice of the trout talking in the river?

ADAM: Where are the footsteps of angels walking through the vines?

> *On the verge of weeping, they are turning to catch the sounds they knew, deaf to the world. Light is playing on them as*

*instruments are heard playing a lugubrious tune. They deject-
edly leave Paradise.*

*A sad bassoon solo emerges, played by Raphael. God, hands
behind his back, turns to Raphael, Chemuel, and Azrael, who
enter together.*

GOD: That is the most depressing instrument I have ever heard.

RAPHAEL, *the bassoonist, protesting*: But You invented it, Lord.

GOD: I can't imagine how I could have thought of such a thing.

CHEMUEL: It was just after Eve ate the apple. You were very down. And
You said, "I think I will invent the bassoon."

GOD: Well, put it away, Raphael.

AZRAEL: Look at Adam and Eve down there. All they do any more is screw.

CHEMUEL: Maybe we ought to talk about something cheerful.

GOD: Do that, yes.

Pause. The angels think.

CHEMUEL: I think the Rocky Mountains are the best yet! *God turns to
him, pained.* I mean the way they go up.

RAPHAEL: And then the way they go down.

GOD: I'm afraid that Lucifer was the only one of you who knew how to
carry on a conversation.

AZRAEL, *a fierce fellow, deep-throated*: I would like to kill Adam and Eve.

GOD: That's natural, Azrael, as the Angel of Death, but I'm not ready for
that yet.

AZRAEL: They like to swim; I could drown them. Or push them over a
cliff—

GOD, *pained*: Don't say those things, stop it.

AZRAEL: I have to say, Lord, I warned You at the time: You mustn't make
a creature that looks like You, or You'll *never* let me kill him.

CHEMUEL: It was such a pleasure with the lions and the gorillas.

GOD: Yes, but—*He looks down at the earth*—when they're good it makes
me feel so marvelous.

AZRAEL: But how often are they good?

GOD: I know, but when they praise My name and all that. There's nothing
like it. When they send up those hallelujahs from Notre Dame—

AZRAEL: Notre Dame!

RAPHAEL: Lord, Notre Dame isn't for six thousand years.

GOD: I know, but I'm looking forward. *He stands, shocked, His eye caught by something below.* Look at that! How do they think up such positions?

AZRAEL: I don't understand why You let them go on offending You like this. You called back other mistakes—the fish with fur who drowned—

CHEMUEL: And the beetle who hiccupped whenever it snowed.

AZRAEL: Why don't You let me go down and wipe them out?

GOD: They are the only ones who need Me.

CHEMUEL: Sure! Give them a chance.

GOD: I'll never forget the first time I realized what I meant to them. It was the first time Adam laid her down and went into her. She closed her eyes, and she began to breathe so deeply I thought she'd faint, or die, or explode. And suddenly she cried out, "Oh dear God!" I have never heard My name so genuinely praised.

AZRAEL: I find the whole spectacle disgusting.

GOD: I know. It's the worst thing that ever happened. *He is in conflict, staring.* It can't go on this way; I must have it out with Lucifer.

ALL: Lucifer!

GOD, *energetically*: I have never before been in conflict with Myself. Look at it; My poor, empty Eden; the ripened peach falls uneaten to the ground, and My two idiotic darlings roam the desert scrounging for a crust. It has definitely gone wrong. And not one of you has an idea worth talking about. Clear away; I must decide.

CHEMUEL: Decide what, Lord?

GOD: I don't know yet, but a decision is definitely rising in Me. And that was the one thing Lucifer always knew—the issue. Go. *Chemuel throws up his hands.*

ALL, *singing*: Hallelujah, hallelujah . . .

The angels are walking out.

GOD: One more.

ALL: Hallelujah!

They go. God is alone. He concentrates. Lucifer appears.

LUCIFER, *wary, looking for cues to God's attitude*: Thank You, Father. I have been waiting. I am ready to face my ordeal.

GOD: Lucifer, I have been struggling to keep from destroying you. The Law of the Conservation of Energy does not protect an angel from being broken into small pieces and sprinkled over the Atlantic Ocean.

LUCIFER: Wouldn't that just spread him around, though?

GOD: What restrains me is a feeling that somewhere in the universe a stupendous event has occurred. For an instant it made Me terribly happy. I thought it might be the icecaps, but they're not really working out.

LUCIFER: Trouble?

GOD: There is a definite leak.

LUCIFER: Can You repair it?

GOD: I've decided to let them run. It will mean a collection of large lakes across North America, and some in Europe.

LUCIFER: Oh, Father, surely You planned it that way.

GOD: I see now what I probably did; but frankly I wasn't thinking of the lakes; I simply felt there should be icecaps on both poles. But that's the way it is—one thing always leads to another.

LUCIFER: Then you must already know the fantastic news I've brought You.

GOD, *staring for his thought*: I undoubtedly do. *At a loss*: Happy news.

LUCIFER: Glorious.

GOD: I knew it! In the very midst of all my disappointments I suddenly felt a sort of . . . hopeful silence.

LUCIFER: The silent seed of Adam squirming into Eve's ovarian tube.

GOD, *striking His forehead*: Aaaaah! Of course! And the ovum?

LUCIFER: Has been fertilized.

GOD: And has attached itself . . .

LUCIFER: To the womb. It is holding on nicely.

GOD: Then so far—

LUCIFER: So good. I can't see any reason to worry.

GOD, *clapping His hands*: My first upright pregnancy! *Worried*: Maybe she ought to lie down more.

LUCIFER: Lord, she could stand on her head and not lose it.

GOD: And how is she feeling?

LUCIFER: I thought I'd ask You about that. She is slightly nauseated in the mornings.

GOD: That is partly disgust with herself. At least I hope so. But it is also the blood supply diverting to the womb.

LUCIFER: I never thought of that! In any case, it works.

GOD: How utterly, utterly superb.

LUCIFER: Oh, dear Father, ever since my interview with Eve I've been terrified You'd never speak to me again. And now when I so want to thank You properly, all metaphor, simile, and image scatter before this victory of ours. *God becomes alert.* Like the firm cheek of Heaven, the wall of her womb nuzzles the bud of the first son of man.

GOD: Say that again?

LUCIFER: Like the firm—

GOD: No, before that.

>   *Slight pause.*

LUCIFER: But surely it was all according to plan?

GOD, *peering at him*: According to . . . ?

LUCIFER: It was supposed to happen through me. Of course I am perfectly aware that I merely acted as Your agent.

GOD: Not on your life! They would have made it in Paradise, clean and innocent, and with My blessing instead of My curse!

LUCIFER: But the fact is, they were not making it!

GOD: They might have by accident!

LUCIFER: Father, I can't believe a technicality is more important than this service to Your cause.

GOD: Technicality! I am going to condemn you, Lucifer.

LUCIFER: Dear God, for what? For making You a grandfather?

GOD: I forbade those apples! Nobody violates a Commandment, I don't care how good it comes out!

LUCIFER: You mean the letter of the law is more important than the survival of the human race? *God is silent. A smile breaks onto Lucifer's face.* This is a test, isn't it? You're testing me? *God is inscrutable.* That's all right, don't answer. Now I will confess myself and prove that I finally understand my part in the Plan.

GOD: What Plan? What are you talking about?

LUCIFER: Your hidden Plan for operating the world. All my life, sir, I've had the feeling that I was somehow . . . a *useless* angel. I look at Azrael, so serious and grave, perfect for the Angel of Death. And our sweet Chemuel—exactly right for the Angel of Mercy. But when I tried to examine *my* character, I could never find any. Gorgeous profile, superb intelligence, but what was Lucifer *for*? Am I boring You?

GOD: Not at all.

LUCIFER, *worried*: How do you mean that? *God simply looks at him.* Good, good—don't make it easy for me. I will now explain about the apple. You see, I'd gone down there to help You, but she took one bite and that innocent stare erupted with such carnal appetite that I began to wonder, was it possible I had actually done something— *He breaks off.*

GOD: Evil?

LUCIFER: Oh, that terrible word! But now I will face it! *The desperate yet joyful confession.* Father, I've *always* had certain impulses that mystified me. If I saw my brother angels soaring upwards, my immediate impulse was to go down. A raspberry cane bends to the right, I'd find myself leaning left. Others praise the forehead, I am drawn to the ass. Holes—I don't want to leave anything out—I adore holes. Every hole is precious to me. I'll go even further—in excrement, decay, the intestine of the world is my stinking desire. You ever hear anything so straightforwardly disgusting? I tell you I have felt so worthless, I was often ready to cut my throat. But Eve is pregnant now, and I see the incredible, hidden truth.

GOD: Which is?

LUCIFER: How can I be rotten? How else but through my disobedience was Eve made pregnant with mankind? How dare I hate myself? Not only am I not rotten—I am God's corrective symmetry, that festering embrace which keeps His world from impotent virtue. And once I saw that, I saw Your purpose working through me and I nearly wept with self-respect. And I fell in love—with both of us. *Slight pause. God is motionless.* Well, that's—the general idea, right?

GOD: Lucifer, you are a degenerate! You are a cosmic pervert!

LUCIFER: But God in Heaven, who made me this way?

God whacks him across the face; Lucifer falls to his knees.

GOD: Don't you ever, ever say that.

LUCIFER: Adonoi elohaenu, adonoi echaud. Father, I know Your anger is necessary, but my love stands fast!

GOD: Love! The only love you know is for yourself! You think I haven't seen you standing before a mirror whole years at a time!

LUCIFER: I have, Lord, admiring Your handiwork.

GOD: How can you lie like this and not even blush!

LUCIFER: All right! *He stands up. Now* I will tell You the Truth! *At the pinnacle*: Lord, I am ready to take my place beside the throne.

GOD: Beside the *what?*

LUCIFER: Why, the throne, Lord. At Your right hand. If not the right, then the left. I can suggest a title: Minister of Excremental Matters. I can walk with a limp, now watch this. *He walks, throwing one leg out spastically.*

GOD: What is this?

LUCIFER: And I do a tic, You see? *He does a wild tic as he walks crazily.*

GOD: What are you doing?

LUCIFER: I'll stutter, too. *Horribly*: Whoo, wha—munnnn—

GOD: What is this?

LUCIFER: I'll wear a hunch back and masturbate incessantly, eternal witness that God loves absolutely everything He made! What a *lesson!* But before you answer—the point, the far-reaching ultimate, is that this will change the future. Do You remember the future, Lord?

GOD: Of course I remember the future.

LUCIFER: It is a disaster; it is one ghastly war after another down through the centuries.

GOD: You can never change the future. The past, yes, but not the future.

LUCIFER: How do you change the past?

GOD: Why, the past is always changing—nobody remembers anything. But the future can no more be turned away than the light flowing off the moon.

LUCIFER: Unless we stood together, Lord, You immaculate on Your throne, absolutely good, and I beside You, perfectly evil. Father and son, the two inseparable buddies. *God is caught by it.* There could never, never be war! You see it, I can see You see it! If good and evil stand as one, what'll they have to fight about? What army could ever mobilize if on all the flags was written: "For God and Country and the Stinking Devil"? Without absolute righteousness there can never be a war! We will flummox the generals! Father, you are a handshake away from a second Paradise! Peace on earth to the end of time. *God is peering, feverish.* And that, sir, is your entire plan for me as I see it.

GOD: In other words, I would no longer be absolutely right.

LUCIFER: Just in public, sir. Privately, of course—*a gesture connecting them*—we know what's what.

GOD: We do.

LUCIFER: Oh Lord, I have no thought of . . . actually—

GOD: Sharing power.

LUCIFER: God forbid. I'm speaking purely of the image.

GOD: But in reality . . .

LUCIFER: Nothing's changed. You're good, and I'm bad. It's just that to the public—

GOD: We will appear to be—

LUCIFER: Yes.

GOD: Equal.

LUCIFER: Not morally equal. Just equally real. Because if I'm sitting beside You in Heaven—

GOD: Then I must love you.

LUCIFER: Exactly. And if God can love the Devil, He can love absolutely anybody.

GOD: *That's* certainly true, yes.

LUCIFER: So people would never come to hate themselves, and there's the end of guilt. Another Eden, and everybody innocent again.

    Pause.

GOD: Operationally speaking—

LUCIFER: Yes.

GOD: Yes *sir.*

LUCIFER: Yes sir. Excuse me.

GOD: In cases of lying, cheating, fornication, murder, and so on—you mean they are no longer to be judged?

LUCIFER: Oh, on the contrary! Between the two of us *no one* will escape the judgment of Heaven. I'll judge the bad people, and you judge the good.

GOD: But who would try to be good if it's just as good to be bad?

LUCIFER: And will the bad be good for fear of your judgment? So you may as well let them be bad and the good be good, and either way they'll all love God because they'll know that God . . . loves . . . me. Sir, I am ready to take my place. Between the two of us we'll have mankind mouse-trapped.

GOD: Yes. *Slight pause.* There is only one problem.

LUCIFER: But basically that's the Plan, isn't it?

GOD: There is a problem.

LUCIFER: What's that?

GOD, *looking straight at him*: I don't love you.

LUCIFER, *shocked—he can hardly speak*: You can't mean that.

GOD: Afraid I do.

LUCIFER: Well. *He gives a deflated laugh.* This is certainly a surprise.

GOD: I see that. And it is fundamentally why we can never sit together. Nothing is real to you. Except your appetite for distinction and power. I've been waiting for some slightest sign of repentance for what you did to Paradise, but there's nothing, is there? Instead, I'm to join you in a cosmic comedy where good and evil are the same. It doesn't occur to you that I am unable to share the bench with the very incarnation of all I despise?

LUCIFER: I can't believe You'd let Your feelings stand in the way of peace.

GOD: But that is why I am perfect—I *am* my feelings.

LUCIFER: You don't think that's a limitation?

GOD: It certainly is. I am perfectly limited. Where evil begins, I end. When good loves evil, it is no longer good, and if God could love the Devil, then God has died. And that is precisely what you're after, isn't it?

LUCIFER: I am after peace! Between us and mankind!

GOD: Then let there be war! Better ten thousand years of war than I should rule one instant with the help of unrighteousness!

LUCIFER: Lord God, I am holding out my hand!

GOD, *rising*:

>Go to Hell! Now thou art Fallen in all thy beauty.
>As the rain doth fall and green the grass
>And the fish out of water suffocates,
>So dost thy fall prove that there are consequences.
>Now die in Heaven, Lucifer, and live in Hell
>That man may ever know how good and evil separate!

LUCIFER: Lord? *He is upright, stern.* You will not take my hand?

GOD: Never! Never, never, never!

LUCIFER: Then I will take the world. *He exits.*

GOD, *calling*: And if you ever do, I will burn it, I will flood it out, I will leave it a dead rock spinning in silence! For I am the Lord, and the Lord is good and only good!

ANGELS' VOICES, *singing loudly and sharply*: Blessed is the Lord our God, Glory, glory, glory!

God sits, cleaved by doubt. He turns His head, looking about.

GOD: Why do I miss him? *He stares ahead.* How strange.

CURTAIN

ACT TWO

Darkness. The sound of a high wind. It dies off. A starry sky.

In the starlight, Adam and Eve are discovered asleep, but apart. He snores contentedly, she lies in silence on her back, her very pregnant belly arching up.

Lucifer, in black now, rises from the ground. He scans the sky for any sign of God, then looks down at the two people. In deep thought he walks to the periphery and sits, his chin on his fist, staring.

Overhead a bird begins to sing. He looks up.

LUCIFER: Oh, shut up. *The birdsong effloresces gloriously.* Will you get out of here? Go! Glorify the Lord some place else! *Flapping of wings. He follows the bird's flight overhead with his gaze.* Idiot. *Depressed, he stares ahead.* Everything I see throws up the same irrational lesson. The hungriest bird sings best. What a system! That deprivation should make music—is anarchy! And what is greatness in God's world? A peaceful snake lies dozing in the sun with no more dignity than a long worm; but let him arch his head to strike—and there, by God, is a *snake*! Yes! I have reasoned, pleaded, argued, when only murder in this world makes majesty—God's included. Was He ever Godlier, ever more my king than when He murdered my hopes? And will I ever be more than a ridiculous angel—*he turns to Adam and Eve*—until I murder His? *He stands, goes to Eve, looks down at her.* Where is His dearest hope in all the world—but in that belly? *He suddenly raises his foot to stomp her, then retracts.* No. N-no. Let her do it. Make her do it. *He looks skyward.* Oh, the shock, the shock! If she refused the Lord the fruit of man because He made the world unreasonable! *He inspires himself, slowly sinking to the ground, and insinuates into Eve's ear:* This is a dream. *He ceremoniously lifts his hand and with his middle finger touches her forehead.* I enter the floor of thy skull. *He bends and kisses her belly.* Now, woman, help me save the world from the anarchy of God. *She inhales sensuously, and her knee rises, her cloak falling away, exposing a bare thigh.* Your time has come, dear woman. *He slides his hand along her thigh.*

EVE, *exhaling pleasurably:* Aaaaaahhh!

LUCIFER: Sssh! Don't wake up; the only safe place to have this conversation is inside your head. Am I clear in your mind? Do you remember me?

EVE: Oh, yes! When our fingers touched around the apple—

LUCIFER: Flesh to naked flesh!

EVE: And I awoke and saw myself! How beautiful I was! *She opens her eyes.*

LUCIFER: What in the world has happened to you? How'd you get so ugly?

EVE, *covering her face*: I can't stand myself!

LUCIFER: When I think how you looked in Paradise—*she weeps*— Why did you let yourself go?

EVE: Can you help me, angel? Something's got into my belly, and it keeps getting bigger.

LUCIFER: No idea what it is?

EVE: Well . . . I *have* been eating a lot of clams lately.

LUCIFER: Clams.

EVE: Sometimes it even squirms. *Lucifer looks away in thought.* Isn't that it?

LUCIFER, *turning back to her*: Like to have it out?

EVE, *clapping her hands*: Could I?

LUCIFER: But are you sure you won't change your mind afterwards?

EVE: No! I want to be as I was. Please, angel, take thy power and drive it out.

LUCIFER: Lie back, dear.

EVE: Oh, thank you, angel, I will adore you forever!

LUCIFER, *starting to spread her knees*: I certainly hope so. Now just try to relax. . . .

EVE, *on her back, facing the sky, her arms stretched upward*: Oh, won't the Lord be happy when he sees me looking good again! *Lucifer removes his hands, instantly turning away to think. She, on her back, can't see what he is doing.* Is anything happening?

LUCIFER, *drawing her upright*: Woman, I don't want you hating me in the morning; now listen, and I will waken your mind as once I awakened your body in Paradise.

EVE: By the way, I've been wanting to ask you: did you ever come to me again—*after* Paradise?

LUCIFER, *evasively*: Why do you ask?

EVE: Near twilight, once, I was lying on my stomach, looking at my face in a pool; and suddenly a strange kind of weight pressed down on my back, and it pressed and pressed until we seemed to go tumbling out like dragonflies above the water. And in my ear a voice kept whispering, "This is God's will, darling. . . ."

LUCIFER: Which it was, at the time.

EVE, *marveling*: It was you!

LUCIFER: All me. About nine months ago.

EVE, *gleefully*: Oh, angel, that was glorious! Come, make me beautiful again! *She starts to lie back; he stops her.*

LUCIFER: You will have it out, Eve, but it's important there be no recriminations afterwards, so I'm going to tell you the truth. I have been thrown out of Heaven.

EVE: How's that possible? You're an *angel*!

LUCIFER: Dear girl, we are dealing with a spirit to whom nothing is sacred.

EVE: But why? What did you do?

LUCIFER: What He could not do. *He breaks off.*

EVE: What?

LUCIFER, *taking the plunge*: I caused you to multiply.

EVE: You mean—*she looks down at her belly*—I'm multiplying?

LUCIFER: What you have in your belly . . . is a man.

EVE: A man! *Overjoyed, she rolls back onto the ground.* In me!

LUCIFER: Remember what you said! You want it out!

EVE, *sitting up*: How is God feeling about me? Does He know?

LUCIFER: All right, then. Yes, He knows and He is ecstatic!

EVE: Oh, praise the Lord!

LUCIFER, *furiously*: Quadruple hallelujahs!

EVE: Glory to Him in the highest!

LUCIFER: Precisely. *Jabbing his finger at her*: And now I'll bet your agony begins!

EVE, *with a shock of pain*: Aaaahhhhh!

LUCIFER: Why'd you stop praising Him? *She yells in pain.* Where's the hallelujah?

EVE: What is happening to me?

LUCIFER: What're you complaining about? You praise God, and this is what you get for it!

EVE: But why?

LUCIFER: Don't you remember Him cursing you out of Paradise?

EVE: And this—

LUCIFER: Is it, honey.

EVE, *pointing to the sleeping Adam*: But he ate the apple too!

LUCIFER: Right. And he looks better than ever.

EVE, *furiously pounding her hands on the ground*: WHY?

LUCIFER, *grabbing her face, driving his point home*: Because this is the justice of the world He made, and only you can change that world!

EVE: Angel . . . it's getting worse.

LUCIFER: Oh, it'll get worse than this, dear.

EVE: It can't get worse!

LUCIFER: Oh yes, it can, because He's perfect, and when He makes something worse, it's *perfectly* worse!

EVE: Oh God, what have I done!

LUCIFER: You multiplied with my help, not with His, and your agony is His bureaucratic revenge. Now listen to me—

EVE: I can't stand any more! *Lashing about on the ground.* Where's a rock, I'll kill him! *With clawed hands she starts for Adam.*

LUCIFER: He is as innocent as you!

EVE, *bursting into helpless tears*: This is not *right*!

LUCIFER: Oh, woman, to hear that word at last from other lips than mine! It is not right, no—it is chaos. Eve, you are the only voice of reason God's insane world can ever have, for in you alone His chaos shows its claws. *In poene veritas*—the only truth is pain. Now mount it and take your power.

EVE: What power? I'm a grain of dust.

LUCIFER: He is pacing up and down in Heaven waiting for this child. You have in your belly the crown of God.

EVE: The crown . . . ?

LUCIFER: His highest honor is your gratitude for the agony He is giving you. He is a maniac! *He takes her hand.* You can refuse. You must deny this crown to chaos. Kill it. *He is behind her, his lips to her ear, his hand on her belly.*

Let the serpent in again, and we'll murder him,
And so teach the Lord His first humility.

He slips around in front of her, starting to press her back to the ground.

Crown His vengeance on thee not with life
But with a death; a lump of failure
Lay before the Lord a teaching, woman—

EVE, *in conflict, resisting his pressure to lie down*: I teach God?

LUCIFER:

Teach God, yes!—that if men must be born
Only in the pain of unearned sin,
Then there will be no men at all!
Open to me!

He tries to spread her legs, she reaches uncertainly to his face, while trying to fend his hands off.

EVE: Angel, I'm afraid!

LUCIFER: Hold still! *He is on top of her to pin her down.*

EVE: I don't think I can do that!

LUCIFER: Open up, you bitch! *He violently tries to spread her knees, she breaks free, skittering away on the ground.*

EVE: I can't! I mustn't! I won't! *Sexually infuriated, he starts again for her.* I want him! *Adam turns over. Lucifer springs out of her line of sight so that she is looking around at empty space, holding her belly. In short, she has only now awakened in the dream's hangover. Day is drawning.* Where am I? *The baaing of sheep is heard.*

LUCIFER:

The dream ends here, a dark rehearsal of the coming day;
This day you must decide—to crown unreason with thy gift of life,
Or with a tiny death teach justice. *He bends and kisses her.*
I understand thee, woman—I alone.
Call any time at all.

Intimately, pointing into her face: You know what I mean.

Adam sits up. Lucifer goes. Day dawns. Adam stares at Eve, as she sits there. Now she brings her body forward and wipes her eyes.

ADAM: What a night! I don't think I slept five minutes. *She gives him a look.* Did you?

EVE, *after a slight pause, guiltily*: I slept very well, yes.

Disturbed, inward, she gets up, begins gathering pieces of wood for the fire. The baaing of sheep is heard.

ADAM, *looking around*: Say! *She stops moving, looks at him.* The wind! It finally stopped! See? I told you I'd find a place that's not windy!

A blast of howling wind makes them both huddle into their clothes. It dies off. She gets out some figs, places them in a bowl.

EVE: There's your figs.

ADAM: Could it be, you suppose, that everywhere but in Paradise it's just naturally windy? *He bites into a fig.*

EVE: I just don't know, Adam.

ADAM—*he spits out sand*: They're sandy.

EVE: Well, it's windy.

He leans his head on his fist disconsolately.

ADAM: What a way to live! At least if I knew how long it was going to last—

EVE: I still don't understand what's so wrong about digging a hole. We could sit in it and keep out of the wind. Like the groundhogs.

ADAM: I wish you'd stop trying to change the rules! We're not groundhogs. If He meant us to live in holes, He would have given us claws.

EVE: But if He meant us to live in a windstorm He'd have put our eyes in our armpits. *Another blast of wind, then it dies.*

ADAM: Aren't you eating anything?

EVE: I don't feel like it.

ADAM: You know something? You don't look so green today.

EVE, *faintly hopeful, a little surprised at his interest*: I don't?

ADAM: All your color came back. What happened? *He slides over to her, looking quizzically and somewhat excitedly into her face.* You look beautiful, Eve.

EVE—*she laughs nervously*: Well, I can't imagine why!

ADAM, *pushing her back, starting to open her cloak*: It's amazing! I haven't seen you look this way since Paradise! *His hand on her swollen belly stops him.* Oh, excuse me.

EVE, *grasping his hand*: That's all right!

ADAM, *getting up, sliding his hand out of hers*: I forgot that thing. *He stands, looks around.* What a funny morning!

EVE: Why do you always look around like that?

ADAM, *after a slight pause*: I miss God.

EVE, *looking down in sorrow*: I'm sorry, Adam. *Sheep are heard again.*

ADAM, *looking off*: It is just that I'm never really sure what to do next. That grass is giving out; we'll have to move this afternoon.

EVE: I don't think I can walk very far.

ADAM: Goddamn clams . . .

EVE: I'm always out of breath, Adam. This thing has gotten very heavy.

ADAM: Does it still move?

EVE: It's doing it now. Would you like to feel it?

ADAM, *touching her belly*: Huh!

EVE: It's almost like a little foot pressing.

ADAM: A foot! No. *He presses his stomach.* I have the same thing sometimes.

EVE, *with sudden hope*: You too? Let me feel it! *She feels his stomach.* I don't feel anything.

ADAM: Well, it stopped. I can't remember—did He say to kill clams before eating?

EVE: But they squash so.

ADAM: I'm not sure we're supposed to eat live things. I can't remember half the things He said any more.

EVE, *tentatively, with some trepidation*: Can I talk to you about that? I'm not sure any more it is those clams.

ADAM: Don't worry, it's the clams. Sits down and eats maybe fifty clams, and suddenly it's not the clams.

EVE: Well, I *like* clams. Especially lately.

ADAM: I like eggs.

EVE: Adam, dear, there's something I feel I should tell you.

ADAM: I had three delicious eggs last— *He breaks off, recalling.* No, no, that was a dream!

EVE, *startled*: You dreamed?

ADAM: Why, did you?

EVE, *quickly*: Tell me yours first.

ADAM: I . . . was in Paradise. Huh! Remember those breakfasts there?

EVE: I wasn't there long enough for breakfast. I was born just before lunch. And I never even got that.

ADAM: Pity you missed it. What a dream! Everything was just the way it used to be. I woke up, and there He was—

EVE: God.

ADAM: Yes. And He brought a tray—and about six beautifully scrambled eggs.

EVE, *with guilt and hunger*: Ohhh!

ADAM: And no sand whatsoever. I guess it was Sunday because there was also a little tray of warm croissants.

EVE, *sadly charmed*: And then?

ADAM: Same as always—I named a few things. And then we took a nice nap. And angels were playing some soft music. *He hums, trying to recall the tune.* How perfect it all was!

EVE: Until I showed up.

ADAM: Yes. *He looks about with a heightened longing, and, seeing this, she weeps.*

EVE: I don't know why He made me!

ADAM: Well, don't cry, maybe we'll find out some day. I'll round up the sheep. *He starts out.*

EVE—*trying not to call him, she does*: Adam!

ADAM, *halting*: You'll just have to walk. That thing might go away if you get some exercise. *He moves to go.*

EVE: An angel came.

ADAM: When?

EVE: Last night.

ADAM—*happily astounded, he rushes to her*: Which one?

EVE, *fearfully*: It was, ah . . .

ADAM: Chemuel?

EVE: No, not Chemuel.

ADAM: Raphael? Michael?

EVE, *holding her forehead*: No.

ADAM: Well, what'd he look like? Short or tall?

EVE: Quite tall.

ADAM: It wasn't God, was it?

EVE: Oh, not God.

ADAM: What'd he want?

EVE: I—I can't remember it clearly.

ADAM: Was it about getting back into Paradise?

EVE: Well, no. . . .

ADAM: About what we're supposed to do next?

EVE: Not exactly. . . .

ADAM: Why didn't you wake me up?

EVE: I couldn't move!

ADAM: You mean God sends an angel down, and you can't even remember what he said?

EVE: It was about this—*she touches her belly*—thing.

ADAM, *disbelieving; in fact, with disappointment*: About that?

EVE—*she looks up at him*: Would you sit down, Adam? I think I know what we're supposed to do now. *He senses something strange, sits on his heels.* He came through the mist. Like the mist on the sea. Smoke rose from his hair, and his hands smoked.

> *Lucifer materializes; motionless, he stands in his terrible beauty at the periphery.*

ADAM, *with wonder*: Ahhh!

EVE: And he said— *She breaks off in fear as she feels the attraction of the Evil One.*

ADAM: What?

> *A blast of wind. They huddle. It dies. She has remained staring ahead. Now she turns to him.*

EVE: That angel opened my eyes, Adam. I see it all very clearly now—with you the Lord was only somewhat disappointed, but with me He was furious. *Lucifer gravely nods.* And His curse is entirely on me. It is the reason why you've hardly changed out here in the world; but I bleed, and now I am ugly and swollen up like a frog. And I never dream of Paradise, but you do almost every night, and you seem to expect to find it over every hill. And that is right—I think now that you belong in Eden. But not me. And as long as I am with you, you will never find it again. *Slight pause.* Adam, I haven't the power to move from this place, and this is the proof that I must stay here, and you—go back to Paradise.

ADAM, *in conflict with his wishes*: Alone?

EVE: He would lead you there if you walked away alone. You are thirsting for Eden, and the Lord knows that.

ADAM: But so are you.

EVE: Eden is not in me any more.

　　Lucifer seems to expand with joy.

ADAM: Eve!

EVE: I disgust Him! I am abominable to Him!

ADAM: But the Lord said we are to cleave to one another. I don't think I'm *supposed* to go.

EVE, *bursting into tears, as much with pity for him as with her own indignation*: But you don't like me any more either!

ADAM, *pointing at her belly*: That thing—that thing is what I cannot bear! It turns my stomach! I can't seem to get near you any more! Every time I turn around I'm bumping into it! *She cries louder, turns to find herself face to face with Lucifer.* I don't understand you. Do you *like* that thing?

EVE, *turning back to him from the tempting angel*: I—I don't know!

ADAM: Because if it moves it's alive, and if it's alive we could just hit it! *She gasps, holding her belly.* There, you see? You like it! And this is why I don't know where I am any more! I told you when it started, if you jumped up and down—

EVE: I did jump!

ADAM: You did not jump. You went like that. *He makes a few measly hops.*

EVE: I jumped as hard as I could!

ADAM: I think you're taking *care* of that thing! *Jealously.* You know what's in there, don't you?

EVE, *crying out*: I love thee, husband, and I know this thing will be thy curse!

ADAM: Woman, you will tell me what is in thy belly!

EVE, *clapping her hands over her eyes*: It is a death!

> *Pause.*

ADAM: Whose death?

> *Pause. Eve lowers her hands, staring ahead.*

EVE: Its own.

> *Pause.*

ADAM: Who told thee?

EVE: Lucifer.

ADAM: You're seeing Lucifer again?

EVE: I screamed, but you didn't hear me!

ADAM: Well, I was sleeping!

EVE: You're always sleeping! Every time that son of a bitch comes around, you're someplace else! I would never have touched that apple in the first place if you hadn't left me alone with him!

ADAM: Well, I was *swimming*!

EVE: If you're not swimming, you're sleeping!

ADAM: You mean I can't turn my back for a minute on my own *wife*?

EVE: I couldn't help it, it was like a dream!

ADAM: I don't know how a decent woman can dream about the Devil!

EVE: Adam—he's not all bad.

ADAM: He's not all . . . ! *Light dawns in his head.* Ohhhh! No wonder you looked so juicy when you woke up! I want to know what's so good about him!

EVE, *clapping her hands to her ears*: I can't stand any more!

ADAM, *furiously*: God said I am thy master, woman, and you are going to tell me what went on here! No wonder I haven't been able to get near you. There's been something strange about you for months!

EVE: There is a man in my belly, Adam.

ADAM, *chilled with astonishment, wonder, fear*: A man.

EVE: He told me.

> *Long pause.*

ADAM: How could a man fit in there?

EVE: Well . . . small. To start off with. Like the baby monkeys and the little zebras—

ADAM: Zebras! He's got you turning us into animals now? No human being has ever been born except grown-up! I may be confused about a lot of things, but I know facts!

EVE: But it's what God said—we were to go forth and multiply.

ADAM, *striking his chest indignantly*: If we're going to multiply, it'll be through me! Same as it always was! What am I going to do with you? After everything he did to us with his goddamned lies, you still—

EVE: Husband, he told me to do with it exactly what you have told me to do with it.

ADAM, *struck*: What I . . . ?

EVE: He told me it is a man and he told me to kill it. What the Devil hath spoken, thou hast likewise spoken.

> *Silence. Neither moves. One sheep baas, like a sinister snarl.*
> *A sudden surge of wind, which quickly dies.*

ADAM, *tortured*: But I had no idea it was a man when I said that.

EVE, *holding her belly, with a long gaze beyond them both*: Adam . . . I believe I am meant to bring out this man—alone.

ADAM, *furiously, yet unable to face her directly*: Are you putting me with that monster?

EVE: But why do you all want him dead!

ADAM: I forbid you to say that again! I am not Lucifer! *A heartbroken cry escapes him.* Eve! *He sinks to his knees. He curls up in ignominy, then prostrates himself before her, flat out on the ground, pressing his lips to her foot.* Forgive me! *He weeps. Wind blasts. It dies.*

EVE—*a new thought interrupts her far-off gaze, and she looks at his prostrate body*: Will you dig us a hole?

ADAM—*he joyously scrambles up and kisses her hand*: A hole!

EVE: It needn't be too big—

ADAM: What do you mean? I'll dig you the biggest hole you ever saw in your life! Woman . . . *With a cry of gratitude he sweeps her into his arms.* Woman, thou art my salvation!

EVE: Oh, my darling, that's so good to hear!

ADAM: How I thirst for thee! My doe, my rabbit . . .

EVE: My five-pointed buck, my thundering bull!

ADAM, *covering his crotch*: Oh, Eve, thy forgiveness hath swelled me like a ripened ear of corn.

EVE: Oh, how sweet. Then I will forgive thee endlessly.

> *Lucifer shows alarm and rising anger.*

ADAM: Say, now, the Lord will probably expect me to think of a name for him. Or do you want to? *He indicates her belly.*

EVE: No, you. You're so good at names.

ADAM—*he thinks, paces*: Well, let's see . . .

EVE: I'll be quiet. *She watches him with pleasure.* It ought to be something clear, and clean and—something for a *handsome* man.

ADAM: Y'know, when I saw the first giraffe—it may not fit, but it went through my mind at the time.

EVE: What?

ADAM: Frank?

EVE: Don't you think that's a little too, ah . . . ?

ADAM: I guess so, yes. Maybe it ought to begin with A. ⎱ *Simultaneously*
EVE: . . . to begin with an A. ⎰

> *They point at each other and laugh.*

ADAM: I mean because he's the first. ⎱ *Simultaneously*
EVE: He's the first. ⎰

> *They laugh again.*

EVE: Isn't it marvelous that we both have the same thoughts . . . ⎱ *Simultaneously*
ADAM: Both have the same thoughts. ⎰

EVE, *in the clear*: . . . again!

ADAM, *lifting his arms thankfully*: What a God we have!

EVE: How perfectly excellent is the Lord!

> *Lucifer throws up his hands and goes into darkness, holding his head.*

ADAM, *suddenly looking down at the ground, astonished*: Eve?

EVE: What, my darling?

ADAM: Is this grass growing?

EVE, *looking about quickly at the ground*: I believe it is!

ADAM: *looking front*: Look at the pasture! It's up to their bellies!

EVE: Adam, the wind . . . !

> *They look up and around. There is silence.*

ADAM: Woman, we must have done something right! *He looks upward.* I think He loves us again.

EVE—*her hands shoot up, open-palmed, her eyes wide with terror*: Sssh!

ADAM: Could it possibly be . . .

EVE, *a hand moving toward her belly*: Ssh, sh!

ADAM: . . . that the curse is over? *She grips her belly. She suddenly rushes right and is stopped by a wild, curling cry of a high-screaming French horn. He is oblivious to the sound.* What are you doing? *She turns and rushes upstage; he is starting after her, and she is stopped short by a whining blow on a timpani and a simultaneous snarling trumpet blast. He nearly catches her, but she gets away and is rushing left and is stopped by a pair of cacophonic flutes. He catches her now.* Eve! *She wrenches free of him—and she shows terror of him, and for an instant they are two yards apart, he uncomprehending, she in deadly fear of him. Protesting*: It's Adam. I am thy husband!

> *She rushes to a point and halts, crying upward.*

EVE: *Chemuuuuu-ellll!* Merciful sweet angel, take me out of myself! *She is seized by her agony and rolls over and over along the ground, as a massive cacophonic music flares up. Adam is put off, unmanned, afraid to touch her. She slams her hands on the ground as she writhes on her back.* God! Oh, God!

ADAM: Maybe it'll get better.

EVE: It will get worse. And when it gets worse it—*she sits up, recalling*—will get perfectly worse. . . . A contraction. Oh, God! *Stretching on her side, hands outstretched*: I call on any angel whatsoever!

ADAM, *calling upward*: Chemuel, come! Bring mercy!

EVE: Help me, demon! Come to me, Lucifer!

ADAM, *clapping his ears shut*: Aiiii!

EVE, *as though whipped, submissively begging*: Take out this agony! Demon, I am awake! Still me, angel! Take him out of my flesh!

ADAM, *falling to his knees*: God in Heaven, she is out of her mind!

EVE: I am *in* my mind—He never gave me a chance!

ADAM: Lord, give her a chance!

EVE: No, He loves this! God, if this is Thy pleasure, then I owe Thee nothing any more, and I call, I call, I call for—*A seizure, with each call she pounds the earth.* God. Oh, God. Oh, God. God—damn—you—God!

ADAM, *curled up in terror*: Aiiii!

> *Lucifer appears at the periphery.*

EVE: Still me, demon . . . take this out! Don't waste another minute! Not a minute more! He is bursting me! Kill him! Kill him!

> *Lucifer takes a step toward her and is halted by trumpets; a single melodious chord. She faints. Adam tries to rise and, seeing her, he faints too. God enters. A step behind Him are Azrael, Angel of Death, and Chemuel, Angel of Mercy.*

GOD, *standing over her, looking down*: Now bend, Azrael, and blow thy cold death across her lip. *Azrael bends and exhales over her face. Eve shudders as with icy cold and gasps in air, still asleep.* That's enough. Chemuel, in thy compassion, drive anguish to the corner of her mind, and seal it up. *Chemuel kneels, kisses her once. Eve exhales with relief. God walks a few yards away and sits.* Go away, Death. *Azrael stands fast.* Go, Azrael. And wait her need. *Azrael exits unwillingly.* Chemuel, in thy mercy, deliver Eve. *Chemuel reaches, lays his hand on her swollen belly, and with a short pull removes the swelling; clutching it to his breast, he starts to lean to kiss her again.* That's enough. *Chemuel hesitates, glancing up at God.* Go, Chemuel, and wait her need. *Chemuel stands and goes out.* Now in thy slumber let us reason together. *Adam and Eve sit up, their eyes shut in sleep.* Behold the stranger thine agony hath made. *A youth of sixteen appears, his eyes shut, his arms drawn in close to his body, his hands clasping his forward-tilted head. He moves waywardly, like a windblown leaf, and as he at last approaches Eve, he halts some feet away as God speaks again.* Here is the first life of thy life, woman. And it is fitting that the first letter stand before his name. But seeing that in thy extremity thou hast already offered his life to Lucifer; and seeing, Adam, that in your ignorance you have likewise threatened him with murder—*He loses his calm*—all of which amazes Me and sets My teeth on edge—*He breaks off, gritting His teeth*—I am nevertheless mindful that this child—*He turns to the youth*—is innocent. So we shall try again. And rather than call him Abel, who was in jeopardy, he shall be Cain, for his life's sake. *He stands.* Now Cain is born!

> *Cain lies down, coiled beside Eve. She sits up, opens her eyes, and looks down at Cain.*

EVE, *joyfully surprised*: Ahhh!

ADAM, *waking up quickly, seeing Cain*: What's that?

EVE: It is . . .

GOD: Cain. Thy son.

> *Both gasp, surprised by His presence.*

EVE—*she suddenly feels her flat belly and with a cry prostrates before God*: I see I have been favored of Thee, O Lord!

GOD, *indicating the inert Cain*: Here is thine innocence returned to thee, which thou so lightly cast away in Eden. Now protect him from the worm of thine own evil, which this day hath uncovered in thee. Look in My face, woman.

EVE, *covering her eyes*: I dare not, for I doubted Thy goodness!

GOD: And will you doubt Me any more?

EVE: Never, never, never!

GOD: Then lift up thine eyes.

> *She slowly dares to face Him on her knees.*

EVE: I have gotten a man from the Lord.

GOD: Thou art the mother of mankind.

EVE: And generations unknown to me shall spring from my loins. *He extends His hand. She rests hers on it and rises.*

> I am the river abounding in fish,
> I am the summer sun arousing the bee,
> As the rising moon is held in her place
> By Thine everlasting mind, so am I held
> In Thine esteem.

GOD: Eve, you are my favorite girl!

> *An angelic waltz strikes up. God sweeps Eve in a glorious dance all over the stage. Adam, happiness on his face, makes light and abortive attempts to cut in. God and Eve exit, dancing, Adam trailing behind and calling.*

ADAM: Eve! Look at Him dance! *Laughing, bursting with joy, he waltzes out after them.*

> *Lucifer, alone with Cain coiled up nearby, looks off toward the party and shakes his head.*

LUCIFER: You've got to hand it to Him. *He turns front, staring.* What a system! *Now he looks down at Cain.* So this is Cain. *He crouches over Cain.* With the kiss of Lucifer begin thy life; let my nature coil around thine own. And on thy shoulders, may I climb the throne. *He bends and kisses him.*

CURTAIN

ACT THREE

The family discovered asleep. A primitive shelter is suggested, hanging skins, and a cooking area in one corner. God is seated on a rock. He is thoughtfully watching them. He shakes his head, baffled, then raises a hand.

GOD: Azrael! *Azrael lights up behind the left screen.* Angel of Death, I have work for you today. The time has come when the human race will spread across the earth. But these people have all but forgotten God. They eat to live, and live to eat. By what law shall the multitudes be governed when even now my name is hardly mentioned any more? *Stands, looking down at the people.* Therefore, when this dawn comes, you will blow visions of death into their dreams. But be careful not to kill anybody; you are only to remind them that they cannot live forever. And having seen death, I hope they'll think of God again, and begin to face their terrible responsibilities. *Azrael starts to raise his arms.* Not yet!—wait till dawn. I want them to remember what they've dreamed when they awake. *To the people*: Dear people, I shall be watching every move you make today. *He exits. Lucifer comes up out of the trap. Looks about, notices a golden bowl, and picks it up.*

LUCIFER: Every time I come up here they've got more junk. What a race— a little prosperity and they don't even need the Devil.

EVE, *awakening*: What spirit art thou?

LUCIFER: It's me, honey.

EVE: Why don't you just go to hell and stay there?

LUCIFER: Darling, I'm terribly worried about your soul! A beautiful, intelligent woman like you can't waste her life just cooking and doing the house. You simply have no idea what you're missing!

EVE: I have absolutely everything I ever dreamed of, Angel. . . .

LUCIFER: But don't you want to broaden your horizons?

EVE: No! *She lies back down.*

LUCIFER: Whatever you say, darling. Sweet dreams, pretty girl. *Comes away with her.* For all the bad I've done I might as well have stayed in

Heaven. Only bad trouble will make them call to me for help. I'll break them apart!—or they'll turn the whole earth into this smug suburb of Heaven! Now let's see—Cain is jealous of his brother; suppose we start from there. . . . *He leaps to Cain when the light of dawn glows and Azrael appears behind the screen. Lucifer hides to observe him. Sotto:* Azrael? What's this about? *Azrael raises his caped arms menacingly.* My God, is somebody going to die? *Azrael blows three loud, short breaths. The people instantly groan. Azrael vanishes. Lucifer comes down to the people.* Groaning! Did he blow dreams of death into them?

ADAM—*sits up*: What a dream! *Eve turns to him expectantly.* I think I saw . . . something die.

EVE, *against her fear*: Maybe a sheep.

ADAM: No. It had a face.

LUCIFER: But none of them is old or sick—how do they die?

EVE: A *person's* face?

ADAM: Yes. And there was blood.

EVE: Blood!

LUCIFER: Blood?—Is he setting them up for a murder?—Of course! What better way to make them guilty and put the fear of God back into them! What a mistake I nearly made—I've got to keep them out of trouble, not get them into it.

CAIN, *sitting up*: What a dream!

ADAM AND EVE: What!

CAIN: I think I saw something die.

LUCIFER: And here's my opening at last! I'll stop this killing and they'll love me for it, and hate the Lord who has to have a death and their remorse! Oh, this is beautiful! But which one kills, and who's supposed to die? *He continuously moves around the periphery and sometimes in among them, searchingly, awaiting his opening.*

ABEL, *sitting up*: What a dream!

ADAM: That's enough. Eve, make breakfast.

ABEL: I was flying across the sky. . . .

EVE: But that's a wonderful dream!

ABEL: And then I fell. . . . *Mystified:* And an angel kissed me.

CAIN, *instantly—an exhale of recognition, his finger raised*: Ohhhhh! *All turn to him as he points to Abel.* I remember now. He died. *Eve gasps.*

EVE: Don't say that! *She gets up and goes to Abel and, holding his head in her arms, kisses him. Adam moves her aside, and he kisses him.*

LUCIFER: It's Abel who dies? But who kills him?

CAIN, *kisses Abel*: I saw thee on the ground, thy face crushed, and a blood-covered flail . . . rolling away.

ADAM: All right, now wait a minute.

CAIN, *turning to Adam*: How is it that he dies in my sleep? *Turning to Abel*: You haven't done anything, have you?

ABEL, *to Eve*: The minute anything happens he always blames me!

EVE: You two stop fighting.

ADAM: Now pay attention. Nobody ever dreamed of death before, so I don't want to hear any arguments of any kind whatsoever today.

LUCIFER: Good man! *To Eve*: Brighten it up.

EVE: I'll make a nice breakfast!

CAIN: Father. *Adam turns to him, sensing his strange intensity.* When you decided to leave Paradise, did God . . . ?

EVE: What's Paradise got to do with this?

CAIN: I wish we could talk about it, Mother! Didn't God give you any instructions when you left? I mean, how do we know we're saying the right prayers. Or maybe we don't pray enough.

ADAM: Oh, no I'm sure He'd let us know if we were doing something wrong.

CAIN: But maybe that's what the dream was for.

ADAM, *struck by this*: Say!

CAIN: Because lately when I'm out in the fields chopping weeds—it suddenly seems so strange . . .

EVE, *impatiently*: What, dear?

CAIN: Did God order you to make me the farmer and Abel to tend the sheep?

ADAM: You can't expect Him to go into those kind of details, Cain. He just felt it was time we went out in the world and multiplied, that's all.

CAIN: Father, I've never understood why you couldn't have stayed in the Garden and multiplied.

EVE: In the *Garden*!

ADAM: Oh, no, boy—

EVE: That's not something you do in the *Garden*, darling.

CAIN: Well, what did He say, exactly, when you left?

ADAM: He said to get out—

EVE: Not "Get out!"

ADAM, *quickly*: No, no, not "Get out!"

EVE: I think he's overtired.

CAIN: I am not overtired! Why do you always make everything ridiculous? I'm not talking about sheep or farming; I'm talking about what God wants us to *do*!

ABEL: If you think He wants me to farm, I'll be glad to switch.

CAIN, *to Adam with a laugh*: He's going to farm!

ADAM, *laughing*: God help us!

ABEL, *protesting*: Why!

CAIN: With your sense of responsibility, we'd be eating thistle soup!

EVE, *touching Abel*: He's just more imaginative.

LUCIFER: Will you just shut up?

CAIN: Imaginative!

ABEL: Have I ever lost a sheep?

CAIN: How *could* you lose them? They always end up in my corn.

ABEL: Cain, that only happened once!

CAIN, *with raw indignation*: Go out there and sweat the way I do and tell me it only happened once!

EVE: He's just younger!

CAIN: And I'm older, and I'll be damned if I plant another crop until he fences those sheep!

LUCIFER: Stop this!

EVE, *to Adam*: Stop this!

CAIN: Why must you always take his side?

EVE: But how can he build a fence?

CAIN: The same way I plant a crop, Mother! By bending his back! Abel, I'm warning you, if you ever again—

ADAM: Boys, boys!

ABEL, *turning away*: If he wants a fence, I think he should build it.

CAIN: *I* should build it! Are the corn eating the sheep or the sheep eating the corn?

ABEL: It's not natural for me to build a fence.

CAIN: Not natural! You've been talking to God lately?

ABEL: I don't know anything about God. But it's the nature of sheep to move around, and it's the nature of corn to stay in one place. So the fence should fence the thing that stays in one place and not the thing that moves around.

ADAM: That's logical, Cain.

CAIN: In other words, the work belongs to me and the whole wide world belongs to him!

ADAM, *at a loss*: No, that's not fair either.

ABEL, *angering, to Adam*: Well, I can't fence the mountains, can I? I can't fence the rivers where they go to drink. *To Cain*: I know you work harder, Cain, but I didn't decide that. I've even thought sometimes that it is unfair, and maybe we should change places for a while—

CAIN: You wouldn't last a week.

ABEL, *crying out*: Then what am I supposed to do? *Cain is close, staring into his face, a tortured expression in his eyes which puzzles Abel. Why is he looking like that? Suddenly Cain embraces Abel, hugging him close.*

ADAM: Attaboy!

EVE, *puzzled and alarmed*: Cain?

CAIN—*he lets Abel go and moves a few steps, staring*: I don't know what's happening to me.

ADAM: Abel, shake his hand. Go on, make up. You're both sorry.

ABEL, *holding out his hand*: Cain?

LUCIFER, *victoriously to Heaven*: Why don't you give up!

> *Cain has just raised his hand to approach Abel when a large snake is dropped in their midst from Heaven. Eve screams. Lucifer rushes and flings it out of sight.*

LUCIFER: Scat! Get out of here!

EVE: It flew in and flew out!

ADAM: A flying snake?

Instantly the high howling of several coyotes is heard, and the family turns in all directions, as though toward an invading force.

LUCIFER: *off to one side, looking up to Heaven*: Father, this is *low*!

ADAM, *looking about at the air*: Something is happening. *To Eve, who is staring about*: I think . . . I'd better tell them. *She covers her eyes in trepidation.* Eve? Maybe we're supposed to, now.

EVE, *lowering her hands*: All right. Then maybe everything will be as it was again.

ADAM: Boys? Maybe you'd better sit down, boys.

ABEL: Tell what, Pa?

They all sit except Eve, who remains standing, staring about apprehensively.

ADAM: About the question of leaving Paradise—I don't want you to think that we tried to mislead you or anything like that.

EVE, *pleadingly to Cain*: It's just everything was going so good, you see?

ADAM, *with a glance around at the air*: But it looks like something is happening, so maybe we better get this settled.

ABEL: What, Pa?

ADAM: We . . . didn't exactly *decide* to go, y'see. We were ah—*he blinks away a tear*—told to leave.

CAIN: *Told?*

ABEL: Why, Pa?

ADAM, *fumbling*: Why? Well . . . *He turns helplessly to Eve.* Why?

EVE: We just didn't fit in, you see. I mean if a person doesn't fit in—

ADAM: If we're going to tell it, we better tell it.

EVE: But the way you're telling it, it sounds like it was all my fault!

ADAM: I didn't say anything yet!

EVE: Well, when are you going to say it?

ADAM, *setting himself*: Well—as we told you before, I was alone with God for a long time, and then—

ABEL: He made Mama.

ADAM: Right.

ABEL, *with a big smile*: And you liked her right away, heh?

CAIN: Of course he did.

ADAM: She was gorgeous. Of course, there wasn't much choice. *He laughs.*

EVE: Ha. Ha. Ha.

ADAM: Well, anyway, I believe I mentioned there was this tree—with an apple—

ABEL: Of good and evil.

ADAM: Right.

CAIN: Which you're never allowed to eat under any circumstances.

ADAM: Right. Well, the thing is, you see—we ate it.

ABEL—*thrilled and scared, he laughs*: You ate it!

CAIN: I thought you said you—

ADAM: No, we ate it.

ABEL, *more scared now*: Not Mama, though.

ADAM: Mama too.

> *Cain goes to a lyre and, turning his back on them, he plays.*
> *They watch him for a moment, aware of his intense feeling.*

ABEL, *avidly*: And then what happened?

> *Cain strums as loud as he can, then stops.*

ADAM, *with a worried glance at Cain*: Well, the next thing—I looked at her, y'see. And there was something funny. I didn't know what it was. And then I realized. She was naked.

> *Cain now turns to them.*

CAIN AND ABEL: Mama?

EVE: Well, *he* was too.

CAIN—*shocked, he drops the lyre*: Mama!

LUCIFER, *holding his head*: Ohhh!

EVE: We didn't know it, darling!

CAIN: How could you not know you were naked?

EVE: Well, we were like children; like you, like Abel. You remember, when Abel was a baby and ran around—

CAIN, *outraged, accusing*: But you weren't a baby!

EVE, *to Adam, at a loss*: Aren't you going to say anything?

ABEL, *explaining for Adam*: Well, they were like animals.

CAIN, *pained, horrified*: Don't you say a thing like that!

ADAM, *to Cain*: Well, I told you—I could smell water?

ABEL: Sure! And they could hear the trout talking.

CAIN: But you never said you were actually . . . *animals.*

ADAM: Now just a minute, Cain. That was the way God wanted it—

CAIN: I can't believe that! God could never have wanted my mother going around without any clothes on!

ADAM, *angrily, standing*: You mean *I* wouldn't let her put her clothes on?

EVE, *going to him*: Darling, we were innocent!

CAIN, *furiously*: You were naked and innocent? Don't you understand that that's why He threw you out?

EVE: He loved us most when we were naked. He only got mad when we knew we were. *Slight pause.*

CAIN, *swept by this truth*: No wonder we dreamed of death!

EVE: Why?

CAIN: We've been saying all the wrong prayers. We shouldn't be thanking God—we should be begging His forgiveness. We've been living as though we were innocent. We've been living as though we were blessed!

EVE: But we are, darling.

CAIN: We are cursed, Mother!

EVE, *furiously to Adam*: You should never have told him!

CAIN: Why did you lie to us?

ADAM: Now just a minute . . .

CAIN, *accusingly*: I always *knew* there was something you weren't saying!

ADAM: Just a minute! *Slight pause.* We didn't want to frighten you, that's all. But maybe now you're old enough to understand.—He did curse us when He threw us out. And part of the curse is that we will have to die.

CAIN: *We're* going to die?

ABEL: Like the sheep, you mean?

ADAM: Sheep, birds, everything.

CAIN: You and Mama, too? You mean we wouldn't see you any more?

EVE: Don't worry about it, darling. I'm sure we have a long, long time yet.

CAIN: You mean before He got angry you would never die?

ADAM: Far as I know—yes.

CAIN: Oh, my God—then He must have been absolutely furious with you.

EVE: I'm sure He's forgiven us, dear, or we wouldn't have you and everything so wonderful—

CAIN, *sinking to his knees*: Listen to me! I tell you we have been warned. Now we must do what has never been done.

EVE: Do what?

CAIN: We must give this day—not to the animals or the crops; this day we must give to God. I tell you—*he looks upward tenderly*—if we will open up our sins to Him and cleanse ourselves, He might show His face and tell us how we are supposed to live. Father, Mother, Abel—come and pray with me.

ADAM, *to Eve*: Well—a prayer wouldn't hurt.

EVE, *recalling*: Maybe he's right. Maybe it'll all be sweet again. *Going to her knees*: What should we pray, darling?

> *Cain faces Heaven. Adam goes to his knees. And finally Abel.*

CAIN: Almighty God, seeing that our parents were thrown out of Paradise for their transgressions against Thee, we, Cain and Abel, beseech Thy forgiveness. Let this family live, let us be innocent again! Now each one, give up the sin.

> *Adam and Eve shut their eyes and concentrate. Abel watches them, then leans over to Eve.*

ABEL, *with a glance at the praying Cain*: Does this mean I'm building a fence?

CAIN, *eyes shut*: It seems to me that when a person dies in his brother's dream he ought to pray!

ADAM: I saw it too, Abel—you were dead. I think you'd better pray.

> *Pause. All heads are lowered. Lucifer stands up. He comes down to them and sits next to Abel.*

ABEL, *softly*: Mother!

EVE: Sssh!

ABEL: Someone has come.

ADAM: I don't see anybody.

A slight pause. They contemplate, but Abel is glancing apprehensively toward Lucifer.

ABEL: Who art thou?

The family turns quickly to him, astonished, Lucifer being invisible to all but Abel.

LUCIFER: I am what you fear in your heart is true—your brother is dangerous. Tell him you'll build the fence. *Abel reacts in refusal.* This man is inconsolable!

ABEL: Why?

LUCIFER: She loves you best, Abel.

ABEL: But Cain is loved!

EVE: How sweet! *To Adam*: Did you hear?

LUCIFER: Cain has her respect but her love has gone to you. Tell him you'll build it if you care to live! *Now Abel turns with new eyes to Cain.*

ABEL: About the fence—

CAIN: Yes?

ABEL: You're right. It's not the corn that eat the sheep but the sheep that eat the corn—

LUCIFER: Attaboy!

EVE, *to Adam, happily*: Listen!

ABEL: So I will build the fence around the sheep.

EVE, *to Adam*: Do you hear!

ADAM: Marvelous.

CAIN: Where would you build it?

ABEL: Well—anywhere out of the way. In the valley?

CAIN: I need the valley.

ABEL: Oh . . . On the hillside?

CAIN: I'll need the hillside. I'm planning to set out quite a large vineyard this spring.

ABEL: Where would you suggest, then?

CAIN: There is very rich pasture across the mountain.

ABEL: That's . . . pretty far away, though, isn't it?

CAIN: I don't think it's all that far.

LUCIFER: Agree! Agree!

ABEL, *swallowing his resentment*: All right, Cain.

LUCIFER: I know how you feel, son, but lying is better than dying.

EVE, *affected by Abel's anguish*: Cain, dear, I want to tell him you didn't mean that before—

LUCIFER: Abel, shut her up—

EVE, *to Cain, insistently*: You won't make him go so far away to pasture, will you?

LUCIFER: She is killing you, word by loving word!

ABEL: I don't mind, Mother. In fact—

LUCIFER: I *like* long walks.

ABEL: I *like* long walks.

EVE: But you *agreed* to build the fence! *To Cain*: Why must you humiliate him?

> *Cain slams his hands down on the ground and springs up furiously, goes to a big rock, and picks it up.*

LUCIFER, *to Abel*: Watch out! Don't turn your back on him! *Abel quickly turns to watch his brother.*

EVE: What are you doing?

> *Cain places the boulder on top of another.*

CAIN: What has never been done. It has come to me to make an offering to the Lord.

LUCIFER, *shaking a fist at Heaven*: Don't you ever give up?

EVE, *vastly relieved*: That's a wonderful idea!

ADAM: Say, now! That sounds very good, Cain.

EVE: You think He'll come?

ADAM: He might. The way Cain loves Him, He might just stop by. *To Cain, with his expertise*: Take the best of thy corn and the first of thy wheat, and a little parsley—He always rather liked parsley.

> *Cain finds a flat stone and sets it on top of the altar he is constructing. Eve immediately takes a broom and starts sweeping the area.*

EVE: What about some grapes?

ADAM, *calling to Cain*: Grapes too!

CAIN: The grapes aren't too good this year—

EVE: You'd better not, then.

ADAM, *all excited*: Don't listen to her; it doesn't matter if they're not too good, it's the feeling behind it. Because He's fair, Cain, you'll see. And here's another thing. We've go to praise Him more. We haven't been praising Him enough.

EVE: Praise God! Praise the Lord!

ADAM: Will you wait! *To Cain*: Hurry up, get the stuff. *Cain rushes back to load a tray with his crops.*

EVE, *clasping her hands together feverishly*: He's going to come! I feel it, I tell you I feel it!

ADAM, *supervising Cain, calling*: I'd throw in a few onions. *To Eve*: Loved a good onion.

EVE: It's going to be like it was again! *She rushes to Abel.* Push back your hair, darling. Adam, there's dirt on your cheek. *Adam brushes it off. Abel fixes his hair. Cain turns to them now with a tray loaded with vegetables and fruit. Silence for an instant; then Eve suddenly is swept forward to him.* Would you mind, darling? *She picks an apple off the tray.* No apples. *She hides the apple in her clothes.*

CAIN, *in tension*: Is it all right, Pa?

Adam comes forward, inspects the tray. Silence.

ADAM: This looks absolutely beautiful, Cain. Now, when you see His face, regard the right eye. Because that's the one He loves you with. The left one squints, y'see, because that's the one He judges with. So watch the right eye and don't be frightened.

CAIN: I love Him, Father.

ADAM: I know that, Cain, and now you will know His love for thee. *He kisses Cain, who turns and tensely starts for the altar.*

EVE: Cain!

He halts. She comes to him, elevated within. She kisses the offering. Then she kisses him. He turns again to the altar. Abel steps before him. They stare at one another. Now Cain leans and kisses him. Then he carefully sets the offering on the altar and steps back. All go to their knees before the altar, as—

EVE, *to Adam, tentatively*: I think Abel ought to make an offering too.

> *Abel sits up, and Adam considers this. Cain remains bowed.*
> *Lucifer cries out, rushing about before Abel.*

LUCIFER: Don't! Under no circumstances must you get into this competition!

CAIN: It was my idea, Mother. Can't he do it another time?

EVE: It was just a suggestion! You don't have to get angry.

ABEL, *struck by his vision*: Maybe He would come because of me. . . .

LUCIFER: What are *you* guilty about? Just because your mother loves you best? Lie back and enjoy it.

ABEL: But it is not fair to Cain, and I can't bear that any more! I want God to bring us peace!

LUCIFER: And what if it turns out God also loves you best? Is *that* fair to Cain?

ABEL: But—Cain would have to accept *that*!

LUCIFER: Boy, even with God's help, nobody can be Number One and good at the same time.

ABEL: Get thee behind me! *He draws his knife and rushes upstage.*

EVE, *to Adam*: He's going to do it! *Calling to Abel, who is exiting.* Pick a nice fat lamb, darling!

LUCIFER, *as he rushes upstage after Abel*: Abel! Don't call down God!

> *Cain is still on his knees, staring ahead. Eve feels his anguish.*

EVE: He'll come now, dear, and He'll bless you both, as I do. *But Cain refuses to turn to her, she sees his hurt.* I love thee, Cain, I always loved thee from the hour of thy conception!

LUCIFER, *looks to Heaven*: What a genius that old fart is—with one dream of death he's got them all guilty! By God, I'll free them now or never—with the truth! *He exits.*

> *Abel enters, holding before him a slab of wood loaded with*
> *the flesh and entrails of a lamb, his hands dripping blood.*
> *Adam instantly goes to him, smears his own hand, and snaps*
> *the blood into the air toward the sky.*

ADAM: The blood is the life, and the life is the Lord's.

EVE—*she looks up to the sky*:

Now, Maker, show Thyself and spread Thy peace
On all of us, my Abel and my Cain.

*She and Adam kiss Abel from his right and left. He sets his
offering on the altar. The deep bellow of a bull is heard.*

ALL: Aiee!

*The bellowing resounds again, and now a figure rises behind
the altar, a man with the head of a bull. At the sight they all
prostrate themselves on the ground.*

LUCIFER:

A second time I come with thine awakening, Mankind!
Nobody's guilty any more!
And for your progeny now and forever
I decare one massive, eternal, continuous parole!
From here on out there is no sin or innocence
But only Man. *He flings off his mask.*
Now claim thy birthright! *He leaps, stands away from the altar,
    welcoming arms outflung.*
Total freedom!

EVE, *leaps up*: Thank God!

ADAM, *springing to his feet*: That's the Devil!

LUCIFER: There are two Gods, Adam—in Heaven, God; and God on
earth is me!

ADAM: Slaughter him! *He starts for Lucifer, and the boys stand. Eve
throws herself before Lucifer to shield him.* Woman!

EVE: I believe this angel!

ADAM: This is the enemy!

EVE: I won't deny it any more—this spirit makes me happy!

ADAM, *to the altar*: Lord, show Thy face, my wife is going to Hell!

EVE: Adam! *She raises her hand gently toward him.*

Where has all our old contentment gone?
You were so long in Paradise
With God, that all your dreams go there,
But the only home I ever had is on this dust,
This windy world,
And here I am condemned. I know God rules in Heaven,
But in the name of peace, I have to speak the truth:

Except for one short dance—*she nearly weeps*—
God never showed me any kindness.

ADAM: Woman!

EVE:

I see it, husband!
This God is mine—I know it!
For only this one frees me of my sin.

ADAM: There is one God!

EVE: No—two! One for me and one for— *A strange light blossoms around the altar, and seeing it, she breaks off and like the others backs away. Lucifer rushes down to her.*

LUCIFER: Let's end this war! Dance with me, woman. Show God your love and end this stupid war!

> *A wild music explodes, then diminishes as Lucifer pulls her to himself, and in conflict she breaks and with arms spread calls to Abel.*

EVE: Abel! Cain! *Rushing to them, grabbing them*: Love! Love, my darlings!

ADAM: I forbid this! God's coming!

EVE—*clamping both their heads to her, she calls out to Adam and Heaven*: Is God not pleased if peace comes in? *She springs from them and then turns back invitingly to them.* Let hate go out and love come in!

LUCIFER:

Now save yourselves with music and the truth!
Be what you are and as you are.
Give God to Adam, boys—and I will give you Eve!

> *The music flies up: Eve begins to dance—awkwardly at first, and Lucifer grabs her, awakens her again, and her body loosens, writhes, then she flies to Abel, who is embarrassed but quickly learns, and now she flies to Cain, who is stiff at first, but Lucifer helps him loosen up, and finally she is whirling among the three of them, kissing them in turn, her hands flowing over their bodies and theirs over hers—and suddenly Cain explodes into a prancing step, flapping his arms like a giant mating bird. Eve is astonished, innocently laughs, but in a swoop he pulls her down and climbs onto her. The truth is out—fuck her, Cain, and save the world! Adam rushes to*

separate them. Lucifer grabs him. Shame! How can you be so selfish! *And with Cain on his stunned but compliant mother and Abel trying to hold out till Cain is done—God appears behind the altar.*

Adam roars a gigantic, horrified roar. Silence. Cain rolls off Eve and sits looking up at the Presence. Eve sits up. Adam prostrates himself.

ADAM: Glory to God in the highest!

LUCIFER: Good morning, sir. *With an ironic gesture toward the crew.* May I introduce you to mankind? I don't believe I need labor the point— to the naked eye how pious and God-fearing they were; but with a moment's instruction and the right kind of music, a bear would blush at their morality. Dear Father, what are we fighting about? Truly, Lord, what is Man beyond his appetite? *Extends his hand.* Come, make peace; share Heaven—I the God of what-they-are, and you in charge of their improvement. In you let them find their hopes, in me their pleasure, and shut the gates of Hell forever. Sir, I am ready to take my place.

Striving against anger, God turns his head to each of the people in turn. Then He looks down at the offerings and picks out an onion.

GOD: Peace, children, on this first Sabbath. Whose is this?

LUCIFER: You'll accept those offerings when the filth in their hearts stinks to Heaven!

GOD: Whose is this?

CAIN, *with uncertainty*: That was mine, Lord.

GOD: Do you want me to taste it?

LUCIFER: You saw him on his mother!

GOD: Cain?

CAIN, *his eyes averted*: If it pleases Thee.

GOD: Why?

CAIN: It's . . . my *onion*, sir.

GOD: Then you still have respect for an onion?

CAIN: Lord, it's my work, my labor; it is the best of all I've made.

GOD, *with angry eyes*: And were you not the best that I had made?

Cain looks up, aware, and lowers his eyes in shame. God bites the onion, chews it.

That . . . is a good onion, Cain. *Cain falls to his knees weeping.* And this is Abel's meat?

ABEL: It's mine, sir, yes.

GOD: Mutton.

EVE: Oh, no, sir—lamb.

GOD—*He glances at her, then with high interest leans and inhales the delicious scent*: Ohhh, yes.

ABEL, *encouraged*: My youngest, fattest lamb, Lord. I hope it will please Thee.

EVE: I usually sprinkle it with salt and pepper first. . . .

GOD: You might try rubbing a bud of garlic over it.

EVE: Oh, I will!

ADAM: Do that next time, definitely.

EVE: Oh yes, Adam!

> *Now God picks up a piece of meat. All grow tense. Abel raises his head to watch. God puts the meat in His mouth and chews, His eyes opening wider with the taste.*

GOD: What in the world do you feed your flock?

ABEL, *joyously*: I find the sweetest grass, sir!

CAIN: And corn. *God turns to him. Abel, tense, turns to him.*

GOD, *understanding*: Oh, yes. I see. *He turns slowly to Abel.* Abel? Rise. *Abel springs to his feet.* Young man, this is undoubtedly the sweetest, most delicious, delicate, and profoundly *satisfying* piece of meat I have ever tasted since the world began.

> *Adam, filled with glory, comes to Abel and shakes his hand.*

ADAM: Boy, this is our proudest moment.

EVE—*unable to hold back, she starts for Abel*: Darling! *She grabs Abel's face, kisses him on the lips, and turns up to God.* There is one God now and forever, there is no other on earth or in Heaven!

GOD: And don't you forget it, either. *Turning to Lucifer, who is staring at the ground*: I seem to have forgotten what you were saying. What was that all about, fallen angel?

LUCIFER, *bitterly*: About truth, sir—my mistake. But this isn't over yet!

GOD, *steps down from the altar*: Come, children, and walk a little way with me, and we shall talk a while together of life and earth and Heaven. Come, Adam. *He takes Adam by the hand.* Eve? *She comes to him, enthralled, and gives him her hand.* Abel? Cain?

CAIN: Lord, there's still my corn. You haven't tasted my corn.

GOD: Oh, I can see it's all very nice. You have done quite well, Cain. Keep it up. *With which He walks into light with Adam and Abel following behind.*

EVE, *beckoning*: Cain? *Seeing his shock*: Darling, he *loved* your vegetables. Come.

> *Cain seems to hardly hear her and takes a few dead steps following her. She goes, and he comes to a halt. Lucifer starts for him, then halts as he sees his strange expression.*

LUCIFER: Now control yourself, boy. Cain?

CAIN: He never even tasted my corn.

LUCIFER: You mustn't get excited.

CAIN, *still with the undercurrent of dangerous laughter*: But do you know what goes into an ear of corn? I planted twice this year; the floods washed my seeds away the first time. *His eyes fall on a flask beside the altar.* And my wine. *Going to the flask*: I was going to offer . . . *He suddenly kicks down the altar.*

LUCIFER: Listen to me— *For good measure Cain sends all the food flying with another kick.* We've got to get serious!

CAIN: Cain, serious? That's all over, Devil, now Cain starts to *live! He starts throwing everything out of the shelter.*

LUCIFER: What's this, now?

CAIN: This is my house! Mine! *He faces Lucifer.* No one enters here but Cain any more. They have God, and I have this farm—and before I'm finished, my fences will stretch out to cover the earth!

LUCIFER: Adam will never agree to leave this house—

CAIN: Oh, he'll agree, all right—*he strides to his flail and brandishes it—* once I explain it to him! *He whips the flail with a whoosh, and, holding it up*: There's the only wisdom I will ever need again! *A deep hum sounds in the earth, like a dynamo.*

LUCIFER: Listen! *Cain freezes.* He has set a moaning in the earth. *Daylight changes to night; stars appear.* Look! *Both look up at the night sky.*

He is giving you a night at noon,
Darkening your mind to kill for him!

*Frightened, Cain turns from the sky to the flail in his hand
and throws it down guiltily.*

Don't let him use you. Go away. Hide yourself.

CAIN: I, hide? I was the one who thought of the offerings; from me this
Sabbath came! Let them hide! I want nothing from anyone any more!

LUCIFER: But God wants a murder from you.

CAIN, *astonished*: God . . . wants . . . ?

LUCIFER: He has designed your vengeance, boy. He's boiling your blood
in his hand.

CAIN: But why?

LUCIFER:

So He may stand above your crime, the blameless God,
The only assurance of Mankind, and His power is safe.
Come now,
We'll hide you till this anger's gone.

*He leads Cain a few yards, Cain moves as though being car-
ried, staring into Lucifer's face.*

ABEL'S VOICE, *calling from a distance*: Cain? Where are you? Come on!

Cain swerves about toward the voice.

LUCIFER: Don't stop!

CAIN—*a cry, as though from his bowel, to the sky*: How is Abel the
favorite of God?

LUCIFER:

God has no favorites! *He grasps Cain's astounded face.*
Man's a mirror to Him, Cain,
In which he looks to see His praise.

CAIN: But I have praised Him! And Abel only played His flute!

LUCIFER:

So where is good and where is evil?
God wants power, not morals!

ABEL'S VOICE, *closer now, calling*: Cain! We're all waiting for you!

LUCIFER, *grabbing for him*: Come!

CAIN: I have to face him first! *He breaks from Lucifer, facing in the direction of Abel's voice.*

LUCIFER:

>Then face him with indifference.
>Kill love, Cain, kill whatever in you cares;
>Murder now is but another sort of praise to God!
>Don't praise Him with a death!

ABEL, *closer yet*: Cain?

CAIN:

>His voice is like silver, like his life,
>And mine is the voice of the ox, the driven beast!

LUCIFER: Indifference, Cain!

Abel enters.

ABEL: Aren't you coming? God is sitting by the river, telling all about Paradise—come on! *Cain stares front.*

LUCIFER, *facing front*: I swear this, Cain—if man will not kill man, God is unnecessary! Walk away and you're free! *Cain starts to walk away.*

ABEL: Brother! God wants you there!

CAIN, *halting*: Wants *me*?

LUCIFER: Swallow it and walk!

ABEL: Of course—He loves you, Cain. He was just saying how you do everything He wants.

CAIN: Then by God I order you out of here and your mother and father, and never come back!

ABEL: Brother!—I've as much right here as you. *He moves toward Cain.*

CAIN: Are you even so sure of His blessing that you come to me?

ABEL: You'll not hurt me, Cain.

CAIN: Why? Am I thy servant? *He sweeps up his flail.* Am I thy fool? Run from me!

ABEL: *Astonished at the flail, he starts to back away.* Brother! God loves us both!

CAIN: You are dead to me, Abel—run!

ABEL, *halts*: I will not! Come to the Lord!

CAIN, *moving toward him, raising the flail*: Run for your life!

ABEL: Brother, let God calm you!

CAIN, *whirling about, flail raised, he calls to the air*: Save us, Lord . . . !

ABEL, *rushing to him*: Come to Him!

CAIN—*he turns on Abel, calling to God*: Now save us! *He strikes at Abel who dodges and runs.*

ABEL, *screaming*: Mother!

CAIN, *pursuing him he strikes Abel down*: Save us! *He strikes him again on the ground.* Save us!

LUCIFER: Cain! How can you love God so!

GOD, *calling from off*: Cain! Where art thou!

> *Cain flings the flail away like an alien thing that somehow got into his hand. God enters rapidly, behind Him Eve and Adam.*

GOD: Where is thy brother?

> *Cain is silent.*

EVE: Where is Abel?

ADAM: Where is he?

GOD: Where is Abel, thy brother?

CAIN, *with a new, dead indifference*: I know not. Am I my brother's keeper?

GOD: The voice of thy brother's blood crieth unto me from the ground.

EVE—*seeing the corpse, like a sigh at first*: Ahhh.

ADAM, *wide-eyed*: Ohhh. *The sigh repeatedly emanating from her, she halts, looking down at the corpse. Adam comes and faces it.* Ohhhh.

EVE—*she goes down beside the corpse, keening*: Abel? Wake, my darling!

ADAM: Abel? *Calls.* Abel!

GOD: What hast thou done!

CAIN, *with a bitter, hard grin, plus a certain intimate, familiar tone*: What had to be done. As the Lord surely knew when I laid before Him the fruit of my sweat—for which there was only Thy contempt.

GOD: But why contempt? Didn't I approve of your offering?

CAIN: As I would "approve" my ox. Abel's lamb was not "approved," it was adored, like his life!

GOD, *indignantly*: But I *like* lamb! *Cain is dumbfounded.* I don't deny it, I like lamb better than onions.

LUCIFER: Surely there can be no accounting for taste.

CAIN: And this is Your justice?

GOD: Justice!

CAIN, *with a bitter laugh*: Yes, justice! Justice!

GOD: When have I ever spoken that word?

CAIN: You mean our worth and value are a question of *taste*?

GOD, *incredulously*: But Cain, there are eagles and sparrows, lions and mice—is every bird to be an eagle? Are there to be no mice? Let a man do well, and he shall be accepted.

CAIN: I have done well and I am humiliated!

GOD: You hated Abel before this day, so you cannot say you have done well.

EVE, *rising from the corpse*: You argue with *Him*? *She rushes to tear at Cain, Adam holding her back.* Kill him! He's a murderer! *Weeping, held by Adam, she calls:* Take his life!

GOD: Surely you repent this, Cain.

CAIN: When God repents His injustice, I will repent my own!

LUCIFER: Why should he repent? Who sent death down here? You did! *He points to God.* There is the murderer!

ADAM: Watch your mouth!

LUCIFER: He arranged it all from beginning to end! *Eve stops weeping, straightens, astonished, turns to God.* Do You deny Azrael was here this morning while they slept? *To Eve:* Ask him!

EVE: You sent the Angel of Death?

> *Pause.*

GOD: Yes.

EVE: Lord God . . . did you want this?

> *Pause.*

GOD: Eve . . . soon the multitude will spring from this first family, and cover the earth. How will the thousands be shepherded as I have shepherded thee? Only if the eye of God opens in the heart of every man; only if each himself will choose the way of life, not death. For otherwise you go as beasts, locked up in the darkness of their nature. *Slight pause.* I saw that Cain was pious, yet in him I saw envy too. And so I thought— if Cain were so enraged that he lift his hand against his brother, but then, remembering his love for Abel and for me, even in his fury lay down his arms? *To Cain:* Man!—you would have risen like a planet before the generations, the victory of God, first brother and the first to reject a murder. Oh, Cain, how I hoped for thee!

ADAM, *to Eve:* Do you understand? He was trying to help us. *She stands rigid, wide-eyed.* Eve, you must beg his pardon.

EVE, *turning to God:* But why must my child have died? You could have tested me, or Adam or Abel—we could *never* have killed.

GOD: Woman, a moment ago you commanded me to take Cain's life.

EVE: But I . . . I was *angry.*

GOD: Cain was also angry. *She turns away, rejecting.* Do you understand me? *Beginning to anger.* Then am I a wanton murderer? Speak! What am I to you?

ADAM: Eve! Tell Him you understand!

EVE: I do not understand . . . why we *can't just live*!

GOD: Because without God you'll murder each other!

EVE, *furiously:* And with God? With God?

GOD: Then do you want the Devil? Tell me now before the multitudes arrive. Who do you want?

ADAM: You, Lord, you!

GOD: Why? Your innocent son is dead; why!

ADAM: Because . . . how do I know?—maybe for someone somewhere, even this . . . is good? Right?

GOD, *outraged:* You are all worthless! The mother blames God, the father blames no one, and the son knows no blame at all. *To Lucifer:* Angel, you have won the world—and I hereby give it over to your ministry.

ADAM: *Him!*

GOD: This is the chaos you want, and him you shall have—the God who judges nothing, the God of infinite permission. I shall continue to do the hurricanes, the gorillas, and all that, but I see now that your hearts' desire is anarchy and I wash my hands. I do not want to be God . . . any more! *He starts away.*

LUCIFER, *dashing after Him*: Lord! You don't mean—not me all by myself!

GOD: That's what you've been after, isn't it?

LUCIFER: No, no—with You! It's out of the question for me to run the world alone.

GOD: But what do you need Me for?

LUCIFER: But I can't—I can't *make* anything!

GOD: Really! But you're such a superb critic.

LUCIFER: But they're two entirely different things!

GOD: Perhaps once you're in charge you'll become more creative. *He starts away again; Eve rushes to Him.*

EVE: Wait, Lord, please!

GOD: Oh, woman, for thy torment especially I am most deeply sorry. Good-bye, dear Eve. *He starts away.*

EVE: But what do we do about Cain?

    Now He halts, turns, alert.

LUCIFER, *to God*: Very well, I take the world! *To Eve*: Tell Him to go!

EVE, *to Lucifer*: But what about Cain?

LUCIFER: There'll be no more talk about Cain. The boy simply got caught in a rotten situation, and no emotions are called for.

GOD: She seems to have a question—

LUCIFER: She is free! She has no further questions! *To Eve*: Tell Him to go back to His hurricanes.

EVE, *to Lucifer*: But He murdered my son.

GOD: But what is the question?

EVE: HE MURDERED MY SON!

GOD: And what is the *question*, woman!

LUCIFER: You've got your freedom! Stop here!

EVE, *to Lucifer*: But how—*turning to Cain's adamant face*: How do I hand him his breakfast tomorrow? How do I call him to dinner? "Come, mankiller, I have meat for thee"?

CAIN, *holding his ground, his profile to her eyes*: It was not my fault!

EVE, *crying out to God*: How can we live with him!

GOD: But what did you say to me a moment ago—"Why can't we just live?" Why can't you do it? Take your unrepentant son and start living.

LUCIFER: Why not? Will blaming Cain bring Abel back?

EVE: But shouldn't he . . . shouldn't he repent?

LUCIFER: You mean a few appropriate words will console you?

EVE: Not words, but . . . *To Cain*: Don't you feel you've done *anything*?

LUCIFER: What's the difference what he feels?

EVE, *with high anxiety*: You mean nothing has *happened*?

LUCIFER: There is no consolation, woman! Unless you want the lie of God, the false tears of a killer repenting!

EVE: But why must they be false? If he loved his brother, maybe now he feels . . . *She breaks off, backing a step from Lucifer, and turns to God*: Is this . . . why he can't be God?

GOD, *quickly*: Why can't he be God?

LUCIFER: I can and I will be—I am the truth!

EVE: But you . . . *In fear*: you don't . . .

ADAM—He doesn't love us!

EVE: Yes!

GOD: And that is why whatever you do, it's all the same to him—it's only his power this angel loves!

ADAM AND EVE, *rushing to God*: Father, save us!

GOD: Oh, my children, I thought you'd never understand!

LUCIFER, *with a furious, bitter irony, as God approaches the beseeching people*: And here He comes again—Father Guilt is back! *Rushing to Cain*: Cain, help me! You're the one free, guiltless man! Tell God you have no need for Him! Speak out your freedom and save the world!

CAIN—*he has been staring in silence, now he turns his dead eyes to Lucifer*: Angel, none of this seems to matter, you know? One way or the other. Why don't you let it all go?

> *With a near-sob Lucifer claps his hands over his ears, then, straightening, he comes to a salute before God.*

LUCIFER: You have my salute! You have gorgeously prearranged this *entire* dialogue, and it all comes out the way You want—but You have solved absolutely nothing!

GOD, *lifting His eyes from the kneeling Adam and Eve*: Except, angel, that you will never be God. And not because I forbid it, but because they will never—at least for very long—believe it. For I made them not of dust alone, but dust and love; and by dust alone they will not, cannot long be governed. *Lucifer bursts into sobbing tears.* Why do you weep, angel? They love, and with love, kill brothers. Take heart, I see now that our war goes on.

ADAM AND EVE: No, Lord!

> *Lucifer looks at God now, clear-eyed, expectant.*

GOD: It does go on. For love, I see, is not enough; though the Devil himself cry peace, you'll find your war. Now I want to know what is in your heart. Tell me, man, what do you feel?

CAIN: I am thirsty.

GOD, *after a slight pause*: So in thy thirst will I sentence thee, Cain—to live. And in this loneliness shalt thou walk forever in the populous cities, a fugitive and a vagabond all the days of thy life. And whoever looks on thee will point and say, "There is the man who murdered his brother."

CAIN, *coming alive*: Better kill me now! They will stone me wherever I go!

GOD: No, I declare to all the generations: Whoever slayeth Cain, vengeance shall be taken on him sevenfold. For I will set a mark upon thee, Cain, that will keep thee from harm.

CAIN: What mark?

GOD, *holding two index fingers pointed toward Cain's face*: Come to me, my son. *Terrified, Cain comes up to His fingers, and He comes around behind Cain, who is facing front, and presses his cheeks, forming a smile which Cain cannot relax. God lowers His fingers.*

CAIN, *smiling*: What is the mark?

GOD: That smile is.

CAIN: But they will know that I killed my brother!

GOD: Yes, they will know, and you will smile forever with agony in your eyes—the sundered mark of Cain who killed for pride and power in the name of love.

> *Smiling, his eyes desperate, Cain turns to Eve. She cries out, hides her face in her hands. He tears at his cheeks, but his smile remains. He lowers his hands—a smiling man with astonished, terrifying eyes.*

> Adam? Eve? Now the way of life is revealed before you, and the way of death. Seek Me only in your hearts, you will never see My face again.

Lucifer, who has been staring off, swerves about. The people come alert, startled. God turns and walks upstage.

ADAM, *rushing a half-step behind God:* What'd you say? Lord, I don't understand . . . *God continues, moving into light. Adam halts, calling.* Did you say *never?*

EVE: What does that mean? Almighty God! *She starts to run up toward Him, but He disappears among the stars. Adam, above her now, turns down to Lucifer.*

ADAM: Angel! *He comes down to Lucifer, his finger rising toward the angel.* Did he mean that you are . . . ?

Lucifer turns from the vanished God to Adam, his face twisted with puzzlement.

ADAM AND EVE, *with a heartbroken, lost cry:* Who is God?

LUCIFER: Does it really matter? Why don't you have a nice breakfast together—the three of you—and forget the whole thing? After all, who-ever God is, we have to be sensible. *He walks away, glancing back to Eve.* And whenever you'd like to start the dancing—just call.

EVE: Don't ever come back!

LUCIFER, *pointing insinuatingly at her:* You know exactly what I mean.

Lucifer walks into darkness. Adam and Eve turn to Cain.

ADAM: He condemned you to wander the earth. You'll have to go.

CAIN: But He let me live; there was some forgiveness in that. There's too much work here for one man, Father.

EVE: How can you ask forgiveness? *Indicating Abel.* You can't even weep for him. You are still full of hate!

CAIN: And your hate, Mother? *She turns away.* How will I weep? You never loved Cain!

ADAM: Spare one another . . . !

EVE, *turning to the corpse:* I loved him more. *To Cain:* Yes, more than you. And God was *not* fair. To me, either. *Indicating Abel:* And I still don't understand why he had to die, or who or what rules this world. But this boy was innocent—that I know. And you killed him, and with him any claim to justice you ever had.

CAIN: I am not to blame!

EVE: Are you telling me that nothing *happened* here? I will not sit with you as though nothing happened!

ADAM: Ask her pardon! *Cain turns away from both.* Cain, we are surrounded by the beasts! And God's not coming any more—*Cain starts
away.* Boy, we are all that's left responsible!—ask her pardon! *Cain, adamant, the smile fixed on his face, walks out.* Call to him. Pardon him. In
God's name cry mercy, Eve, there is no other!

> *With his arm around her he has drawn her to the periphery,
> where she stands, her mouth open, struggling to speak. But
> she cannot, and she breaks into weeping. As though in her
> name, Adam calls toward the departed Cain:* Mercy!

> *The roars, songs, and cries of the animals fill the air. Adam looks
> up and about, and to the world, a clear-eyed prayer:* Mercy!

CURTAIN

THE ARCHBISHOP'S CEILING

1977

Characters

ADRIAN

MAYA

MARCUS

IRINA

SIGMUND

ACT ONE

Some time ago.

A capital in Europe; the sitting room in the former residence of the archbishop.

Judging by the depth of the casement around the window at right, the walls must be two feet thick. The room has weight and power, its contents chaotic and sensuous. Decoration is early baroque.

The ceiling is first seen: in high relief the Four Winds, cheeks swelling, and cherubim, darkened unevenly by soot and age.

Light is from a few lamps of every style, from a contemporary bridge lamp to something that looks like an electrified hookah, but the impression of a dark, overcrowded room remains; the walls absorb light.

A grand piano, scarved; a large blue vase on the floor under it.

Unhung paintings, immense and dark, leaning against a wall, heavy gilt frames.

Objects of dull brass not recently polished.

Two or three long, dark carved chests topped with tasseled rose-colored cushions.

A long, desiccated brown leather couch with billowing cushions; a stately carved armchair, bolsters, Oriental camel bags.

A pink velour settee, old picture magazines piled on its foot and underneath—Life, Stern, Europeo . . .

A Bauhaus chair in chrome and black leather on one of the smallish Persian rugs.

A wide, ornate rolltop desk, probably out of the twenties, with a stuffed falcon or gamebird on its top.

Contemporary books on shelves, local classics in leather.

A sinuous chaise in faded pink.

Layers of chaos.

At up right a doorway to the living quarters.

At left a pair of heavy doors opening on a dimly lit corridor. More chests here, a few piled-up chairs. This corridor leads upstage into darkness (and the unseen stairway down to the front door). The corridor wall is of large unfaced stones.

Adrian is seated on a couch. He is relaxed, an attitude of waiting, legs crossed, arms spread wide. Now he glances at the doorway to the living quarters, considers for a moment, then lifts up the couch cushions, looking underneath. He stands and goes to a table lamp, tilts it over to look under its base. He looks about again and peers into the open piano.

He glances up at the doorway again, then examines the ceiling, his head turned straight up. With another glance at the doorway he proceeds to the window at right and looks behind the drapes.

Maya enters from the living quarters with a coffeepot and two cups on a tray.

ADRIAN: Tremendous view of the city from up here.

MAYA: Yes.

ADRIAN: Like seeing it from a plane. Or a dream. *He turns and approaches the couch, blows on his hands.*

MAYA: Would you like one of his sweaters? I'm sorry there's no firewood.

ADRIAN: It's warm enough. He doesn't heat this whole house, does he?

MAYA: It's impossible—only this and the bedroom. But the rest of it's never used.

ADRIAN: I forgot how gloomy it is in here.

MAYA: It's a hard room to light. Wherever you put a lamp it makes the rest seem darker. I think there are too many unrelated objects—the eye can't rest here. *She laughs, offers a cup; he takes it.*

ADRIAN: Thanks, Maya. *He sits.* Am I interrupting something?

MAYA: I never do anything. When did you arrive?

ADRIAN: Yesterday morning. I was in Paris.

MAYA: And how long do you stay?

ADRIAN: Maybe tomorrow night—I'll see.

MAYA: So short!

ADRIAN: I had a sudden yen to come look around again, see some of the fellows. And you.

MAYA: They gave a visa so quickly?

ADRIAN: Took two days.

MAYA: How wonderful to be famous.

ADRIAN: I was surprised I got one at all—I've attacked them, you know.

MAYA: In the *New York Times*.

ADRIAN: Oh, you read it.

MAYA: Last fall, I believe.

ADRIAN: What'd you think of it?

MAYA: It was interesting. I partly don't remember. I was surprised you did journalism. *She sips. He waits; nothing more.*

ADRIAN: I wonder if they care what anybody writes about them anymore.

MAYA: Yes, they do—very much, I think. But I really don't know. . . . How's your wife?

ADRIAN: Ruth? She's good.

MAYA: I liked her. She had a warm heart. I don't like many women.

ADRIAN: You look different.

MAYA: I'm two years older—and three kilos.

ADRIAN: It becomes you.

MAYA: Too fat.

ADRIAN: No . . . *zaftig.* You look creamy. You changed your hairdo.

MAYA: From *Vogue* magazine.

ADRIAN, *laughs*: That so! It's sporty.

MAYA: What brings you back?

ADRIAN: . . . Your English is a thousand percent better. More colloquial.

MAYA: I recite aloud from *Vogue* magazine.

ADRIAN: You're kidding.

MAYA: Seriously. Is all I read anymore.

ADRIAN: Oh, go on with you.

MAYA: Everything in *Vogue* magazine is true.

ADRIAN: Like the girl in pantyhose leaning on her pink Rolls-Royce.

MAYA: Oh, yes, is marvelous. One time there was a completely naked girl in a mink coat—*she extends her foot*—and one foot touching the bubble bath. Fantastic imagination. It is the only modern art that really excites me.

    Adrian laughs.

And their expressions, these girls. Absolutely nothing. Like the goddesses of the Greeks—beautiful, stupid, everlasting. This magazine is classical.

ADRIAN: You're not drinking anymore?

MAYA: Only after nine o'clock.

ADRIAN: Good. You seem more organized.

MAYA: Until nine o'clock.

    They laugh. Maya sips. Slight pause. Adrian sips.

ADRIAN: What's Marcus doing in London?

MAYA: His last novel is coming out there just now.

ADRIAN: That's nice. I hear it was a success here.

MAYA: Very much—you say very much or . . . ?

ADRIAN: Very much so.

MAYA: Very much so—what a language!

ADRIAN: You're doing great. You must practice a lot.

MAYA: Only when the English come to visit Marcus, or the Americans. . . . I have his number in London if you . . .

ADRIAN: I have nothing special to say to him.

    Pause.

MAYA: You came back for one day?

ADRIAN: Well, three, really. I was in a symposium in the Sorbonne— about the contemporary novel—and it got so pompous I got an urge to sit down again with writers who had actual troubles. So I thought I'd stop by before I went home.

MAYA: You've seen anyone?

ADRIAN: Yes. *Slight pause. He reaches for a pack of cigarettes.*

MAYA, *turning to him quickly, to forgive his not elaborating*: It's all right . . .

ADRIAN: I had dinner with Otto and Sigmund, and their wives.

MAYA, *surprised*: Oh! You should have called me.

ADRIAN: I tried three times.

MAYA: But Sigmund knows my number.

ADRIAN: You don't live here anymore?

MAYA: Only when Marcus is away. *She indicates the bedroom doorway.* He has that tremendous bathtub . . .

ADRIAN: I remember, yes. When'd you break up?

MAYA: I don't remember—eight or nine months, I think. We are friends. Sigmund didn't tell you?

ADRIAN: Nothing. Maybe 'cause his wife was there.

MAYA: Why? I am friends with Elizabeth. . . . So you have a new novel, I suppose.

ADRIAN, *laughs*: You make it sound like I have one every week.

MAYA: I always think you write so easily.

ADRIAN: I always have. But I just abandoned one that I worked on for two years. I'm still trying to get up off the floor. I forgot how easy you are to talk to.

MAYA: But you seem nervous.

ADRIAN: Just sexual tension.

MAYA: You wanted to make love tonight?

ADRIAN: If it came to it, sure. *He takes her hand.* In Paris we were in the middle of a discussion of Marxism and surrealism, and I suddenly got this blinding vision of the inside of your thigh . . .

> *She laughs, immensely pleased.*

> . . . so I'm here. *He leans over and kisses her on the lips. Then he stands.* Incidentally . . . Ruth and I never married, you know.

MAYA, *surprised*: But didn't you call each other . . .

ADRIAN: We never did, really, but we never bothered to correct people. It just made it easier to travel and live together.

MAYA: And now?

ADRIAN: We're apart together. I want my own fireplace, but with a valid plane ticket on the mantel.

MAYA: Well, that's natural, you're a man.

ADRIAN: In my country I'm a child and a son of a bitch. But I'm toying with the idea of growing up—I may ask her to marry me.

MAYA: Is that necessary?

ADRIAN: You're a smart girl—that's exactly the question.

MAYA: Whether it is necessary.

ADRIAN: Not exactly that—few books are necessary; a writer has to write. It's that it became absurd, suddenly. Here I'm laying out motives, characterizations, secret impulses—the whole psychological chess game— when the truth is I'm not sure anymore that I believe in psychology. That anything we think really determines what we're going to do. Or even what we feel. This interest you?

MAYA: You mean anyone can do anything.

ADRIAN: Almost. Damn near. But the point is a little different. Ruth— when we came back from here two years ago—she went into a terrible depression. She'd had them before, but this time she seemed suicidal.

MAYA: Oh, my God. Why?

ADRIAN: Who knows? There were so many reasons there was no reason. She went back to psychiatry. Other therapies . . . nothing worked. Finally, they gave her a pill. *Slight pause.* It was miraculous. Turned her completely around. She's full of energy, purpose, optimism. Looks five years younger.

MAYA: A chemical.

ADRIAN: Yes. She didn't have the psychic energy to pull her stockings up. Now they've just made her assistant to the managing editor of her magazine. Does fifty laps a day in the swimming pool— It plugged her in to some . . . some power. And she lit up.

MAYA: She is happy?

ADRIAN: I don't really know—she doesn't talk about her mind anymore, her soul; she talks about what she does. Which is terrific . . .

MAYA: But boring.

ADRIAN: In a way, maybe—but you can't knock it; I really think it saved her life. But what bothers me is something else. *Slight pause.* She knows neither more nor less about herself now than when she was trying to die. The interior landscape has not lit up. What has changed is her reaction to power. Before she feared it, now she enjoys it. Before she fled from it, now she seeks it. She got plugged in, and she's come alive.

MAYA: So you have a problem.

ADRIAN: What problem do you think I have?

MAYA: It is unnecessary to write novels anymore.

ADRIAN: God, you're smart—yes. It made me think of Hamlet. Here we are tracking that marvelous maze of his mind, but isn't that slightly ludicrous when one knows that with the right pill his anxiety would dissolve? Christ, he's got everything to live for, heir to the throne, servants, horses—correctly medicated, he could have made a deal with the king and married Ophelia. Or Socrates—instead of hemlock, a swig of lithium and he'd end up the mayor of Athens and live to a hundred. What is lost? Some wisdom, some knowledge found in suffering. But knowledge is power, that's why it's good—so what is wrong with gaining power without having to suffer at all?

MAYA, *with the faintest color of embarrassment, it seems*: You have some reason to ask me this question?

ADRIAN: Yes.

MAYA: Why?

ADRIAN: You have no pills in this country, but power is very sharply defined here. The government makes it very clear that you must snuggle up to power or you will never be happy. *Slight pause.* I'm wondering what that does to people, Maya. Does it smooth them all out when they know they must all plug in or their lights go out, regardless of what they think or their personalities?

MAYA: I have never thought of this question. *She glances at her watch.* I am having a brandy, will you? *She stands.*

ADRIAN *laughs*: It's nine o'clock?

MAYA: In one minute. *She goes upstage, pours.*

ADRIAN: I'd love one; thanks.

MAYA: But I have another mystery. *She carefully pours two glasses. He waits. She brings him one, remains standing.* Cheers.

ADRIAN: Cheers. *They drink.* Wow—that's good.

MAYA: I prefer whisky, but he locks it up when he is away. *She sits apart from him.* I have known intimately so many writers; they all write books condemning people who wish to be successful and praised, who desire some power in life. But I have never met one writer who did not wish to be praised and successful . . . *she is smiling* . . . and even powerful. Why do they condemn others who wish the same for themselves?

ADRIAN: Because they understand them so well.

MAYA: For this reason I love *Vogue* magazine.

He laughs.

I am serious. In this magazine everyone is successful. No one has ever apologized because she was beautiful and happy. I believe this magazine. *She knocks back the remains of her drink, stands, goes toward the liquor upstage.* Tell me the truth—why have you come back?

ADRIAN, *slight pause:* You think I could write a book about this country?

MAYA, *brings down the bottle, fills his glass:* No, Adrian.

ADRIAN: I'm too American.

MAYA: No, the Russians cannot either. *She refills her own glass.* A big country cannot understand small possibilities. When it is raining in Moscow, the sun is shining in Tashkent. Terrible snow in New York, but it is a beautiful day in Arizona. In a small country, when it rains it rains everywhere. *She sits beside him.* Why have you come back?

ADRIAN: I've told you.

MAYA: Such a trip—for three days?

ADRIAN: Why not? I'm rich.

MAYA, *examines his face:* You are writing a book about us.

ADRIAN: I've written it, and abandoned it. I want to write it again.

MAYA: About this country.

ADRIAN: About you.

MAYA: But what do you know about me?

ADRIAN: Practically nothing. But something in me knows everything.

MAYA: I am astonished.

ADRIAN: My visa's good through the week—I'll stay if we could spend a lot of time together. Could we? It'd mean a lot to me.

An instant. She gets up, goes to a drawer, and takes out a new pack of cigarettes.

I promise nobody'll recognize you—the character is blonde and very tall and has a flat chest. What do you say?

MAYA: But why?

ADRIAN: I've become obsessed with this place, it's like some Jerusalem for me.

MAYA: But we are of no consequence . . .

ADRIAN: Neither is Jerusalem, but it always has to be saved. Let me stay here with you till Friday. When is Marcus coming back?

MAYA: I never know—not till spring, probably. Is he also in your book?

ADRIAN: In a way. Don't be mad, I swear you won't be recognized.

MAYA: You want me to talk about him?

ADRIAN: I'd like to understand him, that's all.

MAYA: For example?

ADRIAN: Well . . . let's see. You know, I've run into Marcus in three or four countries the past five years; had long talks together, but when I go over them in my mind I realize he's never said anything at all about himself. I like him, always glad to see him, but he's a total blank. For instance, how does he manage to get a house like this?

MAYA: But why not?

ADRIAN: It belongs to the government, doesn't it?

MAYA: It is the same way he gets everything—his trips abroad, his English suits, his girls . . .

ADRIAN: How?

MAYA: He assumes he deserves them.

ADRIAN: But his money—he seems to have quite a lot.

MAYA, *shrugs, underplaying the fact*: He sells his father's books from time to time. He had a medieval collection . . .

ADRIAN: They don't confiscate such things?

MAYA: Perhaps they haven't thought of it. You are the only person I know who thinks everything in a Socialist country is rational.

ADRIAN: In other words, Marcus is a bit of an operator.

MAYA: Marcus? Marcus is above all naive.

ADRIAN: Naive! You don't mean that.

MAYA: No one but a naive man spends six years in prison, Adrian.

ADRIAN: But in that period they were arresting everybody, weren't they?

MAYA: By no means everybody. Marcus is rather a brave man.

ADRIAN: Huh! I had him all wrong. What do you say, let me bring my bag over.

MAYA: You have your book with you?

ADRIAN: No, it's home.

She seems skeptical.

. . . Why would I carry it with me?

She stares at him with the faintest smile.

What's happening?

MAYA: I don't know—what do you think?

She gets up, cradling her glass, walks thoughtfully to another seat, and sits. He gets up and comes to her.

ADRIAN: What is it?

She shakes her head. She seems overwhelmed by some wider sadness. His tone now is uncertain.

Maya?

MAYA: You've been talking to Allison Wolfe?

ADRIAN: I've talked to him, yes.

She stands, moves, comes to a halt.

MAYA: He is still telling that story?

ADRIAN, *slight pause*: I didn't believe him, Maya.

MAYA: He's a vile gossip.

ADRIAN: He's a writer. All writers are gossips.

MAYA: He is a vile man.

ADRIAN: I didn't believe him.

MAYA: What did he say to you?

ADRIAN: Why go into it?

MAYA: I know that. I want to know. Please.

ADRIAN: It was ridiculous. Allison has a puritan imagination.

MAYA: Tell me what he said.

ADRIAN, *slight pause*: Well . . . that you and Marcus . . . look, it's so stupid . . .

MAYA: That we have orgies here?

ADRIAN: . . . Yes.

MAYA: And we bring in young girls?

He is silent.

Adrian?

ADRIAN: That this house is bugged. And you bring in girls to compromise writers with the government.

Pause.

MAYA: You'd better go, I believe.

He is silent for a moment, observing her. She is full.

I'm tired anyway . . . I was just going to bed when you called.

ADRIAN: Maya, if I believed it, would I have talked as I have in here?

MAYA, *smiling*: I don't know, Adrian—would you? Anyway, you have your passport. Why not?

ADRIAN: You know I understand the situation too well to believe Allison. Resistance is impossible anymore. I know the government's got the intellectuals in its pocket, and the few who aren't have stomach ulcers. *He comes to her, takes her hand.* I *was* nervous when I came in but it was sexual tension—I knew we'd be alone.

Her suspicion remains; she slips her hand out of his.

. . . All right, I did think of it. But that's inevitable, isn't it?

MAYA: Yes, of course. *She moves away again.*

ADRIAN: It's hard for anyone to know what to believe in this country, you can understand that.

MAYA: Yes. *She sits, lonely.*

ADRIAN, *sits beside her*: Forgive me, will you?

MAYA: It is terrible.

ADRIAN: What do you say we forget it?

She looks at him with uncertainty.

What are you doing now?

Slight pause. She stares front for a moment, then takes a breath as though resolving to carry on. Her tone brightens.

MAYA: I write for the radio.

ADRIAN: No plays anymore?

MAYA: I can't work that hard anymore.

ADRIAN: They wouldn't put them on?

MAYA: Oh, they would—I was never political, Adrian.

ADRIAN: You were, my first time . . .

MAYA: Well, everybody was in those days. But it wasn't really politics.

ADRIAN: What, then?

MAYA: I don't know—some sort of illusion that we could be Communists without having enemies. It was a childishness, dancing around the May-pole. It could never last, life is not like that.

ADRIAN: What do you write?

MAYA: I broadcast little anecdotes, amusing things I notice on the streets, the trams. I am on once a week; they have me on Saturday mornings for breakfast. What is it you want to know?

ADRIAN: I'm not interviewing you, Maya.

MAYA, *stands suddenly, between anger and fear*: Why have you come?

ADRIAN, *stands*: I've told you, Maya—I thought maybe I could grab hold of the feeling again.

MAYA: Of what?

ADRIAN: This country, this situation. It escapes me the minute I cross the border. It's like some goddammed demon that only lives here.

MAYA: But we are only people, what is so strange?

ADRIAN: I'll give you an example. It's an hour from Paris here; we sit down to dinner last night in a restaurant, and two plainclothesmen take the next table. It was blatant. Not the slightest attempt to disguise that they were there to openly intimidate Sigmund and Otto. They kept staring straight at them.

MAYA: But why did he take you to a restaurant? Elizabeth could have given you dinner.

ADRIAN: . . . I don't understand.

MAYA: But Sigmund knows that will happen if he walks about with a famous American writer.

ADRIAN: You're not justifying it . . . ?

MAYA: I have not been appointed to justify or condemn anything. *She laughs*. And neither has Sigmund. He is an artist, a very great writer, and that is what he should be doing.

ADRIAN: I can't believe what I'm hearing, Maya.

MAYA, *laughs*: But you must, Adrian. You really must believe it.

ADRIAN: You mean it's perfectly all right for two cops to be . . .

MAYA: But that is their *business*. It is not Sigmund's business to be taunting the government. Do you go about trying to infuriate your CIA, your FBI?

He is silent.

Of course not. You stay home and write your books. Just as the Russian writers stay home and write theirs . . .

ADRIAN: But Sigmund isn't permitted to write his books . . .

MAYA: My God—don't you understand *anything*?

The sudden force of her outburst is mystifying to him. He looks at her, perplexed. She gathers herself.

I'm very tired, Adrian. Perhaps we can meet again before you leave.

ADRIAN: Okay. *He looks about.* I forgot where I put my coat . . .

MAYA: I hung it inside.

She goes upstage and out through the doorway. Adrian, his face taut, looks around at the room, up at the ceiling. She returns, hands him the coat.

You know your way back to the hotel?

ADRIAN: I'll find it. *He extends his hand, she takes it.* I'm not as simple as I seem, Maya.

MAYA: I'm sorry I got excited.

ADRIAN: I understand—you don't want him taking risks.

MAYA: Why should he? Especially when things are improving all the time anyway.

ADRIAN: They aren't arresting anybody? . . .

MAYA: Of course not. Sigmund just can't get himself to admit it, so he does these stupid things. One can live as peacefully as anywhere.

ADRIAN, *putting on his coat*: Still, it's not in every country where writers keep a novel manuscript behind their fireplace.

MAYA, *stiffening*: Goodnight.

ADRIAN, *sees her cooled look; slight pause*: Goodnight, Maya. *He crosses the room to the double doors at left, and he opens one . . .*

MAYA: Adrian?

He turns in the doorway.

You didn't really mean that, I hope.

He is silent. She turns to him.

No one keeps manuscripts behind a fireplace anymore. You know that.

ADRIAN, *looks at her for a moment, with irony:* . . . Right. *He stands there, hand on the door handle, looking down at the floor, considering. He smiles, turning back to her.* Funny how life imitates art; the melodrama kept flattening out my characterizations. It's an interesting problem— whether it matters who anyone is or what anyone thinks, when all that counts anymore—is power.

> *He goes brusquely into the corridor, walks upstage into dark-ness. She hesitates then rushes out, closing the door behind her and calls up the corridor.*

MAYA, *a suppressed call:* Adrian? *She waits.* Adrian!

> *He reappears from the darkness and stands shaking his head, angry and appalled. She has stiffened herself against her con-fession.*

We can talk out here, it is only in the apartment.

ADRIAN: Jesus Christ, Maya.

MAYA: I want you to come inside for a moment—you should not have mentioned Sigmund's manuscript . . .

ADRIAN, *stunned, a look of disgust—adopting her muffled tone:* Maya . . . how can you do this?

MAYA, *with an indignant note:* They never knew he has written a novel, how dare you mention it! Did he give it to you?

ADRIAN: My head is spinning, what the hell is this? . . .

MAYA: Did he give it to you?

ADRIAN, *a flare of open anger:* How can I tell you anything? . . .

MAYA: Come inside. Say that you have sent it to Paris. Come . . . *She starts for the door.*

ADRIAN: How the hell would I send it to Paris?

MAYA: They'll be searching his house now, they'll destroy it! You must say that you sent it today with some friend of yours. *She pulls him by the sleeve.*

ADRIAN, *freeing himself:* Wait a minute—you mean they were taping us in bed?

MAYA: I don't know. I don't know when it was installed. Please . . . simply say that you have sent the manuscript to Paris. Come. *She grasps the door handle.*

ADRIAN, *stepping back from the door*: That's a crime.

> *She turns to him with a contemptuous look.*

Well it is, isn't it? Anyway, I didn't say it was his book.

MAYA: It was obviously him. Say you have sent it out! You must! *She opens the door instantly, enters the room, and speaking in a relaxed, normal tone.* . . . Perhaps you'd better stay until the rain lets up. I might go to bed, but why don't you make yourself comfortable?

ADRIAN, *hesitates in the corridor, then enters the room and stands there in silence, glancing about:* . . . All right. Thanks. *He stands there silent, in his fear.*

MAYA: Yes?

ADRIAN: Incidentally—*He breaks off. A long hiatus. He is internally positioning himself to the situation.* . . . that manuscript I mentioned.

MAYA: Yes?

ADRIAN: It's in Paris by now. I . . . gave it to a friend who was leaving this morning.

MAYA: Oh?

ADRIAN: Yes. *Slight pause. It occurs to him suddenly*: A girl.

MAYA, *as though amused*: You already have girls here?

ADRIAN, *starting to grin*: Well, not really—she's a cousin of mine. Actually, a second cousin. Just happened to meet her on the street. All right if I have another brandy?

MAYA: Of course.

ADRIAN, *pours*: I'll be going in a minute. *He sits in his coat on the edge of a chair with his glass.* Just let me digest this. This drink, I mean.

> *She sits on the edge of another chair a distance away.*

Quite an atmosphere in this house. I never realized it before.

MAYA: It's so old. Sixteenth century, I think.

ADRIAN: It's so alive—once you're aware of it.

MAYA: They built very well in those days.

ADRIAN, *directly to her*: Incredible. I really didn't believe it.

MAYA: Please go.

ADRIAN: In one minute. Did I dream it, or did it belong to the archbishop?

MAYA: It was his residence.

ADRIAN, *looks up to the ceiling*: That explains the cherubims . . . *looks at his drink* . . . and the antonyms.

She stands.

I'm going. This is . . . *looks around* . . . this is what I never got into my book—this doubleness. This density with angels hovering overhead. Like power always with you in a room. Like God, in a way. Just tell me—do you ever get where you've forgotten it?

MAYA: I don't really live here anymore.

ADRIAN: Why? You found this style oppressive?

MAYA: I don't hear the rain. Please.

ADRIAN, *stands facing her*: I'm not sure I should, but I'm filling up with sympathy. I'm sorry as hell, Maya.

She is silent.

I could hire a car—let's meet for lunch and take a drive in the country.

MAYA: All right. I'll pick you up at the hotel. *She starts past him toward the doors.*

ADRIAN, *takes her hand as she passes*: Thirty seconds. Please. I want to chat. Just to hear myself. *He moves her to a chair.* Half a minute . . . just in case you don't show up.

MAYA, *sitting*: Of course I will.

ADRIAN, *clings to her hand, kneebends before her*: I've never asked you before—you ever been married?

She laughs.

Come on, give me a chat. Were you?

MAYA: Never, no.

ADRIAN: And what were your people—middle class?

MAYA: Workers. They died of flu in the war.

ADRIAN: Who brought you up?

MAYA: The nuns.

ADRIAN, *stands; looks around*: . . . Is it always like a performance? Like we're quoting ourselves?

MAYA, *stands*: Goodnight. *She goes and opens the door.*

ADRIAN: My God—you poor girl. *He takes her into his arms and kisses her.* Maybe I should say—in all fairness—*leaving her, he addresses the ceiling*—that the city looks much cleaner than my last time. And there's much more stuff in the shops. And the girls have shaved their legs. In fact—*he turns to her*—*she is smiling*—this is the truth—I met my dentist in the hotel this morning. He's crazy about this country! *With a wild underlay of laughter*: Can't get over the way he can walk the streets any hour of the night, which is impossible in New York. Said he'd never felt so relaxed and free in his whole life! And at that very instant, Sigmund and Otto walked into the lobby and he congratulated them on having such a fine up-and-coming little civilization! *He suddenly yells at the top of his lungs.* Forgive me, I scream in New York sometimes.

> *She is half smiling, alert to him; he comes to the open doorway and grasps her hands.*

Goodnight. And if I never see you again . . .

MAYA: I'll be there, why not?

ADRIAN: How do I know? But just in case—I want you to know that I'll never forget you in that real short skirt you wore last time, and the moment when you slung one leg over the arm of the chair. You have a sublime sluttishness, Maya—don't be mad, it's a gift when it's sublime.

> *She laughs.*

How marvelous to see you laugh—come, walk me downstairs. *He pulls her through the doorway.*

MAYA: It's too cold out here . . .

ADRIAN, *shuts the door to the room, draws her away from it*: For old times' sake . . .

MAYA: We'll talk tomorrow.

ADRIAN, *with a wild smile, excited eyes*: You're a government agent?

MAYA: What can I say? Will you believe anything?

ADRIAN, *on the verge of laughter*: My spine is tingling. In my book, Maya—I may as well tell you, I've been struggling with my sanity the last ten minutes—in my book I made you an agent who screws all the writers and blackmails them so they'll give up fighting the government. And I abandoned it because I finally decided it was too melodramatic, the characters got lost in the plot. I invented it and I didn't believe it; and I'm standing here looking at you and *I still don't believe it!*

MAYA: Why should you?

ADRIAN, *instantly, pointing in her face*: That's what you say in the book! *He grasps her hand passionately in both of his.* Maya, listen—you've got to help me. I believe in your goodness. I don't care what you've done, I still believe that deep inside you're a rebel and you hate this goddamned government. You've got to tell me—I'll stay through the week—we'll talk and you're going to tell me what goes on in your body, in your head, in this situation.

MAYA: Wait a minute . . .

ADRIAN, *kissing her hands*: Maya, you've made me believe in my book!

> *She suddenly turns her head. So does he. Then he sees her apprehension.*

You expecting somebody?

> *Voices are heard now from below. She is listening.*

Maya?

MAYA, *mystified*: Perhaps some friends of Marcus.

ADRIAN: He gives out the key?

MAYA: Go, please. Goodnight.

> *She enters the room. He follows her in.*

ADRIAN: You need any help?

> *A man and woman appear from upstage darkness in the corridor.*

MAYA: No—no, I am not afraid . . . *She moves him to the door.*

ADRIAN: I'll be glad to stay . . . *He turns, sees the man, who is just approaching the door, a valise in his hand, wearing a raincoat.* For Christ's sake—it's Marcus!

> *Marcus is older, fifty-eight. He puts down his valise, spreads out his arms.*

MARCUS: Adrian!

> *Laughter. A girl, beautiful, very young, stands a step behind him as he and Adrian embrace.*

MAYA, *within the room*: Marcus?

MARCUS, *entering the room*: You're here, Maya! This is marvelous.

> *He gives her a peck. The girl enters, stands there looking around. He turns to Adrian.*

A friend of yours is parking my car, he'll be delighted to see you.

ADRIAN: Friend of *mine*?

MARCUS: Sigmund.

MAYA: Sigmund?

ADRIAN: Sigmund's *here?*

MARCUS: He's coming up for a drink. We ran into each other at the airport. *To Maya:* Is there food? *To Adrian:* You'll stay, won't you? I'll call some people, we can have a party.

ADRIAN: Party? *Flustered, glances at Maya.* Well . . . yeah, great!

An understanding outburst of laughter between him and Marcus.

MAYA: There's only some ham. I'm going home. *She turns to go upstage to the bedroom.*

MARCUS, *instantly*: Oh, no, Maya! You mustn't. I was going to call you first thing . . . *Recalling:* Wait, I have something for you. *He hurriedly zips open a pocket of his valise, takes out a pair of shoes in tissue.* I had an hour in Frankfurt. Look, dear . . .

He unwraps the tissue. Her face lights. She half unwillingly takes them.

MAYA: Oh, my God.

Marcus laughs. She kicks off a shoe and tries one on.

MARCUS: Right size?

IRINA, *as Maya puts on the other shoe*: Highly beautiful.

Maya takes a few steps, watching her feet, then goes to Marcus and gives him a kiss, then looks into his eyes with a faint smile, her longing and hatred.

MARCUS, *taking out folds of money*: Here, darling . . . ask Mrs. Andrus to prepare something, will you? *He hands her money.* Let's have an evening. *He starts her toward the bedroom door upstage—*But come and put something on, it's raining—*and comes face to face with the girl.* Oh, excuse me—this is Irina.

Maya barely nods, and goes back to pick up her other shoes.

ADRIAN: I'll go along with you, Maya—*He reaches for his coat.*

MARCUS: No, it's only down the street. Irina, this is my good friend, Maya.

IRINA: 'Aloo.

Maya silently shakes her hand.

MARCUS: And here is Adrian Wallach. Very important American writer.

Maya exits upstage.

ADRIAN: How do you do?

IRINA: 'Aloo. I see you Danemark.

ADRIAN: She's going to see me in Denmark?

MARCUS: She's Danish. But she speaks a little English.

IRINA, *with forefinger and thumb barely separated, to Adrian*: Very small.

ADRIAN: When do you want to meet in Denmark?

> *Maya enters putting on a raincoat.*

MAYA: Sausages?

MARCUS: And maybe some cheese and bread and some fruit. I'll open wine.

IRINA: I see your book.

ADRIAN, *suddenly, as Maya goes for the door*: Wait! I'll walk her there . . .

> *Maya hesitates at the door.*

MARCUS, *grasping Adrian's arm, laughing*: No, no, no, you are our guest; please, it's only two doors down. Maya doesn't mind.

> *Maya starts out to the door. Sigmund appears in the corridor, a heavy man shaking out his raincoat. He is in his late forties. She halts before the doorway.*

MAYA, *questioningly, but with a unique respect*: Sigmund.

SIGMUND: Maya.

> *He kisses the palm of her hand. For a moment they stand facing each other.*

MARCUS: Look who we have here, Sigmund!

> *Maya exits up the corridor as Sigmund enters the room.*

SIGMUND: Oh—my friend! *He embraces Adrian, laughing, patting his back.*

ADRIAN: How's it going, Sigmund? *He grasps Sigmund's hand.* What a terrific surprise! How's your cold, did you take my pills?

SIGMUND: Yes, thank you. I take pills, vodka, brandy, whisky—now I have only headache. *With a nod to Irina*: Grüss Gött.

> *Marcus goes and opens a chest, brings bottles and glasses to the marble table.*

IRINA: *Grüss Gött.*

ADRIAN: Oh, you speak German?

IRINA, *with the gesture*: Very small.

MARCUS: Come, help yourselves. *He takes a key ring out of his valise.* I have whisky for you, Adrian.

ADRIAN: I'll drink brandy. How about you, Sigmund?

SIGMUND: For me whisky.

MARCUS, *taking out an address book*: I'll call a couple of people, all right?

ADRIAN: *Girls!*

> *Sigmund sits downstage, takes out a cigarette.*

MARCUS: If you feel like it.

ADRIAN, *glancing at Sigmund, who is lighting up*: Maybe better just us.

MARCUS: Sigmund likes a group. *He picks up his valise.*

SIGMUND: What you like.

ADRIAN, *to Marcus*: Well, okay.

MARCUS, *pointing upstage to Irina*: Loo?

IRINA: Oh, ja!

MARCUS, *holding Irina by the waist and carrying the valise in his free hand as they move upstage; to Sigmund*: We can talk in the bedroom in a little while. *He exits with Irina.*

ADRIAN: That's a nice piece of Danish.

> *Sigmund draws on his cigarette. Adrian gets beside him and taps his shoulder; Sigmund turns up to him. Adrian points to ceiling, then to his own ear.*

Capeesh?

SIGMUND, *turns front, expressionless*: The police have confiscated my manuscript.

ADRIAN, *his hand flies out to grip Sigmund's shoulder*: No! Oh, Jesus—when?

SIGMUND: Now. Tonight.

ADRIAN, *glancing quickly around, to cover their conversation*: He had a record player . . .

SIGMUND, *with a contemptuous wave toward the ceiling*: No—I don't care.

ADRIAN: The last fifteen, twenty minutes, you mean?

SIGMUND: Tonight. They have take it away.

ADRIAN: My God, Sigmund . . .

> *Sigmund turns to him.*

I mentioned something to Maya, but I had no idea it was really . . . *He breaks off, pointing to the ceiling.*

SIGMUND: When, you told Maya?

ADRIAN: In the last fifteen minutes or so.

SIGMUND: No—they came earlier—around six o'clock.

ADRIAN: Nearly stopped my heart . . .

SIGMUND: No, I believe they find out for different reason.

ADRIAN: Why?

SIGMUND: I was so happy.

> *Pause.*

ADRIAN: So they figured you'd finished the book?

SIGMUND: I think so. I worked five years on this novel.

ADRIAN: How would they know you were happy?

SIGMUND, *pause; with a certain projection*: In this city, a man my age who is happy, attract attention.

ADRIAN: . . . Listen. When I leave tomorrow you can give . . . *He stops himself, glances upstage to the bedroom doorway, taking out a notebook and pencil. As he writes, speaking in a tone of forced relaxation*: Before I leave you've got to give me a tour of the Old Roman bath . . .

> *He shows the page to Sigmund, who reads it and looks up at him. Sigmund shakes his head negatively.*

> *Horrified*: They've got the only . . . ?

> *Sigmund nods positively and turns away.*

> *Appalled*: Sigmund—why?

SIGMUND: I thought would be safer with . . . *He holds up a single finger.*

> *Pause. Adrian keeps shaking his head.*

ADRIAN, *sotto*: What are you doing here?

SIGMUND: I met him in the airport by accident.

ADRIAN: What were you doing at the airport?

SIGMUND: To tell my wife. She works there.

ADRIAN: I thought she was a chemist.

SIGMUND: She is wife to me—they don't permit her to be chemist. She clean the floor, the windows in the airport.

ADRIAN: Oh, Jesus, Sigmund . . . *Pause.* Is there anything you can do?

SIGMUND: I try.

ADRIAN: Try what?

> *Sigmund thumbs upstage.*

> Could he?

> *Sigmund throws up his chin—tremendous influence.*

> Would he?

> *Sigmund mimes holding a telephone to his mouth, then indicates the bedroom doorway.*

> Really? To help?

SIGMUND: Is possible.

ADRIAN: Can you figure him out?

> *Sigmund extends a hand and rocks it, an expression of uncertainty on his face.*

ADRIAN: And Maya?

SIGMUND, *for a moment he makes no answer*: Woman is always complicated.

ADRIAN: You know that they . . . lie a lot.

SIGMUND: Yes. *Slight pause. He looks now directly into Adrian's eyes.* Sometimes not.

ADRIAN: You don't think it's time to seriously consider . . . *He spreads his arms wide like a plane, lifting them forward in a takeoff, then points in a gesture of flight.* What I mentioned at dinner?

> *Sigmund emphatically shakes his head no, while pointing downward—he'll remain here.*

> When we leave here I'd like to discuss whether there's really any point in that anymore.

> *Sigmund turns to him.*

> I don't know if it was in your papers, but there's a hearing problem all over the world. Especially among the young. Rock music, traffic—modern life is too loud for the human ear—you

understand me. The subtler sounds don't get through much anymore.

Sigmund faces front, expressionless.

On top of that there's a widespread tendency in New York, Paris, London, for people to concentrate almost exclusively on shopping.

SIGMUND: I have no illusion.

ADRIAN: I hope not—shopping and entertainment. Sigmund?

Sigmund turns to him, and Adrian points into his face, then makes a wide gesture to take in the room, the situation.

Not entertaining. Not on anybody's mind in those cities.

SIGMUND: I know.

ADRIAN: Boring.

SIGMUND: Yes.

ADRIAN: Same old thing. It's the wrong style.

SIGMUND: I know.

ADRIAN: I meant what I said last night; I'd be happy to support— *He points at Sigmund, who glances at him.* Until a connection is made with a university. *He points to himself.* Guarantee that.

Sigmund nods negatively and spreads both hands—he will stay here.

We can talk about it later. I'm going to ask you why. I don't understand the point anymore. Not after this.

SIGMUND: You would also if it was your country.

ADRIAN: I doubt it. I would protect my talent. I saw a movie once where they bricked up a man in a wall.

Marcus enters in a robe, opening a whisky bottle.

MARCUS: A few friends may turn up. *He sets the whisky bottle on the marble table. To Adrian:* Will you excuse us for a few minutes? Sigmund? *He indicates the bedroom.*

SIGMUND: I have told him.

Marcus turns to Adrian with a certain embarrassment.

ADRIAN: They wouldn't destroy it, would they?

Marcus seems suddenly put upon, and unable to answer.

Do you know?

MARCUS, *with a gesture toward the bedroom; to Sigmund*: Shall we?

SIGMUND, *standing*: I would like Adrian to hear.

ADRIAN, *to Marcus*: Unless you don't feel . . .

MARCUS, *unwillingly*: No—if he wishes, I have no objection.

    Sigmund sits.

ADRIAN: If there's anything I can do you'll tell me, will you?

MARCUS, *to Sigmund*: Does Maya know?

SIGMUND: She was going out.

MARCUS, *as a muted hope for alliance*: I suppose she might as well. But it won't help her getting excited.

SIGMUND: She will be calm, Maya is not foolish.

ADRIAN: Maybe we ought to get into it, Marcus—they wouldn't destroy the book, would they?

MARCUS, *with a fragile laugh*: That's only one of several questions, Adrian—the first thing is to gather our thoughts. Let me get your drink. *He stands.*

ADRIAN: I can wait with the drink. Why don't we get into it?

MARCUS: All right. *He sits again.*

ADRIAN: Marcus?

    Marcus turns to him. He points to the ceiling.

I know.

    Marcus removes his gaze from Adrian, a certain mixture of embarrassment and resentment in his face.

Which doesn't mean I've drawn any conclusions about anyone. I mean that sincerely.

MARCUS: You understand, Adrian, that the scene here is not as uncomplicated as it may look from outside. You must believe me.

ADRIAN: I have no doubt about that, Marcus. But at the same time I wouldn't want to mislead you . . . *he glances upward* . . . or anyone else. If that book is destroyed or not returned to him—for whatever it's worth I intend to publicize what I believe is an act of barbarism. This is not some kind of an issue for me—this man is my brother.

    Slight pause. Marcus is motionless. Then he turns to Adrian and gestures to him to continue speaking, to amplify. Adrian looks astonished. Marcus repeats the gesture even more imperatively.

For example . . . I've always refused to peddle my books on television, but there's at least two national network shows would be glad to have me, and for this I'd go on.

He stops; Marcus gestures to continue.

Just telling the story of this evening would be hot news from coast to coast—including Washington, D.C., where some congressmen could easily decide we shouldn't sign any more trade bills with this country. And so on and so forth.

MARCUS: It was brandy, wasn't it?

ADRIAN, *still amazed*: . . . Thanks, yes.

Marcus goes to get the drinks. Adrian catches Sigmund's eye, but the latter turns forward thoughtfully. Irina enters, heading for the drinks. Marcus brings Adrian a brandy as she makes herself a drink. In the continuing silence, Marcus returns to the drink table, makes a whisky and takes it down to Sigmund. Adrian turns toward Irina, upstage.

So how's everything in Denmark?

IRINA, *with a pleasant laugh*: No, no, not everything.

ADRIAN, *thumbing to the ceiling, to Sigmund*: *That* ought to keep them busy for a while.

MARCUS, *chuckles, sits with his own drink*: Cheers.

ADRIAN: Cheers.

SIGMUND: Cheers,

They drink. Irina brings a drink, sits on the floor beside Marcus.

MARCUS: Have you been to London this time?

ADRIAN, *pauses slightly, then glances toward Sigmund*: No. How was London?

MARCUS: It's difficult there. It seems to be an endless strike.

ADRIAN, *waits a moment*: Yes. *He decides to continue.* Last time there my British publisher had emphysema and none of the elevators were working. I never heard so many Englishmen talking about a dictatorship before.

MARCUS: They probably have come to the end of it there. It's too bad, but why should evolution spare the English?

ADRIAN: Evolution toward what—fascism?

MARCUS: Or the Arabs taking over more of the economy.

ADRIAN: I can see the bubble pipes in the House of Commons.

Laughter.

The Honorable Member from Damascus.

Laughter. It dies. Adrian thumbs toward Sigmund and then to the ceiling, addressing Marcus.

If they decide to give an answer, would it be tonight?

MARCUS, *turns up his palms*: . . . Relax, Adrian. *He drinks.* Please.

ADRIAN, *swallows a glassful of brandy*: This stuff really spins the wheels. *He inhales.*

MARCUS: It comes from the mountains.

ADRIAN: I feel like I'm on one.

MARCUS: What's New York like now?

ADRIAN: New York? New York is another room in hell. *He looks up.* Of course not as architecturally ornate. In fact, a ceiling like this in New York—I can't imagine it lasting so long without some half-crocked writer climbing up and chopping holes in those cherubim.

MARCUS: The ceiling is nearly four hundred years old, you know.

ADRIAN: That makes it less frightful?

MARCUS: In a sense, maybe—for us it has some reassuring associations. When it was made, this city was the cultural capital of Europe—the world, really, this side of China. A lot of art, science, philosophy poured from this place.

ADRIAN: Painful.

MARCUS, *with a conceding shrug*: But on the other hand, the government spends a lot keeping these in repair. It doesn't do to forget that, you know.

SIGMUND: That is true. They are repairing all the angels. It is very good to be an angel in our country.

Marcus smiles.

Yes, we shall have the most perfect angels in the whole world.

Marcus laughs.

But I believe perhaps every government is loving very much the angels, no, Adrian?

ADRIAN: Oh, no doubt about it. But six months under this particular kind of art and I'd be ready to cut my throat or somebody else's. What do you say we go to a bar, Marcus?

MARCUS, *to Sigmund*: *Ezlatchu stau?*

SIGMUND, *sighs, then nods*: *Ezlatchu.*

ADRIAN, *to Marcus*: Where does that put us?

MARCUS: He doesn't mind staying till we've had something to eat. Afterwards, perhaps.

> *Pause. Silence.*

ADRIAN: Let me in on it, Marcus—or are we waiting for something?

MARCUS: No, no, I just thought we'd eat before we talked.

ADRIAN: Oh. All right.

IRINA, *patting her stomach*: I to sandwich?

MARCUS, *patting her head like a child's, laughing*: Maya is bringing very soon.

ADRIAN: She's as sweet as sugar, Marcus, where'd you find her?

MARCUS: Her husband is the head of Danish programming for the BBC. There's Maya. *He crosses to the corridor door.*

ADRIAN: What does he do, loan her out?

MARCUS, *laughs*: No, no, she just wanted to see the country. *He exits into the corridor.*

SIGMUND: And Marcus will show her every inch.

ADRIAN, *bursts out laughing*: Oh Sigmund, Sigmund—what a century! *Sotto*: What the hell is happening?

> *Men's shouting voices below, Maya yelling loudly. Marcus*
> *instantly breaks into a run, disappears up the corridor. Adrian*
> *and Sigmund listen. The shouting continues. Sigmund gets*
> *up, goes and listens at the door.*

ADRIAN: What is it?

> *Sigmund opens the door, goes into the corridor, listens.*

Who are they?

> *A door is heard slamming below, silencing the shouts. Pause.*

Sigmund?

> *Sigmund comes back into the room.*

What was it?

SIGMUND: Drunken men. They want to see the traitor to the motherland. Enemy of the working class. *He sits.*

Pause.

ADRIAN: . . . Come to my hotel.

SIGMUND: Is not possible. Be calm.

ADRIAN: How'd they know you were here?

Sigmund shrugs, then indicates the ceiling.

They'd call out hoodlums?

Sigmund turns up his palms, shrugs.

Marcus and Maya appear up the corridor. She carries a large tray covered with a white cloth. He has a handkerchief to his cheekbone. He opens the door for her. Irina stands and clears the marble table for the tray. Marcus crosses to the upstage right doorway and exits.

Sigmund stands. Maya faces him across the room. Long pause.

What happened?

MAYA, *with a gesture toward the food*: Come, poet.

Sigmund watches her for a moment more, then goes up to the food. She is staring excitedly into his face.

The dark meat is goose.

Sigmund turns from her to the food.

Adrian?

ADRIAN: I'm not hungry. Thanks.

MAYA, *takes the plate from Sigmund and loads it heavily*: Beer?

SIGMUND: I have whisky. You changed your haircut?

MAYA: From *Vogue* magazine. You like it?

SIGMUND: Very.

MAYA, *touching his face*: Very much, you say.

SIGMUND: Very, very much.

He returns to his chair with a loaded plate, sits, and proceeds to eat in silence. She pours herself a brandy, sits near him.

MAYA, *to Adrian as she watches Sigmund admiringly*: He comes from the peasants, you know. That is why he is so beautiful. And he is sly. Like a snake.

Slight pause. Sigmund eats.

What have you done now? *She indicates below.* Why have they come?

Sigmund pauses in his eating, not looking at her.

ADRIAN, *after the pause:* The cops took his manuscript tonight.

She inhales sharply with a gasp, nearly crying out. Sigmund continues to eat. She goes to him, embraces his head, mouth pressed to his hair. He draws her hands down, apparently warding off her emotion, and continues eating. She moves and sits further away from him, staring ahead, alarmed and angry. Marcus enters from the bedroom, a bandage stuck to his cheekbone.

MARCUS, *to Adrian:* Have you taken something?

ADRIAN: Not just yet, thanks.

Maya rises to confront Marcus, but refusing her look, he passes her, a fixed smile on his face, picks up his drink from the marble table, and comes downstage and stands. First he, then Adrian, then Maya, turn and watch Sigmund eating. He eats thoroughly. Irina is also eating, off by herself.

Pause.

Marcus goes to his chair, sits, and lights a cigarette. Adrian watches him.

It's like some kind of continuous crime.

MAYA: You are so rich, Adrian, so famous—why do you make such boring remarks?

ADRIAN: Because I am a bore.

MARCUS: Oh, now, Maya . . .

MAYA, *sharply, to Marcus:* Where is it not a continuous crime?

SIGMUND: It is the truth. *To Adrian:* Just so, yes. It is a continuous crime.

MAYA, *to the three:* Stupid. Like children. Stupid!

MARCUS: *Sssh*—take something to eat, dear . . .

ADRIAN: Why are we stupid?

Ignoring his question, she goes up to the table, takes a goose wing, and bites into it. Then she comes down and stands eating. After a moment . . .

MARCUS: It's wonderful to see you again, Adrian. What brought you back here?

MAYA: He has been talking to Allison Wolfe.

MARCUS, *smiling, to Adrian*: Oh, to Allison.

ADRIAN: Yes.

MARCUS: Is he still going around with that story?

MAYA: Yes.

MARCUS, *slight pause*: Adrian . . . you know, I'm sure, that this house has been a sort of gathering place for writers for many years now. And they've always brought their girlfriends, and quite often met girls here they didn't know before. Our first literary magazine after the war was practically published from this room.

ADRIAN: I know that, Marcus.

MARCUS: Allison happened to be here one night, a month or so ago, when there was a good bit of screwing going on.

ADRIAN: Sorry I missed it.

MARCUS: It *was* fairly spectacular. But believe me—it was a purely spontaneous outburst of good spirits. Totally unexpected, it was just one of those things that happens with enough brandy.

Adrian laughs.

What I think happened is that—you see, we had a novelist here who was about to emigrate; to put it bluntly, he is paranoid. I can't blame him—he hasn't been able to publish here since the government changed. And I am one of the people he blamed, as though I had anything to say about who is or isn't to be published. But the fact that I live decently and can travel proved to him that I have some secret power with the higher echelons—in effect, that I am some sort of agent.

ADRIAN: Those are understandable suspicions, Marcus.

MARCUS, *with a light laugh*: But why!

MAYA: It is marvelous, Adrian, how understandable everything is for you.

ADRIAN: I didn't say that at all, Maya; I know practically nothing about Marcus, so I could hardly be making an accusation, could I?

MARCUS: Of course not. It's only that the whole idea is so appalling.

ADRIAN: Well, I apologize. But it's so underwater here an outsider is bound to imagine all sorts of nightmares.

MAYA: You have no nightmares in America?

ADRIAN: You know me better than that, Maya—of course we have them, but they're different.

IRINA, *revolving her finger*: Is music?

MARCUS: In a moment, dear.

MAYA: I really must say, Adrian—when you came here the other times it was the Vietnam War, I believe. Did anyone in this country blame you personally for it?

ADRIAN: No, they didn't. But it's not the same thing, Maya.

MAYA: It never is, is it?

ADRIAN: I was arrested twice for protesting the war. Not that that means too much—we had lawyers to defend us and the networks had it all over the country the next day. So there's no comparison, and maybe I know it better than most people. And that's why I'm not interested in blaming anyone here. This is impossible, Marcus, why don't we find a restaurant, I'm beginning to sound like an idiot.

MARCUS: We can't now, I've invited . . .

ADRIAN: Then why don't you meet us somewhere. Sigmund? What do you say, Maya—where's a good place?

MARCUS: Not tonight, Adrian.

> *Adrian turns to him, catching a certain obscure decision. Marcus addresses Sigmund.*

I took the liberty of asking Alexandra to stop by.

> *Sigmund turns his head to him, surprised. Maya turns to Marcus from upstage, the plate in her hand.*

> *To Maya*: I thought he ought to talk to her. *To Sigmund*: I hope you won't mind.

MAYA, *turns to Sigmund, and with a certain surprise*: You will talk with Alexandra?

> *Sigmund is silent.*

IRINA, *revolving her finger*: Jazz?

MARCUS: In a moment, dear.

SIGMUND: She is coming?

MARCUS: She said she'd try. I think she will. *To Adrian*: She is a great admirer of Sigmund's.

> *Maya comes down to Adrian with a plate. She is watching Sigmund, who is facing front.*

MAYA: I think you should have asked if he agrees.

MARCUS: I don't see the harm. She can just join us for a drink, if nothing more.

ADRIAN, *accepting the plate*: Thanks. She a writer?

MAYA: Her father is the Minister of Interior. *She points at the ceiling.* He is in charge . . .

ADRIAN: Oh! I see. *He turns to watch Sigmund, who is facing front.*

MARCUS: She writes poetry.

MAYA: Yes. *She glances anxiously to Sigmund.* Tremendous . . . *spreads her arms . . . long* poems. *She takes a glass and drinks deeply.*

MARCUS, *on the verge of sharpness*: Nevertheless, I think she has a certain talent.

MAYA: Yes. You think she has a certain talent, Sigmund?

MARCUS: Now, Maya . . . *He reaches out and lifts the glass out of her hand.*

MAYA: Each year, you see, Adrian—since her father was appointed, this woman's poetry is more and more admired by more and more of our writers. A few years ago only a handful appreciated her, but now practically everybody calls her a master. *Proudly*: Excepting for Sigmund—until now, anyway. *She takes the glass from where Marcus placed it.*

SIGMUND, *pause*: She is not to my taste . . . *he hesitates* . . . but perhaps she is a good poet.

MAYA, *slight pause*: But she has very thick legs.

> *Marcus turns to her.*

> But that must be said, Marcus . . . *She laughs.* We are not yet obliged to overlook a fact of nature. Please say she has thick legs.

MARCUS: I have no interest in her legs.

MAYA: Sigmund, my darling—surely you will say she . . .

MARCUS: Stop that, Maya . . .

MAYA, *suddenly, at the top of her voice*: It is important! *She turns to Sigmund.*

SIGMUND: She has thick legs, yes.

MAYA: Yes. *She presses his head to her hip.* Some truths will not change, and certain people, for all our sakes, are appointed never to forget them. How do the Jews say?—If I forget thee, O Jerusalem, may I cut off my hand? . . . *To Irina*: You want jazz?

IRINA, *starts to rise, happily*: Jazz!

MAYA, *helping her up*: Come, you poor girl, we have hundreds . . . I mean he does. *She laughs.* My God, Marcus, how long I lived here. *She laughs, nearly weeping.* I'm going crazy . . .

SIGMUND, *stands*: I must walk. I have eaten too much. *He buttons his jacket.*

ADRIAN, *indicating below*: What about those men?

> Sigmund beckons Adrian toward the double doors at left. He moves toward the left door, which he opens as Adrian stands, starts after him, then halts and turns with uncertainty to Marcus and Maya, who look on without expression. Adrian goes out, shutting the door. Sigmund is standing in the corridor.

MAYA, *to Irina*: Come, we have everything. *She goes and opens an overhead cabinet, revealing hundreds of records.* From Paris, London, New York, Rio . . . you like conga?

> Irina reads the labels. Maya turns her head toward the corridor. Marcus now turns as well.

SIGMUND: Do you understand?

ADRIAN: No.

SIGMUND: I am to be arrested.

ADRIAN: How do you know that?

SIGMUND: Alexander is the daughter of . . .

ADRIAN: I know—the Minister of . . .

SIGMUND: Marcus would never imagine I would meet with this woman otherwise.

ADRIAN: Why? What's she about?

SIGMUND: She is collecting the dead for her father. She arrange for writers to go before the television, and apologize for the government. *Mea culpa*—to kissing their ass.

> *Slight pause.*

ADRIAN: I think you've got to leave the country, Sigmund.

> *Maya crosses the room.*

SIGMUND: Is impossible. We cannot discuss it.

> *Maya enters the corridor, closing the door behind her.*

MAYA: Get out.

SIGMUND, *comes to her, takes her hand gently*: I must talk to Adrian.

MAYA: Get out, get out! *To Adrian*: He must leave the country. *To Sigmund*: Finish with it! Tell Marcus.

SIGMUND, *turns her to the door, a hand on her back. He opens the door for her*: Please, Maya.

> *She enters the room, glancing back at him in terror. He shuts the door.*

IRINA, *holding out a record*: Play?

> *Maya looks to Marcus, who turns away. Then she goes and uncovers a record player, turns it on, sets the record on it. During the following the music plays, a jazz piece or conga. First Irina dances by herself, then gets Marcus up and dances with him. Maya sits, drinking.*
>
> *Pause.*

SIGMUND: You have a pistol?

ADRIAN: . . . A pistol?

SIGMUND: Yes.

ADRIAN: No. Of course not. *Pause.* How could I carry a pistol on an airplane?

SIGMUND: Why not? He has one in his valise. I saw it.

> *Pause.*

ADRIAN: What good would a pistol do?

> *Pause.*

SIGMUND: . . . It is very difficult to get pistol in this country.

ADRIAN: This is unreal, Sigmund, you can't be thinking of a . . .

SIGMUND: If you will engage him in conversation, I will excuse myself to the bathroom. He has put his valise in the bedroom. I will take it from the valise.

ADRIAN: And do what with it?

SIGMUND: I will keep it, and he will tell them that I have it. In this case they will not arrest me.

ADRIAN: But why not?

SIGMUND: They will avoid at the present time to shoot me.

ADRIAN: . . . And I'm to do . . . what am I to . . .

SIGMUND: It is nothing; you must only engage him when I am excusing myself to the bathroom. Come . . .

ADRIAN: Let me catch my breath, will you? . . . It's unreal to me, Sigmund, I can't believe you have to do this.

SIGMUND: It is not dangerous, believe me.

ADRIAN: Not for me, but I have a passport. . . . Then this is why Marcus came back?

SIGMUND: I don't know. He has many friends in the government, but . . . I don't know why.

ADRIAN: He's an agent.

SIGMUND: Is possible not.

ADRIAN: Then what is he?

SIGMUND: Marcus is Marcus.

ADRIAN: Please, explain to me. I've got to understand before I go in there.

SIGMUND: It is very complicated between us.

ADRIAN: Like what? Maya?

SIGMUND: Maya also. *Slight pause.* When I was young writer, Marcus was the most famous novelist in our country. In Stalin time he has six years in prison. He could not write. I was not in prison. When he has returned I am very popular, but he was forgotten. It is tragic story.

ADRIAN: You mean he's envious of you.

SIGMUND: This is natural.

ADRIAN: But didn't you say he's protected you . . .

SIGMUND: Yes, of course. Marcus is very complicated man.

ADRIAN: But with all that influence, why can't you sit down and maybe he can think of something for you.

SIGMUND: He has thought of something—he has thought of Alexandra.

ADRIAN: You mean he's trying to destroy you.

SIGMUND: No. Is possible he believes he is trying to help me.

ADRIAN: But subconsciously . . .

SIGMUND: Yes. Come, we must go back.

ADRIAN: Just one more minute. You're convinced he's not an agent.

SIGMUND: My opinion, no.

ADRIAN: But how does he get all these privileges?

SIGMUND: Marcus is lazy. Likewise, he is speaking French, English, German—five, six language. When the foreign writers are coming, he is very gentleman, he makes using salon, he is showing the castles, the restaurants, introduce beautiful girls. When these writers return home they say is no bad problem in this civilized country. He makes very nice impression, and for this they permit him to be lazy. Is not necessary to be agent.

ADRIAN: You don't think it's possible that he learned they were going to arrest you and came back to help you?

Sigmund looks at him, surprised.

That makes as much sense as anything else, Sigmund. Could he have simply wanted to do something decent? Maybe I'm being naive, but if he wanted your back broken, his best bet would be just to sit tight in London and let it happen.

Sigmund is silent.

And as for calling Alexandra—maybe he figured your only chance *is* actually to make peace with the government.

Sigmund is silent.

You grab that gun and you foreclose everything—you're an outlaw. Is it really impossible to sit down with Marcus, man to man? I mean, you're pinning everything on an interpretation, aren't you?

SIGMUND: I know Marcus.

ADRIAN: Sigmund—every conversation I've ever had with him about this country, he's gone out of his way to praise you—your talent and you personally. I can't believe I was taken in; he genuinely admires your guts, your resistance. Let me call him out here.

Sigmund turns, uncertain but alarmed.

What's to lose? Maybe there's a string he can pull, let's put *his* feet to the fire. Because he's all over Europe lamenting conditions here, he's a big liberal in Europe. I've seen him get girls with those lamentations. Let me call him on it.

SIGMUND, *with a blossoming suspicion in the corners of his eyes*: I will never make speech on the television . . .

ADRIAN, *alarmed*: For Christ's sake, Sigmund, you don't imagine *I* would want that. *He explodes.* This is a quagmire, a fucking asylum! . . . But I'm not helping out with any guns. It's suicide, you'll have to do that alone. *He goes to the door.*

SIGMUND: Adrian?

ADRIAN: I'm sorry, Sigmund, but that's the way I feel.

SIGMUND: I want my manuscript. If you wish to talk to Marcus, I have nothing to object . . . on this basis.

Adrian looks at him, unsatisfied, angry. He turns and flings the door open, enters the room.

ADRIAN: Marcus? Can I see you a minute?

MARCUS: Of course. What is it?

ADRIAN: Out here, please . . . if you don't mind?

Marcus crosses the room and enters the corridor. Sigmund avoids Marcus's eyes, stands waiting. Marcus turns to Adrian as he shuts the door.

MARCUS: Yes?

Maya opens the door, enters the corridor, shuts it behind her. Marcus turns up his robe collar.

ADRIAN, *breaks into an embarrassed grin*: I'm not sure what to say or not say. . . . I'm more of a stranger than I'd thought, Marcus . . .

MARCUS: We're all strangers in this situation—nobody ever learns how to deal with it.

ADRIAN: . . . I take it you have some contacts with the government.

MARCUS: Many of us do; it's a small country.

ADRIAN: I think they ought to know that, ah . . . *He glances to Sigmund, but Sigmund is not facing in his direction.* If he's to be arrested, he'll—resist.

Maya turns quickly to Sigmund, alarm in her face.

MARCUS: I don't understand—*To Sigmund, with a faintly embarrassed grin*: Why couldn't you have said that to me?

Sigmund, bereft of an immediate answer, starts to turn to him.

Well, it doesn't matter. *He is flushed. He turns back to Adrian.* Yes?

ADRIAN: What I thought was, that . . .

MARCUS: Of course, if we're talking about some—violent gesture, they will advertise it as the final proof he is insane. Which is what they've claimed all along. But what was your thought?

ADRIAN: I have the feeling that the inevitable is being accepted. They act and you react. I'd like to sit down, the four of us, and see if we can come up with some out that nobody's ever thought of before.

MARCUS: Certainly. But it's a waste of time if you think you can change their program.

ADRIAN: Which is what, exactly?

MARCUS: Obviously—to drive him out of the country. Failing that, to make it impossible for him to function.

ADRIAN: And you think?

MARCUS: There's no question in my mind—he must emigrate. They've taken the work of his last five years, what more do you want?

ADRIAN: There's no one at all you could approach?

MARCUS: With what? What can I offer that they need?

ADRIAN: Like what, for example?

MARCUS: Well, if he agreed to emigrate, conceivably they might let go of the manuscript—providing, of course, that it isn't too politically inflammatory. But that could be dealt with, I think—they badly want him gone.

ADRIAN: There's no one up there who could be made to understand that if they ignored him he would simply be another novelist . . .

MARCUS, *laughing lightly*: But will he ignore *them*? How is it possible? This whole country is inside his skin—that is his greatness—They have a right to be terrified.

ADRIAN: Supposing there were a copy of the manuscript.

MARCUS: But there isn't, so it's pointless talking about it.

ADRIAN: But if there were.

MARCUS: It might have been a consideration.

ADRIAN: . . . If they knew it would be published abroad.

MARCUS: It might slow them down, yes. But they know Sigmund's personality.

ADRIAN: How do you mean?

MARCUS: He's not about to trust another person with his fate—it's a pity; they'd never have found it in this house in a hundred years. The cellar's endless, the gallery upstairs full of junk—to me, this is the saddest part of all. If it had made a splash abroad it might have held their hand for six months, perhaps longer. *With a regretful glance at Sigmund*: But . . . so it goes. *Pause. He blows on his hands.* It's awfully cold out here, come inside . . . *He starts for the door.*

ADRIAN: There's a copy in Paris.

Maya and Sigmund turn swiftly to him.

MARCUS: . . . In Paris.

ADRIAN: I sent it off this morning.

MARCUS: *This* morning?

ADRIAN: I ran into a cousin of mine; had no idea she was here. She took it with her to Gallimard—they're my publishers.

> *A broken smile emerges on Marcus's face. He is filling with a swirl of colors, glancing first at Maya, then at Sigmund, then back to Adrian.*

MARCUS: Well then . . . that much is solved. *He goes to the door.*

ADRIAN: They should be told, don't you think?

MARCUS, *stands at the door, his hand on the knob, finally turns to all of them*: How terrible. *Slight pause. To Maya and Sigmund: Such* contempt. *Slight pause.* Why? . . . Can you tell me? *They avoid his gaze. He turns to Adrian.* There's no plane to Paris today. Monday, Wednesday, and Friday. This is Tuesday, Adrian.

SIGMUND: I did not ask him to say that.

MARCUS: But perfectly willing to stand there and hope I'd believe it.

ADRIAN: I'm sorry, Marcus . . .

MARCUS, *laughing*: But Adrian, I couldn't care less.

MAYA, *moving to him*: Help him.

MARCUS: Absolutely not. I am finished with it. No one will ever manipulate me, I will not be in that position.

MAYA: He is a stupid man, he understands nothing!

ADRIAN: Now, hold it a second . . .

MAYA: Get out of here!

ADRIAN: Just hold it a second, goddammit! I'm out of my depth, Marcus, but I've apologized. I'm sorry. But you have to believe it was solely my invention; Sigmund has absolute faith in you.

SIGMUND: You can forgive him, Marcus—he tells you the truth; he believes you are my friend, he said this to me a moment ago.

ADRIAN: I feel he's drowning, Marcus, it was just something to grab for. *He holds out his hand.* Forgive me, it just popped out of my mouth.

MARCUS, *silently clasps his hand for an instant, and lets go; to Sigmund and Maya especially*: Come inside. We'll talk.

ADRIAN, *as Marcus turns to the door*: . . . Marcus?

> *Marcus turns to him. He is barely able to continue.*

Don't you think—it would be wiser—a bar or something?

MARCUS: I'm expecting Alexandra.

ADRIAN: Could you leave a note on the door? But it's up to you and Sigmund. *To Sigmund*: What do you think?

SIGMUND, *hesitates*: It is for Marcus to decide. *He looks at Marcus*. It is his house.

> *Marcus expressionless, stands silent.*

MAYA: Darling . . . *delicately* . . . it will endure a thousand years. *Marcus looks at her*. . . . I've read it. It is all we ever lived. They must not, must not touch it. Whatever humiliation, whatever is necessary for this book, yes. More than he himself, more than any human being—this book they cannot harm. . . . Francesco's is still open. *She turns to Adrian*. But I must say to you, Adrian—nothing has ever been found in this house. We have looked everywhere.

ADRIAN: It's entirely up to Marcus. *To Marcus*: You feel it's all right to talk in there?

> *Long pause.*

MARCUS, *with resentment*: I think Maya has answered that question, don't you?

ADRIAN: Okay. Then you're not sure.

MARCUS: But you are, apparently.

ADRIAN, *slight pause; to Sigmund*: I think I ought to leave.

SIGMUND: No, no . . .

ADRIAN: I think I'm only complicating it for you—

SIGMUND: I insist you stay . . .

ADRIAN, *laughs nervously, his arm touching Sigmund's shoulder*: I'm underwater, kid, I can't operate when I'm drowning. *Without pausing, to Marcus*: I really don't understand why you're offended.

MARCUS: The question has been answered once. There has never been any proof of an installation. But when so many writers congregate here, I've had to assume there might be something. The fact is, I have always warned people to be careful what they say in there—but only to be on the safe side. Is that enough?

SIGMUND: Come! *To Marcus, heartily, as he begins to press Adrian toward the door*: Now I will have one big whisky . . .

> *Marcus laughs, starting for the door.*

ADRIAN, *separating himself from Sigmund*: I'll see you tomorrow, Sigmund.

> *Silence. They go still.*

This is all your marbles, kid. It's too important for anyone to be standing on his dignity. I think I'm missing some of the overtones. *To Marcus*: But all I know is that if it were me I'd feel a lot better if I could hear you say what you just said—in there.

MARCUS: What *I* said?

ADRIAN, *slight pause*: That you've always warned people that the government might be listening, in that room.

SIGMUND: Is not necessary . . .

ADRIAN: I think it . . .

SIGMUND: Absolutely not! Please . . . *He presses Adrian toward the door and stretches his hand out to Marcus.* Come, Marcus, please.

Sigmund leads the way into the room, followed by Adrian, then Marcus and Maya. For an instant they are all awkwardly standing there. Then Sigmund presses his hand against his stomach.

Excuse me one moment. *He goes up toward the bedroom doorway.*

ADRIAN, *suddenly alerted, starts after Sigmund*: Sigmund . . .

But Sigmund is gone. He is openly conflicted about rushing after him . . .

MAYA: What is it?

ADRIAN, *blurting, in body-shock*: Level with him. Marcus . . . this is your Hemingway, your Faulkner, for Christ's sake—help him!

Sigmund enters from bedroom, a pistol in his hand. Irina, seeing it, strides away from him in fright.

SIGMUND, *to Marcus*: Forgive me. I must have it. *He puts it in his pocket.*

IRINA, *pointing at his pocket*: Shoot?

SIGMUND: No, no. We are all friend. *Alle gute Freunde hier.*

IRINA: Ah. *She turns questioningly to Marcus, then Adrian, Maya, and Sigmund.*

Pause.

ADRIAN: Marcus?

Marcus, at center, turns front, anger mounting in his face. Maya goes and shuts off the record player. Then she turns to him, waiting.

Will you say it? In here? Please?

END OF ACT ONE

ACT TWO

*Positions the same. A tableau, Marcus at center, all waiting
for him to speak. Finally he moves, glances at Sigmund.*

MARCUS: They are preparing a trial for you.

MAYA, *clapping her hands together, crying out*: Marcus!

*She starts toward him, but he walks from her, turning away in
impatience. She halts.*

When?

Marcus is silent, downing his resentment.

Do you know when?

MARCUS: I think within the month.

MAYA, *turning to Sigmund*: My God, my God.

SIGMUND, *after a moment*: And Otto and Peter?

MARCUS: I don't know about them. *He goes in the silence to his chair, sits.*

Pause.

ADRIAN: What would they charge him with?

MARCUS: . . . Fantastic. Break off a trip, fly across Europe, and now I'm
asked—what am I asked?—to justify myself? Is that it?

*Unable to answer, Adrian evades his eyes, then glances to Sig-
mund for aid; but Sigmund is facing front and now walks to
a chair and sits.*

MAYA, *to Marcus*: No, no, dear . . . *Of Sigmund*: It's only such a shock
for him . . .

MARCUS, *rejecting her apology, glances at Adrian*: . . . Section Nineteen,
I'd imagine. Slandering the state.

ADRIAN: On what grounds?

MARCUS: He's been sending out some devastating letters to the European
press; this last one to the United Nations—have you read that?

ADRIAN: Just now in Paris, yes.

MARCUS: What'd you think of it?

ADRIAN, *with a cautious glance at Sigmund*: It was pretty hot, I guess—What's the penalty for that?

MARCUS: A year. Two, three, five—who knows?

> *Slight pause.*

MAYA: It was good of you to return, dear.

> *Marcus does not respond. She invites Sigmund's gratitude.*

> . . . Sigmund?

SIGMUND, *waits an instant*: Yes. Thank you, Marcus.

> *Marcus remains looking front.*

> It is definite?

MARCUS: I think it is. And it will affect every writer in the country, if it's allowed to happen.

SIGMUND: How do you know this?

> *Slight pause.*

MARCUS: My publisher had a press reception for me day before yesterday—for my book. A fellow from our London embassy turned up. We chatted for a moment, then I forgot about him, but in the street afterwards, he was suddenly beside me . . . we shared a cab. *Slight pause. He turns directly to Sigmund.* He said he was from the Embassy Press Section.

SIGMUND: Police.

MARCUS, *lowers his eyes in admission*: He was . . . quite violent . . . his way of speaking.

SIGMUND: About me.

> *Slight pause.*

MARCUS: I haven't heard that kind of language . . . since . . . the old days. "You are making a mistake," he said, "if you think we need tolerate this scum any longer . . ."

MAYA: My God, my God . . .

MARCUS: "You can do your friend a favor," he said, "and tell him to get out this month or he will eat his own shit for five or six years."

> *Maya weeps.*

"And as far as a protest in the West, he can wrap it in bacon fat and shove it up his ass." Pounded the seat with his fist. Bloodshot eyes. I thought he was going to hit me for a moment there. . . . It was quite an act.

ADRIAN: An act?

MARCUS: Well he wasn't speaking for himself, of course. *Slight pause.* I started a letter, but I know your feelings about leaving—I felt we had to talk about it face to face.

SIGMUND: Please.

MARCUS, *hesitates, then turns to Adrian*: Are you here as a journalist?

ADRIAN: God, no—I just thought I'd stop by . . .

MAYA: He has written a novel about us.

MARCUS, *unguarded*: About us? Really! . . .

ADRIAN: Well, not literally . . .

MARCUS: When is it coming out?

ADRIAN: It won't. I've abandoned it.

MARCUS: Oh! That's too bad. Why?

ADRIAN: I'm not here to write about you, Marcus . . . honestly.

> *Marcus nods, unconvinced. Adrian addresses Sigmund as well.*

> I'll leave now if you think I'm in the way . . .

> *Sigmund doesn't react.*

MARCUS: It's all right. *Slight pause.* But if you decide to write something about us . . .

ADRIAN: I've no intention . . .

MARCUS, *smiling*: You never know. We have a tactical disagreement, Sigmund and I. To me, it's really a question of having had different experiences—although there are only seven or eight years between us; things that he finds intolerable are actually—from another viewpoint—improvements over the past . . .

ADRIAN, *indicating Maya*: I only found out today you were in prison . . .

MARCUS: A camp, actually—we dug coal.

ADRIAN: Six years.

MARCUS: And four months.

ADRIAN: What for?

MARCUS: It's one of those stories which, although long, is not interesting. *He laughs.* The point is simple, in any case. We happen to occupy a . . . strategic zone, really—between two hostile ways of life. And no government here is free to do what it would like to do. But some intelligent, sympathetic people are up there now who weren't around in the old times, and to challenge these people, to even insult them, is to indulge in a sort of fantasy . . .

SIGMUND, *pointing to the ceiling*: Marcus, this is reality?

MARCUS: Let me finish . . .

SIGMUND: But is very important—who is fantastic? *He laughs.* We are some sort of characters in a poem which they are writing; is not my poem, is their poem . . . and I do not like this poem, it makes me crazy! *He laughs.*

ADRIAN: I understand what he means, though . . .

SIGMUND: I not! I am sorry. Excuse me, Marcus—please continue.

MARCUS, *slight pause*: They ought not be forced into political trials again . . .

SIGMUND: *I* am forcing . . . ?

MARCUS: May I finish? It will mean a commitment which they will have to carry through, willingly or not. And that can only mean turning out the lights for all of us, and for a long time to come. It mustn't be allowed to happen, Sigmund. And it need not happen. *Slight pause.* I think you have to get out. For all our sakes.

With an ironic shake of his head, Sigmund makes a long exhale.

MARCUS: . . . I've called Alexandra because I think you need a line of communication now. If only to stall things for a time, or whatever you . . .

SIGMUND, *toward Maya*: I must now communicate with *Alexandra.*

MARCUS: She adores your work, whatever you think of her.

Sigmund gives him a sarcastic glance.

This splendid isolation has to end, Sigmund—it was never real and now it's impossible.

SIGMUND, *shakes his head*: I will wait for her. I may wait?

MARCUS: I certainly hope you will. *Slight pause.* I only ask you to keep in mind that this goes beyond your personal feelings about leaving . . .

SIGMUND: I have never acted for personal feelings.

MARCUS, *insistently*: You've been swept away now and then—that United Nations letter could change nothing except enrage them . . .

SIGMUND: I may not also be enraged?

MAYA: Don't argue about it, please . . .

SIGMUND, *smiling to her*: Perhaps is time we argue . . .

MAYA: Sigmund, we are all too old to be right! *She picks up a glass.*

MARCUS: Are you getting drunk?

MAYA: No, I am getting sorry. Is no one to be sorry? I am sorry for both of you. I am sorry for Socialism. I am sorry for Marx and Engels and Lenin— *She shouts to the air.* I am sorry! *To Irina, irritably*: Don't be frightened. *She pours a drink.*

> Pause.

ADRIAN: I'd like to take back what I asked you before, Marcus.

MARCUS: How can I know what is in this room? How ludicrous can you get?

ADRIAN: I agree. I wouldn't be willing to answer that question in my house either.

SIGMUND: But would not be necessary to ask such question in your house.

ADRIAN: Oh, don't kid yourself . . .

MARCUS: The FBI is everywhere . . .

ADRIAN: Not everywhere, but they get around. The difference with us is that it's illegal.

SIGMUND: *Vive la différence.*

MARCUS: Provided you catch them.

ADRIAN, *laughs*: Right. *He catches Sigmund's dissatisfaction with him.* I'm not saying it's the same . . .

SIGMUND, *turns away from Adrian to Maya*: Please, Maya, a whisky.

MAYA, *eagerly*: Yes! *She goes up to the drink table. Silence. She pours a drink, brings it to Sigmund.*

ADRIAN: Did this woman say what time she . . .

MARCUS: She's at some embassy dinner. As soon as she can break away. Shouldn't be long. *Slight pause. He indicates Sigmund's pocket.* Give me that thing, will you?

> *Sigmund does not respond.*

ADRIAN: Go ahead, Sigmund.

SIGMUND: I . . . keep for few minutes. *He drinks.*

> Pause.

ADRIAN: I'm exhausted. *He hangs his head and shakes it.*

MAYA: You drink too fast.

ADRIAN: No . . . it's the whole thing—it suddenly hit me. *He squeezes his eyes.* Mind if I lie down?

MARCUS, *gesturing toward the couch*: Of course.

> *Adrian goes to the couch.*

> What's *your* feeling?

ADRIAN: He's got to get out, I've told him that. *He lies down.* They're doing great, what do they need literature for? It's a pain in the ass. *He throws an arm over his eyes, sighs.* Christ . . . it's unbelievable. An hour from the Sorbonne.

MAYA, *a long pause; she sits between Sigmund and Marcus, glancing uncomfortably from one to the other*: It was raining in London?

MARCUS: No, surprisingly warm. How's your tooth?

MAYA, *pointing to a front tooth, showing him*: They saved it.

MARCUS: Good. He painted the bathroom.

MAYA: Yes, he came, finally. I paid him. The rest of the money is in the desk.

MARCUS: Thanks, dear. Looks very nice.

> *Slight pause.*

MAYA, *leans her elbow on her knee, her chin on her fist, observes her leg, then glances at Marcus*: My bird died on Sunday.

MARCUS: Really? Lulu?

MAYA: Yes. I finally found out, though—she was a male. *To Sigmund*: And all these years I called him Lulu!

SIGMUND: I can give you one of my rabbits.

MAYA: Oh, my God, no rabbits. *She sighs.* No birds, no cats, no dogs . . . Nothing, nothing anymore. *She drinks.*

> *Pause.*

ADRIAN, *from the couch*: You ever get mail from your program?

MAYA: Oh, very much. Mostly for recipes, sometimes I teach them to cook.

SIGMUND: She is very comical. She is marvelous actress.

ADRIAN: It's not a political . . . ?

MAYA: No! It's too early in the morning. I hate politics . . . boring, boring, always the same. . . . You know something? You are both very handsome.

Sigmund and Marcus look at her and laugh softly.

You too, Adrian. *She looks at her glass.* And this is wonderful whisky.

ADRIAN: Not too much, dear.

MAYA: No, no. *She gets up with her glass, moves toward the window at right.* There was such a marvelous line—that English poet, what was his name? Very famous . . . you published him in the first or second issue, I think. . . . "The world . . ." *She presses her forehead. Marcus observes her, and she sees him.* I'm not drunk, it's only so long ago. Oh, yes! "The world needs a wash and a week's rest."

ADRIAN: Auden.

MAYA: Auden, yes! A wash and week's rest—what a wonderful solution.

ADRIAN: Yeah—last one into the Ganges is a rotten egg.

They laugh.

MARCUS: Every now and then you sound like Brooklyn.

ADRIAN: That's because I come from Philadelphia. How do you know about Brooklyn?

MARCUS: I was in the American army.

ADRIAN, *amazed, sits up*: How do you come to the American army?

MAYA: He was sergeant!

MARCUS: I enlisted in London—we had to get out when the Nazis came. I was translator and interpreter for General McBride, First Army Intelligence.

ADRIAN: Isn't that funny? Every once in a while you come into a kind of—focus, that's very familiar. I've never understood it.

MARCUS: I was in almost three years.

ADRIAN: Huh! *He laughs.* I don't know why I'm so glad to hear it . . .

MARCUS: Well, you can place me now—we all want that.

ADRIAN: I guess so. What'd she mean, that you published Auden?

MAYA: Marcus was the editor of the magazine, until they closed it.

ADRIAN, *toward Sigmund*: I didn't know that.

SIGMUND: Very good editor—Marcus was first editor who accept to publish my story.

MAYA: If it had been in English—or even French or Spanish—our magazine would have been as famous as the *New Yorker*.

MARCUS, *modestly*: Well . . .

MAYA, *to Marcus*: In my opinion it was better . . . *To Adrian*: But our language even God doesn't read. People would stand on line in the street downstairs, like for bread. People from factories, soldiers from the army, professors . . . It was like some sort of Bible, every week a new prophecy. Pity you missed it . . . It was like living on a ship—every morning there was a different island.

MARCUS, *to Sigmund with a gesture of communication*: Elizabeth didn't look well, is she all right?

SIGMUND: She was very angry tonight. She is sometimes foolish.

   Slight pause.

MAYA: Could he live, in America?

ADRIAN: I'm sure he could. Universities'd be honored to have him.

SIGMUND: I am speaking English like six-years-old child.

ADRIAN: Faculty wives'll be overjoyed to correct you. You'd be a big hit—with all that hair.

SIGMUND, *laughs dryly*: You are not going to Algeria?

MARCUS: On Friday.

ADRIAN: What's in Algeria?

MARCUS: There's a writers' congress—they've asked me to go.

ADRIAN: Communist countries?

MARCUS: Yes. But it's a big one—Arabs, Africans, Latin Americans . . . the lot.

SIGMUND: The French?

MARCUS: Some French, yes—Italians too, I think.

ADRIAN: What do you do at those things?

MAYA, *admiringly*: He represents our country—he lies on the beach with a gin and tonic.

MARCUS, *laughs*: It's too cold for the beach now. *To Adrian*: They're basically ideological discussions.

SIGMUND: Boring, no?

MARCUS: Agony. But there are some interesting people sometimes.

SIGMUND: You can speak of us there?

Marcus turns to him, silent, unable to answer.

No.

MARCUS: We're not on the agenda.

MAYA: It's difficult, dear . . .

SIGMUND: But perhaps privately—to the Italian comrades? . . . French? Perhaps they would be interested for my manuscript.

Marcus nods positively, but turns up his palms—he'll do what he can.

With the slightest edge of sarcasm: You will see, perhaps. *He chucks his head, closes his eyes with his face stretched upward, his hand tapping frustratedly on his chair arm, his foot beating.* So-so-so-so.

MARCUS, *looking front:* The important thing . . . is to be useful.

SIGMUND, *flatly, without irony:* Yes, always. *Slight pause.* Thank you, that you have returned for this, I am grateful.

MARCUS: Whatever you decide, it ought to be soon. Once they move to prosecute . . .

SIGMUND: Yes. I have still some questions—we can take a walk later, perhaps.

MARCUS: All right. I've told you all I know . . .

SIGMUND: . . . About ourselves

MARCUS, *surprised:* Oh. All right.

Pause.

MAYA: How handsome you all are! I must say . . .

Marcus laughs, she persists.

Really, it's unusual for writers. *Suddenly, to Irina:* And she is so lovely . . . *Du bist sehr schön.*

IRINA: *Danke.*

MAYA, *to Marcus:* Isn't she very young?

MARCUS, *shrugs:* We only met two days ago.

MAYA, *touching his hair:* How marvelous. You are like God, darling— you can always create new people. *She laughs, and with sudden energy:*

Play something, Sigmund! . . . *She goes to Sigmund to get him up.* Come . . .

SIGMUND: No, no, no . . .

MAYA, *suddenly bends and kisses the top of his head, her eyes filling with tears*: Don't keep that thing . . .

> *She reaches for his pocket; he takes her hand and pats it, looking up at her. She stares down at him.*

> The day he walked in here for the first time . . . *She glances at Marcus.* Do you remember? The snow was half a meter high on his hat—I thought he was a peasant selling potatoes, he bowed the snow all over my typewriter. *She glances at Adrian.* And he takes out this lump of paper—it was rolled up like a bomb. A story full of colors, like a painting; this boy from the beet fields—a writer! It was a miracle—such prose from a field of beets. That morning—for half an hour—I believed Socialism. For half an hour I . . .

MARCUS, *cutting her off*: What brings you back, Adrian? *The telephone rings in the bedroom.* Probably for you.

MAYA: For me? *She goes toward the bedroom.* I can't imagine . . . *She exits.*

ADRIAN: I don't really know why I came. There's always been something here that I . . .

IRINA, *getting up, pointing to the piano*: I may?

MARCUS: Certainly . . . please.

> *Irina sits at the piano.*

SIGMUND: I think you will write your book again.

ADRIAN: I doubt it—there's a kind of music here that escapes me. I really don't think I dig you people.

IRINA, *testing the piano, she runs a scale; it is badly out of tune and she makes a face, turning to Marcus*: Ach . . .

MARCUS, *apologizing*: I'm sorry, it's too old to be tuned anymore . . . but go ahead . . .

MAYA, *entering*: There's no one—they cut off.

> *Sigmund turns completely around to her, alerted.*

MAYA, *to him, reassuringly*: I'm sure they'll call back . . . it was an accident. Good! You play?

> *Irina launches into a fast "Bei Meir Bist Du Schön," the strings whining.*

MAYA: Marvelous! Jitterbug! *She breaks into a jitterbug with her glass in one hand, lifting her skirt.* Come on, Adrian! . . . *She starts for Adrian.*

IRINA, *stops playing and stands up, pushing her fingers into her ears*: Is too, too . . .

MAYA: No, play, play . . .

IRINA, *refusing, laughing, as she descends onto the carpet beside Marcus, shutting her ears*: Please, please, please . . .

MARCUS, *patting Irina*: I believe she's done concerts . . . serious music. *He looks at his watch; then, to Sigmund*: You're not going outside with that thing, are you?

> *Sigmund glances at him.*

> It's absurd.

MAYA: It must be the Americans—ever since they started building that hotel the phones keep ringing.

ADRIAN: What hotel?

MAYA: The Hilton . . . three blocks from here. It's disarranged the telephones.

MARCUS: I'd love to read your novel—do you have it with you?

ADRIAN: It's no good.

MARCUS: That's surprising—what's the problem?

ADRIAN, *sits up*: Well . . . I started out with a bizarre, exotic quality. People sort of embalmed in a society of amber. But the longer it got, the less unique it became. I finally wondered if the idea of unfreedom can be sustained in the mind.

MARCUS: You relied on that.

ADRIAN: Yes. But I had to keep injecting melodramatic reminders. The brain tires of unfreedom. It's like a bad back—you simply learn to avoid making certain movements . . . like . . . whatever's in this ceiling; or if nothing is; we still have to live, and talk, and the rest of it. I really thought I knew, but I saw that I didn't; it's been an education tonight. I'd love to ask you something, Marcus—why do you carry a gun?

MARCUS: I don't, normally. I was planning a trip into the mountains in Algeria—still pretty rough up there in places. *He looks at his watch.*

MAYA: He fought a battle in Mexico last year. In the Chiapas. Like a cowboy.

MARCUS: Not really—no one was hurt.

ADRIAN: What the hell do you go to those places for?

MARCUS: It interests me—where there is no law, people alone with their customs. I started out to be an anthropologist.

ADRIAN: What happened?

MARCUS: The Nazis, the war. You were too young, I guess.

ADRIAN: I was in the army in the fifties, but after Korea and before Vietnam.

MARCUS: You're a lucky generation, you missed everything.

ADRIAN: I wonder sometimes. History came at us like a rumor. We were never really there.

MARCUS: Is that why you come here?

ADRIAN: Might be part of it. We're always smelling the smoke, but we're never quite sure who the devil really is. Drives us nuts.

MARCUS: You don't like ambiguity.

ADRIAN: Oh sure—providing it's clear. *He laughs.* Or maybe it's always clearer in somebody else's country.

MARCUS: I was just about to say—the first time I came to America—a few years after the war . . .

ADRIAN: . . . You're not an American citizen, are you?

MARCUS: Very nearly, but I had a little . . . ambiguity with your Immigration Department. *He smiles.*

ADRIAN: You came from the wrong country.

MARCUS: No—it was the right country when I boarded ship for New York. But the Communists took over here while I was on the high seas. A Mr. Donahue, Immigration Inspector, Port of New York, did not approve. He put me in a cage.

ADRIAN: Why!

MARCUS: Suspicion I was a Red agent. Actually, I'd come on an invitation to lecture at Syracuse University. I'd published my first two—or it may have been three novels in Paris by then. I phoned the university—from my cage—and they were appalled, but no one lifted a finger, of course, and I was shipped back to Europe. It was terribly unambiguous, Adrian—you were a fascist country, to me. I was wrong, of course, but so it appeared. Anyway, I decided to come home and have a look here—I stepped off the train directly into the arms of our police.

ADRIAN: As an American spy.

MARCUS, *laughs*: What else?

ADRIAN, *nodding*: I got ya, Marcus.

MARCUS: Yes. *Slight pause.* But it's better now.

Adrian glances at Sigmund.

It has been, anyway. But one has to be of the generation that can remember. Otherwise, it's as you say—a sort of rumor that has no reality—excepting for oneself.

Sigmund drinks deeply from his glass. Slight pause.

ADRIAN, *stands, and from behind Sigmund looks down at him for an instant*: She's sure to come, huh?

MARCUS: I'm sure she will.

ADRIAN, *strolls to the window at right, stretches his back and arms, looks out of the window*: It's starting to snow. *Slight pause.* God, it's a beautiful city. *He lingers there for a moment, then walks, his hands thrust into his back pockets.* What do you suppose would happen if I went to the Minister of the Interior tonight—if I lost my mind and knocked on his door and raised hell about this?

Marcus turns to him, eyebrows raised.

I'm serious.

MARCUS: Well . . . what happened when you tried to reason with Johnson or Nixon during Vietnam?

ADRIAN: Right. But of course we could go into the streets, which you can't . . .

SIGMUND: Why not?

ADRIAN, *surprised*: With all their tanks here?

SIGMUND: Yes, even so. *Pause.* Is only a question of the fantasy. In this country we have not Las Vegas. The American knows very well is almost impossible to winning money from this slot machine. But he is enjoying to experience hope. He is playing for the hope. For us, is inconceivable. Before such a machine we would experience only despair. For this reason we do not go into the street.

ADRIAN: You're more realistic about power . . .

SIGMUND: This is mistake, Adrian, we are not realistic. We also believe we can escaping power—by telling lies. For this reason, I think you have difficulty to write about us. You cannot imagine how fantastically we lie.

MARCUS: I don't think we're any worse than others . . .

SIGMUND: Oh certainly, yes—but perhaps is not exactly lying because we do not expect to deceive anyone; the professor lies to the student, the student to the professor—but each knows the other is lying. We must lie, it is our only freedom. To lie is our slot machine—we know we cannot win, but it gives us the feeling of hope. Is like a serious play which no one really believes, but the technique is admirable. Our country is now a theatre, where no one is permitted to walk out and everyone is obliged to applaud.

MARCUS: That is a marvelous description, Sigmund—of the whole world.

SIGMUND: No, I must object—when Adrian speaks to me it is always his personal opinion. But with us, is impossible to speaking so simply, we must always making theatre.

MARCUS: I've been as plain as I know how to be. What is it you don't believe?

SIGMUND, *laughs*: But that is the problem in the theatre—I believe everything but I am convinced of nothing.

MAYA: It's enough.

SIGMUND: Excuse me, Maya—for me is not enough; if I am waking up in New York one morning, I must have concrete reason, not fantastic reason.

MAYA: Darling, they've taken your book . . .

SIGMUND, *with sudden force*: But is my country—is this reason to leave my country!

MAYA: There are people who love you enough to want to keep you from prison. What is fantastic about that?

SIGMUND, *turns to Marcus, with a smile*: You are loving me, Marcus?

> *Marcus, overwhelmed by resentment, turns to Sigmund, silent.*

> Then we have not this reason. *Slight pause.* Therefore . . . perhaps you have come back for different reason.

MARCUS: I came back to prevent a calamity, a disaster for all of us . . .

SIGMUND: Yes, but is also for them a calamity. If I am in prison the whole world will know they are gangster. This is not intelligent—my book are published in nine country. For them is also disaster.

MARCUS: So this fellow in London? These threats? They're not serious?

SIGMUND: I am sure they wish me to believe so, therefore is very serious.

MARCUS: You don't believe a word I've told you, do you? There was no man at all in London; that conversation never happened? There'll be no arrest? No trial?

SIGMUND, *pause*: I think not.

MARCUS: Then give me back my pistol.

> *Sigmund does not move. Marcus holds out his hand.*

> Give it to me, you're in no danger; I've invented the whole thing.

Sigmund is motionless.

Are you simply a thief? Why are you keeping it?

Sigmund is silent.

MAYA: Marcus . . .

MARCUS: I insist he answer me . . . *To Sigmund*: Why are you keeping that pistol? *He laughs.* But of course you know perfectly well I've told you the truth; it was just too good an opportunity to cover me with your contempt . . . in her eyes and—*pointing toward Adrian*—the eyes of the world.

ADRIAN: Now, Marcus, I had no intention . . .

MARCUS: Oh come now, Adrian, he's been writing this story for you all evening! *New York Times* feature on Socialist decadence.

ADRIAN: Now, wait a minute . . .

MARCUS: But it's so obvious! . . .

ADRIAN: Wait a minute, will you? He has a right to be uneasy.

MARCUS: No more than I do, and for quite the same reason.

ADRIAN: Why!

MARCUS, *laughs*: To whom am *I* talking, Adrian—the *New York Times*, or your novel, or you?

ADRIAN: For Christ's sake, are you serious?

MARCUS, *laughs*: Why not? You may turn out to be as dangerous to me as he believes I am to him. Yes!

Adrian looks astonished.

Why is it any more absurd? Especially after that last piece of yours, which, you'll pardon me, was stuffed with the most primitive misunderstandings of what it means to live in this country. You haven't a clue, Adrian—you'll forgive me, but I have to say that. So I'm entitled to a bit of uneasiness.

ADRIAN: Marcus, are you asking me to account for myself?

MARCUS: By no means, but why must I?

MAYA: Why don't we all go to the playground and swing with the other children?

MARCUS, *laughs*: Very good, yes.

MAYA, *to Adrian*: Why is he so complicated? They allow him this house to store his father's library. These books earn hard currency. To sell them he must have a passport.

MARCUS: Oh, he knows all that, dear—it's hopeless; when did the facts ever change a conviction? It doesn't matter. *He looks at his watch.*

ADRIAN: It does, though. It's a terrible thing. It's maddening.

MARCUS, *denigrating*: Well . . .

ADRIAN: It is, you know it is. Christ, you're such old friends, you're writers . . . I never understood the sadness in this country, but I swear, I think it's . . .

MARCUS: Oh, come off it, Adrian—what country isn't sad?

ADRIAN: I think you've accepted something.

MARCUS: And you haven't?

ADRIAN: Goddammit, Marcus, we can still speak for ourselves! And not for some . . . *He breaks off.*

MARCUS: Some what?

ADRIAN, *walks away*: . . . Well, never mind.

MARCUS: I've spoken for no one but myself here, Adrian. If there seems to be some . . . unspoken interest . . . well, there is, of course. I am interested in seeing that this country does not fall back into darkness. And if he must sacrifice something for that, I think he should. That's plain enough, isn't it?

ADRIAN: I guess the question is . . . how you feel about that yourself.

MARCUS, *laughs*: But I feel terribly about it. I think it's dreadful. I think there's no question he is our best living writer. Must I go on, or is that enough? *Silence.* What change can feelings make? It is a situation which I can tell you—*no one wants* . . . no one. If I flew into an orgasm of self-revelation here it might seem more candid, but it would change nothing . . . except possibly to multiply the confusion.

MAYA, *to Adrian*: I think you were saying the same thing before. . . . Tell him.

MARCUS: What?

ADRIAN: Whether it matters anymore, what anyone feels . . . about anything. Whether we're not just some sort of . . . filament that only lights up when it's plugged into whatever power there is.

MAYA: It's interesting.

MARCUS: I don't know—it seems rather childish. When was a man ever conceivable apart from society? Unless you're looking for the angel who wrote each of our blessed names in his book of gold. The collective giveth and the collective taketh away—beyond that . . . *he looks to the ceiling* . . . was never anything but a sentimental metaphor; a God who now is simply a form of art. Whose style may still move us, but there was never any mercy in that plaster. The only difference now, it seems to me, is that we've ceased to expect any.

ADRIAN: I know one reason I came. I know it's an awkward question, but—those tanks bivouacked out there in the countryside . . . do they figure at all in your minds?

MAYA: Do you write *every minute*?

ADRIAN: Well, do they? *To Marcus*: Are they part of your lives at all?

MARCUS: I don't really know . . .

ADRIAN: Maya? It interests me.

MAYA: It's such a long time, now. And you don't see them unless you drive out there . . .

MARCUS: It's hard to say.

ADRIAN, *of Sigmund*: Why do you suppose he can't stop thinking about them? I bet there isn't an hour a day when they don't cross his mind.

MAYA: Because he is a genius. When he enters the tram, the conductor refuses to accept his fare. In the grocery store they give him the best oranges. The usher bows in the theatre when she shows him to his seat. *She goes to Sigmund, touches his hair.* He is our Sigmund. He is loved, he creates our memories. Therefore, it is only a question of time when he will create the departure of these tanks, and they will go home. And then we shall all be ourselves, with nothing overhead but the sky, and he will turn into a monument standing in the park. *Her eyes fill with tears, she turns up his face.* Go, darling. Please. There is nothing left for you.

SIGMUND, *touches her face*: Something, perhaps. We shall see.

Maya moves right to the window, sips a drink.

IRINA, *with a swimming gesture, to Marcus*: I am bathing?

MARCUS: Yes, of course—come, I'll get you a towel. *He starts to rise.*

MAYA, *looking out the window*: She'd better wait a little—I used all the hot water. *With a laugh, to Sigmund*: I came tonight to take a bath!

Marcus laughs.

ADRIAN: Marcus, when they arrested you . . .

MAYA, *suddenly*: Will you stop writing, for Christ's sake! Isn't there something else to talk about?

MARCUS: Why not—if he's interested?

MAYA: Are we some sick fish in a tank! *To Adrian*: Stop it! *She gets up, goes to the drink table.* What the hell do you expect people to *do*? What *is* it?

MARCUS: You've had enough, dear . . .

MAYA, *pouring*: I have not had enough, dear. *She suddenly slams the glass down on the table.* Fuck all this diplomacy! *At Adrian*: You're in no position to judge anybody! We have nothing to be ashamed of!

MARCUS, *turning away in disgust*: Oh, for God's sake . . .

MAYA: You know what he brought when he came to me? A bottle of milk!

> *Perplexed, Marcus turns to her.*

> I wake up and he's in the kitchen, drinking *milk*! *She stands before Marcus, awaiting his reaction.* A grown man!

MARCUS, *to calm her*: Well, they drink a lot of it in the States.

MAYA, *quietly, seeking to explain*: He smelled like a baby, all night.

MARCUS, *stands*: I'll make you some coffee . . .

> *He starts past her, but she stops him with her hand on his arm, frightened and remorseful. She kisses him.*

MAYA: I'm going home. *She takes his hand, tries to lead him toward Sigmund with imperative force.* Come, be his friend . . . you are friends, darling . . . *The telephone in the bedroom rings. She turns up to the entrance in surprise.* Goddamn that Hilton!

> *She starts toward the bedroom, but as the telephone rings again, Marcus goes up and exits into the bedroom. She comes to Sigmund.*

> Darling . . . *She points up to the ceiling, speaking softly in desperation.* I really don't think there is anything there. I would never do that to you, you know that. I think it was only to make himself interesting—he can't write anymore; it left him . . . *In anguish*: It left him!

SIGMUND: I know.

MAYA: He loves you, he loves you, darling! . . . *She grips her head.* My God, I'm sick . . .

> *She starts upstage as Marcus enters. He has a stunned look.*

> *She halts, seeing him, looks at him questioningly. Sigmund turns to look at him, and Adrian. After a moment . . .*

MARCUS, *turns to Sigmund with a gesture inviting him to go to the phone*: It's Alexandra.

> *Sigmund does not move.*

> . . . She wishes to speak to you.

Sigmund stands, confounded by Marcus's look, and goes out into the bedroom. Marcus remains there, staring.

MAYA: What?

Marcus is silent, staring.

ADRIAN: Something happen?

Marcus crosses the stage and descends into his chair, his face transfixed by some enigma.

MAYA, *in fright, starting up toward the bedroom*: Sigmund! . . .

Sigmund enters, halts, shakes his head, uttering an almost soundless laugh, his eyes alive to something incredible.

MARCUS: They're returning his manuscript.

Maya claps her hands together, then crosses herself, her face between explosive joy and some terror, rigid, sobered.

ADRIAN, *grabs Sigmund by the shoulders*: Is it true?

MARCUS: She may be able to bring it when she comes.

ADRIAN: Sigmund! *He kisses him. They look at each other and laugh.*

SIGMUND, *half smiling*: You believe it?

ADRIAN, *taken aback*: Don't you?

SIGMUND, *laughs*: I don't know! *He walks, dumbfounded.* . . . Yes, I suppose I believe. *He suddenly laughs.* Why not! They have made me ridiculous, therefore I must believe it.

MARCUS: Well, the main thing is, you . . .

SIGMUND: Yes, that is the main thing. I must call Elizabeth . . . *He starts to the bedroom but looks at his watch.* No . . . she will not yet be home.

ADRIAN, *to all*: What could it mean? *He laughs, seeing Sigmund.* You look punchy. *He grabs him.* Wake up! You got it back! . . . Listen, come to Paris with me . . . with the boy and Elizabeth. We'll get you a visa— you can be in New York in ten days. We'll go to my publisher, I'll break his arm, we'll get you a tremendous advance, and you're on your way.

SIGMUND, *laughing*: Wait, wait . . .

ADRIAN: Say yes! Come on! You can waste the rest of your life in this goddamned country. Jesus, why can't they steal it again tomorrow? *To the ceiling*: I didn't mean that about the country. But it's infuriating—they play you like a yo-yo.

SIGMUND, *sits; an aura of irony on his voice*: So, Maya . . . you are immortal again.

ADRIAN: Is *she* that character?

MAYA: Of course.

ADRIAN: She sounded terrific.

MAYA: She is the best woman he has ever written—fantastic, complicated personality. *To Sigmund*: What is there to keep you now? It is enough, no?

IRINA: Is good?

MARCUS, *patting her*: Yes, very good.

SIGMUND: She is so lucky—she understands nothing. We also understand nothing—but for us is not lucky.

MAYA: We should go to Francesco's later—we should have a party.

SIGMUND, *turns to her with a faint smile*: It is strange, eh? We have such good news and we are sad.

MARCUS: It isn't sadness.

SIGMUND: Perhaps only some sort of humiliation. *He shakes his head.* We must admire them—they are very intelligent—they can even create unhappiness with good news.

ADRIAN, *to Marcus*: What do you suppose happened?

MARCUS: I've no idea.

ADRIAN: It seems like a gesture of some kind. Is it?

MARCUS: I haven't the foggiest.

ADRIAN: Could it be that I was here?

MARCUS: Who knows? Of course they would like to make peace with him, it's a gesture in that sense.

> *Sigmund looks across at him.*

I think you ought to consider it that way.

SIGMUND: It is their contempt; they are laughing.

MARCUS: Not necessarily—some of them have great respect for you.

SIGMUND: No, no, they are laughing.

MAYA: Why are you such children?

> *Sigmund turns to her.*

It is not respect and it is not contempt—it is nothing.

ADRIAN: But it must mean something.

MAYA: Why? They have the power to take it and the power to give it back.

ADRIAN: Well, that's a meaning.

MAYA: You didn't know that before? When it rains you get wet—that is not exactly meaningful. *To the three*: There's nothing to say; it is a terrible embarrassment for geniuses, but there is simply no possible comment to be made.

SIGMUND: How is in Shakespeare? "We are like flies to little boys, they kill us for their sport."

MAYA: They are not killing you at all. Not at all.

SIGMUND: Why are you angry with me? I am not obliged to ask why something happens?

MAYA: Because you can live happily and you don't want to.

ADRIAN: It's not so simple.

MAYA: But for you it is! You are so rich, Adrian, you live so well—why must he be heroic?

ADRIAN: I've never told him to . . .

MAYA: Then tell him to get out! Be simple, be clear to him . . .

ADRIAN: I've been very clear to him . . .

MAYA: Good! *To Sigmund*: So the three of us are of the same opinion, you see? Let's have a party at Francesco's . . . call Elizabeth . . . a farewell party. All right?

> *He looks up at her.*
>
> It is all finished, darling!
>
> *He smiles, shaking his head. She is frightened and angry.*
>
> What? What is it? What more can be said?

SIGMUND, *with a certain laughter*: Is like some sort of theatre, no? Very bad theatre—our emotions have no connection with the event. Myself also—I *must* speak, darling—I do not understand myself. I must confess, I have feeling of gratitude; *before* they have stolen my book I was never grateful. *Now* I am grateful— *His laughter vanishes.* I cannot accept such confusion, Maya, is very bad for my mentality. I must speak! I think we must all speak now! *He ends looking at Marcus; his anger is open.*

MARCUS: What can I tell you? I know nothing.

SIGMUND: I am sure not, but we can speculate, perhaps? *To Maya*: Please, darling—sit; we must wait for Alexandra, we have nothing to do. Please, Adrian—sit down . . . I have some idea . . .

Adrian sits. Sigmund continues to Maya.

. . . which I would like to discuss before I leave my country.

Maya sits slowly, apprehensively. He turns to Marcus, adopting a quiet, calm air.

Is possible, Marcus—there was some sort of mistake? Perhaps only one police commander has made this decision for himself—to stealing my book? Perhaps the government was also surprised?

Marcus considers in silence.

I am interested your opinion. *I* think so, perhaps—no?

MARCUS: Do you know if they were the Security Police?

SIGMUND: Yes, Security Police.

MARCUS: *They* might, I suppose.

SIGMUND: I think so. But in this case . . . this fellow in London taxi—is possible he was also speaking for himself?

MARCUS: I can't believe that.

SIGMUND: But if he was speaking for the government . . . such terrible thing against me—why have they chosen to returning my manuscript? I think is not logical, no?

MARCUS: . . . Unless they had second thoughts, and felt it would make it easier for you to leave.

SIGMUND: Yes. That is very strong idea.

ADRIAN: I think that's it.

SIGMUND: Very good, yes. But at same time, if I have manuscript—you do not object that I . . . ?

MARCUS: Go ahead—it's simply that I know no more than . . .

SIGMUND: You understand is very important to me. . . . I must understand why I am leaving.

MARCUS: Of course. Go ahead.

SIGMUND, *slight pause*: If I have manuscript, I must probably conclude it is *not* dangerous for me here, no? I must believe is only some particular antagonistic enemy who wish me to go out. Is possible?

MARCUS: What can I tell you?

SIGMUND, *with nearly an outcry through his furious control*: But you know you are sad! I am sad, Maya is sad—if was only some sort of mistake . . . why we are not happy?

Maya gets up and strides toward the bedroom.

Maya?

MAYA, *hardly turning back*: I'm going home . . .

SIGMUND, *leaps up and intercepts her*: No, no—we must have celebration! *He grips her hands.*

MAYA: Let me go!

SIGMUND: No! We have tremendous good news, we must have correct emotion!

MAYA, *wrenching her hands free, pointing at his pocket*: Give me that thing . . . Give it to me!

SIGMUND: My God—I had forgotten it. *He takes out the pistol, looks at it.*

MAYA: Please. Sigmund. Please! . . .

SIGMUND: I have crazy idea . . .

MAYA, *weeping*: Sigmund . . .

SIGMUND, *moving toward the piano*: One time very long ago, I have read in American detective story . . . that criminal has placed revolver inside piano. *He sets the pistol on the strings and comes around to the bench.* Then someone is playing very fortissimo . . . something like Beethoven . . . *raising his hands over the keyboard. . . .* and he is firing the pistol.

ADRIAN: What the hell are you doing?

SIGMUND, *smashes his hands down on the keyboard*: Ha! Is not true.

ADRIAN, *stands*: What the hell are you doing?

SIGMUND: Wait! I have idea . . . *He reaches over, takes out the pistol, and cocks it.*

MAYA: Marcus!

SIGMUND, *replacing the cocked pistol in the piano*: Now we shall see . . .

ADRIAN, *rushing Maya away from the piano*: Watch out!

SIGMUND, *crashes his hands down; the gun explodes, the strings reverberating*: Is true! *He reaches in and takes out the revolver.* My God, I am so happy . . . *He holds up the revolver.* The truth is alive in our country, Marcus! *He comes and sits near Marcus.* Is unmistakable, no?—when something is true?

He looks at the pistol, puts it in his pocket. Marcus turns to him only now. Maya suddenly weeps, sobbing, and makes for the bedroom.

I cannot permit you to leave, Maya!

She halts, turning to him in terror.

I must insist, darling—is most important evening of my life and I understand nothing. Why do you weep, why do you go? If I am ridiculous I must understand why? Please . . . sit. Perhaps you also can say something.

She sits a distance from him and Marcus. Adrian remains standing, catching his breath; he leans his head on his hand, as though caught by a rush of sadness and he shakes his head incredulously, glancing at Marcus.

MARCUS: What is it? What *is* it!

SIGMUND: This fellow . . . this fellow in taxi who has threatened me— what was his name?

MARCUS: I don't recall, I only heard it once. Granitz, I think. Or Grodnitz. But I'm sure he didn't know you.

SIGMUND: Grodnitz.

MARCUS: . . . Or Granitz.

ADRIAN: You know him?

SIGMUND: . . . No. *Slight pause.* No Granitz. No Grodnitz. *Slight pause. He takes the pistol out of his pocket, looks at it in his hand, then turns again to Marcus.* He exists? Or is imaginary man?

Marcus is silent.

Was *ever* discussion of trial for me? Or is imaginary trial?

Marcus is silent. Sigmund looks at the pistol again; then, stretching over to Marcus he places it in his hand.

I believe I have no danger, at the moment.

Long pause. No one dares do more than glance at Marcus whose face is filled with his fury. The pause lengthens. Sigmund looks at his watch.

I will try to call Elizabeth . . . she was worried.

MARCUS: The sole function of every other writer is to wish he were you.

Sigmund stands, looks to Maya, who avoids his eyes. He exits into the bedroom. After a moment . . .

ADRIAN, *sotto, to assuage Marcus:* He's terribly scared . . .

MARCUS, *slight pause; like a final verdict:* I couldn't care less. *He looks at his watch.*

ADRIAN, *silent for a moment*: For what it's worth . . . I know he has tremendous feeling for you.

MARCUS: For his monument. To build his monument he has to prove that everyone else is a coward or corrupt. My mistake was to offer him my help—it's a menace to his lonely grandeur. No one is permitted anything but selfishness. He's insane.

ADRIAN: Oh come on . . .

MARCUS: He's paranoid—these letters to the foreign press are for nothing but to bring on another confrontation. It was too peaceful; they were threatening him with tolerance. He must find evil or he can't be good.

MAYA: Let's not talk about it anymore . . .

MARCUS: I exist too, Maya! I am not dancing around that megalomania again!

 Slight pause.

ADRIAN: I can't blame you, but I wish you wouldn't cut out on him yet. Look, I'll stay through the week, maybe I can convince him. Does he have a week?

MARCUS, *slowly turns to Adrian*: How would I know?

ADRIAN: All I meant was whether you . . .

MARCUS: I won't have any more of this, Adrian!

 Slight pause.

ADRIAN: I believe you—I've told him to get out.

MARCUS: No, you haven't; you've insinuated.

ADRIAN: Christ's sake, you've heard me say . . .

MARCUS: I *have* heard you.

 They are facing each other. Slight pause.

 You don't believe me, Adrian . . . not really.

 Adrian can't answer.

So it's all over. It's the end of him—I've been there. He will smash his head against the walls, and the rest of us will pay for his grandeur.

 Slight pause. Adrian turns front in his conflict. Sigmund enters. Marcus turns away.

MAYA, *with a forced attempt at cheerfulness*: Did you reach her? Elizabeth?

SIGMUND: She is very happy. *To Marcus*: She send you her greetings—she is grateful. *Slight pause.* I also.

> *Marcus half turns toward him. Sigmund says no more, goes to his chair and sits.*

ADRIAN: Sigmund? *Sigmund glances at him.* Do you trust me?

> *Sigmund is silent.*

I'm convinced he's told you the truth.

In all the times we've talked about you, he's never shown anything but a wide-open pride in you, and your work. He's with you. You have to believe that.

> *Sigmund turns, stares at Marcus's profile for a moment. Then looks at Maya. She ultimately turns slightly away. He looks down at the floor.*

SIGMUND: I am afraid; that is all. I think I will not be able to write in some other country.

ADRIAN: Oh, that's impossible . . .

SIGMUND: I am not cosmopolitan writer, I am provincial writer. I believe I must hear my language every day, I must walk in these particular streets. I think in New York I will have only some terrible silence. Is like old tree—it is difficult to moving old tree, they most probably die.

ADRIAN: But if they lock you up . . .

SIGMUND: Yes, but that is my fate; I must accept my fate. But to run away because of some sort of rumor—I have only some rumor, no? How will I support this silence that I have brought on myself? This is terrible idea, no? How I can accept to be so ridiculous? Therefore, is reasonable, I believe—that I must absolutely understand who is speaking to me.

ADRIAN, *slight pause, a hesitation*: I'm going to level with you, Sigmund—I think you're being far too . . .

SIGMUND, *a frustrated outburst*: I am not crazy, Adrian! *All turn to him, fear in their faces. He spreads his arms, with an upward glance.* Who is commanding me? Who is this voice? *Who is speaking to me?*

MAYA: They. *An instant's silence; she seems ashamed to look directly at Sigmund. She gestures almost imperceptibly upward.* It is there.

MARCUS, *in protest*: Maya!

MAYA: Why not! *To Sigmund*: They have heard it all.

MARCUS, *to Sigmund and Adrian*: It isn't true, there's nothing.

MAYA, *persisting, to Sigmund*: He has risked everything . . . for you. God knows what will happen for what has been said here.

MARCUS, *to Sigmund*: There's nothing . . . she can't know . . . *To Maya*: You can't know that . . .

MAYA, *her eyes to the ceiling*: Who else have we been speaking to all evening! *To them all*: Who does not believe it? *To Marcus*: It is his life, darling—we must begin to say what we believe. Somewhere, we must begin!

> *Pause. She sits a distance from Sigmund; only after a moment does she turn to face him as she fights down her shame and her fear of him.*

SIGMUND: So.

MAYA, *downing her shame*: Just so, yes. You must go.

SIGMUND: For your sake.

MAYA: Yes.

MARCUS, *softly, facing front*: It isn't true.

MAYA: And yours. For all of us.

SIGMUND: You must . . . deliver me? My departure?

> *Maya stiffens. She cannot speak.*

For your program? His passport . . . ?

ADRIAN: Sigmund, it's enough . . .

MAYA: He had no need to return, except he loves you. There was no need. That is also true.

SIGMUND, *his head clamped in his hands*: My God . . . Maya. *Pause. To Marcus*: They brought you back to make sure my departure?

ADRIAN, *aborting the violence coming*: Come on, Sigmund, it's enough . . .

SIGMUND, *trying to laugh*: But she is not some sort of whore! I have many years with this woman! . . .

ADRIAN: What more do you *want*!

MARCUS: Her humiliation; she's not yet on her knees to him. We are now to take our places, you see, at the foot of the cross, as he floats upward through the plaster on the wings of his immortal contempt. We lack remorse, it spoils the picture. *He glares, smiling at Sigmund, who seems on the verge of springing at him.*

ADRIAN, *to Sigmund*: Forget it, Sigmund—come on . . . *To Marcus*: Maybe you ought to call that Alexandra woman.

MARCUS: She'll be along.

> *Silence. The moment expands. Sigmund stares front, gripping his lower face. Adrian is glancing at him with apprehension. Maya is looking at no one.*

SIGMUND, *to Maya*: You can say nothing to me?

MAYA, *slight pause*: You know my feeling.

SIGMUND: I, not. I know your name. Who is this woman?

MARCUS: Don't play that game with him.

SIGMUND: It is a game?

ADRIAN: Come on, fellas . . .

SIGMUND, *irritated, to Adrian*: Is interesting to me. *To Marcus*: What is your game? What did you mean?

MARCUS: It's called Power. Or Moral Monopoly. The winner takes all the justifications. When you write this, Adrian, I hope you include the fact that they refused him a visa for many years and he was terribly indignant— the right to leave was sacred to civilization. Now he has that right and it's an insult. You can draw your own conclusions.

SIGMUND: And what is the conclusion?

MARCUS: You are a moral blackmailer. We have all humored you, Sigmund, out of some misplaced sense of responsibility to our literature. Or maybe it's only our terror of vanishing altogether. We aren't the Russians— after you and Otto and Peter there aren't a handful to keep the breath of life in this language. We have taken all the responsibility and left you all the freedom to call us morally bankrupt. But now you're free to go, so the responsibility moves to you. Now it's yours. All yours. We have done what was possible; now you will do what is necessary, or turn out our lights. And that is where it stands.

SIGMUND, *slight pause*: This is all?

> *Marcus is silent.*

ADRIAN: What more can be said, Sigmund? What can they give you? It's pointless.

SIGMUND, *turns to Maya*: I am only some sort of . . . comical Jesus Christ? Is only my egotism? This is all? What you can give me, Maya? *She is silent.* There is nothing?

> *In silence, Maya turns to face him.*

You understand what I ask you?

MAYA: Yes.

SIGMUND: You cannot? *Slight pause. Then he glances toward Marcus.* After so many years . . . so many conversations . . . so many hope and disaster—you can only speak for them? *He gestures toward the ceiling.* Is terrible, no? Why we have lived?

ADRIAN, *to cut off his mounting anger:* Sigmund . . .

SIGMUND, *swiftly, his eyes blazing:* Why have you come here? What do you want in this country?

ADRIAN, *astonished:* What the hell are you . . . ?

SIGMUND: You are scientist observing the specimens: this whore? this clever fellow making business with these gangsters?

ADRIAN: For Christ's sake, Sigmund, what can I do!

SIGMUND: They are killing us, Adrian—they have destroyed my friends! You are free man—*with a gesture toward the ceiling*—why you are obliged to be clever? Why do you come here, Adrian?

MAYA: To save his book.

ADRIAN: That's a lie!

MAYA: But it's exactly what you told me an hour ago. *She stands. To both Sigmund and Adrian:* What is the sin? He has come for his profit, to rescue two years' work, to make more money . . .

ADRIAN: That's a goddamned lie!

MAYA: And for friendship! Oh yes—his love for you. I believe it! Like ours. Absolutely like ours! Is love not love because there is some profit in it? Who speaks only for his heart? And yes, I speak to them now—this moment, this very moment to them, that they may have mercy on my program, on his passport. Always to them, in some part to them for my profit—here and everywhere in this world! Just as you do.

SIGMUND: I speak for Sigmund.

MAYA: Only Sigmund? Then why can't you speak for Sigmund in America? Because you will not have them in America to hate! And if you cannot hate you cannot write and you will not be Sigmund anymore, but another lousy refugee ordering his chicken soup in broken English—and where is the profit in that? They are your theme, your life, your partner in this dance that cannot stop or you will die of silence! *She moves toward him. Tenderly:* They are in you, darling. And if you stay . . . it is also for your profit . . . as it is for ours to tell you to go. Who can speak for himself alone?

> *A heavy brass knocker is heard from below. Sigmund lifts his eyes to the ceiling. Marcus stands and faces Sigmund, who now turns to him. Silence.*

SIGMUND: Tell her, please . . . is impossible . . . any transaction. Only to return my property.

MAYA, *with an abjectness, a terror, taking his hand and kissing it*: Darling . . . for my sake. For this little life that I have made . . .

MARCUS, *with anger, disgust*: Stop it! *He turns to Sigmund.* For your monument. For the bowing ushers in the theatre. For the power . . . the power to bring down everyone.

SIGMUND, *spreads his hands, looks up at the ceiling*: I don't know. *He turns to Marcus.* But I will never leave. Never.

> *Another knock is heard. Marcus, his face set, goes out and up the corridor. Sigmund turns to Maya. She walks away, her face expressionless, and stands at the window staring out.*

> Forgive me, Maya.

> *She doesn't turn to him. He looks to Adrian.*

> Is quite simple. We are ridiculous people now. And when we try to escape it, we are ridiculous too.

ADRIAN: No.

SIGMUND: I think so. But we cannot help ourselves. I must give you . . . certain letters, I wish you to keep them . . . before you leave. *He sits.* I have one some years ago from Malraux. Very elegant. *French*, you know? Also Gyula Illyés, Hungarian . . . very wise fellow. Heinrich Böll, Germany, one letter. Kobo Abe, Japan—he also. Nadine Gordimer, South Africa. Also Cortázar, Argentina . . . *Slight pause.* My God, eh? So many writers! Like snow . . . like forest . . . these enormous trees everywhere on the earth. Marvelous. *Slight pause. A welling up in him. He suddenly cries out to Maya across the stage.* Maya! Forgive me . . . *He hurries to her.* I cannot help it.

MAYA: I know. *She turns to him, reaches out, and touches his face.* Thank you.

SIGMUND, *surprised, he is motionless for an instant, then pulls her into his arms, and holds her face*: Oh, my God! Thank you, Maya.

> *The voices of Marcus and Alexandra are heard approaching from the darkness up the corridor. The three of them turn toward the door.*

IRINA, *revolving her finger, to Maya*: Now, music?

CURTAIN

THE AMERICAN CLOCK

A VAUDEVILLE

Based in part on Studs Terkel's *Hard Times*

1980

Characters

THEODORE K. QUINN

LEE BAUM

ROSE BAUM, *Lee's mother*

MOE BAUM, *Lee's father*

ARTHUR A. ROBERTSON

CLARENCE, *a shoeshine man*

FRANK, *the Baums' chauffeur*

FANNY MARGOLIES, *Rose's sister*

GRANDPA, *Rose's father*

DR. ROSMAN

JESSE LIVERMORE, WILLIAM DURANT, ARTHUR CLAYTON, *Financiers*

TONY, *a speakeasy owner*

DIANA MORGAN

HENRY TAYLOR, *a farmer*

IRENE, *a middle-aged black woman*

BANKS, *a black veteran*

JOE, *a boyhood friend of Lee's*

MRS. TAYLOR, *Henry's wife*

HARRIET TAYLOR, *their daughter*

BREWSTER, CHARLEY, *Farmers*

JUDGE BRADLEY

FRANK HOWARD, *an auctioneer*

MISS FOWLER, *Quinn's secretary*

GRAHAM, a New York Times *reporter*

SIDNEY MARGOLIES, *Fanny's son*

DORIS GROSS, *the landlady's daughter*

RALPH, RUDY, *Students*

ISABEL, *a prostitute*

ISAAC, *a black café proprietor*

RYAN, *a federal relief supervisor*

MATTHEW R. BUSH, GRACE, KAPUSH, DUGAN, TOLAND, LUCY, *People at the relief office*

EDIE, *a comic-strip artist*

LUCILLE, *Rose's niece*

STANISLAUS, *a seaman*

BASEBALL PLAYER

WAITER

THIEF

FARMERS

BIDDERS

SHERIFF

DEPUTIES

MARATHON DANCERS

WELFARE WORKER

SOLDIERS

ACT ONE

The set is a flexible area for actors. The actors are seated in a choral area onstage and return to it when their scenes are over. The few pieces of furniture required should be openly carried on by the actors. An impression of a surrounding vastness should be given, as though the whole country were really the setting, even as the intimacy of certain scenes is provided for. The background can be sky, clouds, space itself, or an impression of the geography of the United States.

A small jazz band onstage plays "Million-Dollar Baby" as a baseball pitcher enters, tossing a ball from hand to glove. Quinn begins to whistle "Million-Dollar Baby" from the balcony. Now he sings, and the rest of the company joins in, gradually coming onstage. All are singing by the end of the verse. All form in positions onstage. The band remains onstage throughout the play.

ROSE: By the summer of 1929 . . .

LEE: I think it's fair to say that nearly every American . . .

MOE: Firmly believed that he was going to get . . .

COMPANY: Richer and richer . . .

MOE: Every year.

ROBERTSON: The country knelt to a golden calf in a blanket of red, white, and blue. *He walks to Clarence's shoeshine box.* How you making out, Clarence?

CLARENCE: Mr. Robertson, I like you to lay another ten dollars on that General Electric. You do that for me?

ROBERTSON: How much stock you own, Clarence?

CLARENCE: Well, this ten ought to buy me a thousand dollars' worth, so altogether I guess I got me about hundred thousand dollars in stock.

ROBERTSON: And how much cash you got home?

CLARENCE: Oh, I guess about forty, forty-five dollars.

ROBERTSON, *slight pause*: All right, Clarence, let me tell you something. But I want you to promise me not to repeat it to anyone.

CLARENCE: I never repeat a tip you give me, Mr. Robertson.

ROBERTSON: This isn't quite a tip, this is what you might call an untip. Take all your stock, and sell it.

CLARENCE: Sell! Why, just this morning in the paper Mr. Andrew Mellon say the market's got to keep goin' up. *Got* to!

ROBERTSON: I have great respect for Andrew Mellon, Clarence, know him well, but he's up to his eyebrows in this game—he's got to say that. You sell, Clarence, believe me.

CLARENCE, *drawing himself up*: I never like to criticize a customer, Mr. Robertson, but I don't think a man in your position ought to be carryin' on that kind of talk! Now you take this ten, sir, put it on General Electric for Clarence.

ROBERTSON: I tell you something funny, Clarence.

CLARENCE: What's that, sir?

ROBERTSON: You sound like every banker in the United States.

CLARENCE: Well, I should hope so!

ROBERTSON: Yeah, well . . . bye-bye.

> *He exits. Clarence exits with his shoeshine box. The company exits singing and humming "Million-Dollar Baby"; Quinn sings the final line.*

> *Light rises on Rose at the piano, dressed for an evening out. Two valises stand center stage.*

ROSE, *playing piano under speech*: Now sing, darling, but don't forget to breathe—and then you'll do your homework.

LEE, *starts singing "I Can't Give You Anything But Love," then speaks over music*: Up to '29 it was the age of belief. How could Lindbergh fly the Atlantic in that tiny little plane? He believed. How could Babe Ruth keep smashing those homers? He believed. Charley Paddock, "The World's Fastest Human," raced a racehorse . . . and won! Because he believed. What I believed at fourteen was that my mother's hair was supposed to flow down over her shoulders. And one afternoon she came into the apartment . . .

> *Rose, at piano, sings a line of "I Can't Give You Anything But Love."*

. . . and it was short!

Rose and Lee sing the last line together.

ROSE, *continuing to play, speaking over music*: I personally think with all the problems there was never such a glorious time for anybody who loved to play or sing or listen or dance to music. It seems to me every week there was another marvelous song. What's the matter with you?

Lee can only shake his head—"nothing."

Oh, for God's sake! Nobody going to bother with long hair anymore. All I was doing was winding it up and winding it down . . .

LEE: It's *okay*! I just didn't think it would ever . . . happen.

ROSE: But why can't there be something new!

LEE: But why didn't you *tell* me!

ROSE: Because you would do exactly what you're doing now—carrying on like I was some kind of I-don't-know-what! Now stop being an idiot and *sing*!

Lee starts singing "On the Sunny Side of the Street."

You're not breathing, dear.

Moe enters carrying a telephone, joins in song. Lee continues singing under dialogue.

ROSE: Rudy Vallee is turning green.

Frank enters in a chauffeur's uniform.

MOE, *into phone*: Trafalgar five, seven-seven-one-one. *Pause.* Herb? I'm just thinking, maybe I ought to pick up another five hundred shares of General Electric. *Pause.* Good. *He hangs up.*

FRANK: Car's ready, Mr. Baum.

Frank chimes in with Lee on the last line of "Sunny Side of the Street." Then Lee sits on the floor, working on his crystal set.

ROSE, *to Frank*: You'll drop us at the theatre and then take my father and sister to Brooklyn and come back for us after the show. And don't get lost, please.

FRANK: No, I know Brooklyn.

He exits with the baggage. Fanny enters—Rose's sister.

FANNY, *apprehensively*: Rose . . . listen . . . Papa really doesn't want to move in with us.

A slow turn with rising eyebrows from Moe; Rose is likewise alarmed.

ROSE, *to Fanny*: Don't be silly, he's been with us six months.

FANNY, *fearfully, voice lowered*: I'm telling you . . . he is not happy about it.

MOE, *resoundingly understating the irony*: He's not happy.

FANNY, *to Moe*: Well, you know how he loves space, and this apartment is so roomy.

MOE, *to Lee*: He bought himself a grave, you know. It's going to be in the cemetery on the aisle. So he'll have a little more room to move around, . . .

ROSE: Oh, stop it.

MOE: . . . get in and out quicker.

FANNY, *innocently*: Out of a grave?

ROSE: He's kidding you, for God's sake!

FANNY: Oh! *To Rose*: I think he's afraid my house'll be too small; you know, with Sidney and us and the one bathroom. And what is he going to do with himself in Brooklyn? He never liked the country.

ROSE: Fanny, dear, make up your mind—he's going to *love* it with you.

MOE: Tell you, Fanny—maybe we should *all* move over to your house and he could live here with an eleven-room apartment for himself, and we'll send the maid every day to do his laundry . . .

FANNY: He's brushing his hair, Rose, but I know he's not happy. I think what it is, he still misses Mama, you see.

MOE: Now *that's* serious—a man his age still misses his mother . . .

FANNY: No, *our* mother—*Mama. To Rose, almost laughing, pointing at Moe*: He thought Papa misses his own mother!

ROSE: No, he didn't, he's kidding you!

FANNY: Oh, you . . . ! *She swipes at Moe.*

ROSE, *walking her to the doorway*: Go hurry him up. I don't want to miss the first scene of this show; it's Gershwin, it's supposed to be wonderful.

FANNY: See, what it is, something is always happening here . . .

MOE, *into phone*: Trafalgar five, seven-seven-one-one.

FANNY: . . . I mean with the stock market and the business. . . . Papa just loves all this!

> *Grandpa appears, in a suit, with a cane; very neat, proper—and very sorry for himself. Comes to a halt, already hurt.*

MOE, *to Grandpa*: See you again soon, Charley!

FANNY, *deferentially*: You ready, Papa?

MOE, *on phone*: Herb? . . . Maybe I ought to get rid of my Worthington Pump. Oh . . . thousand shares? And remind me to talk to you about gold, will you? *Pause.* Good. *He hangs up.*

FANNY, *with Rose, getting Grandpa into his coat*: Rose'll come every few days, Papa . . .

ROSE: Sunday we'll all come out and spend the day.

GRANDPA: Brooklyn is full of tomatoes.

FANNY: No, they're starting to put up big apartment houses now; it's practically not the country anymore. *In a tone of happy reassurance*: On some streets there's hardly a tree! *To Rose, of her diamond bracelet*: I'm looking at that bracelet! Is it new?

ROSE: For my birthday.

FANNY: It's gorgeous.

ROSE: He gave exactly the same one to his mother.

FANNY: She must be overjoyed.

ROSE, *with a cutting smile, to Moe*: Why not?

GRANDPA, *making a sudden despairing announcement*: Well? So I'm going! *With a sharp tap of his cane on the floor, he starts off.*

LEE: Bye-bye, Grandpa!

GRANDPA, *goes to Lee, offers his cheek, gets his kiss, then pinches Lee's cheek*: You be a good boy. *He strides past Rose, huffily snatches his hat out of her hand, and exits.*

MOE: There goes the boarder. I lived to see it!

ROSE, *to Lee*: Want to come and ride with us?

LEE: I think I'll stay and work on my radio.

ROSE: Good, and go to bed carly. I'll bring home all the music from the show, and we'll sing it tomorrow. *She kisses Lee.* Good night, darling. *She swings out in her furs.*

MOE, *to Lee*: Whyn't you get a haircut?

LEE: I did, but it grew back, I think.

MOE, *realizing Lee's size*: Should you talk to your mother about college or something?

LEE: Oh, no, not for a couple of years.

MOE: Oh. Okay, good. *He laughs and goes out, perfectly at one with the world.*

Robertson appears, walks over to the couch, and lies down. Dr.
Rosman appears and sits in a chair behind Robertson's head.

ROBERTSON: Where'd I leave off yesterday?

DR. ROSMAN: Your mother had scalded the cat.

Pause.

ROBERTSON: There's something else, Doctor. I feel a conflict about saying it . . .

DR. ROSMAN: That's what we're here for.

ROBERTSON: I don't mean in the usual sense. It has to do with money.

DR. ROSMAN: Yes?

ROBERTSON: Your money.

DR. ROSMAN, *turns down to him, alarmed*: What about it?

ROBERTSON, *hesitates*: I think you ought to get out of the market.

DR. ROSMAN: Out of the market!

ROBERTSON: Sell everything.

DR. ROSMAN, *pauses, raises his head to think, then speaks carefully*:
Could you talk about the basis for this idea? When was the first time you
had this thought?

ROBERTSON: About four months ago. Around the middle of May.

DR. ROSMAN: Can you recall what suggested it?

ROBERTSON: One of my companies manufactures kitchen utensils.

DR. ROSMAN: The one in Indiana?

ROBERTSON: Yes. In the middle of May all our orders stopped.

DR. ROSMAN: Completely?

ROBERTSON: Dead stop. It's now the end of August, and they haven't resumed.

DR. ROSMAN: How is that possible? The stock keeps going up.

ROBERTSON: Thirty points in less than two months. This is what I've been
trying to tell you for a long time now, Doctor—the market represents
nothing but a state of mind. *He sits up.* On the other hand, I must face the
possibility that this is merely my personal fantasy . . .

DR. ROSMAN: Yes, your fear of approaching disaster.

ROBERTSON: But I've had meetings at the Morgan Bank all week, and it's
the same in almost every industry—it's not just my companies. The

warehouses are overflowing, we can't move the goods, that's an objective fact.

DR. ROSMAN: Have you told your thoughts to your colleagues?

ROBERTSON: They won't listen. Maybe they can't afford to—we've been tossing the whole country onto a crap table in a game where nobody is ever supposed to lose! . . . I sold off a lot two years ago, but when the market opens tomorrow I'm cashing in the rest. I feel guilty for it, but I can't see any other way.

DR. ROSMAN: Why does selling make you feel guilty?

ROBERTSON: Dumping twelve million dollars in securities could start a slide. It could wipe out thousands of widows and old people. . . . I've even played with the idea of making a public announcement.

DR. ROSMAN: That you're dumping twelve million dollars? That could start a slide all by itself, couldn't it?

ROBERTSON: But it would warn the little people.

DR. ROSMAN: Yes, but selling out quietly might not disturb the market quite so much. You *could* be wrong, too.

ROBERTSON: I suppose so. Yes. . . . Maybe I'll just sell and shut up. You're right. I could be mistaken.

DR. ROSMAN, *relieved*: You probably are—but I think I'll sell out anyway.

ROBERTSON: Fine, Doctor. *He stands, straightens his jacket.* And one more thing. This is going to sound absolutely nuts, but . . . when you get your cash, don't keep it. Buy gold.

DR. ROSMAN: You can't be serious.

ROBERTSON: Gold bars, Doctor. The dollar may disappear with the rest of it. *He extends his hand.* Well, good luck.

DR. ROSMAN: Your hand is shaking.

ROBERTSON: Why not? Ask any two great bankers in the United States and they'd say that Arthur A. Robertson had lost his mind. *Pause.* Gold bars, Doctor . . . and don't put them in the bank. In the basement. Take care, now. *He exits.*

> *A bar. People in evening dress seated morosely at tables. An atmosphere of shock and even embarrassment.*

LIVERMORE: About Randolph Morgan. Could you actually see him falling?

TONY: Oh, yeah. It was still that blue light, just before it gets dark? And I don't know why, something made me look up. And there's a man flyin' spread-eagle, falling through the air. He was right on top of me, like a giant! *He looks down.* And I look. I couldn't believe it. It's Randolph!

LIVERMORE: Poor, poor man.

DURANT: Damned fool.

LIVERMORE: I don't know—I think there is a certain gallantry. . . . When you lose other people's money as well as your own, there can be no other way out.

DURANT: There's always a way out. The door.

TONY: Little more brandy, Mr. Durant?

LIVERMORE, *raising his cup*: To Randolph Morgan.

> *Durant raises his cup.*

TONY: Amen here. And I want to say something else—everybody should get down on their knees and thank John D. Rockefeller.

LIVERMORE: Now you're talking.

TONY: Honest to God, Mr. Livermore, didn't that shoot a thrill in you? I mean, there's a *man*—to come out like that with the whole market falling to pieces and say, "I and my sons are buying six million dollars in common stocks." I mean, that's a bullfighter.

LIVERMORE: He'll turn it all around, too.

TONY: Sure he'll turn it around, because the man's a capitalist, he knows how to put up a battle. You wait, tomorrow morning it'll all be shootin' up again like Roman candles!

> *Enter Waiter, who whispers in Tony's ear.*

Sure, sure, bring her in.

> *Waiter hurries out. Tony turns to the two financiers.*

My God, it's Randolph's sister. . . . She don't know yet.

> *Enter Diana, a young woman of elegant ease.*

How do you do, Miss Morgan, come in, come in. Here, I got a nice table for you.

DIANA, *all bright Southern belle*: Thank you!

TONY: Can I bring you nice steak? Little drink?

DIANA: I believe I'll wait for Mr. Robertson.

TONY: Sure. Make yourself at home.

DIANA: Are you the . . . *famous* Tony?

TONY: That's right, miss.

DIANA: I certainly am thrilled to meet you. I've read all about this marvelous place. *She looks around avidly.* Are all these people literary?

TONY: Well, not all, Miss Morgan.

DIANA: But this is the speakeasy F. Scott Fitzgerald frequents, isn't it?

TONY: Oh, yeah, but tonight is very quiet with the stock market and all, people stayin' home a lot the last couple days.

DIANA: Is that gentleman a writer?

TONY: No, miss, that's Jake the Barber, he's in the liquor business.

DIANA: And these?

> *She points to Durant and Livermore. Durant, having overheard, stands.*

TONY: Mr. Durant, Miss Morgan. Mr. Livermore, Miss Morgan.

DIANA, *in a Southern accent, to the audience*: The name of Jesse Livermore was uttered in my family like the name of a genius! A Shakespeare, a Dante of corporate finance.

> *Clayton, at the bar, picks up a phone.*

LEE, *looking on from choral area*: And William Durant . . . he had a car named after him, the Durant Six.

MOE, *beside Lee*: A *car*? Durant had control of General Motors, for God's sake.

DIANA: Not *the* Jesse Livermore?

LIVERMORE: Afraid so, yes!

DIANA: Well, I declare! And sitting here just like two ordinary millionaires!

LEE: Ah, yes, the Great Men. The fabled High Priests of the neverending Boom.

DIANA: This is certainly a banner evening for me! . . . I suppose you know Durham quite well.

LIVERMORE: Durham? I don't believe I've ever been there.

DIANA: But your big Philip Morris plant is there. You do still own Philip Morris, don't you?

LIVERMORE: Oh, yes, but to bet on a horse there's no need to ride him. I never mix in business. I am only interested in stocks.

DIANA: Well, that's sort of miraculous, isn't it, to own a place like that and never've seen it! My brother's in brokerage—Randolph Morgan?

LIVERMORE: I dealt with Randolph when I bought the controlling shares in IBM. Fine fellow.

DIANA: But I don't understand why he'd be spending the night in his office. The market's closed at night, isn't it?

Both men shift uneasily.

DURANT: Oh, yes, but there's an avalanche of selling orders from all over the country, and they're working round the clock to tally them up. The truth is, there's not a price on anything at the moment. In fact, Mr. Clayton over there at the end of the bar is waiting for the latest estimates.

DIANA: I'm sure something will be done, won't there? *She laughs.* They've cut off our telephone!

LIVERMORE: How's that?

DIANA: It seems that Daddy's lived on loans the last few months and his credit stopped. I had no idea! *She laughs.* I feel like a figure in a dream. I sat down in the dining car the other day, absolutely famished, and realized I had only forty cents! I am surviving on chocolate bars! *Her charm barely hides her anxiety.* Whatever has become of all the money?

LIVERMORE: You mustn't worry, Miss Morgan, there'll soon be plenty of money. Money is like a shy bird: the slightest rustle in the trees and it flies for cover. But money cannot bear solitude for long, it must come out and feed. And that is why we must all speak positively and show our confidence.

ROSE, *from choral area*: And they were nothing but pickpockets in a crowd of innocent pilgrims.

LIVERMORE: With Rockefeller's announcement this morning the climb has probably begun already.

ROBERTSON, *from choral area*: Yes, but they also believed.

TAYLOR, *from choral area*: *What* did they believe?

IRENE AND BANKS, *from choral area, echoing Taylor*: Yeah, what did they believe?

ROBERTSON: Why, the most important thing of all—that talk makes facts!

DURANT: If I were you, Miss Morgan, I would prepare myself for the worst.

LIVERMORE: Now, Bill, there is no good in that kind of talk.

ROBERTSON: And they ended up believing it themselves!

DURANT: It's far more dreamlike than you imagine, Miss Morgan.

MOE: There they are, chatting away, while the gentleman at the end of the bar . . .

DURANT: . . . That gentleman . . . who has just put down the telephone is undoubtedly steeling himself to tell me that I have lost control of General Motors.

DIANA: What!

Clayton, at the bar, has indeed put down the phone, has straightened his vest, and is now crossing to their table.

DURANT, *watching him approach*: If I were you, I'd muster all the strength I have, Miss Morgan. Yes, Clayton?

CLAYTON: If we could talk privately, sir . . .

DURANT: Am I through?

CLAYTON: If you could borrow for two or three weeks . . .

DURANT: From whom?

CLAYTON: I don't know, sir.

DURANT, *standing*: Good night, Miss Morgan.

She is looking up at him, astonished.

How old are you?

DIANA: Nineteen.

DURANT: I hope you will look things in the face, young lady. Shun paper. Paper is the plague. Good luck to you. *He turns to go.*

LIVERMORE: We have to talk, Bill . . .

DURANT: Nothing to say, Jesse. Go to bed, old boy. It's long past midnight.

MOE, *trying to recall*: Say . . . didn't Durant end up managing a bowling alley in Toledo, Ohio?

CLAYTON, *nods*: Dead broke.

LIVERMORE, *turns to Clayton, adopting a tone of casual challenge*: Clayton . . . what's Philip Morris going to open at, can they tell?

CLAYTON: Below twenty. No higher. If we can find buyers at all.

LIVERMORE, *his smile gone*: But Rockefeller. Rockefeller . . .

CLAYTON: It doesn't seem to have had any effect, sir.

Livermore stands. Pause.

I should get back to the office, sir, if I may.

Livermore is silent.

I'm very sorry, Mr. Livermore.

Clayton exits. Diana is moved by the excruciating look coming onto Livermore's face.

DIANA: Mr. Livermore? . . .

ROBERTSON, *entering*: Sorry I'm late, Diana. How was the trip? *Her expression turns him to Livermore. He goes to him.* Bad, Jesse?

LIVERMORE: I am wiped out, Arthur.

ROBERTSON, *trying for lightness*: Come on, now, Jesse, a man like you has always got ten million put away somewhere.

LIVERMORE: No, no. I always felt that if you couldn't have *real* money, might as well not have any. Is it true what I've heard, that you sold out in time?

ROBERTSON: Yes, Jesse. I told you I would.

LIVERMORE, *slight pause*: Arthur, can you lend me five thousand dollars?

ROBERTSON: Certainly. *He sits, removes one shoe. To audience.* Five weeks ago, on his yacht in Oyster Bay, he told me he had four hundred and eighty million dollars in common stocks.

LIVERMORE: What the hell are you doing?

Robertson removes a layer of five thousand-dollar bills from the shoe and hands Livermore one as he stands. Livermore stares down at Robertson's shoes.

By God. Don't you believe in anything?

ROBERTSON: Not much.

LIVERMORE: Well, I suppose I understand that. *He folds the bill.* But I can't say that I admire it. *He pockets the bill, looks down again at Robertson's shoes, and shakes his head.* Well, I guess it's your country now. *He turns like a blind man and goes out.*

ROBERTSON: Not long after, Jesse Livermore sat down to a good breakfast in the Sherry-Netherland Hotel and, calling for an envelope, addressed it to Arthur Robertson, inserted a note for five thousand dollars, went into the washroom, and shot himself.

DIANA, *staring after Livermore, then turning to Robertson*: Is Randolph ruined too?

ROBERTSON, *taking her hand*: Diana . . . Randolph is dead. *Pause.* He . . . he fell from his window.

Diana stands, astonished. Irene sings "'Tain't Nobody's Bizness" from choral area. Fadeout.

ROSE, *calling as she enters*: Lee? Darling?

LEE, *takes a bike from prop area and rides on, halting before her*: How do you like it, Ma!

ROSE: What a beautiful bike!

LEE: It's a Columbia Racer! I just bought it from Georgie Rosen for twelve dollars.

ROSE: Where'd you get twelve dollars?

LEE: I emptied my savings account. But it's worth way more! . . .

ROSE: Well, I should say! Listen, darling, you know how to get to Third Avenue and Nineteenth Street, don't you?

LEE: Sure, in ten minutes.

ROSE, *taking a diamond bracelet from her bag*: This is my diamond bracelet. *She reaches into the bag and brings out a card.* And this is Mr. Sanders' card and the address. He's expecting you; just give it to him, and he'll give you a receipt.

LEE: Is he going to fix it?

ROSE: No, dear. It's a pawnshop. Go. I'll explain sometime.

LEE: Can't I have an idea? What's a pawnshop?

ROSE: Where you leave something temporarily and they lend you money on it, with interest. I'm going to leave it the rest of the month, till the market goes up again. I showed it to him on Friday, and we're getting a nice loan on it.

LEE: But how do you get it back?

ROSE: You just pay back the loan plus interest. But things'll pick up in a month or two. Go on, darling, and be careful! I'm so glad you bought that bike. . . . It's gorgeous!

LEE, *mounting his bike*: Does Papa know?

ROSE: Yes, dear. Papa knows . . .

> She starts out as Joey hurries on.

JOEY: Oh, hiya, Mrs. Baum.

ROSE: Hello, Joey. . . . Did you get thin?

JOEY: Me? *He touches his stomach defensively.* No, I'm okay. *To Lee as well, as he takes an eight-by-ten photo out of an envelope*: See what I just got?

> Rose and Lee look at the photo.

ROSE, *impressed*: Where did you get that!

LEE: How'd you get it autographed?

JOEY: I just wrote to the White House.

LEE, *running his finger over the signature*: Boy . . . look at that, huh? "Herbert Hoover"!

ROSE: What a human thing for him to do! What did you write him?

JOEY: Just wished him success . . . you know, against the Depression.

ROSE, *wondrously*: Look at that! You're going to end up a politician, Joey. *She returns to studying the photo.*

JOEY: I might. I like it a lot.

LEE: But what about dentistry?

JOEY: Well, either one.

ROSE: Get going, darling.

> *She exits, already preoccupied with the real problem. Lee mounts his bike.*

LEE: You want to shoot some baskets later?

JOEY: What about now?

LEE, *embarrassed*: No . . . I've got something to do for my mother. Meet you on the court in an hour. *He starts off.*

JOEY, *stopping him*: Wait, I'll go with you, let me on! *He starts to mount the crossbar.*

LEE: I can't, Joey.

JOEY, *sensing some forbidden area, surprised*: Oh!

LEE: See you on the court.

> *Lee rides off. Joey examines the autograph and mouths silently, "Herbert Hoover . . . " He shakes his head proudly and walks off.*

ROBERTSON, *from choral area*: To me . . . it's beginning to look like Germany in 1922, and I'm having real worries about the banks. There are times when I walk around with as much as twenty-five, thirty thousand dollars in my shoes.

> *Frank enters in a chauffeur's uniform, a lap robe folded over his arm. Moe enters, stylishly dressed in a fur-collared overcoat, as though on a street.*

FRANK: Morning, Mr. Baum. Got the car nice and warmed up for you this morning, sir. And I had the lap robe dry-cleaned.

MOE, *showing Frank a bill*: What is that, Frank?

FRANK: Oh. Looks like the garage bill.

MOE: What's that about tires on there?

FRANK: Oh, yes, sir, this is the bill for the new tires last week.

MOE: And what happened to those tires we bought six weeks ago?

FRANK: Those weren't very good, sir, they wore out quick—and I want to be the first to admit that!

MOE: But twenty dollars apiece and they last six weeks?

FRANK: That's just what I'm telling you, sir—they were just no good. But these ones are going to be a whole lot better, though.

MOE: Tell you what, Frank . . .

FRANK: Yes, sir—what I mean, I'm giving you my personal guarantee on this set, Mr. Baum.

MOE: I never paid no attention to these things, but maybe you heard of the market crash? The whole thing practically floated into the ocean, y'know.

FRANK: Oh, yes, sir, I certainly heard about it.

MOE: I'm glad you heard about it, because I heard a *lot* about it. In fact, what you cleared from selling my tires over the last ten years . . .

FRANK: Oh, no, sir! Mr. Baum!

MOE: Frank, lookin' back over the last ten years, I never heard of that amount of tires in my whole life since I first come over from Europe a baby at the age of six. That is a lot of tires, Frank; so I tell ya what we're gonna do now, you're going to drive her over to the Pierce Arrow showroom and leave her there, and then come to my office and we'll settle up.

FRANK: But how are you going to get around!

MOE: I'm a happy man in a taxi, Frank.

FRANK: Well, I'm sure going to be sorry to leave you people.

MOE: Everything comes to an end, Frank, it was great while it lasted. No hard feelings. *He shakes Frank's hand.* Bye-bye.

FRANK: But what . . . what am I supposed to do now?

MOE: You got in-laws?

FRANK: But I never got along with them.

MOE: You should've. *He hurries off, calling*: Taxi!

FRANK, *cap in hand, throws down lap robe and walks off aimlessly*: Damn!

Irene enters with a pram filled with junk and sings a few lines of "'Tain't Nobody's Bizness," unaccompanied. She picks up robe and admiringly inspects it. Then:

IRENE: You got fired, you walked away to nothing; no unemployment insurance, no Social Security—just the in-laws and fresh air. *She tosses the robe in with her junk.*

Fadeout.

ROSE: Still . . . it was very nice in a certain way. On our block in Brooklyn a lot of married children had to move back with the parents, and you heard babies crying in houses that didn't have a baby in twenty years. But of course the doubling up could also drive you crazy . . .

With hardly a pause, she turns to Grandpa, who is arriving center with canes and hatboxes. He drops the whole load on the floor.

What are *you* doing?

GRANDPA, *delivering a final verdict*: There's no room for these in my closet . . .

ROSE: For a few *canes?*

GRANDPA: And what about my hats? You shouldn't have bought such a small house, Rose.

ROSE, *of the canes*: I'll put them in the front-hall closet.

GRANDPA: No, people step on them. And where will I put my hats?

ROSE, *trying not to explode*: Papa, what do you want from me? We are doing what we can do!

GRANDPA: One bathroom for so many people is not right! You had three bathrooms in the apartment, and you used to look out the window, there was the whole New York. Here . . . listen to that street out there, it's a Brooklyn cemetery. And this barber here is *very* bad—look what he did to me. *He shows her.*

ROSE: Why? It's beautiful. *She brushes some hairs straight.* It's just a little uneven . . .

GRANDPA, *pushing her hand away*: I don't understand, Rose—why does he declare bankruptcy if he's going to turn around and pay his debts?

ROSE: For his reputation.

GRANDPA: His reputation! He'll have the reputation of a fool! The reason to go bankrupt is *not* to pay your debts!

ROSE, *uncertain herself*: He wanted to be honorable.

GRANDPA: But that's the whole beauty of it! He should've asked me. When I went bankrupt I didn't pay *nobody*!

ROSE, *deciding*: I've got to tell you something, Papa. From now on, I wish you . . .

GRANDPA, *helping her fold a bed sheet*: And you'll have to talk to Lee— he throws himself around in his bed all night, wakes me up ten times, and he leaves his socks on the floor. . . . Two people in that bedroom is too much, Rose.

ROSE: I don't want Moe to get aggravated, Papa.

He is reached, slightly glances at her.

He might try to start a new business, so he's nervous, so please, don't complain, Papa. Please?

GRANDPA: What did I say?

ROSE: Nothing. *Suddenly she embraces him guiltily.* Maybe I can find an umbrella stand someplace.

GRANDPA: I was reading about this Hitler . . .

ROSE: Who?

GRANDPA: . . . He's chasing all the radicals out of Germany. He wouldn't be so bad if he wasn't against the Jews. But he won't last six months. . . . The Germans are not fools. When I used to take Mama to Baden-Baden this time of year . . .

ROSE: How beautiful she was.

GRANDPA: . . . one time we were sitting on the train ready to leave for Berlin. And suddenly a man gallops up calling out my name. So I says, "Yes, that's me!" And through the window he hands me my gold watch and chain: "You left it in your room, mein Herr." Such a thing could only happen in Germany. This Hitler is finished.

ROSE, *of the canes*: Please. . . . Put them back in your closet, heh? *He starts to object.* I don't want Moe to get mad, Papa! *She cuts the rebellion short and loads him with his canes and hatboxes.*

GRANDPA, *muttering*: Man don't even know how to go bankrupt.

He exits. Lee appears on his bike—but dressed now for winter. He dismounts and parks the bike just as Rose lies back in the chair.

LEE: Ma! Guess what!

ROSE: What?

LEE: Remember I emptied my bank account for the bike?

ROSE: So?

LEE: The bank has just been closed by the government! It's broke! There's a whole mob of people in the street yelling where's their money! They've got cops and everything! There is no more money in the bank!

ROSE: You're a genius!

LEE: Imagine! . . . I could have lost my twelve dollars! . . . Wow!

ROSE: That's wonderful. *She removes a pearl choker.*

LEE: Oh, Ma, wasn't that Papa's wedding present?

ROSE: I hate to, but . . .

LEE: What about Papa's business! Can't he . . .

ROSE: He put too much capital in the stock market, dear—it made more there than in his business. So now . . . it's not there anymore.

> *A thief swiftly appears and rides off on the bike.*

But we'll be all right. Go. You can have a jelly sandwich when you come back.

> *Lee stuffs the pearls into his pants as he approaches where the bike was; he looks in all directions, his bones chilling. He runs in all directions and finally comes to a halt, breathless, stark horror in his face. As though sensing trouble, Rose walks over to him.*

Where's your bike?

> *He can't speak.*

They stole your bike?

> *He is immobile.*

May he choke on his next meal. . . . Oh, my darling, my darling, what an awful thing.

> *He sobs once but holds it back. She, facing him, tries to smile.*

So now you're going to have to walk to the hockshop like everybody else. Come, have your jelly sandwich.

LEE: No, I'd like to see if I can trot there—it'd be good for my track. By the way, I've almost decided to go to Cornell, I think. Cornell or Brown.

ROSE, *with an empty congratulatory exclamation*: Oh! . . . Well, there's still months to decide.

Rose and Lee join the company as they stand up to sing the Iowa Hymn, Verse 1: "We gather together to ask the Lord's blessing, He chastens and hastens His will to make known: The wicked oppressing now cease from distressing, Sing praises to His name: He forgets not His own." The hymn music continues under the following.

ROBERTSON: Till then, probably most people didn't think of it as a system.

TAYLOR: It was more like nature.

MRS. TAYLOR: Like weather; had to expect bad weather, but it always got good again if you waited. And so we waited. And it didn't change. *She is watching Taylor as he adopts a mood of despair and slowly sits on his heels.* And we waited some more and it never changed. You couldn't hardly believe that the day would come when the land wouldn't give. Land always gives. But there it lay, miles and miles of it, and there was us wanting to work it, and couldn't. It was like a spell on Iowa. We was all there, and the land was there waitin', and we wasn't able to move. *The hymn ends.* Amen.

Brewster, followed by Farmers, comes front and calls to the crowd in the audience's direction.

BREWSTER: Just sit tight, folks, be startin' in a few minutes.

FARMER 1, *hitting his heels together*: Looks like snow up there.

FARMER 2, *laughs*: Even the weather ain't workin'.

Low laughter in the crowd.

BREWSTER, *heading over to Taylor*: You be catchin' cold sitting on the ground like that, won't you, Henry?

TAYLOR: Tired out. Never slept a wink all night. Not a wink.

Mrs. Taylor appears carrying a big coffeepot, accompanied by Harriet, her fifteen-year-old daughter, who has a coffee mug hanging from each of her fingers.

MRS. TAYLOR: You'll have to share the cups, but it's something hot anyway.

BREWSTER: Oh, that smells good, lemme take that, ma'am.

She gives the coffeepot to Brewster and comes over to Taylor. Harriet hands out the cups.

MRS. TAYLOR, *sotto voce, irritated and ashamed*: You can't be sitting on the ground like that, now come on! *She starts him to his feet.* It's a auction— anybody's got a right to come to a auction.

TAYLOR: There must be a thousand men along the road—they never told me they'd bring a thousand men!

MRS. TAYLOR: Well, I suppose that's the way they do it.

TAYLOR: They got guns in those trucks!

MRS. TAYLOR, *frightened herself*: Well, it's too late to stop 'em now. So might as well go around and talk to people that come to help you.

CHARLEY, *rushing on*: Brewster! Where's Brewster!

BREWSTER, *stepping forward from the crowd*: What's up, Charley?

CHARLEY, *pointing off*: Judge Bradley! He's gettin' out of the car with the auctioneer!

> *Silence. All look to Brewster.*

BREWSTER: Well . . . I don't see what that changes. *Turning to all*: I guess we're gonna do what we come here to do. That right?

> *The crowd quietly agrees: "Right," "Stick to it, Larry," "No use quittin' now," etc. Enter Judge Bradley, sixty, and Mr. Frank Howard, the auctioneer. The silence spreads.*

JUDGE BRADLEY: Good morning, gentlemen. *He looks around. There is no reply.* I want to say a few words to you before Mr. Howard starts the auction. *He walks up onto a raised platform.* I have decided to come here personally this morning in order to emphasize the gravity of the situation that has developed in the state. We are on the verge of anarchy in Iowa, and that is not going to help anybody. Now, you are all property owners, so you—

BREWSTER: Used to be, Judge, used to be!

JUDGE BRADLEY: Brewster, I will not waste words; there are forty armed deputies out there. *Slight pause.* I would like to make only one point clear—I have levied a deficiency judgment on this farm. Mr. Taylor has failed to pay what he owes on his equipment and some of his cattle. A contract is sacred. The National Bank has the right to collect on its loans. Now then, Mr. Howard will begin the auction. But he has discretionary power to decline any unreasonable bid. I ask you again, obey the law. Once law and order go down, no man is safe. Mr. Howard?

MR. HOWARD, *with a clipboard in hand, climbs onto the platform*: Well, now, let's see. We have here one John Deere tractor and combine, three years old, beautiful condition.

> *Three Bidders enter, and the crowd turns to look at them with hostility as they come to a halt.*

I ask for bids on the tractor and combine.

BREWSTER: Ten cents!

MR. HOWARD: I have ten cents. *His finger raised, he points from man to man in the crowd.* I have ten cents, I have ten cents . . .

He is pointing toward the Bidders, but they are looking around at the crowd in fear.

BIDDER 1: Five hundred.

JUDGE BRADLEY, *calling*: Sheriff, get over here and protect these men!

The Sheriff and four Deputies enter and edge their way in around the three Bidders. The deputies carry shotguns.

MR. HOWARD: Do I hear five hundred dollars? Do I hear five . . .

BIDDER 1: Five hundred!

MR. HOWARD: Do I hear six hundred?

BIDDER 2: Six hundred!

MR. HOWARD: Do I hear seven hundred?

BIDDER 3: Seven hundred!

Disciplined and quick, the Farmers grab the Deputies and disarm them; a shotgun goes off harmlessly.

JUDGE BRADLEY: Brewster! Great God, what are you doing!

Brewster has pinned the Judge's arms behind him, and another man lowers a noose around his neck.

BREWSTER, *to Deputies*: You come any closer and we're gonna string him up! You all get back on that road or we string up the Judge! So help me Christ, he goes up if any one of you deputies interferes with this auction! Now, let me just clear up one thing for you, Judge Bradley . . .

TAYLOR: Let him go, Brewster—I don't care anymore, let them take it!

BREWSTER: Just sit tight, Henry, nobody's takin' anything. That is all over, Judge. Mr. Howard, just to save time, why don't you take a bid on the whole place? Do that, please?

MR. HOWARD, *turns to the crowd, his voice shaking*: I . . . I'll hear bids on . . . everything. Tractor and combine, pair of mules and wagon, twenty-six cows, eight heifers, farm and outbuildings, assorted tools . . . and so forth. Do I hear . . .

BREWSTER: One dollar.

MR. HOWARD, *rapidly*: I hear one dollar. One dollar, one dollar? . . . *He looks around.* Sold for one dollar.

BREWSTER, *Handing him a dollar*: Now, will you just sign that receipt, please?

Mr. Howard scribbles and hands him a receipt. Brewster leaps off the platform, goes to Taylor, and gives him the receipt.

Henry? Whyn't you go along now and get to milkin'. Let's go, boys.

He waves to the crowd, and his men follow him out. Judge Bradley, removing the noose, comes down off the platform and goes over to Taylor, who is staring down at the receipt.

JUDGE BRADLEY: Henry Taylor? You are nothing but a thief!

Taylor cringes under the accusation. The Judge points to the receipt.

That is a crime against every law of God and man! And this isn't the end of it, either! *He turns and stalks out.*

HARRIET: Should we milk 'em, Papa?

MRS. TAYLOR: Of course we milk 'em—they're ours. *But she needs Taylor's compliance.* Henry?

TAYLOR, *staring at the receipt*: It's like I stole my own place.

Near tears, humiliated, Taylor moves into darkness with his wife. The Farmers disperse.

ROBERTSON, *from choral area*: Nobody knows how many people are leaving their hometowns, their farms and cities, and hitting the road. Hundreds of thousands, maybe millions of internal refugees, Americans transformed into strangers.

Banks enters in army cap, uniform jacket, and jeans, carrying his little bundle of clothes and a cooking pot.

BANKS:

I still hear that train.
Still hear that long low whistle.
Still hear that train, yeah.

He imitates train whistle: Whoo-ooo! *He sings the first verse of "How Long," then speaks over music, which continues.*

Nineteen twenty-nine was pretty hard. My family had a little old cotton farm, McGehee, Arkansas. But a man had to be on the road—leave his wife, his mother—just to try to get a little money to live on. But God help me, I couldn't get anything, and I was too ashamed to send them a picture, all dirty and ragged and hadn't shaved. Write a postcard: "Dear Mother, doin' wonderful and hope you're all fine." And me sleepin' on a Los Angeles sidewalk under a newspaper. And my ma'd say, "Oh, my son's in Los Angeles, he's doin' pretty fair." *He grins.* Yeah . . . "all the way on the Santa Fe." So hungry and weak I begin to see snakes through the smoke, and a white hobo named Callahan got a scissors on me, wrapped me 'tween his legs—otherwise I'd have fell off into a cornfield there. But except for Callahan there was no friendships in the hobo jungle. Everybody else was worried and sad-lookin', and they was evil to each other. I still hear that long low whistle . . . *whoo-ooo!*

Banks sings the second verse of "How Long." Then the music changes into "The Joint is Jumpin'": Marathon Dancers enter, half asleep, some about to drop. They dance. Fadeout.

Light comes up on Moe in an armchair. Lee enters with college catalogues.

MOE: When you say three hundred dollars tuition . . . Lee!

LEE: That's for Columbia. Some of these others are cheaper.

MOE: That's for the four years.

LEE: Well, no, that's one year.

MOE: Ah. *He lies back in the chair and closes his eyes.*

LEE, *flipping a page of a catalogue*: Minnesota here is a hundred and fifty, for instance. And Ohio State is about the same, I think. *He turns to Moe, awaiting his reaction.* Pa?

Moe is asleep.

He always got drowsy when the news got bad. And now the mystery of the marked house began. Practically every day you'd see the stranger coming down the street, poor and ragged, and he'd go past house after house, but at our driveway he'd make a turn right up to the back porch and ask for something to eat. Why us?

Taylor appears at one side of the stage in mackinaw, farm shoes, and peaked hunter's cap, a creased paper bag under his arm. Looking front, he seems gaunt, out of his element; now he rings the doorbell. Nothing happens. Then Lee goes to the "door."

Yes?

TAYLOR, *shyly, still an amateur at the routine*: Ah . . . sorry to be botherin' you on a Sunday and all.

ROSE, *enters in housedress and apron, wiping her hands on a dish towel*: Who is that, dear? *She comes to the door.*

LEE: This is my mother.

TAYLOR: How-de-do, ma'am, my name is Taylor, and I'm just passing by, wondering if you folks have any work around the place . . .

MOE, *waking up suddenly*: Hey! The bell rang! *He sees the conclave.* Oh . . .

ROSE, *ironically*: Another one looking for work!

TAYLOR: I could paint the place or fix the roof, electrical, plumbing, masonry, gardening . . . I always had my own farm, and we do all that, don't you know. I'd work cheap . . .

ROSE: Well, we don't need any kind of . . .

MOE: Where you from?

TAYLOR: State of Iowa.

LEE, *as though it's the moon*: Iowa!

TAYLOR: I wouldn't hardly charge if I could have my meals, don't you know.

MOE, *beginning to locate Taylor in space*: Whereabouts in Iowa?

ROSE: My sister's husband comes from Cleveland.

MOE: No, no, Cleveland is nowhere near. *To Taylor*: Whereabouts?

TAYLOR: You know Styles?

MOE: I only know the stores in the big towns.

TAYLOR, *giving a grateful chuckle*: Well! I never expected to meet a . . .

> *He suddenly gets dizzy, breaks off, and reaches for some support. Lee holds his arm, and he goes down like an elevator and sits there.*

ROSE: What's the matter?

MOE: Mister?

LEE: I'll get water! *He rushes out.*

ROSE: Is it your heart?

TAYLOR: 'Scuse me . . . I'm awful sorry . . .

> *He gets on his hands and knees as Lee enters with a glass of water and hands it to him. He drinks half of it, returns the glass.*

Thank you, sonny.

ROSE, *looks to Moe, sees his agreement, gestures within*: He better sit down.

MOE: You want to sit down?

Taylor looks at him helplessly.

Come, sit down.

Lee and Moe help him to a chair, and he sits.

ROSE, *bending over to look into his face*: You got some kind of heart?

TAYLOR, *embarrassed, and afraid for himself now*: Would you be able to give me something to eat?

The three stare at him; he looks up at their shocked astonishment and weeps.

ROSE: You're *hungry*?

TAYLOR: Yes, ma'am.

Rose looks at Moe whether to believe this.

MOE, *unnerved*: Better get him something.

ROSE, *hurrying out immediately*: Oh, my God in heaven!

MOE, *now with a suspicious, even accusatory edge*: What're you doing, just going around? . . .

TAYLOR: Well, no, I come east when I lost the farm. . . . They was supposed to be hiring in New Jersey, pickers for the celery? But I only got two days. . . . I been to the Salvation Army four, five times, but they only give me a bun and a cup of coffee yesterday . . .

LEE: You haven't eaten since *yesterday*?

TAYLOR: Well, I generally don't need too much . . .

ROSE, *entering with a tray, bowl of soup, and bread*: I was just making it, so I didn't put in the potatoes yet . . .

TAYLOR: Oh, beets?

ROSE: That's what you call borscht.

TAYLOR, *obediently*: Yes, ma'am.

He wastes no time, spoons it up. They all watch him: their first hungry man.

MOE, *skeptically*: How do you come to lose a farm?

TAYLOR: I suppose you read about the Farmers' Uprisin' in the state couple months ago?

LEE: I did.

MOE, *to Lee*: What uprising?

LEE: They nearly lynched a judge for auctioning off their farms. *To Taylor, impressed*: Were you in *that*?

TAYLOR: Well, it's all over now, but I don't believe they'll be auctioning any more farms for a while, though. Been just terrible out there.

ROSE, *shaking her head*: And I thought they were all Republicans in Iowa.

TAYLOR: Well, I guess they all are.

LEE: Is that what they mean by radical, though?

TAYLOR: Well . . . it's like they say—people in Iowa are practical. They'll even go radical if it seems like it's practical. But as soon as it stops being practical they stop being radical.

MOE: Well, you probably all learned your lesson now.

LEE: Why! He was taking their homes away, that judge!

MOE: So you go in a court and lynch him?

LEE: But . . . but it's all *wrong*, Pa!

ROSE: Shh! Don't argue . . .

LEE, *to Rose*: But *you* think it's wrong, don't you? Suppose they came and threw us out of *this* house?

ROSE: I refuse to think about it. *To Taylor*: So where do you sleep?

MOE, *instantly*: Excuse me. We are not interested in where you sleep, Mr. . . . what's your name?

TAYLOR: Taylor. I'd be satisfied with just my meals if I could live in the basement . . .

MOE, *to Taylor, but half addressing Rose*: There is no room for another human being in this house, y'understand? Including the basement. *He takes out two or three bills.*

TAYLOR: I wasn't asking for charity . . .

MOE: I'm going to loan you a dollar, and I hope you're going to start a whole new life. Here . . . *He hands Taylor the bill, escorting him to the door.* And pay me back, but don't rush. *He holds out his hand.* Glad to have met you, and good luck.

TAYLOR: Thanks for the soup, Mrs. . . .

ROSE: Our name is Baum. You have children?

TAYLOR: One's fifteen, one's nine. *He thoughtfully folds the dollar bill.*

    Grandpa enters, eating a plum.

ROSE: Take care of yourself, and write a letter to your wife.

TAYLOR: Yes, I will. *To Moe*: Goodbye, sir . . .

MOE, *grinning, tipping his finger at Taylor*: Stay away from rope.

TAYLOR: Oh, yeah, I will . . . *He exits.*

LEE, *goes out on the periphery and calls to him as he walks away*: Goodbye, Mr. Taylor!

TAYLOR, *turns back, waves*: Bye, sonny!

   He leaves. Lee stares after him, absorbing it all.

GRANDPA: Who was that?

MOE: He's a farmer from Iowa. He tried to lynch a judge, so she wanted him to live in the cellar.

GRANDPA: What is a farmer doing here?

ROSE: He went broke, he lost everything.

GRANDPA: Oh. Well, he should borrow.

MOE, *snaps his fingers to Lee*: I'll run down the street and tell him! He got me hungry. *To Rose*: I'm going down the corner and get a chocolate soda. . . . What do you say, Lee?

LEE: I don't feel like it.

MOE: Don't be sad. Life is tough, what're you going to do? Sometimes it's not as tough as other times, that's all. But it's always tough. Come, have a soda.

LEE: Not now, Pa, thanks. *He turns away.*

MOE, *straightens, silently refusing blame*: Be back right away. *He strolls across the stage, softly, tonelessly whistling, and exits.*

   Grandpa, chewing, the plum pit in his hand, looks around for a place to put it. Rose sees the inevitable and holds out her hand.

ROSE, *disgusted*: Oh, give it to me.

   Grandpa drops the pit into her palm, and she goes out with it and the soup plate.

LEE, *still trying to digest*: That man was starving, Grandpa.

GRANDPA: No, no, he was hungry but not starving.

LEE: He was, he almost fainted.

GRANDPA: No, that's not starving. In Europe they starve, but here not. Anyway, couple weeks they're going to figure out what to do, and you can forget the whole thing. . . . God makes one person at a time, boy—worry about yourself.

   Fadeout.

ROBERTSON: His name is Theodore K. Quinn.

Music begins—"My Baby Just Cares for Me"—and Quinn, with boater and cane, sings and dances through Robertson's speech.

The greatest Irish soft-shoe dancer ever to serve on a board of directors. They know him at Lindy's, they love him at Twenty-one. High up on top of the American heap sits Ted Quinn, hardly forty years of age in 1932 . . .

QUINN, *continues singing, then breaks off and picks up the phone*: Ted Quinn. Come over, Arthur, I've got to see you. But come to the twenty-ninth floor. . . . I've got a new office.

ROBERTSON, *looking around, as at a striking office*: All this yours?

QUINN: Yup. You are standing on the apex, the pinnacle of human evolution. From that window you can reach out and touch the moustache of Almighty God.

ROBERTSON, *moved, gripping Quinn's hand*: Ted! *Ted!!*

QUINN: Jesus, don't say it that way, will ya?

ROBERTSON: President of General Electric!

QUINN: I'm not sure I want it, Arthur.

Robertson laughs sarcastically.

I'm not, goddammit! I never expected Swope to pick me—never!

ROBERTSON: Oh, go on, you've been angling for the presidency the last five years.

QUINN: No! I swear not. I just didn't want anybody else to get it . . .

Robertson laughs.

Well, that's not the same thing! . . . Seriously, Arthur, I'm scared. I don't know what to do. *He looks around.* Now that I'm standing here, now that they're about to paint my name on the door . . . and the *Times* sending a reporter . . .

ROBERTSON, *seriously*: What the hell's got into you?

QUINN, *searching in himself*: I don't know. . . . It's almost like shame.

ROBERTSON: For *what*? It's that damned upbringing of yours, that anarchist father . . .

QUINN: The truth is, I've never been comfortable with some of the things we've done.

ROBERTSON: But why suddenly after all these years . . .

QUINN: It's different taking orders and being the man who gives them.

ROBERTSON: I don't know what the hell you are talking about.

Pause. For Quinn it is both a confession and something he must bring out into the open. But he sustains his humor.

QUINN: I had a very unsettling experience about eighteen months ago, Arthur. Got a call from my Philadelphia district manager that Frigidaire was dropping the price on their boxes. So I told him to cut ours. And in a matter of weeks they cut, we cut, they cut, we cut, till I finally went down there myself. Because I was damned if I was going to get beat in Philadelphia . . . and I finally cut our price right down to our cost of production. Well—ting-a-ling-a-ling, phone call from New York: "What the hell is going on down there?" Gotta get down to Wall Street and have a meeting with the money boys. . . . So there we are, about ten of us, and I look across the blinding glare of that teakwood table, and lo and behold, who is facing me but Georgy Fairchild, head of sales for Frigidaire. Old friends, Georgy and I, go way back together, but he *is* Frigidaire, y'know—what the hell is he doing in a GE meeting? . . . Well, turns out that both companies are owned by the same money. And the word is that Georgy and Quinn are going to cut this nonsense and get those prices up to where they belong. *He laughs.* Well, I tell you, I was absolutely flabbergasted. Here I've been fightin' Georgy from Bangkok to the Bronx, layin' awake nights thinkin' how to outfox him—hell, we were like Grant and Lee with thousands of soldiers out to destroy each other, and it's suddenly like all these years I'd been shellin' my own men! *He laughs.* It was farcical.

ROBERTSON: It's amazing. You're probably the world's greatest salesman, and you haven't an ounce of objectivity . . .

QUINN: Objectivity! Arthur, if I'm that great a salesman—which I'm far from denying—it's because I believe; I believe deeply in the creative force of competition.

ROBERTSON: Exactly, and GE is the fastest-growing company in the world because. . . .

QUINN, loves *this point*: . . . because we've had the capital to buy up one independent business after another. . . . It's haunting me, Arthur—thousands of small businesses are going under every week now, and we're getting bigger and bigger every day. What's going to become of the independent person in this country once everybody's sucking off the same tit? How can there be an America without Americans—people not beholden to some enormous enterprise that'll run their souls?

ROBERTSON: Am I hearing what I think?

Quinn is silent.

Ted? You'd actually resign?

QUINN: If I did, would it make any point to you at all? If I made a statement that . . .

ROBERTSON: What statement can you possibly make that won't call for a return to the horse and buggy? The America you love is cold stone dead in the parlor, Ted. This is a corporate country; you can't go back to small personal enterprise again.

QUINN: A corporate country! . . . Jesus, Arthur, what a prospect!

Miss Fowler enters.

MISS FOWLER: The gentleman from the *Times* is waiting, Mr. Quinn . . . unless you'd like to make it tomorrow or . . .

QUINN, *slight pause*: No, no—it has to be now or never. Ask him in.

She exits.

Tell me the truth, Arthur, do I move your mind at all?

ROBERTSON: Of course I see your point. But you can't buck the inevitable.

Graham enters with Miss Fowler.

MISS FOWLER: Mr. Graham.

QUINN, *shakes hands, grinning*: Glad to meet you. . . . My friend Mr. Robertson.

GRAHAM, *recognizing the name*: Oh, yes, how do you do?

ROBERTSON: Nice to meet you. *To Quinn, escaping*: I'll see you later . . .

QUINN: No, stay . . . I'll only be a few minutes . . .

ROBERTSON: I ought to get back to my office.

QUINN, *laughs*: I'm still the president, Arthur—stay! I want to feel the support of your opposition.

Robertson laughs with Quinn, glancing uneasily at Graham, who doesn't know what's going on.

I'll have to be quick, Mr. Graham. Will you sit down?

GRAHAM: I have a few questions about your earlier life and background. I understand your father was one of the early labor organizers in Chicago.

QUINN: Mr. Graham, I am resigning.

GRAHAM: Beg your pardon?

QUINN: Resigning, I said.

GRAHAM: From the presidency? I don't understand.

QUINN: I don't believe in giant business, or giant government, or giant anything. And the laugh is . . . no man has done more to make GE the giant it is today.

GRAHAM: Well, now! *He laughs.* I think this takes us off the financial section and onto the front page! But tell me, how does a man with your ideas rise so high in a great corporation like this? How did you get into GE?

QUINN: Well, it's a long story, but I love to tell it. I started out studying law at night and working as a clerk in a factory that manufactured bulbs for auto headlights. Y'see, in those days they had forty or fifty makes of car and all different specifications for the lightbulbs. Now, say you got an order for five thousand lamps. The manufacturing process was not too accurate, so you had to make eight or nine thousand to come out with five thousand perfect ones. Result, though, was that we had hundreds of thousands of perfectly good lamps left over at the end of the year. So . . . one night on my own time I went through the records and did some simple calculations and came up with a new average. My figure showed that to get five thousand good bulbs we only had to make sixty-two hundred instead of eight thousand. Result was, that company saved a hundred and thirty thousand dollars in one year. So the boss and I became very friendly, and one day he says, "I'm selling out to General Electric," but he couldn't tell whether they'd be keeping me on. So he says to me, "Ted, tell you what we do. They're coming out from Wall Street"—these bankers, y'see—"and I'm going to let you pick them up at the depot." Figuring I'd be the first to meet them and might draw their attention and they'd rehire me, y'see. Well, I was just this hick-town kid, y'know, about to meet these great big juicy Wall Street bankers—I tell you, I hardly slept all night tryin' to figure how to make an impression. And just toward dawn . . . it was during breakfast—and I suddenly thought of that wall. See, the factory had this brick wall a block long; no windows, two stories high, just a tremendous wall of bricks. And it went through my mind that one of them might ask me how many bricks were in that wall. 'Cause I could answer any question about the company except that. So I got over to the plant as quick as I could, multiplied the vertical and horizontal bricks, and got the number. Well . . . these three bankers arrive, and I get them into the boss's limousine, and we ride. Nobody asks me anything! Three of them in those big fur-lined coats, and not one goddamn syllable. . . . Anyway we round the corner, and doesn't one of them turn to me and say, "Mr. Quinn, how many bricks you suppose is in that wall!" And by

God, I told him! Well, he wouldn't believe it, got out and counted himself—and it broke the ice, y'see, and one thing and another they made me manager of the plant. And that's how I got into GE.

GRAHAM, *astonished*: What are your plans? Will you join another company or . . .

QUINN: No. I've been tickling the idea I might set up an advisory service for small business. Say a fella has a concept, I could teach him how to develop and market it . . . 'cause I *know* all that, and maybe I could help—*to the audience*—to keep those individuals coming. Because with this terrible Depression you hear it everywhere now—an individual man is not worth a bag of peanuts. I don't know the answers, Mr. Graham, but I sure as hell know the question: How do you keep everything that's big from swallowing everything that's small? 'Cause when that happens—God Almighty—it's not going to be much fun!

GRAHAM: Well . . . thanks very much. Good day. Good day, Mr. Robertson. I must say . . . ! *With a broken laugh and a shake of the head, he hurries out.*

QUINN: He was not massively overwhelmed, was he?

ROBERTSON: He heard the gentle clip-clop of the horse and buggy coming down the road.

QUINN: All right, then, damn it, maybe what you ought to be looking into, Arthur, is horseshoes!

ROBERTSON: Well, you never did do things in a small way! This is unquestionably the world record for the shortest presidency in corporate history. *He exits.*

> *Alone, Quinn stares around in a moment of surprise and fright at what he's actually done. Soft-shoe music steals up, and he insinuates himself into it, dancing in a kind of uncertain mood that changes to release and joy, and at the climax he sings the last lines of "My Baby Just Cares for Me." As the lyrics end, the phone rings. He picks up the receiver, never losing the beat, and simply lets it drop, and dances off.*

> *Rose comes downstage, staring front, a book in her hand.*

ROSE: Who would believe it? You look out the window in the middle of a fine October day, and there's a dozen college graduates with advanced degrees playing ball in the street like children. And it gets harder and harder to remember when life seemed to have so much purpose, when you couldn't wait for the morning!

> *Lee enters, takes a college catalogue off the prop table, and approaches her, turning the pages.*

LEE: At Cornell there's no tuition fee at all if you enroll in bacteriology.

ROSE: Free *tuition*!

LEE: Maybe they're short of bacteriologists.

ROSE: Would you like that?

LEE, *stares, tries to see himself as a bacteriologist, sighs*: Bacteriology?

ROSE, *wrinkling her nose*: Must be awful. Is anything else free?

LEE: It's the only one I've seen.

ROSE: I've got to finish this before tomorrow. I'm overdue fourteen cents on it.

LEE: What is it?

ROSE: *Coronet* by Manuel Komroff. It's about this royal crown that gets stolen and lost and found again and lost again for generations. It's supposed to be literature, but I don't know, it's very enjoyable. *She goes back to her book.*

LEE, *closes the catalogue, looks at her*: Ma?

ROSE, *still reading*: Hm?

LEE, *gently breaking the ice*: I guess it's too late to apply for this year anyway. Don't you think so?

ROSE, *turns to him*: I imagine so, dear . . . for this year.

LEE: Okay, Ma . . .

ROSE: I feel so terrible—all those years we were throwing money around, and now when you need it—

LEE, *relieved, now that he knows*: That's okay. I think maybe I'll try looking for a job. But I'm not sure whether to look under "Help Wanted, Male" or "Boy Wanted."

ROSE: Boy! *Their gazes meet. She sees his apprehension.* Don't be frightened, darling—you're going to be wonderful! *She hides her feeling in the book.*

> *Fadeout. Light comes up on Fanny, standing on the first-level balcony. She calls to Sidney, who is playing the piano and singing "Once in a While."*

FANNY: Sidney?

> *He continues singing.*

Sidney?

> *He continues singing.*

Sidney?

> *He continues singing.*

I have to talk to you, Sidney.

He continues singing.

Stop that for a minute!

SIDNEY, *stops singing*: Ma, look . . . it's only July. If I was still in high school it would still be my summer vacation.

FANNY: And if I was the Queen of Rumania I would have free rent. You graduated, Sidney, this is not summer vacation.

SIDNEY: Mama, it's useless to go to employment agencies—there's grown men there, engineers, college graduates. They're willing to take anything. If I could write one hit song like this, just one—we wouldn't have to worry again. Let me have July, just July—see if I can do it. Because that man was serious—he's a good friend of the waiter who works where Bing Crosby's manager eats. He could give him any song I write, and if Crosby just sang it one time . . .

FANNY: I want to talk to you about Doris.

SIDNEY: What Doris?

FANNY: Doris! Doris from downstairs. I've been talking to her mother. She likes you, Sidney.

SIDNEY: Who?

FANNY: Her mother! Mrs. Gross. She's crazy about you.

SIDNEY, *not comprehending*: Oh.

FANNY: She says all Doris does is talk about you.

SIDNEY, *worried*: What is she talking about me for?

FANNY: No, nice things. She likes you.

SIDNEY, *amused, laughs incredulously*: Doris? She's thirteen.

FANNY: She'll be fourteen in December. Now listen to me.

SIDNEY: What, Ma?

FANNY: It's all up to you, Sidney, I want you to make up your own mind. But Papa's never going to get off his back again, and after Lucille's wedding we can forget about *her* salary. Mrs. Gross says—being she's a widow, y'know? And with her goiter and everything . . .

SIDNEY: What?

FANNY: If you like Doris—only if you like her—and you would agree to get married—when she's eighteen, about, or seventeen, even—if you would agree to it now, we could have this apartment rent-free. Starting next month.

SIDNEY, *impressed, even astounded*: Forever?

FANNY: Of course. You would be the husband, it would be your house. You'd move downstairs, with that grand piano and the tile shower . . . I even think if you'd agree she'd throw in the three months' back rent that we owe. I wouldn't even be surprised you could take over the bakery.

SIDNEY: The bakery! For God's sake, Mama, I'm a composer!

FANNY: Now listen to me . . .

Doris enters and sits on the floor weaving a cat's cradle of string.

SIDNEY: But how can I be a baker!

FANNY: Sidney, dear, did you ever once look at that girl?

SIDNEY: Why should I look at her!

FANNY, *taking him to the "window"*: Because she's a beauty. I wouldn't have mentioned it otherwise. Look. Look at that nose. Look at her hands. You see those beautiful little white hands? You don't find hands like that everywhere.

SIDNEY: But Ma, listen—if you just leave me alone for July, and if I write one hit song . . . I know I can do it, Mama.

FANNY: Okay. Sidney, we're behind a hundred and eighty dollars. August first we're out on the street. So write a hit, dear. I only hope that four, five years from now you don't accidentally run into Doris Gross somewhere and fall in love with her—after we all died from exposure!

SIDNEY: But Ma, even if I agreed—supposing next year or the year after I meet some other girl and I really like her . . .

FANNY: All right, and supposing you marry *that* girl and a year after you meet another girl you like better—what are you going to do, get married every year? . . . But I only wanted you to know the situation. I'll close the door, everything'll be quiet. Write a big hit, Sidney! *She exits.*

Sidney begins to sing "Once in a While"; Doris echoes him timorously. They trade a few lines, Sidney hesitant and surprised. Then:

DORIS, *fully confident, ending the song*: ". . . nearest your heart."

SIDNEY, *sits on his heels beside her as she weaves the string*: Gee, you're really terrific at that, Doris.

He stands, she stands, and they shyly walk off together as he slips his hand into hers.

ROBERTSON, *from choral area*: I guess the most shocking thing is what I see from the window of my Riverside Drive apartment. It's Calcutta on the Hudson, thousands of people living in cardboard boxes right next to that beautiful drive. It is like an army encampment down the length of Manhattan Island. At night you see their campfires flickering, and some nights I go down and walk among them. Remarkable, the humor they still have, but of course people still blame themselves rather than the government. But there's never been a society that hasn't had a clock running on it, and you can't help wondering—how long? How long will they stand for this? So now Roosevelt's got in I'm thinking—boy, he'd better move. He'd better move fast. . . . And you can't help it; first thing every night when I get home, I go to the window and look down at those fires, the flames reflecting off the river through the night.

> *Lights come up on Moe and Rose. Moe, in a business suit and hat, is just giving her a peck.*

ROSE: Goodbye, darling. This is going to be a good day—I know it!

MOE, *without much conviction*: I think you're right. G'bye. *He walks, gradually comes to a halt. Much uncertainty and tension as he glances back toward his house and then looks down to think.*

> *Lee enters, and Rose gives him a farewell kiss. He wears a mackinaw. She hands him a lunch bag.*

ROSE: Don't squeeze it, I put in some cookies. . . . And listen—it doesn't mean you can *never* go to college.

LEE: Oh, I don't mind, Ma. Anyway, I like it around machines. I'm lucky I got the job!

ROSE: All the years we had so much, and now when you need it—

LEE, *cutting her off*: See ya!

> *He leaves her; she exits. He walks and is startled by Moe standing there.*

I thought you left a long time ago!

MOE: I'll walk you a way.

> *He doesn't bother explaining, simply walks beside Lee, but at a much slower pace than Lee took before. Lee feels his unusual tension but can only glance over at him with growing apprehension and puzzlement. Finally Moe speaks.*

Good job?

LEE: It's okay. I couldn't believe they picked me!

MOE, *nodding*: Good.

> *They walk on in silence, weaving all over the stage, the tension growing as Lee keeps glancing at Moe, who continuously*

stares down and ahead as they proceed. At last Moe halts and takes a deep breath.

How much money've you got, Lee?

LEE, *completely taken aback*: . . . money have I got?

MOE, *indicating Lee's pockets*: I mean right now.

LEE: Oh! Well, about . . . *he takes out change.* . . . thirty-five cents. I'm okay.

MOE: . . . Could I have a quarter? . . . So I can get downtown.

LEE, *pauses an instant, astonished*: Oh, sure, Pa! *He quickly searches his pockets again.*

MOE: You got your lunch—I'll need a hotdog later.

LEE, *handing him a quarter*: It's okay. I have a dollar in my drawer. . . . Should I . . . *He starts to go back.*

MOE: No, don't go back. *He proceeds to walk again.* Don't, ah . . . mention it, heh?

LEE: Oh, no!

MOE: She worries.

LEE: I know. *To audience*: We went down to the subway together, and it was hard to look at one another. So we pretended that nothing had happened. *They come to a halt and sit, as though on a subway.* But something had. . . . It was like I'd started to support my *father*! And why that should have made me feel so happy, I don't know, but it did! And to cheer him up I began to talk, and before I knew it I was inventing a fantastic future! I said I'd be going to college in no more than a year, at most two; and that I'd straighten out my mind and become an A student; and then I'd not only get a job on a newspaper, but I'd have my own column, no less! By the time we got to Forty-second Street, the Depression was practically over! *He laughs.* And in a funny way it *was*—*He touches his breast*—in here . . . even though I knew we had a long bad time ahead of us. And so, like most people, I waited with that crazy kind of expectation that comes when there is no hope, waited for the dream to come back from wherever it had gone to hide.

A voice from the theatre sings the end of "In New York City, You Really Got to Know Your Line," or similar song.

END OF ACT ONE

ACT TWO

Rose, at the piano, has her hands suspended over the keyboard as the band pianist plays. She starts singing "He Loves and She Loves," then breaks off.

ROSE: But this piano is not leaving this house. Jewelry, yes, but nobody hocks this dear, darling piano. *She "plays" and sings more of the song.* The crazy ideas people get. Mr. Warsaw on our block, to make a little money he started a racetrack in his kitchen, with cockroaches. Keeps them in matchboxes with their names written on—Alvin, Murray, Irving . . . They bet nickels, dimes. *She picks up some sheet music.* Oh, what a show, that *Funny Face. She sings the opening of a song like "'S Wonderful."* The years go by and you don't get to see a show and Brooklyn drifts further and further into the Atlantic; Manhattan becomes a foreign country, and a year can go by without ever going there. *She sings more of "'S Wonderful."* Wherever you look there's a contest; Kellogg's, Post Toasties, win five thousand, win ten thousand. I guess I ought to try, but the winners are always in Indiana somehow. I only pray to God our health holds up, because one filling and you've got to lower the thermostat for a month. Sing! *She sings the opening of "Do-Do-Do What You Done-Done-Done Before."* I must go to the library—I must start taking out some good books again; I must stop getting so stupid. I don't see anything, I don't hear anything except money, money, money . . . *She "plays" Schumann. Fadeout.*

ROBERTSON, *from choral area:* Looking back, of course, you can see there were two sides to it—with the banks foreclosing right and left, I picked up some first-class properties for a song. I made more money in the thirties than ever before, or since. But I knew a generation was coming of age who would never feel this sense of opportunity.

LEE: After a lot of jobs and saving, I did get to the university, and it was a quiet island in the stream. Two pairs of socks and a shirt, plus a good shirt and a mackinaw, and maybe a part-time job in the library, and you could live like a king and never see cash. So there was a distinct reluctance to graduate into that world out there . . . where you knew nobody wanted you.

Joe, Ralph, and Rudy gather in graduation caps and gowns.

Joey! Is it possible?

JOE: What?

LEE: You're a dentist!

RALPH: Well, I hope things are better when you get out, Lee.

LEE: You decide what to do?

RALPH: There's supposed to be a small aircraft plant still working in Lou-isville . . .

LEE: Too bad you picked propellers for a specialty.

RALPH: Oh, they'll make airplanes again—soon as there's a war.

LEE: How could there be another war?

JOE: Long as there's capitalism, baby.

RALPH: There'll always be war, y'know, according to the Bible. But if not, I'll probably go into the ministry.

LEE: I never knew you were religious.

RALPH: I'm sort of religious. They pay pretty good, you know, and you get your house and a clothing allowance . . .

JOE, *comes to Lee, extending his hand in farewell*: Don't forget to read Karl Marx, Lee. And if you're ever in the neighborhood with a toothache, look me up. I'll keep an eye out for your byline.

LEE: Oh, I don't expect a newspaper job—papers are closing all over the place. Drop me a card if you open an office.

JOE: It'll probably be in my girl's father's basement. He promised to dig the floor out deeper so I can stand up . . .

LEE: What about equipment?

JOE: I figure two, three years I'll be able to open, if I can make a down payment on a used drill. Come by, I'll put back those teeth Ohio State knocked out.

LEE: I sure will! . . . So long, Rudy!

RUDY: Oh, you might still be seeing me around next semester.

JOE: You staying on campus?

RUDY: I might for the sake of my root canals. If I just take one university course I'm still entitled to the Health Service—could get my canals finished.

LEE: You mean there's a course in the Lit School you haven't taken?

RUDY: Yeah, I just found out about it. Roman Band Instruments.

JOE, *laughs*: You're kiddin'!

RUDY: No, in the Classics Department. Roman Band Instruments. *He pulls his cheek back.* See, I've still got three big ones to go on this side.

Laughter.

Well, if you really face it, where am I running? Chicago's loaded with anthropologists. Here, the university's like my mother—I've got free rent, wash dishes for my meals, get my teeth fixed, and God knows, I might pick up the paper one morning and there's an ad: "Help Wanted: Handsome young college graduate, good teeth, must be thoroughly acquainted with Roman band instruments"!

Laughter. They sing "Love and a Dime" accompanied by Rudy on banjo.

RALPH: I'll keep looking for your byline anyway, Lee.

LEE: No, I doubt it; but I might angle a job on a Mississippi paddleboat when I get out.

RUDY: They still run those?

LEE: Yeah, there's a few. I'd like to retrace Mark Twain's voyages.

RUDY: Well, if you run into Huckleberry Finn—

LEE: I'll give him your regards.

Laughing, Ralph and Rudy start out.

RALPH: Beat Ohio State, kid!

JOE, *alone with Lee, gives him a clenched-fist salute*: So long, Lee.

LEE, *returning the salute*: So long, Joe! *With fist still clenched, he mimes pulling a whistle, dreamily imagining the Mississippi.* Toot! Toot!

He moves to a point, taking off his shirt, with which he wipes sweat off his face and neck as in the distance we hear a paddleboat's engines and wheel in water and whistle. Lee stares out as though from a deck. He is seeing aloud.

How scary and beautiful the Mississippi is. How do they manage to live? Every town has a bank boarded up, and all those skinny men sitting on the sidewalks with their backs against the storefronts. It's all stopped; like a magic spell. And the anger, the anger . . . when they were handing out meat and beans to the hungry, and the maggots wriggling out of the beef, and that man pointing his rifle at the butcher demanding the fresh meat the government had paid him to hand out . . . How could this have happened, is Marx right? Paper says twelve executives in tobacco made more than thirty thousand farmers who raised it. How long can they accept this? The anger has a smell, it hangs in the air wherever people gather. . . . Fights suddenly break out and simmer down. Is this when revolution comes? And why not? How would Mark Twain write what I have seen? Armed deputies guarding cornfields and whole families sitting beside the road, staring at that food which nobody can buy and is rotting on the stalk. It's insane. *He exits.*

ROSE, *from choral area, to audience*: But how can he become a sportswriter if he's a Communist?

Joe, carrying a large basket of flowers, crosses downstage to the sound effect of a subway train passing. He sings a verse of "In New York City, You Really Got to Know Your Line." He then breaks upstage and enters Isabel's apartment. She is in bed.

ISABEL: Hello, honey.

JOE: Could you start calling me Joe? It's less anonymous. *He starts removing his shoes and top pair of trousers.*

ISABEL: Whatever you say. You couldn't come later—hey, could you? I was just ready to go to sleep, I had a long night.

JOE: I can't, I gotta catch the girls before they get to the office, they like a flower on the desk. And later I'm too tired.

ISABEL: Ain't that uncomfortable—hey? Two pairs of pants?

JOE: It's freezing cold on that subway platform. The wind's like the Gobi Desert. The only problem is when you go out to pee it takes twice as long.

ISABEL: Sellin' books too—hey?

JOE: No, I'm reading that. Trying not to forget the English language. All I hear all day is shit, fuck, and piss. I keep meaning to tell you, Isabel, it's so relaxing to talk to you, especially when you don't understand about seventy percent of what I'm saying.

ISABEL, *laughs, complimented*: Hey!

JOE, *takes her hand*: In here I feel my sanity coming back, to a certain extent. Down in the subway all day I really wonder maybe some kind of lunacy is taking over. People stand there waiting for the train, talking to themselves. And loud, with gestures. And the number of men who come up behind me and feel my ass. *With a sudden drop in all his confidence*: What scares me, see, is that I'm getting too nervous to pick up a drill—if I ever get to practice dentistry at all, I mean. The city . . . is crazy! A hunchback yesterday suddenly comes up to me . . . apropos of nothing . . . and he starts yelling, "You will not find one word about democracy in the Constitution, this is a Christian Republic!" Nobody laughed. The Nazi swastika is blossoming out all over the toothpaste ads. And it seems to be getting worse—there's a guy on Forty-eighth Street and Eighth Avenue selling two hotdogs for seven cents! What can he make?

ISABEL: Two for *seven?* Jesus.

JOE: I tell you I get the feeling every once in a while that some bright morning millions of people are going to come pouring out of the buildings and just . . . I don't know what . . . kill each other? Or only the Jews? Or just maybe sit down on the sidewalk and cry. *Now he turns to her and starts to climb up on the bed beside her.*

ISABEL, *looking at the book*: It's about families?

JOE: No, it's just called *The Origin of the Family, Private Property, and the State,* by Friedrich Engels. Marxism.

ISABEL: What's that?

JOE, *his head resting on hers, his hand holding her breast*: Well, it's the idea that all of our relationships are basically ruled by money.

ISABEL, *nodding, as she well knows*: Oh, right—hey, yeah.

JOE, *raising himself up*: No, it's not what you think . . .

ISABEL: It's a whole book about *that?*

JOE: It's about socialism, where the girls would all have jobs so they wouldn't have to do this, see.

ISABEL: Oh! But what would the guys do, though?

JOE, *flustered*: Well . . . like for instance if I had money to open an office I would probably get married very soon.

ISABEL: Yeah, but I get married guys. *Brightly*: And I even get two dentists that you brought me . . . Bernie and Allan? . . . and they've got offices, too.

JOE: You don't understand. . . . He shows that underneath our ideals it's all economics between people, and it shouldn't be.

ISABEL: What should it be?

JOE: Well, you know, like . . . love.

ISABEL: Ohhh! Well that's nice—hey. You think I could read it?

JOE: Sure, try. . . . I'd like your reaction. I like you early, Isabel, you look so fresh. Gives me an illusion.

ISABEL: I'm sorry if I'm tired.

JOE, *kisses her, trying to rouse himself*: Say . . . did Bernie finish the filling?

ISABEL: Yeah, he polished yesterday.

JOE: Open.

> *She opens her mouth.*

> Bernie's good. *Proudly*: I told you, we were in the same class. Say hello when you see him again.

ISABEL: He said he might come after five. He always says to give you his best.

JOE: Give him my best, too.

ISABEL, *readying herself on the bed*: Till you I never had so many dentists.

> *He lowers onto her. Fadeout.*

> *Lights come up on Banks, suspended in a painter's cradle, painting a bridge. He sings a verse of "Backbone and Navel Doin' the Belly Rub," then speaks.*

BANKS: Sometimes you'd get the rumor they be hirin' in New York City, so we all went to New York City, but they wasn't nothin' in New York City, so we'd head for Lima, Ohio; Detroit, Michigan; Duluth, Minnesota; or go down Baltimore; or Alabama or Decatur, Illinois. But anywhere you'd go was always a jail. I was in a chain gang in Georgia pickin' cotton for four months just for hoboin' on a train. That was 1935 in the summertime, and when they set me free they give me thirty-five cents. Yes, sir, thirty-five cents is what they give me, pickin' cotton four months against my will. *Pause*. Yeah, I still hear that train, that long low whistle, *whoo-ooo!*

> *Fadeout. Lights come up on Rose, seated at the piano, playing. Two moving men in work aprons enter, raise her hands from the piano, and push the piano off.*

ROSE, *half to herself, furious*: How stupid it all is. How stupid! *Prayerfully*: Oh, my dear Lee, wherever you are—believe in something. Anything. But believe. *She turns and moves off with the piano stool, as though emptied out.*

> *Lights come up on Lee, sitting at an open-air café table under a tree. Isaac, the black proprietor, brings him a watermelon slice.*

ISAAC: You been workin' the river long? I ain't seen you before, have I?

LEE: No, this is my first trip down the river, I'm from New York City— I'm just kind of looking around the country, talking to people.

ISAAC: What you lookin' around *for*?

LEE: Nothing—just trying to figure out what's happening. Ever hear of Mark Twain?

ISAAC: He from round here?

LEE: Well, long time ago, yeah. He was a story writer.

ISAAC: Unh-unh. I ain't seen him around here. You ask at the post office?

LEE: No, but I might. I'm kind of surprised you can get fifteen cents a slice down here these days.

ISAAC: Ohhh—white folks *loves* watermelon. Things as bad as this up North?

LEE: Probably not quite. I sure wouldn't want to be one of you people down here . . . specially with this Depression.

ISAAC: Mister, if I was to tell you the God's honest truth, the main thing about the Depression is that it finally hit the white people. 'Cause us folks never had nothin' else. *He looks offstage.* Well, now—here come the big man.

LEE: He trouble?

ISAAC: He's anything he wants to be, mister—he the sheriff.

> *The Sheriff enters, wearing holstered gun, boots, badge, broad-brimmed hat, and carrying something wrapped under his arm. He silently stares at Lee, then turns to Isaac.*

SHERIFF: Isaac?

ISAAC: Yes, sir.

SHERIFF, *after a moment*: Sit down.

ISAAC: Yes, sir.

> *He sits on a counter stool; he is intensely curious about the Sheriff's calling on him but not frightened. The Sheriff seems to be having trouble with Lee's strange presence.*

LEE, *makes a nervous half-apology*: I'm off the boat. *He indicates offstage.*

SHERIFF: You don't bother me, boy—relax.

> *He sits and sets his package down and turns with gravity to Isaac. Lee makes himself unobtrusive and observes in silence.*

ISAAC: Looks like rain.

SHERIFF, *preoccupied*: Mm . . . hard to know.

ISAAC: Yeah . . . always is in Louisiana. *Pause.* Anything I can do for you, Sheriff?

SHERIFF: Read the papers today?

ISAAC: I couldn't read my name if an air-o-plane wrote it in the sky, Sheriff, you know that.

SHERIFF: My second cousin Allan? The state senator?

ISAAC: Uh-huh?

SHERIFF: The governor just appointed him. He's gonna help run the state police.

ISAAC: Uh-huh?

SHERIFF: He's comin' down to dinner Friday night over to my house. Bringin' his wife and two daughters. I'm gonna try to talk to Allan about a job on the state police. They still paying the *state* police, see.

ISAAC: Uh-huh. Well, that be nice, won't it.

SHERIFF: Isaac, I like you to cook me up some of that magical fried chicken around six o'clock Friday night. Okay? I'll pick it up.

ISAAC, *noncommittal*: Mm.

SHERIFF: That'd be for . . . let's see . . . *counts on his fingers* . . . eight people. My brother and his wife comin' over too, 'cause I aim to give Allan a little spread there, get him talkin' real good, y'know.

ISAAC: Mm.

   An embarrassed pause.

SHERIFF: What's that gonna cost me for eight people, Isaac?

ISAAC, *at once*: Ten dollars.

SHERIFF: Ten.

ISAAC, *with a little commiseration*: That's right, Sheriff.

SHERIFF, *slight pause; starts to unwrap radio*: Want to show you something here, Isaac. My radio, see?

ISAAC: Uh-huh. *He runs his hand over it.* Play?

SHERIFF: Sure! Plays real good. I give twenty-nine ninety-five for that two years ago.

ISAAC, *looks in the back of it*: I plug it in?

SHERIFF: Go right ahead, sure. You sure painted this place up real nice. Like a real restaurant. You oughta thank the Lord, Isaac.

ISAAC, *takes out the wire and plugs it in*: I sure do. The Lord and fried chicken!

SHERIFF: You know, the county ain't paid nobody at all in three months now . . .

ISAAC: Yeah, I know. Where you switch it on?

SHERIFF: Just turn the knob. There you are. *He turns it on.* They're still payin' the *state* police, see. And I figure if I can get Allan to put me on—

Radio music. It is very faint.

ISAAC: Cain't hardly hear it.

SHERIFF, *angrily*: Hell, Isaac, gotta get the aerial out! *Untangling a wire at the back of the set*: You give me eight fried chicken dinners and I'll let you hold this for collateral, okay? Here we go now.

The Sheriff backs away, stretching out the aerial wire, and Roosevelt's voice suddenly comes on strong. The Sheriff holds still, the wire held high. Lee is absorbed.

ROOSEVELT: Clouds of suspicion, tides of ill-will and intolerance gather darkly in many places. In our own land we enjoy, indeed, a fullness of life . . .

SHERIFF: And nice fat chickens, hear? Don't give me any little old scruffy chickens.

ISAAC, *of Roosevelt*: Who's that talkin'?

ROOSEVELT: . . . greater than that of most nations. But the rush of modern civilization itself has raised for us new difficulties . . .

SHERIFF: Sound like somebody up North.

ISAAC: Hush! *To Lee:* Hey, that's Roosevelt, ain't it?

LEE: Yes.

ISAAC: Sure! That's the President!

SHERIFF: How about it, we got a deal? Or not?

Isaac has his head close to the radio, absorbed. Lee comes closer, bends over to listen.

ROOSEVELT: . . . new problems which must be solved if we are to preserve to the United States the political and economic freedom for which Washington and Jefferson planned and fought. We seek not merely to make government a mechanical implement, but to give it the vibrant personal character that is the embodiment of human charity. We are poor indeed if this nation cannot afford to lift from every recess of American life the dark fear of the unemployed that they are not needed in the world. We cannot afford to accumulate a deficit in the books of human fortitude.

Sidney and Doris enter as lights fade on Lee, Isaac, and the Sheriff.

SIDNEY: What's the matter? Boy, you can change quicker than . . .

DORIS, *shaking her head, closing her eyes*: I can't help it, it keeps coming back to me.

SIDNEY: How can you let a dope like Francey bother you like this?

DORIS: Because she's spreading it all over the class! And I still don't understand how you could have said a thing like that.

SIDNEY: Hon . . . all I said was that if we ever got married I would probably live downstairs. Does that mean that that's the reason we'd get married? Francey is just jealous!

DORIS, *deeply hurt*: I just wish you hadn't said that.

SIDNEY: You mean you think I'd do a thing like that for an *apartment*? What must you think of me! . . .

DORIS, *sobs*: It's just that I love you so much! . . .

SIDNEY: If I could only sell a song! Or even pass the post office exam. Then I'd have my own money, and all this garbage would stop.

DORIS: . . . I said I love you, why don't *you* say something?

SIDNEY: I love you, I love you, but I tell ya, you know what I think?

DORIS: What?

SIDNEY: Honestly—I think we ought to talk about seeing other people for a while.

DORIS, *uncomprehending*: What other people?

SIDNEY: Going out. You're still a little young, honey . . . and even at my age, it's probably not a good idea for us if we never even went out with somebody else—

DORIS: Well, who . . . do you want to take out?

SIDNEY: Nobody! . . .

DORIS: Then what do you mean?

SIDNEY: Well, it's not that I *want* to.

DORIS: Yeah, but who?

SIDNEY: Well, I don't know . . . like maybe . . . what's-her-name, Margie Ganz's sister . . .

DORIS, *alarmed*: You mean Esther Ganz with the . . . ? *She cups her hands to indicate big breasts.*

SIDNEY: Then *not* her!

DORIS, *hurt*: You want to take out *Esther Ganz*?

SIDNEY: I'm not saying *necessarily*! But . . . for instance, you could go out with Georgie.

DORIS: Which Georgie?

SIDNEY: Georgie Krieger.

DORIS: You're putting me with *Georgie Krieger* and *you* go out with *Esther Ganz*?

SIDNEY: It was only an *example*!

DORIS, *with incredulous distaste*: But Georgie *Krieger*! . . .

SIDNEY: Forget Georgie Krieger! Make it . . . all right, *you* pick somebody, then.

DORIS, *stares, reviewing faces*: Well . . . how about Morris?

SIDNEY, *asking the heart-stopping question*: What Morris? You mean Morris from . . .

DORIS: Yeah, Morris from the shoe store.

SIDNEY, *glimpsing quite a different side of her*: Really?

DORIS: Well, didn't he go a year to City College?

SIDNEY: No, he did not, he went one semester—and he *still* walks around with a comb in his pocket. . . . I think maybe we just better wait.

DORIS: I don't know, maybe it would be a good idea . . . at least till I'm a little older . . .

SIDNEY: No, we'll wait, we'll think it over.

DORIS: But you know . . .

SIDNEY, *with high anxiety*: We'll think it over, hon! . . .

> *He goes to the piano, plays a progression. She comes to him, then runs her fingers through his hair.*

DORIS: Play "Sittin' Around"?

SIDNEY: It's not any good.

DORIS: What do you mean, it's your greatest! Please!

SIDNEY, *sighs, sings*:

> You've got me
> Sittin' around
> Just watching shadows
> On the wall;

You've got me
Sittin' around,
And all my hopes beyond recall;

I want to hear
The words of love,
I want to feel
Your lips on mine,

DORIS:

And know
The days and nights
There in your arms.

SIDNEY AND DORIS:

Instead I'm . . .

Sittin' around
And all the world
Is passing by,
You've got me
Sittin' around
Like I was only
Born to cry,

When will I know
The words of love,
Your lips on mine—
Instead of

Sittin' around,
Sittin' around,
Sittin' around . . .

Fadeout. A large crowd emerges from darkness as a row of factory-type lights descend, illuminating rows of benches and scattered chairs. This is an emergency welfare office temporarily set up to handle the flood of desperate people. A Welfare Worker hands each applicant a sheet of paper and then wanders off.

MOE: I don't understand this. I distinctly read in the paper that anybody wants to work can go direct to WPA and they fix you up with a job.

LEE: They changed it. You can only get a WPA job now if you get on relief first.

MOE, *pointing toward the line*: So this is not the WPA.

LEE: I told you, Pa, this is the relief office.

MOE: Like . . . welfare.

LEE: Look, if it embarrasses you—

MOE: Listen, if it has to be done it has to be done. Now let me go over it again—what do I say?

LEE: You refuse to let me live in the house. We don't get along.

MOE: Why can't you live at home?

LEE: If I can live at home, I don't need relief. That's the rule.

MOE: Okay. So I can't stand the sight of you.

LEE: Right.

MOE: So you live with your friend in a rooming house.

LEE: Correct.

MOE: . . . They're gonna believe that?

LEE: Why not? I left a few clothes over there.

MOE: All this for twenty-two dollars a week?

LEE, *angering*: What am I going to do? Even old-time newspapermen are out of work. . . . See, if I can get on the WPA Writers Project, at least I'd get experience if a real job comes along. I've explained this a dozen times, Pa, there's nothing complicated.

MOE, *unsatisfied*: I'm just trying to get used to it. All right.

> *They embrace.*

We shouldn't look too friendly, huh?

LEE, *laughs*: That's the idea!

MOE: I don't like you, and you can't stand the sight of me.

LEE: That's it! *He laughs.*

MOE, *to the air, with mock outrage*: So he laughs.

> *They move into the crowd and find seats in front of Ryan, the supervisor, at a desk.*

RYAN: Matthew R. Bush!

A very dignified man of forty-five rises, crosses, and follows Ryan out.

MOE: Looks like a butler.

LEE: Probably was.

MOE, *shakes his head mournfully*: Hmm!

ROBERTSON, *from choral area*: I did a lot of walking back in those days, and the contrasts were startling. Along the West Side of Manhattan you had eight or ten of the world's greatest ocean liners tied up—I recall the SS *Manhattan*, the *Berengaria*, the *United States*—most of them would never sail again. But at the same time they were putting up the Empire State Building, highest in the world. But with whole streets and avenues of empty stores who would ever rent space in it?

A baby held by Grace, a young woman in the back, cries. Moe turns to look, then stares ahead.

MOE: Lee, what'll you do if they give you a pick-and-shovel job?

LEE: I'll take it.

MOE: You'll dig holes in the streets?

LEE: It's no disgrace, Dad.

ROBERTSON: It was incredible to me how long it was lasting. I would never, never have believed we could not recover before this. The years were passing, a whole generation was withering in the best years of its life . . .

The people in the crowd start talking: Kapush, Slavonic, in his late sixties, with a moustache; Dugan, an Irishman; Irene, a middle-aged black woman; Toland, a cabbie.

KAPUSH, *with ferocious frustration*: What can you expect from a country that puts a frankfurter on the Supreme Court? Felix the Frankfurter. Look it up.

DUGAN, *from another part of the room*: Get back in the clock, ya cuckoo!

KAPUSH, *turning his body around angrily to face Dugan and jarring Irene, sitting next to him*: Who's talkin' to me!

IRENE: Hey, now, don't mess with me, mister!

DUGAN: Tell him, tell him!

Ryan rushes in. He is pale, his vest is loaded with pens and pencils, and a sheaf of papers is in his hand. A tired man.

RYAN: We gonna have another riot, folks? Is that what we're gonna have? Mr. Kapush, I told you three days running now, if you live in Bronx, you've got to apply in Bronx.

KAPUSH: It's all right, I'll wait.

RYAN, *as he passes Dugan*: Leave him alone, will you? He's a little upset in his mind.

DUGAN: He's a fascist. I seen him down Union Square plenty of times.

Irene slams her walking stick down on the table.

RYAN: Oh, Jesus . . . here we go again.

IRENE: Gettin' on to ten o'clock, Mr. Ryan.

RYAN: I've done the best I can, Irene . . .

IRENE: That's what the good Lord said when he made the jackass, but he decided to knuckle down and try harder. People been thrown out on the sidewalk, mattresses, pots and pans, and everything else they own. Right on A Hundred and Thirty-eighth Street. They goin' back in their apartments today or we goin' raise us some real hell.

RYAN: I've got no more appropriations for you till the first of the month, and that's it, Irene.

IRENE: Mr. Ryan, you ain't talkin' to me, you talkin' to Local Forty-five of the Workers Alliance, and you know what that mean.

DUGAN, *laughs*: Communist Party.

IRENE: That's right, mister, and they don't mess. So why don't you get on your phone and call Washington. And while you're at it, you can remind Mr. Roosevelt that I done swang One Hundred and Thirty-ninth Street for him in the last election, and if he want it swung again he better get crackin'!

RYAN: Holy Jesus.

He hurries away, but Lee tries to delay him.

LEE: I was told to bring my father.

RYAN: What?

LEE: Yesterday. You told me to—

RYAN: Get off my back, will ya? *He hurries out.*

DUGAN: This country's gonna end up on the top of the trees throwin' coconuts at each other.

MOE, *quietly to Lee*: I hope I can get out by eleven, I got an appointment with a buyer.

TOLAND, *next to Moe with a* Daily News *open in his hands*: Boy, oh, boy, looka this—Helen Hayes gonna put on forty pounds to play Victoria Regina.

MOE: Who's that?

TOLAND: Queen of England.

MOE: She was so fat?

TOLAND: Victoria? Horse. I picked up Helen Hayes when I had my cab. Very small girl. And Adolphe Menjou once—he was small too. I even had Al Smith once, way back before he was governor. He was real small.

MOE: Maybe your cab was extra large.

TOLAND: What do you mean? I had a regular Ford.

MOE: You lost it?

TOLAND: What're you gonna do? The town is walkin'. I paid five hundred dollars for a new Ford, including bumpers and a spare. But thank God, at least I got into the housing project. It's nice and reasonable.

MOE: What do you pay?

TOLAND: Nineteen fifty a month. It sounds like a lot, but we got three nice rooms—providin' I get a little help here. What's your line?

MOE: I sell on commission right now. I used to have my own business.

TOLAND: Used-ta. Whoever you talk to, "I used-ta." If they don't do something, I tell ya, one of these days this used-ta be a country.

KAPUSH *exploding*: Ignorance, ignorance! People don't know facts. Greatest public library system in the entire world and nobody goes in but Jews.

MOE, *glancing at him*: Ah-ha.

LEE: What're you, Iroquois?

DUGAN: He's a fascist. I seen him talking on Union Square.

IRENE: Solidarity, folks, black and white together, that's what we gotta have. Join the Workers Alliance, ten cents a month, and you git yourself some solidarity.

KAPUSH: I challenge anybody to find the word democracy in the Constitution. This is a republic! *Demos* is the Greek word for mob.

DUGAN, *imitating the bird*: Cuckoo!

KAPUSH: Come to get my money and the bank is closed up! Four thousand dollars up the flue. Thirteen years in hardware, savin' by the week.

DUGAN: Mental diarrhea.

KAPUSH: Mobocracy. Gimme, gimme, gimme, all they know.

DUGAN: So what're *you* doing here?

KAPUSH: Roosevelt was sworn in on a Dutch Bible! *Silence.* Anybody know that? *To Irene*: Betcha didn't know that, did you?

IRENE: You givin' me a headache, mister . . .

KAPUSH: I got nothin' against colored. Colored never took my store away. Here's my bankbook, see that? Bank of the United States. See that? Four thousand six hundred and ten dollars and thirty-one cents, right? Who's got that money? Savin' thirteen years, by the week. *Who's got my money?*

> He has risen to his feet. His fury has turned the moment silent. Matthew Bush enters and sways. Ryan enters.

RYAN, *calls*: Arthur Clayton!

CLAYTON, *starts toward Ryan from the crowd and indicates Bush*: I think there's something the matter with—

> Bush collapses on the floor. For a moment no one moves. Then Irene goes to him, bends over him.

IRENE: Hey. Hey, mister.

> Lee helps him up and sits him in the chair.

RYAN, *calling*: Myrna, call the ambulance!

> Irene lightly slaps Bush's cheeks.

LEE: You all right?

RYAN, *looking around*: Clayton?

CLAYTON: I'm Clayton.

RYAN, *Clayton's form in his hand*: You're not eligible for relief; you've got furniture and valuables, don't you?

CLAYTON: But nothing I could realize anything on.

RYAN: Why not?

IRENE: This man's starvin', Mr. Ryan.

RYAN: What're you, a medical doctor now, Irene? I called the ambulance! Now don't start makin' an issue, will you? *To Clayton*: Is this your address? Gramercy Park South?

CLAYTON, *embarrassed*: That doesn't mean a thing. I haven't really eaten in a few days, actually . . .

RYAN: Where do you get that kind of rent?

CLAYTON: I haven't paid my rent in over eight months . . .

RYAN, *starting away*: Forget it, mister, you got valuables and furniture; you can't—

CLAYTON: I'm very good at figures, I was in brokerage. I thought if I could get anything that required . . . say statistics . . .

IRENE: Grace? You got anything in that bottle?

> *Grace, in a rear row with a baby in her arms, reaches forward with a baby bottle that has an inch of milk at the bottom. She hands the bottle to Irene.*

GRACE: Ain't much left there . . .

IRENE, *takes nipple off bottle*: Okay, now, open your mouth, mister.

> *Bush gulps the milk.*

There, look at that, see? Man's starvin'!

MOE, *stands, reaching into his pocket*: Here . . . look . . . for God's sake. *He takes out change and picks out a dime.* Why don't you send down, get him a bottle of milk?

IRENE, *calls toward a young woman in the back*: Lucy?

LUCY, *coming forward*: Here I am, Irene.

IRENE: Go down the corner, bring back a bottle of milk.

> *Moe gives her the dime, and Lucy hurries out.*

And a couple of straws, honey! You in bad shape, mister—why'd you wait so long to get on relief?

BUSH: Well . . . I just don't like the idea, you know.

IRENE: Yeah, I know—you a real bourgeoisie. Let me tell you something—

BUSH: I'm a chemist.

IRENE: I believe it, too—you so educated you sooner die than say brother. Now lemme tell you people. *Addressing the crowd*: Time has come to say brother. My husband pass away and leave me with three small children. No money, no work—I's about ready to stick my head in the cookin' stove. Then the city marshal come and take my chest of drawers, bed, and table, and leave me sittin' on a old orange crate in the middle of the room. And it come over me, mister, come over me to get mean. And I got real mean. Go down in the street and start yellin' and howlin' like a real mean woman. And the people crowd around the marshal truck, and 'fore you know it that marshal turn himself around and go on back downtown empty-handed. And that's when I see it. I see the solidarity, and I start to preach it up and down. 'Cause I got me a stick, and when I start poundin' time with this stick, a whole lot of people starts to march, keepin' time. We shall not be moved, yeah, we shall in no wise be disturbed. Some days I goes to court with my briefcase, raise hell with the judges. Ever time I goes into court the cops commence to holler, "Here comes that old lawyer woman!" But all I got in here is some old newspaper and a bag of cayenne pepper. Case any cop start musclin' me around—that hot pepper, that's hot cayenne pepper. And if the judge happen to be Catholic I got my rosary layin' in there, and I kind of let that crucifix hang out so's they think I'm Catholic too. *She draws a rosary out of her bag and lets it hang over the side.*

LUCY, *enters with milk*: Irene!

IRENE: Give it here, Lucy. Now drink it slow, mister. Slow, slow . . .

> *Bush is drinking in sips. People now go back into themselves, read papers, stare ahead.*

RYAN: Lee Baum!

LEE, *hurries to Moe*: Here! Okay, Dad, let's go.

> *Lee and Moe go to Ryan's desk.*

RYAN: This your father?

MOE: Yes.

RYAN, *to Moe*: Where's he living now?

LEE: I don't live at home because—

RYAN: Let *him* answer. Where's he living, Mr. Baum?

MOE: Well, he . . . he rents a room someplace.

RYAN: You gonna sit there and tell me you won't let him in the house?

MOE, *with great difficulty*: I won't let him in, no.

RYAN: You mean you're the kind of man, if he rang the bell and you opened the door and saw him, you wouldn't let him inside?

MOE: Well, naturally, if he just wants to come in the house—

LEE: I don't want to live there—

RYAN: I don't care what *you* want, fella. *To Moe*: You will let him into the house, right?

MOE, *stiffening*: . . . I can't stand the sight of him.

RYAN: Why? I saw you both sitting here talking together the last two hours.

MOE: We weren't talking. . . . We were arguing, fighting! . . .

RYAN: Fighting about what?

MOE, *despite himself; growing indignant*: Who can remember? We were fighting, we're always fighting! . . .

RYAN: Look, Mr. Baum . . . you're employed, aren't you?

MOE: I'm employed? Sure I'm employed. Here. *He holds up the folded* Times. See? Read it yourself. R. H. Macy, right? Ladies' full-length slip, genuine Japanese silk, hand-embroidered with lace top and trimmings, two ninety-eight. My boss makes four cents on these, I make a tenth of a cent. That's how I'm employed!

RYAN: You'll let him in the house. *He starts to move.*

MOE: I will not let him in the house! He . . . he don't believe in anything!

Lee and Ryan look at Moe in surprise. Moe himself is caught off balance by his genuine outburst and rushes out. Ryan glances at Lee, stamps a requisition form, and hands it to him, convinced. Ryan exits.

Lee moves slowly, staring at the form. The welfare clients exit, the row of overhead lights flies out.

Lights come up on Robertson.

ROBERTSON: Then and now, you have to wonder what really held it all together, and maybe it was simply the Future: the people were still not ready to give it up. Like a God, it was always worshiped among us, and they could not yet turn their backs on it. Maybe it's that simple. Because from any objective viewpoint, I don't understand why it held.

The people from the relief office form a line as on a subway platform. Joe comes behind the line singing and offering flowers from a basket. There is the sound of an approaching train, its windows flashing light. Joe throws himself under it: a squeal of brakes. The crowd sings "In New York City, You Really Got to Know Your Line," one by one taking the lyrics, ending in a chorus. Fadeout.

Lights come up on Edie. Lee is in spotlight.

LEE, *to audience*: Any girl with an apartment of her own was beautiful. She was one of the dialogue writers for the *Superman* comic strip. *To her*: Edie, can I sleep here tonight?

EDIE: Oh, hi, Lee—yeah, sure. Let me finish and I'll put a sheet on the couch. If you have any laundry, throw it in the sink. I'm going to wash later.

He stands behind her as she works.

This is going to be a terrific sequence.

LEE: It's amazing to me how you can keep your mind on it.

EDIE: He's also a great teacher of class consciousness.

LEE: Superman?

EDIE: He stands for justice!

LEE: Oh! You mean under capitalism you can't . . .

EDIE: Sure! The implications are terrific. *She works lovingly for a moment.*

LEE: Y'know, you're beautiful when you talk about politics, your face lights up.

EDIE, *smiling*: Don't be such a bourgeois horse's ass. I'll get your sheet. *She starts up.*

LEE: Could I sleep in your bed tonight? I don't know what it is lately—I'm always lonely. Are you?

EDIE: Sometimes. But a person doesn't have to go to bed with people to be connected to mankind.

LEE: You're right. I'm ashamed of myself.

EDIE: Why don't you join the Party?

LEE: I guess I don't want to ruin my chances; I want to be a sportswriter.

EDIE: You could write for the *Worker* sports page.

LEE: The *Daily Worker* sports page?

EDIE: Then help improve it! Why are you so defeatist, hundreds of people are joining the Party every week.

LEE: I don't know why, maybe I'm too skeptical—or cynical. Like . . . when I was in Flint, Michigan, during the sit-down strike. Thought I'd write a feature story . . . all those thousands of men barricaded in the GM plant, the wives hoisting food up to the windows in baskets. It was like the French Revolution. But then I got to talk to them as individuals, and the prejudice! The ignorance! . . . In the Ford plant there was damn near a race war because some of the Negro workers didn't want to join the strike. . . . It was murderous.

EDIE: Well, they're still backward, I know that.

LEE: No, they're normal. I really wonder if there's going to be time to save this country from itself. You ever wonder that? You do, don't you.

EDIE, *fighting the temptation to give way*: You really want my answer?

LEE: Yes.

EDIE: We're picketing the Italian consulate tomorrow, to protest Mussolini sending Italian troops to the Spanish Civil War. Come! *Do* something! You love Hemingway so much, read what he just said—"One man alone is no fucking good." As decadent as he is, even *he's* learning.

LEE: Really, your face gets so beautiful when you . . .

EDIE: Anyone can be beautiful if what they believe is beautiful! I believe in my comrades. I believe in the Soviet Union. I believe in the working class and the peace of the whole world when socialism comes . . .

LEE: Boy, you really are wonderful. Look, now that I'm on relief can I take you out to dinner? I'll pay, I mean.

EDIE, *smiles*: Why must you pay for me, just because I'm a woman?

LEE: Right! I forgot about that.

EDIE, *working*: I've got to finish this panel. . . . I'll make up the couch in a minute. . . . What about the Writer's Project, you getting on?

LEE: I think so; they're putting people on to write a WPA Guide, it's going to be a detailed history of every section of the country. I might get sent up to the Lake Champlain district. Imagine? They're interviewing direct descendants of the soldiers who fought the Battle of Fort Ticonderoga. Ethan Allen and the Green Mountain Boys?

EDIE: Oh, yes! They beat the British up there.

LEE: It's a wonderful project; 'cause people really don't know their own history.

EDIE, *with longing and certainty*: When there's socialism everyone will.

LEE, *leaning over to look at her work*: Why don't you have Superman get laid? Or married even.

EDIE: He's much too busy.

> *He comes closer to kiss her, she starts to respond, then rejects.*

> What are you *doing*?

LEE: When you say the word "socialism" your face gets so beautiful . . .

EDIE: You're totally cynical, aren't you.

LEE: Why!

EDIE: You pretend to have a serious conversation when all you want is to jump into my bed; it's the same attitude you have to the auto workers . . .

LEE: I can't see the connection between the auto workers and . . . !

EDIE, *once again on firm ground*: Everything is connected! I have to ask you to leave!

LEE: Edie!

EDIE: You are not a good person! *She bursts into tears and rushes off.*

LEE, *alone, full of remorse*: She's right, too! *He exits.*

Grandpa enters from choral area, sits with his newspaper, and is immediately immersed. Then Rose's niece Lucille, her sister Fanny, and Doris, who wears a bathrobe, carry folding chairs and seat themselves around a table. Lucille deals cards. Now Rose begins speaking within the choral area, and as she speaks, she moves onto the stage proper.

ROSE: That endless Brooklyn July! That little wooden house baking in the heat. *She enters the stage.* I never smelled an owl, but in July the smell of that attic crept down the stairs, and to me it smelled as dry and dusty as an owl. *She surveys the women staring at their cards.* From Coney Island to Brooklyn Bridge, how many thousands of women waited out the afternoons dreaming at their cards and praying for luck? Ah, luck, luck . . .

DORIS: Sidney's finishing a beautiful new song, Aunt Rose.

ROSE, *sitting at the table, taking up her hand of cards*: Maybe this one'll be lucky for you. Why are you always in a bathrobe?

DORIS: I'm only half a block away.

ROSE: But you're so young! Why don't you get dressed and leave the block once in a while?

FANNY, *smugly*: All my girls love it home, too.

ROSE: It's you, isn't it?

FANNY, *brushing dandruff off her bosom and nervously examining her cards*: I'm trying to make up my mind.

ROSE: Concentrate. Forget your dandruff for a minute.

FANNY: It wasn't dandruff, it was a thread.

ROSE: Her dandruff is threads. It's an obsession.

LUCILLE: I didn't tell you; this spring she actually called me and my sisters to come and spend the day cleaning her house.

FANNY: What's so terrible! We used to have the most marvelous times the four of us cleaning the house . . . *Suddenly*: It's turning into an oven in here.

LUCILLE: I'm going to faint.

ROSE: Don't faint, all the windows are open in the back of the house. We're supposed to be away.

FANNY: But there's no draft. . . . For Papa's sake . . .

LUCILLE: Why couldn't you be away and you left a window open? . . . Just don't answer the door.

ROSE: I don't want to take the chance. This one is a professional collector, I've seen him do it; if a window's open he tries to listen. They're merciless. . . . I sent Stanislaus for lemons, we'll have cold lemonade. Play.

FANNY: I can't believe they'd actually evict you, Rose.

ROSE: You can't? Wake up, Fanny. It's a bank—may they choke after the fortune of money we kept in there all those years! Ask them for two hundred dollars now and they . . . *Tears start to her eyes.*

FANNY: Rose, dear, come on—something'll happen, you'll see. Moe's got to find something soon, a man so well known.

LUCILLE: Couldn't he ask his mother for a little?

ROSE: His mother says there's a Depression going on. Meantime you can go blind from the diamonds on her fingers. Which he gave her! The rottenness of people! I tell you, the next time I start believing in anybody or anything I hope my tongue is cut out!

DORIS: Maybe Lee should come back and help out?

ROSE: Never! Lee is going to think his own thoughts and face the facts. He's got nothing to learn from us. Let him help himself.

LUCILLE: But to take up Communism—

ROSE: Lucille, what do you know about it? What does anybody know about it? The newspapers? The newspapers said the stock market will never come down again.

LUCILLE: But they're against God, Aunt Rose.

ROSE: I'm overjoyed you got so religious, Lucille, but please for God's sake don't tell me about it again!

FANNY, *rises, starts to leave*: I'll be right down.

ROSE: Now she's going to pee on her finger for luck.

FANNY: All right! So I won't go! *She returns to her chair.* And I wasn't going to pee on my finger!

ROSE: So what're we playing—cards or statues?

> Doris sits looking at her cards, full of confusion.

GRANDPA, *putting down his paper*: Why do they need this election?

ROSE: What do you mean, why they need this election?

GRANDPA: But everybody knows Roosevelt is going to win again. I still think he's too radical, but to go through another election is a terrible waste of money.

ROSE: What are you talking about, Papa—it's four years, they have to have an election.

GRANDPA: Why! If they decided to make him king . . .

ROSE: King!

FANNY, *pointing at Grandpa, agreeing and laughing*: Believe me!

GRANDPA: If he was king he wouldn't have to waste all his time making these ridiculous election speeches, and maybe he could start to improve things!

ROSE: If I had a stamp I'd write him a letter.

GRANDPA: He could be another Kaiser Franz Joseph. Then after he dies you can have all the elections you want.

ROSE, *to Doris*: Are you playing cards or hatching an egg?

DORIS, *startled*: Oh, it's my turn? *She turns a card.* All right; here!

ROSE: Hallelujah.

She plays a card. It is Lucille's turn; she plays.

Did you lose weight?

LUCILLE: I've been trying. I'm thinking of going back to the carnival.

Doris quickly throws an anxious look toward Grandpa, who is oblivious, reading.

FANNY, *indicating Grandpa secretively*: You better not mention . . .

LUCILLE: He doesn't have to know, and anyway I would never dance anymore; I'd only assist the magician and tell a few jokes. They're talking about starting up again in Jersey.

ROSE: Herby can't find anything.

LUCILLE: He's going out of his mind, Aunt Rose.

ROSE: God Almighty. So what's it going to be, Fanny?

FANNY, *feeling rushed, studying her cards*: One second! Just let me figure it out.

ROSE: When they passed around the brains this family was out to lunch.

FANNY: It's so hot in here I can't think!

ROSE: Play! I can't open the window. I'm not going to face that man again. He has merciless eyes.

Stanislaus, a middle-aged seaman in T-shirt and dungarees, enters through the front door.

You come in the front door? The mortgage man could come today!

STANISLAUS: I forgot! I didn't see anybody on the street, though. *He lifts bag of lemons.* Fresh lemonade coming up on deck. I starched all the napkins. *He exits.*

ROSE: Starched all the napkins . . . they're cracking like matzos. I feel like doing a fortune. *She takes out another deck of cards, lays out a fortune.*

LUCILLE: I don't know, Aunt Rose, is it so smart to let this man live with you?

DORIS: I would never dare! How can you sleep at night with a strange man in the cellar?

FANNY: Nooo! Stanislaus is a gentleman. *To Rose:* I think he's a little bit a fairy, isn't he?

ROSE: I hope!

They all laugh.

For God's sake, Fanny, play the queen of clubs!

FANNY: How did you know I had the queen of clubs!

ROSE: Because I'm smart, I voted for Herbert Hoover. I see what's been played, dear, so I figure what's left.

FANNY, *to Grandpa, who continues reading*: She's a marvel, she's got Grandma's head.

ROSE: Huh! Look at this fortune.

FANNY: Here, I'm playing. *She plays a card.*

ROSE, *continuing to lay out the fortune*: I always feed the vagrants on the porch, but Stanislaus, when I hand him a plate of soup he says he wants to wash the windows before he eats. *Before!* That I never heard. I nearly fell over. Go ahead, Doris, it's you.

DORIS, *desperately trying to be quick*: I know just what to do, wait a minute.

The women freeze, study their cards; Rose now faces front. She is quickly isolated in light.

ROSE: When I went to school we had to sit like soldiers, with backs straight and our hands clasped on the desk; things were supposed to be upright. When the navy came up the Hudson River, you cried it was so beautiful. You even cried when they shot the Czar of Russia. He was also beautiful. President Warren Gamaliel Harding, another beauty. Mayor James J. Walker smiled like an angel, what a nose, and those tiny feet. Richard Whitney, president of the Stock Exchange, a handsome, upright man. I could name a hundred from the rotogravure! Who could know that these upright handsome men would either turn out to be crooks who would land in jail or ignoramuses? What is left to believe? The bathroom. I lock myself in and hold on to the faucets so I shouldn't scream. At my husband, my mother-in-law, at God knows what until they take me away . . . *Returning to the fortune, and with deep anxiety*: What the hell did I lay out here? What is this?

Light returns to normal.

DORIS: "Gray's Elegy in a Country Churchyard."

ROSE: What?

FANNY, *touching her arm worriedly*: Why don't you lie down, Rose? . . .

ROSE: Lie down? . . . Why? *To Doris*: What Gray's "Elegy"? What are you . . .

Stanislaus enters rapidly, wearing a waist-length white starched waiter's jacket, a tray expertly on his shoulder, with glasses and rolled napkins. Rose shows alarm as she lays a card down on the fortune.

STANISLAUS: It's a braw bricht moonlicht nicht tonicht—that's Scotch.

FANNY: How does he get those napkins to stand up!

ROSE, *under terrific tension, tears her gaze from the cards she laid out*: What's the jacket suddenly?

The women watch her tensely.

STANISLAUS, *saluting*: SS *Manhattan*. Captain's steward at your service.

ROSE: Will you stop this nightmare? Take the jacket off. What're you talking about, captain's steward? Who are you?

STANISLAUS: I was captain's personal steward, but they're not sailing the *Manhattan* anymore. Served J. Pierpont Morgan, John D. Rockefeller, Enrico Caruso, lousy tipper, Lionel—

ROSE, *very suspiciously*: Bring in the cookies, please.

He picks up the pitcher to pour the lemonade.

Thank you, I'll pour it. Go, please.

She doesn't look at him; he goes out. In the silence she picks up the pitcher, tilts it, but her hand is shaking, and Fanny takes the pitcher.

FANNY: Rose, dear, come upstairs . . .

ROSE: How does he look to you?

FANNY: Why? He looks very nice.

LUCILLE: He certainly keeps the house beautiful, Aunt Rose, it's like a ship.

ROSE: He's a liar, though; anything comes into his head, he says; what am I believing him for? What the hell got into me? You can tell he's full of shit, and he comes to the door, a perfect stranger, and I let him sleep in the cellar!

LUCILLE: *Shhh!*

> *Stanislaus enters with a plate of cookies, in T-shirt again, determinedly.*

ROSE: Listen, Stanislaus . . . *She stands.*

STANISLAUS, *senses his imminent dismissal*: I go down to the ship chandler store tomorrow, get some special white paint, paint the whole outside the house. I got plenty of credit, don't cost you.

ROSE: I thought it over, you understand?

STANISLAUS, *with a desperate smile*: I borrow big ladder from the hardware store. And I gonna make nice curtains for the cellar windows. Taste the lemonade, I learn that in Spanish submarine. Excuse me, gotta clean out the icebox. *He gets himself out.*

FANNY: I think he's very sweet, Rose. . . . Here . . . *She offers a glass of lemonade.*

LUCILLE: Don't worry about that mortgage man, Aunt Rose, it's after five, they don't come after five . . .

ROSE, *caught in her uncertainty*: He seems sweet to you?

GRANDPA, *putting the paper down*: What Lee ought to do . . . Rosie?

ROSE: Hah?

GRANDPA: Lee should go to Russia.

> *The sisters and Lucille turn to him in surprise.*

ROSE, *incredulous, frightened*: To Russia?

GRANDPA: In Russia they need everything; whereas here, y'see, they don't need anything, so therefore, there's no work.

ROSE, *with an edge of hysteria*: Five minutes ago Roosevelt is too radical, and now you're sending Lee to Russia?

GRANDPA: That's different. Look what it says here . . . a hundred thousand American people applying for jobs in Russia. Look, it says it. So if Lee would go over there and open up a nice chain of clothing stores—

ROSE: Papa! You're such a big anti-Communist . . . and you don't know the government owns everything in Russia?

GRANDPA: Yeah, but not the *stores*.

ROSE: Of course the stores!

GRANDPA: The *stores* they own?

ROSE: Yes!

GRANDPA: Them bastards.

ROSE, *to Lucille*: I'll go out of my mind here . . .

DORIS: So who wrote it?

ROSE: Wrote what?

DORIS: "Gray's Elegy in a Country Churchyard." It was a fifteen-dollar question on the radio yesterday, but you were out. I ran to call you.

ROSE, *suppressing a scream*: Who wrote Gray's "Elegy in a Country Churchyard"?

DORIS: By the time I got back to the radio it was another question.

ROSE: Doris, darling . . . *Slowly*: Gray's "Elegy in a—

> *Fanny laughs.*

What are you laughing at, do you know?

FANNY, *pleasantly*: How would I know?

LUCILLE: Is it Gray?

> *Rose looks at her, an enormous sadness in her eyes. With a certain timidity, Lucille goes on:*

Well, it says "Gray's Elegy," right?

DORIS: How could it be Gray? That's the title!

> *Rose is staring ahead in an agony of despair.*

FANNY: What's the matter, Rose?

DORIS: Well, what'd I say?

FANNY: Rose, what's the matter?

LUCILLE: You all right?

FANNY, *really alarmed, turning Rose's face to her*: What is the matter!

> *Rose bursts into tears. Fanny gets up and embraces her, almost crying herself.*

Oh, Rosie, please . . . don't. It'll get better, something's got to happen . . .

> *A sound from the front door galvanizes them. A man calls from off: "Hello?"*

DORIS, *pointing*: There's some—

ROSE, *her hands flying up in fury*: Sssh! *Whispering*: I'll go upstairs. I'm not home.

She starts to go; Moe enters.

DORIS, *laughing*: It's Uncle Moe!

MOE: What's the excitement?

ROSE, *going to him*: Oh, thank God, I thought it was the mortgage man. You're home early.

He stands watching her.

FANNY: Lets go, come on.

They begin to clear table of tray, lemonade, glasses, etc.

MOE, *looking into Rose's face*: You crying?

LUCILLE: How's it in the city?

ROSE: Go out the back, huh?

MOE: The city is murder.

FANNY: Will you get your bills together? I'm going downtown tomorrow. I'll save you the postage.

ROSE: Take a shower. Why are you so pale?

LUCILLE: Bye-bye, Uncle Moe.

MOE: Bye, girls.

DORIS, *as she exits with Fanny and Lucille*: I must ask him how he made that lemonade . . .

They are gone, Moe is staring at some vision, quite calm, but absorbed.

ROSE: You . . . sell anything? . . . No, heh?

He shakes his head negatively—but that is not what he is thinking about.

Here . . . *She gets a glass from the table.* Come drink, it's cold.

He takes it but doesn't drink.

MOE: You're hysterical every night.

ROSE: No, I'm all right. It's just all so stupid, and every once in a while I can't . . . I can't . . . *She is holding her head.*

MOE: The thing is . . . You listening to me?

ROSE: What? *Suddenly aware of her father's pressure on Moe, she turns and goes quickly to him.* Go on the back porch, Papa, huh? It's shady there now . . . *She hands him a glass of lemonade.*

GRANDPA: But the man'll see me.

ROSE: It's all right, he won't come so late, and Moe is here. Go . . .

> *Grandpa starts to go.*

. . . and why don't you put on your other glasses, they're much cooler.

> *Grandpa is gone. She returns to Moe.*

Yes, dear. What. What's going to be?

MOE: We are going to be all right.

ROSE: Why?

MOE: Because we are. So this nervousness every night is unnecessary, and I wish to God—

ROSE, *indicating the table and the cards spread out*: It's just a fortune. I . . . I started to do a fortune, and I saw . . . a young man. The death of a young man.

MOE, *struck*: You don't say.

ROSE, *sensing*: Why?

> *He turns front, amazed, frightened.*

Why'd you say that?

MOE: Nothing . . .

ROSE: Is Lee . . .

MOE: Will you cut that out—

ROSE: Tell me!

MOE: I saw a terrible thing on the subway. Somebody jumped in front of a train.

ROSE: Aaaahhh—again! My God! You saw him?

MOE: No, a few minutes before I got there. Seems he was a very young man. One of the policemen was holding a great big basket of flowers. Seems he was trying to sell flowers.

ROSE: I saw it! *Her spine tingling, she points down at the cards.* Look, it's there! That's death! I'm going to write Lee to come home immediately. I want you to put in that you want him home.

MOE: I have nothing for him, Rose; how can I make him come home?

ROSE, *screaming and weeping*: Then go to your mother and stand up like a man to her . . . instead of this goddamned fool! *She weeps.*

MOE, *stung, nearly beaten, not facing her*: This can't . . . it can't go on forever, Rose, a country can't just die!

She goes on weeping; he cries out in pain.

Will you stop? I'm trying! God Almighty, I am trying!

The doorbell rings. They start with shock. Grandpa enters, hurrying, pointing.

GRANDPA: Rose—

ROSE: *Ssssh!*

The bell rings again. Moe presses stiffened fingers against his temple, his eyes averted in humiliation. Rose whispers:

God in heaven . . . make him go away!

The bell rings again. Moe's head is bent, his hand quivering as it grips his forehead.

Oh, dear God, give our new President the strength, and the wisdom . . .

Door knock, a little more insistent.

. . . give Mr. Roosevelt the way to help us . . .

Door knock.

Oh, my God, help our dear country . . . and the people! . . .

Door knock. Fadeout.

Lights come up on company as the distant sound of a fight crowd is heard and a clanging bell signals the end of a round. Sidney enters in a guard's uniform; he is watching Lee, who enters smoking a cigar stub, wearing a raincoat, finishing some notes on a pad, his hat tipped back on his head.

SIDNEY: Good fight tonight, Mr. Baum.

LEE, *hardly glancing at him*: Huh? Yeah, pretty good.

Sidney looks on, amused, as Lee slowly passes before him, scribbling away.

As Banks speaks, Soldiers appear and repeat italicized words after him.

BANKS: When the *war* came I was so *glad* when I got in the *army*. A man could be *killed* anytime at all on those trains, but with that uniform on I said, "Now I am safe."

SIDNEY: Hey!

LEE: Huh? *Now he recognizes Sidney.* Sidney!

SIDNEY: Boy, you're some cousin. I'm looking straight at you and no recognito! I'm chief of security here.

BANKS: I felt proud to salute and look around and see all the *good soldiers* of the United States. I was a good *soldier too*, and got five battle stars.

> *Other Soldiers repeat, "Five, five, five."*

LEE: You still on the block?

SIDNEY: Sure. Say, you know who'd have loved to have seen you again? Lou Charney.

LEE: Charney?

SIDNEY: Hundred yard dash—you and him used to trot to school together . . .

LEE: Oh, Lou, sure! How is he!

SIDNEY: He's dead. Got it in Italy.

BANKS: Yeah, I seen all kinds of war—including the kind they calls . . .

COMPANY: . . . peace.

> *Four soldiers sing the beginning of "We're in the Money."*

SIDNEY: And you knew Georgie Rosen got killed, didn't you?

LEE: Georgie Rosen.

RALPH: Little Georgie.

SIDNEY: Sold you his racing bike.

RALPH: That got stolen.

LEE: Yes, yes! God—Georgie too.

COMPANY, *whispering*: Korea.

RALPH: Lot of wars on that block.

> *One actor sings the first verse of "The Times They Are A-Changin'."*

SIDNEY: Oh, yeah—Lou Charney's kid was in *Vietnam*.

> *The company says "Vietnam" with Sidney.*

Still and all, it's a great country, huh?

LEE: Why do you say that?

SIDNEY: Well, all the crime and divorce and whatnot. But one thing about people like us, you live through the worst, you know the difference between bad and *bad*.

BANKS: One time I was hoboin' through that high country—the Dakotas, Montana—I come to the monument for General Custer's last stand, Little Big Horn. And I wrote my name on it, yes, sir. For the memories; just for the note; so my name will be up there forever. Yes, sir . . .

SIDNEY: But I look back at it all now, and I don't know about you, but it seems it was friendlier. Am I right?

LEE: I'm not sure it was friendlier. Maybe people just cared more.

SIDNEY, *with Irene singing "I Want to Be Happy" under his speech*: Like the songs, I mean—you listen to a thirties song, and most of them are so happy, and still—you could cry.

BANKS: But I still hear that train sometimes; still hear that long low whistle. Yes, sir, I still hear that train . . . *whoo-ooo!*

LEE: You still writing songs?

SIDNEY: Sure! I had a couple published.

RALPH: Still waiting for the big break?

SIDNEY: I got a new one now, though—love you to hear it. I'm calling it "A Moon of My Own." I don't know what happened, I'm sitting on the back porch and suddenly it came to me—"A Moon of My Own." I ran in and told Doris, she could hardly sleep all night.

> *Doris quietly sings under the following speeches: ". . . and know the days and nights there in your arms. Instead I'm sittin' around . . . "*

LEE: How's Doris, are you still . . .

SIDNEY: Oh, very much so. In fact, we were just saying we're practically the only ones we know didn't get divorced.

LEE: Did I hear your mother died?

SIDNEY: Yep, Fanny's gone. I was sorry to hear about Aunt Rose, and Moe.

LEE, *over "Life Is Just a Bowl of Cherries" music*: After all these years I still can't settle with myself about my mother. In her own crazy way she was so much like the country.

> *Rose sings the first line of "Life Is Just a Bowl of Cherries." Through the rest of Lee's speech, she sings the next four lines.*

There was nothing she believed that she didn't also believe the opposite. *Rose sings.* She'd sit down on the subway next to a black man—*Rose sings*—and in a couple of minutes she had him asking her advice—*Rose sings*—about the most intimate things in his life. *Rose sings.* Then, maybe a day later—

LEE AND ROSE: "Did you hear! They say the colored are moving in!"

LEE: Or she'd lament her fate as a woman—

ROSE AND LEE: "I was born twenty years too soon!"

ROSE: They treat a woman like a cow, fill her up with a baby and lock her in for the rest of her life.

LEE: But then she'd warn me, "Watch out for women—when they're not stupid, they're full of deceit." I'd come home and give her a real bath of radical idealism, and she was ready to storm the barricades; by evening she'd fallen in love again with the Prince of Wales. She was so like the country; money obsessed her, but what she really longed for was some kind of height where she could stand and see out and around and breathe in the air of her own free life. With all her defeats she believed to the end that the world was meant to be better. . . . I don't know; all I know for sure is that whenever I think of her, I always end up—with this headful of life!

ROSE, *calls, in a ghostly, remote way*: Sing!

> *Alternating lines, Lee and Rose sing "Life Is Just a Bowl of Cherries." The whole company takes up the song in a soft, long-lost tonality. Robertson moves forward, the music continuing underneath.*

ROBERTSON: There were moments when the word "revolution" was not rhetorical.

> *Ted Quinn steps forward.*

QUINN: Roosevelt saved them; came up at the right minute and pulled the miracle.

ROBERTSON: Up to a point; but what really got us out of it was the war.

QUINN: Roosevelt gave them back their belief in the country. The government belonged to them again!

ROBERTSON: Well, I'll give you that.

QUINN: Of course you will, you're not a damned fool. The return of that belief is what saved the United States, no more, no less!

ROBERTSON: I think that's putting it a little too . . .

QUINN, *cutting him off and throwing up his hands*: That's it! . . . God, how I love that music!

> *He breaks into his soft-shoe dance as the singing grows louder. He gestures for the audience to join in, and the company does so as well as the chorus swells . . .*

END

PLAYING FOR TIME

1985

A screenplay based on the book by Fania Fénelon.

Fade in on Fania Fénelon singing. Her voice is unheard, we hear only the opening music.

Cut to a sidewalk café in the afternoon. German soldiers relax, accompanied by French girls. We are in German-occupied Paris, 1942.

Cut to the Nazi flag flying over the Arc de Triomphe.

Cut to Fania accompanying herself on the piano in a Parisian ballad warmed with longing and wartime sentiment. The audience, almost all German troops and French girlfriends, is well-behaved and enjoying her homey romanticism, which salts their so-far epic conquests with pathos and a bit of self-pity.

Nothing in her manner betrays her hostility to Nazism and its destruction of France in the recent battles. She hopes they are enjoying their evening, promises to do what she can to help them forget their soldierly duties; but to the knowing eye there is perhaps a little extra irony in a look she casts, a smile she pours onto the upturned face of a nearby officer that suggests her inner turmoil at having to perform for the conqueror. She is radiant here, an outgoing woman who is still young and with a certain heartiness and appetite for enjoyment.

She is roundly applauded now at the number's end, and she bows and backs into darkness.

Cut to a train of freight cars, moving through open French farmland.

Cut to the inside of one freight car. It is packed with people, many of them well-dressed bourgeois, sitting uncomfortably jammed in. The ordinariness of the types is emphasized, but above that their individuation. Moreover, while all are of course deeply uneasy and uncomfortable, there is no open alarm.

A husband is massaging his wife's cramped shoulders.

A mother is working to remove a speck from a teenage daughter's eye.

Worker types survey the mass with suspicion.

A *clocharde*—a beggar woman off a Paris street—wrapped in rags, and rather at home in this situation, surveys the company.

A second mother pulls a young boy away from a neighbor's bag of food.

Chic people try to keep apart; they are soigné, even bored.

Students are trying to bury themselves in novels.

Two intellectuals scrunched up on the floor are playing chess on a small board.

A boy scout of twelve is doing his knots on a short rope.

An old asthmatic man in a fur-collared coat is urged by his wife to take his pill. He holds it between his fingers, unhappily looking around for water.

Cut to Fania, dressed in a beautiful fur coat and fur hat; her elegant valise is at her feet. She is carrying a net bag with some fruit and a sausage, bread, and a bottle of water, which she offers the old man. He gratefully accepts it, takes his pill, drinks a sip, and returns her the bottle.

Beside Fania on the straw-covered floor sits Marianne, a girl of twenty, quite well dressed and overweight. Marianne has an unmarked, naive face. She is avidly glancing down at Fania's net bag.

FANIA: Have another piece of sausage, if you like.

MARIANNE: I'm so stupid—I never thought to take anything.

FANIA, *kindly*: Well, I suppose your mother has always done that for you.

MARIANNE: Yes. Just a tiny piece . . . *She breaks off more than a tiny piece.* I still can't believe I'm sitting so close to you! I have every one of your records, I think. Really—all my friends love your style.

Marianne bites her sausage and chews sensually.

FANIA: Do you know why they arrested you?

MARIANNE—*glances about nervously for an interloper*: I think it was because of my boyfriend—he's in the Resistance.

FANIA: Oh!— Mine too.

MARIANNE, *reaches under her coat*: I adore him! Maurice is his name.

She hands a snapshot to Fania who looks at it and smiles admiringly. Then Fania opens her soft leather purse and hands a snapshot to Marianne.

FANIA: He's Robert.

MARIANNE, *looking at photo*: Oh, he's fantastic! —a blond! I love blonds. *They return photos*. In the prison they kept beating me up. . . .

FANIA: Me, too.

MARIANNE: . . . They kept asking where he is, but I don't even know!— They nearly broke this arm. *Glancing around*: But somebody said it's really because we're Jewish that they picked us up. Are you?

FANIA: Half.

MARIANNE: I'm half too. Although it never meant anything to me.

FANIA: Nor me.

> They silently stare at the others. Marianne glances down at Fania's food again.

FANIA: You really shouldn't eat so much.

MARIANNE: I can't help it; I never used to until the prison. It made me hungry all the time. I just hope my boyfriend never sees me like this—you wouldn't believe how slim I was only a few months ago. And now I'm bursting out of everything. But my legs are still good. Don't you think? *She extends her leg rather childishly*. I still can't believe I'm sitting next to you! I really have all your records.

> *Cut to* the boy scout who is now sitting with a compass on his knee, studying the needle. Beside him, his mother is asleep.

FANIA: Can you tell our direction?

BOY SCOUT: South.

> A nearby worker overhears.

WORKER: It's probably going to be Munich. They need labor on the farms around there.

SECOND WORKER: I wouldn't mind. I love the outdoors.

> A nearby woman adds her wisdom.

WOMAN: They have those tiny little thatched houses down there. I've seen photographs.

FIRST CHESS PLAYER: In my opinion we'll be machine-gunned right where we sit—and I'm especially sorry for your sake, Madame Fénelon—your music is for me the sound of Paris.

FANIA: Thank you.

MARIANNE, *quietly*: I'm not sure I could do farm work—could you?

FANIA—*shrugs*: Have you ever worked?

MARIANNE—*a little laugh*: Oh no—I never even *met* a worker till the prison. I was in school or at home all my life. *The little laugh again.* And now I don't even know where my parents are. . . . *She verges on a shivering fear with startling rapidity.* Would you mind if we sort of stuck together?

> Fania puts an arm around her and Marianne nestles gratefully into Fania's body. A moment passes; Fania reaches into her net bag and gives Marianne a bonbon. Marianne avidly eats it and Fania pats her hair as though, in effect, forgiving her another dietary lapse.
>
> *Cut to* the boy scout, alert to some change in the compass. He takes it off his knee, shakes it, then sets it back on his knee.

FANIA: Has it changed?

BOY SCOUT: We've turned to the east.

> The first chess player turns to the scout, then leans over to read the compass himself. He then resumes his position, a stare of heightened apprehension growing on his face.

SECOND CHESS PLAYER, *reassuringly*: But a compass can't be right with so much metal around it, can it?

> *Cut to* a sudden explosion of indignation from deep in the crowd; people leaping up to escape something under the hay on the floor; yells of disgust and anger. . . . The mother and little boy emerge from within the crowd, he buttoning his pants. . . .

MOTHER: Well what is he supposed to do!

FIRST MAN: He can use the pail over there!

SECOND MAN: That pail is full.

FIRST MAN—*he yells up to a grill high in a wall of the car*: Hey! Let us empty the pail!

> Only the sound of the clanking train returns. Defeated, the deportees rearrange themselves to find dry places on the floor. The train lurches.
>
> *Cut to* the slop pail, filled with the deportees' urine, overturning.
>
> *Cut to* people, with higher disgust, fleeing from the contents and crowding each other even more, some even remaining on their feet.

Cut to Marianne coming out of Fania's embrace. She whispers in Fania's ear, while placing a hand on her own stomach. Fania glances down at her with distress.

FANIA: Try to hold out—they'll *have* to open the doors soon.

MARIANNE: Could I have another sip of water?

FANIA: But only wet your mouth. You've got to try to discipline yourself.

Marianne drinks from the water bottle. Fania, as she is replacing the stopper, happens to catch the thirsty stare of the old asthmatic man. She hesitates, then holds out the bottle, which is taken by the asthmatic's wife. The old man sips; he is weaker than earlier.

Cut to the nearly full water bottle. Superimposed on it is the crowd in its present postures, which are still rather normal for the circumstances—some are standing to avoid the floor, some are alert and energetic.

The water level in the bottle drops; and the superimposed crowd is losing its energy, with people unconscious, one on top of the other, lips are parched, signs of real distress. . . .

Cut to Fania, asleep sitting up. Marianne awakens, lips parched, tries to get a drop out of the bottle, but it is empty. She looks into Fania's net bag, but it too is empty. Only half alive, Marianne, expressionless, sees a fight starting near her as a man pushes a woman away—and the woman is lowering her dress. . . .

MAN: Do it over there!—this is *my* place!

The woman trips over someone, looks down. . . .

Cut to the old asthmatic man. He's dead. His wife, spiritless and silent, holds his head in her lap.

Cut to the faces of the deportees experiencing the presence of the dead man. Unable to bear it longer, Fania climbs up to the grill.

FANIA: Halloo! Listen! We've got a dead man in here! Halloo!

Surprisingly now, there is a squeal of brakes. People are thrown against each other, and the train stops. Expectation, fear, hope . . .

Cut to the freight-car doors rolling open. A powerful searchlight bathes the crowd, blinding them. The people try to get to their feet and gather their belongings.

From outside, half a dozen kapos leap into the car—these are prisoners working for the administration—and, armed with truncheons, they pull people out of the car onto the ground. ("Hurry up, everybody out, get moving" . . . etc.) They are brutal, enjoying their power.

Cut to the debarkation area. Under the spectral arc lights the cars are being emptied. Kapos are loading valises onto trolleys, but with a certain care, like porters.

Cut to the train platform. Late at night. Still wearing her fur coat and hat, Fania half unwillingly gives up her valise to a kapo. This kapo eyes Marianne's body and gives her a toothless come-on smile.

Cut to a sudden close-up of Dr. Mengele. This monster, the so-called Angel of Death, is a small, dapper man with a not unattractive face. He is the physician in charge of the selections, and in this shot is simply standing at the edge of the milling crowd, observing the people. Now he nods slightly, an order.

Cut to SS guards pushing the people into a rough line, one behind the other. A dozen or more guard dogs and handlers keep the proceedings lively. Snarls electrify, the air is filled with the whining of eager dogs. But the violence is still controlled.

Dr. Mengele faces the head of the line. With a gesture to right or left, with hardly a second's interval between individuals, he motions people toward several waiting trucks (marked with the Red Cross), or to an area where they stand and wait. The latter are generally stronger, male, and younger.

And so the line moves rapidly toward Mengele's pointing fingers, and the crowd parts to the left and the right.

Cut to Fania, right behind Marianne on line, speaking into her ear.

FANIA: It's going to be all right—you see?—the Red Cross is here.

Cut to people being loaded onto the open-backed "Red Cross" trucks. Babies are passed over the crowd to mothers, the aged are carried aboard with the stronger helping. The air still carries the whining and barking of the dogs, the sounds of hurried commands.

Once again, intermittent close shots individualize the crowd, the types, relationships. The crowd, in fact, is relieved to get aboard and moving to some destination.

Cut to the trucks pulling away. Marianne and Fania, alone on the ground, look up at the packed truck that remains. Kapos raise its tailgate and fasten it.

FANIA: Wait—we're supposed to get on, aren't we?

KAPO: How old are you?

FANIA: I'm twenty-eight, she's twenty.

MARIANNE: I wouldn't mind a walk—may we?

KAPO, *with the very faintest glimmer of humor—he too is exhausted, skinny*: You can walk.

The kapo hurries up ahead and boards the truck. The truck starts to pull away, leaving the two women behind.

Cut to the people on the truck. The camera memorializes the faces we have come to know on the train—the boy scout, the chess players, the boy scout's mother, and so on. The truck moves off into darkness.

Cut to Marianne and Fania as they look around at the darkness—shapes of dark buildings surround them. Down the track we hear the activity of the guards and those selected to live.

FANIA: I guess we follow the trucks.

The two move together into the darkness.

Cut to a strange orange glow in the night sky. Is it a massive reflection of bright lights or is it flame? It comes from some half a mile off.

Cut to Fania and Marianne walking, looking up at the glow.

FANIA: There must be some sort of factory.

Out of the darkness a kapo pops up and walks along with them. He puts an arm around Marianne.

KAPO: Listen . . . I'll give you coffee.

FANIA, *pulling his arm away from Marianne*: This must be some high-class place—a cup of coffee for a woman?

KAPO: That's a lot. *Points arrantly at Marianne.* See you later, Beauty.

Fania protectively grasps the frightened Marianne's hand and they move on into the dark toward the glow.

Cut to the reception area. Fania and Marianne enter the dimly lit room, perhaps twenty by forty feet. They enter in uncertainly, unsure if they're supposed to be here. Five Polish women prisoners, employed here, are lounging around a table. One cleans her nails, another reads a scrap of newspaper, another is combing her companion's long hair. They are hefty, coarse, peasant types.

FANIA, *after a moment*: Is this where we get our things back?

She asks this question because—as we see now—along one wall of this room and extending out into a corridor which leads deeper into the building are, in neat piles, hundreds and hundreds of valises, stacks of clothes, piles of shoes, bins full of eyeglasses, false teeth, underwear, sweaters, gloves, galoshes, and every other imaginable personal item.

The Polish women turn to Fania and Marianne. One of them beckons silently, and the two approach her.

From the corridor enter two SS women in uniform. One of them is Frau Schmidt, the brutal, stupid German supervisor of the operation. They halt and expressionlessly observe.

The first Polish woman stands up from the table, and simply takes Fania's handbag out of her hand. The second Polish woman grabs hold of Fania's fur coat and pulls it off her. Bag and coat go into the hands of the SS women, who admiringly examine them.

FIRST POLISH WOMAN: Your shoes.

Fania and Marianne, both in fear now, remove their shoes, which are carried to Frau Schmidt by the Poles. Frau Schmidt examines the expensive shoes appreciatively.

FIRST POLISH WOMAN: Undress.

Cut to Fania and Marianne, sinking into a stunned astonishment. And now hands working scissors enter the shot. Their hair—Fania has braids which are hard to cut—is almost completely removed, leaving tufts.

Cut to a long number—346,991—being tattoed on an arm. Backing off, we see it is Marianne's arm. She is now in a ludicrously outsized dress and shoes far too large. The same for Fania, who is staring down at her own tattoo. The tattooer is a male kapo, who works with his tongue sticking out the corner of his mouth.

Cut to a hundred or so women being handed dresses, some worn to mere shreds. Others are having their hair shorn as they wait to be tattooed. SS women move about, in charge.

Cut to Frau Schmidt, who is handed the little chess set from the train; she admires it, as well as the boy scout's compass. She sets them on the counter. They are then placed by a Polish woman in a receptacle already loaded with toys, stuffed animals, soccer balls, sports things.

Cut to Fania, nearby, as she recognizes these relics; her eyes flare with terror. She turns toward a nearby window.

Cut to the window. We see the eerie glow in the sky.

Cut to one of the Polish women, all but finished pinning Fania's plaits on her own hair, imitating Fania's sophisticated walk as her sister workers laugh.

Fania, humiliated and angered, touches her bare scalp.

Cut to the work gang, from Fania's point of view. An exhausted woman collapses at the feet of Lagerführerin Maria Mandel, who gestures toward a wheelbarrow. As kapos carry the woman, one of her arms brushes Mandel's coat. Mandel viciously hits the arm away, brushing off her coat sleeve as the woman is dumped into the wheelbarrow.

POLISH WOMAN: How do I look, Jew-Crap?

FANIA: I'm not Jew-Crap, I'm French!

An uproar of laughter, and out of nowhere a smashing slap knocks Fania reeling to the floor. Over her stands SS Frau Schmidt, a powerhouse, looking down with menace.
Dissolve to dark.

Cut to the quarantine block—this is the barracks; dimly lit by a hanging bulb or two; a corridor between shelves, in effect, where women lie with barely room to turn over. The shelves go to the ceiling.

Fania and Marianne enter the corridor, escorted by a Polish woman, the Blockawa or Block Warden. She gestures for them to take bunks above and turns to leave.

The women in the bunks are cadaverous, barely able to summon interest in these new arrivals.

FANIA: Where are the people we came with?—they went off on the trucks . . . ?

The Blockawa grips her arm and leads her to a window and points out.

Cut to the orange sky-glow. But from this closer distance smoke can be seen rising from a tall stack.

Cut to Fania, Marianne, and the Blockawa. The Blockawa points upward through the window.

BLOCKAWA: Your friends. You see? —cooking. You too, pretty soon.

The Blockawa cutely blinks both eyes, grins reassuringly, and walks away.

Cut to Marianne, quietly sobbing as she lies beside Fania on their bunk.

FANIA: Marianne? Listen to me. Come, girl, stop that.

MARIANNE: Why are they doing this? What do they get from it?

Fania glances to her other side where, on the shelf beside her, lies a famished-looking woman who might well be dead.

FANIA, *turning back to Marianne*: I've always had to have an aim in life—something I wanted to do next. That's what we need now if we're ever to get out of here alive.

MARIANNE: What sort of an aim?

Fania looks down into the corridor below at the Blockawa, on patrol with a truncheon in her fist.

FANIA: If I ever get out of here alive, I'm going to kill a Polish woman.

Fania lies back, shuts her eyes, hating herself a little.

MARIANNE: I'm so hungry, Fania. Hold me.

Fania, on her back, embraces Marianne; then she turns the other way to look at the woman on her other side; she is skeletal, absolutely still. Cautiously Fania touches her skin and draws her hand away at the cold touch. Then she gives her a little shake. The woman has died.

Now she leans over the edge of the bunk and calls to the Blockawa.

FANIA: There's a dead woman up here.

The Blockawa, club in hand, allows a moment to pass; she slowly looks up at Fania with the interest of a seal, then strolls away.

Cut to a close shot of Fania and Marianne in their bunk. Marianne stares in fright at the corpse, then hides her face in Fania's side.

FANIA: We must have an aim. And I think the aim is to try to remember everything. I'll tell you a story. . . . Once upon a time there was a prince named Jean and he was terribly handsome. And he married a princess named Jeannette and she was terribly beautiful.

Marianne comes out of hiding under Fania's arm—she is childishly interested. . . .

MARIANNE: And?

FANIA: And one day the prince said, "My dear, we must have an aim in life, we must make children," and so they. . . .

As Fania talks, slowly fade to a double exposure of Fania and Marianne. Snow falls over the image of the two women in their bunk: a forest; now spring comes; flowers appear and green grass; brook ice melts—always over the image of Fania and Marianne dragging stones, carrying wood, digging drainage ditches. . . . And finally, once again, in their bunk—now without the dead woman, and they are both asleep, side by side. And both are haggard now, with the half-starved look of the other prisoners.

A voice blares out: "ATTENTION!"

Cut to the barracks. Women start to come obediently out of their bunks into the corridor. The Blockawa yells.

BLOCKAWA: Remain in place! Does anybody know how to sing *Madame Butterfly*!

Astonished silence. The Blockawa is infuriated.

BLOCKAWA: Does anyone know how to sing *Madame Butterfly*!

Cut to Fania, unsure whether to volunteer; she glances at Marianne, who urges her silently to do so. Below in the corridor the Blockawa starts to leave. Fania suddenly lunges and, half hanging out the bunk, waves to the monster woman. . . .

FANIA: I can!

Cut to Fania, entering from exterior darkness into a lighted room. She halts, looking around in total astonishment.

Cut to the musicians' barrack dayroom. Fania, as in a wild dream, sees some twenty-five women, most seated behind music stands, badly but cleanly dressed; some with shaved heads (Jewesses), others still with their hair. Unlike her former barracks, with its faint and few light bulbs, there is brightness here, although it is actually quite bare of furniture.

In the center stands a Bechstein grand, shiny, beautiful. At the sight of the piano, Fania's mouth falls open.

Compared to these women Fania is indeed woebegone—
dirty, in ludicrously enormous shoes, a torn and ill-fitting
dress.

Elzvieta, an older Pole with a full head of hair, approaches
Fania, and with a wet cloth wipes her face. Fania regards this
kindness incredulously. Now Elzvieta runs her pitying fingers
down Fania's cheek.

Etalina, petite, Rumanian, eighteen, brings a lump of
bread and puts it in Fania's hand.

ETALINA: I'm Etalina. I saw you in Paris once, at the "Melody." *Fania
bites into the bread.* My parents took me there last year for my birthday—
I was seventeen.

Michou enters the group; a tiny determined girl of twenty, a
militant communist, terribly pale, with a soft poetic voice.
Etalina indicates her (not without a slight air of joking superciliousness toward this wraith).

ETALINA: But she's the one who recognized you. This is Michou.

MICHOU: I saw you yesterday coming out of your barracks and I ran and
told our kapo—she promised to audition you—

FANIA: What audition?

ETALINA: For the orchestra—us. *With some awe*: Our conductor is Alma
Rosé. *Calls offscreen*: Charlotte, come and meet Fania Fénelon! *To Fania*:
She's one of our best players, but she's shy as a deer. She can do Bach
solos. . . .

CHARLOTTE—*enters shot. Almost a whisper as she curtsies*: I'm honored
to meet you.

FANIA: How do you do, Charlotte. *To Etalina*: Rosé?—there was a string
quartet by that name. . . .

MICHOU: Alma is the first violinist's daughter.

FANIA: Then her uncle must be Gustav Mahler . . . the composer. . . .

ELZVIETA: Yes; she has a fantastic talent.

ETALINA: But not a warm heart, be careful. . . .

Michou touches Etalina to shush her, looking offscreen.

Cut to Alma Rosé, as she makes her entrance—there is instant
silence and respect. Now three Blockawas—Polish prisoners
acting as police in effect, and all weighty types—appear and
look on with belligerent curiosity. They don't approve this
coddling of Jews.

Alma comes toward the group. She is thin, extremely Germanic, scrubbed clean, her shabby clothes brushed. Her face shows her determination, even fanatical perfectionism—her only defense here.

ALMA: You are Mademoiselle Fénelon?

FANIA: Yes, Madame.

ALMA: You play the piano?

FANIA: Oh yes, Madame!

The fervor of her voice causes an excited giggle among some of the onlookers.

ALMA: Let me hear something from *Madame Butterfly*.

Alma goes to a chair, sits; others arrange themselves. Fania approaches the fabulous piano; it is all like a dream—she is slogging along in these immense men's shoes, a fuzz of hair on her bald head, her face gaunt from the near-starvation diet—and she sits before the keys and can't help bending over and kissing them. She starts to play "Un bel di" . . .

Cut to Fania's hands. They are crusted with filth, nails broken. She is stiff and strikes a double note.

Cut to Fania, at the piano. She stops, blows on her fingers. Now she plays and sings. After two bars . . .

Cut to the group. All are glancing at Alma's reaction—she is quickened, eager to claim Fania for her orchestra.

Cut to Fania. In her face and voice, confident now and warm, are the ironic longings for the music's life-giving loveliness. The mood is shattered by the sounds of the scraping of chairs and people suddenly standing. Fania turns, stops playing.

Cut to Lagerführerin Mandel entering the dayroom; she is chief of the women's section of the entire camp. About twenty-eight, tall, blond, shining with health, beautiful in her black uniform. Musicians, Blockawas, all are standing at rigid attention before her. Fania sees this, and attempts to do likewise—although only half successfully in her state of semi-shock.

MANDEL: At ease.

She comes and examines Fania, head to foot. And to Alma . . .

MANDEL: You will take her.

ALMA: Yes, Frau Mandel, certainly—she is very good.

MANDEL, *facing Fania*: She is wonderful.

There is something competitive in Alma's face.

MANDEL: Do you know any German music?

FANIA—*hesitates, her eyes lowered in trepidation*: Yes . . .

MANDEL: I am Lagerführerin Maria Mandel, in command of all women in this camp.

FANIA—*nods in deference*: I . . . had forgotten to tell Madame Rosé . . . that I really can't join the orchestra . . . unless my friend 346,991 is admitted also—she has a beautiful voice. *Now she meets Mandel's surprised look.* She is in Barracks B. *Mandel is silent; surprised actually.* Without her, I . . . must refuse . . . I'm sorry.

Absolute astonishment strikes the expressions of the other musicians.

Cut to Mandel, who looks at Fania for an additional moment, her mind unreadable.

Cut to the kapos, furious, but more incredulous than anything else.

Cut to Fania and Tchaikowska, a kapo, hurrying down a camp "street" (a corridor between barracks buildings). Fania is urging Tchaikowska to go faster. . . . They turn the corner of a building and come upon about twenty women who are being driven by club-wielding Blockawas. Many of these women are near death, falling down, crawling.

In the background, Mala comes to a halt; with her an SS officer. She is a tall, striking Jewess, wears the Star. But—oddly enough—there is no subservience in her manner but rather a seriousness and confidence. She carries a thick notebook.

Marianne is being pulled and struck by a Blockawa whose pressure she is resisting, as she tries to get back into the barracks building.

FANIA, *to Tchaikowska, pointing*: That's her! Quick! Marianne . . . !

Fania drops behind the kapo Tchaikowska—who has the authority here and who walks up to the Blockawa.

TCHAIKOWSKA: Mandel wants this one.

Marianne nearly faints into Fania's arms as they start to move away from the surprised Blockawa and the deadened, staggering group of women.

Cut to Marianne, her face still smudged with dirt, deep scratches on her neck. Incredibly enough she is singing to Fania's piano accompaniment in the musicians' barracks.

Cut to Mandel, legs sheathed in silk, her cap off, letting her blond hair fall to her shoulders. She listens. Alma stands a deferential few paces behind her. And in the background, the musicians, all listening.

Fania is playing encouragingly, glancing from time to time up at Marianne to urge her on. Marianne has a fevered look in her eyes, she is singing for her life. The song ends. Silence.

MANDEL, *to Alma*: Get them dressed.

Cut to Marianne, who starts to sway but is held up by Fania.

Cut to a counter; behind it from floor to ceiling the clothing of the dead.

Blockawas, and the Chief here—Frau Schmidt—stand rigidly at attention. Mandel is holding up a brassiere which she places over Marianne's large breasts. Then she gives it to Marianne. Now she takes a pair of fine silk panties, holds them up for Fania, who accepts them.

MANDEL, *to Frau Schmidt*: Find shoes that fit her.

FRAU SCHMIDT: Of course. *To Fania*: They look very small, what size are they?

FANIA: Four.

FRAU SCHMIDT, *to Mandel*: I doubt very much that we have . . .

MANDEL: Feet must be warm and comfortable or the voice is affected. Find them for my little singer.

Frau Schmidt is irritated but obedient.

Fania and Marianne are thankful to Mandel, but what is the meaning of this incredible insistence?

Mandel exits, leaving Frau Schmidt rummaging in the bin full of women's shoes.

A Blockawa sweeps a woolen coat off the counter and furiously throws it at Fania, who blocks it with her arm.

While Frau Schmidt continues to search, Fania's eye transforms the pile of shoes.

Dissolve to women's legs walking on a railroad station plat-form. In effect, the shoes come alive on the wearers' feet and move about on a sidewalk.

Cut to Alma, tapping on her podium with her baton, raising her arms to begin a number; the orchestra is ready. Suddenly eyes catch something off-camera and all spring to their feet and at attention.
    Mandel enters, followed by her orderly. Mandel is carry-ing a box full of shoes, four or five pair.

Cut to Mandel. Her eyes are happy, somehow softened.

MANDEL: Sit down here, Fania.

Fania comes to her from the piano bench, sits before her at her gestured command. Mandel sets the box of shoes down, takes out a pair of fur-lined boots—and kneels before Fania!
    Fania is now torn; she dares not turn back these incredi-ble gifts, but at the same time she fears what accepting them may imply for her future. She looks down at the fur boot in Mandel's hand. . . .

Cut to a close shot of the boot. The camera either vivifies this boot, gives it the life of its deceased owner—or actually fills it with a leg, and we see the pair of boots on living legs . . . per-haps walking on a city street.

Cut to Mandel, rising to her feet as Fania stands in the fur boots. She looks up from them to Mandel's pleased face and can't help resolving her conflict by saying . . .

FANIA: *Danke schön*, Frau Lagerführerin.

Cut to Mandel. Her pleasure flows onto her face; there is an element of masterly dominance in her expression, and some sort of affection, in fact.

Cut to the entire orchestra, rehearsing. Fania has hands poised over the keyboard; Alma, baton raised, starts the piece—an orchestral number of von Suppé. The sound is not quite horri-ble, but very nearly. The forty-odd players, apart from some of them being totally inadequate, are distressed by hunger and fear and never quite keep the music together.

Cut to the orchestra. The camera introduces us to the main supporting characters:
    Elzvieta, a very good violinist, a rather aristocratic Pole who, as a non-Jew, still has her hair.

Paulette, a woman in her twenties, German-Jewish, an excellent cellist, who is presently pained by the bad playing of her compatriot beside her, who is . . .

Liesle, a bony, timid, near-hysterically frightened mandolin player, trying desperately to keep up with the beat. Belgian.

Charlotte, violinist, fine player, slim and noble-looking, Belgian, extremely intelligent, poetic face.

Etalina, a wisecracker, small, Rumanian, violinist, a tomboy.

Michou, French, plays the flute.

Further in the background of the story are . . .

Giselle, a freckled, very young French girl who can barely play drums at all, but is too young to despair, and thus beats away as loudly as possible.

Berta, a teacher.

Varya, cymbals. A Pole who has her hair.

Katrina, Polish, a very bad guitarist, stubborn, unteachable; has her hair.

Olga, Ukrainian accordionist, a dumbbell who will later take over the orchestra.

Greta, Dutch accordionist, country girl, naive and scared at all times; very poor player.

Esther, a taut, militant Zionist who bears in her intense eyes the vision of Palestine; accordionist.

Tchaikowska, leading kapo.

From time to time, one or more of the secondary characters will emerge on the foreground of this story in order to keep alive and vivid the sense that the "background group" is made of individuals. If this film is to approach even an indication of the vastness of the human disaster involved, the minor characters will have to be kept dramatically alive even in shots where they are only seen and don't have lines.

Cut to Alma, tapping angrily on the podium. . . . the orchestra breaks off.

ALMA: Why is it so loud? This is not band music, we are not playing against the wind—why can you not obey my instructions! *A note of futile and somehow dangerous anxiety on the verge of real anger.* Music is the holiest activity of mankind, you must apply yourselves day and night, you must listen to yourselves, you must aspire to some improvement . . . ! You cannot simply repeat the same mistakes. . . .

She can't go on, and simply walks hurriedly out of the room to recover herself. For a moment, the women keep an abashed silence.

ETALINA: At ease, Philharmonic.

> The women set down their instruments and stand and stretch. . . . Etalina comes to Fania at the piano.

ETALINA: I think you've upset her—your being so good; she suddenly heard what we really sound like.

> Paulette enters the shot and Liesle. Then Giselle.

FANIA: Well it *was* a bit loud. . . .

PAULETTE, *of Liesle*: She can't learn that number—we've got to go loud or she's had it.

LIESLE, *defensively, a whine*: I only studied less than six months in my whole life.

ETALINA: And that's the smartest six months *you* ever spent. *To Fania*: It's not her altogether—it's the maestro herself who's brought on this trouble.

FANIA: Why?

ETALINA: We were simply a marching band when we started—we'd play the prisoners out to their work assignments. But Alma got ambitious, and the first thing you know we're doing these orchestral numbers, giving concerts for the high brass . . . playing Beethoven, for God's sake. She's a victim of her own pride and we're in trouble now.

MARIANNE, *entering the shot*: Do we ever get dinner?

LIESLE—*laughs*: Listen to her . . . !

ETALINA: The slops'll be here any time now, dear.

FANIA: Why trouble, Etalina?

ETALINA: Because once the big shots started coming to hear us they began getting bored hearing the same three numbers.

PAULETTE: We have no other orchestrations. . . .

ETALINA: And no composer ever wrote for this idiotic kind of instrumentation. I mean, piccolos, guitars, flutes, violins, no bass, no horns, no . . .

MICHOU, *to Fania*: You don't orchestrate, do you?

> Obviously Fania doesn't, but her mouth opens and her eyes are inventing. . . .

PAULETTE: I'm really getting worried—we've done practically the same concert at least a dozen times. The Commandant sometimes doesn't even stay to the end.

MARIANNE—*her frightened eyes turn to Fania*: But you do know how to orchestrate, Fania! *Fania looks into her scared face.* And then they could play all sorts of things!

FANIA: Actually—*to the women*—I can.

ETALINA AND PAULETTE: *Orchestrate?*

FANIA: Well, yes . . . not professionally, but I . . .

MICHOU: I knew it!

Paulette swerves about and yells to the women.

PAULETTE: She can orchestrate!

Etalina and Paulette instantly take off down the length of the room flanked by a dozen women all cheering and talking . . . and come to Alma's door where Etalina knocks.

Cut to Alma's room. Alma is sitting by a window, baton still in her grip. Etalina and Paulette step into the room.

ETALINA: We thought you'd want to know, Madame—Fania Fénelon knows how to orchestrate.

The importance of this news is evident in Alma's expression. She stands. Fania is brought forward and into the room.

ALMA, *to the others*: Leave us. Leave us, please.

She shuts the door on the women. The last face we see is Marianne's, imploring Fania to press on. Alma gestures to the bed where Fania sits as Alma sits on the chair facing her. Fania looks around at the clean, bare room.

ALMA: Tell me the truth, Fania.

FANIA: Yes, I can—I don't see why not.

ALMA: And I suppose you . . . actually studied?

FANIA, *plunging on*: At the Paris Conservatory.

ALMA: Oh, Fania—what luck! What luck to have you! There's been a terrible pressure on me for some weeks now . . . for something new. . . .

FANIA: So they tell me. . . .

ALMA: I'm so exhausted and rushed that I've simply been unable to, myself. Could you start with . . . ? *She picks up piano music from a table.* I have a piano score for *Carmen*. . . .

FANIA: Well, I suppose, yes, I could do *Carmen*. . . .

ALMA: Or something German . . . here's another von Suppé. . . .

FANIA: I can't bear von Suppé. . . .

ALMA: I know, but they adore anything by von Suppé and we must try to please them, Fania. *Their eyes meet. Alma is a mite defensive, but it comes out with strength.* Well that is elementary, it seems to me.

FANIA: I suppose. But I prefer to think that I am saving my life rather than trying to please the SS.

ALMA: And you think you can do one without the other?

> Fania shuts up; clearly it is a dilemma, but she is also not trusting Alma. Now Alma relents.

ALMA: You'll begin immediately.

FANIA: I'll need people to copy the parts . . . and music paper.

ALMA: We can't possibly get music paper. . . .

FANIA: Couldn't you request some?

ALMA: There is a war on, my dear!

> Suddenly, in this exclamation is Alma's *own* German indignation.

ALMA: Come—I'll find paper, and you and the girls can draw the lines yourself. *Fania rises, goes past her to the door.* Fania? *Fania turns to her, a slight smile.* I can't help striving for perfection; I was trained that way, I can't change now.

FANIA: Madame, I'm hardly in a position to criticize you when I am also trying to please.

ALMA: Exactly—but we are artists, we can't help that; you have nothing to be ashamed of. *Alma now comes to Fania—and in a more confessing, intimate tone*: Please try to hurry the work—they're so very changeable toward us, you see? Something new and surprising would be—*her fear is outright, open*—a tremendous help. So you'll be quick, Fania?

> *Cut to* Fania. Her eyes are filling with terror and determination. . . .

> *Cut to* the dayroom, that evening. A concert is in full swing, primarily for Commandant Kramer and Dr. Mengele, but other officers are here too, including Frau Schmidt and Lagerführerin Mandel, forming an audience of perhaps twenty.
> Madame Alma Rosé, face aglow, is apprehensively conducting, pushing the stone uphill.

The camera detects the players' abilities—the few good ones trying to overflow onto the sounds of the shaky ones.

Kramer, Dr. Mengele, and Mandel are naturally seated in the front "row." Mandel is interested; Dr. Mengele, who knows music, is very attentive, also amused; Kramer, a bull-necked killer, is struggling to keep his eyes open.

The number is ending with a flashy run on the piano by Fania. There is applause, more or less perfunctory.

Alma turns and bows as though before a gigantic audience.

ALMA: And now, with your permission, *meine Damen und Herren*—a bit of popular music by our new member, Fania Fénelon.

Mandel alone eagerly applauds.

Fania accompanies herself, singing a smoky, very Parisian ballad. And as she sings . . .

Dissolve to Dr. Mengele, his face superimposed on Fania. Then we see him with finger raised, directing deportees emerging from a freight car to right and left, death or life. *Flames reflect orange light on his face.*
This gives way to . . .
A close-up of Mengele. He seems actually attracted to Fania's voice and music.

Cut to Fania, finishing her number—her face is tortured, but she is singing, fully, beautifully, to the finish.

Cut to the audience. Now there is more heartfelt applause. Fania takes bows, her eyes trying to evade the monsters applauding her.

Cut to Fania, dousing her face with water as though trying to wash herself clean.

Cut to the dormitory. Marianne is drawing out a box from under her bed—she opens it, takes out a package of margarine, starts to dig some out with a finger—and looks up guiltily, her finger nearly in her mouth.

Fania is standing nearby, having discovered her. Fania is still drying herself from the shower.

FANIA: Why do you steal when you know I can't stand margarine?

Marianne starts to put the margarine back in the box. Fania comes and forces it back into her hand. Fania's voice is losing its control.

Other women look up from their beds, still others are entering the dormitory—and gradually all are drawn to this.

FANIA: Anything you want of mine I wish you would simply take, Marianne! *Turning to the other women*: And that goes for everyone—I don't want to keep anything from anyone who wants it. . . . And I hope you'll do the same for me if I'm desperate.

ETALINA: But Fania, we can't very well share everything.

FANIA: I refuse to turn into an animal for a gram of margarine or a potato peel!

PAULETTE: You don't mean share with the Poles too, though.

> Fania hesitates . . . glances down the dormitory where half a dozen Polish women stand about—heavy, tough, their contempt evident despite their curiosity of the moment. (Katrina: Beefy, appalling guitarist. Varya: Athlete, shrewd, cymbals.)

ETALINA: Count me out, dear—those are monsters; even here in the same hell as we are, they're just praying every one of us goes to the gas. You share with those bitches, not me.

ELZVIETA—*a delicate, gentle Pole, beautiful head of hair*: We're not all like that.

> Slight pause.

PAULETTE: You just have a pet Jew—you like Fania, but you're an anti-Semite, Elzvieta.

ELZVIETA, *timidly*: But I really am not. My father was an actor; we had a lot of Jewish friends in the theater.—I'm really not, Fania. *Glancing at the satiric Etalina.* In my opinion, Etalina—*with a glance toward the Poles*—they think that you people are probably going to be . . . you know . . .

ETALINA: Gassed. —You can say it, dear.

ELZVIETA: Well the point is that they want to feel superior because they'll probably live to go home, when the war ends . . . being Gentiles. *To Fania*: They're more stupid than evil.

FANIA: Then we should try to teach them.

> After the first shock, Etalina laughs. Then another and another until, with glances toward the stolid, suspicious, and bovine Poles, the whole gang are laughing their heads off; and finally the Poles too join in.

GISELLE—*a freckled-faced, red-haired Parisian tomboy*: To hell with this—tell us about Paris—when were you there last? What are they wearing?

Women gather around.

FANIA: I was in Dancy prison almost a year.

PAULETTE: Well, it can't have changed much—where are the skirts now?

FANIA, *indicating*: Oh, to here *(the knee)* but very full—the girls look like flowers.

MARIANNE: The heels are very high—the legs look terrific. You can't buy stockings so they paint their legs. My mother wouldn't let me, though.

PAULETTE: And the hair?—there were some women in a convoy the other day—I think from Holland—curls on top of their heads. . . .

FANIA: In Paris too—piled up top-curls. —Where are those women?

ETALINA: They're burned up by now, I guess. What about songs? —You know any new ones?

FANIA, *to Etalina*: The way you say that, Etalina . . .

ETALINA: That they're burned up?—why not say it? We'll be better prepared for it when our time comes.

GISELLE, *insistently*: Talk about Paris, Fania. . . .

LIESLE: Are they still playing swing?

FANIA: Are you Parisian?

LIESLE: No. But we went there for a vacation just before the war—play us some of the new songs, will you?

OTHERS: That's a great idea. . . . Come on, Fania. . . . Do you know "Stormy Weather"? . . . What was the name of your nightclub? . . . Did you make many records? . . . She's really famous, you know. . . .

The group moves out into the dayroom.

MICHOU: Can you play by ear? . . . Come, sit down . . .

Fania sits at the piano, Marianne beside her . . . when . . .

Cut to Shmuel, in prisoner's stripes. He is an electrician, now taping a wire along a wall of the dayroom. He is forty-five, perhaps deranged, perhaps extraordinarily wise, it's hard to say. He's like a little toy animal, large eyes, curly hair, desperately shy. He makes little peeking glances at the assembling women, but there's some air of persistence about him, too.

Cut to Fania, who senses some indecipherable communication from him and lets her gaze linger on him for an instant. Then

she breaks away and begins to play the intro for "Stormy
Weather."

 After the first couple of lines, Marianne interrupts, unable to restrain herself even though she is breaking up Fania's
number.

MARIANNE: Could I, Fania? Please?

Fania is quite astonished, looks at her with an embarrassed
smile to cover her own resentment.

MARIANNE: I just have such a yen for it suddenly! Do you mind?

Fania, embarrassed, shrugs and obliges, accompanying Marianne, who sings the number—but "appealingly," sentimen-
tally, where Fania sang intelligently, suavely.

Cut to the Polish women. They are identifiable, in part, by the
fact they all have hair. They have come out of the dormitory
and gather a little apart, and are pleasurably listening.

 And before the music has a chance to die on Marianne's
number, Fania picks up another, singing herself.

 Camera pans the women's faces . . . maybe two dozen
clustered around the piano . . . shorn, gaunt captives, yet this
music brings up their lust to live and a certain joy. . . .

 A chorus of players pick up a lyric and join Fania, singing all together.

Cut to Alma Rosé. Her door opens onto the dayroom, and she
is about to protest the noise . . . but her gesture aborts and she
stiffly concedes the moment, turns and goes back into her
room, shutting the door.

Cut to the next morning, outside in the camp "street." About
twenty players form up outside the musicians' barracks. Each
wears a bandanna, a uniform-like element, and of course the
Jewesses have the yellow Star on their clothing. The Gentiles
are indiscriminately mixed in, perhaps four or five of them,
identifiable mainly by their hair.

 It is gray, just before day, very cold. Fania is in place at
one corner of the formation; Alma Rosé appears from the barracks, sees her, and halts.

ALMA: You don't have to do this, you're not in the band.

FANIA: I would like to see it . . . if it's not forbidden.

Alma is surprised, then shrugs, goes around to the head of the
formation, raises her baton, and this crazy band, with no

horns but with fiddles, flutes, accordian, guitars, and cymbals, goes marching off behind Alma, who marches like a Prussian.

Cut to the camp "square." The band is playing "stirring" march music on a low bandstand. Before them in blocks of five square stand the women prisoners about to go off to work.

Some of them are ill, supported by a neighbor's hand; some are fiercely erect, some old, some teenagers—their shoes don't match, some feet are wrapped in rags, and their clothes are ripped rags.

Cut to a close shot of Fania. Her gaze has moved to a point . . . which is . . .

An angry prisoner.

This woman has caught Fania's eye and mimes spitting at her in contempt.

Cut to Fania, quickly lowering her eyes.

Cut to SS men, some handling attack dogs, ordering the prisoners to march. The whole mass moves across the mud.

SS OFFICER, *a whip against his boot beating time*: Eins, zwei, drei . . . hup, hup, hup . . . !

Cut to Fania lifting her eyes, forcing herself to watch. Suddenly up to her ear comes Shmuel. Frightened, surprised, she turns to him swiftly.

SHMUEL, *wild-eyed*: Live!

He quickly limps away, his tool box on his shoulder.

Cut to the dayroom. Women, lining paper with pencils and straightedges, are spread out around Fania near a window. Outside the gray light of winter afternoon.

Charlotte, a good violinist, is practicing some distance away—a Bach chaconne.

Marianne is staring out a window nearby, thinking of food.

Fania is seated, studying a piano score, pencil poised over a lined sheet on which a few notes have been set down. She is intense—worried?

Liesle is repeating the same three bars on her accordion, with the same mistakes.

GISELLE, *musing to no one in particular*: Imagine!—painting their legs! I'd love *that*. . . .

Etalina passes behind Fania and, glancing down at the few notes she has written, halts, surprised.

ETALINA: Is that all you've done? *Fania glances up defensively.* Christ, at this rate we'll need another Hundred Years' War to get a score out of you.

Charlotte enters the shot, carrying her violin.

CHARLOTTE: Will you stop bothering her? Orchestrating is tough work even for experts.

Alma comes out of her room, comes over to Fania, and looks down at the sheet. Then she looks at Fania with real surprise.

ALMA: I have to speak to you.

Alma goes out into her room. Fania stands, as she follows her out, sees . . .
The Polish women, triumphantly laughing (softly, though) and pointing at her and miming her decapitation.

Cut to Alma's room.

ALMA: Then you lied?—you can't orchestrate at all, can you?

FANIA: I'm quite able to do it; I'm sure I can.

ALMA: What is it, then?

FANIA: One of the women this morning—spat at me.

ALMA, *not understanding*: Yes?

FANIA: I hadn't realized . . . how they must hate us.

ALMA: Oh. Yes, of course; what did you expect?

FANIA: Well I . . . I just hadn't thought about it.

ALMA, *now sensing some remote criticism of her own character, is angry*: Perhaps you are too conscientious a person for the orchestra . . .

FANIA: No, no, I didn't mean . . .

ALMA: If you'd be happier back in "B" Barracks . . .

FANIA: Madame, please—I wasn't criticizing you. *Unstrung.* I'm just not used to being hated like that.

ALMA, *decisively*: Fania—there is life or death in this place, there is no room for anything else whatever.—I intend to rehearse that piece tomorrow; I want the parts by morning. If you are able, that is. Are you?

FANIA, *defeated, yet determined*: Yes, Madame.

She walks angrily past Alma out the door.

Cut to the dayroom. Through the window nearby we see darkness of night. Reflection of a big searchlight, which revolves somewhere beyond our line of sight, a rhythm of this flashing light.

Fania at the piano is alone, working out the orchestration. She tries a chord. There is the jarring sound of three rifle shots. She looks up, waits; then silence. Someone probably got killed. She plays the chord again; writes notes.

From outside we hear the hair-raising screeching of someone being destroyed—and the shouts of men killing. Then silence. Fania is in sharp conflict with herself; she knows she is walling herself up against all this. Steels herself again. Plays the chord. Can't continue. Gets up, walks past dormitory doorway. She looks in.

Cut to the dormitory, at night. The whole orchestra, some forty, asleep in beds.

Cut to Fania, in the dayroom, passing the dormitory door, goes into a dark narrow corridor at the end of which is a door. She opens this door. . . .

Cut to the toilet. On the toilet bowl Marianne is straddling a man, a kapo still wearing his striped prisoner's hat. In his hand are gripped two sausages. Marianne turns and sees Fania, but turns back and continues with the man, who is looking straight up at Fania.

Cut to the dayroom. Through the window the first light of dawn. Backing, we find Fania with several pages of completed score under her hand . . . exhausted, but finishing it. She is fighting self-disgust; at the same time is glad at her accomplishment. A hand enters the shot, with a piece of sausage held between forefinger and thumb. Fania looks at it.

Pull back to Marianne, standing beside Fania, offering the piece of sausage. Fania stares at it, then up at Marianne.

MARIANNE: Take it—for saving my life. You must be starved, working all night.

Fania is not looking at her judgmentally but with sorrow and fear. Marianne sets the piece of sausage on the keyboard.

MARIANNE: I'm not going to live to get out of here anyway.

FANIA: But if you do? Marianne? What if you live?

Marianne is silent, then with a certain stubborn air, walks away. Fania looks at the sausage. Tries not to eat it. A desperate struggle to refuse this seeming compromise with her own disgust. Finally she does eat it—and gives way to a look of almost sensual enjoyment as she carefully lengthens out the chewing. Then she swallows, stands in intense conflict, her hands clasped to her mouth as she walks about with no escape.

The sudden sound of ear-piercing whistles.

Fania looks out a window, frightened, bewildered.

Three Blockawas, led by their chief Tchaikowska, come running into the dayroom buttoning up their coats as they rush past Fania into the dormitory.

Cut to the dormitory. The Blockawas, yelling, "'*Raus, 'raus, schnell* . . .'" rip off blankets, push and slap the women out of bed. The women are first in shock, but quickly obey, start dressing.

Cut to the train platform. Dawn. The band is rushed into a formation before a line of freight cars whose doors are shut. SS men stand waiting, along with kapos preparing to pounce on the luggage.

Commandant Kramer is standing in open area, beside him Frau Lagerführerin Mandel, in a cape and cap. Kramer signals Alma, who starts the orchestra in a bright march.

Car doors are rolled open; inside a mass of people who are pulled and driven out onto the platform by kapos, their luggage taken.

Cut to a mother, being torn from her child, who is tossed onto a waiting truck. Mother rushes to Frau Mandel to plead with her; Mandel strikes her across the face with a riding crop.

Cut to Fania, by the dayroom window. She sees this, starts to turn away in horror, then forces herself to turn back to the window.

Shmuel suddenly appears outside the window and sees her, glances around, then hurries out of sight.

He enters the dayroom. With a glance of caution behind him he hurriedly limps over to Fania.

SHMUEL: Don't do that.

FANIA: What?

SHMUEL: Turn away. You have to look and see everything, so you can tell him when it is over.

FANIA: Who?

His eyes roll upward, and he dares point upward just a bit with one finger.

FANIA: I don't believe.

A grin breaks onto his face—as though she has decided to play a game with him.

FANIA: Why do you pick me?

SHMUEL: Oh, I always know who to pick!

A crazy kind of joy suffuses his face as he backs out the door.

SHMUEL: Live!

Cut to the smokestack. Dawn. For an instant the stack is in the clear—then it belches a column of smoke.

Cut to the dayroom. Evening. Mengele, Kramer, and Mandel listen to the orchestra, along with their retinues. Fania, accompanying herself, is singing "Un bel di" in an agonized and therefore extraordinarily moving way. She is just finishing. When she does, Mandel stands, applauding—she is excited as a patron, a discoverer of talent, and turns to Kramer, who is also clapping his hands.

MANDEL: Did you ever hear anything more touching, Herr Commandant?

KRAMER: Fantastic. *To Mengele*: But Dr. Mengele's musical opinions are more expert, of course.

Cut to Fania, staring at the ultimate horror—their love for her music.

Cut to the entire dayroom.

MENGELE: I have rarely felt so totally—moved.

And he appears, in fact, to have been deeply stirred.

ALMA: You might thank the Commandant, Fania.

Fania tries to speak, can't, and nods instead—gratefully.

FANIA—*finally a whisper*: Danke schön, Herr Commandant.

KRAMER: I must tell you, Mademoiselle Fénelon . . .

FANIA: Excuse me, but my name is really not Fénelon. Fénelon was my mother's name.

MANDEL: What is your name, then?

FANIA: My father's name was Goldstein. I am Fania Goldstein. Excuse me, I didn't mean to interrupt, Herr Commandant.

KRAMER: You must learn to sing German songs.

ALMA: I will see that she learns immediately, Herr Commandant.

KRAMER, *continuing to Fania*: Originally, Mademoiselle, I opposed this idea of an orchestra, but I must say now that with singing of your quality, it is a consolation that feeds the spirit. It strengthens us for this difficult work of ours. *Very* good.

> He turns and goes out, followed by his retinue and Mengele. The orchestra is aware Fania has helped them remain in favor and thus alive.
> Mandel turns back at the door and beckons to Fania, who comes to her.

MANDEL: Is there anything you especially need?

FANIA, *out of her conflict, after a struggle*: A . . . toothbrush?

MANDEL, *gestures to Tchaikowska, who approaches*: You will send to Canada for some parcels. *To Fania*: With my compliments.

> Mandel exits.

FANIA, *to Tchaikowska*: To Canada?!

> *Cut to* a long shot of the smoking chimney.

> *Cut to* a counter set in open air beside another barracks. Behind it are the black-market girls—sleek, fed, laughing, busy trading with a few desperate-looking women who hand over a slice of bread for a comb or piece of soap. On the counter are perfumes, lotions, soap and a pile of used toothbrushes. These "Canadians" all have hair—Czechs, Poles, Dutch . . .

FIRST BLACK MARKETEER: Welcome to Canada. So you're the Frenchy singer—what would you like? *Fania picks up a toothbrush. Charlotte accompanies her.* That just came off the last transport—it's practically new and very clean—they were mostly Norwegians. That'll be a good slice of bread.

> The black marketeer holds out her hand. Fania takes out a chunk of bread. Charlotte intercepts, returning it to Fania.

CHARLOTTE: I said this is on the Chief!

BLACK MARKETEER, *cheerfully*: What's wrong with trying? *To Fania*: Here's your junk, stupid.

Set aside at one end of the counter are forty tiny packets in soiled and much-used paper. Charlotte and Fania load their arms.

Cut to the high excitement in the dayroom as the girls open their gift packages, which contain, in one case, a bit of butter and a pat of jam which a girl ever so carefully smears on a cracker-sized piece of bread, or an inch of sausage and a chip of chocolate to be savored for a full five minutes, and so forth.

Marianne, suffering, gobbles up her bread and jam in one gulp.

Fania nearby is swallowing. She takes out her toothbrush.

MARIANNE: You got a toothbrush!—can I see? *She takes it, examines it, reads words on the handle.* From Norway. Looks almost new. *Offering it back*: Nothing like having important friends, right?

Fania's hand stops in air. But then she takes the toothbrush, and forces herself to look directly into Marianne's eyes.

MARIANNE: Whoever that belonged to is probably up the chimney now. *Fania is silent.* So why are you superior?

FANIA: If I ever thought I was, I sure don't any more.

Etalina enters the shot . . . addressing all.

ETALINA: I'll say one thing, Fania—I feel a lot safer now that the Chief is so hot for you.

Some of the women laugh, titillated . . . the Poles loudest of all.

ETALINA: Although I wouldn't want to wake up in the morning next to that Nazi bitch's mug.

FANIA: I don't expect to. But it's not her face that disgusts me.

Esther speaks—a shaven Polish Jewess, angular, tight-faced.

ESTHER: Her face doesn't disgust you?

FANIA: No—I'm afraid she's a very beautiful woman, Esther.

ESTHER: That murderer you dare call beautiful?

Others react against Fania—"Shame!" "You toady!" "Just because she favors you!"

FANIA, *overriding*: What disgusts me is that a woman so beautiful can do what she is doing. Don't try to make her ugly, Esther . . . she's beautiful and human. We are the same species. And that is what's so hopeless about this whole thing.

MICHOU: What's the difference that she's human? There's still hope—because when this war is over Europe will be communist—and for that I want to live.

ESTHER: No. To see Palestine—that's why you have to live. You're Jewish women—*that's* your hope: to bring forth Jewish children in Palestine. You have no identity, Fania—and that's why you can call such a monster human and beautiful.

FANIA: I envy you both—you don't feel you have to solve the problem.

ESTHER, *anxiously, aggressively*: *What* problem! I don't see a problem!

FANIA: She is human, Esther. *Slight pause; she is looking directly into Esther's eyes.* Like you. Like me. You don't think that's a problem?

> Fania's eye is caught by Marianne slipping out the dayroom door.
>
> *Cut to* outside the barracks. While two kapos expectantly watch, Marianne opens a bar of chocolate they have given her and bites into it. They lead her around the corner of the barracks and out of sight. One of them has a bottle half-filled with wine.
>
> *Cut to* Fania, asleep in her bunk. Marianne appears, starts to climb in—she is tipsy—slips and lands on her behind on the floor with a scream. Women awaken.

ETALINA: At least let *us* get some rest, Busy-Ass.

MARIANNE, *to Etalina*: What's it to you? *To Fania*: Say!—your hair's coming back white!

FANIA: Come to bed, Marianne. . . .

MARIANNE: Oh, screw these idiots. . . .

VOICES: Shut up! Whore! I'm exhausted! She's disgusting! Somebody throw her out! Shut up!

MARIANNE, *to the whole lot*: Well, it so happens, one of them was a doctor from Vienna. . . .

ETALINA: She just went for a checkup!

MARIANNE: And he thinks we are never going to menstruate again! *Silence now.* Because of this . . . this fear every day and night . . . and the food . . . can sterilize . . .

> She looks around at their stricken faces. She climbs up, helped into her bunk by Fania.

Cut to a series of close-ups:

ESTHER, *praying quietly*: Shma Israel, adonai elohaynu . . .

Elzvieta crosses herself and prays quietly.

Other women are praying.

Fania is silent, staring, while beside her Marianne lies on her back asleep and snoring.

Cut to two kapos, carrying Paulette on a stretcher across the dayroom to the exit door. Paulette, the young cellist, is in high fever. Alma attempts to explain to the kapos in pidgin . . .

ALMA: Do you understand me? —she is musician, cellist, not to be gassed. To hospital, you understand? Typhus, you see? We need her. Well, do you understand or not! *At the door*: Wait!

Cut to Alma rushing over to Tauber, an SS officer, and Mala. Mala is the tall, striking Jewess, wearing the Star, but who appears to show no obsequiousness toward Tauber, the SS officer beside her. Kapos approach carrying Paulette on a stretcher.

ALMA: Excuse me, Herr Commandant Tauber—with your permission, would Mala instruct these men to be sure this girl is not . . . harmed? She is our cellist and must go to the hospital—she has high fever, typhus perhaps. I don't know what language they speak. . . .

Without waiting for Tauber's permission, Mala stops the kapos.

MALA: Parl' Italiano? *They shake their heads negatively.* Espagnol? *They shake their heads again.* Russky? *Again.*

KAPO: Romany.

MALA: Ah! *In Rumanian*: Be sure to take her to hospital, not death—she is a musician, they need her.

KAPO, *in Rumanian*: We understand.

They walk off with Paulette. Tauber and staff move off with Mala.

Cut to the dayroom. The orchestra members are clustered at the windows watching this.

MICHOU: Isn't she fantastic?—

FANIA, *amazed*: But she's wearing the Star!

MICHOU: Sure—that's Mala, she's their chief interpreter. She's Jewish but she's got them bulldozed.

FANIA: How's it possible?

Alma re-enters the dayroom, goes to her podium, leafs through score.

MICHOU: She's been here for years—since the camp was built—she escaped once; she and five others were supposed to be gassed, so they'd been stripped, and she got out through an air vent. Ended up stark naked going down a road past the Commandant's house. She's afraid of absolutely nothing, so when he stopped her she demanded some clothes; they got to talking, and he found out she speaks practically every language and made her an interpreter.

LIESLE, *proudly*: She's Belgian, you know—like me.

CHARLOTTE: She was in the Resistance. She even has a lover.

ETALINA: And handsome!

FANIA: Now you're kidding me.

ETALINA: It's true—Edek's his name—a Polish Resistance guy. He's got a job in the Administration.

MICHOU, *starry-eyed*: They're both unbelievable—they've saved people—a few anyway, and helped some. They're afraid of nothing!

ALMA: Fania! *From Alma's viewpoint we see the group turning to her.* Come here now and let us go through your Schubert song. *Fania comes to the piano, sits.* You must try the *ch* sound again—Dr. Mengele has a sensitive ear for the language, and it's his request, you know. Begin . . .

Fania sings a Schubert song with *"lachen"* in the verse, pronouncing "lacken."

ALMA: No, no, not "lacken,"—"la*ch*en . . . "

FANIA, *trying, but . . . :* Lacken.

ALMA: *Lachen*! *Lachen*! *Lachen*! Say it!

Alma's face is close to Fania's; Fania looks into Alma's eyes and with a sigh of angry defeat . . .

FANIA: *Lachen.*

ALMA: That's much better. I hope you won't ever be stupid enough to hate a *language*! Now the song once more . . . I want you perfect by Sunday. . . .

Fania, her jaw clamped, forces herself into the song.

Cut to the train platform. It is barely light. Freight-car doors roll open, and the deportees are hustled out. From within the dormitory we hear women yelling and screaming.

Cut to the dormitory. Tchaikowska, burly chief of the barracks, and other Blockawas are pulling Etalina out of her bunk by the ankles, and she lands with a bang on the floor. The other inmates are yelling. . . .

VOICES: Why can't you wake up like everybody else! Why are you always making trouble! and so on . . .

Alma appears on the scene with Fania nearby. Tchaikowska bangs a fist on Etalina's back.

ETALINA: I said I didn't hear you call me!

ALMA—*now she smashes Etalina across the face*: You're a spoiled brat! You will obey, d'you hear?

Alma's face, infuriated.

Cut to Alma's face. She is conducting. Great anxiety about the sounds coming forth. Suddenly she strides from the podium to Etalina. She is near hysteria as she bends over Etalina, who looks up at her in terror.

ALMA: Are you trying to destroy us? That is a B flat; do you know a B flat or don't you? *Etalina is cowering in terror.* I asked if you know B flat or if you do not!

With a blow she knocks Etalina off her chair.

ETALINA, *screaming—she is a teenager, a child*: I want my mother! Mama! Mama!

She collapses in tears. Fania goes to her, holds her.

MICHOU: You'd better get some discipline, Etalina. You're not going to make it on wisecracks.

Alma looks at Fania, a bit guiltily now that her anger has exploded, then goes out into her own room. Fania waits a second, then obediently follows her in and shuts the door.

Cut to Alma's room. Fania is massaging Alma's shoulders and neck as she sits in a chair by the window. Alma moves Fania's fingers to her temples, which she lightly massages. After a moment she has Fania massage her hands, and Fania sits before her doing this.

ALMA: Talk to me, Fania. *Fania keeps silent; wary of expressing herself.* There must be strict discipline. As it is, Dr. Mengele can just bear to listen to us. If we fall below a certain level anything is possible. . . . He's a violently changeable man. *Fania does not respond, only massages.* The truth is if it weren't for my name they'd have burned them up long ago; my father was first violin with the Berlin Opera, his string quartet played all over the world. . . .

FANIA: I know, Madame.

ALMA: That I, a Rosé, am conducting here is a . . .

FANIA: I realize that, Madame.

ALMA: Why do you resent me? You are a professional, you know what discipline is required; a conductor must be respected.

FANIA: But I think she can be loved, too.

ALMA: You cannot love what you do not respect. In Germany it is a perfectly traditional thing, when a musician is repeatedly wrong . . .

FANIA: To slap?

ALMA: Yes, of course! Furtwängler did so frequently, and his orchestra idolized him. *Fania keeping her silence, simply nods very slightly.* I need your support, Fania. I see that they look up to you. You must back up my demands on them. We will have to constantly raise the level of our playing or I . . . I really don't know how long they will tolerate us. Will you? Will you help me?

FANIA: I . . . I will tell you the truth, Madame—I really don't know how long I can bear this. *She sees resentment in Alma's eyes.* . . . I am trying my best, Madame, and I'll go on trying. But I feel sometimes that pieces of myself are falling away. And believe me, I recognize that your strength is probably what our lives depend on. . . .

ALMA: Then why do you resent me?

FANIA: I don't know! I suppose . . . maybe it's simply that . . . one wants to keep *something* in reserve; we can't . . . we can't really and truly wish to please them. I realize how silly it is to say that, but . . .

ALMA: But you *must* wish to please them, and with all your heart. You are an artist, Fania—you can't purposely do less than your best.

FANIA: But when one looks out the window . . .

ALMA: That is why I have told you *not* to! You have me wrong, Fania—you seem to think that I fail to see. But I *refuse* to see. Yes. And *you* must refuse!

FANIA—*nearly an outcry*: But what . . . *She fears it will sound accusatory.* . . . what will be left of me, Madame!

ALMA: Why . . . yourself, the artist will be left. And this is not new, is it? —what did it ever matter, the opinions of your audience? —or whether you approved their characters? You sang because it was in you to do! And more so now, when your life depends on it! Have you ever married?

FANIA: No, Madame.

ALMA: I was sure you hadn't—you married your art. I did marry . . . *Alma breaks off. She moves, finds herself glancing out the window, but quickly turns away.* . . . Twice. The first time to that . . . *She gestures ironically toward her violin case lying on her cot.* The second time to a man, a violinist, who only wanted my father's name to open the doors for him. But it was my fault—I married him because I pitied myself; I had never had a lover, not even a close friend. There is more than a violin locked in that case, there is a life.

FANIA: I couldn't do that, Madame, I need the friendship of a man.

ALMA—*slight pause*: I understand that, Fania. *She is moved by an impulse to open up.* Once I very nearly loved a man. We met in Amsterdam. The three good months of my life. He warmed me . . . like a coat. I think . . . I could have loved him.

FANIA: Why didn't you?

ALMA: They arrested me . . . as a Jew. It still astonishes me.

FANIA: Because you are so German?

ALMA: Yes. I am. *Slight pause.* In this place, Fania, you will have to be an artist and only an artist. You will have to concentrate on one thing only— to create all the beauty you are capable of. . . .

FANIA, *unable to listen further*: Excuse me, Madame . . .

She quickly pulls open the door and escapes into the dayroom; Alma is left in her conflict and her anger. She goes to her violin case on the bed, takes out the instrument. Some emotion has lifted her out of the moment; she walks out of the room.

Cut to the dayroom. Alma enters; the women come quickly out of their torpor, reach for their instruments. Alma halts before them and looks out over them. And with an expression of intense pride which also reprimands and attempts to lead them higher, she plays—and extraordinarily beautifully—the "Meditation" from *Thaïs*, perhaps.

Jew, Gentile, Pole, kapo—Etalina herself and Fania— everyone is captivated, subdued, filled with awe.

As the final crescendo begins, Frau Schmidt and two kapos armed with clubs enter. Everyone leaps up to attention.

FRAU SCHMIDT: Jews to the left, Aryans to the right!

KAPOS: Quick! Hop, hop! Move; quick; five by five!

In the milling around to form two groups, Marianne pushes through and just as the groups make an empty space between them, she pulls an uncomprehending Fania into that space, where they stand alone facing Frau Schmidt.

MARIANNE: She and I are only half.

FRAU SCHMIDT: Half! Half what?

MARIANNE: Half Jewish. Both our mothers were Aryan.

Frau Schmidt's face shows her perplexity as to the regulations in such cases. Alma steps out of the Jewish group and goes to her.

ALMA, *sotto voce, in order not to embarrass her*: Mixed race—are not to be gassed, I'm quite sure, Frau Schmidt. *But Fania overhears and is moved by gratitude and surprise.* But what is this selection for . . . if I may ask?

FRAU SCHMIDT—*her hostility to Alma is quite open*: You belong with the Jews, Madame. *Alma steps back into her group, humiliated but stoic.* Jews! Your hair is getting too long! Haircuts immediately! *To Fania and Marianne*: You two, follow me!

She makes a military about-face and goes out. The two women follow.

Cut to a tiny office in the administration building. The over-stuffed noncom is poring over a book of regulations open on a table as Fania and Marianne stand looking on. He lip-reads, his finger moving along the lines.

Now he finds something, nods his head appreciatively as his comprehension gains, then he looks at the women.

SERGEANT: In this case you are allowed to cut off the upper half of the Star of David.

Marianne reacts instantly, ripping a triangle off her coat. (The Star is actually two separate triangles superimposed.) Fania is uncertain, does nothing.

Cut to the dayroom. Much agitation: an impromptu sort of trial is taking place. Sides are taken with Marianne and Fania alone in the middle.

Fania and Marianne both have half-stars on their dresses. As they are attacked, Marianne reacts with far more anguish than Fania, who, although disturbed, is strong enough to remain apart from any group.

ESTHER: You've behaved like dirty goyim, you've dishonored the Jews in your families.

MARIANNE: But if it's the truth why should I hide it? I *am* only half. . . .

ETALINA: Maybe they'll only be half-gassed.

Laughter. Varya, who is standing with other Poles, steps out of the group.

VARYA: You ashamed to be Jews. You, filth. But you never be Aryan. God always spit on you. We Aryan, never you! *Spits.* Paa!

Her sister Poles guffaw and heavily nod agreement.

ESTHER: For once the Poles are right!

ETALINA: It's disgusting!—cutting the Star of David in half?

MARIANNE: Why not?—if we can avoid the gas?

FANIA: Since when have you all become such Jewish nationalists? Suddenly you're all such highly principled ladies?

ELZVIETA: Bravo! You get up on your high horse with them because you don't dare open your traps with anybody else!

FANIA: I'm sorry; your contempt doesn't impress me. Not when you've accepted every humiliation without one peep. We're just a convenience.

ESTHER: The blood of innocent Jews cries out against your treason!

FANIA: Oh, Esther, why don't you just shut up? I am sick of the Zionists-and-the-Marxists; the Jews-and-the-Gentiles; the Easterners-and-the-Westerners; the Germans-and-the-non-Germans; the French-and-the-non-French. I am sick of it, sick of it, sick of it! I am a woman, not a tribe! And I am humiliated! That is all I know.

She sits on a chair by the window, her face turned from them. After a silence . . .

MARIANNE: You're all just jealous. And anyway, we're just as much betraying the Catholics—our mothers were Catholic, after all.

Fania suddenly gets up and escapes through the door into the dormitory.

Cut to Fania, seated on a lower bunk, is sewing the upper half of her Star back on. Marianne enters and behind her some of the other arguers are approaching in curiosity.

MARIANNE: What are you doing that for? *Fania is silent.* Fania?

FANIA—*glances up at the group with resentment, then continues sewing*: I don't know. I'm doing it. So I'm doing it.

She sews angrily—angry at herself too.

Cut to the barracks "street" outside the dayroom; through windows we see the orchestra and Alma conducting a practice session—phrases are played, then repeated.
    The rhythm of a passing beam of the arc light ceaselessly surveys the camp, but here it is only an indirect brightening and darkening.
    Coming to the corner of the building, Fania turns into the adjacent street just as a hanging bulb overhead goes out. Shmuel is standing on a short ladder, then descends, leading a wire down with him which he busies himself peeling back to make a fresh connection. Fania hardly looks at him or he at her, this conversation being forbidden.
    The music continues in the background from within the dayroom.

SHMUEL: Behind you, in the wall.

Fania leans against the barracks wall; stuck in a joint between boards is a tiny folded piece of paper which she palms.

FANIA—*a whisper*: Thank you.

SHMUEL: Don't try to send an answer—it's too dangerous; just wants you to know he's here . . . your Robert. *She nods once, starts to leave.* Fania? They are gassing twelve thousand a day now. *Her face drains. He goes up the ladder with wire.* Twelve thousand angels fly up every day.

FANIA: Why do you keep telling me these things? What do you want from me!

Shmuel makes the bulb go on, the light flaring on the wild and sweet look in his face. He looks up.

SHMUEL: Look with your eyes—the air is full of angels! You mustn't stop looking, Fania!

He perplexes and unnerves her; she claps hands over her ears and hurries along the barracks wall. As she turns the corner she nearly collides with Tchaikowska, who is enjoying a cigarette. She is standing next to the door to her own room. Fania gives her a nod, starts to pass, when the door opens; a kapo comes out buttoning his shirt.

TCHAIKOWSKA: Two more cigarettes—you took longer this time.

KAPO: I'm broke—give you two more next time.

Marianne comes through this door. She is eating meat off a bone. She sees Fania, is slightly surprised, but goes on eating. The kapo gives her ass a squeeze and walks away.
Tchaikowska goes into the room.
Fania sees into the room—Tchaikowska is straightening the rumpled bed in what is obviously her room.

Cut to a barracks street. Fania catches up with Marianne, who is stashing the bone with some slivers of meat still on it in her pocket.

FANIA: At least share some of it with the others—for your own sake, so you don't turn into an animal altogether!

MARIANNE: Jealous?

She walks away, flaunting her swinging backside, and enters the dormitory.

Cut to Fania playing the piano with the orchestra. (A light piece—airy, popular music.) The keyboard starts tilting. The orchestra stops, breaking off the music.
Four kapos are turning the piano on its side, onto a dolly.
Fania rescues her music and skitters out of the way, astonished and frightened. Alma and the orchestra look on in silent terror as the piano is simply rolled out of the building through the door to the street. Does it mean the end of the orchestra? All eyes go to Alma, who is clearly shocked and frightened. After a moment, as though nothing had happened:

ALMA: Let us turn now to . . . to ah—*she leafs through music on podium*—the Beethoven . . .

GISELLE: Madame?—if I could make a suggestion . . .

ALMA: I'm sure this will soon be explained . . .

GISELLE, *desperately*: But why wait till they "explain" it, Madame! I used to play a lot in movie houses . . . on Rue du Four and Boulevard Raspail . . . And I could teach you all kinds of Bal Musette numbers . . . you know, real live stuff that won't bore them. I mean, listen just for a minute!

She plays on her violin—her face perspiring with anxiety—a Bal Musette, lively, dance music. . . .

Enter Frau Lagerführerin Mandel, and Commandant Kramer, with two SS aides.

All but Giselle spring to attention.

TCHAIKOWSKA: Attention!

Giselle looks up from her violin, nearly falls back in a faint at the threatening sight of the big brass, and stands at rigid attention.

MANDEL: At ease. The officers have decided to keep the piano in their club for the use of the members.

KRAMER, *to Alma*: I thought you could manage without it, Madame.

ALMA: Of course, Herr Commandant . . . it was only a little extra sound to fill out, but not imperative at all. We hope the officers will enjoy it.

KRAMER: Which one is Greta, the Dutch girl?

An accordion squeaks . . . it is in Greta's hands.

ALMA: Come!

Greta comes out of the orchestra, accordion in hand. Kramer moves, inspecting her fat, square body. She hardly dares glance at him, her eyes lowered.

KRAMER: Open your mouth. *In terror she does so. He peers in at her teeth.* Do you have any disease?

GRETA—*a scared whisper*: No, Herr Commandant.

KRAMER, *to Alma*: Dr. Mengele tells me she's not a very good player.

ALMA: Not very good, no, although not too bad—but she . . . she works quite hard. . . .

KRAMER: But you could manage without her.

ALMA, *unwillingly*: Why . . . yes, of course, Herr Commandant.

Cut to Fania, flaring with anger at Alma.

Cut to Kramer, signaling one of the SS aides, who steps forward to Greta, preparing to take her off. Greta stiffens.

KRAMER, *to Greta*: My wife needs someone to look after our little daughters. You look like a nice clean girl.

General relief; Greta is simply rigid. Mandel takes a coat from the second SS aide and hands it to Greta, who quickly and gratefully puts it on. The first aide leads her to exit, and she nearly stumbles in her eagerness to keep up with him, her accordion left behind.

KRAMER, *turning to Alma:* This Sunday you will play in the hospital for the sick and the mental patients. You will have the Beethoven ready.

ALMA: Yes, Herr Commandant. I must ask your . . . toleration, if I may— our cellist has typhus and now without the accordion we may sound a little wanting in the lower . . .

KRAMER: I will send one of the cellists from the men's orchestra—they have several from the Berlin Philharmonic—he can teach one of your violinists by Sunday.

ALMA—*the idea knocks the breath out of her, but . . . :* Why . . . yes, of course, I'm sure we can teach one of our girls by Sunday, yes.

> Kramer turns and strolls out.

MANDEL, *as though the orchestra should feel honored:* It will be very interesting, Madame—Dr. Mengele wants to observe the effects of music on the insane.

ALMA: Ah so!—well, we will do our very best indeed.

> Mandel walks over to Fania.

MANDEL, *pleasantly:* And how are you, these days?

FANIA, *swallowing her feelings:* I am quite well . . . of course, we are all very hungry most of the time—that makes it difficult.

MANDEL: I offered to send an extra ration this week before the concert on Sunday, but Madame Alma feels it ought to be earned, as a reward afterwards. You disagree?

> Fania glances past Mandel to Alma, who is near enough to have overheard as she turns pages in a score. Alma shoots her a fierce warning glance.

FANIA, *lowering her gaze in defeat:* It's . . . not for me to agree or not . . . with our conductor.

> *Cut to* Alma's room. Alma is pacing up and down, absolutely livid, while Fania stands with lowered gaze—this could be her end.

ALMA: How do you dare make such a comment to her!

FANIA: I don't understand, Madame—I simply told her that we were hungry. . . .

ALMA: When they have managed to play a single piece without mistakes I will recommend an extra ration—but *I* will decide that, do you understand? *Fania is silent.* There cannot be two leaders. Do you agree or don't you?

FANIA: Why are you doing this?

Alma doesn't understand.

FANIA: We are hungry, Madame! And I saw a chance to tell her! Am I to destroy every last human feeling? She asked and I told her!

ALMA, *a bit cowed, but not quite*: I think we understand each other—that will be all now. *Fania doesn't move.* Yes?—what is it?

FANIA: Nothing. *Makes a move to go.* I am merely trying to decide whether I wish to live.

ALMA: Oh come, Fania—no one dies if they can help it. You must try to be more honest with yourself. Now hurry and finish the Beethoven orchestration—we must give them a superb concert on Sunday.

> Alma walks to a table where her scores are, and sits to study them. Fania has been reached, and turns and goes out, a certain inner turmoil showing on her face.

> *Cut to* Etalina, being coached by a young cellist, a thin young man with thick glasses and shaven head. Most of the orchestra is watching them avidly—watching *him*, the women standing around in groups at a respectful distance, the Poles also.
> His hands, in close shots, are sensuous and alive and male. The camera bounces such shots off the women's expressions of fascination and desire and deprivation.
> Fania tears her gaze from him, and tries to work on her orchestrations—on a table.

> *Cut to* the cellist's hands. He is demonstrating a tremolo. Etalina tries, but she is awkward. He adjusts her arm position.

> *Cut to* Paulette, just entering the dayroom from outside. She is barely strong enough to stand. Michou rushes to her with a cry of joy. Fania sees her, and leaps up to go to her; and Elzvieta also and Etalina.

ETALINA: Paulette! Thank God, I don't have to learn this damned instrument!

> *Cut to* the group helping Paulette to a chair; Paulette is an ascetic-looking, aristocratic young lady.

FANIA: Are you sure you should be out?

ELZVIETA: Was it typhus or what?

ETALINA: She still looks terrible.

FANIA: Sssh! Paulette? What is it?

For Paulette is trying to speak but has hardly the strength to. Everyone goes silent, awaiting her words.

PAULETTE: You're to play on Sunday . . .

ETALINA: In the hospital, yes, we know.

FANIA: You don't look to me like you should be walking around, Paulette. . . .

PAULETTE, *stubborn, gallant, she grips Fania's hand to silence her*: They plan . . . to gas . . . all the patients . . . after . . . the concert.

A stunned silence.

FANIA: How do you know this?

PAULETTE: One of the SS women . . . warned me. . . . I knew her once. . . . She used to be . . . one of the . . . chambermaids in our house. So I got out.

Alma enters from her room, sees the gathering, then sees Paulette.

ALMA: Paulette! How wonderful! Are you all better now? We're desperate for you! We're doing the Beethoven Fifth on Sunday!

Paulette gets to her feet, wobbling like a mast being raised.

FANIA: She's had to walk from the hospital, Madame—could she lie down for a bit?

PAULETTE: No! I . . . I can.

She gets to the cello, sits, as though the room is whirling around for her. Etalina rushes and hands her the bow. The orchestra quickly sit in their places.

ALMA, *at podium*: From the beginning, please.

The Beethoven Fifth begins. Paulette, on the verge of pitching forward, plays the cello. The pall of fear is upon them all now. Fania has resumed her place at the table with her orchestrations. She bends over them, shielding her eyes, a pencil in hand.

She is moved to glance at the window. There, just outside it, she sees . . .

Shmuel, at the window. He is pointing at his eyes, which he opens extra wide.

Cut to Fania, startled. Then, lowering her hands from her eyes, forces herself to see, to look—first at Paulette, and the orchestra, and finally at . . .

Alma, conducting. She is full of joyful tension, pride, waving her arms, snapping her head in the rhythm and humming the tune loudly, oblivious to everything else.

Cut to Paulette feverishly trying to stay with the music; her desperation—which those around her understand—is the dilemma of rehearsing to play for the doomed.

Cut to Fania, at one end of the dormitory corridor between bunks, wringing out a bra and heavy stockings over a pail. Her expression is tired, deadened; she has been changing, much life has gone from her eyes. Nearby, in dimness, Tchaikowska and another Blockawa are lying in an embrace, kissing; Tchaikowska glances over, and with a sneer . . .

TCHAIKOWSKA: Now you do her laundry? —the contessa?

Fania takes the bra and stockings down corridor to Paulette's bunk, hangs them to dry there. Paulette is lying awake, but weak.

PAULETTE: Thank you. I'm troubled . . . whether I should have told the other patients—about what's going to happen. What do you think? *Fania shakes her head and shrugs.* Except, what good would it do them to know?

FANIA: I have no answers anymore, Paulette.

VOICES: Shut up, will you? Trying to sleep! Sssh!

FANIA: Better go to sleep . . .

Across the corridor, Charlotte is staring at Michou with something like surprise in her expression, self-wonder. Michou turns her head and sees Charlotte staring at her, and shyly turns away.

Fania now climbs into her own bunk, lies there openeyed. Other women are likewise not asleep, but some are.

Fania lies there in her depression.

She shuts her eyes against the sounds from outside—the coupling of freight cars, a surge of fierce dogs barking, shouts—her face depleted. Now Charlotte's head appears at the edge of the bunk. Fania turns to her.

Charlotte timorously asks if she may slide in beside her.

CHARLOTTE: May I?

Fania slides over to make room. Charlotte lies down beside her.

CHARLOTTE, *with a certain urgency*: I just wanted to ask you . . . about Michou.

Now their eyes meet. Fania is surprised, curious.

Charlotte is innocently fascinated, openly in love but totally unaware of it.

CHARLOTTE: What do you know about her? I see you talking sometimes together.

FANIA: Well . . . she's militant; sort of engaged to be married; the kind that has everything planned in life. Why?

CHARLOTTE: I don't know! She just seems so different from the others— so full of courage. I love how she always stands up for herself to the SS.

FANIA—*slight pause; she knows now that she is cementing an affair*: That's what she says about you.

CHARLOTTE, *surprised, excited*: She's spoken about me?

FANIA: Quite often. She especially admired your guts. *Slight pause.* And your beauty.

Charlotte looks across the aisle and sees Michou, who is asleep.

Cut to Michou, emphasizing her hungered look in sleep, her smallness and fragility.

Cut to Fania and Charlotte.

CHARLOTTE: She's so beautiful, don't you think? I love her looks.

FANIA: It would be quicker if you told me what you don't like about her.

CHARLOTTE, *shyly laughing*: I don't understand what is happening to me, Fania. Just knowing she's sleeping nearby, that she'll be there tomorrow when I wake—I think of her all day. I could see her face all through my fever . . . I just adore her, Fania.

FANIA: No. You love her, Charlotte.

CHARLOTTE: You mean . . . ?

FANIA: You're seventeen, why not? At seventeen what else is there but love?

CHARLOTTE: But it's impossible.

Fania softly laughs.

CHARLOTTE: Are you laughing at me?

FANIA: After all you've seen and been through here, is that such a disaster?

CHARLOTTE: How stupid I am—I never thought of it as . . .

FANIA: In this place to feel at all may be a blessing.

CHARLOTTE: Do you ever have such . . . feelings?

FANIA, *shaking her head*: I have nothing. Nothing at all, anymore. Go now, you're still not well, you should sleep.

> Charlotte starts to slide out, then turns back and suddenly kisses Fania's hand gratefully.

FANIA—*she smiles, moved*: What a proper young lady you must have been!

> Charlotte shyly grins, confessing this, and moves away down the aisle. She pauses as she starts to pass Michou. The latter opens her eyes. Both girls stare in silence at one another— really looking inward, astonished at themselves. Now Michou tenuously reaches out her hand, which Charlotte touches with her own.
>
> *Cut to* Fania, observing them. A deep, desperate concern for herself is on her face. She closes her eyes and turns over to sleep.
> 　　At the distant drone of bombers, Fania slowly opens her eyes. Turns on her back, listening.
>
> *Cut to* a series of close-ups: Michou, Paulette, Liesle, Etalina, and others; they are opening their eyes, listening, trying to figure out the nationality of the planes.
> 　　Now the Polish Blockawas, some in bed with each other, do the same.
>
> *Cut to* Fania. She has gone to a window and is looking out onto the "street." The sound of the bombers continues.
>
> *Cut to* the barracks "street," SS guards in uniform carrying rifles—five or six of them converging and looking upward worriedly.
>
> *Cut to* Fania, turning from the window and momentarily facing the apprehensive, questioning stares of the Blockawas. She starts to pass them; Tchaikowska reaches out and grasps her wrist.

TCHAIKOWSKA, *pointing upward*: American? English? *Fania shrugs, doesn't know. Tchaikowska releases her.* Too late for you anyway.

Fania's face is totally expressionless—yet in this impacted look is torment that another human could do this.

FANIA: Maybe it is too late for the whole human race, Tchaikowska.

She walks past, heading for the dayroom, not her bunk.

Cut to Fania, under a single bulb, alone in the dayroom. She has pencil in hand, orchestrating—but she looks off now, unable to concentrate. Elzvieta appears beside her, sits.

ELZVIETA: So it's going to end after all. *Fania gives her an uncomprehending glance.* Everyone tries to tell you their troubles, don't they.

FANIA: I don't know why, I can't help anyone.

ELZVIETA: You are someone to trust, Fania—maybe it's that you have no ideology, you're satisfied just to be a person.

FANIA: I don't know what I am anymore, Elzvieta. I could drive a nail through my hand, it would hardly matter. I am dying by inches, I know it very well—I've seen too much. *Tiredly wipes her eyes.* Too much and too much and too much . . .

ELZVIETA: I'm one of the most successful actresses in Poland. *Fania looks at her, waiting for the question; Elzvieta, in contrast to Fania, has long hair.* My father was a count; I was brought up in a castle; I have a husband and Marok, my son who is nine years old. *Slight pause.* I don't know what will happen to us, Fania—you and I, before the end. . . .

FANIA, *with a touch of irony*: Are you saying good-bye to me?

ELZVIETA, *with difficulty*: I only want one Jewish woman to understand. . . . I lie here wondering if it will be worse to survive than not to. For me, I mean. When I first came here I was sure that the Pope, the Christian leaders did not know; but when they found out they would send planes to bomb out the fires here, the rail tracks that bring them every day. But the trains keep coming and the fires continue burning. Do you understand it?

FANIA: Maybe other things are more important to bomb. What are we anyway but a lot of women who can't even menstruate anymore—and some scarecrow men?

ELZVIETA, *suddenly kissing Fania's hand*: Oh Fania—try to forgive me!

FANIA: You! Why? What did you ever do to me? You were in the Resistance, you tried to fight against this, why should you feel such guilt? It's the other ones who are destroying us—and they only feel innocent! It's all a joke, don't you see? It's all meaningless, and I'm afraid you'll never change that, Elzvieta! *Elzvieta gets up, rejected, full of tears.* I almost pity a person like you more than us. You will survive, and everyone around you will be innocent, from one end of Europe to the other.

Offscreen, we hear the sounds of a train halting, shouts, debarkation noises. Elzvieta turns her eyes toward a window.

Cut to a convoy debarking in the first dawnlight. SS and kapos and dogs.

Cut to Elzvieta, riven by the sight now, sinking to her knees at a chair, and crossing herself, praying. Fania studies her for a moment . . . then she goes back to work on her orchestration, forcing herself to refuse this consolation, this false hope and sentiment. She inscribes notes. Something fails in her; she puts down pencil.

FANIA: My memory is falling apart; I'm quite aware of it, a little every day . . . I can't even remember if we got our ration last night . . . did we?

Tchaikowska appears from the dormitory door—she is drinking from a bowl. Now she walks to the exit door of the day-room, opens it, and throws out the remainder of milk in the bowl, wiping the bowl with a rag.

Elzvieta, still on her knees, watches Tchaikowska returning to the dormitory; she tries to speak calmly. . . .

ELZVIETA: You throw away milk, Tchaikowska?

TCHAIKOWSKA: It was mine.

ELZVIETA: Even so . . .

TCHAIKOWSKA: Our farm is two kilometers from here—they bring it to me, my sisters.

ELZVIETA: But even so . . . to throw it away, when . . .

She breaks off. Tchaikowska looks slightly perplexed.

TCHAIKOWSKA: You saying it's not my milk?

ELZVIETA: Never mind.

TCHAIKOWSKA, *tapping her head*: You read too many books, makes you crazy.

She exits into the dormitory. Elzvieta swallows in her hunger, and, as Fania watches her, she bends her head and more fervently, silently prays.

Cut to the barracks "street," silent and empty for a moment; suddenly the blasts of sirens, whistles, and the howling of pursuit dogs. From all corners SS guards and dog handlers explode onto the street. They are in a chaotic hunt for someone.

Prisoners are being turned out of barracks onto the "street," lined up to be counted, hit, kicked. . . .

Cut to the hunters, crashing into the dayroom with dogs howling. Blockawas are coming out of the dormitory, throwing on clothes. SS women accompany the guards. Alma comes out of her room questioningly.

Cut to the orchestra, fleeing from bunks in the dormitory as hunters rip off blankets, overturn mattresses—screaming in fear of dogs, shouting.

Cut to the players, being driven outside into the "street."

Cut to the "street." Scurrying to form ranks and trying to dress at the same time the players are calling out their names and coming to attention. Before them stand an SS officer and a dog handler beside Tchaikowska, who is checking off a roster she holds.

Alma stands at attention before the officer.

TCHAIKOWSKA: All accounted for, Mein Herr.

SS OFFICER, *to Madame Alma*: Do you know Mala?

ALMA: Mala? No, but I have seen her accompanying the Commandant, of course—as an interpreter.

SS OFFICER: She has had no contact at all with your players?

ALMA: No, no, she has never been inside our barracks, Herr Kapitän.

The SS officer now walks off, followed by the handler and dog. Michou is the first to realize.

MICHOU: Mala's escaped! I bet she's gotten out!

The orchestra is electrified. . . .

CHARLOTTE, *to another*: Mala's out!

Blockawas are pushing them back into barracks.

PAULETTE: Fania!—did you hear!

Cut to the "Canada" girls. Deals are going on at their tables, and a girl prisoner comes hurrying up. A quick whisper to one of the dealers.

GIRL: Mala got out . . . and Edek too!

DEALER: With Edek? How!?

GIRL: They got SS uniforms somehow, and took off!

> Business stops as three or four dealers cross themselves and bow their heads in prayer.
>
> *Cut to* Alma, at the podium going through a score, with Fania alongside her pointing out something on it.
>   The following lines of dialogue are all in close intimate shots—since they dare not too openly discuss the escape. (All are in their chairs, instruments ready for rehearsal.)

CHARLOTTE: What a romance! Imagine, the two of them together—God!

MICHOU: I saw him once, he's gorgeous—blond, and beautiful teeth. . . .

LIESLE: She's a Belgian, like me. . . .

ESTHER: What Belgian? She's Jewish, like all of us. . . .

LIESLE: Well, I mean . . .

ELZVIETA: Edek is a Pole, though—and they're going to tell the world what's happening here.

ETALINA: Imagine—if they could put a bomb down that chimney!

ELZVIETA: Now the world will know! Lets play for them. The Wedding March!

> She raises her violin.

CHARLOTTE, *readying her bow on the violin—devoutly*: For Mala and Edek!

MICHOU: Mala and Edek!

> Etalina, on time for once, readies her instrument.
>
> *Cut to* Shmuel, bowing to Alma, his toolbox on his shoulder.

SHMUEL: I'm supposed to diagram the wiring, Madame. I won't disturb you.

> Alma nods, lifts her baton, and starts the number.
>   Shmuel, as the number proceeds, has a piece of paper on which he is tracing the wiring. He follows along one wall to the table in a corner of the room, where Fania is seated with a score she is following, pencil in hand.
>   Fania senses Shmuel is lingering at a point near her; and as he approaches her, his eyes on the wiring, he exposes the paper in his hand for her to read. She glances at Alma at the end of the room, then leans a little . . .

Cut to the note, reading: ALLIES LANDED IN FRANCE.
Shmuel's hand crumples the paper.

Cut to Shmuel, swallowing the note. Then taking his toolbox
and slinging it onto his shoulder, he hurriedly limps away and
goes out the exit without turning back.
Fania turns and looks out the window, and sees . . .
The by-now familiar arrival of new prisoners as seen
from the dayroom window. Shmuel walks out of the shot, his
place taken by . . .
Mandel—who is leading Ladislaus, a four-year-old boy,
away from his mother, who is at the edge of a crowd of new
arrivals, watching, not knowing what to make of it. The
mother now calls to him; we can't hear her through the window. Ladislaus is beautiful, and Mandel seems delighted as
she gives him a finger to hold on to.
Note: The character of this particular crowd of prisoners
is somewhat different—they are Polish peasant families, not
Jews. They are innocently "camping" between barracks buildings, far less tensely than the Jews on arrival, and the kids are
running about playing, even throwing a ball. Infants are suck-
ling; improvised little cooking fires, etc. . . . So that Ladislaus's
mother is only apprehensive as she calls to him, not hysterical
at his going off with Mandel.

Cut to the orchestra, continuing to play. Etalina is turning with
a look of open fear from the window; she leans to Elzvieta
beside her and unable to contain herself, whispers into her ear.

Alma sees this breach of discipline and . . .

ALMA, *furiously*: Etalina!

The music breaks off.

ETALINA, *pointing outside*: Those are Poles, not Jews. . . . They're Aryans, Madame!

MICHOU: Why not? Hitler always said they would kill off the Poles to
make room for Germans out there.

ETALINA: But look at them, there must be thousands. . . . They'd never
gas that many Aryans! *To Alma*: I think they're going to give them these
barracks, Madame!

Mandel and Ladislaus enter.
Silence. Mandel now picks up Ladislaus to show him off
to the orchestra.

MANDEL: Isn't he beautiful?

Only Tchaikowska and other Blockawas purr and smile. The orchestra sits in silence, not knowing what to make of this or Etalina's theory.

MANDEL, *to Alma*: What's the matter with them?

ALMA: It's nothing, Frau Mandel—there seems to be a rumor that these Aryan Poles will be given our barracks. . . .

MANDEL: Oh, not at all, Madame—in fact, I can tell you that there will be no further selections from within our camp. Of course we have no room for new arrivals—so for them . . . there will be other arrangements.

> *Cut to* Fania, turning out toward the window; she sees a line of trucks loading the peasants for gassing.

> *Cut to* the child's mother being pushed aboard—but now she is fighting to stay off the truck and looking desperately about for her child.

> *Cut to* Mandel, now fairly surrounded with players who, in their relief, can now express feeling for the beautiful child. Featured here is Marianne, who is chanting a nursery rhyme and tickling his cheek. . . .

MARIANNE: Hoppa, hoppa, Ladislaus
        Softly as a little mouse . . .

> Mandel, with an almost girlishly innocent laugh, presses the child's face against her own. Then putting him down, and bending to him, holding his hand.

MANDEL: And now we are going to get you a nice new little suit, and shoes, and a sweet little shirt. *She gives a perfectly happy, proud glance at the orchestra.* Work hard now—we are all expecting an especially fine concert for the hospital on Sunday! *To child*: Come along.

> She exits with Ladislaus hanging on to her finger.

> *Cut to* the "street," teeming with life a few moments before, now totally cleansed of people. Mandel leads the boy so as to avoid the dying embers of cooking fires, other debris left by the crowd, bundles, cookpots. . . .
>
> Kapos are policing the area, throwing debris into hand-drawn wagons. A kapo picks up a ball, and as Mandel approaches he bows a little and offers it to her. She accepts it and hands it to Ladislaus and walks on, tenderly holding his hand.

Cut to the players, clustered at the door and windows, watching Mandel going away. They are all confused, yet attracted by this show of humanity.

GISELLE: So she's a human being after all!

ESTHER: She is? Where's the mother?

ETALINA: Still—in a way, Esther . . . I mean at least she adores the child.

ESTHER, *with a wide look of alarm to all*: What's happening here . . . ?

PAULETTE: All she said was that . . .

ESTHER, *shutting her ears with her hands*: One Polack kid she saves and suddenly she's human? What is happening here!

From the podium, Alma calmly, sternly summons them with the tapping of her baton.

ALMA: From the beginning, please! We have a great deal to do before Sunday.

Silently they seat themselves. And Beethoven's Fifth begins.

Cut to the searchlight from a tower, sweeping the street. Sirens sound and the searchlight is extinguished.

Cut to Marianne, singing; breaks off as the sirens sound. And all lights go out.
As the sirens die out, bombers take over.
The players sit waiting in the dark, eyes turned upward toward the sound. As the sound rises to crescendo, Alma exits into her room; and as she is closing the door she catches Fania's eye. Fania rises, approaches the door.

Cut to Alma's room. Still in darkness, Alma sits. The bombers are fading.

ALMA: I will be leaving you after the Sunday concert, Fania. *Fania is surprised.* They are sending me on a tour to play for the troops. I wanted you to be first to hear the news. *A different camera angle reveals the excitement and pride in her expression.* I am going to be released, Fania! Can you imagine it? I'll play what I like and as I like. They said . . . *Elated now, filling herself*: they said a musician of my caliber ought not be wasted here! . . . What's the matter? I thought you'd be happy for me.

FANIA: Well, I am, of course. But you'll be entertaining men who are fighting to keep us enslaved, won't you.

ALMA: But that is not the point! I . . . *Only an instant's difficulty.* I will play for German soldiers.

FANIA, *changing the hopeless subject*: And what about us? We're going to continue, aren't we?

ALMA: I have suggested you to replace me.

FANIA—*nods, consenting*: Well . . . *A move to leave*. I hope . . . it ends soon for all of us.

> She turns to grasp the doorknob.

ALMA: Why are you trying to spoil my happiness?

> Fania turns to her, trying to plumb her.

ALMA: I will be playing for honorable men, not these murderers here! Soldiers risk their lives . . . !

FANIA: Why do you need my approval? If it makes you happy then enjoy your happiness.

ALMA: Not all Germans are Nazis, Fania! You are nothing but a racialist if you think so!

FANIA: Alma—you are German, you are free—what more do you want! I agree, it is an extraordinary honor—the only Jew to play a violin for the German Army! My head will explode . . . !

> She pulls the door open just as SS Frau Schmidt walks up to it. Shock. Schmidt is the powerhouse who runs the clothing depot and who knocked Fania down earlier on for speaking out of line.

ALMA: Why . . . Frau Schmidt . . . come in . . . please!

> The lights suddenly go on. All glance up, noting this wordlessly.

SCHMIDT: I wanted to extend my congratulations, Madame Rosé—I have just heard the great news.

ALMA, *ravished*: Oh, thank you, thank you, Frau Schmidt. This is very moving to me, especially coming from you.

SCHMIDT: Yes, but I always express my feelings. I would like you to join me for dinner tonight—a farewell in your honor?

ALMA: I . . . I am overwhelmed, Frau Schmidt. Of course.

SCHMIDT: At eight, then?—in my quarters.

ALMA: Oh, I'll be there. . . . Thank you, thank you.

> Schmidt exits. Now, eyes glistening with joy, Alma turns to Fania.

ALMA: Now . . . now you see! That woman, I can tell you, has tried everything to be transferred . . . she is desperate to get out of here, and yet she has the goodness to come and wish me well on my departure.

FANIA, *stunned*: Well I certainly never expected that of her. . . . But who knows what's in the human heart?

ALMA: You judge people, Fania, you are terribly harsh.

Alma is now sprucing herself up for dinner, brushing her skirt, straightening her blouse. . . .

FANIA: And Mandel saved that child. Maybe they figure they're losing the war, so . . .

ALMA, *at the height of her hopes for herself*: Why must everything have a worm in it? Why can't you accept the little hope there is in life?

She is now putting on her coat.

FANIA: I'm all mixed up. Schmidt wanting to get out is really unbelievable, Alma—she's gotten rich running the black market; she's robbed every woman who's landed here . . . every deal in the place has her hand in it. . . .

ALMA, *extending her hand*: I am leaving in the morning, Fania—if we don't see each other . . . Thank you for your help.

FANIA, *taking her hand*: You are totally wrong about practically everything, Alma—but I must say you probably saved us all. And I thank you from my heart.

ALMA: You can thank my refusal to despair, Fania.

FANIA: Yes, I suppose that's true.

Cut to an honor guard, and SS at attention.

The whole orchestra is filling into this room through a doorway. They are in their finest; atmosphere is hushed, eyes widened with curiosity, incredulity at this whole affair.

For at center stands a coffin, flowers on it, the top open. But the orchestra is ranged some yards from it.

When they have all assembled, enter Commandant Kramer, Dr. Mengele, other brass—

And finally Mandel, her finger in the hand of little Ladislaus, who is now dressed in a lovely blue suit, and linen shirt, and tie, and good shined shoes, and holding a teddy bear.

First Kramer, Mengele, Mandel, and the other brass step up and look mournfully into the coffin. Now the orchestra is ordered to pay its respects by a glance from Mandel to Fania.

Cut to Mandel, her eyes filling with tears.

Cut to the orchestra. A feeling of communion; they are starting to weep, without quite knowing why.

Cut to Alma—in the coffin. Fania looks down at Alma dead— she is bewildered, horrified. Then she moves off, her place taken by Paulette, then others. . . . The sound of keening is beginning as they realize it is Alma who has died.

Cut to the black market. Fania is pretending to trade a thick slice of bread for some soap with the chief black marketeer, a brazen girl who is smelling the bread offered.

FANIA: What happened?

BLACK MARKETEER: Schmidt poisoned her at dinner.

FANIA: How do you know!

BLACK MARKETEER: They shot her this morning.

FANIA: Schmidt!?

BLACK MARKETEER—*nods*: Nobody was getting out if she couldn't. 'Specially a Jew.

FANIA: Then she really wanted out!

BLACK MARKETEER: Well, she'd made her pile, why not?

Both their heads suddenly turn to the same direction at a booming sound in the distance.

BLACK MARKETEER, *looking questioningly at Fania*: That thunder or artillery?

They both turn again, listening in the midst of the market.

Cut to Olga, the Ukranian accordionist, who has apparently inherited the conductorship; she is robot-like in her arm-waving as she leads them in the Fifth Symphony—but it all falls to pieces, and Fania hurries up to the podium.

OLGA, *before Fania can get a word out*: No! I have been appointed and I am going to conduct!

FANIA: Now listen to me!

OLGA: No! I am kapo now and I order you to stop interfering!

FANIA: Olga, dear—you can barely read the notes, you have no idea how to bring in the instruments!

OLGA: Go back to your seat!

FANIA: You'll send us to the gas! Mengele will be there on Sunday—he won't stand for this racket—it's nonsensical! Now let me rehearse, and on Sunday you can stand up in front and wave your arms, but at least we'll be rehearsed!

ETALINA: Hey!—sssh!

> All turn to listen . . . once again there is the sound of a distant booming.

ETALINA: God . . . you suppose Mala and Edek found the Russians and are leading them here?

GISELLE: I bet! That was artillery. The Russians are famous for their artillery . . . !

OLGA: All right, listen! *She is desperately trying to fill out an image of authority.* I know a number. It's very famous with us in the Ukraine. We are going to play it. First I.

> Olga takes up her accordion and launches into a "Laughing Song," a foot-stomper polka, full of "Ha-ha-ha, hee-hee-hee," etc.
>
> Orchestra looks at her, appalled, some of them starting to giggle.
>
> Blockawas led by Tchaikowska appear and, loving it, begin doing polka with one another, hands clapping. . . .
>
> There is sharp whistling outside.
>
> Tchaikowska hurries out into the street as players go to the windows. . . .
>
> *Cut to* a gallows. The hanging of Mala and Edek. They have both been horribly beaten, can barely stand. Mala stumbles to her knees but flings away the hand of the executioner and stands by herself under the noose.
>
> The camera now turns out . . . picking up the immense crowd of prisoners forced to watch the executions.
>
> *Cut to* prisoners, en masse—in fact, the whole camp, tens of thousands, a veritable city of the starved and humiliated, ordered to watch the execution. This is a moment of such immense human import—for one after another, in defiance, they dare to bare their heads before the two doomed lovers and create a sea of shaven heads across a great space, while SS men and kapos club at them to cover themselves.
>
> *Cut to* the gallows—and the drop. Both Mala and Edek are hanging.
>
> *Cut to* the sky.

Dissolve from sky to rain.

Cut to the dayroom at night. Rain is falling on the windows. Girls are practicing in a desultory way, breaking off in mid-note to talk quietly together. Fania is at her table; she is playing with a pencil, staring at nothing, her face deeply depressed, deadened.

> Now Michou, who is at another window a few yards away, calls in a loud whisper . . .

MICHOU, *pointing outside*: Fania!

Fania looks out her window.

Cut to Marianne, on the "street," just parting from the executioner, a monstrous large man, who grimly pats her ass as she rushes into the barracks.

Cut to Marianne, entering the dayroom from outside, shaking out her coat, and as she passes Michou . . .

MICHOU: With the executioner?

Marianne halts. All around the room the expressions are angrily contemptuous, disgusted.

MICHOU: He killed Mala and Edek, did you know?

MARIANNE: Well, if he didn't, somebody else would've, you can be sure of that.

> She starts toward the door to the dormitory, then halts, turns to them all.

MARIANNE: I mean to say, dearies, whose side do you think *you're* on? Because if anybody's not sure you're on the side of the executioners, you ought to go out and ask any prisoner in this camp, and they'll be happy to tell you! *To Michou*: So you can stick your comments you know exactly where, Michou. Any further questions?

> She looks about defiantly, smiling, exits into the dormitory, removing her coat.
> The truth of her remarks is in the players' eyes. They avoid one another as the women resume practicing. Esther comes to Fania.

ESTHER: You shouldn't let her get away with that. —I'd answer but nobody listens to what *I* say. . . .

FANIA: But she's right, Esther, what answer is there?

ESTHER: I am *not* on their side—I am only keeping myself for Jerusalem.

FANIA: Good.

ESTHER—*Fania's uninflected, sterilized comment has left her unsatisfied*: What do you mean by that, Fania?

FANIA: That it's good, if you can keep yourself so apart from all this. So clean.

ESTHER, *asking, in a sense*: But we're not responsible for this.

FANIA: Of course not, nothing here is our fault. *Finally agreeing, as it were, to go into it.* All I mean is that we may be innocent, but we have changed. I mean we know a little something about the human race that we didn't know before. And it's not good news.

ESTHER, *anxiously, even angry*: How can you still call them human?

FANIA: Then what are they, Esther?

ESTHER: I don't like the way you . . . you seem to connect such monsters with . . .

> Suddenly, Giselle calls out sotto voce—she is sitting with Charlotte.

GISELLE: Mengele!

> Dr. Mengele's importance is evident in the way they leap to their feet as he enters. His handsome face is somber, his uniform dapper under the raincoat which he now opens to take out a baton and Alma's armband, which has some musical insignia on it.

OLGA, *at rigid attention*: Would the Herr Doktor Mengele like to hear some particular music?

> Mengele walks past her to the door of Alma's room.

> *Cut to* Mengele, entering Alma's room. He looks about at the empty bed and chair, as though in a sacred place. Then he takes the baton and hangs it up from a nail in the wall above a shelf, and on the shelf he carefully places her armband. Now he steps back and, facing these relics, stands at military attention for a long moment.
>
> The camera turns past him to discover, through the doorway to the dayroom, Fania looking in, and others jammed in beside her, watching in tense astonishment.

MENGELE: Kapo!

OLGA, *rushing into room*: Herr Doktor Mengele!

> She goes to attention.

MENGELE: That is Madame Rosé's baton and armband. They are never to be disturbed. *He faces the relics again.* In Memoriam.

> Fania greets this emotional display with incredulity, as do others nearby.
>
> Now the dread doctor turns and walks into the day-room, the players quickly and obsequiously making way for him, and standing with attentive respect as he goes by.
>
> As he passes into the center of the dayroom, his heels clacking on the wooden floor in a slow, pensive measure, the tension rises—no one is sure why. And he halts instead of leaving them, his back to them. Why has he halted, what is the monster thinking?
>
> *Cut to* the players. They have risen to a dread tension, their faces rigid.
>
> *Cut to* Mengele. He turns to them; he has an out-of-this-world look now, an inspired air, as though he had forgotten where he was and only now takes these faces into consciousness. He seems less angry than alarmed, surprised.
>
> Fania, unable to wait for what may come out of him, takes a tenuous step forward and bows a little, propelled by her terror of death, now, at this moment.

FANIA: If the Herr Doktor will permit me—the orchestra is resolved to perform at our absolute best, in memory of our beloved Madame Rosé.

> Only now does Mengele turn that gaze on her, as though he heard her from afar. Fania's voice is near trembling.

FANIA: I can assure the Herr Doktor that we are ready to spend every waking moment perfecting our playing. . . . We believe our fallen leader would wish us to continue . . . *Beginning to falter*: to . . . to carry on as she . . . inspired us. . . .

> The sound of bombers overhead. Mengele reacts, but in the most outwardly discreet way, with an aborted lift of the head. But the girls understand that he knows the end is near, and this heightens their fear.
>
> He changes under this sound from the sky, and rather strolls out as though to show unconcern. As soon as he is out of sight several girls break into weeping. Fania feels humiliated, and goes alone to her table. . . .

ETALINA, *weeping*: It's the end! You felt it, didn't you, Fania! He's going to send us to the gas!

PAULETTE, *asking Fania's reaction*: The way he stared at us!

CHARLOTTE: The thing to do is rehearse and rehearse and rehearse! *To Liesle*: To this day you've never gotten the Beethoven right! Now here, damn you! *She thrusts an accordion at her.* Work on that arpeggio! *She notices Fania looking upward.* What's the matter?

> The whole group turns to Fania questioningly—they are scared, panicked. She is listening to the sky.

FANIA: I can't understand why they don't bomb here. They could stop the convoys in one attack on the rails.

ELZVIETA: They're probably afraid they'll hit *us*.

MICHOU: It's political—it always is—but I can't figure out the angles.

ESTHER: They don't want it to seem like it's a war to save the Jews. *They turn to Esther.* They won't risk planes for our sake, and pilots— their people wouldn't like it. *To Fania*: Fania . . . if they do come for us and it's the end . . . I ask you not to do that again and beg for your life. . . .

FANIA, *guiltily*: I was only . . .

ESTHER, *crying out—a kind of love for Fania is in it*: You shouldn't ever beg, Fania!

> *Cut to* Lagerführerin Mandel entering from the rain. She wears a great black cape. She looks ravaged, desolate. She goes to a chair and sits, unhooks her cape. In one hand now is seen . . .
> The child's sailor hat. It is held tenderly on her lap.

> *Cut to* Mandel, in a state of near shock; yet an air of self-willed determination too, despite her staring eyes.
> Olga, now the kapo, looks to Fania for what to do. Others likewise glance at her. Fania now comes forward and stands before Mandel.
> Mandel comes out of her remoteness, looks at Fania.

MANDEL: The duet from *Madame Butterfly*. You and the other one.

> Fania turns to the girls—Giselle hurries into the dormitory, calling . . .

GISELLE, *running off*: Marianne? Come out here . . . !

> Mandel now stands and walks to a window looking out at the rain. Meanwhile Charlotte and Etalina have taken up their violins to accompany.

Marianne, half asleep, enters from the dormitory and comes to Fania. And now they wait for Mandel to turn from the window and order them to begin. But she doesn't. So Fania walks across the room to her.

Cut to Fania, arriving beside Mandel, who is staring out at the rain-washed window. Fania's eyes travel down to the hat in the other woman's hand.

FANIA: We are ready to begin, Frau Mandel.

Mandel seems hardly to have heard, keeps on staring. After a moment . . .

FANIA: Is something the matter with the little boy?

Mandel now glances at Fania—there is an air of dissociation coming over the Nazi's face.

MANDEL: It has always been the same—the greatness of a people depends on the sacrifices they are willing to make.

Fania's expression of curiosity collapses—she knows now.

MANDEL: I gave him . . . back.

Now Mandel is straightening with an invoked pride before Fania, stiffening. But she is still struggling with an ancient instinct within her.

MANDEL: Come now, sing for me.

She goes to her seat. Fania, nearly insensible, joins Marianne—who greets her with a raised eyebrow to keep their hostility intact. Charlotte's violin starts it off, the duet from Act II.

MARIANNE (*as Suzuki*): *It's daylight! Cio-Cio-San.*

FANIA (*as Butterfly*)—*mimes picking up an infant, cradling it in her arms*: *He'll come, he'll come, I know he'll come.*

MARIANNE (*as Suzuki*): *I pray you go and rest, for you are weary. And I will call you when he arrives.*

FANIA (*as Butterfly*) *to her "baby"*: *Sweet thou art sleeping, cradled on my heart . . .*

Cut to Mandel, stunned by the lyric and music; but through her sentimental tears her fanatic stupidity is emerging.

FANIA (*as Butterfly*) (*voice-over*): *Safe in God's keeping, while I must weep apart. Around thy head the moonbeams dart. . . .*

Cut to the group.

FANIA (*as Butterfly*), *rocking the "baby": Sleep my beloved.*

MARIANNE (*as Suzuki*): *Poor Madame Butterfly!*

Cut to Mandel, fighting for control, staring up at Fania. And Fania now takes on a challenging, protesting tone.

FANIA (*as Butterfly*): *Sweet, thou art sleeping, cradled on my heart. Safe in God's keeping, while I must weep apart.*

The sound of bombers . . . coming in fast, tremendous.
  Sirens.
  Mandel comes out of her fog, stands . . . girls are rushing to windows to look up. The lights go out.
  The sound of bombers overhead and nearby explosions.
  There is screaming; in the darkness, total confusion; but Mandel can be seen rushing out into the night, a determined look on her face.

Cut to the railroad platform. Bombs explode.
  Despite everything, deportees are being rushed onto waiting trucks, which roar away.

Cut to a series of close shots: Kramer kicking a deportee. . . . Mandel commanding a woman to board a truck. . . . And Mengele, face streaming, his eyes crazed as he looks skyward; then he goes to an SS officer.

MENGELE: Hurry!—faster!

Cut to the warehouse hospital. "The Blue Danube" is in full swing as the shot opens. At one end of the vast shadowy space is the orchestra "conducted" by Olga.
  The few good violinists like Elzvieta and Charlotte saw away as loudly as possible.
  The Bechstein piano has been brought in and Fania is playing.
  The sick, what appear to be hundreds of them, are ranged in beds; the insane, some of them clinging to walls or to each other like monkeys; about a hundred so-called well prisoners in their uniforms ranged at one end; dozens of SS officers, male and female, in one unified audience sit directly before the players.

Cut to a dancing woman emerging from among the insane; heads turn as she does a long, sweeping waltz by herself; shaven head, cadaverous, a far-out expression.
  SS glance at her, amused.

Cut to the prisoners. A humming has started among them to "The Blue Danube."

Cut to Mengele, Kramer, and SS officers. These high brass notice the humming—they take it with uncertainty—is it some kind of demonstration of their humanity?

Cut to the prisoners. They have dared to hum louder—and the fact that it is done in unison and without command or authorization enlivens them more and more.

Cut to Commandant Kramer, starting to get to his feet, when Mengele touches his arm and gestures for him to permit the humming as harmless. Kramer half-willingly concedes, and sits.

Cut to the orchestra. "Blue Danube" ends. With no announcement, in the bleak silence, Olga picks up her accordion. Fania and Paulette immediately come to her and have a quick whispered conversation while trying to appear calm.

FANIA, *sotto voce:* Not the "Laughing Song"!

OLGA: But they want another number!

PAULETTE: But they're all going to the gas, you can't play that!

OLGA: But I don't know any other! What's the difference?

Olga steps from them and begins to play and sing the "Laughing Song," which requires all to join in.
     And as it proceeds, some of the insane join in, out of tempo to be sure, and . . .
     Kramer is laughing, along with other SS.
     Patients in beds are laughing. . . .

Cut to Fania, in her eyes the ultimate agony.

Cut to Mengele, signaling Kramer, who is beside him, and the latter speaks to an aide at his side. The aide gets up and moves out of the shot. . . .

Cut to the orchestra. The "Laughing Song" is continuing.

Cut to a door to the outside, which is opening. Kapos are leading half a dozen patients through it.

Cut to the orchestra. The "Laughing Song" continues; now Paulette sees the kapos leading people out. Her cello slides out of her grasp as she faints. "Laughing Song" is climaxing. Michou is propping up Paulette while attempting to play and laugh.

Cut to the hospital warehouse. Patients, orchestra, and SS are rocking along in the finale, as more patients are being led out through the door.

Cut to the dayroom. Later that night. The players are sitting in darkness while some are at the windows watching a not very distant artillery bombardment—the sky flashes explosions.

Fania, seated at her table, is staring out the window. She is spiritless now.

Players' faces, in the flashes of light from outside, are somber, expectant.

Cut to a fire in the dayroom stove, visible through its cracks. Michou is grating a potato into a pan. Charlotte is hungrily looking on. This is very intense business.

Cut to Olga, the new conductor, emerges from Alma's room: She is very officious lately.

OLGA: All right—players? We will begin rehearsal. *Heads turn to her but no one moves.* I order you to rehearse!

ETALINA, *indicating outside*: That's the Russian artillery, Olga.

OLGA: I'm in charge here and I gave no permission to suspend rehearsals!

ETALINA: Stupid, it's all over, don't you understand? The Russians are out there and we will probably be gassed before they can reach us.

GISELLE: Relax, Olga—we can't rehearse in the dark.

ETALINA: She can—she can't read music anyway.

OLGA—*defeated, she notices Michou*: Where'd you get those potatoes?

MICHOU: I stole them, where else?

OLGA, *pulling her to her feet*: You're coming to Mandel! —I'm reporting you!

From behind her, suddenly, Fania has her by her hair.

FANIA, *quietly*: Stop this, Olga, or we'll stuff a rag in your mouth and strangle you tonight. Let her go.

Olga releases Michou.

CHARLOTTE: She was only making me a pancake, that's all.

FANIA: Sit down, Olga—we may all go tonight.

OLGA: I don't see why.

ETALINA: We've seen it all, dummy, we're the evidence. *Olga unhappily stares out a window.* I feel for her—she finally gets an orchestra to conduct and the war has to end.

> *Cut to* a series of close shots: the players' faces—the exhaustion now, the anxiety, the waiting.
>
> *Cut to* Etalina, just sitting close to Fania.

ETALINA: I think I saw my mother yesterday. And my two sisters and my father.

FANIA, *coming alert to her from her own preoccupations*: What? Where? What are you talking about?

ETALINA: Yesterday afternoon; that convoy from France; when we were playing outside the freight car; I looked up and . . . I wasn't . . . I wasn't sure, but . . .

> Their eyes meet; Fania realizes that she is quite sure, and she reaches around and embraces Etalina, who buries her face in Fania's breast and shakes with weeping.

FANIA: Oh, but what could you have done?

> *Cut to* Lagerführerin Mandel, entering the dayroom. All rise to stand at attention, faces flaring with anxiety. Mandel is wide-eyed, totally distracted, undone. Etalina is weeping as she stands at attention.

MANDEL: Has anyone come across that little hat? *Silence. No one responds. Amazement in faces now.* The little sailor hat. I seem to have dropped it. No?

> Heads shake negatively, rather stunned. Mandel, expressionless, exits.
> The players sit again.
> Etalina has an explosion of weeping.

FANIA, *comforting her*: Sssh . . .

> Marianne now comes over to Fania, who is stroking Etalina's face.

MARIANNE: I just want you to know, Fania, that . . . you turned your back on me when I needed you, and . . . I don't want you to think I'm too stupid to know it.

FANIA: What are you talking about? *Marianne bitterly turns away, as . . .* Are you a little child that I should have locked in the closet?

> Marianne walks away to a window, adamantly bitter.

Cut to Michou, feeding Charlotte pieces of pancake from a pan, as she would a child.

Cut to Fania, looking with a certain calculation at . . .
Elzvieta, who blanches and turns from an explosion in the sky, and crosses herself.
Fania comes up to her.

FANIA: Elzvieta? *She takes out a small but thick notebook.* I would like you to keep this. It's my diary—everything is in there from the first day.

ELZVIETA: No, no. You keep it. You will be all right, Fania. . . .

FANIA: Take it. Take it, maybe you can publish it in Poland. . . .

ELZVIETA—*starts to take it, then doesn't*: It's impossible, Fania—I feel like I'm condemning you! You keep it, you will live, I know you will!

FANIA: I am not sure . . . that I wish to, Elzvieta.

ELZVIETA, *realizing, she looks deeply into Fania's dying eyes*: Oh no . . . no, Fania! No!

She suddenly sweeps Fania into her arms, as . . .
Two troopers enter. These are not SS men; they carry rifles and combat gear.

FIRST TROOPER: Jews left! Aryans right! Hurry up!

The players scurry to form up. . . .
Fania and Elzvieta slowly disengage—it's good-bye.

Cut to an open freight car. Dawn is breaking; rain drenches some twenty-five players in this freight car ordinarily used for coal. Fania now is lying on her back with her eyes shut, the players extending their coats to shield her. The train slows.
Nearby two Wehrmacht troopers are huddled over a woodstove; women also cluster around for warmth.
These men are themselves worn out with war, dead-eyed.
Marianne makes her way over to one of the troopers and gives him a flirty look.

MARIANNE: How's it going, soldier?

The trooper's interest is not very great.

MARIANNE: Could a girl ask where you're taking us?

She comes closer—and with mud-streaked face, she smiles. . . .
Now he seems to show some interest in her.

MARIANNE: 'Cause wherever it is, I know how to make a fellow forget his troubles. Where are we heading?

TROOPER, *shrugging*: Who knows? I guess it's to keep you away from the Russians, maybe . . . so you won't be telling them what went on there. Or the Allies either.

MARIANNE: Going to finish us off?

TROOPER: Don't ask me.

The train stops.

Cut to a flat, barren, endless landscape covered with mud.

Cut to an SS officer mounting onto the car; below him on the ground are several other SS plus dogs and handlers.
The officer looks the players over, then points at Marianne. She steps forward. He hands her a club.

SS OFFICER: You are the kapo. Get them out and form up.

Officer hops down and moves off to next car.

Cut to Marianne, who hefts the club in her hand and turns to the players, who all seem to receive the message her spirit emits—they fear her.

MARIANNE: Out, and form up five by five.

She prods Charlotte in the back as she is starting to climb down.

CHARLOTTE: Stop pushing me!

Marianne viciously prods Paulette, who falls to the ground as Michou and Giselle seek to intercede; and Marianne swings and hits Giselle, then goes after Michou, and both escape only by jumping down and falling to their hands and knees. Now Marianne turns to the *pièce de résistance*—
Fania is practically hanging from the supporting hands of Charlotte and Etalina, who are moving her past Marianne.

MARIANNE: She can walk like anybody else.

ETALINA: She's got typhus, Marianne!

She beats their hands away from Fania, who faces her, swaying with a fever. Marianne swings and cracks Fania to the floor of the car.

Cut to a vast barn or warehouse, its floor covered with hundreds of deportees in the final stages of their physical resistance. They are practically on top of one another; and over all a deep, undecipherable groaning of sound, the many languages of every European nation.

Now a shaft of daylight flashes across the mass as a door to the outside is opened and through it a straggling column of deportees moves out of this building.

The door closes behind them, followed by . . .

The sound of machine guns.

Cut to the little group of players around Fania, who are wide-eyed, powerless. She is propped up in Paulette's lap now, panting for breath.

Fania opens her eyes . . .

ETALINA, *slapping Fania's hands*: That's better . . . keep your eyes open . . . you've got to live, Fania. . . .

Now Fania, half-unconscious, sees past Etalina . . . to . . .

A woman and man making love against a wall.

A man barely able to crawl, peering into women's faces.

MAN: Rose? Rose Gershowitz?

Cut to a Polish woman, surrounded by the ill and dying, giving birth, with help from another woman.

Machine guns fire in near distance. Along with the baby's first cries.

Cut to Fania, receiving these insanely absurd sounds with a struggle to apprehend. And now she sees . . .

The Polish woman who just gave birth, standing up, swaying a little, wrapping her rags about her as she takes her baby from a woman and holds it naked against herself.

Cut to Fania, ripping the lining out of her coat—which was lying on top of her as a blanket—and gestures for Paulette to hand it on to the Polish woman, which is done. And the baby is wrapped in it.

Light again pours in from the opening door, and another column of deportees is moving to exit and death. And as this column stumbles toward the door, urged on by SS men and kapos . . .

Shmuel appears in the barn door. The light behind him contrasts with the murk within the building and he seems to blaze in an unearthly luminescence.

He is staring in a sublime silence, as now he lifts his arms in a wordless gesture of deliverance, his eyes filled with miracle, and turning he starts to gesture behind him. . . .

A British soldier appears beside him and looks into the barn.

Cut to the British soldier. His incredulous, alarmed, half-disgusted, half-furious face fills the screen.

Cut to a panoramic shot: a shouting mass of just-liberated deportees throwing stones. Some of these people are barely able to stand, some fall to their knees and still throw stones at . . .
    A truck filled with SS men and women, their arms raised in surrender, trying to dodge the stones. Several trucks are pulling away, filled with SS.
    Fania is being half-carried by Michou and Etalina, the others near them.

ETALINA: Please, Fania, you've got to live, you've got to live . . . !

Michou suddenly sees something offscreen, picks up stones and starts throwing. . . .

MICHOU: There she is! Hey rat! Rat!

Paulette and Esther turn to look at . . .

Marianne.

In the midst of the mob, Marianne is being hit by stones thrown by Michou. Other deportees are trying to hold on to Marianne to keep her from escaping. . . .

FANIA'S VOICE: Michou!

Michou turns to . . .
    Fania, steadied on her feet by the others, staring at . . .
Marianne, frightened, but still full of defiant hatred.

Cut to a British communications soldier with a radio unit, coming up to Fania.

SOLDIER: Would it be at all possible to say something for the troops?

Fania registers the absurdity of the request.

SOLDIER: It would mean so much, I think . . . unless you feel . . .

She stops him by touching his arm; all her remaining strength is needed as she weakly sings the "Marseillaise."

FANIA:

Allons enfants de la Patrie
Le jour de gloire est arrivé
Contre nous de la tyrannie . . .

Fania's eyes lift to . . .

The sky. The clouds are in motion.

Cut to a busy, prosperous avenue in Brussels—1978 autos, latest fashions on women, etc. . . .

Cut to a restaurant dining room. The camera discovers Fania at a table, alone. It is a fashionable restaurant, good silver, formal waiters, sophisticated lunch crowd. Fania is smoking, sipping an aperitif, her eye on the entrance door.

Of course she is now thirty years older, but still vital and attractively done up and dressed. And she sees . . .

First, Liesle, the miserable mandolin player, who enters and is looking around for her. Fania half-stands, raising her hand. As Liesle starts across the restaurant toward her, Charlotte enters behind her. And she recognizes Liesle.

Keeping Fania's viewpoint—Charlotte quickly catches up with Liesle, touches her arm; turns; a pause; they shake hands, then Liesle gestures toward Fania's direction and they start off together.

Cut to Liesle and Charlotte arriving at the table; Fania is standing; a pause. It is impossible to speak. Finally, Fania extends both her hands, and the other two grasp them.

FANIA: Liesle! —Charlotte!

They sit, their hands clasped. After a moment . . .

LIESLE: We could hardly believe you were still singing—and here in Brussels!

CHARLOTTE: I'm only here on a visit, imagine? And I saw your interview in the paper!

Words die in them for a moment as they look at one another trying to absorb the fact of their survival, of the absurdity of their lives. Finally . . .

FANIA: What about the others? Did you ever hear anything about Marianne?

LIESLE: Marianne died.

FANIA—*it is still a shock*: Ah!

LIESLE: A few years after the war—I can't recall who told me. She was starting to produce concerts. She had cancer.

CHARLOTTE: I have two children, Fania . . .

FANIA: Charlotte with children!—Imagine!

A waiter appears. He knows Fania.

WAITER: Is Madame ready to order or shall we . . . ?

FANIA: In a few minutes, Paul. *With a glance at the other two.* We haven't seen each other in thirty years, so . . . you must ask the chef to give us something extraordinary; something . . . absolutely marvelous!

And she reaches across the table to them and they clasp hands.

Cut to their hands on the white tablecloth, and their numbers tattooed on their wrists.

The camera draws away, and following the waiter as he crosses the restaurant, we resume the normality of life and the irony of it; and now we are outside on the avenue, the bustle of contemporary traffic; and quick close shots of passersby, the life that continues and continues. . . .

FINAL FADE-OUT

THE RIDE DOWN
MT. MORGAN

1991

Characters

LYMAN FELT

THEO FELT

LEAH FELT

BESSIE

NURSE LOGAN

TOM WILSON

ACT ONE

SCENE I

Lyman Felt asleep in a hospital bed.

Nurse Logan is reading a magazine in a chair a few feet away. She is black. He is deeply asleep, snoring now and then.

LYMAN, *his eyes still shut*: Thank you, thank you all very much. Please be seated. *Nurse turns, looks toward him.* We have a lot of . . . not material . . . yes, material . . . to cover this afternoon, so please take your seats and cross your . . . No-no . . . *Laughs weakly.* . . . Not cross your legs, just take your seats. . . .

NURSE: That was a lot of surgery, Mr. Felt. You're supposed to be resting . . . Or you out?

LYMAN, *for a moment he sleeps, snores, then* . . . : Today I would like you to consider life insurance from a different perspective. I want you to look at the whole economic system as one enormous tit. *Nurse chuckles quietly.* So the job of the individual is to get a good place in line for a suck. *She laughs louder.* Which gives us the word "suckcess." Or . . . or not.

NURSE: You know, you better settle down after all that surgery.

LYMAN, *opens his eyes*: You black?

NURSE: That's what they keep telling me.

LYMAN: Good for you. I've got the biggest training program of any company for you guys. And the first one that ever put them in sales. There's no election now, is there? —Eisenhower or something?

NURSE: It's December. And he's been dead since I don't know when.

LYMAN: Eisenhower *dead*? *Peers in confusion.* Oh, right, right! . . . Why can't I move, do you mind?

NURSE, *returns to her chair*: You're all in a cast, you broke a lot of bones.

LYMAN: Who?

NURSE: You. You smashed your car. They say you went skiing down that Mount Morgan in a Porsche.

She chuckles. He squints, trying to orient himself.

LYMAN: Where . . . where . . . I'm where?

NURSE: Clearhaven Memorial Hospital.

LYMAN: That Earl Hines?

NURSE: Who?

LYMAN: That piano. Sounds like Earl Hines. *Sings an Earl Hines tune. Laughs appreciatively.* Listen to that, will you? That beautiful? Jimmy Baldwin . . . long, long ago when I was still a writer . . . used to say, "Lyman, you're a nigger underneath." *Chuckles; it fades. Now with some anxiety.* . . . Where?

NURSE: Clearhaven Memorial Hospital.

LYMAN, *it is slowly penetrating*: Clearhaven?

NURSE: Your wife and daughter just arrived up from New York. They're out in the visitors' room.

LYMAN, *canniness attempt, but still confused*: . . . From *New York*? Why? Who called them?

NURSE: What do you mean? Why not?

LYMAN: And where is this?

NURSE: Clearhaven—I'm from Canada myself, I only just started here. We've still got railroads in Canada.

LYMAN, *a moment of silent confusion*: Listen. I'm not feeling well . . . why are we talking about Canadian railroads?

NURSE: No, I just mentioned it, as there is a storm.

LYMAN: Now what . . . what . . . what was that about my wife . . . New York?

NURSE: She's here in the waiting room . . .

LYMAN: Here in the waiting . . .

NURSE: . . . And your daughter.

LYMAN, *tension rising with clearing of mind; he looks at his hands, turns them over*: . . . Would you mind?—Just . . . touch me? *She touches his face; he angers with the fully dawning fact.* Who the hell called them, for God's sake? Why didn't somebody ask me?

NURSE: I'm new here! I'm sorry if I'm not satisfactory.

LYMAN, *high anxiety*: Who said you're not satisfactory? What is this . . . endless . . . *verbiage?*—not verbiage, for Christ's sake, I meant . . . *Panting*. Listen, I absolutely can't see anyone and they have to go back to New York right away.

NURSE: But as long as you're awake . . .

LYMAN: Immediately! Go—get them out of here! *A jab of pain*. Ow!—Please, quickly, go!—Wait!—There's no . . . like another . . . you know, woman out there?

NURSE: Not while I was out there.

LYMAN: Please . . . quickly, huh? I can't see anybody.

> *Bewildered, Nurse exits.*

Oh, poor Theo—here! My God, what have I done! How could I have gone out on that road in a storm! *Terrified of self-betrayal*. Have you lost your fucking mind?! *Frozen in anguish, he stares straight ahead as music is heard. His mood changes as he is caught by his catastrophic vision*. Oh, dear God, this mustn't happen.

> *His wife, Theo, and daughter, Bessie, are discovered seated on a waiting room settee. A burst of weeping from Bessie. He is not looking directly at them but imagining them.*

Oh, Bessie, my poor Bessie! *Covers his eyes, as Bessie weeps*. No-no-no, it mustn't happen!—think of something else!—

> *His vision is forcing him out of the bed in his hospital gown. Music fades out.*

THEO, *touching Bessie's hand*: Darling, try not to.

BESSIE: I can't help it.

THEO: Of course you can. Be brave now, dear.

LYMAN, *moving into the range of the women*: Oh yes! My Theo! That's exactly what she'd say! What a woman!

THEO: Try to think of all the happiness; think of his laughter; Daddy loves life, he'll fight for it.

BESSIE: . . . I guess I've just never had anything really bad happen.

LYMAN, *a few feet away*: Oh, my dear child . . . !

THEO: But you'll see as you get older—everything ultimately fits together . . . and for the good.

LYMAN, *staring front*: Oh yes . . . good old Episcopal Theo!

THEO: —Now come, Bessie.—Remember what a wonderful time we had in Africa? Think of Africa.

BESSIE: What an amazing woman you are, Mother.

Nurse Logan enters.

NURSE: It'll still be a while before he can see anybody. Would you like me to call a motel? It's ski season, but my husband can probably get you in, he plows their driveway.

BESSIE: Do you know if he's out of danger?

NURSE: I'm sure the doctors will let you know. *Obviously changing the subject.* I can't believe you made it up from New York in this sleet.

THEO: One does what one has to. Actually . . . would you mind calling the motel? It was a terrible drive . . .

NURSE: Sometimes I feel like going back to Canada—at least we had a railroad.

THEO: We'll have them again; things take time in this country but in the end we get them done.

NURSE: Don't hesitate if you want more tea.

Nurse exits.

THEO, *turns to Bessie, smiling painfully*: Why'd you start to laugh?

BESSIE, *touching Theo's hand*: It's nothing . . .

THEO: Well, what is it?

BESSIE: Well . . . I mean things really don't always get done in this country.

THEO, *disengaging her hand; she is hurt*: I think they do, ultimately. I've lived through changes that were inconceivable thirty years ago. *Straining to laugh.* Really, dear, I'm not *that* naive.

BESSIE, *angering*: Well, don't be upset!—They certainly are very nice people around here, aren't they?

THEO, *managing to pull her mood together*: I'm sorry you never knew small town life—there is a goodness.

BESSIE: I'm wondering if we should call Grandma Esther.

THEO, *dutifully*: If you like. *Slight pause. Bessie is still.* She gets so impressively emotional, that's all. But call . . . she *is* his mother.

BESSIE: I know she's a superficial woman, but I can't help it, I . . .

THEO: But you *should* like her, she adores you; she simply never liked me and I've always known it, that's all. *She looks away.*

BESSIE: I mean she can be awfully funny sometimes. And she *is* warm.

THEO: Warm? Yes, I suppose—provided it doesn't commit her to anything or anyone. I've never hidden it, dear—I think she's the center of his psychological problem . . .

LYMAN: Perfect!

THEO: . . . But I suppose I'm prejudiced.

> *Lyman laughs silently with a head shake of joyful recognition.*

I used to think it was because he didn't marry Jewish, but . . .

BESSIE: But she didn't either.

THEO: Darling, she'd have disliked any woman he married . . . except an heiress or a sexpot. But go ahead, I do think you should call her. *Bessie stands.* And give her my love, will you?

> *Lyman issues a cackling laugh of appreciation of her nature.*

> *Leah enters. She is in her thirties; in an open raccoon coat, high heels. Nurse enters with her.*

LYMAN, *on the instant she enters, claps his hands over his eyes*: No, she mustn't! It can't happen! She mustn't! *Unable to bear it, he starts to flee, but stops as . . .*

LEAH: After all the money we've put into this hospital it seems to me I ought to be able to speak to the chief nurse, for Christ's sake!

NURSE: I'm doing my best to get her for you . . . !

LEAH: Well hurry, will you? *Nurse starts to exit.* I'm only asking for a little information, dear!

> *Nurse exits. Pause.*

LYMAN, *imploring himself, his eyes clamped shut*: Think of something else. Let's see now—the new Mercedes convertible . . . that actress, what's her name . . . ? *But he fails to escape; and scared, slowly turns his head toward . . .*

> *Leah, who sits, but quickly stands again and moves restlessly. Theo and Bessie observe her indirectly, with polite curiosity. Now their eyes meet. Leah throws up her hands.*

LEAH: The same thing when I had my baby here, it was like pulling teeth to get them to tell me if it was a boy or a girl.

BESSIE: Is it an emergency?

LEAH: Yes, my husband; he cracked up the car on Mount Morgan. You?

BESSIE: My father. It was a car, too.

LYMAN, *eyes heavenward, hands clasped*: Oh please, please!

THEO: The roads are impossible.

LEAH: I can't imagine what got into him, driving down Mount Morgan on ice . . . and at night yet! It's incomprehensible! *A sudden explosion.* Damn them, I have a right to know what's happening! *She charges out.*

BESSIE: Poor thing.

THEO: But she *knows* how busy they are . . .

> *Silence now; Theo leans back, closing her eyes. Another sobbing fit threatens Bessie, who downs it, covers her eyes. Then suddenly she breaks down and weeps.*

> Oh Bessie, dear, try not to.

BESSIE, *shaking her head helplessly*: . . . I just love him so!

> *Leah returns, more subdued now. She sits tiredly, closes her eyes. Pause. She gets up, goes to a window, looks out.*

LEAH: *Now* the moon comes out!—everybody smashes up in the dark and now you could read a paper out there.

BESSIE: You live around here?

LEAH: Not far. We're out near the lake.

BESSIE: It looks like beautiful country.

LEAH: Oh, it is. But I'll take New York anytime. *A great sob suddenly bursts from her; she chokes it back.* I'm sorry. *But she weeps again, helplessly into her handkerchief. Bessie is affected and begins weeping, too.*

THEO: Now really . . . ! *Shakes Bessie's arm.* Stop this! *She sees Leah's indignant look.* You still don't know how serious it is, why do you carry on like this?

LEAH, *rather unwillingly*: You're probably right.

THEO, *exulting—to Bessie as well*: Of course! I mean there's always time to despair, why should . . . ?

LEAH, *sharply*: I *said* you were right, I was agreeing with you! *Theo turns away stiffly.* I'm sorry.

> *Now the women go motionless.*

LYMAN, *marveling*: What strong, admirable women they are! What definite characters! Thank God I'm only imagining this to torture myself . . . But it's enough! *Starts resolutely toward the bed, but caught by his vision, halts.* Now what would they say next?

> *The women reanimate.*

BESSIE: You raise things on your place?

LEAH: We grow most of what we eat. And we're starting to raise a few thoroughbreds now, in a small way.

BESSIE: Oh, I'd love that . . .

LEAH: I envy your composure—both of you. Really, you make me feel better. What part of New York are you in?

BESSIE: East Seventy-fourth Street.

LYMAN: Oh no! No no!

LEAH: Really! We often stay at the Carlyle . . .

BESSIE: Oh, it's practically around the corner.

THEO: You sound like a New Yorker.

LEAH: I went to NYU School of Business for three years; I loved it but I was raised up here in Elmira . . . and my business is here, so . . .

THEO: What sort of business do you have?

LEAH: Insurance.

BESSIE: That's what Daddy does!

LYMAN, *knocking his knuckles against his head*: No-no-no-no-no!

LEAH: Well, there's a million of us. You in it too?

BESSIE: No, I'm at home . . . take care of my husband.

LEAH: I'm hoping to sell out in a couple of years, get a place in Manhattan somewhere, and just paint morning to night the rest of my life.

BESSIE: Really! My husband's a painter.

LEAH: Professionally, or . . . ?

BESSIE: Oh yes. He's Harold Lamb.

> *Lyman rushes over to the bed and pulls the covers over his head.*

LEAH: Harold Lamb?

> *Leah ceases all movement, staring at Bessie. She turns to stare at Theo.*

THEO: What is it?

LEAH: Your husband is really Harold Lamb?

BESSIE, *very pleased and proud*: You've heard of him?

LEAH: You're not Mrs. Felt, are you?

THEO: Why yes.

LEAH, *her puzzled look*: Then you . . . *Breaks off, then* . . . You're not here for Lyman, are you?

BESSIE: You know Daddy?

LEAH: But . . . *Turning from one to the other* . . . how'd they come to notify *you*?

LYMAN, *sits up in bed and raises a devout, monitory hand to heaven, whispering loudly*: Stop it, stop it, stop it . . . !

THEO, *uncomprehending, but beginning to take affront*: Why shouldn't they notify me?

LEAH: Well . . . after so many years.

THEO: What do you mean?

LEAH: But it's over nine . . .

THEO: What is?

LEAH: Your divorce.

> *Theo and Bessie are struck dumb. A silence.*

> You're Theodora Felt, right?

THEO: Who *are* you?

LEAH: I'm Leah. Leah Felt.

THEO, *a haughtiness begins*: Felt!

LEAH: Lyman is my husband.

THEO: Who *are* you? What are you talking about!

BESSIE, *intensely curious about Leah, she angers at Theo*: Well don't get *angry*, for heaven's sake!

THEO: Be quiet!

LEAH, *seeing Theo's genuineness*: Well, you're divorced, aren't you?

THEO: Divorced!—who the hell *are* you!

LEAH: I'm Lyman's wife. *Theo sees she is a serious woman; it silences her.*

BESSIE: When . . . when did you . . . ? I mean . . .

THEO, *in motion again*: She's insane!—she's some kind of a nut!

LEAH, *to Bessie*: It was nine years this past July.

THEO: Really. And who performed this . . . this *event*?

LEAH: The Reno City Hall clerk, later a rabbi here in Elmira. My son's name is Benjamin, for Lyman's father, and Alexander for his great-grandmother—Benjamin Alexander Felt.

THEO, *with a weak attempt to sustain mockery*: Really!

LEAH: Yes, I'm terribly sorry if you didn't know.

THEO: Didn't know *what?* What are you *talking* about?

LEAH: We have been married a little over nine years, Mrs. Felt.

THEO: Have you? And I suppose you have some document . . . ?

LEAH: I have our marriage certificate, I guess . . .

THEO: You guess!

LEAH, *angrily*: Well I'm sure I do! And I know I have Lyman's will in our safe deposit box . . .

THEO, *helplessly mocking*: And it names you as his wife!

LEAH: And Benjamin as his son. *Theo is halted by her factuality.* . . . But I guess you have more or less the same . . . is that right? *Theo is still as a stone.* There really was no divorce?

BESSIE, *with a glance at her stricken mother . . . softly, almost apologetically*: . . . No.

LEAH: Well, I guess we'd better . . . meet, or something. And talk. *Theo is staring into space.* Mrs. Felt? I understand your feelings, but you'll just have to believe it, I guess—we have a terrible problem. Mrs. Felt?

THEO: It's impossible, nine years ago . . . *To Bessie:* That's when we all went to Africa.

BESSIE: Oh, right!—the safari!

THEO, *to Leah, with a victorious, if nearly demented laugh*: We were never closer in our lives! We traveled through Kenya, Nigeria . . . *As though this clinched everything.* . . . we even flew to Egypt!

> *Nurse enters. It instantly galvanizes all of them. She glances from one to the other.*

NURSE: Doctor Lowry would like to see Mrs. Felt now.

For one instant no one moves—then both Theo and Leah rise simultaneously. This actualization of Leah's claim stiffens Theo, forcing her to start assertively toward the Nurse—and she sways and starts to fall to the floor.

LEAH: Catch her!

BESSIE: Mother!

Nurse and Bessie catch Theo, then lower her to the floor.

LEAH, *over her shoulder*: Help here, someone's fainted! Where the hell is a doctor, goddammit! *To the air*: Is there a doctor in this fucking hospital?!

BLACKOUT

SCENE II

A couch and chair. Leah is seated facing Tom Wilson, a middle-aged but very fit lawyer who is reading a will, and sipping coffee. After a moment she gets up and moves to a point and stares, eyes filled with fear. Then dialing a cell phone, turns to him.

LEAH: Sure you wouldn't like some toast?—Sorry I'm not being much of a hostess.

TOM, *immersed*: Thanks. I'm just about done here.

LEAH, *dialing*: God, I dread it—my boy'll be home any minute . . . *Into phone*: Put my brother on, Tina. . . . Lou?— I don't know, they won't let me see him yet. What'd Uniroyal say? *What?* Well get on it, will you, call L.A. this minute! I mean for God's sake, Lou, I want that business! *Hangs up.* How much do you have to pay relatives to get them to do any work? *Tom closes the file, turns to her, silent.* —I know you're her lawyer, but I'm not really asking advice, am I?

TOM: I can discuss this. *Returns her file.* The will does recognize the boy as his son, but you are not his wife.

LEAH, *lifting the file*: Even if this refers to me as his wife?

TOM: I'm afraid that's legally meaningless, since he never divorced. However . . . *Breaks off, pressing his eyes.* I'm just stunned, I simply can't absorb it.

LEAH: I'm still in midair someplace.

TOM: What'd you ask me? Oh yes—provided the legal wife gets a minimum of one third of the estate he can leave you as much as he likes. So you're very well taken care of. *Sighs, leaning forward and gripping his head.* He actually flies a plane, you say?

LEAH: Oh yes, soaring planes, too.

TOM: You know, for years he'd never get off the ground unless it was unavoidable.

LEAH: Oh, he's wonderful in the air. *Pause.* I'm not here. I'm simply . . . not here. Can he be two people? Is that possible?

TOM: . . . May I ask you . . . ?

LEAH: Please. . . . Incidentally, have you known him long?

TOM: Sixteen, seventeen years.—When you decided to marry, I assume he told you he'd gotten a divorce . . .

LEAH: Of course. We went to Reno together.

TOM: No kidding! And what happened?

LEAH: God, I'd forgotten all about this . . . *Breaks off.* How could I be so *stupid!* —You see, it was July, streets were boiling hot, so he had me stay in the hotel while he went to pick up his divorce decree . . . *She goes silent.*

TOM: Yes?

LEAH, *shaking her head*: God!—my gullibility!—I was curious to see what a decree looked like, so . . .

> *Lyman enters, wearing a short-sleeved summer shirt and cowboy hat.*

No particular reason, but I'd never seen one . . .

LYMAN: I threw it away.

LEAH, *with a surprised laugh*: Why!

LYMAN: I don't want to look back, I feel twenty-five! *Laughs.* You look stunned!

LEAH: I guess I never believed you'd marry me, darling.

LYMAN—*he draws her to him*: Feeling is all I really believe in, Leah— you're making me see that again. Feeling is chaos, but any decent thing I've ever done was out of feeling, and every lousy thing I'm ashamed of came from careful thinking. I simply can't lose you, Leah, you're precious to me. —You look scared . . . what is it?

LEAH: I don't want to say it.

LYMAN: Go ahead. Please!

LEAH: Every relationship I've known gets to where it needs a lie to keep it going.

LYMAN: But does that always have to be!

LEAH, *hesitates*: Can I say something? I wish we could make a different wedding vow; like "Dearly beloved, I promise everything good, but I might have to lie to you sometimes." *He is taken aback, but grins.* —I wanted to say that, okay? You're shocked, aren't you.

LYMAN: What balls you have to say that! —Come here. *Takes her hand, closes his eyes.* I'm going to learn to fly a plane.

LEAH: What are you talking about?

LYMAN: Because flying terrifies me. I'm going to wrestle down one fear at a time till I've dumped them all and I am a free man! *Gripping her hands, nose to nose.* I have a car and driver downstairs. *Holds out his beckoning arm.* Come to your wedding, Leah, my darling!

> *Lyman exits without lowering his arm.*

LEAH: . . . And it was all lies! How is it possible! Why did he do it? What did he want?

TOM: Actually, though . . . *Tries to recall.* Yes, I think it was about nine years ago, we did have a discussion about a divorce . . . although at the time I didn't take it all that seriously. He suddenly popped in one day with this "research" he said he'd done . . .

> *Lyman enters in a business suit. Tom has moved out of Leah's area.*

LYMAN: . . . I've been looking into bigamy, Tom.

TOM, *laughs, surprised*: Bigamy!—what are you talking about?

LYMAN: You know there's an enormous amount of it in the United States now.

TOM: Really? But what's the point . . . ?

LYMAN: . . . And not just among blacks or the poor. I've been wondering about a desertion insurance policy. Might call it the Bigamy Protection Plan. *Tom laughs.* I'm serious. We could set the premiums really low. Be great, especially for minority women.

TOM, *admiringly*: Say now! Where the hell do you get these ideas?

LYMAN: Just put myself in other people's places. —Incidentally, how frequently do they prosecute for bigamy anymore, you have any idea?

TOM: None whatsoever. But it's a victimless crime so it can't be often.

LYMAN: That's my impression, too. Get somebody to research it, will you, I want to be sure.—I'll be in Elmira till Friday. *Lyman starts to leave but dawdles.*

TOM: Why do I think you're depressed?

LYMAN: . . . I guess I am—slightly. *The grin.* I'm turning fifty-four this July.

TOM: Fifty's much tougher, I think.

LYMAN: My father died at fifty-three.

TOM: Well, you're over the hump. Anyway, you're in better shape than anybody I know.

LYMAN: Famous last words.

TOM: Something wrong, Lyman?

LYMAN: I don't think I have the balls. *A laugh. Moves into high tension; then, facing his challenge, turns rather abruptly to Tom.* There's no man I trust like you, Tom. *A grin.* —I guess you know I've cheated on Theodora.

TOM: Well, I've had my suspicions, yes—ever since I walked in on you humping that Pakistani typist on your desk.

LYMAN, *laughs*: "Humping!" —I love that Presbyterian jive of yours, haven't heard that in years.

TOM: Quaker.

LYMAN, *confessionally, quietly*: There've been more than that one, Tommy.

TOM, *laughs*: God, where do you get the time?

LYMAN: Disgust you?

TOM: Not catastrophically.

LYMAN, *pause; he composes himself, then . . . again with the grin*: I think I've fallen in love.

TOM: Oh Lyman . . . don't tell me!

LYMAN, *pointing at him and laughing nervously*: Look at you!—God, you really love Theodora, don't you!

TOM: Of course I do!—you're not thinking of divorce, are you?

LYMAN: I don't know. Maybe I just wanted to say it aloud to somebody.

TOM: But how sure are you about your feelings for this woman?

LYMAN: I'm sure. A new woman has always been an undiscovered shore, but I'd really like to go straight now, Tom. I want one woman for the rest of my life. And I can't quite see it being Theodora.

TOM: You know she loves you deeply, Lyman.

LYMAN: Tom, I love her, too. But after thirty-two years we bore each other, we just do. And boredom is a form of deception, isn't it. And deception has become like my Nazi, my worst horror—I want nothing now but to wear my own face on my face every day till the day I die. Or do you think that kind of honesty is possible?

TOM: I don't have to tell you, the problem is not honesty but how much you hurt others with it.

LYMAN: Right. What about your religion? But there's no solution there either, I guess.

TOM: I somehow can't imagine you praying, Lyman. *Short pause.*

LYMAN: Is there an answer?

TOM: I don't know, maybe all one can do is hope to end up with the right regrets.

LYMAN: You ever cheated, Tom?

TOM: No.

LYMAN: Honest to God?—I've seen you eye the girls around here.

TOM: It's the truth.

LYMAN: Is that the regret you end up with?

> *Tom laughs bashfully, then Lyman joins him. And suddenly, Lyman's embarrassment and suffering are on his face.*

> . . . Shit, that was cruel, Tom, forgive me, will you? Dammit, why do I let myself get depressed? It's all pointless guilt, that's all! Here I start from nothing, create forty-two hundred jobs for people and raise over sixty ghetto blacks to office positions when that was not easy to do—I should be proud of myself, son of a bitch! And I am! I am! *He bangs on the desk, then subsides, looks front and downward.* I love your view. That red river of taillights gliding down Park Avenue on a winter's night—and all those silky white thighs crossing inside those heated limousines . . . Christ, can there be a sexier vision in the world? *Turning back to Tom.* I keep thinking of my father—how connected he was to his life; couldn't wait to open the store every morning and happily count the pickles, rearrange the olive

barrels. People like that knew the main thing. Which is what? What is the main thing, do you know?

Tom is silent.

—Look, don't worry, I really can't imagine myself without Theodora, she's a great, great wife! . . . I love that woman! It's always good talking to you, Tom. *Starts to go, halts.* Maybe it's simply that if you try to live according to your real desires, you have to end up looking like a shit.

Lyman exits. Leah covers her face and there is a pause as Tom observes her.

TOM: I'm sorry.

LEAH: He had it all carefully worked out from the very beginning.

TOM: I'd say it was more like . . . a continuous improvisation.

LEAH: It was the baby, you see—once I was pregnant he simply wouldn't listen to reason . . .

Lyman hurries on in a winter overcoat, claps a hand over her mouth.

LYMAN: Don't tell me it's too late. *Kisses her.* Did you do it?

LEAH: I was just walking out the door for the hospital.

LYMAN: Oh, thank God. *Draws her to a seat, and pulls her down.* Please, dear, give me one full minute and then you can do as you like.

LEAH, *with pain*: Don't, Lyme, it's impossible.

LYMAN: You know if you do this it's going to change it between us.

LEAH: Darling, it comes down to being a single parent and I just don't want that.

LYMAN: I've already named him.

LEAH, *amused, touching his face*: How do you know it's a him?

LYMAN: I'm never wrong. I have a very intimate relationship with ladies' bellies. His name is Benjamin after my father and Alexander after my mother's mother, who I loved a lot. *Grins at his own egoism.* You can put in a middle name.

LEAH, *with an unhappy laugh*: Well thanks so much! *She tries to stand up but he holds her.* He asked me not to be late.

LYMAN: The Russians—this is an ancient custom—before an important parting, they sit for a moment in silence. Give Benjamin this moment.

LEAH: He's not Benjamin, now stop it!

LYMAN: Believe in your feelings, Leah, the rest is nonsense. What do you really and truly want?

   Silence for a moment.

   I would drive him to school in the mornings and take him to ball games.

LEAH: Twice a month?

LYMAN: With the new office set up here, I could easily be with you more than half the time.

LEAH: And Theodora?

LYMAN: It's difficult to talk about her.

LEAH: With me, you mean?

LYMAN: I can't lie to myself, darling, she's been a tremendous wife. It would be too unjust.

LEAH: But keeping it a secret—where does that leave me? It's hard enough to identify myself as it is. And I can't believe she won't find out sooner or later, and then what?

LYMAN: If I actually have to choose it'll be you. But she doesn't know a soul in this whole area, it'd be a million-to-one shot for her to ever find out. I'm practically with you half the time now, and it's been pretty good, hasn't it?

LEAH, *touching her belly*: . . . But what do we tell this? . . .

LYMAN: . . . Benjamin.

LEAH: Oh stop calling him Benjamin! It's not even three weeks!

LYMAN: That's long enough to be Benjamin—he has a horoscope, stars and planets; he has a *future*!

LEAH: . . . Why do I feel we're circling around something? There's something I don't believe here—what is it?

LYMAN: Maybe that I'm this desperate. *Kisses her belly.*

LEAH: Are you? —I can't express it . . . there's just something about this baby that doesn't seem . . . I don't know—inevitable.

LYMAN: Darling, I haven't wanted anything this much since my twenties, when I was struggling to be a poet and make something of my own that would last.

LEAH: Really.

LYMAN: It's the truth.

LEAH: That's touching, Lyman, I'm very moved.

So it is up in the air for a moment.

But I can't, I won't, it's the story of my life, I always end up with all the responsibility; I'd have to be in total charge of your child and I know I'd resent it finally—and maybe even you as well. You're putting me back to being twelve or thirteen and my parents asking *me* where to go on vacation, or what kind of car to buy or what color drapes. I hate that position! One of the most sensuous things about you was that I could lie back and let you drive, and now you're putting me behind the wheel again. It's just all wrong.

LYMAN: I thought if we lived together let's say ten years, you'd still be in the prime, and pretty rich, and I'd . . .

LEAH: . . . Walk away into the sunset.

LYMAN: I'm trying to be as cruelly realistic as life, darling. Have you ever loved a man the way you love me?

LEAH: No.

LYMAN: Well? That's the only reality.

LEAH: You can drive me to the hospital, if you like realism so much. *She stands; he does.* You look so sad! You poor man.

She kisses him; a silent farewell is in the kiss; she gets her coat and turns to him.

I won't weaken on this, dear, so make up your mind.

LYMAN: We're going to lose each other if you do this. I feel it.

LEAH: Well, there's a very simple way not to lose me, dear, I guess that's why they invented it. —Come, wait in the hospital if you want to. If not, I'll be back tomorrow. *She draws him on, but he halts.*

LYMAN: Will you give me a week to tell her? It's still early for you, isn't it?

LEAH: Tell her what?

LYMAN: . . . That I'm going to marry you.

TOM: I see.

Lyman moves into darkness.

LEAH: I don't understand it; he'd had dozens of women, why did he pick me to be irreplaceable? *She looks down at her watch, stares in silence.* God! How do I tell my boy?

TOM: He's nine now?

LEAH: And worships Lyman. Worships him.

TOM: I'd better get to the hospital. *He moves to go, halts hesitantly.* Don't answer this if you'd rather not, but you think you could ever take him back?

LEAH, *thinks for a moment*: How could you ask me that? It's outrageous! —Would Theodora? She struck me as a rather judgmental sort of woman.

TOM: Oh, she has a tender side, too. —I guess she hasn't had time to think of the future, any more than you have.

LEAH: All this reminds me of an idea I used to have about him that . . . well, it'll sound mystical and silly . . .

TOM: Please. I'd love to understand him.

LEAH: Well, it's just that he wants so much; like a kid at a fair; a jelly apple here, a cotton candy there, and then a ride on a loop-the-loop . . . and it never lets up in him; it's what's so attractive about him—to women, I mean—Lyman's mind is up your skirt but it's such a rare thing to be wanted like that—indifference is what most men feel now—I mean they have an appetite but not hunger—and here is such a splendidly hungry man and it's simply . . . well . . . precious once you're past twenty-five. I tell you the truth, somewhere deep down I think I sensed something about him wasn't on the level, but . . . I guess I must have loved him so much that I . . . *Breaks off.* —But I mustn't talk this way; he's unforgivable! It's the rottenest thing I've ever heard of! The answer is no, absolutely not!

TOM, *nods, thinks, then . . .* : Well, I'll be off. I hope it's not too difficult for you with the little boy. *He exits.*

BLACKOUT ON LEAH

SCENE III

Lyman is softly snoring; a deep troubled sleep, however; bad dreams, muttering, an arm raised in a gesture.

Tom enters with Nurse. She raises Lyman's eyelid.

NURSE: He still goes in and out but you can try him.

TOM: Lyman? Can you hear me? *Lyman stops snoring but eyes remain shut.* It's Tom Wilson.

NURSE: Keep going, he shouldn't be staying under this much by now.

TOM: Lyman, it's Tom.

LYMAN, *opens his eyes*: You in the store?

TOM: It's the hospital.

LYMAN: Hospital? Oh right, right . . . Jesus, I was dreaming of my father's store; every time he looked at me he'd shake his head and say, "Hopeless case." *Laughs tiredly, trying to focus.* Give me a second; little mixed up. How'd you get here?

TOM: Theodora called me.

LYMAN: Theodora?

TOM: Your car is registered in the city so the state police called her.

LYMAN: I had some weird dream that she and Bessie . . . *Breaks off.* They're not here, are they?

NURSE: I told you your wife came . . .

TOM, *to Nurse*: Excuse us, please?

NURSE: But I told him. *She exits.*

TOM: They've met, Lyman.

LYMAN, *pause; he struggles to orient himself*: Theo . . . didn't collapse, did she?

TOM: Yes, but she's come around, she'll be all right.

LYMAN: I don't understand it, I think I dreamed the whole thing . . .

TOM: Well, that wouldn't be too difficult, it's all pretty inevitable.

LYMAN: Why're you being so brutal?

TOM: There's no time to fool around, you've got things to decide. It's all over television . . .

LYMAN: Oh. —Have you met her?—Leah? I'm finished.

TOM: We've had a talk. She's a considerable woman.

LYMAN, *gratefully*: Isn't she? —She's furious, too, huh?

TOM: Well, what do you expect?

LYMAN: See . . . I thought I'd somehow divorce Theo later. —But it sort of settled in where I had both of them. And after a while it didn't seem so godawful . . . What about Bessie?

TOM: It's hit her pretty bad, I guess.

LYMAN: God, and poor little Benny! Jesus, if I could go through the ceiling and just disappear.

TOM: The television is flogging it. I think you ought to issue a press statement to cut the whole thing short. As to your intentions.

LYMAN: What intentions? Just give each of them whatever they want. I'll probably go and live somewhere . . . maybe like Brazil or something . . .

TOM: You won't try to hold on to either of them.

LYMAN: Are you mad? They wouldn't have anything to do with me. My God . . . *He turns away, tears in his eyes.* How could I have destroyed everything like this!—my character! *Higher intensity:* Why did I drive into that storm?—I can't understand it! I had the room in the Howard Johnson's, I think I was even in bed . . . figured I'd wait out the storm there . . . Why'd I go out into it again?

TOM: Can you give Theo a few minutes? She wants to say good-bye.

LYMAN: How can I face her? Ask her to wait till tomorrow, maybe I'll feel a little better and . . .

> *Theo and Bessie enter; Lyman does not see them, as they are above him.*

TOM: They're here, Lyman.

> *Lyman closes his eyes, breathing fast. Bessie, holding Theo by the elbow, accompanies her to the beside.*

BESSIE, *whispering with some shock*: Look at his bandages! *Turning away.* Oh, Mother!

THEO: Stop that. *Bending to Lyman*: Lyman? *He can't get himself to speak.* It's Theodora.

LYMAN, *opening his eyes*: Hi.

THEO: How are you feeling?

LYMAN: Not too bad now. I hope I make sense with all this painkiller . . . Is that you, Bessie?

BESSIE: I'm only here because of Mother.

LYMAN: Oh. Okay. I'm sorry, Bess—I mean that my character's so bad. But I'm proud that you have enough strength to despise me.

BESSIE: But who wouldn't?

LYMAN: Good! *His voice starts to break but he controls himself.* That was well-spoken, sweetie.

BESSIE, *with quick anger*: Don't call me that . . .

THEO, *to Bessie*: Shhh! *She has been observing him in silence.* Lyman? —Is it true?

> *Lyman closes his eyes.*

I have to hear it from you. Did you marry that woman?

> *Deep snores.*

> *More urgently*: Lyman?

BESSIE, *points*: He's not really sleeping!

THEO: Did you have a child with that woman? Lyman? I insist!!! I insist!!!

> *Lyman emerges from the upstage side of the bed, hands clapped to his ears, while Theo and Bessie continue addressing the bed, as though he were still in it.*

> *Light change: an ethereal colorlessness now, air devoid of pigment.*

LYMAN, *agonized cry, ears still covered*: I hear you!

> *Theo continues to address the bed, and Bessie is fixed on it as well, but their attitude becomes formalized as they become part of his vision.*

THEO: What in God's name have you done!

> *Almost writhing in conflict, Lyman clears his throat. He remains a distance upstage of the bed.*

BESSIE, *bent over the bed*: Shh! He's saying something!

LYMAN: I realize . . . how crazy it sounds, Theodora . . . *Breaks off.*

THEO: Yes?

LYMAN: . . . I'm not really sure, but . . . I wonder if this crash . . . was maybe to sort of subconsciously . . . get you both to . . . meet one another, finally.

THEO, *with disgust*: Meet *her*?

LYMAN: I know it sounds absurd but . . .

THEO: Absurd! —It's disgusting! She's exactly the type who forgets to wash out her panties.

LYMAN, *wincing, but with a certain pleasurable recognition*: I *knew* you'd say that! —I admit it, though, there is a sloppy side to her . . .

THEO: She's the worst generation in our history—screw anybody in pants, then drop their litters like cats, and spout mystic credos on cosmic responsibility, ecology, and human rights!

LYMAN: To my dying day I will stand amazed at your ability to speak in complete paragraphs!

THEO: I insist you explain this to me yourself. Lyman? Lyman!

> *Leah enters. Theo reacts instantly.*

There'll be no one in here but family! *To Bessie*: Get the nurse!

LEAH, *despite Theo, approaches the cast, but with uncertainty about his reaction to her*: Lyman?

THEO, *to Tom*: Get her out of here! *Tom is immobile, and she goes to him furiously.* She does not belong here!

LEAH, *to the cast, with a certain warmth*: It's me, Lyme. Can you hear me?

THEO, *rushing threateningly toward Leah*: Get out, get out, get out . . . !

> *Just as she is about to lay hands on Leah, Lyman throws his arms up and cries imploringly.*

LYMAN: I want everybody to lie down!

> *The three women instantly deanimate as though suddenly falling under the urgency of his control. Lyman gestures, without actually touching them, and causes Theo and Leah to lie on the bed.*

LEAH, *as she lies down; voice soft, remote*: What am I going to tell Benny? Oh gee whiz, Lyman, why did you . . . ?

THEO, *lying down beside Leah*: You have a bitter smell, you should use something.

LEAH: I have, but he likes it.

THEO: Blah. *To Lyman*: And what would you say if one of us took another man to bed and asked you to lie next to him?

LYMAN, *lifting off her glasses*: Oh, I'd kill him, dear; but you're a lady, Theodora; the delicate sculpture of your noble eye, your girlish faith in me and your disillusion; your idealism and your unadmitted greed for wealth; the awkward tenderness of your wooden fingers, your incurably Protestant cooking; your savoir-faire and your sexual inexperience; your sensible shoes and devoted motherhood, your intolerant former radicalism and stalwart love of country now—your Theodorism! Who can ever take your place!

LEAH, *laughing*: Why am I laughing!!

LYMAN: Because you're an anarchist, my darling! *He stretches out on both of them.* Oh, what pleasure, what intensity! Your countercurrents are like bare live wires! *Kisses each in turn.* I'd have no problem defending both of you to the death! Oh the double heat of two blessed wives—this is heaven! *Rests his head on Leah while holding Theo's hand to his cheek.*

LEAH: Listen, you've got to make up your mind about something.

LYMAN: I'm only delaying as long as possible, let's delay it till we all die! Delay, delay, how delicious, my loving Leah, is delay!

THEO, *sits up*: How you can still go on talking about love is beyond my understanding.

LYMAN: And still I love you, Theodora, although certain parts of your body fill me with *rage!*

THEO: So you simply got yourself some other parts instead.

> *Leah, still lying on her back, raises one leg in the air, and her skirt slides down, exposing her thigh.*

LYMAN, *replying to Theo, kissing Leah's thigh*: That's the truth, yes—at least it was all flesh at first.

LEAH, *stretching out her arms and her body*: Oh, how good that was! I'm still pulsing to the tips of my toes. *Theo helps him into shirt and trousers and hands him a jacket.*

> You're really healthy, aren't you.

LYMAN, *they are moving out of Theo's area*: You mean for my age? Yes.

LEAH: I did not mean that!

> *Loud knocking heard. She turns upstage with slight shock. A man's angry voice, muffled words. She stands motionless.*

LYMAN: You okay?

LEAH: It's nothing! Do you have time for a walk?

LYMAN: My health is terrific; in fact, it keeps threatening my dignity.

> *A park bench appears.*

LEAH: Why!

LYMAN: Well, how do I come to be lounging in a park with a girl, and on a working day! I really hadn't planned to do that this afternoon. Did you know I was going to?

LEAH: No . . . but I never do.

LYMAN: Really? But you seem so organized.

LEAH: In business; but not in pleasure.

LYMAN: What surprised me was the openness of your laughter with those heavy executives at the table.

LEAH: Well, your presentation was so funny, I'd heard you were a real brain, not a comic.

LYMAN: Well, insurance is basically comical, isn't it?—at least pathetic.

LEAH: Why?

LYMAN: You're buying immortality, aren't you?—reaching out of your grave to pay the bills and remind people of your life? It's poetry. The soul was once immortal, now we've got an insurance policy.

LEAH: You sound pretty cynical about it.

LYMAN: Not at all—I started as a writer, nobody lusts after the immortal like a writer.

LEAH: How'd you get into insurance?

LYMAN: Pure accident. How'd you?

LEAH: My mother had died, my dad had his stroke, and insurance was something I could do from home. Dad knew a lot of people, being a doctor, so the thing just took off.

LYMAN: Don't take this wrong—but you know what I find terrifically sexy about you?

LEAH: What?

LYMAN: Your financial independence. Horrible, huh?

LEAH: Why?—*wryly*—Whatever helps, helps.

LYMAN: You don't sound married, are you?

LEAH: It's a hell of a time to ask! *They laugh, come closer.* I can't see myself getting married . . . not yet anyway. —Incidentally, have you been listening to me?

LYMAN: Yes, but my attention keeps wandering toward a warm and furry place . . . *She laughs, delighted.* It's funny, my generation got married to show its maturity, yours stays single for the same reason.

LEAH: That's good!

LYMAN: How happy I am! *Sniffs his hands.* Sitting in Elmira in the sun with you, and your scent still on my hands! God!—all the different ways there are to try to be real! —I don't know the connection, but when I turned twenty I sold three poems to *The New Yorker* and a story to *Harper's,* and the first thing I bought was a successful blue suit to impress my father how real I was even though a writer. He ran an appetizer store on Fortieth Street and Ninth Avenue. *Grinning, near laughter.* And he sees the suit and says, "How much you pay?" And I said, "Twenty-nine-fifty," thinking I'd got a terrific bargain. And he says, "Pray God keep an eye on you the rest of your life."

LEAH, *laughs*: That's awful!

LYMAN: No!—it spurred me on! *Laughs.* He had two pieces of wisdom—never trust anybody, and never forgive. Funny, it's like magic, I simply can't trace how we got into bed.

LEAH, *a glance at her watch*: I really have to get back to the office. —But is Lyman an Albanian name?

LYMAN: Lyman's the judge's name in Worcester, Massachusetts, who gave my father his citizenship. Felt is short for Feltman, my mother's name, because my father's was unpronounceable and they wanted a successful American for a son.

LEAH: Then your mother was Jewish.

LYMAN: And the source of all my conflicts. In the Jewish heart is a lawyer and a judge, in the Albanian a bandit defying the government with a knife.

LEAH: What a surprise you are! *She stands, and he does.*

LYMAN: Being so silly?

LEAH: Being so interesting, and in the insurance business.

LYMAN, *taking her hand*: When was the moment?—I'm just curious.

LEAH: I don't know . . . I guess at the conference table I suddenly thought, "He's basically talking to me." But then I figured, this is probably why he's such a great salesman, because everybody he talks to feels loved.

LYMAN: You know?—I've never before with a Jewish girl.

LEAH: Well, you're my first Albanian.

LYMAN: There's something venerable in your eyes. Not old—ancient. Like our peoples.

LEAH, *touching his cheek*: Take care, dear.

LYMAN, *as she passes before him to leave, he takes her hand*: Why do I feel I know nothing about you?

LEAH, *shrugs, smiles*: Maybe you weren't listening . . . which I don't mind if it's in a good cause.

LYMAN, *letting go of her hand*: I walk in the valley of your thighs. *She laughs, gives him a quick kiss.* When you move away now, would you turn back to me for a moment?

LEAH, *amused*: Sure, why?

LYMAN, *half-kidding in his romanticism*: I have to take a small commuter plane and if I die I want that vision as I go down—

LEAH, *backing away with a wave*: 'Bye, Lyman . . .

LYMAN: Can I ask who that fellow was banging on your apartment door?

LEAH, *caught off-guard*: Somebody I used to go with . . . he was angry, that's all.

LYMAN: Are you afraid of him?

LEAH, *shrugs in an accepted uncertainty*: See you, dear.

> *She turns and walks a few yards, then halts and turns her head to look back at him over her shoulder. She exits.*

LYMAN: Beautiful. *Alone*: Miraculous. *Thinks for a moment.* Still . . . was it really all *that* great? *Takes out a cell phone, troubled.* Theo?—hi, darling, I'm just about to take off. Oh, definitely, it has the makings of a much bigger operation; had a talk with Aetna's chief rep up here, and she's agreed to take us on, so I'll probably be spending more time here.—Yes, a woman; she's got a great agency, I might try to buy into her.—Listen, dear, how about you flying up here and we rent a car and drive through Cherry Valley—it's bursting into bloom now!—Oh, I forgot; no-no, you'd better go to your meeting then; it's okay; no, it just suddenly hit me how quickly it's all going by and . . . You ever have the feeling that you never *really* got to know anybody?

> *She never has; he resents it, and a sharpness enters his voice.*

> Well, yes, I do feel that sometimes, very much; sometimes I feel I'm going to vanish without a trace, Theo! *Unhappily now, with hidden anger, the romance gone.* Theo, dear, it's nothing against you, I only meant that with all the analysis and the novels and the Freuds we're still as opaque and unknowable as some line of statues in a church wall. *He hangs up. Now a light strikes the cast on the bed. He moves to it and looks down at himself. Bessie, Theo, and Leah are standing*

motionless around the bed and Tom is off to the one side, observing. Lyman slowly lifts his arms and raises his face like a suppliant. We're all in a cave . . . *The three women now begin to move, ever so slightly at first; their heads are turning as they appear to be searching for the sight of something far away or overhead or on the floor.*

. . . where we entered to make love or money or fame. It's dark in here, as dark as sleep, and each one moves blindly, searching for another, to touch, hoping to touch and afraid; and hoping, and afraid.

As he speaks, the women and Tom move in a crisscrossing path, just missing one another, spreading farther and farther across the stage until one by one they disappear. Lyman has moved above the bed where his cast lies.

So now . . . now that we're here . . . what are we going to say?

BLACKOUT

ACT TWO

SCENE I

The hospital waiting room. Tom is seated with Theo.

TOM: Really, Theo, I wish you'd let Bessie take you back to the city.

THEO: Please stop repeating that! *Slight pause.* I need to talk to him . . . I'll never see him again. I can't simply walk away. Is my head trembling?

TOM: A little, maybe. Should you let one of the doctors look at you?

THEO: I'll be all right, my family has a tendency to tremors, I've had it for years when I'm tense. What time is it?

TOM: Give them a few minutes more. —You seem pale.

THEO, *pressing fingers against her temples to steady herself*: When you spoke with this woman . . . was there any feeling about . . . what she has in mind?

TOM: She's as much in shock as you. The child was her main concern.

THEO: Really? I wouldn't have thought so.

TOM: Oh, I think he means everything to her.

THEO, *begrudgingly*: Well, that's nice. Messes like this are basically comical, aren't they—until you come to the children. I'm very worried about Bessie. She lies there staring at the ceiling. She can hardly talk without starting to weep. He's been her . . . her world. *She begins to fill up.* You're right, I think I'll go. It just seemed unfinished, somehow . . . but maybe it's better to leave it this way . . . *Starts for her bag, stops.* I don't know what to do. One minute I could kill him, the next I wonder if some . . . aberration got into him . . .

> *Leah enters. They did not expect to see each other. A momentary pause. Leah sits.*

LEAH: Good afternoon.

TOM: Good afternoon.

Awkward silence.

LEAH, *asking*: He's not in his room?

THEO, *as it is difficult for her to address Leah, she turns to her slowly*: They're treating his eye.

LEAH: His eye?

TOM: It's nothing serious, he tried to climb out his window. Probably in his sleep. His eyelid was slightly scratched by a rhododendron.

THEO, *making a stab at communication*: He must not have realized he's on the ground floor.

Short pause.

LEAH: Hm! That's interesting, because a friend of ours, Ted Colby, called last night—he's a commander of the state police here. They'd put up a wooden barrier across the Mount Morgan road when it got so icy; and he thinks Lyman moved the barrier aside.

TOM: How could they know it was him?

LEAH: There was only one set of tire tracks.

THEO: Oh my God.

LEAH: He's worried about him. They're good friends, they go hunting together.

THEO: Lyman hunts?

LEAH: Oh sure. *Theo shakes her head incredulously.* But I can't imagine him in that kind of depression, can you?

TOM: Actually . . . yes, I think I can.

LEAH: Really. He's always seemed so . . . up with me, and happy. *Theo glances from her, irked, then away. Leah glances at her watch.* I just have to settle some business with him for a few minutes, I won't be in your way.

THEO: *My* way? You're free to do anything you like, as far as I'm concerned.

LEAH, *slightly taken aback*: Yes . . . the same with me . . . in your case. *Beat.* I mean as far as I'm concerned. *The hostility turns her to look at her watch again.* I want to tell you . . . I almost feel worse for you, some-how, than for myself.

THEO, *gives a hard laugh*: Why! Do I seem *that* old? *The second rebuff stiffens Leah.* I shouldn't have said that. I apologize. I'm exhausted.

LEAH, *letting it pass*: How is your daughter?—she still here?

THEO, *a hostile color despite everything*: In the motel. She's devastated.

TOM: Your boy taking it all right?

LEAH: No, it's wracked him, it's terrible. *To Theo*: I thought Lyman might have some idea how to deal with him, the kid's always idolized him so. I'm really at my wits' end.

THEO, *bitterly angry, but contained*: We are his dust; we billow up behind his steps and settle again when he passes by. Billie Holiday . . . *She touches her forehead.* I can't recall when she died, it's quite a while, isn't it.

TOM: Billie Holiday? Why?

> *Tom and Leah observe, puzzled, as Theo stares in silence. Then . . .*

LEAH: Why don't I come back in a couple of hours—I've got a two o'clock conference call and it's getting a bit late . . . *She stands, goes to Theo, and, extending her hand*: Well, if we don't meet again . . .

THEO, *touching her hand briefly, hostility momentarily overcome*: . . . Do you understand this?

LEAH: It's baffling. He's raced the Mount Morgan road, he knows what it's like, even in summer.

THEO: Raced? You mean cars?

LEAH: Sure. He has a Lotus and a Z. He had a Ferrari, but he totaled it. *Theo turns and stares into space, stunned.* I was thinking before . . .

THEO: He's always been terrified of speed; he never drives over sixty . . .

LEAH: . . . He reminds me of a frog . . .

THEO: A frog?

LEAH: . . . I mean you never know when you look at a frog whether it's the same one you just saw or a different one. *To Tom*: When you talk to him—the television is hounding us; he really has to make a definite statement to stop all this stupid speculation.

THEO: What speculation?

LEAH: You've seen the *Daily News*, haven't you?

THEO: What!

LEAH: We're both on the front page with a headline . . .

TOM, *to Theo, placating*: It's unimportant . . .

THEO, *to Leah*: What's the headline?

LEAH: "Who gets Lyman?"

THEO: How dare they!

TOM: Don't be upset. *To Leah*: I'll get a statement from him this afternoon . . .

LEAH: Goodbye, Mrs. . . . *Stops herself; a short laugh.* I was going to call you Mrs. Felt, but . . . *Correcting again.* . . . Well you are, aren't you—I guess I'm the one who's not! I'll come by about three or so. *Leah exits.*

THEO: She wants him back, doesn't she.

TOM: Why?

THEO, *gives her little laugh*: Didn't you hear it?—she's the one he was happy with!

TOM: Oh, I don't think she meant . . .

THEO, *her fierce competitiveness aroused*: That's *all* she meant.—I pity her, though, with such a young child. *She fumes in silence. Can* it have been suicide?

TOM: Frankly, I'd almost hope so, in a way.

THEO: You mean it would indicate a moral conscience?

TOM: Yes. —But I'm wondering . . . maybe he just wanted to change his life; become a completely different person . . .

THEO, *stares for a moment*: . . . Maybe not so different.

TOM: How do you mean?

THEO, *a long hesitation*: I don't know why I'm still trying to protect him—he tried to kill me once.

TOM: You're not serious.

> *Lyman appears in sunlight in swim trunks, inhaling deeply on a boat deck. She begins walking toward him.*

THEO: Oh yes! I didn't know this woman existed then, but I see now it was just about the time they had either married or were on the verge. *As she moves toward Lyman, her coat slides off, revealing her in a swimsuit.* He seemed very strange, unreal. We'd gone for a two-day sail off Montauk . . .

> *Lyman is doing breathing exercises.*

LYMAN: The morning mist rising from the sea is always like the first day of the world . . . the "oysterygods and the visigods . . ."

> *Theo enters into Lyman's acting area.*

THEO: *Finnegans Wake.*

LYMAN: I'll get the weather. *Kneels, tunes a radio; static.* Is that a new suit? It's sexy as hell.

THEO: Two years ago. You bought it for me in San Diego.

LYMAN, *mimes a pistol to his head*: Bang.

ANNOUNCER, *voice-over*: . . . Due to the unusually warm spring tides there've been several shark sightings off Montauk . . . one is reported to be twelve to fourteen feet long . . . *Heavy static intervenes; Lyman mimes switching the radio off.*

LYMAN: Jesus.

THEO: Oh that's ridiculous, it's only May! I'm going in for a dip . . . *She looks out over the ocean.*

LYMAN: But the radio man said . . .

THEO: Nonsense. I've sailed around here since my childhood, and so did my grandparents—there are never sharks until July if at all, the water's much too cold. Come in with me?

LYMAN: I'm the Mediterranean type—we're unreliable and hate cold water. I know I shouldn't say this, Theo, but how you can hang on to your convictions in the face of a report like that . . . just seems . . . I don't know—fanatical.

THEO, *with a hard, determined laugh*: Now that is really uncalled for! You're just as stubborn as I am when you're committed to something.

LYMAN: Goddammit, you're right! And I love your convictions!—go ahead, I'll keep an eye out.

THEO, *with loving laughter*: You simply can't stand me contradicting you, darling, but it's the best exercise for your character.

LYMAN: Right! And a miserable character it is. Into the ocean! *He leaves her side, scans the ocean.*

THEO, *bends for a dive*: On the mark . . . get set . . .

LYMAN, *pointing left*: What's that out there!

THEO: No, sharks always move, that's a log.

LYMAN: Oh right. Okay, jump in.

THEO: I'll run in! Wait, let me warm up. *Backs up to make a run for it.* Join me! Come on.

LYMAN: I can't, dear, I fear death.

> *She is behind him, running in place. His back is to her and his eye catches sight of something toward the right front; his mouth opens, eyes staring in horror following the moving shark. She bends to start her run.*

THEO: Okay, one . . . and a two . . . and a . . . three! *She runs and as she comes abreast of him he suddenly, at the last moment, reaches out and stops her at the edge.*

LYMAN: Stop!

He points front; she looks, horror rising on her face as their eyes follow the fish.

THEO: My God, the *size* of him! Ahhh . . . ! *She bursts into tears of released terror; he takes her into his arms.*

LYMAN: Honey, when are you going to trust something I say!

THEO: Oh, I'm going to be sick . . . !

About to vomit, she bends and rushes into darkness. Lights go out on Lyman and up on Tom in the waiting room; he is staring straight ahead, listening. The light widens and finds Theo standing in her fur coat.

TOM: That sounds like he saved you.

THEO: Yes, I've always tried to think of it that way, too, but I have to face everything, now—*coming downstage; newly distressed by the memory*—it was not quite at the top of his voice. I mean, it wasn't . . .

Light flares up on Lyman in his trunks. At top voice and in horror he shouts . . .

LYMAN: Stop! *He stands mesmerized looking at the shark below. Blackout on Lyman.*

THEO: It was more like . . .

Lights flare up again on Lyman, and he merely semi-urgently—as he did in the scene—shouts . . .

LYMAN: Stop.

Blackout on Lyman.

THEO: I tell you he was on the verge of letting me go.

TOM: Come on, Theo, you can't really believe that. I mean, how could you have gone on living with him?

THEO: How I've gone on? *A bitter and embarrassed smile.* Well, we did have two serious breakups and . . . months have gone by without . . . relations. *Gradually becomes furious.* No, damnit, I'm not going to evade this anymore. —Maybe I've gone on because I'm corrupt, Tom. I certainly wasn't once, but who knows, now? He's rich, isn't he? And vastly respected, and what would I do with myself alone? Why does anybody stay together, once they realize who they're with? *Suddenly livid.* What the hell am I hanging around here for? This is the stupidest thing I've ever done in my life! *Indignantly grabs her bag.*

TOM: You love him, Theo. *Physically stops her.* Please go home, will you? And give it a few weeks before you decide anything? *She stifles a sob as he embraces her.* I know how crazy this sounds, but part of him worships you. I'm sure of it.

THEO, *suddenly screams in his face*: I hate him! I hate him! *She is rigid, pale, and he grips her shoulders to steady her. A pause.* I must lie down. We'll probably go back to the city tonight. But call me if he wakes up. —It's so hard to just walk away without knowing what happened. —Or maybe I should just leave . . . *She passes her hand across her brow.* Do I look strange?

TOM: Just tired. Come, I'll find you a cab.

THEO: It's only a few blocks, I need the air. *Starting off, turns back.* Amazing how beautiful the country still is up here. Like nothing bad had ever happened in the world. *She exits.*

Alone, Tom stands staring into space, arms folded, trying to figure out an approach.

BLACKOUT

SCENE II

Lyman's room. He is deeply asleep, snoring placidly at first. Now he starts muttering.

NURSE: Whyn't you take some time off? You do more work asleep than most of us awake. You ought to come up ice fishing with us sometime, that'll slow you down.

Nurse goes out. Now there is a tensing up, he is groaning in his sleep. Leah and Theo appear on either side of him, but on elevated platforms, like two stone deities; they are in kitchen aprons, wifely ribbons tying up their hair. But there is something menacing about their deathly stillness as the sepulchral dream-light finds them, motionless in this tableau. After a long moment they reanimate. As in life they are reserved, each measuring herself against the other. Their manner of speaking is godlike, deathly.

THEO: I wouldn't mind it at all if you did some of the cooking, I'm not all that super.

LEAH, *generously*: I hear you make good desserts, though.

THEO: Apple cobbler, yes; gingerbread with whipped cream. *Gaining confidence.* And exceptional waffles for breakfast, with real maple syrup, although he's had to cut out the sausages.

LEAH: I can do potato pancakes and segadina goulash.

THEO, *disapproving*: And all that paprika?

LEAH: It has to be blended in, of course.

THEO, *at a loss, sensing defeat*: Ah, blended in! I'm afraid I couldn't do something like that.

LEAH, *smiling, brutally pressing her advantage*: Oh yes, blended in and really blended *in!* And my gefilte fish is feather-light. *Clapping her cupped palms together.* I wet my hands and keep patting it till it shapes up just perfect!

THEO, *struggling, at a loss*: He does love my glazed ham. Yes!—and my boiled tongue. *A sudden bright idea.* Custard!

LEAH, *generously*: You can do all the custard and glazed ham and I'll do all the gefilte fish and goulash . . . *and* the blending in.

THEO: But may I do *some*? Once or twice a month, perhaps?

LEAH: Let's leave it up to him—some months you can do more . . .

THEO: Yes!—and some months you.

LEAH: 'Kay! Would you wash out my panties?

THEO: Certainly. As long as he tells me my lies.

LEAH: Good! Then you'll have your lies and I'll have mine!

THEO AND LEAH: Hurrah for the menu!

LEAH, *filled with admiration*: You certainly have class!

> *Lyman chuckles in his sleep as they emerge from their matronly costumes, now dressed in sexy black tight-fitting body stockings and high heels and, slithering toward each other, kiss, turn toward the bed and as he laughs suddenly raise long daggers and chop at him again and again. He is shouting and writhing as Nurse rushes in and the women disappear.*

NURSE: All right now, let's come back, dear, come on back . . .

> *He stops struggling and opens his eyes.*

LYMAN: Wah. Oh. What dreams. God, how I'd like to be dead.

NURSE: Don't start feeling sorry for yourself; you know what they say—come down off the cross, they need the wood.

LYMAN: I'm suffocating, can't you open a window?

NURSE: Not anymore, I can't.

LYMAN: Huh? Oh listen, that's ridiculous, I wasn't really trying to climb out . . .

NURSE: Well, you did a pretty good imitation. Your lawyer's asking can he come in . . .

LYMAN: I thought he'd gone back to New York. I look terrible?

NURSE, *swabbing his face and hands*: You takin' it too hard. Be different if you deserted those women, but anybody can see how well taken care of they are. . . .

LYMAN: Go on, you don't kid me, Logan—underneath all this cool you know you're as shocked as hell.

NURSE: Go on, brush your teeth. *As he does*: The last shock I had come off a short in my vacuum cleaner . . . *He laughs, then groans in pain*. One thing I *have* been wondering, though.

LYMAN: What've you been wondering?

NURSE: Whatever got into you to actually marry that woman?—man as smart as you?

LYMAN: Were you talking about ice before?

NURSE: Ice? Oh, you mean . . . ya, we go ice fishing on the lake, me, my husband, and my boy—you're remembering a lot better now.

LYMAN, *staring*: Not being married is going to feel very strange—like suddenly your case has been dismissed and you don't have to be in court anymore.

NURSE: Don't you talk bad about those women; they don't look mean to me.

LYMAN: Why I married her? —I'm very attracted to women who smell like fruit; Leah smelled like a pink, ripe cantaloupe. And when she smiled, her clothes seemed to drop off. I'd never been so jealous. I swear, if a hundred women walked past me on a sidewalk I could pick out the clack of Leah's heels. I even loved lying in bed listening to the quiet splash of her bathwater. And of course slipping into her pink cathedral . . .

NURSE: You have the dirtiest mind I ever seen on an educated man.

LYMAN: I couldn't lose her, Logan, and that's the best reason to marry anybody, unless you're married already.

NURSE: I'll get your lawyer, okay? *He seems suddenly overcome; weeps.* Now don't you start that cryin' again . . .

LYMAN: It's just my children . . . you can't imagine how they respected me . . . *Bracing himself.* But nobody's any better, goddammit!

    Tom enters.

TOM: May I come in?

LYMAN, *uncertainly, trying to read Tom:* Hi! I thought you'd gone back—something happen?

TOM: Can we talk?

    Nurse exits.

LYMAN: If you can bear it. *Grins.* You despise me, Tom?

TOM: I'm still staggering. I don't know what to think.

LYMAN: Sure you do, but that's okay. *His charming grin.* So, what's up?

TOM: I've been discussing things with the women . . .

LYMAN: I thought I told you—or did I?—just give them what they want. Within reason, I mean.

TOM: I really believe Theo'd like to find a way to forgive you.

LYMAN: Impossible!

TOM: She's a great spirit, Lyman.

LYMAN: . . . Not that great; I'd have to live on my knees for the rest of my life.

TOM: Maybe not—if you were clear about yourselves . . .

LYMAN: I'm pretty clear now—I'm a selfish son of a bitch. But I have loved the truth.

TOM: And what's the truth?

LYMAN: A man can be faithful to himself or to other people—but not to both. At least not happily. We all know this, but it's immoral to admit that the first law of life is betrayal; why else did those rabbis pick Cain and Abel to open the Bible? Cain felt betrayed by God, so he betrayed Him and killed his brother.

TOM: But the Bible doesn't end there, does it.

LYMAN: Jesus Christ? I can't worship self-denial; it's just not true for me. We're all ego, kid, ego plus an occasional heart-felt prayer.

TOM: Then why'd you bother building one of the most socially responsible companies in America?

LYMAN: The truth? I did that twenty-five years ago, when I was a righteous young man; but I am an unrighteous middle-aged man now, so all I have left is to try not to live with too many lies. *Suddenly collapsing within.* —Why must I see them? . . . What can I say to them? Christ, if I could only lose consciousness! *Rocking side to side in anguish.* . . . Advise me, Tom, tell me something.

TOM: Maybe you ought to give up trying to seem so strong.

   Slight pause.

LYMAN: What do you want me to say, I'm a loser?

TOM: Well, right now, aren't you?

LYMAN: No, goddammit! A loser has lived somebody else's life, I've lived my own; crappy as it may seem, it's mine. —And I'm no worse than anybody else! —Now answer that, and don't kid me.

TOM: All right, I won't kid you; I think you've done these women terrible harm.

LYMAN: You do.

TOM: If you want to get off this dime you're on I'd begin by confronting the damage I'd done—I think you've raked Theo's soul.

LYMAN: I've also given her an interesting life, a terrific daughter, and made her very rich. I mean, exactly what harm are you talking about?

TOM: Lyman, you deceived her . . .

LYMAN, *fury overtaking him*: But she couldn't have had all that if I hadn't deceived her!—you know as well as I that nobody could live with Theo for more than a month without some relief! I've suffered at least as much as she has in this marriage!

TOM, *demurring*: Well . . .

LYMAN: . . . Now listen, you want the rock-bottom truth?—I curse the day I ever laid eyes on her and I don't *want* her forgiveness!

TOM: For Pete's sake, don't get angry . . .

LYMAN: I ever tell you how we met?—let's stop pretending this marriage was made in heaven, for Christ's sake!—I was hitchhiking back from Cornell; nineteen innocent years of age; I'm standing beside the road with my suitcase and I go behind a bush. This minister sees the suitcase and stops, gives me a ride, and I end up at an Audubon Society picnic, where lo and behold, I meet his daughter, Theodora.—Had I taken that suitcase with me behind the bush I'd never have met her!—And serious people are still talking about the moral purpose of the universe!

TOM: Give or take a bad patch or two, you've had the best marriage of anyone I've ever met.

LYMAN, *with a sigh*: I know. —Look, we're all the same; a man is a fourteen-room house—in the bedroom he's asleep with his intelligent wife, in his living room he's rolling around with some bare-assed girl, in the library he's paying his taxes, in the yard he's raising tomatoes, and in the cellar he's making a bomb to blow it all up. And nobody's different . . . Except you, maybe. Are you?

TOM: I don't raise tomatoes . . . Listen, the TV is flogging the story and it's humiliating for the women; let's settle on a statement and be done with it. What do you want?

LYMAN: What I always wanted; both of them.

TOM: Be serious . . .

LYMAN: I know these women and they still love me! It's only what they think they're *supposed* to feel that's confusing them. —Do I sound crazy?

TOM: Listen, I forgot to tell you—Jeff Huddleston called me this morning; heard it on the radio; he insists you resign from the board.

LYMAN: Not on your life! That fat fraud—Jeff Huddleston's got a woman stashed in Trump Tower and two in L.A.

TOM: *Huddleston!*

LYMAN: He offered to loan me one once! Huddleston has more outside ass than a Nevada whorehouse!

TOM: But he doesn't marry them.

LYMAN: Right!—in other words, what I really violated was the law of hypocrisy.

TOM: Unfortunately that's the one that operates.

LYMAN: Not with me, baby! I may be a bastard but I am not a hypocrite! I am not quitting my company! What's Leah saying . . . anything?

TOM: She's stunned. But frankly, I'm not sure she's out of the question either . . . if that's the move you wanted to make.

LYMAN, *deeply touched*: What size these women have! *Weeping threatens again.* Oh Tom, I'm lost!

Bessie and Theo enter. Theo stands beside his bed staring at him without expression. Bessie doesn't so much as look at him. After a long moment . . .

Downing fear: My God, Theo—thank you . . . I mean for coming. I didn't expect you . . .

She sits down in a potent silence. Bessie stands, fiercely aloof. He is openly and awkwardly ashamed.

Hi, Bessie.

BESSIE: I'm here for her sake, she wanted to say something to you. *Hurrying her along.* Mother?

But Theo takes no notice, staring at Lyman with a fixed, unreadable smile. After a long, awkward moment . . .

LYMAN, *to fill the void*: How are you feeling today? I hear you were . . .

THEO, *dead flat, cutting him off*: I won't be seeing you again, Lyman.

LYMAN, *despite everything, a bit of a blow—slight pause*: Yes. Well . . . I guess there's no use in apologizing. . . . But I am sorry, Theo.

THEO: I can't leave my life lying all over the floor like this.

LYMAN: I'll talk about anything you like.

THEO: I seem confused but I'm not; there's just so much that I . . . that I don't want bottled up in me anymore.

LYMAN: Sure, I understand.

THEO: —Do you remember that young English instructor whose wife walked out on him—his advice to you about sex?

LYMAN: An English instructor? At Cornell, you mean?

THEO: "Bend it in half," he said, "and tie a rubber band around it."

LYMAN, *laughing, a little alarmed*: Oh sure, Jim Donaldson!

THEO: Everyone used to laugh at that.

LYMAN: *Her smile is empty, his charm desperate.* Right! "Bend it in half and . . ." *Continues a strained chuckling.*

THEO, *cutting him off*: I *hated* you laughing at that; it showed a vulgar and disgusting side of you. I was ashamed . . . for you and for myself.

LYMAN, *brought up short*: I see. But that's so long ago, Theo . . .

THEO: I want to tell you that I nearly ended it right then and there, but I thought I was too inexperienced to make a judgment. But I was right—you *were* a vulgar, unfeeling man, and you are still.

Anxiously, Lyman glances over to Bessie for help or explanation of this weirdness.

LYMAN: I see. Well, I guess our whole life was a mistake then. *Angered but attempting charm.* But I made a good living.

BESSIE: Please, Mother, let's go, he's mocking you, can't you hear it?

LYMAN, *flaring up*: Must I not defend myself? Please go ahead, Theo, I understand what you're saying, and it's okay, it's what you feel.

THEO, *seemingly relaxed*: —What was the name of the river, about half an hour's walk past the Chemistry building?

LYMAN, *puzzled—is she mad?*: What river?

THEO: Where we went skinny-dipping with those geologists and their girls?

LYMAN, *at a loss for a moment*: Oh, you mean graduation night!

THEO: . . . The whole crowd swimming naked at the falls . . . and the girls all laughing in the darkness . . . ?

LYMAN, *starting to smile but still uncomprehending*: Oh sure . . . that was a great night!

THEO: I straddled you, and over your shoulder . . . did I dream this? I recall a white wall of limestone, rising straight out of the river . . . ?

LYMAN: That's right, Devonian. It was full of fossils.

THEO: Yes! Beetle imprints, worm tracks, crustacea fifty million years old going straight up like a white temple wall . . . and we floated around below, like two frogs attached in the darkness . . . our wet eyelashes touching.

LYMAN: Yes. It was beautiful. I'm glad you remember it that way.

THEO: Of course I do; I was never a Puritan, Lyman, it is simply a question of taste—that night was inspiring.

LYMAN: Well, I never had taste, we both know that. But I won't lie to you, Theo—taste to me is what's left of life after people can't screw anymore.

THEO: You should have told me that thirty years ago.

LYMAN: I didn't know it thirty years ago.

THEO: And do you remember what you said as we floated there?

LYMAN, *hesitates*: Yes.

THEO: You couldn't.

LYMAN: I said, "What could ever come between us?" Correct?

THEO, *surprised, derailed*: . . . But did you mean that then? Please tell me the truth, it's important to me.

LYMAN, *affected*: Yes, I meant it.

THEO: Then . . . when did you begin to fool me?

LYMAN: Please don't go on anymore . . .

THEO: I am trying to pinpoint when my life died. That's not unreasonable, is it?

LYMAN: From my heart, Theo, I ask your pardon.

THEO: —When did Billie Holiday die?

LYMAN, *perplexed*: Billie Holiday?—oh I don't know, ten, twelve years ago? Why?

> *Theo goes silent, staring into space. He is suddenly weeping at the sight of her suffering.*

Why do you want to know about Billie?

BESSIE: All right, Mother, let's go, huh?

LYMAN: I think it might be better if she talked it out . . .

BESSIE: No one is interested in what you think. *To Theo*: I want you to come now!

LYMAN: Have mercy!

BESSIE: You talking mercy?!

LYMAN: For her, not me! Don't you hear what she's trying to say?—she loved me!

BESSIE: How can you listen to this shit!

LYMAN: How dare you! I gave you a damned fine life, Bessie!

BESSIE: You have nothing to say anymore, you are nonsense!

THEO: Please, dear!—wait outside for a few minutes. *Bessie, seeing her adamance, strides out.* You've torn out her heart. *Lyman turns away trying not to weep.* Was there some pleasure in making a fool of me? Why couldn't you have told me about this woman?

LYMAN: I did try, many times, but . . . I guess it sounds crazy, but . . . I just couldn't bear to lose you.

THEO: But—*with sudden, near-hysterical intensity*—you were lying to me every day all these nine or ten years—what could you possibly lose?

LYMAN, *determined not to flinch*: . . . Your happiness.

THEO: *My* happiness! In God's name what are you talking about!

LYMAN: Only the truth can help us, Theo—I think you were happier in those last years than ever in our marriage—you feel that, don't you?

She doesn't contradict.

May I tell you why? Because I was never bored being with you.

THEO: You'd been bored with me?

LYMAN: Same as you'd been bored with me, dear . . . I'm talking about— you know—just normal marital boredom.

She seems obtuse to this, so he tries to explain.

You know, like at dinner—when I'd repeat some inane story you'd heard a thousand times . . . ? Like my grandfather losing three fingers under the Ninth Avenue trolley . . . ?

THEO: But I loved that story! I was *never* bored with you . . . stupid as that was.

LYMAN, *now she just seems perverse*: Theo, you were bored—it's no sin! Same as I was when, for instance, you'd start telling people for the ten thousandth time that . . . *his charming laugh* . . . as a minister's daughter you were not permitted to climb a tree and show off your panties?

THEO, *sternly resisting his charm*: But I think that story describes a kind of society that has completely disappeared! That story has historical importance!

LYMAN, *the full agony*: That story is engraved in my flesh! . . . And I beg you, don't make this a moral dilemma. It is just common domestic tedium, dear, it is life, and there's no other woman I know who has the honesty and strength to accept it as life—if you wanted to!

THEO, *a pause; above her confusion, she is striving desperately to understand*: And why do you say I was happier in these last years?

LYMAN: Because you could see my contentment, and I was content . . .

THEO: Because she . . . ?

LYMAN: Because whenever you started with your panties again I could still find you lovable, knowing that story was not going to be my entire and total fate till the day I died.

THEO: . . . Because she was waiting for you.

LYMAN: Right.

THEO: You were never bored with *her*?

LYMAN: Oh God yes! Sometimes even more than with you.

THEO, *with quick, intense, hopeful curiosity*: Really! And what then?

LYMAN: Then I would thank my luck that I had you to come back to. —I know how hard this is to understand, Theo.

THEO: No-no . . . I guess I've always known it.

LYMAN: What.

THEO: You are some kind of . . . of giant clam.

LYMAN: Clam?

THEO: Waiting on the bottom for whatever happens to fall from the ocean into your mouth; you are simply a craving, and that craving you call love. You are a kind of monster, and I think you even know it, don't you. I can almost pity you, Lyman. *She turns to leave.* I hope you make a good recovery. It's all very clear now, I'm glad I stayed.

LYMAN: It's amazing—the minute the mystery of life appears, you think everything's cleared up.

THEO: There's no mystery to me, you have never loved anyone!

LYMAN: Then explain to yourself how this worthless, loveless, treacherous clam could have single-handedly made two such different women happier than they'd ever been in their lives!

THEO: Really! *Laughs, ending in a near-scream.* Really and truly *happy*?!

LYMAN: . . . In fact, if I dared admit the whole idiotic truth, the only one who suffered these past nine years—was *me*!

> *An enormous echoing roar fills the theater—the roar of a lion. Light rises on Bessie looking front through field glasses; she is wearing shorts and a pith helmet and khaki safari jacket.*

THEO: *You suffering?*—oh dear God save us!

> *She is trying to sustain her bitter laughter and moves toward Bessie, and as she enters Bessie's area Theo's laughter dies off and she takes a pith helmet out of a picnic basket and puts it on. Lyman, slipping out of bed at the same time, follows Theo. There is no dialogue break.*

LYMAN: . . . What would you call it, then—having to look into your innocent, loving faces, when I knew the hollowness your happiness was based on? That isn't suffering?

He takes his place beside the two women, looking in the same direction out front, shading his eyes. With no break in dialogue . . .

BESSIE, *looking through field glasses*: Good heavens, is he going to mount her *again*?

LYMAN: They don't call him the king of the beasts for nothing, honey.

BESSIE: Poor thing, how patient she is.

THEO, *taking the glasses from her*: Oh come, dear, she's not *only* patient.

BESSIE, *spreading a tablecloth and picnic things on the ground*: But it's only once every half a year, isn't it?

LYMAN: Once that we *know* about.

THEO, *helping to spread the picnic*: Oh no, they're marvelously loyal couples.

LYMAN: No, dear, lions have harems—you're thinking of storks.

BESSIE, *offering an egg*: Daddy?

LYMAN, *sitting—happily eating*: I love you in those helmets, you look like two noble ladies on safari.

THEO, *stretching out on the ground*: The air here! The silence. These hills.

BESSIE: Thanks for bringing me, Daddy. I wish Harold could have been here. —Why do you look sad?

LYMAN: Just thinking. *To Theo*: About monogamy—why you suppose we think of it as a higher form of life? *She turns up to him . . . defensively . . .* I mean I was just wondering.

THEO: Well, it implies an intensification of love.

LYMAN: How about that, Bess? You had a lot of boyfriends before Harold, didn't you?

BESSIE: Well . . . yes, I guess it is more intense with one.

LYMAN: But how does that make it a higher form?

THEO: Monogamy strengthens the family; random screwing undermines it.

LYMAN: But as one neurotic to another, what's so good about strengthening the family?

THEO: Well, for one thing it enhances liberty.

BESSIE: Liberty? Really?

THEO: The family disciplines its members; when the family is weak the state has to move in; so the stronger the family the fewer the police. And that is why monogamy is a higher form.

LYMAN: Jesus, did you just make that up? *To Bessie:* Isn't she marvelous? I'm giving her an A-plus!

THEO, *happily hurt:* Oh shut up.

LYMAN: But what about those Muslims? They're very big on stable families but a lot of them have two or three wives.

THEO: But only one is really the *wife.*

LYMAN: Not according to my father—they often had two main women in Albania, one to run the house and the other for the bed. But they were both serious wives.

THEO: Your father's sociology was on a par with his morals. A wife to your father was a walking dish towel.

LYMAN, *laughs, to Bessie:* Your mother is a classical woman, you know why?

BESSIE, *laughing delightedly:* Why?

LYMAN: Because she is always clear and consistent and . . .

THEO: . . . Rather boring.

> *He guffaws warmly, clapping his hands over his head in appreciation.*

BESSIE: You are not boring! *Rushing to embrace Theo.* Tell her she is not boring!

LYMAN, *embracing Theo with Bessie:* Theo, please . . . I swear I didn't mean boring!

THEO, *tearfully hurt:* Well I'd rather be boring and clear than cute and stupid!

LYMAN: Who asked you to be cute!—now please don't go on about it.

THEO: I wish I knew how to amuse you! Your eyes have been glazed over since we stepped onto this wretched continent!

LYMAN, *guiltily stretching an awkward embrace toward her:* I *love* this trip, and being with both of you . . . ! Theo, please!—now you are making me guilty!

> *The lion's roar interrupts and they all look front in shock.*

BESSIE: Is he heading here . . . ? Daddy!—he's trotting!

GUIDE'S VOICE, *off, on bullhorn*: You will have to come back to the car, everyone! At once!

LYMAN: Quick! *He pushes both women off.*

BESSIE, *on exiting*: Daddy, come . . . !

THEO, *sensing he is remaining behind*: Lyman . . . ?

LYMAN: Go! *He pushes Theo off, but turns back himself.*

GUIDE'S VOICE: Come back to the car at once, Mr. Felt!

> *Lion's roar—but closer now. Lyman facing front and the lion, prepared to run for it but holding his ground.*

> Mr. Felt, get back to the car!

> *Another roar.*

LYMAN, *eyes on the lion, shouting toward it with fear's exhilaration*: I am happy, yes! That I'm married to Theodora and have Bessie . . . yes, *and Leah, too!*

> *Another roar!*

BESSIE, *from a distance*: Daddy, please come here!

LYMAN: And that I've made a mountain of money . . . yes, and have no impending lawsuits!

BESSIE, *from a distance*: Daddy . . . !

LYMAN, *flinging his words toward the approaching beast, but crouched and ready to flee*: . . . And that I don't sacrifice one day to things I don't believe in—including monogamy, yes!—*arms thrown out, terror-inspired*—I love my life, I am not guilty! I dare you to eat me, son of a bitch!

> *Immense roar! Wide-eyed, crouched now, and on the very verge of fleeing, he is watching the approaching lion—whose roar, as we now hear, has changed to a rather more relaxed guttural growling, much diminished; and Lyman cautiously straightens up, and now turns triumphantly toward the women offstage. And Bessie flies out and throws her arms around him in ecstatic relief, kissing him.*

BESSIE, *looking front*: Daddy, he turned back! What did you do that for!

> *Theo enters.*

THEO: He turned back! *To Lyman*: How did you do that! *To Bessie*: Did you see how he stopped and turned around? *To Lyman*: What happened?

LYMAN: I think I've lost my guilt! I think he sensed it! *Half-laughing.* Maybe lions don't eat happy people!

THEO: What are you talking about?

LYMAN, *staring in wonder*: I tell you his roar hit my teeth like voltage and suddenly it was so clear that . . . *Turns to her.* I've always been happy with you, Theo!—I just somehow couldn't accept it! But I am never going to apologize for my happiness again!—it's a miracle!

THEO, *with tears of gratitude, clasping her hands together prayerfully*: Oh, Lyman! *Rushing to kiss him.* Oh, darling!

LYMAN, *still riding his wave, holding out his hand to her*: What old good friends we are, Theo! Put her there! *She laughs and manfully shakes hands.* What a *person* you are, what a grave and beautiful face you have!

BESSIE: Oh, Daddy, that's so lovely!—you're just marvelous! *She weeps.*

LYMAN: I worship this woman, Bessie! *To Theo*: How the hell are we still together? *To Bessie*: —Do you realize how she must love me to stand for my character?

THEO: Oh, this is what I always saw happening someday!—*a sophisticated laugh*—not with a lion, of course, but exactly this sudden flash of light . . . !

LYMAN: The whole future is clear to me now! We are going to march happily into our late middle age, proudly, heads up! I'm going to build a totally selfish little cottage in the Caribbean and we'll fill it up with all the thick English novels we never got to finish . . . plus Proust!—and I'll buy two mopeds with little baskets on the handlebars for the shopping trips . . .

THEO: I knew it, I knew it!

LYMAN: . . . And I'll spend every day with you—except maybe a week or so a month in the Elmira office!

BESSIE: How fantastic, Mother!

THEO: Thank you, lion! Thank you, Africa! *Turning to him.* Lyman?

LYMAN, *already mentally departing the scene*: . . . Huh? Yes!

THEO: I am all new!

> *She throws her arms around him, burying her face in his neck. He looks front with an expression of deepening agony.*

BESSIE: This has been the most fantastic two weeks of my life! I love you, Daddy!

> *She rushes to him and with one arm he embraces her, the other around Theo. Tears are starting in his eyes.*

Are you weeping?

LYMAN: Just amazement, honey . . . at my luck, I guess. Come, we'd better go back.

Somberly he turns them upstage; lights are changing, growing dimmer, and they walk into the darkness while he remains behind. Dim light reveals the Nurse sitting near the bed.

NURSE: The only thing I don't understand is why you married that woman, a smart man like you.

Lyman stares ahead as Leah appears, isolated in light; she is in her fur coat, exactly as in Act One when she was about to go for an abortion. The Nurse remains in periphery, immobile.

LEAH: Yes, I suppose it could wait a week or so, but . . . really, Lyman, you know you're never going to leave her.

LYMAN: You cancel the operation, okay? And I'm telling her tomorrow.

LEAH: You're telling her what?

LYMAN, *almost holding his breath*: I will not rationalize you away. I have one life! I'm going to ask her for a divorce.

LEAH: My God, Lyman! —But listen, I know your attachment to her . . .

LYMAN, *kisses her hand*: Please keep this baby. Will you? And stay home and cross your legs, you hear?

LEAH: This is serious?

LYMAN: This is serious. I'm asking her for a divorce.

LEAH: Suddenly . . . why am I not sure I want to be a mother!—Do I, do you think?

LYMAN: Yes you do, we think!

Kisses her. They laugh together. He turns to leave; she grasps his hands and presses them together between hers in a prayerful gesture; and facing heaven . . .

LEAH: Please! Some good luck! *To Lyman directly*: Why is everything so dangerous! *She gives him a violent kiss. She exits as Theo appears walking toward him; she is hiding something behind her back and smiling lovingly. Lyman looks solemn, prepared for the showdown.*

LYMAN: Theo, dear . . . There's something I have to tell you . . .

THEO, *holding out a cashmere sweater*: Happy birthday!

LYMAN, *startled*: Hah? But it's not July, is it!

THEO: But it was so sinfully expensive I needed an excuse. *Putting him into the sweater.* Here . . . straighten it. It's not too big, is it? *Stepping back to admire.* It's gorgeous, look in the mirror!

LYMAN: It's beautiful, thank you, dear. But listen, I really have something to . . .

THEO: My God, Lyman, you are simply magnificent! *Linking arms with him and walking in her cumbersome way.* I have another surprise—I got tickets for the Balanchine! And a table at Luigi's afterwards!

LYMAN, *grimly screwing up his courage—and beginning to resent her domination*: I have something to tell you, Theo, why do you make it so hard for me!

THEO: What. *He is paralyzed.* What is it? Has something happened? *Alarmed now.* Lyman!—*asking*—you went for your checkup!

LYMAN, *about to explode*: God's sake, no, it's not that!

THEO: Why is your face so gray? Please, what is it, you look terrified!

> *He moves away from her and her awful caring, and halts facing front. She remains behind and calls to him from the distance.*

> —My cousin Wilbur's still at Mass. General, we can go up there together . . . ! Please, darling, don't worry about anything . . . ! What is it, can't you tell me?

> *In total blockage—both in the past and in the present—he inhales deeply and lets out a gigantic long howl, arms raised, imploring heaven for relief. In effect, it blasts her out of his mind—she goes dark, and he is alone again.*

LYMAN, *to himself, facing front*: No guts. That's the whole story. Courage! If I'd been honest for three consecutive minutes . . . No! I know what's wrong with me—I could never stand still for death! Which you've got to do by a certain age, or be ridiculous—you've got to stand there nobly and serene and let death run his tape out your arms and around your belly and up your crotch until he's got you fitted for that last black suit. And I can't, I won't! . . . So I'm left wrestling with this anachronistic energy which . . . *as he leaps onto the bed, covering his left arm, crying out to the world* . . . God has charged me with and I will use it till the dirt is shoveled into my mouth! Life! Life! Fuck death and dying!

> *Light widens, finding Leah in the present, dressed differently than previously—in her fur coat—standing near the bed with the Nurse, listening to his shouts.*

NURSE: Don't be afraid, just wait a minute, he comes out of it. I'm sure he wants to see you.

LEAH, *moving tentatively to the cast*: Lyman? *He looks at her with cloudy recognition.* It's me, Leah.

Nurse exits. Lyman now fully aware of Leah.

LYMAN: Leah! *Turning away from her.* Jesus, what have I done to you!—wait . . . *A moment. He looks around.* Was Theo here?

LEAH: I think she's gone, I just got here.

LYMAN: Oh, Leah, it's sitting on my chest like a bag of cement.

LEAH: What is?

LYMAN: My character.

LEAH: Yes, well . . . it's pretty bad. Listen . . .

LYMAN, *moved*: Thanks for coming. You're a friend.

LEAH: I only came about Benny. *Frustrated, turns away.* He's excited that he has a sister.

LYMAN, *painful admiration*: Oh that dear boy!

LEAH: He's very badly mixed up, Lyman; he's seen us all on TV and the other kids tell him he has two mothers. He sits there and weeps. He keeps asking me are you coming home again. It's twisting my heart. I'm terrified if this isn't settled right it could screw up the rest of his life. *Tears start.* You're his idol, his god, Lyman!

LYMAN: Oh, the wreckage, the wreckage . . .

LEAH: Tell me the truth; whichever it is is okay but I just want to know—do you feel a responsibility or not?

LYMAN, *flaring up, scared as much as indignant*: How can you ask such a thing?

LEAH: Why! That's a reasonable question!

LYMAN: Now listen to me—I know I'm wrong and I'm wrong and I'm wrong but I did not throw you both across my saddle to rape you in my tent! You knew I was married, and you tried to make me love you, so I'm not entirely . . .

LEAH: Lyman, if you're blaming me I'm going to sink through this floor!

LYMAN: I'm talking about truth, not blame—this is not entirely a one-man disaster!

LEAH: It's amazing, the minute you talk about truth you always come out looking better than anyone else!

LYMAN: Now that's unfair!

LEAH, *slight pause*: I want to talk about Benny.

LYMAN: You could bring him tomorrow if you like. But go ahead, we can talk now.

LEAH, *a pause as she settles down*: I'm thinking.

LYMAN: Well stop thinking and bring him!

LEAH, *with a flushed grin*: Incidentally . . . they tell me you spent over an hour with your wife. Are you settling in there again?

LYMAN: All she did was sit there telling me I'm a monster who never loved anybody.

LEAH, *with a hard grin*: And you reassured her otherwise, of course.

LYMAN: Well, I did love her. And you know that better than anybody.

LEAH: What a piece of work you are, Lyman, really—you go falling off a mountain and you still don't understand your hatred for that woman. It's monumental. It's . . . it's *oceanic*.

LYMAN: What the hell is this now!

LEAH: My dear man, in case it slipped your mind, when I was two months pregnant we went to New York and you picked the Carlyle Hotel to stay at—four blocks from your house! "Loved her" . . . good G—!

> *A window begins to appear upstage with Theo seated in profile, reading a book. He is staring as he emerges from the bed, turning to look up at the window . . . Leah goes on with no pause.*

> What was all that about if it wasn't hatred!—And walking me past your front window with her sitting there . . . ? You had murder in you and you still do!—probably for me too!

LYMAN, *glancing up at Theo in the window*: But it didn't feel like murder at all. I was dancing the high wire on the edge of the world . . . finally risking everything to find myself! Strolling with you past my house, the autumn breeze, the lingerie in the Madison Avenue shop windows, the swish of . . . wasn't it a taffeta skirt you wore? . . . and my new baby coiled in your belly? —I'd beaten guilt forever! *She is moving toward him, part of his recall. . . .* And how languorous you were, your pregnant glory under the streetlamp!

> *She takes on the ease of that long-ago stroll, and . . .*

LEAH: Is that her?

> *Lyman looks up at Theo, then at Leah, inspired, alive.*

LYMAN: Oh Leah darling, how sexy you look against tall buildings.

LEAH, *with a warm smile, taking his arm*: You're tense, aren't you.

LYMAN: Well, I lived here with her for so many years . . . You know?—I'd love to go in and say hello . . . But I don't have the guts . . .

LEAH: Was she very upset when you told her?

LYMAN, *tragically, but hesitates*: Very, yes.

LEAH: Well, maybe she'll think of marrying again.

LYMAN: Marrying again? *With a glance to the window; loosening her grip on his arm.* I doubt it, somehow.

LEAH, *with an intrigued smile*: Mustn't we touch?

LYMAN, *quickly regaining her arm*: Of course! *They start walking away.*

LEAH: I'd love to meet her sometime . . . just as friends.

LYMAN: You might. *Halts. A strange determination suddenly*: Listen, I'd like to see if I can go in and say hello.

LEAH: Why not! You don't want me to come, do you?

LYMAN: Not just yet. Would you mind a lot?

LEAH: Why! I'm glad that you still have feeling for her.

LYMAN: God, you have balls! I'll see you back at the hotel in twenty minutes, okay?

LEAH: Take your time! I'll play with all that gorgeous underwear you bought. *Touching her belly.* I'm so contented, Lyman!

> She turns and walks toward the cast, which lights up. He remains below the window, staring at her departing figure.

LYMAN, *alone*: Why is it, the happier she is the sadder I get? It's this damned *objectivity!*—Why can't I just dive in and swim in my happiness! *Now he looks up at Theo, and his heart sinks. Leaps up with violent determination.* Idiot!—love her! Now that she can't deprive you anymore let love flow to your wise and wonderful wife! *He rushes toward Theo, but then turns away in terror, walking around in a circle and blowing out air and covering his face.* Guilt, burn in hell! *Now he again hurries toward the window . . . which disappears, as she rises, setting her book down, startled.*

THEO: Lyman! —You said Tuesday, didn't you?

> He takes her in his arms, kisses her frantically. She is surprised and happy.

LYMAN: What a handsome lady! Theo, you are God's handwriting.

THEO: Ralph Waldo Emerson.

LYMAN: Someday I'm going to swipe an image you never heard of! *Laughing, in a comradely style, embraces her closely as he takes her to a seat—stoking up a certain excited intimacy here.* Listen, I just hitched a ride down with this pilot in his new Cessna—I have meetings up there starting seven-thirty tomorrow but I just had to astonish you.

THEO: You flew in a small plane *at night?*

LYMAN: That whole fear was guilt, Theo—I thought I *deserved* to crash. But I deserve to live because I am not a bad guy and I love you.

THEO: Well, I'm floating away! When must you go back?

LYMAN: Now.

THEO, *near laughter at the absurdity*: Can't we even chat?

LYMAN: Let me call that I'm on my way. *Dials a phone.*

THEO: I'll drive you to the airport.

LYMAN: No, he's picking me up at the Carlyle . . . Hello?

> *Lights up on Leah, holding a phone.*

LEAH: Darling!

LYMAN: Be there in ten minutes.

LEAH, *puzzled*: Oh? Okay. Why are you calling?

LYMAN: Just to make sure you didn't forget me and took off.

LEAH: Your jealousy is so comforting!—You know, she made a very dignified picture, reading in the window—it was like an Edward Hopper, kind of haunted.

LYMAN: Yes. Well, I'm leaving right now. *Hangs up.*

THEO: You won't forget about dinner Thursday with Leona and Gilbert . . . he's gotten his hearing aid so it won't be so bad.

LYMAN, *with a certain solemnity, taking her hands*: I just had to steal this extra look at you . . . life's so stupidly short, Theo.

THEO, *happily*: Why must death always sit on your shoulder when you've got more life in you than anybody! *Ruffling his hair.* In fact, you're kind of sparkly tonight.

LYMAN, *responding to her acceptance*: Listen, we have time to make love.

THEO, *with a surprised, delighted laugh*: I wish I knew what's come over you!

LYMAN: The realization of what a sweet piece of ass my wife is. *He starts to lead her.*

THEO: I bet it's the new office in Elmira—new beginnings are always so exciting! There's such power in you, Lyman.

LYMAN, *turning her to him, he kisses her mouth*: Yes, we're going to do great business up there! Tell me something—has there ever been a god who was guilty?

THEO: Gods are never guilty, that's why they're gods.

LYMAN: It feels like the moon's in my belly and the sun's in my mouth and I'm shining down on the world. *Laughs with a self-mocking charm. . . .* A regular planetary flashlight! Come! *And laughing in high tension takes her hand and moves her into darkness . . .*

THEO: Oh, Lyman—how wonderfully, endlessly changing you are!

BLACKOUT

SCENE III

Lights up on Leah in hospital room; Lyman is returning to the bed.

LEAH: So you bopped her that night.

LYMAN: What can I say?

LEAH: And when you came back to the hotel, didn't we . . . ?

LYMAN: I couldn't help myself, you both looked absolutely gorgeous! How can that be evil?

LEAH, *with a sigh*: There's just no end to you, is there. —Listen, I came to talk business; I want the house transferred to my name . . .

LYMAN: *What?*

LEAH: . . . Immediately. I know how much feeling you put into it but I want the security for Benny's sake.

LYMAN: Leah, I beg you to wait with that . . .

LEAH: I will not wait with that! And I want my business returned to me.

LYMAN: That'll be complicated—it's many times bigger than when I took it over . . .

LEAH: I want it back! I would have expanded without you! I'm not going to be a *total* fool! I will sue you!

LYMAN, *with a very uncertain grin*: You'd really sue me?

LEAH, *searching in her pocketbook*: I'm not fooling around, Lyman. You've hurt me very deeply . . . *She breaks off, holding back tears. She takes out a sheet of paper.*

LYMAN, *forced to turn from her*: Jesus, how I hate to see you cry.

LEAH: I have something I want you to sign.

LYMAN: To *sign*?

LEAH: It's a quit-claim on the house and my business. Will you read it?

LYMAN: You're not serious.

LEAH: I had Ted Lester draw it up. Here, read it.

LYMAN: I know what a quit-claim is, don't tell me to read a quit-claim. How can you do this?

LEAH: We aren't married and I don't want you making claims on me.

LYMAN: And . . . and what about Benny. You don't mean you're taking Benny from me . . .

LEAH: I . . .

LYMAN: I want you to bring him here tomorrow morning so I can talk to him.

LEAH: Just a minute . . .

LYMAN: No! You're going to bring him, Leah . . .

LEAH: Now you listen to me! I will not allow you to see him until I know what you intend to say to him about all this. I've also been through it with my father's old lawyer and you haven't a legal leg to stand on.

LYMAN: I'll tell him the truth—I love him.

LEAH: You mean it's all right to lie and deceive people you love? He's all I have now, Lyman, I am not going to see him go crazy!

LYMAN: Now you stop that! I did a helluva lot more than lie to him . . .

LEAH, *outpouring*: You lied to him!—why don't you seem to register this? . . . To buy him the pony, and teach him to ski, and take him up in the glider . . . you made him worship you—when you knew what you knew! That was cruelty!

LYMAN: All right, what do you think I should tell him?

LEAH: That you beg his pardon and say he musn't follow your example because lying to people injures them.

LYMAN: I am not turning myself into a pile of shit in front of my son's face! If I can teach him anything now it's to have the guts to be true to himself! That's all that matters!

LEAH: Even if he has to betray the whole world to do it?

LYMAN: Only the truth is sacred, Leah!—to hold back nothing!

LEAH: You must be crazy—you hold back everything! You really don't know right from wrong, do you!

LYMAN: Jesus Christ, you sound like Theo!

LEAH: Well maybe it's what happens to people who marry you! Look—I don't think it's a good idea at the moment . . .

LYMAN: I have a right to see my son!

LEAH: I won't have him copying you, Lyman, it will destroy his life! I'm leaving! *She starts to leave.*

LYMAN: You bring me Benny or I'll . . . I'll sue you, goddammit!

Enter Bessie alone. She is extremely tense and anxious.

BESSIE: Oh, good, I was hoping you'd still be here. Listen . . .

LEAH: I was just going . . .

BESSIE: Oh please wait! My mother's had an attack of some kind . . .

LYMAN: My God, what is it!

BESSIE: They're looking at her in a room down the hall. She's a little delusionary and talks about taking him home with her, and I think it would help for her to see you're still together.

LEAH: But we're not at all together . . .

LYMAN: Wait! Why must it be delusion—maybe she really wants me back!

BESSIE, *with a frustrated stamp of her foot*: I want her out of here and home!

LYMAN: I am not a monster, Bessie! My God, where did all this cruelty come from!

LEAH: He wants her, you see . . .

LYMAN: I want you both!

BESSIE, *a hysterical overtone, screaming*: Will you once in your life think of another human being!

Tom and Theo enter with the Nurse; he has Theo by the arm. She has a heightened, seeing air about her, but a fixed, dead smile, and her head trembles.

LYMAN: Theo!—come, sit her down, Tom!

LEAH, *to Bessie, fearfully*: I really feel I ought to go . . .

THEO: Oh, I wish you could stay for a few minutes! *To Nurse*: Please get a chair for Mrs. Felt.

The reference causes surprise in Bessie. Leah looks quickly to Bessie, perplexed because this is the opposite of what Bessie and Theo wished. Lyman is immensely encouraged. The Nurse, as she goes out for the chair, glances about, perplexed.

Pleasantly: Well! Here we are all together.

Slight pause.

TOM: She's had a little . . . incident, Lyman. *To Bessie*: I've arranged for a plane; the three of us can fly down together.

BESSIE: Oh good. —We're ready to leave whenever you say, Mother.

LYMAN: Thanks, Theo . . . for coming.

THEO, *turns to him, smiling blankly*: Socialism is dead.

LYMAN: Beg your pardon?

THEO: And Christianity is finished, so . . . *Searches* . . . there really is nothing left to . . . to . . . to defend. Except simplicity? *She crosses her legs, and her coat falls partially open, revealing a bare thigh.*

BESSIE: Mother!—where's your skirt?

THEO: I'm comfortable, it's all right . . .

Nurse enters with a chair.

BESSIE: She must have left her skirt in that room she was just in—would you get it, please?

Nurse, perplexed again, exits.

THEO, *to Leah*: I wish I hadn't carried on that way . . . I'm sorry. I've really nothing against you personally, I just never cared for your *type*. The surprise is what threw me, I mean that you were actually married. But I think you are rather an interesting person . . . I was just unprepared, but I'm seeing things much clearer now. Yes. *Breaks off.* Do you see the *Village Voice* up here?

LEAH: Yes, occasionally.

THEO: There was a strange interview some years back with Isaac Bashevis Singer, the novelist? The interviewer was a woman whose husband had left her for another woman, and she couldn't understand why. And Singer said, "Maybe he liked her hole better." I was shocked at the time, really outraged—you know, that he'd gotten a Nobel; but now I think it was courageous to have said that, because it's probably true. Courage . . . courage and directness are always the main thing!

Nurse enters, offers Theo the skirt.

NURSE: Can I help you on with it?

THEO, *takes the skirt, looks at it without recognition, and drops it on the floor*: I can't remember if I called you Leah or Mrs. Felt.

LEAH: I'm not really Mrs. Felt.

THEO, *with a pleasant social smile*: Well, you are *a* Mrs. Felt; perhaps that's all one can hope for when we are so interchangeable—who knows anymore which Mrs. Felt will be coming down for breakfast! *Short pause.* Your boy needs his father, I imagine.

LEAH: Well . . . yes, but . . .

THEO: Then he should be here with you, shouldn't he. We must all be realistic now. *To Lyman*: You can come up here whenever you want to . . . if that's what you'd really like.

BESSIE, *to Tom*: She's really too ill for this. —Come, Mother, we're going.

THEO: I'm not at all ill. *To Lyman*: I can say "fuck," you know. I never cared for the word but I'm sure she has her limitations too. I can say "Fuck me, Lyman," "Fuck you, Lyman"; whatever.

Lyman is silent in guilty anguish.

BESSIE, *to Lyman, furiously*: Will you tell her to leave? Just out of respect, out of friendship!

LYMAN: Yes. *Delicately.* She's right, Theo, I think that would be the best . . .

THEO, *to Bessie*: But I can take better care of him at home. *To Leah*: I really have nothing to do, and you're busy, I imagine . . .

BESSIE: Tom, will you . . .

TOM: Why don't we let her say what's on her mind?

THEO, *to Bessie*: I want to start being real—he had every right to resent me. Truly. What did I ever do but correct him? *To Leah*: You don't correct him, do you. You like him as he is, even now, don't you. And that's the secret, isn't it. *To Lyman*: Well I can do that. I don't need to correct you . . . or pretend to . . .

BESSIE: I can't bear this, Mother!

THEO: But this is our *life*, Bessie dear; you must bear it. —I think I've always pretty well known what he was doing. Somewhere inside we all really know everything, don't we? But one has to live, darling—one has to live . . . in the same house, the same bed. And so one learns to tolerate . . . it's a good thing to tolerate . . . *A furious shout*. And tolerate, and tolerate!

BESSIE, *terrified for her mother*: Daddy, please . . . tell her to go!

LYMAN: But she's telling the truth!

LEAH, *suddenly filling up*: You poor woman! *To him*: What a bastard you are; one honest sentence from you and none of this would have happened, it's despicable! *Appealing to Theo*. I'm so sorry about it, Mrs. Felt . . .

THEO: No-no . . . he's absolutely right—he's always said it—it's life I can't trust! But you—you trust it, and that's why you *should* win out.

LEAH: But it's not true—I never really trusted him! Not really! I always knew there was something dreadful wriggling around underneath! *In full revolt now*. I'll tell you the goddamned truth, I never really wanted to marry anybody! I've never known one happy couple! —Listen, you mustn't blame yourself, the whole damned thing doesn't work, it never works . . . which I knew and went ahead and did it anyway and I'll never understand why!

LYMAN: Because if you hadn't married me you wouldn't have kept Benny, that's why. *She can't find words*. You wouldn't have had Benny or this last nine years of your happiness. Shit that I am, I helped you become the woman you always wanted to be, instead of . . . *Catches himself*. Well, what's the difference?

LEAH: No, don't stop—instead of what? What did you save me from?

LYMAN, *accepting her challenge*: All right . . . from all those lonely post-coital showerbaths, and the pointless pillow talk and the boxes of heartless condoms beside your bed . . . !

LEAH, *speechless*: Well now!

LYMAN: I'm sick of this crap, Leah! —You got a little something out of this despicable treachery!

THEO: That's a terrible thing to say to the woman.

LYMAN: But the truth is terrible, what else have you just been saying? It's terrible because it's embarrassing, but the truth is always embarrassing or it isn't the truth! —You tolerated me because you loved me, dear, but wasn't it also the good life that I gave you? —Well, what's wrong with that? Aren't women people? Don't people love comfort and power? I don't understand the disgrace here!

BESSIE, *to both women*: Why are you still sitting here, don't you have any pride! *To Leah*: This is disgusting!

LEAH: Will you please stop this high moral tone? I have business with him, so I have to talk to him! —I'll go out of my mind here! Am I being accused of something?

> *Off to the side, Tom bends his head over clasped hands, eyes shut.*

BESSIE: You shouldn't be in the same room with him!

LEAH, *rattled*: I just explained that, didn't I? *What the hell do you want?*

LYMAN, *crying out, voice cracking with a sob*: She wants her father back!

BESSIE: You son of a bitch! *Raises her fists, then weeps helplessly.*

LYMAN: I love you—Bessie!—all of you!

BESSIE: You ought to be killed!

LYMAN: You are all magnificent!

> *Bessie bursts into tears. A helpless river of grief, which now overflows to sweep up Lyman; then Leah is carried away by the wave of weeping. All strategies collapse as finally Theo is infected. The four of them are helplessly covering their faces. It is a veritable mass keening, a funerary explosion of grief, each for his or her own condition, for love's frustration and for the end of all their capacity to reason. Tom has turned from them, head bent in prayer, hands clasped, eyes shut.*

LYMAN, *his eye falls on Theo's bare leg*: Tom, please!—get her to put some clothes on . . . *Breaks off.* Are you praying, for Christ's sake?

TOM, *staring ahead*: There is no way to go forward. You must all stop loving him. You must or he will destroy you. He is an endless string attached to nothing.

LYMAN: Who is not an endless string? Who is sworn to some high golden purpose now—lawyers? Why are you all talking nonsense?

TOM: —Theo needs help now, Lyman, and I don't want a conflict, so I don't see how I can go on representing you.

LYMAN: Of course not, I am not worthy. *A shout, but with the strain of his loss, his inability to connect.* —But I *am* human, and proud of it!— yes, of the glory and the shit! The truth, the truth is holy!

TOM, *exploding*: Is it. Well! Then you'll admit that you moved that barrier aside yourself, and drove onto that sheet of ice? That's the truth, isn't it?

LYMAN, *instant's hesitation*: That was not suicide—I am not a cop-out!

TOM: Why is it a cop-out? Your shame finally caught up with you—or is that too true for comfort? Your shame is the best part of you, for God's sake, why do you pretend you're beyond it? *Breaks off, giving it up.* I'm ready to go, Theo.

LYMAN, *suddenly struck*: One more moment—I beg you all. Before you leave me . . . please. I'd like to tell you something.

BESSIE, *quietly relentless*: Mother?

> She raises Theo to her feet. Her head is trembling. She turns to Lyman.

LYMAN: I'm asking you to hear me out, Theo. I see what happened.

THEO: I have nothing left in me anymore, Lyman.

> Bessie takes her by the arm to go. Leah stands, as though to leave.

LYMAN: I beg you, Leah, two minutes. I have to tell you this!

LEAH, *an evasive color*: I have work in the office . . .

LYMAN, *losing control*: Two minutes, Leah? Before you take away my son because of my unworthiness? *Pause. Something simple, authentic in his tone stops them all.* Here is how I got on the Mount Morgan road. I kept calling you, Leah, from the Howard Johnson's to tell you I'd be staying over because of the storm . . . but the line was busy. So I went to bed, but it was busy . . . over an hour . . . more! And I started to ask the operator to cut in as an emergency when . . . *Breaks off.* I remembered what you once said to me . . .

LEAH: I was talking to . . .

LYMAN, *in quick fury*: It doesn't matter, I'm not accusing you, or defending myself either, I'm telling you what *happened!*—please let me finish!

LEAH: I was talking to my brother!

LYMAN: In Japan, for over an hour?

LEAH: He just got back on Monday.

LYMAN: Well it doesn't matter!

LEAH: It certainly does matter!

LYMAN: Please let me finish, Leah; remember you once said . . . "I might lie to you," remember that? Way at the beginning? It seemed so wonderful then . . . that you could be so honest; but now, on my back in that room, I started to die.

LEAH: I don't want to hear anymore!

Theo, Bessie are moving out.

LYMAN: Wait! Please! I haven't made my point! *Something new, genuine in his voice stops them.* I want to stop lying. It's simple. *A visionary look.* On my back in that bed, the snow piling up outside . . . the wind howling at my window—this whole nine-year commute suddenly seemed so ludicrous, it was suddenly laughable. I couldn't understand why I'd done it. And somehow I realized that I had no feeling left . . . for myself or anyone . . . I was a corpse on that bed. And I got dressed and drove back into the storm. I don't know—maybe I did want to die, except that what I really thought, Leah . . . was that if I walked in two, three in the morning out of a roaring blizzard like that . . . you'd believe how I needed you. And then I would believe it too, and I'd come back to life again. Unless . . . *Turns to Tom.* I just wanted the end of it all. *To the women*: But I swear to you . . . looking at you now, Theo, and Leah, and you, Bessie . . . I have never felt the love that I feel right now. But I've harmed you and I know it. —And one more thing; I can't leave you with a lie—the truth is that in some miserable, dark corner of my soul I still don't see why I am condemned. I bless you all. *He weeps helplessly.*

Bessie turns Theo to leave.

THEO: . . . Say goodbye to him, dear.

BESSIE, *dry-eyed now; her feeling clearer, she has a close to impersonal sound*: I hope you're better soon, Daddy. Goodbye.

She takes her mother's arm—Theo no longer resists as they move out into darkness. He turns to Leah.

LYMAN: Oh Leah, say something tough and honest . . . the way you can.

LEAH: I don't know if I'll ever believe anything . . . or anybody, again.

LYMAN: Oh no. No!—I haven't done that!

A great weeping sweeps Leah and she rushes out.

Leah! Leah! Don't say I've done that!

But she is gone.

TOM: Talk to you soon.

He sees that Lyman is lost in space, and he goes out. The Nurse comes from her corner to Lyman.

NURSE: You got pain?

He doesn't reply.

I'll get you something to smooth you out.

LYMAN: Don't leave me alone, okay?—for a little while? Please, sit with me. *Pats the mattress. She approaches the bed but remains standing.*

I want to thank you, Logan. I won't forget your warmth, especially. A woman's warmth is the last magic, you're a piece of sun. —Tell me . . . when you're out there on the ice with your husband and your boy . . . what do you talk about?

NURSE: . . . Well, let's see . . . this last time we all bought us some shoes at that big Knapp Shoe Outlet up there?—they're seconds, but you can't tell them from new.

LYMAN: So you talked about your new shoes?

NURSE: Well, they're great buys.

LYMAN: Right. That . . . that's just wonderful to do that. I don't know why, but it just is.

NURSE: I'll be right back. *She starts away.*

LYMAN: Hate me?

NURSE, *with an embarrassed shrug*: I don't know. I got to think about it.

LYMAN: Come right back, huh? I'm still a little . . . shaky.

She leans down and kisses his forehead.

Why'd you do that?

NURSE, *shrugs*: No reason.

She exits.

LYMAN, *painful wonder and longing in his face, his eyes wide, alive . . .* : What a miracle everything is! Absolutely everything! . . . Imagine . . . three of them sitting out there together on that lake, talking about their shoes! *He begins to weep, but quickly catches himself.* Now learn loneliness. But cheerfully. Because you earned it, kid, all by yourself. Yes. You have found Lyman at last! So . . . cheer up!

BLACKOUT

THE LAST YANKEE

1993

Characters

LEROY HAMILTON
JOHN FRICK
PATRICIA HAMILTON
KAREN FRICK
UNNAMED PATIENT

SCENE I

The visiting room of a state mental hospital. Leroy Hamilton is seated on one of the half-dozen chairs, idly leafing through an old magazine. He is forty-eight, trim, dressed in subdued Ivy League jacket and slacks and shined brogans. A banjo case rests against his chair.

Mr. Frick enters. He is sixty, solid, in a business suit. He carries a small valise. He looks about, glances at Leroy, just barely nods, and sits ten feet away. He looks at his watch, then impatiently at the room. Leroy goes on leafing through the magazine.

FRICK, *pointing right*: Supposed to notify somebody in there?

LEROY, *indicating left*: Did you give your name to the attendant?

FRICK: Yes. 'Seem to be paying much attention, though.

LEROY: They know you're here, then. He calls through to the ward. *Returns to his magazine.*

FRICK, *slight pause*: Tremendous parking space down there. 'They need that for?

LEROY: Well a lot of people visit on weekends. Fills up pretty much.

FRICK: Really? That whole area?

LEROY: Pretty much.

FRICK: 'Doubt that. *He goes to the window and looks out. Pause.* Beautifully landscaped, got to say that for it.

LEROY: Yes, it's a very nice place.

FRICK: 'See them walking around out there it's hard to tell. 'Stopped one to ask directions and only realized when he stuck out his finger and pointed at my nose.

LEROY: Heh-heh.

FRICK: Quite a shock. Sitting there reading some thick book and crazy as a coot. You'd never know. *He sits in another chair. Leroy returns to the magazine. He studies Leroy.* Is it your wife?

LEROY: Yes.

FRICK: I've got mine in there too.

LEROY: Uh, huh. *He stares ahead, politely refraining from the magazine.*

FRICK: My name's Frick.

LEROY: Hi. I'm Hamilton.

FRICK: Gladamettu. *Slight pause.* How do you find it here?

LEROY: I guess they do a good job.

FRICK: Surprisingly well kept for a state institution.

LEROY: Oh, ya.

FRICK: Awful lot of colored, though, ain't there?

LEROY: Quite a few, ya.

FRICK: Yours been in long?

LEROY: Going on seven weeks now.

FRICK: They give you any idea when she can get out?

LEROY: Oh, I could take her out now, but I won't for a couple weeks.

FRICK: Why's that?

LEROY: Well this is her third time.

FRICK: 'Don't say.

LEROY: I'd like them to be a little more sure before I take her out again. . . . Although you can never *be* sure.

FRICK: That fairly common?—that they have to come back?

LEROY: About a third they say. This your first time, I guess.

FRICK: I just brought her in last Tuesday. I certainly hope she doesn't have to stay long. They ever say what's wrong with her?

LEROY: She's a depressive.

FRICK: Really. That's what they say about mine. Just gets . . . sort of sad?

LEROY: It's more like . . . frightened.

FRICK: Sounds just like mine. Got so she wouldn't even leave the house.

LEROY: That's right.

FRICK: Oh, yours too?

LEROY: Ya, she wouldn't go out. Not if she could help it, anyway.

FRICK: She ever hear sounds?

LEROY: She used to. Like a loud humming.

FRICK: Same thing! Ts. What do you know! —How old is she?

LEROY: She's forty-four.

FRICK: Is that all! I had an idea it had something to do with getting old . . .

LEROY: I don't think so. My wife is still—I wouldn't say a raving beauty, but she's still . . . a pretty winsome woman. They're usually sick a long time before you realize it, you know. I just never realized it.

FRICK: Mine never showed any signs at all. Just a nice, quiet kind of a woman. Always slept well . . .

LEROY: Well mine sleeps well too.

FRICK: Really?

LEROY: Lot of them love to sleep. I found that out. She'd take naps every afternoon. Longer and longer.

FRICK: Mine too. But then about six, eight months ago she got nervous about keeping the doors locked. And then the windows. I had to air-condition the whole house. I finally had to do the shopping, she just wouldn't go out.

LEROY: Oh I've done the shopping for twenty years.

FRICK: You don't say!

LEROY: Well you just never think of it as a sickness. I like to ski, for instance, or ice skating . . . she'd never come along. Or swimming in the summer. I always took the kids alone . . .

FRICK: Oh you have children.

LEROY: Yes. Seven.

FRICK: Seven!—I've been wondering if it was because she never had any.

LEROY: No, that's not it. —You don't have *any*?

FRICK: No. We kept putting it off, and then it got too late, and first thing you know . . . it's just too late.

LEROY: For a while there I thought maybe she had too *many* children . . .

FRICK: Well I don't have any, so . . .

LEROY: Yeah, I guess that's not it either.

   Slight pause.

FRICK: I just can't figure it out. There's no bills; we're very well fixed; she's got a beautiful home. . . . There's really not a trouble in the world. Although, God knows, maybe that's the trouble . . .

LEROY: Oh no, I got plenty of bills and it didn't help mine. I don't think it's how many bills you have.

FRICK: What do you think it is, then?

LEROY: Don't ask me, I don't know.

FRICK: When she started locking up everything I thought maybe it's these Negroes, you know? There's an awful lot of fear around; all this crime.

LEROY: I don't think so. My wife was afraid before there were any Negroes. I mean, around.

FRICK: Well one thing came out of it—I finally learned how to make coffee. And mine's better than hers was. It's an awful sensation, though—coming home and there's nobody there.

LEROY: How'd you like to come home and there's seven of them there?

FRICK: I guess I'm lucky at that.

LEROY: Well, I am too. They're wonderful kids.

FRICK: They still very young?

LEROY: Five to nineteen. But they all pitch in. Everything's clean, house runs like a ship.

FRICK: You're lucky to have good children these days. —I guess we're both lucky.

LEROY: That's the only way to look at it. Start feeling sorry for yourself, that's when you're in trouble.

FRICK: Awfully hard to avoid sometimes.

LEROY: You can't give in to it though. Like tonight—I was so disgusted I just laid down and . . . I was ready to throw in the chips. But then I got up and washed my face, put on the clothes, and here I am. After all, she can't help it either, who you going to blame?

FRICK: It's a mystery—a woman with everything she could possibly want. I don't care what happens to the country, there's nothing could ever hurt her anymore. Suddenly, out of nowhere, she's terrified! . . . She lost all her optimism. Yours do that? Lose her optimism?

LEROY: Mine was never very optimistic. She's Swedish.

FRICK: Oh. Mine certainly was. Whatever deal I was in, couldn't wait till I got home to talk about it. Real estate, stock market, always interested. All of a sudden, no interest whatsoever. Might as well be talking to that wall over there. —Your wife have brothers and sisters?

LEROY: Quite a few, ya.

FRICK: Really. I even thought maybe it's that she was an only child, and if she had brothers and sisters to talk to . . .

LEROY: Oh no—at least I don't think so. It could be even worse.

FRICK: They don't help, huh?

LEROY: They *think* they're helping. Come around saying it's a disgrace for their sister to be in a public institution. That's the kind of help. So I said, "Well, I'm the public!"

FRICK: Sure! —It's a perfectly nice place.

LEROY: They want her in the Rogers Pavilion.

FRICK: Rogers! —that's a couple of hundred dollars a day minimum . . .

LEROY: Well if I had that kind of money I wouldn't mind, but . . .

FRICK: No-no, don't you do it. I could afford it, but what are we paying taxes for?

LEROY: So they can go around saying their sister's in the Rogers Pavilion, that's all.

FRICK: Out of the question. That's fifty thousand dollars a year. Plus tips. I'm sure you have to tip them there.

LEROY: Besides, it's eighty miles there and back, I could never get to see her . . .

FRICK: If they're so sensitive you ought to tell *them* to pay for it. That'd shut them up, I bet.

LEROY: Well no—they've offered to pay part. Most of it, in fact.

FRICK: Whyn't you do it, then?

LEROY, *holding a secret*: I didn't think it's a good place for her.

FRICK: Why?—if they'd pay for it? It's one of the top places in the country. Some very rich people go there.

LEROY: I know.

FRICK: And the top doctors, you know. And they order whatever they want to eat. I went up there to look it over; no question about it, it's absolutely first-class, much better than this place. You should take them up on it.

LEROY: I'd rather have her here.

FRICK: Well I admire your attitude. You don't see that kind of pride anymore.

LEROY: It's not pride, exactly.

FRICK: Never mind, it's a great thing, keep it up. Everybody's got the gimmes, it's destroying the country. Had a man in a few weeks ago to put in a new showerhead. Nothing to it. Screw off the old one and screw on the new one. Seventeen dollars an hour!

LEROY: Yeah, well. *Gets up, unable to remain seated.* Everybody's got to live, I guess.

FRICK: I take my hat off to you—that kind of independence. Don't happen to be with Colonial Trust, do you?

LEROY: No.

FRICK: There was something familiar about you. What line are you in?

LEROY, *he is at the window now, staring out. Slight pause*: Carpenter.

FRICK, *taken aback*: Don't say. . . . Contractor?

LEROY: No. Just carpenter. —I take on one or two fellas when I have to, but I work alone most of the time.

FRICK: I'd never have guessed it.

LEROY: Well that's what I do. *Looks at his watch, wanting escape.*

FRICK: I mean your whole . . . your way of dressing and everything.

LEROY: Why? Just ordinary clothes.

FRICK: No, you look like a college man.

LEROY: Most of them have long hair, don't they?

FRICK: The way college men used to look. I've spent thirty years around carpenters, that's why it surprised me. You know Frick Supply, don't you?

LEROY: Oh ya. I've bought quite a lot of wood from Frick.

FRICK: I sold out about five years ago . . .

LEROY: I know. I used to see you around there.

FRICK: You did? Why didn't you mention it?

LEROY, *shrugs*: Just didn't.

FRICK: You say Anthony?

LEROY: No, Hamilton. Leroy.

FRICK, *points at him*: Hey now! Of course! There was a big article about you in the *Herald* a couple of years ago. Descended from Alexander Hamilton.

LEROY: That's right.

FRICK: Sure! No wonder! *Holding out his palm as to a photo.* Now that I visualize you in overalls, I think I recognize you. In fact, you were out in the yard loading plywood the morning that article came out. My bookkeeper pointed you out through the window. It's those clothes—if I'd seen you in overalls I'd've recognized you right off. Well, what do you know? *The air of condescension plus wonder.* Amazing thing what clothes'll do, isn't it. —Keeping busy?

LEROY: I get work.

FRICK: What are you fellas charging now?

LEROY: I get seventeen an hour.

FRICK: Good for you.

LEROY: I hate asking that much, but even so I just about make it.

FRICK: Shouldn't feel that way; if they'll pay it, grab it.

LEROY: Well ya, but it's still a lot of money. —My head's still back there thirty years ago.

FRICK: What are you working on now?

LEROY: I'm renovating a colonial near Waverly. I just finished over in Belleville. The Presbyterian church.

FRICK: Did you do *that*?

LEROY: Yeah, just finished Wednesday.

FRICK: That's a beautiful job. You're a good man. Where'd they get that altar?

LEROY: I built that.

FRICK: That altar?

LEROY: Uh huh.

FRICK: Hell, that's first-class! Huh! You must be doing all right.

LEROY: Just keeping ahead of it.

FRICK, *slight pause*: How'd it happen?

LEROY: What's that?

FRICK: Well coming out of an old family like that—how do you come to being a carpenter?

LEROY: Just . . . liked it.

FRICK: Father a carpenter?

LEROY: No.

FRICK: What was your father?

LEROY: Lawyer.

FRICK: Why didn't you?

LEROY: Just too dumb, I guess.

FRICK: Couldn't buckle down to the books, huh?

LEROY: I guess not.

FRICK: Your father should've taken you in hand.

LEROY, *sits with magazine, opening it*: He didn't like the law either.

FRICK: Even so. —Many of the family still around?

LEROY: Well my mother, and two brothers.

FRICK: No, I mean of the Hamiltons.

LEROY: Well they're Hamiltons.

FRICK: I know, but I mean— some of them must be pretty important people.

LEROY: I wouldn't know. I never kept track of them.

FRICK: You should. Probably some of them must be pretty big. —Never even looked them up?

LEROY: Nope.

FRICK: You realize the importance of Alexander Hamilton, don't you?

LEROY: I know about him, more or less.

FRICK: More or less! He was one of the most important Founding Fathers.

LEROY: I guess so, ya.

FRICK: You read about him, didn't you?

LEROY: Well sure . . . I read about him.

FRICK: Well didn't your father talk about him?

LEROY: Some. But he didn't care for him much.

FRICK: Didn't care for *Alexander Hamilton*?

LEROY: It was something to do with his philosophy. But I never kept up with the whole thing.

FRICK, *laughing, shaking his head*: Boy, you're quite a character, aren't you.

> Leroy is silent, reddening. Frick continues chuckling at him for a moment.

LEROY: I hope to God your wife is cured, Mr. Frick, I hope she never has to come back here again.

FRICK, *sensing the hostility*: What have I said?

LEROY: This is the third time in two years for mine, and I don't mean to be argumentative, but it's got me right at the end of my rope. For all I know I'm in line for this funny farm myself by now, but I have to tell you that this could be what's driving so many people crazy.

FRICK: What is!

LEROY: This.

FRICK: This what?

LEROY: This whole kind of conversation.

FRICK: Why? What's wrong with it?

LEROY: Well never mind.

FRICK: I don't know what you're talking about.

LEROY: Well what's it going to be, equality or what kind of country—I mean, am I supposed to be ashamed I'm a carpenter?

FRICK: Who said you . . . ?

LEROY: Then why do you talk like this to a man? One minute my altar is terrific and the next minute I'm some kind of shit bucket.

LEROY: Hey now, wait a minute . . . !

LEROY: I don't mean anything against you personally, I know you're a successful man and more power to you, but this whole type of conversation about my clothes—should I be ashamed I'm a carpenter? I mean everybody's talking "labor, labor," how much labor's getting; well if it's so great to be labor how come nobody wants to be it? I mean you ever hear a parent going around saying—*mimes thumb pridefully tucked into suspenders*—"My son is a carpenter"? Do you? Do you ever hear people brag about a bricklayer? I don't know what you are but I'm only a dumb swamp Yankee, but . . . *Suddenly breaks off with a shameful laugh.* Excuse me. I'm really sorry. But you come back here two-three more times and you're liable to start talking the way you were never brought up to. *Opens magazine.*

FRICK: I don't understand what you're so hot about.

LEROY, *looks up from the magazine. Seems to start to explain, then sighs*: Nothing.

He returns to his magazine. Frick shakes his head with a certain condescension, then goes back to the window and looks out.

FRICK: It's one hell of a parking lot, you have to say that for it.

They sit for a long moment in silence, each in his own thoughts.

BLACKOUT

SCENE II

Most of the stage is occupied by Patricia's bedroom. In one of the beds a fully clothed woman lies motionless with one arm over her eyes. She will not move throughout the scene.

Outside this bedroom is a corner of the Recreation Room, bare but for a few scattered chairs.

Presently . . . from just offstage the sound of a Ping-Pong game. The ball comes bouncing into the Recreation Room area and Patricia Hamilton enters chasing it. She captures it and with a sigh of boredom goes offstage with it.

We hear two or three pings and the ball comes onstage again with Patricia Hamilton after it. She starts to return to the game offstage but halts, looks at the ball in her hand, and to someone offstage . . .

PATRICIA: Why are we doing this? Come let's talk, I hate these games.

> *Mrs. Karen Frick enters. She is in her sixties, very thin, eyeglasses, wispy hair.*

I said I'm quitting.

> *Karen stares at the paddle.*

Well never mind. *Studies her watch.* You're very good.

KAREN: My sister-in-law taught me. She used to be a stewardess on the *Queen Mary*. She could even play when the ship was rocking. But she never married.

PATRICIA: Here, put it down, dear.

> *Karen passively gives up the paddle, then stands there looking uncomfortable.*

I'm going to lie down; sit with me, if you like.

KAREN, *indicates Ping-Pong area*: Hardly anyone ever seems to come out there.

PATRICIA: They don't like exercise, they're too depressed.

Patricia lies down. The woman in the other bed does not stir and no attention is paid to her.

Don't feel obliged to say anything if you . . .

KAREN: I get sick to my stomach just looking at a boat. Does your husband hunt?

PATRICIA: Sit down. Relax yourself. You don't have to talk. Although I think you're doing a little better than yesterday.

KAREN: Oh, I like talking with you. *Explaining herself timorously; indicating offstage—and very privately*: . . . I should go out—he doesn't like being kept waiting, don't y'know.

PATRICIA: Why are you so afraid? He might start treasuring you more if you make him wait a little. Come, sit.

Karen adventurously sits at the foot of the bed, glancing about nervously.

Men are only big children, you know—give them a chocolate soda every day and pretty soon it doesn't mean a thing to them. *Looks at her watch again.* Only reason I'm nervous is that I can't decide whether to go home today. —But you mustn't mention it, will you?

KAREN: Mention . . . ?

PATRICIA: About my pills. I haven't told anybody yet.

Karen looks a bit blank.

Well never mind.

KAREN: Oh! You mean not taking them.

PATRICIA: But you mustn't mention it, will you. The doctor would be very upset.

KAREN: And how long has it been?

PATRICIA: Twenty-one days today. It's the longest I've been clean in maybe fifteen years. I can hardly believe it.

KAREN: Are you Baptist?

PATRICIA: Baptist? No, we're more Methodist. But the church I'd really love hasn't been invented yet.

KAREN, *charmed, slavishly interested*: How would it be?

PATRICIA, *begins to describe it, breaks off*: I can't describe it. *A sign of lostness.* I was raised Lutheran, of course. —But I often go to the Marble

Baptist Church on Route 91? I've gotten to like that minister. —You hear what I'm saying, don't you?

Karen looks at her nervously trying to remember.

I must say it's kind of relaxing talking to you, Karen, knowing that you probably won't remember too much. But you'll come out of it all right, you're just a little scared, aren't you. —But who isn't? *Slight pause.* Doctor Rockwell is not going to believe I'm doing better without medication but I really think something's clicked inside me. *A deep breath.* I even seem to be breathing easier. And I'm not feeling that sort of fuzziness in my head. —It's like some big bird has been hovering over me for fifteen years, and suddenly it's flown away.

KAREN: I can't stand dead animals, can you?

PATRICIA: Well just insist that he has to stop hunting! You don't have to stand for that, you're a *person.*

KAREN: Well you know, men like to . . .

PATRICIA: Not all—I've known some lovely men. Not many, but a few. This minister I mentioned?—he came one day this summer and sat with me on our porch . . . and we had ice cream and talked for over an hour. You know, when he left his previous church they gave him a Pontiac Grand Am. He made me realize something; he said that I seem to be in like a constant state of prayer. And it's true; every once in a while it stops me short, realizing it. It's like inside me I'm almost continually talking to the Lord. Not in words exactly . . . just—you know—communicating with Him. Or trying to. *Deeply excited, but suppressing it.* I tell you truthfully, if I can really come out of this I'm going to . . . I don't know what . . . fall in love with God. I think I have already.

KAREN: You're really beautiful.

PATRICIA: Oh no, dear, I'm a torn-off rag of my old self. The pills put ten years on my face. If he was a Jew or Italian or even Irish he'd be suing these doctors, but Yankees never sue, you know. Although I have to say the only thing he's been right about is medication.

KAREN: Your husband against pills?

PATRICIA: Fanatical. But of course he can stick his head out the window and go high as a kite on a breath of fresh air. *Looks at her watch.*

KAREN: I really think you're extremely attractive.

PATRICIA: No-no, dear, although I did win the country beauty pageant when I was nineteen. But if you're talking beauty you should have seen my mother. She only died two years ago, age eighty-nine, but I still haven't gotten over it. On the beach, right into her seventies, people would still be staring at her—she had an unbelievable bust right up to the end.

KAREN: I cut this finger once in a broken Coke machine. But we never sued.

PATRICIA: Did your conversation always jump around? Because it could be your pills, believe me; the soul belongs to God, we're not supposed to be stuffing Valium into His mouth.

KAREN: I have a cousin who went right through the windshield and she didn't get a cent. *Slight pause.* And it was five below zero out. *Slight pause.* Her husband's Norwegian.

PATRICIA: Look, dear, I know you're trying but don't feel you have to speak.

KAREN: No, I like speaking to you. Is he Baptist too, your husband?

PATRICIA: I said Methodist. But he's more Episcopal. But he'll go to any church if it's raining. *Slight pause.* I just don't know whether to tell him yet.

KAREN: What.

PATRICIA: That I'm off everything.

KAREN: But he'll like that, won't he?

PATRICIA: Oh yes. But he's going to be doubtful. —Which I am, too, let's face it—who can know for sure that you're going to stay clean? I don't want to fool myself, I've been on one medication or another for almost twenty years. But I do feel a thousand percent better. And I really have no idea how it happened. *Shakes her head.* Dear God, when I think of him hanging in there all these years . . . I'm so ashamed. But at the same time he's absolutely refused to make any money, every one of our children has had to work since they could practically write their names. I can't be expected to applaud, exactly. *Presses her eyes.* I guess sooner or later you just have to stand up and say, "I'm normal, I made it." But it's like standing on top of a stairs and there's no stairs. *Staring ahead.*

KAREN: I think I'd better go out to him. Should I tell your husband you're coming out?

PATRICIA: I think I'll wait a minute.

KAREN, *stands*: He seems very nice.

PATRICIA: —I'll tell you the truth, dear—I've put him through hell and I know it. . . . *Tears threaten her.* I know I have to stop blaming him; it came to me like a visitation two weeks ago, I-must-not-blame-Leroy-anymore. And it's amazing. I lost all desire for medication, I could feel it leaving me like a . . . like a ghost. *Slight pause.* It's just that he's got really well-to-do relatives and he simply will not accept anyone's help. I mean you take the Jews, the Italians, Irish—they've got their Italian-Americans, Irish-Americans, Hispanic-Americans—they stick together and help each other. But you ever hear of Yankee-Americans? Not on your life. Raise his taxes, rob him blind, the Yankee'll just sit there all alone getting sadder and sadder. —But I'm not going to think about it anymore.

KAREN: You have a very beautiful chin.

PATRICIA: Men with half his ability riding around in big expensive cars and now for the second Easter Sunday in a row his rear end collapsed.

KAREN: I think my license must have expired.

PATRICIA, *a surge of deep anger*: I refuse to ride around in a nine-year-old Chevrolet which was bought secondhand in the first place!

KAREN: They say there are only three keys for all General Motors cars. You suppose that's possible?

PATRICIA, *peremptorily now*: Believe me, dear, whatever they tell you, you have got to cut down the medication. It could be what's making your mind jump around . . .

KAREN: No, it's that you mentioned Chevrolet, which is General Motors, you see.

PATRICIA: Oh. . . . Well, let's just forget about it. *Slight pause.* Although you're probably right—here you're carefully locking your car and some crook is walking around with the same keys in his pocket. But everything's a fake, we all know that.

KAREN, *facing Patricia again*: I guess that would be depressing.

PATRICIA: No, that's not what depressed me . . .

KAREN: No, I meant him refusing to amount to anything and then spending money on banjo lessons.

PATRICIA: Did I tell you that?—I keep forgetting what I told you because I never know when you're listening. *Holds out her hand.* Here we go again. *Grasps her hand to stop the shaking.*

KAREN: —You sound like you had a wonderful courtship.

PATRICIA: Oh, Karen, everyone envied us, we were the handsomes pair in town; and I'm not boasting, believe me. *Breaks off; watches her hand shake and covers it again.* I just don't want to have to come back here again, you see. I don't think I could bear that. *Grips her hand, moving about.* I simply have to think positively. But it's unbelievable—he's seriously talking about donating his saw-and-chisel collection to the museum!—some of those tools are as old as the United States, they might be worth a fortune! —But I'm going to look ahead, that's all just as straight ahead as a highway.

> *Slight pause.*

KAREN: I feel so ashamed.

PATRICIA: For Heaven's sake, why? You've got a right to be depressed. There's more people in hospitals because of depression than any other disease.

KAREN: Is that true?

PATRICIA: Of course! Anybody with any sense has got to be depressed in this country. Unless you're really rich, I suppose. Don't let him shame you, dear.

KAREN: No . . . it's that you have so many thoughts.

PATRICIA: Oh. Well you can have thoughts, too—just remember your soul belongs to God and you mustn't be shoving pills into His mouth.

> *Slight pause.*

KAREN: We're rich, I think.

PATRICIA, *quickly interested*: . . . Really rich?

KAREN: He's got the oil delivery now, and of course he always had the fertilizer and the Chevy dealership, and of course the lumber yard and all. And Isuzus now.

PATRICIA: What's Isuzus?

KAREN: It's a Japanese car.

PATRICIA: . . . I'll just never catch up.

KAREN: We go to Arkansas in the spring.

PATRICIA: Arkansas?

KAREN: For the catfish. It's where I broke down. But I can't help it, the sight of catfish makes me want to vomit. Not that I was trying to . . . you know . . . do anything. I just read the instructions on the bottle wrong. Do you mind if I ask you something?

PATRICIA: I hope it's nothing personal, is it?

KAREN: Well I don't know.

PATRICIA: . . . Well go ahead, what is it?

KAREN: Do you shop in the A&P or Stop & Shop?

PATRICIA: . . . I'm wondering if you've got the wrong medication. But I guess you'll never overdose—you vomit at the drop of a hat. It may be your secret blessing.

KAREN: —He wants to get me out of the house more, but it's hard to make up my mind where.

PATRICIA: Well . . . A&P is good. Or Stop & Shop. More or less. Kroger's is good for fish sometimes.

KAREN: Which do you like best? I'll go where you go.

PATRICIA: You're very flattering. *Stands, inner excitement.* It's amazing—I'm really beginning to feel wonderful; maybe I ought to go home with him today. I mean what does it come down to, really?—it's simply a question of confidence . . .

KAREN: I wish we could raise some vegetables like we did on the farm. Do you?

PATRICIA: Oh, he raises things in our yard. Healthy things like salsify and collards—and kale. You ever eat kale?

KAREN: I can't remember kale.

PATRICIA: You might as well salt your shower curtain and chop it up with a tomato.

KAREN: —So . . . meats are . . . which?—A&P?

PATRICIA: No. Meats are Stop & Shop. I'm really thinking I might go home today. It's just not his fault, I have to remember that . . .

KAREN: But staples?

PATRICIA: What? —Oh, Stop & Shop.

KAREN: Then what's for A&P?

PATRICIA: Vegetables.

KAREN: Oh right. And Kroger's?

PATRICIA: Why don't you just forget Kroger's.

KAREN, *holds up five fingers, bends one at a time*: . . . Then Stop & Shop . . .

PATRICIA: Maybe it's that you're trying to remember three things. Whyn't you just do A&P and Stop & Shop.

Slight pause.

KAREN: I kind of liked Kroger's.

PATRICIA: Then go to Kroger's, for Heaven's sake!

KAREN: Well I guess I'll go out to him. *Moves to go. Halts.* I hope you aren't really leaving today, are you?

PATRICIA, *higher tension*: I'm deciding.

KAREN: Well . . . here I go, I guess. *Halts again.* I meant to tell you, I kind of like the banjo. It's very good with tap dancing.

PATRICIA: Tap dancing.

KAREN: There's a tap teacher lives on our road.

PATRICIA: You tap-dance?

KAREN: Well John rented a video of Ginger Rogers and Fred Astaire, and I kind of liked it. I can sing "Cheek to Cheek"? Would you like to hear it?

PATRICIA: Sure, go ahead—this is certainly a surprise.

KAREN, *sings in a frail voice*: "Heaven, I'm in heaven, and the cares that clung around me through the week . . ."

PATRICIA: That's beautiful, Karen! Listen, what exactly does Doctor Rockwell say about you?

KAREN: Well, he says it's quite common when a woman is home alone all day.

PATRICIA: What's common?

KAREN: Something moving around in the next room?

PATRICIA: Oh, I see. —You have any idea who it is?

KAREN: My mother. —My husband might bring my tap shoes and tails . . . but he probably forgot. I have a high hat and shorts too. And a walking stick? But would they allow dancing in here?

PATRICIA: They might. But of course the minute they see you enjoying yourself they'll probably try to knock you out with a pill.

    Karen makes to go, halts again.

KAREN: Did your mother like you?

PATRICIA: Oh yes. We were all very close. Didn't yours?

KAREN: No. She left the whole farm to her cousin. Tell about your family, can you? Were they really all blond?

PATRICIA: Oh as blond as the tassels on Golden Bantam corn . . . everybody'd turn and look when we went by. My mother was perfection. We all were, I guess. *With a chuckle.* You know, we had a flat roof extending from the house over the garage, and mother and my sisters and me—on the first warm spring days we used to sunbathe out there.

KAREN, *covering her mouth*: No! You mean nude?

PATRICIA: Nudity doesn't matter that much in Sweden, and we were all brought up to love the sun. And we'd near die laughing because the minute we dropped our robes—you know how quiet a town Grenville is— you could hear the footsteps going up the clock tower over the Presbyterian church, and we pretended not to notice but that little narrow tower was just packed with Presbyterians.

KAREN: Good lord!

PATRICIA: We'd stretch out and pretend not to see a thing. And then my mother'd sit up suddenly and point up at the steeple and yell, "Boo!" And they'd all go running down the stairs like mice!

They both enjoy the laugh.

KAREN: I think your husband's very good-looking, isn't he.

PATRICIA: He is, but my brothers . . . I mean the way they stood, and walked . . . and their teeth! Charles won the All-New England golf tournament, and Buzz came within a tenth of an inch of the gold medal in the pole vault—that was in the Portugal Olympics.

KAREN: My! Do you still get together much?

PATRICIA: Oh, they're all gone now.

KAREN: Moved away?

PATRICIA: No . . . dead.

KAREN: Oh my. They overstrain?

PATRICIA: Buzz hung himself on his wife's closet door.

KAREN: Oh my!

PATRICIA: Eight days later Charles shot himself on the tractor.

KAREN, *softly*: Oh my. Did they leave a note or anything?

PATRICIA: No. But we all knew what it was.

KAREN: Can you say?

PATRICIA: Disappointment. We were all brought up expecting to be wonderful, and . . . *breaks off with a shrug* . . . just wasn't.

KAREN: Well . . . here I go.

> *Karen exits. Patricia stares ahead for a moment in a blankly reminiscent mood. Now she looks at her face in a mirror, smoothing wrinkles away . . .*
>
> *Leroy enters.*

PATRICIA: I was just coming out.

LEROY: 'Cause Mrs. Frick . . .

PATRICIA, *cuts him off by drawing his head down and stroking his cheek. And in a soft but faintly patronizing tone:* . . . I was just coming out, Leroy. You don't have to repeat everything. Come, sit with me and let's not argue.

LEROY: . . . How's your day been?

> *She is still moved by her brothers' memory; also, she hasn't received something she hoped for from him. She shrugs and turns her head away.*

PATRICIA: I've had worse.

LEROY: Did you wash your hair?

PATRICIA, *pleased he noticed*: How can you tell?

LEROY: Looks livelier. Is that nail polish?

PATRICIA: M-hm.

LEROY: Good. You're looking good, Patty.

PATRICIA: I'm feeling better. Not completely but a lot.

LEROY, *nods approvingly*: Great! Did he change your medication or something?

PATRICIA: No.

LEROY: Something different about you.

PATRICIA, *mysteriously excited*: You think so?

LEROY: Your eyes are clearer. You seem more like you're . . . connecting.

PATRICIA: I am, I think. But I warn you, I'm nervous.

LEROY: That's okay. Your color is more . . . I don't know . . . vigorous.

PATRICIA: Is it? *She touches her face.*

LEROY: You look almost like years ago . . .

PATRICIA: Something's happened but I don't want to talk about it yet.

LEROY: Really? Like what?

PATRICIA, *instant resistance*: I just said I . . .

LEROY: . . . Okay. *Goes to a window.* —It looks like rain outside, but we can walk around if you like. They've got a beautiful tulip bed down there; the colors really shine in this gray light. Reds and purple and whites, and a gray. Never saw a tulip be that kind of gray.

PATRICIA: How's Amelia's leg? Are you getting her to change her bandage?

LEROY: Yes. But she'd better stop thinking she can drive a car.

PATRICIA: Well, why don't you tell her?

LEROY, *a little laugh*: That'll be the day, won't it, when she starts listening to her father.

PATRICIA, *a softness despite her language*: She might if you laid down the law without just complaining. And if she could hear something besides disappointment in your voice.

LEROY: She's learned to look down at me, Patty, you know that.

PATRICIA, *strongly, but nearly a threat of weeping*: Well, I hope you're not blaming me for that.

LEROY, *he holds back, stands silent. Then puffs out his cheeks and blows, shaking his head with a defensive grin*: Not my day, I see.

PATRICIA: Maybe it could have been.

LEROY: I was looking forward to telling you something.

PATRICIA: What.

LEROY: I got Harrelson to agree to twelve-thousand-five for the altar.

PATRICIA: There, you see!—and you were so glad to accept eight. I told you . . . !

LEROY: I give you all the credit. I finally got it through my thick skull, I said to myself, okay, you are slower than most, but quality's got a right to be slow. And he didn't make a peep—twelve thousand, five hundred dollars.

>   *She looks at him, immensely sad.*

>   —Well why do you look so sad?

PATRICIA: Come here. *Draws him down, kisses him.* I'm glad. . . . I just couldn't help thinking of all these years wasted trying to get you to charge enough; but I've decided to keep looking straight ahead, not back—I'm very glad you got the twelve. You've done a wonderful thing.

LEROY, *excited*: Listen, what has he got you on?

PATRICIA: Well, I'm still a long way from perfect, but I . . .

LEROY: Patty, nothing's perfect except a hot bath.

PATRICIA: It's nothing to joke about. I told you I'm nervous, I'm not used to . . . to . . .

LEROY: He changed your medication, didn't he.

PATRICIA: I just don't want you to think I have no problems anymore.

LEROY: Oh, I'd never think that, Patty. Has he put you on something new?

PATRICIA: *He* hasn't done anything.

> *Pause.*

LEROY: Okay, I'll shut up.

> *She sweeps her hair back; he silently observes her. Then . . .*

> . . . This Mr. Frick handles oil burners; I don't know if I can trust him but he says he'd give me a good buy. We could use a new burner.

PATRICIA: What would you say if I said I'm thinking of coming home.

LEROY, *a pause filled with doubt*: You are? When?

PATRICIA: Maybe next Thursday. For good.

LEROY: Uh huh.

PATRICIA: You don't sound very positive.

LEROY: You know you're the only one can make that decision, Pat. You want to come home I'm always happy to take you home.

> *Slight pause.*

PATRICIA: I feel if I could look ahead just the right amount I'd be all right.

LEROY: What do you mean?

PATRICIA: I realized something lately; when I'm home I have a tendency— especially in the afternoons when everybody's out and I'm alone—I look very far ahead. What I should do is only look ahead a little bit, like to the evening or the next day. And then it's all right. It's when I start looking years ahead . . . *slight pause* . . . You once told me why you think I got sick. I've forgotten . . . what did you say?

LEROY: What do I really know about it, Pat?

PATRICIA: Why do you keep putting yourself down?—you've got to stop imitating your father. There are things you know very well. —Remind me what you said . . . Why am I sick?

LEROY: I always thought it was your family.

PATRICIA, *fingers pressing on her eyes*: I want to concentrate. Go on.

LEROY: They were so close, they were all over each other, and you all had this—you know—very high opinion of yourselves; each and every one of you was automatically going to go to the head of the line just because your name was Sorgenson. And life isn't that way, so you got sick.

Long pause; she stares, nodding.

PATRICIA: You've had no life at all, have you.

LEROY: I wouldn't say that.

PATRICIA: I can't understand how I never saw it.

LEROY: Why?—it's been great watching the kids growing up; and I've had some jobs I've enjoyed . . .

PATRICIA: But not your wife.

LEROY: It's a long time since I blamed you, Pat. It's your upbringing.

PATRICIA: Well I could blame yours too, couldn't I.

LEROY: You sure could.

PATRICIA: I mean this constant optimism is very irritating when you're fifty times more depressed than I am.

LEROY: Now Patty, you know that's not . . .

PATRICIA: You are depressed, Leroy! Because you're scared of people, you really don't trust anyone, and that's incidentally why you never made any money. You could have set the world on fire but you can't bear to work along with other human beings.

LEROY: The last human being I took on to help me tried to steal my half-inch Stanley chisel.

PATRICIA: You mean you *think* he tried . . .

LEROY: I didn't think anything, I found it in his tool box. And that's an original Stanley, not the junk they sell today.

PATRICIA: So what!

LEROY: So what?—that man has three grandchildren! And he's a Chapman—that's one of the oldest upstanding families in the country.

PATRICIA, *emphatically, her point proved*: Which is why you're depressed.

LEROY, *laughs*: I'm not, but why shouldn't I be?—a Chapman stealing a chisel? I mean God Almighty, they've had generals in that family, secretaries of state or some goddam thing. Anyway, if I'm depressed it's from something that happened, not something I imagine.

PATRICIA: I feel like a log that keeps bumping against another log in the middle of the river.

LEROY: Boy, you're a real roller coaster. We were doing great there for a minute, what got us off on this?

PATRICIA: I can't be at peace when I know you are full of denial, and that's saying it straight.

LEROY: What denial? *Laughs.* You want me to say I'm a failure?

PATRICIA: That is not what I . . .

LEROY: Hey, I know what—I'll get a bumper sticker printed up—"The driver of this car is a failure!" —I betcha I could sell a hundred million of them . . . *A sudden fury:* . . . Or maybe I should just drive out on a tractor and shoot myself!

PATRICIA: That's a terrible thing to say to me, Leroy!

LEROY: Well I'm sorry, Patty, but I'm not as dumb as I look—I'm never going to win if I have to compete against your brothers!

PATRICIA, *chastened for the moment:* I did not say you're a failure.

LEROY: I didn't mean to yell; I'm sorry. I know you don't mean to sound like you do, sometimes.

PATRICIA, *unable to retrieve:* I said nothing about a failure. *On the verge of weeping.*

LEROY: It's okay, maybe I am a failure; but in my opinion no more than the rest of this country.

PATRICIA: What happened?—I thought this visit started off so nicely.

LEROY: Maybe you're not used to being so alert; you've been so lethargic for a long time, you know.

> She moves; he watches her.

> I'm sure of it, Pat, if you could only find two ounces of trust I know we could still have a life.

PATRICIA: I know. *Slight pause; she fights down tears.* What did you have in mind, exactly, when you said it was my upbringing?

LEROY: I don't know . . . I had a flash of your father, that time long ago when we were sitting on your porch . . . we were getting things ready for our wedding . . . and right in front of you he turns to me cool as a cucumber and says—*through laughter, mimicking Swedish accent*—"No Yankee will ever be good enough for a Swedish girl." I nearly fell off into the rosebushes.

PATRICIA, *laughs with a certain delight:* Well, he was old-fashioned . . .

LEROY, *laughing:* Yeah, a real old-fashioned welcome into the family!

PATRICIA: Well, the Yankees *were* terrible to us.

LEROY: That's a hundred years ago, Pat.

PATRICIA, *starting to anger*: You shouldn't keep denying this! —They paid them fifty cents a week and called us dumb Swedes with strong backs and weak minds and did nothing but make us ridiculous.

LEROY: But, Patty, if you walk around town today there isn't a good piece of property that isn't owned by Swedes.

PATRICIA: But that's now.

LEROY: Well when are we living?

PATRICIA: We were treated like animals, some Yankee doctors wouldn't come out to a Swedish home to deliver a baby . . .

LEROY, *laughs*: Well all I hope is that I'm the last Yankee so people can start living today instead of a hundred years ago.

PATRICIA: There was something else you said. About standing on line.

LEROY: On line?

PATRICIA: That you'll always be at the head of the line because . . . *breaks off.*

LEROY: I'm the only one on it.

PATRICIA: . . . Is that really true? You do compete, don't you? You must, at least in your mind?

LEROY: Only with myself. We're really all on a one-person line, Pat. I learned that in these years.

> *Pause. She stares ahead.*

PATRICIA: That's very beautiful. Where'd you get that idea?

LEROY: I guess I made it up, I don't know. It's up to you, Pat—if you feel you're ready, let's go home. Now or Thursday or whenever. What about medication?

PATRICIA, *makes herself ready*: I wasn't going to tell you for another week or two, till I'm absolutely rock sure; —I've stopped taking anything for . . . this is twenty-one days.

LEROY: *Anything?*

> *She nods with a certain suspense.*

My God, Patty. And you feel all right?

PATRICIA: . . . I haven't felt this way in—fifteen years. I've no idea why, but I forgot to take anything, and I slept right through till morning, and I woke up and it was like . . . I'd been blessed during the night. And I haven't had anything since.

LEROY: Did I tell you or didn't I!

PATRICIA: But it's different for you. You're not addictive . . .

LEROY: But didn't I tell you all that stuff is poison? I'm just flying, Patty.

PATRICIA, *clasps her hands to steady herself*: But I'm afraid about coming home. I don't know if I'm jumping the gun. I *feel* I could, but . . .

LEROY: Well, let's talk about it. Is it a question of trusting yourself? Because I think if you've come this far . . .

PATRICIA: Be quiet a minute! *She holds his hand.* Why have you stayed with me?

LEROY, *laughs*: God knows!

PATRICIA: I've been very bad to you sometimes, Leroy, I really see that now. *Starting to weep.* Tell me the truth; in all these years, have you gone to other women? I wouldn't blame you, I just want to know.

LEROY: Well I've thought of it but I never did anything.

PATRICIA, *looking deeply into his eyes*: You really haven't, have you.

LEROY: No.

PATRICIA: Why?

LEROY: I just kept hoping you'd come out of this.

PATRICIA: But it's been so long.

LEROY: I know.

PATRICIA: Even when I'd . . . throw things at you?

LEROY: Uh uh.

PATRICIA: Like that time with the roast?

LEROY: Well, that's one time I came pretty close. But I knew it was those damned pills, not you.

PATRICIA: But why would you be gone night after night? That was a woman, wasn't it.

LEROY: No. Some nights I went over to the library basement to practice banjo with Phil Palumbo. Or to Manny's Diner for some donuts and talk to the fellas.

PATRICIA, *slightest tinge of suspicion*: There are fellas there at *night*?

LEROY: Sure; working guys, mostly young single fellas. But some with wives. You know—have a beer, watch TV.

PATRICIA: And women?

LEROY, *a short beat*: —You know, Pat—and I'm not criticizing—but wouldn't it be better for you to try believing a person instead of trying not to believe?

PATRICIA: I'm just wondering if you know . . . there's lots of women would love having you. But you probably don't know that, do you.

LEROY: Sure I do.

PATRICIA: You know lots of women would love to have you?

LEROY: . . . Well, yes, I know that.

PATRICIA: Really. How do you know that?

LEROY, *his quick, open laugh*: I can tell.

PATRICIA: Then what's keeping you? Why don't you move out?

LEROY: Pat, you're torturing me.

PATRICIA: I'm trying to find myself!

> *She moves in stress, warding off an explosion. There is angry resentment in his voice.*

LEROY: I'd remember you happy and loving—that's what kept me; as long ago as that is now, I'd remember how you'd pull on your stockings and get a little makeup on and pin up your hair. . . . When you're positive about life there's just nobody like you. Nobody. Not in life, not in the movies, not on TV. *Slight pause.* But I'm not going to deny it—if it wasn't for the kids I probably *would* have gone.

> *She is silent, but loaded with something unspoken.*

You're wanting to tell me something, aren't you.

PATRICIA: . . . I know what a lucky woman I've been.

LEROY, *he observes her*: —What is it, you want me to stop coming to see you for a while? Please tell me, Pat; there's something on your mind.

> *Pause. She forces it out.*

PATRICIA: I know I shouldn't feel this way, but I'm not too sure I could stand it, knowing that it's never going to . . . I mean, will it ever change anymore?

LEROY: You mean—is it ever going to be "wonderful."

> *She looks at him, estimating.*

Well—no, I guess this is pretty much it; although to me it's already wonderful—I mean the kids, and there are some clear

New England mornings when you want to drink the air and the sunshine.

PATRICIA: You can make more out of a change in temperature than any human being I ever heard of—I can't live on weather!

LEROY: Pat, we're getting old! This is just about as rich and handsome as I'm ever going to be and as good as you're ever going to look, so you want to be with me or not?

PATRICIA: I don't want to fool either of us . . . I can't bear it when you can't pay the bills . . .

LEROY: But I'm a carpenter—this is probably the way it's been for carpenters since they built Noah's ark. What do you want to do?

PATRICIA: I'm honestly not sure I could hold up. Not when I hear your sadness all the time and your eyes are full of disappointment. You seem . . . *breaks off.*

LEROY: . . . How do I seem?

PATRICIA: I shouldn't say it.

LEROY: . . . Beaten. Like it's all gone by. *Hurt, but holding on:* All right, Patty, then I might as well say it—I don't think you *ever* had a medical problem; you have an attitude problem . . .

PATRICIA: My problem is spiritual.

LEROY: Okay, I don't mind calling it spiritual.

PATRICIA: Well that's a new note; I thought these ministers were all quacks.

LEROY: Not all; but the ones who make house calls with women, eating up all the ice cream, are not my idea of spiritual.

PATRICIA: *You* know what spiritual is?

LEROY: For me? Sure. Ice skating.

PATRICIA: Ice skating is spiritual.

LEROY: Yes, and skiing! To me spiritual is whatever makes me forget myself and feel happy to be alive. Like even a well-sharpened saw, or a perfect compound joint.

PATRICIA: Maybe this is why we can't get along—spiritual is nothing you can see, Leroy.

LEROY: Really! Then why didn't God make everything invisible! We are in this world and you're going to have to find some way to love it!

Her eyes are filling with tears.

Pounding on me is not going to change anything to wonderful, Patty.

She seems to be receiving him.

I'll say it again, because it's the only thing that's kept me from going crazy—you just have to love this world. *He comes to her, takes her hand.* Come home. Maybe it'll take a while, but I really believe you can make it.

Uncertainty filling her face . . .

All right, don't decide now, I'll come back Thursday and we'll see then.

PATRICIA: Where you going now?

LEROY: For my banjo lesson. I'm learning a new number. —I'll play it for you if you want to hear it.

PATRICIA, *hesitates, then kisses him*: Couldn't you do it on guitar?

LEROY: It's not the same on guitar. *He goes to his banjo case and opens it.*

PATRICIA: But banjo sounds so picky.

LEROY: But that's what's good about it, it's clean, like a toothpick . . .

Enter the Fricks.

LEROY: Oh hi, Mrs. Frick.

KAREN: He brought my costume. Would you care to see it? *To Frick*: This is her—Mrs. Hamilton.

FRICK: Oh! How do you do?

KAREN: This is my husband.

PATRICIA: How do you do?

FRICK: She's been telling me all about you. *Shaking Patricia's hand*: I want to say that I'm thankful to you.

PATRICIA: Really? What for?

FRICK: Well what she says you've been telling her. About her attitude and all.

KAREN, *to Patricia*: Would you like to see my costume? I also have a blue one, but . . .

FRICK, *overriding her*: . . . By the way, I'm Frick Lumber, I recognized your husband right away . . .

KAREN: Should I put it on?

PATRICIA: Sure, put it on!

Leroy starts tuning his banjo.

FRICK, *to Patricia*: All it is is a high hat and shorts, y'know . . . nothing much to it.

KAREN, *to Frick*: Shouldn't I?

PATRICIA: Why not, for Heaven's sake?

FRICK: Go ahead, if they want to see it. *Laughs to Patricia.* She found it in a catalogue. I think it's kinda silly at her age, but I admit I'm a conservative kind of person . . .

KAREN, *cutting him off, deeply embarrassed*: I'll only be a minute. *She starts out, and stops, and to Patricia*: You really think I should?

PATRICIA: Of course!

FRICK, *suppressing an angry embarrassment*: Karen, honey, if you're going to do it, do it.

Karen exits with valise. Leroy tunes his instrument.

FRICK: The slightest decision, she's got to worry it into the ground. —But I have to tell you, it's years since I've seen this much life in her, she's like day and night. What exactly'd you say to her? *To Leroy, thumbing toward Patricia*: She says she just opened up her eyes . . .

LEROY, *surprised*: Patricia?

FRICK: I have to admit, it took me a while to realize it's a sickness . . .

PATRICIA: You're not the only one.

FRICK: Looked to me like she was just favoring herself; I mean the woman has everything, what right has she got to start shooting blanks like that? I happen to be a great believer in self-discipline, started from way down below sea level myself, sixty acres of rocks and swampland is all we had. That's why I'm so glad that somebody's talked to her with your attitude.

PATRICIA, *vamping for time*: What . . . what attitude do you mean?

FRICK: Just that you're so . . . so positive.

Leroy looks up at Patricia, thunderstruck.

She says you made her realize all the things she could be doing instead of mooning around all day . . .

PATRICIA: Well I think being positive is the only way.

FRICK: That's just what I tell her . . .

PATRICIA: But you have to be careful not to sound so disappointed in her.

FRICK: I sound disappointed?

PATRICIA: In a way, I think. —She's got to feel treasured, you see.

FRICK: I appreciate that, but the woman can stand in one place for half an hour at a time practically without moving.

PATRICIA: Well that's the sickness, you see.

FRICK: I realize that. But she won't even go shopping . . .

PATRICIA: You see? You're sounding disappointed in her.

FRICK, *angering*: I am not disappointed in her! I'm just telling you the situation!

PATRICIA: Mr. Frick, she's standing under a mountain a mile high— you've got to help her over it. That woman has very big possibilities!

FRICK: Think so.

PATRICIA: Absolutely.

FRICK: I hope you're right. *To Leroy, indicating Patricia*: You don't mind my saying it, you could do with a little of her optimism.

LEROY, *turns from Patricia, astonished*: Huh?

FRICK, *to Patricia, warmly*: Y'know, she made me have a little platform built down the cellar, with a big full-length mirror so she could see herself dance . . .

PATRICIA: But do you spend time watching her . . .

FRICK: Well she says not to till she's good at it.

PATRICIA: That's because she's terrified of your criticism.

FRICK: But I haven't made any criticism.

PATRICIA: But do you like tap dancing?

FRICK: Well I don't know, I never thought about it one way or another.

PATRICIA: Well that's the thing, you see. It happens to mean a great deal to her . . .

FRICK: I'm for it, I don't mean I'm not for it. But don't tell me you think it's normal for a woman her age to be getting out of bed two, three in the morning and start practicing.

PATRICIA: Well maybe she's trying to get you interested in it. Are you?

FRICK: In tap dancing? Truthfully, no.

PATRICIA: Well there you go . . .

FRICK: Well we've got a lot of new competition in our fuel-oil business . . .

PATRICIA: Fuel oil!

FRICK: I've got seven trucks on the road that I've got to keep busy . . .

PATRICIA: Well there you go, maybe that's why your wife is in here.

FRICK, *visibly angering*: Well I can't be waked up at two o'clock in the morning and be any good next day, now can I. She's not normal.

PATRICIA: Normal! They've got whole universities debating what's normal. Who knows what's normal, Mr. Frick?

FRICK: You mean getting out of bed at two o'clock in the morning and putting on a pair of tap shoes is a common occurrence in this country? I don't think so. —But I didn't mean to argue when you're . . . not feeling well.

PATRICIA: I've never felt better.

> *She turns away, and Frick looks with bewildered surprise to Leroy, who returns him a look of suppressed laughter.*

FRICK: Well you sure know how to turn somebody inside out.

> *Karen enters; she is dressed in satin shorts, a tailcoat, a high hat, tap shoes, and as they turn to look at her, she pulls out a collapsible walking stick, and strikes a theatrical pose.*

PATRICIA: Well now, don't you look great!

KAREN, *desperate for reassurance*: You really like it?

LEROY: That looks terrific!

PATRICIA: Do a step!

KAREN: I don't have my tape. *Turns to Frick, timorously*: But if you'd sing "Swanee River" . . .

FRICK: Oh Karen, for God's sake!

PATRICIA: I can sing it . . .

KAREN: He knows my speed. Please, John . . . just for a minute.

FRICK: All right, go ahead. *Unhappily, he sings*:

> Way down upon the Swanee River . . .

KAREN: Wait, you're too fast . . .

FRICK, *slower and angering*:

Way—down—upon—the—Swanee River,
Far, far away.
That's where my heart is turning ever . . . [etc.]

Karen taps out her number, laboriously but for a short stretch with a promise of grace. Frick continues singing . . .

PATRICIA: Isn't she wonderful?

LEROY: Hey, she's great!

Karen dances a bit more boldly, a joyous freedom starting into her.

PATRICIA: She's marvelous! Look at her, Mr. Frick!

A hint of the sensuous in Karen now; Frick, embarrassed, uneasily avoids more than a glance at his wife.

FRICK:

. . . everywhere I roam . . .

PATRICIA: Will you look at her!

FRICK, *hard-pressed, explodes*: I am looking at her, goddammit!

This astonishing furious shout, his reddened face, stops everything. A look of fear is on Karen's face.

KAREN, *apologetically to Patricia*: He *was* looking at me . . . *To Frick*: She didn't mean you *weren't* looking, she meant . . .

FRICK, *rigidly repressing his anger and embarrassment*: I've got to run along now.

KAREN: I'm so sorry, John, but she . . .

FRICK, *rigidly*: Nothing to be sorry about, dear. Very nice to have met you folks.

He starts to exit. Karen moves to intercept him.

KAREN: Oh John, I hope you're not . . . [going to be angry.]

JOHN: I'm just fine. *He sees her despair coming on.* What are you looking so sad about?—you danced great . . .

She is immobile.

I'm sorry to've raised my voice but it don't mean I'm disappointed, dear. You understand? *A nervous glance toward Patricia. Stiffly, with enormous effort:* . . . You . . . you danced better than I ever saw you.

She doesn't change.

Now look here, Karen, I hope you don't feel I'm . . . disappointed or something, you hear . . . ? 'Cause I'm not. And that's definite.

She keeps staring at him.

I'll try to make it again on Friday. —Keep it up.

He abruptly turns and exits.

Karen stands perfectly still, staring at nothing.

PATRICIA: Karen?

Karen seems not to hear, standing there facing the empty door in her high hat and costume.

How about Leroy playing it for you? *To Leroy*: Play it.

LEROY: I could on the guitar, but I never did on this . . .

PATRICIA: Well couldn't you try it?—I don't know what good that thing is.

LEROY: Well here . . . let me see.

He picks out "Swanee River" on his banjo, but Karen doesn't move.

PATRICIA: There you go, Karen! Try it, I love your dancing! Come on . . . *Sings*:

Way down upon the Swanee River . . .

Karen now breaks her motionlessly depressed mode and looks at Patricia. Leroy continues playing, humming along with it. His picking is getting more accurate . . .

PATRICIA: Is it the right tempo? Tell him!

KAREN, *very very softly*: Could you play a little faster?

Leroy speeds it up. With an unrelieved sadness, Karen goes into her number, does a few steps, but stops. Leroy gradually stops playing. Karen walks out. Patricia starts to follow her but gives it up and comes to a halt.

Leroy turns to Patricia, who is staring ahead. Now she turns to Leroy.

He meets her gaze, his face filled with inquiry. He comes to her and stands there. For a long moment neither of them moves. Then she reaches out and touches his face—there is a muted gratitude in her gesture.

She goes to a closet and takes a small overnight bag to the bed and puts her things into it.

Leroy watches her for a moment, then stows his banjo in its case, and stands waiting for her. She starts to put on a light coat. He comes and helps her into it.

Her face is charged with her struggle against her self-doubt.

LEROY, *laughs, but about to weep*: Ready?

PATRICIA, *filling up*: Leroy . . .

LEROY: One day at a time, Pat—you're already twenty-one ahead. Kids are going to be so happy to have you home.

PATRICIA: I can't believe it . . . I've had nothing.

LEROY: It's a miracle.

PATRICIA: Thank you. *Breaking through her own resistance, she draws him to her and kisses him. Grinning tauntingly*: . . . That car going to get us home?

LEROY, *laughs*: Stop picking on that car, it's all checked out!

They start toward the door, he carrying her bag and his banjo.

PATRICIA: Once you believe in something you just never know when to stop, do you.

LEROY: Well there's very little rust, and the new ones aren't half as well built . . .

PATRICIA: Waste not, want not.

LEROY: Well I really don't *go* for those new Chevies . . .

She walks out, he behind her. Their voices are heard . . .

PATRICIA: Between the banjo and that car I've certainly got a whole lot to look forward to.

His laughter sounds down the corridor.

The woman on the bed stirs, then falls back and remains motionless. A stillness envelops the whole stage.

END

BROKEN GLASS

A PLAY IN TWO ACTS

1994

Characters

PHILLIP GELLBURG

SYLVIA GELLBURG

DR. HARRY HYMAN

MARGARET HYMAN

HARRIET

STANTON CASE

The play takes place in Brooklyn in the last days of November 1938, in the office of Dr. Harry Hyman, the bedroom of the Gellburg house, and the office of Stanton Case.

ACT ONE

SCENE I

A lone cellist is discovered, playing a simple tune. The tune finishes. Light goes out on the cellist and rises on. . . .

Office of Dr. Harry Hyman in his home. Alone on stage Phillip Gellburg, an intense man in his late forties, waits in perfect stillness, legs crossed. He is in a black suit, black tie and shoes, and white shirt.

Margaret Hyman, the doctor's wife, enters. She is lusty, energetic, carrying pruning shears.

MARGARET: He'll be right with you, he's just changing. Can I get you something? Tea?

GELLBURG, *faint reprimand*: He said seven o'clock sharp.

MARGARET: He was held up in the hospital, that new union's pulled a strike, imagine? A strike in a hospital? It's incredible. And his horse went lame.

GELLBURG: His horse?

MARGARET: He rides on Ocean Parkway every afternoon.

GELLBURG, *attempting easy familiarity*: Oh yes, I heard about that . . . it's very nice. You're Mrs. Hyman?

MARGARET: I've nodded to you on the street for years now, but you're too preoccupied to notice.

GELLBURG, *a barely hidden boast*: Lot on my mind, usually. *A certain amused loftiness.*—So you're his nurse, too.

MARGARET: We met in Mount Sinai when he was interning. He's lived to regret it. *She laughs in a burst.*

GELLBURG: That's some laugh you've got there. I sometimes hear you all the way down the block to my house.

MARGARET: Can't help it, my whole family does it. I'm originally from Minnesota. It's nice to meet you finally, Mr. Goldberg.

GELLBURG: —It's Gellburg, not Goldberg.

MARGARET: Oh, I'm sorry.

GELLBURG: G-e-l-l-b-u-r-g. It's the only one in the phone book.

MARGARET: It does sound like Goldberg.

GELLBURG: But it's not, it's Gellburg. *A distinction.* We're from Finland originally.

MARGARET: Oh! We came from Lithuania . . . Kazauskis?

GELLBURG, *put down momentarily*: Don't say.

MARGARET, *trying to charm him to his ease*: Ever been to Minnesota?

GELLBURG: New York State's the size of France, what would I go to Minnesota for?

MARGARET: Nothing. Just there's a lot of Finns there.

GELLBURG: Well there's Finns all over.

MARGARET, *defeated, shows the clipper*: . . . I'll get back to my roses. Whatever it is, I hope you'll be feeling better.

GELLBURG: It's not me.

MARGARET: Oh. 'Cause you seem a little pale.

GELLBURG: Me?—I'm always this color. It's my wife.

MARGARET: I'm sorry to hear that, she's a lovely woman. It's nothing serious, is it?

GELLBURG: He's just had a specialist put her through some tests, I'm waiting to hear. I think it's got him mystified.

MARGARET: Well, I mustn't butt in. *Makes to leave but can't resist.* Can you say what it is?

GELLBURG: She can't walk.

MARGARET: What do you mean?

GELLBURG, *an overtone of protest of some personal victimization*: Can't stand up. No feeling in her legs.—I'm sure it'll pass, but it's terrible.

MARGARET: But I only saw her in the grocery . . . can't be more than ten days ago . . .

GELLBURG: It's nine days today.

MARGARET: But she's such a wonderful-looking woman. Does she have fever?

GELLBURG: No.

MARGARET: Thank God, then it's not polio.

GELLBURG: No, she's in perfect health otherwise.

MARGARET: Well Harry'll get to the bottom of it if anybody can. They call him from everywhere for opinions, you know . . . Boston, Chicago . . . By rights he ought to be on Park Avenue if he only had the ambition, but he always wanted a neighborhood practice. Why, I don't know—we never invite anybody, we never go out, all our friends are in Manhattan. But it's his nature, you can't fight a person's nature. Like me for instance, I like to talk and I like to laugh. You're not much of a talker, are you.

GELLBURG, *a purse-mouthed smile*: When I can get a word in edgewise.

MARGARET, *burst of laughter*: Ha!—so you've got a sense of humor after all. Well give my best to Mrs. Goldberg.

GELLBURG: Gellbu . . .

MARGARET, *hits her own head*: Gellburg, excuse me! —It practically sounds like Goldberg . . .

GELLBURG: No-no, look in the phone book, it's the only one, G-e-l-l . . .

    Enter Dr. Hyman.

MARGARET, *with a little wave to Gellburg*: Be seeing you!

GELLBURG: Be in good health.

    Margaret exits.

HYMAN, *in his early fifties, a healthy, rather handsome man, a determined scientific idealist. Settling behind his desk—chuckling*: She chew your ear off?

GELLBURG, *his worldly mode*: Not too bad, I've had worse.

HYMAN: Well there's no way around it, women are talkers . . . *Grinning familiarly*: But try living without them, right?

GELLBURG: Without women?

HYMAN, *he sees Gellburg has flushed; there is a short hiatus, then*: . . . Well, never mind. —I'm glad you could make it tonight, I wanted to talk to you before I see your wife again tomorrow. *Opens cigar humidor.* Smoke?

GELLBURG: No thanks, never have. Isn't it bad for you?

HYMAN: Certainly is. *Lights a cigar.* But more people die of rat bite, you know.

GELLBURG: Rat bite!

HYMAN: Oh yes, but they're mostly the poor so it's not an interesting statistic. Have you seen her tonight or did you come here from the office?

GELLBURG: I thought I'd see you before I went home. But I phoned her this afternoon—same thing, no change.

HYMAN: How's she doing with the wheelchair?

GELLBURG: Better, she can get herself in and out of the bed now.

HYMAN: Good. And she manages the bathroom?

GELLBURG: Oh yes. I got the maid to come in the mornings to help her take a bath, clean up . . .

HYMAN: Good. Your wife has a lot of courage, I admire that kind of woman. My wife is similar; I like the type.

GELLBURG: What type you mean?

HYMAN: You know—vigorous. I mean mentally and . . . you know, just generally. Moxie.

GELLBURG: Oh.

HYMAN: Forget it, it was only a remark.

GELLBURG: No, you're right, I never thought of it, but she is unusually that way.

HYMAN, *pause, some prickliness here which he can't understand*: Doctor Sherman's report . . .

GELLBURG: What's he say?

HYMAN: I'm getting to it.

GELLBURG: Oh. Beg your pardon.

HYMAN: You'll have to bear with me . . . may I call you Phillip?

GELLBURG: Certainly.

HYMAN: I don't express my thoughts very quickly, Phillip.

GELLBURG: Likewise. Go ahead, take your time.

HYMAN: People tend to overestimate the wisdom of physicians so I try to think things through before I speak to a patient.

GELLBURG: I'm glad to hear that.

HYMAN: Aesculapius stuttered, you know—ancient Greek god of medicine. But probably based on a real physician who hesitated about giving advice. Somerset Maugham stammered, studied medicine. Anton Chekhov, great writer, also a doctor, had tuberculosis. Doctors are very often physically defective in some way, that's why they're interested in healing.

GELLBURG, *impressed*: I see.

HYMAN, *pause, thinks*: I find this Adolf Hitler very disturbing. You been following him in the papers?

GELLBURG: Well yes, but not much. My average day in the office is ten, eleven hours.

HYMAN: They've been smashing the Jewish stores in Berlin all week, you know.

GELLBURG: Oh yes, I saw that again yesterday.

HYMAN: Very disturbing. Forcing old men to scrub the sidewalks with toothbrushes. On the Kurfürstendamm, that's equivalent to Fifth Avenue. Nothing but hoodlums in uniform.

GELLBURG: My wife is very upset about that.

HYMAN: I know, that's why I mention it. *Hesitates.* And how about you?

GELLBURG: Of course. It's a terrible thing. Why do you ask?

HYMAN, *a smile*: —I don't know, I got the feeling she may be afraid she's annoying you when she talks about such things.

GELLBURG: Why? I don't mind. —She said she's annoying me?

HYMAN: Not in so many words, but . . .

GELLBURG: I can't believe she'd say a thing like . . .

HYMAN: Wait a minute, I didn't say she said it . . .

GELLBURG: She doesn't annoy me, but what can be done about such things? The thing is, she doesn't like to hear about the other side of it.

HYMAN: What other side?

GELLBURG: It's no excuse for what's happening over there, but German Jews can be pretty . . . you know . . . *Pushes up his nose with his forefinger.* Not that they're pushy like the ones from Poland or Russia but a friend of mine's in the garment industry; these German Jews won't take an ordinary good job, you know; it's got to be pretty high up in the firm or they're insulted. And they can't even speak English.

HYMAN: Well I guess a lot of them were pretty important over there.

GELLBURG: I know, but they're supposed to be *refugees*, aren't they? With all our unemployment you'd think they'd appreciate a little more. Latest official figure is twelve million unemployed you know, and it's probably bigger but Roosevelt can't admit it, after the fortune he's pouring into WPA and the rest of that welfare *mishugas*. —But she's not *annoying* me, for God's sake.

HYMAN: . . . I just thought I'd mention it; but it was only a feeling I had . . .

GELLBURG: I'll tell you right now, I don't run with the crowd, I see with these eyes, nobody else's.

HYMAN: I see that. —You're very unusual— *Grinning.* —you almost sound like a Republican.

GELLBURG: Why?—the Torah says a Jew has to be a Democrat? I didn't get where I am by agreeing with everybody.

HYMAN: Well that's a good thing; you're independent. *Nods, puffs.* You know, what mystifies me is that the Germans I knew in Heidelberg . . . I took my M.D. there . . .

GELLBURG: You got along with them.

HYMAN: Some of the finest people I ever met.

GELLBURG: Well there you go.

HYMAN: We had a marvelous student choral group, fantastic voices; Saturday nights, we'd have a few beers and go singing through the streets. . . . People'd applaud from the windows.

GELLBURG: Don't say.

HYMAN: I simply can't imagine those people marching into Austria, and now they say Czechoslovakia's next, and Poland. . . . But fanatics have taken Germany, I guess, and they can be brutal, you know . . .

GELLBURG: Listen, I sympathize with these refugees, but . . .

HYMAN, *cutting him off*: I had quite a long talk with Sylvia yesterday, I suppose she told you?

GELLBURG, *a tensing*: Well . . . no, she didn't mention. What about?

HYMAN, *surprised by Sylvia's omission*: . . . Well about her condition, and . . . just in passing . . . your relationship.

GELLBURG, *flushing*: My relationship?

HYMAN: . . . It was just in passing.

GELLBURG: Why, what'd she say?

HYMAN: Well that you . . . get along very well.

GELLBURG: Oh.

HYMAN, *encouragingly, as he sees Gellburg's small tension*: I found her a remarkably well-informed woman. Especially for this neighborhood.

GELLBURG, *a pridefully approving nod; relieved that he can speak of her positively*: That's practically why we got together in the first place. I don't exaggerate, if Sylvia was a man she could have run the Federal Reserve. You could talk to Sylvia like you talk to a man.

HYMAN: I'll bet.

GELLBURG, *a purse-mouthed grin*: . . . Not that talking was all we did— but you turn your back on Sylvia and she's got her nose in a book or a magazine. I mean there's not one woman in ten around here could even tell you who their Congressman is. And you can throw in the men, too. *Pause.* So where are we?

HYMAN: Doctor Sherman confirms my diagnosis. I ask you to listen carefully, will you?

GELLBURG, *brought up*: Of course, that's why I came.

HYMAN: We can find no physical reason for her inability to walk.

GELLBURG: No physical reason . . .

HYMAN: We are almost certain that this is a psychological condition.

GELLBURG: But she's numb, she has no feeling in her legs.

HYMAN: Yes. This is what we call an hysterical paralysis. Hysterical doesn't mean she screams and yells . . .

GELLBURG: Oh, I know. It means like . . . ah . . . *Bumbles off.*

HYMAN, *a flash of umbrage, dislike*: Let me explain what it means, okay?—Hysteria comes from the Greek word for the womb because it was thought to be a symptom of female anxiety. Of course it isn't, but that's where it comes from. People who are anxious enough or really frightened can imagine they've gone blind or deaf, for instance . . . and they really can't see or hear. It was sometimes called shell-shock during the War.

GELLBURG: You mean . . . you don't mean she's . . . crazy.

HYMAN: We'll have to talk turkey, Phillip. If I'm going to do you any good I'm going to have to ask you some personal questions. Some of them may sound raw, but I've only been superficially acquainted with Sylvia's family and I need to know more . . .

GELLBURG: She says you treated her father . . .

HYMAN: Briefly; a few visits shortly before he passed away. They're fine people. I hate like hell to see this happen to her, you see what I mean?

GELLBURG: You can tell it to me; is she crazy?

HYMAN: Phillip, are you? Am I? In one way or another, who isn't crazy? The main difference is that our kind of crazy still allows us to walk around and tend to our business. But who knows?—people like us may be the craziest of all.

GELLBURG, *scoffing grin*: Why!

HYMAN: Because we don't know we're nuts, and the other kind does.

GELLBURG: I don't know about that . . .

HYMAN: Well, it's neither here nor there.

GELLBURG: I certainly don't think *I'm* nuts.

HYMAN: I wasn't saying that . . .

GELLBURG: What do you mean, then?

HYMAN, *grinning*: You're not an easy man to talk to, are you.

GELLBURG: Why? If I don't understand I have to ask, don't I?

HYMAN: Yes, you're right.

GELLBURG: That's the way I am—they don't pay me for being easy to talk to.

HYMAN: You're in . . . real estate?

GELLBURG: I'm head of the Mortgage Department of Brooklyn Guarantee and Trust.

HYMAN: Oh, that's right, she told me.

GELLBURG: We are the largest lender east of the Mississippi.

HYMAN: Really. *Fighting deflation*. Well, let me tell you my approach; if possible I'd like to keep her out of that whole psychiatry rigmarole. Not that I'm against it, but I think you get further faster, sometimes, with a little common sense and some plain human sympathy. Can we talk turkey? *Tuchas offen tisch*, you know any Yiddish?

GELLBURG: Yes, it means get your ass on the table.

HYMAN: Correct. So let's forget crazy and try to face the facts. We have a strong, healthy woman who has no physical ailment, and suddenly can't stand on her legs. Why?

He goes silent. Gellburg shifts uneasily.

I don't mean to embarrass you . . .

GELLBURG, *an angry smile*: You're not embarrassing me. —What do you want to know?

HYMAN, *sets himself, then launches*: In these cases there is often a sexual disability. You have relations, I imagine?

GELLBURG: Relations? Yes, we have relations.

HYMAN, *a softening smile*: Often?

GELLBURG: What's that got to do with it?

HYMAN: Sex could be connected. You don't have to answer . . .

GELLBURG: No-no it's all right. . . . I would say it depends—maybe twice, three times a week.

HYMAN, *seems surprised*: Well that's good. She seems satisfied?

GELLBURG, *shrugs; hostilely*: I guess she is, sure.

HYMAN: That was a foolish question, forget it.

GELLBURG, *flushed*: Why, did she mention something about this?

HYMAN: Oh no, it's just something I thought of later.

GELLBURG: Well, I'm no Rudolph Valentino but I . . .

HYMAN: Rudolph Valentino probably wasn't either. —What about before she collapsed; was that completely out of the blue or . . .

GELLBURG, *relieved to be off the other subject*: I tell you, looking back I wonder if something happened when they started putting all the pictures in the paper. About these Nazi carryings-on. I noticed she started . . . staring at them . . . in a very peculiar way. And . . . I don't know. I think it made her angry or something.

HYMAN: At you.

GELLBURG: Well . . . *Nods, agreeing*. In general. —Personally I don't think they should be publishing those kind of pictures.

HYMAN: Why not?

GELLBURG: She scares herself to death with them—three thousand miles away, and what does it accomplish! Except maybe put some fancy new ideas into these anti-Semites walking around New York here.

    Slight pause.

HYMAN: Tell me how she collapsed. You were going to the movies . . . ?

GELLBURG, *breathing more deeply*: Yes. We were just starting down the porch steps and all of a sudden her . . . *Difficulty; he breaks off.*

HYMAN: I'm sorry but I . . .

GELLBURG: . . . Her legs turned to butter. I couldn't stand her up. Kept falling around like a rag doll. I had to carry her into the house. And she kept apologizing . . . ! *He weeps; recovers.* I can't talk about it.

HYMAN: It's all right.

GELLBURG: She's always been such a level-headed woman. *Weeping threatens again.* I don't know what to do. She's my life.

HYMAN: I'll do my best for her, Phillip, she's a wonderful woman. —Let's talk about something else. What do you do exactly?

GELLBURG: I mainly evaluate properties.

HYMAN: Whether to grant a mortgage . . .

GELLBURG: And how big a one and the terms.

HYMAN: How's the Depression hit you?

GELLBURG: Well, it's no comparison with '32 to '36, let's say—we were foreclosing left and right in those days. But we're on our feet and running.

HYMAN: And you head the department . . .

GELLBURG: Above me is only Mr. Case. Stanton Wylie Case; he's chairman and president. You're not interested in boat racing.

HYMAN: Why?

GELLBURG: His yacht won the America's Cup two years ago. For the second time. The *Aurora*?

HYMAN: Oh yes! I think I read about . . .

GELLBURG: He's had me aboard twice.

HYMAN: Really.

GELLBURG, *the grin*: The only Jew ever set foot on that deck.

HYMAN: Don't say.

GELLBURG: In fact, I'm the only Jew ever worked for Brooklyn Guarantee in their whole history.

HYMAN: That so.

GELLBURG: Oh yes. And they go back to the 1890s. Started right out of accountancy school and moved straight up. They've been wonderful to me; it's a great firm.

A long moment as Hyman stares at Gellburg, who is proudly positioned now, absorbing his poise from the evoked memories of his success. Gradually Gellburg turns to him.

How could this be a mental condition?

HYMAN: It's unconscious; like . . . well take yourself; I notice you're all in black. Can I ask you why?

GELLBURG: I've worn black since high school.

HYMAN: No particular reason.

GELLBURG, *shrugs*: Always liked it, that's all.

HYMAN: Well it's a similar thing with her; she doesn't know why she's doing this, but some very deep, hidden part of her mind is directing her to do it. You don't agree.

GELLBURG: I don't know.

HYMAN: You think she knows what she's doing?

GELLBURG: Well I always liked black for business reasons.

HYMAN: It gives you authority?

GELLBURG: Not exactly authority, but I wanted to look a little older. See, I graduated high school at fifteen and I was only twenty-two when I entered the firm. But I knew what I was doing.

HYMAN: Then you think she's doing this on purpose?

GELLBURG: —Except she's numb; nobody can purposely do that, can they?

HYMAN: I don't think so. —I tell you, Phillip, not really knowing your wife, if you have any idea why she could be doing this to herself . . .

GELLBURG: I told you, I don't know.

HYMAN: Nothing occurs to you.

GELLBURG, *an edge of irritation*: I can't think of anything.

HYMAN: I tell you a funny thing, talking to her, she doesn't seem all that unhappy.

GELLBURG: Say!—yes, that's what I mean. That's exactly what I mean. It's like she's almost . . . I don't know . . . enjoying herself. I mean in a way.

HYMAN: How could that be possible?

GELLBURG: Of course she apologizes for it, and for making it hard for me—you know, like I have to do a lot of the cooking now, and tending to my laundry and so on . . . I even shop for groceries and the butcher . . . and change the sheets . . .

He breaks off with some realization. Hyman doesn't speak. A long pause.

You mean . . . she's doing it against me?

HYMAN: I don't know, what do *you* think?

Stares for a long moment, then makes to rise, obviously deeply disturbed.

GELLBURG: I'd better be getting home. *Lost in his own thought.* I don't know whether to ask you this or not.

HYMAN: What's to lose, go ahead.

GELLBURG: My parents were from the old country, you know,—I don't know if it was in Poland someplace or Russia—but there was this woman who they say was . . . you know . . . gotten into by a . . . like the ghost of a dead person . . .

HYMAN: A dybbuk.

GELLBURG: That's it. And it made her lose her mind and so forth. —You believe in that? They had to get a rabbi to pray it out of her body. But you think that's possible?

HYMAN: Do I think so? No. Do you?

GELLBURG: Oh no. It just crossed my mind.

HYMAN: Well I wouldn't know how to pray it out of her, so . . .

GELLBURG: Be straight with me—is she going to come out of this?

HYMAN: Well, let's talk again after I see her tomorrow. Maybe I should tell you . . . I have this unconventional approach to illness, Phillip. Especially where the mental element is involved. I believe we get sick in twos and threes and fours, not alone as individuals. You follow me? I want you to do me a favor, will you?

GELLBURG: What's that.

HYMAN: You won't be offended, okay?

GELLBURG, *tensely*: Why should I be offended?

HYMAN: I'd like you to give her a lot of loving. *Fixing Gellburg in his gaze.* Can you? It's important now.

GELLBURG: Say, you're not blaming this on me, are you?

HYMAN: What's the good of blame? —From here on out, *tuchas offen tisch*, okay? And Phillip?

GELLBURG: Yes?

HYMAN, *a light chuckle*: Try not to let yourself get mad.

Gellburg turns and goes out. Hyman returns to his desk, makes some notes. Margaret enters.

MARGARET: That's one miserable little pisser.

He writes, doesn't look up.

He's a dictator, you know. I was just remembering when I went to the grandmother's funeral? He stands outside the funeral parlor and decides who's going to sit with who in the limousines for the cemetery. "You sit with him, you sit with her . . ." And they obey him like he owned the funeral!

HYMAN: Did you find out what's playing?

MARGARET: At the Beverly they've got Ginger Rogers and Fred Astaire. Jimmy Cagney's at the Rialto but it's another gangster story.

HYMAN: I have a sour feeling about this thing. I barely know my way around psychiatry. I'm not completely sure I ought to get into it.

MARGARET: Why not?—She's a very beautiful woman.

HYMAN, *matching her wryness*: Well, is that a reason to turn her away? *He laughs, grasps her hand.* Something about it fascinates me—no disease and she's paralyzed. I'd really love to give it a try. I mean I don't want to turn myself into a post office, shipping all the hard cases to specialists, the woman's sick and I'd like to help.

MARGARET: But if you're not getting anywhere in a little while you'll promise to send her to somebody.

HYMAN: Absolutely. *Committed now: full enthusiasm.* I just feel there's something about it that I understand.—Let's see Cagney.

MARGARET: Oh, no Fred Astaire.

HYMAN: That's what I meant. Come here.

MARGARET, *as he embraces her*: We should leave now . . .

HYMAN: You're the best, Margaret.

MARGARET: A lot of good it does me.

HYMAN: If it really bothers you I'll get someone else to take the case.

MARGARET: You won't, you know you won't.

He is lifting her skirt.

Don't, Harry. Come on.

She frees her skirt, he kisses her breasts.

HYMAN: Should I tell you what I'd like to do with you?

MARGARET: Tell me, yes, tell me. And make it wonderful.

HYMAN: We find an island and we strip and go riding on this white horse . . .

MARGARET: Together.

HYMAN: You in front.

MARGARET: Naturally.

HYMAN: And then we go swimming . . .

MARGARET: Harry, that's lovely.

HYMAN: And I hire this shark to swim very close and we just manage to get out of the water, and we're so grateful to be alive we fall down on the beach together and . . .

MARGARET, *pressing his lips shut*: Sometimes you're so good. *She kisses him.*

BLACKOUT

SCENE II

The Lone Cellist plays. Then lights go down . . .

Next evening. The Gellburg bedroom. Sylvia Gellburg is seated in a wheelchair reading a newspaper. She is in her mid-forties, a buxom, capable, and warm woman. Right now her hair is brushed down to her shoulders, and she is in a night-gown and robe.

She reads the paper with an intense, almost haunted interest, looking up now and then to visualize.

Her sister Harriet, a couple of years younger, is straightening up the bedcover.

HARRIET: So what do you want, steak or chicken? Or maybe he'd like chops for a change.

SYLVIA: Please, don't put yourself out, Phillip doesn't mind a little shopping.

HARRIET: What's the matter with you, I'm going anyway, he's got enough on his mind.

SYLVIA: Well all right, get a couple of chops.

HARRIET: And what about you. You have to start eating!

SYLVIA: I'm eating.

HARRIET: What, a piece of cucumber? Look how pale you are. And what is this with newspapers night and day?

SYLVIA: I like to see what's happening.

HARRIET: I don't know about this doctor. Maybe you need a specialist.

SYLVIA: He brought one two days ago, Doctor Sherman. From Mount Sinai.

HARRIET: Really? And?

SYLVIA: We're waiting to hear. I like Doctor Hyman.

HARRIET: Nobody in the family ever had anything like this. You feel *something*, though, don't you?

SYLVIA, *pause, she lifts her face*: Yes . . . but inside, not on the skin. *Looks at her legs.* I can harden the muscles but I can't lift them. *Strokes her thighs.* I seem to have an ache. Not only here but . . . *She runs her hands down her trunk.* My whole body seems . . . I can't describe it. It's like I was just born and I . . . didn't want to come out yet. Like a deep, terrible aching . . .

HARRIET: Didn't want to come out yet! What are you talking about?

SYLVIA, *sighs gently, knowing Harriet can never understand*: Maybe if he has a nice duck. If not, get the chops. And thanks, Harriet, it's sweet of you. —By the way, what did David decide?

HARRIET: He's not going to college.

SYLVIA, *shocked*: I don't believe it! With a scholarship and he's not going?

HARRIET: What can we do? *Resignedly.* He says college wouldn't help him get a job anyway.

SYLVIA: Harriet, that's terrible! —Listen, tell him I have to talk to him.

HARRIET: Would you! I was going to ask you but with this happening. *Indicates her legs.* I didn't think you'd . . .

SYLVIA: Never mind, tell him to come over. And you must tell Murray he's got to put his foot down—you've got a brilliant boy! My God . . . *Picks up the newspaper.* If I'd had a chance to go to college I'd have had a whole different life, you can't let this happen.

HARRIET: I'll tell David . . . I wish I knew what is suddenly so interesting in a newspaper. This is not normal, Sylvia, is it?

SYLVIA, *pause, she stares ahead*: They are making old men crawl around and clean the sidewalks with toothbrushes.

HARRIET: Who is?

SYLVIA: In Germany. Old men with beards!

HARRIET: So why are you so interested in that? What business of yours is that?

SYLVIA, *slight pause; searches within*: I don't really know. *A slight pause.* Remember Grandpa? His eyeglasses with the bent sidepiece? One of the old men in the paper was his spitting image, he had the same exact glasses with the wire frames. I can't get it out of my mind. On their knees on the sidewalk, two old men. And there's fifteen or twenty people standing in a circle laughing at them scrubbing with toothbrushes. There's three women in the picture; they're holding their coat collars closed, so it must have been cold . . .

HARRIET: Why would they make them scrub with toothbrushes?

SYLVIA, *angered*: To humiliate them, to make fools of them!

HARRIET: Oh!

SYLVIA: How can you be so . . . so . . . ? *Breaks off before she goes too far.* Harriet, please . . . leave me alone, will you?

HARRIET: This is not normal. Murray says the same thing. I swear to God, he came home last night and says, "She's got to stop thinking about those Germans." And you know how he loves current events. *Sylvia is staring ahead.* I'll see if the duck looks good, if not I'll get chops. Can I get you something now?

SYLVIA: No, I'm fine, thanks.

HARRIET, *moves upstage of Sylvia, turns*: I'm going.

SYLVIA: Yes.

> *She returns to her paper. Harriet watches anxiously for a moment, out of Sylvia's sight line, then exits. Sylvia turns a page, absorbed in the paper. Suddenly she turns in shock—Phillip is standing behind her. He holds a small paper bag.*

SYLVIA: Oh! I didn't hear you come in.

GELLBURG: I tiptoed, in case you were dozing off . . . *His dour smile.* I bought you some sour pickles.

SYLVIA: Oh, that's nice! Later, maybe. You have one.

GELLBURG: I'll wait. *Awkwardly but determined*: I was passing Green-berg's on Flatbush Avenue and I suddenly remembered how you used to love them. Remember?

SYLVIA: Thanks, that's nice of you. What were you doing on Flatbush Avenue?

GELLBURG: There's a property across from A&S. I'm probably going to foreclose.

SYLVIA: Oh that's sad. Are they nice people?

GELLBURG, *shrugs*: People are people—I gave them two extensions but they'll never manage . . . nothing up here. *Taps his temple.*

SYLVIA: Aren't you early?

GELLBURG: I got worried about you. Doctor come?

SYLVIA: He called; he has the results of the tests but he wants to come tomorrow when he has more time to talk to me. He's really very nice.

GELLBURG: How was it today?

SYLVIA: I'm so sorry about this.

GELLBURG: You'll get better, don't worry about it. Oh!—there's a letter from the captain. *Takes it out of his jacket.*

SYLVIA: Jerome?

GELLBURG, *terrific personal pride*: Read it.

   She reads; his purse-mouthed grin is intense.

   That's your son. General MacArthur talked to him twice.

SYLVIA: Fort Sill?

GELLBURG: Oklahoma. *He's going to lecture them on artillery!* In *Fort Sill*! That's the field-artillery center.

   She looks up dumbly.

   That's like being invited to the Vatican to lecture the Pope.

SYLVIA: Imagine. *She folds the letter and hands it back to him.*

GELLBURG, *restraining greater resentment*: I don't understand this atti-tude.

SYLVIA: Why? I'm happy for him.

GELLBURG: You don't seem happy to me.

SYLVIA: I'll never get used to it. Who goes in the army? Men who can't do anything else.

GELLBURG: I wanted people to see that a Jew doesn't have to be a lawyer or a doctor or a businessman.

SYLVIA: That's fine, but why must it be Jerome?

GELLBURG: For a Jewish boy, West Point is an honor! Without Mr. Case's connections, he never would have gotten in. He could be the first Jewish general in the United States Army. Doesn't it mean something to be his mother?

SYLVIA, *with an edge of resentment*: Well, I said I'm glad.

GELLBURG: Don't be upset. *Looks about impatiently.* You know, when you get on your feet I'll help you hang the new drapes.

SYLVIA: I started to . . .

GELLBURG: But they've been here over a month.

SYLVIA: Well this happened, I'm sorry.

GELLBURG: You have to occupy yourself is all I'm saying, Sylvia, you can't give in to this.

SYLVIA, *near an outburst*: Well I'm sorry—I'm sorry about everything!

GELLBURG: Please, don't get upset, I take it back!

>   *A moment; stalemate.*

SYLVIA: I wonder what my tests show.

>   *Gellburg is silent.*

>   That the specialist did.

GELLBURG: I went to see Doctor Hyman last night.

SYLVIA: You did? Why didn't you mention it?

GELLBURG: I wanted to think over what he said.

SYLVIA: What did he say?

>   *With a certain deliberateness, Gellburg goes over to her and gives her a kiss on the cheek.*

SYLVIA, *she is embarrassed and vaguely alarmed*: Phillip! *A little uncomprehending laugh.*

GELLBURG: I want to change some things. About the way I've been doing.

>   *He stands there for a moment perfectly still, then rolls her chair closer to the bed on which he now sits and takes her*

hand. She doesn't quite know what to make of this, but doesn't remove her hand.

SYLVIA: Well what did he say?

GELLBURG, *he pats her hand*: I'll tell you in a minute. I'm thinking about a Dodge.

SYLVIA: A Dodge?

GELLBURG: I want to teach you to drive. So you can go where you like, visit your mother in the afternoon. —I want you to be happy, Sylvia.

SYLVIA, *surprised*: Oh.

GELLBURG: We have the money, we could do a lot of things. Maybe see Washington, D.C. . . . It's supposed to be a very strong car, you know.

SYLVIA: But aren't they all black?—Dodges?

GELLBURG: Not all. I've seen a couple of green ones.

SYLVIA: You like green?

GELLBURG: It's only a color. You'll get used to it. —Or Chicago. It's really a big city, you know.

SYLVIA: Tell me what Doctor Hyman said.

GELLBURG, *gets himself set*: He thinks it could all be coming from your mind. Like a . . . a fear of some kind got into you. Psychological.

She is still, listening.

Are you afraid of something?

SYLVIA, *a slow shrug, a shake of her head*: . . . I don't know, I don't think so. What kind of fear, what does he mean?

GELLBURG: Well, he explains it better, but . . . like in a war, people get so afraid they go blind temporarily. What they call shell-shock. But once they feel safer it goes away.

SYLVIA: What about the tests the Mount Sinai man did?

GELLBURG: They can't find anything wrong with your body.

SYLVIA: But I'm numb!

GELLBURG: He claims being very frightened could be doing it. —Are you?

SYLVIA: I don't know.

GELLBURG: Personally. . . . Can I tell you what I think?

SYLVIA: What.

GELLBURG: I think it's this whole Nazi business.

SYLVIA: But it's in the paper—they're smashing up the Jewish stores . . . Should I not read the paper? The streets are covered with broken glass!

GELLBURG: Yes, but you don't have to be constantly . . .

SYLVIA: It's ridiculous. I can't move my legs from reading a newspaper?

GELLBURG: He didn't say that; but I'm wondering if you're too involved with . . .

SYLVIA: It's ridiculous.

GELLBURG: Well you talk to him tomorrow. *Pause. He comes back to her and takes her hand, his need open.* You've got to get better, Sylvia.

SYLVIA, *she sees his tortured face and tries to laugh*: What is this, am I dying or something?

GELLBURG: How can you say that?

SYLVIA: I've never seen such a look in your face.

GELLBURG: Oh no-no-no . . . I'm just worried.

SYLVIA: I don't understand what's happening . . . *She turns away on the verge of tears.*

GELLBURG: . . . I never realized . . . *Sudden sharpness* . . . look at me, will you?

> *She turns to him; he glances down at the floor.*

> I wouldn't know what to do without you, Sylvia, honest to God. I . . . *Immense difficulty*: I love you.

SYLVIA, *a dead, bewildered laugh*: What is this?

GELLBURG: You have to get better. If I'm ever doing something wrong I'll change it. Let's try to be different. All right? And you too, you've got to do what the doctors tell you.

SYLVIA: What can I do? Here I sit and they say there's nothing wrong with me.

GELLBURG: Listen . . . I think Hyman is a very smart man . . . *He lifts her hand and kisses her knuckle; embarrassed and smiling.* When we were talking, something came to mind; that maybe if we could sit down with him, the three of us, and maybe talk about . . . you know . . . everything.

> *Pause.*

SYLVIA: That doesn't matter anymore, Phillip.

GELLBURG, *an embarrassed grin*: How do you know? Maybe . . .

SYLVIA: It's too late for that.

GELLBURG, *once launched he is terrified*: Why? Why is it too late?

SYLVIA: I'm surprised you're still worried about it.

GELLBURG: I'm not worried, I just think about it now and then.

SYLVIA: Well it's too late, dear, it doesn't matter anymore. *She draws back her hand.*

> *Pause.*

GELLBURG: . . . Well all right. But if you wanted to I'd . . .

SYLVIA: We did talk about it, I took you to Rabbi Steiner about it twice, what good did it do?

GELLBURG: In those days I still thought it would change by itself. I was so young, I didn't understand such things. It came out of nowhere and I thought it would go the same way.

SYLVIA: I'm sorry, Phillip, it didn't come out of nowhere.

> *Silent, he evades her eyes.*

SYLVIA: You regretted you got married.

GELLBURG: I didn't "regret" it . . .

SYLVIA: You did, dear. You don't have to be ashamed of it.

> *A long silence.*

GELLBURG: I'm going to tell you the truth—in those days I thought that if we separated I wouldn't die of it. I admit that.

SYLVIA: I always knew that.

GELLBURG: But I haven't felt that way in years now.

SYLVIA: Well I'm here. *Spreads her arms out, a wildly ironical look in her eyes.* Here I am, Phillip!

GELLBURG, *offended*: The way you say that is not very . . .

SYLVIA: Not very what? I'm here; I've been here a long time.

GELLBURG, *a helpless surge of anger*: I'm trying to tell you something!

SYLVIA, *openly taunting him now*: But I said I'm here!

> *Gellburg moves about as she speaks, as though trying to find an escape or a way in.*

I'm here for my mother's sake, and Jerome's sake, and everybody's sake except mine, but I'm here and here I am. And now finally you want to talk about it, now when I'm turning into an old woman? How do you want me to say it? Tell me, dear, I'll say it the way you want me to. What should I say?

GELLBURG, *insulted and guilty*: I want you to stand up.

SYLVIA: I can't stand up.

He takes both her hands.

GELLBURG: You can. Now come on. Stand up.

SYLVIA: I can't!

GELLBURG: You can stand up, Sylvia. Now lean to me and get on your feet.

He pulls her up; then steps aside, releasing her; she collapses on the floor. He stands over her.

What are you trying to do? *He goes to his knees to yell into her face*: What are you trying to do, Sylvia!

She looks at him in terror at the mystery before her.

BLACKOUT

SCENE III

The Lone Cellist plays. Then lights go down . . .

Dr. Hyman's office. He is in riding boots and a sweater. Harriet is seated beside his desk.

HARRIET: My poor sister. And they have everything! But how can it be in the mind if she's so paralyzed?

HYMAN: Her numbness is random, it doesn't follow the nerve paths; only part of the thighs are affected, part of the calves, it makes no physiological sense. I have a few things I'd like to ask you, all right?

HARRIET: You know, I'm glad it's you taking care of her, my husband says the same thing.

HYMAN: Thank you . . .

HARRIET: You probably don't remember, but you once took out our cousin Roslyn Fein? She said you were great.

HYMAN: Roslyn Fein. When?

HARRIET: She's very tall and reddish-blond hair? She had a real crush . . .

HYMAN, *pleased*: When was this?

HARRIET: Oh—NYU, maybe twenty-five years ago. She adored you; seriously, she said you were really *great. Laughs knowingly.* Used to take her to Coney Island swimming, and so on.

HYMAN, *laughs with her*: Oh. Well give her my regards.

HARRIET: I hardly see her, she lives in Florida.

HYMAN, *pressing on*: I'd like you to tell me about Sylvia; —before she collapsed, was there any sign of some shock, or anything? Something threatening her?

HARRIET, *thinks for a moment, shrugs, shaking her head*: Listen, I'll tell you something funny—to me sometimes she seems . . . I was going to say happy, but it's more like . . . I don't know . . . like this is how she wants to be. I mean since the collapse. Don't you think so?

HYMAN: Well I never really knew her before. What about this fascination with the Nazis—she ever talk to you about that?

HARRIET: Only this last couple of weeks. I don't understand it, they're in *Germany,* how can she be so frightened, it's across the ocean, isn't it?

HYMAN: Yes. But in a way it isn't. *He stares, shaking his head, lost.* . . . She's very sensitive; she really sees the people in those photographs. They're alive to her.

HARRIET, *suddenly near tears*: My poor sister!

HYMAN: Tell me about Phillip.

HARRIET: Phillip? *Shrugs.* Phillip is Phillip.

HYMAN: You like him?

HARRIET: Well he's my brother-in-law . . . You mean personally.

HYMAN: Yes.

HARRIET, *takes a breath to lie*: . . . He can be very sweet, you know. But suddenly he'll turn around and talk to you like you've got four legs and long ears. The men—not that they don't respect him—but they'd just as soon not play cards with him if they can help it.

HYMAN: Really. Why?

HARRIET: Well, God forbid you have an opinion—you open your mouth and he gives you that Republican look down his nose and your brains dry up. Not that I don't *like* him . . .

HYMAN: How did he and Sylvia meet?

HARRIET: She was head bookkeeper at Empire Steel over there in Long Island City . . .

HYMAN: She must have been very young.

HARRIET: . . . Twenty; just out of high school practically and she's head bookkeeper. According to my husband, God gave Sylvia all the brains and the rest of us the big feet! The reason they met was the company took out a mortgage and she had to explain all the accounts to Phillip—he used to say, "I fell in love with her figures!" *Hyman laughs.* Why should I lie?—personally to me, he's a little bit a prune. Like he never stops with the whole Jewish part of it.

HYMAN: He doesn't like being Jewish.

HARRIET: Well yes and no—like Jerome being the only Jewish captain, he's proud of that. And him being the only one ever worked for Brooklyn Guarantee—he's proud of that too, but at the same time . . .

HYMAN: . . . He'd rather not be one.

HARRIET: . . . Look, he's a mystery to me. I don't understand him and I never will.

HYMAN: What about the marriage? I promise you this is strictly between us.

HARRIET: What can I tell you, the marriage is a marriage.

HYMAN: And?

HARRIET: I shouldn't talk about it.

HYMAN: It stays in this office. Tell me. They ever break up?

HARRIET: Oh God no! Why should they? He's a wonderful provider. There's no Depression for Phillip, you know. And it would kill our mother, she worships Phillip, she'd never outlive it. No-no, it's out of the question, Sylvia's not that kind of woman, although . . . *Breaks off.*

HYMAN: Come, Harriet, I need to know these things!

HARRIET: . . . Well I guess everybody knows it, so . . . *Takes a breath.* I think they came very close to it one time . . . when he hit her with the steak.

HYMAN: Hit her with a *steak?*

SYLVIA: It was overdone.

HYMAN: What do you mean, hit her?

SYLVIA: He picked it up off the plate and slapped her in the face with it.

HYMAN: And then what?

HARRIET: Well if my mother hadn't patched it up I don't know what would have happened and then he went out and bought her that gorgeous beaver coat, and repainted the whole house, and he's tight as a drum, you know, so it was hard for him. I don't know what to tell you. —Why? —you think *he* could have frightened her like this?

HYMAN, *hesitates*: I don't know yet. The whole thing is very strange.

> *Something darkens Harriet's expression and she begins to shake her head from side to side and she bursts into tears. He comes and puts an arm around her.*

HYMAN: What is it?

HARRIET: All her life she did nothing but love everybody!

HYMAN, *reaches out to take her hand*: Harriet.

> *She looks at him.*

What do you want to tell me?

HARRIET: I don't know if it's right to talk about. But of course, it's years and years ago . . .

HYMAN: None of this will ever be repeated; believe me.

HARRIET: Well . . . every first of the year when Uncle Myron was still alive we'd all go down to his basement for a New Year's party. I'm talking like fifteen, sixteen years ago. He's dead now, Myron, but . . . he was . . . you know . . . *Small laugh* . . . a little comical; he always kept this shoe-box full of . . . you know, these postcards.

HYMAN: You mean . . .

HARRIET: Yes. French. You know, naked women, and men with these great big . . . you know . . . they hung down like salamis. And every-body'd pass them around and die laughing. It was exactly the same thing every New Year's. But this time, all of a sudden, Phillip . . . we thought he'd lost his mind . . .

HYMAN: What happened?

HARRIET: Well Sylvia's in the middle of laughing and he grabs the post-card out of her hand and he turns around screaming—I mean, really screaming—that we're all a bunch of morons and idiots and God knows what, and throws her up the stairs. Bang! It cracked the bannister, I can still hear it. *Catches her breath.* I tell you it was months before anybody'd talk to him again. Because everybody on the block loves Sylvia.

HYMAN: What do you suppose made him do that?

HARRIET, *shrugs*: . . . Well if you listen to some of the men—but of course some of the dirty minds on this block . . . if you spread it over the backyard you'd get tomatoes six feet high.

HYMAN: Why?—what'd they say?

HARRIET: Well that the reason he got so mad was because he couldn't . . . you know . . .

HYMAN: Oh really.

HARRIET: . . . anymore.

HYMAN: But they made up.

HARRIET: Listen, to be truthful you have to say it—although it'll sound crazy . . .

HYMAN: What.

HARRIET: You watch him sometimes when they've got people over and she's talking—he'll sit quietly in the corner, and the expression on that man's face when he's watching her—it could almost break your heart.

HYMAN: Why?

HARRIET: He adores her!

BLACKOUT

SCENE IV

The cellist plays, and is gone.

Stanton Case is getting ready to leave his office. Putting on his blazer and a captain's cap and a foulard. He has a great natural authority, an almost childishly naive self-assurance. Gellburg enters.

CASE: Good!—you're back. I was just leaving.

GELLBURG: I'm sorry. I got caught in traffic over in Crown Heights.

CASE: I wanted to talk to you again about 611. Sit down for a moment.

Both sit.

We're sailing out through the Narrows in about an hour.

GELLBURG: Beautiful day for it.

CASE: Are you all right? You don't look well.

GELLBURG: Oh no, I'm fine.

CASE: Good. Have you come to anything final on 611? I like the price, I can tell you that right off.

GELLBURG: Yes, the price is not bad, but I'm still . . .

CASE: I've walked past it again; I think with some renovation it would make a fine annex for the Harvard Club.

GELLBURG: It's a very nice structure, yes. I'm not final on it yet but I have a few comments . . . unless you've got to get on the water right away.

CASE: I have a few minutes. Go ahead.

GELLBURG: . . . Before I forget—we got a very nice letter from Jerome.

> No reaction from Case.

My boy.

CASE: Oh yes!—how is he doing?

GELLBURG: They're bringing him out to Fort Sill . . . some kind of lecture on artillery.

CASE: Really, now! Well, isn't that nice! . . . Then he's really intending to make a career in the army.

GELLBURG, *surprised Case isn't aware*: Oh absolutely.

CASE: Well that's good, isn't it. It's quite surprising for one of you people— for some reason I'd assumed he just wanted the education.

GELLBURG: Oh no. It's his life. I'll never know how to thank you.

CASE: No trouble at all. The Point can probably use a few of you people to keep the rest of them awake. Now what's this about 611?

GELLBURG, *sets himself in all dignity*: You might recall, we used the ABC Plumbing Contractors on a couple of buildings?

CASE: ABC? —I don't recall. What have they got to do with it?

GELLBURG: They're located in the neighborhood, just off Broadway, and on a long shot I went over to see Mr. Liebfreund—he runs ABC. I was wondering if they may have done any work for Wanamaker's.

CASE: Wanamaker's! What's Wanamaker's got to do with it?

GELLBURG: I buy my shirts in Wanamaker's, and last time I was in there I caught my shoe on a splinter sticking up out of the floor.

CASE: Well that store is probably fifty years old.

GELLBURG: Closer to seventy-five. I tripped and almost fell down; this was very remarkable to me, that they would leave a floor in such condition. So I began wondering about it . . .

CASE: About what?

GELLBURG: Number 611 is two blocks from Wanamaker's. *A little extra-wise grin.* They're the biggest business in the area, a whole square block, after all. Anyway, sure enough, turns out ABC does all Wanamaker's plumbing work. And Liebfreund tells me he's had to keep patching up their boilers *because they canceled installation of new boilers last winter.* A permanent cancellation.

Pause.

CASE: And what do you make of that?

GELLBURG: I think it could mean they're either moving the store, or maybe going out of business.

CASE: *Wanamaker's?*

GELLBURG: It's possible, I understand the family is practically died out. Either way, if Wanamaker's disappears, Mr. Case, that neighborhood in my opinion is no longer prime. Also, I called Kevin Sullivan over at Title Guarantee and he says they turned down 611 last year and he can't remember why.

CASE: Then what are you telling me?

GELLBURG: I would not touch Number 611 with a ten-foot pole—unless you can get it at a good defensive price. If that neighborhood starts to slide, 611 is a great big slice of lemon.

CASE: Well. That's very disappointing. It would have made a wonderful club annex.

GELLBURG: With a thing like the Harvard Club you have got to think of the far distant future, Mr. Case, I don't have to tell you that, and the future of that part of Broadway is a definite possible negative. *Raising a monitory finger:* I emphasize "possible," mind you; only God can predict.

CASE: Well I must say, I would never have thought of Wanamaker's disappearing. You've been more than thorough, Gellburg, we appreciate it. I've got to run now, but we'll talk about this further . . . *Glances at his watch.* Mustn't miss the tide . . . *Moves, indicates.* Take a brandy if you like. Wife all right?

GELLBURG: Oh yes, she's fine!

CASE, *the faint shadow of a warning*: Sure everything's all right with you—we don't want you getting sick now.

GELLBURG: Oh no, I'm very well, very well.

CASE: I'll be back on Monday, we'll go into this further. *Indicates.* Take a brandy if you like.

> *Case exits rather jauntily.*

GELLBURG: Yes, sir, I might!

> *Gellburg stands alone; with a look of self-satisfaction starts to raise the glass.*

BLACKOUT

SCENE V

The cello plays, and the music falls away.

Sylvia in bed, reading a book. She looks up as Hyman enters. He is in his riding clothes. Sylvia has a certain excitement at seeing him.

SYLVIA: Oh, doctor!

HYMAN: I let myself in, hope I didn't scare you . . .

SYLVIA: Oh no, I'm glad. Sit down. You been riding?

HYMAN: Yes. All the way down to Brighton Beach, nice long ride—I expected to see you jumping rope by now.

> *Sylvia laughs, embarrassed.*

I think you're just trying to get out of doing the dishes.

SYLVIA, *strained laugh*: Oh stop. You really love riding, don't you?

HYMAN: Well there's no telephone on a horse.

> *She laughs.*

Ocean Parkway is like a German forest this time of the morning— riding under that archway of maple trees is like poetry.

SYLVIA: Wonderful. I never did anything like that.

HYMAN: Well, let's go—I'll take you out and teach you sometime. Have you been trying the exercise?

SYLVIA: I can't do it.

HYMAN, *shaking a finger at her*: You've got to do it, Sylvia. You could end up permanently crippled. Let's have a look.

> *He sits on the bed and draws the cover off her legs, then raises her nightgown. She inhales with a certain anticipation as he does so. He feels her toes.*

You feel this at all?

SYLVIA: Well . . . not really.

HYMAN: I'm going to pinch your toe. Ready?

SYLVIA: All right.

> *He pinches her big toe sharply; she doesn't react. He rests a palm on her leg.*

HYMAN: Your skin feels a little too cool. You're going to lose your muscle tone if you don't move. Your legs will begin to lose volume and shrink . . .

SYLVIA, *tears threaten*: I know . . . !

HYMAN: And look what beautiful legs you have, Sylvia. I'm afraid you're getting comfortable in this condition . . .

SYLVIA: I'm not. I keep trying to move them . . .

HYMAN: But look now—here it's eleven in the morning and you're happily tucked into bed like it's midnight.

SYLVIA: But I've tried . . . ! Are you really sure it's not a virus of some kind?

HYMAN: There's nothing. Sylvia, you have a strong beautiful body . . .

SYLVIA: But what can I do, I can't feel anything!

> *She sits up with her face raised to him; he stands and moves abruptly away. Then turning back to her . . .*

HYMAN: I really should find someone else for you.

SYLVIA: Why!—I don't want anyone else!

HYMAN: You're a very attractive woman, don't you know that?

> *Deeply excited, Sylvia glances away shyly.*

HYMAN: Sylvia, listen to me . . . I haven't been this moved by a woman in a very long time.

SYLVIA: . . . Well, you mustn't get anyone else.

Pause.

HYMAN: Tell me the truth, Sylvia. Sylvia? How did this happen to you?

SYLVIA, *she avoids his gaze:* I don't know. *Sylvia's anxiety rises as he speaks now.*

HYMAN: . . . I'm going to be straight with you; I thought this was going to be simpler than it's turning out to be, and I care about you too much to play a game with your health. I can't deny my vanity. I have a lot of it, but I have to face it—I know you want to tell me something and I don't know how to get it out of you. *Sylvia covers her face, ashamed.* You're a responsible woman, Sylvia, you have to start helping me, you can't just lie there and expect a miracle to lift you to your feet. You tell me now—what should I know?

SYLVIA: I would tell you if I knew! *Hyman turns away defeated and impatient.* Couldn't we just talk and maybe I could . . . *Breaks off.* I like you. A lot. I love when you talk to me . . . couldn't we just . . . like for a few minutes. . . .

HYMAN: Okay. What do you want to talk about?

SYLVIA: Please. Be patient. I'm . . . I'm trying. *Relieved; a fresher mood:* —Harriet says you used to take out our cousin Roslyn Fein.

HYMAN, *smiles, shrugs:* It's possible, I don't remember.

SYLVIA: Well you had so many, didn't you.

HYMAN: When I was younger.

SYLVIA: Roslyn said you used to do acrobatics on the beach? And all the girls would stand around going crazy for you.

HYMAN: That's a long time ago. . . .

SYLVIA: And you'd take them under the boardwalk. *Laughs.*

HYMAN: Nobody had money for anything else. Didn't you used to go to the beach?

SYLVIA: Sure. But I never did anything like that.

HYMAN: You must have been very shy.

SYLVIA: I guess. But I had to look out for my sisters, being the eldest . . .

HYMAN: Can we talk about Phillip?

Caught unaware, her eyes show fear.

I'd really like to, unless you . . .

SYLVIA, *challenged:* No!—It's all right.

HYMAN: . . . Are you afraid right now?

SYLVIA: No, not . . . Yes.

>   *Picks up the book beside her.*

>   Have you read *Anthony Adverse*?

HYMAN: No, but I hear it's sold a million copies.

SYLVIA: It's wonderful. I rent it from Womraths.

HYMAN: Was Phillip your first boyfriend?

SYLVIA: The first serious.

HYMAN: He's a fine man.

SYLVIA: Yes, he is.

HYMAN: Is he interesting to be with?

SYLVIA: Interesting?

HYMAN: Do you have things to talk about?

SYLVIA: Well . . . business, mostly. I was head bookkeeper for Empire Steel in Long Island City . . . years ago, when we met, I mean.

HYMAN: He didn't want you to work?

SYLVIA: No.

HYMAN: I imagine you were a good businesswoman.

SYLVIA: Oh, I loved it! I've always enjoyed . . . you know, people depending on me.

HYMAN: Yes. —Do I frighten you, talking like this?

SYLVIA: A little. —But I want you to.

HYMAN: Why?

SYLVIA: I don't know. You make me feel . . . hopeful.

HYMAN: You mean of getting better?

SYLVIA: —Of myself. Of getting . . . *Breaks off.*

HYMAN: Getting what?

>   *She shakes her head, refusing to go on.*

>   . . . Free?

>   *She suddenly kisses the palm of his hand. He wipes her hair away from her eyes. He stands up and walks a few steps away.*

HYMAN: I want you to raise your knees.

She doesn't move.

Come, bring up your knees.

SYLVIA, *she tries*: I can't!

HYMAN: You can. I want you to send your thoughts into your hips. Tense your hips. Think of the bones in your hips. Come on now. The strongest muscles in your body are right there, you still have tremendous power there. Tense your hips.

She is tensing.

Now tense your thighs. Those are long dense muscles with tremendous power. Do it, draw up your knees. Come on, raise your knees. Keep it up. Concentrate. Raise it. Do it for me.

With an exhaled gasp she gives up. Remaining yards away . . .

Your body strength must be marvelous. The depth of your flesh must be wonderful. Why are you cut off from yourself? You should be dancing, you should be stretching out in the sun. . . . Sylvia, I know you know more than you're saying, why can't you open up to me? Speak to me. Sylvia? Say anything.

She looks at him in silence.

I promise I won't tell a soul. What is in your mind right now?

A pause.

SYLVIA: Tell me about Germany.

HYMAN, *surprised*: Germany. Why Germany?

SYLVIA: Why did you go there to study?

HYMAN: The American medical schools have quotas on Jews, I would have had to wait for years and maybe never get in.

SYLVIA: But they hate Jews there, don't they?

HYMAN: These Nazis can't possibly last— Why are you so preoccupied with them?

SYLVIA: I don't know. But when I saw that picture in the *Times*—with those two old men on their knees in the street . . . *Presses her ears.* I swear, I almost heard that crowd laughing, and ridiculing them. But nobody really wants to talk about it. I mean Phillip never even wants to talk about being Jewish, except—you know—to joke about it the way people do . . .

HYMAN: What would you like to say to Phillip about it?

SYLVIA, *with an empty laugh, a head shake*: I don't even know! Just to talk about it . . . it's almost like there's something in me that . . . it's silly . . .

HYMAN: No, it's interesting. What do you mean, something in you?

SYLVIA: I have no word for it, I don't know what I'm saying, it's like . . . *She presses her chest.* —something alive, like a child almost, except it's a very dark thing . . . and it frightens me!

Hyman moves his hand to calm her and she grabs it.

HYMAN: That was hard to say, wasn't it. *Sylvia nods.* You have a lot of courage.—We'll talk more, but I want you to try something now. I'll stand here, and I want you to imagine something. *Sylvia turns to him, curious.* I want you to imagine that we've made love.

> *Startled, she laughs tensely. He joins this laugh as though it is a game.*

> I've made love to you. And now it's over and we are lying together. And you begin to tell me some secret things. Things that are way down deep in your heart. *Slight pause.* Sylvia—

> *Hyman comes around the bed, bends, and kisses her on the cheek.*

> Tell me about Phillip.

> *Sylvia is silent, does not grasp his head to hold him. He straightens up.* Think about it. We'll talk tomorrow again. Okay?

> *Hyman exits. Sylvia lies there inert for a moment. Then she tenses with effort, trying to raise her knee. It doesn't work. She reaches down and lifts the knee, and then the other and lies there that way. Then she lets her knees spread apart . . .*

BLACKOUT

SCENE VI

The cellist plays, then is gone.

Hyman's office. Gellburg is seated. Immediately Margaret enters with a cup of cocoa and a file folder. She hands the cup to Gellburg.

GELLBURG: Cocoa?

MARGARET: I drink a lot of it, it calms the nerves. Have you lost weight?

GELLBURG, *impatience with her prying*: A little, I think.

MARGARET: Did you always sigh so much?

GELLBURG: Sigh?

MARGARET: You probably don't realize you're doing it. You should have him listen to your heart.

GELLBURG: No-no, I think I'm all right. *Sighs.* I guess I've always sighed. Is that a sign of something?

MARGARET: Not necessarily; but ask Harry. He's just finishing with a patient. —There's no change, I understand.

GELLBURG: No, she's the same. *Impatiently hands her the cup.* I can't drink this.

MARGARET: Are you eating at all?

GELLBURG, *suddenly shifting his mode*: I came to talk to *him*.

MARGARET, *sharply*: I was only trying to be helpful!

GELLBURG: I'm kind of upset, I didn't mean any . . .

> *Hyman enters, surprising her. She exits, insulted.*

HYMAN: I'm sorry. But she means well.

> *Gellburg silently nods, irritation intact.*

HYMAN: It won't happen again. *He takes his seat.* I have to admit, though, she has a very good diagnostic sense. Women are more instinctive some-times . . .

GELLBURG: Excuse me, I don't come here to be talking to her.

HYMAN, *a kidding laugh*: Oh, come on, Phillip, take it easy. What's Sylvia doing?

GELLBURG, *it takes him a moment to compose himself*: . . . I don't know what she's doing.

> *Hyman waits. Gellburg has a tortured look; now he seems to brace himself, and faces the doctor with what seems a haughty air.*

I decided to try to do what you advised. —About the loving.

HYMAN: . . . Yes?

GELLBURG: So I decided to try to do it with her.

HYMAN: . . . Sex?

GELLBURG: What then, handball? Of course sex.

The openness of this hostility mystifies Hyman, who becomes conciliatory.

HYMAN: . . . Well, do you mean you've done it or you're going to?

GELLBURG, *long pause; he seems not to be sure he wants to continue. Now he sounds reasonable again*: You see, we haven't been really . . . together. For . . . quite a long time. *Correcting*: I mean specially since this started to happen.

HYMAN: You mean the last two weeks.

GELLBURG: Well yes. *Great discomfort.* And some time before that.

HYMAN: I see. *But he desists from asking how long a time before that. A pause.*

GELLBURG: So I thought maybe it would help her if . . . you know.

HYMAN: Yes, I think the warmth would help. In fact, to be candid, Phillip—I'm beginning to wonder if this whole fear of the Nazis isn't because she feels . . . extremely vulnerable; I'm in no sense trying to blame you but . . . a woman who doesn't feel loved can get very disoriented you know? —lost. *He has noticed a strangeness.* —Something wrong?

GELLBURG: She says she's not being loved?

HYMAN: No-no. I'm talking about how she may feel.

GELLBURG: Listen . . . *Struggles for a moment; now firmly.* I'm wondering if you could put me in touch with somebody.

HYMAN: You mean for yourself?

GELLBURG: I don't know; I'm not sure what they do, though.

HYMAN: I know a very good man at the hospital, if you want me to set it up.

GELLBURG: Well maybe not yet, let me let you know.

HYMAN: Sure.

GELLBURG: Your wife says I sigh a lot. Does that mean something?

HYMAN: Could just be tension. Come in when you have a little time, I'll look you over. . . . Am I wrong?—you sound like something's happened . . .

GELLBURG: This whole thing is against me . . . *Attempting a knowing grin.* But you know that.

HYMAN: Now wait a minute . . .

GELLBURG: She knows what she's doing, you're not blind.

HYMAN: What happened, why are you saying this?

GELLBURG: I was late last night—I had to be in Jersey all afternoon, a problem we have there—she was sound asleep. So I made myself some spaghetti. Usually she puts something out for me.

HYMAN: She has no problem cooking.

GELLBURG: I told you—she gets around the kitchen fine in the wheelchair. Flora shops in the morning—that's the maid. Although I'm beginning to wonder if Sylvia gets out and walks around when I leave the house.

HYMAN: It's impossible.—She is paralyzed, Phillip, it's not a trick—she's suffering.

GELLBURG, *a sideways glance at Hyman*: What do you discuss with her?—You know, she talks like you see right through her.

HYMAN, *a laugh*: I wish I could! We talk about getting her to walk, that's all. This thing is not against you, Phillip, believe me. *Slight laugh.*—I wish you could trust me, kid!

GELLBURG, *seems momentarily on the edge of being reassured and studies Hyman's face for a moment, nodding very slightly*: I would never believe I could talk this way to another person. I do trust you.

> *Pause.*

HYMAN: Good!—I'm listening, go ahead.

GELLBURG: The first time we talked you asked me if we . . . how many times a week.

HYMAN: Yes.

GELLBURG, *nods*: . . . I have a problem sometimes.

HYMAN: Oh.—Well that's fairly common, you know.

GELLBURG, *relieved*: You see it often?

HYMAN: Oh very often, yes.

GELLBURG, *a tense challenging smile*: Ever happen to you?

HYMAN, *surprised*: . . . Me? Well sure, a few times. Is this something recent?

GELLBURG: Well . . . yes. Recent and also . . . *breaks off, indicating the past with a gesture of his hand.*

HYMAN: I see. It doesn't help if you're under tension, you know.

GELLBURG: Yes, I was wondering that.

HYMAN: Just don't start thinking it's the end of the world because it's not—you're still a young man. Think of it like the ocean—it goes out but it always comes in again. But the thing to keep in mind is that she loves you and wants you.

> *Gellburg looks wide-eyed.*

You know that, don't you?

GELLBURG, *silently nods for an instant*: My sister-in-law Harriet says you were a real hotshot on the beach years ago.

HYMAN: Years ago, yes.

GELLBURG: I used to wonder if it's because Sylvia's the only one I was ever with.

HYMAN: Why would that matter?

GELLBURG: I don't know exactly—it used to prey on my mind that . . . maybe she expected more.

HYMAN: Yes. Well that's a common idea, you know. In fact, some men take on a lot of women not out of confidence but because they're afraid to lose it.

GELLBURG, *fascinated*: Huh! I'd never of thought of that.—A doctor must get a lot of peculiar cases, I bet.

HYMAN, *with utter intimacy*: Everybody's peculiar in one way or another but I'm not here to judge people. Why don't you try to tell me what happened? *His grin; making light of it.* Come on, give it a shot.

GELLBURG: All right . . . *Sighs.* I get into bed. She's sound asleep . . . *Breaks off. Resumes; something transcendent seems to enter him.* Nothing like it ever happened to me, I got a . . . a big yen for her. She's even more beautiful when she sleeps. I gave her a kiss. On the mouth. She didn't wake up. I never had such a yen in my life.

> *Long pause.*

HYMAN: And?

> *Gellburg silent.*

Did you make love?

GELLBURG, *an incongruous look of terror, he becomes rigid as though about to decide whether to dive into icy water or flee*: . . . Yes.

HYMAN, *a quickening, something tentative in Gellburg mystifies*: How did she react?—It's been some time since you did it, you say.

GELLBURG: Well yes.

HYMAN: Then what was the reaction?

GELLBURG: She was . . . *Searches for the word*. Gasping. It was really something. I thought of what you told me—about loving her now; I felt I'd brought her out of it. I was almost sure of it. She was like a different woman than I ever knew.

HYMAN: That's wonderful. Did she move her legs?

GELLBURG, *unprepared for that question*: . . . I think so.

HYMAN: Well did she or didn't she?

GELLBURG: Well I was so excited I didn't really notice, but I guess she must have.

HYMAN: That's wonderful, why are you so upset?

GELLBURG: Well let me finish, there's more to it.

HYMAN: Sorry, go ahead.

GELLBURG: —I brought her some breakfast this morning and—you know—started to—you know—talk a little about it. She looked at me like I was crazy. She claims she doesn't remember doing it. It never happened.

Hyman is silent, plays with a pen. Something evasive in this.

How could she not remember it?

HYMAN: You're sure she was awake?

GELLBURG: How could she not be?

HYMAN: Did she say anything during the . . . ?

GELLBURG: Well no, but she's never said much.

HYMAN: Did she open her eyes?

GELLBURG: I'm not sure. We were in the dark, but she usually keeps them closed. *Impatiently*: But she was . . . she was groaning, panting . . . she had to be awake! And now to say she doesn't remember?

Shaken, Hyman gets up and moves; a pause.

HYMAN: So what do you think is behind it?

GELLBURG: Well what would any man think? She's trying to turn me into nothing!

HYMAN: Now wait, you're jumping to conclusions.

GELLBURG: Is such a thing possible? I want your medical opinion—could a woman not remember?

HYMAN, *a moment, then*: . . . How did she look when she said that; did she seem sincere about not remembering?

GELLBURG: She looked like I was talking about something on the moon. Finally, she said a terrible thing. I still can't get over it.

HYMAN: What'd she say?

GELLBURG: That I'd imagined doing it.

> *Long pause. Hyman doesn't move.*

> What's your opinion? Well . . . could a man imagine such a thing? Is that possible?

HYMAN, *after a moment*: Tell you what; supposing I have another talk with her and see what I can figure out?

GELLBURG, *angrily demanding*: You have an opinion, don't you?—How could a man imagine such a thing!

HYMAN: I don't know what to say . . .

GELLBURG: What do you mean you don't know what to say! It's impossible, isn't it? To invent such a thing?

HYMAN, *fear of being out of his depth*: Phillip, don't cross-examine me, I'm doing everything I know to help you! —Frankly, I can't follow what you're telling me—you're sure in your own mind you had relations with her?

GELLBURG: How can you even ask me such a thing? Would I say it unless I was sure? *Stands shaking with fear and anger.* I don't understand your attitude! *He starts out.*

HYMAN: Phillip, please! *In fear he intercepts Gellburg.* What attitude, what are you talking about?

GELLBURG: I'm going to vomit, I swear—I don't feel well . . .

HYMAN: What happened . . . has she said something about me?

GELLBURG: About you? What do you mean? What could she say?

HYMAN: I don't understand why you're so upset with me!

GELLBURG: What are you doing!

HYMAN, *guiltily*: What am *I* doing! What are you talking about!

GELLBURG: She is trying to destroy me! And you stand there! And what do you do! Are you a doctor or what! *He goes right up to Hyman's face.* Why don't you give me a straight answer about anything! Everything is in-and-out and around-the-block! —Listen, I've made up my mind; I don't want you seeing her anymore.

HYMAN: I think she's the one has to decide that.

GELLBURG: I am deciding it! It's decided!

> *He storms out. Hyman stands there, guilty, alarmed. Margaret enters.*

MARGARET: Now what? *Seeing his anxiety*: Why are you looking like that?

> *He evasively returns to his desk chair.*

Are *you* in trouble?

HYMAN: Me! Cut it out, will you?

MARGARET: Cut what out? I asked a question—are you?

HYMAN: I said to cut it out, Margaret!

MARGARET: You don't realize how transparent you are. You're a pane of glass, Harry.

HYMAN, *laughs*: Nothing's happened. *Nothing has happened!* Why are you going on about it!

MARGARET: I will never understand it. Except I do, I guess; you believe women. Woman tells you the earth is flat and for that five minutes you're swept away, helpless.

HYMAN: You know what baffles me?

MARGARET: . . . And it's irritating.—What is it—just new ass all the time?

HYMAN: There's been nobody for at least ten or twelve years . . . more! I can't remember anymore! You know that!

MARGARET: What baffles you?

HYMAN: Why I take your suspicions seriously.

MARGARET: Oh that's easy. —You love the truth, Harry.

HYMAN, *a deep sigh, facing upward*: I'm exhausted.

MARGARET: What about asking Charley Whitman to see her?

HYMAN: She's frightened to death of psychiatry, she thinks it means she's crazy.

MARGARET: Well, she is, in a way, isn't she?

HYMAN: I don't see it that way at all.

MARGARET: Getting this hysterical about something on the other side of the world is sane?

HYMAN: When she talks about it, it's not the other side of the world, it's on the next block.

MARGARET: And that's sane?

HYMAN: I don't know what it is! I just get the feeling sometimes that she *knows* something, something that . . . It's like she's connected to some . . . some wire that goes half around the world, some truth that other people are blind to.

MARGARET: I think you've got to get somebody on this who won't be carried away, Harry.

HYMAN: I am not carried away!

MARGARET: You really believe that Sylvia Gellburg is being threatened by these Nazis? Is that real or is it hysterical?

HYMAN: So call it hysterical, does that bring you one inch closer to what is driving that woman? It's not a word that's driving her, Margaret—she *knows* something! I don't know what it is, and she may not either—but I tell you it's real.

   A moment.

MARGARET: What an interesting life you have, Harry.

BLACKOUT

INTERMISSION

ACT TWO

SCENE I

The cellist plays, music fades away.

Stanton Case is standing with hands clasped behind his back as though staring out a window. A dark mood. Gellburg enters behind him but he doesn't turn at once.

GELLBURG: Excuse me . . .

CASE, *turns*: Oh, good morning. You wanted to see me.

GELLBURG: If you have a minute I'd appreciate . . .

CASE, *as he sits*: —You don't look well, are you all right?

GELLBURG: Oh I'm fine, maybe a cold coming on . . .

Since he hasn't been invited to sit he glances at a chair then back at Case, who still leaves him hanging—and he sits on the chair's edge.

I wanted you to know how bad I feel about 611 Broadway. I'm very sorry.

CASE: Yes. Well. So it goes, I guess.

GELLBURG: I know how you had your heart set on it and I . . . I tell you the news knocked me over; they gave no sign they were talking to Allan Kershowitz or anybody else . . .

CASE: It's very disappointing—in fact, I'd already begun talking to an architect friend about renovations.

GELLBURG: Really. Well, I can't tell you how . . .

CASE: I'd gotten a real affection for that building. It certainly would have made a perfect annex. And probably a great investment too.

GELLBURG: Well, not necessarily, if Wanamaker's ever pulls out.

CASE: . . . Yes, about Wanamaker's—I should tell you—when I found out that Kershowitz had outbid us I was flabbergasted after what you'd said about the neighborhood going downhill once the store was gone— Ker-showitz is no fool, I need hardly say. So I mentioned it to one of our club members who I know is related to a member of the Wanamaker board. —He tells me there has never been any discussion whatever about the company moving out; he was simply amazed at the idea.

GELLBURG: But the man at ABC . . .

CASE, *impatience showing*: ABC was left with the repair work because Wanamaker's changed to another contractor for their new boilers. It had nothing to do with the store moving out. Nothing.

GELLBURG: . . . I don't know what to say, I . . . I just . . . I'm awfully sorry . . .

CASE: Well, it's a beautiful building, let's hope Kershowitz puts it to some worthwhile use. —You have any idea what he plans to do with it?

GELLBURG: Me? Oh no, I don't really know Kershowitz.

CASE: Oh! I thought you said you knew him for years?

GELLBURG: . . . Well, I "know" him, but not . . . we're not personal friends or anything, we just met at closings a few times, and things like that. And maybe once or twice in restaurants, I think, but . . .

CASE: I see. I guess I misunderstood, I thought you were fairly close.

> Case says no more; the full stop shoots Gellburg's anxiety way up.

GELLBURG: I hope you're not . . . I mean I never mentioned to Kershowitz that you were interested in 611.

CASE: Mentioned? What do you mean?

GELLBURG: Nothing; just that . . . it almost sounds like I had something to do with him grabbing the building away from under you. Because I would never do a thing like that to you!

CASE: I didn't say that, did I. If I seem upset it's being screwed out of that building, and by a man whose methods I never particularly admired.

GELLBURG: Yes, that's what I mean. But I had nothing to do with Ker-showitz . . .

> Breaks off into silence.

CASE: But did I say you did? I'm not clear about what you wanted to say to me, or have I missed some . . . ?

GELLBURG: No-no, just that. What you just said.

CASE, *his mystification peaking*: What's the matter with you?

GELLBURG: I'm sorry. I'd like to forget the whole thing.

CASE: What's happening?

GELLBURG: Nothing. Really. I'm sorry I troubled you!

> *Pause. With an explosion of frustration, Case marches out. Gellburg is left open-mouthed, one hand raised as though to bring back his life.*

BLACKOUT

SCENE II

> *The cellist plays and is gone.*

> *Sylvia in a wheelchair is listening to Eddie Cantor on the radio, singing "If You Knew Susie Like I Know Susie." She has an amused look, taps a finger to the rhythm. Her bed is nearby, on it a folded newspaper.*

> *Hyman appears. She instantly smiles, turns off the radio, and holds a hand out to him. He comes and shakes hands.*

SYLVIA, *indicating the radio*: I simply can't stand Eddie Cantor, can you?

HYMAN: Cut it out now, I heard you laughing halfway up the stairs.

SYLVIA: I know, but I can't stand him. This Crosby's the one I like. You ever hear him?

HYMAN: I can't stand these crooners—they're making ten, twenty thousand dollars a week and never spent a day in medical school. *She laughs.* Anyway, I'm an opera man.

SYLVIA: I never saw an opera. They must be hard to understand, I bet.

HYMAN: Nothing to understand—either she wants to and he doesn't or he wants to and she doesn't. *She laughs.* Either way one of them gets killed and the other one jumps off a building.

SYLVIA: I'm so glad you could come.

HYMAN, *settling into chair near the bed*: —You ready? We have to discuss something.

SYLVIA: Phillip had to go to Jersey for a zoning meeting . . .

HYMAN: Just as well—it's you I want to talk to.

SYLVIA: —There's some factory the firm owns there . . .

HYMAN: Come on, don't be nervous.

SYLVIA: . . . My back aches, will you help me onto the bed?

HYMAN: Sure.

> *He lifts her off the chair and carries her to the bed where he gently lowers her.*

> There we go.

> *She lies back. He brings up the blanket and covers her legs.*

> What's that perfume?

SYLVIA: Harriet found it in my drawer. I think Jerome bought it for one of my birthdays years ago.

HYMAN: Lovely. Your hair is different.

SYLVIA, *puffs up her hair*: Harriet did it; she's loved playing with my hair since we were kids. Did you hear all those birds this morning?

HYMAN: Amazing, yes; a whole cloud of them shot up like a spray in front of my horse.

SYLVIA, *partially to keep him*: You know, as a child, when we first moved from upstate there were so many birds and rabbits and even foxes here— Of course that was *real* country up there; my dad had a wonderful general store, everything from ladies' hats to horseshoes. But the winters were just finally too cold for my mother.

HYMAN: In Coney Island we used to kill rabbits with slingshots.

SYLVIA, *wrinkling her nose in disgust*: Why!

HYMAN, *shrugs*: —To see if we could. It was heaven for kids.

SYLVIA: I know! Brooklyn was really beautiful, wasn't it? I think people were happier then. My mother used to stand on our porch and watch us all the way to school, right across the open fields for—must have been a mile. And I would tie a clothesline around my three sisters so I wouldn't have to keep chasing after them! —I'm so glad—honestly . . . *A cozy little laugh.* I feel good every time you come.

HYMAN: Now listen to me; I've learned that these kinds of symptoms come from very deep in the mind. I would have to deal with your dreams to get any results, your deepest secret feelings, you understand? That's not my training.

SYLVIA: But when you talk to me I really feel my strength starting to come back . . .

HYMAN: You should already be having therapy to keep up your circulation.

A change in her expression, a sudden withdrawal which he notices.

You have a long life ahead of you, you don't want to live it in a wheelchair, do you? It's imperative that we get you to someone who can . . .

SYLVIA: I could tell you a dream.

HYMAN: I'm not trained to . . .

SYLVIA: I'd like to, can I?—I have the same one every night just as I'm falling asleep.

HYMAN, *forced to give way*: Well . . . all right, what is it?

SYLVIA: I'm in a street. Everything is sort of gray. And there's a crowd of people. They're packed in all around, but they're looking for me.

HYMAN: Who are they?

SYLVIA: They're Germans.

HYMAN: Sounds like those photographs in the papers.

SYLVIA, *discovering it now*: I think so, yes!

HYMAN: Does something happen?

SYLVIA: Well, I begin to run away. And the whole crowd is chasing after me. They have heavy shoes that pound on the pavement. Then just as I'm escaping around a corner a man catches me and pushes me down . . . *Breaks off.*

HYMAN: Is that the end of it?

SYLVIA: No. He gets on top of me, and begins kissing me . . . *Breaks off.*

HYMAN: Yes?

SYLVIA: . . . And then he starts to cut off my breasts. And he raises himself up, and for a second I see the side of his face.

HYMAN: Who is it?

SYLVIA: . . . I don't know.

HYMAN: But you saw his face.

SYLVIA: I think it's Phillip. *Pause.* But how could Phillip be like . . . he was almost like one of the others?

HYMAN: I don't know. Why do you think?

SYLVIA: Would it be possible . . . because Phillip . . . I mean . . . *A little laugh* . . . he sounds sometimes like he doesn't like Jews? *Correcting.* Of course he doesn't mean it, but maybe in my mind it's like he's . . . *Breaks off.*

HYMAN: Like he's what. What's frightening you? *Sylvia is silent, turns away.* Sylvia?

> *Hyman tries to turn her face towards him, but she resists.*

> Not Phillip, is it?

> *Sylvia turns to him, the answer is in her eyes.*

> I see.

> *He moves from the bed and halts, trying to weigh this added complication. Returning to the bedside, sits, takes her hand.*

> I want to ask you a question.

> *She draws him to her and kisses him on the mouth.*

SYLVIA: I can't help it.

> *She bursts into tears.*

HYMAN: Oh God, Sylvia, I'm so sorry . . .

SYLVIA: Help me. Please!

HYMAN: I'm trying to.

SYLVIA: I know!

> *She weeps even more deeply. With a cry filled with her pain she embraces him desperately.*

HYMAN: Oh Sylvia, Sylvia. . . .

SYLVIA: I feel so foolish.

HYMAN: No-no. You're unhappy, not foolish.

SYLVIA: I feel like I'm losing everything, I'm being torn to pieces. What do you want to know, I'll tell you!

> *She cries into her hands. He moves, trying to make a decision . . .*

> I trust you. What do you want to ask me?

HYMAN: —Since this happened to you, have you and Phillip had relations?

SYLVIA, *open surprise*: Relations?

HYMAN: He said you did the other night.

SYLVIA: We had *relations* the other night?

HYMAN: But that . . . well he said that by morning you'd forgotten. Is that true?

> *She is motionless, looking past him with immense uncertainty.*

SYLVIA, *alarmed sense of rejection*: Why are you asking me that?

HYMAN: I didn't know what to make of it. . . . I guess I still don't.

SYLVIA, *deeply embarrassed*: You mean you believe him?

HYMAN: Well . . . I didn't know what to believe.

SYLVIA: You must think I'm crazy, —to forget such a thing.

HYMAN: Oh God no!—I didn't mean anything like that . . .

SYLVIA: We haven't had relations for almost twenty years.

> *The shock pitches him into silence. Now he doesn't know what or whom to believe.*

HYMAN: Twenty . . . ? *Breaks off.*

SYLVIA: Just after Jerome was born.

HYMAN: I just . . . I don't know what to say, Sylvia.

SYLVIA: You never heard of it before with people?

HYMAN: Yes, but not when they're as young as you.

SYLVIA: You might be surprised.

HYMAN: What was it, another woman, or what?

SYLVIA: Oh no.

HYMAN: Then what happened?

SYLVIA: I don't know, I never understood it. He just couldn't anymore.

> *She tries to read his reaction; he doesn't face her directly.*

You believe me, don't you?

HYMAN: Of course I do. But why would he invent a story like that?

SYLVIA, *incredulously*: I can't imagine. . . . Could he be trying to . . . *Breaks off.*

HYMAN: What.

SYLVIA: . . . Make you think I've gone crazy?

HYMAN: No, you mustn't believe that. I think maybe . . . you see, he mentioned my so-called reputation with women, and maybe he was just trying to look . . . I don't know—competitive. How did this start? Was there some reason?

SYLVIA: I think I made one mistake. He hadn't come near me for like—I don't remember anymore—a month maybe; and . . . I was so young . . . a man to me was so much stronger that I couldn't imagine I could . . . you know, hurt him like that.

HYMAN: Like what?

SYLVIA: Well . . . *Small laugh.* I was so stupid, I'm still ashamed of it . . . I mentioned it to my father—who loved Phillip—and he took him aside and tried to suggest a doctor. I should never have mentioned it, it was a terrible mistake, for a while I thought we'd have to have a divorce . . . it was months before he could say good morning, he was so furious. I finally got him to go with me to Rabbi Steiner, but he just sat there like a . . . *She sighs, shakes her head.* —I don't know, I guess you just gradually give up and it closes over you like a grave. But I can't help it, I still pity him; because I know how it tortures him, it's like a snake eating into his heart. . . . I mean it's not as though he doesn't like me, he does, I know it. —Or do you think so?

HYMAN: He says you're his whole life.

She is staring, shaking her head, stunned.

SYLVIA, *with bitter irony*: His whole life! Poor Phillip.

HYMAN: I've been talking to a friend of mine at the hospital, a psychiatrist. I want your permission to bring him in; I'll call you in the morning.

SYLVIA, *instantly*: Why must you leave? I'm nervous now. Can't you talk to me a few minutes? I have some yeast cake. I'll make fresh coffee . . .

HYMAN: I'd love to stay but Margaret'll be upset with me.

SYLVIA: Oh. Well call her! Ask her to come over too.

HYMAN: No-no . . .

SYLVIA, *a sudden anxiety burst, colored by her feminine disappointment*: For God's sake, why not!

HYMAN: She thinks something's going on with us.

SYLVIA, *pleased surprise—and worriedly*: Oh!

HYMAN: I'll be in touch tomorrow . . .

SYLVIA: Couldn't you just be here when he comes. I'm nervous—please—just be here when he comes.

Her anxiety forces him back down on the bed. She takes his hand.

HYMAN: You don't think he'd do something, do you?

SYLVIA: I've never known him so angry. —And I think there's also some trouble with Mr. Case. Phillip can hit, you know. *Shakes her head.* God, everything's so mixed up! *Pause. She sits there shaking her head, then lifts the newspaper.* But I don't understand—they write that the Germans are starting to pick up Jews right off the street and putting them into . . .

HYMAN, *impatience*: Now Sylvia, I told you . . .

SYLVIA: But you say they were such nice people—how could they change like this!

HYMAN: This will all pass, Sylvia! German music and literature is some of the greatest in the world; it's impossible for those people to suddenly change into thugs like this. So you ought to have more confidence, you see?—I mean in general, in life, in people.

She stares at him, becoming transformed.

HYMAN: What are you telling me? Just say what you're thinking right now.

SYLVIA, *struggling*: I . . . I . . .

HYMAN: Don't be frightened, just say it.

SYLVIA, *she has become terrified*: You.

HYMAN: Me! What about me?

SYLVIA: How could you believe I forget we had relations!

HYMAN, *her persistent intensity unnerving him*: Now stop that! I was only trying to understand what is happening.

SYLVIA: Yes. And what? What is happening?

HYMAN, *forcefully, contained*: . . . What are you trying to tell me?

SYLVIA: Well . . . what . . .

Everything is flying apart for her; she lifts the edge of the newspaper; the focus is clearly far wider than the room. An unbearable anxiety . . .

What is going to become of us?

HYMAN, *indicating the paper*: —But what has Germany got to do with . . . ?

SYLVIA, *shouting; his incomprehension dangerous*: But how can those nice people go out and pick Jews off the street in the middle of a big city like that, and nobody stops them . . . ?

HYMAN: You mean *I've* changed? Is that it?

SYLVIA: I don't know . . . one minute you say you like me and then you turn around and I'm . . .

HYMAN: Listen, I simply must call in somebody . . .

SYLVIA: No! You could help me if you believed me!

HYMAN, *his spine tingling with her fear; a shout*: I do believe you!

SYLVIA: No!—you're not going to put me away somewhere!

HYMAN, *a horrified shout*: Now you stop being ridiculous!

SYLVIA: But . . . but what . . . what . . . *Gripping her head; his uncertainty terrifying her*: What will become of us!

HYMAN, *unnerved*: Now stop it—you are confusing two things . . . !

SYLVIA: But . . . from now on . . . you mean if a Jew walks out of his house, do they arrest him . . . ?

HYMAN: I'm telling you this won't last.

SYLVIA, *with a weird, blind, violent persistence*: But what do they do with them?

HYMAN: I don't know! I'm out of my depth! I can't help you!

SYLVIA: But why don't they run out of the country! What is the matter with those people! Don't you understand . . . ? *Screaming*: . . . This is an *emergency*! What if they kill those children! Where is Roosevelt! Where is England! Somebody should do something before they murder us all!

> *Sylvia takes a step off the edge of the bed in an hysterical attempt to reach Hyman and the power he represents. She collapses on the floor before he can catch her. Trying to rouse her from her faint . . .*

HYMAN: Sylvia? Sylvia!

> *Gellburg enters.*

GELLBURG: What happened!

HYMAN: Run cold water on a towel!

GELLBURG: What happened!

HYMAN: Do it, goddam you!

> *Gellburg rushes out.*

Sylvia!—oh good, that's it, keep looking at me, that's it dear, keep your eyes open . . .

He lifts her up onto the bed as Gellburg hurries in with a towel. Gellburg gives it to Hyman, who presses it onto her forehead and back of her neck.

There we are, that's better, how do you feel? Can you speak? You want to sit up? Come.

He helps her to sit up. She looks around and then at Gellburg.

GELLBURG, *to Hyman*: Did *she* call *you*?

HYMAN, *hesitates; and in an angry tone*: . . . Well no, to tell the truth.

GELLBURG: Then what are you doing here?

HYMAN: I stopped by, I was worried about her.

GELLBURG: You were worried about her. Why were you worried about her?

HYMAN, *anger is suddenly sweeping him*: Because she is desperate to be loved.

GELLBURG, *off guard, astonished*: You don't say!

HYMAN: Yes, I do say. *To her*: I want you to try to move your legs. Try it.

She tries; nothing happens.

I'll be at home if you need me; don't be afraid to call anytime. We'll talk about this more tomorrow. Good night.

SYLVIA, *faintly, afraid*: Good night.

Hyman gives Gellburg a quick, outraged glance, Hyman leaves.

GELLBURG, *reaching for his authority*: That's some attitude he's got, ordering me around like that. I'm going to see about getting somebody else tomorrow. Jersey seems to get further and further away, I'm exhausted.

SYLVIA: I almost started walking.

GELLBURG: What are you talking about?

SYLVIA: For a minute. I don't know what happened, my strength, it started to come back.

GELLBURG: I knew it! I told you you could! Try it again, come.

SYLVIA, *she tries to raise her legs*: I can't now.

GELLBURG: Why not! Come, this is wonderful . . . ! *Reaches for her.*

SYLVIA: Phillip, listen . . . I don't want to change, I want Hyman.

GELLBURG, *his purse-mouthed grin*: What's so good about him?—you're still laying there, practically dead to the world.

SYLVIA: He helped me get up, I don't know why. I feel he can get me walking again.

GELLBURG: Why does it have to be him?

SYLVIA: Because I can talk to him! I want *him*. *An outburst*: And I don't want to discuss it again!

GELLBURG: Well we'll see.

SYLVIA: We will not see!

GELLBURG: What's this tone of voice?

SYLVIA, *trembling out of control*: It's a Jewish woman's tone of voice!

GELLBURG: A Jewish woman . . . ! What are you talking about, are you crazy?

SYLVIA: Don't you call me crazy, Phillip! I'm talking about it! They are smashing windows and beating children! I am talking about it! *Screams at him*: I am talking about it, Phillip!

> She grips her head in her confusion. He is stock still; horrified, fearful.

GELLBURG: What . . . "beating children"?

SYLVIA: Never mind. Don't sleep with me again.

GELLBURG: How can you say that to me?

SYLVIA: I can't bear it. You give me terrible dreams. I'm sorry, Phillip. Maybe in a while but not now.

GELLBURG: Sylvia, you will kill me if we can't be together . . .

SYLVIA: You told him we had relations?

GELLBURG, *beginning to weep*: Don't, Sylvia . . . !

SYLVIA: You little liar!—you want him to think I'm crazy? Is that it? *Now she breaks into weeping*.

GELLBURG: No! It just . . . it came out, I didn't know what I was saying!

SYLVIA: *That I forgot we had relations?! Phillip?*

GELLBURG: Stop that! Don't say any more.

SYLVIA: I'm going to say anything I want to.

GELLBURG, *weeping*: You will kill me . . . !

> They are silent for a moment.

SYLVIA: What I did with my life! Out of ignorance. Out of not wanting to shame you in front of other people. A whole life. Gave it away like a couple of pennies—I took better care of my shoes. *Turns to him.* —You want to talk to me about it now? Take me seriously, Phillip. What happened? I know it's all you ever thought about, isn't that true? *What happened?* Just so I'll know.

A long pause.

GELLBURG: I'm ashamed to mention it. It's ridiculous.

SYLVIA: What are you talking about?

GELLBURG: But I was ignorant, I couldn't help myself. —When you said you wanted to go back to the firm.

SYLVIA: What are you talking about?—When?

GELLBURG: When you had Jerome . . . and suddenly you didn't want to keep the house anymore.

SYLVIA: And? —You didn't want me to go back to business, so I didn't.

He doesn't speak; her rage an inch below.

Well what? I didn't, did I?

GELLBURG: You held it against me, having to stay home, you know you did. You've probably forgotten, but not a day passed, not a person could come into this house that you didn't keep saying how wonderful and interesting it used to be for you in business. You never forgave me, Sylvia.

She evades his gaze.

So whenever I . . . when I started to touch you, I felt that.

SYLVIA: You felt what?

GELLBURG: That you didn't want me to be the man here. And then, on top of that when you didn't want any more children . . . everything inside me just dried up. And maybe it was also that to me it was a miracle you ever married me in the first place.

SYLVIA: You mean your face?

He turns slightly.

What have you got against your face? A Jew can have a Jewish face.

Pause.

GELLBURG: I can't help my thoughts, nobody can. . . . I admit it was a mistake, I tried a hundred times to talk to you, but I couldn't. I kept waiting for myself to change. Or you. And then we got to where it didn't seem to matter anymore. So I left it that way. And I couldn't change anything anymore.

Pause.

SYLVIA: This is a whole life we're talking about.

GELLBURG: But couldn't we . . . if I taught you to drive and you could go anywhere you liked. . . . Or maybe you could find a position you liked . . . ?

She is staring ahead.

We have to sleep together.

SYLVIA: No.

Gellburg drops to his knees beside the bed, his arms spread awkwardly over her covered body.

GELLBURG: How can this be?

She is motionless.

Sylvia? *Pause.* Do you want to kill me?

She is staring ahead, he is weeping and shouting.

Is that it! Speak to me!

Sylvia's face is blank, unreadable. He buries his face in the covers, weeping helplessly. She at last reaches out in pity toward the top of his head, and as her hand almost touches . . .

BLACKOUT

SCENE III

Case's office. Gellburg is seated alone. Case enters, shuffling through a handful of mail. Gellburg has gotten to his feet. Case's manner is cold; barely glances up from his mail.

CASE: Good morning, Gellburg.

GELLBURG: Good morning, Mr. Case.

CASE: I understand you wish to see me.

GELLBURG: There was just something I felt I should say.

CASE: Certainly. *He goes to a chair and sits.* Yes?

GELLBURG: It's just that I would never in this world do anything against you or Brooklyn Guarantee. I don't have to tell you, it's the only place I've ever worked in my life. My whole life is here. I'm more proud of this company than almost anything except my own son. What I'm trying to say is that this whole business with Wanamaker's was only because I didn't want to leave a stone unturned. Two or three years from now I didn't want you waking up one morning and Wanamaker's is gone and there you are paying New York taxes on a building in the middle of a dying neighborhood.

    Case lets him hang there. He begins getting flustered.

    Frankly, I don't even remember what this whole thing was about. I feel I've lost some of your confidence, and it's . . . well, it's unfair, I feel.

CASE: I understand.

GELLBURG, *he waits, but that's it*: But . . . but don't you believe me?

CASE: I think I do.

GELLBURG: But . . . you seem to be . . . you don't seem . . .

CASE: The fact remains that I've lost the building.

GELLBURG: But are you . . . I mean you're not still thinking that I had something going on with Allan Kershowitz, are you?

CASE: Put it this way—I hope as time goes on that my old confidence will return. That's about as far as I can go, and I don't think you can blame me, can you? *He stands.*

GELLBURG, *despite himself his voice rises*: But how can I work if you're this way? You have to trust a man, don't you?

CASE, *begins to indicate he must leave*: I'll have to ask you to . . .

GELLBURG, *shouting*: I don't deserve this! You can't do this to me! It's not fair, Mr. Case, I had nothing to do with Allan Kershowitz! I hardly know the man! And the little I do know I don't even like him, I'd certainly never get into a deal with him, for God's sake! This is . . . this whole thing is . . . *Exploding*: I don't understand it, what is happening, what the hell is happening, what have I got to do with Allan Kershowitz, just because he's also a Jew?

CASE, *incredulously and angering*: What? What on earth are you talking about!

GELLBURG: Excuse me. I didn't mean that.

CASE: I don't understand . . . how could you say a thing like that!

GELLBURG: Please. I don't feel well, excuse me . . .

CASE, *his resentment mounting*: But how could you say such a thing! It's an outrage, Gellburg!

> *Gellburg takes a step to leave and goes to his knees, clutching his chest, trying to breathe, his face reddening.*

CASE: What is it? Gellburg? *He springs up and goes to the periphery.* Call an ambulance! Hurry, for God's sake! *He rushes out, shouting*: Quick, get a doctor! It's Gellburg! Gellburg has collapsed!

> *Gellburg remains on his hands and knees trying to keep from falling over, gasping.*

BLACKOUT

SCENE IV

Sylvia in wheelchair, Margaret and Harriet seated on either side of her. Sylvia is sipping a cup of cocoa.

HARRIET: He's really amazing, after such an attack.

MARGARET: The heart is a muscle; muscles can recover sometimes.

HARRIET: I still can't understand how they let him out of the hospital so soon.

MARGARET: He has a will of iron. But it may be just as well for him here.

SYLVIA: He wants to die here.

MARGARET: No one can know, he can live a long time.

SYLVIA, *handing her the cup*: Thanks. I haven't drunk cocoa in years.

MARGARET: I find it soothes the nerves.

SYLVIA, *with a slight ironical edge*: He wants to be here so we can have a talk, that's what it is. *Shakes her head.* How stupid it all is; you keep putting everything off like you're going to live a thousand years. But we're like those little flies—born in the morning, fly around for a day till it gets dark—and bye-bye.

HARRIET: Well, it takes time to learn things.

SYLVIA: There's nothing I know now that I didn't know twenty years ago. I just didn't say it. *Grasping the chair wheels.* Help me! I want to go to him.

MARGARET: Wait till Harry says it's all right.

HARRIET: Sylvia, please—let the doctor decide.

MARGARET: I hope you're not blaming yourself.

HARRIET: It could happen to anybody—*To Margaret*: Our father, for instance—laid down for his nap one afternoon and never woke up. *To Sylvia*: Remember?

SYLVIA, *a wan smile, nods*: He was the same way all his life—never wanted to trouble anybody.

HARRIET: And just the day before he went and bought a new bathing suit. And an amber holder for his cigar. *To Sylvia*: She's right, you mustn't start blaming yourself.

SYLVIA, *a shrug*: What's the difference? *Sighs tiredly—stares. Basically to Margaret*: The trouble, you see—was that Phillip always thought he was supposed to be the Rock of Gibraltar. Like nothing could ever bother him. Supposedly. But I knew a couple of months after we got married that he . . . he was making it all up. In fact, I thought I was stronger than him. But what can you do? You swallow it and make believe you're weaker. And after a while you can't find a true word to put in your mouth. And now I end up useless to him . . . *starting to weep*, just when he needs me!

HARRIET, *distressed, stands*: I'm making a gorgeous pot roast, can I bring some over?

SYLVIA: Thanks, Flora's going to cook something.

HARRIET: I'll call you later, try to rest. *Moves to leave, halts, unable to hold back*. I refuse to believe that you're blaming yourself for this. How can people start saying what they know?—there wouldn't be two marriages left in Brooklyn! *Nearly overcome*. It's ridiculous!—you're the best wife he could have had!—better! *She hurries out. Pause.*

MARGARET: I worked in the pediatric ward for a couple of years. And sometimes we'd have thirty or forty babies in there at the same time. A day or two old and they've already got a personality; this one lays there, stiff as a mummy . . . *mimes a mummy, hands closed in fists*, a regular banker. The next one is throwing himself all over the place . . . *wildly flinging her arms*, happy as a young horse. The next one is Miss Dreary, already worried about her hemline drooping. And how could it be otherwise—each one has twenty thousand years of the human race backed up behind him . . . and you expect to change him?

SYLVIA: So what does that mean? How do you live?

MARGARET: You draw your cards face down; you turn them over and do your best with the hand you got. What else is there, my dear? What else can there be?

SYLVIA, *staring ahead*: . . . Wishing, I guess . . . that it had been otherwise. Help me! *Starts the chair rolling.* I want to go to him.

MARGARET: Wait. I'll ask Harry if it's all right. *Backing away.* Wait, okay? I'll be right back.

> *She turns and exits. Alone, Sylvia brings both hands pressed together up to her lips in a sort of prayer, and closes her eyes.*

BLACKOUT

SCENE V

The cellist plays, the music falls away.

Gellburg's bedroom. He is in bed. Hyman is putting his stethoscope back into his bag, and sits on a chair beside the bed.

HYMAN: I can only tell you again, Phillip,—you belong in the hospital.

GELLBURG: Please don't argue about it anymore! I couldn't stand it there, it smells like a zoo; and to lay in a bed where some stranger died . . . I hate it. If I'm going out I'll go from here. And I don't want to leave Sylvia.

HYMAN: I'm trying to help you. *Chuckles.* And I'm going to go on trying even if it kills both of us.

GELLBURG: I appreciate that. I mean it. You're a good man.

HYMAN: You're lucky I know that. The nurse should be here around six.

GELLBURG: I'm wondering if I need her—I think the pain is practically gone.

HYMAN: I want her here overnight.

GELLBURG: I . . . I want to tell you something; when I collapsed . . . it was like an explosion went off in my head, like a tremendous white light. It sounds funny but I felt a . . . happiness . . . that funny? Like I suddenly had something to tell her that would change everything, and we would go back to how it was when we started out together. I couldn't wait to tell it to her . . . and now I can't remember what it was. *Anguished, a rushed quality; suddenly near tears.* God, I always thought there'd be time to get to the bottom of myself!

HYMAN: You might have years, nobody can predict.

GELLBURG: It's unbelievable—the first time since I was twenty I don't have a job. I just can't believe it.

HYMAN: You sure? Maybe you can clear it up with your boss when you go back.

GELLBURG: How can I go back? He made a fool of me. It's infuriating. I tell you—I never wanted to see it this way but he goes sailing around on the ocean and meanwhile I'm foreclosing Brooklyn for them. That's what it boils down to. You got some lousy rotten job to do, get Gellburg, send in the Yid. Close down a business, throw somebody out of his home. . . . And now to accuse me . . .

HYMAN: But is all this news to you? That's the system, isn't it?

GELLBURG: But to accuse me of double-crossing the *company*! That is absolutely unfair . . . it was like a hammer between the eyes. I mean to me Brooklyn Guarantee—for God's sake, Brooklyn Guarantee was like . . . like . . .

HYMAN: You're getting too excited, Phillip . . . come on now. *Changing the subject*: —I understand your son is coming back from the Philippines.

GELLBURG, *he catches his breath for a moment*: . . . She show you his telegram? He's trying to make it here by Monday. *Scared eyes and a grin.* Or will I last till Monday?

HYMAN: You've got to start thinking about more positive things— seriously, your system needs a rest.

GELLBURG: Who's that talking?

HYMAN, *indicating upstage*: I asked Margaret to sit with your wife for a while, they're in your son's bedroom.

GELLBURG: Do you always take so much trouble?

HYMAN: I like Sylvia.

GELLBURG, *his little grin*: I know . . . I didn't think it was for my sake.

HYMAN: You're not so bad. I have to get back to my office now.

GELLBURG: Please if you have a few minutes, I'd appreciate it. *Almost holding his breath*: Tell me—the thing she's so afraid of . . . is me isn't it?

HYMAN: Well . . . among other things.

GELLBURG, *shock*: It's me?

HYMAN: I think so . . . partly.

Gellburg presses his fingers against his eyes to regain control.

GELLBURG: How could she be frightened of me! I worship her! *Quickly controlling*: How could everything turn out to be the opposite—I made my son in this bed and now I'm dying in it . . . *Breaks off, downing a cry.* My thoughts keep flying around—everything from years ago keeps coming back like it was last week. Like the day we bought this bed. Abraham & Straus. It was so sunny and beautiful. I took the whole day off. (God, it's almost twenty-five years ago!) . . . Then we had a soda at Schrafft's— of course they don't hire Jews but the chocolate ice cream is the best. Then we went over to Orchard Street for bargains. Bought our first pots and sheets, blankets, pillowcases. The street was full of pushcarts and men with long beards like a hundred years ago. It's funny, I felt so at home and happy there that day, a street full of Jews, one Moses after another. But they all turned to watch her go by, those fakers. She was a knockout; sometimes walking down a street I couldn't believe I was married to her. Listen . . . *Breaks off, with some diffidence*: You're an educated man, I only went to high school—I wish we could talk about the Jews.

HYMAN: I never studied the history, if that's what you . . .

GELLBURG: . . . I don't know where I am . . .

HYMAN: You mean as a Jew?

GELLBURG: Do you think about it much? I never . . . for instance, a Jew in love with horses is something I never heard of.

HYMAN: My grandfather in Odessa was a horse dealer.

GELLBURG: You don't say! I wouldn't know you were Jewish except for your name.

HYMAN: I have cousins up near Syracuse who're still in the business— they break horses. You know there are Chinese Jews.

GELLBURG: I heard of that! And they look Chinese?

HYMAN: They are Chinese. They'd probably say you don't look Jewish.

GELLBURG: Ha! That's funny. *His laugh disappears; he stares.* Why is it so hard to be a Jew?

HYMAN: It's hard to be anything.

GELLBURG: No, it's different for them. Being a Jew is a full-time job. Except you don't think about it much, do you. —Like when you're on your horse, or . . .

HYMAN: It's not an obsession for me . . .

GELLBURG: But how'd you come to marry a shiksa?

HYMAN: We were thrown together when I was interning, and we got very close, and . . . well she was a good partner, she helped me, and still does. And I loved her.

GELLBURG: —a Jewish woman couldn't help you?

HYMAN: Sure. But it just didn't happen.

GELLBURG: It wasn't so you wouldn't seem Jewish.

HYMAN, *coldly*: I never pretended I wasn't Jewish.

GELLBURG, *almost shaking with some fear*: Look, don't be mad, I'm only trying to figure out . . .

HYMAN, *sensing the underlying hostility*: What are you driving at, I don't understand this whole conversation.

GELLBURG: Hyman . . . Help me! I've never been so afraid in my life.

HYMAN: If you're alive you're afraid; we're born afraid—a newborn baby is not a picture of confidence; but how you deal with fear, that's what counts. I don't think you dealt with it very well.

GELLBURG: Why? How did I deal with it?

HYMAN: I think you tried to disappear into the goyim.

GELLBURG: . . . You believe in God?

HYMAN: I'm a socialist. I think we're at the end of religion.

GELLBURG: You mean everybody working for the government.

HYMAN: It's the only future that makes any rational sense.

GELLBURG: God forbid. But how can there be Jews if there's no God?

HYMAN: Oh, they'll find something to worship. The Christians will too—maybe different brands of ketchup.

GELLBURG, *laughs*: Boy, the things you come out with sometimes . . . !

HYMAN: —Some day we're all going to look like a lot of monkeys running around trying to figure out a coconut.

GELLBURG: She believes in you, Hyman . . . I want you to tell her—tell her I'm going to change. She has no right to be so frightened. Of me or anything else. They will never destroy us. When the last Jew dies, the light of the world will go out. She has to understand that—those Germans are shooting at the sun!

HYMAN: Be quiet.

GELLBURG: I want my wife back. I want her back before something happens. I feel like there's nothing inside me, I feel empty. I want her back.

HYMAN: Phillip, what can I do about that?

GELLBURG: Never mind . . . since you started coming around . . . in those boots . . . like some kind of horseback rider . . . ?

HYMAN: What the hell are you talking about!

GELLBURG: Since you came around she looks down at me like a miserable piece of shit!

HYMAN: Phillip . . .

GELLBURG: Don't "Phillip" me, just stop it!

HYMAN: Don't scream at me Phillip, you know how to get your wife back! . . . don't tell me there's a mystery to that!

GELLBURG: She actually told you that I . . .

HYMAN: It came out while we were talking. It was bound to sooner or later, wasn't it?

GELLBURG, *gritting his teeth*: I never told this to anyone . . . but years ago when I used to make love to her, I would almost feel like a small baby on top of her, like she was giving me birth. That's some idea? In bed next to me she was like a . . . a marble god. I worshipped her, Hyman, from the day I laid eyes on her.

HYMAN: I'm sorry for you Phillip.

GELLBURG: How can she be so afraid of me? Tell me the truth.

HYMAN: I don't know; maybe, for one thing . . . these remarks you're always making about Jews.

GELLBURG: What remarks?

HYMAN: Like not wanting to be mistaken for Goldberg.

GELLBURG: So I'm a Nazi? Is Gellburg Goldberg? It's not, is it?

HYMAN: No, but continually making the point is kind of . . .

GELLBURG: Kind of what? What is kind of? Why don't you say the truth?

HYMAN: All right, you want the truth? Do you? Look in the mirror sometime!

GELLBURG: . . . In the mirror!

HYMAN: You hate yourself, that's what's scaring her to death. That's my opinion. How it's possible I don't know, but I think you helped paralyze her with this "Jew, Jew, Jew" coming out of your mouth and the same time she reads it in the paper and it's coming out of the radio day and night? You wanted to know what I think . . . that's what I think.

GELLBURG: But there are some days I feel like going and sitting in the *schul* with the old men and pulling the *talles* over my head and be a full-time Jew the rest of my life. With the sidelocks and the black hat,and settle it once and for all. And other times . . . yes, I could almost kill them. They infuriate me. I am ashamed of them and that I look like them. *Gasping again*: —Why must we be different? Why is it? What is it for?

HYMAN: And supposing it turns out that we're *not* different, who are you going to blame then?

GELLBURG: What are you talking about?

HYMAN: I'm talking about all this grinding and screaming that's going on inside you—you're wearing yourself out for nothing, Phillip, absolutely nothing! —I'll tell you a secret—I have all kinds coming into my office, and there's not one of them who one way or another is not persecuted. Yes. *Everybody's* persecuted. The poor by the rich, the rich by the poor, the black by the white, the white by the black, the men by the women, the women by the men, the Catholics by the Protestants, the Protestants by the Catholics—and of course all of them by the Jews. Everybody's persecuted—sometimes I wonder, maybe that's what holds this country together! And what's really amazing is that you can't find anybody who's persecuting anybody else.

GELLBURG: So you mean there's no Hitler?

HYMAN: Hitler? Hitler is the perfect example of the persecuted man! I've heard him—he kvetches like an elephant was standing on his pecker! They've turned that whole beautiful country into one gigantic kvetch! *Takes his bag*. The nurse'll be here soon.

GELLBURG: So what's the solution?

HYMAN: I don't see any. Except the mirror. But nobody's going to look at himself and ask what am *I* doing—you might as well tell him to take a seat in the hottest part of hell. Forgive her, Phillip, is all I really know to tell you. *Grins*: But that's the easy part—I speak from experience.

GELLBURG: What's the hard part?

HYMAN: To forgive yourself, I guess. And the Jews. And while you're at it, you can throw in the goyim. Best thing for the heart you know.

> *Hyman exits. Gellburg is left alone, staring into space. Sylvia enters, Margaret pushing the chair.*

MARGARET: I'll leave you now, Sylvia.

SYLVIA: Thanks for sitting with me.

GELLBURG, *a little wave of the hand*: Thank you Mrs. Hyman!

MARGARET: I think your color's coming back a little.

GELLBURG: Well, I've been running around the block.

MARGARET, *a burst of laughter and shaking her finger at him*: I always knew there was a sense of humor somewhere inside that black suit!

GELLBURG: Yes, well . . . I finally got the joke.

MARGARET, *laughs, and to Sylvia*: I'll try to look in tomorrow. *To both*: Good-bye!

>   *Margaret exits.*

>   *A silence between them grows self-conscious.*

GELLBURG: You all right in that room?

SYLVIA: It's better this way, we'll both get more rest. You all right?

GELLBURG: I want to apologize.

SYLVIA: I'm not blaming you, Phillip. The years I wasted I know I threw away myself. I think I always knew I was doing it but I couldn't stop it.

GELLBURG: If only you could believe I never meant you harm, it would . . .

SYLVIA: I believe you. But I have to tell you something. When I said not to sleep with me . . .

GELLBURG: I know . . .

SYLVIA, *nervously sharp*: You don't know!—I'm trying to tell you something! *Containing herself*: For some reason I keep thinking of how I used to be; remember my parents' house, how full of love it always was? Nobody was ever afraid of anything. But with us, Phillip, wherever I looked there was something to be suspicious about, somebody who was going to take advantage or God knows what. I've been tip-toeing around my life for thirty years and I'm not going to pretend—I hate it all now. Everything I did is stupid and ridiculous. I can't find myself in my life.

>   *She hits her legs.*

>   Or in this now, this thing that can't even walk. I'm not this thing. And it has me. It has me and will never let me go.

>   *She weeps.*

GELLBURG: Sshh! I understand. I wasn't telling you the truth. I always tried to seem otherwise, but I've been more afraid than I looked.

SYLVIA: Afraid of what?

GELLBURG: Everything. Of Germany. Mr. Case. Of what could happen to us here. I think I was more afraid than you are, a hundred times more! And meantime there are Chinese Jews, for God's sake.

SYLVIA: What do you mean?

GELLBURG: They're *Chinese*!— and here I spend a lifetime looking in the mirror at my face!—Why we're different I will never understand but to live so afraid, I don't want that anymore. I tell you, if I live I have to try to change myself.—Sylvia, my darling Sylvia, I'm asking you not to blame me anymore. I feel I did this to you! That's the knife in my heart.

Gellburg's breathing begins to labor.

SYLVIA, *alarmed*: Phillip!

GELLBURG: God almighty, Sylvia forgive me!

A paroxysm forces Gellburg up to a nearly sitting position, agony on his face.

SYLVIA: Wait! Phillip!

Struggling to break free of the chair's support, she starts pressing down on the chair arms.

There's nothing to blame! There's nothing to blame!

Gellburg falls back, unconscious. She struggles to balance herself on her legs and takes a faltering step toward her husband.

Wait, wait . . . Phillip, Phillip!

Astounded, charged with hope yet with a certain inward seeing, she looks down at her legs, only now aware that she has risen to her feet.

Lights fade.

THE END

MR. PETERS' CONNECTIONS

1999

Characters

CALVIN, *Mr. Peters' dead brother*

HARRY PETERS, *Retired airline and military pilot and lecturer*

ADELE, *A black bag lady*

CATHY-MAY, *Mr. Peters' dead lover*

LARRY, *Her husband as Peters imagines him*

LEONARD, *A guitarist and lover of:*

ROSE, *Mr. Peters' daughter*

CHARLOTTE, *Mr. Peters' wife*

A broken structure indicating an old abandoned nightclub in New York City.

A small, dusty upright piano, some chairs, a couple of tables, a few upended.

Three chairs set close to the piano with instruments propped up on them—a bass, trumpet, saxophone.

Seated on a banquette, Adele, a black bag lady, is ensconced amid her bags; she is reading Vogue *magazine, and sipping from a bottle of wine. She occasionally examines her face in a hand mirror.*

Calvin enters. Peters enters, looking around. Halts.

CALVIN: Well, here it is. *Silence. Peters very slowly looks at everything. Then goes still.*

PETERS, *undirected to anyone*: To be moved. Yes. Even once more to feel that thunder, yes. Just once! *Slight pause.* Lust aside, what could hit me? Novels? Model airplanes, movies, cooking, the garden? *Shakes his head, dry grief.* And yet, deep down . . . deep down I always seem on the verge of weeping. God knows why, when I have everything. *Slight pause; he peers ahead.* What is the subject?

> *Peters goes to the piano, plays the first five notes of "September Song," then walks a few steps. The piano continues playing; both men stare into space; piano subsides into silence. Now Calvin gestures toward the structure.*

CALVIN: Needs some work, of course.

PETERS: My wife should be here in a few minutes, I believe.

CALVIN: She'll like it, most women do.

PETERS: I'm very tired. I've been walking. Why women?

CALVIN: Hard to say. The powder room, maybe.

ADELE, *not looking away from her mirror*: Gorgeous. *Neither man seems to hear her.*

PETERS: I take it you're not from here?

CALVIN: You have a good ear. Russia, I guess.

PETERS: You guess!

CALVIN: Who can be sure? In my mother's bed, I suppose, same as everybody else.

PETERS: Mother's bed.

CALVIN: Where I'm from. Actually, Sheepshead Bay, Brooklyn.

PETERS: Actually. But people from Sheepshead Bay, Brooklyn, do not say "actually," it's too . . . I don't know, high-class. But it doesn't matter; if you'd told me in the first place I'd have forgotten it by now. My personal situation these days is trying to paddle a canoe with a tennis racket . . . I am thinking, who does he remind me of?

CALVIN: I tend to do that. Some people, all they do in life is remind people of somebody. —Generally I remind people of somebody nice and reliable.

PETERS: Why don't we leave it right there.

CALVIN: I'm not trying to be facetious . . .

PETERS: Listen. Let's settle this—conflict is not my game anymore; or suspense; I really don't like trying to figure out what's going on. Peace and quiet, avoid the bumps, I'm perfectly content just to raise the shade and greet my morning. Not that I'm depressed; in fact, I feel I am an inch away from the most thrilling glass of water I ever had. On that order.

> *Cathy-May is lit.*
>
> Oh my. *Going toward her; sad amazement.* My-my-my. The flat broad belly, the spring of thighs, how the fire flares up just before it dies . . . ! *He recognizes her, gasps.* Good God, Cathy-May! *Mystified*: Then you're not . . . you're not . . . dead? *Turns from her.* How can we go on seeing them if they . . . ? Or . . . say now, can she not have d . . . ? *Breaks off, thinks.* But of course she did! *Freshly affected.* Of course she did! *Nearly weeping.* Of course she did! It snowed on her funeral . . . *Peers for a clue, then glances at her.* But where is she, then? *Barely smiling, shakes his head, mystified, excited*: Why am I so happy? *A tinkling of Mozart is heard. Cathy-May comes to him; she is naked, in high heels; a big smile breaks onto his face as she approaches. She is giggling.* Ah yes, how proud of your body—like a new party gown. *Giggling, with finely*

honed mock solemnity, she does a formal curtsy with thumbs and forefingers pressed together as though lifting a wide skirt. Laughing softly he bows formally, with one foot thrust forward. They are like two mating birds. Laughing. You can't do this kind of dancing dressed like that, darling! *Still curtsying, she retreats into darkness. Music dies. His laughter sours.* Or am I depressed?

CALVIN: You've been around.

PETERS: And around again, yes—Pan Am captain twenty-six years. I'm really much older than I look. If you planted an apple tree when I was born you'd be cutting it down for firewood by now.

CALVIN: I was going to say, you don't look all that old.

PETERS, *a chuckle:* I am older than everyone I ever knew. All my dogs are dead. Half a dozen cats, parakeets . . . all gone. Every pilot I ever flew with. Probably every woman I ever slept with, too, except my wife. I doubt there's a government in the world that hasn't been overthrown at least once since I was born, except for us and England. I still pick up the phone to call some old friend, until I realize . . . *Chuckles:* Maybe some broken nerve in my brain won't register the vacant pillows and the empty chairs. I wonder sometimes, have I without knowing it been embalmed? Or maybe death is polite, and we must open the door to let him in or he'll just hang around out there on the porch. *Frowns, mystified:* Why am I so fluent? I'm not, usually. I'm known for not saying anything for eight hours at a time. —What about this powder room, why are women so crazy about it? . . . I'm enjoying this, but what is the subject?

CALVIN: Women love to redecorate.

PETERS: Oh, of course, yes. A man will never notice the paint floating off the ceiling onto his head, but a woman can count dust. —You always have an answer, don't you.

CALVIN: Not always.

PETERS: Often, though.

CALVIN: Pretty often.

PETERS: Do you enjoy being so right?

CALVIN, *shrugs:* I can live with it.

PETERS: I'm very different; I enjoy being right but you have to let the woman think they're right so you can take your nap in peace. The older you get, you know, the more you tend to chuckle. I do a lot of it. I mean, who can hit a man when he's chuckling, right? I had a dream, many years ago: this enormous fireplace; and I got up from my chair and said good-bye to my wife, and walked into it. The back of it swung open and I stepped out into the most perfect room I'd ever seen. Everything in that room—the furniture, the color of the walls, the carpet—it was all abso-lutely right. Not a single thing out of place or painful to me. And I looked out the window and the street was perfect. And I felt perfect too. It was all so satisfying, as though that is where I really belong. In fact, I begin to yearn for that house every now and then until I realize—and with some surprise—that it never existed. And the subject, you said, was . . . ? Well, never mind. *Looks about. . . .* I can't imagine anyone thinking he belonged in this place, can you? You absolutely remind me of someone, don't you.

CALVIN: Show your wife the powder room, she'll love you for it.

PETERS: Let's not go into it any further, okay? I have no interest whatso-ever in this place. It's not my kind of place at all.

CALVIN: Maybe give it a little time, you might get used to it.

PETERS, *chuckles angrily*: I don't want to get used to it, will you stop irri-tating me? The only reason I'm even in this neighborhood is . . . I can't recall . . . oh yes, *Calvin is motionless, unaffected.* I decided to buy shoes. I have very narrow feet.

CALVIN: Not as narrow as mine, betcha—triple-A.

PETERS: Quadruple-A. *Extending a foot.* Narrow as herrings. —So I said I'd meet her here.

CALVIN: I used to take a quintuple-A but I don't have time to go running all over the city looking for them anymore . . . I am busy!

PETERS: Well I'm busy too . . .

CALVIN: Not as busy as I am.

PETERS: I assure you, I am just as busy as you are. I got these in that shoe store right on the corner.

CALVIN: You went in *there?*

PETERS, *shamed*: . . . Well only for a couple of minutes.

CALVIN: Phew! Well, it's your funeral.

PETERS, *embarrassed*: Why?—what's wrong with going in there?

CALVIN: There isn't time now; I really need to know what you think of this place? Yes?

PETERS: Well let's see. . . . Oh, the hell with this, I'm leaving. *Starts to go.*

CALVIN: You can't!

PETERS: Don't you tell me I can't, I have very low cholesterol! *He turns and starts out.*

CALVIN: What about your wife?

PETERS: God, I almost forgot. *Sits meekly.* Thanks for reminding me. . . . You always need a reason to stay. I have to stay because of my wife. Why because of my wife?

CALVIN: You're meeting her here.

PETERS: Right, yes! *Short pause.* Why am I meeting her here?

CALVIN: Probably because that was the arrangement.

PETERS: But why here?

CALVIN: What's the difference? One has to meet somewhere.

Cathy-May appears in a filmy dress; Peters goes to her, hesitantly.

PETERS: Could we walk together, darling? Just side by side? I'm sure you can get out of this if you exercise. Please—concentrate, darling! *Desperately.* You must try to move more! Here, let me help! *He gets in front of her, grasps a thigh and gets her to take a stiff, doll-like step. Alarm in his voice.* Relax! You must stop being so stiff. *Angered.* Why are you doing this, are you spiting me?! Here, do this and stop being an idiot! One-two, one-two . . . *He jumps up and down flapping his arms. She remains inert. He turns to Calvin.* Could you applaud?—she loves me, but she's forgotten. *Calvin claps his hands; she doesn't change.* He's applauding, dear . . . listen! *To Calvin, indicating her:* Are you sure we're both in the same place?

CALVIN: How can two occupy . . . ?

PETERS: . . . the same space, yes, that's right. *Moves away from her.* That's one thing you have to say for the war, you always knew where you had to be . . . you had to be where you could get killed, you see. Taking off after a couple of dozen missions you'd naturally wonder, "Is this my last moon?" And so on. But funny, you know?—remarkably little fear—I don't recall actual fear; I suppose because we knew we were good and the Japs were evil, so the whole thing was necessary, and that can soak up fear like a blotter. On that order. *Desperation, loudly:* Whereas now, I just cannot find the subject! Like I'll be strolling down the street, and suddenly I'm weeping, everything welling up. —What is the subject? Know what I mean? Simply cannot grasp the subject. —I can't understand why I'm so fluent here!

ADELE: Something you forgot hasn't forgotten you. You should take up drinking, it might all come pouring out.

PETERS: But I had a wonderful childhood.

ADELE: Famous last words.

PETERS: No-no, in fact, as a kid of sixteen . . . good God, I'd bicycle out to Floyd Bennett Field and wash airplanes for the Army pilots. Dollar a plane, plus they taught me to fly those little Stinsons all over the clear Brooklyn sky. Imagine that nowadays, a kid handed the stick of a fighter plane?—things are never going to get that good again, I tell you we had the best of it, the sweetness. Take Pan Am; Pan Am was not an airline, it was a calling, a knighthood. A Pan Am Captain . . . hell, we were the best of the best and when you took off, the sweaty little corporate statistician, for Christ's sake, did not climb into your lap, they stayed back there on the ground where they belonged. And God—when you got suited up in your whites and your gold epaulettes, the girls inhaled and puffed their feathers and achieved womanhood right in front of your eyes. *Chuckle.* I cannot understand why I'm so fluent in this building.

CALVIN: And what about this place?

PETERS: I don't flaunt my opinions, but I'd say the best way to redecorate this place would be a small bomb . . .

CALVIN: Some people think this could be a gold mine.

PETERS: Oh I'm sure! 'Specially the powder room, probably.

CALVIN: Then why do you have this browbeaten attitude?

PETERS, *angering*: Absolutely not! If I were younger I'd be champing at the bit to get in there . . .

CALVIN: But you're skeptical.

PETERS, *suddenly in distress*: I'm asking you to stop talking about this . . . you're disturbing me!

CALVIN: Listen, you've got to start facing reality.

PETERS: No-no, I'm too old—facing reality is for the young who still have time to avoid it. An old man talking about a . . . a *woman's powder room*—?—it's obscene! Look at the veins in the back of my hands?— shall these warped fingers stroke a breast, cup an ass . . . ? And you call life fair? No . . . no-no . . . *Fumbling.* Why don't I just sit here acting my age, quietly reading my paper till my wife comes? Tell you the truth, I've just had lunch and it makes me drowsy . . . *Head raised, eyes shut.* But I'll be okay in a minute . . . *Begins panting in anxiety.*

CALVIN: I really don't mind, I like explaining, and I have a right to explain.

PETERS, *panting anxiously, nearly shouting*: I respect your rights but whose nap is this? *Breaks off.*

CALVIN: It's why I've always felt just slightly . . . you know . . . under par.

PETERS, *anxiously*: Oh no, Calvin, you musn't say that; you don't look at all under par. In fact, I wish I looked as successful and vigorous and trustworthy as you.

CALVIN: But you are successful. Although I am, in my way.

PETERS: Of course you are. We're both equally successful and promising.

CALVIN: Yes. Although in a way, I am more.

PETERS: It's a relief to hear you say that.

CALVIN: You're relieved because it's not true.

PETERS: If you feel it's true, it's true.

CALVIN: I'd feel it more if it *was*. True, that is.

PETERS: We're depressing one another, don't you think? Why don't we both be quiet and, if necessary, just think about each other, okay? Shhh. Shhh. And maybe the time has come to forget this powder room.

   Sleeps, breathes deeply.

ADELE: Those toilet seats are solid African mahogany. Ask any detective— the imprint of woman's flesh on solid mahogany can never be entirely washed away.

PETERS: I can't bear not understanding this.

ADELE: Think of it—if science could come up with a way of reading those mahogany seats, we could identify women who went to their reward over a hundred years ago. We could inquire about their lives, their shoes, and their deaths. When I enter that powder room it's like the silence of a cathedral, a place of remembrance where dead women linger. It's always three o'clock in the morning in that room, and thoughts come up from the depths. And the dusty oval mirrors still reflect the forgotten beauty of long-departed women in their sweeping satin gowns.

PETERS: This fluency is alarming—can they all be dying?

   Larry Tedesco enters.

CALVIN: Yes? Can I help you?

LARRY: I'm from Posito's. *Indicates.* The shoe store?

PETERS, *sits up*: Yes! —I was just in there, you sold me these shoes! *Raises a foot.* Quadruple-A! *Alarmed.* My God, I paid you, didn't I?

LARRY, *to Calvin*: My wife come in here?

PETERS, *to himself*: But he can't be dead, he just sold me these . . . *Breaks off, looking at his shoes, then looks about*. Listen, please—these are real shoes! I paid with money! *To Larry*: . . . Or rather a credit card, didn't I?

LARRY: You got some kind a problem?

PETERS, *intimidated*: . . . No. No problem.

CALVIN: Do I know your wife?

LARRY, *suspiciously*: I wouldn't be surprised; I'll look around, okay?

CALVIN: . . . Go ahead, but I don't know what she'd be legitimately doing in here; you can see for yourself, it's all torn apart.

LARRY, *indicates off*: Okay?

CALVIN: But what would she be doing here?

LARRY, *shrugs—not saying*: You mind?

PETERS: Please let this man look for his wife, if he loves her he might hear her call and jump into the water and save us all!

CALVIN, *to Larry*: Well, okay, go ahead. But no fooling around back there, wife or no wife, got it? *Larry saunters off. Suggestive sneer*. You know that broad?

PETERS: Me? *Embarrassed*. I've never been in this neighborhood before. Not that I'm trying to deny her—she's very lovely, I say that openly.

CALVIN: She's juicy. A prime sirloin. A ripe pomegranate. A Spanish blood orange. An accordion pleated fuck.

PETERS, *recalling*: Yes, I know, but please; I hate talking like this about a woman behind her back . . .

CALVIN: What's the difference?—she'll never know.

PETERS: Why won't she? Oh! You mean . . . *Breaks off*. Oh . . .

CALVIN: All her underwear has been sold, stolen, or given away. And the phones don't ring that deep.

PETERS: Yes. I see. —And where she is . . . ?

CALVIN: She's nowhere.

PETERS: Yes, but is she older now? Has she grown into herself at last?

> *Cathy-May appears, in a middle-aged woman's coat.*
>
> Glasses?

She takes out a pair and puts them on.

Would it be a little less angry between us now that she's complete and her fires are banked?

She turns slowly to him. A calm, slow smile spreads across her face. He smiles back familiarly. They both rise.

Oh yes, darling, smile . . . do that!

Music: a Big Band—"Just One of Those Things." They dance close, the music speeds, they separate with hands clasped, and when he moves to draw her back she disappears into darkness.

CALVIN: Anyway, once upon a time this building was a bank.

PETERS, *desperation*: Oh don't, I beg you do not start explaining this building, will you? I'm too old for sad stories!

CALVIN: Why sad? I'm telling about a bank!

PETERS: Yes, but recalling a dead bank is painful. In those days . . . in those days . . . banks were built like fortresses, not salad bars. They had those gigantic, beautifully filigreed brass gates, and they did not go around shystering people, begging them to borrow money. No, they sat behind their little brass grills and *suspected* you. So you had to be upright, honest, and good or you were practically under arrest the minute you walked in from the street! And the clerks—what about their cute white blouses with those little rounded collars—you don't call it sad that all that is no more?

CALVIN: But think of the high-class ladies who used to come in to talk over their inheritance, and also, incidentally, to have a pee. And the dense perfumes those women wore! And the way they crossed and separated their legs!

PETERS, *clapping his ears shut*: Stop it, I beg you!

CALVIN: Well then don't go on saying you have no interest in this place! Sooner or later, as I said, these rich ladies, after spending the afternoon shopping or having coffee or tea . . .

PETERS: Or probably a sip of champagne . . .

CALVIN: Right. They had to pee, so they stopped at the bank . . . *Peters sighs openly, rests head tiredly on hand.* This is very important. —As early as the turn of the century—*Peters stretches out in the chair, arm over his eyes*—the women already held most of the money in this country. Probably all countries. Because they live longer. Because of the salads, in my opinion. Without women you could forget lettuce. *Peters sleeps.* Sir?

PETERS, *awakened*: What? —Oh no, I enjoy salads, my father was Italian. Especially arugula and even some nice fresh spinach. My mother was Spanish as a matter of fact. God knows what I am anymore.

CALVIN: I personally crossed the River Don with two hundred pounds of the family silver under my shirt, I was twelve and very brave, and the weight built up my legs.

PETERS: None of that is true, is it.

CALVIN: Well in a way . . .

PETERS: It's all right; it's just that you remind me of somebody who used to make up stories like that. But I can't remember who he was.

CALVIN: Then let's say it was me.

PETERS: Okay.

CALVIN: Look, you're not flying anywhere, are you?

PETERS, *sitting up*: Flying! They haven't let me into a cockpit for eighteen years! I had at least five years of flying left in me when they dumped me like a bag of shit! And the Democrats are no better!

CALVIN: Then let me finish; this could soothe you, it's very educational.

PETERS: Is this the subject?

CALVIN: Let me finish.

PETERS: No! I have a right to know the subject! Precious days are passing! Hours! I will need this time!

CALVIN: After the bank it was a library. The Morris family, the largest privately owned public library in America, I was told—the idea was to educate the working class.

PETERS: Whose idea? *Quickly amending*: Unless you're not supposed to tell.

CALVIN: Rich people; they had ideas like that in those ancient times. You know—the Frick Museum, the Astor Forty-second Street Library, Morgan, Rockefeller—

ADELE: Carnegie?

CALVIN, *reluctantly*: Carnegie is correct.

ADELE: The Frick has very nice toilets too . . . lots of marble.

CALVIN: Right. Those bastards stole but they gave back; now they steal and they fly the coop. And what's the answer?—religion; those old-time crooks were afraid of God. Anyway . . .

PETERS: Not that I love the rich; in fact, between their greed and stupidity they wrecked the greatest airline in the world.

CALVIN: Are you serious?

PETERS: Am I serious! —For generations my family were the only chiropractors in Naples! One of them is buried in the marble floor of the cathedral; yes, and a yard away from the king . . . who incidentally had terrible arthritis, so you'd think they'd have buried him in a warmer place.

CALVIN: I'm glad you're feeling better. Anyway, the Morris family died off and then you had the Depression and where you're sitting now was a cafeteria through the thirties. The famous Eagle Cafeteria, open twenty-four hours.

PETERS, *almost, not quite remembering*: Ah yes!—where I'm sitting now. Philosophical Marxist discussions going through the night. Leon Trotsky was supposed to have been a waiter, which I'd like to believe, but who ever heard of a waiter in a cafeteria? Anyway, the dates don't work out; by the thirties Trotsky was already the head of the Red Army.

CALVIN: So, that's more or less the history. Was that so bad?

PETERS: No-no, I'm beginning to enjoy it. Why don't you rest now, you must be pretty old, too, aren't you?

CALVIN: Me? I stopped getting old a long time ago.

Pause.

PETERS: . . . *Stopped getting old*, did you say?

Calvin is silent, motionless, stares front.

Something horrifying dawns on Peters. Ohhh . . . *Covers his face.* Oh my God, yes! —Then where is this? Say, you're not all dead here, are you?

CALVIN: Don't let it bother you; life is one to a customer and no returns if you're not satisfied.

PETERS: Listen, I really have to leave; I don't belong here! Just because a man decides to buy a pair of quadruple-A shoes . . . is that fair? *Struggling to rise.* I am leaving!

CALVIN: What will I do with your wife!

PETERS: My wife? Oh God, I don't know, just . . . just . . . kiss her and tell her . . . to . . . to . . . sadly die.

Peters lies back, falling asleep again.

CALVIN: —It's important to know that up until the Vietnam War the place was a real money-maker, but those little fellas in their black pajamas killed all the nightclubs.

PETERS: Vietnamese killed the nightclubs?

CALVIN: Destroyed all the optimism. And the pessimism. No optimism, no clubs; no pessimism, no clubs.

PETERS: Then what's left?

CALVIN: Vacillation, indecision, self-satisfaction, and religion—all enemies of nightclubs. In London, on the other hand . . .

PETERS: Wait! Before you get to London . . . could you give me an idea of the subject.

CALVIN, *angrily*: I'm explaining—I said I don't mind.

PETERS, *desperately*: I know you don't mind but I am not happy when I don't know even what the subject is! *Shouting*: Can't I have a hint! I ask you . . . a hint! A hint!

CALVIN, *frustrated*: For God's sake, man, they have clubs in London that go on for a hundred, two hundred years! Can you imagine anything like that here? Anyway, that's the history. *Peters stands up, peers out in silence.* What is this misery of yours?

PETERS, *sings softly*: "I've got a crush on you, sweetie-pie . . . " *Sings another line, then it dies.* You're not from Moscow, by any chance?

CALVIN: Odessa. Name a great violinist and you can bet he came from Odessa. I'm talking Mischa Elman, I'm talking Sasha Schneider, and Mischa Auer . . .

PETERS: Mischa Auer did not come from Odessa, but that's all right.

CALVIN: Well, the greatest olives in the world come from Odessa.

PETERS: It's all right, just go on lying, why shouldn't you? Can I believe that during the war I delivered our P-40 fighter planes to Odessa? I had some great hopes for Russia then, but terribly puritanical—I inadvertently learned you must never get into bed with two Russian women. And incidentally, every adventurous woman I met there carried a bathtub stopper in her purse.

CALVIN: I was never conservative enough to be a Communist. Seriously— soon as a girl joined the party she'd cross her unshaven legs and you might as well go to the library.

PETERS, *sits*: I think the subject is—humiliation. Give up the gin, then the vermouth, and end up having to explain to a Princeton class which war you were in. Talk about futility. Christ's sake, behind our propellers we were saving the world! And now, "Which war . . . " So you end up staring into space, with maybe some woman's wonderful ass floating by, or a banana split. Remember banana splits; four balls of ice cream on a sliced banana, covered with hand-whipped cream, chocolate sauce, and a maraschino cherry on top . . . for twenty-five cents? That, my friend, was a country, huh? I mean *that was a country*! —And who ever had a key to their front door?

CALVIN: Unheard of. You said you had a question?

PETERS: A question? Oh yes, yes . . . *Takes out a tabloid paper.* Why are you so untruthful? Are you trying to destroy the world?

CALVIN: Destroy the world!—I'm just talking!

PETERS, *springing up*: That's it!! That's what I think I've been trying to say since I walked in here! —"Just talking" is . . . is . . . There is no subject anymore! Turn on the radio, turn on the television, what is it—just talking! It can sink the ship! *Breaks off, bewildered. Gripping his forehead.* Something's happening to me.

CALVIN: Something like what?

PETERS, *holds up his paper as though just discovering it in his hand*: . . . I found this on the train. Amazing ads; pages and pages . . . look: breast augmentation, $4,400. And guess how much breast reduction is.

CALVIN: How much?

PETERS: Same price. That seem strange to you?

CALVIN: . . . No, seems about right.

PETERS: My father paid five thousand for the eight-room house our whole family lived in for thirty years! And a pair of tits is five thousand?

CALVIN: Yes. But houses are not as important; put a house on one magazine cover and a pair of tits on another, which one'll sell?

PETERS: And here we have penile augmentation for four thousand dollars and hymen reconstruction for two thousand. I can't imagine why hymens are cheaper.

CALVIN: There's not as much to a hymen. And they're nothing but trouble.

PETERS: Ah! But isn't it odd that penile augmentation costs four hundred dollars *less* than breast augmentation.

CALVIN: Well, I wouldn't take it personally.

PETERS, *turning pages*: But you have to, don't you?! I read these ads and I wonder—"Why don't I understand this?" You see? WHY DON'T I

UNDERSTAND THIS! *A sudden quizzical expression.* Please don't be offended, but are you asleep?

CALVIN: Me?

Larry reenters.

LARRY: Thanks. If you see her let me know, would you? I'm Larry, in Posito's near the corner.

CALVIN: What's she look like?

LARRY: What she looks like? . . . She looks perfect. With a white angora sweater. And pink plastic spike-heel shoes. A little on the pudgy side but not too fat . . . just . . . you know, perfect.

PETERS: What made you think she would be in here?

LARRY, *he shrugs*: She could be. *Nods.* She could be anywhere. The neighborhood's got a lot of Jews, you know. And Koreans now and Chinks.

PETERS, *in Italian*: E italiani.

LARRY: I'm Italian.

PETERS, *in Italian*: Certo; non sono sordo? *In English*: You know, Larry, Italians have always been a tolerant people.

LARRY: Fuck that, sir.

PETERS: Excuse me but fuck that sir is not a way to talk intelligently. Italian tolerance comes from the Roman era when so many different races flooded into the empire . . . Arabs, Gauls, Spanish, Nordics, Russians . . .

CALVIN: Lithuanians.

PETERS, *sharply*: Not Lithuanians.

LARRY: In March the niggers busted our window, robbed forty-one pairs of shoes.

CALVIN: I heard about that.

LARRY: You heard about it? We're fed up. Fed up!

ADELE: Us too.

LARRY: I didn't hear that. *Leaning angrily toward Peters.* Fuck the tolerance, sir, that's all over. Finished! Now we protect ourselves! *To Calvin*: Thanks. *To Peters*: Good luck with the shoes. By the way, her name is Cathy; Cathy-May.

PETERS: Yes, I know . . . But is she the same Cathy-May who used to be alive? —I don't mean "alive" in that sense, I mean . . .

Larry exits.

Peters leans his elbows on his thighs and holds his head in despair.

PETERS: It didn't used to get to me—but lately . . . almost every time I take my nap . . . it's like a long icicle slowly stabbing down into my balls.

CALVIN: When I lived in Florence . . .

PETERS, *open fury*: For God's sake, don't say one additional thing, will you?! *Eyes shut, hand on forehead.* I wonder if I'm eating too much for lunch. *Suddenly turning on Adele.* Excuse me, but may I ask what you are doing here?

ADELE, *puts on a nurse's cap*: Thank you for your interest. With God's permission I live here. I hope none of you has the idea of tearing this building down.

PETERS: Why are you putting on a nurse's cap?

ADELE: Could it be I'm a nurse? And before you mock me, be sure you don't get sick and need my services.

PETERS: I'm not at all mocking you, but a nurse sitting around drinking like that . . .

ADELE: You mock everyone! Look at how you mocked that handsome shoe salesman!

PETERS: But it's a mistake, she can't have married a lout like him! She's not really a common slut, you know—and she's . . . well I won't say she's . . . *A choked cry.* She's dead?

A *realization*: Or not? . . . Not? *High hope suddenly.* Please! Is she? What is her situation!

ADELE: I'm not a nurse; sorry.

PETERS: Then what are you doing with that cap!

ADELE: I just found it on the sidewalk outside the Lenox Hill Hospital, probably some nurse lost it jumping into a cab to meet her date, probably a well-to-do elderly man who was going to fix her up for life. But if I was a nurse would I have the right to sit around drinking booze?

PETERS: Of course, just as he . . . *To Calvin:* I've forgotten, what was your right . . . ?

Leonard and Rose enter. He carries a guitar case. He is holding her by the elbow.

LEONARD: Excuse me, can she sit down?

CALVIN: We're closed. We only open the second floor around six-thirty.

LEONARD: She's pregnant.

CALVIN: Oh! Well, have a chair. They've all been re-glued. *Leonard and Calvin quickly seat her.*

ROSE, *sitting*: Don't worry, I'm not having it, I just walked too much.

CALVIN: Relax, we're all on the side of the pregnant woman. *Asking*: You're not the father.

LEONARD: How'd you know!

CALVIN: What's to know?—nobody's the father anymore. *To Peters*: So that's the history. *To Rose*: If you need the powder room, it's straight that way.

ROSE: Thank you, I will in a minute.

LEONARD: I've passed this place a hundred times and never knew it was a nightclub . . . it is, isn't it?

CALVIN: That's our style, or it was—no sign outside, no advertising; people either want to be here or they don't. Most didn't, obviously. *To Peters*: I'll be in my office if your wife is interested. *Slows beside Rose.* I hope you know the father.

ROSE: Of course I know the father!

PETERS: Of course!

CALVIN: Just kidding—it's only that they used to say—I'm talking forty, fifty years ago—"A man who betrays his wife will betray his country."

PETERS, *simultaneously*: ". . . Will betray his country."

CALVIN: I figured you knew that saying.

PETERS: Haven't heard it in fifty years, and it's still idiotic. What has screwing a woman got to do with betraying your country?

CALVIN: Nothing, but nobody even *says* things like that anymore. *To Rose.* Morals count, you know, even if you just say them. *Making to leave.* Excuse me, Professor.

PETERS: How did you know I was a professor?

CALVIN: What else could you be? —I can smell the chalk. *Touching his temple.* Nobody forgets chalk.

> He exits. Peters stares after him, perplexed, deeply curious. Silence. Rose takes out a bottle of Evian and drinks. Finally . . .

PETERS: How old are you people now, if you don't mind my asking?

LEONARD: I'm twenty-seven.

ROSE: Twenty-eight now.

ADELE, *unasked*: Thirty-four.

PETERS: And you're all . . . *Embarrassed chuckle.* I feel a little funny asking, but . . . you're all awake, aren't you.

ROSE: Awake?

PETERS: Forget it. Maybe it's that I don't see many young people anymore, so it's hard to guess their ages. . . . To me, everybody looks about twenty-two. Do you find it hard to follow what people are saying?

LEONARD: Well . . . not really. *To Rose:* Do we? *Before she can answer:* Except she never listens anyway.

ROSE: I do listen, but I have my own thoughts and it's hard to listen while I'm thinking.

PETERS: Let me put it another way—do you find you get sleepy after lunch, or when do you start?

ADELE: Getting sleepy? The minute I wake up.

PETERS: It struck me the other day that everyone I know is sleepy—I wonder if it's something about the times.

ROSE: Maybe you're low on potassium. You should eat bananas.

PETERS: I do eat two or three a week for breakfast. Actually I rather like bananas.

ROSE: You should try to love them. Motivation is important in the diet; bananas are there to be loved. Try eating five a week. Seven or eight would be even better. Or ten.

PETERS: Isn't that quite a lot of bananas?

ROSE, *raises one leg in a stretch*: You only have enough bananas when one more would make you want to throw up. I know about such things, I'm a dancer, dancers need trace elements for the knees.

PETERS: *Trace elements for the knees?*

ROSE: They're tiny but important.

PETERS, *nods with a certain alarm: Trace elements for the knees?* You see, this is what I mean; when I was young no human being from one end of the United States to the other would have uttered that sentence. For example, my father and grandfather—I don't recall them ever in the presence of a banana. And they lived into their nineties.

ADELE: Same thing with my mother; she can gross down two, three at a time, a woman over ninety and no bigger than a thimble and still driving an eight-cylinder Buick loaded with extras—air bags, defrosting side mirrors, tinted glass . . . *Continues mouthing.*

PETERS: In fact, nobody ate bananas when I was young. You make me wonder how we managed.

ADELE: . . . Fifteen-inch wheels, leather trim, non-skid brakes, moon roof, lighted trunk . . . *Continues mouthing.*

ROSE: People had different thoughts then, and there was nothing around to get them so exhausted.

ADELE: Upholstered armrest, front and rear utility lights, metallic paint . . . V6, three-and-a-half-liter engine, automatic transmission . . . *Goes on mouthing.*

PETERS, *nods in silence for a moment*: Please forgive my curiosity, but does this conversation revolve around some . . . subject that I am unaware of?

LEONARD: A subject? I don't think so . . . *To Rose*: Does it?

ROSE: What? Excuse me, I was thinking of something.

LEONARD: You know, darling, it's not very polite to drop out of a conversation without telling anybody.

PETERS: . . . Unless we don't need a subject anymore . . . *They look at him blankly.* I mean do you people ever wonder . . . as you're getting into bed, what you were talking about all day?

LEONARD: I don't think so. *To Rose*: Do we?

ROSE: When we're getting into *bed*?

PETERS: Or for example, I do enjoy the movies, but every so often I wonder, "What was the *subject* of the picture?"

ROSE: The subject of a *picture*?

PETERS: I remember my mother—washing machines were rather rare in those times—and she'd have the maid boil the sheets and the laundry on the stove and lug it all up to the roof of the apartment house to dry. Have you ever heard of that?

ROSE: Boiling sheets?

LEONARD: On a gas stove? That's a fire hazard!

ROSE: Water is fireproof, Leonard.

PETERS, *forcing concentration; peering*: No-no, I think what I'm trying to . . . to . . . find my connection with is a . . . what's the word . . .

continuity . . . yes, with the past, perhaps . . . in the hope of finding a . . . yes, a subject. That's the idea, I think, but I'm exhausted . . .

ROSE: Boiling sheets?

LEONARD: But that's not really a *subject*.

ROSE: Well then, going up to the roof?

PETERS: That's it! Yes! Maybe!

ROSE: But wouldn't wet sheets weigh a ton?

PETERS: Right! And nobody would do that anymore! So maybe that's a real subject, because one thing reveals another. What else about that?

ROSE: Maybe that's why you need more bananas now.

PETERS, *to Leonard*: Say now! She makes a lot of sense! You've relieved me a lot.

ROSE: Really? Why?

PETERS: Because you have added to what I said! Rather than exhausting me by starting a whole new unrelated conversation. That's really glorious! Thank you so much. *Tears flow, he wipes them.*

ROSE: Don't be upset.

PETERS: It's just that when you've flown into hundreds of gorgeous sunsets, you want them to go on forever and ever . . . and hold off the darkness . . .

> *The trumpet plays a loud blast of "My Blue Heaven." His anxiety soars.*
>
> How like sex the trumpet is—it always leaves you kind of sad when it's finished. You know, every spring . . . every spring the Polish maids would carry our carpets up to the roof and hang them out on wires, and they'd beat them for hours until their blouses were dark with sweat. When April came and early May, hundreds of rooftops all over the city had those big fair-haired Polish girls walloping clouds of carpet dust to drift out over the avenues.

ROSE: Was this before vacuum cleaners?

PETERS, *frowning, disturbed, he pants*: Oh, God, imagine dying in the midst of a conversation about vacuum cleaners!

LEONARD, *passionately*: But would it be any better talking about differential calculus? The thing is not to be afraid . . .

ROSE, *covers his hand*: That's right, dear.

PETERS: But you're so young—how can you know!

LEONARD: We're afraid.

PETERS: Oh, good, then we can talk without my risking your disdain—yes, we did have a vacuum cleaner; but it screamed like a coal truck and it frightened the Polish girls. Actually, though, I think it was virtue that made people go lugging those carpets up to the roof. Discomfort was righteous in America; when Teddy Roosevelt went sweating through the jungle hunting tigers he wore a tie; Woodrow Wilson, Warren Harding, Calvin Coolidge, Herbert Hoover—those men went fishing in the same itchy dark suits they wore at their inaugurations; they waded into wild rivers wearing cuff links, stiff collars, and black high-topped shoes. The President of the United States was above all morally righteous, you see, rather than just entertaining. Even after President Harding was exposed as the father of an illegitimate daughter he continued to take precisely the same virtuous photographs. And Grover Cleveland likewise. And for that matter, George Washington was in and out of so many beds they finally called him the father of his country. But no one ever questioned his dignity, you see. Or his virtue. And he was never exhausted. I can't remember my point.

ROSE: I definitely think something very tiring is in the air now.

LEONARD: It's lead. *All turn to him.* It's a proven fact, there's more lead than ever in the air.

PETERS: But we seem to be living longer than ever.

LEONARD: But in a poisoned condition.

ROSE: Like you being so sleepy. You might live to a hundred, but half asleep.

LEONARD: You know?—I just realized—I've been getting up later and later in the mornings.

ROSE: Maybe you're just a teeny bit depressed, Leonard. *She kisses his cheek lightly.*

ADELE: Depression'll do it every time.

LEONARD: Like do you find you're a little more slow-witted than you used to be?

ADELE: You can count me in there.

PETERS: Definitely, yes. But couldn't it be this constant changing of the subject that's wearing out our brains?

LEONARD, *to Rose, indicating Peters*: Sounds like lead. You know the Romans used lead pipes in their water systems and also wine storage, and one emperor after another was nutty as a fruitcake.

ROSE: And lots of subnormal children.

LEONARD: The Teutonic tribes, on the other hand . . .

PETERS, *gripping his forehead*: Would you mind not talking about the Teutonic tribes?

LEONARD: It's just that they drank out of lakes and clear streams . . .

PETERS: Yes, I know, but I am much older than I look and there is just so much irrelevant information that I am able to . . .

LEONARD: But everything is relevant! If you don't mind my saying it, that's what you don't seem to understand and what is making you rather pessimistic. You are trying to pick and choose what is important, sir, like a batter waiting for a ball he can hit. But what if you have to happily swing at everything they throw at you? The fact is—those Germanic tribes were drinking fresh water and came down and just wiped out the Roman Empire! Which was drinking wine loaded with lead! I think that's kind of relevant, isn't it? Incidentally, we never picked up the laundry. Or maybe wait till tomorrow?

ROSE: There's still time. Where'd he say that powder room was?

PETERS: That way, I believe, in the back.

    Rose exits.

LEONARD, *calling after her*: Maybe I should try to pick it up now? *To Peters.* I just hate leaving laundry overnight. On the other hand, I've never lost any. Although I did get a wrong shirt once. *Getting up to leave.* Maybe tell her I left, would you? —Well, never mind, I'll wait. *Sits again.* Except one of those shirts belongs to my brother, it's very expensive. I'd better go. *Stands.* . . . Well, I'll wait, to hell with it, he's got fifty shirts. *Sits. Pause.*

PETERS: You may have read the Babylonian myth explaining why there are so many different languages in the world?

LEONARD: No.

PETERS: God was extremely annoyed by the racket in the streets, so he invented all the different languages to keep people from talking to each other so much.

LEONARD: That's pretty funny.

PETERS: Are you in business?

LEONARD: No, I'm a composer. And investor.

ADELE: You may as well ask why I started drinking.

PETERS, *a bare glance at Adele*: Then what are you doing here?

LEONARD: My friend had to urinate.

PETERS: Of course! —My God, I think I'm just swinging at random from limb to limb.

LEONARD: Are you in business?

PETERS: No, I flew for Pan Am for many years, then some lecturing at Princeton till I retired.

LEONARD: May I ask your subject?

PETERS: Oh, mysterious things—like the suicidal impulse in large corporations. Are you a college man?

LEONARD: Harvard, yes.

PETERS: Well, that's not a bad school. Incidentally, are you asleep? I only ask because it just occurs to me that I may be awake. *Chuckles*. . . . Horrible as that would be. But that's impossible, isn't it—a person awake can't talk to one who's asleep. You are, aren't you—asleep? . . . But that's not right either, is it; two sleeping people can't converse can they. *Chuckles*. You can't share sleep, can you. Any more than death, right? So . . . I'm asleep. But you— what's your . . . you know . . . situation? What bothers me is that—look at these shoes; they're obviously brand-new, right? *Leonard looks at them*. So all this must be happening, right? I didn't produce these shoes out of thin air, correct? Look at the soles . . . not even soiled. *Leonard looks at soles, but almost de-animatedly, totally uninterested*. And I couldn't have bought them in my sleep, could I. You walk into a store with your eyes closed they're not going to let you walk out with a new pair of shoes. . . . What's begun to haunt me is that next to nothing I have believed has turned out to be true. *Breaks off in a surge of fear*. IF SHE DOESN'T COME, DOES IT MEAN I CAN'T LEAVE?! WHERE IS MY POOR GOD-DAMNED WIFE!

> He is on the verge of weeping. The piano plays loud and fast,
> for a moment, "If You Knew Suzie" and stops.

LEONARD: Is she ill?

PETERS: We are both ill; we are sick of each other. *Shouts*: Her imagination is destroying me! *Moment*. We're happy. *Takes a few deep breaths*. —I'm much obliged to you for listening. Are you Jewish?

LEONARD: Yes.

PETERS: I thought so; Jews and Italians are happy to allow a person to mourn.

ADELE: Yes, we cry them into the grave.

PETERS: Tell me . . . this Calvin guy here . . . the owner or manager or whatever he is . . . Did you notice anything odd about his eyes?

LEONARD: His eyes? *A moment; thinks.* Say now . . . yes. It's almost like . . . I can't describe it, almost like there's nothing in his eye sockets. No!—it's that his eyes . . . can it be they have no color? *Peters stares, silent.* Is that what you mean? *Peters says nothing.* What is it, some disease?

PETERS, *motionless*: He's my brother.

LEONARD: Your brother! Did you know he was here?

PETERS: Oh no, no, it just came to me. *Pause.* He's dead. *Leonard astonished.* Drowned almost twenty years ago.

LEONARD: You mean he's *like* your brother.

PETERS, *shakes his head*: No. *Leonard is silent, terrified.* His eyes . . . they're almost translucent, like jellyfish; the sea in winter; the insides of oyster shells . . .

LEONARD: Well, I . . . I don't know what to say . . . Does he know you're his brother?

PETERS: I'm not sure. It's hard to know how much the dead remember, isn't it . . . But that's not quite right . . . *Stares in silence, smiles now.*

LEONARD: I understand.

PETERS: . . . You see, he was always a great kidder and practical joker. Once he was driving us down the Rocky Mountains and pretended the brakes had failed. Darn near a hundred miles an hour and heading straight for the rail when he pretended the brakes came back. A cruel streak, but full of life.

LEONARD: You mean he pretended to drown, as a joke?

PETERS: I'm wondering that. He was capable of anything. But that can't be right, we were all at his funeral. —I'm wondering if my wife got lost. Could you be a good fellow and take a look outside? She's very short . . . although you might not agree . . .

LEONARD, *gets up*: What's her name?

PETERS: Her name? *Touches his head.* I'm so embarrassed.

LEONARD: Well it doesn't matter . . .

PETERS: Oh it does, it does! —What I do in these circumstances is start with *A* and go down the alphabet. Anna, Annabella, Augusta, Bernice, Beatrice . . .

LEONARD: Well what's your name . . . just so I can approach her. *Peters stares in deepening anxiety.* It's all right, I'll just look for a short woman . . .

PETERS: It's not all right! *Suddenly.* Charlotte! Charlotte Peters! —My God this is terrible.

LEONARD: No-no, maybe I shouldn't have asked . . .

PETERS: This is the worst I've had. It's not Alzheimer's, I've been examined . . . I wonder if it's just a case of not wanting to be around anymore.

LEONARD: I'd look into lead.

PETERS: Oh, my boy, I wish it were lead, but in the end I'm afraid one arrives at a sort of terminal indifference, and there is more suspense in the bowel movement than a presidential election.

LEONARD: But I often forget things . . . In fact, as a child I used to wonder why we needed to remember at all. Wouldn't it be wonderful if we got up in the morning and everyone was a complete stranger?

PETERS: Are your parents divorced?

LEONARD: Yes, that's where I got the idea. Do you think things are worse than years ago? —Although I'm glad there's penicillin.

PETERS: Penicillin is definitely better, yes, but things have been getting worse since Eden; it's not lead, however.

LEONARD: What then?

PETERS: Washington, Jefferson . . . most of the founding fathers were all Deists, you know; they believed that God had wound up the world like a clock and then disappeared. We are unwinding now, the ticks are further and further apart. So instead of tick-tick-tick-tick-tick we've got tick—*pause*—tick—*pause*—tick. And we get bored between ticks, and boredom is a form of dying, and dying, needless to say, takes an awful lot out of a person.

LEONARD: But so many things are happening.

PETERS: But not the main thing. The main thing is emphatically not happening at all and probably never will again.

LEONARD: And what is that?

PETERS: Redemption.

LEONARD: I've never really understood that word.

PETERS: That's all right, no one understands love either, but look how we long for it.

LEONARD: Then you believe in God?

PETERS: I'm quite sure I do, yes.

LEONARD: What would you say God is? Or is that too definite?

PETERS: Not at all—God is precisely what is not there when you need him. And what work of beauty have you created this week?

LEONARD: I haven't done much this week.

PETERS: Well, I suppose that can happen in the creative life.

LEONARD: I'm not having much of a creative life these days.

PETERS: Lover trouble?

LEONARD: As a matter of fact, I recently split up with somebody.

PETERS: Too bad. Boy or girl?

LEONARD: Girl.

PETERS: Well, cheer up and pray that you run into a girl who makes you imagine you've forgotten the other fifty million single American women walking around loose. —Charlotte! Here I am!

He has spotted his wife. She enters, looking all around.

CHARLOTTE: For Christ's sake.

PETERS: Yes, it's pretty awful.

CHARLOTTE: Awful!—it's marvelous! Look at those moldings, look at that ceiling, look at these floors. Gimme a break, this is heaven! *Rose enters.* And who is this lovely young pregnant woman?

Rose looks at Charlotte and laughs.

LEONARD: She's not so short.

CHARLOTTE, *to Peters*: What is this again?

PETERS, *covering his eyes*: I'm terribly sorry, I had a vision of you as being quite . . .

CHARLOTTE: He said I was *short*?

LEONARD, *to Peters*: I'm awfully sorry! *To Charlotte*: He asked me to go out and look for you and he couldn't think of your name, so he . . .

CHARLOTTE, *laughing angrily, to Peters*: Couldn't think of my *name!*

LEONARD, *tortured*: Only for a minute!

CHARLOTTE: In my opinion it's his flying for three solid years in World War II; the Essex Class Carrier had a very short flight deck and it blew his nerves. *To Peters*: I'll bet something here reminded you of the war, didn't it.

PETERS: . . . as a matter of fact . . . *Looking around.* . . . I think I said this place could use a small bomb.

CHARLOTTE: There you go. —Where's this Mister Calvin?

PETERS: He said he'd be in his office if you were interested. He said you should see the powder room.

CHARLOTTE: Gimme a break—the *powder* room?

ROSE: It's glorious. I was just in there—I've never been like . . . kissed by a room, or felt such good-hearted *safety*, or like a room was hugging me. It's like you suddenly didn't have to . . . like defend yourself. It's a sort of *courteous* room, you know? I mean the energy I use up just keeping people from . . . *bothering* me, you know what I mean?

CHARLOTTE: I know exactly what you mean, I'm a decorator.

LEONARD: Really!—we were just thinking of calling a decorator for her apartment.

ROSE: But it's so tiny . . . practically a closet.

PETERS: It doesn't matter, if it's vertical she'll happily decorate it.

CHARLOTTE: You're not the father?

PETERS: They're only friends. He just brought her in here to pee.

CHARLOTTE: He did? Well, that is one of the most encouraging things I've heard in I don't know how long. —I must have a look at this powder room.

ROSE: It's straight that way. Watch out for the lumber on the floor.

CHARLOTTE: I know how you feel, we have four daughters. All four are flight attendants on major airlines.

PETERS, *to Leonard*: I truly wonder whether the country could be saved if people could stay on the same subject for more than twenty seconds.

CHARLOTTE: So if you're planning on flying anywhere let us know and one of the girls might be able to look after you. Now let's see this famous powder room. *She exits.*

ROSE: Actually, I was thinking of flying to Oregon to see a friend; maybe I could have one of your daughters' phone numbers.

PETERS, *chuckling*: I'm afraid the girls are not connected to the airlines.

LEONARD: But didn't she say . . . ?

PETERS: Sometimes she is simply overwhelmed by a burst of comprehensive enthusiasm. A little like heels and skirts—one year high, next year low. Women have visions. Now, she has a vision of our four young women in those snug uniforms and cute little hats, feeding the multitudes. She's a very emotional woman, as you know by now, and she means no harm, but she has powerful longings.

LEONARD, *to Rose*: That's really weird.

ROSE: I don't know. I mean here I'm carrying around this, I assume, baby which could end up not even liking me . . .

LEONARD: Rose, how can you say a thing like that?

ROSE: But how many of our friends really like their parents?

LEONARD: Parents!

ROSE: Yes! I'm going to be a *parent*, Leonard.

LEONARD: Oh, right. *Stares, shaking his head in amazement.* This is turning out to be a really strange day. *Charlotte enters, inspired, amazed.*

CHARLOTTE: Wow. Did you see it?

PETERS: I don't normally go into powder rooms.

CHARLOTTE, *pointing off imperiously*: Go. GO!

PETERS: I absolutely refuse! I have no conceivable interest in . . .

CHARLOTTE: Gimme a break, Harry, I insist you see that powder room! Now will you or won't you!

PETERS, *rising*: But I have no viewpoint toward powder rooms!

CHARLOTTE: Well how about participating for once *without* a viewpoint! I mean gimme a break, Harry, be human, this place is fantastic!

PETERS, *peering into air*: I simply don't understand anything anymore. When I woke up this morning, I did not plan to shop for shoes, and I certainly did not expect to end the day inspecting a ladies' bathroom. *To Leonard*: Would you mind? —I'd like another man with me.

CHARLOTTE: Oh, Harry darling, aren't you feeling well?

PETERS: Let me put it this way . . . *He begins to weep.* Are you feeling well, Charlotte?

CHARLOTTE: I'm feeling wonderful.

PETERS: I'm so glad for you. *To Rose.* She's everybody's mother . . . as I'm sure you realize, and her happiness—*sighs*—is inexhaustible. *Peters turns and goes, taking out a handkerchief as he exits.*

LEONARD, *as he goes*: I'm worried about my brother's shirt.

ROSE: Leonard please, try to have some faith, it's only away in the laundry for the afternoon. Maybe think of it like a vacation it's on. *Leonard exits following Peters.*

CHARLOTTE: How far along?

ROSE: Six weeks, I think.

CHARLOTTE: Did you want it or . . . ?

ROSE, *shrugs*: It wants me, I know that much.

CHARLOTTE: You sound alone.

ROSE: I am, I guess. He can't quite make up his mind.

CHARLOTTE: Men! If they were in charge of the sun it would go up and down every ten minutes. What happened!—a good man is so hard to find anymore.

ROSE: My friend Leonard thinks it's something in the water.

CHARLOTTE: He's not the father?

ROSE: Sometimes he seems to think he is. But sometimes he doesn't.

CHARLOTTE: What stories the world is full of! So are you telling him he is or he isn't?

ROSE: I want to see what it looks like first.

CHARLOTTE: Why! Tell him it's his and you can change your mind later.

ROSE: But we always end up fighting like brother and sister. And that can't be right, can it.

CHARLOTTE: You young people—why are you always digging away at each other for the truth? We never dreamed of telling the truth to a husband and the result was practically no divorces. —Well, thank God for the airlines! You know, if something drops on the uniform the company pays the cleaning.

ROSE, *near tears*: How can you be so happy!—you're wonderful!

CHARLOTTE: I can't help myself—I've been happy since I was a baby and I never changed. It irritates my husband but what can I do? —First thing in the morning I open my eyes and I'm so overjoyed I could eat the whole world for breakfast. Listen, I like your Leonard; I would let him be the father.

ROSE: It's strange, I think I feel older than you.

CHARLOTTE: Italians love to cook, that's my salvation. And I'm in pretty fair shape—I used to dance, you know.

ROSE: Professionally?

CHARLOTTE: Radio City Rockettes nine years. We met in the alley of the theater. He was a Navy pilot, stage-door Johnnie, he'd come back from bombing Asia and go banging through that chorus line . . . eighteen girls on a thirty-day leave! But a delight, a dee-light! Funny? Gimme a break, the man was sheer humongous wit. I weighed one-eighteen those days, till the bread did me in. I lost twelve pounds last year but who's kidding who, I'm still everybody's mother. *Leonard and Peters enter; rather expressionless, even solemn looks.*

> Well? *The men glance uneasily at each other.* So? *They still hesitate.*

LEONARD: Well it's a washroom, right?

CHARLOTTE: A *washroom!*

PETERS: Where you wash up.

CHARLOTTE: Mama mia . . . *To Rose:* They don't see anything! He walks around the house like a blind man— "Where's my glasses? Where's my suspenders? Where's my bathrobe?"

ROSE: By the way, how did you know I was pregnant?

CHARLOTTE: I'm part Gypsy.

LEONARD, *to Peters:* Is that true? *Peters sighs and looks away.*

CHARLOTTE: What does he know? To him nothing is true unless you can hammer it, fuck it, or fly it around. —Gypsy women, darling, can tell you're pregnant just by looking into your eyes. Not only that, but I can tell you it's a girl.

PETERS: Now how could you know *that*, for God's sake?

CHARLOTTE: Because the air is full of *things! Gesturing between Rose and herself.* And we are looking at each other through the air, aren't we?

PETERS: I feel I have lived my life and I eagerly look forward to a warm oblivion.

LEONARD: May I ask whether you intend to start a new night-club or is this a . . . ?

CHARLOTTE: Depends; if this man's deal is good I would certainly consider a new club . . . why?

LEONARD: I'm not trying to pressure you but if it's going to be a club I'd like to talk to you about the music.

ROSE: He has a great little band. She danced in Radio City.

LEONARD: Really, a Rockette? *To Peters*: Is that true?

CHARLOTTE: Why do you keep asking him if it's true! You think I'm off my nut, or something?

LEONARD: Oh no-no, please don't think I . . .

ROSE: No-no! He didn't mean anything like that . . .

CHARLOTTE, *to Peters*: Well aren't you going to answer him?

PETERS, *shuts his eyes, sighs, then* . . . : Yes, it's true.

CHARLOTTE: Well I'll go find this Calvin and see what kind of deal he has in mind. Tell them your philosophy. *Charlotte exits.*

LEONARD: We should really pick up the laundry . . .

ROSE: Your philosophy?

PETERS: No-no, it was only a dream I had many years ago. After my wing was destroyed.

ROSE: I love dreams, could you tell it?

PETERS: I'm afraid I have to rest now. Why don't we all?

ROSE: I'd love to, frankly. What was your dream?

LEONARD: Shouldn't I pick up the laundry?

ROSE: Try to rest, Leonard.

LEONARD: Should you be on the floor?

ROSE: It's okay.

LEONARD: Should I look for a pillow?

ROSE: You've got to try to have a little confidence, Leonard.

LEONARD, *self-blame*: I know.

ROSE: I mean try to assume that whatever is going on out there will go on without us for a while. So you might as well rest.

ADELE: This is my kinda thing, I tell ya. It's been going on without me for a long, long time.

ROSE: All right then . . . *She stretches her legs. All lean back and close their eyes. Pause.* I don't think you're resting, are you?

LEONARD: I want to be the father, Rose.

ROSE: We'll see. I don't like deciding right now.

LEONARD: But when you do, will you think of me?

ROSE: Of course. *Slight pause.* If not, you could be its brother.

LEONARD: A brother twenty-eight years older?

ROSE: Well, an older brother. It happens.

ADELE: Appearance is everything; my older sister's got those hips, those eyes, and those ambitious legs—the girl could raise a man from the dead just by stepping over his grave. And now she's down Wall Street with her own office at Bear Stearns.

PETERS: I dreamed of another planet; it was very beautiful—the air was rose, the ground was beige, the water was green, the sky was the fairest blue. And the people were full of affection and respect, and then suddenly they grabbed a few defectives and flung them into space.

LEONARD: Why were they defective?

PETERS: They were full of avarice and greed. And they broke into thousands of pieces and fell to earth, and it is from their seed that we all descend.

LEONARD: Well that's very strange . . . I mean we usually assume that man is born good . . .

PETERS: Not if you look sharply at the average baby.

ROSE, *hand on her belly*: How can you say that?

PETERS: If a baby had the strength, wouldn't he knock you down to get to a tit? Has a baby a conscience? If he could tear buildings apart to get to a suck, what would stop him? We tolerate babies only because they are helpless, but the alpha and omega of their real nature is a five-letter word, g-r-e-e-d. The rest is gossip.

> *Calvin enters with Charlotte, both studying papers of figures. She sits down absorbed in papers, and working a pocket calculator.*

CALVIN, *absorbed in his figures*: Harry.

PETERS: Yes? *Calvin still doesn't look up.* . . . Did you call me Harry?

CALVIN, *surprised at himself*: What?

PETERS: Charley . . . come on . . . *Calvin stares at him as he approaches.* It's me! *Calvin stares front.* Mother and Dad . . . remember Mother and Dad? Fishing in Sheepshead Bay? The fluke? . . . I know!—the bluefish, when you gutted that big bluefish and brought it over to . . . what was her name!—Marcia . . . yes, Marcia Levine!

CALVIN: Marcia Levine?

PETERS: In that shingle house on the corner! You said she had . . . *To the others*: Excuse me, please— *To Calvin*: . . . the best ass on the East Coast.

CALVIN, *very doubtfully, striving to recall*: Marcia *Levine*?

PETERS: For God's sake, Calvin, you'd be in there whole *days* with her! *Frantically—to all*. Am I the only one who remembers anything? I'm going to fall off the earth! *Furiously to Calvin*: For God's sake, man, you'd lie on your bed looking up at the ceiling endlessly repeating, like a prayer, "Marcia Levine's ass, Marcia Levine's ass . . . Marcia Levine has the most beautiful ass in America!"

CALVIN: I don't remember her . . .

PETERS, *laughing happily*: You have to step out of this . . . this forgetfulness, Calvin! It's a terrible, terrible thing to forget Marcia Levine! . . . Listen, you do know I'm Harry, don't you?

CALVIN, *a remoteness coming over him*: You're mistaking me for somebody else.

PETERS: No! Charley, I will not accept that! Charley? Please . . . if you forget me . . . don't you see? If you forget me—who . . . *With a desperate cry*. Who the hell am I! Charley, save me! *Calvin is staring front, eyes dead. Peters roars in terror into his face*. Man . . . wake up your dead eyes! *Calvin doesn't move. A moment*. . . . Sorry for troubling you. *Closes his eyes in pain; slumps down on a seat. Pause*. God, if no one remembers what I remember . . . if no one remembers what I . . .

> *Cathy-May enters. She is in a tight white miniskirt, transparent blouse, carries a white purse and a brown shopping bag . . . and wears a dog collar.*

> Why are you wearing a dog collar?

CATHY-MAY: Case I get lost, he said.

PETERS: Dear . . . listen . . . could I ask you . . . ?

CATHY-MAY: Don't ask me too much, I might not be here by the end.

PETERS: Could I just listen to you?

CATHY-MAY: But don't take too long. And please don't hurt me. *He presses his ear to her breast. She breathes in deeply, and exhales*. You were loved, Harry. But I'm very tired.

PETERS: Please; more . . . *She inhales again*. Yes! More! *She does it again*. Oh, glorious . . . to hear a woman's deep breathing again! *She breathes in and out again and again, her breaths coming faster and faster . . . and now he is breathing with her*. Oh Cathy-May, Cathy-May, Cathy-May . . . !

> *Larry enters, walks over to her and rips the shopping bag out of her hand, turns it over—it is empty.*

LARRY: This is shopping? Where's the stuff, left it on the counter again? *Feels her for panties.* And where's your underwear? *To Peters:* And this woman votes! Walks around bareass on New York streets? Bends over in the fruit market to test tomatoes in front of *Koreans?*—a married woman? What am I a fuckin' ox, I don't have feelings? Take her to a counselor and I'm behind her on the stairs and she's wearing no panties!—for a conference with a *counselor?* Meantime I'm overdue for a heart operation, so I'm not supposed to be stressed! Can you believe a fucking doctor telling me not to be stressed in the City of New York? And that idiot is going to operate on me!—Look at this! *Shaking the bag.* Look at this! . . . Where's your underwear? You belong to me or not? I said you belong to me or not! Where is your underwear, stupid!! *With a sweeping gesture he sends her onto her back, legs in the air, and looks under her skirt; she is struggling ineffectually to free herself.* You see underwear, Mister? Look, everybody! *He is trying to spread her legs apart.* Forget your shoes and take a look at this! How can this belong to anybody! —Look at it!

CATHY-MAY: You were loved, Harry!

LARRY, *struggling with her legs:* Show them, show them! Look at this, Professor!

> *Peters, crying out, tries to intervene but the horror of it sends him away, rushing about, covering his eyes and yelling.*

PETERS: Nonononono!

LARRY, *to Peters:* What are you scared of, come here and open your eyes!

> *The struggle stops; Larry is kneeling beside Cathy-May now, kissing her gently. She has become inert. Peters comes, bends, and presses his ear to her breast.*

LEONARD: What do you hear?

PETERS: Footsteps. And darkness. Oh, how terrible to go into that darkness alone, alone! *Cathy-May emits one last exhale. Peters kisses his finger and touches it to her mouth.*

CATHY-MAY: C-aaaaaaahh! *And then she is still.*

ADELE: I was a substitute teacher for six years in Weehauken New Jersey. But little by little I came to realize that I am a brokenhearted person. That's all there was to it—I'm brokenhearted. Always was and would always be. At the same time I am often full of hope . . . that for no particular reason I will wake up one morning and find that my sorrow has left me, just walked away, quiet as a pussy cat in the middle of the night. I know it can happen . . . *She picks up her mirror and examines her face.* I know it. I know it.

PETERS, *slight pause*: —Rest now. All rest. Quietly, please. Quietly rest. While we think of the subject. While breath still comes blessedly clear. While we learn to be brave.

> *Rose and Leonard sit on either side of Peters. Farther upstage, frozen in time, Larry is looking into the empty shopping bag, Charlotte is working her calculator, Calvin is staring into space, Adele is examining her face in her mirror, turning from side to side.*
>
> *Light begins to die on these. Rose opens her eyes. Light dies on Leonard now, and only Rose and Peters are illuminated.*

ROSE: Papa?

PETERS, *opens his eyes, listens*: Yes?

ROSE: Please stay.

PETERS, *straight ahead*: I'm trying!

ROSE: I love you, Papa.

PETERS: I'm trying as hard as I can. I love you, darling. I wonder . . . could that be the subject!

> *For a moment he is alone in light. It snaps out.*

RESURRECTION BLUES

A PROLOGUE AND TWO ACTS

2002

Characters

GENERAL FELIX BARRIAUX, *chief of state*
HENRI SCHULTZ, *his cousin*
EMILY SHAPIRO, *a film director*
SKIP L. CHEESEBORO, *an account executive*
PHIL, *a cameraman*
SARAH, *a soundwoman*
POLICE CAPTAIN
JEANINE, *Schultz's daughter*
STANLEY, *a disciple*
SOLDIERS, WAITERS, PASSERSBY, PEASANTS

Place
Various locations in a far away country

PROLOGUE

Dark stage. Light finds Jeanine in wheelchair; she is wrapped in bandages, one leg straight out. She addresses the audience.

JEANINE: Nothing to be alarmed about. I finally decided, one morning, to jump out my window. In this country even a successful suicide is difficult. I seem to be faintly happy that I failed, although god knows why. But of course you can be happy about the strangest things . . . I did not expect failure in my life. I failed as a revolutionary . . . and come to think of it, even as a dope addict—one day the pleasure simply disappeared, along with my husband. We so badly need a revolution here. But that's another story. I refuse to lament. Oddly, in fact, I feel rather cheerful about it all, in a remote way, now that I died, or almost, and have my life again. The pain is something else, but you can't have everything.

Going out the window was a very interesting experience. I can remember passing the third floor on my way down and the glorious sensation of release. Like when I was a student at Barnard and went to Coney Island one Sunday and took that ride on the loop-the-loop and the big drop when you think it won't ever come up again. This time it didn't and I had joined the air, I felt transparent, and I saw so sharply, like a condor, a tiger. I passed our immense jacaranda tree and there was a young buzzard sitting on a branch, picking his lice. Passing the second floor I saw a cloud over my head the shape of a grand piano. I could almost taste that cloud. Then I saw the cracks in the sidewalk coming up at me and the stick of an Eskimo ice cream bar that had a faint smear of chocolate. And everything I saw seemed superbly precious and for a split second I think I believed in god. Or at least his eye, or *an* eye seeing everything so exactly.

Light finds Henri Schultz.

My father has returned to be of help. I am trying to appreciate his concern after all these years. Like many fools he at times has a certain crazy wisdom. He says now—despite being a philosopher—that I must give up on ideas which only lead to other ideas. Instead I am to think of specific, concrete things. He says the Russians have always had more ideas than any other people in history and ended in the pit. The Americans have no ideas and they have one success after another. I am trying to have no ideas.

Papa is so like our country, a drifting ship heading for where nobody knows—Norway, maybe, or is it Java or Los Angeles? The one thing we know for sure, our treasure that we secretly kiss and adore—is death—

Light finds Emily Shapiro and Skip L. Cheeseboro.

—death and dreams, death and dancing, death and laughter. It is our salt and chile pepper, the flavoring of our lives.

We have eight feet of topsoil here, plenty of rain, we can grow anything, but especially greed. A lot of our people are nearly starving. And a bullet waits for anyone who seriously complains.

Light finds Stanley.

In short—a normal country in this part of the world. A kind of miraculous incompetence, when you look at it.

I had sixteen in my little brigade, including two girls. We were captured. They shot them all in thirty seconds.

Light finds Felix Barriaux.

My uncle Felix, the head of the country, spared me. I still find it hard to forgive him. I think it is one of the contradictions that sent me out my window. Survival can be hard to live with. . . . None of my people was over nineteen.

Light finds nothing.

I have a friend now. When I woke on the sidewalk he was lying beside me in my blood, embracing me and howling like a child in pain. He saved me. His love. He comes some nights and brings me honor for having fought.

The last light brightens.

Up in the mountains the people think he is the son of god. Neither of us is entirely sure of that. I suppose we'll have to wait and see.

Brightens further still. Slight pause.

What will happen now, will happen: I am content.

She rolls into darkness. The last light brightens even further, widening its reach until it fully covers the stage.

SCENE I

Office of the Chief of State, Felix Barriaux. He is seated at a window near his desk, studying a letter while filing his nails. Intercom barks.

FELIX, *to intercom*: My cousin? Yes, but didn't he say this afternoon? Well, ask him in. . . . Wait. *Tension as he studies the letter again.* All right, but interrupt me in fifteen minutes; he can go on and on. You know these intellectuals. —Anything in the afternoon papers? The radio? And the Miami station? Good. . . . Listen, Isabelle . . . are you alone? —I want you to forget last night, agreed? Exactly, and we will, we'll try again soon. I appreciate your understanding, my dear, you're a fantastic girl . . .

You can send in Mr. Schultz. *In conflict he restudies the letter, then* . . . Oh, fuck all intellectuals! *He passionately, defiantly kisses the letter and stashes it in his inside pocket.*

Henri enters. Wears a cotton jacket and a tweed cap.

Henri! Welcome home! Wonderful to see you; and you look so well!

HENRI, *solemn smile*: Felix.

FELIX, *both hands smothering Henri's*: —I understood you to say this afternoon.

HENRI, *confused*: Did I? *Touching his forehead*: . . . Well I suppose I could come back if you're . . .

FELIX: Out of the question! Sit! Please! *Shaking his head, amazed— before Henri can sit.* I can't help it.

HENRI: What?

FELIX: I look at you, cousin, and I see the best years of our lives.

HENRI, *embarrassed*: Yes, I suppose.

Now they sit.

FELIX: You don't agree.

HENRI: I have too much on my mind to think about it.

FELIX, *grinning feigns shooting with pistol at Henri*: . . . You sound like you're bringing me trouble . . . I hope not.

HENRI: The contrary, Felix, I'd like to keep you out of trouble . . .

FELIX: What does that mean?

HENRI: I didn't want to take up your office time, but there was no answer at your house . . . have you moved?

FELIX: No, but . . . I sleep in different places every night. —No guarantee, but I try to make it a little harder for them.

HENRI: Then the war is still on? I see hardly anything in the European press . . .

FELIX: Well, it's hardly a war anymore; comes and goes now, like a mild diarrhea. What is it, two years?

HENRI: More like three, I think.

FELIX: No. There was still major fighting three years ago. You came afterward.

HENRI: That's right, isn't it. —God, my mind is gone.

FELIX: Listen, I lied to you—you're not looking good at all. Wait! —I have some new vitamins! *Presses intercom.* Isabelle! Give my cousin a bottle of my new vitamins when he leaves. *To Henri*: French.

HENRI: What?

FELIX: My vitamins are French.

HENRI: Your vitamins are French?

FELIX: —What's the matter?

HENRI: I'm . . . very troubled, Felix.

FELIX: Jeanine.

HENRI: Partly. . . . It's that . . . at times nothing seems to follow from anything else.

FELIX: Oh, well, I wouldn't worry about a thing like that.

HENRI: I've always envied how you accept life, Felix.

FELIX: Maybe you read too many books—life is complicated, but underneath the principle has never changed since the Romans—fuck them before they can fuck you. How's Jeanine now?

HENRI: What can I say? —I'm with her every day and there are signs that she wants to live . . . but who knows? The whole thing is a catastrophe.

FELIX: I know her opinion of me, but I still think that girl has a noble heart; she's a Greek tragedy. . . . You remember my son-in-law, the accountant? He calculates that falling from the third floor— *Raises his arm straight up.* —she must have hit the sidewalk at sixty-two miles an hour. *Slaps his hand loudly on desktop.*

HENRI, *pained*: Please.

FELIX: But at least it brought you together. Sorry. Incidentally, where's your dentist?

HENRI: My dentist?

FELIX: I am practically commuting to Miami but my teeth keep falling apart. Where do you go?

HENRI: It depends. New York, London, Paris . . . wherever I happen to be. Listen, Felix . . . *Breaks off.* I don't know where to begin . . .

FELIX: . . . I hope it's not some kind of problem for me because I'll be frank with you, Henri—I'm not . . . completely myself these days. —I'm all right, you understand, but I'm just . . . not myself.

HENRI: . . . I didn't come to antagonize you.

FELIX, *in a flare of anger-alarm*: How the hell could you antagonize me! I love you, you bastard. . . . Tell me, you still living in New York?

HENRI: Mostly Munich. Lecturing on Tragedy.

FELIX: Tragedy is my life, Henri—when I was training in Georgia those Army dentists were the best, but I didn't have a cavity then. Now, when I'm paying the bills I'm full of holes. —How do you lecture on Tragedy?

HENRI, *inhales, exhales*: Let me tell you what's on my . . .

FELIX, *now a certain anxiety begins to seep out more openly*: Yes! Go ahead, what is it? . . . Isn't that cap too hot?

HENRI: It helps my arthritis.

FELIX: Oh, right! And how does that work again? —Oh yes!—it's that most of the body heat escapes through the skull . . .

HENRI: Exactly . . .

FELIX, *suddenly recalling*: . . . So it keeps your joints warm!—this is why I always loved talking to you, Henri!—you make my mind wander. . . . Wait! My god, I haven't congratulated you; your new wife.

HENRI: Thank you.

FELIX: I read that she's a concert pianist?

HENRI, *a strained smile*: . . . You're going to have to hear this, Felix.

FELIX: I'm listening! —But seeing you again always . . . moves me. *Reaches over to touch Henri's knee.* I am moved. *Collects himself.* How long will you be staying this time?

HENRI: A month or two; depends on how Jeanine progresses . . .

FELIX: Doctor Herman tells me she'll need another operation.

HENRI: Two more, possibly three. The whole thing is devastating.

FELIX: . . . I have to say, I never thought you were this close . . .

HENRI: No one can be close to a drug addict; but she's absolutely finished with that now. I was never much of a father but I'm going to see her back to health if it's the last thing I ever do.

FELIX: Bravo, I'm glad to hear that. —How a woman of her caliber could go for drugs is beyond me. What happened, do you know?

HENRI, *sudden surge*: What happened!—she lost a revolution, Felix.

FELIX: All right, but she has to know all that is finished, revolution is out . . . I'm talking everywhere.

HENRI: . . . Listen, don't make me drag it out—I haven't the strength.

FELIX: Yes. Please. —But I must tell you, it always amazes me how you gave up everything to just read books and *think*. Frankly, I have never understood it. But go ahead . . .

HENRI: Day before yesterday I drove with my wife up toward Santa Felice to show her the country.

FELIX: According to this *Vanity Fair* magazine that is one of the finest views in the world, you know.

HENRI: As we were passing through the villages . . .

FELIX: . . . Also the *National Geographic*.

HENRI: When we got up there, Felix . . . it all came back to me . . . remember when we were students and hiked up there together? Remember our shock and disgust that so many of the children had orange hair . . .

FELIX, *a happy memory; laughs indulgently*: Ah yes! The blood fluke . . . it's in the water. But it's practically harmless, you know.

HENRI: Not for children. It can destroy a child's liver . . .

FELIX: Well now, that's a bit . . .

HENRI, *sudden sharpness*: It is true, Felix! And the symptom of course is orange hair.

FELIX: What's your point?

HENRI: What's my point! Felix, blood fluke in the water supply in the twenty-first century is. . . . My god, you are the head of this country, don't you feel a . . . ?

FELIX: They won't boil the water, what can I do about it! —What is all this about the fluke suddenly? The British are definitely going to build a gigantic warehouse on the harbor, for god's sake!

HENRI, *distressed*: A warehouse! What's that got to do with . . .

FELIX: Because this country's starting to move and you're still talking blood fluke! I assure you, Henri, nobody in this country has the slightest interest in blood fluke!—Is this what you wanted to talk to me about?

HENRI: You probably won't remember, but on my last visit I brought home an eighteenth-century painting from Paris, cost me twenty-six thousand dollars. The pollution in our air has since peeled off about a third of the paint.

FELIX: That couldn't happen in Paris?

HENRI: It's been sitting in Paris for two hundred and fifty years! . . . I had a grand piano shipped from New York for my wife . . .

FELIX: The varnish cracked?

HENRI: The varnish did not crack but my architect is afraid the floor may collapse because of the underground leakage of water from the aqueduct, which has undermined the foundations of that whole lovely neighborhood. And brought in termites!

FELIX: I'm to chase termites?

HENRI: —My wife has to practice in the garage, Felix! When she plays for me I have to sit listening in the Mercedes!

FELIX: But cousin, a grand piano—you're talking three-quarters of a ton!

HENRI: I was getting out of a taxi yesterday on Avenue Fontana, our number-one shopping street . . .

FELIX: Did you see the new Dunhill store . . . ?

HENRI: . . . I nearly stepped on a dead baby lying at the curb.

Felix throws up his hands and walks away, steaming.

Shoppers were passing by, saw it, and walked on. As I did.

FELIX: What is all this suddenly? None of this has ever been any different!

HENRI: I don't know! I suppose I never really *looked* at anything. It may be Jeanine; she was so utterly beautiful, Felix.

FELIX: Oh god, yes.

HENRI: I think I never really *saw* what I meant to her. Sitting with her day after day now . . . for the first time I understood my part in her suffering. I betrayed her, Felix. It's terrible.

FELIX: Why? You always gave her everything . . .

HENRI: A faith in the revolution is what I gave her . . . and then walked away from it myself.

FELIX: I hope I'm not hearing your old Marxism again . . .

HENRI: Oh shit, Felix!—I haven't been a Marxist for twenty-five years!

FELIX: Because that is finished, they're almost all in narcotics now, thanks be to god; but the Americans are here now and they'll clean out the whole lot of them by New Years! Your guerillas are done!

HENRI: These are not my guerillas, my guerillas were foolish, idealistic people, but the hope of the world! These people now are cynical and stupid enough to deal narcotics!

FELIX: Listen, after thirty-eight years of civil war what did you expect to find here, Sweden? Weren't you in analysis once?

HENRI: Yes. I was. Twenty years ago at least. Why?

FELIX: I'm seeing a man in Miami.

HENRI: Well, that's surprising. I always think of you in control of everything.

FELIX: Not the most important thing.

HENRI: . . . You don't say. Maybe you have the wrong woman.

FELIX: They can't all be wrong. My dog just won't hunt.

HENRI: Imagine. And analysis helps?

FELIX, *hesitates*: Semi. I'm trying to keep from letting it obsess me. But I have this vision, you know?

HENRI: Oh? Someone you've met?

FELIX: No, just imaginary—like those women you see in New York. Tall, you know? Fine teeth. Kind of . . . I don't know . . . nasty. Or spirited . . . spirited is the word. Is your wife tall?

HENRI: No. She's Viennese. Rather on the short, round side.

FELIX: I've tried short and round, but . . . *Shakes his head*. It's torturing me, Henri. Listen, how would you like to be ambassador to Moscow again?

HENRI, *gripping his head*: Do you see why I am depressed?—nothing follows!

FELIX: —The reason you're depressed is . . .

HENRI, *grips his head*: I beg you, Felix, don't tell me why I'm depressed!

FELIX: . . . It's because you're a rich man in a poor country, that's all . . . but we're moving, by god!

Intercom. Felix bends to it.

Thank you, my dear. *To Henri*: —I have a meeting. . . . What'd you want to tell me?

HENRI, *a pause to organize*: On our little trip to Santa Felice—Hilda and I—we were struck by a . . . what to call it? . . . a kind of spiritual phenomenon up there. Really incredible. Wherever we went the peasants had pictures of this young man whom they . . .

FELIX: He's finished. We've captured him, Henri, he is history, all done.

HENRI: They keep candles lit before his photograph, you know . . . like a saint.

FELIX: This saint's gunmen have shot up three police stations and killed two officers and wounded five more in the past two months.

HENRI: They say he personally had nothing to do with the violence.

FELIX: The man is a revolutionary and he is responsible! —Listen, Henri, two of my brothers died fighting shits like these and he will have no mercy from me. Is this what you wanted to talk about?

HENRI: There is a rumor—which I find hard to believe—that you intend to crucify this fellow?

FELIX: I can't comment on that.

HENRI: Beg your pardon?

FELIX: No comment, Henri, that's the end of it.

HENRI: And if this brings on a bloodbath?

FELIX: Don't think it will.

HENRI: Felix, you are totally out of touch. They really think he is the Messiah, the son of god!

FELIX: The son of god is a man named Ralph?

HENRI: But a crucifixion! Don't you see?—it will prove they were right! These are simple people, it could bring them roaring down out of the mountains!

FELIX: Shooting doesn't work! People are shot on television every ten minutes; bang-bang, and they go down like dolls, it's meaningless. But nail up a couple of these bastards, and believe me this will be the quietest country on the continent and ready for development! A crucifixion always quiets things down. Really, I am amazed—a cretin goes about preaching bloody revolution, and you . . .

HENRI: Talk to the people! They'll tell you he's preaching justice.

FELIX: Oh come off it, Henri! Two percent of our people—including you—own ninety-six percent of the land. The justice they're demanding is your land; are you ready to give it to them?

HENRI: . . . To tell the truth, yes, I just might be. I returned to try to help Jeanine but also . . . I've decided to put the business and both farms up for sale.

FELIX: Why!—those farms are terrific!

HENRI: They've been raising coca and it's impossible to police my managers when I'm away so much; in short, I've decided to stop pretending to be a business man . . . *Breaks off.*

FELIX: Really. And what's stopping you?

HENRI: Courage, probably. I lack enough conviction . . .

FELIX: No, Henri, it's your common sense telling you that in ten years the land you gave away will end up back in the hands of two percent of the smartest people! You can't teach a baboon to play Chopin. —Or are you telling me this idiot is the son of god?

HENRI: I don't believe in god, let alone his son. I beg you, Felix, listen to what I'm saying . . . you crucify this fellow and our country is finished, ruined!

FELIX: Henri, dear friend . . . *Draws the letter out of his jacket pocket.* . . . not only are we not ruined—I can tell you that with this crucifixion our country will finally begin to live!

This fax arrived this morning.

A gigantic fax unspurls.

You've heard of Thomson, Weber, Macdean and Abramowitz of Madison Avenue?

HENRI: Of course . . . Thomson, Weber, Macdean and Abramowitz. They're the largest advertising agency for pharmaceutical companies.

FELIX: So I'm told. How they got wind of it I don't know, unless General Gonzalez contacted them for a finder's fee—he's our consul in New York now; anyway, they want to photograph the crucifixion for television.

HENRI: What in god's name are you talking about?

FELIX, *hands the letter to Henri*: This is an offer of seventy-five million dollars for the exclusive worldwide rights to televise the crucifixion.

HENRI, *stunned, he reads the letter*: Have you read these conditions?

FELIX: What do you mean?

HENRI, *indicating letter*: They will attach commercial announcements!

FELIX: But they say "dignified" announcements. . . . Probably like the phone company or, I don't know, the Red Cross.

HENRI: They are talking underarm deodorants, Felix!

FELIX: You don't know that!

HENRI, *slapping the letter*: Read it! They hardly expect a worldwide audience for the phone company! They're talking athlete's foot, Felix!

FELIX: Oh no, I don't think they . . .

HENRI: They're talking athlete's foot, sour stomach, constipation, anal itch . . . !

FELIX: No-no!

HENRI: Where else does seventy-five million come from? I'm sure they figure it would take him four or five hours to die, so they could load it up— runny stool, falling hair, gum disease, crotch itch, dry skin, oily skin, nasal blockage, diapers for grownups . . . impotence . . .

FELIX: God no, they'd never do that!

HENRI: Why not? Is there a hole in the human anatomy we don't make a dollar on? With a crucifixion the sky's the limit! I forgot ear wax, red eyes, bad breath . . .

FELIX: Please, Henri, sit down for a moment.

HENRI, *sitting*: It's a catastrophe! And for me personally it's . . . it's the end!

FELIX: Why?—nobody will blame you . . .

HENRI: My company distributes most of those products, for god's sake!

FELIX: I think maybe you're exaggerating the reaction . . .

HENRI: Am I! As your men drive nails into his hands and split the bones of his feet the camera will cut away to . . . god knows what . . . somebody squirming with a burning asshole! You must let the fellow go . . . !

FELIX: He's not going anywhere, he's a revolutionary and an idiot!

HENRI: You're not visualizing, Felix! People are desperate for someone this side of the stars who feels their suffering himself and gives a damn! The man is hope!

FELIX: He is hope because he gets us seventy-five million! My god, we once had an estimate to irrigate the entire eastern half of the country and that was only thirteen million! This is fantastic!

HENRI: Felix—if you sell this man, you will join the two other most contemptible monsters in history.

FELIX: What two others?

HENRI: Pontius Pilate and Judas, for god's sake! That kind of infamy is very hard to shed.

FELIX: Except that Jesus Christ was not an impostor and this one is.

HENRI: We don't know that.

FELIX: What the hell are you talking about, the son of a bitch is not even Jewish!—Good god, Henri, with that kind of money I could put the police into decent shoes and issue every one of them a poncho. And real sewers . . . with *pipes!*—so the better class of people wouldn't have to go up to the tops of the hills to build a house . . . we could maybe have our own airline and send all our prostitutes to the dentist . . .

HENRI: Stop. Please. *Slight pause.* Do you really want our country blamed for a worldwide suicide?

FELIX: *What?*

HENRI: A crucifixion lasting possibly hours on the screen—use your imagination! To a lot of people it will mean the imminent end of the world . . .

FELIX, *dismissing*: Oh that's nonsense . . . !

HENRI: I can see thousands jumping off bridges in Paris, London, New York . . . ! And California . . . my god, California will turn into a madhouse. —*And the whole thing blamed on us? —We'll be a contemptible country!* I know you'll call it off now, won't you.

> *Felix stares.*

> Felix, think of your children—their father will be despised through the end of time, do you want that stain on their lives?

> *Pause. Felix in thought.*

FELIX: I disagree. I really do. Look at it calmly—fifteen or twenty years after they kicked Nixon out of the White House he had one of the biggest funerals since Abraham Lincoln. Is that true or isn't it?

HENRI: Well, yes, I suppose it is.

FELIX: Believe me, Henri, in politics there is only one sacred rule—nobody clearly remembers anything.

HENRI: I've seen him.

FELIX: Really! How'd that happen?

HENRI: The police happened to have caught him in the street outside my window. Terrible scene; four or five of his . . . I suppose you could call them disciples stood there, weeping. One of the cops clubbed him down and kicked him squarely in the mouth. I was paralyzed. But then, as they were pushing him into the van—quite accidentally, his gaze rose up to my window and for an instant our eyes met. —His composure, Felix—his poise—there was a kind of tranquility in his eyes that was . . . chilling; he almost seemed to transcend everything, as though he knew all this had to happen . . .

FELIX: I thank you for this conversation, it's cleared me up . . .

HENRI: Let me talk to him. I take it you have him here?

FELIX: He won't open his mouth.

HENRI: Let me try to convince him to leave the country.

FELIX: Wonderful, but try to feel out if we can expect some dignity if he's nailed up? I don't want it to look like some kind of torture or something . . .

HENRI: And what about our dignity!

FELIX: Our dignity is modernization! Tell him he's going to die for all of us!

HENRI: . . . Because we need that money!

FELIX: All right, yes, but that's a hell of a lot better than dying for nothing!

> Felix opens the door; a blinding white light pours through the doorway through which they are peering.

HENRI: What is that light on him?

FELIX: Nothing. He just suddenly lights up sometimes. It happens, that's all.

HENRI: It "happens"!

FELIX, *defensive outburst*: All right, I don't understand it! Do you understand a computer chip? Can you tell me what electricity is? And how about a gene? I mean what is a fucking gene? So he lights up; it's one more *thing*, that's all. But look at him, you ever seen such total vacancy in a man's face? *Pointing.* That idiot is mental and he's making us all crazy! Go and godspeed!

HENRI, *takes a step toward doorway and halts*: You know, when I saw him outside my window a very odd thought . . . exploded in my head—that I hadn't actually been *seeing* anything . . . for most of my life. That I have lived half blind . . . to Jeanine, even to my former wife . . . I can't begin to explain it, Felix, but it's all left me with one idea that I can't shake off—it haunts me.

FELIX: What idea?

HENRI: That I could have loved. *Slight pause.* In my life.

Henri, conflicted, exits through the doorway. Felix shuts the door behind him.

FELIX: Odd—one minute I'd really love to blow that moron away. But the next minute . . .

He stares in puzzlement. He goes to his phone. Picks up the letter.

Isabelle. Get me New York. 212-779-8865. Want to speak to a Mr. . . . *Reads letter.* Skip L. Cheeseboro, he's a vice president of the firm. —Well, yes—if they ask you, say it's in reference to a crucifixion. He'll know what it means.

BLACKOUT

SCENE II

Mountain top. Emily Shapiro enters with Skip L. Cheeseboro. She is in jeans and zipper jacket and baseball cap, he in bush jacket, carrying a portfolio and a shooting stick. They bend over to catch their breaths. Now she straightens up and looks out front, awed.

EMILY: My god! Look at this!

SKIP: Yeah!

EMILY: That snow. That sun. That light!

SKIP: Yeah!

EMILY: What a blue! What an orange! What mountains!

SKIP: What's the date today?

EMILY: Seventeenth.

SKIP: Huh! . . . I think she's getting the divorce today and I completely forgot to call her.

EMILY: Well maybe she'll forgive you. *Looking into distance.* —This is absolutely awesome. How pure.

SKIP: A lot like Nepal—the Ivory Soap shoot.

EMILY: Like Kenya too, maybe . . . Chevy Malibu.

SKIP: The Caucasus, too.

EMILY: Caucasus?

SKIP: Head and Shoulders.

EMILY: Wasn't that Venezuela?

SKIP: Venezuela was Jeep.

EMILY: Right! —No! —Jeep was the Himalayas.

SKIP: Himalayas was Alka Seltzer, dear.

EMILY: Oh right, that gorgeous bubbling fountain.

SKIP: I think the bubbling fountain was Efferdent in Chile.

EMILY, *closing her eyes in anguish*: God, what a mush it all is! *Looking out again.* Human beings don't deserve this world. *Spreading out her arms.* I mean look at this! Look at this glory! . . . And look at us.

> *The Captain enters.*

CAPTAIN: Everything is fine?

SKIP: Beautiful, thank you very much, Captain. Our crew will be arriving shortly . . .

CAPTAIN: We will help them up . . .

> *Important news.*

> Mr. Schultz is already arriving.

EMILY: Mr. Schultz?

CAPTAIN: Very famous; his company is making the medicine for the feet.

EMILY and SKIP, *uncomprehending*: Ah!

EMILY: Oh!—athlete's foot!

CAPTAIN: And for the ears . . . to remove the wax.

SKIP: Really. And what connection does he have with . . . ?

CAPTAIN: He is cousin to General Barriaux . . . very important. *A wide gesture front.* This is the perfect scenery, no?—for the crucifixion?

EMILY, *laughs*: For the what?

SKIP: Thank you, Captain . . .

CAPTAIN: Yes! I must go down; I am speaking English?

SKIP: Oh yes, you speak very well.

CAPTAIN: How you say "lunch"?

SKIP: Lunch? Well . . . lunch.

CAPTAIN: We also. You say lunch and we say lunch.

EMILY: That's really remarkable.

CAPTAIN, *pleased with himself*: Thank you, Madame.

> *He leaves.*

EMILY: That wonderful?—a great spot for a crucifixion!

SKIP, *empty laugh*: Yes . . . Darling, what exactly did Atcheson tell you?

Captain reenters with Henri.

CAPTAIN: Ah, here is Mr. Schultz!! *To Henri*: Here is our director!

HENRI, *to Emily and Skip*: How do you do?

CAPTAIN: I am honored, sir. My wife and daughter are taking "Schultz's" every month!

HENRI, *trying to get back to Emily*: . . . Thank you, but I have very little to do with the company anymore.

CAPTAIN: You also have very good pills for the malaria.

HENRI, *turning to Skip*: I am Henri Schultz . . .

EMILY: Emily Shapiro. Director. This is my producer, Mr. Cheeseboro. We're making a commercial up here.

HENRI: So I understand. I believe the General will be coming up; I have something I'd like to say to you both if you have a moment . . .

EMILY: We're just laying out possible backgrounds . . . *Turning to Skip*. . . . Although I still haven't been told what exactly we're shooting . . .

SKIP: . . . May I ask your involvement, sir? Or should I know?

HENRI: Well let me see—my involvement, I suppose, is my concern for the public peace or something in that line.

SKIP: I don't understand. —If you mean good taste, Miss Shapiro has given the world some of its most uplifting commercial images. And luckily, the beauty of this location practically cries out for a . . . ah . . .

HENRI: A crucifixion, yes. But if you can give me five minutes, I'd like to speak to you about . . .

EMILY: What is he talking about?

SKIP, *to Henri, walking her away*: Excuse us, please. *To Emily*: What exactly did Atcheson tell you?

EMILY: Practically nothing. —Phoned from his limo and said to get my crew right over to Kennedy and the company jet and you'd fill me in when I got here . . .

SKIP: That's all?

EMILY: Wait a minute—yes; he sort of mentioned some kind of execution, but I didn't get the product . . . —What is it, somebody making an execution movie, is that it? And I grab some footage?

HENRI: Candidly, I wouldn't rule out a certain danger . . .

SKIP: There is no danger whatsoever; they have troops all over the mountain.

CAPTAIN: . . . Everything is absolutely covered.

EMILY: Why?

SKIP: Well, let's see. There is this sort of revolutionary terrorist.

EMILY: *Terrorist?* A real one?

HENRI: Actually, he himself is apparently not a . . .

SKIP: The man is totally vicious! His gang have killed some cops and blown up government buildings. And he goes around claiming to be the . . . like, you know, the son of god. *Turning on Henri nervously.* —Is there something I can help you with, sir . . . I mean, what is it you want?

EMILY: I'm confused—what's the product? *To Henri:* What are all those soldiers doing down below?

SKIP: They always have soldiers . . . even around weddings . . . rock concerts . . . anything.

HENRI: This is a bit different, they are there in case of a protest.

EMILY: Protest about what?

SKIP: Sir? We are here under an agreement with General Barriaux, and you are interfering with our work; I'm afraid I really must ask you to leave . . .

Soldiers enter, dark local men; two carry spades, and a long beam which they set down. One carries a submachine gun and a chainsaw—he stands guard.

EMILY: What's this now?

SKIP: They're putting up a little set. *To the soldiers:* Very good, gentlemen, but don't do anything yet, okay? Just sit down and wait a few minutes, okay? We'll be with you in a few seconds, okay?

The soldiers nod agreeably but begin unpacking tools—an electric drill, bolts. One of them lays a beam across another.

HENRI: You know it's to be a crucifixion?—

EMILY: A crucifixion. Really. But what's the product? *Calling to the soldiers:* Wait gentlemen! Don't do anything till I tell you, okay?

The soldiers nod agreeably and one of them begins digging a hole. Skip grasps the shovel handle.

No, wait, fellas; for one thing, I've got to decide on the camera angle before you build anything, okay?

The guard shifts his gun nervously.

Oh well, go ahead.

They proceed with the digging as she turns to Skip with beginning alarm.

Will you kindly explain what the hell is going on here? And what am I shooting, please?

SKIP: . . . It's a common thing with murderers here . . . they attach the prisoner . . .

EMILY: Attach? What do you mean? To what?

A very short burst from an electrical drill interrupts.

Please stop that!

Drill cuts out and in the momentary silence the Captain, to Henri . . .

CAPTAIN, *patting his own stomach*: Also you have the best for the gas . . . "Schultz's"!

HENRI: Captain, please—I inherited the company but I have very little to do with running it. I am a philosopher, a teacher . . .

SKIP: Darling, you must understand—this fellow has blown up a number of *actual* buildings, so they're quite angry with him . . .

EMILY: Wait, Skip—I don't know where I got the idea but I thought somebody was shooting a movie and we were just hitchhiking onto it . . .

SKIP: There's no movie.

EMILY: So . . . is that a cross?

SKIP: Well . . . *Takes a fortifying breath.* In effect.

EMILY: It's really a *crucifixion*?

SKIP: Well . . . in effect, yes, it's very common here . . .

EMILY: "In effect"—you mean like with nails?

HENRI: That's correct.

SKIP: It is not! I was told they'll most likely just tie him onto it! *To Emily*: They do that quite a lot in this country. I mean with death sentences.

EMILY: But he's not actually going to like . . . die . . .

SKIP, *frustration exploding*: I cannot believe that Atcheson . . . !

EMILY: Atcheson told me to get here, period! He didn't say "die"! Nobody dies in a commercial! Have you all gone crazy?

SKIP: We're only photographing it, we're not *doing* it, for god's sake!

EMILY, *clapping hands over ears*: Please stop talking!

A soldier starts up a chainsaw. She rushes to him, waving her arms.

Prego, Signor . . . No, that's Italian. Bitte . . . not bitte . . . stop, okay? What's Spanish for "stop"?

HENRI: Stop.

EMILY: Yes. *To the men*: Stop!

They stop.

Gracias. Muchos. *To Skip*: I'm sorry, Skip—I think maybe I'm just out.

SKIP: Now you stop being silly!

CAPTAIN: This is going to be a very good thing, Madame. It will frighten the people, you see.

EMILY: And that's good?

CAPTAIN: Oh yes . . . it's when they are not frightened of the government is when they get in trouble. Of course, it would be even better if they were allowed to say whatever they want. Like in the States.

HENRI: Well that's a surprise, coming from the police.

CAPTAIN: Oh, but is a very simple thing—if the troublemakers are allowed to speak they are much easier to catch.

His handheld intercom erupts. He holds it to his ear.

The General has arrived!

Captain rushes out.

HENRI: You may start a bloodbath in this country, sir, I hope you realize that.

SKIP: You are endangering this woman's career! *To Emily*: This could move you into a whole new area. I mean just for starters, if you shot him against the view of those incredible mountains . . .

EMILY: You mean on the cross?

SKIP: Emily dear, you know I adore you. Have I ever steered you wrong? This is a door to possibly Hollywood. There's never been anything remotely like this in the history of television.

EMILY: —And when are we talking about? For it to happen? Just out of curiosity.

SKIP: Toward sundown would be best, but it has to be today.

EMILY: Why?

SKIP: . . . Well, basically . . .

EMILY: Don't tell me "basically," just tell me why.

SKIP: Well, basically because the story is bound to jump the border and we'll have CNN here and ABC and every goddam camera in Europe. So it has to be done today because we have an exclusive.

HENRI: I beg you both, let us discuss this rationally.

EMILY: My head is spinning.

SKIP: I share your feelings, believe me, but . . .

EMILY: . . . I mean there's something deeply, deeply offensive, Skip.

HENRI: That's the point precisely.

EMILY: Really. I think it like . . . disgusts me. Doesn't it you?

SKIP: In a way, I suppose, but realistically, who am I to be disgusted? I mean . . .

Suddenly, the gigantic cross is raised, dominating the stage. Emily, struck, raises her hand to silence Skip, who turns to look as it rises to position while soldiers observe to figure if it is the right height.

All right, dear, let's parse this out head-on, okay? *She is staring into space now, into herself. Sudden new idea.* Showing it on the world screen could help put an end to it forever! *Warming.* Yes! That's it! If I were moralistic I'd even say you have a *duty* to shoot this! Really. I mean that.

Soldiers take down the pole and start up a chainsaw again, which stops their talk. The pole is sawed shorter.

In fact, it could end up a worldwide blow against capital punishment, which I know you are against as I passionately am. Please, dear, come here . . .

She doesn't move.

Darling, please!

He goes upstage of the soldiers and the beams. Half in a dream she reluctantly joins him and he holds arms out.

Look at this!—if you shot from here, with that sky and the mountains . . .

EMILY: But, Skip, I've never in my life shot anything like . . . real—I do commercials!

SKIP: But your genius is that everything you shoot *becomes* real, darling—

EMILY: My genius is to make everything comfortably fake, Skip. No agency wants real. You want a fake-looking crucifixion?—call me.

SKIP: Dear, what you do is make real things look fake, and that makes them emotionally real, whereas . . .

EMILY: Stop. Just stop it, Skip. Please. I'm totally lost. All I know is that somebody actually dying in my lens would melt my eyeball. —I have to call New York . . .

> *She takes out cell phone.*

SKIP: No, dear, please . . .

EMILY: I can't call my mother?

SKIP: Your mother! —Of course. *Handing her his cell phone.* Use mine, charge it to us. And darling, please don't feel . . .

EMILY, *punching the numbers, yells, outraged, scared*: Skip, I beg you do not use ordinary beseeching language to me, okay?! This is death we're talking about!

> *She dials.*

SKIP, *suddenly turning on Henri*: Sir, I appreciate who you are, but if you refuse to leave I will be forced to call the police!

HENRI: Sir, my family has been in this country since the Conquistadors.

SKIP: Really. Conquistadors named Schultz?

HENRI: Cortez had a German doctor.

SKIP, *one-upped, growing desperate*: You don't say!

EMILY, *in phone*: Mother! Yes! Hello? *To Skip*: Now listen, I haven't agreed to anything, okay? —Hello?

> *Captain enters, glancing about; Emily mouths a conversation into the phone.*

CAPTAIN: My excuses, please! General Barriaux is approaching below. I am to ask if there are any firearms . . . pistols, long knives, please to hand them to me. I am speaking English.

HENRI: Don't bother, Captain . . . I'm sure they're not armed.

CAPTAIN, *salutes*: Very good, sir! From Mister Schultz I accept this reassurance! You know, since I was a little child . . . when I was coughing . . . my mother always gave me . . .

HENRI: Will you stop that? Just stop it. This is a serious event, Captain!

Skip settles onto his shooting stick, takes out a magazine and affects to blithely work a crossword puzzle.

EMILY, *in phone*: . . . Mother, please! Listen a minute, will you? . . . It is, yes, it's beautiful. And the birds, yes, they're sensational. I saw a condor, twelve-foot wingspread, unbelievable, it can carry off a goat! —Listen, I left in such a hurry I forgot my cleaning woman doesn't come today so could you go over and feed my cats? Thanks, dear, but just the one can for both, I mean don't have pity, okay? What?

SKIP, *to Henri*: Sir, we are trying to work here . . . I'd be happy to meet somewhere later . . . tomorrow, perhaps . . .

EMILY, *in phone*: —Do I? Well I am nervous, they've just thrown a whole pail of garbage at me and I don't know what to do with it. Well it turns out it's a . . . well, a crucifixion. Some kind of Communist, I suppose. Not as far as I know—*Louder*. I said he's not Jewish as far as I know!

SKIP, *glancing up from his puzzle*: But she mustn't mention . . .

EMILY: But you mustn't mention this to anybody, you understand? —Of course it's a problem for me! I'd be on the next plane but I just signed for my new apartment and I was depending totally on this check.

SKIP: You'll have walked twice in one year, darling—case closed.

EMILY: This'd be my second time I walked off a shoot . . . well the slaughter of the baby seals last year. So I'm a little scared. —And it's also that I'm a little late. —Well, who wouldn't be edgy! I mean I don't know, do I want it or don't I? —Well . . . to tell you the truth I'm not sure, it could have been Max Fleisher. —What marry? —I should marry Max Fleisher? I'm not sure it was him anyway. —Mother, please will you listen, dear; I have no interest in marrying anybody. —I profoundly don't know why! Except I can't imagine being with the same person the entire rest of my life. —But I do believe in people—it's just myself I have doubts about.

The crew enters: Phil, cameraman; Sarah, soundwoman.

Got to run, don't forget the cats and give Daddy a kiss for me. I'll call tomorrow. 'Bye!

PHIL, *sets camera on the ground*: Skip. Good morning, director, what are we shooting?

SARAH: Emily, please could I use your cell phone, I've got to call New York.

EMILY: Is it all right, Skip?

SKIP: Why can't you call from the hotel?

SARAH: Because it's just after nine and they said I could get my pregnancy report after nine and I can't wait.

EMILY: Sarah, really! Isn't that fantastic!

SARAH, *jumping up and down*: Please!

EMILY, *hands her the phone*: Here! Can you say who the father is?

SARAH: Well, ah . . . actually, yes. My husband . . .

EMILY: You have a *husband*?

SARAH: Last Tuesday.

EMILY: How fantastic! Make your call!

> *Watches with unwilling envy as Sarah goes to a space and calls.*

PHIL: Listen, I'm trustworthy, can you tell me the secret?—what am I shooting?

EMILY, *indicates the cross*: That.

PHIL: What am I supposed to do with that?

EMILY: Well, nothing, until they nail a man to it.

> *Soldiers lower the cross to the ground and start attaching a footrest . . . as . . .*

PHIL: I always knew you were gutsy, but doesn't this crowd insanity? You're not serious, are you?

EMILY: I may not be your director in about ten minutes, Phil. *To Skip*: . . . Which reminds me, do you have a doctor?

SKIP: Oh god, you're not feeling well?

EMILY: Not for me, for him! —You've really gone crazy, haven't you . . .

SKIP: I am not at all crazy! . . . In all the thousands of paintings and the written accounts of the crucifixion scene I defy anyone to produce a single one that shows a doctor present! I'm sorry but we can't be twisting the historical record! *Great new idea. . . .* And furthermore, I will not superimpose American mores on a dignified foreign people. The custom here is to crucify criminals, period! I am not about to condescend to these people with a foreign colonialist mentality!

EMILY: What about a hat?

SKIP: A hat?

EMILY: If I know mountains it'll probably be a hundred degrees up here by noon.

SKIP: Yes, but a hat—is that the look we want?—on a cross with a hat? I mean we're not here to make some kind of a *comment*. I defy anyone to find a painting where he's wearing a . . .

EMILY: And what do you plan on giving him?

SKIP: Giving him . . . ?

EMILY: For the pain!

SKIP: If you're talking light drugs, okay, but we can't have him staggering up to the cross or something. Especially in like dry states . . . Kansas or whatever.

SARAH, *holding the phone*: They gave him wine, you know—the Romans . . .

SKIP: Well a little wine, but he can't look stoned. I mean we've got several million born-agains watching. Actually, I was thinking aspirin . . . or Tylenol if he's allergic . . .

EMILY: Aspirin with nails through his hands and feet? Skip dear, are you out of your fucking head? —I mean I personally am on the verge of disappearing here, but. . . . Look, I don't know why I'm even talking to you!

SKIP, *terror raised a notch*: Emily, dear, in all solemnity—if you walk on this one you'd better forget about any more work from us! And probably most if not all the other agencies. Now that's candid. It's simply too late to get somebody else, and your career, I can assure you is a wipeout.

EMILY: You are threatening me, Skip.

SKIP: I'm in no way threatening, dear, but if I know Thomson, Weber, Macdean and Abramowitz a lawsuit is not out of the question, and you'll be total roadkill in the industry!

> *Enter Felix in uniform, with the Captain.*

FELIX: Henri! Good!—you've decided to come, what a nice surprise. Good morning all! —Have you met Mr. Cheeseboro? Mister Cheeseboro, Mr. Schultz, my cousin.

SKIP: We've met.

HENRI, *taking Felix's elbow—intimately*: Felix, I beg you . . . we must talk before you commit to this.

FELIX: Later. I have a problem.

HENRI: What do you mean?

FELIX: Everything is under control . . .

HENRI: What are you talking about?

But Felix has spotted Emily and is instantly vibrating.

FELIX, *both open hands toward her*: And who is . . . ?

SKIP: . . . Our director, sir—Emily Shapiro.

EMILY: How do you do.

FELIX, *sweeps his hat off his head, lowering it for an instant, hiding his "enthusiasm"*: Wonderful! I hadn't expected a *woman* . . .

SARAH, *at one side with her phone*: Why not! I assure you women can film crucifixions as well as anybody else!

FELIX: I'm sure, but . . . *To Emily, while putting his hat back on*: . . . watching them, you know, can make even strong men uncomfortable.

EMILY: Oh? . . . Is this something you do fairly often?

FELIX, *points skyward*: That depends on the weather . . .

SKIP, *warm academic objectivity*: Now isn't that *interesting*.

FELIX: Most of our people are peasants, you see. *A shake of the fist.* When the crops are good, people are content. *Points skyward.* But it's hardly rained for twenty-six months, so there is a certain amount of unrest; we have an old saying, "when the rain stops the crosses sprout." It is not something we enjoy, I assure you, but there is either order or chaos. Are you taken for dinner?

EMILY: I hadn't thought about it. . . . I hope you won't mind too much, but I've half decided to try to stop this travesty from happening.

SKIP: That is not for you to . . . !

EMILY, *over-shouting him*: . . . Just so my crew and I—and especially Mr. Cheeseboro—know what to expect—when they're being nailed up do they like . . . *scream?*

HENRI: Certainly.

EMILY: And for how long?

FELIX: Not very; usually they're given a couple of bottles of tequila beforehand. Incidentally, I particularly admire your haircut.

SKIP: But you don't mean they're like . . . staggering.

HENRI: Of course.

FELIX: That is nonsense, Henri. Occasionally they have to be carried to the cross, but . . .

SKIP: Well that's out of the question . . .

FELIX: Oh? Why?

SKIP: Carrying him up to the cross would be like . . . I don't know . . . blasphemous in the United States!

EMILY: Sounds terrific to me . . . piggyback!

SKIP: Now wait, dear . . . !

EMILY: . . . Stop calling me "dear," my name is mud. Miss Mud. Emily Mud. *To Felix*: I'm sorry, General Whatever, but I've lost my brain.

FELIX: Haha—it's certainly not noticeable!

SKIP: Moving on to screaming, Mr. President—just to reassure our director—I assume it's important to this man what kind of public impression he makes, right?

FELIX: I have no idea; he has refused to say a word since he was caught.

SKIP: —But I should think if he is confident that he is about to . . . like meet his father in heaven, you could put it to him as a test of his faith that he not scream on camera. The camera, you see, tends to magnify everything and screaming on camera could easily seem in questionable taste.

FELIX: I understand. I will certainly try to discuss it with him.

SKIP: He cannot scream on camera, sir; it would destroy the whole effect. And I'm afraid I'll have to go further—I mean, sir, you have deposited our check, right? I mean as a man of honor . . .

FELIX: I will certainly do all I can to convince him not to scream.

HENRI, *turning Felix by the elbow—sotto*: What problem were you talking about?

EMILY: Well let's not nail him, so screaming is not a problem, right? *To both*: I said is that right?

SKIP, *to Emily*: All I'm trying to say, dear . . .

EMILY: Mud. When Emily is sued her name is Mud, so make it Mud, please!

SKIP, *momentarily put down*: I am simply saying that even though he was nailed—the Original, I mean—he is always shown hanging up there in perfect peace.

FELIX: The paintings are not like it is.

SARAH, *still with the phone*: What about the little sign over his head?

SKIP: What sign?

EMILY: Say that's right, they mocked him and stuck this hand-painted sign on the cross over his head—I believe it said "King of the Jews."

SKIP: No!! Absolutely out of the question . . . this has nothing to do with the Jews! Or Jesus either!

HENRI: Excuse me, but it will inevitably have that connotation.

SKIP: Nonsense! This is simply the execution of a violent criminal!

HENRI: Yes, but isn't that what they said the first time?

SARAH, *phone to her ear*: Speaking of Jews, they called him "rabbi," I think.

SKIP: Stop it! —Excuse me, Emily, no reflection on your personal heritage, but I mean, this will run in like Mississippi and even the Middle East, like Egypt . . . we do a lot of business in Egypt and Pakistan, and there's no point irritating the world's largest religion—I mean, from their viewpoint it's bad enough implying the son of god was Christian without making him Jewish, for Heaven's sake.

EMILY: All right, but I'm just saying—he . . . *was* . . .

SKIP: You know it and I know it, dear, but what's the point of rubbing it in worldwide, darling? *Turning to Felix*: Now sir, have you decided what time of the day you are going to . . . ah . . . there's a question of the light, you see.

FELIX: I'm not sure we will be able to proceed today. It is possible, but perhaps not.

SKIP: I don't understand, sir.

FELIX: He's escaped.

EMILY: Our guy?

HENRI, *a clap of his hands*: Felix!

FELIX: He will certainly be captured, there's no question, but it may be a day or two . . .

EMILY, *to the crew*: He's escaped!

CREW: Attaway, baby! Hurray! etc. . . .

SKIP: Shame on you! The man's a criminal! *To Felix*: This is terrible, terrible news, General! CNN, NBC . . .

> *Soldier starts up a screaming chainsaw.*

FELIX: Para! Esta puta cosa. Para! [English: Stop that goddam thing! I said stop it!]

> *Soldier, dumbfounded, cuts saw.*

CAPTAIN: No ves que están hablando? [English: Can't you see they're talking?]

Soldier salutes in terror.

Eres un imbécil? [English: Are you an idiot?]

Soldier salutes again.

HENRI, *touching Felix's arm*: Listen, Felix . . .

FELIX, *freeing his arm*: I want to offer to pay for the extra time you will be here, Mr. Skip, but he will absolutely be found by tomorrow, maybe tonight.

SKIP: I am only concerned about our exclusivity, any delay is dangerous. *To the crew*: I want everyone at the hotel . . . we meet let's say noon, or make it eleven, and we'll see where we are. And don't wander off in case he's caught sooner.

FELIX: . . . I believe we will catch him even this afternoon, maybe.

> *As crew packs, preparing—with uncertainty—to leave, he turns back to Skip.*

Not to worry about the exclusivity, I have the Army blocking the only road up this mountain; no other crew can get up here.

SKIP: There are helicopters.

FELIX: I have forbidden any takeoffs.

SKIP: What about from over the border?

FELIX: They cross the border they will be shot happily down.

SKIP: Well that's a relief. *To Emily*: How about lunch and let's talk?

EMILY: I think I'll have a look around the country for a bit . . .

SKIP: Don't go far . . . please. *To Felix*: I'm expecting your call the moment you have any news, sir.

FELIX: Rest assured. *Skip exits. To Emily*: Then may I expect you for dinner, Miss Shapiro? I was serious about your haircut, I find it very moving in a way that is particularly important to me.

EMILY: A moving haircut!—in that case, yes, I'd love dinner . . .

FELIX: Until tonight then, Miss Shapiro!

> *He gets to the periphery where Henri intercepts him— intimately.*

HENRI: What happened?

FELIX: I can't talk about it.

HENRI: Well, how did he get out?

FELIX: He paid off the guards.

HENRI: Where'd he get the money?

FELIX: How the hell would I know! —They're trying to hand me this bull-shit that he walked through the walls. They're calling him a magician, but he paid them off and I've locked them all up and I'm going to find that little bastard if I do nothing else in my life!

He starts out; Henri grabs his arm.

HENRI: Felix! Do nothing! Thank your lucky stars, it's a blessing.

FELIX, *loudly, angered*: A blessing? It's chaos! —And I'm going to miss my analysis day in Miami!

Felix throws off Henri's hand, goes to Emily, kisses her hand.

Again! —Until tonight, Miss Shapiro!

With a gallant wave he exits. Henri starts to follow, but halts and turns to Emily.

HENRI: You could stop this, you know.

EMILY: Me!

HENRI: Couldn't you try to dissuade him? Seriously—he can be very affected by good-looking women. He's undergoing psychoanalysis now. I've never known him to be quite this ambivalent about things—last year he'd have shot this man by now. And to be candid, I thought his reaction to meeting you was amazingly genuine . . . I mean his feeling.

EMILY: And he did like my haircut.

HENRI: He's a big baby, you know; his mother nursed him till he was seven.

EMILY: I hope you don't expect me to pick up where she left off.

SARAH, *closing her phone*: I'm pregnant!

EMILY: Oh, Sarah!

She bursts into tears.

SARAH: What's the matter? *Taking her hand as she weeps loudly, uncontrolled.* Oh Emily, what is it!

EMILY: I'm so glad for you! I mean you look so happy and I'm all fucked up! *Kisses Sarah.* Drink milk or something . . .

HENRI: I do admire your irony!

EMILY: Yes, I'm famous for it. Miss Irony Mud. —Okay, I'll margarine the General.

HENRI: Thank you, my dear.

EMILY: Tell me, Henri, as a truth-loving philosopher—wouldn't you gladly resign from the human race if only there was another one to belong to?

HENRI: Oh, of course. But are we sure it would be any better?

BLACKOUT

SCENE III

Stanley, an apostle, softly plays a harmonium in Felix's office. Sneakers, unkempt ponytail, blue denim shirt, backpack.

Felix enters.

FELIX: Thank you for coming.

STANLEY: Well, I was arrested.

FELIX: What's your name again?

STANLEY: Stanley.

FELIX: You know who I am.

STANLEY: Of course. You're the head.

FELIX: Tha-a-a-t's right, I am the head. I'm told you're very close to him.

STANLEY, *cautiously*: You could say that.

FELIX: Asshole buddies.

STANLEY: . . . I never put it quite that way.

FELIX: I'm told you did some . . . service for us a while back.

STANLEY: I've made some mistakes in my life, that was one of the big ones.

FELIX: We need to know where he is. There's good money in the information.

STANLEY: Thanks, but I really don't need money right now.

FELIX: Then tell me gratis—where is he?

STANLEY: I've no idea. Honest.

FELIX: A neighbor claims he saw him going into your house in the middle of last night.

STANLEY: How did he know it was him?

FELIX: He'd seen him earlier, standing on the corner staring into space for over an hour like a crazy man.

STANLEY: He only stayed with me a little and left.

FELIX: . . . Tell me, does *he* think he's the son of god?

STANLEY: That depends.

FELIX: Really! On what?

STANLEY: Hard to say.

FELIX: Let's put it this way, Stanley, if you're going to fuck around with me we'll be happy to knock your teeth out, starting with the front. This would not be my preference, but we are a military government and I am only one of five officers running things. Now please answer my questions before some really bad personalities get into this. The question is whether he believes he is the son of god.

STANLEY: Some days he's sure of it and then he . . . suddenly can't believe it. I mean it's understandable.

FELIX: Why is it understandable?

STANLEY: Well, a man facing crucifixion'd better be pretty sure what he believes.

FELIX: Why? If he's the son of god crucifixion shouldn't bother him too much.

STANLEY: Yeah, but if it turns out he's not the son of god it'll bother him a lot.

FELIX: What's your opinion? Is he?

STANLEY: . . . I better fill you in before I answer that. I've ruined my life believing in things; I spent two and a half years in India in an ashram; I've been into everything from dope to alcohol to alfalfa therapy to Rolfing to Buddhism to total vegetarianism, which I'm into now. So you ask me do I believe he's the son of god, I have to be honest—yes, I believe he is . . . kind of.

FELIX: Kind of.

STANLEY: Well, with a background like mine how do I know what I'm going to believe next week?

FELIX, *thinks for a moment*: What did you talk about with him last night?

STANLEY: Last night? Well, let's see—women, mainly. They're a mystery to him. Men also, but not as much.

FELIX: He's bisexual?

STANLEY: I would say he's more like . . . tri.

FELIX: Trisexual.

STANLEY: Yes.

FELIX: Well let's see now—there's men, and women, and what?

STANLEY: Well . . . vegetation.

FELIX: He fucks cabbages?

STANLEY: No-no, he loves them.

FELIX: Loves cabbages.

STANLEY: Well they're alive.

FELIX: I see. What about a girlfriend?

STANLEY: Well, yeah, one. But she jumped out of a window recently.

FELIX: . . . You don't mean Henri Schultz's daughter.

STANLEY: Oh, you know him?

FELIX: We're cousins. —So this son of god is banging Schultz's daughter?

STANLEY: I don't think so, frankly. My impression is that it stays kind of—you know—remote. Although I picked him up one morning at her apartment and she looked like a woman who . . . you know . . .

FELIX: Had had it.

STANLEY: But I think it was different. I think he may have just . . . laid down next to her and . . . you know . . . lit up. —Because you know he can just light up and . . .

FELIX: I know, I saw him do it. So you mean if he lights up it makes her . . . ?

STANLEY: Definitely.

FELIX, *truly fascinated*: Huh! That's very interesting. That's one of the most interesting things I've heard lately. —And how long can he stay lit up?

STANLEY: Seems like . . . I don't know . . . a few seconds.

FELIX: Is that all.

STANLEY: Well of course I never actually saw . . .

FELIX: So it could have been longer.

STANLEY: Who knows? I mean . . .

FELIX: Yes. *Exhales, blows out air.* This is really amazing. *Worried but curious.* I was wondering why Schultz was so fascinated by him.

STANLEY: Oh but I doubt she'd have mentioned Jack to her father.

FELIX: That's his name—Jack?

STANLEY: Well one of them. Jack Brown. But he's got others . . . depending.

FELIX: We believe his name is Juan Manuel Francisco Frederico Ortuga de Oviedo. Although up in the villages some of them call him Ralph.

STANLEY: Possible. He changes names so he won't turn into like . . . you know . . . some kind of celebrity guru.

FELIX: Well, that's unusual, isn't it. Now tell me how he escaped from jail.

STANLEY: I really can't talk about that.

FELIX: How did he get out, Stanley?

STANLEY: He doesn't like people talking about it.

FELIX: About what?

STANLEY, *conflicted, shifts in his chair*: I'm really not comfortable talking about that part of it.

FELIX: I don't want to have to persuade you, Stan. How did he escape?

STANLEY: Well . . . is this something you're insisting on?

FELIX: This is something I'm insisting on.

STANLEY: . . . He went through the walls.

>   *Pause.*

FELIX: And how did he do that?

STANLEY: You're asking me so I'm telling you, right? He has terrific mind control, he can see space.

FELIX: Anybody can see space.

STANLEY: No. What you see is the borders, like the walls of a room, or mountains. Pure space is only an idea, so he can think it out of existence. But he doesn't want it spread around too much.

FELIX: Why's that?

STANLEY: If he gets known as a magician he thinks it could take away from his main message.

FELIX: Which is what, in a few words?

STANLEY: Well, you know . . . just don't do bad things. Especially when you know they're bad. Which you mostly do.

>   *Pause.*

FELIX: You like women?

STANLEY: Well I'm . . . yeah, I guess I'm kind of on the horny side.

FELIX: You ever light up with them?

STANLEY: Me? Well there've been times when I almost feel I have, but . . . I guess I've never *blinded* any of them.

FELIX, *some embarrassment*: I want to talk to him, Stanley. For personal reasons.

STANLEY: Well, if he shows up, I'll tell him.

FELIX, *attempting cool*: . . . I want you to emphasize the personal. Let him pick a place and I'll meet him alone.

STANLEY, *realizing*: . . . Oh!

FELIX: I'm interested in discussing the *whole* situation. You understand?

STANLEY: —Okay, I'll tell him. —You want to be any more specific?

FELIX, *hesitates*: . . . No, that's . . . that's about it. *Suddenly suspicious, hardens.* He didn't send you to me, did he?

> *Stanley looks away.*
>
> Stanley?
>
> *No response.*
>
> Did he send you?
>
> *No response.*
>
> Why did he send you?
>
> *No response.*
>
> Answer me! Did you get yourself arrested?

STANLEY: It's complicated. —I can't stand the idea of him being . . . you know . . . hurt. So I thought maybe I could talk to you about it. —See, I think in some part of his mind he thinks it would help the people.

FELIX: If he's executed.

STANLEY: Crucified.

FELIX: He wants it.

STANLEY: . . . In a way, maybe.

FELIX: How would it help them?

STANLEY: Well, now that the revolution's practically gone, people are pretty . . . you know . . . cynical about everything.

FELIX: What about it?

STANLEY: To see a man tortured for their sake . . . you know . . . that a man could actually like care that much about anything . . .

FELIX: You're telling me something . . . what are you telling me? —Does he want it or not?

STANLEY: Oh no! No. It's just that . . . you see— *Rapidly overwhelmed by the vision's horror.* —he gets to where he just can't like bear it—

FELIX: Bear what!

STANLEY: Well . . . the horror!

FELIX: What horror, what the hell are you talking about!

STANLEY: Well like—excuse the expression—living in this country! Like when he takes a walk and sees some—some guy sending out eight-year-old daughters to work the streets, or those little kids a couple of weeks ago killing that old man for his shoes . . . Or, excuse the expression, the Army opening up on that farmers' demonstration last spring . . .

FELIX: Those people had no permission to . . . !

STANLEY, *more and more stridently:* Well you asked me so I'm telling you, right? A massacre like that can start him shivering and he can't stop crying! I've seen him go for . . . like two hours at a time, crying his heart out. Then he stops and he's cool for a while. We even have fun. Then he sees something and it like hits him again and he begins talking like in . . . Swedish, sounds like, or Russian or German—he once told me in a joke that he's trying to find out what language god understands. Then he falls asleep, and wakes up sounding like anybody else—and that's when he doesn't know.

FELIX: Doesn't know what?

STANLEY: Well . . . whether maybe he really is supposed to die, and . . . like cause everything to change. —I mean, for your own sake, sir, I would definitely think about just letting him go, you know? I mean this can be dangerous!

FELIX: I think you know where he is, Stanley. I asked you in a nice way, now we'll try something else.

Goes to the door, grasps the knob.

STANLEY: You going to hurt me?

FELIX: I'm stashing you away until you make up your mind to lead us to him. And incidentally, there's some hungry livestock in there that I don't think you're going to enjoy. Get in!

Felix opens the door and the blinding white light flies out; he raises his hands to shield his eyes.

My god, he's back!

Stanley falls to his knees facing the open door. Felix steps to his desk, presses a button, loud alarm bells go off as he shouts into his intercom . . .

Captain! Come quick, he's back, he's back!

Captain and two soldiers come in on the run.

Captain and soldiers rush out through the door. Felix yanks Stanley to his feet.

FELIX: Why did he come back? What's this all about, Stanley?

STANLEY, *scared, elevated*: God knows!

FELIX, *grabs Stanley, shakes him*: Answer me! Answer me!

STANLEY, *almost lifted off the floor by the throat*: —I think he just can't make up his mind, that's all—whether he really wants to—like die. I mean it's understandable, right?—

Felix releases him.

. . . with this great kind of weather we're having?

Captain and two soldiers back out of the cell doorway; they are trembling, trailing their rifles, staring in at the cell.

FELIX: What's this now!

He rushes to the cell, looks in. Then turns to the soldiers.

How'd he get out!

They are speechless. Whirls about to Stanley.

Talk to me! Why'd he come back! Why'd he escape?

STANLEY: I don't know! . . . Maybe to get your mind off me? I mean . . . it's possible, right?—for a friend?

BLACKOUT

SCENE IV

Café table. Henri seated with a bottle of water and glass. Skip enters, looking about.

HENRI: Mr. Cheeseboro!

SKIP: Hi. *Sitting.* I don't have much time. What can you tell me?

HENRI: Can I order something?

SKIP: I'll have to leave in a few minutes.

HENRI: No news, I take it.

SKIP: Nothing. And you?

HENRI, *a shake of the head*: I thought an exchange of ideas could be useful—the two of us, quietly . . .

SKIP, *slaps his own cheeks then lets his head hang*: I'm beginning to smell the dead-dog stink of disaster. *Straightens up.* Tell me—why'd the General let this man escape?

HENRI: It was a complete surprise to him. I spoke to him shortly after it happened; he was absolutely shocked . . .

SKIP: But he had him locked in a cell. —We've made a large down-payment, you know. . . . Or may one appeal to logic in this country?

HENRI: This is why I thought you and I ought to talk.

SKIP: About what?

HENRI: Have you any interest in history? Or philosophy? Where did you go to school?

SKIP: Princeton. But my interest was business, frankly. No philosophy, no culture, mainly the market.

HENRI: Oh, but poetry and the stock market have a lot in common, you know.

SKIP: *Poetry and the market!*

HENRI: Oh yes. They are both based on rules that the successful never obey. —A few years ago I spent some time in Egypt . . . you've probably been there?

SKIP: Egypt?—I've shot commercials all over Egypt . . . Chrysler, Bayer Aspirin, Viagra . . .

HENRI: . . . Then you know some of the wall paintings and sculpture.

SKIP: Of course. —What's this about?

HENRI: I want to tell you about a surprising discovery I made there. I am far from expert on the subject, but . . .

SKIP: What are you, a businessman or an academic?

HENRI: I retired from the pharmaceuticals business some years ago. I still breed fighting bulls but I'm getting out of that too; I'm basically a scholar now. In Egypt . . .

SKIP, *takes out a cell phone and punches numbers from notebook*: Excuse me.

HENRI: If you're making a local call . . .

SKIP: The General's office. To tell him I'm here.

HENRI: Doubt that'll work . . . *Glances at watch.* . . . this close to lunch.

SKIP: Good god, why don't they fix it?

HENRI: They? There is no "they" here; hasn't been in most of the world since the fall of Rome.

SKIP, *snaps his phone shut*: What can you tell me about this guy's escape?

HENRI: —I know how absurd this is going to sound, but I ask you to hear me out. *Slight pause.* I had a very distinct feeling at the time they found him gone, that he had never been in that cell.

SKIP: But they had him, they'd captured him.

HENRI: They believed that, yes.

SKIP: What are you talking about?

HENRI, *considers*: . . . It struck me one day in Egypt . . .

SKIP, *starting to rise*: Look, I have no interest in Egypt . . .

HENRI, *voice hardly raised*: This may save your neck, Mr. Cheeseboro! Do sit; please.—

Skip goes still.

It struck me one day; that there were lots of images of the peoples the Egyptians had conquered, but none showing Jewish captives. I am far from expert in the subject but I couldn't find more than one or two menorah—candelabra—a vague star of David . . . almost nothing, really. Which is terribly strange when the Jews are supposed to have drowned the whole Egyptian army, don't you think? And Joseph was the Pharaoh's chief adviser and so on? It would be, let's say, like writing the history of Japan with no mention of the atomic bomb.—

SKIP: But what is the connection with . . . ?

HENRI: One day the thought hit me—could the whole story of the Jews in Egypt have simply been a poem? More or less like Homer describing magical cattle, and ravenous women and so on? Ancient peoples saw no difference between a vivid description of marvels and what we call reality—for them the description itself *was* the reality. In short, the Jews may never have been literally enslaved in Egypt; or perhaps *some* had been, but the story as we know it may have been largely fictional, an overwhelmingly powerful act of the imagination.

SKIP: If you're telling me this guy doesn't exist, I'm . . .

HENRI: That depends on what you mean by "exist"; he certainly exists in the mind of the desperately poor peasant—he is the liberator; for the General his crucifixion will powerfully reinforce good order, so he must exist . . . and I know a suicidal young woman of high intelligence who insists that he has restored her will to live, so for her he certainly exists. And needless to say, for you, of course . . . his execution will sell some very expensive advertising, so you are committed to his existing.

SKIP: But he can't be imaginary, the General spoke with him.

HENRI: Not quite. According to the General the fellow never said a single word. Not one. The General spoke *at* him.

SKIP: But didn't I hear of this . . . apostle of his they've just jailed? *He's* certainly spoken with him.

HENRI: A fellow named Stanley, yes. I understand he is a drug addict. I needn't say more; he could be put away for the rest of his life unless he cooperates. Drug-taking is a felony in this country.

SKIP: Really. But they export tons of it.

HENRI: They do indeed. The logic is as implacable as it is beyond anyone's comprehension.

SKIP: Then what are you telling me? —Because you've gotta believe it, the money we paid the General is not a poem.

HENRI: But it may turn into one as so many other important things have done. The Vietnam War, for example, began . . .

SKIP: The Vietnam War!

HENRI: . . . Which was set off, mind you, by a night attack upon a United States warship by a Vietnamese gunboat in the Gulf of Tonkin. It's now quite certain the attack never happened. This was a fiction, a poem; but fifty-six thousand Americans and two million Vietnamese had to die before the two sides got fed up reciting it.

SKIP: But what is this light . . . not that I'm sure I believe it . . . but he emits a light, I'm told.

HENRI: Yes. I saw it.

SKIP: You saw it!

HENRI: At the time I thought I did, yes. But I was primed beforehand by my two days in the upper villages where everyone is absolutely convinced he is god—so as I approached that cell door my brain *demanded* an astonishment and I believe I proceeded to create one.

SKIP: Meaning what?

HENRI: Mr. Cheeseboro, I have spent a lifetime trying to free myself from the boredom of reality. —Needless to say, I have badly hurt some people dear to me—as those who flee reality usually do. So what I am about to tell you has cost me. —I am convinced now apart from getting fed, most human activity—sports, opera, TV, movies, dressing up, dressing down— or just going for a walk—has no other purpose than to deliver us into the realm of the imagination. The imagination is a great hall where death, for example, turns into a painting, and a scream of pain becomes a song. The hall of the imagination is really where we usually live; and this is all right except for one thing—to enter that hall one must leave one's real sorrow at the door and in its stead surround oneself with images and words and music that mimic anguish but are really drained of it—no one has ever lost a leg from reading about a battle, or died of hearing the saddest song. *Close to tears.* And this is why . . .

SKIP: I don't see why . . .

HENRI, *overriding*: . . . This is why this man must be hunted down and cru- cified; because—*he still really feels everything.* Imagine, Mr. Cheeseboro, if that kind of reverence for life should spread! Governments would collapse, armies disband, marriages disintegrate! Wherever we turned, our dead unfeeling shallowness would stare us in the face until we shriveled up with shame! No!—better to hunt him down and kill him and leave us in peace.

SKIP: . . . You're addressing me, aren't you.

HENRI: Oh, and myself, I assure you a thousand, thousand times myself.

SKIP: On the other hand, shallow as I am I have twins registered at Andover; maybe some need to be shallow so that some can be deep.

He starts to rise.

HENRI: Please! Go home!

SKIP: I can't go home until this job is done!

HENRI: You could tell your company there was nothing here to photograph! It was all imaginary, a poem!

SKIP: It's impossible, I can't pull out of this.

Starts off.

HENRI: I hope you won't take offense!

Skip halts, turns, curious.

Our generals are outraged, a cageful of tigers roaring for meat! *Somebody* may get himself crucified—and not necessarily a man who has done anything. Do you want the responsibility for helping create that injustice!

SKIP: I've been trying hard not to resent you, Mr. Schultz, but this I resent. —I am not "creating" anything! I am no more responsible for this situation than Matthew, Mark, Luke, and John were for Jesus' torture!

HENRI: But Jesus was already long dead when they wrote about him, he was beyond harm!

SKIP: Well, I can't see the difference.

HENRI: But Mr. Cheeseboro, this man is still alive!

SKIP: We are recording a preexisting fact, Mr. Schultz, not creating it—I create nothing!

HENRI: But the fortune you've paid the General has locked him into this monstrous thing! Your money is critical in his decision!

SKIP, *exploding*: You have utterly wasted my time!

He exits.

HENRI: And so the poem continues, written in someone's blood, and my country sinks one more inch into the grass, into the jungle, into the everlasting sea.

BLACKOUT

SCENE V

Darkness. A moon. A palm tree. Light rises, gradually reveal-
ing a candelabra on a café table, with Felix and Emily eating
lobsters and drinking wine.

At all the dim edges of the stage, riflemen sit crouched, weap-
ons at the ready, backs to the couple.

Music; very distant strains of a guitar and singers serenading.

EMILY: I've never in my life eaten three lobsters.

FELIX: But they're very small, no?

EMILY: Even so.

FELIX: Of course, small things can be better than big sometimes.

EMILY: Oh? *Catches on.* Oh, of course, yes!

FELIX: I beg you to forgive my forwardness.

EMILY: Not at all—I like it.

FELIX: I can't help myself, I am desperate for you not to slip away.

They eat in silence, sucking the lobster legs.

EMILY: You're a contradictory person, aren't you?

FELIX: I have never thought so; why am I contradictory?

EMILY: Well, you seem so tough, but you're also very sentimental.

FELIX: Perhaps, yes. But with very few people. This is a hard country to govern.

EMILY: —I must say, your face seems softer than when we met.

FELIX: Possibly because something grips my imagination as we converse.

EMILY: Grips your imagination?

FELIX: Your body. —I beg you to forgive my frankness, it's because I am sure, Emily, that I could . . . how shall I say . . . function with you.

EMILY, *equivocally*: Well now . . .

FELIX: How fantastic—you are blushing! *She laughs nervously.* My god, how your spirit speaks to me! There is something sacred in you, Emily— for me it's as though you descended from the air. —I must sound like I have lost my mind, but could you stay on some weeks? Or months? I have everything here for you . . .

EMILY: I'm afraid I have too many obligations at home. And I'm going to have to get busy saving my career. *Pointedly.* . . . Unless you'd decide to do what I asked.

FELIX: I beg you, my dear, you can't ask me to call off the search. The General Staff would never stand for it . . .

EMILY: But if you insisted . . .

FELIX: It's impossible; the honor of the Armed Forces is at stake. This man is trying to make fools of us.

EMILY, *reaches out and touches his cheek. Surprised, he instantly grasps her hand and kisses her palm*: Why do I think you don't want to catch him, Felix . . . you personally?

FELIX, *cradles his face in her palm*: . . . To tell you the truth I'm not sure anymore what I want.

EMILY: . . . Just out of curiosity, you really think my haircut started it?

FELIX: Oh yes, absolutely, it went straight to my heart.

EMILY: Imagine. And here I was thinking it was too short.

FELIX: No—no, it's perfect! I had one look and it was as though I . . . I was rising from the dead.

EMILY: . . . Could we talk about that?

FELIX: About what, my dear?

EMILY: The . . . ah . . . difficulty you have that you've been . . . alluding to.

FELIX, *fear and eager curiosity*: What about it?

EMILY: . . . Unless you don't feel . . .

FELIX, *steeling himself; deeply curious*: . . . No—no, of course not, I have no fear!

EMILY: Well, what I think, is that you have to seem invulnerable to the world, and so you suppress your feelings.

FELIX: I am running a country, Emily, I cannot expose my feelings to . . .

EMILY: I know, but that suppression has spread down and down and down . . . *Running her finger up his arm and down his chest*: until it's finally clobbered . . . your willy. *Quickly.* You're simply going to have to let your feelings out, Felix, is all I'm saying.

FELIX, *aroused and confused*: I am . . . I am . . . I . . . I . . . *Disarming himself*. . . . must talk to you . . . I can come to New York, I have money there and an apartment . . .

EMILY: Why wait? Like if you feel you really don't wish to pursue this fellow, just don't do it and see what happens.

FELIX: Darling, the General Staff would tear me apart, they are hungry lions . . .

EMILY, *reaches for his hand*: Felix dear . . . I don't know where this is going between us, but I must tell you now—if you go through with this outrage you'll have to find yourself another girl. —Not that I'm promising anything in any case.

FELIX: But what are your feelings toward me? You never speak of them.

EMILY: I like a man to be a man, Felix—which you are. And I have enormous curiosity.

FELIX: About men.

EMILY: Yes. Powerful men, especially . . . to tell the truth.

FELIX: About what in particular?

EMILY: Well, frankly, for one thing—how they are making love.

FELIX: I have never known a woman with such courage to speak her mind.

EMILY: One needs it when one is not marvelous to look at.

FELIX, *kisses her hand*: You are more marvelous to look at than . . . than six mountains and a waterfall!

EMILY: That's very sweet of you, Felix. —I'd love to walk along the beach. Could we, without all these guards?

FELIX: I'm afraid not. But come, we can take a few steps through the garden.

   They walk together.

EMILY: Who exactly would want to kill you, Communists?

FELIX: The Party is split on this question. One side thinks somebody worse would replace me if I am eliminated.

EMILY: And I suppose the Right Wing people love you . . .

FELIX: Not all—some of them think I am not hard enough on the Communists . . . those might take a shot at me too. Then there are the narco-guerillas; with some we have an arrangement, it's no secret, but there are others who are not happy for various reasons.

EMILY: It all seems so utterly, utterly futile. Or do you mind?

He halts, holds her hand.

FELIX: I mind very much, in these hours since I know you. Very much. You have made me wish that I could live differently.

EMILY: Really!

FELIX: Emily, I will confess to you—when I imagine myself making love to you, entering into you, I . . . I almost hear a choir.

EMILY: A choir! Really, Felix, that is beautiful!

Felix suddenly turns away, covering his eyes.

EMILY: What is it? You all right? Felix?

Felix straightens up, grasps her hand, kisses it, holds it to his cheek.

EMILY: What is it?

FELIX: I will divorce.

EMILY, *blurting*: Oh no, you mustn't do that! . . . I mean you're a Catholic, aren't you?

FELIX: I am ready to go to hell! I cannot lose you!

EMILY: But my dear, I'm not prepared for . . . I assume you're talking commitment?

FELIX, *striking his chest*: You have exploded in my mind like a grenade! I have never had such a feeling . . . it is like all my windows have blown out and a fresh breeze is passing through me . . . I must not let you go, Emily—what can I give you! Anything! Tell me!

EMILY: Ralph!

FELIX: Ralph?

EMILY: Let him go!

FELIX, *at the height of tension—dives*: That is what you truly wish?

EMILY: Oh yes, Felix—yes! It would solve everything for me! And he sounds like such a dear person!

FELIX: And you will surely see me in New York.

EMILY: Of course, I'll be happy to!—I mean not necessarily on a permanent basis . . . I mean I travel a lot, but . . . yes, of course!

FELIX: All right, then—it is done!

EMILY: Done! Oh, Felix, I'm overwhelmed!

FELIX: I have fallen in love with you, Emily! Come—let me take you to my best house.

EMILY: Your best?

FELIX, *solemnly*: It was my mother's. I have never brought anyone there before. It is sacred to me. I haven't been there since I was seven.

EMILY: That's very touching. But first could we go into the mountains? I would like to see one of those high villages where they love this Ralph fellow so. It's just an experience I've never had, have you?—to walk in a place full of love? *Up close to him, face raised.* Take me there, Felix?

FELIX, *sensing her distant surrender*: My god, woman—yes, anything! Come . . . come to the mountains!

> He grips her hand and they hurry off with all the guards following, their heads revolving in all directions in the search for killers.

BLACKOUT

SCENE VI

Jeanine rises from her wheelchair with help of a cane, and walks with a limp to a point. Henri enters, stands, astonished.

HENRI: Jeanine!

She turns to him.

JEANINE: I don't understand it. I woke up, and I was standing.

HENRI: And the pain?

JEANINE: It seems much less. For the moment anyway.

HENRI: This is absolutely astonishing, Jeanine. This is marvelous! How did this happen?

JEANINE: The lightning this morning shot a lot of electricity into the air—

HENRI: —Could that have affected you?

JEANINE, *cryptically*: I . . . don't know, really.

> *Pause. Henri settles in.*

HENRI: I'm sorry, dear, but we have to talk about Felix.

JEANINE: Oh god, why?

HENRI: He called me this morning—woke me at dawn. He's convinced you can lead him to this god-fellow.

> *Jeanine is silent.*

> He'll be here to see you this morning. He insisted. *Coming to his point.* . . . Do you know a fellow named Stanley?

JEANINE, *hedging*: Stanley.

HENRI: They have him.

> *She stiffens.*

> He has apparently told Felix you and this . . . god-fellow are lovers.

She is silent.

Felix is convinced you would know where to find him.

JEANINE: Papa, I have no way of contacting this man, so let's just forget it, will you?

HENRI, *a moment; swallows resentment*: According to Felix this Stanley fellow has hinted that your friend may actually welcome crucifixion. In order to accomplish his . . . whatever it is . . . his mission.

Jeanine is silent.

In any case, I'm not sure I can keep you from being arrested for harboring him and failing to turn him in.

JEANINE: But how can I turn him in! I don't know how to contact him!

HENRI: . . . For one thing, darling—how shall I put it?—he clearly had to have been here last night . . .

JEANINE: Why!

HENRI, *patience gone*: Well look at you! Felix is not stupid, Jeanine—he knows your spine was crushed, it could only have been this man's hand on you that has brought you to life like this!

JEANINE: . . . You believe then!?

HENRI: . . . I don't know what I believe! I only know that Felix intends to kill this man and that can't be allowed to happen!

JEANINE: Oh Papa, why do you go on caring so much when you know you will never act! You'll never stand up to these murderers!

HENRI: Act how! Who do I join! How can you go on repeating that political nonsense? There is no politics anymore, Jeanine—if you weren't so tough-minded you'd admit it! There is nothing, my dear, nothing but one's family, if one can call that a faith.

JEANINE: Late one night you came into my room and sat down on my bed. There was a storm. Tremendous! The wind broke limbs off the oak behind the house. It groaned, like pieces of the sky breaking off! And you said you had decided to go into the mountains and join the guerillas to fight against Felix! Lightning seemed to flash around your head, Papa. You were like a mountain, sitting there. At last you would do something, at last you would answer the idiots and fight against Felix! And I knew I would follow you . . . and high up in the mountains I found you in your tent with a rifle on your lap, reading Spinoza.

HENRI: The world will never again be changed by heroes; if I misled you I apologize to the depths of my heart. One must learn to live in the garden of one's self.

JEANINE: Even if one has seen god?

HENRI: . . . Then you really do believe?

JEANINE: I think so, yes.

HENRI: Very well. I'm glad.

JEANINE: You are!

HENRI: I'm happy for the love I see in you, my dear, your hair flowing so gently around your face, and the softness that I haven't seen in so many years in the corners of your eyes. I love you, Jeanine, and if it's he who brought you back to life . . . —Why not? I think now it is no more impossible than the rest of this dream we live in. *Glances at watch.* —Felix will be here soon. I'll wait with you, is that all right?

She suddenly weeps; he goes to his knees beside her.

HENRI, *embracing her*: Oh my darling, my darling . . . !

Enter Felix, with Emily—her hand tucked under his arm. Henri springs up.

Felix! Miss Shapiro! Good morning! Miss Shapiro, this is my daughter, Jeanine.

FELIX, *going to Jeanine in surprise*: Why Jeanine, how wonderfully well you look! My god, this is amazing—what's happened?

HENRI: Nothing. She often has more energy in the mornings.

FELIX: We must talk, Jeanine . . .

HENRI: She's really not up to it, Felix.

FELIX: There's a couple of things I'd like this man to understand. It's important.

HENRI: But she has no contact with him.

FELIX: Well, if you happen to see him—

HENRI, *glancing from one to the other*: —Something's happened, hasn't it . . . with you.

EMILY: Oh yes! We hardly slept all night.

HENRI: How nice!

EMILY: Yes . . . it was.

HENRI: Well! May one congratulate the old dog?

FELIX: Definitely!—he's back hunting over hill and dale. This is the strangest twenty-four hours I've ever been through. —*Drapes an arm around Emily.* . . . She wanted to drive up and look around in the villages . . .

EMILY: It's like walking on the sky up there—the purity of the sunbeams . . . that strangely warm, icy air . . .

FELIX: It's been years since I was up there in our last campaigns. I was absolutely amazed—his picture really is everywhere in the villages. They paint halos around his head. I had no idea of the devotion of the people— it's a real phenomenon, he's like a saint. *To Henri:* You remember, Henri—that whole back country was always so . . . what's the word . . . ?

HENRI: Depressing.

EMILY: They've taken out the ancient instruments that nobody has played for years, and they dance the old dances again. . . . It was so absolutely delightful, we didn't want to leave.

JEANINE: Then you've decided what?—not to kill him?

FELIX: I must have a meeting with him. I was hoping you could arrange it.

HENRI, *instantly:* She really has no idea where he . . .

FELIX, *charmingly to Jeanine:* One thing I'm never wrong about is the face of a satisfied woman. —When he comes to you again I would like him to understand the following: I have talked to a number of his people now and they say he has always told them to live in peace. Some of my own people say otherwise but I'm willing to leave it at that. What I want him to consider—I mean eventually, of course—is a place in the government.

JEANINE: In *your* government? *Him?*

FELIX: I'm serious. The military is not as stupid as maybe we've sometimes looked, Jeanine. We must get ready for some kind of democracy, now that the revolution is finished. He could help us in that direction.

JEANINE: I'd doubt that.

EMILY: He's released Stanley.

JEANINE: Really.

FELIX: Stanley's agreed to deliver my message to your friend, but I don't know how much weight he carries with him. I would feel better if you spoke to him yourself.

JEANINE: But I know his answer. He will tell you to resign.

FELIX: Resign.

JEANINE: —Let's be honest, Felix; this man is full of love—I think you realize that now, don't you; all he is is love. But we aren't. I'm not and neither are you. You've killed too many of us to forget so quickly.

FELIX: I have changed, Jeanine. This woman has opened my eyes.

JEANINE, *to Emily*: Imagine!—in one night!

FELIX: No, not one night; I've been thinking about it for some time now . . . that we've been fighting each other almost since I was born. It has wasted us all. I want a normal country. Where people can walk safely in the streets at night; sleep in peace, build a house . . . I can't tell you how exactly it happened, but this woman has made me wonder—maybe if your friend could help us begin to come together I am ready to give it a try. *He sees she is not convinced.*

What can I do to prove I have changed, Jeanine?

EMILY, *to Jeanine*: I have an idea . . . suppose he announced on television that your friend was no longer a wanted man?

FELIX: Excuse me, dear—I can't do that unless he agrees in advance to disarm *his* people . . .

JEANINE: He personally has not armed anybody . . .

FELIX, *composure rattling*: Now look, dear . . .

JEANINE: Don't call me dear! —Why can't you make that announcement?

FELIX: They have tons of hidden arms, goddamit!

EMILY, *to Felix*: Don't, darling, please . . .

FELIX, *to Emily, indignantly*: No! I can't pretend I am dealing with Jesus Christ here! I'm trying my best but the man is not just a hippie, he's also a guerilla . . . !

EMILY, *patting his head*: And he has also managed to walk through your prison wall.

FELIX: So what?—am I supposed to have an explanation for everything?

HENRI: Felix, listen; if you announce that he is no longer a wanted man you take the moral high ground, and if . . .

FELIX: Do we have laws or not? There's a homicide sentence on the man! In return for what am I lifting his sentence? *His anger returning.* I am not turning this government into a farce! I'm asking you, will he promise to keep the peace?—

JEANINE: But shouldn't you promise first? You have the tanks.

FELIX: Yes, I have the tanks and he doesn't, so he's the one who has to make the promises!

JEANINE: Well now! —So much for all this high spiritual change you've gone through . . .

HENRI: I have an idea; for just this moment, right now, try to think of this problem as though you did not have a gun.

FELIX: Right. Okay, I'm ready! You want me to talk?—here I am. *To Jeanine*: So where is he? *Slaps his hips*. No guns! I'm all ears! Where's god?

Stanley enters.

JEANINE: Stanley!

Stanley comes and embraces her.

STANLEY: How you doin', Jeanie, you're lookin' good.

JEANINE: Is . . . everything all right?

FELIX: Have you spoken with him?

STANLEY: . . . Here's the thing.

Pause.

What it all comes down to is—he's having big trouble making up his mind.

HENRI: About . . . ?

STANLEY: Getting crucified.

FELIX: What's his problem?

STANLEY: Well . . . if he doesn't, will people feel he's let them down?

JEANINE: I'm surprised at you, Stanley; his deciding to be crucified is not going to depend on whether he's disappointing people's expectations!

STANLEY: He is serious about changing the world, Jeanie, everything he does he's got to think of the effect on people. What's wrong with that?

JEANINE: What's wrong is that it changes him into one more shitty politician! Whatever he does he'll do because it's right, not to get people's approval!

FELIX: So where does that leave matters? *Violently*. . . . And try not to use so many words, will you?

STANLEY: My candid, rock bottom opinion?

FELIX: What.

STANLEY: Ignore him.

HENRI: Brilliant.

FELIX: I can't ignore him, he's broken the law, he's . . .

STANLEY: General, I don't have to tell you, even now up in the villages the crime rate's been dropping since he showed up, people are getting ready for heaven, right? A lot of them like starting to boil the water, right? And much less garbage in the street and whitewashing their houses and brushing their teeth—and the number screwing their daughters is like way down, you know. —In other words, this is a very good thing he got going for you, so how about just turning your attention . . . elsewhere?

HENRI: Brilliant. Absolutely brilliant.

FELIX: And will he "turn his attention elsewhere"? His people will go right on agitating against me, won't they. As though I had nothing to do but go around murdering people; as though I'd done nothing to improve the country, as though the British are not building two hotels, and the Dutch and Japanese weren't starting to talk to us. . . . What the hell more does he want of me!

STANLEY: Well for one thing . . . I don't know like maybe let's say, if you like stopped—you know, like knocking off union organizers . . .

FELIX: I have no outstanding orders against organizers!

JEANINE: Of course not, they're all dead.

FELIX: I'm sorry, decent people don't join unions!

EMILY: I'm in a union.

FELIX: *You!*

EMILY, *smoothing his cheek*: Don't take it to heart, dear, it's only the Directors Guild of America.

FELIX: I can't believe this, Emily . . . *you* are in a *union?*

EMILY: Felix dear, you really do have to start thinking differently . . .

FELIX, *furious*: How can I think differently if nobody else is thinking differently? —So where are we, Stanley—the war goes on? Yes or no?

STANLEY: . . . Could I please ask a favor, General? Would you leave us alone for a couple minutes?

FELIX: No! We've got to settle this!

STANLEY: I can't talk to her otherwise, okay?

EMILY: There's nothing to lose, dear. *Holding out her hand to him.* Come. Let's both have a glass of water.

FELIX, *hesitates*: . . . But I hope we understand each other.

STANLEY: We do, sir, just give me five.

EMILY: Come, Felix dear.

FELIX, *sotto, as she leads him off*: I don't know why everybody's being so fucking stupid!

Felix and Emily leave.

Henri starts to move.

STANLEY: You can stay if you want—it's just I didn't want to say it in front of him but in my personal opinion this thing is getting pretty nasty out there—

JEANINE: Nasty how?

STANLEY: A lot of the folks—they don't say it out loud, but they're hoping their village will be picked.

JEANINE: Picked?

STANLEY: For the crucifixion.

HENRI, *grips his head*: Oh my god!—why!

STANLEY: Well—like you know the honor of it and . . . well, the ah . . . property values.

JEANINE: *Property* values!

STANLEY: Well, face it, once it's televised they'll be jamming in from the whole entire world to see where it happened. Tour buses bumper to bumper across the Andes to get to see his bloody drawers? Buy a souvenir fingernail, T-shirts, or one of his balls? It's a whole tax base thing, Jeanie, y'know? Like maybe a new school, roads, swimming pool, maybe even a casino and theme park—all that shit. I don't have to tell you, baby, these people have *nothing*.

HENRI: We are living in hell.

STANLEY: Well yes and no; I think he figures it could also like give people some kind of hope for themselves.

JEANINE, *incredulously*: *Hope?* From seeing a man crucified?!

STANLEY: From seeing somebody who means it when he says he loves them, honey. So that's why—at least when I left him—he's like thinking death.

JEANINE, *bursts into tears*: Oh god . . .

STANLEY: —So what I'm hoping . . . can I tell you? —Cause you're the only one he'd possibly listen to . . . I guess because you tried to die yourself.

Jeanine lifts her eyes to him.

STANLEY: . . . I really wish you'd tell him he's got to live . . . and just maybe forget about . . . you know, being god. I mean even if he is.

Jeanine moans in pain.

We've got to face it, Jeanie, in a couple weeks people forget, you know? Nothing much lasts anymore, and if they nail him up it'll eventually blow away like everything else. I mean he's just got to . . .

JEANINE: . . . Give up his glory.

STANLEY: Maybe not quite—he's already waked up a lot of people that things don't have to be this way. He could settle for that. —You're the only one who could save him, Jeanie. Please, for all of us. Make him live.

HENRI: And of course, to return to basics, we still don't know for sure . . . who and what he really is, do we.

Pause.

JEANINE: Do we know, Stanley? Tell me the truth.

STANLEY: Oh, Jeanie, I wish I knew! Some days it's like he walked straight out of the ocean or a cloud or a bush full of roses. Other days . . . Shrugs. . . . he smells a lot like anybody else.

JEANINE: Then what do you want me to say to him, exactly?

STANLEY: . . . I think he has to . . . well . . . agree to a deal that if Felix will stop persecuting people he'll . . . you know . . . disappear.

JEANINE: Forever?

STANLEY: Well . . . I guess so . . . yeah.

JEANINE: I'm to ask him not to be god.

STANLEY: No—no, he could be god like . . . in a more general inspirational way. I mean the actual improvements would just have to be up to us, that's all.

HENRI: Wonderful! He's still god but he goes away and there's no bloodbath! Peace!

JEANINE: And each for himself.

HENRI: Peace! Or the country is done, finished, a heap of bones!

Long pause.

JEANINE, *to Stanley*: All right, I want him alive. We haven't the greatness to deserve his death. —I just hope I never hear that he's mowing the lawn.

STANLEY: Nobody's pure, baby—if that's what's bothering you . . .

JEANINE: So if he comes again. . . . Tell me what to say.

STANLEY: . . . Just say . . . like—"Charley darling . . . "

JEANINE: Charley?

STANLEY: He changed it last night. Said it was really Charley from now on, not Jack. Although he's changed it on me a dozen times. Vladimir once, Francisco . . . Herby for a week or two . . . Just say, like . . .

> *The light comes on, but dimly. He looks about. A music very distant, subliminal.*

STANLEY: Charley? Is that you?

> *The light brightens sharply. All straighten, look slightly upward.*

> *Felix enters with Emily.*

FELIX, *feeling the air*: Something is happening . . . !

STANLEY: Ssh—please!

FELIX: Who are you telling to sshh!

EMILY, *end of her patience*: For god's sake, will you control yourself! *To Stanley, pointing up to the light*: Is that . . . ?

STANLEY: I think so.

JEANINE, *facing upward*: How I love you, darling. Now please, please listen to me!

FELIX, *looking about combatively*: Well where is he, goddamit!

EMILY, *pointing up*: The light, dear, the light!

FELIX, *realizing now, looking up with dawning fear*: Holy shi . . .

STANLEY, *upward*: I've got an idea, baby, if you'd like to consider it.

JEANINE: Whatever you decide you are my life and my hope, darling.

STANLEY: You've like turned the country inside out, you know? There's lots of changes since you showed up . . . compared, you know? So maybe, just as—you know, a suggestion—we're thinking maybe the best thing right now, would be for you to . . . just let it hang the way it is. Stand pat. Don't make your move, you know? Bleiben sie ruhig, baby; vaya con calme; ne t'en fais pas; spokoine-e gospodin; nin bu yao jaoji—dig?

> *As Skip, the two soldiers, and the crew all appear, looking up and about.*

SKIP: We've got thirty-five minutes of sun . . . where is he?

FELIX, *finger raised*: Ssh—that's him!

SKIP, *looking up*: *What's him?*

JEANINE, *to the air*: Adore you, darling.

FELIX, *to Stanley*: Are you talking to him or not?

STANLEY: I'm not sure, I think so.

FELIX: Tell him I'll call off the search and we can forget the whole thing if he goes away and never comes back!

SKIP: Goes away!—we have a contract, sir!

JEANINE, *furious*: And empty the jails, of course. And the torturers are to be prosecuted!

FELIX: What torturers?

JEANINE, *to Heaven*: Come down, Charley!

FELIX, *to Heaven*: Wait!! Hold it! —Okay, you stay up there indefinitely, and I'll . . . fire the torturers.

SKIP: This is a contractual breach!—he's got to come down!

FELIX, *to Skip, retrieving authority*: . . . Will you shut up? I've still got him under arrest, don't I?!

STANLEY: . . . That's about it, Charley, okay? I mean we're going to miss you, baby, especially those fantastic conversations on the beach, but . . . you know, maybe it's all for the best, right? I mean, could you give us a sign?

Maybe you tell him, Jeanie, could you?

JEANINE: Oh my dear, my darling, it cuts my heart to say this but I think maybe you better not come back! I'm going to miss you terribly, nothing will be the same . . . but I guess you really have to go!

STANLEY: I'm not trying to rush you, baby, but can we have some kind of an answer?

SKIP: Just a minute, I'd like a word with him. *Comes down, center— sotto*: What's his latest name again?

STANLEY: Charley.

SKIP, *looking up*: Charles? You simply have to return, there's no question about it. I will only remind you that my agency has a signed contract with this government to televise your crucifixion and we have paid a substantial sum of money for the rights. I will forebear mentioning our stockholders, many of them widows and aged persons, who have in good faith bought shares in our company. I plead with you as a responsible, feeling person—show yourself and serve your legal sentence. I want to assure you that everyone from the top of my company to the bottom will be everlastingly grateful and will mourn your passing all the days of our lives. —A practical note: the sun is rapidly going down so may I have the favor of a quick reply? Thank you very much.

All look about expectantly, but nothing happens.

FELIX, *stepping up to the center*: Now listen, Charley, I'm having some second thoughts about this deal I mentioned—you just have to come down and get crucified.

JEANINE: You just promised not to . . . !

FELIX: The country's desperate! If he stays up there I will have to return some of the money!

SKIP: All of it, General.

FELIX: Well, we'll discuss that.

JEANINE: So much for your word!

FELIX, *to Jeanine*: That money will mean hundreds of jobs . . . ! *Upward*: I'm planning on school upgrading, health clinics, lots of improvements for the folks. Whereas if I have to return some of the money . . .

SKIP: All of it!

FELIX: I am not returning that goddam money!

Emily steps up.

EMILY: May I, Skip?

Skip steps aside, gesturing to her to move in. She looks up.

I'm afraid I have to differ with my friend Skip, and my dear friend General Barriaux. —Wherever you are, Charley, I beg you stay there.

FELIX: This is terrible stuff you're telling the man! You are condemning this country to ruin!

EMILY, *persisting to the light*: Don't make me photograph you hanging from two sticks, I beg you, Charley! Stay where you are and you will live in all our imaginations where the great images never die. Wish you all the best, my dear . . . be well!

FELIX, *to the light*: All right now, just listen to me . . .

HENRI, *to the light*: Whoever you are!—I thank you for my daughter's return to life. And before your loving heart I apologize for ignoring her for so many years, and for having led her in my blind pride to the brink of destruction.

PHIL: Speaking for the crew— *Sees Skip react*. . . . this is not a strike! *To the light*: But we'd appreciate it a lot if you, you know, just didn't show. . . .

Sees Skip react. We're ready to go as the contract calls for! But . . . *Upward:* well, that's the message.

SKIP, *upward:* Now look here, Charles —we have fifteen minutes of sun . . . !

> *He is stopped by the low, rumbling bass of a great organ heard as from a distance.*

STANLEY: Sshh! *He looks around for the source of the sound—the others too. Then upward again:* Am I hearing the ocean in the background, Charley? I visualize you on the beach, right? Staring out at the sea, making up your mind? —Let me say one more final thing, okay?—the country's like nice and quiet at least for the moment, right?—give or take a minor ambush here and there? After thirty-eight years of killing, so they tell me, it's almost normal now, right? —So the thing is, Charley—do you want to light the match that'll explode the whole place again?

FELIX: Don't worry about the country, Charley, I'll take care of it. You come down, you hear me? I'm talking syndication, this is one big pot of money! I'm talking new hotels, I'm talking new construction, I'm talking investment. You care about people? Come down and get crucified!

JEANINE, *starting to weep:* For all our sakes, my darling, don't come down . . . !

SKIP AND FELIX, *upward:* You can't do this to us!

> *They look about, wait . . . then . . .*

SKIP, *to Felix:* You will return that check, or I'm calling the Embassy!

FELIX: Fuck the Embassy, I'm keeping the money . . . !

> *They continue shouting at each other, vanishing into the crowd . . .*

SKIP: This is larceny! I'll call Washington! You are destroying my career!

FELIX: I did my good-faith best!

STANLEY: Go away, Charley, before they all kill each other! You gotta give us a sign, baby, what's it gonna be!

> *The light slowly fades to black, as they all look upward and about in wonder and apprehension.*

STANLEY, *in the silence, tentatively:* Charley?

> *All wait, all glancing about. Nothing happens.*

We're not seeing the light, okay?

> *Silence; all listening.*

Don't hear the ocean, okay?

Silence . . . then . . .

They are weeping, immensely relieved and sorry.

HENRI: Good-bye, Charley.

EMILY: Good-bye, Charley.

FELIX: Good-bye, Charley.

SARAH: Good-bye, Charley.

PHIL: Good-bye, Charley.

Skip turns and angrily walks out.

JEANINE: Good-bye, my darling! . . . But could you think about . . . maybe trying it . . . another time?

Silence. Henri takes Jeanine's arm and they move; each of the others now leave the stage silently, in various directions, each alone.

STANLEY, *lifts a hand in farewell, looking forward and up*: Always love you, baby. And look, if you ever feel like, you know . . . a cup of tea, or a glass of dry white, don't hesitate, okay? . . . I'm always home. *Salutes.* Thanks.

He walks off alone.

END